About the Author

James Clavell, the son of a Royal Navy family, was educated in Portsmouth before, as a young artillery officer, he was captured by the Japanese at the Fall of Singapore. He spent the rest of World War II in the infamous Changi prison. It was on his experience in Changi that his bestselling novel KING RAT was based. The interest in Asia, its people and culture continued with TAI-PAN, a tale of Canton and Hong Kong in the mid-19th century and the founding of an Anglo-Chinese trading company, Struan's. This was followed by the classic SHOGUN, the story of Japan during the period when Europe began to make an impact on the island people of the Rising Sun. NOBLE HOUSE, the fourth novel in the Asian saga published in 1981, continued the story of Struan's, the Hong Kong trading company, as the winds of change blew through the Far East. WHIRLWIND, set in Iran, continued the saga. His last novel, GAI-JIN, is set in Japan in 1862, when the-Tai Pan of the Noble House seeks to profit from the decline of the Shogunate.

James Clavell lived for many years in Vancouver and Los Angeles, before settling in Switzerland, where he died in 1994.

WHIRLWIND

is the sixth novel in the Asian Saga that consists of:

SHOGUN	1600
TAI-PAN	1841
GAI-JIN	1862
KING RAT	1945
NOBLE HOUSE	1963
WHIRLWIND	1979

Other titles by James Clavell

Escape
The Children's Story
Thrump-O-moto
The Art of War by Sun Tzu
(edited by James Clavell)

JAMES CLAVELL

Whirlwind

HODDER

Copyright © 1986 by James Clavell

First published in Great Britain in 1986 by Hodder & Stoughton
This edition published in 2006 by Hodder and Stoughton
A division of Hodder Headline

A Hodder paperback

6

A CIP catalogue record for this title
is available from the British Library

ISBN 978-0-340-76618-7

Typeset by Hewer Text UK Ltd, Edinburgh
Printed and bound in Great Britain by
Clays Ltd, St Ives plc

Hodder Headline's policy is to use papers that are natural, renewable
and recyclable products and made from wood grown in sustainable
forests. The logging and manufacturing processes are expected to
conform to the environmental regulations of the country of origin.

Hodder and Stoughton
A division of Hodder Headline PLC
338 Euston Road
London NW1 3BH

For
Shigatsu

This adventure story is set in revolutionary Iran, between February 9th and March 3rd, 1979, long before the hostage crisis began. I've tried to make it seem as real as possible – but it is fiction, peopled with imaginary characters, and many places, and no reference to any living person or company that was or is part of the era exists or is intended. Of course, those shadows of the opposing giants, HIH Shah Mohammed Pahlavi – and his father Reza Shah – and of Imam Khomeini that are cast upon my imaginary characters are a vital part of this story. They, personally, are not portrayed, though I have tried to present an accurate but fictional picture of those times, of the different kinds of people who endured them, the sort of opinions that existed and would have been expressed, but nothing herein is meant, by me, in disrespect.

This is a story, not as things really happened, but as I imagined came to pass within those twenty-four days . . .

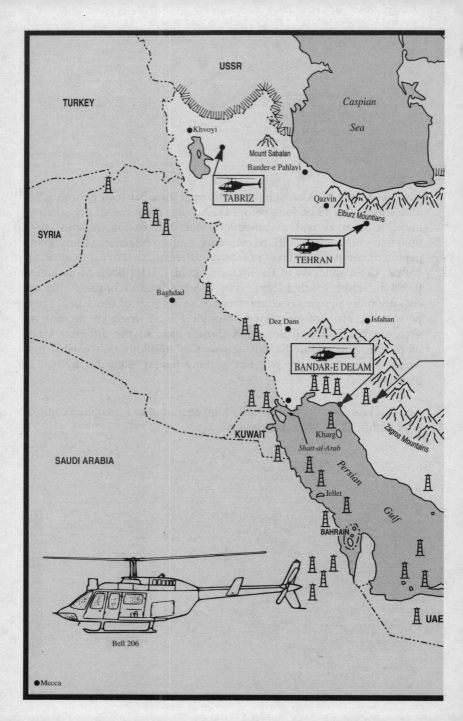

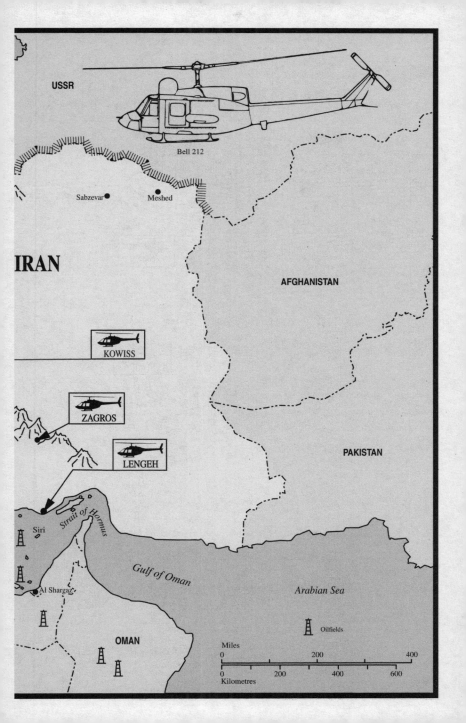

Contents

BOOK ONE

Friday
February 9, 1979

In the Zagros Mountains: Sunset. Now the sun touched the horizon and the man reined in his horse tiredly, glad that the time for prayer had come.

His name was Hussain Kowissi, and he was a powerfully built Iranian of thirty-four, his skin light and his eyes and beard very dark. Over his shoulder was a Soviet AK47 assault rifle. He was bundled against the cold and wore a white turban and travel-stained dark robes with a rough, nomad Kash'kai sheepskin jacket belted over them, and well-used boots. Because his ears were muffled he did not hear the distant scream of the approaching jet helicopter. Behind him his weary pack camel tugged at the halter, impatient for food and rest. Absently he cursed her as he dismounted.

The air was thin at this height, almost 8,000 feet, and cold, very cold, a heavy snow on the ground that the wind took into drifts, making the way slippery and treacherous. Below, the little-known track curled towards distant valleys, at length to Isfahan where he had been. Ahead the path wound dangerously upwards through the crags, then to other valleys facing the Persian Gulf and to the town of Kowiss where he had been born, where he now lived and from which he had taken his name when he had become a mullah.

He did not mind the danger or the cold. The danger felt clean to him as the air was clean.

It's almost as though I was once more a nomad, he thought, my grandfather leading us as in the old days when all our tribes of the Kash'kai could roam from winter pasture to summer pasture, a horse and a gun for every man and herds to spare, our flocks of sheep and goats and camels a multitude, our women unveiled, our tribes living free as our forefathers had done for tens of centuries, subject to no one but the Will of God – the old days that were ended barely sixty years ago, he told himself, his anger rising, ended by Reza Khan, the upstart soldier who with the help of the vile British usurped the throne, proclaimed himself Reza Shah, first of the Pahlavi Shahs, and then, with the support of his Cossack regiment, curbed us and tried to stamp us out.

God's work that in time Reza Shah was humiliated and exiled by his foul British masters to die forgotten, God's work that Mohammed Shah was forced to flee a few days ago, God's work that Khomeini has returned to lead His revolution, the Will of God that tomorrow or the next day I will be martyred, God's pleasure that we're swept by His whirlwind and that now there will be a final reckoning on all Shah lackeys and all foreigners.

The helicopter was closer now but still he did not hear it, the whine of the gusting wind helping to bury the sound. Contentedly he pulled out his prayer rug and spread it on the snow, his back still aching from the weals that the whip had caused, then scooped up a handful of snow. Ritually he washed his hands and face, preparing for the fourth prayer of the day, then faced southwest towards the Holy City of Mecca that lay a thousand miles away in Saudi Arabia, and put his mind to God.

'Allah-u Akbar, Allah-u Akbar, La illah illa Allah . . .' As he repeated the Shahada he prostrated himself, letting the Arabic words embrace him: God is most Great, God is most Great. I testify there is no other God but God and Mohammed is His Prophet. God is most Great, God is most Great, I testify there is no other God but God and Mohammed is His Prophet . . .

The wind picked up, colder now. Then through his earmuffs he caught the pulse of the jet engine. It grew and grew and went into his head and drove away his peace and ruined his concentration. Angrily he opened his eyes. The approaching helicopter

6

was barely two hundred feet above the ground, climbing straight towards him.

At first he thought it might be an army aircraft and a sudden fear went into him that they were searching for him. Then he recognised the British red, white and blue colours and familiar markings of the bold S-G around the red lion of Scotland on the fuselage – the same helicopter company that operated from the air base at Kowiss and all over Iran – so his fear left him but not his rage. He watched it, hating what it represented. Its course was almost directly overhead but it presented no danger to him – he doubted if those aboard would notice him, here in the lee of an outcrop – even so, with all of his being, he resented the intrusion into his peace, and destruction of his prayers. And as the ear-shattering scream increased, his anger soared.

'La illah illa Allah . . .' He tried to go back into prayer but now the thrust of the blades whirled the snow into his face. Behind him his horse whinnied and cavorted in sudden panic, the hobble making him slip and slide. The pack camel, jerked by the halter, equally in panic, reeled to her feet, bellowing, and stumbled this way and that on three legs, shaking her load and fouling the bindings.

His rage burst. 'Infidel!' he bellowed at the airplane that now was almost over the lip of the mountain, leaped to his feet, and grabbed his gun, slipped the safety and let off a burst, then corrected and emptied the magazine.

'SATAN!' he shrieked in the sudden silence.

When the first bullets splashed the chopper, the young pilot, Scot Gavallan, was momentarily paralysed and he stared stupidly at the holes in the plastic canopy ahead. 'Christ Almighty . . .' he gasped, never having been fired on before, but his words were drowned by the man in the front seat beside him whose reactions were honed and battle fast: 'Hit the deck!' The command roared in his headphones.

'Hit the deck,' Tom Lochart shouted again into his boom mike, then, because he had no controls of his own, he overrode the pilot's left hand and shoved the collective lever down, cutting lift and power abruptly. The chopper reeled drunkenly, instantly losing height. At that moment the second burst sprayed them. There was an ominous crack above and behind, somewhere else a bullet howled off metal, the jets coughed, and the chopper fell out of the sky.

She was a 206 Jet Ranger, one pilot, four passengers, one in front, three in the back and she was full. An hour ago Scot had routinely picked up the others back from a month's home leave at Shiraz airport fifty-odd miles southeast, but now routine was nightmare and the mountain rushed at them until just over a ridge the earth tumbled away miraculously and the chopper sank into a depression giving him a split second of respite to get back air power and partial control.

'Watch out for crissake!' Lochart said.

Scot had seen the hazard but not as quickly. Now his hands and feet slid the plane into a shuddering swerve around the jutting outcrop; the left skid of the undercarriage caught the rocks a glancing blow, howled in protest, and once more they plunged away barely a few feet above the uneven surface of rocks and trees that fell and reeled up again.

'Low and fast,' Lochart said, 'that way, Scot – no, that way, over there, down that crest into the ravine . . . Are you hit?'

'No, no, I don't think so. You?'

'No, you're fine now, drop into the ravine, come on, hurry!'

Scot Gavallan banked obediently and fled, too low and too fast and his mind not quite normal yet. There was still the taste of bile in his mouth and his heart was pumping. From behind the partition he could hear the shouts and curses of the others in the back above the roar of the engines, but he could not risk turns and said anxiously into the intercom, 'Anyone hurt back there, Tom?'

'Forget them, concentrate, watch the ridge, I'll deal with them!' Tom Lochart said urgently, his eyes searching everywhere. He was forty-two, Canadian, ex-RAF, ex-mercenary, and now chief pilot of their base, Zagros Three. 'Watch the ridge and get ready to evade again. Hug the deck and keep her low. Watchitt!'

The ridge was slightly above them and it came at them too fast. Gavallan saw the fang of rocks directly in his path. He just had time to lurch around it when a violent gust shoved him perilously near to the sheer side of the ravine. He overcorrected and heard the obscenity in his earphones, got back control. Then ahead he saw the trees and the rocks and the sudden end to the ravine and he knew they were lost.

Abruptly everything seemed to slow down for him. 'Christ Al –'

'Hard aport . . . watch the rock!'

Scot felt his hands and feet obey and saw the chopper pirouette the rocks by inches, slam for the trees, ride over them, and escape into free air.

'Set her down over there, fast as you can.'

He gaped at Lochart, his insides still churning. 'What?'

'Sure. We better take a look; check her out,' Lochart said urgently, hating not having the controls. 'I heard something go.'

'So did I, but what about the undercart, it might be torn off?'

8

'Just keep her weight off. I'll slip out and check it, then if it's all right, set her down and I'll make a quick inspect. Safer to do that: Christ only knows if the bullets chopped an oil line or nicked a cable.' Lochart saw Scot take his eyes off the clearing to glance around at his passengers. 'The hell with them for crissake, I'll deal with them,' he said sharply. 'You concentrate on the landing.' He saw the younger man flush but obey, then, trying to contain his sudden nausea, Lochart turned around expecting blood splashed everywhere and entrails and someone scream-ing – screams drowned by the jet engines – knowing there was nothing he could do until they reached sanctuary and landed, always the first duty to land safely.

To his aching relief the three men in the backseat – two mechanics and another pilot – were seemingly unhurt though they were all hunched down, and Jordon, the mechanic directly behind Scot, was white-faced, holding his head with both hands. Lochart turned back.

They were about fifty feet now, on a good approach, coming in fast. In the clearing the surface was stark and white and flat with no tufts of grass showing through, the snow banked high at the sides. Seemingly a good choice. Easily enough room to manoeuvre and land. But how to judge the depth of snow and the hidden level of the earth beneath? Lochart knew what he would do if he had the controls. But he did not have control, he was not the captain though he was senior. 'They're okay in the back, Scot.'

'Thank God for that,' Scot Gavallan said. 'You set to get out?'

'How's the surface look to you?'

Scot heard the caution in Lochart's voice, instantly aborted the landing, put on power and went into a hover. Christ, he thought, almost in panic at his stupidity, if Tom hadn't nudged me I'd've put down there and Christ only knows how deep the snow is or what's underneath! He steadied at a hundred feet and searched the mountain-side. 'Thanks, Tom. What about over there?'

The new clearing was smaller, a few hundred yards away across the other side of the valley, lower down with a good escape route if they needed one, and protected from the wind. The ground was almost clear of snow, rough but serviceable.

'Looks better to me too.' Lochart slid one earphone away and looked back. 'Hey, Jean-Luc,' he shouted over the engines, 'you all right?'

'Yes. I heard something go.'

'So did we. Jordon, you all right?'

'Course I'm all effing right, for Gawd's sake,' Jordon shouted back sourly. He was a lean, tough Australian and he was shaking his head like a dog. 'Just banged my bleeding head, didn't I? Bloody effing bullets! I thought Scot said things were getting bleeding better with the bleeding Shah gone and Khomeini bleeding back. Better? Now they're bleeding firing at us! They've never done that before – what the eff's going on?'

'How the hell do I know? Probably just a trigger-happy nutter. Sit tight, I'm going to take a quick look. If the undercart's okay we'll set down and you and Rod can make a check.'

'How's the effing oil pressure?' Jordon shouted.

'In the green.' Lochart settled back, automatically scanning the dials, the clearing, the sky, left, right, overhead, and below. They were descending nicely, two hundred feet to go. Through his headset he heard Gavallan humming tonelessly. 'You did very well, Scot.'

'The hell I did,' the younger man said, trying to sound matter-of-fact. 'I'd've pranged. I was bloody paralysed when the bullets hit, and if it hadn't been for you I'd've gone in.'

'Most of it was my fault. I bashed the collective without warning. Sorry about that but I had to get us out of the bastard's line of fire fast. I learned that in Malaya.' Lochart had spent a year there with the British Forces in their war against communist insurgents. 'No time to warn you. Set down as fast as you can.' He watched approvingly as Gavallan went into a hover, searching the terrain carefully.

'Did you see who fired at us, Tom?'

'No, but then I wasn't looking for hostiles. Where you going to land?'

'Over there, well away from the fallen tree. Okay?'

'Looks fine to me. Quick as you can. Hold her off about a foot.'

The hover was perfect. A few inches above the snow, as steady as the rocks below though the wind was gusting. Lochart opened the door. The sudden cold chilled him. He zipped up his padded flight jacket, slid out carefully, keeping his head well down from the whirling blades.

The front of the skid was scraped and badly dented and a little twisted but the rivets holding it to the undercarriage mounts were firm. Quickly he checked the other side, rechecked the damaged skid, then gave the thumbs-up. Gavallan eased off the throttle a hair and set her down, soft as thistledown.

At once the three men in the back piled out. Jean-Luc Sessonne, the French pilot, ducked out of the way to let the two mechanics begin their inspection, one port, the other starboard, working back from nose to tail. The wind from the rotors tore at their clothes, whipping them. Lochart was under the helicopter now looking for oil or petrol seepage

10

but he could find none, so he got up and followed Rodrigues. The man was American and very good – his own mechanic who, for a year now, had serviced the 212 he normally flew. Rodrigues unclipped an inspection panel and peered inside, his grey-flecked hair and clothes tugged by the airflow.

S-G safety standards were the highest of all Iranian helicopter operators, so the maze of cables, pipes, and fuel lines was neat, clean, and optimum. But suddenly Rodrigues pointed. There was a deep score on the crankcase where a bullet had ricocheted. Carefully they backtracked the line of the bullet. Again he pointed into the maze, this time using a flash. One of the oil lines was nicked. When he brought out his hand it was oil heavy. 'Shit,' he said.

'Shut her down, Rod?' Lochart shouted.

'Hell no, there may be more of those trigger-happy bastards around, an' this's no place to spend the night.' Rodrigues pulled out a piece of waste and a spanner. 'You check aft, Tom.'

Lochart left him to it, uneasily looked around for possible shelter in case they had to overnight. Over the other side of the clearing, Jean-Luc was casually peeing against a fallen tree, a cigarette in his mouth. 'Don't get frostbite, Jean-Luc!' he called out and saw him wave the stream good-naturedly.

'Hey, Tom.'

It was Jordon beckoning. At once he ducked under the tail boom to join the mechanic. His heart skipped a beat. Jordon also had an inspection panel off. There were two bullet holes in the fuselage, just over the tanks. Jesus, just a split second later and the tanks would have blown, he thought. If I hadn't shoved the collective down we'd all've bought it. Absolutely. But for that we'd be sprayed over the mountainside. And for what?

Jordon tugged him and pointed again, following the line of the bullets. There was another score on the rotor column. 'How the effer missed the effing blades I'm effed if I know,' he shouted, the red wool hat that he always wore pulled down over his ears.

'It wasn't our time.'

'What?'

'Nothing. Have you found anything else?'

'Not effing yet. You all right, Tom?'

'Sure.'

A sudden crash and they all whirled in fright, but it was only a huge tree limb, overloaded with snow, tumbling earthward.

'*Espèce de con*,' Jean-Luc said and peered up into the sky, very

11

conscious of the falling light, then shrugged to himself, lit another cigarette, and wandered off, stamping his feet against the cold.

Jordon found nothing else amiss on his side. The minutes ticked by. Rodrigues was still muttering and cursing, one arm reaching awkwardly into the bowels of the compartment. Behind him the others were huddled in a group, watching, well away from the rotors. It was noisy and uncomfortable, the light good but not for long. They still had twenty miles to go and no guidance systems in these mountains other than the small homer at their base which sometimes worked and sometimes didn't. 'Come on, for Christ's sake,' someone muttered.

Yes, Lochart thought, hiding his disquiet.

At Shiraz the outgoing crew of two pilots and two mechanics they were replacing had hurriedly waved goodbye and rushed for their company 125 – an eight-place, twin-engined private jet airplane for transportation or special freighting – the same jet that had brought them from Dubai's International Airport across the Gulf and a month's leave, Lochart and Jordon in England, Jean-Luc in France, and Rodrigues from a hunting trip in Kenya. 'What the hell's the hurry?' Lochart had asked as the small twin jet closed its doors and taxied off.

'The airport's only still partially operational, everyone's still on strike, but not to worry,' Scot Gavallan had said. 'They've got to take off before the officious, bloody little burk in the tower who thinks he's God's gift to Iranian Air Traffic Control cancels their bloody clearance. We'd better get the lead out too before he starts to sod us around. Get your gear aboard.'

'What about customs?'

'They're still on strike, old boy. Along with everyone else – banks're still closed. Never mind, we'll be normal in a week or so.'

'*Merde*,' Jean-Luc said. 'The French papers say Iran is *une catastrophe* with Khomeini and his mullahs on one side, the armed forces ready to stage a coup any day, the communists winding everyone up, the government of Bakhtiar powerless, and civil war inevitable.'

'What do they know in France, old boy?' Scot Gavallan had said airily as they loaded their gear. 'The Fr –'

'The French know, *mon vieux*. All the papers say Khomeini'll never cooperate with Bakhtiar because he's a Shah appointee and anyone connected with the Shah is finished. Finished. That old fire-eater's said fifty times he won't work with anyone Shah appointed.'

Lochart said, 'I saw Andy three days ago in Aberdeen, Jean-Luc, and he was bullish as hell that Iran'll come back to normal soon, now that Khomeini's back and the Shah gone.'

Scot beamed. 'There, you see. If anyone should know it's the Old Man. How is he, Tom?'

Lochart grinned back at him. 'In great shape, his usual ball of fire.' Andy was Andrew Gavallan, Scot's father, chairman and managing director of S-G. 'Andy said Bakhtiar has the army, navy, and air force, the police, and SAVAK, so Khomeini's got to make a deal somehow. It's that or civil war.'

'Jesus,' Rodrigues said, 'what the hell we doing back here anyway?'

'It's the money.'

'*Bullmerde!*'

They had all laughed, Jean-Luc the natural pessimist, then Scot said, 'What the hell does it matter, Jean-Luc? No one's ever bothered us here, have they? All through the troubles no one's really ever bothered us. All our contracts are with IranOil which's the government – Bakhtiar, Khomeini or General Whoever. Doesn't matter whoever's in power, they've got to get back to normal soon – any government'll need oil dollars desperately, so they've got to have choppers, they've got to have us. For God's sake, they're not fools!'

'No, but Khomeini's fanatic and doesn't care about anything except Islam – and oil's not Islam.'

'What about Saudi? The Emirates, OPEC, for God's sake? They're Islamic and they know the price of a barrel. The hell with that, listen!' Scot beamed. 'Guerney Aviation have pulled out of all the Zagros Mountains and are cutting all their Iranian ops to zero. To zero!'

This caught the attention of all of them. Guerney Aviation was the huge American helicopter company and their major rival. With Guerney gone, work would be doubled and all expat S-G personnel in Iran were on a bonus system that was tied to Iranian profits.

'You sure, Scot?'

'Sure, Tom. They had a helluva row with IranOil about it. The upshot was that IranOil said, If you want to leave, leave, but all the choppers are on licence to us so they stay – and all spares! So Guerney told them to shove it, closed their base at Gash, and put all the choppers in mothballs and left.'

'I don't believe it,' Jean-Luc said. 'Guerney must have fifty choppers on contract; even they can't afford to write off that lot.'

'Even so, we've already flown three missions last week which were all Guerney exclusives.'

Jean-Luc broke through the cheers. 'Why did Guerney pull out, Scot?'

'Our Fearless Leader in Tehran thinks they haven't the bottle, can't

13

stand the pressure, or don't want to. Let's face it, most of Khomeini's vitriol's against America and American companies. McIver thinks they're cutting their losses and that's great for us.'

'*Mon Dieu*, if they can't take out their planes and spares, they're in dead trouble.'

'Ours not to reason why, old boy, ours just to do and fly. So long as we sit tight we'll get all their contracts and more than double our pay this year alone.'

'*Tu en parles à mon cul, ma tête est malade!*'

They had all laughed. Even Jordon knew what that meant: speak to my backside, my head is sick. 'Not to worry, old chap,' Scot said.

Confidently, Lochart nodded to himself, the cold on the mountain-side not hurting him yet. Andy and Scot're right, everything's going to be normal soon, has to be, he thought. The newspapers in England were equally confident the Iranian situation'd normalise itself quickly now. Provided the Soviets didn't make an overt move. And they had been warned. It was hands off, Americans and Soviets, so now Iranians can settle their affairs in their own way. It's right that whoever's in power needs stability urgently, and revenue – and that means oil. Yes. Everything's going to be all right. She believes it and if she believed everything would be wonderful once the Shah was overthrown and Khomeini back, why shouldn't I?

Ah, Sharazad, how I've missed you.

It had been impossible to phone her from England. Phones in Iran had never been particularly good, given the massive overload of too-fast industrialisation. But in the past eight months since the troubles began, the almost constant telecommunication strikes had made inter-nal and external communication worse and worse and now was almost non-existent. When he was at Aberdeen HQ for his biannual medical he had managed to send her a telex after eight hours of trying. He had sent it care of Duncan McIver in Tehran where she was now. You can't say much in a telex except see you soon, miss you, love.

Not long now, my darling, and th –

'Tom?'

'Oh, hi, Jean-Luc? What?'

'It's going to snow soon.'

'Yes.' Jean-Luc was thin-faced, with a big Gallic nose and brown eyes, spare like all the pilots who had serious medicals every six months with no excuses for overweight. 'Who fired at us, Tom?'

Lochart shrugged. 'I saw no one. Did you?'

'No. I hope it was just one crazy.' Jean-Luc's eyes bored into him.

14

'For a moment I thought I was back in Algiers, these mountains are not so different, back in the air force fighting the fellagha and the FLN, may God curse them for ever.' He ground the cigarette stub out with his heel. 'I've been in one civil war and hated it. At least then I had bombs and guns. I don't want to be a civilian caught in another with nothing to rely on except how fast I can run.'

'It was just a lone crazy.'

'I think we're going to have to deal with a lot of crazies, Tom. Ever since I left France I've had a bad feeling. It's worse since I got back. We've been to war, you and I, most of the others haven't. We've a nose, you and I, and we're in for bad trouble.'

'No, you're just tired.'

'Yes, that's true. Andy was really bullish?'

'Very. He sends his best and said to keep it up!'

Jean-Luc laughed and stifled a yawn. '*Mon Dieu*, I'm starving. What's Scot planned for our homecoming?'

'He's got a welcome home sign up over the hangar.'

'For dinner, *mon vieux*. Dinner.'

'Scot said he and some villagers went hunting so he's got a haunch of venison and a couple of hares ready for your tender mercies – and the barbecue'll be all set to go.'

Jean-Luc's eyes lit up. 'Good. Listen, I've brought Brie, garlic, a whole kilo, smoked ham, anchovies, onions, also a few kilos of pasta, cans of tomato puree, and my wife gave me a new recipe for matriciana from Gianni of St. Jean that is merely incredible. And the wine.'

Lochart felt his juices quicken, Jean-Luc's hobby was cooking and he was inspired when he wanted to be. 'I brought tins of everything I could think of from Fortnums and some whisky. Hey, I've missed your cooking.' And your company, he thought. When they had met at Dubai they had shaken hands and he had asked, 'How was leave?'

'I was in France,' Jean-Luc had said grandly.

Lochart had envied him his simplicity. England had not been good, the weather, food, leave, the kids, her, Christmas – much as he had tried. Never mind. I'm back and soon I'll be in Tehran. 'You'll cook tonight, Jean-Luc?'

'Of course. How can I live without proper food?'

Lochart laughed. 'Like the rest of the world.' They watched Rodrigues still working hard. The sound of the jets was muted, the rotors whipping him. Lochart gave a thumbs-up to Scot Gavallan waiting patiently in the cockpit. Scot returned the signal, then pointed at the sky. Lochart nodded, shrugged, then put his attention back on Ro-

15

drigues, knowing there was nothing he could do to help but wait stoically.

'When do you go to Tehran?' Jean-Luc asked.

Lochart's heart quickened. 'Sunday, if it doesn't snow. I've a report for McIver and mail for them there. I'll take a 206; it'll take all tomorrow to check everything. Scot said we're to stand by to start up full operations.'

Jean-Luc stared at him. 'Nasiri said full ops?'

'Yes.' Nasiri was their Iranian liaison and base manager, an employee of IranOil – the government monopoly that owned all oil above and below the ground – that channelled and authorised all their flights. S-G worked under contract to this company, surveying, supplying personnel, supplies and equipment to the oil rigs that were scattered over the mountain range, and dealing with the inevitable CASEVACS – casualty evacuations – accidents and emergencies. 'I doubt if we'll be doing much flying over the next week because of weather but I should be able to get out in the 206.'

'Yes. You will need a guide. I will come too.'

Lochart laughed. 'No way, old friend. You're next in command and on duty for the next two weeks.'

'But I will not be needed. For three days, eh? Look at the sky, Tom. I must see that our apartment is all right.' In normal times Tehran was where all pilots with families would be based, who would fly two weeks on, one week off. Many pilots opted for two months on and one month off on leave at home, particularly the English. 'It's very important I get to Tehran.'

'I'll check out your apartment if you like, and if you promise to cook three nights a week, I'll sneak you two days when I get back. You've just had a month's leave.'

'Ah, but that was at home. Now I must think of *mon amie*. Of course she is desolate without me in Tehran, it's been a whole month for her without me. Of course.' Jean-Luc was watching Rodrigues. Then again he looked at the sky. 'We can wait ten minutes more, Tom, then we should prepare a camp while there is light.'

'Yes.'

'But back to more important things. Tom –'

'No.'

'*Merde*, be French and not Anglo-Saxon. A whole month, consider her feelings!'

Rodrigues clipped the panel back in place and wiped his hands. 'Let's get the hell outta here,' he called out and climbed aboard. They

16

followed quickly. He was still fastening his seat belt, his back and head and neck aching, when they were airborne and scudding for their base over the next range. Then he saw Jordon staring at him. 'What's with you, Effer?'

'How'd you fix that effing pipe, sport? She was effing holed to bust.'

'Gum.'

'What?'

'Chewing gum. Sure, goddammit. It worked in goddam-Vietnam, so it'll goddam work here. Maybe. Because it was only a goddam-little bit but it was all I got so start goddam-praying. Can't you stop cursing for crissake?'

They landed safely at their base, snow was just beginning. The ground staff had switched on the landing lights, just in case.

Their base consisted of four trailer huts, a cookhouse, hangar for the 212 – a fourteen-place passenger transport or freight helicopter – and two 206s, and landing pads. Storage sheds for oil drilling spares, sacks of cement, pumps, generators, and all manner of support equipment for the rigs, along with drilling pipe. It was on a small plateau at 7,500 feet, wooded and very picturesque, in a bowl half surrounded by snow-capped peaks that soared to twelve thousand feet and more. Half a mile away was the village of Yazdek. The villagers were from a minor tribe of nomad Kash'kai who had settled here a century ago around this crossroads of two of the minor caravan routes that had crisscrossed Iran for three, perhaps four thousand years.

S-G had had a base here for seven years under contract to IranOil, first to survey a pipeline and make topographical maps of the area, then to help build and service the rigs of the rich oil fields nearby. It was a lonely, wild and beautiful place, the flying interesting and good, the hours easy – throughout Iran only daylight flying was allowed by Iranian regulations. Summers were wonderful. Most of the winter they were snowed in. Close by were crystal lakes with good fishing, and in the forests game was plentiful. Their relations with the villagers of Yazdek were excellent. Apart from mail they were well supplied, usually, and wanted for nothing. And, important for all of them, they were well away from HQ in Tehran, out of radio contact most of the time, and left happily to their own devices.

The moment the rotors had stopped and the airplane shut down, Rodrigues and Jordon unclipped the panel again. They were aghast. The floor of the compartment was awash with oil. With it was the heavy smell of petrol. Shakily Rodrigues searched, then pointed the flash. In one of the seams at the edge of a petrol tank was a tiny rupture they could not possibly have detected on the mountainside. A thin stream of fuel came out to mix with the oil below.

'Jesus, Effer! Lookit, she's a goddam time bomb,' he croaked. Behind him, Jordon almost fainted. 'One spark and . . . Effer, get me a hose for crissake, I'll flood her out now before we go sky-high . . .'

'I'll get it,' Scot said, then added queasily, 'Well, I guess that's one of our lives gone. Eight more to go.'

'You musta been born lucky, Captain,' Rodrigues said, feeling very sick. 'Yeah, you must've been born lucky. This baby . . .' He stopped abruptly, listening. So did everyone nearby – Lochart and Jean-Luc near the HQ hut with Nasiri, the half-dozen Iranian ground staff, cooks, and labourers. It was very quiet. Then again came a burst of machine-gun fire from the direction of the village.

'Goddam –!' Rodrigues muttered. 'What the hell'd we come back to this lousy dump for?'

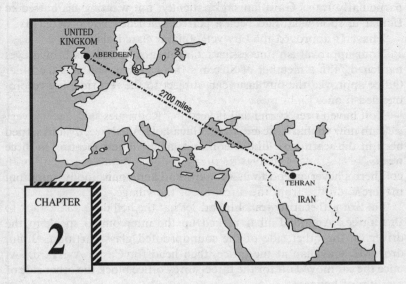

Aberdeen, Scotland – McCloud Heliport: 5:15 P.M. The great helicopter came down out of the gloaming, blades thrashing, and landed near the Rolls that was parked near one of the rainswept helipads – the whole heliport busy, other helicopters arriving or leaving with shifts of oil riggers, personnel and supplies, all airplanes and hangars proudly displaying the S-G symbol. The cabin door opened and two men wearing flight overalls and Mae Wests came down the hydraulic steps, leaning against the wind and the rain. Before they reached the car the uniformed chauffeur had opened the door for them.

'Smashing ride, wasn't it?' Andrew Gavallan said happily, a tall man, strong and very trim for his sixty-four years. He slipped out of his Mae West easily, shook the rain from his collar, and got in beside the other man. 'She's marvellous, everything the makers claim. Did I tell you we're the first outsiders to test-fly her?'

'First or last, makes no difference to me. I thought it was bloody bumpy and bloody noisy,' Linbar Struan said irritably, fighting off the Mae West. He was fifty, sandy-haired and blue-eyed, head of Struan's, the vast conglomerate based in Hong Kong, nicknamed the Noble House, that secretly owned the controlling interest in S-G Helicopters. 'I still think the investment is too much per aircraft. Much too much.'

'The X63's as good a bet economically as you can get; she'll be perfect for the North Sea, Iran, and anywhere we have heavy loads,

19

particularly Iran,' Gavallan said patiently, not wanting his hatred of Linbar to spoil what had been a perfect test ride. 'I've ordered six.'

'I haven't approved the buy yet!' Linbar flared at him.

'Your approval isn't necessary,' Gavallan said and his brown eyes hardened. 'I'm a member of Struan's Inner Office; you and the Inner Office approved the buy last year, subject to the test ride, if *I* recommended it an –

'You haven't recommended it yet!'

'I am now so that's the end of it!' Gavallan smiled sweetly and settled back in the seat. 'You'll have contracts at the board meeting in three weeks.'

'There's never an end to it, Andrew, you and your bloody ambition, is there?'

'I'm not a threat to you, Linbar, let's –'

'I agree.' Angrily Linbar picked up the intercom to speak to the driver on the other side of the soundproofed glass partition. 'John, drop Mr. Gavallan at the office, then head for Castle Avisyard.' At once the car moved off for the three-storey office block the other side of a group of hangars.

'How is Avisyard?' Gavallan asked strangely.

'Better than in your day – so sorry you and Maureen weren't invited for Christmas, perhaps next year.' Linbar's lips curled. 'Yes, Avisyard is much better.' He glanced out of the window and jerked a thumb at the jumbo helicopter. 'And better you don't fail with that. Or anything else.'

Gavallan's face tightened; the jibe about his wife had slipped under his constant guard. 'Talking about failure, what about your disastrous South American investments, your stupid fracas with Toda Shipping over their tanker fleet, what about losing the Hong Kong tunnel contract to Par-Con/Toda, what about betraying our old friends in Hong Kong with your stock manipul –'

'Betray, bullshit! "Old friends", bullshit! They're all over twenty-one and what've they done for us recently? Shanghainese are supposed to be smarter than us – Cantonese, mainlanders, all of them, you've said it a million times! Not my fault there's an oil crisis or the world's in turmoil or Iran's up the spout or the Arabs are nailing us to the cross along with the Japs, Koreans and Taiwanese!' Linbar was suddenly choked with rage. 'You forget we're in a different world now, Hong Kong's different, the world's different! I'm taipan of Struan's, I'm committed to look after the Noble House, and every taipan has had reverses, even your God-cursed Sir bloody Ian Dunross, and he'll have more with his delusions of oil riches in China. Ev –'

'Ian's right ab –'

'Even Hag Struan had reverses, even our bloody founder, the great Dirk himself, may he rot in hell too! Not my fault the world's sodded up. You think you can do better?' Linbar shouted.

'Twenty times!' Gavallan slammed back.

Now Linbar was shaking with rage. 'I'd fire you if I could but I can't! I've had you and your treachery. You married into the family, you're not a real part of it. If there's a God in heaven you'll destroy yourself! I'm taipan and by God you'll never be!'

Gavallan hammered on the glass partition and the car stopped abruptly. He tore the door open and got out. '*Dew neh loh moh*, Linbar!' he said through his teeth and stormed off into the rain.

Their hatred stemmed from the late fifties and early sixties when Gavallan was working in Hong Kong for Struan's, prior to coming here at the secret order of the then taipan, Ian Dunross, the brother of his late wife, Kathy. Linbar had been frantically jealous of him because he had had Dunross's confidence while Linbar had not, and mostly because Gavallan had always been in the running to succeed as taipan one day, whereas Linbar was considered to have no chance.

It was Struan's ancient company law for the taipan to have total, undisputed executive power, and the inviolate right to choose the timing of his own retirement and successor – who had to be a member of the Inner Office and therefore in some way, family – but once the decision was made, to relinquish all power. Ian Dunross had ruled wisely for ten years then had chosen a cousin, David MacStruan, to succeed him. Four years ago, in his prime, David MacStruan – an enthusiastic mountaineer – had been killed in a climbing accident in the Himalayas. Just before he died and in front of two witnesses he had, astonishingly, chosen Linbar to succeed him. There had been police inquiries into his death – British and Nepalese. His ropes and climbing gear had been tampered with.

The inquiries finalised with 'accident'. The mountain face they had been climbing was remote, the fall sudden, no one knew exactly what had happened, neither climbers nor guides, conditions were only fair, and, yes, the sahib was in good health and a wise man, never one to take a foolish risk, 'But, sahib, our mountains in the High Lands are different from other mountains. Our mountains have spirits and get angry from time to time, sahib, and who can foretell what a spirit may do?' No finger was pointed at any one man, the rope and gear 'might' not have been tampered with, just badly serviced. Karma.

Apart from Nepalese guides all twelve climbers in the party were men from Hong Kong, friends and business associates, British, Chinese, one American, and two Japanese, Hiro Toda, head of Toda Shipping Industries – a longtime personal friend of David MacStruan's – and one of his associates, Nobunaga Mori. Linbar was not among them.

At great personal risk two men and a guide climbed down the fault and reached David MacStruan before he died, Profitable Choy, an enormously wealthy director of Struan's, and Mori. Both testified that, just before he died, David MacStruan had formally made Linbar Struan his successor. Shortly after the distraught party had returned to Hong Kong, MacStruan's executive secretary going through his desk had found a simple typewritten page signed by him, dated a few months before, witnessed by Profitable Choy, that confirmed it.

Gavallan remembered how shocked he had been, they all had – Claudia Chen, who had been executive secretary to the taipan for generations, cousin to his own executive secretary, Liz Chen, most of all. 'It wasn't like the taipan, Master Andrew,' she had told him – an old lady but still sharp as a needle. 'The taipan would never have left such an important piece of paper here, he would have put it in the safe in the Great House along with . . . with all the other private documents.'

But David MacStruan had not. And the dying command and the supporting paper had made it legal and now Linbar Struan was taipan of the Noble House and that was the end of it but *dew neh loh moh* on Linbar even so, his foul wife, his devil Chinese mistress, and his rotten friends. I'll still bet my life if David wasn't murdered, he was manipulated somehow. But why should Profitable Choy lie, or Mori, why should they – they've nothing to gain by that . . .

A sudden rain squall battered him and he gasped momentarily, brought out of his reverie. His heart was still pumping and he cursed himself for losing his temper and letting Linbar say what should not have been said. 'You're a bloody fool, you could have contained him like always, you've got to work with him and his ilk for years – you were also to blame!' he said aloud, then muttered, 'Bastard shouldn't't've jibed about Maureen . . .' They had been married for three years and had a daughter of two. His first wife, Kathy, had died nine years ago of multiple sclerosis.

Poor old Kathy, he thought sadly, what bad luck you had.

He squinted against the rain and saw the Rolls turn out of the heliport gate and vanish. Damn shame about Avisyard, I love that place, he thought, remembering all the good times and the bad that he had lived there with his Kathy and their two children, Scot and Melinda. Castle Avisyard was the ancestral estate of Dirk Struan and left by him to the following taipan, during his tenure, to be passed on again, rambling and beautiful, more than a thousand hectares in Ayrshire. Shame we'll never go there, Maureen and I and little Electra, certainly as long as Linbar's taipan. Pity, but that's life.

'Well, the sod can't last for ever,' he said to the wind and felt all the better for the saying of it aloud. Then he strode into the building and into his office.

'Hi, Liz,' he said. Liz Chen, his executive secretary, was a good-looking Eurasian woman in her fifties who had come with him from Hong Kong in '63 and knew all the secrets of Gavallan Holdings – his original cover operation – S-G, and Struan's. 'What's new?'

'You had a row with the taipan, never mind.' She offered him the cup of tea, her voice lilting.

'Dammit, yes. How the hell did you know?' When she just laughed he laughed with her. 'The hell with him. Have you got through to Mac yet?' This was Duncan McIver, head of S-G's Iran operations and his oldest friend.

'We've a laddie dialling from dawn to dusk but the Iran circuits are still busy. Telex isn't answering either. Duncan must be just as anxious as you to talk.' She took his coat and hung it on the peg in his office. 'Your wife called – she's picking up Electra from nursery school and wanted to know if you'd be home for dinner. I told her I thought yes but it might be late – you've the conference call with ExTex in half an hour.'

'Yes.' Gavallan sat down behind his desk and made sure the file was ready. 'Check if the telex to Mac's working yet, would you, Liz?'

At once she began to dial. His office was large and tidy, looking out on the airfield. On the clean desk there were some framed family photographs of Kathy with Melinda and Scot, when they were small, the great Castle Avisyard behind them, and another of Maureen holding up their baby. Nice faces, smiling faces. Just one oil painting on the wall by Aristotle Quance of a corpulent Chinese mandarin – a gift from Ian Dunross to celebrate their first successful landing on a North Sea rig that McIver had done, and the start of an era.

'Andy,' Dunross had said, beginning it all, 'I want you to take Kathy and the kids and leave Hong Kong and go home to Scotland. I want you to pretend to resign from Struan's – of course you'll still be a member of the Inner Office but that'll be secret for the time being. I want you to go to Aberdeen and quietly buy the best property, wharfs, factory areas, a small airfield, potential heliports – Aberdeen's still a backwater so you can get the best cheaply. This's a secret operation, just between us. A few days ago I met a strange fellow, a seismologist called Kirk who convinced me the North Sea's over an enormous oil field. I want the Noble House to be ready to supply the rigs when they're developed.'

'My God, Ian, how could we do that? The North Sea? Even if there's oil there, which sounds impossible, those seas are the worst in the world for most of the year. Wouldn't be possible, all the year round – and anyway the expense'd be prohibitive! How could we do it?'

'That's your problem, laddie.'

Gavallan remembered the laugh and the brimming confidence and, as always, he was warmed. So he had left Hong Kong, Kathy delighted to leave, and he had done everything asked of him.

Almost at once, like a miracle, North Sea oil began to blossom and the major U.S. companies – headed by ExTex, the enormous Texas oil conglomerate, and BP, British Petroleum – rushed in with huge investments. He had been superbly positioned to take advantage of the new El Dorado and the first to recognise that the only efficient way to service the vast discoveries in those violent waters was by helicopter, the first – with Dunross's power – to raise the massive funds needed for helicopter leasing, the first to shove major helicopter manufacturers into size, safety, instrumentation and performance standards undreamed of, and the first to prove that all-weather flying in those foul seas was practical. McIver had done that for him, the flying and developing the necessary techniques quite unknown then.

The North Sea had led to the Gulf, Iran, Malaysia, Nigeria, Uruguay, South Africa – Iran the jewel in his crown, with its enormous potential, vastly profitable, with the very best connections into the ultimate seat of power, the Court, that his Iranian partners had assured him would be equally powerful even though the Shah had been deposed. 'Andy,' General Javadah, the senior partner, stationed in London, had told him yesterday, 'there's nothing to worry about. One of our partners is related to Bakhtiar and, just in case, we've the highest level of contacts with Khomeini's inner circle. Of course, the new era will be more expensive than before . . .'

Gavallan smiled sardonically. Never mind the added expense and that each year the partners become a little more greedy, there's still more than enough left over to keep Iran as our flagship – just so long as she gets back to normal quickly. Ian's gamble paid off a thousandfold for the Noble House – pity he resigned when he did, but then he'd carried Struan's for ten years. That'd be enough for any man – even me. Linbar's right that I want that slot. If I don't get it, by God, Scot will.

24

Meanwhile, onward and upward, the X63s'll put us way out ahead of Imperial and Guerney and make us one of the biggest helicopter-leasing companies in the world. 'In a couple of years, Liz, we'll be the biggest,' he said with total confidence. 'The X63's a smash! Mac'll be fractured when I tell him.'

'Yes,' she said and put down the phone. 'Sorry, Andy, the circuits are still busy. They'll let us know the very moment. Did you tell the taipan the rest of the good news?'

'It wasn't exactly a perfect moment, never mind.' They laughed together. 'I'll reserve that for the board meeting.' An old ship's clock on a bureau began to chime six o'clock. Gavallan reached over and switched on the multiband radio that was on the filing cabinet behind him. Sound of Big Ben tolling the hour . . .

Tehran – McIver's Apartment: Last of the chimes dying away, radio reception minimal, heavy with static: 'This is the BBC World Service, the time is 1700 hours Greenwich Mean Time . . .' 5 p.m. GMT was 8.30 p.m. local Iranian time.

The two men automatically checked their watches. The woman just sipped her vodka martini. The three of them were huddled around the big shortwave battery radio, the broadcast signal faint and heterodyning badly. Outside the apartment the night was dark. There was a distant burst of gunfire. They took no notice. She sipped again, waiting. Inside the apartment it was cold, the central heating off weeks ago. Their only source of warmth now was a small electric fire that, like the dimmed electric lights, was down to half power.

'. . . at 1500 hours GMT there will be a special report on Iran "From Our Own Correspondent" . . .'

'Good,' she muttered and they all nodded. She was fifty-one, young for her age, attractive, blue-eyed and fair-haired, trim, and she wore dark-rimmed glasses. Genevere McIver, Genny for short.

'. . . but first a summary of the world news: in Britain 19,000 workers again went on strike at the Birmingham plant of British Leyland, the country's largest motor car manufacturer, for higher pay: union negotiators representing public-service workers reached an agreement for pay increases of sixteen percent though Prime Minister James Callaghan's Labour government wants to maintain eight point eight percent: the Queen will fly to Kuwait on Monday to begin a three-week visit of the Persian Gulf states: in Washington, Pres –'

The transmission faded completely. The taller man cursed.

25

'Be patient, Charlie,' she said gently. 'It'll come back.'

'Yes, Genny, you're right,' Charlie Pettikin answered. Another burst of machine-gun fire in the distance.

'A bit dicey sending the Queen to Kuwait now, isn't it?' Genny said. Kuwait was an immensely wealthy oil sheikdom just across the Gulf, flanking Saudi Arabia and Iraq. 'Pretty stupid at a time like this, isn't it?'

'Bloody stupid. Bloody government's got its head all the way up,' Duncan McIver, her husband, said sourly. 'All the bloody way to Aberdeen.'

She laughed. 'That's a pretty long way, Duncan.'

'Not far enough for me, Gen!' McIver was a heavyset man of fifty-eight, built like a boxer, with grizzled grey hair. 'Callaghan's a bloody twit and th—' He stopped, hearing faint rumbles of a heavy vehicle going past in the street below. The apartment was on the top floor, the fifth, of the modern residential building in the northern suburbs of Tehran. Another vehicle passed.

'Sounds like more tanks,' she said.

'They're tanks, Genny,' Charlie Pettikin said. He was fifty-six, ex-RAF, originally from South Africa, his hair dark and grey flecked, senior pilot, Iran, and chief of S-G's Iranian Army and Air Force helicopter training programme.

'Perhaps we're in for another bad one,' she said.

For weeks now every day had been bad. First it was martial law in September when public gatherings had been banned and a 9.00 p.m. to 5.00 a.m. curfew imposed by the Shah that had only further inflamed the people. Particularly in the capital Tehran, the oil port of Abadan, and the religious cities of Qom and Meshed. There had been much killing. Then the violence had escalated, the Shah vacillating, then abruptly cancelling martial law in the last days of December and appointing Bakhtiar, a moderate, prime minister, making concessions, and then, incredibly, on January 16 leaving Iran for 'a holiday'. Then Bakhtiar forming his government and Khomeini – still in exile in France – decrying it and anyone who supported it. Riots increasing, the death toll increasing. Bakhtiar trying to negotiate with Khomeini, who refused to see him or talk to him, the people restive, the army restive, then closing all airports against Khomeini, then opening them to him. Then, equally incredibly, eight days ago on February 1, Khomeini returning.

Since then the days have been very bad, she thought.

*　　*　　*

26

That dawn she, her husband and Pettikin had been at Tehran's International Airport. It was a Thursday, very cold but crisp with patches of snow here and there, the wind light. To the north the Elburz Mountains were white-capped, the rising sun blooding the snow. The three of them had been beside the 212 that was standing on the airport apron, well away from the tarmac in front of the terminal. Another 212 was on the other side of the airfield, also ready for instant takeoff – both ordered here by Khomeini's supporters.

This side of the terminal was deserted, except for twenty or so nervous airport officers, most of whom carried submachine guns, waiting near a big black Mercedes and a radio car that was tuned to the tower. It was quiet here – in violent contrast to the inside of the terminal and outside the perimeter fence. Inside the terminal building was a welcoming committee of about a thousand specially invited politicians, ayatollahs, mullahs, newsmen, and hundreds of uniformed police and special Islamic guards with green armbands – nicknamed Green Bands – the mullahs' illegal revolutionary private army. Everyone else had been kept away from the airport, all access roads blocked, guarded and barricaded. But just the other side of these barricades were tens of thousands of anxious people of all ages. Most women wore the chador, the long, shroudlike robe that covered them from head to foot. Beyond these people, lining the ten-mile route, all the way to Behesht-Zahra Cemetery where the Ayatollah was to make his first speech, were five thousand armed police, and around them, crammed together on balconies, in windows, on walls, and in the streets was the biggest gathering of people Iran had ever known, a sea of people – most of Tehran's population. Nearly five million lived in and around the city. All anxious, all nervous, all afraid that there would be a last-moment delay or that perhaps the airport would be closed once more against *him* or that perhaps the air force would shoot *him* down – with or without orders.

Prime Minister Shahpur Bakhtiar, his cabinet and the generals of all the armed services were not at the airport. By choice. Nor were there any of their officers or soldiers. These men waited in their barracks or airfields or ships – all equally anxious and impatient to move.

'I wish you'd stayed at home, Gen,' McIver had said uneasily.

'I wish we'd all stayed at home,' Pettikin said, equally ill at ease.

A week before, McIver had been approached by one of Khomeini's supporters to supply the helicopter to take Khomeini from the airport to Behesht-Zahra. 'Sorry, that's not possible, I haven't the authority to do that,' he had said, aghast. Within an hour the man was back with

Green Bands, McIver's office and the outer offices jammed with them, young, tough, angry-looking men, two with Soviet AK47 automatic rifles over their shoulders, one with a U.S. M16.

'You will supply the helicopter as I have said,' the man told him arrogantly. 'In case crowd control becomes too difficult. Of course all Tehran will be there to greet the Ayatollah, the Blessings of God be upon him.'

'Much as I would like to do that, I can't,' McIver had told him carefully, trying to buy time. He was in an untenable position. Khomeini was being allowed to return, but that was all; if the Bakhtiar government knew that S-G was supplying their arch-enemy with a chopper for a triumphal entry into their capital, they would be very irritated indeed. And even if the government agreed, if anything went wrong, if the Ayatollah was hurt, S-G would be blamed and their lives not worth a bent farthing. 'All our aircraft are leased and I don't have the necessary authority to g –'

'I give you the necessary authority on behalf of the Ayatollah,' the man had said angrily, his voice rising. 'The Ayatollah is the only authority in Iran.'

'Then it should be easy for you to get an Iranian Army or Air Force helicopter –'

'Quiet! You have had the honour to be asked. You will do as you are told. In the Name of Allah, the komiteh has decided you will supply a 212 with your best pilots to take the Ayatollah to where we say, when we say, as we say.'

This was the first time McIver had been confronted by one of the komitehs – small groups of young fundamentalists – that had appeared, seemingly miraculously, the moment the Shah had left Iran, in every village, hamlet, town, and city to seize power. attacking police stations, leading mobs into the streets, taking control wherever they could. Most times a mullah led them. But not always. In the Abadan oil fields the komitehs were said to be left-wing fedayeen – literally 'those who are prepared to sacrifice themselves'.

'You will obey!' the man shook a revolver in his face.

'I'm certainly honoured by your confidence,' McIver had said, the men crowding him, the heavy smell of sweat and unwashed clothes surrounding him. 'I will ask the government for perm –'

'The Bakhtiar government is illegal and not acceptable to the people,' the man had bellowed. At once the others took up the shout and the mood became ugly. One man unslung his automatic rifle. 'You will agree or the komiteh will take further action!'

28

McIver had telexed Andrew Gavallan in Aberdeen, who gave immediate approval provided S-G's Iranian partners approved. The partners could not be found. In desperation McIver contacted the British embassy for advice: 'Well, old boy, you can certainly ask the government, formally or informally, but you'll never get an answer. We're not even certain they'll really allow Khomeini to land, or that the air force won't take matters into their own hands. After all the bloody fellow's an out-and-out revolutionary, openly calling for insurrection against the legal government that everyone else recognises – Her Majesty's Government to boot. Either way, if you're silly enough to ask, the government will certainly remember you embarrassed them and you're damned either way.'

Eventually McIver had worked out an acceptable compromise with the komiteh. 'After all,' he had pointed out with enormous relief, 'it would look very strange if a British aircraft ferried your revered leader into town. Surely it would be better if he was in an Iranian Air Force plane, flown by an Iranian. I'll certainly have one of ours standing by, two in fact, in case of accidents. With our best pilots. Just call us on the radio, call for a CASEVAC and we'll respond at once . . .'

And now he was here, waiting, praying that there was no CASEVAC to which they would have to respond.

The Air France 747 jumbo jet appeared out of the pink haze. For twenty minutes she circled, waiting for clearance to land.

McIver was listening to the tower on the 212's radio. 'Still some problem about security,' he told the other two. 'Wait a minute . . . she's cleared!'

'Here we go,' Pettikin muttered.

They watched her come on to final. The 747 was gleaming white, the French colours sparkling. She inched her way earthward on a perfect approach, then, at the last moment, the pilot put on full power, aborting the landing. 'What the hell's he playing at?' Genny said, her heart fluttering.

'Pilot says he wanted to take a closer look,' McIver told her. 'I think I would too – just to make sure.' He looked at Pettikin who would fly any CASEVAC call from the komiteh. 'I hope to Christ the air force don't do anything crazy.'

'Look!' Genny said.

The jet came on to final and touched down, smoke belched from the tyres, her massive engines roaring into reverse thrust to slow her. At once a Mercedes rushed to intercept her, and as the news spread to those in the terminal, thence to the barricades, thence to the streets, the multitudes went berserk with joy. The chant began: 'Allah-u Akbar . . . Agha uhmad,' God is Great . . . the Master has returned . . .

It seemed to take for ever for the steps to arrive and the doors to open and the stern-faced, black-turbaned, heavily bearded old man to come down the steps, helped by one of the French stewards. He walked through the hastily assembled honour guard of a few mullahs and the Iran Air France crew, to be surrounded by his top aides and the nervous officials and quickly bundled into the car which headed for the terminal. There he was greeted by bedlam as the cheering, screaming, frenzied guests fought with one another to get near him, to touch him, newspapermen from all the world fighting each other for the best-position with their barrage of flash cameras, TV cameras – everyone shouting, Green Bands and police trying to protect him from the crush. Genny could just see him for a moment, a graven statue among the frenzy, then he was swallowed up.

She sipped her martini, remembering, her eyes fixed on the radio, trying to will the broadcast to continue, to blot out the memory of that day and Khomeini's speech at Behesht-Zahra Cemetery, chosen because so many of those massacred on Bloody Friday – martyrs he called them – were buried there.

To blot out the TV pictures they had all seen later of the raging sea of bodies surrounding the motorcade as it inched along – all ideas of security gone – tens of thousands of men, women and young people shouting, struggling, shoving to get closer to him, scrambling all over the Chevy van that he was in, trying to reach him, to touch him, the Ayatollah sitting in the front seat in seeming serenity, occasionally raising his hands at the adulation. People clambering on the bonnet and on the roof, weeping and shouting, calling to him, fighting to keep others off – impossible for the driver to see, at times braking hard to shake people off, at others simply accelerating blindly. To blot out the memory of a youth in a rough brown suit who had scrambled on to the bonnet but could not get a proper grip and slowly rolled off and under the wheels.

Dozens like the youth. Eventually Green Bands had fought their way around and on to the van and called down the helicopter and she remembered the way the helicopter carelessly plummeted down on to the mob that scattered from the blades, bodies everywhere, injured everywhere, then the Ayatollah walking in the centre of his pack of Islamic guards to be helped into the copter, stern-faced, impassive, then the helicopter taking off into the skies to the never-ending torrent of 'Allah-uuuuu Akbar . . . Agha uhmad . . .'

30

'I need another drink,' she said and got up to hide a shiver. 'Can I fix yours, Duncan?'

'Thanks, Gen.'

She went towards the kitchen for some ice. 'Charlie?'

'I'm fine, Genny, I'll get it.'

She stopped as the radio came back strongly: '. . . China reports that there have been serious border clashes with Vietnam and denounces these attacks as further evidence of Soviet hegemony: in Fran . . .' Again the signal vanished, leaving only static.

After a moment Pettikin said, 'I had a drink at the club on the way here. There's a rumour amongst the journalists that Bakhtiar's preparing a showdown. Another was that there's heavy fighting in Meshed after a mob strung up the chief of police and half a dozen of his men.'

'Terrible,' she said, coming back from the kitchen. 'Who's controlling the mobs, Charlie, really controlling them? Is it the communists?'

Pettikin shrugged. 'No one seems to know for certain but the communist Tudeh've got to be stirring it up, outlawed or not. And all the leftists, particularly the mujhadin-al-Khalq, who believe in a sort of marriage between the religions of Islam and Marx, Soviet sponsored. The Shah, the U.S., and most Western governments *know* it's them, aided and heavily abetted by the Soviets north of the border, so of course all the Iranian press agree. So do our Iranian partners, though they're scared out of their pants, not knowing which way to jump, trying to support the Shah and Khomeini equally. I wish to God they'd all settle down. Iran's a great place and I don't plan to move.'

'What about the press?'

'The foreign press're mixed. Some of the Americans agree with the Shah as to who is to blame. Others say it's pure Khomeini, purely religious, and led by him and the mullahs. Then there're those who blame the left-wing fedayeen, or the hard-core fundamentalist Muslim Brotherhood – there was even one sport, I think he was French, who claimed Yasser Arafat and the PLO're . . .' He stopped. The radio came in for a second then went back to emitting static. 'It must be sunspots.'

'Enough to make you want to spit blood,' McIver said. Like Pettikin, he was ex-RAF. He had been the first pilot to join S-G, and now as director of Iran operations, he was also managing director of IHC – Iran Helicopters Company – the fifty-fifty joint venture with the obligatory Iranian partners that S-G leased their helicopters to, the company that got their contracts, made their deals, held the money –

without whom there would be no Iranian operations. He leaned forward to adjust the tuning, changed his mind.

'It'll come back, Duncan,' Genny said confidently. 'I agree Callaghan's a twit.'

He smiled at her. They had been married thirty years. 'You're not bad, Gen. Not bad at all.'

'For that you can have another whisky.'

'Thanks, but this time put some in with the wat –'

'. . . partment of Energy spokesman says that the new fourteen percent OPEC hike will cost the U.S. fifty-one billion for imported oil next year. Also in Washington, President Carter announced, because of the deteriorating situation in Iran, a carrier force has been ordered to proceed from the Philip—' The announcer's voice was drowned by another station, then both faded.

In silence they waited, very tense. The two men glanced at each other, trying to hide their shock. Genny walked over to the whisky bottle that was on the sideboard. Also on the sideboard, taking up most of the space, was the HF radio, McIver's communicator with their helicopter bases all over Iran – conditions permitting. The apartment was big and comfortable, with three bedrooms and two sitting rooms. For the last few months, since martial law and the subsequent escalating street violence, Pettikin had moved in with them – he was single now, divorced a year ago – and this arrangement pleased them all.

A slight wind rattled the windowpanes. Genny glanced outside. There were a few dim lights from the houses opposite, no streetlamps. The low rooftops of the huge city stretched away limitlessly. Snow on them, and on the ground. Most of the five to six million people who lived here lived in squalor. But this area, to the north of Tehran, the best area, where most foreigners and well-to-do Iranians lived, was well policed. Is it wrong to live in the best area if you can afford it? she asked herself. This world's a very strange place, whichever way you add it up.

She made the drink light, mostly soda, and brought it back. 'There's going to be civil war. There's no way we can continue here.'

'We'll be all right, Carter can't let . . .' Abruptly the lights died and the electric fire went out.

'Bugger,' Genny said. 'Thank God we've the butane cooker.'

'Maybe the power cut'll be a short one.' McIver helped her light the candles that were already in place. He glanced at the front door. Beside it was a five-gallon can of petrol – their emergency fuel. He hated the idea of having petrol in the apartment, they all did, particularly when they had to use candles most evenings. But for weeks now it had taken from five to twenty-four hours of lining up at a petrol station and even then the Iranian attendant would more than likely turn you away because you were a foreigner. Many times their car had had its tank drained – locks made no difference. They were luckier than most because they had access to airfield supplies, but for the normal person, particularly a foreigner, the queues made life miserable. Black-market petrol cost as much as 160 rials a litre – $2 a litre, $8 a gallon, when you could get it. 'Mind the iron rations,' he said with a laugh.

'Mac, maybe you should stand a candle on it, just for old times' sake,' Pettikin said.

'Don't tempt him, Charlie! You were saying about Carter?'

'The trouble is if Carter panics and puts in even a few troops – or planes – to support a military coup, it will blow the top off everything. Everyone'll scream like a scalded cat, the Soviets most of all, and they'll have to react and Iran'll become the set piece for World War Three.'

McIver said, 'We've been fighting World War Three, Charlie, since forty-five . . .'

A burst of static cut him off, then the announcer came back again. '. . . for illicit intelligence work: It is reported from Kuwait by the chief of staff of the armed forces that Kuwait has received shipments of arms from the Soviet Union . . .'

'Christ,' both men muttered.

'. . . In Beirut, Yasser Arafat, the PLO leader, declared his organisation will continue to actively assist the revolution of Ayatollah Khomeini. At a press conference in Washington, President Carter reiterated the U.S. support for Iran's Bakhtiar government and the "constitutional process". And finally from Iran itself, Ayatollah Khomeini has threatened to arrest Prime Minister Bakhtiar unless he resigns, and has called on the people to "destroy the terrible monarchy and its illegal government", and on the army "to rise up against their foreign-dominated officers and flee their barracks with their weapons". Throughout the British Isles exceptionally heavy snow, gales and floods have disrupted much of the country, closing Heathrow Airport and grounding all aircraft. And that ends the news summary. The next full report will be at 1800 hours, GMT. You're listening to the World Service of the BBC. And now a report from our farm correspondent, "Poultry and pigs". We begin . . .'

McIver reached over and snapped it off. 'Bloody hell, the whole world's falling apart and the BBC gives us pigs.'

Genny laughed. 'What would you do without the BBC, the telly, and the football pools? Gales and floods.' She picked up the phone on the off chance. It was dead as usual. 'Hope the kids are all right.' They had a son and a daughter, Hamish and Sarah, both married now and on their own and two grandchildren, one from each. 'Little Karen catches colds so badly and Sarah! Even at twenty-three she needs reminding to dress properly! Will that child never grow up?'

Pettikin said, 'It's rotten not being able to phone when you want.'

'Yes. Anyway, it's time to eat. The market was almost empty today for the third day on the trot. So it was a choice of roast ancient mutton again with rice, or a special. I chose the special and used the last two cans. I've corned beef pie, cauliflower au gratin, and treacle tart, and a surprise hors d'oeuvre.' She took a candle and went off to the kitchen and shut the door behind her.

'Wonder why we always get cauliflower au gratin?' McIver watched the candlelight flickering on the kitchen door. 'Hate the bloody stuff! I've told her fifty times . . .' The nightscape suddenly caught his attention. He walked over to the window. The city was empty of light because of the power cut. But southeastward now a red glow lit up the sky. 'Jaleh, again,' he said simply.

On September 8, five months ago, tens of thousands of people had taken to the streets of Tehran to protest against the Shah's imposition of martial law. There was widespread destruction, particularly in Jaleh – a poor, densely populated suburb – where bonfires were lit and barricades of burning tyres set up. When the security forces arrived, the raging, milling crowd shouting 'Death to the Shah' refused to disperse. The clash was violent. Tear gas didn't work. Guns did. Estimates of the death toll ranged from an official 97 to 250 according to some witnesses, to 2,000 to 3,000 by the militant opposition groups.

In the following crackdown to that 'Bloody Friday', a vast number of opposition politicians, dissidents and hostiles were arrested and detained – later the government admitted 1,106 – along with two ayatollahs, which further inflamed the multitudes.

McIver felt very sad, watching the glow. If it weren't for the ayatollahs, he thought, particularly Khomeini, none of it would have happened. Years ago when McIver had first come to Iran he had asked a friend in the British embassy what ayatollah meant. 'It's an Arabic word, ayat'Allah, and means "Reflection of God".'

'He's a priest?'

'Not at all, there are no priests in Islam, the name of their religion – that's another Arabic word, it means "submission", submission to the will of God.'

'What?'

34

'Well,' his friend had said with a laugh, 'I'll explain but you've got to be a little patient. First, Iranians are not Arabs but Aryans, and the vast majority are Shi'ite Muslims, a volatile sometimes mystical breakaway sect. Arabs are mostly orthodox Sunni – they make up most of the world's billion Muslims – and the sects are somewhat like our Protestants and Catholics and they've fought each other just as viciously. But all share the same overarching belief, that there is one God, Allah – the Arabic word for God – that Mohammed, a man of Mecca who lived from A.D. 570 to 632, was His Prophet, and that the words of the Koran proclaimed by him and written down by others over many years after his death came directly from God and contain all instruction that is necessary for an individual or society to live by.'

'Everything? That's not possible.'

'For Muslims it is, Mac, today, tomorrow, for ever. But "ayatollah" is a title peculiar to Shi'ites and granted by consensus and popular acclaim by the congregation of a mosque – another Arabic word meaning "meeting place", which is all it is, a meeting place, absolutely not a church – to a mullah who exhibits those characteristics most sought after and admired amongst the Shi'ites: piety, poverty, learning – but only the Holy Books, the Koran and the Sunna – and leadership, with a big emphasis on leadership. In Islam there's no separation between religion and politics, there can be none, and the Shi'ite mullahs of Iran, since the beginning, have been fanatic guardians of the Koran and Sunna, fanatic leaders and whenever necessary fighting revolutionaries.'

'If an ayatollah or mullah's not a priest, what is he?'

'Mullah means "leader", he who leads prayers in a mosque. Anyone can be a mullah, providing he's a man, and Muslim. Anyone. There's no clergy in Islam, none, no one between you and God, that's one of the beauties of it, but not to Shi'ites. Shi'ites believe that, after the Prophet, the earth should be ruled by a charismatic, semi-divine infallible leader, the Imam, who acts as an intermediary between the human and the divine – and that's where the great split came about between Sunni and Shi'ite, and their wars were just as bloody as the Plantagenets'. Where Sunnis believe in consensus, Shi'ites accept an Imam's authority.'

'Then who chooses the man to be Imam?'

'That was the whole problem. When Mohammed died – by the way he never claimed to be anything other than mortal although last of the Prophets – he left neither sons nor a chosen successor, a caliph. Shi'ites believed leadership should remain with the Prophet's family and the Caliph could only be Ali, his cousin and son-in-law who had married

35

Fatima, his favourite daughter. But the orthodox Sunnis, following historic tribal custom which applies even today, believed a leader should only be chosen by consensus. They proved to be stronger, so the first three Caliphs were voted in – two were murdered by other Sunnis – then, at long last for the Shi'ites, Ali became Caliph, in their fervent belief the first Imam.'

'They claimed he was semi-divine?'

'Divinely guided, Mac. Ali lasted five years, then he was murdered – Shi'ites say martyred. His eldest son became Imam, then was thrust aside by a usurping Sunni. His second son, the revered, twenty-five-year-old Hussain, raised an army against the usurper but was slaughtered – martyred – with all his people, including his brother's two young sons, his own five-year-old son, and suckling babe. That happened on the tenth day of Muhrarram, in A.D. 650 by our counting, 61 by theirs, and they still celebrate Hussain's martyrdom as their most holy day.'

'That's the day they have the processions and whip themselves, stick hooks into themselves, mortify themselves?'

'Yes, mad from our point of view. Reza Shah outlawed the custom. But Shi'ism is a passionate religion, needing outward expressions of penitence and mourning. So martyrdom is deeply embedded in Shi'ites, and in Iran venerated. Also rebellion against usurpers.'

'So the battle is joined – the Faithful against the Shah?'

'Oh, yes. Fanatically on both sides. For the Shi'ites, the mullah is the sole interpreting medium which therefore gives him enormous power. He is leader, interpreter, lawgiver, judge, and leader. And the greatest of mullahs are ayatollahs.'

And Khomeini is the Grand Ayatollah, McIver was thinking, staring at the bloody nightscape over Jaleh. He's it, and like it or not, all the killing, all the bloodshed and suffering and madness has to be laid at his doorstep, justified or not . . .

'Mac!'

'Oh, sorry, Charlie,' he said, coming back to himself. 'I was miles away. What?' He glanced at the kitchen door. It was still closed.

'Don't you think you should get Genny out of Iran?' Pettikin asked quietly. 'It's getting pretty smelly.'

'She won't bloody go. I've told her fifty times, asked her fifty times, but she's as obstinate as a bloody mule,' McIver replied as quietly. 'She just bloody smiles and says: "When you go, I go." ' He finished his whisky, glanced at the door, and hastily poured himself another. Stronger. 'Charlie, you talk to her. She'll listen to y –'

'The hell she will.'

'You're right. Bloody women. Bloody obstinate. They're all the bloody same.' They laughed.

After a pause, Pettikin said, 'How's Sharazad?'

McIver thought a moment. 'Tom Lochart's a lucky man.'

'Why didn't she go back with him on leave and stay in England until Iran settles down?'

'There's no reason for her to go – she has no family or friends there. She wanted him to see his kids, Christmas and all that. She said she felt she'd stir things up and be in the way if she went along. Deirdre Lochart's still very pissed off with the divorce, and anyway Sharazad's family's here and you know how strong Iranians are on family. She won't leave until Tom goes and even then I don't know. And as for Tom, if I tried to post him I think he'd quit. He'll stay for ever. Like you.' He smiled. 'Why do you stay?'

'Best posting I've ever had, when it was normal. Can fly all I want, ski winters, sail summers . . . but let's face it, Mac, Claire always hated it here. For years she spent more time in England than here, so she could be near Jason and Beatrice, her own family, and our grandchild. At least the parting of the ways was friendly. Chopper pilots shouldn't be married anyway, have to move about too much. I'm a born expatriate, I'll die one. Don't want to go back to Cape Town – hardly know that place anyway – and can't stand those bloody English winters.' He sipped his beer in the semi-darkness. 'Insha' Allah,' he said with finality. In God's hands. The thought pleased him.

Unexpectedly the telephone jangled, startling them. For months now the phone system had been unreliable – for the last few weeks impossible and almost non-existent, with perpetually crossed lines, wrong numbers, and no dial tones that miraculously cleared for no apparent reason for a day or an hour, to fall back like a shroud again, equally for no reason.

'Five pounds it's a bill collector,' Pettikin said, smiling at Genny who came out of the kitchen, equally startled at hearing the bell.

'That's no bet, Charlie!' Banks had been on strike and closed for two months in response to Khomeini's call for a general strike, so no one – individuals, companies, or even the government – had been able to get any cash out and most Iranians used cash and not cheques.

McIver picked up the phone not knowing what to expect. Or who. 'Hello.'

'Good God, the bloody thing's working,' the voice said. 'Duncan, can you hear me?'

'Yes, yes, I can. Just. Who's this?'

'Talbot, George Talbot at the British embassy. Sorry, old boy, but the stuff is hitting the fan. Khomeini's named Mehdi Bazargan prime minister and called for Bakhtiar's resignation or else. About a million people are in the streets of Tehran right now looking for trouble. We've just heard there's a revolt of airmen at Doshan Tappeh – and Bakhtiar's said if they don't quit he'll order in the Immortals.' The Immortals were crack units of the fanatically pro-Shah Imperial Guards. 'Her Majesty's Government, along with the U.S., Canadian, et al., are advising all non-essential nationals to leave the country at once . . .'

McIver tried to keep the shock off his face and mouthed to the others, 'Talbot at the embassy.'

'. . . Yesterday an American of ExTex Oil and an Iranian oil official were ambushed and killed by "unidentified gunmen" in the southwest, near Ahwaz' – McIver's heart skipped another beat – '. . . you're operating down there still, aren't you?'

'Near there, at Bandar-e Delam on the coast,' McIver said, no change in his voice.

'How many British nationals do you have here, excluding dependents?'

McIver thought a moment. 'Forty-five, out of our present complement of sixty-seven, that's twenty-six pilots, thirty-six mechanic/engineers, five admin, which's pretty basic for us.'

'Who're the others?'

'Four Americans, three German, two French, and one Finn – all pilots. Two American mechanics. We'd treat all our lads as British if necessary.'

'Dependants?'

'Four, all wives, no children. We got the rest out three weeks ago. Genny's still here, one American at Kowiss and two Iranians.'

'You'd better get both the Iranian wives into their embassies tomorrow – with their marriage certificates. They're in Tehran?'

'One is, one's in Tabriz.'

'You'd better get them new passports as fast as possible.'

By Iranian law all Iranian nationals coming back into the country had to surrender their passports to Immigration at the point of entry, to be held until they wished to leave again. To leave they had to apply in person to the correct government office for an exit permit for which they needed a valid identity card, a satisfactory reason for wanting to go abroad, and, if by air, a valid prepaid ticket for a specific flight. To get this exit permit might take days or weeks. Normally.

'Thank God we don't have that problem,' McIver said.

'We can thank God we're British,' Talbot went on. 'Fortunately we don't have any squabbles with the Ayatollah, Bakhtiar, or the generals. Still, any foreigners are liable for a lot of flak so we're formally advising you to send dependants off, lickety-split, and cut the others down to basic – for the time being. The airport's going to be a mess from tomorrow on – we estimate there are still about five thousand expats, most of them American – but we've asked British Airways to cooperate and increase flights for us and our nationals. The bugger of it is that all civilian air traffic controllers are still totally out on strike, Bakhtiar's ordered in the military controllers and they're even more punctilious if that's possible. We're sure it's going to be the exodus over again.'

'Oh, God!'

A few weeks ago, after months of escalating threats against foreigners – mostly against Americans because of Khomeini's constant attacks on American materialism as 'the Great Satan' – a rampaging mob went berserk in the industrial city of Isfahan, with its enormous steel complex, petrochemical refinery, ordnance and helicopter factories, and where a large proportion of the 50,000-odd American expats and their dependants worked and lived. The mobs burned banks – the Koran forbade lending money for profit – liquor stores – the Koran forbade the drinking of alcohol – and two movie houses – places of 'pornography and Western propaganda', always particular targets for the fundamentalists – then attacked factory installations, peppered the four-storey Grumman Aircraft HQ with Molotov cocktails, and burned it to the ground. That precipitated the 'exodus'.

Thousands converged on Tehran Airport, mostly dependants, clogging it as would-be passengers scrambled for the few available seats, turning the airport and its lobbies into a disaster area with men, women and children camping there, afraid to lose their places, barely enough room to stand, patiently waiting, sleeping, pushing, demanding, whining, shouting, or just stoic. No schedules, no priorities, each airplane overbooked twenty times, no computer ticketing, just slowly handwritten by a few sullen officials – most of whom were openly hostile and non-English-speaking. Quickly the airport became foul and the mood ugly.

In desperation some companies chartered their own airplanes to pull out their own people. United States Air Force transports came to take out the military dependants while all embassies tried to play down the extent of the evacuation, not wanting to further embarrass the Shah, their stalwart ally of twenty years. Adding to the chaos were thousands of Iranians, all hoping to flee while there was still time to flee. The unscrupulous and the wealthy jumped the queues. Many an official became rich and then more greedy and richer still. Then the air traffic controllers struck, shutting down the airport completely.

For two days no flights came in or left. The crowds streamed away or stayed. Then some of the controllers went back to work and it began again. Rumours of incoming flights. Rushing to the airport with the kids and the luggage of years, or with no luggage, for a guaranteed seat that never was, back to Tehran again, half a thousand waiting in the taxi rank ahead of you, most taxis on strike – back to the hotel at length, your hotel room long since sold to another, all banks closed so no money to grease the ever-open hands.

At length most foreigners who wanted to leave left. Those who stayed to keep the businesses running, the oil fields serviced, airplanes flying, nuclear plants abuilding, chemical plants working, tankers moving – and to protect their gigantic investments – kept a lower profile, particularly if they were American. Khomeini had said, 'If the foreigner wants to leave, let him leave; it is American materialism that is the Great Satan . . .'

McIver held the phone closer to his ear as the volume slipped a fraction, afraid that the connection would vanish. 'Yes, George, you were saying?'

Talbot continued: 'I was just saying, Duncan, we're quite sure everything's going to work out eventually. There's no way in the world the pot will completely blow up. An unofficial source says a deal's already in place for the Shah to abdicate in favour of his son Reza – the compromise HM Government advocates. The transition to constitutional government may be a bit wobbly but nothing to worry about. Sorry, got to dash – let me know what you decide an –'

The phone went dead.

McIver cursed, jiggled the connectors to no avail, and told Genny and Charlie what Talbot had said. Genny smiled sweetly. 'Don't look at me, the answer's no. I agr –'

'But, Gen, Tal –'

'I agree the others should go but this one's staying. Food's almost ready.' She went back to the kitchen and closed the door, cutting off further argument.

'Well she's bloody going and that's it,' McIver said.

'My year's salary says she won't – until you leave. Why don't you go for God's sake? I can look after everything.'

'No. Thanks, but no.' Then McIver beamed in the semi-darkness. 'Actually it's like being back in the war, isn't it? Back in the bloody blackout. Nothing to worry about except get with it and look after the troops and obey orders.' He watched Pettikin for a while, trying to raise their base at Bandar-e Delam. 'Did you know the American who was killed, Stanson?'

'No. You?'

'Yes. Just an ordinary sort of fellow, an area manager for ExTex. I met him once. There was a story he was CIA but I think that was just a rumour.' McIver frowned at his glass. 'Talbot was right about one thing: we're bloody lucky to be British. Tough on the Yanks. Not fair.'

'Yes, but you've covered ours as best you can.'

'Hope so.' When the Shah had left and violence everywhere increased, McIver had issued British IDs to all Americans. 'They should be all right unless the Green Bands, police, or SAVAK check them against their licences.' By Iranian law all foreigners had to have a current visa, which had to be cancelled before they could leave the country, a current ID card giving their corporate affiliate – and all pilots a current annual Iran pilot's licence. For a further measure of safety McIver had had corporate IDs made and signed by the chief of their Iranian partners in Tehran, General Valik. So far there had been no problems. To the Americans, McIver had said, 'Better you have these to show if necessary,' and had issued orders for all personnel to carry photographs of both Khomeini and the Shah. 'Make sure you use the right one if you're stopped!'

Pettikin was trying to call Bandar-e Delam on the HF with no success. 'We'll try later,' McIver said. 'All bases'll be listening out at 0830 – that'll give us time to decide what to do. Christ, it's going to be bloody difficult. What do you think? Status quo, except for dependants?'

Very concerned, Pettikin got up and took a candle and peered at the operations map pinned to the wall. It showed the status of their bases, crew, ground staff, and aircraft. The bases were scattered over Iran, from air force and army training bases at Tehran and Isfahan, to high-altitude oil-rig support in the Zagros, a logging operation in Tabriz in the northwest, a uranium survey team near the Afghan border, from a pipeline survey on the Caspian, to four oil operations on or near the Gulf, and the last, far to the southeast, another at Lengeh on the Strait of Hormuz. Of these only five were operational now: Lengeh, Kowiss, Bandar-e Delam, Zagros and Tabriz. 'We've fifteen 212s, including two non-operational on their two-thousand-hour checks, seven 206s, and three Alouettes, all supposed to be working at the moment . . .'

'And all leased on binding legal contracts, none of which have been

41

rescinded, but none of which we're being paid for,' McIver said testily. 'There's no way we can base them all at Kowiss – we can't even legally remove any one of them without the approval of the contractor, or our dear partners' approval – not unless we could declare *force majeure*.'

'There isn't any yet. It has to be status quo, as long as we can. Talbot sounded confident. Status quo.'

'I wish it was status quo, Charlie. My God, this time last year we had almost forty 212s working and all the rest.' McIver poured himself another whisky.

'You'd better go easy,' Pettikin said quietly. 'Genny'll give you hell. You know your blood pressure's up and you're not to drink.'

'It's medicinal, for Christ's sweet sake.' A candle guttered and went out. McIver got up and lit another and went back to staring at the map. 'I think we'd better get Azadeh and the Flying Finn back. His 212's on its fifteen-hundred-hour so he could be spared for a couple of days.' This was Captain Erikki Yokkonen and his Iranian wife, Azadeh, and their base was near Tabriz in East Azerbaijan Province, to the far northwest, near the Soviet border. 'Why not take a 206 and fetch them? That'd save him three hundred and fifty miles of lousy driving and we've got to take him some spares.'

Pettikin was beaming. 'Thanks, I could do with an outing. I'll file a flight plan by HF tonight and leave at dawn, refuel at Bandar-e Pahlavi, and buy us some caviar.'

'Dreamer. But Gen'd like that. You know what I think of the stuff.' McIver turned away from the map. 'We're very exposed, Charlie, if things got dicey.'

'Only if it's in the cards.'

McIver nodded. Absently his eyes fell on the telephone. He picked it up. Now there was a dialling tone. Excitedly he began to dial: 00, international; 44, British Isles; 224, Aberdeen in Scotland; 765–8080. He waited and waited, then his face lit up. 'Christ, I'm through!'

'S-G Helicopters, hold the line, please,' the operator said before he could interrupt and put him on hold. He waited, fuming. 'S-G Helico –'

'This's McIver in Tehran, give me the Old Man, please.'

'He's on the phone, Mr. McIver.' The girl sniffed. 'I'll give you his secretary.'

'Hello, Mac!' Liz Chen said almost at once. 'Hang on a tick, I'll get Himself. You all right? We've been trying to get you for days, hang on.'

'All right, Liz.'

A moment, then Gavallan said happily, 'Mac? Christ, how did you get through? Wonderful to hear from you – I've got a laddie permanently dialling you, your office, your apartment, ten hours a day. How's Genny? How did you get through?'

'Just luck, Andy. I'm at home. I'd better be fast in case we're cut off.' McIver told him most of what Talbot had said. He had to be circumspect because rumour had it that SAVAK, the Iranian secret police, often tapped telephones, particularly of foreigners. It was standing company procedure for the last two years to presume someone was listening – SAVAK, CIA, MI5, KGB, someone.

There was a moment's silence. 'First, obey the embassy and get all our dependants out at once. Alert the Finnish embassy for Azadeh's passport. Tell Tom Lochart to expedite Sharazad's – I got him to apply two weeks ago, just in case. He's, er, got some mail for you, by the way.'

McIver's heart picked up a beat. 'Good, he'll be in tomorrow.'

'I'll get on to BA and see if I can get them guaranteed seating. As backup I'll send our company 125. She's scheduled for Tehran tomorrow. If you've any problem with BA, send all dependants and spare bods out by her, starting tomorrow. Tehran's still open, isn't it?'

'It was today,' McIver said carefully.

He heard Gavallan say equally carefully, 'The authorities, thank God, have everything under control.'

'Yes.'

'Mac, what do you recommend about our Iranian ops?'

McIver took a deep breath. 'Status quo.'

'Good. All indications here, up to the highest levels, say it should be business as usual soon. We've got lots of face in Iran. And future. Listen, Mac, that rumour about Guerney was correct.'

McIver brightened perceptibly. 'You're sure?'

'Yes. A few minutes ago I got a telex from IranOil confirming we'll get all Guerney contracts at Kharg, Kowiss, Zagros and Lengeh to begin with. Apparently the order to squeeze came from on high, and I did have to make a generous pishkesh contribution to our partners' slush fund.' A pishkesh was an ancient Iranian custom, a gift given him in advance for a favour that might be granted. It was also ancient custom for any official legitimately to keep pishkesh given him in the course of his work. How else could he live? 'But never mind that, we'll quadruple our Iranian profits, laddie.'

'That's wonderful, Andy.'

'And that's not all: Mac, I've just ordered another twenty 212s and today I confirmed the order for six X63s – she's a smasher!'

'Christ, Andy, that's fantastic – but you're pushing it, aren't you?'

'Iran may be, er, in temporary difficulties, but the rest of the world's

43

scared fartless about alternate sources of oil. The Yanks have their knickers in a twist, laddie.' The voice picked up another beat. 'I've just confirmed another huge deal with ExTex for new contracts in Nigeria, Saudi and Borneo, another with All-Gulf Oil in the Emirates. In the North Sea it's just us, Guerney, and Imperial Helicopters.' Imperial Helicopters was a subsidiary of Imperial Air, the second semi-government airline in opposition to British Airways. 'It's paramount you keep everything stable in Iran – our contracts, aircraft and spares're part of our collateral for the new aircraft. For God's sake keep our dear partners on the straight and narrow. How are the dear sweet people?'

'Just the usual.'

Gavallan knew this meant rotten as usual. 'I've just had a session with General Javadah in London myself.' Javadah had left Iran with all his family a year ago, just before the troubles became overt. For the past three months two of their other Iranian partners, and families, had been visiting London 'for medical reasons', four others were in America also with their families. Three remained in Tehran. 'He's bullish – though expensive. What about Kharg? Can we get back in yet?' Kharg Island was the enormously important and immense offshore terminal in the Gulf, through which Iran exported most of its oil – this time last year almost 6 million barrels a day, now down to a mere trickle of 600,000 barrels a day. Kharg had been a giant source of revenue for S-G but three weeks ago the S-G crew and airplanes under the command of Captain Rudiger Lutz had been ordered off the island by the military commander to the nearby coast port of Bandar-e Delam. 'Any chance of our getting back?'

'Not yet but we can still service all our seaborne rigs from Bandar-e Delam when the strikes are over.' McIver wanted to add, urgently: Andy, I saw Rudiger and he told me privately he was glad to be off the island, that it was a time bomb waiting to explode – so easy to sabotage. Instead he said gruffly, 'I'll send a report with the dependants. The authorities have everything under control.'

'Yes. How's young Scot?'

'Doing very well. He'll be operational on the 212 any day now.' McIver smiled. He had been Scot's first instructor.

'Good. I may pull him back to train for the X63s.'

'No, give him time, Andy. He's good but he needs time. Let him fly the 212 for a year.'

'Whatever you say. How're things at Lengeh?' This was their most southeasterly base that serviced the whole Strait of Hormuz area.

'Good. Scragger reported the new Siri rigs are on stream, their

44

tanks're full to brimming, and at last report the strikes haven't affected them at all – we think that's because Siri's French developed and because they gave Khomeini sanctuary when he got expelled from Iraq a few months ago.'

'Good. I'll pass that on. When you talk to that old bugger Scrag give him my best.'

'Andy, don't you think it's time you talked to him about retiring an –'

'How's his medical?'

'Perfect, but h –'

'It's every three months and as tough and serious as we can make it?'

'Yes, but h –'

'Then he flies until it isn't.'

'Yes but he's sixty-three and it's about ti –'

'So long as he's legal he's a captain – that's what I promised him.'

'All right but how that cantankerous, lecherous, independent old sod stays perfect I'm damned if I know. I swear to God I still believe he's cheating somehow though there's no way he can fiddle his medical. No way. I've even flown with him and there's no way even I wouldn't pass him A1.'

McIver put him away for more important problems. 'Andy, I've got to have some money. Cash.'

'It's in the post.'

McIver heard the rich laugh and felt the warmer for it. 'Up yours, Chinaboy!' he said. Chinaboy was his private nickname for Gavallan who, before going to Aberdeen, had spent most of his previous life as a China trader, based first in Shanghai, then with Struan's in Hong Kong where they had first met. At that time McIver had had a small, struggling helicopter service in the colony. 'For God's sake, we're way behind paying our ground crews, there's all the pilots' expenses, almost everything's got to be bought on the . . .' He stopped himself in time. In case someone was listening. He was going to say black market. 'The bloody banks are still closed and the little cash I've left is for *heung yau*.' He used the Cantonese expression, literally meaning 'fragrant grease', the money used to grease palms.

'Javadah's promised that General Valik in Tehran'll give you half a million rials tomorrow. I've got a telex confirming.'

'But that's barely $6,000 and we've bills for twenty times that amount.'

'I know that, laddie, but he says both Bakhtiar and the Ayatollah want the banks open so they'll open within the week. As soon as they're open he swears IHC will pay us everything they owe.'

'Meanwhile has he released A stock yet?' This was a code that McIver and Gavallan used for funds held outside Iran by IHC, almost six million dollars. IHC was almost four million dollars behind on payments to S-G.

'No. He claims that he has to have the partners' formal approval. The standoff stays.'

Thank God for that, McIver thought. Three signatures were needed on this account, two from the partners, one from S-G, so neither side could touch this particular fund without the other. 'It's pretty dicey, Andy. With the down payment on the new aircraft, lease payments on our equipment here, you're on the edge, aren't you?'

'All life's on the edge, Mac. But the future's rosy.'

Yes, McIver thought, for the helicopter business. But here in Iran? Last year the partners had forced Gavallan to assign real ownership of all S-G helicopters and spares in Iran to IHC. Gavallan had agreed, providing he could buy everything back at a moment's notice, without a refusal on their part, and provided they kept up the lease payments on the equipment on time and made good any bad debts. Since the crisis began and the banks closed, IHC had been in default and Gavallan had been making the lease payments on all Iranian-based helicopters from S-G funds in Aberdeen – the partners claiming it was not their fault the banks had closed, Javadah and Valik saying as soon as everything's normal of course we'll repay everything – don't forget, Andrew, we've got you all the best contracts for years: we got them, we did; without us S-G can't operate in Iran. As soon as everything's normal . . .

Gavallan was saying, 'Our Iranian contracts're still very profitable, we can't fault our partners on that, and with Guerney's we'll be like pigs in waller!' Yes, McIver thought, even though they're squeezing and squeezing and each year our share gets smaller and theirs fatter. '. . . They've a lock on the country, always have had, and they swear by all that's holy, it'll all settle down. They have to have choppers to service their fields. Everyone here says it'll blow over. The minister, their ambassador, ours. Why shouldn't it? The Shah did his best to modernise, the people's income's up, illiteracy down. Oil revenues are huge – and'll go higher once this mess's over, the minister says. So do my contacts in Washington, even old Willie in ExTex, for God's sake, and he should know if anyone does. The betting's fifty to one it'll all be normal in six months, with the Shah abdicating in favour of his son Reza and a constitutional monarchy. Meanwhile I think we sh –'

The line went dead. McIver jigged the plunger anxiously. When the line came back it was just a constant busy signal. Angrily he slammed the receiver down. The lights came on suddenly.

'Bugger,' Genny said, 'candlelight's so much prettier.'

Pettikin smiled and switched the lights off. The room was prettier, more intimate, and the silver sparkled on the table she had laid earlier. 'You're right, Genny, right again.'

'Thanks, Charlie. You get an extra helping. Dinner's almost up. Duncan, you can have another whisky, not as strong as the one you sneaked – don't look so innocent – but after speaking to our Fearless Leader even I need extra sustenance. You can tell me what he said over dinner.' She left them.

McIver told Pettikin most of what Gavallan had said – Pettikin was not a director of S-G or IHC so, of necessity, McIver had to keep his own counsel on much of it. Deep in thought, he wandered over to the window, glad to have talked to his old friend. It's been a lot of years, he thought. Fourteen.

In the summer of '65 when the Colony was poised on revolution with Mao Tse-tung's Red Guards rampaging all over mainland China, tearing the motherland apart and now spilling over into the streets of Hong Kong and Kowloon, Gavallan's letter had arrived. At that time McIver's helicopter business was on the edge of disaster, he was behind on lease payments on his small chopper, and Genny was trying to cope with two teenage children in a tiny, noisy flat in Kowloon where the riots were the worst.

'For God's sake, Gen, look at this!' The letter said: 'Dear Mr. McIver, You may remember we met once or twice at the races when I was with Struan's a few years back – we both won a bundle on a gelding called Chinaboy. The taipan, Ian Dunross, suggested I write to you as I have great need of your expertise immediately – I know that you taught him to fly a chopper, and he recommends you highly. North Sea oil is a fait accompli. I have a theory that the only way to supply the rigs in all weather conditions is by helicopter. That is presently not possible – I think you'd call it Instrument Flight Rules, IFR. We could make it possible. I've got the weather, you've got the skill. One thousand pounds a month, a three-year contract to prove or disprove, a bonus based on success, transportation for you and your family back to Aberdeen, and a case of Loch Vay whisky at Christmas. Please phone as soon as possible . . .'

Without saying a word Genny had casually handed him back the

47

letter and started out of the room, the constant noise of the great city –
traffic, Klaxons, street vendors, ships, jets, blaring discordant Chinese
music through the windows that rattled in the wind.

'Where the hell're you going?'

'To pack.' Then she laughed and ran back and hugged him. 'It's a gift
from heaven, Duncan, quick, call him, call him now . . .'

'But Aberdeen? IFR in all weather? My God, Gen, it's never been
done. There isn't the instrumentation, I don't know if it's poss –'

'For you it is, my lad. Of course. Now, where the devil have Hamish
and Sarah gone?'

'Today's Saturday, they've gone to the movies an –'

A brick crashed through one of the windows, and the tumult of a riot
began again. Their apartment was on the second floor and faced a
narrow street in the heavily populated Mong Kok area of Kowloon.
McIver pulled Genny to safety then cautiously looked out. In the street
below, five to ten thousand Chinese, all shouting, Mao, Mao, Kwai
Loh! Kwai Loh – Foreign Devil, Foreign Devil – their usual battle cry,
were surging towards the police station a hundred yards away where a
small detachment of uniformed Chinese police and three British
officers waited silently behind a barricade.

'My God, Gen, they're armed!' McIver gasped. Usually the police
just had batons. Yesterday the Swiss consul and his wife had been
burned to death nearby when a mob had overturned their car and set it
on fire. Last night on radio and television the governor had warned that
he had ordered the police to take whatever steps necessary to stop all
rioting. 'Get down, Gen, out of the way . . .'

His words were drowned by police loudspeakers as the superintendent commanded the massed rioters in Cantonese and English to
disperse. The mob paid no attention and attacked the barricade. Again
the order to stop was disregarded. Then the firing began and those in
front panicked and were trampled as others fought to get away. Soon
the street was clear except for the dozen or so bodies lying in the dirt. It
was the same on Hong Kong island. The next day the whole Colony
was once more at peace, there were no more serious riots, only a few
pockets of hard-core Red Guards trying to whip up the crowds who
were quickly deported.

Within the week McIver sold his interest in his helicopter business,
flew to Aberdeen ahead of Genny, and hurled himself into his new job
with gusto. It had taken her a month to pack, settle their apartment,
and sell what they didn't need. By the time she arrived he had an found
an ideal apartment near the McCloud heliport that she promptly

declined: 'For goodness sake, Duncan, it's a million miles away from the nearest school. An apartment in Aberdeen? Now that you're as rich as Dunross, we, my lad, we are renting a house . . .'

He smiled to himself, thinking about those early days, Genny loving being back in Scotland – she had never really liked Hong Kong, life so difficult there with little money and children to care for – he loving his work, Gavallan a great man to work for and with, but hating the North Sea, all the cold and the wet and the aches that the salt-heavy air brought. But the five-odd years there had been worth it, renewing and increasing his old contacts in the still tiny international helicopter world – most of the pilots ex-RAF, RCAF, RAAF, USAF, and all the allied services – against the day they could expand. Always a generous bonus at Christmas, carefully put away for retirement, and always the case of Loch Vay: 'Andy, that was the one condition that really got me!' Gavallan always the driving force, living up to his motto for the company, Be Bold. In East Scotland nowadays, Gavallan was known as 'the Laird', from Aberdeen to Inverness and south as far as Dundee, with tentacles reaching to London, New York, Houston – wherever there was oil power. Yes, old Chinaboy's great and he can also wrap you and most men around his little finger, McIver thought without rancour. Look how you got here . . .

'Listen, Mac,' Andrew Gavallan had said one day in the late sixties, 'I've just met a top general in the Iranian General Staff at a shoot. General Beni-Hassan. Great shot, he got twenty brace to my fifteen! Over the weekend I spent a lot of time with him and sold him on close-support helicopters for infantry and tank regiments along with a whole programme for training their army and air force – as well as helicopters for their oil business. We, laddie, are in like Flynn.'

'But we're not equipped to do half of that.'

'Beni-Hassan's a smashing fellow and the Shah's a really go-ahead monarch – with great plans for modernisation. You know anything about Iran?'

'No, Chinaboy,' McIver had said, suspiciously, recognising the twinkling exuberance. 'Why?'

'You're booked on Friday for Bahrain, you and Genny . . . now wait a moment, Mac! What do you know about Sheik Aviation?'

'Genny's happy in Aberdeen, she doesn't want to move, the kids are finishing school, we've just put the down payment on a house, we're not moving and Genny'll kill you.'

'Of course,' Gavallan said airily. 'Sheik Aviation?'

'It's a small but good helicopter company that services the Gulf. They've three 206s and a few fixed-wing feeder airplanes, based in Bahrain. Well thought of and they do a lot of work for ARAMCO, ExTex, and I think IranOil. Owned and operated by Jock Forsyth, ex-paras and pilot who formed the company in the fifties with an old chum of mine, Scrag Scragger, an Aussie. Scrag's the real owner, ex-RAAF, AFC and Bar, DFC and Bar, now a chopper fanatic. First they were based in Singapore where I first met Scrag. We, er, we were on a bender and I don't remember who started it but the others said it was a draw. Then they moved to the Gulf with an ex-ExTex executive who happened to have a great contract to launch them there. Why?'

'I've just bought them. You take over as managing director on Monday. Scragger and all their pilots and personnel will stay on or not, as you suggest, but I think we'll need their knowledge – I found them all good fellows – Forsyth's happy to retire to Devon. Curious, Scragger didn't mention he knew you, but then I only spent a few moments with him and dealt with Forsyth. From now on we're S-G Helicopters Ltd. Next Friday I want you to go to Tehran . . . listen, for Christ's sake . . . on Friday to set up an HQ there. I've made a date for you to meet Beni-Hassan and sign the papers for the air force deal. He said he'd be glad to introduce us to the right people, all over. Oh, yes, you've ten percent of all profits, ten percent of the stock in the new Iran subsidiary, you're managing director of Iran – which includes the rest of the Gulf for the time being . . .'

Of course McIver had gone. He could never resist Andrew Gavallan and he had enjoyed every moment, but he had never found out how Gavallan had persuaded Genny. When he had gone home that night she had his whisky and soda ready and wore a sweet smile. 'Hello, dear, did you have a nice day?'

'Yes, what's up?' he asked suspiciously.

'You're what's up. Andy says there's a wonderful new opportunity for us in some place called Tehran in some place called Persia.'

'Iran. It used to be called Persia, Gen, modern word's Iran. I, er, I th –'

'How exciting! When are we leaving?'

'Er, well, Gen, I thought we'd talk it over and if you like I've fixed it so that I could do two months on and one month off back here an –'

'And what do you plan to do for the two months, nights and Sundays?'

'I, er, well I'll be working like the devil and there wo –'

'Sheik Aviation? You and old Scragger east of Suez together drinking and cavorting?'

'Who, me? Come on, there'll be so much to do we won't ha –'

'No, you won't, my lad. Huh! Two on and one off? Over Andy's dead body and I mean dead. We go as a family by God or we don't go by God!' Even more sweetly, 'Don't you agree, darling heart?'

'Now look here, Gen . . .'

Within a month they were once more starting afresh, but it had been exciting and the best time he had ever had, meeting all sorts of interesting people, laughing with Scrag and the others, finding Charlie and Lochart and Jean-Luc and Erikki, making the company into the most efficient, the safest flying operation in Iran and the Gulf, moulding it the way he alone decided. His baby. His alone.

Sheik Aviation was the first of many acquisitions and amalgamations Gavallan made. 'Where the hell do you get all the money, Andy?' he had once asked.

'Banks. Where else? We're a triple-A risk and Scots to boot.'

It wasn't until much later that he discovered, quite by chance, that the S of S-G Helicopters really stood for Struan's that was also the secret source of all their financing and civilian intelligence, and S-G their subsidiary.

'How did you find out, Mac?' Gavallan had asked gruffly.

'An old friend in Sydney, ex-RAF, who's in mining, wrote to me and said he'd heard Linbar spouting about S-G being part of the Noble House – I didn't know but it seems Linbar's running Struan's in Australia.'

'He's trying to. Mac, between us, Ian wanted Struan's involvement kept quiet – David wants to continue the pattern so I'd prefer you to keep it to yourself,' Gavallan had said quietly. David was David MacStruan, the then taipan.

'Of course, not even Genny. But it explains a lot and gives me a grand feeling to know the Noble House's covering us. I often wondered why you left.'

Gavallan had smiled but hadn't answered. 'Liz knows about Struan's, of course, the Inner Office, and that's all.'

McIver had never told anyone. S-G had thrived and grown as the oil business had grown. So had his profits. So had the value of his stock in the Iran venture. When he retired in six or seven years he would be comfortably well off. 'Isn't it time to quit?' Genny would say every year. 'There's more than enough money, Duncan.'

'It's not the money,' he would always say . . .

*   *   *

McIver was staring at the red glow to the southeast over Jaleh that now had deepened and spread. His mind was in turmoil. Jaleh's got to make it hit the fan again all over Tehran, he thought.

He sipped his whisky. No extra need to be nervous, he thought, the weight of it all bearing down. What the devil was Chinaboy going to say when we were cut off? He'll get me word if it was important – he's never failed yet. Terrible about Stanson. That's the third civilian, all American, to be murdered by 'unknown gunmen' in the last few months – two ExTex and one from Guerney. Wonder when they'll start on us – Iranians hate the British just as much as the Yanks. Where to get more cash? We can't operate on half a million rials a week. Somehow I'll have to lean on the partners, but they're as devious as anyone on earth and past masters at looking after number one.

He took the last swallow of his whisky. Without the partners we're stymied, even after all these years – they're the ones who know who to talk to, which palm to touch with how much or what percentage, who to flatter, who to reward. They're the Farsi speakers, they've the contacts. Even so, Chinaboy was right: whoever wins, Khomeini, Bakhtiar, or the generals, they have to have choppers . . .

In the kitchen Genny was almost in tears. The secret tin of haggis that she had kept hidden so carefully for half a year and had just opened was defective and the contents ruined. And Duncan loved it so. How could he, a mess-up of minced sheep heart and liver and lungs and oatmeal, onion, suet, seasonings, and stock, all stuffed into a bag made from the poor bloody sheep's stomach, then boiled for several hours. 'Ugh! Bugger everything.' She had had young Scot Gavallan – sworn to secrecy – bring the tin back after his last leave for this special occasion.

Today was their wedding anniversary and this was her secret surprise for Duncan. Sod everything!

It's not Scot's fault the bloody tin's defective, she thought in misery. Even so, shit shit shit! I've planned this whole bloody dinner for months and now it's ruined. First the bloody butcher lets me down even though I'd paid twice as much as usual in advance, sod his 'Insha's Allah,' and then because the bloody banks are closed I've no cash to bribe the rotten sod's rival to sell me the leg of good fresh lamb not old mutton he'd promised, then the grocery store pulls a sudden strike, then . . .

The window of the small kitchen was half open and she heard another burst of machine-gun fire. Closer this time. Then wafted on the wind came the distant, deep-throated sound of the mobs: 'Allahhh-u Akbarrr . . . Allahhh-u Akbarrr . . .' repeated over and over. She shivered, finding it curiously menacing. Before the troubles began she used to find the muezzin's call to prayer five times daily from the minarets reassuring. But not now, not from the throats of the mobs.

I hate this place now, she thought. Hate the guns and hate the threats. There was another in the mailbox, their second – like the other, badly typed and copied on the cheapest of paper: 'On December 1 we gave you and family one month to leave our country. You are still here. You are now our enemies and we will fight you categorically.' No signature. Almost every expat in Iran got one.

Hate the guns, hate the cold and no heat and no light, hate their rotten toilets and squatting like an animal, hate all the stupid violence and destruction of something that was really very nice. Hate standing in queues. Sod all queues! Sod the rotten bugger who screwed up the tin of haggis, sod this rotten little kitchen and sod corned beef pie! For the life of me I can't understand why the men like it. Ridiculous! Tinned corned beef mixed with boiled potatoes, a little onion, butter and milk if you have it, bread crumbs on top, and baked till it's brown. Ugh! And as for cauliflower, the smell of it cooking makes me want to puke but I read it's good for diverticulitis and anyone can see Duncan's not as well as he should be. So silly to think he can fool me. Has he fooled Charlie? I doubt it. And as for Claire, what a fool to leave such a good man! I wonder if Charlie ever found out about the affair she had with that Guerney pilot. No harm in that I suppose if you're not caught – difficult being left so much alone and if that's what you want. But I'm glad they parted friends though I thought she was a selfish bitch.

She caught sight of herself in the mirror. Automatically she straightened her hair and stared at her reflection. Where's all your youth gone? I don't know, but it's gone. At least mine has, Duncan's hasn't, he's still young, young for his age – if only he'd look after himself. Damn Gavallan! No, Andy's all right. So glad he remarried such a nice girl. Maureen'll keep him in line and so will little Electra. I was so afraid he was going to marry that Chinese secretary of his. Ugh! Andy's all right and so was Iran. Was. Now it's time to leave and to enjoy our money. Definitely. But how?

She laughed out loud. More of the same, I suppose.

Carefully she opened the oven, blinked against the heat and smell, then shut the door again. Can't stand corned beef pie, she told herself irritably.

Dinner was very good, the corned beef pie golden brown on top, just as they liked it. 'Will you open the wine, Duncan? It's Persian, sorry, but it's the last bottle.' Normally they were well stocked with both French and Persian wines but the mobs had smashed and burned all Tehran's liquor shops, encouraged by the mullahs, following Khomeini's strict fundamentalism – drinking any form of alcohol being prohibited by the Koran. 'The man in the bazaar told me there's none officially on sale anywhere and even drinking in the Western hotels is officially forbidden now.'

'That won't last, the people won't stand for it – or fundamentalism – for long,' Pettikin said. 'Can't, not in Persia. Historically, the Shahs've always been tolerant and why not? For almost three thousand years Persia's been famous for the beauty of its women – look at Azadeh and Sharazad – and their vineyards and wines. What about the *Rubáiyát of Omar Khayyám*, isn't that a hymn to wine, women and song? Persia for ever, I say.'

' "Persia" sounds so much better than "Iran", Charlie, so much more exotic, as it used to be when we first came here, so much nicer,' Genny said. For a moment she was distracted by more firing, then went on, talking to cover her nervousness. 'Sharazad told me they've always called it Iran, or Ayran themselves. Seems that Persia was what the ancient Greeks called it, Alexander the Great and all that. Most Persians were happy when Reza Shah decreed Persia was to be henceforth Iran. Thank you, Duncan,' she said and accepted the glass of wine, admiring its colour, and smiled at him.

'Everything's grand, Gen,' he said and gave her a little hug.

The wine had been savoured. And the pie. But they were not merry. Too much to wonder about. More tanks going by. More firing. The red glow over Jaleh spreading. The chant of distant mobs. Then halfway through the dessert – trifle, another McIver favourite – one of their pilots, Nogger Lane, staggered in, his clothes badly torn, his face deeply bruised, helping a girl. She was tall and dark-haired and dark-eyed, rumpled and in shock, mumbling pathetically in Italian, one sleeve almost ripped out of her coat, her clothes and face and hands and hair filthy, as though she had fallen in the gutter.

'We got caught between . . . between the police and some bastard mobs,' he said in a rush, almost incoherently. 'Some bugger'd siphoned my tank so . . . but the mob, there were thousands of them, Mac. One moment the street was normal, then everyone else started running and they . . . the mobs, they came out of a side street and a lot had guns . . . it was the God-cursed chanting over and over, Allah-u Akbar, Allah-u Akbar, that made your blood curdle . . . I'd never . . . then stones, firebombs, tear gas – the lot – as the police and troops arrived. And tanks. I saw three, and I thought the bastards were going to open up. Then someone started firing from the crowd, then there were guns everywhere and . . . and bodies all over the place. We ran for our lives, then a swarm of the bastards saw us and started shrieking 'American Satan' and charged after us and cornered us in an alley. I tried to tell 'em I was English and Paula, Italian, and not . . . but they were crowding me and . . . and if it hadn't been for a mullah, a big bastard with a black beard and black turban, this . . . this bugger called them off and Christ, they let us go. He cursed us and told us to piss off . . .' He accepted the whisky and gulped it, trying to catch his breath, his hands and knees shaking uncontrollably now, quite unnoticed by him. McIver, Genny and Pettikin were listening aghast. The girl was sobbing quietly.

'Never, never been in the middle of a nightmare like that, Charlie,' Nogger Lane continued shakily. 'Troops were all as young as the mobs and they all seemed scared shitless, too much to take night after night, mobs screaming and throwing stones . . . A Molotov cocktail caught a soldier in the face and he burst into flames, screaming through the flames with no . . . and then those bastards cornered us and started manhandling Paula, trying to get at her, pawing her, tearing at her clothes, . . . I went a bit mad myself and got hold of one bastard and smashed his face in, I know I hurt him because his nose went into his head and if it hadn't been for this mullah . . .'

'Take it easy, laddie,' Pettikin said worriedly, but the youth paid no attention and rushed onward.

'. . . if it hadn't been for this mullah who pulled me off I'd've gone on smashing until that bugger was pulp, I wanted to claw out his eyes, Jesus Christ, I tried to, I know I did . . . Jesus Christ, I've never killed anything with my hands, never wanted to until tonight but I did and would have . . .' His hands were trembling as he brushed his fair hair out of his eyes, his voice edged now and rising. 'Those bastards, they had no right to touch us but they were grabbing Paula and . . . and . . .' The tears began gushing, his mouth worked but no words came out, a fleck of foam was at the corners of his lips, 'and . . . and kill . . . I wanted to Killlll –'

Abruptly Pettikin leaned over and belted the young man backhanded across the face, knocking him spread-eagled on the sofa. The others almost leapt out of themselves at the suddenness. Lane was momentarily stunned, then he groped to his feet to hurl himself at his attacker.

'Hold it, Nogger!' Pettikin roared. The command stopped the youth in his tracks. He stared at the older man stupidly, fists bunched. 'What the bloody hell's the matter with you, you damn near broke my bloody jaw,' he said furiously. But the tears had stopped and his eyes were clean again. 'Eh?'

'Sorry, lad, but you were going, flipping, I've seen it aco –'

'The bloody hell I was,' Lane said menacingly, his senses back, but it took them time to explain and to calm him and calm her. Her name was Paula Giancani, a tall girl, a stewardess from an Alitalia flight.

'Paula, dear, you'd better stay here tonight,' Genny said. 'It's past curfew. You understand?'

'Yes, understand. Yes, I speak English, I th –'

'Come along, I'll lend you some things. Nogger, you take the sofa.'

Later Genny and McIver were still awake, tired but not sleepy, gunfire somewhere in the night, chanting somewhere in the night. 'Like some tea, Duncan?'

'Good idea.' He got up with her. 'Oh, dammit, I forgot.' He went over to the bureau and found the little box, badly wrapped. 'Happy anniversary. It's not much, just a bracelet I got in the bazaar.'

'Oh, thank you, Duncan.' As she unwrapped it she told him about the haggis.

'What a bugger! Never mind. Next year we'll have it in Scotland.'

The bracelet was rough amethysts set in silver. 'Oh, it's so pretty, just what I wanted. Thank you, darling.'

'You too, Gen.' He put his arm around her and kissed her absently.

She didn't mind about the kiss. Most kisses nowadays, hers as well, were just affectionate, like patting a beloved dog. 'What's troubling you, dear?'

'Everything's fine.'

She knew him too well. 'What – that I don't know yet?'

'It's getting hairier and hairier. Every hour on the hour. When you were out of the room with Paula, Nogger told us they'd come from the airport. Her Alitalia flight – it'd been chartered by the Italian government to evacuate their nationals and had been grounded for two days – had got clearance to leave at midday, so he'd gone to see her off. Of course takeoff was delayed and delayed, as usual, then just before dusk the flight was grounded again, the whole airport closed down, and everyone told to leave. All Iranian staff just vanished. Then almost immediately a group of heavily armed, and he meant heavily armed, revolutionaries, started spreading out all over the place. Most of 'em were wearing green armbands, but some had IPLO on them, Gen, the first Nogger'd seen. "Iranian Palestine Liberation Organisation".'

'Oh, my God,' she said, 'then it's true that the PLO's helping Khomeini?'

'Yes, and if they're helping, it's a different game, civil war's just started, and we're in the bloody middle.'

At Tabriz One: 11:05 P.M. Erikki Yokkonen was naked, lying in the sauna that he had constructed with his own hands, the temperature 107 degrees Fahrenheit, the sweat pouring off him, his wife Azadeh nearby, also lulled by the heat. Tonight had been grand with lots of food and two bottles of the best Russian vodka that he had purchased black market in Tabriz and had shared with his two English engineers, and their station manager, Ali Dayati. 'Now we'll have sauna,' he had said to them just before midnight. But they had declined, as usual, with hardly enough strength to reel off to their own cabins. 'Come on, Azadeh!'

'Not tonight, please, Erikki,' she had said, but he had just laughed and lifted her in his great arms, wrapped her fur coat around her clothes, and carried her through the front door of their cabin, out past the pine trees heavy with snow, the air just below freezing. She was easy to carry, and he went into little hut that abutted the back of their cabin, into the warmth of the changing area and then, un-clothed, into the sauna itself. And now they lay there, Erikki at ease,

58

Azadeh, even after a year of marriage, still not quite used to the nightly ritual.

He lay on one arm and looked at her. She was lying on a thick towel on the bench opposite. Her eyes were closed and he saw her breast rising and falling and the beauty of her – raven hair, chiselled Aryan features, lovely body, and milky skin – and as always he was filled with the wonder of her, so small against his six foot four.

Gods of my ancestors, thank you for giving me such a woman, he thought. For a moment he could not remember which language he was thinking in. He was quadrilingual, Finnish, Swedish, Russian and English. What does it matter he told himself, giving himself back to the heat, letting his mind waft with the steam that rose from the stones he had laid so carefully. It satisfied him greatly that he had built his sauna himself – as a man should – hewing the logs as his ancestors had done for centuries.

This was the first thing he had done when he was posted here four years ago – to select and fell the trees. The others had thought him crazy. He had shrugged good-naturedly. 'Without a sauna life's nothing. First you build the sauna, then the house; without sauna a house is not a house; you English, you know nothing – not about life.' He had been tempted to tell them that he had been born in a sauna, like many Finns – and why not, how sensible when you think of it, the warmest place in the home, the cleanest, quietest, most revered. He had never told them, only Azadeh. She had understood. Ah, yes, he thought, greatly content, she understands everything.

Outside, the threshold of the forest was silent, the night sky cloudless, the stars very bright, snow deadening sound. Half a mile away was the only road through the mountains. The road meandered northwest to Tabriz, ten miles away, thence northwards to the Soviet border a few miles farther on. Southeast it curled away over the mountains, at length to Tehran, 350 miles away.

The base, Tabriz One, was home for two pilots – the other was on leave in England – two English engineers, the rest Iranians: two cooks, eight day labourers, the radio op, and the station manager. Over the hill was their village of Abu-Mard and, in the valley below, the wood-pulp factory belonging to the forestry monopoly, Iran-Timber, they serviced under contract. The 212 took loggers and equipment into the forests, helped build camps and plan the few roads that could be built, then serviced the camps with replacement crews and equipment and flew the injured out. For most of the landlocked camps the 212 was their only link with the outside, and the pilots were venerated. Erikki loved the life and the land, so much like Finland that sometimes he would dream he was home again.

His sauna made it perfect. The tiny, two-room hut at the back of their cabin was screened from the other cabins, and built traditionally with lichen between the logs for insulation, the wood fire that heated the stones well ventilated. Some of the stones, the top layer, he had brought from Finland. His grandfather had fished them from the bottom of a lake, where all the best sauna stones come from, and had given them to him on his last home leave eighteen months ago. 'Take them, my son, and with them surely there'll go a good Finnish sauna tonto—' the little brown elf that is the spirit of the sauna – 'though what you want to marry one of those foreigners for and not your own kind, I really don't know.'

'When you see her, Grandfather, you'll worship her also. She has blue-green eyes and dark-dark hair an –'

'If she gives you many sons – well, we'll see. It's certainly long past the time you should be married, a fine man like you, but a foreigner? You say she's a schoolteacher?'

'She's a member of Iran's Teaching Corps, they're young people, men and women, volunteers as a service to the state, who go to villages and teach villagers and children how to read and write, but mostly the children. The Shah and the Empress started the corps a few years ago, and Azadeh joined when she was twenty-one. She comes from Tabriz where I work, teaches in our village in a makeshift school and I met her seven months and three days ago. She was twenty-four then . . .'

Erikki glowed, remembering the first time he ever saw her, neat in her uniform, her hair cascading, sitting in a forest glade surrounded by children, then her smiling up at him, seeing the wonder in her eyes at his size, knowing at once that this was the woman he had waited his life to find. He was thirty-six then. Ah, he thought, watching her lazily, once more blessing the forest tonto – spirit – that had guided him to that part of the forest. Only three more months then two whole months of leave. It will be good to be able to show her Suomi – Finland.

'It's time, Azadeh, darling,' he said.

'No, Erikki, not yet, not yet,' she said half asleep, drowsed by the heat but not by alcohol, for she did not drink. 'Please, Erikki, not y –'

'Too much heat isn't good for you,' he said firmly. They always spoke English together, though she was also fluent in Russian – her mother was half Georgian, coming from the border area where it was useful and wise to be bilingual. Also she spoke Turkish, the language most used in this part of Iran, Azerbaijan, and of course Farsi. Apart from a few words, he spoke no Farsi or Turkish. He sat up and wiped the sweat off, at peace with the world, then leaned over and kissed her. She kissed him back and trembled as his hands sought her and hers sought him back. 'You're a bad man, Erikki,' she said, then stretched gloriously.

'Ready?'

'Yes.' She clung to him as he lifted her so easily into his arms, then walked out of the sauna into the changing area, then opened the door and went outside into the freezing air. She gasped as the cold hit her and hung on as he scooped up some snow and rubbed it over her, making her flesh tingle and burn but not painfully. In seconds she was glowing within and without. It had taken her a whole winter to get used to the snow bath after the heat. Now, without it, the sauna was incomplete. Quickly she did the same for him, then rushed happily back into the warm again, leaving him to roll and thrash in the snow for a few seconds. He did not notice the group of men and the mullah standing in a shocked group up the rise, half-hidden under the trees beside the path, fifty yards away. Just as he was closing the door he saw them. Fury rushed through him. He slammed the door.

'Some villagers are out there. They must have been watching us. Everyone knows this is off limits!' She was equally enraged and they dressed hurriedly. He pulled on his fur boots and heavy sweater and pants and grabbed the huge axe and rushed out. The men were still there and he charged them with a roar, his axe on high. They scattered as he whirled at them, then one of them raised the machine gun and let off a burst into the air that echoed off the mountainside. Erikki skidded to a halt, his rage obliterated. Never before had he been threatened with guns, or had one levelled at his stomach.

'Put axe down,' the man said in halting English, 'or I kill you.'

Erikki hesitated. At that moment Azadeh came charging between them and knocked the gun away and began shouting in Turkish: 'How dare you come here! How dare you have guns – what are you, bandits? This is our land – get off our land or I'll have you put in jail!' She had wrapped her heavy fur coat over her dress but was shaking with rage.

'This is the land of the people,' the mullah said sullenly, keeping out of range. 'Cover your hair, woman, cover y –'

'Who're you, mullah? You're not of my village! Who are you?'

'I'm Mahmud, mullah of the Hajsta mosque in Tabriz. I'm not one of your lackeys,' he said angrily and jumped aside as Erikki lunged at him. The man with the gun was off balance but another man, safely away, cocked his rifle: 'By God and the Prophet, stop the foreign pig or I'll blow you both to the hell you deserve!'

61

'Erikki, wait! Leave these dogs to me!' Azadeh called out in English, then shouted at them, 'What do you want here? This is our land, the land of my father Abdollah Khan, Khan of the Gorgons, kin to the Qajars who've ruled here for centuries.' Her eyes had adjusted to the darkness now and she peered at them. There were ten of them, all young men, all armed, all strangers, all except one, the kalandar – chief – of their village. 'Kalandar, how dare you come here!'

'I'm sorry, Highness,' he said apologetically, 'but the mullah said I was to lead him here by this trail and not by the main path and so –'

'What do you want, parasite?' she said, turning on the mullah.

'Show respect, woman,' the mullah said even more angrily. 'Soon we'll be in command. The Koran has laws for nakedness and loose living: stoning and the lash.'

'The Koran has laws for trespass and bandits and threatening peaceful people, and rebellion against their chiefs and liege lords. I'm not one of your frightened illiterates! I know you for what you are and what you've always been, the parasites of the villages and the people. *What do you want?*'

From the base, people were hurrying up with flashlights. At their head were the two bleary-eyed engineers, Dibble and Arberry, with Ali Dayati carefully in tow. All were sleep ruffled, hastily dressed, and anxious. 'What's going on?' Dayati demanded, thick glasses on his nose, peering at them. His family had been protected by and had served the Gorgon Khans for years. 'Who ar –'

'These dogs,' Azadeh began hotly, 'came out of the nigh –'

'Hold your tongue, woman,' the mullah said angrily, then turned on Dayati. 'Who're you?'

When Dayati saw the man was a mullah, his demeanour changed and at once he became deferential. 'I'm . . . I'm Iran-Timber's manager here, Excellency. What's the matter, please, what can I do for you?'

'The helicopter. At dawn I want it for a flight around the camps.'

'I'm sorry, Excellency, the machine is in pieces for an overhaul. It's the foreigner's policy an –'

Azadeh interrupted angrily, 'Mullah, by what right do you dare to come here in the middle of the night to –'

'Imam Khomeini has issued ord –'

'Imam?' she echoed, shocked. 'By what right do you call Ayatollah Khomeini that?'

'He is Imam. He has issued orders an –'

'Where does it say in the Koran or the Sharia that an ayatollah can claim to be Imam, can order one of the Faithful? Where does it sa –'

62

'Aren't you Shi'ite?' the mullah asked, enraged, conscious of his followers listening silently.

'Yes, I'm Shi'ite, but not an illiterate fool, Mullah!' The way she used the word it was a curse. 'Answer!'

'Please, Highness,' Dayati said, pleading with her. 'Please leave this to me, please, I beg you.'

But she began to rage and the mullah to rage back, and the others joined in, the mood becoming ugly, until Erikki raised his axe and let out a bellow of rage, infuriated that he could not understand what was being said. The silence was sudden, then another man cocked his machine pistol.

'What's this bastard want, Azadeh?' Erikki said.

She told him.

'Dayati, tell him he can't have my 212 and to get off our land now or I'll send for the police.'

'Please, Captain, please allow me to deal with it, Captain,' Dayati said, sweating with anxiety, before Azadeh could interrupt. 'Please, Highness, please leave now.' Then turned to the two engineers, 'It's all right, you can go back to bed. I'll deal with it.'

It was then that Erikki noticed Azadeh was still barefoot. He scooped her up into his arms. 'Dayati, you tell that *matyeryebyets* and all of them if they come here again at night I'll break their necks – and if he or anyone touches one hair of my woman's head I'll crawl into hell after him if need be.' He went off, massive in his rage, the two engineers following.

A voice in Russian stopped him. 'Captain Yokkonen, perhaps I could have a word with you in a moment?'

Erikki looked back. Azadeh, still in his arms, was tense. The man stood at the back of the pack, difficult to see, seemingly not very different from the others, wearing a nondescript parka. 'Yes,' Erikki told him in Russian, 'but don't bring a gun into my house, or a knife.' He stalked off.

The mullah went closer to Dayati, his eyes stony. 'What did the foreign devil say, eh?'

'He was rude, all foreigners are rude, Her High – the woman was rude too.'

The mullah spat in the snow. 'The Prophet set laws and punishments against such conduct, the People have laws against hereditary wealth and stealing lands, the land belongs to the People. Soon correct laws and punishments will govern us all, at long last, and Iran will be at peace.' He turned to the others. 'Naked in the snow! Flaunting herself

63

in the open against all the laws of modesty. Harlot! What are the Gorgons but lackeys of the traitor Shah and his dog Bakhtiar, eh?' His eyes went back to Dayati. 'What lies are you telling about the helicopter?'

Trying to hide his fear, Dayati said at once that the fifteen-hundred-hour check was according to foreign regulations imposed upon him and the aircraft and further ordered by the Shah and the government.

'Illegal government,' the mullah interrupted.

'Of course, of course illegal,' Dayati agreed at once and nervously led them into the hangar and lit the lights – the base had its own small generating system and was self-contained. The engines of the 212 were laid out neatly, piece by piece, in regimented lines. 'It's nothing to do with me, Excellency, the foreigners do what they like.' Then he added quickly, 'And although we all know Iran-Timber belongs to the People, the Shah took all the money. I've no authority over them, foreigner devils or their regulations. There's nothing I can do.'

'When will it be airworthy?' the Russian-speaking man asked in perfect Turkish.

'The engineers promise two days,' Dayati said and prayed silently, very afraid, though he tried hard not to show it. It was clear to him now that these men were leftist mujhadin believers in the Soviet-sponsored theory that Islam and Marx were compatible. 'It's in the hands of God. Two days; the foreign engineers are waiting for some spares that're overdue.'

'What are they?'

Nervously he told him. They were some minor parts and a tail rotor blade.

'How many hours do you have on the rotor blade?'

Dayati checked the log book, his fingers trembling. '1073.'

'God is with us,' the man said, then turned to the mullah. 'We could safely use the old one for fifty hours at least.'

'But the life of the blade . . . the airworthy certificate's invalidated,' Dayati said without thinking. 'The pilot wouldn't fly because air regulations requi –'

'Satan's regulations.'

'True,' the Russian speaker interrupted, 'some of them. But laws for safety are important to the People, and even more important, God laid down rules in the Koran for camels and horses and how to care for them, and these rules can apply equally to airplanes which also are the gift of God and also carry us to do God's work. We must, therefore, care for them correctly. Don't you agree, Mahmud?'

'Of course,' the mullah said impatiently and his eyes bore into Dayati who began to tremble. 'I will return in two days, at dawn. Let the helicopter be ready and the pilot ready to do God's work for the People. I will visit every camp in the mountains. Are there other women here?'

'Just . . . just two wives of the labourers and . . . my wife.'

'Do they wear chador and veil?'

'Of course,' Dayati lied instantly. To wear the veil was against the law of Iran. Reza Shah had outlawed the veil in 1936, made the chador a matter of choice and Mohammed Shah had further enfranchised women in '64.

'Good. Remind them God and the People watch, even in the foreigner's vile domain.' Mahmud turned on his heel and stomped off, the others going with him.

When he was alone, Dayati wiped his brow, thankful that he was one of the Faithful and that now his wife would wear the chador, would be obedient, and act as his mother with modesty and not wear jeans like Her Highness. What did the mullah call her to her face? God protect him if Abdollah Khan hears about it. . . . even though, of course, the mullah's right, and, of course, Khomeini's right, God protect him.

In Erikki's Cabin: 11:23 P.M. The two men sat at the table opposite each other in the main room of the cabin. When the man had knocked on the door, Erikki had told Azadeh to go into the bedroom but he had left the inner door open so that she could hear. He had given her the rifle that he used for hunting. 'Use it without fear. If he comes into the bedroom, I am already dead,' he had said, his pukoh knife sheathed under his belt in the centre of his back. The pukoh knife was a haft knife and the weapon of all Finns. It was considered unlucky – and dangerous – for a man not to carry one. In Finland it was against the law to wear one openly – that might be considered a challenge. But everyone carried one, and always in the mountains. Erikki Yokkonen's matched his size.

'So, Captain, I apologise for the intrusion.' The man was dark-haired, a little under six feet, in his thirties, his face weather-beaten, his eyes dark and Slavic – Mongol blood somewhere in his heritage. 'My name is Fedor Rakoczy.'

'Rakoczy was a Hungarian revolutionary,' Erikki said curtly. 'And from your accent you're Georgian. Rakoczy's not Georgian. What's your real name – and KGB rank?'

The man laughed. 'It is true my accent is Georgian and that I am

Russian from Georgia, from Tbilisi. My grandfather came from Hungary but he was no relation to the revolutionary who in ancient times became prince of Transylvania. Nor was he Muslim, like my father and me. There, you see, we both know a little of our history, thanks be to God,' he said pleasantly. 'I'm an engineer on the Iran-Soviet natural gas pipeline, based just over the border at Astara on the Caspian – and pro-Iran, pro-Khomeini, blessings be upon him, anti-Shah and anti-American.'

He was glad that he had been briefed about Erikki Yokkonen. Part of his cover story was true. He certainly came from Georgia, from Tbilisi, but he was not a Muslim, nor was his real name Rakoczy. His real name was Igor Mzytryk and he was a captain in the KGB, a specialist attached to the 116th Airborne Division that was deployed just across the border, north of Tabriz, one of the hundreds of undercover agents who had infiltrated northern Iran for months and now operated almost freely. He was thirty-four, a KGB career officer like his father and he had been in Azerbaijan for six months. His English was good, his Farsi and Turkish fluent, and although he could not fly he knew much about the piston-driven Soviet army close support helicopters of his division. 'As to my rank,' he added in his most gentle voice, 'it is friend. We Russians are good friends of Finns, aren't we?'

'Yes, yes that's true. Russians are, not communists – Soviets. Holy Russia was a friend in the past, yes when we were a Grand Duchy of Russia. Atheist Soviet Russia was friendly after 1917 when we became independent. Soviet Russia is now. Yes, now. But not in '39. Not in the Winter War. No, not then.'

'Nor were you in '41,' Rakoczy said sharply. 'In'41 you went to war against us with the stinking Nazis, you sided with them against us.'

'True, but only to take back our land, our Karelian, our province you'd stolen from us. We didn't walk on to Leningrad as we could have done.' Erikki could feel the knife in the centre of his back and he was very glad of it. 'Are you armed?'

'No. You said not to come armed. My gun is outside the door. I have no pukoh knife nor need to use one. By Allah, I'm a friend.'

'Good. A man has need of friends.' Erikki watched the man, loathing what he represented: the Soviet Russia that, unprovoked, had invaded Finland in '39 the moment Stalin had signed the Soviet-German non-aggression pact. Finland's little army had fought back alone. They had beaten off the Soviet hordes for one hundred days in the Winter War and then they had been overrun. Erikki's father had been killed defending Karelian, the southern and eastern province, where the

Yokkonens had lived for centuries. At once Soviet Russia had annexed the province. At once all Finns left. All of them. Not one would stay under a Soviet flag so the land became barren of Finns. Erikki was just ten months old then and in that exodus thousands died. His mother had died. It was the worst winter in living memory.

And in '45, Erikki thought, bottling his rage, in '45 America and England betrayed us and gave our lands to the aggressor. But we've not forgotten. Nor have the Estonians, Latvians, Lithuanians, East Germans, Czechs, Hungarians, Bulgars, Slavs, Rumanians – the list endless. There will be a day of reckoning with the Soviets, oh yes, one day there will surely be a day of reckoning with the Soviets – most of all by Russians who suffer their lash most of all. 'For a Georgian you know a lot about Finland,' he said calmly.

'Finland is important to Russia. The détente between us works, is safe and a lesson to the world that anti-Soviet American Imperialistic propaganda is a myth.'

Erikki smiled. 'This is not the time for politics, eh? It's late. What do you want with me?'

'Friendship.'

'Ah, that's easily asked, but as you would know, for a Finn, given with difficulty.' Erikki reached over to the sideboard for an almost empty vodka bottle and two glasses. 'Are you Shi'ite?'

'Yes, but not a good one, God forgive me. I drink vodka sometimes if that's what you ask.'

Erikki poured two glasses. 'Health.' They drank. 'Now, please come to the point.'

'Soon Bakhtiar and his American lackeys will be thrown out of Iran. Soon Azerbaijan will be in turmoil, but you will have nothing to fear. You are well thought of here, so is your wife and her family, and we would like your . . . your cooperation in bringing peace to these mountains.'

'I'm just a helicopter pilot, working for a British company, contracted to Iran-Timber, and I'm without politics. We Finns have no politics, don't you remember?'

'We're friends, yes. Our interests of world peace are the same.'

Erikki's great right fist slammed down on the table, the sudden violence making the Russian flinch as the bottle skittered away and fell to the floor. 'I've asked you politely twice to come to the point,' he said in the same calm voice. 'You have ten seconds.'

'Very well,' the man said through his teeth. 'We require your services to ferry teams into the camps within the next few days. We . . .'

'What teams?'

'The mullahs of Tabriz and their followers. We requ –'

'I take my orders from the company, not mullahs or revolutionaries or men who come with guns in the night. Do you understand?'

'You will find it is better to understand us, Captain Yokkonen. So will the Gorgons. All of them,' Rakoczy said pointedly and Erikki felt the blood go into his face. 'Iran-Timber is already struck and on our side. They will provide you with the necessary orders.'

'Good. In that case I will wait and see what their orders are.' Erikki got up to his great height. 'Good night.'

The Russian got up too and stared at him angrily. 'You and your wife are much too intelligent not to understand that without the Americans and their fornicating CIA Bakhtiar's lost. That motherless madman Carter has ordered U.S. marines and helicopters into Turkey, an American war fleet into the Gulf, a task force with a nuclear carrier and support vessels, with marines and nuclear armed aircraft – a war fleet an –'

'I don't believe it!'

'You can. By God, of course they're trying to start a war, for of course we have to react, we have to match war game with war game for of course they'll use Iran against us. It's all madness – we don't want nuclear war . . .' Rakoczy meant it with all his heart, his mouth running away with him. Only a few hours ago his superior had warned him by code radio that all Soviet forces on the border were on Yellow Alert – one step from Red – because of the approaching carrier fleet, all nuclear missiles on equal alert. Worst of all, vast Chinese troop movements had been reported all along the 5,000 miles of shared border with China. 'That motherfucker Carter with his motherfucking Friendship Pact with China's going to blow us all to hell if he gets half a chance.'

'If it happens it happens,' Erikki said.

'Insha'Allah, yes, but why become a running dog for the Americans, or their equally filthy British allies? The People are going to win, we are going to win. Help us and you won't regret it, Captain. We only need your skills for a few da –'

He stopped suddenly. Running footsteps were approaching. Instantly Erikki's knife was in his hand and he moved with catlike speed between the front door and the bedroom door as the front door burst open.

'SAVAK!' a half-seen man gasped, then took to his heels.

Rakoczy jumped for the doorway, scooped up his machine pistol.

'We require your help, Captain. Don't forget!' He vanished into the night.

Azadeh came out into the living room. With the gun ready, her face white. 'What was that about a carrier? I didn't understand him.'

Erikki told her. Her shock was clear. 'That means war, Erikki.'

'Yes, if it happens.' He put on his parka. 'Stay here.' He closed the door after him. Now he could see lights from approaching cars that were racing along the rough dirt road that joined the base to the main Tabriz-Tehran road. As his eyes adjusted to the darkness, he could make out two cars and an army truck. In a moment the lead vehicle stopped and police and soldiers fanned out into the night. The officer in charge saluted. 'Ah, Captain Yokkonen, good evening. We heard that some revolutionaries were here, or communist Tudeh – firing was reported,' he said, his English perfect. 'Her Highness is all right? There's no problem?'

'No, not now, thank you, Colonel Mazardi.' Erikki knew him quite well. The man was a cousin of Azadeh, and chief of police in this area of Tabriz. But SAVAK? That's something else, he thought uneasily. If he is, he is, and I don't want to know. 'Come in.'

Azadeh was pleased to see her cousin and thanked him for coming and they told him what had occurred.

'The Russian said his name was Rakoczy, Fedor Rakoczy?' he asked.

'Yes, but it was obviously a lie,' Erikki said. 'He had to be KGB.'

'And he never told you why they wanted to visit the camps?'

'No.'

The colonel thought a moment, then sighed. 'So the mullah Mahmud wishes to go flying, eh? Foolish for a so-called man of God to go flying. Very dangerous, particularly if he's an Islamic Marxist – that sacrilege! Flying helicopters, you can easily fall out, so I'm told. Perhaps we should accommodate him.' He was tall and very good-looking, in his forties, his uniform immaculate. 'Don't worry. These rabble-rousers will soon be back in their flea-bitten hovels. Soon Bakhtiar'll give the orders for us to contain these dogs. And that rabble-rouser Khomeini – we should muzzle that traitor quickly. The French should have muzzled him the moment he arrived there. Those weak fools. Stupid! But then they've always been weak, meddling, and against us. The French've always been jealous of Iran.' He got up. 'Let me know when your aircraft is airworthy. In any event we'll be back just before dawn in two days. Let's hope the mullah and his friends, particularly the Russian, return.'

He left them. Erikki put the kettle on to boil for coffee. Thoughtfully he said, 'Azadeh, pack an overnight bag.'

She stared at him. 'What?'

'We're going to take the car and drive to Tehran. We'll leave in a few minutes.'

'There's no need to leave, Erikki.'

'If the chopper was airworthy we'd use that but we can't.'

'There's no need to worry, my darling. Russians have always coveted Azerbaijan, always will, Tsarist, Soviet, it makes no difference. They've always wanted Iran and we've always kept them out and always will. No need to worry about a few fanatics and a lone Russian, Erikki.'

He looked at her. 'I'm worried about American marines in Turkey, the American task force and why the KGB think "you and your wife are much too intelligent", why that one was so nervous, why they know so much about me and about you and why they "require" my services. Go and pack a bag, my darling, while there's time.'

Saturday
February 10, 1979

At Kowiss Air Base: 3:32 A.M. Led by the mullah, Hussain Kowissi, the shouting mob was pressing against the barred, floodlit main gate and the nearby barbed-wire fence that surrounded the huge base, the night dark, very cold, with snow everywhere. There were three to four thousand of them, youths mostly, a few armed, some young women in chadors well to the front, adding their cries to the tumult: 'God is Great . . . God is Great . . .'

Inside the gate, facing the mob, platoons of nervous soldiers were spread out on guard, their rifles ready, other platoons in reserve, all officers with revolvers. Two Centurion tanks, battle ready, waited in the centre of the roadway, engines growling, the camp commander and a group of officers nearby. Behind them were trucks filled with more soldiers, headlights trained on the gate and the fence – soldiers outnumbered twenty or thirty to one. Behind the trucks were the hangars, base buildings, barracks, and the officers' mess, knots of milling, anxious servicemen everywhere, all hastily dressed, for the mob had arrived barely half an hour

73

ago demanding possession of the base in the name of Ayatollah Khomeini.

Again the voice of the camp commander came over the loudspeakers. 'You will disperse at once!' His voice was harsh and threatening, but the mob's chant overpowered him, 'Allah-u Akbarrr . . .'

The night was overcast, obscuring even the southern foothills of the snowcapped Zagros Mountains that towered behind the base. The base was S-G's main HQ in southern Iran as well as home for two Iranian Air Force squadrons of F 4s and, since martial law, a detachment of Centurions and the soldiers. Outside the fence, eastwards, the giant oil refinery sprawled over hundreds of acres, the tall stacks belching smoke, many sending jets of flame into the night as the excess gas was burned off. Though the whole plant was on strike and shut down, parts were floodlit: a skeleton staff of Europeans and Iranians permitted by the strike komiteh to try to keep the refinery and its feeder pipelines and storage tanks safe.

'God is Great . . .' Hussain shouted again and at once the mob took up the cry and again the cry went into the heads and hearts of the soldiers. One of those in the front rank was Ali Bewedan, a conscript like all the others, young like all the others, not so long ago a villager like all the others and those outside the fence. Yes, he thought, his head hurting, heart pounding, I'm on the side of God and ready to be martyred for the Faith and for the Prophet, Whose name be praised! Oh God let me be a martyr and go straight to Paradise as promised to the Faithful. Let me spill my blood for Islam and Khomeini but not for protecting the evil servants of the Shah!

The living words of Khomeini kept pounding in his ears, words from the cassette their mullah had played in the mosque two days ago: . . . 'Soldiers: join with your brothers and sisters doing God's work, flee your barracks with your arms, disobey the illegal orders of the generals, tear down the illegal government! Do God's work, God is Great . . .'

His heart picked up tempo as he heard the voice again, the rich, deep peasant voice of the leader of leaders, that made everything clear. 'God is Great, God is Great . . .'

The young soldier did not realise that now he was shouting with the mob, his eyes fixed on his mullah who was outside the gate, on God's side, outside, clawing at the gate, leading what he knew were his brothers and sisters, trying to break it down. His brother soldiers nearby shifted, even more nervously, staring at him, not daring to say anything, the baying going into their heads and hearts equally. Many of those inside the fence wished to open the gate. Most would have done

74

so if it were not for their officers and sergeants and the inevitable punishments, even death, that all knew was the reward for mutiny.

'On God's side, *outside* . . .'

The young man's brain seemed to explode with the words and he did not hear the sergeant shouting at him, nor see him, but only the gate that was closed against the Faithful. He flung down his rifle and ran for the gate, fifty yards away. For an instant there was a vast silence, all eyes within and without riveted on him, transfixed.

Colonel Mohammed Peshadi, the camp commander, stood near his lead tank, a lithe man with greying hair, his uniform immaculate. He watched the youth screaming, 'Allahhhh-u Akkbarrr . . .' the only voice now.

When the youth was five yards from the fence, the colonel motioned to the senior sergeant beside him. 'Kill him,' he said quietly.

The sergeant's ears were filled with the battle cry of the youth who now was tearing at the bolts. In one fluid motion, he jerked the rifle from the nearest soldier, cocked it, leaned momentarily on the side of the tank, put the sights on the back of the youth's head and pulled the trigger. He saw the face blow outward, showering those on the other side of the gate. Then the body slumped and hung obscenely on the barbed wires.

For a moment there was an even vaster silence. Then, as one, Hussain leading, the mob surged forward, a roaring, senseless, mindless being. Those in front tore at the wires, careless of the barbs that ripped their hands to shreds. Urged on by those behind, they began to climb the wires.

A submachine gun began to chatter among them. At that moment the colonel stabbed a finger at the officer in the tank.

At once a tongue of flame leapt from the barrel of the four-inch gun that was aimed just over the heads of the crowd and loaded with a blank charge, but the suddenness of the explosion sent attackers reeling from the gate in panic, half a dozen soldiers dropped their rifles in equal shock, a few fled, and many of the unarmed watchers scattered in fright. The second tank fired, its barrel closer to the ground, the shaft of flame lower.

The mob broke. Men and women fled from the gate and the fence, trampling one another in their haste. Again the lead tank fired and again the tongue of flame and again the earsplitting detonation and the mob redoubled its effort to get away. Only the mullah Hussain remained at the gate. He reeled drunkenly, momentarily blinded and deafened, then his hands caught the stanchions of the gate and he hung on. Immediately, instinctively, many went forward to help him, soldiers, sergeants, and one officer.

'Stay where you are!' Colonel Peshadi roared, then took the microphone on the long lead and switched to full power. His voice blasted the night. 'All soldiers stay where you are! Safety catches on! SAFETY CATCHES ON! All officers and sergeants take charge of your men! Sergeant, come with me!'

Still in shock, the sergeant fell into step beside his commander who went forward towards the gate. Scattered in front of the gates were thirty or forty who had been trampled on. The mass of rioters had stopped a hundred yards away and was beginning to re-form. Some of the more zealous began to charge. Tension soared.

'STOP! Everyone STAND STILL!'

This time the commander was obeyed. At once. He could feel the sweat on his back, his heart pumping in his chest. He glanced briefly at the corpse impaled on the barbs, glad for him – hadn't the youth been martyred with the Name of God on his lips, and wasn't he therefore already in Paradise? – then spoke harshly into the mouthpiece. 'You three . . . yes, you three, help the mullah. NOW!' Instantly, the men outside the fence he had pointed at rushed to do his bidding. He jerked an angry thumb at some soldiers. 'You! Open the gate! You, take the body away!'

Again he was obeyed instantly. Behind him, some groups of men began to move, and he roared, 'I said, STAND STILL! THE NEXT MAN WHO MOVES WITHOUT MY ORDER'S A DEAD MAN!' Everyone froze. Everyone.

Peshadi waited a moment, almost daring someone to move. No one did. Then he glanced back at Hussain whom he knew well. 'Mullah,' Peshadi said quietly, 'are you all right?' He was standing beside him now. The gate was open. A few yards away the three villagers waited, petrified.

There was a monstrous ache in Hussain's head and his ears hurt terribly. But he could hear and he could see and though his hands were bloody from the barbs, he knew he was undamaged and not yet the martyr he had expected and had prayed to be. 'I demand . . .' he said weakly, 'I demand this . . . this base in the name of Khomeini.'

'You will come to my office at once,' the colonel interrupted, his voice and face grim. 'So will you three, as witnesses. We will talk, mullah. I will listen and then you will listen.' He turned on the loudspeaker again and explained what was going to happen, his voice even grimmer, the words echoing, cutting the night apart. 'He and I will talk. We will talk peacefully and then the mullah will return to the mosque and you will all go to your homes to pray. The gate will remain open. The gate will be guarded by my soldiers and my tanks, and, by God and the Prophet on Whose name be praise, if one of you sets foot inside the gate or comes over the fence uninvited, my soldiers will kill him. If twenty or more of you charge into my base I will lead my tanks into your villages and I will burn your villages with you in them! Long live the Shah!' He turned on his heel and strode off, the mullah and the three frightened villagers following slowly. No one else moved.

And on the veranda of the officers' mess, Captain Conroe Starke, leader of the S-G contingent, sighed. 'Good sweet Jesus,' he muttered with vast admiration to no one in particular, 'what cojones!'

5:21 A.M. Starke stood at the window of the officers' mess, watching Peshadi's HQ building across the street. The mullah had not yet come out. Here in the main lounge of the officers' mess it was very cold. Freddy Ayre hunched deeper into his easy chair, pulling his flight jacket closer around him, and looked up at the tall Texan who rocked gently on his heels. 'What do you think?' he asked wearily, stifling a yawn.

'I think it'll be dawn in an hour odd, old buddy,' Starke said absently. He also wore a flight jacket and warm flying boots. The two pilots were in a corner window of the second-floor room overlooking most of the base. Scattered around the room were a dozen of the senior Iranian officers who had also been told to stand by. Most were asleep in easy chairs, bundled in their flight jackets or army greatcoats – heating throughout the base had been off for weeks to conserve fuel. A few weary orderlies, also in overcoats, were clearing up the last of the debris from the party that the mob had interrupted.

'I feel wrung out. You?'

'Not yet, but how come I always seem to draw duty on high days and holidays, Freddy?'

'It's the Fearless Leader's privilege, old chum,' Ayre said. He was second-in-command of the S-G contingent, ex-RAF, a good-looking man of twenty-eight, with sloe blue eyes, his accent Oxford English. 'Sets a good example to the troops.'

Starke glanced towards the open main gate. No change: it was still well guarded. Outside, half a thousand of the villagers still waited, huddled together for warmth. He went back to staring at the HQ building. No change there either. Lights were on in the upper floor where Peshadi had his offices. 'I'd give a month's pay to be kibitzing on that one, Freddy.'

'What? What's that mean?'

'To be listening to Peshadi and the mullah.'

'Oh!' Ayre looked across the street at the offices. 'You know, I thought we'd had it when those miserable buggers started climbing the wire. Bloody hell! I was all set to hare off to old Nellie, crank her up and say farewell to Kublai Khan and his Mongol hordes!' He chuckled to himself as he imagined himself running for his 212. 'Of course,' he added dryly, 'I'd have waited for you, Duke.' He used their nickname for Starke who was Texan like John Wayne and built like John Wayne and just as handsome.

Starke laughed. 'Thanks, old buddy. Come to think of it, if they'd bust in I'd've been ahead of you.' His blue eyes crinkled with the depth of his smile, his accent slight. Then he turned back to the window, hiding his concern. This was the base's third confrontation with a mob, always led by the mullah, each more serious than the last. And now the first deliberate death. Now what? That death'll lead to another and to another. If it hadn't been for Colonel Peshadi someone else would have gone for the gate and been shot and now there'd be bodies all over. Oh, Peshadi would've won – this time. But soon he won't, not unless he breaks the mullah. To break Hussain he'll have to kill him – can't jail him, the mob'll bust a gut, and if he kills him, they'll bust a gut, if he exiles him, they'll bust a gut, so he's on to a no-win play. What would I do?

I don't know.

He looked around the room. The Iranian officers didn't seem concerned. He know most of them by sight, not one of them intimately. Though S-G had shared the base since it was built some eight years before, they had had little to do with the military or air force personnel. Since Starke had taken over as chief pilot last year, he had tried to expand S-G's contacts with the rest of the base but without success. The Iranians preferred their own company.

That's okay too, he thought. It's their country. But they're tearing it apart and we're in the middle and now Manuela's here. He had been overjoyed to see his wife when she arrived by helicopter five days ago – McIver not trusting her to the roads – though a little angry that she had talked her way on to a lone incoming BA flight and had slipped back into Tehran. 'Dammit, Manuela, you're in danger here!'

'No more than in Tehran, Conroe darlin'. Insha'Allah,' she had said with a beam.

'But how'd you talk Mac into letting you come down here?'

'I just smiled at him, honey, and promised to go on the first available flight back to England. Meanwhile, darlin', let's go to bed.'

He smiled to himself and let his mind drift. This was his third two-year tour in Iran and his eleventh year with S-G. Eleven good years, he thought. First Aberdeen and the North Sea, then Iran, Dubai, and Al Shargaz just across the Gulf, then Iran again where he'd planned to stay. The best years here, he thought. But not any more. Iran's changed since '73 when the Shah quadrupled the price of oil – from $1 to $4 or thereabouts. It was like B.C. and A.D. for Iran. Before, they were friendly and helpful, good to live among and to work with. After? Increasingly arrogant, more and more puffed up by the Shah's constant overriding message about the 'inherent superiority of Iranians' because of their three thousand years of civilisation and how within twenty years Iran would be a world leader as was her divine right – would be the fifth industrial power on earth, sole guardian of the crossroads between East and West, with the best army, the best navy, the best air force, with more tanks, helicopters, refrigerators, factories, telephones, roads, schools, banks, businesses than anyone else here in the centre of the world. And based on all of this, with the rest of the world listening attentively, Iran under his leadership would be the real arbiter of East and West, and real fountain of all wisdom – his wisdom.

Starke sighed. He had come to understand the message, loud and clear over the years, but he blessed Manuela for agreeing to hurl themselves into the Iranian way of life, learning Farsi, going everywhere and seeing everything – new sights and tastes and smells, learning about Persian carpets and caviar, wines and legends and making friends – and not living their life out like many of the expat pilots and engineers who elected to leave their families at home, to work two months on and one off and sat on their bases on days off, saving money, and waiting for their leaves home – wherever home was.

'Home's here from now on,' she had said. 'This's where we'll be, me and the kids,' she had added with the toss of her head he admired so much, and the darkness of her hair, the passion of her Spanish heritage.

'What kids? We haven't got any kids and we can't afford them yet on what I make.'

Starke smiled. That had been just after they had been married, ten years ago. He had gone back to Texas to marry her as soon as his place with S-G was confirmed. Now they had three children, two boys and a girl, and he could afford them all, just. Now? Now what's going to happen? My job here's threatened, most of our Iranian friends've gone, there're empty shops where there was plenty – and fear where there'd only been laughter.

Goddam Khomeini and these goddam mullahs, he thought. He's certainly messed up a great way of life and a great place. I wish Manuela'd take the kids and leave London and fly home to Lubbock until Iran stabilises. Lubbock was a small country town in the Panhandle of Texas where his father still ran the family ranch. Five hundred acres, a few cattle, some horses, some farming, enough for the family to live comfortably. I wish she was there already, but then there'd be no mail for weeks and the phones're sure to be out. Goddam Khomeini for frightening her with his speeches – wonder what he'll say to God and God'll say to him when they meet, as they will.

He stretched and sat back in the easy chair. He saw Ayre watching him, his eyes bleary. 'You really hung one on.'

'It was my day off, my two days in fact, and I hadn't planned on the hordes. Actually I had intended to drink to oblivion, I miss my Better Half, bless her, and anyway Hogmanay's important to us Scots an –'

'Hogmanay was New Year's Eve and today's February 10th and you're no more Scots than I am.'

'Duke, I'll have you know the Ayres are an ancient clan and I can play the bagpipes, old boy.' Ayre yawned mightily. 'Christ, I'm tired.' He burrowed deeper into the chair, trying to settle himself more comfortably, then glanced out of the window. At once his tiredness dropped away. An Iranian officer was hurrying out of the HQ entrance, heading across the street towards them. It was Major Changiz, the base adjutant.

When he came in, his face was taut. 'All officers will report to the commandant at seven o'clock,' he said in Farsi. 'All officers. There will be a full parade of all military and air force personnel at eight o'clock in the square. Anyone absent – anyone,' he added darkly, 'except for medical reasons approved by me in advance – can expect immediate and severe punishment.' His eyes searched the room until he found Starke. 'Please follow me, Captain.'

Starke's heart skipped a beat. 'Why, Major?' he asked in Farsi.

'The commandant wants you.'

'What for?'

The major shrugged and walked out.

Starke said quietly to Ayre, 'Better alert all our guys. And Manuela. Huh?'

'Got it,' Ayre said, then muttered, 'Christ.'

As Starke walked across the street and up the stairs, he felt the eyes on him as a physical weight. Thank God I'm a civilian and work for a British company and not in the U.S. Army any more, he thought fervently. 'God damn—' he muttered, remembering his year's stint in Vietnam in the very early days when there were no U.S. forces in Vietnam, 'only a few advisers'. Shit! And that sonofabitching spit-and-polish meathead Captain Ritman who ordered all our base's helicopters – in our jungle base a million miles from anywhere, for crissake – to be painted with bright red, white, and blue stars and stripes: 'Yes, goddammit, all over! Let the gooks know who we are and they'll rush their asses all the way to goddam Russia.' The Viet Cong could see us coming from fifty miles and I got peppered to hell and back and we lost three Hueys with full crews before the sonofabitch was posted to Saigon, promoted and posted. No wonder we lost the goddam war.

He went into the office building and up the stairs, past the three petrified villagers who had been banished to the outer office, into the camp commandant's lair. 'Morning, Colonel,' he said cautiously in English.

'Morning, Captain Starke.' Peshadi switched to Farsi. 'I'd like you to meet the mullah, Hussain Kowissi.'

'Peace be upon you,' Starke said in Farsi, very conscious of the speckles of blood from the dead youth that still marred the man's white turban and black robe.

'Peace be upon you.'

Starke put out his hand to shake hands as was correct custom. Just in time he noticed the coagulated rips in the man's palms that the barbed wire had caused. He made his grip gentle. Even so he saw a shaft of pain go across the mullah's face. 'Sorry,' he said in English.

The mullah just stared back and Starke felt the man's hatred strongly.

'You wanted me, Colonel?'

'Yes. Please sit down.' Peshadi motioned at the empty chair opposite his desk. The office was spartan, meticulously tidy. A photograph of the Shah and Farah, his wife, in court dress was the only wall decoration. The mullah sat with his back towards it. Starke took the chair facing the two men.

Peshadi lit another cigarette and saw Hussain's disapproving eyes drop to the cigarette, then glare into his face. He stared back. Smoking was forbidden in the Koran – according to some interpretation. They had argued this point for over an hour. Then he had said with finality, 'Smoking is not forbidden in Iran, not yet. I am a soldier. I have sworn to obey orders. Ir –'

'Even the illegal ord –'

'I repeat: the orders of His Imperial Majesty, Shahinshah Mohammed Pahlavi or his representative, Prime Minister Bakhtiar, are still legal according to the law of Iran. Iran is not yet an Islamic state. Not yet. When it is I will obey the orders of whoever leads the Islamic state.'

'You will obey the Imam Khomeini?'

'If Ayatollah Khomeini becomes our legal ruler, of course.' The colonel had nodded agreeably, but he was thinking: before that day comes there's going to be a lot of blood spilled. 'And me, if I'm elected leader of this possible Islamic state, will you obey me?'

Hussain had not smiled. 'The leader of the Islamic state will be the Imam, the Whirlwind of God, and after him another ayatollah, then another.'

And now the stony, uncompromising eyes still glared at him, and Peshadi wanted to smash the mullah into the ground and take his tanks and smash everyone else who would not obey the orders of the Shahinshah, their God-given ruler. Yes, he thought, our God-given leader who like his father stood against you mullahs and your grasp for power, who curbed your archaic dogmatism and brought Iran out of the Dark Ages into our rightful greatness, who single-handedly bulldozed OPEC to stand up to the enormous power of the foreign oil companies, who slung the Russians out of Azerbaijan after World War II and has kept even them at bay, licking his hands like lap dogs.

By God and the Prophet, he told himself, enraged, staring back at Hussain, I cannot understand why fornicating mullahs don't recognise the truth about that senile old man Khomeini who screams lies from his deathbed, won't realise that the Soviets are sponsoring him, feeding him, protecting him, to stir them up to inflame the peasants to wreck Iran and make it a Soviet protectorate.

We only need one single order: Stamp out rebellion forthwith!

With that order, by God, within three days I'd have Kowiss and a hundred miles around quiet, peaceful and prosperous, mullahs happily in the mosques where they belong, the Faithful praying five times a day – within a month the armed forces'd have all Iran as it was last year and Khomeini solved permanently. Within minutes of the order I'd arrest him, publicly shave off half his beard, strip him naked, and trundle him through the streets in a dung cart. I'd let the people see him for what he is: a broken, beaten old man. Make him a loser and all the people would turn their faces and ears from him. Then accusers would come from the ayatollahs who adore life and love and power and land and talking, accusers would come from the mullahs and bazaaris and from the people and together they would snuff him out.

So simple to deal with Khomeini or any mullah – by God if I'd been in charge I'd've dragged him from France months ago. He puffed his cigarette and very carefully kept his thoughts off his face and out of his eyes. 'Well, mullah, Captain Starke is here.' Then he added, as though it was unimportant, 'You can speak to him in Farsi or English, as you wish – he speaks Farsi as you speak English. Fluently.'

The mullah turned on Starke. 'So,' he said, his English American-accented, 'you are CIA.'

'No,' Starke said, instantly on his guard. 'You were at school in the States?'

'I was a student there, yes,' Hussain said. Then, because of his pain and tiredness, his temper snapped. He switched to Farsi and his voice harshened. 'Why did you learn Farsi if not to spy on us for the CIA – or your oil companies, eh?'

'For my interest, just for my interest,' Starke replied politely in Farsi, his knowledge and accent good. 'I'm a guest in your country, invited here by your government to work for your government in partnership with Iranians. It's polite for guests to be aware of their hosts' taboos and customs, to learn their language, particularly when they enjoy the country and hope to be guests for many years.' His voice edged. 'And they're not my companies.'

'They're American. You're American. The CIA's American. All our problems come from America. The Shah's greed's American. All our problems come from America. For years Iran's been spat on by Americans.'

'Bullshit,' Starke said in English, now equally angry, knowing the only way to deal with a bully was to come out swinging. At once. He saw the man flush. He looked back, unafraid, letting the silence hang. The seconds ticked by. His eyes held the mullah's. But he couldn't dominate him. Unsettled but trying to appear calm, he glanced at Peshadi who waited and watched, smoking quietly. 'What's this all about, Colonel?'

'The mullah has asked for one of your helicopters to visit all the oil installations in our area. As you're aware we don't plan your routes or participate in your operations. You will arrange for one of your best pilots to do this. Today, starting at midday.'

'Why not use one of your airplanes? Perhaps I could supply a navi –'

'No. One of your helicopters with your personnel. At midday.'

Starke turned to the mullah. 'Sorry, but I only take orders from

IranOil, through our base manager and their area rep, Esvandiary. We're under contract to them and they're exclus –'

'The airplanes you fly, they're Iranian,' the mullah interrupted harshly, his exhaustion and pain welling up again, wanting a finish. 'You will provide one as required.'

'They're Iranian registry, but owned by S-G Helicopters Ltd of Aberdeen.'

'Iranian registry, in Iranian skies, filled with Iranian gasoline, authorised by Iranians, servicing Iranian rigs pumping Iranian oil, by God. They're Iranian!' Hussain's thin mouth twisted. 'Esvandiary will give the necessary flight orders by noon. How long will it take you to visit all your sites?'

After a pause Starke said, 'Airtime, maybe six hours. How long do you plan to spend at each setdown?'

The mullah just looked at him. 'After that I want to follow the pipeline to Abadan and land where I choose.'

Starke's eyes widened. He glanced at the colonel but saw that the man was still pointedly watching the spirals of smoke from his cigarette. 'That one's more difficult, mullah. We'd need clearances. Radar's not working, most of that airspace's controlled by Kish Air Traffic Control and that's er, air force controlled.'

'Whatever clearance is needed you will get,' Hussain said with finality and turned his eyes inflexibly on Peshadi. 'In the Name of God, I come back at noon: if you stand in my way, the guns begin.'

Starke could feel his heart pumping and the mullah could feel his heart pumping and so could Peshadi. Only the mullah was content – there was no need for him to worry, he was in the Hands of God, doing God's work, obeying orders: 'Press the enemy in every way. Be like water flowing downhill to the dam. Press against the dam of the usurper Shah, his lackeys, and the armed forces. We have to win them over with courage and blood. Press them in every way, you do God's work . . .'

A wind rattled the window and, involuntarily, they glanced at it and at the night beyond. The night was still black, the stars brilliant, but to the east there was the glimmer of dawn, the sun just under the rim of the sky.

'I will return at noon, Colonel Peshadi, alone or with many. You choose,' Hussain said quietly, and Starke felt the threat – or promise – with all of his being. 'But now, now it is time for prayer.' He forced himself to his feet, his hands still burning with pain, his back and head and ears still aching monstrously. For a moment he felt he was going to faint but he fought off the giddiness and the pain and strode out.

Peshadi got up. 'You will do as he asks. Please,' he added as a great concession. 'It is a temporary truce and temporary compromise – until we have final orders from His Imperial Majesty's legal government when we will stop all this nonsense.' Shakily he lit a cigarette from the butt of the last. 'You will have no problem. He will provide the necessary permissions so it will be a routine VIP flight. Routine. Of course you must agree because of course I can't allow one of my military airplanes to service a mullah, particularly Hussain who's renowned for his sedition! Of course not! It was a brilliant finesse on my part and you will not destroy it.' Angrily he stubbed out the cigarette, the ashtray full now, the air nicotine-laden, and he almost shouted, 'You heard what he said. At noon! Alone or with many. Do you want more blood spilled? Eh?'

'Of course not.'

'Good. Then do what you're told!' Peshadi stormed off.

Grimly Starke went to the window. The mullah had taken his place near the gate, raised his arms, and, like every muezzin from every minaret at every dawn in Islam, called the Faithful to first prayer in the time-honoured Arabic: 'Come to prayer, come to progress, prayer is better than sleep. There is no other God but God . . .'

And as Starke watched, Peshadi devoutly took his place at the head of all the men of the base, all ranks, who obediently, and with obvious gladness, had streamed out of their barracks, soldiers laying down their rifles on the ground beside them, villagers outside the fence equally devout. Then, following the lead of the mullah, they all turned towards Mecca, and began the obligatory movements, prostrations and Shahada litany: 'I testify there is no other God but God, and Mohammed is the Prophet of God . . .'

When the prayer was finished there was a great silence. Everyone waited. Then the mullah called out loudly, 'God, the Koran, and Khomeini!' Then he went through the gates towards Kowiss. Obediently, the villagers followed him.

Starke shivered in spite of himself. That mullah's so full of hate it's coming out of his pores. And so much hate's got to blow something or someone to hell. If I fly maybe it'll make him worse. If I assign someone or ask a volunteer that's ducking it because it's my responsibility.

'I have to fly him,' he muttered. 'Have to.'

Off Lengeh: 6:42 A.M. The 212, with two pilots and a full load of thirteen passengers, was on a routine flight, outward bound into the Strait of Hormuz from her S-G base at Lengeh, heading over the placid water of the Gulf for the French-developed Siri oil field. The sun just over the horizon with the promise of another fine cloudless day, though haze, routine over the Gulf, brought visibility down to a few miles.

'Chopper EP-HST, this is Kish Radar Control, turn to 260 degrees.'

Obediently, she went on to her new heading. '260 at 1,000,' Ed Vossi answered.

'Maintain 1,000. Report overhead Siri.' Unlike most of Iran, radar here was good, with stations at Kish Island and Lavan Island, manned by excellent USAF-trained Iranian Air Force operators – both ends of the Gulf were equally strategic and equally well serviced.

'HST.' Ed Vossi was an American – ex-USAF, thirty-two, and built like a linebacker. 'Radar's jumpy today, huh, Scrag?' he said to the other pilot.

'Too right. Must be their piles.'

Ahead now was the small island of Siri. It was barren, desolate, and low lying, with a small dirt airstrip, a few barracks for oil personnel, and a cluster of huge storage tanks that were fed by pipes laid on the seabed from rigs that were westward in the Gulf. The island lay about sixty miles off the Iranian coast, just inside the international boundary that bisected the Strait of Hormuz and separated Iranian waters from those of Oman and the United Arab Emirates.

Directly over the oil tanks, the chopper banked smoothly, heading westward, her first stop some miles away on the oil rig called Siri Three. At present the field had six working rigs, all operated by the French semi-government consortium, EPF, that had developed the field for IranOil against future shipments of oil. 'Kish Radar Control, HST over Siri at 1,000 feet,' Ed Vossi said into the boom mike.

'Roger HST. Maintain 1,000,' came back instantly. 'Report before you let down. You have outbound traffic ahead of you at ten o'clock, climbing.'

'We have them in sight.' The two pilots watched the flight of four closely packed fighter jets soaring into the high skies, going past them for the mouth of the strait.

'They're in a hurry,' the older man said and shifted in his seat.

'You can say that again. Lookit! Jesus, they're USAF, F15s!' Vossi was astonished. 'Shit, I didn't know any were in this area. You seen any before, Scrag?'

'No, mate,' Scrag Scragger said, equally concerned, making a slight adjustment to the volume of his headset. At 63, he was the oldest pilot in S-G, senior pilot at Lengeh, a wizened little man, very thin, very tough, with grizzled grey hair and deep-set, light blue Australian eyes that always seemed to be searching the horizon. His accent was interesting. 'I'd like to know what the hell's up. Radar's as itchy as a roo in a twiddle and that's the third flight we've seen since we got airborne, though the first Yankee.'

'Gotta be a task force, Scrag. Or maybe they're escort fighters the U.S. sent to Saudi Arabia with the AWACs.'

Scragger was sitting in the left seat, acting as training captain. Normally the 212 used a single-pilot configuration, the pilot in the right seat, but Scragger had had this airplane fitted with dual controls for training purposes. 'Well,' he said with a laugh, 'so long as we don't spot MIGs we're in good shape.'

'The Reds won't send equipment down here, much as they want the strait.' Vossi was very confident. He was barely half Scragger's age and almost twice his size. 'They won't so long as we tell them they'd better the hell not – and have airplanes and task forces and the will to use them.' He squinted down through the haze. 'Hey, Scrag, lookit.'

The huge supertanker was heavily burdened, low in the water, steaming ponderously outward bound towards Hormuz. 'I'll bet she's 500,000 tons or more.' They watched her for a moment. Sixty percent of the free world's oil went through this shallow, narrow waterway between Iran and Oman, barely fifteen miles across where the neck was navigable. Twenty million barrels a day. Every day.

'You think they'll ever build a million-ton tanker, Scrag?'

'Sure. Sure they'll build her if they want, Ed.' The ship passed below them. 'She was flying a Liberian flag,' Scragger said absently.

'You got eyes like an eagle.'

'It's all my clean living, sport.' Scragger glanced around into the cabin. All the passengers were in their seats, belts on, regulation Mae West life jackets on, ear protectors on, reading or looking out of the windows. Everything normal, he thought. Yes, and instruments're normal, sounds're normal, I'm normal and so's Ed. Then why am I itchy he asked himself, turning back once more.

Because of the task force, because of Kish radar, because of the passengers, because it's your birthday, and most of all because you're airborne and the only way you stay alive airborne is to be itchy. Amen. He laughed out loud.

'What's up, Scrag?'

'You're up, that's what. So you think you're a pilot, right?'

'Sure, Scrag,' Vossi said cautiously.

'Okay. You've pegged Siri Three?'

Vossi grinned and pointed at the distant rig that was barely visible in the haze, slightly east of the cluster.

Scragger beamed. 'Then close your eyes.'

'Aw c'me on, Scrag, sure this's a check flight but how about le –'

'I got control,' Scragger said happily. Instantly Vossi relinquished the controls. 'Now close your eyes 'cause you're under training.' Confidently, the young man took a last careful look at the target rig, adjusted his headset, took off his dark glasses, and obeyed.

Scragger handed Vossi the special pair of dark goggles he had had made. 'Here, put 'em on and don't open your eyes till I say. Get ready to take control.'

Vossi put on the goggles, and smoothly, still with his eyes closed, his hands and feet reached out, barely touching the controls as he knew Scragger liked. 'Okay. Ready, Scrag.'

'You got her.'

At once Vossi took over the controls, firmly and lightly, and was pleased that the transition was smooth, the airplane staying straight and level. He was flying now with only his ears to guide him, trying to anticipate the slightest variation in engine note – slowing down or speeding up – that would indicate he was climbing or descending. Now a small change. He anticipated nicely, almost sensing it before it happened, that the pitch was rising, therefore the engines were gathering speed and therefore the chopper was diving. He made the correction and brought her level again.

'Good on you, sport,' Scragger said approvingly. 'Now open your eyes.'

Vossi had expected the usual training glasses that excluded outside visibility but allowed you to see the instruments. He found himself in total blackness. In sudden panic, his concentration vanished and with it his coordination. For a split second he was totally disoriented, his stomach reeling as he knew the airplane would reel. But it didn't. The controls stayed rock firm in Scragger's hands that he had not felt on the controls.

'Jessus,' Vossi gasped, fighting his nausea, automatically reaching up to tear off the goggles.

'Keep 'em on! Ed, this's an emergency, you're the pilot, the only pilot aboard and you're in trouble – you can't see. What're you going to do? Take the controls! Come on! Emergency!'

There was bile in Vossi's mouth and he spat it out, his hands and feet nervous. He took the controls, overcorrected, and almost cried out in panic as they lurched, for he was expecting that Scragger would still be monitoring them. But he wasn't. Again Vossi overcorrected, totally disoriented. This time Scragger minimised the mistake.

'Settle down, Ed,' he ordered. 'Listen to the bloody engine! Get your hands and feet in tune.' Then more gently: 'Steady now you're doing fine, steady now. You can vomit later. You're in an emergency, you've got to put her down, and you got thirteen passengers aft. Me, I'm here beside you but I'm not a bleeding pilot, now what you going to do?'

Vossi's hands and feet were together again and his ears listening to the engine. 'I can't see but you can?'

'Right.'

'Then you can talk me down!'

'Right!' Scragger's voice edged. 'Course you got to ask the right questions. Kish Control, HST leaving 1,000 for Siri Three.'

'Roger, HST.'

Scragger's voice became different. 'My name's Burt from now on.

I'm a roustabout off one of the rigs. I know nothing about flying but I can read a dial – if you tell me proper where to look.'

Happily, Vossi hurled himself into the game and asked the right questions, 'Burt' forcing him to use the limits of his knowledge of flight control, cockpit control, where the dials were, making him ask what only an amateur could understand and answer. From time to time when he was not accurate enough, Burt with rising hysteria would screech, 'Jesus, I can't find the dial, which dial for Christ's sake, they're all the bloody same! Explain again, explain slower, oh, God we're all going to die . . .'

For Vossi the darkness fed on darkness. Time became stretched, no friendly dials or needles to reassure him, nothing but the voice forcing him to his own utmost limits.

When they were at fifty feet on their approach, Burt calling out landing advice, Vossi was nauseous, terrified in the darkness, knowing that the tiny landing circle on the oil rig was coming up to meet him. You've still time to abort, to put on power and get to hell out of here and wait it out aloft, but for how long?

'Now you're ten feet up and ten yards away just like you wanted.'

At once Vossi put her into hover, the sweat pouring off him.

'You're perfect, just over the dead centre, just like you wanted.'

The blackness had never been more intense. Nor his fear. Vossi muttered a prayer. Gently he eased off power. It seemed to take a lifetime and another and another and then the skids touched and they were down. For an instant he didn't believe it. His relief was so intense that he almost wept for joy. Then, from a great distance, he heard Scragger's real voice and felt the controls taken over. 'I got her, sport! That was bloody good, Ed. Ten out of ten. I'll take her now.'

Ed Vossi pulled off the goggles. He was soaking, his face chalky, and he slumped in his seat, hardly seeing the activity on the working rig before him, the heavy rope net spread over the landing pad that was a bare thirty yards in diameter. Jesus, I'm down, we're down and safe.

Scragger had put the engines to idle; no need to shut down as this was a short stop. He was humming 'Waltzing Matilda' which he did only when he was very pleased. The lad did very well, he thought, his flying's bonza. But how fast will he recover? Always wise to know, and where his balls are – when you fly with someone.

He turned and gave the thumbs-up to the man in the side front seat of the cabin, one of the French engineers who had to check electrical pumping equipment that had just been installed on this rig. The rest of the passengers waited patiently. Four were Japanese, guests of the

French officials and engineers from EPF. Scragger had been disquieted about carrying Japanese – pulled back to memories of his war days, memories of Australian losses in the Pacific war and thousands who died in the Japanese POW camps and on the Burma railway. Murders more like, he told himself darkly, then turned his attention to the off-loading.

The engineer had opened the door and was now helping Iranian deck labourers take packing cases from the cargo hatch. It was hot and humid on the deck, enervating, and the air stank of oil fumes. In the cockpit it was scorching as usual, humidity bad, but Scragger was comfortable. He glanced at Vossi, still slumped in his seat, his hands behind his neck, gathering himself.

He's a good lad, Scragger thought, then the dominating voice in the cabin behind him attracted his attention. It was Georges de Plessey, chief of the French officials and EPF's area manager. He was sitting on the arm of one of the seats, delivering another of his interminable lectures, this time to the Japanese. Better them'n me, Scragger told himself, amused. He had known de Plessey for three years and liked him – for the French food he provided and the quality of his bridge which they both enjoyed, but not for his conversation. Oil men're all the same, oil's all they know and all they want to know, and as far as they're concerned all the rest of us are here on earth to consume the stuff, pay through the bloody nose for it till we're dead – and even then most crematoria're oil fired. Bloody hell! Oil's skyrocketed to $14.80 a barrel, $4.80 a couple of years ago, and $1.80 a few years before that. Bloody highway robbers, the bloody lot, OPEC, the Seven Sisters, and even North Sea oil!

'All these rigs're on legs that sit on the sea floor,' de Plessey was saying, 'all French built and operated, serving one well each . . .' He wore khakis, and had sparse sandy hair, his face sunburned. The other Frenchmen were chattering and arguing among themselves – and that's all they do, Scragger thought, except eat and drink wine and romance the pants off any sheila without so much as a by-your-leave. Like that old bugger Jean-Luc, king cocksman of them all! Still, they're all individualists, every one of them – not like those other buggers. The Japanese were all short, lithe, and well groomed, all dressed the same: short-sleeved white shirt and dark tie and dark trousers and dark shoes, same digital watches, dark glasses; the only difference was in their ages. Like sardines in a can, Scragger thought.

'. . . The water here, as in all of the Gulf, is very shallow, M'sieur Kasigi,' de Plessey was saying. 'Here it's just about a hundred feet –

oil's easy to reach at about a thousand feet. We've six wells in this part of the field we call Siri Three, they're all on stream, that is, connected by pipes and pumping oil into our storage tanks on Siri Island – tank capacity is three million barrels and all tanks are full now.'

'And the docking on Siri, Monsieur de Plessey?' Kasigi, the greying Japanese spokesman asked, his English clear and careful. 'I could not see when we were over the island.'

'We load offshore at the moment. A wharf's planned for next year. Meanwhile there'll be no problem to load your medium tankers. Monsieur Kasigi. We guarantee quick service, quick loading. After all, we are French. You'll see tomorrow. Your *Rikomaru* hasn't been delayed?'

'No. She will be there at noon. What's the final capacity of the field?'

'Limitless,' the Frenchman said with a laugh. 'We're only pumping 75,000 barrels a day now but, *mon Dieu*, under the seabed here is a lake of oil.'

'Capit'an Excellency!' At Scragger's side window was the beaming face of young Abdollah Turik, one of the fire crew. 'I very good, ver very good. You?'

'Tip-top, young feller. How're things?'

'I pleased you to see, Capit'an Excellency.'

About a year ago Scragger's base at Lengeh had been alerted by radio – there was a CASEVAC on this rig. It was in the middle of a dirty night and the Iranian manager said perhaps the fireman had a burst appendix and could they get there as quick as possible after dawn – night flying being forbidden in Iran except for emergencies. Scragger had been duty officer and he had gone at once – it was company policy to go immediately, even in minimum conditions, and part of their special service. He had fetched the young man, taken him direct to the Iranian Naval Hospital at Bandar-e Abbas and talked them into accepting the youth. But for that the youth would have died.

Ever since then the young man would be there to welcome him, and once a month there was a haunch of fresh goat's meat at the base, much as Scragger tried to prevent it, because of the expense. Once he had visited the village in the hinterland of Lengeh where the youth had come from. It was usual: no sanitation, no electricity, no water, dirt floors, mud walls. Iran was very basic outside the cities but, even so, better than most of the Gulf states outside the cities. Abdollah's family was like all the others, no better, no worse. Many children, clouds of flies, a few goats and chickens, a few scrubby acres and soon, his father had said, one day soon we'll have our own school, Excellency pilot, and our own water supply and one day electricity, and yes it is true we are much better off with work from our oil that foreigners exploit – thanks be to God for giving us oil. Thanks be to God that my son Abdollah lived. It was the Will of God that Abdollah lived, the Will of God that persuaded the Excellency pilot to take so much trouble. Thanks be to God!

'How're things, Abdollah?' Scragger repeated, liking the youth who was modern, not like his father.

'Good.' Abdollah came closer, put his face almost into the window. 'Capit'an,' he said haltingly, no longer smiling, his voice so soft Scragger had to bend forwards to hear. 'Soon much trouble . . . communist Tudeh, mujhadin, perhaps fedayeen. Guns and explosives – perhaps a ship at Siri. Danger. Please please say not anything who says, yes?' Then he put back the smile on his face and called out loudly, 'Happy landings and come again soon, agha.' He waved once and, hiding his nervousness, went back to join the others.

'Sure, sure, Abdollah,' Scragger muttered. There were a number of Iranians watching but that was usual. Pilots were appreciated because they were the only link on a CASEVAC. He saw the landing master give him the thumbs-up. Automatically he turned around and re-checked that all was locked and everyone back in his place. 'Shall I take her, Ed?'

'Yeah, sure, Scrag.'

At a thousand feet Scragger levelled off, heading for Siri One where the rest of the passengers were due to disembark. He was very perturbed. Stone the crows, he thought. One bomb could blow Siri Island into the Gulf. This was the first time there had been any whisper of trouble. The Siri field had never been subjected to any of the strikes that had closed down all other fields, mostly, expats believed, because the French had given sanctuary to Khomeini.

Sabotage? Didn't the Jap say he's got a tanker due tomorrow? Yes, he did. What to do? Nothing at the moment, just put Abdollah aside for later – now's not the time, not when you're flying.

He glanced at Vossi. Ed did good, very good, better than . . . better than who? His mind ranged over all the pilots he had helped train over the years. Hundreds. He had been flying since he was fifteen, Royal Australian Air Force at seventeen in '33, Spitfires in '39 and flight lieutenant, then converting to choppers in '45, Korea '49, and out after twenty years' service, still a flight lieutenant, still ornery, and only thirty-seven. He laughed. In the air force he was always on the mat.

'For Christ's sake, Scragger, why pick on the air vice-marshal? You've done it this time . . .'

'But, Wingco, the Limey started it, the bastard said all us Aussies were thieves, had chain marks around our wrists, and were descended from convicts!'

'He did? Fucking Limeys're all the same, Scrag, even though in your case he was probably right as your family's been Down Under for ever, but even so you're still busted a rank again and if you don't behave I'll ground you for ever!'

But they never did. How could they? DFC and Bar, AFC and Bar, sixteen kills, and three times as many missions, happily, than anyone in the whole RAAF. And today still flying which was all he wanted in the world, still trying to be the best and safest, and still wanting to walk away from a prang, all passengers safe. If you fly choppers you can't not have equipment failures, he thought, knowing he had been very, very lucky. Not like some, equally good pilots, whose luck ran out. You've got to be lucky to be a good pilot.

Again he glanced across at Vossi, glad there wasn't a war on which was a pilot's great testing ground. I wouldn't like to lose young Ed, he's one of the best in S-G. Now who's better that you've flown with? Charlie Pettikin, of course, but then he should be, he's been bush pilot and through the wringer too. Tom Lochart the same. Dirty Duncan McIver's still the best of the lot even though he's grounded, may he rot with his bleeding three-month medicals – but I'd be just as mean and just as careful with him if I was grounded and he was flying around at sixty-three like a junior birdman. Poor bugger.

Scragger shuddered. If the CAA bring in the new regs about age and enforced retirement, I've had it. The day I'm grounded I'm for the pearly gates and no doubt about it.

Siri One was still well ahead. He had landed there three times a week for a year or more. Even so he was planning his approach as though it were the first time: 'Safety's no accident, it has to be prepared.' Today we'll do a nice gentle low approach an –

'Scrag.'

'Yes, me son?'

'You scared the bejesus outta me.'

'That's lesson number one. What else did you learn?'

'I guess how goddam easy it is to panic, how lonely you feel, helpless, and to bless your eyes.' Vossi almost burst out, 'I guess I learned how mortal I am, goddammit. Jesus, Scrag. I was scared – shit scared.'

'When it happened to me I did it in my pants.'

'Huh?'

'I was flying out of Kuwait, a 47G2 in the old days, the sixties.' The 47G2 was the small, three-seat, bubble-shaped, piston-engined Bell, now the workhorse of most traffic control and police forces. 'The charter was for a doc and an engineer in ExTex. They wanted to go out to an oasis, past Wafrah, where they had a CASEVAC – some poor sod mixed his leg up with the drill. Well, we were flying with the doors off as usual 'cause it was summer, about a hundred and twenty degrees, and dry and rotten for man and chopper as only the desert can be – worse'n our Outback by a long shot. But we'd been promised double charter and a bonus, so my old pal Forsyth volunteered me. It wasn't a bad day as desert days go, Ed, though the winds were red-hot'n gusting'n playing tricks, you know, the normal: sudden eddies whipping the sand into dust clouds, the usual whirlwinds in the eddies. I was at around three hundred feet on the approach when we hit the dust cloud – the dust so fine you couldn't see it. How it got through my goggles God only knows but one moment we were okay and the next coughing and spluttering and I had both eyes full and was as blind as an old Pegleg Pete.'

'You're kidding me!'

'No. It's true, swear to God! Couldn't see a bleeding thing, couldn't open my eyes, and I'm the only pilot with two passengers aboard.'

'Jesus, Scrag. Both eyes?'

'Both eyes and we swung all over the sky to hell until I got her more or less even and my heart back in me chest. The doc couldn't get the dust out, and every time he tried or I tried we near turned belly-up – you know how twitchy the G2 is. They were as panicked as me and that didn't help a bleeding bit. That's when I figured the only chance we got was to set her down blind. You said you was shit-scared, well, when I got our skids on the sand there wasn't a dribble left to come out, not even a dribble.'

'Jesus, Scrag, you got her down for real? Just like today but for real, both eyes full of dust? No shit?'

'I got 'em to talk me down, just like I did to you, 'least the doc did, the other poor sod'd fainted.' Scragger's eyes had never left his landfall. 'How's she look to you?'

'No sweat.' Siri One was dead ahead, the landing pad esplanaded over the water. They could see the landing master and his obligatory fire crew standing by. The wind sock was half full and steady.

Normally Scragger would report into radar and begin their gradual descent. Instead he said, 'We'll stay high today, sport, a high-angle approach and let her settle in.'

'Why, Scrag?'

'Make a change.'

Vossi frowned but said nothing. He rescanned the dials, seeking something amiss. There was nothing. Except a slight strangeness about the old man.

When they were in position high over the rig, Scragger clicked on the transmit: 'Kish Radar, HST, leaving 1,000 for Siri One.'

'Okay, HST. Report when ready for takeoff.'

'HST.'

They were set up for a steep-angle approach, normally used when high buildings or trees or pylons surrounded the point of touchdown. Scragger took off the exact amount of power. The chopper began to settle nicely, perfectly controlled. Nine hundred, eight seven six five . . . four . . . three . . . They both felt the vibration in the controls at the same time.

'Jesus,' Vossi gasped, but Scragger had already put her nose down sharply and floored the collective lever. Immediately she began to go down very fast. Two hundred feet, one fifty, one, vibrations increasing. Vossi's eyes leaped from dial to dial to landing point and back again. He was rigid in his seat, his mind shouting, Tail rotor's gone or tail rotor gearbox . . .

The landing pad was rushing at them, the ground crew scattering in panic, passengers hanging on in sudden fright at the untoward steepness, Vossi holding on to the side of his seat to steady himself. Now the whole instrument panel was vibrating, the engine pitch different. Any second he expected them to lose the tail rotor completely and then they'd be lost. The altimeter read sixty feet . . . fifty . . . forty . . . thirty . . . twenty, and his hands reached to grab the controls to begin the flare but Scragger anticipated him by a fraction of a second, gave her full power and flared perfectly. For a second she seemed poised motionless three feet up, engines screaming, then she touched down hard but not too hard on the near edge of the circle, skidded forward, and came to rest six feet off centre.

'Fuck,' Scragger muttered.

'Jesus, Scrag.' Vossi was hardly able to talk. 'That was perfect.'

'Oh, no, no, it wasn't, I'm off six feet.' With an effort Scragger unlocked his hands from the controls. 'Shut her down, Ed, quick as you can!' Scragger opened his door and slid out fast, the airflow from the blades whipping him, and went back to the cabin door, opening it. 'Stay where you are a moment,' he shouted over the dying scream of the jets, wet with relief that everyone was still belted in and no one hurt.

96

Obediently they stayed put, two of them pasty grey. The four Japanese stared at him impassively. Cold bloody lot, he thought.

'*Mon Dieu*, Scrag,' Georges de Plessey called out. 'What happened?'

'Don't know, think it's the tail rotor – soon's the rotors slow we c –'

'What the hell are you playing at, Vossi!' It was Ghafari, the Iranian landing manager, and he had shoved his face near the pilot's window, taut with rage. 'How dare you pull a practice engine out on this rig? I'll report you for dangerous flying!'

Scragger whirled on him. 'I was flying, not Capt'n Vossi!' Abruptly, Scragger's enormous relief that he had got down safely, mixed with his long-standing detestation of this man, snapped his temper. 'Piss off, Ghafari, piss off, or I'll thump you once and for all!' His fists bunched and he was ready. 'PISS OFF!'

The others watched, appalled. Vossi blanched. Ghafari, bigger and heavier than Scragger, shook his fist in Scragger's face, cursing him in Iranian, then shouted in English, wanting to provoke him: 'Foreign pig! How dare you swear at me, threaten me? I'll have you grounded for dangerous flying and thrown out of Iran. You dogs think you own our skies . . .'

Scragger lunged forward but Vossi was suddenly between them and he blocked the lunge with his great chest. 'Well what you know, old buddy? Hey, sorry, Scrag,' he said easily, 'but we'd better look at the tail rotor. Scrag, Scrag, old buddy, the tail rotor, huh?'

It took a few seconds for Scragger's eyes to clear. His heart was pumping and he saw them all staring at him. With a great effort he fought down his rage. 'You're . . . you're right, Ed. Yes.' Then he turned on Ghafari. 'We had a . . . we had an emergency.' Ghafari began to scoff and Scragger's rage soared but this time he controlled it.

They went aft. Many of the oil riggers, European and Iranian, were crowding around. The tail rotor stopped. About four inches were missing from one blade, the break jagged. When Vossi tried the main bearing, it was completely loose – the enormous torque caused by the imbalance of the blades had wrecked it. Behind him one of the passengers went to the side of the rig and was violently sick.

'Jesus,' Vossi muttered, 'I could break it off with two fingers.'

Ghafari broke the silence with his bluster. 'Clearly bad servicing, endangering the li –'

'Shut up, Ghafari,' de Plessey said angrily. '*Merde*, we are all alive and we owe our lives to Captain Scragger. No one could forecast this, S-G's standards are the highest in Iran.'

'It will be reported, Mr. de Plessey, an –'

'Yes, please do that and remember that I will be commending him for his airmanship.' De Plessey was imposing in his rage. He loathed Ghafari, considering him a rabble-rouser, openly pro-Khomeini one moment, inciting the workers to strike – provided there were no pro-Shah military or police nearby – the next fawningly pro-Shah and punishing the riggers for a minor infraction. Foreign pig, eh? 'Remember, too, this is a French-Iranian co-venture and France is not, how shall I put it, France has not been unfriendly to Iran in her hour of need.'

'Then you should insist Siri be serviced only by Frenchmen and not by old men! I will report this incident at once.' Ghafari walked off.

Before Scragger could say or do anything, de Plessey put his hands on his shoulders and kissed him on both cheeks and shook his hand with equal warmth. 'Thank you, *mon cher ami*!' There were loud cheers from the French as they congratulated themselves and crowded Scragger, formally embracing him. Then Kasigi stepped forward. '*Domo*,' he said formally, and to Scragger's further acute embarrassment, the four Japanese bowed to him in unison to more French cheers and much backslapping.

'Thank you, Captain,' Kasigi said formally. 'Yes, we understand and thank you.' He smiled and offered his card with both hands and another little bow. 'Yoshi Kasigi, Toda Shipping Industries. Thank you.'

'It wasn't a bad one, Mr. er Mr. Kasigee,' Scragger said, trying to get over his embarrassment – over his rage now and back in control though he promised himself that one day soon he'd get Ghafari alone ashore. 'We've, er, we've flotation gear, we'd plenty of space and we could have put her down in the water. It's our job, our job to get her down safely. Ed here,' he beamed at Vossi genially, knowing that by getting in the way the young man had saved him from a matting he would not have won, 'Captain Vossi would've done the same. Easy. It wasn't a bad one – I just wanted to save you getting wet though the water's nice and warm but you never know about Jaws . . .'

The tension broke and they all laughed, albeit a little nervously, for most of the Gulf and the mouths of the rivers that fed it were shark-infested. The warm waters and the abundance of food waste and untreated sewage that the Gulf nations had poured into it for millennia encouraged fish of all kinds. Particularly sharks. And because all food waste and human waste from the rigs went overboard, sharks would usually be nearby.

'Have you ever seen a big one, Captain?'

'Too right. There's a hammerhead that lurks off Kharg Island. I was stationed there for a couple of years and I'd spot him, oh, once or twice every few months. He's maybe twenty-five, maybe thirty feet. I've seen plenty of giant stingrays but he's the only big one.'

De Plessey shuddered. '*Merde* on all sharks. I was almost caught once on Siri and I was, how you say it, ah, yes, I was only paddling but the shark came racing at me in the shallows and going so fast it beached itself. It was about eight feet long. We shot it six times but it still thrashed around and tried to get us and took hours to die and even then not one of us wanted to get within range of it. Eh, sharks!' He glanced back at the broken blade. 'Me, I am very happy to be on the rig.'

They all agreed. The Frenchmen started chattering among themselves, gesticulating, two went to unload some hampers and another went to help the man who was still being sick. Riggers wandered off. The Japanese waited and watched.

Superstitiously Vossi touched the blade. 'Just for luck, huh, Scrag?'

'Why not? So long as you and the passengers walk away, it was a good landing.'

'What caused it?' de Plessey asked.

'Don't know, mate,' Scragger said. 'There was a flock of small seabirds, terns I think, at Siri Three. One of them might have gone into the rotor and caused a stress point – I never felt anything, but then you wouldn't. I know the rotor was perfect this morning because we both checked her as routine.' He shrugged. 'Act of God.'

'*Oui. Espèce de con*! Me, I don't like to be that close to an act of God.' He frowned at the landing pad. 'Can a 206 or Alouette get in to take us out by stages?'

'We'll send for another 212 and park our bird over there.' Scragger pointed to the inside of the landing pad near the tall stack of the working derrick. 'We've wheels in the baggage compartment, so it'll be no sweat, and no delay for you.'

'Good. Good, then we'll leave you to it. Come along the rest of you,' de Plessey said importantly. 'I think we all need some coffee and then a glass of iced Chablis.'

'I thought all rigs were dry,' Kasigi said.

De Plessey's eyebrows soared. 'They are, *monsieur*. Of course. For Iranians and non-French. Of course. But our rigs are French and subject to the Code Napoleon.' He added grandly, 'We should celebrate our safe arrival, and today you are guests of la Belle France so we can be civilised and bend the rules – what are rules for if not to be bent? Of course. Come along, then we'll begin the tour and have the briefing.'

They all followed him, except Kasigi. 'And you, Captain?' he asked. 'What will you do?'

'We'll wait. The chopper'll bring out spares and engineers,' Scragger said, ill at ease, not liking to be so near to any Japanese, unable to crush the memory of so many friends lost in the war so young with him still alive, and the constant, nagging question, why them and not me? 'We'll wait till she's repaired, then we'll go home. Why?'

'When will that be?'

'Before sundown. Why?'

Kasigi glanced back at the blade. 'With your permission I would like to fly back with you.'

'That's . . . that's up to Capt'n Vossi. He's formally captain on this flight.' Kasigi turned his attention to Vossi. The young pilot knew Scragger's dislike for Japanese but could not understand it. Just before takeoff he had said, 'Hell, Scrag, World War II was a million years ago. Japan's our ally now – the only big one we've got in Asia.' But Scragger had said, 'Just leave it, Ed,' so he had left it.

'You'd, er, best go back with the others, Mr. Kasigi, there's no telling how long we'll be.'

'Choppers make me nervous. I'd prefer to fly with you, if you don't mind.' Kasigi looked back at Scragger, hard eyes in a lived-in face. 'It was a bad one. You had almost no time, yet you autorotate at barely three hundred feet to make a perfect setdown on this flyspot. That was incredible flying. Incredible. One thing I don't understand: why were you high angle, on a high-angle approach?' He caught Vossi's glance at Scragger. Ah, he thought, you're wondering too. 'There's no reason on a day like today, is there?'

Scragger stared at him, even more unsettled. 'You fly choppers?'

'No, but I've been in enough to know when there's bad trouble. My business is tankers, so oil fields, here in the Gulf, Iraq, Alaska, everywhere – even Australia.' Kasigi let the hatred pass over him. He was used to it. He knew the reason, for he did a great deal of business now in Australia, a very great deal. Some of the hatred's merited, he thought. Some. Never mind, Australians will change, they'll have to. After all, we own a considerable section of her raw materials for years to come and soon we'll own more. Curious that we can do economically so easily what we failed to do militarily. 'Please, why did you choose a high-angle approach today? On a normal approach we'd be under the sea right now, on the bottom. Why?'

Scragger shrugged, wanting to end it.

'Skipper,' Vossi said, 'why did you?'

100

'Luck.'

Kasigi half smiled. 'If you'll allow me I would like to fly back with you. A life for a life, Captain. Please keep my card. Perhaps one day I can be of service to you.' He bowed politely and left.

11:56 A.M. 'Explosives on Siri, Scrag?' De Plessey was shocked.

'There might be,' Scragger replied, equally softly. They were on the far side of the platform, well away from everyone, and he had just told him what Abdollah had whispered.

The second 212 was long since there, waiting for de Plessey to give the word to start up and take him and his party on to Siri where they were due to have lunch. Mechanics had already stripped most of the tail section of Scragger's 212 and were well into repairs, Vossi watching attentively. The new rotor and gearbox were already in place.

After a moment, de Plessey said helplessly, 'Explosives could be anywhere, anywhere. Even a little explosive could wreck our whole pumping system. *Mon Dieu*, it would be a perfect ploy to further wreck Bakhtiar's chances – or Khomeini's – of getting back to normal.'

'Yes. But be careful how you use the info – and for God's sake keep it to yourself.'

'Of course. This man was on Siri Three?'

'At Lengeh.'

'Eh? Then why didn't you tell me this morning?'

'There was no time.' Scragger glanced around, making sure they were still not overheard. 'Be careful, whatever you do. Those fanatics don't give a twopenny damn for anything or anyone and if they think there's been a leak, that someone's ratted . . . there'll be bodies floating from here to Hormuz.'

'I agree.' De Plessey was very worried. 'Did you tell anyone else?'

'No, cobber.'

'*Mon Dieu*, what can I do? Security is . . . how can you have security in Iran? Like it or not we're in their power.' Then he added, 'Thank you a second time. I must tell you I've been expecting major sabotage on Kharg, and at Abadan; it's to the leftist advantage to create even more chaos, but I never thought they'd come here.'

Moodily he leaned on the rail and looked down at the sea sluggishly washing the legs of the platform. Sharks were circling and feeding. Now we've terrorists threatening us. Siri's tanks and pumps are a good target for sabotage. And if Siri's interfered with, we lose years of planning, years of oil that France desperately needs. Oil we may have to buy from the shit-stenched English and their shit-stenched North

101

Sea oil fields – how dare they be so lucky with their 1.3 million barrels a day and rising!

Why isn't there oil off our coasts or off Corse? God-cursed English with their two-faced, two-hearted approach to life! De Gaulle was right to keep them out of Europe, and now that we, out of the goodness of our hearts, have accepted them, even though we all know they're lying bastards, they care nothing to share their windfall with us, their partner. They only pretend to be with us in the EEC – they've always been against us and always will be. The Great Charles was right about them but incredibly wrong about Algeria. If we still had our Algeria, our soil and therefore our oil, we'd be rich, content, with Britain and Germany and all the rest licking the grime from between our toes.

Meanwhile, what to do?

Go to Siri and have lunch. After lunch you will think better. Thank God we can still get supplies from sensible, civilised Dubai, Sharyah and Al Shargaz: Brie, Camembert, Boursin, fresh garlic and butter from France daily, and real wine without which we might as well be dead. Well, almost, he added cautiously and saw Scragger staring at him. 'Yes, *mon brave*?'

'I said, what're you going to do?'

'Order a security exercise,' he said majestically. 'It seems that I had forgotten clause 56/976 of our original French-Iran contract that says every six months for a period of several days security must be checked against any and all intruders for . . . for the great glory of France and, er, Iran!' De Plessey's fine eyes lit up with the beauty of his ruse. 'Yes. Of course my subordinates forgot to remind me but now we will all hurl ourselves into the exercise with perfect French enthusiasm. Everywhere, on Siri, on the rigs, ashore, even at Lengeh! *Les crétins*! How dare they think they could sabotage the work of years.' He glanced around. There was still no one near. The rest of the party was assembled now near the second 212. 'I'll have to tell Kasigi because of his tanker,' he said quietly. 'That might be the target.'

'Can you trust him? I mean, to do everything quietly.'

'Yes. We will have to, *mon ami*. We will have to warn him, yes, we'll have to do that.' De Plessey felt his stomach rumbling. My God, he thought, very perturbed, I hope it's just hunger and that I'm not in for a bilious attack – though I wouldn't wonder with all that's happened today. First we almost have an accident, then our top pilot almost has a fight with that barrelful of dung Ghafari, and now the revolution may come to us. 'Kasigi asked if he could fly back with you. When will you be ready?'

'Before sundown, but there's no need for him to wait for us, he can go back with you.'

De Plessey frowned. 'I understand why you don't like Japanese – me, I still can't stand the Germans. But we must be practical. He's a good customer and since he asked, I'd appreciate it if you'd, you'd, er, ask Vossi to fly him, *mon cher ami*. Yes, now we are intimate friends, you saved our lives, and we shared an Act of God! Now we ca—' He brightened. 'Yes, and if he's with you it would be a perfect opportunity for you to tell him about security – I'm sure you could put it perfectly.'

'But th –'

'He's one of our very good customers,' de Plessey said firmly. 'Very good. Thank you, *mon ami*. I'll leave him at Siri. When you're ready, pick him up there. Excellent, then that's decided, and rest assured I will commend you to the authorities and to the Laird Gavallan himself.' He beamed again. 'We'll be off and I'll see you tomorrow.'

Scragger watched him go. He cursed silently. De Plessey was the top man so there was nothing he could do and that afternoon on the way to Siri he sat back in the cabin, sweating and hating it.

'Jesus, Scrag,' Vossi had said, in shock, when he had told him he was riding in the back. 'Passenger? You all right? You sure y –'

'I just want to see what it feels like,' Scragger had said irritably. 'Get your arse in the captain's seat, fetch that bugger from Siri, and set her down like a bleeding feather at Lengeh or it's in your bleeding report.'

Kasigi was waiting at the helipad. There was no shade and he was hot, dusty and sweating. Dunes stretched back to the pipelines and tank complex, all dirty brown from the dust. Scragger watched the dust devils, little whirlwinds, dance over the ground, and he thanked his stars that he could fly and didn't have to work in such a place. Yes, choppers are noisy and always vibrating and maverick, he thought, and yes, I miss flying the high skies, flying fixed wing alone in the high skies, diving and turning over and falling like an eagle to rise up again – but flying is flying and I still hate sitting in the bleeding cabin. For God's sake, here it's even worse than a regular aircraft! He hated flying without the controls and never felt safe and this added to his discomfort as he beckoned Kasigi to sit beside him and slammed the door shut. The two mechanics were dozing in their seats opposite, their white overalls stained with sweat. Kasigi adjusted the Mae West and snapped his seat belt tight.

Once airborne Scragger leaned closer to him. 'There's no way to tell you but quickly, so here it is: there may be a terrorist attack on Siri, one of the rigs, perhaps even your ship. De Plessey asked me to warn you.'

103

The air hissed out of Kasigi's mouth. 'When?' he asked over the heavy cabin noise.

'I don't know. Nor does de Plessey. But it's more than possible.'

'How? How will they sabotage?'

'No idea. Guns or explosives, maybe a time bomb, so you'd better tighten security.'

'It is already optimum,' Kasigi replied at once, and then saw the flash of anger in Scragger's eyes. For a second he could not fathom the why, then he remembered what he had just said. 'Ah, so sorry, Captain, I did not mean to be boastful. It is just that we have always very high standards and in these waters my ships are . . .' He had almost said 'on a war footing' but stopped himself in time, containing his irritation at the other's sensitivity. 'In these waters everyone is more than careful. Please excuse me.'

'De Plessey wanted you to know. And also to keep the tip mum – to keep it to yourself – and not get any Iranian backs up.'

'I understand. The tip is safe with me. Again, thank you.' Kasigi saw Scragger nod briefly then settle back in his seat. The bigger half of him also wanted to nod briefly and end everything there, but because the Australian had saved his companions' lives as well as his own, therefore enabling them to give further service to the company and their leader, Hiro Toda, he felt it his duty to attempt a healing.

'Captain,' he said as quietly as he could over the thunder of the jets, 'I understand why we Japanese are hated by Australians and I apologise for all the Changis, all the Burma Roads, and all the atrocities. I can only tell you the truth: these happenings are well taught in our schools and not forgotten. It is to our national shame that these things happened.'

It's true, he thought angrily. To commit those atrocities was stupid even though those fools did not understand they were committing atrocities – after all, the enemy were cowards, most of them, and meekly surrendered in tens of thousands and so forfeited their rights as human beings according to our Bushido, our code, that stipulates for a soldier to surrender is the worst dishonour. A few mistakes by a few sadists, a few ill-educated peasants of prison guards – most of whom were the garlic eaters, Koreans – and all Japanese have to suffer for ever. It is a shame of Japan. And another, the worst of all shames, that our supreme war-leader failed in his duty and so forced the emperor into the shame of having to terminate the war. 'Please accept my apology for all of us.'

Scragger stared at him. After a pause he said simply, 'Sorry, but I

104

can't. For one thing my ex-partner Forsyth was the first man into Changi; he never got over what he saw; for another too many of my cobbers, not just POWs, bought it. Too many. I can't forget. An' more than that, I won't. I won't because if I did, that'd be their last betrayal. We've betrayed them in the peace – what peace? We've betrayed 'em all, that's what I think. Sorry, but there it is.'

'I understand. Even so we can make a peace, you and I. No?'

'Maybe. Maybe in time.'

Ah, time, Kasigi thought, bemused. Today I was again on the edge of death. How much time do we have, you and I? Isn't time an illusion and all life just illusions within illusions? And death? His revered samurai ancestor's death poem had summed it up perfectly: What are clouds, But an excuse for the sky? What is life, But an escape from Death?

The ancestor was Yabu Kasigi, daimyo of Izu and Baka and supporter of Yoshi Toronaga, first and greatest of the Toronaga shoguns who, from father to son, ruled Japan from 1603 until 1871 when the Meiji emperor finally obliterated the shogunate and outlawed the entire samurai class. But Yabu Kasigi was not remembered for his loyalty to his liege lord or his courage in battle – as was his famous nephew Omi Kasigi, who fought for Toronaga at the great battle of Sekigahara, had his hand blown off but still led the charge that broke the enemy.

Oh, no, Yabu betrayed Toronaga, or tried to betray him, and so was ordered by him to commit seppuku – ritual death by disembowelment. Yabu was revered for the calligraphy of his death poem, and his courage when he committed seppuku. On that day, kneeling before the assembled samurai, he contemptuously dispensed with the second samurai who would stand behind him with a long sword to end his agony quickly by cutting off his head and so preventing the shame of crying out. He took the short knife and plunged it deep into his stomach, then leisurely made the four cuts, the most difficult seppuku of all – across and down, across again and up – then lifted out his own entrails to die at length, never having cried out.

Kasigi shivered at the thought of having to do the same, knowing he would not have had the courage. Modern war's nothing to those days when you could be ordered to die thus at the whim of your liege lord . . .

He saw Scragger watching him.

'I was in the war, too,' he said involuntarily. 'Fixed wing. I flew Zeros in China, Malaya and Indonesia. And New Guinea. Courage in war is different from . . . from courage alone . . . I mean, not in war, isn't it?'

'I don't understand.'

I haven't thought about my war for years, Kasigi was thinking, a sudden wave of fear going through him, remembering his constant terror of dying or being maimed, terror that had consumed him – like today when he was certain they were all going to die and he and his companions had been frozen with fear. Yes, and we all did today what we did all those war years: remembered our heritage in the Land of the Gods, swallowed our terror as we had been taught from childhood, pretended calm, pretended harmony so as not to shame ourselves before others, flew missions for the emperor against the enemy as best we could and then, when he said lay down your arms, thankfully laid down our arms, however much the shame.

A few found the shame unbearable and killed themselves in the ancient way with honour. Did I lose honour because I didn't? Never. I obeyed the emperor who ordered us to bear the unbearable, then joined my cousin's firm as was ordained and have served him loyally for the greater glory of Japan. From the ruins of Yokohama I helped rebuild Toda Shipping Industries into one of Japan's greatest firms, constructing great ships, inventing the supertankers, bigger every year – soon the keel of the first million-tonner to be laid. Now our ships are everywhere, carrying bulk raw materials into Japan and finished goods out. We Japanese are rightly the wonder of the world. But, oh, so vulnerable – we must have oil or we perish.

Out of one of the windows he noticed a tanker steaming up the Gulf, another going towards Hormuz. The bridge continues, he thought. At least one tanker every hundred miles all the way from here to Japan, day in day out, to feed our factories without which we starve. All OPEC knows it, they're gouging us and gloating. Like today. Today it took all my willpower to pretend outward calm dealing with that . . . that odious Frenchman, stinking of garlic and that revolting, stinking, oozing vomit mess called Brie, blatantly demanding $2.80 over and above the already outrageous $14.80, and me, of ancient samurai lineage, having to haggle with him like a Hong Kong Chinese.

'But, M'sieur de Plessey, surely you must see that at that price, plus freight an –'

'So sorry, m'sieur, but I have my instructions. As agreed the three million barrels of Siri oil are on offer to you first. ExTex have asked for a quote and so have four other majors. If you wish to change your mind . . .'

'No, but the contract specifies "the current OPEC price" and w –'

'Yes, but you surely know that all OPEC suppliers are charging a premium. Don't forget the Saudis plan to cut back production this month, that last week all the majors ordered another sweeping wave of *force majeur* cutbacks, that Libya's cutting her production too. BP's increased its cutback to forty-five percent . . .'

Kasigi wanted to bellow with rage as he remembered that when at length he had agreed, provided he could have all three million barrels at the same price, the Frenchman had smiled sweetly and said, 'Certainly, provided you load within seven days,' both of them knowing it was impossible. Knowing too that a Rumanian state delegation was presently in Kuwait seeking three million tons of crude, let alone three million barrels, to compensate for the cut-off of their own Iranian supplies that came to them through the Iran-Soviet pipelines. And that there were other buyers, dozens of them, waiting to take over his Siri option and all his other options – for oil, liquid natural gas, naphtha, and other petrochemicals.

'Very well, seventeen sixty a barrel,' Kasigi had said agreeably. But inside he swore to even the score somehow.

'For this one tanker, *m'sieur*.'

'Of course for this tanker,' he had said even more agreeably.

And now this Australian pilot whispers to me that even this one tanker may not be safe. This strange old man, far too old to be flying yet so skilled, so knowledgeable, so open, and so foolish – foolish to be so open, for then you put yourself into another's power.

He looked back at Scragger. 'You said we could make a peace maybe in time. We both ran out of time today – but for your skill, and luck, though we call that karma. I truly don't know how much time we have. Perhaps my ship is blown up tomorrow. I will be aboard her.' He shrugged. 'Karma. But let us be friends, just you and I – I don't think we betray our war comrades, yours and mine.' He put out his hand. 'Please.'

Scragger looked at the hand. Kasigi willed himself to wait. Then Scragger conceded, half nodded and shook the hand firmly. 'Okay, sport, let's give it a go.'

At that moment he saw Vossi turn and beckon him. At once Scragger went forward to the cockpit. 'Yes, Ed?'

'There's a CASEVAC, Scrag, from Siri Three. One of the deck crew's fallen overboard . . .'

They went at once. The body was floating near the legs of the rig. They winched it aboard. Sharks had already fed on the lower limbs and one arm was missing. The head and face were badly bruised and curiously disfigured. It had been Abdollah Turik.

Near Bandar-e Delam: 4:52 P.M. Shadows were lengthening. Beyond the road the land was scrubby, and beyond that stony foothills rose to snowcapped mountains – the northern end of the Zagros. This side, beside the stream and marshes that led at length to the port a few miles away, was one of the numerous oil pipelines that crisscrossed this whole area. The pipeline was steel, twenty inches in diameter, and set on a concrete trestle that led down into a culvert under the road, then went underground. A mile or so to the east was a village – low lying, dust-covered, earth-coloured, made from mud bricks – and coming from that direction was a small car. It was old and battered and travelled slowly, the engine sounding good, too good for the body.

In the car were four Iranians. They were young and clean-shaven shaven and better dressed than usual, though all were sweat-stained and very nervous. Near the culvert the car stopped. One young man wearing glasses got out from the front seat and pretended to urinate on the side of the road, his eyes searching all around.

'It's all clear,' he said.

At once the two youths in the back came out swiftly, a rough, heavy bag between them, and ducked down the dirt embankment into the culvert. The young man with glasses fastened his buttons, then casually went to the boot of the car and opened it. Under a piece of torn canvas he saw the snub nose of the Czech-made machine pistol. A little of his nervousness left him.

The driver got out and urinated into the ditch, his stream strong.

'I wanted to, Mashoud, but couldn't,' the youth with glasses said, envying him. He wiped the sweat off his face and pushed at his glasses.

'I can never do it before an exam,' Mashoud said and laughed. 'God grant university will open again soon.'

'God! God's the opiate of the masses,' the youth with glasses said witheringly, then turned his attention to the road. It was still empty as far in both directions. South a few miles away, the sun reflected off the waters of the Gulf. He lit a cigarette. His fingers trembled. Time passed very slowly. Flies swarmed, making the silence seem more silent. Then he noticed a dust cloud on the road, the other side of the village. 'Look!'

Together they squinted into the distance. 'Are they lorries – or trucks, army trucks?' Mashoud said anxiously, then ran to the side of the culvert and shouted, 'Hurry up, you two. There's something coming!'

'All right,' a voice called from below.

'We're almost done,' another voice said.

The two youths in the culvert had the sack open and were already packing the flat bags of explosive haphazardly against the welded steel pipe and along its length. The pipe was covered with a sheath of canvas and pitch to protect it from erosion. 'Give me the detonator and fuse, Ali,' the older one said throatily. Both of them were filthy now, the dirt streaked with sweat.

'Here.' Ali handed it to him carefully, his shirt clinging to his skin. 'Are you sure you know how to do it, Bijan?'

'We've studied the pamphlet for hours. Didn't we practise doing it with our eyes closed?' Bijan forced a smile. 'We're like Robert Jordan in *For Whom the Bell Tolls*. Just like him.'

The other shivered. 'I hope the bell's not tolling for us.'

'Even if it does, what does that matter? The party will conquer, and the Masses will have victory.' Bijan's inexperienced fingers awkwardly jammed the highly volatile, nitroglycerine detonator against one of the explosives, connected one end of the fuse beside it, and piled the last of the bags on top to hold it in place.

Mashoud's voice called out even more urgently, 'Hurry, they're . . . we think they're army trucks with soldiers!'

For a moment both young men were paralysed, then they unreeled the length of fuse, tripping over each other in their nervousness. Unnoticed, the fuse end near the detonator came away. They laid the ten-foot length along the ground, lit the far end, and took to their heels. Bijan glanced back to check everything, saw that one end was spluttering nicely, and was aghast to notice the other end dangling free. He rushed back, shakily stuffed it near the detonator, slipped, and slammed the detonator against the concrete.

The nitroglycerine exploded and blew the bag of explosives next to it and that blew the next and the next and they all went and tore Bijan to pieces with twenty feet of the pipe, blowing off the culvert roof and overturning the car, killing two of the other youths and ripping a leg off the last.

Oil began gushing from the pipe. Hundreds of barrels a minute. The oil should have ignited but it did not – the explosives had been wrongly placed and detonated – and by the time the two army trucks had stopped cautiously a hundred yards away, the oil slick had already reached the stream. The lighter oils, gaseous, volatile, floated on the surface, and the heavier crude began to seep into the banks and marshes and soil, making the whole area highly dangerous.

In the two commandeered trucks were some twenty of Khomeini's Green Bands, most of them bearded, the rest unshaven, all wearing their characteristic armbands – peasants, a few oil-field workers, a PLO-trained leader, and a mullah – all armed, all battle-stained, a few wounded, the uniformed police captain bound and gagged and still alive lying on the floor. They had just attacked and overwhelmed a police station to the north and were now heading into Bandar-e Delam to continue the war. Their assignment was to help others subdue the civilian airport that was a few miles to the south.

The mullah leading, they came to the edge of the blown-up culvert. For a moment they watched the oil gushing, then a moaning attracted them. They unslung their guns and went carefully to the overturned car. The youth missing a leg was lying half under it, dying fast. Flies swarmed and settled and swarmed again, blood and entrails everywhere.

'Who are you?' the mullah asked, shaking him roughly. 'Why did you do this?'

The youth opened his eyes. Without his glasses everything was misted. Blindly he groped for them. The terror of dying engulfed him. He tried to say the shahada but only a petrified scream came forth. Blood welled into his throat, choking him.

110

'As God wants,' the mullah said, turning away. He noticed the broken glasses in the dirt and picked them up. One lens was fractured, the other missing.

'Why should they do this?' one of the Green Bands asked. 'We've no orders to sabotage the pipes – not now.'

'They must be communists, or Islamic-Marxist carrion.' The mullah tossed the glasses away. His face was bruised and his long robe torn in places and he was starving. 'They look like students. May God kill all His enemies as quickly.'

'Hey, look at these,' another called out. He had been searching the car and found three machine pistols and some grenades. 'All Czech made. Only leftists are so well armed. These dogs're enemy all right.'

'God be praised. Good, we can use the arms. Can we get the trucks around the culvert?'

'Oh, yes, easily, thanks be to God,' his driver, a thickset bearded man said. He was a worker in one of the oil fields and knew about pipelines. 'We'd better report the sabotage,' he added nervously. 'This whole area could explode. I could phone the pumping station if there's a phone working – or send a message – then they can cut the flow. We'd better be fast. This whole area's deadly and the spill will pollute everything downstream.'

'That's in the Hands of God.' The mullah watched the oil spreading. 'Even so it's not right to waste the riches God gave us. Good, you will try to phone from the airport.' Another bubbling scream for help came from the youth. They left him to die.

Bandar-e Delam Airport: 5:30 P.M. The civilian airport was unguarded, abandoned, and not operational except for the S-G contingent that had come here a few weeks ago from Kharg Island. The airport had two short runways, a small tower, some hangars, a two-storey office building, and some barracks, and now a few modern trailers – S-G's property – for temporary housing and HQ. It was like any one of the dozens of civilian airports that the Shah had had built for the feeder airlines that used to service all Iran: 'We will have airports and modern services,' he had decreed and so it was done. But since the troubles had begun six months ago and all internal feeder airlines struck, airplanes had been grounded throughout Iran and the airports closed down. Ground crews and staff had vanished. Most of the aircraft had been left in the open, without service or care. Of the three twin jets that were parked on the apron, two had flat tyres, one, a cockpit window broken. All had had their tanks drained by looters. All were filthy, almost derelict. And sad.

In great contrast to these were the five sparkling S-G helicopters, three 212s and two 206s lined up meticulously, being given their daily bath and final check of the day. The sun was low now and cast long shadows.

Captain Rudiger Lutz, senior pilot, moved to the last helicopter and inspected it as carefully as he had the others. 'Very good,' he said at length. 'You can put them away.' He watched while the mechanics and their Iranian ground crew wheeled the airplanes back into the hangars that were also spotless. He knew that many of the crew laughed at him behind his back for his meticulousness, but that didn't matter – so long as they obeyed. That's our most difficult problem, he thought. How to get them to obey, how to operate in a war situation when we're not governed by army rules and just noncombatants in the middle of a war situation whether Duncan McIver wants to admit it openly or not.

This morning Duke Starke at Kowiss had relayed by HF McIver's terse message from Tehran about the rumoured attack on Tehran Airport and the revolt of one of the air bases there – because of distance and mountains Bandar-e Delam could not talk direct to Tehran nor to their other bases, only to Kowiss. Worriedly Rudi had assembled all his expat crew, four pilots, seven mechanics – seven English, two Americans, one German, and one Frenchman – where they could not be overheard and had told them. 'It wasn't so much what Duke said but the way he said it – kept calling me "Rudiger" when it's always "Rudi". He sounded itchy.'

'Not like Duke Starke to be itchy – unless it's hit the fan,' Jon Tyrer, Rudi's American second-in-command, had said uneasily. 'You think he's in trouble? You think maybe we should go take a look at Kowiss?'

'Perhaps. But we'll wait till I talk to him tonight.'

'Me, I think we'd better get ready to do a midnight skip, Rudi,' mechanic Fowler Joines had said with finality. 'Yes. If old Duke's nervous . . . we'd best be ready to scarper, to get lost.'

'You're crazy, Fowler. We've never had trouble,' Tyrer said. 'This whole area's more or less quiet, police and troops disciplined and in control. Shit, we've five air force bases within twenty miles and they're all elite and pro-Shah. There's bound to be a loyalist coup soon.'

'You ever been in the middle of a coup for crissake? They bloody shoot each other and I'm a civilian!'

'Okay, say the stuff hits the fan, what do you suggest?'

They had discussed all sorts of possibilities. Land, air, sea. Iraq's border was barely a hundred miles away – and Kuwait within easy range across the Gulf.

'We'll have plenty of notice.' Rudi was very confident. 'McIver'll know if there's a coup coming.'

'Listen, old son,' Fowler had said, more sourly than usual, 'I know companies – same as bloody generals! If it gets really tough we'll be on our tod – on our bloody own – so we'd better have a plan. I'm not going to get my head shot off for the Shah, Khomeini or even the Laird-god Gavallan. I say we just scarper – fly the coop!'

'Bloody hell, Fowler,' one of the English pilots had burst out, 'are you suggesting we hijack one of our own planes? We'd be grounded for ever!'

'Maybe that's better than the pearly gates!'

'We could get shot down, for God's sake. We'd never get away with it – you know how all our flights are monitored, how twitchy radar is here – bloody sight worse than at Lengeh! We can't get off the ground without asking permission to start engines . . .'

At length Rudi had asked them to give him contingency suggestions in case sudden evacuation was necessary, by land, by air, or by sea, and had left them arguing.

All day he had been worrying what to do, what was wrong at Kowiss, and at Tehran. As senior pilot he felt responsible for his crew – apart from the dozen Iranian labourers and Jahan, his radio op, none of whom he had been able to pay for six weeks now – along with all the aircraft and spares. We were damned lucky to get out of Kharg so well, he thought, his stomach tightening. The withdrawal had gone smoothly with all airplanes, all important spares, and some of their transport brought here over four days without interfering with their heavy load of contract flying and CASEVACs.

Getting out of Kharg had been easy because everyone had wanted to go. As quickly as possible. Even before the troubles, Kharg was an unpopular base with nothing to do except work and look forward to R and R in Tehran or home. When the troubles began everyone knew that Kharg was a prime target for revolutionaries. There had been a great deal of rioting, some shooting. Recently more of the IPLO armbands had been seen among the rioters and the commander of the island had threatened that he'd shoot every villager on the island if the rioting didn't stop. Since they had left a few weeks ago the island had been quiet, ominously quiet.

And that retreat wasn't a real emergency, he reminded himself. How to operate in one? Last week he had flown to Kowiss to pick up some special spares and had asked Starke how he planned to operate at Kowiss if there was real trouble.

'The same as you, Rudi. You'd try to operate within company rules which won't apply then,' the tall Texan had said. 'We got a couple of things going for us: just about all of our guys're ex-service of some sort so there's a kinda chain of command – but hell, you can plan all you want and then you still won't sleep nights because when the stuff hits the fan, it'll be the same as ever: some of the guys'll fall apart, some won't, and you'll never know in advance who's gonna do what, or even how you'll react yourself.'

Rudi had never been in a shooting war, though his service with the German army in the fifties had been on the East German borders, and in West Germany you're always conscious of the Wall, the Curtain, and of all your brothers and sisters behind it – and of the waiting, brooding Soviet legions and satellite legions with their tens of thousands of tanks and missiles also behind it, just yards away. And conscious of German zealots on both sides of the border who worship their messiah called Lenin and the thousands of spies gnawing at our guts.

Sad.

How many from my hometown?

He had been born in a little village near Plauen close to the Czecho-slovakian border, now part of East Germany. In '45 he had been twelve, his brother sixteen and already in the army. The war years had not been bad for him and his younger sister and mother. In the country there was enough to eat. But in '45 they had fled before the Soviet hordes, carrying what they could, to join the vast German migrations westward: two million from Prussia, another two from the north, four from the centre, another two from the south – along with other millions of Czechs, Poles, Hungarians, Rumanians, Austrians, Bulgarians, of all Europe – all starving now, all petrified, all fighting to stay alive.

Ah, staying alive, he thought.

On the trek, cold and weary and almost broken, he remembered going with his mother to a garbage dump, somewhere near Nürnberg, the countryside war-ravaged and even towns rubbled, his mother frantic to find a kettle – their own stolen in the night – impossible to buy one, even if they had had the money. 'We've got to have a kettle to boil water or we'll all die, we'll get typhus or dysentery like the others – we can't live without boiled water,' she had cried out. So he had gone with her, in tears, convinced it was a waste of time, but they had found one. It was old and battered, the spout bent and the handle loose but the top was with it and it did not leak. Now the kettle was clean and sparkling and in a place of honour on the mantelpiece in the kitchen of their farmhouse near Freiburg in the Black Forest where his wife and sons and mother were. And once a year, each New Year's Eve, his mother would still make tea from water boiled in the kettle. And, when he was there, they would smile together, he and she. 'If you believe enough, my son, and try,' she would always whisper, 'you can find your kettle. Never forget, you found it, I didn't.'

There were sudden warning shouts. He whirled around to see three army trucks burst through the gate, one racing for the tower, the other towards his hangars. The trucks skidded to a halt and Green Band revolutionaries fanned out over the base, two men charging at him, their guns levelled, screaming Farsi which he did not understand, as others started rounding up his men in the hangar. Petrified, he raised his hands, his heart pounding at the suddenness. Two Green Bands, bearded and sweating with excitement-fear, shoved gun barrels at his face and Rudi flinched.

'I'm not armed,' he gasped. 'What do you want? Eh?'

Neither man answered, just continued to threaten him. Behind them he could see the rest of his crew being herded out of their barrack trailers on to the apron. Other attackers were jumping in and out of the helicopters, searching them, carelessly overturning gear, one man hurling neatly rolled life jackets out of their seat pockets. His rage overcame his terror. 'Hey, *Sie verrückten Dummkopfe*,' he shouted. '*Lass'n Sie meine verrückten Flugzeuge allein!*' Before he knew what he was doing he had brushed the guns aside and rushed towards them. For a moment it looked as though the two Iranians would shoot, but they just went after him, caught up with him, and pulled him around. One lifted a rifle by the butt to smash his face in.

'Stop!'

The men froze.

The man who shouted out the command in English was in his early thirties, heavyset, wearing rough clothes, with a green armband, a stubbled beard, dark wavy hair, and dark eyes. 'Who is in charge here?'

'I am!' Rudi Lutz tore his arms out of his assailants' grasp. 'What are you doing here? What do you want?'

'We are possessing this airport in the name of Islam and the revolution.' The man's accent was English English. 'How many troops are here, air staff?'

'There's none. No troops – there's no tower staff, there's no one here but us,' Rudi said, trying to catch his breath.

115

'No troops?' The man's voice was dangerous.

'No, none. We've had patrols here since we came here a few weeks ago – they come from time to time. But none are stationed here. And no military airplanes.' Rudi stabbed a finger at the hangar. 'Tell those . . . those men to be careful of my airplanes, lives depend on them, Iranian as well as ours.'

The man turned and saw what was happening. He shouted another command, cursing them. The men shouted back at him carelessly, then after a moment came out into the sunset, leaving chaos in their wake.

'Please excuse them,' the man said. 'My name is Zataki. I am chief of the Abadan komiteh. With the help of God, we command Bandar-e Delam now.'

Rudi's stomach was churning. His expats and Iranian staff were in a frozen group beside the low office building, guns surrounding them. 'We're working for a British comp –'

'Yes, we know about S-G Helicopters.' Zataki turned and shouted again. Reluctantly, some of his men went to the gate and began to take up defensive positions. He looked back at Rudi. 'Your name?'

'Captain Lutz.'

'You have nothing to fear, Captain Lutz, you and your men. Do you have arms here?'

'No, except Verey Light pistols, aircraft stores. For signalling, distress signalling.'

'You will fetch them.' Zataki turned and went nearer to the S-G group and stood there, examining faces. Rudi saw the fear of his Iranians, cooks, ground staff, fitters, Jahan, and Yemeni, the IranOil manager.

'These are all my people,' he said, trying to sound firm. 'All S-G employees.'

Zataki looked at him, then came very close, and Rudi had to steel himself not to flinch again. 'Do you know what Mujhadin-al-Khalq means? Fedayeen? Tudeh?' he asked softly, heavier than Rudi, and with a gun.

'Yes.'

'Good.' After a pause, Zataki went back to staring at the Iranians. One by one. The silence grew. Suddenly he stabbed a finger at one man, a fitter. The man sagged, then began to run frantically, screaming in Farsi. They caught him easily and beat him senseless.

'The komiteh will judge him and sentence him in God's Name.' Zataki glanced at Rudi. 'Captain,' he said, his lips a thin line, 'I asked you to fetch your Verey pistols.'

'They're in the safe, and quite safe,' Rudi said, just as toughly, not feeling brave inside. 'You may have them whenever you want. They're only in the airplane during a mission. I . . . I want that man released!'

Without warning, Zataki reversed his machine gun and slammed the butt at Rudi's head but Rudi caught it with one hand, deflecting it, tore it out of the man's grasp, his reflexes perfect, and before the gun crashed to the ground, the hardened edge of his other, open hand was axing into Zataki's unprotected throat. But he stopped the death blow, barely touching the man's skin. Then he stepped back, at bay now. All guns were trained on him.

The silence grew. His men watched, appalled. Zataki was staring at Rudi, enraged. The shadows were long, and a slight wind toyed with the wind sock, crackling it slightly.

'Pick up the gun!'

In the bigger silence, Rudi heard the threat and the promise and he knew that his life – all of theirs – was in the balance. 'Fowler, do it!' he ordered and prayed that he had chosen correctly.

Reluctantly Fowler came forward. 'Yessir, coming right up!' It seemed to take a long time for him to cover the twenty yards, but no one stopped him and one of the guards moved out of his way. He picked the gun up, automatically put the safety on, carefully handed it back to Zataki, butt first. 'It's not bent and, er, good as new, me son.'

The leader took the gun and slipped the safety off and everyone heard the click as though it were a thunderclap. 'You know guns?'

'Yes . . . oh, yes. We . . . all mechanics were . . . we all had to have a course in the RAF . . . Royal Air Force,' Fowler said, keeping his eyes on the man's eyes and he thought, What the fuck am I doing here, standing up to this smelly son of a whore's left tit? 'Can we dismiss? We're civilians, me son, we're noncombatants, begging your pardon. Neutral.'

Zataki jerked a thumb at the line. 'Go back there.' Then he turned to Rudi. 'Where did you learn karate?'

'In the army – the German army.'

'Ah, German. You're German? Germans have been good to Iran. Not like the British, or Americans. Which are your pilots, their names and their nationalities?'

Rudi hesitated, then pointed. 'Captain Dubois, French, Captains Tyrer, Block, and Forsyth, English.'

'No Americans?'

Rudi had another great sinking in his stomach. Jon Tyrer was American and had false identity cards. Then his ears heard the sound

117

of the approaching chopper, recognised the thrunk-thrunk of a 206, and automatically he searched the skies, along with all of them. Then one of the Green Bands let out a cry and pointed as others rushed into defensive positions, everyone scattering except the expats. They had recognised the markings.

'Everyone into the hangar,' Zataki ordered. The chopper came over the airfield at a thousand feet and began to circle. 'It's one of yours?'

'Yes. But not from this base.' Rudi squinted into the sun. His heart picked up when he read the markings. 'It's EP-HXT, from Kowiss, from our base in Kowiss.'

'What's he want?'

'Obviously to land.'

'Find out who's aboard. And don't try any tricks.'

Together they went to the UHF in his office. 'HXT, do you read?'

'HXT, loud and clear. This is Captain Starke of Kowiss.' A pause, then, 'Captain Lutz?'

'Yes, it's Captain Lutz, Captain Starke,' he said, knowing by the formality that there must be hostiles aboard, as Starke would know something was wrong here.

'Request permission to land. I'm low on gas and require refuelling. I'm cleared by Abadan radar.'

Rudi glanced at Zataki. 'Ask who's in that airplane?' the man said.

'Who've you got aboard?'

There was a pause. 'Four passengers. What's the problem?'

Rudi waited. Zataki did not know what to do. Any of the military bases might be listening in. 'Let him land . . . near the hangar.'

'Permission to land, HXT. Set her down near the east hangar.'

'HXT.'

Zataki leaned over and switched off the set. 'In future you will only use the radio with permission.'

'There are routine reports to give to Abadan and Kharg radar. My radio op's been with us f –'

Blood soared into Zataki's face and he shouted, 'Until further orders your radio's only to be used with one of us listening in. Nor will any airplanes take off, nor land here without permission. You are responsible.' Then the rage evaporated as quickly as it had arrived. He lifted his gun. The safety was still off. 'If you'd continued the blow you would have broken my neck, my throat, and I would have died. Yes?'

After a pause, Rudi nodded. 'Yes.'

'Why did you stop?'

'I've . . . I've never killed anyone. I did not want to start.'

'I've killed many – doing God's work. Many – thanks be to God. Many. And will kill many more enemies of Islam, with God's help.' Zataki clicked on the safety. 'It was the Will of God the blow was stopped, nothing more. I cannot give you that man. He is Iranian, this is Iran, he is an enemy of Iran and Islam.'

They watched from the hangar as the 206 came in. There were four passengers aboard, all civilians, all armed with submachine guns. In the front seat was a mullah and some of Zataki's tension left him, but not his anger. The moment the chopper touched down his revolutionaries swarmed out of hiding, guns levelled, and surrounded her.

The mullah Hussain got out. His face tightened seeing Zataki's hostility. 'Peace be with you. I am Hussain Kowissi of the Kowiss komiteh.'

'Welcome to my area in the Name of God, mullah,' Zataki said, his face even grimmer. 'I am Colonel Zataki of the Abadan komiteh. We rule this area and do not approve of men putting themselves between us and God.'

'Sunni and Shi'as are brothers, Islam is Islam,' Hussain said. 'We thank our Sunni brethren of the Abadan oil fields for their support. Let us go and talk, our Islamic revolution is not yet won.'

Tautly Zataki nodded and called his men off and beckoned the mullah to follow him out of earshot.

At once Rudi hurried under the rotors.

'What the hell's going on, Rudi?' Starke said from the cockpit, his shoulders aching, finishing shutdown procedures.

Rudi told him. 'What about you?'

As rapidly Starke told him what had happened during the night and in Colonel Peshadi's office. 'The mullah and these thugs came back at midday and they near bust a gut when I refused to fly armed men. Man, I liked to die, but I'm not flying armed men, that makes us accessories to revolution, and the revolution's nowhere near settled yet – we saw hundreds of troops and roadblocks coming here.' His hard eyes went over the base and the pockets of Green Bands here and there, the rest of the crew still standing near their barracks under guard, and the fitter still senseless. 'Bastards,' he said and got out. He stretched against the ache in his back and felt better. 'Eventually we compromised. They kept their weapons but I kept their magazines and stowed them in the baggage compart . . .' He stopped. The tall mullah, Hussain, was approaching them, the blade above circling leisurely now.

'The baggage key, please, Captain,' Hussain said.

Starke gave it to him. 'There's no time to get back to Kowiss and no time to get into Abadan.'

'Can't you night fly?'

'I can but it's against your regulations. You had a headset, you heard how radar is here. You'll have military choppers and airplanes buzzing us like hornets before we're halfway airborne. I'll refuel and we'll overnight here – least I will. You can always grab some transport from your buddies here if you need to go into town.'

Hussain flushed. 'Your time is very short, American,' he said in Farsi. 'You and all your imperialist parasites.'

'If it is the Will of God, mullah, if it's the Will of God. I'll be ready to leave after first prayer. Then I leave, with or without you.'

'You will take me to Abadan and wait and then return to Kowiss as I wish and as Colonel Peshadi ordered!'

Starke snapped in English, 'If you're ready to leave after first prayer! But Peshadi didn't order it – I'm not under his orders, or yours or IranOil – IranOil asked me to fly you on this charter. I'll have to refuel on the way back.'

Hussain said irritably, 'Very well, we will leave at dawn. As to refuelling . . .' He thought a moment. 'We will do that at Kharg.'

Both Starke and Rudi were startled. 'How we going to get cleared into Kharg? Kharg's loyal, er, still air force controlled. You'd have your heads blown off.'

Hussain just looked at them. 'You will wait here until the komiteh has decided. In one hour I want to talk to Kowiss on the HF.' He stormed off.

Starke said quietly, 'These bastards're too well organised, Rudi. We're up shit creek.'

Rudi could feel the weakness in his legs. 'We'd better get ourselves organised, prepare to get to hell out of here.'

'We'll do that after food. You okay?'

'I thought I was dead. They're going to kill us all, Duke.'

'I don't think so. For some reason we're VIPs to them. They need us and that's why Hussain backs off, your Zataki too. They might rough us up to keep us in line but I figure at least for the short haul we're important in some way.' Again Starke tried to ease the tiredness out of his back and shoulders. 'I could use one of Erikki's saunas.' They both looked at a burst of exuberant gunfire into the air from some Green Bands. 'Crazy sonsofbitches. From what I overheard this operation's part of a general uprising to confront the armed forces – guns against guns. How's your radio reception? BBC or Voice of America?'

'Bad to very bad and jammed most days and nights. Of course Radio Free Iran's loud and clear as always.' This was the Soviet station based just over the border at Baku on the Caspian Sea. 'And Radio Moscow's like it was in your back garden, as always.'

TABRIZ

CHAPTER

7

Near Tabriz: 6:05 P.M. In the snow-covered mountains far to the north, not far from the Soviet border, Pettikin's 206 came over the rise fast, continuing to climb up the pass, skimming the trees, following the road.

'Tabriz One, HFC from Tehran. Do you read?' he called again.

Still no answer. Light was closing in, the late afternoon sun hidden by deep cloud cover that was only a few hundred feet above him, grey and heavy with snow. Again he tried to raise the base, very tired now, his face badly bruised and still hurting from the beating he had taken. His gloves and the broken skin over his knuckles made it awkward for him to press the transmit button. 'Tabriz One. HFC from Tehran. Do you read?'

Again there was no answer but this did not worry him. Communication in the mountains was always bad, he was not expected, and there was no reason for Erikki Yokkonen or the base manager to have arranged a radio watch. As the road climbed, the cloud cover came down but he saw, thankfully, that the crest ahead was still clear, and once over it, the road fell away and there, half a mile farther on, was the base.

This morning it had taken him much longer than expected to drive to the small military air base at Galeg Morghi, not far from Tehran's international airport, and though he had left the apartment before dawn, he did not arrive there until a bleak sun was well into the polluted, smoke-filled sky. He had had to divert many times. Street battles were still going on with many roads blocked – some deliberately with barricades but more with burned-out wrecks of cars or buses. Many bodies sprawled on the snow-covered sidewalks and roadways, many wounded, and twice, angry police turned him back. But he persevered and took an even more circuitous route. When he arrived, to his surprise the gate to their section of the base where they operated a training school was open and unguarded. Normally air force sentries would be there. He drove in and parked his car in the safety of the S-G hangar but found none of the day skeleton crew of mechanics or ground personnel on duty.

It was a cold brisk day and he was bundled in winter flight gear. Snow covered the field and most of the runway. While he waited he ground-checked the 206 that he was going to take. Everything was fine. The spares that Tabriz needed, tail rotor and two hydraulic pumps, were in the baggage compartment. Tanks were full which gave it two and a half to three hours' range – two to three hundred miles depending on wind, altitude, and power settings. He would still have to refuel en route. His flight plan called for him to do this at Bandar-e Pahlavi, a port on the Caspian. Without effort he wheeled the airplane on to the apron. Then all hell let loose and he was on the edge of a battle.

Trucks filled with soldiers raced through the gate and headed across the field to be greeted with a hail of bullets from the main part of the base with its hangars, barracks and administration buildings. Other trucks raced down the perimeter road, firing as they went, then a tracked armoured Bren carrier joined the others, its machine guns blazing. Aghast, Pettikin recognised the shoulder badges and helmet markings of the Immortals. In their wake came armoured buses filled with paramilitary police and other men who spread out over his side of the base, securing it. Before he knew what was happening, four of them grabbed him and dragged him over to one of the buses, shouting Farsi at him.

'For Christ's sake, I don't speak Farsi,' he shouted back, trying to fight out of their grasp. Then one of them punched him in the stomach and he retched, tore himself free, and smashed his attacker in the face.

At once another man pulled out a pistol and fired. The bullet went into the neck of his parka, ricocheted violently off the bus, speckles of burning cordite in its wake. He froze. Someone belted him hard across the mouth and the others started punching and kicking him. At that moment a police officer came over. 'American? You American?' he said angrily in bad English.

'I'm British,' Pettikin gasped, the blood in his mouth, trying to free himself from the men who pinioned him against the hood of the bus. 'I'm from S-G Helicopters and that's my –'

'American! Saboteur!' The man stuck his gun in Pettikin's face and Pettikin saw the man's finger tighten on the trigger. 'We SAVAK know you Americans cause all our troubles!'

Then through the haze of his terror he heard a voice shout in Farsi and he felt the iron hands holding him loosen. With disbelief he saw the young British paratroop captain, dressed in a camouflage jumpsuit and red beret, two small, heavily armed soldiers with Oriental faces, grenades on their shoulder belts, packs on their backs, standing in front of them. Nonchalantly the captain was tossing a grenade up and down in his left hand as though it were an orange, the pin secured. He wore a revolver at his belt and a curiously shaped knife in a holster. Abruptly he stopped and pointed at Pettikin and then at the 206, angrily shouted at the police in Farsi, waved an imperious hand, and saluted Pettikin.

'For Christ's sake, look important, Captain Pettikin,' he said quickly, his Scots accent pleasing, then knocked a policeman's hand away from Pettikin's arm. One of the others started to raise his gun but stopped as the captain jerked the pin out of his grenade, still holding the lever tight. At the same time his men cocked their automatic rifles, held them casually but very ready. The older of the two beamed, loosened his knife in its holster. 'Is your chopper ready to go?'

'Yes . . . yes it is,' Pettikin mumbled.

'Crank her up, fast as you can. Leave the doors open and when you're ready to leave, give me the thumbs-up and we'll all pile in. Plan to get out low and fast. Go on! Tenzing, go with him.' The officer jerked his thumb at the chopper fifty yards away and turned back, switched to Farsi again, cursed the Iranians, ordering them away to the other side where the battle had waned a little. The soldier called Tenzing went with Pettikin who was still dazed.

'Please hurry, sahib,' Tenzing said and leaned against one of the doors, his gun ready. Pettikin needed no encouragement.

More armoured cars raced past but paid no attention to them, nor did other groups of police and military who were desperately intent on securing the base against the mobs who could now be heard approaching. Behind them the police officer was angrily arguing with the paratrooper, the others nervously looking over their shoulders at the advancing sound of 'Allah-uuuu Akbarrrr!' Mixed with it was more gunfire now and a few explosions. Two hundred yards away on the perimeter road outside the fence, the vanguard of the mob set fire to a parked car and it exploded.

The helicopter's jet engines came to life and the sound enraged the police officer, but a phalanx of armed civilian youths came charging through the gate from the other direction. Someone shouted 'Mujhadin!' At once everyone this side of the base grouped to intercept them and began firing. Covered by the diversion, the captain and the other soldier rushed for the chopper, jumped in, Pettikin put on full power and fled a few inches above the grass, swerved to avoid a burning truck, then barrelled drunkenly into the sky. The captain lurched, almost dropped his grenade, couldn't put the pin back in because of Pettikin's violent evading action. He was in the front seat and hung on for his life, held the door open, tossed the grenade carefully overboard and watched it curve to the ground.

It exploded harmlessly. 'Jolly good,' he said, locked the door and his seat belt, checked that the two soldiers were okay, and gave a thumbs-up to Pettikin.

Pettikin hardly noticed. Once clear of Tehran he put her down in scrubland, well away from any roads or villages, and checked for bullet damage. When he saw there was none, he began to breathe. 'Christ, I can't thank you enough, Captain,' he said, putting out his hand, his head aching. 'I thought you were a bloody mirage at first. Captain . . . ?'

'Ross. This's Sergeant Tenzing and Corporal Gueng.'

Pettikin shook hands and thanked both of them. They were short, happy men, hard and lithe. Tenzing was older, in his early fifties. 'You're heaven sent, all of you.'

Ross smiled, his teeth very white in his sunburned face. 'I didn't quite know how we were going to get out of that one. Wouldn't have been very good form to knock off police, anyone for that matter – even SAVAK.'

'I agree.' Pettikin had never seen such blue eyes in a man, judging him to be in his late twenties. 'What the hell was going on back there?'

'Some air force servicemen had mutinied, and some officers, and

125

loyalists were there to put a stop to it. We heard Khomeini supporters and leftists were coming to the help of the mutineers.'

'What a mess! Can't thank you enough. How'd you know my name?'

'We'd, er, got wind of your approved flight plan to Tabriz via Bandar-e Pahlavi and wanted to hitch a ride. We were very late and thought we'd missed you – we were diverted to hell and gone. However, here we are.'

'Thank God for that. You're Gurkhas?'

'Just, er, odd bods, so to speak.'

Pettikin nodded thoughtfully. He had noticed that none of them had shoulder patches or insignias – except for Ross's captain's pips and their red berets. 'How do "odd bods" get wind of flight plans?'

'I really don't know,' Ross said airily. 'I just obey orders.' He glanced around. The land was flat and stony and open, and cold with snow on the ground. 'Don't you think we should move on? We're a bit exposed here.'

Pettikin got back into the cockpit. 'What's on in Tabriz?'

'Actually, we'd like to be dropped off just this side of Bandar-e Pahlavi, if you don't mind.'

'Sure.' Automatically Pettikin had begun start-up procedures. 'What's going on there?'

'Let's say we have to see a man about a dog.'

Pettikin laughed, liking him. 'There's lots of dogs all over! Bandar-e Pahlavi it is, then, and I'll stop asking questions.'

'Sorry, but you know how it is. I'd also appreciate it if you'd forget my name and that we were aboard.'

'And if I'm asked – by authority? Our departure was a little public.'

'I didn't give any name – just ordered you,' Ross grinned, 'with vile threats!'

'All right. But I won't forget your name.'

Pettikin set down a few miles outside the port of Bandar-e Pahlavi. Ross had picked the landing from a map that he carried. It was a duned beach, well away from any village, the blue waters of the Caspian Sea placid. Fishing boats dotted the sea, great cumulus clouds in the sunny sky. Here the land was tropical and the air humid with many insects and no sign of snow though the Elburz Mountains behind Tehran were heavily covered. It was highly irregular to land without permission, but twice Pettikin had called Bandar-e Pahlavi Airport where he was to refuel and had got no answer so he thought that he would be safe enough – he could always plead an emergency.

'Good luck, and thanks again,' he said and shook all their hands. 'If you ever need a favour – anything – you've got it.' They got out quickly, shouldered their packs, heading up the dunes. That was the last he had seen of them.

'Tabriz One, do you read?'

He was circling uneasily at the regulation seven hundred feet, then came lower. No sign of life – nor were any lights on. Strangely disquieted he landed close to the hangar. There he waited, ready for instant takeoff, not knowing what to expect – the news of servicemen mutinying in Tehran, particularly the supposedly elite air force, had disturbed him very much. But no one came. Nothing happened. Reluctantly, he locked the controls with great care and got out, leaving the engines running. It was very dangerous and against regulations – very dangerous because if the locks slipped it was possible for the chopper to ground-loop and get out of control.

But I don't want to get caught short, he thought grimly, rechecked the locks and quickly headed for the office through the snow. It was empty, the hangars empty except for the disembowelled 212, trailers empty, with no sign of anyone – or any form of a battle. A little more reassured, he went through the camp as quickly as he could. On the table in Erikki Yokkonen's cabin was an empty vodka bottle. A full one was in the refrigerator – he would dearly have loved a drink but flying and alcohol never mix. There was also bottled water, some Iranian bread, and dried ham. He drank the water gratefully. I'll eat only after I've gone over the whole place, he thought.

In the bedroom the bed was made but there was a shoe here and another there. Gradually his eyes found more signs of a hasty departure. The other trailers showed other clues. There was no transport on the base and Erikki's red Range Rover was gone too. Clearly the base had been abandoned somewhat hastily. But why?

His eyes gauged the sky. The wind had picked up and he heard it whine through the snow-laden forest over the muted growl of the idling jet engines. He felt the chill through his flying jacket and heavy pants and flying boots. His body ached for a hot shower – even better, one of Erikki's saunas – and food and bed and hot grog and eight hours' sleep. The wind's no problem yet, he thought, but I've got an hour of light at the most to refuel and get back through the pass and down into the plains. Or do I stay here tonight?

Pettikin was not a forest man, not a mountain man. He knew desert and bush, jungle, veld, and the Dead Country of Saudi. The vast reaches on the flat never fazed him. But cold did. And snow. First refuel, he thought.

127

But there was no fuel in the dump. None. Many forty-gallon drums but they were all empty. Never mind, he told himself, burying his panic, I've enough in my tanks for the hundred and fifty miles back to Bandar-e Pahlavi. I could go on to Tabriz Airport, or try to scrounge some from the ExTex depot at Ardabil, but that's too bloody near the Soviet border.

Again he measured the sky. Bloody hell! I can park here or somewhere en route. What's it to be?

Here. Safer.

He shut down and put the 206 into the hangar, locking the door. Now the silence was deafening. He hesitated, then went out, closing the hangar door after him. His feet crunched on the snow. The wind tugged at him as he walked to Erikki's trailer. Halfway there he stopped, his stomach twisting. He sensed someone watching him. He looked around, his eyes and ears searching the forest and the base. The wind sock danced in the eddies that trembled the treetops, creaking them, whining through the forest, and abruptly he remembered Tom Lochart sitting around a campfire in the Zagros on one of their skiing trips, telling the Canadian legend of the Wendigo, the evil demon of the forest, borne on the wild wind, that waits in the treetops, whining, waiting to catch you unawares, then suddenly swoops down and you're terrified and begin to run but you can't get away and you feel the icy breath behind you and you run and run with bigger and ever bigger steps until your feet are bloody stumps and then the Wendigo catches you up on to the treetops and you die.

He shuddered, hating to be alone here. Curious, I've never thought about it before but I'm almost never alone. There's always someone around, mechanic or pilot or friend or Genny or Mac or Claire in the old days.

He was still watching the forest intently. Somewhere in the distance dogs began to bark. The feeling that there was someone out there was still very strong. With an effort he dismissed his unease, went back to the chopper, and found the Verey Light pistol. He carried the huge-calibre, snub-nosed weapon openly as he went back to Erikki's cabin and felt happier having it with him. And even happier when he had bolted the door and closed the curtains.

Night came quickly. With darkness animals began to hunt.

Tehran: 7:05 P.M. McIver was walking along the deserted, tree-lined residential boulevard, tired and hungry. All streetlights were out and he picked his way carefully in the semi-darkness, snow banked against the

128

walls of fine houses on both sides of the roadway. Sound of distant guns and, carried on the cold wind, 'Allahhh-u Akbarrr.' He turned the corner and almost stumbled into the Centurion tank that was parked half on the sidewalk. A flashlight momentarily blinded him. Soldiers moved out of ambush.

'Who're you, agha?' a young officer said in good English. 'What're you doing here?'

'I'm Captain . . . I'm Captain McIver, Duncan . . . Duncan McIver, I'm walking home from my office, and . . . and my flat's the other side of the park, around the next corner.'

'ID please.'

Gingerly McIver reached into his inner pocket. He felt the two small photos beside his ID, one of the Shah, the other of Khomeini, but with all the day's rumours of mutinies, he could not decide which would be correct so produced neither. The officer examined the ID under the flashlight. Now that McIver's eyes had adjusted to the darkness, he noticed the man's tiredness and stubble beard and crumpled uniform. Other soldiers watched silently. None were smoking which McIver found curious. The Centurion towered over them, malevolent, almost as though waiting to pounce.

'Thank you.' The officer handed the well-used card back to him. More firing, nearer this time. The soldiers waited, watching the night. 'Better not to be out after dark, agha. Good night.'

'Yes, thank you. Good night.' Thankfully McIver walked off, wondering if they were loyalist or mutineers – Christ, if some units mutiny and some don't there's going to be hell to pay. Another corner, this road and the park also dark and empty that, not so long ago, was always busy and brightly lit with more light streaming from windows, servants and people and children, all happy and lots of laughter among themselves, hurrying this way and that. That's what I miss most of all, he thought. The laughter. Wonder if we'll ever get those times back again.

His day had been frustrating, no phones, radio contact with Kowiss bad, and he had not been able to raise any of his other bases. Once again none of his office staff had arrived which further irritated him. Several times he had tried to telex Gavallan but could not get a connection. 'Tomorrow'll be better,' he said, then quickened his pace, the emptiness of the streets unpleasant.

Their apartment block was five storeys and they had one of the penthouses. The staircase was dimly lit, electricity down to half power again, the lift out of action for months. He went up the stairs wearily, the paucity of light making the climb more gloomy. But inside his apartment, candles were already lit and his spirits rose. 'Hi, Genny!' he called out, relocked the door, and hung up his old British warm. 'Whisky time!'

'Duncan! I'm in the dining room, come here for a minute.'

He strode down the corridor, stopped at the doorway, and gaped. The dining table was laden with a dozen Iranian dishes and bowls of fruit, candles everywhere. Genny beamed at him. And so did Sharazad. 'Bless my soul! Sharazad, this's your doing? How nice to see you wh –'

'Oh, it's nice to see you too, Mac, you get younger every day, both of you are, so sorry to intrude,' Sharazad said in a rush, her voice bubbling and joyous, 'but I remember that yesterday was your wedding anniversary because it's five days before my birthday, and I know how you like lamb horisht and polo and the other things, so we brought them, Hassan, Dewa and I, and candles.' She was barely five foot three, the kind of Persian beauty that Omar Khayyám had immortalised. She got up. 'Now that you're back, I'm off.'

'But wait a second, why don't you stay and eat with us an –'

'Oh but I can't, much as I'd like to, Father's having a party tonight and I have to attend. This is just a little gift and I've left Hassan to serve and to clean up and oh I do hope you have a lovely time! Hassan! Dewa!' she called out, then hugged Genny and hugged McIver and ran down to the door where her two servants were now waiting. One held her fur coat for her. She put it on, then wrapped the dark shroud of her chador around her, blew Genny another kiss, and, with the other servant, hurried away. Hassan, a tall man of thirty, wearing a white tunic and black trousers and a big smile, relocked the door. 'Shall I serve dinner, madam?' he asked Genny in Farsi.

'Yes, please, in ten minutes,' she replied happily. 'But first the master will have a whisky.' At once Hassan went to the sideboard and poured the drink and brought the water, bowed, and left them.

'By God, Gen, it's just like the old days,' McIver said with a beam.

'Yes. Silly, isn't it, that that's only a few months ago?' Up to then they had had a delightful live-in couple, the wife an exemplary cook of European and Iranian food who made up for the lighthearted malingering of her husband whom McIver had dubbed Ali Baba. Both had suddenly vanished, as had almost all expat servants. No explanation, no notice. 'Wonder if they're all right, Duncan?'

'Sure to be. Ali Baba was a grafter and had to have enough stashed away to keep them for a month of Sundays. Did Paula get off?'

'No, she's staying the night again – Nogger isn't. They went to dinner with some of her Alitalia crew.' Her eyebrows arched. 'Our Nogger's sure she's ripe for nogging, but I hope he's wrong. I like Paula.' They could hear Hassan in the kitchen. 'That's the sweetest sound in the world.'

McIver grinned back at her and raised his glass. 'Thank God for Sharazad and no washing up!'

'That's the best part.' Genny sighed. 'Such a nice girl, so thoughtful. Tom's so lucky. Sharazad says he's due tomorrow.'

'Hope so, he'll have mail for us.'

'Did you get hold of Andy?'

'No, no, not yet.' McIver decided not to mention the tank. 'Do you think you could borrow Hassan or one of her other servants for a couple of days a week? It'd help you tremendously.'

'I wouldn't ask – you know how it is.'

'I suppose you're right, bloody annoying.' Now it was almost impossible for any expats to find help, whatever you were prepared to pay. Up to a few months ago it had been easy to get fine, caring servants and then, with a few words of Farsi and their help, running a happy home, shopping, was usually a breeze.

'That was one of the best things about Iran,' she said. 'Made such a difference – took all the agony out of living in such an alien country.'

'You still think of it as alien – after all this time?'

'More than ever. All the kindness, politeness, of the few Iranians we'd meet, I've always felt it was only on the surface – that their real feelings are the ones out in the open now – I don't mean everyone, of course, not our friends; Annoush, for instance, now she's one of the nicest, kindest people in the world.' Annoush was the wife of General Valik, the senior of the partners in Tehran. 'Most of the wives felt that, Duncan,' she added, lost in her musing. 'Perhaps that's why expats flock together, all the tennis parties and skiing parties, boating, weekends on the Caspian – and servants to carry the picnic baskets and clean up. I think we had the life of Riley, but not any more.'

'It'll come back – hope to God it does, for them as well as us. Walking home I suddenly realised what I missed most. It was all the laughter. No one seems to laugh any more, I mean on the streets, even the kids.' McIver was drinking his whisky sparingly.

'Yes, I miss the laughter very much. I miss the Shah too. Sorry he had to go – everything was well ordered, as far as we were concerned, up to such a short time ago. Poor man, what a rotten deal we've given him now, him and that lovely wife of his – after all the friendship he gave our side. I feel quite ashamed – he certainly did his best for his people.'

'Unfortunately, Genny, for most of them it seems it wasn't good enough!'

'I know. Sad. Life is very sad sometimes. Well, no point in crying over spilt milk. Hungry?'

'I'll say.'

Candles made the dining room warm and friendly and took the chill off the apartment. Curtains were drawn against the night. At once Hassan brought the steaming bowls of various horisht – literally meaning soup but more like a thick stew of lamb or chicken and vegetables, raisins and spices of all kinds – and polo, the delicious Iranian rice that is parboiled, then baked in a buttered dish until the crust is firm and golden brown, a favourite of both of them. 'Bless Sharazad, she's a sight for sore eyes.'

Genny smiled back at him. 'Yes, she is, so's Paula.'

'You're not so bad either, Gen.'

'Get on with you, but for that you can have a nightcap. As Jean-Luc would say, *Bon appétit!*' They ate hungrily, the food exquisite, reminding both of them of meals they had had in the houses of their friends.

'Gen, I ran into young Christian Tollonnen at lunch, you remember Erikki's friend from the Finnish embassy? He told me Azadeh's passport was all ready. That's good, but the thing that shook me was he said, in passing, about eight out of every ten of his Iranian friends or acquaintances are no longer in Iran and if it kept up in the new exodus, pretty soon there'd only be mullahs and their flocks left. Then I started counting and came up with about the same proportion – those in what we'd call the middle and upper class.'

'I don't blame them leaving. I'd do the same.' Then she added involuntarily, 'Don't think Sharazad will.'

McIver had heard an undercurrent and he studied her. 'Oh?'

Genny toyed with a little piece of the golden crust and changed her mind about not telling him. 'For the love of God don't say anything to Tom who'd have a fit – and I don't know how much is fact and how much a young girl's idealistic make-believe – but she happily whispered she's spent most of the day at Doshan Tappeh where, she says, there's been a real insurrection, guns, grenades, the lot . . .'

'Christ!'

'. . . militantly on the side of what she called "our Glorious Freedom Fighters" who turn out to be mutinying air force servicemen, some officers, Green Bands supported by thousands of civilians – against police, loyalist troops, and the Immortals . . .'

At Bandar-e Delam Airport: 7: 50 P.M. With the going down of the sun, more armed revolutionaries had arrived and now there were guards on all hangars and approaches to the airport. Rudi Lutz had been told by Zataki that no S-G peronnel could leave the field without permission and they were to continue as usual and one or more of his men would accompany every flight. 'Nothing will happen providing you all obey orders,' Zataki had said. 'This is a temporary situation during the change from the Shah's illegal government to the new government of the people.' But his nervousness and that of all his ill-disciplined reabble belied his attempt at confidence.

Starke had heard mutterings among them and told Rudi they expected troops loyal to the Shah to arrive any moment and the counterattack to begin. By the time he, Rudi, and the other American pilot, John Tyrer, had managed to get to the radio in Rudi's trailer, most of the news was over. The little they heard of it was all bad.

'. . . and the Saudi, Kuwait, and Iraqi governments fear that the political turmoil in Iran will destabilise the entire Persian Gulf, with the

133

Sultan of Oman reported as saying the problem is more than just a contagion, it's another convenient umbrella for Soviet Russia to use its string of client states to create nothing less than a colonial empire in the Gulf with the end goal of possessing the Strait of Hormuz . . .

'In Iran it is reported that there was heavy fighting during the night between mutinying, pro-Khomeini air cadets at the Tehran air base of Doshan Tappeh – supported by thousands of armed civilians – against police, loyalist troops and units of the Immortals, the Shah's elite Imperial Guard. Joining the insurgents later were over 5,000 leftists of the Saihkal Marxist Group, some of whom broke into the base's armoury and carried away its weapons . . .'

'Jesus!' Starke said.

'. . . Meanwhile Ayatollah Khomeini again demanded total resignation of the whole government and called on the people to support his choice of prime minister, Mehdi Bazargan, exhorting all soldiers, airmen and navy personnel to support him. Prime Minister Bakhtiar discounted rumours of an imminent military coup, but confirmed a big buildup of Soviet forces on the border . . .

'Gold went to an all-time high of $254 per ounce and the dollar slumped sharply against all currencies. That is the end of the news from London.'

Rudi switched the set off. They were in the sitting room of his trailer. In one of the cabinets was a spare HF that, like the radio, he had built in himself. On the sideboard was a telephone that was hooked up to the base system. The telephone was not working.

'If Khomeini wins at Doshan Tappeh, then the armed forces will have to choose,' Starke said with finality. 'Coup, civil war, or concede.'

'They won't concede, that'd be suicide, why the hell should they?' Tyrer said. He was a loose-limbed American from New Jersey. 'And don't forget the air force is elite, the ones we've met, for crissake. The mutiny's just a bunch of local meathead discontents. The real kicker's about the Marxists joining in, 5,000 of them! Jesus! If they're out in the open now with guns! We're goddam crazy to be here right now, huh?'

Starke said, 'Except we're here by choice; the company says no one loses seniority if they want out. We've got it in writing. You want out?'

'No, no, not yet,' Tyrer said irritably. 'But what we gonna do?'

'Stay out of the way of Zataki for one thing,' Rudi said. 'That bastard's psycho.'

'Sure,' Tyrer said, 'but we've gotta make a plan.'

There was an abrupt knock and the door opened. It was Mohammed Yemeni, their IranOil base manager – a good-looking, clean-shaven man in his forties who had been in their area for a year. With him were two guards. 'Agha Kyabi is on the HF. He wants to speak to you at once,' he said with an untoward imperiousness. Kyabi was IranOil's senior area manager and the most important official in southern Iran.

At once Rudi switched on the HF which interlinked with Kyabi's HQ near Ahwaz, north of Bandar-e Delam. To his astonishment the set did not activate. He jiggled the switch a few times, then Yemeni said with an open sneer, 'Colonel Zataki ordered the current cut off and the set disconnected. You will use the main office set. At once.'

None of them liked the tone of voice. 'I'll be there in a minute,' Rudi said.

Yemeni scowled and said to the guards in coarse Farsi, 'Hurry the dog of a foreigner!'

Starke snapped in Farsi, 'This is our ruler's tent. There are very particular laws in the Holy Koran about defending the leader of your tribe in his tent against armed men.' The two guards stopped, nonplussed. Yemeni gaped at Starke, not expecting Farsi, then backed a pace as Starke got up to his full height and continued: 'The Prophet, Whose Name be praised, laid down rules of manners among friends, and also among enemies, and also that dogs are vermin. We are People of the Book and not vermin.'

Yemeni flushed, turned on his heel, and left. Starke wiped the sweat from his hands on his trousers. 'Rudi, let's see what's with Kyabi.'

They followed Yemeni across the tarmac, the guards with them. The night was clean and the air tasted good to Starke after the closeness of the little office.

'What was all that about?' Rudi asked.

Starke explained, his mind elsewhere, wishing he was back at Kowiss. He had hated leaving Manuela but thought she was safer there than in Tehran. 'Honey,' he had said, just before he had left, 'I'll get you out the soonest.'

'I'm safe here, darlin', safe as Texas. I've got lots of time, the kids are safe in Lubbock – I didn't leave England till I knew they were home – and you know Granddaddy Starke won't let them come to harm.'

'Sure. The kids'll be fine, but I want you out of Iran as soon as possible.'

He heard Rudi saying, 'Who're "People of the Book"?'

'Christians and Jews,' he replied, wondering how he could get the 125 into Kowiss. 'Mohammed considered our Bible and their Torah as Holy Books too – a lot of what's in them's also in the Koran. Lots of scholars, our scholars, think he just copied them, though Muslim

135

legend says that Mohammed couldn't read or write. He recited the Koran, all of it, can you imagine that?' he said, still awed by the accomplishment. 'Others wrote it all down – years after he was dead. In Arabic it's fantastically beautiful, his poetry, so they say.'

Ahead now was the officer trailer, guards outside smoking, and Starke felt good within himself and pleased that he had dealt satisfactorily with Yemeni and all day with the mullah Hussain – fifteen landings, all perfect, waiting at the rigs while the mullah harangued the workers for Khomeini with never a soldier or policeman of SAVAK in sight, expecting them any second and always at the next setdown. Yemeni's chicken shit compared to Hussain, he thought.

Zataki and both mullahs were waiting in the office trailer. Jahan, the radio op, was on the HF. Zataki sat behind Rudi's desk. The office had been very neat. Now it was a mess, with files open and papers spilled everywhere, dirty cups, cigarette stubs in the cups and on the floor, half-eaten food on the desk – rice and goat meat. And the air stank of cigarette smoke.

'*Mein Gott!*' Rudi said, enraged. 'It's a *Verrückte* pigsty and y –'

'SHUT UP!' Zataki exploded. 'This is a war situation, we need to search,' then added, more quietly, 'You . . . you can send one of your men to clean up. You will not tell Kyabi about us. You will act normally and take my instructions, you will watch me. Do you understand, Captain?'

Rudi nodded, his face set. Zataki motioned to the radio op who said into the mike, 'Excellency Kyabi, here is Captain Lutz.'

Rudi took the mike. 'Yes, Boss?' he said, using their nickname for him. Both he and Starke had known Yusuf Kyabi for a number of years. Kyabi had been trained at Texas A&M, then by ExTex before taking over the southern sector, and they were on good terms with him.

'Evening, Rudi,' the voice said in American English. 'We've a break in one of our main pipelines, somewhere north of you. It's a bad one – it's only just shown up in our pumping stations. God knows how many barrels have been pumped out already, or how much is left in the pipe. I'm not calling for a CASEVAC but want a helicopter at dawn to find it. Can you pick me up early?'

Zataki nodded agreement so Rudi said, 'Okay, Boss. We'll be there as soon after dawn as possible. Would you want a 206 or 212?'

'A 206, there'll be me and my chief engineer. Come yourself, will you? It may be sabotage – may be a break. You had any problems at Bandar-e Delam?'

Rudi and Starke were very conscious of the guns in the room. 'No,

136

no more than usual. See you tomorrow,' Rudi said, wanting to cut him off because Kyabi was usually very outspoken about revolutionaries. He did not approve of insurrection or of Khomeini's fanaticism, and hated the interference with their oil complex.

'Hold on a moment, Rudi. We heard there're more riots in Abadan, and we could hear shooting in Ahwaz. Did you know that an American oilman and one of our own people were ambushed and killed near Ahwaz, yesterday?'

'Yes, Tommy Stanson. Lousy.'

'Very. God curse all murderers! Tudeh, mujhadin, fedayeen, or whom the hell ever!'

'Sorry, Boss, got to go, see you tomorrow.'

'Yes. Good, we can talk tomorrow. Insha' Allah, Rudi. Insha' Allah!'

The transmission went dead. Rudi breathed a sigh of relief. He did not think that Kyabi had said anything that could harm him. Unless these men were secretly Tudeh – or one of the other extremists – and not Khomeini supporters as they claimed. 'All our extremists use mullahs as a cover, or try to use them,' Kyabi had told him. 'Sadly most mullahs are impoverished, dull-witted peasants, and easy prey for trained insurgents. God curse Khomeini . . .'

Rudi felt the sweat on his back.

'One of my men will go with you, and this time you will not remove his magazine,' Zataki said.

Rudi's jaw came out and tension in the room soared. 'I will not fly armed men. It is against all company rules, air rules, and particularly Iranian CAA orders. Disobeying ICAA rules invalidates our licences,' he said, loathing them.

'Perhaps I will shoot one of your men unless you obey.' Furiously Zataki slammed a cup off the desk and it skittered across the room.

Starke came forward, as angry. Zataki's gun covered him. 'Are the followers of Ayatollah Khomeini murderers? Is this the law of Islam?'

For a moment Starke thought Zataki was going to pull the trigger, then the mullah Hussain got up. 'I will go in the airplane.' Then to Rudi, 'You swear you will play no tricks and return here without tricks?'

After a pause Rudi said shakily, 'Yes.'

'You are Christian?'

'Yes.'

'Swear by God you will not cheat us.'

Again Rudi paused. 'All right. I swear by God I won't cheat you.'

'How can you trust him?' Zataki asked.

'I don't,' Hussain said simply. 'But if he cheats God, God will punish him. And his companions. If we don't return or if he brings back trouble . . .' He shrugged.

Aberdeen – Gavallan's Mansion: 7:23 P.M. They were in the TV room watching on a big screen a replay of today's rescheduled Scotland versus France rugby match – Gavallan, his wife Maureen, John Hogg who normally flew the company 125 jet, and some other pilots. The score was 17–11 in France's favour deep in the second half. All the men groaned as a Scot fumbled, a French forward recovered and gained forty yards. 'Ten pounds that Scotland still wins!' Gavallan said.

'I'll take that,' his wife said and laughed at his look. She was tall and red-haired and wore elegant green that matched her eyes.

'After all I'm half French.'

'A quarter – your grandmother was Norman, *quelle horreur*, and sh –' An enormous cheer that was echoed in the room drowned his pleasantry as the Scottish scrum half grabbed the ball from the scrimmage, threw it to a wing half who threw it to another who broke loose of the pack, smashed two enemy out of his way and hurtled for the goal line fifty yards away, weaving, brilliantly changing direction to rush onward again, then stumble but somehow stay upright, then charge in a last, chest-heaving glorious run to dive over the line – to be buried at once by bodies and thunderous applause. Touchdown! 17 to 15 now. A successful goal kick will make it 17 all. 'Scotland for everrrr . . .'

The door opened and a manservant stood there. At once Gavallan got up, achingly watched the kick that was good and breathed again. 'Double or nothing, Maureen?' he asked over the pandemonium, grinning at her as he hurried off.

'Taken!' she called out after him.

She's down twenty quid, he thought, very pleased with himself, and crossed the corridor of the big, rambling old house that was well furnished with old leather and good paintings and fine antiques, many of them from Asia, and went into his study opposite. In it, his chauffeur, also his gun bearer and trusty, who had been dialling McIver in Tehran for three hours and monitoring his incoming calls, held up one of the two phones. 'Sorry to interrupt, sir, th –'

'You got him, Williams? Great – score's seventeen all.'

'No, sir, sorry, circuits're still busy but I thought this one was important enough – Sir Ian Dunross.'

Gavallan's disappointment vanished. He took the phone. Williams went out and closed the door. 'Ian, how wonderful to hear from you – this is a pleasant surprise.'

'Hello, Andy, can you speak up, I'm phoning from Shanghai?'

'I thought you were in Japan; I can hear you very well. How's it going?'

'Grand. Better than I expected. Listen, have to be quick but I heard a buzz, two in fact, the first that the taipan needs some financial success to get himself and Struan's out of the hole this year. What about Iran?'

'Everyone advises that it will cool down, Ian. Mac's got things under control, as much as possible; we've been promised all of Guerney's contracts so we should be able to more than keep our end up, even double our profits, presuming there's no act of God.'

'Perhaps you should presume there might be.'

Gavallan's bonhomie vanished. Time and again his old friend had privately given him a warning or information that had later proved to be astonishingly correct – he never knew where Dunross obtained the information, or from whom, but he was rarely wrong. 'I'll do that right away.'

'Next, I've just heard that a secret, very high-level – even perhaps cabinet level – shuffle has been ordered, financial as well as management, for Imperial Air. Will that affect you?'

Gavallan hesitated. Imperial Air owned Imperial Helicopters, his main competition in the North Sea. 'I don't know, Ian. In my opinion they squander taxpayers' money; they could certainly use reorganisation – we beat them hands down in every area I can think of, safety, tenders, equipment – I've ordered six X63s by the way.'

'Does the taipan know?'

'The news almost broke his sphincter.' Gavallan heard the laugh, and for a moment he was back in Hong Kong in the old days when Dunross was taipan and life was hairy but wildly exciting, when Kathy was Kathy and not sick. Joss, he thought, and again concentrated. 'Anything to do with Imperial's important – I'll check at once. Other business news from here is very good – new contracts with ExTex – I was going to announce them at the next board meeting. Struan's isn't in danger, is it?'

Again the laugh. 'The Noble House is always in danger, laddie! Just wanted to advise you – got to go – give my love to Maureen.'

'And to Penelope. When do I see you?'

'Soon. I'll call when I can, give my best to Mac when you see him, 'bye.'

Lost in thought, Gavallan sat on the edge of his fine desk. His friend always said 'soon' and that could mean a month or a year, even two years. It's over two years since I last caught up with him, he thought. Pity he's not taipan still – damn shame he retired, but then we all have to move on and move over sometime. 'I've had it, Andy,' Dunross had said, 'Struan's is in cracking good shape, the seventies promise to be a fantastic era for expansion and . . . well, now there's no excitement any more.' That was in '70, just after his hated main rival, Quillan Gornt, taipan of Rothwell-Gornt, had drowned in a boating accident off Sha Tin in Hong Kong's New Territories.

Imperial Air? Gavallan glanced at his watch, reached for the phone, but stopped at the discreet knock. Maureen stuck her head in, beamed when she saw he wasn't on the phone. 'I won – twenty-one to seventeen – busy?'

'No, come in, darling.'

'Can't, have to check dinner's ready. In ten minutes? You can pay me now if you like!'

He laughed, caught her in his arms, and gave her a hug. 'After dinner! You're a smashing bird, Mrs. Gavallan.'

'Good, don't forget.' She was comfortable in his arms. 'Everything all right with Mac?'

'It was Ian – he just called to say hello. From Shanghai.'

'Now there's a lovely man too. When do we see him?'

'Soon.'

Again she laughed with him, dancing eyes and creamy skin. They had first met seven years ago at Castle Avisyard where the then taipan, David MacStruan, was giving a Hogmanay Ball. She was twenty-eight, just divorced, and childless. Her smile had blown the cobwebs from his head and Scot had whispered, 'Dad, if you don't drag that one off to the altar, you're crazy.' His daughter Melinda had said the same. And so, somehow, three years ago it had happened, and every day since then a happy day.

'Ten minutes, Andy? You're sure?'

'Yes, just have to make one call.' Gavallan saw her frown and added quickly, 'Promise. Just one and then Williams can monitor the calls.'

She gave him a quick kiss and left. He dialled. 'Good evening, is Sir Percy free – this is Andrew Gavallan.' Sir Percy Smedley-Taylor, director of Struan's Holdings, an MP, and slated as the probable minister for defence if the Conservatives won the next election.

'Hullo, Andy, nice to hear from you – if it's about the shoot next Saturday, I'm on. Sorry not to have told you before but things have been rather busy with the so-called government shoving the country up the creek, and the poor bloody unions as well, if they only knew it.'

'I quite agree. Am I disturbing you?'

'No, you just caught me – I'm off to the House for another late-night vote. The stupid twits want us out of NATO, among other things. How did the X63 test out?'

'Wonderful! Better than they claimed. She's the best in the world!'

'I'd love a ride in her if you could fix it. What can I do for you?'

'I heard a buzz that there's a secret, high-level reorganisation of Imperial Air going on. Have you heard anything?'

'My God, old man, your contacts are bloody good – I only heard the rumour myself this afternoon, whispered in absolute secrecy by an unimpeachable Opposition source. Damn curious! Didn't mean much to me at the time – wonder what they're up to. Have you anything concrete to go on?'

'No. Just the rumour.'

'I'll check. I wonder . . . I wonder if the burks might be positioning Imperial to formally nationalise it, therefore Imp Helicopters, therefore you and all the North Sea?'

'God Almighty!' Gavallan's worry increased. This thought had not occurred to him. 'Could they do that if they wanted?'

'Yes. Simple as that.'

Sunday
February 11, 1979

IRAN

BANDAR-E DELAM

AFGHANISTAN

Caspian Sea

Khvoy
Tabriz   Mount Sabalan
Bandar-e Pahlavi
Sadzevar
Meshed
Qazvin
Tehran
Baghdad
Dez Dam
Isfahan
IRAQ
Abadan
Kowiss
KUWAIT
Kharg Island
PAKISTAN
Zagros
Jellet
SAUDI ARABIA
Lengeh
Persian Gulf
Strait of Hormuz
BAHRAIN
Siri
QATAR
Al Shargaz
Gulf of Oman
UAE

CHAPTER

9

Outside Bandar-e Delam: 6:55 A.M. It was just after dawn and Rudi had landed away from the culvert and now the four of them were standing on the lip. The early sun was good, and so far no problems. Oil still poured out of the pipe but it was no longer under pressure. 'It's just what's left in the line,' Kyabi said. 'It should stop entirely in an hour.' He was a strong-faced man in his fifties, clean-shaven with glasses, and he wore used khakis and a hard hat. Angrily he looked around. The earth was soaked with oil and the fumes almost overpowering. 'This whole area's lethal.' He led the way to the overturned car. Three bodies were twisted in or near the wreckage and already beginning to smell.

'Amateurs?' Rudi said, waving away the flies. 'Premature explosion?'

Kyabi did not answer. He went below into the culvert. It was hard to breathe but he searched the area carefully, then climbed back on to the road. 'I'd say you were right, Rudi.' He glanced at Hussain, his face set. 'Yours?'

The mullah took his eyes off the car. 'It is not the Imam's orders to sabotage pipelines. This is the work of enemies of Islam.'

'There are many enemies of Islam who claim to be Followers of the Prophet, who have taken His words and twisted them,' Kyabi said bitterly, 'betraying Him and betraying Islam.'

'I agree, and God will seek them out and punish them. When Iran is ruled according to Islamic law we will seek them out and punish them for Him.' Hussain's dark eyes were equally hard. 'What can you do about the oil spill?'

It had taken them two hours backtracking to find the break. They had circled at a few hundred feet, appalled at the extent of the spill that had inundated the small river and its marshlands and, carried by the current, was already some miles downstream. A thick black scum covered the surface from bank to bank. So far only one village was in its path. A few miles south there were many others. The river supplied drinking water, washing water, and was the latrine.

'Burn it off. As soon as possible.' Kyabi glanced at his engineer. 'Eh?'

'Yes, yes, of course. But what about the village, Excellency?' The engineer was a nervous, middle-aged Iranian who watched the mullah uneasily.

'Evacuate the villagers – tell them to leave until it's safe.'

'And if the village catches fire?' Rudi asked.

'It catches fire. The Will of God.'

'Yes,' Hussain said. 'How will you burn it off?'

'One match would do most of it. Of course you'd burn up too.' Kyabi thought a moment. 'Rudi, you've your Verey pistol aboard?'

'Yes.' Rudi had insisted on taking the pistol, saying it was essential equipment in case of an emergency. All the pilots had backed him though all knew it was not essential. 'With four signal flares. Do you –'

They all looked into the sky at the scream of approaching jets. Two fighters, low and very fast, slashed over the terrain heading out into the Gulf. Rudi judged their path as leading directly to Kharg. They were attack fighters and he had seen the air-to-ground missiles in their racks. Are the missiles for Kharg Island? he asked himself, a new tightness in his throat. Has the revolution hit there too? Or is it just a routine flight?

'What do you think, Rudi? Kharg?' Kyabi asked.

'Kharg's that way, Boss,' Rudi said, not wanting to be involved. 'If so it'd be a routine flight. We'd have dozens of takeoffs and landings a day when we were there. You want to use flares to set the fire?'

Kyabi hardly heard him. His clothes were stained with sweat, his desert boots black with the oil ooze. He was thinking about the air force revolt at Doshan Tappeh. If those two pilots are also in revolt and attack Kharg and sabotage our facilities there, he thought,

146

almost choked with rage and frustration, Iran will go back twenty years.

When Rudi had come to collect him early this morning, Kyabi had been astonished to see the mullah. He had demanded an explanation. When the mullah angrily said that Kyabi should close down all facilities and declare for Khomeini at once, he was almost speechless. 'But that's revolution. That means civil war!'

Hussain had said, 'It is the Will of God. You're Iranian, not a foreign lackey. The Imam has ordered confrontation with the armed forces to subdue them. With God's help, the first true Islamic republic on earth since the days of the Prophet, the Blessing of God be upon Him, begins in a few days.'

Kyabi had wanted to say what he had said privately many times: 'It's a madman's dream, and your Khomeini's an evil, senile old man, driven by a personal vendetta against the Pahlavis – Reza Shah whose police he believes murdered his father, and Mohammed Shah whose SAVAK he believes murdered his son in Iraq a few years ago; he's nothing but a narrow-minded fanatic who wants to put us, the people, and particularly women, back into the Dark Ages . . .'

But he had said none of this today to this mullah. Instead, he put his mind back on to the problem of the village. 'If the village catches fire, they can easily rebuild it. Their possessions are the important things.' He hid his hatred. 'You can help, if you want, Excellency. I would appreciate your help. You can talk to them.'

The villagers refused to go. For the third time Kyabi explained that fire was the only way to save their water and to save the other villages. Then Hussain talked to them, but still they would not go. By now it was time for the midday prayer and the mullah led them in prayer and again told them to leave the banks of the river. The elders consulted with one another and said, 'It is the Will of God. We will not leave.'

'It is the Will of God,' Hussain agreed. He turned on his heel and led the way back to the helicopter.

Once more they landed near the culvert. Now oil just seeped out of the pipe, no more than a trickle. 'Rudi,' Kyabi said, 'go upwind, far as you can, and put a flare into the culvert. Then put one smack in the middle of the stream. Can you do that?'

'I can try. I've never fired a Verey pistol before.' Rudi plodded out into the scrub desert. The others went back to the chopper which he had parked safely away. When he was in position he put the large cartridge into the pistol, aimed, and pulled the trigger. The gun kicked, more than he expected. The burning phosphorus signal flare arched low over the ground, bounced as it came down short, then skipped into the air again and fell into the culvert. For a moment nothing happened, then the earth exploded and fire gushed upward and outward, making the overturned car into a funeral pyre. The superheated shock wave enveloped him but passed by safely. Acrid black smoke billowed skyward. Fire began spreading, racing towards the stream.

The second red flare arced high and then went into the river. The river caught fire. They knew it more from the sound than sight, but when they were airborne once more, skirting the river upwind, they saw the fire spreading rapidly downstream. Vast clouds of black smoke marked its path. Near the village they circled. Men, women, and children were fleeing with what they could carry. As they watched, the village was consumed.

The four men flew home.

Home for Kyabi was the area HQ of IranOil just outside Ahwaz, a neat complex of white concrete buildings with well-watered lawns and a helipad, enclosed by a tall fence.

'Thanks, Rudi,' he said, sick at heart. Around the chopper was a ring of armed men who had rushed out of hiding the moment they had landed, shouting and pointing their guns. Behind Kyabi the mullah toyed with his string of prayer beads.

Kyabi unbuckled his seat belt. The Will of God, he thought. I've done what I could, prayed correctly, and know that there is no other God but God and Mohammed is the Prophet of God. When I die I will die cursing the enemies of God, chief among them, Khomeini, False Prophet, murderer, and all those who follow him.

He turned around. His engineer was grey-faced and rigid in his seat beside Hussain. 'Mullah, I commend you to God's vengeance.' Kyabi got out.

They shot Kyabi and dragged the engineer away. Then, because the mullah asked it, they allowed the chopper to leave.

148

At Kowiss Air Base: 5:09 P.M. Manuela was hurrying across the S-G compound towards the one-storey office building that was tidy under the afternoon sun, the radio tower jutting above as a second floor. She wore flight overalls with the S-G emblem on the back and her auburn hair was bundled into a long peaked flight cap, but her walk shouted her femininity.

In the outer office were three of their Iranian staff. Politely they got up and smiled, watching her under heavy-lidded eyes.

'Good afternoon, Excellency Pavoud,' she said in Farsi with a smile. 'Captain Ayre wanted to see me?'

'Yes, Madam Lady. His Excellency's in the tower,' the chief clerk replied. 'May I have the honour of escorting you?' She declined with thanks, and when she had gone along the corridor and up the spiral staircase, Pavoud said contemptuously, 'Scandalous the way she flaunts herself at us – she does it just to taunt us.'

'Worse than a public woman from the Old Quarter, Excellency,' another said, equally disgusted. 'By God, of all Infidels Americans are the worst and their women the worst. And that one, that one's asking, that one's begging for trouble . . .'

'She's begging for a good Iranian cock,' a small man said, scratching himself.

Pavoud said, 'She should wear a chador and cover herself and walk modestly. We are all men here. We've all sired children. Does she think we're eunuchs?'

'She should be whipped for taunting us.'

Pavoud picked his nose delicately. 'With God's help, soon she will be – publicly. Everyone will be subject to Islamic law, and punishments.'

'They say that American women have no pubics.'

'No, it's just that they shave those parts.'

'Pubics or no, Excellency Chief Clerk, I'd like to thrust it into her, until she squealed – with joy,' the small man said, and they laughed together.

'That great oaf of her husband has every night since she's been here.' The chief clerk's eyes glittered. 'I've heard them moaning in the night.' He lit a cigarette from the butt of the last, then got up and looked out of the window. He wore glasses and peered into the sky until he saw the distant chopper turn on to final. Death to all foreigners, he thought, then added in his most secret heart: And death to Khomeini and his parasites! Long live the Tudeh and the revolution of the Masses!

The tower was small with glass windows on all sides and well equipped. This had been their permanent base for many years, so S-G had had time to fit it out with some modern air safety and all-weather landing aids. Freddy Ayre, senior pilot in Starke's absence, was waiting for Manuela.

'HXB's on final,' he said as she came up the stairs. 'He –'

'Oh, wonderful,' she interrupted happily. They had been trying to contact Starke all day without success: 'Not to worry,' Ayre had told her, 'their HF often goes out, same's ours.' Since last night, just after dark, the only communication had been Starke's terse report that he was overnighting at Bandar-e Delam and would contact them today.

'Sorry, Manuela, but Duke's not aboard. Marc Dubois's flying her.'

'There's been an accident?' she burst out, her world tumbling. 'He's hurt?'

'Oh, no, nothing like that. When Marc reported in a few minutes ago, he said Duke had stayed at Bandar-e Delam and he'd been told to fly the mullah and his team on the return trip.'

150

'Is that all? You're sure?'

'Yes. Look,' Ayre said, pointing out of the window, 'there she is.'

The 206 was coming in out of the sun nicely. Behind her the Zagros Mountains reached skyward. Below were the chimney stacks of the vast refinery, plumes of fire from waste gases perpetually burning off. She touched down in the exact centre of Landing Pad One. 'HXB shutting down,' Marc Dubois said over the radio.

'Roger, HXB,' S-G's duty tower operator, Massil Tugul, a Palestinian and longtime employee replied. He switched to the main base frequency. 'Base, we have no birds in the system now. I confirm HVU and HCF will return before sunset.'

'Okay, S-G.' There was a moment of quiet, then over the main base channel, they heard a voice cut in harshly in Farsi, transmitting from the 206. It went on for half a minute, then ceased.

Massil muttered, 'Insha' Allah!'

'Who the hell was that?' Ayre said.

'The mullah Hussain, agha.'

'What the hell did he say?' Ayre asked him, forgetting Manuela could speak Farsi.

Massil hesitated. Manuela answered for him, her face white. 'The mullah said, "In the Name of God and in the Name of the Whirlwind of God, Strike!" over and over, just ov—' She stopped.

From the other side of the airfield came the muted sound of gunfire. At once Ayre took the mike. '*Marc, à la tour, vite, immediatement,*' he ordered, his accent excellent, then squinted at the base, half a mile away. Men were running from their barracks now. Some carried guns. Several fell as other men opposed them. Ayre opened one of the windows to hear better. Faint shouts of 'Allah-u Akbarr' mixed with the coarse thranggg-thranggg-thranggg of automatic rifles.

'What's that? Near the gate, the main gate?' Manuela said, Massil on his feet beside her, equally shocked and not a little frightened.

Ayre reached for the binoculars and focused them. 'Christ Almighty, soldiers're firing into the base and . . . and trucks're storming the gate . . . half a dozen of them . . . Green Bands and mullahs and soldiers jumping out of them . . .'

Over the base channel came an excited voice shouting in Farsi that was abruptly cut off. Again Manuela translated: ' "In the Name of God, kill all officers who oppose Imam Khomeini and take possession –" It's revolution!'

Below they saw the mullah Hussain and his two Green Bands pile out of the 206, guns unslung. The mullah motioned Dubois out of the

151

cockpit, but the pilot just shook his head and pointed at the whirling blades, continued shutdown procedure. Hussain hesitated.

All over the S-G compound work had stopped. People were leaning out of windows or had come out on to the tarmac and were standing there in silent little groups, looking across the field. Sounds of gunfire increased. Nearby, the jeep and fuel truck that were to service the 206 had skidded to a halt the moment the guns had started. Hussain hailed the jeep, left one man to guard the chopper. The driver saw him coming, jumped out, and took to his heels. The mullah cursed him and, with a Green Band, got into the driver's seat, gunned the engine and tore off down the boundary road, heading for the far barracks.

Dubois came up the steps, three at a time. He was thirty-six, tall and skinny, with dark hair and a roguish smile. At once he stuck out his hand and shook with Ayre. '*Mon Dieu*, what a day, Freddy! I . . . Manuela!' He kissed her fondly on both cheeks. 'The Duke is fine, *chérie*. He just had a row with the mullah who told him that he would no longer fly with him. Bandar-e Delam's not . . .' He stopped, very conscious now of Massil, not trusting him. 'I need a drink, eh? Let's go to the mess, eh?'

They did not go to the mess. Marc led them out on to the tarmac and into the lee of a building where they could watch with safety and not be overheard. 'There's no way of telling which side Massil's on, eh, or even most of our staff – if they even know themselves, poor people.'

On the other side of the field there was a loud explosion. Fire gushed from one of the sheds and smoke billowed. '*Mon Dieu*, is that the fuel dump?'

'No, just near it.' Ayre was filled with disquiet. Another explosion distracted him, then mixed with sporadic gunfire came the heavy, deep-throated detonation of a tank's big gun.

The jeep with the mullah in it had disappeared behind the barracks. Near the main gate, the army trucks had stopped haphazardly: their attacking soldiers and Green Bands vanished into hangars and barracks. A few bodies lay in the dust. Tank soldiers guarding Camp Commandant Peshadi's office block crouched near the doorway, their guns ready. Others waited at the second-floor windows. One of the men there let off a burst of automatic fire as half a dozen screaming soldiers and airmen charged in attack across the square. Another burst of fire and they were all dead or dying or badly wounded. One of the wounded half crawled, half scrambled for safety. The tank guards let him get almost to safety. Then they filled him with bullets.

152

Manuela moaned and they both took her deeper into the lee of their building. 'I'm all right,' she said. 'Marc, when's Duke coming back?'

'Rudi or Duke will call tonight or tomorrow, guarantee it. *Pas problème*! Le Grand Duke is fine. *Mon Dieu*, now I am ready for a drink!'

They waited a moment, the firing lessening. 'Come on,' Ayre said, 'we'll be safer in the bungalows.'

They scurried across the compound into one of the fine bungalows surrounded by whitewashed fences and tidy gardens. There were no married quarters at Kowiss. Usually two pilots shared the two-bedroom bungalows.

Manuela left them to get the drinks. 'Now, what really happened?' Ayre asked softly.

Rapidly the Frenchman told him about the attack and Zataki and Rudi's bravery. 'That old Kraut really deserves a medal,' he said admiringly. 'But listen, last night the revs shot one of our day labourers. They tried him and shot him in four minutes for being fedayeen. This morning other bastards shot Kyabi.'

Ayre was appalled. 'But why?'

Dubois told him about the pipeline sabotage, then added, 'When Rudi and the mullah got back, Zataki paraded us all and said it was correct Kyabi had been shot as "a supporter of the Shah, a supporter of Satanic Americans and British who had despoiled Iran for years and was therefore an enemy of God" .'

'Poor old Boss. Christ, I liked him a lot, he was a good fellow!'

'Yes. And openly anti-Khomeini, and now those bastards have guns – never seen so many guns and they're all *stupide*, crazy.' Dubois tightened. 'Old Duke began raving in Farsi at them all: he'd already had a confrontation with Zataki and the mullah last night. We don't know what he said but it all became ugly, the bastards fell on him, started to kick and scream at him. Of course we all began to charge, then there was an explosion of automatic fire and we froze. Them too, because it was Rudi. Somehow he'd taken a gun from one of them and let another short burst into the air. He shouted, "Leave him alone or I'll kill you all," keeping the gun trained on Zataki and the group near Duke. They left him. After cursing them – *ma foi, quel homme* – he made a deal: they leave us alone, we leave them to their revolution, I was to fly the mullah here and Duke has to stay, and Rudi keeps the gun. He made Zataki and the mullah swear by Allah not to break the contract, but I still wouldn't trust them. *Merde*, they're all *merde, mon ami*. But Rudi, Rudi was fantastic. He should be French, that one. I tried to call them all day but no answer . . .'

The other side of the field, a Centurion tank came charging out of one of the streets in the far barracks complex, whirled across the open and went into the main street opposite base HQ and the officers' mess. It stopped there, engines growling, fat, squat and deadly. The long gun swivelled, seeking a target. Then suddenly the tracks spun, the tank twirled on its axis and fired and the shell demolished the second floor where Colonel Peshadi had his offices. The defenders reeled from the sudden treachery. Again the tank fired. Great slabs of masonry tore off and half the roof collapsed. The building began to burn.

Then from the ground floor and part of the second storey a fusillade of bullets surrounded the tank. At once two of the loyalists charged out of the main door with grenades, tossed them through the tank slits, and fled for cover. Both men crumpled under a hail of automatic fire from across the roadway, but there was a terrible explosion inside the tank and flames and smoke gushed forth. The metal top flipped open and a burning man tried to clamber out. His body was almost ripped out of the tank by the hail of automatic fire from the broken building. On the wind that blew from across the base there was the smell of cordite and fire and meat burning.

The battle continued for more than an hour, then ended. The lowering sun cast a bloody hue and there were dead and dying throughout the base, but the insurrection had failed because they had not killed Colonel Peshadi or his chief officers in the first sneak attack, because not enough of the airmen and soldiers went over to their side – and only one of three tank crews.

Peshadi had been in the lead tank, and he held the tower and all radio communications. He had gathered loyal forces and led the ruthless drive that gouged the revolutionaries out of the hangars and out of the barracks. And once the cautious majority, the fence-sitting, unsure – in this case airmen and troops – perceived that the revolt was lost, they hesitated no longer. Immediately and zealously they declared their undying and historic loyalty to Peshadi and the Shah, picked up discarded weapons, and, equally zealously, in the name of God, began firing at the 'enemy'. But few fired to kill and though Peshadi knew it, he left an escape route open and allowed a few of the attackers to escape. His only secret order to his most trusted men was, Kill the mullah Hussain.

But, somehow, Hussain escaped.

'This is Colonel Peshadi,' came over the main base frequency and all loudspeakers. 'Thanks be to God the enemy is dead, dying, or captured. I thank all loyal troops. All officers and men will collect our glorious dead who died doing God's work and report numbers, and also numbers of enemy killed. Doctors and medics! Attend to all wounded without favour. God is Great . . . God is Great! It is almost the time for evening prayer. Tonight I am mullah and I will lead it. All will attend to give thanks to God.'

In Starke's bungalow, Ayre, Manuela and Dubois were listening on the base intercom. She finished translating Peshadi's Farsi. Now there was just static. Smoke hung over the base and the air was heavy with the smell. The two men were sipping vodka and canned orange juice, she soda water. A portable butane gas fire warmed the room pleasantly.

'That's curious,' she said thoughtfully, steeling herself not to think of all the killing or about Starke at Bandar-e Delam. 'Curious that Peshadi didn't end: Long live the Shah. Surely it's a victory for him? He must be scared out of his wits.'

'I would be too,' Ayre said. 'He's g –' They all jumped as the base intercom telephone jangled. He picked it up. 'Hello?'

'This is Major Changiz. Ah, Captain Ayre, did they come your side of the base? What happened with you?'

'Nothing. No insurgents came over here.'

'Praise be to God. We were all worried for your safety. You're sure there are no dead or wounded?'

'None – to my knowledge.'

'Thanks be to God. We've plenty. Fortunately there're no enemy wounded.'

'None?'

'None. You won't mind if I mention that you will not report or relate this incident to anyone on the radio – to no one, Captain. Top security. Do you understand?'

'Loud and clear, Major.'

'Good. Please listen out on our base frequency – as for safety we will monitor yours. Please do not use your HF radio until first clearing it with us during the emergency.' Ayre felt the blood in his face but he said nothing. 'Please stand by for a briefing by Colonel Peshadi at 2000 and now send Esvandiary and all your Faithful to evening prayers – at once.'

'Certainly, but Hotshot – Esvandiary's on leave for a week.' Esvandiary was their IranOil station manager.

'Very well. Send the rest with Pavoud in charge.'

'Right away.' The phone went dead. He told them what had been said, then went to pass the word.

In the tower Massil was very uneasy. 'But, Captain, Excellency. I'm on duty till sunset. We've our two 212s to come home yet and th –'

'He said all Faithful. At once. Your papers are in order, you've been in Iran for years. He knows you're here so you'd better go – unless you've something to fear?'

'No. No, not at all.'

Ayre saw the sweat on the man's forehead. 'Don't worry, Massil,' he said, 'I'll see the lads in. No sweat. And I'll stay here until you get back. It won't take you long.'

He saw his two 212s to bed, waiting with growing impatience, Massil long overdue now. To pass the time he had tried to do some paperwork but gave up, his mind in turmoil. The only thought that cheered him was that his wife and infant son were safe in England – even with the lousy weather there, the gales and blizzards and rains and lousy cold and lousy strikes and lousy government.

The HF came to life. It was just after dark. 'Hello, Kowiss, this is McIver in Tehran . . .'

Tehran – at the S-G Office: 6:50 P.M. McIver said again, 'Hello, Kowiss, this is McIver in Tehran, do you read?'

'Tehran, this is Kowiss, Standby One,' – one minute – vernacular for 'Please wait a moment.'

'All right, Freddy,' McIver said and put the HF mike back on the desk. He and Tom Lochart, who had arrived from Zagros that afternoon, were in his office on the top floor of the building that had been HQ for S-G ever since it had opened operations in Iran almost ten years before. The building had five storeys with a flat roof where Genny had made a delightful, screened roof garden with chairs and tables and barbecue. General Beni-Hassan, Andrew Gavallan's friend, had recommended the building highly: 'Nothing but the best for Andy Gavallan's company. There's space for half a dozen offices, the price's reasonable, you've space on the roof for your own generator and radio antenna, you're near the main highway that goes to the airport, bazaar's convenient, my HQ's around the corner, parking's convenient, projected hotels convenient, and here's the *pièce de résistance!*' Proudly

157

the general had shown McIver the toilet. It was ordinary and not very clean.

'What's so special about that?' McIver had asked, nonplussed.

'It's the only one in the building, the rest are squatters – just a hole in the floor over a sewer – and if you're not used to squatting it's a tricky operation – in fact it's a pain in the ass, particularly for the ladies, who've been known to slip into the hole with messy results,' the general had said jovially. He was a fine-looking man, very strong, very fit.

'Squatters are everywhere?'

'Even in the best houses, everywhere outside of modern hotels. When you think about it, Mac, squatting's more hygienic, nothing sensitive touches anything alien. Then there's this.' The general had pointed to a small hose attached to the toilet spigot. 'We use water to clean ourselves – always use the left hand, that's the shit hand, the right's for eating, which is why you never offer anything with your left hand. Very bad manners, Mac. Never eat or drink with your left hand in the Islamic world, and don't forget most toilets and squatters don't have hoses so you have to use water from a bucket, if there happens to be one. As I said it's a tricky op, but a way of life. By the way we've no left-handed people in Islam.' Again the good-natured chuckle. 'Most Muslims can't perform comfortably unless they squat – it's the muscles – so a lot will squat on the Western seat when they relieve themselves. Strange, isn't it, but then outside of most cities, even in them, throughout most of Asia, the Middle East, China India, Africa, South America there's not even running water . . .'

'A penny for your thoughts, Mac?' Lochart said. The tall Canadian sat opposite him, both of them in old easy chairs. Their electric light and fire were at full power from their own generator.

McIver grunted. 'I was thinking about squatters. Hate squatters and bloody water. Just can't get used to them.'

'Doesn't bother me now, hardly notice it. We've squatters in our apartment – Sharazad said she'd have a "Western" toilet put in if I wanted it as a wedding present, but I said I could deal with it.' Lochart smiled wryly. 'Doesn't bother me now but, my God, that was the one thing that sent Deirdre around the bend.'

'Same for all the wives. That's their biggest bitch, all of them, Genny too. Not my bloody fault most of the world does it that way. Thank God we've a real loo in the flat. Gen'd mutiny otherwise.' McIver fiddled with the volume on the receiver. 'Come on, Freddy,' he muttered. There were many charts on the walls, no pictures, though there was the heavy dust mark of one taken down recently – the obligatory photograph of the Shah. Outside, the night sky was lit with fires that dotted the skyline of the darkened city, no lights or streetlamps anywhere except here. Gunfire, rifle and automatic, mixed with the ever-present sound of the city – mobs roaring 'Allahhh-u Akbarrrrr . . .'

Now over the loudspeaker: 'This is Kowiss, Captain Ayre speaking. I read you loud and clear, Captain McIver.'

Both men were startled and Lochart sat upright. 'Something's wrong, Mac, he can't talk openly – someone's listening.'

McIver clicked on the send switch. 'You're doing your own radio, Freddy,' he said deliberately to make sure there was no mistake, 'as well as putting in the hours?'

'Just happened to be here, Captain McIver.'

'Everything five by five?' This meant maximum radio signal strength, or in the vernacular of pilots, Everything okay?

After a deliberate pause that told them no, 'Yes, Captain McIver.'

'Good, Captain Ayre,' McIver said, to tell him at once that he understood. 'Put Captain Starke on, will you?'

'Sorry, sir, I can't. Captain Starke's still at Bandar-e Delam.'

McIver said sharply, 'What's he doing there?'

'Captain Lutz ordered him to stop over and ordered Captain Dubois to complete the VIP journey requested by IranOil – and approved by you.'

Starke had managed to get through to Tehran before taking off to explain the problem of the mullah Hussain to McIver. McIver had approved the trip as long as Colonel Peshadi okayed it, and told him to keep him advised.

'Is the 125 due in Kowiss tomorrow, Captain McIver?'

'It's possible,' McIver replied, 'but you never know.' The 125 had been scheduled for Tehran yesterday, but because of the insurrection surrounding the airport, all inbound traffic had been provisionally cancelled until tomorrow, Monday. 'We're working on getting clearances for a direct into Kowiss. It's dicey because military air traffic control are . . . are undermanned. The airport at Tehran is, er, jammed so we can't get any of our dependants out. Tell Manuela to stand by in case we can get a clearance.' McIver grimaced, trying to decide how much he should say over the open airwaves, then saw Lochart motioning to him.

'Let me, Mac. Freddy can speak French,' Lochart said softly.

McIver brightened and gratefully leaned over and gave him the mike. '*Écoute*, Freddy,' Lochart began in Canadian French that he knew even

Ayre, whose French was excellent, had difficulty in understanding. 'Marxists still hold the International Airport, helped by Khomeini insurgents, supposedly with some PLO, and still hold the tower. Tonight's major rumour is that there's going to be a coup, that the Prime Minister's approved it, that troops are finally on the move all over Tehran with orders to quell the riots and shoot to kill. What's your problem down there? Are you all right?'

'Yes, no sweat,' they heard him reply in gutter French and innuendo; 'I'm under orders to say nothing, but no real problems here, bet on it, but they're listening. At Smelly' – their nickname for Bandar-e Delam where the air stank constantly of petrol – 'lots of problems and Boss was sent upward before his allotted span . . .'

Lochart's eyes widened. 'Kyabi's been shot,' he muttered to McIver. '. . . but old Rudi's got everything under control and the Duke's okay. We'd better stop this, old one. They're listening.'

'Understand. Sit tight and tell the others if you can; also that we're okay,' adding in English without missing a beat, 'and I repeat we'll be sending down cash for your people tomorrow.'

Ayre's voice brightened. 'No shit, old chap.'

Involuntarily Lochart laughed. 'No shit. Keep a duty radio op on and we'll call back progress. Here's Captain McIver again. Insha'Allah!' He handed the mike back.

'Captain, have you heard from Lengeh, yesterday or today?'

'No, we tried them but couldn't raise them. Might be the sunspots. I'll try again now.'

'Thanks. Give my regards to Captain Scragger and remind him his medical's due next week.' McIver smiled grimly, then added, 'Make sure Captain Starke calls the moment he returns.' He signed off. Lochart told him what Ayre had said. He poured himself another whisky.

'What about me, for God's sake?' McIver said irritably.

'But Mac, you kn –'

'Don't you start. Make it a light one.' As Lochart poured, McIver got up, went to the window, and stared out, seeing nothing. 'Poor old Kyabi. Now there was a good man if ever there was one, good for Iran and fair to us. What'd they murder him for? Madmen! Rudi "ordering" Duke and "ordering" Marc – what the hell does that mean?'

'Only that there was trouble but Rudi's got it in control. Freddy would have told me if Rudi hadn't – he's very sharp and his French's good so he could've found a way. There was plenty of time, even

160

though "they" were listening, whoever the hell "they" were,' Lochart said. 'Maybe it was like at Zagros.'

At Zagros the villagers from Yazdek had come at dawn the day after Lochart had arrived back from leave. Their village mullah had received Khomeini's orders to begin the insurrection against 'the illegal government of the Shah', and to take control of his area. The mullah had been born in the village and was wise in the ways of the mountains that were snow-locked in winter and only accessible with great difficulty the rest of the year. And, too, the chief of police against whom he should lead the revolt was his nephew, and Nasiri, the base manager who was also a target, was married to his wife's sister's daughter who now lived in Shiraz. Even more important, they were all Galezan, a minor tribe of the nomad Kash'kai who had settled protectively – centuries ago – athwart this tiny crossroads, and the chief of police whose name was Nitchak Khan was also their kalandar, their elected tribal leader.

So, correctly, he had consulted Nitchak Khan and the Khan had agreed that a revolt should take place against their hereditary enemy the Pahlavi Shah, that to celebrate the revolution any who cared to could fire their arms at the stars and that, at dawn, he would lead the necessary investiture of the foreigners' airfield.

They had arrived at dawn. Armed. Every man in the village. Nitchak Khan no longer wore his police uniform but tribal clothes. He was much shorter than Lochart, a hard-bodied man, spare, with hands of iron and legs of steel, a cartridge belt over his chest and rifle in his hands. By prearrangement, Lochart, accompanied by Jean-Luc Sessonne – at the Khan's request – met them at two hastily erected columns of stones that symbolised the gate to the base. Lochart saluted and agreed that Nitchak Khan had jurisdiction over the base, the two tiers of stones were formally knocked down, there were loud cheers from all sides and many guns were fired into the air. Then Nitchak Khan presented bouquets of flowers to Jean-Luc Sessonne as a representative of France, thanking him on behalf of all the Galezan-Kash'kai for succouring and helping Khomeini who had rid them of their enemy, the Pahlavi Shah. 'Thanks be to God that this self-dubbed Great King of Kings who dared sacrilege to try to connect his line back to Kings Cyrus and Darius the Great, men of courage and pride – this Light of the Aryans, this lackey of foreign devils – fled like a painted paramour from his Iraqi pasha!'

Then there were brave speeches from both sides and the feast began and Nitchak Khan, the mullah beside him, had asked Tom Lochart,

161

tribal chief of the foreigners at Zagros Three, to continue as before under the new regime. Lochart had gravely agreed.

'Let's hope Rudi and his lads're as lucky as you at Zagros, Tom.' McIver turned back to the windows, knowing there was nothing he could do to help them. 'Things get worse and worse,' he muttered. Kyabi's murder's terrible, and a very bad sign for us, he thought. How the hell can I get Genny out of Tehran and where the hell's Charlie?

They had not heard from Pettikin since he had left yesterday morning for Tabriz. From their ground staff at Galeg Morghi they had had garbled reports – that Pettikin had been kidnapped and forced to fly off with 'three unknown persons', or that 'three Iranian Air Force pilots hijacked the 206 and fled for the border,' or that 'the three passengers were high-ranking officers fleeing the country.' Why three passengers in every story? McIver had asked himself. He knew Pettikin must have got to the airfield safely because his car was still there, though the tanks were dry, the radio torn out and the car vandalised. Bandar-e Pahlavi, where he was to have refuelled, was silent – Tabriz was hardly ever in range. He cursed silently. It had been a bad day for McIver.

All day irate creditors had arrived to harass him, the phones weren't working, the telex got jammed and took hours to clear, and his meeting at noon with General Valik, who Gavallan had promised would supply cash weekly, was a disaster.

'As soon as the banks open we'll pay what is owed.'

'For God's sake, you've been saying that for weeks,' McIver said coldly, 'I need money now.'

'So do we all,' the general had hissed back, shaking with rage, but very conscious of the Iranian employees in the outer office who would be sure to be listening. 'There's civil war going on and I can't open the banks. You'll have to wait.' He was a rotund man, balding, with darkish skin, an ex-army general, his clothes expensive, his watch expensive. He dropped his voice even lower. 'If it wasn't for stupid Americans who betrayed the Shah and persuaded him to curb our glorious armed forces, we wouldn't be in this mess!'

'I'm British as you well know and you brought the mess on yourself.'

'British, American, what's the difference? It's all your fault. You both betrayed our Shah and Iran and now you're going to pay for it!'

'With what?' McIver asked sourly. 'You've got all our money.'

'If it wasn't for your Iranian partners – me particularly – you wouldn't have any money. Andy's not complaining. I had a telex from my revered colleague, General Javadah, that Andy was signing the new Guerney contracts this week.'

'Andy said he had a telex from you confirming that you promised him you'd provide us with cash.'

'I promised I'd try.' The general curbed his rage with an effort, for he needed McIver's cooperation. He mopped his forehead and opened his briefcase. It was stuffed with high-denomination rials but he held the top carefully so it was impossible for McIver to see inside, then brought out a small sheaf of notes, closing the briefcase. With great deliberation he counted out 500,000 rials – about $6,000. 'There,' he said with a great flourish, putting the rials on the table and the rest away again. 'Next week I or one of my colleagues will bring some more. A receipt, please.'

'Thank you.' McIver signed the receipt. 'When can we exp –'

'Next week. If the banks open we can settle everything. We're always good as our word. Always. Haven't we arranged the Guerney contracts?' Valik leaned forward and dropped his voice even more. 'Now, I have a special charter. Tomorrow I want a 212, to leave sometime in the morning.'

'To go where?'

'I need to inspect some facilities at Abadan,' Valik said and McIver noticed the sweat.

'And how will I get the necessary permissions, General? With all your airspace controlled by the military and w –'

'Don't bother with permission, just hav –'

'Unless we've a flight plan, approved by the military in advance, it's an illegal flight.'

'You can always say you asked for permission and it was given verbally. What's so difficult about that?'

'First it's against Iranian law, General, your law, second, even if cleared verbally and the aircraft got out of Tehran airspace, you've still got to give the next military air traffic controller your recorded number – all flight plans are recorded at your air force HQ and they're even more twitchy about helicopters than civilians – and if you don't have one the controller will say get your tail down at the next military base and report to the tower. And when you land, they'll meet you very irritably – and correctly – in force, my aircraft will be impounded, and the passengers and crew put in jail.'

'Then find a way. It's a very important charter. The, er, the Guerney contracts depend on it. Just have the 212 ready at nine o'clock, say at Galeg Morghi.'

'Why there? Why not at the International Airport?'

'It's more convenient . . . and quiet now.'

McIver frowned. It was well within Valik's authority to ask for and authorise such a flight. 'Very well, I'll try.' He pulled out the pad of blank flight plan forms, noticed that the last copy referred to Pettikin's flight to Tabriz and again his anxiety mounted – where the devil is he? Under 'passengers' he put General Valik, chairman of IHC, and handed it to him. 'Please sign under authority.'

Valik shoved the form back imperiously. 'There's no need for my name to be put on it – just put four passengers – my wife and two children will be with me, and some luggage. We will be staying in Abadan for a week, then returning. Just have the 212 ready at 9 p.m. At Galeg Morghi.'

'Sorry, General, the names have to be on the clearance or the air force won't even accept the flight plan. All passengers have to be named. I'll apply for clearance but I don't hold out much hope for you.' McIver began to add the other names.

'No, stop! No need to give our names. Just put down the trip's to send some spares to Abadan. Surely there are some spares you need to send there?' The sweat was beading him.

'All right, but first please sign the authority, with the name of all passengers and your final destination.'

The general's face reddened. 'Just arrange it without involving me. At once!'

'I can't.' McIver was becoming equally impatient. 'I repeat, the military will want to know all the "who" and the "where" – they're as sticky now as flypaper. We'll get even more searching enquiries than usual because we haven't had any traffic in weeks going that way. Tehran's not like in the south where we're flying all day.'

'This is a special flight for spares. Simple.'

'It isn't simple at all. Sentries at Galeg Morghi wouldn't let you aboard without papers, nor would the tower. They'd see you going aboard, for God's sake.' McIver stared at him, exasperated. 'Why don't you arrange the clearance yourself, General? You've the best connections in Iran. You've certainly made that clear. For you it should be simple.'

'They're all our planes. We own them – own them!'

'Yes, you do,' McIver said as grimly. 'When you've paid for them – you owe us almost four million U.S. in back payments. If you want to go to Abadan that's your business, but if they catch you doing it in an S-G chopper with false papers which I must countersign, you'll land in jail, your family'll be in jail along with me and the pilot, and they'll impound our aircraft and close us down for ever.' Just the thought of jail made him feel bilious. If a tenth of the stories about SAVAK and Iranian jails were true, they were no places to be.

Valik choked back his rage. He sat down and put a sickly smile on his face. 'There's no need for us to quarrel, Mac, we've been through too much together. I, I will make it very worthwhile, eh? Both to you and the pilot.' He opened the briefcase. 'Eh? Twelve million rials – between you.'

McIver looked at the money blankly. Twelve million was about $150,000 – over 100,000 pounds sterling. Numbly, he shook his head.

At once Valik said, 'All right, twelve million each – and expenses – half now and half when we're safe at Kuwait Airport, eh?'

McIver was in shock, not only because of the money but because Valik had openly said 'Kuwait' which McIver had suspected but had not wished to think about. This was a complete 180-degree turn from everything that Valik had been saying for months: for months he had been bullish about the Shah crushing the opposition, then Khomeini. And even after the Shah's unbelievable departure and Khomeini's astonishing return to Tehran – my God, was that only ten days ago? – Valik had said a dozen times that there was nothing to worry about, for Bakhtiar and the generals of the Imperial Staff held the complete balance of power and would never permit 'this Khomeini-covert communist revolution to succeed'. Nor would the United States permit it. Never. At the right time the services would seize power and take over. Only yesterday Valik had confidently repeated it and said he'd heard that any hour the army was going to move in force and that the Immortals at Doshan Tappeh, putting down the small air force mutiny, was the first sign.

McIver tore his gaze off the money and looked at the eyes of the man opposite. 'What do you know that we don't know?'

'What're you talking about?' Valik began to bluster. 'I don't know an –'

'Something's happened, what is it?'

'I've got to get out, with my family,' Valik said, on the edge of desperation now. 'Rumours are terrible – coup or civil war, Khomeini or not, I'm, we're, we're marked. Do you understand? It's my family, Mac, I've got to get out, until things quiet down. Twelve million each, eh?'

'What rumours?'

'Rumours!' Valik almost spat at him. 'Get the clearance any way you can. I pay in advance.'

'However much money you offer I won't do it. It has to be straight.'

'You stupid hypocrite! Straight? How have you been operating all these years in Iran? Pishkesh! How much have you yourself paid under the counter – or to customs men? Pishkesh! How do you think we get contracts, eh? The Guerney contracts? Pishkesh! By putting cash, quietly, into the right hands. Are you so stupid you still don't know Iranian ways?'

McIver said as grimly, 'I know pishkesh, I'm not stupid, and I know Iran has its own ways. Oh, yes, Iran has its own ways. The answer's no.'

'Then the blood of my children and my wife are on your head. And mine.'

'What're you talking about?'

'Are you afraid of the truth?'

McIver stared at him. Valik's wife and two children were favourites of Genny's and his. 'What makes you so sure?'

'I've . . . I've a cousin in the police. He saw a . . . a secret SAVAK list. I am to be arrested the day after tomorrow along with many other prominent persons as a sop to the . . . the opposition. And my family. And you know how they treat . . . how they can treat women and children in front of the . . .' Valik's words trailed off.

McIver's defences crumbled. They had all heard horrendous stories of wives and children being tortured in front of the arrested man to force compliance with whatever they wanted, or just for devilment. 'All right,' he said helplessly, feeling rotten, knowing he was trapped. 'I'll try, but don't expect to get a clearance, and you shouldn't go south to Abadan. Your best bet would be Turkey. Perhaps we could chopper you to Tabriz, then you could buy your way over the border in a truck. You must have friends there. And you can't make the pickup Galeg Morghi – there's no way you could sneak aboard with Annoush and the children or even get into that military field without being stopped. You'd . . . you'd have to be picked up outside of Tehran. Somewhere off the roads and out of sight of radar.'

'All right, but it has to be Abadan.'

'Why? You lessen your chances by half.'

'Has to be. My family . . . my father and mother got there by road. Of course you're right about Galeg Morghi. We could be picked up outside Tehran at . . .' Valik thought for a moment, then rushed on: 'at the junction of the pipeline south and the river Zehsan . . . it's away from the road and safe. We'll be there in the morning at eleven o'clock. God will thank you, Mac. If . . . if you apply for a clearance for spares, I . . . I will arrange that it's approved. Please, I beg you.'

'But what about refuelling? When you land for refuelling, the landing officer's bound to spot you and you'll be arrested in seconds.'

'Request refuelling at the air force base at Isfahan. I . . . I will arrange Isfahan.' Valik wiped the sweat off his face.

'And if anything goes wrong?'

'Insha' Allah! You'll apply for clearance for spares – no names on the clearance or I'm dead or worse and so are Annoush, Jalal, and Setarem. Please?'

McIver knew it was madness. 'I'll apply for clearance: spares only for Bandar-e Delam. I should know by midnight if it's approved – I'll send someone to wait for it and bring it to me at the apartment. Phones are out so you'll have to come to me for confirmation. That'll give me time to think this out and decide yes or no.'

'But you –'

'Midnight.'

'Yes, very well, I shall be there.'

'What about the other partners?'

'They – they know nothing of this. Emir Paknouri or one of the others will act for me.'

'What about weekly monies?'

'They will provide it.' Again Valik wiped his forehead. 'The Blessings of God on you.' He put on his overcoat and walked for the door. The briefcase stayed on the desk.

'Take that with you.'

Valik turned back. 'Ah, you want me to pay in Kuwait? Or Switzerland? In what currency?'

'There's no payment. You can authorise a charter. Maybe we can get you to Bandar-e Delam – then you're on your own.'

Valik stared at him with disbelief. 'But . . . but even so, you'll need expense money to pay for the, er, pilot or whatever.'

'No, but you can give me an advance of five million rials against the money the partnership owes which we desperately need.' McIver scrawled out a receipt and handed it to him. 'If you're not here, the Emir or the others may not be so generous.'

'The banks will open next week, we're sure of it. Oh, yes, quite sure.'

'Well, let's hope so and we can be paid what's owing.' He saw Valik's expression, saw him count out the money, knowing that Valik thought him mad not to have accepted the pishkesh, knowing also that inevitably the man would try to bribe the pilot, whoever the pilot was, to take them the last stretch if the chopper ever got out of Tehran airspace – and that would be a disaster.

167

And now, in his office, staring blankly out of the window at the night, not hearing the gunfire or seeing the occasional flare light the darkened city, he thought, My God, SAVAK? I have to try to help him, have to. Those poor bloody kids and poor woman. I have to! And when Valik offers the pilot a bribe, even though I'll warn the pilot in advance, will he resist? If Valik offered twelve million now, at Abadan it would be doubled. Tom could use that money, Nogger Lane, so could I, anyone. Just for a short trip across the Gulf – short but one way and no return. Where the hell did Valik get all that cash anyway? Of course from a bank.

For weeks there had been rumours that for a fee certain well-connected people could get monies out of Tehran even though the banks – formally – were closed. Or for an even larger fee get monies transferred to a numbered account in Switzerland, and that now Swiss banks were groaning under the weight of money fleeing the country. Billions. A few million in the right palm and anything's possible. Isn't that the same over the whole of Asia? Be honest, why just Asia? Isn't it true over the whole world?

'Tom,' he said wearily, 'try military air traffic control and see if the 212's cleared, will you?' As far as Lochart was concerned, this was just a routine delivery – McIver had told him only that he had seen Valik today and that the general had given him some cash, but nothing else. He still had to decide the pilot he would send, wishing he could do it himself and so put no one else at risk. God-cursed medical! God-cursed rules!

Lochart went to the HF. At that moment there was a scuffle in the outer office, and the door swung open. Standing there was a youth with an automatic rifle over his shoulder and a green band on his arm. Half a dozen other youths were with him. The Iranian staff waited, paralysed. The young man stared at McIver and Lochart then consulted a list.

'Salaam, agha. Capta'n McIver?' he asked Lochart, his English hesitant and heavily accented.

'Salaam, agha. No, I am Captain McIver,' McIver said uneasily, his first thought, Are these more of the same group who murdered poor Kyabi? His second, Gen should have left with the others, I should have insisted. His third about the stacks of rials in his open attaché case on the floor beside the hatstand.

'Ah, good,' the young man said politely. There were dark rings under his eyes, his face strong, and though McIver judged him to be twenty-five at the most, he had an old man's look about him. 'Danger here. For you here. Now. Please to go. We are komiteh for this block. Please you to go. Now.'

'All right. Certainly, er, thank you.' Twice before, McIver had thought it prudent to evacuate the offices because of riots and mobs in the streets around them even though, astonishingly, considering their vast numbers, the mobs had been very disciplined with little damage to property or to Europeans – except for cars parked on the streets. This was the first time anyone had come here to warn him personally. Obediently McIver and Lochart put on their overcoats, McIver closed his attaché case, and, with the others, began to leave. He switched off the lights.

'How lights when no one else?' the leader asked.

'We've our own generator. On the roof.'

The youth smiled strangely, his teeth very white. 'Foreigners have generators and warm, Iranians not.'

McIver was going to answer but thought better of it.

'You got message? Message about leaving? Message today?'

'Yes,' McIver said. One message in the office, one at the apartment that Genny had found in their letter box. They just said, 'On December 1 you were warned to leave. Why are you still here if not as an enemy? You have little time left. (signed) The University supporters for Islamic Republic in Iran.'

'You, er, you are representatives of the university?'

'We are your komiteh. Please to leave now. Enemies better not come back ever. No?'

McIver and Lochart walked out. The revolutionaries followed them down the stairs. For weeks the lift had not worked.

The street was still clear, no mobs, or fires, and all gunfire distant.

'Not come back. Three days.'

McIver stared at them. 'That's not possible. I've got many th –'

'Danger.' The young man and the others, equally young, waited silently and watched. Not all were armed with guns. Two had clubs. Two were holding hands. 'Not come back. Very bad. Three days, komiteh says. Understand?'

'Yes, but one of us has to refuel the generator or the telex will stop and then we'll be out of touch an –'

'Telex unimportant. Not come back. Three days.' The youth patiently motioned them to leave. 'Danger here. Not forget, please. Good night.'

McIver and Lochart got into their cars that were locked in the garage below the building, very conscious of the envious stares. McIver was driving his '65 four-seat Rover coupe that he called Lulu and kept in mint condition. Lochart had borrowed Scot Gavallan's car, a small battered old Citroën that was deliberately low key though the engine was souped up, the brakes perfect, and if need be, she was very fast.

They drove off, and around the second corner stopped alongside one another.

'Those buggers really meant it,' McIver said angrily. 'Three days? I can't stay out of the office three days!'

'Yes. What now?' Lochart glanced into his rearview mirror. The young men had rounded the far corner and stood watching them. 'We better get going. I'll meet you at your apartment,' he said hurriedly.

'Yes, but in the morning, Tom, nothing we can do now.'

'But I was going to go back to Zagros – I should have left today.'

'I know. Stay tomorrow, go the next day. Nogger can do the charter, if the clearance comes through, which I doubt. Come around ten.'

McIver saw the youths begin to walk towards them. 'Around ten, Tom,' he said hurriedly, let in the clutch and drove off cursing.

The youths saw them go and their leader, Ibrahim, was glad, for he did not want to clash with foreigners or to kill them – or to bring them to trial. Only SAVAK. And guilty police. And enemies of Iran, inside Iran, who wanted to bring back the Shah. And all traitorous Marxist totalitarianists who opposed democracy and freedom of worship and the freedom of education and universities.

'Oh, how I'd like that car,' one of them said, almost sick with envy. 'It was a sixty-eight, wasn't it, Ibrahim?'

'A sixty-five,' Ibrahim answered. 'One day you'll have one, Ali, and the petrol to put in it. One day you'll be the most famous writer and poet in all Iran.'

'Disgusting of that foreigner to flaunt so much wealth when there's so much poverty in Iran,' another said.

'Soon they'll all be gone. For ever.'

'Do you think those two will come back tomorrow, Ibrahim?'

'I hope not,' he said with a tired laugh. 'If they do I don't know what we'll do. I think we scared them enough. Even so, we should visit this block at least twice a day.'

A young man holding a club put his arm around him affectionately. 'I'm glad we voted you leader. You were our perfect choice.'

They all agreed. Ibrahim Kyabi was very proud, and proud to be part of the revolution that would end all of Iran's troubles. And proud too of his father who was an oil engineer and important official in IranOil who had patiently worked over the years for democracy in Iran, opposing the Shah, who now would surely be a powerful voice in the new and glorious Iran. 'Come along, friends,' he said contentedly. 'We've several more buildings to investigate.'

170

At Siri Island: 7:42 P.M. A little over seven hundred miles southwest from Tehran, the loading of the 50,000-ton Japanese tanker, the *Rikomaru*, was almost complete. A good moon lit up the Gulf, the night was balmy with many stars above and Scragger had agreed to join de Plessey and go aboard for dinner with Yoshi Kasigi. Now the three of them were on the bridge with the captain, the deck floodlit, watching the Japanese deckhands and the chief engineer near the big intake pipe that led overboard to the complex of valves on the permanently anchored, floating oil-landing barge that was alongside and also flood-lit.

They were about two hundred yards off the low-lying Siri island, the tanker anchored securely with her two bow chains fixed to buoys ahead and two anchors aft from the stern. Oil was pumped from the shore storage tanks through a pipe laid on the seabed up to the barge, thence aboard through their own pipe system into their tanks. Loading and unloading were dangerous operations because volatile, highly explosive gases built up in the tanks in the space over the crude – emptied tanks

171

being even more dangerous until they were washed out. In the most modern tankers, for increased safety, nitrogen – an inert gas – was pumped into the space built up in the tanks, to be expelled at leisure. The *Rikomaru* was not so equipped.

They heard the chief engineer shout down to the men on the barge, 'Close the valve,' then turn to the bridge and give a thumbs-up that the captain acknowledged and said to Kasigi in Japanese, 'Permission to sail as soon as we can?' He was a thin, taut-faced man in starched white shirt and shorts, with white socks and shoes, epaulets, and a naval style, peaked cap.

'Yes, Captain Moriyama. How long will that be?'

'Two hours at the most – to clean up and to cat the moorings.' This meant sending out their motorboat to unshackle their bow anchor chains that were bolted to the permanent buoys, then reattach them to the ship's anchors.

'Good.' To de Plessey and Scragger, Kasigi said in English, 'We're full now and ready to leave. About two hours and we'll be on our way.'

'Excellent,' de Plessey said, equally relieved. 'Now we relax.'

The whole operation had gone very well. Security had been tightened throughout the island and throughout the ship. Everything that could be checked was checked. Only three essential Iranians had been allowed aboard. Each had been searched and were being carefully monitored by a Japanese crewman. There had been no signs of any hostilities among any of the other Iranians ashore. Every likely place had been searched that could hide explosives or arms. 'Perhaps that poor young man off Siri One was mistaken, Scrag, *mon ami.*'

'Perhaps,' Scragger replied. 'Even so, cobber, I think young Abdollah Turik was murdered – no one gets face and eye mutilation like that from falling off a rig in a calm sea. Poor young bugger.'

'But the sharks, Captain Scragger,' Kasigi said, equally disquieted, 'the sharks could have caused those wounds.'

'Yes, they could. But I'll bet my life it was because of what he told me.'

'I hope you're wrong.'

'I'll bet we'll never know the truth,' Scragger said sadly. 'What was your word, Mr. Kasigi? Karma. That poor young bugger's karma was short and not sweet.'

The others nodded. In silence they watched the ship being detached from the barge's umbilical cord.

To see better, Scragger went to the side of the bridge. Under more floodlights oilmen were laboriously unscrewing the twelve-inch pipe

172

from the barge's complex of valves. Six men were there. Two Japanese crew, three Iranians, and a French engineer.

Ahead of him was the expanse and length of the flat deck. In the middle of the deck was his 206. He had landed there at de Plessey's suggestion and with Kasigi's permission. 'Beaut,' Scragger had told the Frenchman; 'I'll fly you back to Siri, or Lengeh, just as you want.'

'Yoshi Kasigi suggests we both stay overnight, Scrag, and return in the morning. It'll make a change for you. We can leave at dawn and return to Lengeh. Come aboard. I'd appreciate it.'

So he had landed on the tanker at sunset, not sure why he had accepted the invitation but he had made a pact with Kasigi and felt he should honour it. Too, he felt sickeningly responsible for young Abdollah Turik. The sight of the youth's corpse had rocked him badly and made him want to be at Siri until the tanker left. So he had arrived and had tried to be a good guest, half-heartedly agreeing with de Plessey that perhaps, after all, the youth's death was just a coincidence and that their security precautions would stop any sabotage attempt.

Since the loading had begun the day before, they had all been edgy. Tonight more so. The BBC news had again been very bad with reports of greatly increased confrontations in Tehran, Meshed and Qom. Added to this was McIver's report that Ayre had carefully relayed from Kowiss in French – news of the continuing investiture of Tehran's International Airport, of the possible coup and about Kyabi. Kyabi's murder had also shocked de Plessey. And all of this, along with the floods of rumours and counter-rumours among the Iranians had made the evening sombre. Rumours of imminent U.S. military intervention, of imminent Soviet intervention, of assassination attempts on Khomeini, on Bazargan his chosen prime minister, on Bakhtiar the legal prime minister, on the U.S. ambassador, rumours that the military coup d'état would happen in Tehran tonight, that Khomeini was arrested already, that all the armed services had capitulated and Khomeini was already de facto ruler of Iran and that General Nassiri, chief of SAVAK, had been captured, tried and shot.

'All the rumours can't be true,' Kasigi had said for all of them. 'There's nothing we can do except wait.'

He had been a fine host. All the food was Japanese. Even the beer. Scragger had tried to hide his distaste for the hors d'oeuvre of sushi but he greatly enjoyed the barbecued chicken in a salty sweet sauce, the rice, and the deep-fried prawns and vegetables in batter. 'Another beer, Captain Scragger?' Kasigi had offered.

'No, thanks. One's all I allow myself though I'll admit it's good. Maybe not as good as Foster's but close.'

De Plessey had smiled, 'You don't know what a compliment that is, Mr. Kasigi. For an Australian to say a beer's "close to Foster's" is praise indeed.'

'Oh, yes, indeed I know, Mr. de Plessey. Down Under I prefer Foster's.'

'You spend a lot of time there?' Scragger had asked him.

'Oh, yes. Australia's one of Japan's main sources of all kinds of raw materials. My company has bulk cargo freighters for coal, iron ore, wheat, rice, soya bean,' Kasigi had said. 'We import huge amounts of your rice though much of that goes into the manufacture of our national drink, saké. Have you tried saké, Captain?'

'Yes, yes I did once. But warm wine . . . saké's not to my taste.'

'I agree,' de Plessey said, then added hurriedly, 'except in winter, like hot toddy. You were saying about Australia?'

'I enjoy the country very much. My eldest son goes to Sydney University too, so we visit him from time to time. It's a wonderland – so vast, so rich, so empty.'

Yes, Scragger had thought grimly. You mean so empty and just waiting to be filled up by your millions of worker-ants? Thank the Lord we're a few thousand miles away and the U.S.'ll never allow us to be taken over.

'Bollocks!' McIver had said to him once during a friendly argument, when he, McIver and Pettikin were on a week's leave two years ago in Singapore. 'If some time in the future Japan picked the right time, say when the U.S. was having at Russia, the States wouldn't be able to do a thing to help Australia. I think they'd make a deal an –'

'Dirty Duncan's lost his marbles, Charlie,' Scragger had said.

'You're right,' Pettikin had agreed. 'He's just needling you, Scrag.'

'Oh, no, I'm not. Your real protector's China. Come hell or strawberries, China's always going to be there. And only China will always be in a position to stop Japan if ever Japan got militant and strong enough to move south. My God, Australia's the great prize in the whole Pacific, the treasure chest of the Pacific, but none of you buggers down there care to plan ahead or use your loaf. All you bloody want's three days' holiday a week, with more pay for less bloody work, free bloody school, free medical, free welfare, and let some other bugger man the ramparts – you're worse than poor old bloody England who's got nothing! The real tr –'

'You've got North Sea oil. If that's not the luck of the devil I do –'

174

'The real trouble is you bloody twits Down Under don't know your arse from a hole in the wall.'

'Sit down, Scrag!' Pettikin had said warningly. 'You agreed no fighting. None. Both of you – you did it once but that was friendly. You try and thump Mac when he's not smashed you'll end up in the sewer. He may have high blood pressure but he's still a black belt.'

'Me thump Dirty Duncan? You must be joking, cobber. I don't pick on old buggers . . .'

Scragger smiled to himself, remembering that bender to end all benders. Singapore's a good place, he thought, then turned his attention back to the ship, feeling better now, well fed and very glad that the loading was done.

The night was grand. Far above him he saw the blinking navigation lights of an airplane heading westward and wondered briefly where its landfall was, what airline it was and how many passengers were aboard. His night vision was excellent and he could see that now the men on the barge had almost unscrewed the pipe. Once it had been winched aboard, the tanker could leave. At dawn the *Rikomaru* would be in the Strait of Hormuz and he would take off and fly home to Lengeh with de Plessey.

Then his sharp eyes saw some men running away from the semi-floodlit pumping junction just ashore. His attention zeroed on them.

There was a small explosion, then a gush of flame as the oil caught fire. Everyone aboard watched aghast. The flames began to spread, and they heard shouting – Iranian and French – ashore. Men were running down from the barracks and storage tanks area. A sudden flicker of a machine gun in the darkness, the sharp ugly crackle following. Over the ship's loudspeaker system came the captain's voice in Japanese: 'Action stations!'

At once the men on the barge redoubled their efforts, petrified that somehow the fire might spread through the pipe to the barge and blow it up. The moment the nozzle fell away from the valve, the Iranians hastily jumped into their small motorboat and fled, their work completed. The French engineer and Japanese seamen ran up the gangplank as the tanker's deck winch rattled into life, dragging the pipe aboard.

Below decks the crew had scurried to emergency positions, some to the engine room, some to the bridge, others to the main gangways. Momentarily the three Iranians monitoring the fuel flow in various parts of the ship were left alone. They rushed for the deck.

One of them, Saiid, pretended to stumble and fall near the main tank

175

inlet. When he was sure he was not observed he hastily opened his trousers and brought out the small plastic explosive device that had been missed in the body search when he had come aboard. It had been taped to the inside of a thigh, high up between his legs. Hastily he activated the chemical detonator that would explode in about one hour, stuck the device behind the main valve and ran for the gangway. When he came on deck he was appalled to find that the men on the barge had not waited and that now the motorboat was almost ashore. The other two Iranians were chattering excitedly, equally enraged to be left aboard. Neither were members of his leftist cell.

Onshore the oil spill was blazing out of control but the oil supply had been cut and the break isolated. Three men had been badly burned, one French and two Iranians. The mobile fire-fighting truck poured sea-water into the flames, sucking it up from the Gulf. There was no wind and the choking black smoke made fire-fighting even more difficult.

'Get some foam on to it,' Legrande, the French manager, shouted. Almost beside himself with rage, he tried to get order, but everyone was still milling about in the floodlights not knowing what to do. 'Jacques, round up everyone and let's count heads. Fast as you can.' Their full complement was seven French and thirty Iranians on the island. The security force of three men hurried off into the darkness, unarmed except for hastily made batons, not knowing what further sabotage to expect or from where.

'*M'sieur!*' the Iranian medic was beckoning Legrande.

He went down towards the shore to the complex of pipes and valves that joined the tanks to the barge. The medic was kneeling beside two of the injured men who lay on a piece of canvas, unconscious and in shock. One of them had had his hair completely singed off and most of his face severely burned; the other had been sprayed with oil in the initial explosion that had instantly conflagrated his clothes, causing first-degree burns over most of the front of his body.

'*Mon Dieu*,' Legrande muttered and crossed himself, seeing the ugly charred skin, barely recognising his Iranian foreman.

One of his French engineers sat hunched over and was moaning softly, his hands and arms burned. Mixed with his agony was a constant stream of expletives.

'I'll get you to the hospital, fast as I can, Paul.'

'Find those fornicators and burn them,' the engineer snarled, then went back into his pain.

'Of course,' Legrande said helplessly, then to the medic, 'Do what you can, I'll call for a CASEVAC.' He hurried away from the shore for the radio room that was in one of the barracks, his eyes adjusting to the darkness. Then he noticed two men on the far side of the tiny airstrip, running up the track on the slight bluff. Over the bluff was a cove with a small wharf used for sailing and swimming. I'll bet the bastards have a boat there, he thought at once. Then, almost berserk with rage, he shouted after them into the night, 'Bastardsssss!'

When the first explosion had occurred, de Plessey had rushed for the ship-to-shore radio that was on the bridge. 'Have you found that machine gun yet?' he asked the base submanager in French. Behind him, Scragger, Kasigi and the captain were equally grim. Lights on the bridge were dimmed. Outside, the moon was high and strong.

'No, *m'sieur*. After the first burst, the attackers vanished.'

'What about the damage to the pumping system?'

'I don't know. I'm waiting for a . . . ah, just a moment, here's M'sieur Legrande.' After a moment again in French: 'This's Legrande. Three burned, two Iranians very badly, the other's Paul Beaulieu, hands and arms – call for a CASEVAC at once. I saw a couple of men heading for the cove – probably the saboteurs, and they've probably a boat there. I'm assembling everyone so we can see who's missing.'

'Yes, at once. What about the damage?'

'Not major. With luck we'll have that fixed in a week – certainly by the time the next tanker arrives.'

'I'll come ashore as soon as I can. Wait a moment!' De Plessey looked at the others and told them what Legrande had said.

Scragger said at once, 'I'll take the CASEVAC, no need to call for one.'

Kasigi said, 'Bring the injured aboard – we've a surgery and a doctor. He's very skilled, particularly with burns.'

'Good on you!' Scragger rushed off.

Into the mike de Plessey said, 'We'll deal with the CASEVAC from here. Get the men on to stretchers. Captain Scragger will bring them aboard at once. There's a doctor here.'

A young Japanese deck officer came and spoke briefly to the captain who shook his head and replied curtly, then explained in English to de Plessey: 'The three Iranians who were left aboard when the others on the barge fled want to be taken ashore at once. I said they could wait,' then he called down to the engine room preparing to make way.

Kasigi was staring at the island. And at the tanks there. I need that oil, he thought, and I need the island safe. But it's not safe and nothing I can do to make it safe.

'I'm going ashore,' de Plessey said and left.

Scragger was already at the 206, unhooking the rear doors.

'What're you doing, Scrag?' de Plessey said, hurrying up to him.

'I can lay the stretcher on the backseat and lash it safe. Quicker than rigging an outside carry sling.'

'I'll come with you.'

'Hop in!' They glanced around at the noise behind them. The three Iranians had run over and were jabbering at him. It was clear they wanted to go ashore in the helicopter. 'Shall we take them, Scrag?'

Scragger was already in the pilot's seat, his fingers dancing over the switches. 'No. You're an emergency, they're not. Get in, old sport.' He pointed at the right seat then waved the Iranians away. '*Nah, ajaleh daram*' – No, I'm in a hurry – he said, using one of the few expressions in Farsi he knew. Two of them backed off obediently. The third, Saiid, slid into the backseat and started to buckle up. Scragger shook his head, motioning him to get out. The man took no notice and spoke rapidly and forced a smile and pointed at the shore.

Impatiently Scragger motioned him out, one finger pressing the Engine Start button switch. The whine began instantly. Again the man refused and, angry now, pointed at the shore, his voice drowned by the cranking engine. For a moment Scragger thought, Okay, why not?, then he noticed the man's face, his sweat-soaked overalls, and seemed to smell his fear. 'Out!' he said, studying him very carefully.

Saiid paid no attention to him. Above them the blade was turning slowly, gaining speed.

'Let him stay,' de Plessey called out over. 'We'd better hurry.'

Abruptly Scragger aborted the engine start and with very great strength for such a small man, had Saiid's belt unbuckled and the man out on the deck, half unconscious, before anyone knew what was happening. He cupped his hands around his mouth and shouted up at the bridge. 'Hey there, aloft! Kasigi! This joker's too bloody anxious to go ashore – wasn't he below decks?' Without waiting for an answer, he jumped back into the cockpit and jabbed Engine Start.

De Plessey watched him silently. 'What did you see in that man?'

Scragger shrugged. Long before the engine came to full power, seamen had grabbed the man and the other two and were herding them up to the bridge.

The 206 went like an arrow for the shore. The two injured men were already on stretchers. Rapidly a spare stretcher was lashed in place across the backseat and the first stretcher lashed to this. Scragger helped the injured Frenchman, arms and hands bandaged, into the front seat alongside him, and trying to close his nostrils to the stench, eased her airborne and flew back, landing like gossamer. Medics and the doctor were waiting, plasma ready, morphine hypodermic ready.

In seconds Scragger darted shoreward again. In more seconds the last stretcher was in place and he was away, again to land delicately. Once more the doctor was waiting, needle ready, and again he ducked down and ran for the stretcher under the whirling blades. This time he did not use the needle. 'Ah so sorry,' he said in halting English. 'This man dead.' Then, keeping his head low, he scurried for his surgery. Medics took the body away.

When Scragger had shut down and had everything locked and safe, he went to the side of the ship and was violently sick. Ever since he had seen and heard and smelled a pilot in a crashed, burning biplane, years upon years ago, it had been an abiding horror of his to be caught in the same way. He had never been able to stomach the smell of burned human hair and skin.

After a while he wiped his mouth, breathing the good air, and blessed his luck. Three times he had been shot down, twice in flames, but each time he had got out safely. Four times he had had to autorotate to save himself and his passengers, twice over jungle and into the trees, once with an engine on fire. 'But my name wasn't on the list,' he muttered. 'Not those times.' Footsteps were approaching. He turned to see Kasigi walking across the deck, an ice-cold bottle of Kirin beer in each hand.

'Please excuse me, but here,' Kasigi said gravely, offering the beer. 'Burns do the same for me. I was sick too. I . . . I went down to the surgery to see how the injured were and . . . I was very sick.'

Scragger drank gratefully. The cool, hop-flavoured liquid, bubbles tingling as he swallowed, rebirthed him. 'Christ Jesus that was good. Thanks, cobber.' And having said it once it became easier to say it the second time, 'Thanks, cobber.' Kasigi heard it both times and considered it a major victory. Both of them looked at the seaman hurrying up to them with a teleprinter message in his hand. He gave it to Kasigi who went to the nearest light, put on his glasses and peered at it. Scragger heard him suck in his breath and saw him become even more ashen.

'Bad news?'

After a pause Kasigi said, 'No – just, just problems.'

'Anything I can do?'

Kasigi did not answer him. Scragger waited. He could see the turmoil written in the man's eyes though not his face, and he was sure Kasigi was trying to decide whether to tell him. Then Kasigi said, 'I don't think so. It's . . . it's about our petrochemical plant at Bandar-e Delam.'

'The one Japan's building?' Along with almost everyone else in the Gulf Scragger knew about the enormous $3.5 billion endeavour that, when completed, would easily be the biggest petrochemical complex in Asia Minor and the Middle East, with a 300,000-ton ethylene plant as its heart. It had been building since '71 and was almost finished, 85 percent complete. 'That's some plant!'

'Yes. But it's being built by Japanese private industry, not by the Japanese government,' Kasigi said, 'The Iran-Toda plant's privately financed.'

'Ah,' Scragger said, the connection falling into place. '*Toda* Shipping – Iran-*Toda*! You're the same company?'

'Yes, but we're only part of the Japanese syndicate that put up the money and technical advice for the Shah . . . for Iran,' Kasigi corrected himself. All gods great and small curse this land, curse everyone in it, curse the Shah for creating all the oil crises, curse OPEC, curse all the misbegotten fanatics and liars who live here. He glanced at the message again and was pleased to see his fingers were not shaking. It was in private code from his chairman, Hiro Toda.

It read: 'URGENT. Due to absolute and continuous Iranian intransigence, I have finally had to order all construction at Bandar-e Delam to cease. Present cost overruns total $500 million and would probably go to 1 billion before we could begin production. Present interest payments are $495,000 daily. Due to infamous secret pressure by "Broken Sword", our Contingency Plan 4 has been rejected. Go to Bandar-e Delam urgently and give me a personal report. Chief Engineer Director Watanabe is expecting you. Please acknowledge.'

It's impossible to get there, Kasigi thought crestfallen. And if Plan 4 is rejected, we're ruined.

Contingency Plan 4 called for Hiro Toda to approach the Japanese government for low-interest loans to take up the shortfall, and at the same time, discreetly, to petition the prime minister to declare the Iran-Toda complex at Bandar-e Delam a 'National Project'. 'National Project' meant that the government formally accepted the vital nature of the endeavour and would see it through to completion. 'Broken Sword' was their code name for Hiro Toda's personal enemy and chief rival, Hidiyoshi Ishida, who headed the enormously powerful group of trading companies under the general name of Mitsuwari.

All gods curse that jealous, lying son of vermin, Ishida, Kasigi was thinking, as he said, 'My company is only one of many in the Syndicate.'

'I flew over your plant once,' Scragger said. 'Going from our base to Abadan. I was on a ferry, ferrying a 212. You've trouble there?'

'Some temporary . . .' Kasigi stopped and stared at him. Pieces of a plan fell into place. 'Some temporary problems . . . important but temporary. As you know we've had more than our fair share of problems since the beginning, none of them our fault.' First there was February '71 when twenty-three oil producers signed the OPEC price agreement, formed their cartel, and doubled the price to $2.16 . . . then the Yom Kippur War of '73 when OPEC cut shipments to the United States and raised the price to $5.12. Then the catastrophe of '74 when OPEC shipments were resumed but again at over double the price, $10.95, the world recession began. 'Why the U.S. allowed OPEC to wreck the economy of the world when they alone had the power to smash it, we'll never know. *Baka!* And now we're all in a perpetual pawn to OPEC, now our major supplier Iran is in revolution, oil's almost $20 a barrel and we have to pay it, have to.' He bunched his fist to smash it on the gunnel, then unclenched, disgusted with his lack of control. 'As to Iran-Toda,' he said, forcing outward calm, 'like everyone else we found Iranians very . . . very difficult to deal with in recent years.' He motioned to the message. 'My chairman asked me to go to Bandar-e Delam.'

Scragger whistled. 'That's going to be dicey – difficult.'

'Yes.'

'Is it important?'

'Yes. Yes, it is.' Kasigi left that hanging in the air, sure that Scragger would suggest the solution. Ashore the oil-soaked earth around the sabotaged valve complex still burned brightly. The fire truck was spreading foam now. They could see de Plessey nearby, talking to Legrande.

Scragger said, 'Listen, old sport, you're an important client of de Plessey, eh? He could fix a charter for you. We've a spare 206. If he agreed, all our aircraft are contracted to IranOil but to him in truth, perhaps we could get permission from air traffic control to fly you up the coast – or if you could clear Immigration and Customs at Lengeh, maybe we could nip you across the Gulf to Dubai or Al Shargaz. From there perhaps you could get a flight into Abadan or Bandar-e Delam. Whichever, old sport, he could let us get you started.'

'Do you think he would?'

'Why not? You're important to him.'

Kasigi was thinking. Of course we're very important to him and he knows it. But I'll never forget that iniquitous two-dollar-a-barrel premium. 'Sorry? What did you say?'

'I said, what made you start the project anyway? It's a long way from home and had to be nothing but trouble. What started you?'

'A dream.' Kasigi would like to have lit a cigarette but smoking was only allowed in certain fireproofed areas. 'Eleven years ago, in '68, a man called Banjiro Kyama, a senior engineer working for my company and kinsman of our president, Hiro Toda, was driving through the oil fields around Abadan. It was his first visit to Iran and everywhere he went he saw jets of natural gas being flared off. He had a sudden thought: why can't we turn that wasted gas into petrochemicals? We've the technology and the expertise and a long-range planning attitude. Japanese skill and money married to Iranian raw materials that presently are totally wasted! A brilliant idea – unique and another first! The feasibility planning took three years, quite long enough, though jealous rivals claimed we went too quickly, at the same time they tried to steal our ideas and tried to poison others against us. But the Toda plan correctly went forward and the $3.5 billion raised. Of course, we're only a part of the Gyokotomo-Mitsuwari-Toda syndicate, but Toda ships will carry Japan's share of the products that our industries desperately need.' If ever we can finish the complex, he thought disgustedly.

'And now the dream's a nightmare?' Scragger asked. 'Didn't I hear . . . wasn't it reported that the project was running out of money?'

'Enemies spread all sorts of rumours.' Under the ever-present drone of the ship's generators, his ears heard the beginning of a scream that he had been expecting – surprised it had been so long arriving. 'When de Plessey comes back aboard, will you help me?'

'Glad to. He's the man who c—' Scragger stopped. Again the thin edge of the scream. 'Burns must be terrible painful.'

Kasigi nodded.

Another gush of flame took their attention to the shore. They watched the men there. Now the fire was almost under control. Another scream. Kasigi dismissed it, his mind on Bandar-e Delam and the teleprinter reply he should make at once to Hiro Toda. If anyone can solve our problem it's Hiro Toda. he has to solve it – if he doesn't, I'm ruined, his failure becomes mine.

'Kasigi-san!' It was the captain calling from the bridge.

'*Hai?*'

Scragger listened to the stream of Japanese from the captain, the sound of the Japanese not pleasing to his ears.

Kasigi gasped. '*Domo*,' he shouted back, then, urgently to Scragger, all else forgotten, 'Come on!' He led the rush to the gangway. 'The Iranian – you remember, the one you threw out of the chopper? He's a saboteur and he's planted an explosive device below.'

Scragger followed Kasigi through the hatchway, down the gangway two steps at a time, rushed along the corridor, and down another deck and another and then he remembered the screams. I thought they came from the bridge and not from below! he told himself. What did they do to him?

They caught up with the captain and his chief engineer. Two angry seamen half shoved, half dragged the petrified Saiid ahead of them. Tears ran down his face and he was jabbering incoherently, one hand holding his pants up. He stopped, trembling and moaning, and pointed at the valve. The captain squatted on his haunches. Very carefully he reached behind the huge valve. Then he stood up. The plastic explosive just covered his hand. The timing device was chemical, a vial embedded in it and taped strongly in place.

'Turn it off,' he said angrily in hesitant Farsi and held it out to the man who backed off, jabbering and screaming, 'You can't turn it off. It's overdue to explode . . . don't you understanddd!'

The captain froze. 'He says it's overdue!'

Before he could move, one of the seamen grabbed it out of his hand and half dragging Saiid with him, half smashing him ahead, rushed for the gangway – there were no portholes on this deck but there were on the next. The nearest porthole was in a corner of the corridor, clamped shut by two heavy metal wing nuts. He almost flung Saiid at it, shouting at him to open it. With his free hand he began unscrewing one of them. The swing bolt fell away, then Saiid's. The seaman swung the port open. At that second the device exploded and blew both his hands off and most of his face and tore Saiid's head apart and splattered the far bulkhead with blood.

The others charging up from below were almost blown backward down the gangway. Then Kasigi went forward and knelt beside the bodies. Numbly he shook his head.

The captain broke the silence. 'Karma,' he muttered.

At Tehran: 8:33 P.M. After Tom Lochart had left McIver near their office he had driven home – a few diversions, some angry police but nothing untoward. Home was a fine penthouse apartment in a modern six-storey building, in the best residential area – a wedding present from his father-in-law. Sharazad was waiting for him. She threw her arms around him, kissed him passionately, begged him to sit in front of the fire and take his shoes off, rushed to fetch some wine that was iced exactly as he liked, brought him a snack, told him that dinner would be ready soon, ran into the kitchen and in her lilting, liquid voice, urged their maid and the cook to hurry for the Master was home and hungry, then came back and sat at his feet – the floor beautifully and heavily carpeted – her arms around his knees, adoring him. 'Oh, I'm so happy to see you, Tommy, I've missed you so much,' her English lovely. 'Oh, I've had such an interesting time today and yesterday.'

She wore light silk Persian trousers and a long loose blouse and was, for him, achingly beautiful. And desirable. Her twenty-third birthday was in a few days. He was forty-two. They had been married almost a year and he had been spellbound from the first moment he had seen her.

That had been a little over three years before, at a dinner party in Tehran that was given by General Valik, a cousin of her father. It was early September then, just at the end of English school summer vacations, and Deirdre, his wife, was in England with their daughter, holidaying and partying, and only that morning he had had another irate letter from her, insisting he write to Gavallan for an immediate transfer: 'I hate Iran, don't want to live there any more, England's all I want, all that Monica wants. Why don't you think of us for a change instead of your damned flying and damned company? All my family's here, all my friends are here, and all Monica's friends are here. I'm fed up with living abroad and want my own house, somewhere near London, with a garden, or even in town – there are some super bargains going in Putney and Clapham Common. I'm totally fed up with foreigners and foreign postings, and absolutely chocker with Iranian food, the filth, the heat, the cold, their foul-sounding language, their foul loos and squatting like an animal, and foul habits, manners – everything. It's time we sorted out things while I'm still young . . .'

'Excellency?'

The smiling, starched waiter had deferentially offered him a tray of drinks, soft drinks mostly. Many middle and upper-society Muslims drank in the privacy of their homes, a few in public – liquor and wine of all sorts being on sale in Tehran, and also in bars in all modern hotels. There were no restrictions on foreigners drinking openly or privately, unlike in Saudi Arabia – and some of the Emirates – where anyone caught, anyone, was subject to Koranic punishment of the lash.

'*Mamoonan*,' thank you, he said politely and accepted a glass of the white Persian wine that had been sought after for almost three millennia, hardly noticing the waiter or the other guests, unable to shake off his depression and irritated that he agreed to join this party tonight, substituting for McIver who had had to go to their HQ base at Al Shargaz, the other side of the Gulf. 'But, Tom, you can talk Farsi,' McIver had said airily, 'and someone's got to go . . .' Yes, he thought, but Mac could just as easily have asked Charlie Pettikin.

It was almost nine o'clock, still before dinner, and he had been standing near one of the open doorways that led to the gardens, looking out at the candlelights and at the lawns that were spread with fine rugs on which guests were sitting and reclining, others standing in groups under trees or near the little pond. The night was star-filled and kind, the house rich and spacious – in the district of Shemiran at the foot of the Elburz Mountains – and the party like most of the others that, because he could speak Farsi, he was usually welcomed to. All the Iranians were very well-dressed, there was much laughter and much jewellery, tables piled with an abundance of food, both European and Iranian, hot and cold, the conversation about the latest play in London or New York or 'Are you going to St Moritz for the skiing or Cannes for the season,' and about the price of oil and gossip about the Court and 'His Imperial Majesty this or Her Imperial Majesty that,' all of it spiced with the politeness and flattery and extravagant compliment so necessary in all Iranian society – preserving a calm, polite and gentle surface rarely penetrated by an outsider, let alone by a foreigner.

At the time he was stationed at Galeg Morghi, a military airfield in Tehran, training Iranian Air Force pilots. In ten days he was due to leave for his new posting at Zagros, well aware that this tour with two weeks in Zagros, one week back in Tehran would further inflame his wife. This morning, in a fit of rage, he had answered her letter and sent it special delivery: 'If you want to stay in England, stay in England but stop bitching and stop knocking what you don't know. Get your suburban house wherever you want – but I'm not EVER going to live there. Never. I've a good job and it pays all right and I like it and that's it. We've a good life if you'd open your eyes. You knew I was a pilot when we got married, knew it was the life I'd chosen, knew I wouldn't live in England, know it's all I'm trained for so I can't change now. Stop bitching or else. If you want to change so be it . . .'

The hell with it. I've had it. Christ, she says she hates Iran and everything about it but she knows nothing about Iran, has never been outside Tehran, won't go, will never even try the food and just visits with those few Brit wives – always the same ones, the loud and bigoted minority, insular, equally bored and boring with their interminable bridge parties, interminable teas – 'but darling, how can you stand anything that's not from Fortnums or Marks and Sparks' – who preen for an invitation to the British embassy for another stuffy roast beef and Yorkshire pudding dinner or tea party with cucumber sandwiches and seedcake, all of them totally convinced everything English is the best in the world, particularly English cooking: boiled carrots, boiled cauliflower, boiled potatoes, boiled Brussels sprouts, underdone roast beef or overdone lamb as the acme of goddam perfection . . .

'Oh, poor Excellency, you don't look happy at all,' she had said softly.

He had looked around and his world was different.

'What's the matter?' she asked, a tiny frown on her oval face.

'Sorry,' he gasped, for a moment disoriented by her, his heart thumping and a tightness in his throat he had never experienced before. 'I thought you were an apparition, something out of *A Thousand and One Nights*, a magical—' He stopped with an effort, feeling like a fool. 'Sorry, I was a million miles away. My name's Lochart, Tom Lochart.'

'Yes, I know,' she said laughing. Tawny brown twinkling eyes. Her lips had a sheen to them, teeth very white, long wavy dark hair, and her skin was the colour of Iranian earth, olive brown. She wore white silk and some perfume and she barely came up to his chin. 'You're the nasty training captain who gives my poor cousin Karim roastings at least three times a day.'

'What?' Lochart found it difficult to concentrate. 'Who?'

'There.' She pointed across the room. The young man was in civilians, smiling at them, and Lochart had not recognised him as one of his students. Very handsome, dark curly hair, dark eyes, and well built. 'My special cousin. Captain Karim Peshadi, of the Imperial Iranian Air Force.' She looked back at Lochart, long black lashes. And again his heart turned over.

Get hold of yourself, for crissake! What the hell's wrong with you? 'I 'er, well, I try not to roast them unless, er, unless they deserve it – it's only to save their lives.' He was trying to remember Captain Peshadi's record but couldn't and in desperation switched to Farsi. 'But, Highness, if you'll give me the exquisite honour, if you'll stay and talk to me and favour me by telling me your name I promise I will . . .' He groped for the right word, couldn't find it and substituted, 'I will be your slave for ever and of course I will have to pass His Excellency your cousin one hundred percent before all others!'

She clapped her hands delightedly. 'Oh, revered Excellency,' she replied in Farsi, 'His Excellency my cousin did not tell me you spoke our language! Oh how beautiful the words sound when you say them . . .'

Almost outside himself, Lochart listened to her extravagant compliments that were normal in Farsi and heard himself replying likewise – blessing Scragger who had told him so many years ago when he had joined Sheik Aviation, after he had left the RAF in '65: 'If you want to fly with us, cobber, you'd better learn Farsi 'cause I'm not about to!' For the first time realising how perfect it was as a language of love, of innuendo.

'My name is Sharazad Paknouri, Excellency.'

'Then Her Highness is from the *Thousand and One Nights* after all.'

187

'Ah, but I cannot tell you a story even if you swear you will cut off my head!' Then in English, with a laugh, 'I was bottom of my class in stories.'

'Impossible!' he said at once.

'Are you always so gallant, Captain Lochart?' Her eyes were teasing him.

In Farsi he heard himself say, 'Only to the most beautiful woman I have ever seen.'

Colour came into her face. She dropped her eyes, and he thought, aghast, he had destroyed everything, but when she looked up at him again her eyes were smiling. 'Thank you. You make an old married lady happ –'

His glass slipped out of his hand and he cursed and picked it up and apologised but no one had noticed except her. 'You're married?' burst out of him, for it hadn't occurred to him, but of course she would be married and anyway he was married with a daughter of eight and what right did he have to get upset? For God's sake you're acting like a lunatic. You've gone mad.

Then his ears and eyes focused. 'What? What did you say?' he asked.

'Oh. I said that I *was* married – well, I still am for another three weeks and two days and that my married name is Paknouri. My family name is Bakravan . . .' She stopped a waiter and chose a glass of wine and gave it to him. Again the frown. 'Are you sure you're all right Captain?'

'Oh yes, oh yes,' he said quickly. 'You were saying? Paknouri?'

'Yes. His Highness, Emir Paknouri, was so old, fifty, a friend of my father, and Father and Mother thought it would be good for me to marry him and he consented though I'm skinny, not plump and desirable, however much I eat. As God wants.' She shrugged then beamed and the world seemed to light up for him. 'Of course I agreed, but only on condition that if I didn't like being married after two years then our marriage would cease. So on my seventeenth birthday we were married and I didn't like it at once and cried and cried and then, as there were no children after two years, or the extra year I agreed to, my husband, my Master, gratefully agreed to divorce me and now he is thankfully ready to remarry and I am free but unfortunately so old an –'

'You're not old, you're as youn –'

'Oh, yes, old!' Her eyes were dancing and she pretended to be sad but he could see that she was not and he watched himself talking to her, laughing with her, then beckoning her cousin to join them, petrified that this was the real man of her choice, chatting with them, learning that her father was an important bazaari, that her family was large and cosmopolitan and well connected, that her mother was sick, that she had sisters and brothers and had been to school in Switzerland but only for half a year because she missed Iran and her family so much. Then eating dinner with them, genial and happy, even with General Valik, and it was the best time he had ever had.

When he had left that night he had not gone home but had taken the road up to Darband in the mountains where there were many cafés in beautiful gardens on the banks of the stream with chairs and tables and sumptuously carpeted divans where you could rest or eat or sleep, some of them esplanaded out over the stream so the water chattered and gurgled below you. And he lay there, looking up at the stars, knowing that he was changed, knowing he'd gone mad but that he would scale any hurdle, endure any hardship to marry her.

And he had – though the way had been cruel and many times he had cried out in despair.

'What are you thinking about, Tommy?' she asked now, sitting at his feet on the lovely carpet that had been a wedding gift from General Valik.

'You,' he said, loving her, his cares banished by her tenderness. The living room was warm like all of the huge apartment, and delicately lit, the curtains drawn and many rugs and lounging cushions scattered around, the wood fire burning merrily. 'But then I think about you all the time!'

She clapped her hands. 'That's wonderful.'

'I'm not going to Zagros tomorrow but the next day.'

'Oh, that's even more wonderful!' She hugged his knees and rested her head against them. 'Wonderful!'

He caressed her hair. 'You said you had an interesting day?'

'Yes, yesterday and today. I've been to your embassy and got the passport, just as you told me to do, th –'

'Great. Now you're Canadian.'

'No, Beloved, Iranian – you're Canadian. Listen, the best part is that I went to Doshan Tappeh,' she said proudly.

'Christ,' he said, not meaning to, for she did not like to hear him blaspheme. 'Sorry, but that's – that was crazy, there's fighting going on there, you're crazy to put yourself in such danger.'

'Oh, I wasn't in the fighting,' she told him gaily, and got up and rushed out saying, 'I'll show you.' In a moment she was back in the doorway. She had put on a grey chador that covered her from head to toe and most of her face, and he hated it. 'Ah, Master,' she said in Farsi, pirouetting in front of him. 'You have no need to fear over me. God watches over me, and the Prophet Whose Name be praised.' She stopped, seeing his expression. 'What's the matter?' she asked in English.

'I – I've never seen you in chador. It's – it doesn't suit you.'

'Oh, I know it's ugly and I'd never wear it at home, but in the street I feel better wearing one, Tommy. All those awful stares from men. It's time we all went back to wearing them – and the veil.'

He was shocked. 'What about all the freedoms you've won, freedom to vote, to take off the veil, freedom to go where you please, marry whom you please, no longer the chattel that you used to be? If you agree to the chador, you'll lose everything else.'

'Perhaps, perhaps not, Tommy.' She was glad that they were talking in English so she could argue a little, unthinkable with an Iranian husband. And so glad that she had chosen to marry this man who, unbelievably, allowed her an opinion and, even more astonishing, allowed her to express it openly to him. This wine of freedom is very heady, she thought, very difficult, very dangerous for a woman to drink – like nectar in the Garden of Paradise.

'When Reza Shah took the veil from our faces,' she said, 'he should also have taken the obsession from the minds of men. You don't go to market, Tommy, or ride in a car, not as a woman. You've no idea what it's like. Men on the streets, in the bazaar, in the bank, everywhere. They're all the same. You can see the same thoughts, the same obsession, in all of them – thoughts about me which only you should have.' She took off the chador, put it neatly on a chair, and sat down at his feet again. 'From today on I will wear it on the street, like my mother and hers before me, not because of Khomeini, God protect him, but for you, my beloved husband.'

She kissed him lightly and sat at his knee and he knew it was decided. Unless he ordered her not to. But then there would be trouble in the home, for it was truly her right to decide this matter here. She was Iranian, his home Iranian, and always would be in Iran – that was part of his bargain with her father – so the trouble would be Iranian and the solution Iranian: days of vast sighs and soul-filled glances, a little tear, abject, slavelike service, judicious sobs in the night, more tortured sighs, never a word or look in anger and all murderous to a husband's or father's or brother's peace.

Lochart found her so hard to understand sometimes. 'Do as you want, but no more Doshan Tappeh,' he said, caressing her hair. It was fine and silky and shone as only youth can shine. 'What happened there?'

Her face lit up. 'Oh, it was so exciting. The Immortals – even the Shah's crack troops – couldn't dislodge the Faithful. Guns were going off everywhere. I was quite safe, my sister Laleh was with me, my cousin Ali and his wife. Cousin Karim was there – he's declared for Islam and the revolution with several other officers and he told us where to meet him and how. There were about two hundred other ladies, all of us in chador, and we kept up our chanting, God is Great, God is Great, then some of the soldiers came over to us. Immortals!' Her eyes widened. 'Imagine, even the Immortals are beginning to see the Truth!'

Lochart was appalled at the danger of her going there without asking or telling him, even though she was accompanied. Thus far the insurrection and Khomeini had seemingly passed her by, except initially when the real troubles began and she was petrified over the safety of her father and relations who were important merchants and bankers in the bazaar, and well known for their connections at Court. Thankfully her father had dispelled all their concerns when he had whispered to Lochart that he and his brothers were secretly supporting Khomeini and the revolt against the Shah and had been doing so for years. But now, he thought, now if the Immortals are cracking and top echelon young officers like Karim are openly supporting the revolt the bloodshed will be enormous. 'How many came over?' he asked, trying to decide what to do.

'Only three joined us, but Karim said it's a good beginning and any day Bakhtiar and his scoundrels will flee like the Shah fled.'

'Listen, Sharazad, today the British and Canadian governments've ordered all dependants out of Iran for a while. Mac's sending everyone to Al Shargaz till things cool down.'

'That's very wise, yes, that's wise.'

'Tomorrow the 125'll be in. She'll take Genny, Manuela, you, and Azadeh tomorrow so pack a b –'

'Oh, I won't leave, my darling, no need for me to leave. And Azadeh, why should she go either? There's no danger for us – Father would certainly know if there was any danger. No need for you to worry . . .' She saw his wineglass was nearly empty so she jumped up and refilled it and came back again. 'I'm quite safe.'

'But I think you'd be safer out of Iran for a wh –'

'It's wonderful of you to think of me, my darling, but there's no reason for me to go and I'll certainly ask Father tomorrow, or you can . . .' A small ember of wood fell without danger into the grate. He started to get up but she was already there. 'I'll do it. Rest, my darling, you must be tired. Perhaps you'd have time tomorrow to see Father with me.' Deftly she tidied the fire. Her chador was on a nearby chair. She saw him glance at it. The shadow of a smile washed over her.

'What?'

For answer she just smiled again, picked it up, and ran gaily across the room and down the corridor to the kitchen.

Unsettled, Lochart stared at the fire, trying to marshal his arguments, not wanting to order her. But I will if I have to. My God, so many troubles: Charlie vanished, Kowiss in a mess, Kyabi murdered, and Sharazad in the middle of a riot! She's crazy! Mad to take such a risk! If I lost her I'd die. God, whoever you are, wherever you are, protect her . . .

This living room was large. At the far end was a dining-room table and chairs that could seat twelve. Most times, they would use the room in Iranian style, sitting on the floor, a tablecloth spread for the dishes, lounging against cushions. Rarely did they wear shoes and never high heels that could damage the deep carpets. There were five bedrooms, three bathrooms, two living rooms – this one they used generally or with company, the other, much smaller at the far end of the apartment, was as customary, for her to go to when he had business to discuss, or when her sister or girlfriends or relations were visiting so their chatter would not disturb him. Around Sharazad was always movement, always family nearby, children, nannies – except after sunset, though frequently relations or close friends were staying in the guest bedrooms.

He never minded, they were a happy, gregarious family, in front of him. It was also part of his bargain with her father that he would patiently learn Iranian ways, patiently live Iranian ways for three years and a day. Then he could choose to live outside Iran temporarily with Sharazad if he needed to: 'Because by then,' her father, Jared Bakravan, had said kindly, 'with the help of the One God and the Prophet of God, may His words live for ever, by then you will have enough knowledge to make the correct choice, for surely by then you will have sons and daughters, for though my daughter is thin, divorced, and still childless, I do not think she is barren.'

'But she's still so young, we may decide it is too soon to have children.'

'It is never too soon,' Bakravan had said sharply. 'The Holy Books are quite clear. A woman needs children. A home needs children. Without children a woman will get into idle ways. That's the most of my beloved Sharazad's problem, no children. Some modern ways I approve of. Some I do not.'

'But if we agree, she and I, that it is too soo –'

'Such a decision would not be her business!' Jared Bakravan had been shocked. He was a small, paunchy man with white hair and beard and hard eyes. 'It would be monstrous, an insult, even to discuss it with her. You must think like an Iranian or this possible marriage will never last. Or even begin. Never. Ah, is it that you don't want children?'

'Oh, no, of course I want children, but per –'

'Good, then it's settled thus.'

'Then can it be settled thus: for three years and a day may I decide if it is too soon?'

'Such an idea is foolish. If you don't want chil –'

'Oh, but of course I do, Excellency.'

At length the old man had said, reluctantly, 'One year and a day only – but only if you swear by the One God that you truly want children, that this astonishing request is completely temporary! Your head is truly filled with nonsense, my son. With the help of God, such nonsense will vanish like the snow on desert sand. Of course women need children . . .'

Absently Lochart smiled to himself. That wonderful old man would bargain with God in the Garden of Paradise. And why not? Isn't that the national pastime of Iranians? But what do I say to him in a few days now – the year and a day almost over? Do I want the burden of children? No, not yet. But Sharazad does. Oh, she went along with my decision, and she's never mentioned it but I don't think she ever approved it.

He could hear the muted sounds of her voice and the maid's voice from the kitchen and the quiet it enhanced was, as always, wonderful – such a contrast to the cockpit that was his other life. His cushions were very comfortable and he watched the fire. There was some gunfire in the night but by now it was so commonplace that they hardly heard it.

I've got to get her out of Tehran, he thought. But how? She'll never leave while her family're here. Maybe she's safer here than anywhere, but not if she joints the riots. Doshan Tappeh! She's crazy, but then they all are at the moment. I wish to God I knew if the army's really been ordered to crush the revolt. Bakhtiar has to move soon or he's finished. But if he does there'll be a blood bath because Iranians are a violent people, death seekers – providing it's in the service of Islam.

Ah, Islam! And God. Where's the One God now?

In all the hearts and heads of Believers. Shi'ites are Believers. So's Sharazad. And all her family. And you? No, not yet but I'm working on

193

it. I promised him I'd work on it, promised I'd read the Koran and keep an open mind. And?

Now's not the time to think of that. Be practical, think practically. She's in danger. Chador or not she's not going to get involved, but then, why shouldn't she? It's her country.

Yes, but she's my wife and I'll order her to stay out of it. What about her father's place on the Caspian Sea near Bandar-e Pahlavi? Maybe they'd take her there or send her there – the weather's good now, not as rotten cold as it is here, though our home's warm, the oil tank always full, wood for the fire, food in the icebox, thanks to her old man and the family.

My God, I owe him so much, so very much.

A slight noise distracted him. Sharazad was standing in the doorway wearing the chador and a light veil that he had never seen before. Her eyes were never more alluring. The chador was sibilant as she moved closer. Then she let it fall open. She wore nothing underneath. The sight of her made him gasp.

'So.' Her voice as always soft and throbbing, the Farsi sweet-sounding. 'So, Excellency, my husband, so now my chador pleases you?'

He reached out for her but she darted back a step, laughing. 'In the summer the public women of the night wear their chadors thus, so it is said.'

'Sharazad . . .'

'No.'

This time he caught her easily. The taste of her, the sheen of her, her softness. 'Perhaps, Master,' she said between kisses, gently taunting him, 'perhaps your slave will always wear her chador thus, in the streets, in the bazaar, many women do, so they say.'

'No. The thought would drive me mad.' He began to pick her up but she whispered, 'No, Beloved, let us stay here,' and he replied, 'But the servants . . .' and again she whispered. 'Forget them, they'll not disturb us, forget them, forget everything, I beg you, Beloved, and only remember that this is your house, this is your hearth, and I am your eternal slave.'

They stayed. As always her passion equalled his though he could not understand how or why, only that with her he went to Paradise, truly, stayed in the Gardens of Paradise with this nymph of Paradise and then returned with her safe to earth again.

Later, during dinner, the front doorbell disturbed their peace. Her servant Hassan answered it, then came back into the room, closing the door. 'Master, it's Excellency General Valik,' he said softly. 'He

194

apologises that he arrives so late but it's important and asks if Your Excellency would grant him a few minutes.'

Lochart's irritation soared but Sharazad reached over and touched him gently and it went away. 'See him, Beloved. I will wait for you in bed. Hassan, bring a fresh plate and heat up the horisht, His Excellency's bound to be hungry.'

Valik apologised profusely for arriving so late, refused food twice but of course allowed himself to be persuaded and ate ravenously. Lochart waited patiently, fulfilling his promise to her father to remember Iranian ways – that family came first, that it was good manners to skirt an issue, never to be blunt, never to be direct. In Farsi it was much easier than in English.

As soon as he could, he switched to English. 'I'm very pleased to see you, General. What can I do for you?'

'I only heard half an hour ago that you were back in Tehran. This horisht is easily the best I've had in years. I'm so sorry to disturb you so late.'

'No trouble.' Lochart left the silence to prosper. The older man ate without embarrassment that he ate alone. A piece of lamb attached itself to his moustache and Lochart watched it, fascinated, wondering how long it would remain there, then Valik wiped his mouth. 'My compliments to Sharazad – her cook is well trained. I will tell my favourite cousin, Excellency Jared.'

'Thank you.' Lochart waited.

Again the silence hung between them. Valik sipped some tea. 'Did the clearance for the 212 come through?'

'Not by the time we'd left.' Lochart was unprepared for the question. 'I know Mac sent a messenger to wait for it. I'd phone him but unfortunately our phone's out. Why?'

'The partners would like you to fly the charter.'

'Captain McIver's assigned Captain Lane, presuming there's a clearance.'

'It will be granted.' Valik wiped his mouth again and helped himself to more tea. 'The partners would like you to fly the charter. I'm sure McIver will agree.'

'Sorry, but I've got to get back to Zagros, I want to make sure everything's okay.' He told him briefly what had happened there.

'I'm sure Zagros can wait a few days. I'm sure Jared would be pleased that you thought it important to do what the partners ask.'

Lochart frowned. 'I'm happy to do anything. What's so important to the partners about this charter, a few spares, a few rials?'

'All charters are important. The partners are very concerned to give the best service. So that's all right, then?'

'I'd . . . first I'd have to take it up with Mac, second, I doubt if the 212'll be cleared, third, I really should get back to my base.'

Valik smiled his nicest smile. 'I'm sure Mac will give his approval. You'll have clearance to leave Tehran airspace.' He got up. 'I'm going to see Mac now and I'll tell him you're agreeable. Thank Sharazad – again a thousand apologies for calling so late but these are troubled times.'

Lochart did not move from the table. 'I still want to know what's so important about a few spares and a hundred thousand rials.'

'The partners have decided it is, and so my dear young friend, hearing you were here and knowing your close relationship with my family, I presumed at once that you would be happy to do this if I asked you personally. We're the same family. Aren't we?' It was said flat now, though the smile remained.

Lochart's eyes narrowed. 'I'm glad to do anything to help b –'

'Good, then it's settled. Thank you. I'll see myself out.' From the doorway Valik turned and pointedly looked around at the apartment. 'You are a very lucky man, Captain. I envy you.'

When Valik had gone, Lochart sat by the dying fire, staring at the flames. Hassan and a maid cleared away the dishes, said good night but he did not hear them – nor Sharazad who came back later, peered at him, then went quietly back to bed, dutifully leaving him to his reverie.

Lochart was sick at heart. He knew that Valik was aware that everything of value in the apartment, along with the apartment itself, had been a wedding gift from Sharazad's father. Jared Bakravan had even given him *de facto* ownership of the whole building – at least the rents thereof. Few knew of their argument: 'As much as I appreciate your generosity I can't accept all this, sir,' Lochart had said. 'It's impossible.'

'But these are material things, unimportant things.'

'Yes, but this is too much. I know my pay's not great, but we can manage. Truly.'

'Yes, of course. But why shouldn't my daughter's husband live pleasantly? How else can you be at peace to learn Iranian ways and fulfil your promise? I assure you, my son, these represent little value to me. Now you are part of my family. Family is most important in Iran. Family looks after family.'

'Yes, but *I* must look after her – I must, not you.'

'Of course, and with the Help of God you will, in time, provide for

196

her in the way she is used to. But now this is not possible for you with the support for your ex-wife and child which you must provide. Now it is my wish to arrange matters in a civilised way, our Iranian way. You have promised to live as we live, no?'

'Yes. But please, I cannot accept all this. Give her what you like, not me. I must be allowed to do the best I can.'

'I'm sure you will. Meanwhile, this is all my gift to you, not to her. This makes my gift of her to you possible.'

'Give it to her not t –'

Jared Bakravan had said sharply, 'It is the Will of God that man is the master of the house. If it is not *your* house then you will *not* be the master. I must insist. I am head of the family and Sharazad will do what I say and for Sharazad I must insist, or the wedding cannot take place. I realise your Western dilemma though I don't understand it, my son. But here Iranian ways dominate all else, and family looks after family . . .'

In the vast loneliness of the sitting room Lochart nodded to himself. That's right and I chose Sharazad, chose to accept but . . . but that sonofabitch Valik threw it all in my face and made me feel dirty again and I hate him for it, hate not paying for everything, and know the only gift I can give her is freedom she would never otherwise have and my life if need be. At least she's Canadian now and doesn't have to stay.

Don't fool yourself, she's Iranian and always will be. Would she be at home in Vancouver, B.C., with all that rain, no family, no friends, and nothing Iranian? Yes, yes, I think so; for a time I'd make up for all the other. For a while, of course not for ever.

It was the first time he had confronted the real problem looming between them. Our Iran's gone for ever, the old one, the Shah one. Never mind that perhaps the new will be better. She'll adapt and so will I. I speak Farsi and she's my wife and Jared's powerful. If we have to leave temporarily, I'll make up for the temporary parting, no problem there. The future's still rosy and good and I love her so very much and bless God for her . . .

The fire was almost finished now and he smelled the comforting, burntwood fragrance and, with it, a thread of her perfume. The cushions still held the indentations where they had lain and though he was totally satisfied and spent, he ached for her. She's really one of the houris, the spirits of Paradise, he thought sleepily. I'm in her spell and that's wonderful, I've no complaints and if I died tonight I know what Paradise is like. She's wonderful, Jared's wonderful, in due course her children will be wonderful and her family . . .

Ah, family! Family looks after family, that's the law, I have to do what Valik asked, like it or not. Have to, her father made that clear.

The last of the embers spluttered and, in dying, momentarily blazed up. 'What's so important about a few spares and a few rials?' he asked the flames.

The flames did not answer him.

Monday
February 12, 1979

TABRIZ

IRAN

USSR
Caspian Sea
USSR
Khvoy
Mount Sabalan
Bandar-e Pahlavi
Sadzevar
Meshed
Qazvin
Tehran
AFGHANISTAN
Baghdad
Isfahan
Dez Dam
IRAQ
Abadan
Bandar-e Delam
Kowiss
PAKISTAN
KUWAIT
Kharg Island
Zagros
Jellet
Lengeh
SAUDI ARABIA
Persian Gulf
Strait of Hormuz
CHAPTER
BAHRAIN
Siri
14
QATAR
UAE
Al Shargaz
Gulf of Oman

At Tabriz One: 7:12 A.M. Charlie Pettikin was fitfully asleep, curled up
on a mattress on the floor under a single blanket, his hands tied in front
of him. It was just dawn and very cold. The guards had not allowed him
a portable gas fire and he was locked into the section of Erikki
Yokkonen's cabin that would normally be a storeroom. Ice glistened
on the inside of the panes of glass in the small window. The window was
barred on the outside. Snow covered the sill.

His eyes opened and he jerked upright, startled, not knowing where
he was for the moment. Then his memory flooded back and he hunched
against the wall, his whole body aching. 'What a damned mess!' he
muttered, trying to ease his shoulders. With both hands he awkwardly
wiped the sleep out of his eyes, and rubbed his face, feeling filthy. The
stubble of his beard was flecked with grey. Hate being unshaved, he
thought.

Today's Monday. I got here Saturday at sunset and they caught me
yesterday. Bastards!

On Saturday evening there had been many noises around the cabin

201

trailer that had added to his disquiet. Once he was sure he heard muffled voices. Quietly he doused the lights, slid the bolt back, and stood on the stoop, the Verey pistol in his hand. With great care he had searched the darkness. Then he saw, or thought he saw, a movement thirty yards away, then another farther off.

'Who are you?' he called out, his voice echoing strangely. 'What do you want?'

No one answered him. Another movement. Where? Thirty, forty yards away – difficult to judge distances at night. Look, there's another! Was it a man? Or just an animal or the shadow of a branch. Or perhaps – what was that? Over there by the big pine. 'You! Over there! What do you want?'

No answer. He could not make out if it was a man or not. Enraged and even a little frightened he aimed and pulled the trigger. The bang seemed like a clap of thunder and echoed off the mountains and the red flare ripped towards the tree, ricocheted off it in a shower of sparks, sprayed into another to bury itself spluttering and spitting in a snowdrift. He waited.

Nothing happened. Noises in the forest, the roof of the hangar creaking, wind in the treetops, sometimes snow falling from an over-laden tree branch that sprang back, free once more. Making a big show he angrily stamped his feet against the cold, switched on the light, loaded the pistol again, and rebolted the door. 'You're getting to be an old woman in your old age,' he said aloud, then added, 'Bullshit! I hate the quiet, hate being alone, hate snow, hate the cold, hate being scared and this morning at Galeg Morghi shook me, God curse it and that's a fact – but for young Ross I know that SAVAK bastard would've killed me!'

He checked that the door was barred and all the windows, closed the curtains against the night, then poured a large vodka and mixed it with some frozen orange juice that was in the freezer and sat in front of the fire and collected himself. There were eggs for breakfast and he was armed. The gas fire worked well. It was cosy. After a while he felt better, safer. Before he went to bed in the spare bedroom, he rechecked the locks. When he was satisfied he took off his flying boots and lay on the bed. Soon he was asleep.

In the morning the night fear had disappeared. After a breakfast of fried eggs on fried bread, just as he liked it, he tidied the room, put on his padded flying gear, unbolted the door and a submachine gun was shoved in his face, six of the revolutionaries crowded into the room and the questioning began. Hours of it.

'I'm not a spy, not American. I keep telling you I'm British,' over and over.

'Liar, your papers say you're South African. By Allah, are they false too?' The leader – the man who called himself Fedor Rakoczy – was tough-looking, taller, and older than the others, with hard brown eyes, his English accented. The same questions over and over: 'Where do you come from, why are you here, who is your CIA superior, who is your contact here, where is Erikki Yokkonen?'

'I don't know. I've told you fifty times I don't know – there was no one here when I landed at sunset last night. I was sent to pick him up, him and his wife. They had business in Tehran.'

'Liar! They ran away in the night, two nights ago. Why should they run away if you were coming to pick them up?'

'I've told you. I was not expected. Why should they run away? Where're Dibble and Arberry, our mechanics? Where's our manager Dayati and wh –'

'Who is your CIA contact in Tabriz?'

'I haven't one. We're a British company and I demand to see our consul in Tabriz. I dem –'

'Enemies of the people cannot demand anything! Even mercy. It is the Will of God that we are at war. In war people get shot!'

The questioning had gone on all morning. In spite of his protests they had taken all his papers, his passport with the vital exit and residence permits, and had bound and thrown him in here with dire threats if he attempted to run away.

Later, Rakoczy and two guards had returned. 'Why didn't you tell me you brought the spares for the 212?'

'You didn't ask me,' Pettikin had said angrily. 'Who the hell are you? Give me back my papers. I demand to see the British consul. Undo my hands, God dammit!'

'God will strike you if you blaspheme! Down on your knees and beg God's forgiveness.' They forced him to kneel. 'Beg forgiveness!'

He obeyed, hating them.

'You fly a 212 as well as a 206?'

'No,' he said, awkwardly getting to his feet.

'Liar! It's on your licence.' Rakoczy had thrown it on the table. 'Why do you lie?'

'What's the difference? You believe nothing I say. You won't believe the truth. Of course I know it's on my licence. Didn't I see you take it? Of course I fly a 212 if I'm rated.'

'The komiteh will judge you and sentence you,' Rakoczy had said with a finality that sent a shock wave up his spine. Then they had left him.

At sunset they had brought him some rice and soup and gone away again. He had slept hardly at all and now, in the dawn, he knew how helpless he was. His fear began to rise up. Once in Vietnam he had been shot down and caught and sentenced to death by Viet Cong but his squadron had come back for him with gunships and Green Berets and they had shot up the village and the Viet Cong with it. That was another time that he had escaped a certainty. 'Never bet on death until you're dead. Thataway, old buddy,' his young American commander had said, 'thataway you sleep nights.' The commander had been Conroe Starke. Their helicopter squadron had been mixed, American and British and some Canadian, based at Da-nang. What another bloody mess that was!

Wonder how Duke's doing now? he thought. Lucky bastard. Lucky to be safe at Kowiss and lucky to have Manuela. Now there's one smasher and built like a koala bear – cuddly, with those big brown eyes of hers, and just the right amount of curves.

He let his mind wander, wondering about her and Starke, about where were Erikki and Azadeh, about that Vietnam village – and about the young Captain Ross and his men. But for him! Ross was another saviour. In this life you have to have saviours to survive, those curious people who miraculously come into your life for no apparent reason just in time to give you the chance you desperately need, or to extract you from disaster or danger or evil. Do they appear because you prayed for help? At the very edge you always pray, somehow, even if it's not to God. But God has many names.

He remembered old Soames at the embassy with his, 'Don't forget, Charlie, Mohammed the Prophet proclaimed that Allah – God – has three thousand names. A thousand are known only to the angels, a thousand only to the prophets, three hundred are in the Torah, the old Testament, another three hundred in the Zabur, that's the Psalms of David, another three hundred in the New Testament, and ninety-nine in the Koran. That makes two thousand nine hundred and ninety-nine. One name has been hidden by God. In Arabic it's called: Ism Allah ala'zam: the Greatest Name of God. Everyone who reads the Koran will have read it without knowing it. God is wise to hide His Greatest Name, eh?'

Yes, if there is a God, Pettikin thought, cold and aching.

Just before noon Rakoczy returned with his two men. Astonishingly, Rakoczy smiled, politely helped him to his feet and began undoing his bonds. 'Good morning, Captain Pettikin. So sorry for the mistake. Please follow me.' He led the way into the main room. Coffee was on the table. 'Do you drink coffee black or English style with milk and sugar?'

Pettikin was rubbing his chafed wrists, trying to get his mind working. 'What's this? The prisoner was offered a hearty breakfast?'

'Sorry, I don't understand.'

'Nothing.' Pettikin stared at him, still not sure. 'With milk and sugar.' The coffee tasted wonderful and revived him. He helped himself to more. 'So it's a mistake, all a mistake?'

'Yes. I, er, checked your story and it was correct, God be praised. You will leave immediately. To return to Tehran.'

Pettikin's throat felt tight at his sudden reprieve – apparent reprieve, he thought suspiciously. 'I need fuel. All our fuel's been stolen, there's no fuel in our dump.'

'Your aircraft has been refuelled. I supervised it myself.'

'You know about choppers?' Pettikin was wondering why the man appeared so nervous.

'A little.'

'Sorry, but I, er, I don't know your name.'

'Smith. Mr. Smith.' Fedor Rakoczy smiled 'You will leave now, please. At once.'

Pettikin found his flying boots and pulled them on. The other men watched him silently. He noted they were carrying Soviet machine pistols. On the table by the door was his overnight bag. Beside it were his documents. Passport, visa, work permit, and Iranian CAA-issued flying licence. Trying to keep the astonishment off his face, he made sure they were all there and stuck them in his pocket. When he went for the refrigerator, one of the men stood in his way and motioned him away. 'I'm hungry,' Pettikin said, still very suspicious.

'There's something to eat in your plane. Follow me, please.'

Outside, the air smelled very good to him, the day crisp and fine with a clean, very blue sky. To the west more snow clouds were building. Eastward, the way over the pass was clear. All around him the forest sparkled, the light refracted by the snow. In front of the hangar was the 206, windshield cleaned, all windows cleaned. Nothing had been touched inside though his map case was now in a side pocket, not beside his seat where he normally left it. Very carefully he began a preflight check.

'Please to hurry,' Rakoczy said.

'Of course.' Pettikin made a great show of hurrying but he didn't, missing nothing in his inspection, all his senses tuned to find a subtle sabotage, or even a crude one. Gas checked out, oil, everything. He could see and feel their growing nervousness. There was still no one else on the base. In the hangar he could see the 212 with its engine parts still neatly spread out. The spares that he had brought had been put on a bench nearby.

'Now you are ready.' Rakoczy said it as an order. 'Get in, you will refuel at Bandar-e Pahlavi as before.' He turned to the others, embraced both of them hastily and got into the right seat. 'Start up and leave at once. I am coming to Tehran with you.' He gripped his machine gun with his knees, buckled himself in, locked the door neatly, then lifted the headset from its hook behind him and put it on, clearly accustomed to the inside of a cockpit.

Pettikin noticed that the other two had taken up defensive positions facing the road. He pressed the Engine Start. Soon the whine and the familiarity – and the fact that 'Smith' was aboard and therefore sabotage unlikely – made him light-headed. 'Here we go,' he said into the boom mike and took off in a scudding rush, banked sweetly and climbed for the pass.

'Good,' Rakoczy said, 'very good. You fly very well.' Casually he put the gun across his knees, muzzle pointing at Pettikin. 'Please don't fly too well.'

'Put the safety catch on – or I won't fly at all.'

Rakoczy hesitated. He clicked it in place. 'I agreed it is dangerous while flying.'

At six hundred feet Pettikin levelled off, then abruptly went into a steep bank and came back towards the field.

'What're you doing?'

'Just want to get my bearings.' He was relying on the fact that though Smith clearly knew his way around a cockpit, he couldn't fly a 206 or he would have taken her. His eyes were searching below for a clue to the man's nervousness and his haste to leave. The field seemed the same. Near the junction of the narrow base road with the main road that went northwest to Tabriz were two trucks. Both headed for the base. From this height he could easily see they were army trucks.

'I'm going to land to see what they want,' he said.

'If you do,' Rakoczy said without fear, 'it will cost you much pain and permanent mutilation. Please go to Tehran – but first to Bandar-e Pahlavi.'

'What's your real name?'

206

'Smith.'

Pettikin left it at that, circled once, then followed the Tehran road southeast, heading for the pass and biding his time – confident now that somewhere en route his time would come.

At Tehran: 8:30 A.M. Tom Lochart eased his old Citroen through the debris of the night's battles, heading for Galeg Morghi. The morning was sour and freezing and he was already late though he had started out just after dawn.

He had passed many bodies and wailing mourners, many burned-out wrecks of cars and trucks, some still smouldering – flotsam from the night's riots. Knots of armed or semi-armed civilians still manned balconies or barricades and he had had to make a dozen diversions. Many men wore the Khomeini green armband now. All Green Bands were armed. The streets were ominously empty of traffic. From time to time police trucks screamed past, a few cars and trucks, but they paid no attention to him except to sound their horns, cursing him out of the way. He cursed them back, almost not caring if he ever reached the airport that would be a perfect solution to his dilemma.

He swerved to avoid a car that charged out of a side street on the wrong side of the road. The car did not stop and he cursed it, and

Tehran and Iran and Valik and said, 'Insha'Allah,' out loud but it did not help him.

Overhead was a dirty, snow-filled overcast that he did not like at all, and he had hated to leave the warmth of his bed and Sharazad. Just before dawn the alarm had startled them awake.

'I thought you weren't going, my darling. I thought you said you were leaving tomorrow.'

'I've got a sudden charter, at least I think I have. That's what Valik came about. I've got to see Mac first, but if I go I'll be away for a few days. Go back to sleep, my darling.' He had shaved, dressed hurriedly, had a quick cup of coffee, and left. Outside it was still dark with just a sullen wisp of dawn, the air acrid and smoke-heavy. In the distance was the inevitable, sporadic gunfire. Suddenly he was filled with foreboding.

McIver lived only a few blocks away. Lochart had been surprised to find him fully dressed. 'Hello, Tom. Come on in. The clearance came through at midnight, delivered by hand. Valik's got power – I never believed we'd get it. Coffee?'

'Thanks. Did he see you last night?'

'Yes.' McIver led the way into the kitchen. Coffee was perking nicely. No sign of Genny, Paula or Nogger Lane. He poured for Lochart. 'Valik told me he'd seen you and that you'd agreed to go.'

Lochart grunted. 'I said I'd go after you approved it and after I'd seen you – if we got the clearance. Where's Nogger?'

'Back in his flat. I cancelled him last night. He's still pretty shook from being involved in that riot.'

'I can imagine. What happened to the girl? Paula?'

'She's in the spare room, her Alitalia flight's still grounded but she'll probably be off today. George Talbot of the embassy dropped by last night and said he heard the airport's been cleared of revolutionaries and today, with any luck, there'll be a few flights in and out.'

Lochart nodded thoughtfully. 'Then maybe Bakhtiar will win after all.'

'Let's hope, eh? The BBC this morning said Doshan Tappeh's still in Khomeini hands and the Immortals are just ringing it, sitting on their tails.'

Lochart shuddered at the thought of Sharazad there. She had promised not to go again. 'Did Talbot say anything about a coup?'

'Only that the rumour is that Carter's opposed to it – if I was Iranian, and a general, I wouldn't hesitate. Talbot agreed, said the coup'll happen in the next three days, it'll have to, the revs are getting too many guns.'

209

Lochart could almost see Sharazad chanting with the thousands, young Captain Karim Peshadi declaring for Khomeini and three Immortals deserting. 'Don't know what I'd do, Mac, if I was one of them.'

'Thank God we're not and this's Iran, not England, with us at the barricades. Anyway, Tom, if the 125 comes in today I'll put Sharazad on her. She'll be better off in Al Shargaz, at least for a couple of weeks. Did she get her Canadian passport?'

'Yes, but, Mac, but I don't think she'll go.' Lochart told him about her joining the insurrection at Doshan Tappeh.

'My God, she needs her head examined. I'll get Gen to see her.'

'Is Genny going to Al Shargaz?'

McIver said testily, 'No. If it was up to me she'd've been there a week already. I'll do what I can. Sharazad's all right?'

'Wonderful, but I wish to God Tehran'd settled down. I get worried sick about her here and me in Zagros.' Lochart gulped some coffee. 'If I'm going I'd better get with it. Keep an eye on her, will you?' He looked at McIver, hard and straight. 'What's this charter about, Mac?'

Stonily McIver looked back at him. 'Tell me exactly what Valik said to you last night.'

Lochart told him. Exactly.

'He's a right bastard, to try to make you lose face like that.'

'He succeeded very well. Unfortunately he's still family and in Iran – well, you know.' Lochart kept the bitterness out of his voice. 'I asked him what's so important about a few spares and a few rials and he sloughed me off.' He saw that McIver's face was set and seemed older and heavier than he had ever known, yet tougher. 'Mac, what *is* so important about a few spares and a few rials?'

McIver finished his coffee and poured some more. He dropped his voice, 'Don't want to wake Genny or Paula, Tom. This's between us.' He told Lochart what had happened in the office. Exactly.

Lochart felt the sudden rush of blood to his face. 'SAVAK? Him and Annoush and little Setarem and Jalal? Jesus wept!'

'That's why I agreed to try. Have to. I'm equally trapped. We're both trapped. But there's more.' McIver told him about the money.

Lochart gasped. 'Twelve million rials, cash? Or the equivalent in Switzerland?'

'Keep your voice down. Yes, twelve for me, and another twelve for the pilot. Last night he said his offer still stands and not to be "naive". ' McIver added grimly, 'If Gen hadn't been here, I'd've thrown him out.'

Lochart was hardly listening. Twelve million rials or cash elsewhere?

Mac's right. If Valik offered that here in Tehran what would he really pay when he's in sight of the border? 'Christ!'

McIver watched him. 'What do you think, Tom? Do you still want to go?'

'I can't refuse. I can't. Not now we've got the clearance.' It was on the kitchen table and he picked it up. It read: 'EP-HBC cleared to Bandar-e Delam. Priority flight for urgent spares. Refuel at IIAF Base Isfahan. One crew: Captain Lane.' Lane had been crossed out, and marked, 'Sick. Substitute pilot,' then a blank and it was not yet countersigned by McIver.

McIver glanced at the kitchen door that was closed, then back to Lochart. 'Valik wants to be picked up outside of Tehran, privately.'

'This gets smellier and smellier. Where's the pickup point?'

'If you get to Bandar-e Delam, Tom, and that's not even probable, he'll pressure you to take them on to Kuwait.'

'Of course.' Lochart stared back at McIver.

'He'll use any pressure, family, Sharazad, the lot. Particularly money.'

'Millions. In cash – which we both know I can use.' Lochart's voice was level. 'But if I fly on to Kuwait without Iranian clearance, in an Iranian registered chopper, without Iranian or company approval, with unauthorised Iranian passengers trying to escape their still legal government, I'm a hijacker, subject to God knows how many criminal charges here and in Kuwait – the Kuwait authorities'd impound the chopper, shove me in jail, and certainly extradite me to Iran. In any event I'd've blown my future as a pilot and could never come back to Iran and Sharazad – SAVAK might even grab her so I'm not about to do that.'

'Valik's a dangerous sod. He'll come armed. He could put a gun to your head and force you to fl –'

'That's possible.' Lochart's voice stayed calm, but his insides were churning. 'I have no option. I've got to help him, and I will – but I'm not goddam stupid.' After a pause, he added, 'Does Nogger know about this?'

'No.' In the watches of the night, after weighing possible plans, McIver had decided to go himself and not risk Nogger Lane or Lochart. The hell with the medical and that I'd be illegal, he had told himself – the whole flight's mad so a little extra madness won't hurt.

His plan was simple: after talking it out with Tom Lochart he would just say he had decided not to authorise the flight and would not countersign the clearance, that he would drive to the pickup point with

211

enough petrol for Valik to make the journey by road. Even if Lochart wanted to come with him, it would be easy to fix a rendezvous, then never go to it but just drive to Galeg Morghi, put his own name on the clearance as pilot and take off. At the pickup point . . .

'What?' he asked.

'There are only three possibilities,' Lockhart said again. 'You refuse to authorise me or you authorise someone else. You've cancelled Nogger, Charlie's not here, so that leaves you or me. You can't go, Mac. You just can't, it's too dangerous.'

'Of course I wouldn't go, my licence h –'

'You can't go, Mac,' Lochart said firmly. 'Sorry. You just can't.'

McIver sighed, his wisdom overcame his obession to fly and he decided on his second plan. 'Yes. Yes, you're right. I agree. So listen carefully: if you want to do it, that's up to you, I'm not ordering it. I will authorise you if you want but there are conditions. If you get to the pickup point and it seems clean, pick them up. Then go on to Isfahan. Valik said he'd fix that. If Isfahan's okay, go on. Maybe Mr. Fixit Iran can do just that, all the way. That's what we'd have to gamble on.'

'That's what I'm gambling on.'

'Bandar-e Delam's the end of the line. You don't go over the border. Agreed?' McIver put out his hand.

'Agreed,' Lochart said, shaking hands with a prayer that he could keep his promise.

McIver told him the pickup point, signed the clearance, and noticed his hands were trembling. If anything goes wrong, guess who SA-VAK'll come after? Both of us. And even maybe Gen, McIver thought, again filled with dread. He did not tell Lochart that she had overheard Valik last night and figured out the rest. 'But I agree, Duncan,' she had said gravely. 'It's terribly risky but you've got to try to help them, Tom too, he's equally trapped. There isn't any option.'

McIver handed Lochart the clearance. 'Tom, you're specifically ordered not to go over the border. If you do, I think you really will lose everything, including Sharazad.'

'This whole scheme's crackpot, but, there you are.'

'Yes. Good luck.'

Lochart nodded, smiled back at him, and left.

McIver closed the front door. I hope that's the right decision, he thought, his head aching. Madness to go myself, and yet . . . I wish I was going and not him. I wish . . .

'Oh,' he said, startled. Genny was standing by the kitchen door, a

212

warm robe over her nightdress. She was not wearing her glasses and she peered at him.

'I'm . . . I'm awfully glad you didn't go, Duncan,' she said in a tiny voice.

'What?'

'Oh, come on, silly, I know you too well. You hardly slept a wink trying to decide – nor did I, worrying about it for you. I know if I'd been you I'd've gone, or wanted to go. But, Duncan, Tom's strong and he'll be all right and I do so hope he takes Sharazad and never comes back . . .' The tears began running down her cheeks. 'I'm ever so glad you didn't go.' She brushed the tears away and went to the stove and put on the kettle. 'Damn, sorry, I really do get into a tizzy sometimes. Sorry.'

He put his arms around her. 'Gen, if the 125 comes today, will you get on it? Please.'

'Certainly, dear. If you get on it too.'

'But Gen. Y –'

'Duncan, listen a moment, please.' She turned and put her arms around him and rested her head against his chest and continued in the same small voice that troubled him greatly, 'Three of your partners have already fled with their families and all the money they can, the Shah and his family've gone with all their money, thousands of others, most of the people we know've gone, you said so yourself and now if even the great General Valik's running away, even with all his contacts and they've got to be on both sides of the fence, and . . . and if even the Immortals haven't squashed the little rebellion at Doshan Tappeh of a few air force cadets and badly armed civilians – practically on their home ground – it's time we should close down and leave.'

'We can't, Gen,' he burst out, and she could hear his heart grinding in his chest and her concern for him increased. 'That'd be a disaster.'

'It'd only be for a short time, until things get better.'

'If I scuttled Iran it'd ruin S-G.'

'I don't know about that, Duncan, but surely the decision's up to Andy, not you – he sent us here.'

'Yes, but he'd ask me what I thought and I couldn't recommend quitting and leaving twenty to thirty-odd million dollars' worth of choppers and spares behind – in this mess they wouldn't last a week, they'd be looted or damaged, we'd lose everything, everything – don't forget, Gen, all our retirement money's tied up in S-G, everything.'

'But, Duncan, don't you think th –'

'I won't leave our choppers and spares.' McIver felt flushed and in momentary panic at the thought. 'I just can't.'

213

'Then take them with you.'

'For God's sake, we can't get 'em out, we can't get the clearances, can't get off Iranian registry – we can't – we're stuck here until the war's over.'

'We're not. Duncan, not you or me or our lads, you've got to think of them too. We have to get out. They'll throw us out anyway, whoever wins, most of all Khomeini.' A tremor went through her as she thought of his first speech at the cemetery: 'I pray God to cut off the hands of all foreigners . . .'

At Tabriz One: 9:30 A.M. The red Range Rover came out of the gates of the Khan's palace and headed down the rise towards Tabriz and the road for Tehran. Erikki was driving, Azadeh beside him. It had been her cousin, Colonel Mazardi, the chief of police, who had persuaded Erikki not to drive to Tehran on Friday: 'The road would be highly dangerous – it's bad enough during the day,' he said. 'The insurgents won't return now, you're quite safe. Much better to go and see His Highness the Khan and ask his advice. That would be much wiser.'

Azadeh had agreed. 'Erikki, of course we will do whatever you want but I would really feel happier if we went home for the night and saw Father.'

'My cousin's right, Captain; of course you may do as you wish, but I swear by the Prophet, God keep His words safe for ever, that her Highness's safety is just as important to me as to you. If you still feel so inclined, leave tomorrow. I can assure you there's no danger here. I'll post guards. If this so-called Rakoczy or any other foreigner or this

215

mullah comes within half a mile of here or the Gorgon palace they'll regret it.'

'Oh, yes, Erikki, please,' Azadeh said enthusiastically. 'Of course, my darling, we'll do whatever you like but it might be you would want to consult His Highness, my father, about what you plan to do.'

Reluctantly Erikki had agreed. Arberry and the other mechanic Dibble had decided to go into Tabriz to the International Hotel and spend the weekend there. 'Spares're due Monday, Captain. Old Skinflint McIver knows our 212's got to be working by Wednesday or he'll have to send another one and he won't like that. We'll just sit tight and get the job done and get her airborne. Our apology for a base manager can come and fetch us. We're British, we've nothing to worry about – no one's going to touch us. And don't forget we're working for their guver'ment, whoever's the bleeding guver'ment and we've no quarrel with any of these bleeding wo – these bleeders, begging your pardon. Now don't you worry about us, you and the Missus. We'll just sit tight and expect you back by Wednesday. Have a fun time in Tehran.'

So Erikki had gone in convoy with Colonel Mazardi to the outskirts of Tabriz. The sprawling palace of the Gorgon Khans was set in mountain foothills, in acres of gardens and orchards behind high walls. When they arrived, the whole house awoke and congregated – stepmother, half sisters, nieces, nephews, servants, and children of servants, but not Abdollah Khan, her father. Azadeh was received with open arms and tears and happiness and more tears, and immediate plans were made for a luncheon feast the next day to celebrate their good fortune in having her home at long last – 'But, oh, how terrible! Bandits and a rogue mullah daring to come on your land? Hasn't His Highness, our revered father, donated barrels of rials and hundreds of acres of land to various mosques in and around Tabriz!'

Erikki Yokkonen was welcomed politely, and guardedly. All of them were afraid of him, the enormity of his size, his quickness with a knife, the violence of his temper, and could not understand his gentleness towards his friends and the vast love he radiated for Azadeh. She was the fifth of six half sisters, and an infant half brother. Her mother, dead now many years, had been Abdollah Khan's second, concurrent wife. Her own adored blood brother, Hakim, a year older than she, had been banished by Abdollah Khan and was still in disgrace at Khvoy to the northwest – banished for crimes against the Khan that both Hakim and Azadeh swore he was not guilty of.

'First a bath,' her half sisters said gaily, 'and you can tell us all that happened, every detail, *every detail*.' Happily, they dragged Azadeh away. In the privacy of their bathhouse, warm and intimate and luxurious and completely outside the domain of all men, they chatted and gossiped until the dawn. 'My Mahmud hasn't made love to me for a week,' Najoud, Azadeh's eldest half sister, said with a toss of her head.

'It has to be another woman, darling Najoud,' someone said.

'No, it's not that. His erection is giving him trouble.'

'Oh, you poor darling! Have you tried giving him oysters . . .'

'Or tried using oil of roses on your breasts . . .'

'Or rubbed him with extract of jacaranda, rhino horn, and musk . . .'

'Jacaranda, musk with rhino horn? I haven't heard of that one, Fazulia.'

'It's brand new from an ancient recipe from the time of Cyrus the Great. This is a secret but the Great King's penis was quite small as a young man, but after he conquered the Medes, miraculously it became the envy of the host! It seems that he obtained a magic potion from the Medes that if rubbed on over a period of a month . . . their high priest gave it to Cyrus in return for his life, providing the Great King swore to keep the secret in his family alone. It's come down from father to son over the centuries and now, dear sisters, the secret's in Tabriz!'

'Oh who, dearest darling Sister Fazulia, who? The Blessings of God be upon thee for ever, who? My rotten husband Abdullah, may his three remaining teeth fall out, he hasn't had an erection for years. Who?'

'Oh be quiet, Zadi, how can she talk if you talk! Go on, Fazulia.'

'Yes, be quiet, Zadi, and bless your good fortune – my Hussan is erect morning, noon and night and so filled with desire for me he gives me no time to even wash my teeth!'

'Well, the secret of the elixir was bought by the great-great-grandfather of the present owner at a huge cost, I was told for a fistful of diamonds . . .'

'Eeeeeeeeee . . .'

'. . . but now you can buy a small vial for fifty thousand rials!'

'Oh, that's too much! Where on earth can I get so much cash?'

'As always you'll find it in his pockets, and you can always bargain. Is anything too much for such a potion when we can't have other men?'

'If it works . . .'

'Of course it works, oh, where do we buy it, dearest dearest Fazulia?'

'In the bazaar, in the shop of Abu Bakra bin Hassan bin Saiidi. I know the way! We'll go tomorrow. Before lunch. You will come with us, darling Azadeh!'

'No thank you, dear sister.'

Then there was lots of laughter and one of the young ones said, 'Poor Azadeh doesn't need jacaranda and muck – she needs the opposite!'

'Jacaranda and *musk*, child, with rhino horn,' Fazulia said.

Azadeh laughed with them. They had all asked her, overtly or covertly, if her husband was equally proportioned and how did she, so skinny and so fragile, deal with it and bear his weight? 'By magic,' she had told the young ones, 'easily,' the serious ones, and 'with unbelievable ecstasy as it must be in the Garden of Paradise,' the jealous ones and those she hated and secretly wanted to taunt.

Not everyone had approved of her marriage to this foreign giant. Many had tried to influence her father against him and against her. But she had won and she knew who her enemies were: her sex-mad half sister, Zadi, lying Cousin Fazulia with her nonsense exaggerations, and, most of all, the honeyed viper of the pack, eldest sister Najoud and her vile husband Mahmud, may God punish them for their evil ways. 'Dearest Najoud, I'm so happy to be home, but now it's time for sleep.'

And so to bed. All of them. Some happily, some sadly, some angrily, some hating, some loving, some to their husbands and some alone. Husbands could have four wives, according to the Koran, at the same time, provided they treated each with equality in every way – Mohammed the Prophet, alone of all men, had been allowed as many wives as he wished. According to legend, the Prophet had had eleven wives in his lifetime though not all at the same time. Some died, some he divorced, and some outlived him. But all of them honoured him for ever.

Erikki awoke as Azadeh slipped into bed beside him. 'We should leave as early as possible, Azadeh, my darling.'

'Yes,' she said, almost asleep now, the bed so comfortable, him so comfortable. 'Yes, whenever you like, but please not until after lunch because dearest Stepmother will weep buckets . . .'

'Azadeh!'

But she was asleep now. He sighed, also content, and went back to sleep.

They did not leave on Sunday as planned – her father had said it was inconvenient as he wished to talk to Erikki first. At dawn today, Monday, after prayers that her father had led, and after breakfast – coffee and bread and honey and yoghurt and eggs – they had been allowed to leave and now swung off the mountain-side road on to the main Tehran road and there ahead was the roadblock.

'That's weird,' Erikki said. Colonel Mazardi had said he would meet

218

them here but he was nowhere to be seen, nor was the roadblock manned.

'Police!' Azadeh said, with a yawn. 'They're never where you want them.'

The road climbed up to the pass. The sky was blue and clear and the tops of the mountains already washed with sunlight. Down here in the valley, it was still dark and chill and damp, the road slippery, snow banked, but this did not worry him as the Range Rover had four-wheel drive and he carried chains. Later, when he came to the base turnoff he passed it by. He knew the base was empty, the 212 safe and waiting for repairs. Before leaving the palace he had tried unsuccessfully to contact his manager, Dayati. But that did not matter. He settled back in his seat, he had full tanks, and six spare five-gallon cans that he had got from Abdollah's private pump.

I can get to Tehran easily today, he thought. And back by Wednesday – if I come back. That bastard Rakoczy's very bad news indeed.

'Would you like some coffee, darling?' Azadeh asked.

'Thanks. See if you can find the BBC or the VOA on the short-wave.' Gratefully he accepted the hot coffee from the Thermos, listening to the crackle of static and heterodyning and loud Soviet stations and little else. Iranian stations were still strikebound and closed down, except the ones worked by the military.

Over the weekend friends, relations, tradesmen, servants had brought rumours and counter-rumours of everything from imminent Soviet invasion to imminent U.S. invasion, from successful military coups in the capital to abject submission of all the generals to Khomeini and Bakhtiar's resignation.

'Asinine!' Abdollah Khan had said. He was a corpulent man in his sixties, bearded, with dark eyes and full mouth, bejewelled and richly dressed. 'Why should Bakhtiar resign? He gains nothing so there's no reason, yet.'

'And if Khomeini wins?' Erikki had asked.

'It is the Will of God.' The Khan was lounging on carpets in the Great Room, Erikki and Azadeh seated in front of him, his armed bodyguard standing behind him. 'But Khomeini's victory will be only temporary, if he achieves it. The armed forces will curb him and his mullahs, sooner or later. He's an old man. Soon he will die, the sooner the better, for though he has done God's Will and been the instrument to remove the Shah whose time had come, he's vindictive, narrow-sighted, as megalomaniacal as the Shah, if not more so. He will surely murder more Iranians than the Shah ever did.'

'But isn't he a man of God, pious and everything an ayatollah should be?' Erikki asked warily, not knowing what to expect. 'Why should Khomeini do that?'

'It's the habit of tyrants.' The Khan laughed and took another of the halvah, the Turkish sweets he gorged on.

'And the Shah? What will happen now?' As much as Erikki disliked the Khan, he was glad for the opportunity to get his opinion. On him depended much of his and Azadeh's life in Iran and he had no wish to leave.

'As God wants. Mohammed Shah did incredibly well for Iran, like his father before him. But in the last few years he was totally curled up in himself and would listen to no one – not even the Shahbanu, Empress Farah, who was dedicated to him, and wise. If he had any sense he would abdicate at once in favour of his son Reza. The generals need a rallying point, they could train him until he's ready to take power – don't forget Iran's been a monarchy for almost three thousand years, always an absolute ruler, some might say tyrant, with absolute power and removed only by death.' He had smiled, his lips full and sensuous. 'Of the Qajar shahs, our legitimate dynasty who ruled for a hundred and fifty years, only one, the last of the line, my cousin, died of natural causes. We are an Oriental people, not Western, who understand violence and torture. Life and death are not judged by your standards.' His dark eyes had seemed to grow darker. 'Perhaps it is the Will of God that the Qajars will return – under their rule Iran prospered.'

That's not what I heard, Erikki had thought. But he held his peace. It's not up to me to judge what has been or what would be here.

All Sunday the BBC and the VOA had been jammed which was not unusual. Radio Moscow was loud and clear as usual, and Radio Free Iran that broadcast from Tbilisi north of the border also loud and clear as usual. Their reports in Iranian and English told of total insurrection against 'Bakhtiar's illegal government of the ousted Shah and his American masters, headed by the warmonger and liar President Carter. Today Bakhtiar tried to curry favour with the masses by cancelling a total of thirteen billion dollars of usurious military contracts forced on the country by the deposed Shah: eight billion dollars in the USA, British Centurion tank contracts worth two point three billion, plus two French nuclear reactors, and one from Germany worth another two point seven billion. This news has sent Western leaders into panic and will undoubtedly send capitalist stock markets into a well deserved crash . . .'

'Excuse me for asking, Father, but will the West crash?' Azadeh had asked.

'Not this time,' the Khan had said and Erikki saw his face grow colder. 'Not unless the Soviets decide this is the time to renege on the eighty billion dollars they owe Western banks – and even some Oriental banks.' He had laughed sardonically, playing with the string of pearls he wore around his neck. 'Of course Oriental moneylenders are much cleverer; at least they're not so greedy. They lend judiciously and require collaterals and believe no one and certainly not in the myth of "Christian charity". ' It was common knowledge that the Gorgons owned enormous tracts of land in Azerbaijan, good oil land, a large part of Iran Timber, seafront property on the Caspian, much of the bazaar in Tabriz, and most of the merchant banks there.

Erikki remembered the whispers he had heard about Abdollah Khan when he was trying to get permission to marry Azadeh, about his parsimony and ruthlessness in business: 'A quick way to Paradise or hell is to owe Abdollah the Cruel one rial, to not pay, pleading poverty, and to stay in Azerbaijan.'

'Father, please may I ask, cancellation of so many contracts will cause havoc, won't it?'

'No, you may not ask. You've asked enough questions for one day. A woman is supposed to hold her tongue and listen – now you can leave.'

At once she apologised for her error and left obediently. 'Please excuse me.'

Erikki got up to leave too, but the Khan stopped him: 'I have not dismissed you yet. Sit down. Now, why should you fear one Soviet?'

'I don't – just the system. That man has to be KGB.'

'Why didn't you just kill him then?'

'It would not have helped, it would have hurt. Us, the base, Iran Timber, Azadeh, perhaps even you. He was sent to me by others. He knows us – knows you.' Erikki had watched the old man carefully.

'I know lots of them. Russians, Soviet or Tsarist, have always coveted Azerbaijan, but have always been good customers of Azerbaijan – and helped us against the stinking British. I prefer them to British, I understand them.' His smile thinned even more. 'It would be easy to remove this Rakoczy.'

'Good, then do it, please.' Erikki had laughed full-throated. 'And all of them as well. That would really be doing God's work.'

'I don't agree,' the Khan said ill-temperedly. 'That would be doing Satan's work. Without the Soviets against them, the Americans and their dogs the British would dominate us and all the world. They'd certainly eat up Iran – under Mohammed Shah they nearly did. Without Soviet Russia, whatever her failings, there'd be no check on America's foul policies, foul arrogance, foul manners, foul jeans, foul music, foul food and foul democracy, their disgusting attitudes to women, to law and order, their disgusting pornography, naive attitude to diplomacy, and their evil, yes, that's the correct word, their evil antagonism to Islam.'

The last thing Erikki wanted was another confrontation. In spite of his resolve, he felt his own rage gathering. 'We had an agreem –'

'It's true, by God!' the Khan shouted at him. 'It's true!'

'It's not, and we had an agreement before your God and my spirits that we'd not discuss politics – either of your world or mine.'

'It's true, admit it!' Abdollah Khan snarled, his face twisted with rage. One hand went to the ornamental knife at his belt, and at once the guard unslung his machine pistol and covered Erikki. 'By Allah, you call me a liar in my own house?' he bellowed.

Erikki said through his teeth, 'I only remind you, Highness, by your Allah, what we agreed!' The dark bloodshot eyes stared at him. He stared back, ready to go for his own knife and kill or be killed, the danger between them very great.

'Yes, yes, that's also true,' the Khan muttered, and the fit of rage passed as quickly as it had erupted. He looked at the guard, angrily waved him away. 'Get out!'

Now the room was very still. Erikki knew there were other guards nearby and spyholes in the walls. He felt the sweat on his forehead and the touch of his pukoh knife in the centre of his back.

Abdollah Khan knew the knife was there and that Erikki would use it without hesitation. But the Khan had given him perpetual permission to be armed with it in his presence. Two years ago Erikki had saved his life.

That was the day Erikki was petitioning him for permission to marry Azadeh and was imperiously turned down: 'No, by Allah, I want no Infidels in my family. Leave my house! For the last time!' Erikki had got up from the carpet, sick at heart. At that moment there had been a scuffle outside the door, then shots, the door had burst open and two men, assassins armed with machine guns, had rushed in, others fighting a gun battle in the corridor. The Khan's bodyguard had killed one, but the other sprayed him with bullets then turned his gun on Abdollah Khan who sat on the carpet in shock. Before the assassin could pull the trigger a second time, he died, Erikki's knife in his throat. At the same moment Erikki lunged for him, ripped the gun out of his hands and the knife out of his throat as another assassin rushed into the room firing. Erikki had smashed the machine gun into the man's face, killing him, almost tearing off his head with the strength of his blow, then charged into the corridor berserk. Three attackers and two of the bodyguards were dead or dying. The last of the attackers took to their heels but Erikki cut them both down and raced onward. And only when he had found Azadeh and saw that she was safe did the bloodlust go out of his head and he become calm again.

Erikki remembered how he had left her and had gone back to the same Great Room. Abdollah Khan still sat on the carpets. 'Who were those men?'

'Assassins – enemies, like the guards who let them in,' Abdollah Khan had said malevolently. 'It was the Will of God you were here to save my life, the Will of God that I am alive. You may marry Azadeh, yes, but because I do not like you, we will both swear before God and your – whatever you worship – not to discuss religion or politics, either of your world or mine, then perhaps I will not have to have you killed.'

And now the same cold black eyes were staring at him. Abdollah Khan clapped his hands. Instantly the door opened and a servant appeared. 'Bring coffee!' The man hurried away. 'I will drop the subject of your world and go to another we can discuss: my daughter, Azadeh.'

Erikki became even more on guard, not sure of the extent of her father's control over her, or his own rights as her husband while he was in Azerbaijan – very much the old man's fief. If Abdollah Khan really ordered Azadeh back to this house and to divorce him, would she? I think yes, I'm afraid yes – she certainly will never hear a word against him. She even defended his paranoic hatred of America by explaining what had caused it.

'He was ordered there, to university, by his father,' she had told him. 'He had a terrible time in America, Erikki, learning the language and trying to get a degree in economics which his father demanded before he was allowed home. My father hated the other students who sneered at him because he couldn't play their games, because he was heavier than they which in Iran is a sign of wealth but not in America, and was slow at learning. But most of all because of the hazing that he was forced to endure, forced, Erikki – to eat unclean things like pork that are against our religion, to drink beer and wine and spirits that are against our religion, to do unmentionable things and be called unmen-

223

tionable names. I would be angry too if it had been me. Please be patient with him. Don't Soviets make a blood film come over your eyes and heart for what they did to your father and mother and country? Be patient with him, I beg you. Hasn't he agreed to our marriage? Be patient with him.'

I've been very patient, Erikki thought, more patient than with any man, wishing the interview was over. 'What about my wife, Highness?' It was custom to call him that and Erikki did so from time to time out of politeness.

Abdollah Khan smiled a thin smile at him. 'Naturally my daughter's future interests me. What is your plan when you go to Tehran?'

'I have no plan. I just think it is wise to get her out of Tabriz for a few days. Rakoczy said they "require" my services. When the KGB say that in Iran or Finland or even America, you'd better clear the decks and prepare for trouble. If they kidnapped her, I would be putty in their hands.'

'They could kidnap her in Tehran much more easily than here, *if* that is their scheme – you forget this is Azerbaijan' – his lips twisted with contempt – 'not Bakhtiar country.'

Erikki felt helpless under the scrutiny. 'I only know that's what I think is best for her. I said I would guard her with my life, and I will. Until the political future of Iran is settled – by you and other Iranians – I think it's the wise thing to do.'

'In that case, go,' her father had said with a suddenness that had almost frightened him. 'Should you need help send me the code words . . .' He thought a moment. Then his smile became sardonic: 'Send me the sentence: "All men are created equal." That's another truth, isn't it?'

'I don't know, Highness,' he had said carefully. 'If it is or if it isn't, it's surely the Will of God.'

Abdollah had laughed abruptly and got up and left him alone in the Great Room and Erikki had felt a chill on his soul, deeply unsettled by the man whose thoughts he could never read.

'Are you cold, Erikki?' Azadeh asked.

'Oh. No, no, not at all,' he said, coming out of his reverie, the sound of the engine good as they climbed up the mountain road towards the pass. Now they were just below the crest. There had been little traffic either way. Around the corner they came into sunshine and topped the rise; at once Erikki changed down smoothly and picked up speed as they began the long descent, the road – built at the order of Reza Shah, like the railway – a wonder of engineering with cuts and embankments and bridges and steep parts with no railings on the precipice side, the surface slippery, snowbanked. He changed down again, driving fast but prudently, very glad they had not driven by night. 'May I have some more coffee?'

Happily she gave it to him. 'I'll be glad to see Tehran. There's lots of shopping to be done, Sharazad's there, and I have a list of things for my sisters and some face cream for Stepmother . . .'

He hardly listened to her, his mind on Rakoczy, Tehran, McIver and the next step.

The road twisted and curled in its descent. He slowed and drove more cautiously, some traffic behind him. In the lead was a passenger car, typically overloaded, and the driver drove too close, too fast, and with his finger permanently on the horn even when it was clearly impossible to move out of the way. Erikki closed his ears to the impatience that he had never become used to, or to the reckless way Iranians drove, even Azadeh. He rounded the next blind corner, the gradient steepening, and there on the straight, not far ahead, was a heavily laden truck grinding upward with a car overtaking on the wrong side. He braked, hugging the mountainside. At that moment the car behind him accelerated, swerved around him, horn blaring, overtaking blindly, and hurtled down the wrong side of the curving road. The two cars smashed into each other and both careened over the precipice to fall five hundred feet and burst into flames. Erikki swung closer into the side and stopped. The oncoming truck did not stop, just lumbered past and continued up the hill as though nothing had happened – so did the other traffic.

He stood at the edge and looked down into the valley. Burning remains of the cars were spread over the mountainside down six or seven hundred feet, no possibility of survivors, and no chance to get down there without serious climbing gear. When he came back to the car he shook his head unhappily.

'Insha'Allah, my darling,' Azadeh said calmly. 'It was the Will of God.'

'No, it wasn't, it was blatant stupidity.'

'Of course you're right, Beloved, it certainly was blatant stupidity,' she said at once in her most calming voice, seeing his anger though not understanding it as she did not understand much that went on in the head of this strange man who was her husband. 'You're perfectly right, Erikki. It was blatant stupidity but the Will of God that those drivers' stupidity caused their deaths and the deaths of those who travelled with them. It was the Will of God or the road would have been clear. You were quite right.'

'Was I?' he said wearily.

'Oh, yes, of course, Erikki. You were perfectly right.'

They went on. The villages that lay beside the road or straddled it were poor or very poor with narrow dirt streets, crude huts and houses, high walls, a few drab mosques, street stores, goats and sheep and chickens, and flies not yet the plague they would become in summer. Always refuse in the streets and in the joub – the ditches – and the inevitable scavenging packs of scabrous despised dogs that frequently were rabid. But snow made the landscape and the mountains pictur-esque, and the day continued to be good though cold with blue skies and cumulus building.

Inside the Range Rover it was warm and comfortable. Azadeh wore padded, modern ski gear and a cashmere sweater underneath, matching blue, and short boots. Now she took off her jacket and her neat woollen ski cap, and her full-flowing, naturally wavy dark hair fell to her shoulders. Near noon they stopped for a picnic lunch beside a moun-tain stream. In the early afternoon they drove through orchards of apple, pear and cherry trees, now bleak and leafless and naked in the landscape, then came to the outskirts of Qazvin, a town of perhaps a hundred and fifty thousand inhabitants and many mosques.

'How many mosques are there in all Iran, Azadeh?' he asked.

'Once I was told twenty thousand,' she answered sleepily, opening her eyes and peering ahead. 'Ah, Qazvin! You've made good time, Erikki.' A yawn swamped her and she settled more comfortably and went back into half sleep. 'There're twenty thousand mosques and fifty thousand mullahs, so they say. At this rate we'll be in Tehran in a couple of hours . . .'

He smiled as her words petered out. He was feeling more secure now, glad that the back of the journey had been broken. The other side of Qazvin the road was good all the way to Tehran. In Tehran, Abdollah Khan owned many houses and apartments, most of them rented to foreigners. A few he kept for himself and his family, and he had said to Erikki that, this time, because of the troubles, they could stay in an apartment not far from McIver.

'Thanks, thanks very much,' Erikki had said and later Azadeh had said, 'I wonder why he was so kind. It's . . . it's not like him. He hates you and hates me, whatever I try to do to please him.'

'He doesn't hate you, Azadeh.'

'I apologise for disagreeing with you, but he does. I tell you again, my darling, it was my eldest sister, Najoud, who really poisoned him against me, and against my brother. She and her rotten husband. Don't forget my mother was Father's second wife and almost half Najoud's mother's age and twice as pretty and though my mother died when I was seven, Najoud still keeps up the poison – of course not to our face, she's much more clever than that. Erikki, you can never know how subtle and secretive and powerful Iranian ladies can be, or how vengeful behind their oh so sweet exterior. Najoud's worse than the snake in the Garden of Eden! She's the cause of all the enmity.' Her lovely blue-green eyes filled with tears. 'When I was little, my father truly loved us, my brother Hakim and me, and we were his favourites. He spent more time with us in our house than in the palace. Then, when Mother died, we went to live in the palace but none of my half brothers and sisters really liked us. When we went into the palace, everything changed, Erikki. It was Najoud.'

'Azadeh, you tear yourself apart with this hatred – you suffer, not her. Forget her. She's got no power over you now and I tell you again: you've no proof.'

'I don't need proof. I know. And I'll never forget.'

Erikki had left it there. There was no point in arguing, no point in rehashing what had been the source of much violence and many tears. Better it's in the open than buried, better to let her rave from time to time.

Ahead now the road left the fields and entered Qazvin, a city like most every other Iranian city, noisy, cramped, dirty, polluted and traffic-jammed. Beside the road were the joub that skirted most roads in Iran. Here the ditches were three feet deep, in parts concreted, with slush and ice and a little water trickling down them. Trees grew out of them, townsfolk washed their clothes in them, sometimes used them as a source of drinking water, or as a sewer. Beyond the ditches the walls began. Walls that hid houses or gardens, big or small, rich or eyesores. Usually the town and city houses were two floors, drab and boxlike, some brick, adobe, some plastered, and almost all of them hidden. Most had dirt floors, a few had running water, electricity, and some sanitation.

Traffic built up with startling suddenness. Bicycles, motorcycles, buses, lorries, cars of all sizes and makes and ages from ancient to very old, almost all dented and patched, some highly decorated with different coloured paints and small lights to suit the owners' fancy. Erikki had driven this way many times over the last few years and he knew the bottlenecks that could happen. But there was no other way, no detour around the city though one had been planned for years. He smiled scornfully, trying to shut his ears to the noise, and thought, There'll never be a detour, the Qazvinis couldn't stand the quiet. Qazvinis and Rashtians – people from Rasht on the Caspian – were the butts of many Itanian jokes.

He skirted a burned-out wreck, then put in a cassette of Beethoven and turned the volume up to soothe the noise away. But it didn't help much.

'This traffic's worse than usual! Where are the police?' Azadeh said, wide awake now. 'Are you thirsty?'

'No, no thanks.' He glanced across at her, the sweater and tumbling hair enhancing her. He grinned. 'But I'm hungry – hungry for you!'

She laughed and took his arm. 'I'm not hungry – just ravenous!'

'Good.' They were content together.

As usual the road surface was bad. Here and there it was torn up – partially because of wear, partially because of never-ending repairs and road works though these rarely were signposted or had safety barriers. He skirted a deep hole then eased past another wreck that had been shoved carelessly into the side. As he did so a crumpled truck came from the other direction, its horn blaring angrily. It was brightly decorated, the bumpers tied up with wire, the cab open and glassless, a piece of cloth the tank cap. On the flatbed was brushwood, piled high, with three passengers hanging on precariously. The driver was huddled up and wrapped in a ragged sheepskin coat. Two other men were beside him. As Erikki passed he was surprised to see them glaring at him. A few yards further on a battered, overladen bus lumbered towards him. With great care he went closer to the joub, hugging the side to give the bus room, his wheels on the rim, and stopped. Again he saw the driver and all the passengers stare at him as they passed, women in their chadors, young men, bearded and clothed heavily against the cold. One of them shook his fist at him. Another shouted a curse.

We've never had any trouble before, Erikki thought uneasily. Everywhere he looked were the same angry glances. From the street and from the vehicles. He had to go very slowly because of the swarms of rogue motorcycles, bicycles, among the cars, buses and trucks in single lanes that fought for space – obedient to no traffic laws other than those which pleased the individual – and now a flock of sheep poured out of a side street to clutter the road, the motorists screaming abuse at the herdsmen, the herdsmen screaming abuse back and everyone angry and impatient, horns blaring.

'Damned traffic! Stupid sheep!' Azadeh said impatiently, wide awake now. 'Sound your horn, Erikki!'

'Be patient, go back to sleep. There's no way I can overtake anyone,' he shouted over the tumult, conscious of the unfriendliness that surrounded them. 'Be patient!'

Another three hundred yards took half an hour, other traffic coming from both sides to join the stream that got slower and slower. Street vendors and pedestrians and refuse. Now he was inching along behind a bus that took up most of the roadway, almost scraping cars the other side, most times with one wheel half over the lip of the joub. Motorcyclists shoved past carelessly, banging the sides of the Range Rover and other vehicles, cursing each other and everyone else, pushing and kicking the sheep out of the way, stampeding them. From behind, a small car nudged him, then the driver jammed his hand on his horn in a paroxysm of rage that sent a sudden shaft of anger into Erikki's head. Close your ears, he ordered himself. Be calm! There's nothing you can do! Be calm!

But he found it increasingly difficult. After half an hour the sheep turned off into an alley, and traffic picked up a little. Then around the next corner the whole roadway was dug up and an unmarked ten-foot ditch – some six feet deep and half filled with water – barred the way. A group of insolent workmen squatted nearby, hurling back abuse. And obscene gestures.

It was impossible to go forward or back, so all traffic had to detour into a narrow side street, the bus ahead not making the turn, having to stop and reverse to more screams of rage and more tumult, and when Erikki backed to give it room, a battered blue car behind him swerved around him on the opposite side of the road into the small opening ahead and forced the oncoming car to brake suddenly and skid. One of its wheels sank into the joub and the whole car tipped dangerously. Now traffic was totally snarled.

Enraged, Erikki put on his brake, tore his door open, and went over to the car in the ditch and used his great strength to drag it back on the road. No one else helped, just swore and added to the uproar. Then he strode for the blue car. At that moment the bus made the corner and now there was room to move, the driver of the blue car let in his clutch and roared off with an obscene gesture.

With an effort Erikki unclenched his fists. Traffic on both sides of the road honked at him. He got into the driver's seat and let in the clutch.

'Here,' Azadeh said uneasily. She gave him a cup of coffee.

'Thanks.' He drank it, driving with one hand, the traffic slowing again. The blue car had vanished. When he could talk calmly, he said, 'If I'd got my hands on him or his car I'd have torn it and him to pieces.'

'Yes. Yes, I know. Erikki, have you noticed how hostile everyone is to us? So angry?'

'Yes, yes, I have.'

'But why? We've driven though Qazvin twenty tim—' Azadeh ducked involuntarily as refuse suddenly hit her window, then lurched across into his protection, frightened. He cursed and rolled up the windows, then reached across her and locked her door. Dung hit the windshield.

'What the hell's up with these *matyeryebyets*?' he muttered. 'It's as though we've an American flag flying and we're waving pictures of the Shah.' A stone came out of nowhere and ricocheted off the metal sides. Then, ahead, the bus broke out of the narrow side street diversion into the wide square in front of a mosque where there were market stalls and two lanes of traffic either side. To Erikki's relief they picked up some speed. The traffic was still heavy but it was moving and he got into second, heading for the Tehran exit the far side of the square. Halfway around the square the two lanes began to tighten as more vehicles joined those heading for the Tehran road.

'It's never been this bad,' he muttered. 'What the hell's the hold-up for?'

'It must be another accident,' Azadeh said, very unsettled. 'Or road works. Should we turn back – the traffic's not so bad that way?'

'We've plenty of time,' he said, encouraging her. 'We'll be out of here in a minute. Once through the town we'll be fine.' Ahead everything was slowing again, the din picking up. The two lanes were clogging, gradually becoming one again with much hooting, swearing, stopping, starting again and grinding along at about ten miles an hour, street stores and barrows encroaching on the roadway and straddling the joub. They were almost at the exit when some youths ran alongside, began shouting insults, some foul. One of the youths banged on his side window. 'American dog . . .'

'Pig Amer'can . . .'

These men were joined by others and some women in chador, fists raised. Erikki was bottled in and could not get out of the traffic or speed up or slow down nor could he turn around and he felt rage growing at his helplessness. Some of the men were banging on the bonnet and sides of the Range Rover and on his window. Now there was a pack of them and those on Azadeh's side were taunting her, making obscene gestures, trying to open the door. One of the youths jumped on the hood but slipped and fell off and just managed to scramble out of the way before Erikki drove over him.

The bus ahead stopped. Immediately there was a frantic mêlée as would-be passengers fought to get on and others fought to get off. Then Erikki saw an opening, stamped on the accelerator throwing off another man, got around the bus, just missing pedestrians who carelessly flooded through the traffic, and swung into a side street that miraculously was clear, raced up it and cut into another, narrowly avoided a mass of motorcyclists, and continued on again. Soon he was quite lost, for there was no pattern to the city or town except refuse and stray dogs and traffic, but he took his bearings from the sun's shadows and at length came out on to a wider road, shoved his way into the traffic and around it and soon came on to a road that he recognised, one that took him into another square in front of another mosque and then back on the Tehran road. 'We're all right now, Azadeh, they were just hooligans.'

'Yes,' she said shakily. 'They should be whipped.'

Erikki had been studying the crowds near the mosque and on the streets and in the vehicles, trying to find a clue to the untoward hostility. Something's different, he thought. What is it? Then his stomach twisted. 'I haven't seen a soldier or an army truck ever since we left Tabriz – none. Have you?'

'No–no, not now that you mention it.'

'Something's happened, something serious.'

'War? The Soviets have come over the border?' Her face lost even more colour.

'I doubt it – there'd be troops going north, or planes.' He looked at her. 'Never mind,' he said, more to convince himself, 'we're going to have a fine time in Tehran, Sharazad's there and lots of your friends. It's about time you had a change. Maybe I'll take the leave I'm owed – we could go to Finland for a week or two . . .'

They were out of the downtown area and into the suburbs now. The suburbs were ramshackle, with the same walls and houses and the same potholes. Here the Tehran road widened to four lanes, two each side, and though traffic was still heavy and slow, barely fifteen miles an hour, he was not concerned. A little way ahead, the Abadan–Kermanshah road branched off southwest, and he knew that this would bleed off a lot of the congestion. Automatically his eyes scanned the gauges as he would his cockpit instruments and, not for the first time, he wished he was airborne, over and out of all this mess. The petrol gauge registered under a quarter full. Soon he would have to refuel but that would be no problem with plenty of spare fuel aboard.

They slowed to ease past another truck parked with careless arrogance near some street vendors, the air heavy with the smell of diesel. Then more refuse came out of nowhere to splatter their windshield. 'Perhaps we should turn around, Erikki, and go back to Tabriz. Perhaps we could skirt Qazvin.'

'No,' he said, finding it eerie to hear fear in her voice – normally she was fearless. 'No,' he repeated even more kindly. 'We'll go to Tehran and find out what the problem is, then we'll decide.'

She moved closer to him and put a hand on his knee. 'Those hooligans frightened me, God curse them,' she muttered, her other fingers toying nervously with the turquoise beads she wore around her neck. Most Iranian women wore turquoise or blue beads, or a single blue stone against the evil eye. 'Those sons of dogs! Why should they be like that? Devils. May God curse them for ever!' Just outside the city was a big army training camp and an adjoining air base. 'Why aren't soldiers here?'

'I'd like to know too,' he said.

The Abadan–Kermanshah turnoff came up on his right. Much of the traffic headed down it. Barbed-wire fences skirted both roads – as on most of the main roads and highways in Iran. The fences were needed to keep sheep and goats and cattle and dogs – and people – from straying across the roads. Accidents were very frequent and mortality high.

But that's normal for Iran, Erikki thought. Like those poor fools who went over the side in the mountains – no one to know, no one to report them or even to bury them. Except the buzzards and the wild animals and packs of rotten dogs.

With the city behind them, they felt better. The country opened up again, orchards once more beyond the joub and the barbed wire, the Elburz Mountains north and undulating country south. But instead of speeding up, his two lanes slowed even more and congested, then reluctantly became one again, with more jostling, hooting and rage. Wearily he cursed the inevitable roadworks that must be causing the bottleneck, shifted down, his hand and feet working smoothly of their own volition, hardly noticing the stopping and starting, stopping and starting, inching along again, engines grinding and overheating, noise and frustration building in every vehicle. Abruptly Azadeh pointed ahead. 'Look!'

A hundred yards ahead was a roadblock. Groups of men surrounded it. Some were armed, all were civilians and poorly dressed. The road-block was just this side of a nondescript village with street stalls beside the road and in the meadow opposite. Villagers, women and children mingled with the men. All the women wore the black or grey chador. As

232

each vehicle stopped, papers were checked and then it was allowed to pass. Several cars had been pulled off the road into the meadow where knots of men interrogated the occupants. Erikki saw more weapons among them.

'They're not Green Bands,' he said.

'There aren't any mullahs. Can you see any mullahs?'

'No.'

'Then they're Tudeh or mujhadin – or fedayeen.'

'Better get your identity card ready,' he said and smiled at her. 'Put on your parka so you won't catch cold when I open the windows, and your hat.' It wasn't the cold that worried him. It was the curve of her breasts, proud under the sweater, the delicacy of her waist and her free-flowing hair.

In the glove compartment was a small, sheathed pukoh knife. This he concealed in his right boot. The other one, his big knife, was under his parka, in the centre of his back.

When at last their turn came, the surly, bearded men surrounded the Range Rover. A few had U.S. rifles, one an AK47. Among them were some women, just faces in the chador. They peered up at her with beady eyes and grim disapproval. 'Papers,' one of the men said in Farsi, holding out his hand, his breath reeking, the pervading smell of unwashed clothes and bodies coming into the car. Azadeh stared ahead, trying to dismiss the leers and mutterings and closeness that were totally outside her experience.

Politely Erikki passed over his ID card and Azadeh's. The man accepted them, stared at them, and passed them to a youth who could read. All the others waited silently, staring, stamping their feet in the cold. At length the youth said, his Farsi coarse, 'He's a foreigner from somewhere called Finland. He comes from Tabriz. He's not American.'

'He looks American,' someone else said.

'The woman's called Gorgon, she's his wife . . . at least that's what the papers say.'

'I'm his wife,' Azadeh said curtly. 'Ca –'

'Who asked you?' the first man said rudely. 'Your family name's Gorgon which is a landowning name and your accent's high and mighty like your manner and more than likely you're an enemy of the people.'

'I'm an enemy of no one. Pl –'

'Shut up. Women are supposed to know manners and be chaste and cover themselves and be obedient even in a socialist state.' The man turned on Erikki. 'Where are you going?'

233

'What's he say, Azadeh?' Erikki asked.

She translated.

'Tehran,' he said quietly to the thug. 'Azadeh, tell him we go to Tehran.' He had counted six rifles and one automatic. Traffic hemmed him in, no way to break out. Yet.

She did so, adding, 'My husband does not speak Farsi.'

'How do we know that? And how do we know you're married? Where is your marriage certificate?'

'I don't have it with me. That I'm married is attested on my identity card.'

'But this is a Shah card. An illegal card. Where is your new card?'

'A card from whom? Signed by whom?' she said fiercely. 'Give us back our cards and allow us to pass!'

Her strength had an effect on him and the others. The man hesitated. 'You will understand, please, that there are many spies and enemies of the people that must be caught . . .'

Erikki could feel his heart pumping. Sullen faces, people out of the Dark Ages. Ugly. More men joined the group around them. One of them angrily and noisily waved the cars and trucks behind him ahead to be checked. No one was honking. Everyone waited their turn. And over the whole traffic jam was a silent brooding dread.

'What's going on here?' A squat man shouldered his way through the crowd. The others gave way to him deferentially. Over his shoulder was a Czechoslovakian machine gun. The other man explained and gave over the papers. The squat man's face was round and unshaven, his eyes dark, his clothes poor and filthy. A sudden shot rang out and all heads turned to look at the meadow.

A man was lying on the ground beside a small passenger car that had been pulled over by the hostiles. One of these men stood over him with an automatic. Another passenger was pressed against the side of the car with his hands over his head. Abruptly this man burst through the cordon and dashed away. The man with the gun raised it and fired, missed and fired again. This time the running man screamed and fell, writhing in agony, tried to scramble away, his legs useless now. Leisurely the man with the gun came up to him, emptied the magazine into him, killing him by stages.

'Ahmed!' the squat man shouted out. 'Why waste bullets when your boots would do just as well? Who are they?'

'SAVAK!' A murmur of satisfaction swept the crowd and villagers and someone cheered.

'Fool! Then why kill them so quickly, eh? Bring me their papers.'

'The sons of dogs had papers claiming they were Tehrani business-men but I know a SAVAK man when I see one. Do you want the false papers?'

'No. Tear them up.' The squat man turned back to Erikki and Azadeh. 'So it is that enemies of the people will be smoked out and done with.'

She did not reply. Their own IDs were in the grubby hand. What if our papers are also considered false? Insha'Allah!

When the squat man finished scrutinising the IDs he stared at Erikki. Then at her. 'You claim you're Azadeh Gorgon Yok . . . Yokkonen – his wife?'

'Yes.'

'Good.' He stuffed their IDs in his pocket and jerked a thumb at the meadow. 'Tell him to drive over there. We will search your car.'

'But th –'

'Do it. NOW!' The squat man climbed on to the bumpers, his boots scratching the paintwork. 'What's that?' he asked, pointing to the blue cross on a white background that was painted on the roof.

'It's the Finnish flag,' Azadeh said. 'My husband's Finnish.'

'Why is it there?'

'It pleases him to have it there.'

The squat man spat, then pointed again towards the meadow. 'Hurry up! Over there.' When they were in an empty spot, the crowd following them, he slid off. 'Out. I want to search your car for arms and contraband.'

Azadeh said, 'We have no guns or contr –'

'Out! And you, woman, you hold your tongue!' The crones in the crowd hissed approvingly. Angrily he jerked a thumb at the two bodies left crumpled in the trampled slush. 'The people's justice is quick and final and don't forget it.' He stabbed a finger at Erikki. 'Tell your monster husband what I said – if he is your husband.'

'Erikki, he says, the people's . . . the people's justice is quick and final and don't forget it. Be careful, my darling. We, we have to get out of the car – they want to search the car.'

'All right. But slide over and come out my side.' Towering above the crowd, Erikki got out. Protectively, he put his arm around her, men, women and some children crowding them, giving them little space. The stench of unwashed bodies was overpowering. He could feel her trembling, as much as she tried to hide it. Together they watched the squat man and others clambering into their spotless car, muddy boots on the seats. Others unlocked the rear door, carelessly removing

235

and scattering their possessions, grubby hands reaching into pockets, opening everything – his bags and her bags. Then one of the men held up her filmy underclothes and night things to catcalls and jeers. The crones muttered their disapproval. One of them reached out and touched her hair. Azadeh backed away but those behind her would not give her room. At once Erikki moved his bulk to help but the mass of the crowd did not move though those nearby cried out, almost crushed by him, their cries infuriating the others who moved closer, threateningly, shouting at him.

Suddenly Erikki knew truly, for the first time, he could not protect Azadeh. He knew he could kill a dozen of them before they overpowered and killed him, but that would not protect her.

The realisation shattered him.

His legs felt weak and he had an overpowering wish to urinate and the smell of his own fear choked him and he fought the panic that pervaded him. Dully he watched their possessions being defiled. Men were staggering away with their vital cans of petrol without which he could never make Tehran as all petrol stations were on strike and closed. He tried to force his legs into motion but they would not work, nor would his mouth. Then one of the crones shouted at Azadeh who numbly shook her head and men took up the cry, jostling him and jostling her, men closing on him, their fetid smell filling his nostrils, his ears clogged with the Farsi.

His arm was still around her, and in the noise she looked up and he saw her terror but could not hear what she said. Again he tried to ease more room for the two of them but again he failed. Desperately he tried to contain the soaring, claustrophobic, panic-savagery and need to fight beginning to overwhelm him, knowing that once he began it would start the riot that would destroy her. But he could not stop himself and lashed out blindly with his free elbow as a thickset peasant woman with strange, enraged eyes pushed though the cordon and thrust the chador into Azadeh's chest, spitting out a paroxysm of Farsi at her, diverting attention from the man who had collapsed behind him, and now lay under their feet, his chest caved in from Erikki's blow.

The crowd were shouting at her and at him, clearly telling her to put on the chador, Azadeh crying out, 'No, no, leave me alone . . .' completely disoriented. In her whole life she had never been threatened like this, never been in a crowd like this, never experienced such closeness of peasants, or such hostility.

'Put it on, harlot . . .

'In the Name of God, put on the chador . . .

'Not in the Name of God, woman, in the name of the People . . .

'God is Great, obey the word . . .

'Piss on God, in the name of the revolution . . .

'Cover your hair, whore and daughter of a whore . . .

'Obey the Prophet Whose Name be praised . . .'

The shouting increased and the jostling, their feet trampling the dying man on the ground, then someone tore at Erikki's arm that was around Azadeh and she felt his other hand go for the big knife and she screamed out, 'Don't, don't, Erikki, they'll kill you . . .'

In panic she pushed the peasant woman away and fought the chador into place, calling out repeatedly, 'Allah-u Akbarrr,' and this mollified those nearby somewhat, their jeers subsiding, though people at the back shoved forward to see better, crushing others against the Range Rover. In the mêlée Erikki and Azadeh gained a little more space around them though they were still trapped on all sides. She did not look up at him, just clutched him, shivering like a frozen puppy, enveloped in the coarse shroud. A roar of laughter as one of the men held her bra against his chest and minced around.

The vandalism went on until, suddenly, Erikki sensed a newness surrounding them. The squat man and his followers had stopped and they were looking fixedly towards Qazvin. As he watched he saw them begin to melt into the crowd. In seconds they had vanished. Other men near the roadblock were getting into cars and heading off down the Tehran road, picking up speed. Now villagers also stared towards the city, then others, until the whole crowd was transfixed. Approaching up the road, through the snarled lines of traffic, was another mob of men, mullahs at their head. Some of the mullahs and many of the men were armed. 'Allah-u Akbar,' they shouted, 'God and Khomeiniiiii!' then broke into a run, charging the roadblock.

A few shots rang out, the fire was returned from the roadblock, the opposing forces clashed with staves, stones, iron bars, and some guns. Everyone else scattered. Villagers rushed from the protection of their homes, drivers and passengers fled from their cars for the ditches or lay on the ground.

The cries and counter-cries and shots and noise and screams of this minor skirmish snapped Erikki's paralysis. He shoved Azadeh towards their car, hastily picking up the nearest of their scattered possessions, throwing them into the back, and slammed the rear door. Half a dozen of the villagers began scavenging too but he shoved them out of the way, jumped into the driver's seat and gunned the engine, jerked the car into reverse, then ahead, then roared off across the meadow, paralleling

237

the road. Just ahead and to the right he saw the squat man with three of his followers getting into a car and remembered that the man still had their papers. For a split second he considered stopping but instantly rejected the thought and held course for the trees that skirted the road. But then he saw the squat man pull the machine gun off his shoulder, aim, and fire. The burst was a little high and Erikki's maddened reflexes swung the wheel over and shoved his foot on the accelerator as he charged the gun. Their massive bumper rammed the man against the car broadside, crushing him and it, the machine gun firing until the magazine was spent, bullets howling off metal, splaying through the windshield, the Range Rover now a battering ram. Berserk, Erikki backed off then charged again, overturning the wreckage, killing them, and he would have got out and continued the carnage with his bare hands but then, in the rearview mirror, he saw men running for him and so he reversed and fled.

The Range Rover was built for this sort of terrain, its snow tyres gripping the surface of the rough ground. In a moment they were in the trees and safe from capture, and he turned for the road, shifted into low, locked both differentials and clambered over the deep joub, ripping the barbed-wire fence apart. Once on the road he unlocked the differentials, changed gear and whirled away.

Only when he was well away did the blood clear from his eyes. Aghast, he remembered the howl of the bullets spraying the car, and that Azadeh was with him. In panic he looked across at her. But she was all right though paralysed with fear and hunched down in the seat, hanging on with both hands to the side, bullet holes in the glass and roof nearby, but all right though he did not recognise her for a moment, saw just an Iranian face made ugly by the chador – like any one of the tens of thousands they had all seen in the mobs.

'Oh, Azadeh,' he gasped, then reached over and pulled her to him, driving with one hand. In a moment he slowed and pulled over to the side and held her to him as the sobs tore her. He did not notice that the fuel gauge read near empty, or that the traffic was building up, or the hostile looks of the passers, or that many cars contained revolutionaries fleeing their roadblock for Tehran.

The map shows IRAN and surrounding countries including USSR, AFGHANISTAN, PAKISTAN, IRAQ, KUWAIT, SAUDI ARABIA, BAHRAIN, QATAR, UAE. Cities and locations marked include Khvoy, Tabriz, Mount Sabalan, Bandar-e Pahlavi, Caspian Sea, Sadzevar, Meshed, Qazvin, Tehran, Baghdad, Dez Dam, Isfahan, Abadan, Bandar-e Delam, Kowiss, Kharg Island, Jellet, Lengeh, Siri, Al Shargaz, Persian Gulf, Strait of Hormuz, Gulf of Oman, and ZAGROS.

At Zagros Three: 3:18 P.M. The four men were lying on toboggans, racing down the slope behind the base, Scot Gavallan slightly in the lead of Jean-Luc Sessonne who was neck and neck with Nasiri, their base manager, with Nitchak Khan trailing some twenty yards. This was a challenge match arranged by Jean-Luc, Iran against the World, and all four men were excitedly trying to maximise their speed. The snow was virgin powder – very light snow on top of hard pack – and trackless. They had all climbed to the crest behind the base with Rodrigues and a villager as starting marshals. The winner's prize was five thousand rials – about sixty dollars – and one of Lochart's bottles of whisky: 'Tom won't mind,' Jean-Luc had said grandly. 'He's having extra leave, enjoying the fleshpots of Tehran while we have to stay on base! Me, am I not in command? Of course. This commander is commandeering the bottle for the glory of France, the good of my troops, and our glorious overlords, the Yazdek Kash'kai,' he added to general cheers.

It was a wonderful, sunny afternoon, here at 7,500 feet, the sky

239

cloudless and deep blue, air crisp. In the night the snow had stopped. Ever since Lochart had left to go to Tehran three days before, it had been snowing. Now the base and the bowl of mountains were a fairyland of pine and snow and crests soaring to 13,000 feet – with about twenty-four inches of fresh powder.

As the racers came lower the slope steepened even more, a few unseen moguls bouncing them from time to time. They picked up speed, sometimes almost disappearing under the spray of snow-flakes, all exhilarated, flat-out, and determined to win.

Ahead now were clumps of pine trees. Scot braked neatly with the toes of his ski boots, his mittened hands gripping the curved front supports, and arced gracefully around the trees, banked again, and began to swoop down the last great slope towards the finish line far below where the rest of the base and villagers were cheering them on. Nasiri and Jean-Luc braked a fraction later, came around the trees just a fraction faster, banked in a cascade of snow and gained on him, now only inches between the three of them.

Nitchak Khan did not brake at all, or make the diversion. He commended himself to God for the hundredth time, closed his eyes and went barrelling into the pines. 'Insha' Allahhhh!'

He passed the first tree safely by a foot, the next by half a foot, opened his eyes just in time to avoid a head-on collision by an inch, ploughed through a dozen saplings gaining speed, abruptly soared into the air over a bump to clear miraculously a fallen tree, and slam back to earth once more in a chest-aching thump that almost crushed the air out of him. But he hung on, rearing up, heeled over on one runner for a second, got his balance back and now he burst out of the forest faster than the others, straighter than the others, ten yards ahead of the others to a roar from all the villagers.

The four racers were converging now, hugging their toboggans for just that extra little speed, Scot, Nasiri, and Jean-Luc gaining on Nitchak Khan, closer and closer. Here the snow was not so good and some small moguls bounced them, making them hold on tighter. Two hundred yards to go, one hundred – the men from the base and the villagers cheering and begging God for victory – now eighty, seventy, sixty, fifty, and then . . .

The great mogul was well hidden. In the lead Nitchak Khan was the first to sail up out of control and come down broadside, the wind knocked out of him, then Scot and Jean-Luc both whirled into the air to sprawl equally helpless, their toboggans upended in clouds of spray. Nasiri desperately tried to avoid them and the mogul and wrenched his

240

craft into a violent skidding turn but lost it and went tumbling down the mountainside to end up a little ahead of the others, gasping for breath.

Nitchak Khan sat up and wiped the snow out of his face and beard. 'Praise be to God,' he muttered, astonished that no limbs were broken, and he looked around at the others. They were also picking themselves up, Scot helpless with laughter at Jean-Luc who was also unhurt but still lying on his back letting out a paroxysm of French invective. Nasiri had ended up almost headfirst into a snowdrift and Scot, still laughing, went to help him. He, too, was a little battered but no damage.

'Hey, you lot up there,' someone was shouting from the crowd below. It was Effer Jordon. 'What about the bleeding race? It's not over yet!'

'Come on, Scot – come on, Jean-Luc, for crissake! Get the lead out!'

Scot forgot Nasiri and started to run for the winning post fifty yards away but he slipped and fell in the heavy snow, lurched up and slipped again, feet leaden. Jean-Luc reeled up and charged in pursuit, closely followed by Nasiri and Nitchak Khan. The cheers of the crowd redoubled as the men fought through the snow, falling, scrambling, getting up and falling again, the going very rough, aches forgotten. Scot was still slightly in the lead, now Nitchak Khan, now Jean-Luc, now Nasiri – Fowler, red in the face, urging them on, the villagers as excited.

Ten yards to go. The old Khan was three feet in the lead when he tripped and sprawled face forward. Scot took the lead, Nasiri almost beside him, Jean-Luc just inches behind. They were all at a labouring, faltering, stumbling walk, dragging their boots up out of the heavy snow, then there was a mighty cheer as Nitchak Khan began to scuttle forward on all fours the last few yards, Jean-Luc and Scot made one last desperate headlong dive for the line, and they all collapsed in a heap amid cheers and counter-cheers.

'Scot won . . .'

'No, it was Jean-Luc . . .'

'No, it was old Nitchak . . .'

When he had collected his breath, Jean-Luc said, 'As there is no clear opinion and even our revered mullah is not sure, I, Jean-Luc, declare Nitchak Khan the winner by a nostril.' There were cheers and even more as he added, 'And as the losers lost so bravely, I award them with another of Tom's bottles of whisky which I will commandeer to be shared by all expats at sundown!'

Everyone shook hands with everyone. Nitchak Khan agreed to another challenge match next month and, as he honoured the law

241

and did not drink, he haggled voraciously but sold the whisky he had won to Jean-Luc at half its value. Everyone cheered again, then someone shouted a warning.

Northwards, far up in the mountains, a red signal flare was falling into the valley. The silence was sudden. The flare vanished. Then another arced up and outwards to fall again: SOS Urgent.

'CASEVAC,' Jean-Luc said, squinting into the distance. 'Must be Rig Rosa or Rig Bellissima.'

'I'm on my way.' Scot Gavallan hurried off.

'I'll come with you. We'll take a 212 and make it a check ride for you.'

In minutes they were airborne. Rig Rosa was one of the rigs they had acquired from the old Guerney contract. Bellissima one of their regulars. All eleven rigs in this area had been developed by an Italian company for IranOil, and though all were radio linked with Zagros Three, the connection was not always solid because of the mountains and scatter effect. Flares were a substitute.

The 212 climbed steadily, passing through 10,000 feet, snow-locked valleys sparkled in the sunshine, their operational ceiling 17,000 depending on their load. Now Rig Rosa was ahead in a clearing on a small plateau at 11,470. Just a few trailers for housing and sheds scattered haphazardly around the tall derrick. And a helipad.

'Rig Rosa, this is Jean-Luc. Do you read?' He waited patiently.

'Loud and clear, Jean-Luc!' It was the happy voice of Mimmo Sera, the 'company man' – the highest rank on the site, an engineer in charge of all operations. 'What you got for us, eh?'

'*Niente*, Mimmo! We saw a red flare and we're just checking.'

'*Mon Dieu*, CASEVAC? It wasn't us.' At once Scot broke off his approach, banked, and went on to the new heading, climbing further into the mountain range. 'Bellissima?'

'We're going to check.'

'Let us know, eh? We haven't been in contact since the storm came. What's the latest news?'

'The last we heard was two days ago: the BBC said the Immortals at Doshan Tappeh had put down a rebellion of air force cadets and civilians. We haven't heard from our Tehran HQ or anyone. If we do I'll radio you.'

'Eh, radio! Jean-Luc, we'll need another dozen loads of six-inch pipe and the usual of cement starting tomorrow. Okay?'

'*Bien sûr!*' Jean-Luc was delighted with the extra business and the opportunity to prove they were better than Guerney. 'How's it going?'

'We've drilled to 8,000 feet and everything looks like another bonanza. I want to run the well next Monday, if possible. Can you order up Schlumberger for me?' Schlumberger was the worldwide firm that manufactured and supplied down-hole tools that sampled and electronically measured, with vast accuracy, oil-bearing capabilities and qualities of the various strata, tools to guide the drilling bits, tools to fish up broken bits, tools to perforate, by explosion, the steel casings of the hole to allow oil to flow into the pipe – along with the experts to work them. Very expensive but totally necessary. To run a well was the last job before cementing the steel casing in place and bringing the well on stream.

'Wherever they are, Mimmo, we'll bring them Monday – Khomeini willing!'

'*Mamma mia*, tell Nasiri we have to have them.'

Reception was fading rapidly.

'No problem. I'll call you on the way back.' Jean-Luc glanced out of the cockpit. They were passing over a ridge, still climbing, the engines beginning to labour. '*Merde*, I'm hungry,' he said, and stretched in his seat. 'I feel like I've been massaged with a pneumatic drill – but that was a great race!'

'You know, Jean-Luc, you were at the line a second before Nitchak Khan. Easily.'

'Of course, but we French are magnanimous, *diplomatique*, and very practical. I knew he'd sell us back our whisky for half price; if he'd been declared the loser, it would have cost us a fortune.' Jean-Luc beamed. 'But if it hadn't been for that mogul, I would not have hesitated – I would have won easily.'

Scot smiled and said nothing, breathing easily, but conscious of his breathing. Above 12,000, according to regulations, pilots should be on oxygen if they were to stay up for more than half an hour. They carried none and never, yet, had any of the pilots felt any discomfort other than a headache or two, though it took a week or so to get acclimatised to living at 7,500 feet. It was harder for the riggers at Bellissima.

Their own stopovers at Bellissima were usually very short. Just lumber up with maximum payload, inside or out, of 4,000 pounds. Pipes, pumps, diesel, winches, generators, chemicals, food, trailers, tanks, men, mud – the all-purpose name for the liquid that was pumped into the drill hole to remove waste, to keep the bit lubricated, in due course to tame the oil or gas, and without which deep drilling was impossible. Then lumber out, light, or with a full load of men or equipment for repair or replacement.

We're just a jumped-up delivery van, Scot thought, his eyes scanning the skies, instruments, and all around. Yes, but how grand to be flying and not driving. Below, the crags were close, the treeline long since passed. They mounted the last ridge. Now they could see the rig.

'Bellissima, this is Jean-Luc. Do you read?'

Rig Bellissima was the highest of the chain, at exactly 12,450 feet above sea level. The base was perched on a ledge just below the crest. The other side of the ledge the mountain fell away 7,000 feet, almost sheer, into a valley ten miles wide and thirty miles long, a vast gash in the surface of the earth.

'Bellissima, this is Jean-Luc. Do you read?'

Rig Bellissima was the highest of the chain, at exactly 12,450 feet above sea level. The base was perched on a ledge just below the crest. The other side of the ledge the mountain fell away 7,000 feet, almost sheer, into a valley ten miles wide and thirty miles long, a vast gash in the surface of the earth.

'Bellissima, this is Jean-Luc. Do you read?'

Again no answer. Jean-Luc switched channels. 'Zagros Three, do you read?'

'Loud and clear, Captain,' came the immediate answer of their Iranian base radio op Aliwani. 'Excellency, Nasiri's beside me.'

'Stand by on this frequency. The CASEVAC's at Bellissima, but we've no radio contact. We're going in to land.'

'Roger. Standing by.'

As always at Bellissima, Scot was awed at the vastness of the earth's convulsion that had caused the valley. And, like all who visited this rig, again he wondered at the enormity of the gamble, labour and wealth necessary to find the oil field, select the site, erect the rig, then to drill the thousands of feet to make the wells profitable. But they were, immensely so, as was this whole area with its huge oil and gas deposits trapped in limestone cones between 7,500 and 11,000 feet below the surface. And then the further huge investment and more gambling to connect this field to the pipeline that straddled the Zagros Mountains, joining the refineries at Isfahan in the centre of Iran to those at Abadan on the Gulf – another extraordinary engineering feat of the old Anglo-Iranian Oil Company, now nationalised and renamed IranOil. 'Stolen, Scot, laddie, stolen's the correct word,' his father had told him many times.

Scot Gavallan smiled to himself, thinking about his father, feeling a warm glow. I'm bloody lucky to have him, he thought. I still miss Mother but I'm glad she died. Terrible for a lovely, active woman to become a helpless, chair-ridden, palsied shell, still with her mind intact even at the end, the best mother a guy could have. Rotten luck, her death, particularly for Dad. But I'm glad he remarried, Maureen's super, and Dad's super and I've a smashing life and the future's rosy – plenty of flying, plenty of birds and in a couple of years I'll get married: how about Tess? His heart picked up a beat. Bloody nuisance Linbar's her uncle and she his favourite niece, but bloody lucky I don't have anything to do with him, she's only eighteen so there's plenty of time . . .

'Which way will you land, *mon vieux*?' came through his earphones.

'From the west,' he said, collecting himself.

'Good.' Jean-Luc was peering ahead. No sign of life. The site was heavily covered with snow, almost buried. Only the helipad was cleared. Threads of smoke came up from the trailer huts. 'Ah! There!'

They saw the tiny figure of a man, bundled up, standing near the helipad and waving his arms. 'Who is it?'

'I think it's Pietro.' Scot was concentrating on the landing. At this height and because of the position on the ledge there were sudden gusts, turbulences, and whirlwinds within them – no room for mistakes. He came in over the abyss, the eddies rocking them, then corrected beautifully as he swooped over the land and touched down.

'Good.' Jean-Luc turned his attention back to the bundled-up man he now recognised as Pietro Fieri, one of the 'tool pushers', next in importance to the company man. They saw him motion with his hand across his throat, the sign to cut engines, indicating the CASEVAC was not an immediate takeoff situation. Jean-Luc beckoned the man to his side window and opened it. 'What's up, Pietro?' he shouted over the engines.

'Guineppa is sick,' Pietro shouted back – Mario Guineppa was the company man – and thumped the left side of his chest. 'We think it may be his heart and that's not all. Look there!' He pointed aloft. Jean-Luc and Scot craned to see better but could not see what was agitating him.

Jean-Luc unbuckled and got out. The cold hit him and he winced, his eyes watering in the eddies caused by the rotors, his dark glasses helping only a little. Then he saw the problem, and his stomach twisted nastily. A few hundred feet above and almost directly over the camp, just under the crest, was an enormous overhang of snow and ice. '*Merde!*'

'If that goes, it'll avalanche the whole mountainside and maybe take us and everything into the valley along with it!' Pietro's face was bluish in the cold. He was thickset and very strong with a dark grizzled beard, his eyes brown and keen but squinting now against the wind. 'Guineppa wants to confer with you. Come to his trailer, eh?'

245

'And that?' Jean-Luc jerked a thumb upwards.

'If it goes, it goes,' Pietro said with a laugh, his teeth white against the darkness of his oil-stained parka. 'Come on!' He ducked away from the rotors and trudged away. 'Come on!'

Uneasily, Jean-Luc gauged the overhang. It could be there weeks, or fall any second. Above the crest the sky was peerless, but little warmth came from the afternoon sun. 'Stay here, Scot, keep her idling,' he called out, then followed Pietro awkwardly, the snow very deep.

Mario Guineppa's two-room trailer was warm and untidy, charts on the walls, oil-stained clothes, heavy gloves, and hard hats on pegs with an oilman's paraphernalia scattered about the office/living room. He was in the bedroom, lying on his bed fully dressed but for his boots, a big tall man of forty-five with an imposing nose, normally ruddy and weathered, but now pallid, a curious bluish tinge to his lips. The tool pusher from the other shift, Enrico Banastasio, was with him – a small, dark man with dark eyes and thin face.

'Ah, Jean-Luc! Good to see you,' Guineppa said wearily.

'And you, *mon ami*.' Very concerned, Jean-Luc unzipped his flying jacket and sat beside the bed. Guineppa had been in charge of Bellissima for two years – twelve hours on, twelve off, two months on site, two off – and had brought in three major producing wells here with space to drill another four. 'It's the hospital in Shiraz for you.'

'That's not important, first there's the overhang. Jean-Luc, I was –'

'We evacuate and leave that *stronzo* to the Hands of God,' Banastasio said.

'*Mamma mia*, Enrico,' Guineppa said irritably, 'I tell you again I think we can give God a hand – with Jean-Luc's help. Pietro agrees. Eh, Pietro?'

'Yes,' Pietro said from the doorway, a toothpick in his mouth. 'Jean-Luc, I was brought up in Aosta in the Italian Alps so I know mountains and avalanches and I th –'

'*Si, e vos fijamete*.' Yes, and you're crazy, Banastasio said curtly.

'*In vos alimente*.' In your backside. Pietro casually made an obscene gesture. 'With your help, Jean-Luc, it's easy to shift that *stronzo*.'

'What do you want me to do?' Jean-Luc asked.

Guineppa said, 'Take Pietro and fly up over the crest to a place he'll show you on the north face. He'll drop a stick of dynamite into the snow from there and that'll avalanche the danger away from us.'

Pietro beamed. 'Just like that and the overhang will vanish.'

Banastasio said even more angrily, his English-American accented,

'For crissake, I tell you again it's too goddam risky. We should evacuate first – then if you must, try your dynamite.'

Guineppa's face screwed up as a spasm of pain went through him. One hand went to his chest. 'If we evacuate we have to close everything down an –'

'So? So we close down. So what? If you don't care about your own life, think of the rest of us. I say we evacuate pronto. Then dynamite. Jean-Luc, isn't it safer?'

'Of course it's safer,' Jean-Luc replied carefully, not wanting to agitate the older man. 'Pietro, you say you know avalanches. How long will that hold?'

'My nose says it will go soon. Very soon. There are cracks below. Perhaps tomorrow, even tonight. I know where to blow her – and be very safe.' Pietro looked at Banastasio. 'I can do it whatever this *stronzo* thinks.'

Banastasio got up. 'Jean-Luc, me and my shift're evacuating. Pronto. Whatever is decided.' He left.

Guineppa shifted in his cot. 'Jean-Luc, take Pietro aloft. Now.'

'First we'll evacuate everyone to Rig Rosa, you first,' Jean-Luc said crisply, 'then dynamite. If it works you're back in business, if not there's enough temporary space at Rig Rosa for you.'

'Not first, last . . . there's no need to evacuate.'

Jean-Luc hardly heard him. He was estimating numbers of men to move. Each of the two shifts contained nine men – tool pusher, assistant, mudman who monitored the mud and decided on its chemical constituents and weight, driller, who looked after the drilling, motor-man, responsible for all winches, pumps, and so on, and four roust-abouts to attach or unhook the pipes and drills. 'You've seven Iranian cooks and labourers?'

'Yes. But I tell you it's not necessary to evacuate,' Guineppa said exhaustedly.

'Safer, *mon vieux*,' Jean-Luc turned to Pietro. 'Tell everyone to travel light and be fast.'

Pietro glanced down at Guineppa. 'Yes or no?'

Disgustedly, Guineppa nodded, the effort tiring him. 'Ask for a volunteer crew to stay. If no one will, Mother of God, close down.'

Pietro was clearly disappointed. Still picking his teeth, he went out. Guineppa shifted in the cot again, trying to get more comfortable, and began to curse. He seemed more frail than before.

Jean-Luc said quietly, 'It's better to evacuate, Mario.'

'Pietro is wise and clever but that *porco miserio*, Banastasio, he's fart up to his nostrils, always trouble, and it was his fault the radio was smashed, I know it!'

'What?'

'It was smashed on his shift. Now we need a new one, do you have a spare?'

'No, but I'll see if I can get one. Is it repairable? Perhaps one of our mechanics c –'

'Banastasio said he slipped and fell on it, but I heard he hit it with a hammer when it wouldn't work . . . *Mamma mia!*' Guineppa winced and clutched his chest and began to curse again.

'How long have you been having pains?'

'Since two days. Today has been the worst. That *stronzo* Banastasio!' Guineppa muttered. 'But what can you expect, it runs in his family. Eh! His family are half-American, no? I heard the American side has mafioso connections.'

Jean-Luc smiled to himself, not believing it, half listening to the tirade. He knew that they hated each other – Guineppa, the Portuguese-Roman patrician, and Banastasio, Sicilian-American peasant. But that's not so surprising, he thought, locked up here, twelve hours on, twelve off, day after day, month after month, however good the pay.

Ah, the pay! How I could use their pay! Why, even the lowest roustabout gets as much in one week as I get in a month – a miserable £1,200 sterling monthly for me, a senior captain and training captain, with 4,800 hours! Even with the miserly £500 monthly overseas allowance, that's not enough for the kids, school fees, my wife, the mortgage and filthy taxes . . . let alone the best food and wine and my darling Sayada. Ah, Sayada, how I've missed you!

But for Lochart . . .

Piece of shit! Tom Lochart could have let me go with him and I could be in Tehran in her arms right now! My God how I need her. And money. Money! May the balls of all taxmen shrivel into dust and their cocks vanish! I've barely enough as it is and if Iran goes down the sewer, what then? I'll bet S-G won't survive. That's their bad luck – there'll always be chopper work for a pilot as excellent as I am somewhere in the world.

He saw Guineppa watching him. 'Yes, *mon vieux?*'

'I'll go with the last load.'

'Better to go first, there's a medic at Rosa.'

'I'm fine – honestly.'

Then Jean-Luc heard his name being called and put on his parka. 'Can I do anything for you?'

The man smiled wearily. 'Just take Pietro aloft with the dynamite.'

'I'll do that, but last, with any luck, before dusk. Don't worry.'

Outside the cold hit him again. Pietro was waiting for him. Men were already grouped near the idling helicopter, with packs and duffle bags of various sizes. Banastasio went past leading a big German shepherd.

'The man said to travel light,' Pietro told him.

'I am,' Banastasio said equally sourly. 'I've my papers, my dog and my shift. The rest's replaceable, on the goddam company.' Then to Jean-Luc, 'You've a full load, Jean-Luc, let's get with it.'

Jean-Luc checked the men aboard, and the dog, then called Nasiri on the radio and told him what they were going to do. 'Okay, Scot, off you go. You take her,' he said and got out and saw Scot's eyes widen.

'You mean by myself?'

'Why not, *mon brave*? You've the hours. This's your third check ride. You've got to start sometime. Off you go.'

He watched Scot lift off. In barely five seconds the chopper was over the abyss with a clear 7,500 feet below and he knew how eerie and wonderful that first solo takeoff from Bellissima would be, envying the young man the thrill. Young Scot's worth it, he thought, watching him critically.

'Jean-Luc!'

He took his eyes off the distant chopper and glanced around, wondering suddenly what was so different. Then he realised it was the silence, so vast that it almost seemed to deafen him. For a moment he felt weirdly unbalanced, even a little sick, then the whine of the wind picked up and he became whole again.

'Jean-Luc! Over here!' Pietro was in a shadow with a group of men on the other side of the camp, beckoning him. Laboriously, he picked his way over to them. They were strangely silent.

'Look there,' Pietro said nervously and pointed aloft. 'Just under the overhang. There! Twenty, thirty feet below. You see the cracks?'

Jean-Luc saw them. His testicles heaved. They were no longer cracks in the ice but fissures. As they watched, there was a vast groaning. The whole mass seemed to shift a fraction. A small chunk of ice and snow fell away. It gathered speed and substance and thundered down the steep slope. They were shock-still. The ava-

249

lanche, now tons of snow and ice, came to rest barely fifty yards away from them.

One of the men broke the silence. 'Let's hope the chopper doesn't come barrelling back like a kamikaze – that could be the detonator, *amico*. Even a little noise could trigger that whole *stronzo* apart.'

In the skies near Qazvin: 3:17 P.M. From the moment Charlie Pettikin had left Tabriz almost two hours ago with Rakoczy – the man he knew as Smith – he had flown the 206 as straight and level as possible, hoping to lull the KGB man to sleep, or at least off guard. For the same reason he had avoided conversation by slipping his headset on to his neck. At length Rakoczy had given up, just watched the terrain below. But he stayed alert with his gun across his lap, his thumb on the safety catch. And Pettikin wondered about him, who he was, what he was, what band of revolutionaries he belonged to – army or SAVAK, and if so why it was so important to get to Tehran. It had never occurred to Pettikin that the man was Russian not Iranian.

At Bandar-e Pahlavi where refuelling had been laboriously slow, he had done nothing to break the monotony, just paid over his last remaining U.S. dollars and watched while the tanks were filled, then signed the official IranOil chit. Rakoczy had tried to chat with the refueller but the man was hostile, clearly frightened of being seen

251

refuelling this foreign helicopter, and even more frightened of the machine gun that was on the front seat.

All the time they were on the ground Pettikin had gauged the odds of trying to grab the gun. There was never a chance. It was Czech. In Korea they had been plentiful. And Vietnam. My God, he thought, those days seem a million years ago.

He had taken off from Bandar-e Pahlavi and was now heading south at 1,000 feet, following the Qazvin road. East he could see the beach where he had set down Captain Ross and his two paratroopers. Again he wondered how they had known he was making a flight to Tabriz and what their mission had been. Hope to God they make it – whatever they had to make. Had to be urgent and important. Hope I see Ross again, I'd like that . . .

'Why do you smile, Captain?'

The voice came through his earphones. Automatically on takeoff this time he had put them on. He looked across at Rakoczy and shrugged, then went back to monitoring his instruments and the ground below. Over Qazvin he banked southeast following the Tehran road, once more retreating into himself. Be patient, he told himself, then saw Rakoczy tense and put his face closer to the window, looking downward.

'Bank left . . . a little left,' Rakoczy ordered urgently, his concentration totally on the ground. Pettikin put the chopper into a gentle bank – Rakoczy on the low side. 'No more! Make a one eighty.'

'What is it?' Pettikin asked. He steepened the bank, suddenly aware the man had forgotten the machine gun in his lap. His heart picked up a beat.

'There, below on the road. That truck.'

Pettikin paid no attention to the ground below. He kept his eyes on the gun, gauging the distance carefully, his heart racing. 'Where? I can't see anything.' He steepened the bank even more to come around quickly on to the new heading. 'What truck? You mean . . .'

His left hand darted out and grabbed the gun by the barrel and awkwardly jerked it through the sliding window into the cabin behind them. At the same time his right hand on the stick went harder left, then quickly right and left-right again, rocking the chopper viciously. Rakoczy was taken completely unaware and his head slammed against the side, momentarily stunning him. At once Pettikin clenched his left fist and inexpertly slashed at the man's jaw to put him unconscious. But Rakoczy, karate-trained, his reflexes good, managed to stop the blow with his forearm. Groggily he held on to Pettikin's wrist, gaining strength every second as the two men fought for supremacy, the chopper dangerously heeled over, Rakoczy still on the downside. They grappled with each other, cursing, seat belts inhibiting them. Both became more frenzied, Rakoczy with two hands free beginning to dominate.

Abruptly Pettikin gripped the stick with his knees, took his right hand off it, and smashed again at Rakoczy's face. The blow was not quite true but the strength of it shifted him off balance, destroyed the grip of his knees shoving the stick left and overrode the delicate balance of his feet on the rudder pedals. At once the chopper reeled on to its side, lost all lift – no chopper can fly itself even for a second – the centrifugal force further throwing his weight askew and in the mêlée the collective lever was shoved down. The chopper fell out of the sky, out of control.

In panic, Pettikin abandoned the fight. Blindly he struggled to regain control, engines screaming and instruments gone mad. Hands and feet and training against panic, overcorrecting, then overcorrecting again. They dropped nine hundred feet before he got her straight and level, his heart unbearable, the snow-covered ground fifty feet below.

His hands were trembling. It was difficult to breathe. Then he felt something hard shoved in his side and heard Rakoczy cursing. Dully he realised the language was not Iranian but did not recognise it. He looked across at him and saw the face twisted with anger and the grey metal of the automatic and cursed himself for not thinking of that. Angrily he tried to shove the gun away but Rakoczy stuck it hard into the side of his neck.

'Stop or I'll blow your head off, you *matyeryebyets!*'

At once Pettikin put the plane into a violent bank, but the gun pressed harder, hurting him. He felt the safety catch go off and the gun cock.

'Your last chance!'

The ground was very near, rushing past sickeningly. Pettikin knew he could not shake him off. 'All right – all right,' he said, conceding, and straightened her and began to climb. The pressure from the gun increased and with it, the pain. 'You're hurting me for God's sake and shoving me off balance! How can I fly if y –'

Rakoczy just jabbed the gun harder, shouting at him, cursing him, jamming his head against the door frame.

'For Christ's sake!' Pettikin shouted back in desperation, trying to adjust his headset that had been torn off in the struggle. 'How the hell can I fly with your gun in my neck?' The pressure eased off a fraction and he righted the plane. 'Who the hell are you, anyway?'

'Smith!' Rakoczy was equally unnerved. A split second later, he thought, and we would have been splattered like a pat of fresh cow dung. 'You think you deal with a *matyeryebyets* amateur?' Before he could stop himself his reflexes took his hand and backhanded Pettikin across the mouth.

Pettikin was rocked by the blow, and the chopper twisted but came back into control. He felt the burn spreading over his face. 'You do that again and I'll put her on her back,' he said with a great finality.

'I agree,' Rakoczy said at once. 'I apologise for . . . for that . . . for that stupidity, Captain.' Carefully he eased back against his door but kept the gun cocked and pointed. 'Yes, there was no need. I'm sorry.'

Pettikin stared at him blankly. 'You're sorry?'

'Yes. Please excuse me. It was unnecessary. I am not a barbarian.' Rakoczy gathered himself. 'If you give me your word you'll stop trying to attack me, I'll put my gun away. I swear you're in no danger.'

Pettikin thought a moment. 'All right,' he said. 'If you tell me who you are and what you are.'

'Your word?'

'Yes.'

'Very well, I accept your word, Captain.' Rakoczy put the safety on and the gun in his far pocket: 'My name is Ali bin Hassan Karakose and I'm a Kurd. My home – my village – is on the slopes of Mount Ararat on the Iranian-Soviet border. Through the Blessings of God I'm a Freedom Fighter against the Shah, and anyone else who wishes to enslave us. Does that satisfy you?'

'Yes–yes it does. Then if y –'

'Please, later. First go there – quickly.' Rakoczy pointed below. 'Level off and go closer.'

They were at 800 feet to the right of the Qazvin-Tehran road. A village straddled the road a mile back and he could see the smoke whirled away by a stiff breeze. 'Where?'

'There, beside the road.'

At first Pettikin could not see what the man pointed at – his mind jumbled with questions about the Kurds and their historic centuries of wars against the Persian shahs. Then he saw the collection of cars and trucks pulled up to one side, and men surrounding a modern truck with a blue cross on a rectangular white background on the roof, other traffic grinding past slowly. 'You mean there? You want to go over those trucks and cars?' he asked, his face still smarting and his neck aching. 'The bunch of trucks near the one with the blue cross on its roof?'

'Yes.'

Obediently Pettikin went into a descending bank. 'What's so important about them, eh?' he asked, then glanced up. He saw the man staring at him suspiciously. 'What? What the hell's the matter now?'

'You really don't know what a blue cross on a white background signifies?'

'No. What about it? What is it?' Pettikin had his eyes on the truck that was much closer now, close enough to see it was a red Range Rover, an angry crowd surrounding it, one of the men smashing at the back windows with the butt of a rifle. 'It's the flag of Finland' came through his earphones and Erikki leaped into Pettikin's mind. 'Erikki had a Range Rover,' he burst out and saw the rifle butt shatter the window. 'You think that's Erikki?'

'Yes . . . yes it's possible.'

At once he went faster and lower, his pain forgotten, his excitement overriding all the sudden questions of how and why this Freedom Fighter knew Erikki. Now they could see the crowd turning towards them and people scattering. His pass was very fast and very low but he did not see Erikki. 'You see him?'

'No. I couldn't see inside the cab.'

'Nor could I,' Pettikin said anxiously, 'but a few of those buggers are armed and they were smashing the windows. You see them?'

'Yes. They must be fedayeen. One of them fired at us. If you . . .' Rakoczy stopped, hanging on tightly as the chopper skidded into a 180-degree turn, twenty feet off the ground, and hurtled back again. This time the crowd of men and the few women fled, falling over one another. Traffic in both directions tried to speed away or shuddered to a halt, one overloaded truck skidding into another. Several cars and trucks turned off the road and one almost overturned in the joub.

Just abreast of the Range Rover, Pettikin swung into a sliding 90-degree turn to face it – snow boiling into a cloud – for just enough time to recognise Erikki, then into another 90 degrees to barrel away into the sky. 'It's him all right. Did you see the bullet holes in the windscreen?' he asked, shocked. 'Reach in the back for the machine gun. I'll steady her and then we'll go and get him. Hurry, I want to keep them off balance.'

At once Rakoczy unbuckled his seat belt, reached back through the small intercommunicating window but could not get the gun that lay on the floor. With great difficulty he twisted out of his seat and clambered head first, half through the window, groping for it, and Pettikin knew

255

the man was at his mercy. So easy to open the door now and shove him out. So easy. But impossible.

'Come on!' he shouted and helped pull him back into the seat. 'Put your belt on!'

Rakoczy obeyed, trying to catch his breath, blessing his luck that Pettikin was a friend of the Finn, knowing that if their positions had been reversed he would not have hesitated to open the door. 'I'm ready,' he said, cocking the gun, appalled at Pettikin's stupidity. The British are so stupid the mother-eating bastards deserve to lose. 'Wh –'

'Here we go!' Pettikin spun the chopper into a diving turn at maximum speed. Some armed men were still near the truck, guns pointing at them. 'I'll soften them up and when I say "fire" put a burst over their heads!'

The Range Rover rushed up at them, hesitated, then swirled away drunkenly – no trees nearby – hesitated again and came at them as the chopper danced around it. Pettikin flared to a sudden stop twenty yards away, ten feet off the ground. 'Fire,' he ordered.

At once Rakoczy let off a burst through the open window, aiming not over heads but at a group of men and women ducked down behind the back end of Erikki's truck, out of Pettikin's line of sight, killing or wounding some of them. Everyone nearby fled panic-stricken – screams of the wounded mingling with the howl of the jets. Drivers and passengers jumped out of cars and trucks, scrambling away in the snowdrifts as best they could. Another burst and more panic, now everyone rushing in retreat, all traffic snarled. On the road some youths came from behind a truck with rifles. Rakoczy sprayed them and those nearby. 'Make a three-sixty!' he shouted.

Immediately the helicopter pirouetted but no one was near. Pettikin saw four bodies in the snow. 'I said over their heads, for God's sake,' he began, but at that moment the door of the Range Rover swung open and Erikki jumped out, his knife in one hand. For a moment he was alone, then a chador-clad woman was beside him. At once Pettikin set the chopper down on the snow but kept her almost airborne. 'Come on,' he shouted, beckoning them. They began to run, Erikki half carrying Azadeh whom Pettikin did not yet recognise.

Beside him Rakoczy unlocked his side door and leaped out, opened the back door and whirled on guard. Another short burst towards the traffic. Erikki stopped, appalled to see Rakoczy. 'Hurry!' Pettikin shouted, not understanding the reason for Erikki's hesitation. 'Erikki, come on!' Then he recognised Azadeh. 'My God . . .' he muttered, then shouted, 'Come on, Erikki!'

256

'Quick, I've not much ammunition left!' Rakoczy shouted in Russian.

Erikki whirled Azadeh up into his arms and ran forward. A few bullets hummed past. At the side of the helicopter Rakoczy helped bundle Azadeh into the back, suddenly shoved Erikki aside with the barrel of the gun. 'Drop your knife and get in the front seat!' he ordered in Russian. 'At once.'

Half paralysed with shock, Pettikin watched Erikki hesitate, his face mottled with rage.

Rakoczy said harshly, 'By God, there's more than enough ammunition for her, you, and this mother-fucking pilot. Get in!'

Somewhere in the traffic a machine gun started to fire. Erikki dropped his knife in the snow, eased his great height into the front seat, Rakoczy slid beside Azadeh and Pettikin took off and sped away, weaving over the ground like a panicked grouse, then climbed into the sky.

When he could talk he said, 'What the hell's going on?'

Erikki did not answer. He craned around to make sure Azadeh was all right. She had her eyes closed and was slumped against the side, panting, trying to get her breath. He saw that Rakoczy had locked her seat belt, but when Erikki reached back to touch her the Soviet motioned him to stop with the gun.

'She will be all right, I promise you.' He continued speaking in Russian, 'providing you behave as your friend has been taught to behave.' He kept his eyes on him as he reached into his small bag and brought out a fresh magazine. 'Just so you know. Now face forward, please.'

Trying to contain his fury, Erikki did as he was told. He put on the headset. There was no way they could be overheard by Rakoczy – there was no intercom in the back – and it felt strange for both of them to be so free and yet so imprisoned. 'How did you find us, Charlie, who sent you?' he said into the mouth mike, his voice heavy.

'No one did,' Pettikin said. 'What the hell's with that bastard? I went to Tabriz to pick up you and Azadeh, got kidnapped by the son of a bitch in the back, and then he hijacked me to Tehran. It was just luck for Christ's sake – what the hell happened to you?'

'We ran out of fuel.' Erikki told him briefly what had happened. 'When the engine stopped, I knew I was finished. Everyone seems to have gone mad. One moment it was all right, then we were surrounded again, just like at the roadblock. I locked all the doors but it was only a matter of time . . .' Again he craned around. Azadeh had her eyes open and had pulled the chador off her face. She smiled at him wearily, reached forward to touch him but Rakoczy stopped her. 'Please excuse me, Highness,' he said in Farsi, 'but wait till we land. You will be all right.' He repeated it in Russian, adding to Erikki, 'I have some water with me. Would you like me to give it to your wife?'

Erikki nodded. 'Yes. Please.' He watched while she sipped gratefully. 'Thank you.'

'Do you want some?'

'No thank you,' he said politely even though he was parched, not wishing any favours for himself. He smiled at her encouragingly. 'Azadeh, like manna from heaven, eh? Charlie like an angel!'

'Yes . . . yes. It was the Will of God. I'm fine, fine now, Erikki, praised be to God. Thank Charlie for me . . .'

He hid his concern. The second mob had petrified her. And him, and he had sworn that if he ever got out of this mess alive, never again would he travel without a gun and, preferably, hand grenades. He saw Rakoczy watching him. He nodded and turned back again. '*Matyeryebyets*,' he muttered, automatically checking the instruments.

'That bugger's a lunatic – no need to kill anyone, I told him to fire over their heads.' Pettikin dropped his voice slightly, uneasy at talking so openly even though there was no way Rakoczy could hear. 'The bastard damn near killed me a couple of times. How do you know him, Erikki? Were you or Azadeh mixed up with the Kurds?'

Erikki stared at him. 'Kurds? You mean the *matyeryebyets* back there?'

'Yes, him of course – Ali bin Hassan Karakose. He comes from Mount Ararat. He's a Kurd Freedom Fighter.'

'He's not a Kurd but a turd, Soviet and KGB!'

'Christ Almighty! You're sure?' Pettikin was openly shocked.

'Oh yes. He claims he's Muslim but I bet that's a lie too. "Rakoczy" he called himself to me, another lie. They're all liars – at least why should they tell us, the enemy, anything?'

'But he swore it was the truth and I gave him my word.' Angrily Pettikin told him about the fight and the bargain he had made.

'You're a fool, Charlie, not him – haven't you read Lenin? Stalin? Marx? He's only doing what all KGB and committed communists do: use anything and everything to forward the "sacred" Cause – absolute world power for the USSR Communist party – and get us to hang ourselves to save them the trouble. My God, I could use a vodka!'

'A double brandy'd be better.'

'Both together would be even better.' Erikki studied the ground

258

below. They were cruising easily, the engines sounding good and plenty of fuel. His eyes searched the horizon for Tehran. 'Not long now. Has he said where to land yet?'

'No.'

'Perhaps we'll get a chance then.'

'Yes.' Pettikin's apprehension increased. 'You mentioned a roadblock. What happened there?'

Erikki's face hardened. 'We got stopped. Leftists. Had to make a run for it. We've no papers left, Azadeh and I. Nothing. A fat bastard at the roadblock kept everything and there wasn't time to get them back.' A tremor went through him. 'I've never been so scared, Charlie. Never. I was helpless in that mob and almost shitting with fear because I couldn't protect her. That stinking fat bastard took everything, passport, ID, flying licences, everything.'

'Mac'll get you more, your embassy'll give you passports.'

'I'm not worried about me. What about Azadeh?'

'She'll get a Finnish passport too. Like Sharazad'll get a Canadian one – no need to worry.'

'She's still in Tehran, isn't she?'

'Sure. Tom should be there too. He was due in from Zagros yesterday with mail from home . . .' Strange, Pettikin thought in passing. I still call England home even with Claire gone, everything gone. 'He's just back off leave.'

'That's what I'd like to do, go on leave. I'm overdue. Perhaps Mac can send a replacement.' Erikki punched Pettikin lightly. 'Tomorrow can take care of tomorrow, eh? Hey, Charlie, that was a great piece of flying. When I first saw you, I thought I was dreaming or already dead. You saw my Finnish flag?'

'No, that was Ali – what did you call him? Rekowsky?'

'Rakoczy.'

'Rakoczy recognised it. If he hadn't I wouldn't have been any the wiser. Sorry.' Pettikin glanced across. 'What's he want with you?'

'I don't know but whatever it is, it's for Soviet purposes.' Erikki cursed for a moment. 'So we owe our lives to him too?'

After a moment Pettikin said, 'Yes. Yes, I couldn't have done it alone.' He glanced around. Rakoczy was totally alert, Azadeh dozing, shadows over her lovely face. He nodded briefly, then turned back. 'Azadeh seems okay.'

'No, Charlie, no, she's not,' Erikki said, an ache inside him. 'Today was terrible for her. She said she'd never been that close to villagers ever . . . I mean surrounded, bottled in. Today they got under her guard.

259

Now she's seen the real face of Iran, the reality of her people – that and the forcing of the chador.' Again a shiver went through him. 'That was a rape – they raped her soul. Now I think everything will be different for her, for us. I think she'll have to choose: family or me, Iran or exile. They don't want us here. It's time for us to leave, Charlie. All of us.'

'No, you're wrong. Perhaps for you and Azadeh it's different but they'll still need oil so they'll still need choppers. We're good for a few more years, good years. With the Guerney contracts and all the—' Pettikin stopped, feeling a tap on his shoulder, and he glanced around. Azadeh awake now. He could not hear what Rakoczy said so he slipped one earphone off. 'What?'

'Don't use the radio, Captain, and be prepared to land on the outskirts where I'll tell you.'

'I . . . I'll have to get clearance.'

'Don't be a fool! Clearance from whom? Everyone's too busy down there. Tehran Airport's under siege – so is Doshan Tappeh and so's Galeg Morghi. Take my advice and make your landfall the small airport of Rudrama after you've dropped me.'

'I have to report in. The military insist.'

Rakoczy laughed sardonically. 'Military? And what would you report? That you landed illegally near Qazvin, helped murder five or six civilians, and picked up two foreigners fleeing – fleeing from whom? From the People!'

Grimly Pettikin turned back to make the call but Rakoczy leaned forward and shook him roughly. 'Wake up! The military doesn't exist any more. The generals have conceded victory to Khomeini! The military doesn't exist any more – they've given in!'

They all stared at him blankly. The chopper lurched. Hastily Pettikin corrected. 'What're you talking about?'

'Late last night the generals ordered all troops back to their barracks. All services – all men. They've left the field to Khomeini and his revolution. Now there's no army, no police, no gendarmes between Khomeini and total power – the People have conquered!'

'That's not possible,' Pettikin said.

'No,' Azadeh said, frightened. 'My father would have known.'

'Ah, Abdollah the Great?' Rakoczy said with a sneer. 'He'll know by now – if he's still alive.'

'It's not true!'

'It's . . . it's possible, Azadeh,' Erikki said, shocked. 'That'd explain why we saw no police or troops – why the mob was so hostile!'

'The generals'd never do that,' she said shakily, then turned on

Rakoczy. 'It would be suicide, for them and thousands. Tell the truth, by Allah!'

Rakoczy's face mirrored his glee, delighted to twist words and sow dissension to unsettle them. 'Now Iran's in the hands of Khomeini, his mullahs, and his revolutionary guards.'

'It's a lie.'

Pettikin said, 'If that's true Bakhtiar's finished. He'll nev—'

'That weak fool never even began!' Rakoczy started laughing. 'Ayatollah Khomeini has frightened the balls of the generals and now he'll cut their throats for good measure!'

'Then the war's over.'

'Ah, the war,' Rakoczy said darkly. 'It is. For some.'

'Yes,' Erikki said, baiting him. 'And if what you say is true, it's all over for you too – all the Tudeh and all Marxists. Khomeini will slaughter you all.'

'Oh, no, Captain. The Ayatollah was the sword to destroy the Shah, but the People wielded the sword.'

'He and his mullahs and the People will destroy you – he's as anti-communist as he is anti-American.'

'Better you wait and see and not further delude yourselves, eh? Khomeini's a practical man and exults in power, whatever he says now.'

Pettikin saw Azadeh whiten and he felt an equal chill. 'And the Kurds?' he asked roughly. 'What about them?'

Rakoczy leaned forward, his smile strange. 'I am a Kurd whatever the Finn told you about Soviet and KGB. Can he prove what he says? Of course not. As to the Kurds, Khomeini will try to stamp us out – if he's allowed to – with all tribal or religious minorities, and foreigners and the bourgeoisie, landowners, moneylenders, Shah supporters, and,' he added with a sneer, 'and any and all people who will not accept his interpretation of the Koran – and he'll spill rivers of blood in the name of *his* Allah, *his*, not the real One God – if the bastard's allowed to.' He glanced out of the window below, checking his bearings, then added even more sardonically, 'This heretic Sword of God has served his purpose and now he's going to be turned into a ploughshare – and buried!'

'You mean murdered?' Erikki said.

'Buried' – again the laugh – 'at the whim of the People.'

Azadeh came to life and tried to claw his face, cursing him. He caught her easily and held her while she struggled. Erikki watched, grey-faced. There was nothing he could do. For the moment.

261

'Stop it!' Rakoczy said harshly. 'You of all people should want this heretic gone – he'll stamp out Abdollah Khan and all the Gorgons and you with them if he wins.' He shoved her away. 'Behave, or I shall have to hurt you. It's true, you of all people should want him dead.' He cocked the machine gun. 'Turn around, both of you.'

They obeyed, hating the man and the gun. Ahead, the outskirts of Tehran were about ten miles away. They were paralleling the road and railway, the Elburz Mountains to their left, approaching the city from the west. Overhead the sky was overcast, the clouds heavy, and no sun showed through.

'Captain, you see the stream where the railway crosses it? The bridge?'

'Yes, I can see that,' Pettikin said, trying to make a plan to overcome him, as Erikki was also planning – wondering if he could whirl and grab him but he was on the wrong side.

'Land half a mile south, behind that outcrop. You see it?'

Not far from this outcrop was a secondary road that headed for Tehran. A little traffic. 'Yes. And then?'

'And then you're dismissed. For the moment.' Rakoczy laughed and nudged the back of Pettikin's neck with the barrel of the gun. 'With my thanks. But don't turn around any more. Stay facing ahead, both of you, and keep your seat belts locked and know that I'm watching you both very closely. When you land, land firmly and cleanly and when I'm clear, take off. But don't turn around or I may become frightened. Frightened men pull triggers. Understand?'

'Yes.' Pettikin studied the landing site. He adjusted his headset. 'It look all right to you, Erikki?'

'Yes. Watch the snow dunes.' Erikki tried to keep the nervousness out of his voice.

'We should have a plan.'

'I think he's . . . he's too clever, Charlie.'

'Maybe he'll make a mistake.'

'I only need one.'

The landing was clean and simple. Snow, whipped up by the idling blades, billowed alongside the windows. 'Don't turn around!'

Both men's nerves were jagged. They heard the door open and felt the cold air. Then Azadeh screamed, 'Erikkiiii!'

In spite of the order both craned around. Rakoczy was already out, dragging Azadeh after him, kicking and struggling and trying to hang on to the door, but he overpowered her easily. The gun was slung over his shoulder. Instantly Erikki jerked his door open and darted out, slid under the fuselage, and charged. But he was too late. A short burst at his feet stopped him. Ten yards away, clear of the rotors, Rakoczy had the gun levelled at them with one hand, the other firm in the neck of her chador. For a moment she was equally still, then she redoubled her efforts, shouting and screaming, flailing at him, catching him unawares. Erikki charged.

Rakoczy grabbed her with both hands, shoved her violently at Erikki, breaking the charge and bringing Erikki down with her. At the same moment he leapt backward, turned, and raced away, whirled again, the gun ready, his finger tightening on the trigger. But there was no need to pull it, the Finn and the woman were still on their knees, half stunned. Beyond them the pilot was still in his seat. Then he saw Erikki come to his senses, and shove her behind him protectively, readying another charge.

'Stop!' he ordered, 'or this time I will kill you all. STOP!' He put a warning burst into the snow. 'Get back in the plane – both of you!' Now totally alert, Erikki watched him suspiciously. 'Go on – you're free. Go!'

Desperately afraid, Azadeh scrambled into the backseat. Erikki retreated slowly, his body shielding her. Rakoczy kept the gun unwavering. He saw the Finn sit on the backseat, the door still open, his feet propped against skid. At once the engines picked up speed. The chopper eased a foot off the ground, slowly swung around to face him, the back door closing. His heart pounded even more. Now, he thought, do you all die or do we live to fight another day?

The moment seemed to him to last for ever. The chopper backed away, foot by foot, still so tempting a target. His finger tightened slightly. But he did not squeeze the further fraction. A few more yards then she twisted, hurried away through the snowfields, and went into the sky.

Good, he thought, tiredness almost overcoming him. It would have been better to have been able to keep the woman as a hostage, but never mind. We can grab old Abdollah Khan's daughter tomorrow, or the day after. She can wait and so can Yokkonen. Meanwhile there's a country to possess, generals and mullahs and ayatollahs to kill . . . and other enemies.

At Tehran Airport: 5:05 P.M. McIver was driving carefully along the road that followed the barbed-wire security fence, heading for the gate that led to the freight area. The road was snow-banked, slippery and unploughed. It was just below freezing, the sky heavy and dull, night not more than an hour away. Again he looked at his watch. Not much time, he thought, still seething over the closure of his office last night by the komiteh. Early this morning he had tried to sneak back into the building, but it was still guarded and all of his entreaties to be allowed to check the telex had proved fruitless.

'Damned people!' Genny had said when he had stomped back into their apartment. 'There must be something we can do. What about George Talbot? Could he help?'

'I doubt it, but it's worth a try – if Valik was . . .' McIver stopped. 'Tom would have refuelled by now and be almost there – wherever there is.'

'Let's hope,' she said with a silent prayer, 'hope for the best. Did you see any shops open?'

264

'None, Gen. It's tinned soup for lunch and a bottle of beer.'

'Sorry, we're out of beer.'

He had tried to call Kowiss and the other bases on his HF but could get no answer from them. Neither could he tune into the BBC or AFN. He had listened briefly to the inevitable anti-American tirade from Radio Free Iran in Tabriz and had turned it off in disgust. The phone was dead. He had tried to read, but he could not, his mind beset with worries about Lochart, Pettikin, Starke, and all the others, hating being cut off from his office and telex and, for the moment, out of control. Never happened before, never. Damn the Shah for leaving and letting everything fall apart. Used to be wonderful. Any problem and out to the airport, get on a shuttle to Isfahan, Tabriz, Abadan, Hormuz, Al Shargaz, or wherever, then chopper the rest of the way, wherever you felt like it. Sometimes Genny coming along for the ride – picnic lunches and ice cold beer.

'Sod everything!'

Just after lunch the HF had crackled into life. It was Freddy Ayre at Kowiss relaying a message that the 125 jet would be at Tehran Airport around 5.00 p.m. today, coming from Al Shargaz, a tiny independent sheikdom 800 miles south of Tehran on the other side of the Gulf where S-G had an office.

'Did he say he had clearance, Freddy?' McIver had asked excitedly.

'I don't know. All our HQ in Al Shargaz said was: "ETA Tehran seventeen hundred, tell McIver – can't raise him" repeated several times.'

'How're things with you?'

'Five by five,' Ayre had said. 'Starke's still at Bandar-e Delam and we've had no contact with them other than a snafu half an hour ago.'

'Rudi sent that?' McIver had tried to keep his voice level.

'Yes.'

'Keep in touch with them and with us. What happened to your radio op this morning? I tried calling for a couple of hours but no joy.'

There had been a long pause. 'He's been detained.'

'What the hell for?'

'I don't know, Mac – Captain McIver. As soon as I know I'll report it. Also, as soon as I can I'll get Marc Dubois back to Bandar-e Delam, but, well it's a bit off here. We've all been confined to base, there's . . . there's a charming and friendly armed guard here in the tower, all flights are grounded except for CASEVACs and even then we've been ordered to take guards along – and no flights're authorised out of our area.'

'What's it all about?'

'I don't know. Our revered base commander, Colonel Peshadi, assured me it was temporary, just for today, perhaps tomorrow. By the way, at 1516 hours we had a brief call from Captain Scragger in Charlie Echo Zulu Zulu en route with a special charter for Bandar-e Delam.'

'What the hell's he going there for?'

'I don't know, sir. Old Scr – Captain Scragger said it'd been requested by de Plessey at Siri. I, er, I don't think I've much more time. Our friendly guard's getting nervous but if you can get the 125 here Peshadi said he'd clear her to land. I'll try to send Manuela off but don't expect much, she's as nervous as a rabbit in a kennel full of beagles without real news of Starke.'

'I can imagine. Tell her I'm sending Gen. I'll sign off now, God knows how long it'll take me to get to the airport.' He had turned his attention to Genny. 'Gen, pack a b –'

'What do you want to take with you, Duncan?' she had asked sweetly.

'I'm not going, you are!'

'Don't be silly, dear. If you're going to meet the 125 you'd better hurry, but do be careful and don't forget the photos! Oh, by the way, I forgot to tell you that while you were trying to get into your office, Sharazad sent one of her servants over asking us to dinner.'

'Gen, you are leaving with the 125 and that's that!'

The argument had lasted no time at all. He had left and had used back roads, most of the main intersections clogged with milling crowds. Every time he was stopped he would hold up the Khomeini photograph with LONG LIVE THE AYATOLLAH in Farsi on the bottom and he would be waved through. He saw no troops, gendarmes, or police so he did not need the photo of the Shah with LONG LIVE GLORIOUS IRAN on the bottom. It still took two and a half hours for a journey that would normally take an hour, his anxiety about being late growing minute by minute.

But the 125 wasn't on either of the parallel runways, or the freight area apron, or near the terminal building across the field. Again he glanced at his watch: 5.17. Another hour of light. She's cutting it fine, he told himself, if she arrives at all. God knows, they may have already turned her back.

Near the terminal building several civilian jets were still grounded. One of them, a Royal Iranian Air 747, was a twisted wreck, gutted by fire. The others seemed all right – he was too far away to see all their markings but among them would be the still grounded Alitalia flight. Paula Giancani was still staying with them, Nogger Lane very much in attendance. She's a nice girl that one, he thought absently.

Ahead now was the gate of the freight area and depot. The depot had been closed since last Wednesday – automatically on Thursday and Friday (the Muslim Holy Day) being the Iranian weekend – and there had been no way he or any of his staff could have got there Saturday or Sunday. The gate was open and unguarded. He swung through it into the forecourt. In front of him was the customs freight shed and barriers, signs everywhere in English and Farsi. NO ADMITTANCE, INBOUND, OUTBOUND, KEEP OUT, and company signs of the various international carriers and helicopter companies that had permanent offices here. Normally it was almost impossible to drive into the forecourt. There was work around the clock for half a thousand men, handling the enormous quantity of goods, military and civilian, that poured into Iran in exchange for part of the ninety million dollars' daily oil revenue. But now the area was deserted. Hundreds of crates and cartons of all sizes were scattered in the snow – many broken open and looted, most sodden. A few abandoned cars and trucks, some derelict, and one truck burned out. Bullet holes in the sheds.

The customs gate that barred the way to the apron was closed, held only by a bolt. The sign, in English and Farsi, read: 'No entry without Customs approval.' He waited, then honked and waited again. No one answered him so he got out, opened the gate wide, and got back into his car. A few yards the other side he stopped, rebolted the gate, then drove down the tarmac to the S-G stores and office shed and allied hangars and repair shop with space for four 212s and five 206s, now containing three 206s and one 212.

To his relief the main doors were still closed and locked. He had been afraid the stores and hangar might have been broken into and looted or wrecked. This was their main depot for repairs and spares in Iran. Over two million dollars' worth of spares and specialised tools were on the inventory, along with their own refuelling pumps and underground tanks containing a highly secret cache of 50,000 gallons of helicopter fuel that McIver had 'lost' when the troubles began in earnest.

He scanned the sky. The wind told him the 125 would land from the west on runway 29 Left but there was no sign of it. He unlocked the door, closed it after him, and hurried through the chilly foyer to the main office to the telex. It was switched off. 'Bloody idiots,' he muttered out loud. Standing orders were for it to be on at all times. When he turned it on, nothing happened. He tried the lights but they didn't work either. 'Bloody country.' Irritably he went over to the HF and UHF receiver-transmitters and switched them on. Both were battery-operated for emergencies. Their hum comforted him.

'EchoTangoLimaLima,' he said crisply into the mike, giving the 125's registration letters: ETLL. 'This is McIver, do you read?'

'EchoTangoLimaLima – we certainly do, old boy,' the laconic answer came back at once. 'It's rather lonely up here – we've been calling for half an hour. Where are you?'

'At the freight office. Sorry, Johnny,' he said, recognising the voice of their senior fixed-wing captain. 'Had a hell of a time getting here – I've just arrived. Where are you?'

'Seventeen miles due south – in the soup – passing through nine thousand on standard approach, expecting final on runway 29 Left. What's going on, Mac? We can't raise Tehran tower – in fact we haven't had a single callback ever since we came into Iran airspace.'

'Good God! Not even from Kish radar?'

'Not even from them, old boy. What's amiss?'

'I don't know. The tower was operating yesterday – up to midnight last night. The military gave us a clearance for a flight south.' McIver was astonished, knowing Kish radar was punctilious about all traffic inbound or outbound, particularly trans-Gulf. 'The whole airfield's deserted which is pretty hairy. Coming here there were crowds all over town, a few roadblocks, but nothing out of the ordinary, no riots or anything.'

'Any problem for a landing?'

'I doubt if any landing aids are functional but cloud cover is about four thousand, visibility ten miles. Runway looks all right.'

'What do you think?'

McIver weighed the pros and cons of a landing – without tower assistance or approval. 'You've enough fuel for the return trip?'

'Oh, yes. You've a no-fuel capability?'

'Unless an emergency – for the moment.'

'I'm through the cloud cover at forty-seven hundred and have you in sight.'

'Okay, EchoTangoLimaLima. Wind's from the east at about ten knots. Normally you'd land on 29 Left. The military base seems closed down and deserted so there should be no other traffic – all civilian flights in and outbound have been cancelled. Suggest you make a pass and if it looks okay to you, come straight in – don't hang around in the sky, they're too many trigger-happy jokers about. Once you've landed, turn around for a quick takeoff just in case. I'll drive out to meet you.'

'EchoTangoLimaLima.'

McIver took out a handkerchief and wiped his hands and forehead. But when he got up, his heart seemed to turn in his chest.

Standing in the open doorway was a customs officer, his hand casually on his holstered gun. His uniform was soiled and crumpled, his roundish face grizzled with three or four days' growth of beard.

'Oh,' McIver said, fighting to appear calm. 'Salaam, agha.' Greetings, Excellency. He did not recognise him as one of their regulars.

The man shifted his gun hand ominously, his eyes going from McIver to the radio sets and back to McIver.

Haltingly, for McIver spoke very little Farsi, he said, '*Inglissi me danid agha? Be-bahk-shid man zaban-e shoma ra khoob nami-danan.*' Do you speak English, sir? Please excuse me but I don't speak your language.

The customs officer grunted. 'What you do here?' he said in halting English, his teeth tobacco-stained.

'I'm . . . I'm Captain McIver, head of S-G Helicopters,' he replied, carefully and slowly. 'I'm just . . . just checking my telex and here to meet an incoming plane.'

'Plane – what plane? Wh –'

At that moment the 125 came directly over the airport at one thousand feet. The customs man hurried out of the office on to the tarmac, closely followed by McIver. They saw the lovely clean lines of the twin-engined jet against the murky overcast and watched a moment as she hurtled away to go into a steep bank to join the landing pattern.

'What plane? Eh?'

'It's our regular flight – regular flight from Al Shargaz.'

The name sent the man into a paroxysm of invective.

'*Be bahk shid nana dhan konan.*' Sorry, I don't understand.

'No land . . . no land, understand?' The man angrily pointed from the plane to the office with the HF. 'Tell plane!'

McIver nodded calmly, not feeling calm, and beckoned him back into the office. He counted out ten thousand rials, about $110, and offered it. 'Please accept the landing fee – landing money.'

The man spurned it with more unintelligible Farsi. McIver put the money on the table, then walked past the man into the storeroom. He unlocked a door. In the small room, put there for just this purpose, were odd and ends of spares, and three full five-gallon cans of petrol. He picked up one can and put it outside the door, remembering what General Valik had said: a pishkesh was not a bribe but a gift and a good Iranian custom. After a second, McIver decided to leave the door but

269

left it open – three cans would more than guarantee no problem. '*Be bahk shid, agha.*' Please excuse me, sir. Then he added in English, 'I must meet my masters.'

He went out of the building and got into his car and did not look back. 'Bloody bastard, damn near gave me a heart attack!' he muttered, then put the man out of his mind, drove on to the taxi runway, and headed for the intercept point. The snow was only a few inches deep and not too bad. His were the only tracks, the main runways equally virgin. The wind had picked up, increasing the chill factor. He did not notice it, concentrating on the airplane.

The 125 came around in a tight turn, gear and flaps down, side-slipping deftly to lose height and cut down the approach distance. John Hogg flared and touched down, letting her roll until it was safe and even then using brakes with great caution. He turned on to the taxi runway and increased power to meet McIver. Near the first access path back to the runway, he stopped.

By the time McIver came alongside, the door was open, the steps down, John Hogg waiting at the foot, bundled in a parka, stamping his feet against the cold.

'Hi, Mac!' he called out – a neat, spare man with a lean face and moustache. 'Great to see you. Come on in – it'll be warmer for you.'

'Good idea.' McIver hastily switched off and followed him up the steps. Inside it was snug, lights on, coffee ready, London newspapers in the rack. McIver knew there would be wine and beer in the refrigerator, a sit-down toilet with soft paper in the back – civilisation again. He waved at the co-pilot. 'I'm so glad to see you, Johnny.' His mouth dropped open. Seated in one of the swivel chairs in the eight-place airplane, beaming at him, was Andy Gavallan.

'Hello, Mac!'

'My God! My God, Chinaboy, it's good to see you,' McIver said, pummelling his hand. 'What the hell are you doing – why didn't you tell me you were coming – what's the id –'

'Slow down, laddie. Coffee?'

'My God yes.' McIver sat opposite him. 'How's Maureen – and little Electra?'

'Great – wonderful! Her second birthday coming and already she's a holy terror! Thought we'd better have a chat so I got on the bird and here I am.'

'Can't tell you how glad I am. You're looking great,' McIver said. And he was. 'Thank you, laddie, you're not so bad yoursel'. How are you, really, Mac?' Gavallan asked more pointedly.

'Excellent.' Hogg put down the coffee in front of McIver. With a small tot of whisky and another for Gavallan. 'Ah, thanks, Johnny,' McIver said, brightening. 'Health!' He touched glasses with Gavallan and swallowed the spirit gratefully. 'I'm cold as charity. Just had a run-in with a bloody customs man! Why're you here? Any problem, Andy? Oh, but what about the 125? Both the revs and loyalists are all very twitchy – either of them could arrive in force and impound her.'

'Johnny Hogg's keeping an eye out for them. We'll talk about my problems in a minute but I decided that I'd better come and see for myself. We've too much at risk now, here and outside, with all our new, upcoming contracts and aircraft. The X63's a total smash, Mac, everything and better!'

'Great, wonderful. When do we get her?'

'Next year – more about her later. Iran's my top priority now. We have to have some contingency plans, how to keep in touch and so on. Yesterday I spent hours in Al Shargaz trying to get an Iranian clearance for Tehran but no joy on that. Even their embassy was closed; I went to their Al Mulla building myself but it was closed tighter than a gnat's arse. I got our rep to call the ambassador's home but he was out to lunch – all day. Eventually I went to Al Shargaz Air Traffic Control and chatted them up. They suggested we wait but I talked them into clearning us out and having a stab and here we are. First, what's the state of our ops?'

McIver related what he knew.

Much of Gavallan's good humour vanished. 'So Charlie's vanished, Tom Lochart's risking his neck and our whole Iranian venture – stupidly or bravely depending on your point of view – Duke Starke's up the creek in Bandar-e Delam with Rudi, Kowiss is in a state of siege, and we've been tossed out of our offices.'

'Yes.' McIver added gruffly, 'I authorised Tom's flight.'

'I'd've done the same, probably, if I'd been on the spot, though it doesn't excuse the danger to him, to us, or poor bloody Valik and his family. But I agree, SAVAK's too smelly for anyone's taste.' Gavallan was distinctly rattled though he showed none of it on his face. 'Ian was right again.'

'Ian? Dunross? You saw him? How is the old bugger?'

'He called from Shanghai.' Gavallan told him what he had said. 'What's the latest on the political situation here?'

'You should know more than we do – we only get real news through the BBC or VOA. There're still no newspapers and only rumours,' McIver said, but he was remembering the good times he had had with

Dunross in Hong Kong. He had taught him to fly a small chopper the year before joining Gavallan in Aberdeen, and though they had not socialised very much, McIver had enjoyed his company greatly. 'Bakhtiar's still top man with the forces behind him, but Bazargan and Khomeini're gnawing at his heels . . . Oh, damn, I forgot to tell you, Boss Kyabi's been murdered.'

'Christ Almighty, that's terrible. But why?'

'We don't know the why or how or by whom. Freddy Ayre told us obliqu –'

'Sorry to interrupt, sir,' came over the loudspeaker, a thread of urgency under Hogg's placid voice. 'There're three cars stuffed with men and guns heading our way, coming from the terminal area.'

Both men peered out of the small round windows. They could see the cars now. Gavallan picked up his binoculars and trained them. 'Five or six men in each car. There's a mullah in the front of the first car. Khomeini's people!' He slung the binoculars around his neck and was out of his seat quickly. 'Johnny!'

Hogg was already at the door. 'Yes, sir?'

'Plan B!' At once Hogg gave the thumbs-up and immediately started to open the throttles as Gavallan struggled into a parka and picked up a light travel bag on the run. 'Come on, Mac!' He led the way down the steps two at a time, McIver just behind him. The moment they were clear, the steps pulled back, the door slammed closed, the engines picked up, and the 125 taxied away, gathering speed. 'Put your back to the cars, Mac – don't watch them, watch her leave!'

It had all happened so rapidly McIver hardly had time to zip his parka. One of the cars peeled off to intercept but by now the 125 was careening down the runway. In seconds it took off and was away. Now they faced the oncoming cars.

'Now what, Andy?'

'That depends on the welcoming committee.'

'What the hell was Plan B?'

Gavallan laughed. 'Better than Plan C, laddie. That was a shit or bust. Plan B: I get out, Johnny takes off at once, and tells no one he had to leave in a hurry, tomorrow he comes back to pick me up at the same time; if there's no contact, visually or by radio, then Johnny skips a day and comes an hour earlier – and so on for four days. Then he sits on his tail in Al Shargaz and waits for further instructions.'

'Plan A?'

'That's if we could have safely stayed overnight – them on guard in the plane, me with you.'

272

The cars skidded to a stop, the mullah and Green Bands surrounding them, guns trained on them, everyone shouting. Suddenly Gavallan bellowed, 'Allah-u Akbar,' and everyone stopped, startled. With a flourish he lifted his hat to the mullah who was also armed, took out an official-looking document – written in Farsi – that was heavily sealed with red wax at the bottom. He handed it to him. 'It's permission to land in Tehran from the "new" ambassador in London,' he told McIver airily as men crowded around the mullah peering at the paper. 'I stopped off in London to collect it. It says I'm a VIP – on official business and I can arrive and leave without harm.'

'How the devil did you manage that?' McIver asked, admiringly.

'Influence, laddie. Influence and a large *heung yau*.' He carefully added the Cantonese equivalent of pishkesh.

'You will come with us,' a bearded youth near the mullah said, his accent American. 'You are under arrest!'

'For what, my dear sir?'

'Illegal landings without permiss –'

Gavallan stabbed at the paper. 'Here is an official permission from your very own ambassador in London! Up the revolution! Long live Ayatollah Khomeini!'

The youth hesitated, then translated for the mullah. There was an angry exchange and mutterings among them. 'You will together come with us!'

'We will follow in our car! Come on Mac,' Gavallan said firmly and got into the passenger seat. McIver turned on the ignition. For a moment the men were nonplussed, then the man who could speak English and another got into the back. Both carried an AK47.

'Go to terminal! You under arrest.'

In the terminal, near the immigration barrier, were more hostile men and a very nervous immigration official. At once McIver showed his airport pass, work permit, explained who he and Gavallan were and how they worked under licence for IranOil and tried to talk them past but he was imperiously waved into silence. Meticulously and ponderously the official examined the paper and Gavallan's passport – all the while the youths crowding them, the smell of bodies heavy. Then he opened Gavallan's bag and searched it roughly but it contained just shaving gear, a spare shirt, underclothes, and night clothes. And a fifth of whisky. At once the bottle was confiscated by one of the young men, opened, and poured on the floor.

'*Dew neh loh moh*,' Gavallan said sweetly in Cantonese, and McIver nearly choked. 'Up the revolution.'

The mullah questioned the official, and they could see the fear in him. At length the youth who could speak English said, 'The authorities will keep paper and passport and you explain more later.'

'I will keep my passport,' Gavallan said easily.

'The authorities keep. Enemies of the people will suffer. Those who break the laws – illegal landings and comings here – will suffer Islamic punishments. His Excellency wants to know who on the airplane with you?'

'Just my crew of two. They're on the manifest attached to the Permission to Land. Now, my passport please and that document.'

'The authorities keep. Where you stay?'

McIver gave his address.

The man translated. Again there was a heated discussion. 'I am to tell you: now your airplanes may not fly or landings without permissions first. All Iran airplanes – all airplanes now in Iran belong to the state an –'

'Airplanes belong to their legal owners. Legal owners,' McIver said.

'Yes,' the man said with a sneer, 'our Islamic state is owners. You not like laws, leave. Leave Iran. We not ask you here.'

'Ah, but you're wrong. We, in S-G Helicopters, were invited here. We work for your government and have served IranOil for years.'

The man spat on the floor. 'IranOil Shah company. Islamic state owns oil not foreigners. You soon arrested with all others for great crime: stealing Iran oil!'

'Rubbish! We've stolen nothing!' McIver said. 'We've helped Iran into the twentieth century! We've b –'

'Leave Iran if you want,' the spokesman said again, paying no attention to him. 'Now all orders come from Imam Khomeini, Allah protect him! He says no landings or takeoffs without permission. Each time, one Khomeini guard goes with each airplane. Understand?'

'We understand what you say,' Gavallan replied politely. 'May I ask that we have this in writing, as the Bakhtiar government may not agree.'

The man translated this and there was a roar of laughter. 'Bakhtiar is gone,' the man said through his own laughter. 'That dog of a Shah man is in hiding. Hiding, you understand? The Imam is the government! Him alone.'

'Yes, of course,' Gavallan said, not believing him. 'We can go, then?'

'Go. Tomorrow report the authorities.'

'Where – and what authorities?'

'Tehran authorities.' The man translated for the others and again everyone laughed. The mullah pocketed the passport and paper and strode off importantly. Guards went with him, taking along the sweating immigration officer. Most of the others wandered off, seemingly aimlessly. A few stayed watching them, lounging against the wall, smoking – their army rifles slung carelessly. It was very cold in the terminal. And very empty.

'He's quite right, you know,' a voice said. Gavallan and McIver looked around. It was George Talbot of the British embassy, a short dry man of fifty-five, wearing a heavy raincoat and a Russian style fur hat. He stood in the doorway of a customs office. Beside him was a tall, broad-shouldered man of sixty with hard, pale blue eyes, his moustache grey as his hair and clipped, and dressed casually, scarf, soft hat and an old raincoat. Both were smoking.

'Oh, hello, George, nice to see you,' Gavallan went over to him, offering his hand. He had known him over the years, both in Iran and Malaya – Talbot's previous posting – where S-G also had an extensive oil support operation. 'How long have you been here?'

'Just a few minutes.' Talbot stubbed out his cigarette, coughed absently. 'Hello, Duncan! Well, this is a fine kettle of fish, isn't it?'

'Yes. Yes, it is.' Gavallan glanced at the other man.

'Ah, may I introduce Mr. Armstrong?'

Gavallan shook hands. 'Hello,' he said, wondering where he'd seen him before and who he was – the hardness to the eyes and strong face. Fifty pounds to a bent button he's CIA if he's American, he thought. 'You're embassy too?' he asked casually to find out.

The man smiled and shook his head. 'No, sir,'

Gavallan had tuned his ears and did not detect a pure English or American accent. Might be either, or Canadian, he thought, difficult to tell on two words.

'You're here on official business, George?' McIver asked.

'Yes and no.' Talbot strolled over to the door that led back to the airport apron where McIver's car was parked, guiding them away from prying ears. 'Actually the moment we heard your incoming jet on the air, we, er, we hurried out here hoping you could take out some er, some dispatches for Her Majesty's Government. The ambassador would have been most grateful but, well, we were here just in time to see your plane take off. Pity!'

'I'd be glad to help in any way,' Gavallan said as quietly. 'Perhaps tomorrow?' He saw the sudden glance between the two men and wondered even more what was amiss.

'Is that possible, Mr. Gavallan?' Armstrong asked.

275

'It's possible.' Gavallan pegged him to be English, though not all English.

Talbot smiled, coughed without noticing it. 'You'll leave with or without Iranian permission, an official permit – or a passport?'

'I, er, do have a copy of the paper. And another passport – I applied for a spare, officially, against this eventuality.'

Talbot sighed. 'Irregular but wise. Yes. Oh, by the way, I would very much like a copy of your Official Permission to Land.'

'Perhaps that's not such a good idea – officially. You never know what larceny some people are up to these days.'

Talbot laughed. Then he said, 'If you, er, do leave tomorrow we would appreciate it if you'd kindly take Mr. Armstrong – I presume Al Shargaz will be your first port of call?'

Gavallan hesitated. 'This is a formal request?'

Talbot smiled. 'Formally informal.'

'With or without Iranian permission, permit or passport?'

Talbot chuckled. 'You're perfectly correct to ask. I guarantee that Mr. Armstrong's papers will be perfectly in order.' He added pointedly to finish the conversation, 'As you so correctly pointed out there's no accounting for the larceny some people will get up to these days.'

Gavallan nodded. 'Very well, Mr. Armstrong. I'll be with Captain McIver. It'll be up to you to stay in touch. The earliest ETD'd be about 5 p.m. but I won't wait around for you. All right?'

'Thank you, sir.'

Again Gavallan had been listening carefully but still could not decide. 'George, when we started talking, you said of that arrogant little bastard, "He's quite right, you know." Right about what? That now I've to find or report to some nebulous authorities in Tehran?'

'No. That Bakhtiar's resigned and in hiding.'

Both men gaped at him. 'God Almighty, are you sure?'

'Bakhtiar formally resigned a couple of hours ago and has, somewhat wisely, vanished.' Talbot's voice was soft and calm, cigarette smoke punctuating his words. 'Actually the situation's suddenly rather dicey, hence our, er, anxiety to, er, well, never mind that. Last night the chief of staff, General Ghara-Baghi, supported by the generals, ordered all troops back into their barracks, declaring the armed forces were now "neutral", thus leaving their legal prime minister defenceless and the state to Khomeini.'

' "Neutral"?' Gavallan echoed with disbelief. 'That's not possible – not possible – they'd be committing suicide.'

'I agree. But it is true.'

'Christ!'

'Of course, only some of the units will obey, other will fight,' Talbot said. 'Certainly the police and SAVAK aren't affected; they won't give up though now their battle will be lost eventually. Insha'Allah, old boy. Meanwhile blood will fill the jolly gutters, rest assured.'

McIver broke the silence. 'But . . . if Bakhtiar . . . doesn't that mean it's over. It's over,' he said with growing excitement. 'The civil war's over and thank God for that. The generals have stopped the real blood bath – the total blood bath. Now we can all get back to normal. The trouble's over.'

'Oh no, my dear chap,' Talbot said even more calmly. 'The trouble's just begun.'

At Rig Bellissima: 6:35 P.M. The sunset was glorious, red-tinged clouds low on the horizon, clean, clear sky, the evening star brilliant, a three-quarter moon. But it was very cold here at 12,500 feet, and already dark in the east and Jean-Luc had difficulty in picking out the incoming 212.

'Here she comes, Gianni,' Jean-Luc shouted at the driller.

This would complete Scot Gavallan's third round trip. Everyone – riggers, cooks, labourers, three cats and four dogs and a canary belonging to Gianni Salubrio – had already been safely transported to Rig Rosa, with the exception of Mario Guineppa who had insisted on waiting till last, in spite of Jean-Luc's pleadings, and Gianni, Pietro and two others who were still shutting down the rig.

Jean-Luc kept a wary eye on the overhang that worked from time to time, sending shivers down his spine. When the chopper had come back the first time, everyone had held their breath at the noise even though Pietro had assured them all that was just an old wives' tale – only dynamite would start an avalanche, or an act of God. And then as if to

278

prove him wrong the overhang shifted again, only a little but enough to nauseate those still left on the rig.

Pietro pulled the last switch and the turbines of the diesel generators began to slow. He wiped his face tiredly and left an oil smear. His back ached and his hands hurt in the cold but the well was sealed and as safe as he could make it. Out over the abyss he saw the chopper beginning her careful approach. 'Let's leave,' he said to the others in Italian. 'There's nothing more that we can do here – nothing more to do except blow that shit roll above to hell!'

The others irritably crossed themselves and trudged off towards the helipad and left him. He looked up at the crest. 'You look as though you're alive,' he muttered, 'a shit-roll monster waiting to get me and my beautiful wells. But you won't, you motherless whore!'

He went to the little dynamite storeroom and picked up the two exploders that he had made – six sticks of dynamite in each, wrapped around a thirty-second fuse. Carefully he put them in a small carrying bag, with a lighter and matches as a backup. 'Mother of God,' he prayed simply, 'make these fornicators work.'

'Pietro! Hey, Pietro!'

'I'm coming, I'm coming, there's plenty of time!' Outside he saw the white, pinched face of Gianni. 'What's up?'

'It's Guineppa – better take a look!'

Mario Guineppa lay on his back, his breath rattling in his throat, eyelids flickering. Jean-Luc was beside the bed, his hand on the man's pulse. 'It's rapid . . . then I can't feel it at all,' he said uneasily.

'Mario had a serious medical four weeks ago, his annual – cardiogram, everything. Very serious. He was perfect!' Pietro spat on the floor. 'Doctors!'

'He was a fool to insist on waiting,' Gianni said.

'He's the boss, he does what he likes. Let's put him on the stretcher and get going.' Pietro was grave. 'There's nothing we can do for him here. The hell with the dynamite, we'll do it later or tomorrow.'

Carefully they lifted him, wrapping him warmly, and carried him out of the trailer, through the snow towards the waiting helicopter. Just as they reached the helipad, the mountain groaned. They looked up. Snow and ice began tumbling, gathering weight. In seconds the avalanche was in full flood. There was no time to run, nothing to do but wait. The roar increased. Snow poured down the mountain to carry the far trailer hut and one of the vast steel mud tanks into the abyss. Then it ceased.

'*Mamma mia*,' Gianni gasped, crossing himself. 'I thought we were gone that time.'

279

Jean-Luc, too, had crossed himself. Now the overhang was even more ominous, thousands of tons poised over the site, part of the rock face exposed. Dribbles of snow fell continuously.

'Jean-Luc!' It was Guineppa. His eyes were open. 'Don't . . . don't wait . . . dynamite now . . . must . . . must.'

Pietro said, 'He's right, it's now or never.'

'Please . . . I'm fine . . . *Mamma mia*, do it now! I'm fine.'

They hurried for the chopper. The stretcher went across the forward bank of seats and was quickly lashed into place. The others put on their seat belts. Jean-Luc got into the cockpit left seat and put on his headset. 'Okay, Scot?'

'Terrific, old chap,' Scot Gavallan said. 'How's Guineppa?'

'Not good.' Jean-Luc checked the instruments. Everything was in the green and plenty of fuel. '*Merde!* The overhang's going any second; let's watch the up and down draughts, they're liable to be rough. *Allons-y!*'

'Here – I rigged it for Pietro while I was waiting at Rosa.' Scot gave Jean-Luc the spare headset that was now linked with theirs.

'I'll give it to him when we're airborne. I don't feel safe here! Take off!'

At once Scot opened the throttles and eased the 212 off the ground, backed off a little, turned, and was over the abyss. As he started to climb, Jean-Luc crawled back into the cabin. 'Here, put these on, Pietro, now you're connected with us up front.'

'Good, very good.' Pietro had taken the seat nearest the door.

'When we begin, for the sake of God, my health, and your mother, don't fall out.'

Pietro laughed nervously. Jean-Luc checked Guineppa who seemed more comfortable now, went forward again and put on his headset. 'You hear me, Pietro?'

'*Si. Si, amico.*'

The chopper laboured in a circling climb. Now they were on a level with the crest. From this angle the overhang did not seem so dangerous. They were beginning to bounce a little. 'Go higher, another hundred feet, *amico*,' came through the headsets, 'and more north.'

'Roger, Pietro. You're navigator now,' Scott said.

The two pilots concentrated. Pietro showed them the spot on the north face where the dynamite would undercut the overhang and create an avalanche away from the rig. 'It might work,' Scot muttered.

They circled once to make sure. '*Amico*, when we're over that spot at a hundred feet, hover; I'll light the fuse and throw her out. *Buono*?' They could hear a tremble in Pietro's voice.

'Don't forget to open the door, old chap,' Scot said dryly. There was a stream of Italian expletives in reply. Scot smiled, then a downdraught took them fifty feet before he caught it. In a minute they were to altitude and in position.

'Good, *amico*, keep her there.'

Jean-Luc turned around to watch. Behind in the cabin the other men stared at Pietro, fascinated. He took out the first charge and caressed the fuse straight, humming *Aida*.

'Mother of God, Pietro,' Gianni said. 'Are you sure you know what you're doing?'

Pietro clenched his left fist, put his right with the fused dynamite on his left bicep, and gestured with significance. 'Get ready, up front,' he said into the boom mike, and unlocked his seat belt. He checked the position below, then nodded. 'Good, keep her steady. Gianni, ready on the door. Open the fornicator a crack and I'll do the rest.'

The airplane was pitching with the gyrating air currents, as Gianni unlocked his belt and went to the door. 'Hurry up,' he said, feeling very unsafe, then added to the nearest man, 'hold on to my belt!'

'Open the door, Gianni!' Gianni fought it open a foot and held it there, the sick man on the stretcher forgotten. A roar of air filled the cabin. The airplane swirled, the added suction from the open door making it more difficult for Scot to control her. Pietro held up the fuse and thumbed the lighter. It failed. Again and again, each time more anxious than the last.

'Mother of God, come on!' Sweat was pouring off Pietro's face when the lighter finally caught. The fuse spluttered into life. Holding on with one hand he leaned towards the door, wind eddies tugging at him. The airplane lurched and both men wished they had had the foresight to bring a safety harness. Carefully Pietro tossed the exploder through the opening. At once Gianni slammed the door closed and locked it. Then he began to swear.

'Bombs away! Let's go!' Pietro ordered, his teeth chattering from the cold, and buckled himself in again. At once the chopper peeled off and he was so relieved that it was done, he started to laugh. Hysterically the others joined him and all happily turned to watch below as he began to count down: '. . . six . . . five . . . four . . . three . . . two . . . one!' Nothing happened. As quickly as their laughter had arrived, it vanished. 'Did you see it fall, Jean-Luc?'

'No. No, we saw nothing,' the Frenchman replied gloomily, not wanting to repeat the manoeuvre. 'Perhaps it hit a rock and the fuse got knocked away.' But inside he was saying to himself, Stupid Italian anus eater, can't even fix a few sticks of dynamite to a fornicating fuse. 'We will do it again, yes?'

'Why not?' Pietro said confidently. 'The detonator was perfect. That it did not fire was an act of the Devil. Yes, without a doubt – it happens many times in snow. Many times. Snow is a whore and you can nev –'

'Don't blame the snow, Pietro, and it was an act of God, not of the Devil,' Gianni said superstitiously, crossing himself. 'By my mother, enough of the Devil while we're aloft.'

Pietro took out the second charge and examined it carefully. The wire holding the sticks tight was firm and the fuse firm. 'There, you see, perfect, just like the other.' He tossed it from one hand to the other then banged it hard on his armrest to see if the fuse would dislodge.

'*Mamma mia*,' one of the men said, his stomach turning over. 'Are you mad?'

'This's not like nitro, *amico*,' Pietro told him and banged it even harder. 'There, you see it's tight.'

'It's not as tight as my anus,' Gianni said angrily in Italian. 'Stop it for the love of the Mother of God!'

Pietro shrugged and looked out of the window. The crest was approaching now. He could see the exact spot. 'Get ready, Gianni.' Then into the boom mike, 'Just a little more, Signor Pilot, more to the east. Hold her there . . . steady her . . . can't you keep her steadier? Get ready, Gianni.' He held up the fuse, the lighter near to the end. 'Open the fornicating door!'

Irritably, Gianni unlocked his seat belt and obeyed, the airplane twisted and he cried out, lost his footing, his weight went against the door, opening it wider, and he pitched out. But the man was holding his belt and he held Gianni there on the brink, half in, half out of the doorway, the wind suction tearing at them. The instant Gianni had opened the door, Pietro had thumbed the lighter and the fuse had caught but in the momentary panic over Gianni, Pietro was distracted. Instinctively he, too, had grabbed for Gianni and the dynamite was knocked out of his hand. They all watched appalled as he scrambled on the floor, reaching under the seats for it as it rolled this way and that, the fuse burning merrily – his headset torn off. Almost fainting with fear, Gianni got one hand firmly on the doorjamb and began to drag himself back, petrified that his belt would give way and cursing himself that he had worn this thin one that his wife had given him for Christmas . . .

Pietro's fingers touched the dynamite. The fuse spluttered against his flesh, burning him, but he did not feel the pain. He got a firm grip then, still on the floor, squirmed around, hung on to a chair support and threw the dynamite and what was left of the fuse past Gianni overboard, then reached forward with his free hand and grabbed one of his friend's legs, helping to drag him back. The other man slammed the door closed and the two of them, Pietro and Gianni, collapsed on the floor.

'Take her away, Scot,' Jean-Luc said weakly.

The chopper banked and left the north face two hundred feet below. For a moment the crest was pure and stark and motionless. There was a vast explosion that no one in the chopper felt or heard. Snow spiralled upward and began to settle. Then with a mighty roar, the whole of the north face tumbled away, the avalanche fell into the valley, searing the mountainside with a swatch a quarter of a mile wide until it had ceased.

The chopper came around. 'My God, look!' Scot said, pointing ahead. The overhang had vanished. Above the Bellissima rig was only a gentle slope, the site untouched except where the trailer and the single mud tank had already been carried away by the first avalanche.

'Pietro!' Jean-Luc called out excitedly. 'You've . . .' He stopped. Pietro and Gianni were still on the floor collecting themselves, Pietro's headset vanished. 'Scot, they won't be able to see from their windows – go closer and turn so they can see!'

Excitedly, Jean-Luc climbed back into the cabin and began to pummel Pietro, congratulating him. Blankly everyone stared at him and when they understood what he was shouting over the screech of the engines, they forgot their fears and peered out of the windows. And when they saw how perfectly the explosion had cleaned away the danger, they let out a cheer. Gianni embraced Pietro emotionally, swearing eternal friendship, blessing him for saving him, for saving their lives and saving their jobs.

'*Niente, caro*,' Pietro said expansively. 'Am I not a man of Aosta?'

Jean-Luc stood over the stretcher and gently shook Mario Guineppa. 'Mario! Pietro did it – he did it perfectly. Bellissima's safe . . .'

Guineppa did not answer. He was already dead.

Tuesday
February 13, 1979

On the North Face of Mount Sabalan: 10:00 A.M. The night was bitterly cold under a cloudless sky, stars abundant, the moon strong and Captain Ross and his two Gurkhas were working their way cautiously under a crest following the guide and the CIA man. The soldiers wore cowled, white snow coveralls over their battle dress, and gloves and thermal underwear but still the cold tormented them. They were about 8,000 feet, down wind of their target half a mile away the other side of the ridge. Above them the vast cone shape of the extinct volcano soared over 16,000.

'Meshghi, we'll stop and rest,' the CIA man said in Turkish to the guide. Both were dressed in rough tribesmen's clothes.

'If you wish it, agha, then let it be so.' The guide led the way off the path, through the snow, to a small cave that none of them had noticed. He was old and gnarled like an ancient olive tree, hairy and thin, his clothes ragged, and still the strongest of them after almost two days' climbing.

'Good,' the CIA man said. Then to Ross, 'Let's hole up here, till we're ready.'

287

Ross unslung his carbine, sat, and rested his pack gratefully, his calves and thighs and back aching. 'I'm all one big bloody ache,' he said disgustedly, 'and I'm supposed to be fit.'

'You're fit, sahib,' the Gurkha sergeant called Tenzing said in Gurkhali with a beam. 'On our next leave we go up Everest, eh?'

'Not on your Nelly,' Ross said in English and the three soldiers laughed together.

Then the CIA man said thoughtfully, 'Must be something to stand on top of that mother.'

Ross saw him look out at the night and the thousands of feet of mountain below. When they had first met at the rendezvous near Bandar-e Pahlavi two days ago, if he hadn't been told otherwise he would have thought him part Mongol or Nepalese or Tibetan, for the CIA man was dark-haired with a yellowish skin and Asian eyes and dressed like a nomad.

'Your CIA contact's Rosemont, Vien Rosemont, he's half Vietnamese – half American,' the CIA colonel had said at his briefing. 'He's twenty-six, been here a year, speaks Farsi and Turkish, he's second-generation CIA, and you can trust him with your life.'

'It seems I'm going to have to, sir, one way or another, don't you think?'

'Huh? Oh, sure, yes. Yes, I guess so. You meet him just south of Bandar-e Pahlavi at those coordinates and he'll have the boat. You'll hug the coast until you're just south of the Soviet border, then back-pack in.'

'He's the guide?'

'No. He, er, he just knows about Mecca – that's our code name for the radar post. Getting the guide's his problem – but he'll deliver. If he's not at the rendezvous, wait throughout Saturday night. If he's not there by dawn, he's blown and you abort. Okay?'

'Yes. What about the rumours of insurrection in Azerbaijan?'

'Far as we know there's some fighting in Tabriz and the western part – nothing around Ardabil. Rosemont should know more. We, er, we know the Soviets are massed and ready to move in if the Azerbaijanis throw Bakhtiar supporters out. Depends on their leaders. One of them's Abdollah Khan. If you run into trouble go see him. He's one of ours – loyal.'

'All right. And this pilot, Charles Pettikin, say he won't take us?'

'Make him. One way or another. There's approval way up to the top for this op, both from your guys and ours, but we can't put anything into writing. Right, Bob?'

The other man at the briefing, a Robert Armstrong whom he had also never met before, had nodded agreement. 'Yes.'

'And the Iranians? They've approved it?'

'It's a matter of, er, of national security – yours and ours. Theirs too but they're . . . they're busy. Bakhtiar's, well, he's – he may not last.'

'Then it's true – the U.S. are jerking the rug?'

'I wouldn't know about that, Captain.'

'One last question: why aren't you sending your fellows?'

Robert Armstrong had answered for the colonel. 'They're all busy – we can't get any more here quickly – not with your elite training.'

We're certainly well trained, Ross thought, easing his shoulders cut raw by his backpack straps – to climb, to jump, to ski, to snorkel, to kill silently or noisily, to move like the wind against terrorist or public enemy, and to blow everything sky-high if need be, above or under water. But I'm bloody lucky, I've everything I want: health, university, Sandhurst, paratroopers, special air services, and even my beloved Gurkhas. He beamed at both of them and said a Gurkhali obscenity in a vulgar dialect that sent them into silent fits of laughter. Then he saw Vien Rosemont and the guide looking at him. 'Your pardon, Excellencies,' he said in Farsi. 'I was just telling my brothers to behave themselves.'

Meshghi said nothing, just turned his attention back to the night.

Rosemont had pulled off his boots and was massaging the chill out of his feet. 'The guys I've seen, British officers, they're not friends with their soldiers, not like you.'

'Perhaps I'm luckier than others.' With the side of his eyes Ross was watching the guide who had got up and was now standing at the mouth of the cave, listening. The old man had become increasingly edgy in the last few hours. How far do I trust him? he thought, then glanced at Gueng who was nearest. Instantly the little man got the message, nodded back imperceptibly.

'The captain is one of us, sir,' Tenzing was saying to Rosemont proudly. 'Like his father and grandfather before him – and they were both Sheng'khan.'

'What's that?'

'It's a Gurkhali title,' Ross said, hiding his pride. 'It means Lord of the Mountain. Doesn't mean much outside the regiment.'

'Three generations in the same outfit. That usual?'

Of course it's not usual, Ross wanted to say, disliking personal questions, though liking Vien Rosemont personally. The boat had been on time, the voyage up the coast safe and quick, them hidden under sacking. Easily ashore at dusk and on their way to the next rendezvous where the guide had been waiting, fast into the foothills, and into the mountains, Rosemont never complaining but pressing forward hard, with little conversation and none of the barrage of questions he had expected.

Rosemont waited patiently, noticing Ross was distracted. Then he saw the guide move out of the cave, hesitate, then come back and squat against the cave mouth, rifle cradled on his lap.

'What is it, Meshghi?' Rosemont asked.

'Nothing, agha. There are flocks in the valley, goats and sheep.'

'Good.' Rosemont leaned back comfortably. Lucky to find the cave, he thought, it's a good place to hole up in. He glanced back at Ross, saw him looking at him. After a pause he added, 'It's great to be part of a team.'

'What's the plan from now on?' Ross asked.

'When we get to the entrance of the cave, I'll lead. You and your guys stay back until I make sure, okay?'

'Just as you like, but take Sergeant Tenzing with you. He can protect your tail – I'll cover you both with Gueng.'

After a pause, Rosemont nodded. 'Sure, sounds good. Okay, Sergeant?'

'Yes, sahib. Please tell me what you want simply. My English is not good.'

'It's just fine,' Rosemont said, covering his nervousness. He knew Ross was weighing him like he was weighing them – too much at stake.

'You just blow Mecca to hell,' his director had told him. 'We've a specialist team to help you; we don't know how good they are but they're the goddam best we can get. Leader's a captain, John Ross, here's his photo and he'll have a couple of Gurkhas with him, don't know if they speak English but they come recommended. He's a career officer. Listen, as you've never worked close with Limeys before, a word of warning. Don't get personal or friendly or use first names too fast – they're as sensitive as a cat with a feather up its ass about personal questions, so take it easy, okay?'

'Sure.'

'Far as we know you'll find Mecca empty. Our other posts nearer Turkey are still operating. We figure to stay as long as we can – by that time the brass'll make a deal with the new jokers, Bakhtiar or Khomeini. But Mecca – goddam those bastards who've put us at so much risk.'

'How much risk?'

'We think they just left in a hurry and destroyed nothing. You've been there, for crissake! Mecca's stuffed with enough top secret gizmos, listening gear, seeing gear, long-range radar, locked-in satellite ciphers and codes and computers to get our unfriendly KGB chief Andropov voted Man of the Year – if he gets them. Can you believe it – those bastards just hightailed it out!'

'Treason?'

'Doubt it. Just plain stupid, dumb – there wasn't even a contingency plan at Sabalan, for crissake – anywhere else either. Not all their fault, I guess. None of us figured the Shah'd fold so goddam quick, or that Khomeini'd get Bakhtiar by the balls so fast. We got no warning – not even from SAVAK . . .'

And now we have to pick up the pieces, Vien thought. Or, more correctly, blow them to hell. He glanced at his watch, feeling very tired. He gauged the night and the moon. Better give it another half an hour. His legs ached, and his head. He saw Ross watching him and he smiled inside: I won't fail, Limey. But will you?

'An hour, then we'll move out,' Vien said.

'Why wait?'

'The moon'll be better for us. It's safe here and we've time. You're clear what we do?'

'Mine everything in Mecca you mark, blow it and the cave entrance simultaneously, and run like the clappers all the way home.'

Rosemont smiled and felt better. 'Where's home for you?'

'I don't know really,' Ross said caught unawares. He had never asked himself the question. After a moment, more for himself than the American, he added, 'Perhaps Scotland – perhaps Nepal. My father and mother are in Katmandu, they're as Scots as I am but they've been living there off and on since '51 when he retired. I was even born there though I did almost all my schooling in Scotland.' Both are home, for me, he thought. 'What about you?'

'Washington, D.C. – really Falls Church, Virginia, which is almost part of Washington. I was born there.' Rosemont wanted a cigarette but knew it might be dangerous. 'Pa was CIA. He's dead now but he was at Langley for his last few years, which's close by – CIA HQ's at Langley.' He was happy to be talking. 'Ma's still in Falls Church, haven't been back in a couple of years. You ever been to the States?'

'No, not yet.' The wind had picked up a little and they both studied the night for a moment.

'It'll die down after midnight,' Rosemont said confidently.

Ross saw the guide shift position again. Is he going to make a run for it? 'You've worked with the guide before?'

'Sure. I tramped all over the mountains with him last year – I spent a month here. Routine. Lotta the opposition infiltrate through this area and we try to keep tabs on 'em – like they do us.' Rosemont watched the guide. 'Meshghi's a good joe. Kurds don't like Iranians, or Iraqis or our friends across the border. But you're right to ask.'

Ross switched to Gurkhali. 'Tenzing, watch everywhere and the pathfinder – you eat later.' At once Tenzing slipped out of his pack and was gone into the night. 'I sent him on guard.'

'Good,' Rosemont said. He had watched them all very carefully on the climb up and was very impressed with the way they worked as a team, leapfrogging, always one of them flanking, always seeming to know what to do, no orders, always safety catches off. 'Isn't that kinda dangerous?' he had said early on.

'Yes, Mr. Rosemont – if you don't know what you're doing,' the Britisher had said to him with no arrogance that he could detect. 'But when every tree or corner or rock could hide hostiles, the difference between safety on and off could mean killing or being killed.'

Vien Rosemont remembered how the other had added guilelessly, 'We'll do everything we can to support you and get you out,' and he wondered again if they would get in, let alone out. It was almost a week since Mecca had been abandoned. No one knew what to expect when they got there – it could be intact, already stripped, or even occupied. 'You know this whole op's crazy?'

'Ours not to reason why.'

'Ours but to do or die? I think that's the shits!'

'I think that's the shits too if it's any help.'

It was the first time they had laughed together. Rosemont felt much better. 'Listen, haven't said it before, but I'm happy you three're aboard.'

'We're, er, happy to be here.' Ross covered his embarrassment at the open compliment. 'Agha,' he called out in Farsi to the guide, 'please join us at food.'

'Thank you, agha, but I am not hungry,' the old man replied without moving from the cave mouth.

Rosemont put his boots back on. 'You got a lot of special units in Iran?'

'No. Half a dozen – we're here training Iranians. You think Bakhtiar will weather it?' He opened his pack and distributed the cans of bully beef.

292

'No. The word in the hills among the tribes is that he'll be out – probably shot – within the week.'

Ross whistled, 'Bad as that?'

'Worse: that Azerbaijan'll be a Soviet protectorate within the year.'

'Bloody hell!'

'Sure. But you never know' – Vien smiled – 'that's what makes life interesting.'

Casually Ross offered the flask. 'Best Iranian rotgut money can buy.'

Rosemont grimaced and took a careful sip, then beamed. 'Jesus H. Christ, it's real Scotch!' He prepared to take a real swallow but Ross was ready and he grabbed the flask back.

'Easy does it – it's all we've got, agha.'

Rosemont grinned. They ate quickly. The cave was snug and safe. 'You ever been to Vietnam?' Rosemont asked, wanting to talk, feeling the time right.

'No, never have. Almost went there once when my father and I were en route to Hong Kong but we were diverted to Bangkok from Saigon.'

'With the Gurkhas?'

'No, this was years ago, though we do have a battalion there now. I was,' Ross thought a moment, 'I was seven or eight, my father has some vague Hong Kong relations, Dunross, yes, that was their name, and there was some sort of clan gathering. I don't remember much of Hong Kong except a leper who lay in the dirt by the ferry terminal. I had to pass him every day – almost every day.'

'My dad was in Hong Kong in '63,' Vien said proudly. 'He was Deputy Director of Station – CIA.' He picked up a stone, toyed with it. 'You know I'm half-Vietnamese?'

'Yes, they told me.'

'What else did they tell you?'

'Just that I could trust you with my life.'

Rosemont smiled wryly. 'Let's hope they're right.' Thoughtfully he began checking the action of his M16. 'I've always wanted to visit Vietnam. My pa, my real pa, was Vietnamese, a planter, but he was killed just before I was born – that was when the French owned Indochina. He got clobbered by Viet Cong just outside Dien Bien Phu. Ma . . .' The sadness dropped off him and he smiled. 'Ma's as American as a Big Mac and when she remarried she picked one of the greatest. No real pa could've loved me more . . .'

Abruptly Gueng cocked his carbine. 'Sahib!' Ross and Rosemont grabbed their weapons, then there was a keening on the wind, Ross and Gueng relaxed. 'It's Tenzing.'

The sergeant appeared out of the night as silently as he had left. But now his face was grim. 'Sahib, many trucks on the road below –'

'In English, Tenzing.'

'Yes, sahib. Many trucks, I counted eleven, in convoy, on the road at the bottom of the valley . . .'

Rosemont cursed. 'That road leads to Mecca. How far away were they?'

The little man shrugged. 'At the bottom of the valley. I went the other side of the ridge and there's a . . .' He said the Gurkhali word and Ross gave him the English equivalent. 'A promontory. The road in the valley twists, then snakes as it climbs. If the tail of the snake is in the valley and the head wherever the road ends, then four trucks were already well past tail.'

Rosemont cursed again. 'An hour at best. We'd bett—' At that moment there was a slight scuffle and their attention flashed to the cave mouth. They just had time to see the guide rushing away, Gueng in pursuit.

'What the hell . . .'

'For whatever reason, he's abandoning ship,' Ross said. 'Forget him. does an hour give us a chance?'

'Sure. Plenty.' Quickly they got into their packs and Rosemont armed his light machine gun. 'What about Gueng?'

'He'll catch us up.'

'We'll go straight in. I'll go first – if I run into trouble you abort. Okay?'

The cold was almost a physical barrier they had to fight through but Rosemont led the way well, the snow not bad on the meandering path, the moon helping, their climbing boots giving them good traction. Quickly they topped the ridge and headed down the other side. Here it was more slippery, the mountainside barren, just a few clumps of weeds and plants fighting to get above the snow. Ahead now was the maw of the cave, the road running into it, many vehicle tracks in the snow.

'They could've been made by our trucks,' Rosemont said, covering his disquiet. 'There's been no snow for a couple of weeks.' He motioned the others to wait and went forward, then stepped out on the road and ran for the entrance. Tenzing followed, using the ground for cover, moving as rapidly.

Ross saw Rosemont disappear into the darkness. Then Tenzing. His anxiety increased. From where he was he could not see far down the road, for it curled away, falling steeply. The strong moonlight made the crags and the wide valley more ominous, and he felt naked and lonely and hated the waiting. But he was confident. 'If you've Gurkhas with you, you've always a chance, my son,' his father had said. 'Guard them – they'll always guard you. And never forget, with luck, one day you'll be Sheng'khan.' Ross had smiled to himself, so proud, the title given so rarely: only to one who had brought honour to the regiment, who had scaled a worthy Nepalese peak alone, who had used the kukri and had saved the life of a Ghurka in the service of the Great Raj. His grandfather, Captain Kirk Ross, MC, killed in 1915 at the Battle of the Somme, had been given it posthumously; his father Lieutenant-Colonel Gavin Ross, DSO, was given it in Burma, 1943. And me? Well, I've scaled a worthy peak – K4 – and that's all so far but I've lots of time . . .

His fine-tuned senses warned him and he had his kukri out, but it was only Gueng. The little man was standing over him, breathing hard. 'Not fast enough, sahib,' he whispered happily in Gurkhali. 'I could have taken you moments ago.' He held up the severed head and beamed. 'I bring you a gift.'

It was the first that Ross had seen. The eyes were open. Terror still contorted the face of the old man. Gueng killed him but I gave the order, he thought, sickened. Was he just an old man who was scared fartless and wanted to get out while the going was good? Or was he a spy or a traitor rushing to betray us to the enemy?

'What is it, sahib?' Gueng whispered, his brow furrowed.

'Nothing. Put the head down.'

Gueng tossed it aside. The head rolled a little down the slope then stopped. 'I searched him, sahib, and found this.' He handed him the amulet. 'It was around his throat and this' – he gave him the small leather bag – 'this hung down around his balls.'

The amulet was just a cheap blue stone worn against the evil eye. Inside the little bag was a small card, wrapped in plastic. Ross squinted at it and his heart skipped a beat. At that moment there was another keening on the wind, the note different. Immediately they picked up their guns and ran for the cave mouth, knowing that Tenzing had given them the all clear signal and to hurry. Inside the throat of the cavern the darkness seemed deeper and then, as their eyes adjusted, they saw a fleck of light. It was a flashlight, the lens partially covered.

'Over here, Captain.' Though it was softly said, Rosemont's voice echoed loudly. 'This way.' He led them farther into the cave and when he was sure it was safe he shone the light on the rock walls and all around to get his bearings. 'It's okay to use your flashes.' The cave was immense, many tunnels and passages leading off it, some natural, some man-made, the rock dome fifty feet overhead. 'This's the unloading area,' he said. When he found the tunnel he sought he shone the light down it. At the end was a thick steel door, half open. 'It should be locked,' he whispered, his voice raw. 'I don't know if it was left like that or what, but that's where we have to go.'

Ross motioned to Tenzing. At once the kukri came out and the soldier went forward to vanish inside. Automatically Ross and Gueng took up defensive positions. Against whom? Ross asked himself helplessly, feeling trapped. There could be fifty men hidden in any one of those other tunnels.

The seconds dragged. Again there was the keening. Ross led the rush through the doorway, then Gueng, then Rosemont. As Rosemont passed the door he saw that Tenzing had taken up a position nearby and was covering them. He pulled the door to and switched on the lights. The suddenness made the other gasp.

'Hallelujah!' Rosemont said, openly relieved. 'The brass figured if the generators were still working, we'd have a good shot. This door's lightproof.' He slid heavy bolts into place, hung his flashlight on his belt.

They were in another cave, much smaller, that had been adapted, the floor levelled and carpeted roughly, the walls made more flat. It was a form of anteroom with desks and phones and litter everywhere. 'The guys sure didn't waste any time getting to hell out, did they?' he said bitterly, hurrying across the room to another tunnel, down it and into another caveroom with more desks, a few radar screens, and more phones, grey and green.

'The grey're internal, greens go to the tower and masts on the crest, from there by satellite to Tehran, our HQ switchboard in the embassy, and various top secret places – they've built-in scramblers.' Rosemont picked one up. It was dead. 'Maybe the communications guys did their job after all.' At the far end of the room was a tunnel. 'That goes down to the generator room for this section which has all the gear we've to blow. Living quarters, kitchens, mess halls, repair shops, are in other caves off the unloading area. About eighty guys worked here around the clock.'

'Is there any other way out of here?' Ross asked. His feeling of being closed in was greater than ever.

'Sure, topside, where we're going.'

Rough steps led upward through the domed roof. Rosemont started climbing them. On the landing was a door: TOP SECURITY AREA – NO ADMITTANCE WITHOUT SPECIAL AUTHORITY. It too was open. 'Shit,' he muttered. This cave was well appointed, floor flatter, walls white-washed. Dozens of computers and radar screens, and banked electronic equipment. More desks and chairs and phones, grey and green. And two red on a central desk.

'What're those for?'

'Direct to Langley by military satellite.' Rosemont picked one up. It was dead. So was the other. He pulled out a piece of paper and checked it, then went over to a bank of switches and turned some on. Another obscenity as a soft hum began, computers started chattering, warming up, and three of the radar screens came to life, the central white trace-line turning, leaving a scatter pattern in its wake. 'Bastards! Bastards to leave everything like this.' His finger stabbed at four corner computers. 'Blow those mothers – they're the core.'

'Gueng!'

'Yes, sahib.' The Gurkha took off his pack and began to lay out the plastic explosives and detonators.

'Half-hour fuses?' Rosemont said.

'Half-hour fuses it is.' Ross was staring at one of the screens, fascinated. Northward he could see most of the Caucasus, all of the Caspian, eastward even part of the Black Sea, all with extraordinary clarity. 'That's a lot of space to peer into.'

Rosemont went over to its keyboard and turned a switch.

For a moment Ross was dumbfounded. He tore his eyes off the screen. 'Now I understand why we're here.'

'That's only part.'

'Christ! Then we'd better get cracking. What about the cave mouth?'

'We've no time to do a decent job – and the other side of our door's routine junk they've stolen anyway. We'll blow our tunnels after us and use the escapeway.'

'Where's that?'

The American went over to a door. This one was locked. He took out a bunch of tagged keys and found the one he wanted. The door swung open. Behind the door a narrow flight of stairs spiralled upward steeply. 'It leads out on to the mountain.'

'Tenzing, make sure the way's clear.' Tenzing went up the stairs two at a time. 'Next?'

'Code room and the safes, we'll mine those. Then communications. Generator room last, okay?'

'Yes.' Ross liked the incisive strength more and more. 'Before we do you'd better look at this.' He took out the small, plastic-covered card. 'Gueng caught up with our guide. This was on him.'

All colour left Rosemont's face. On the card was a thumb-print, some writing in Russian script and a signature. 'An ID!' he burst out. 'A commie ID!' Behind them Gueng paused momentarily.

'That's what I thought. What's it say exactly?'

'I don't know, I can't read Russian either but I'll bet my life it's a safe-conduct pass.' A wave of sickness came up from his stomach as he remembered all the days and nights he had spent in the old man's company, wandering the mountains, sleeping alongside him in the open, feeling very safe. And all the time he'd been pegged. Numbly he shook his head. 'Meshghi was with us for years – he was one of Ali bin Hassan Karakose's band – Ali's an underground leader and one of our best contacts in the mountains. Great guy who even operates as far north as Baku. Jesus, maybe he's been betrayed.' He looked at the card again. 'Just doesn't figure.'

'I think it figures we could have been deliberately set up, sitting ducks,' Ross said. 'Perhaps the convoy's part of it, full of troops to track us. We'd better hurry it up, eh?'

Rosemont nodded, fighting to dominate the fear that swept through him, helped by the calmness of the other man. 'Yes, yes, you're right.' Still shattered, he went through a small passage to another door. Locked. As he looked for the key on the tabbed ring of keys he said, 'I owe you and your men an apology. I don't know how we – I – got taken in or how that bastard escaped the security check but he did and you're probably right – we're set up. Sorry, but, shit, that doesn't help a goddam bit.'

'It helps.' Ross grinned and the fear dropped off both of them. 'It helps. Okay?'

'Okay. Thanks, yes, thanks. Gueng killed him?'

'Well,' Ross said dryly. 'He handed me his head. They usually just bring back ears.'

'Jesus. You been with them long?'

'The Gurkhas? Four years.'

The key slid into the lock and the door opened. The code room was pedantically neat. Telex and teleprinter and copy machines. A curious computer printer with a keyboard was on its own desk. 'That's the decoder – worth any money you'd like to ask the opposition.' On the desks pencils were lined up. Half a dozen manuals.

Rosemont picked them up. 'Good sweet Jesus . . .' All were code-books marked MECCA – ONE COPY ONLY. 'Well, at least the master code's locked up.' He went to the modern safe with its electronic, 0–9 digital lock that was set into one wall, read the combination from his piece of paper and touched the digits. But the open light didn't come on. 'Maybe I missed a number. Read them to me, okay?'

'Sure.' Ross began reading out the long series of numbers. Behind them Tenzing came in noiselessly. Neither man heard him . . . then both men felt the presence at the same instant and whirled, momentarily panicked.

Tenzing kept the delight off his face and closed his ears to the profanity. Hadn't the Sheng'khan told him to train the son and make him wise in the ways of stealth and killing? Hadn't he sworn to guard him and be his silent teacher? 'But, Tenzing, for the love of God don't let my son know I told you to. Keep this secret between us . . .' It's been very hard to catch the sahib unawares for weeks, he thought happily. But Gueng caught him tonight and so did I. Much better we do than an enemy – and now they surround us like bees and their queen.

'The staircase leads upward for seventy-five steps to an iron door,' Tenzing said in his best reporting voice. 'The door is rusty but I forced it. Outside is a cave, outside the cave is the night – a good escape route, sahib. Not good is that from there I saw the first of the convoy.' He paused, not wanting to be wrong. 'Perhaps half an hour of time is left.'

'Go back to the first door, Tenzing, the one we barred. Mine the tunnel this side of the door to leave the door unharmed – twenty-minute fuse from now. Tell Gueng to set his fuses the same from now exactly. Tell Gueng what I've ordered.'

'Yes, sahib.'

Ross turned back. He noticed the sweat on Rosemont's forehead. 'Okay?'

'Sure. We got to 103.'

'The last two numbers are 660 and 31.' He saw the American touch the numbers. The Open light began winking. Rosemont's right hand went for the lever. 'Hold it!' Ross wiped the sweat from his own chin, the golden stubble rasping. 'I suppose there's no chance it could be booby-trapped?'

Rosemont stared at him, then at the safe. 'It's possible. Sure, it's possible.'

'Then let's just blow the bugger and not risk it.'

'I – I've gotta check. I've got to check if Mecca's master code's inside or not. That and the decoder are priority.' Again he looked at the light winking at him. 'You go back in the other room, take cover with Gueng, shout when you're ready. I – it's my shot.'

Ross hesitated. Then he nodded, picked up both packs that contained explosives and detonators. 'Where's the communication room?'

'Next door.'

'Is – is the generator room important?'

'No. Just this one, the decoder and those four mothers back there, though it'd be best if this whole goddam floor went to hell.' Rosemont watched Ross walk away then turned his back and looked back at the lever. There was a bad tightness in his chest. That sonofabitch Meshghi! I'd've bet my life – you did, we all did, even Ali Karakose. 'You ready?' he called out impatiently.

'Wait!' Again his stomach surged. Ross was back beside him before he had heard him, in his hands a long, thin, nylon climbing rope that, quickly, he lashed to the lever. 'Turn the lever when I say but don't open the door. We'll jerk it open from back there.' Ross hurried out. 'Now!'

Rosemont took a deep breath to slow his heart and turned the lever to Open then ran through the passage into the other cave. Ross beckoned him down beside the wall. 'I sent Gueng to warn Tenzing. Ready?'

'Sure.'

Ross tightened the rope, then tugged hard. The rope remained taut. He tugged even harder, then it slackened a foot but came no farther. Silence. Nothing. Both men were sweating. 'Well,' Ross said, greatly relieved, and got up. 'Better safe than sorr—' The explosion obliterated his words, a great cloud of dust and bits of metal blew out of the passage into their cave, jerking the air from their lungs, scattering tables and chairs. All radar screens burst, lights vanished, one of the red phones tore loose and hurtled across the room to smash through the steel casing of a computer. Gradually the dust settled, both men coughing their hearts out in the darkness.

Rosemont was the first to recover. His flashlight was still on his belt. He groped for it.

'Sahib?' Tenzing called out anxiously, rushing into the room, his flash on, Gueng beside him.

'I'm all – right,' Ross said, still coughing badly. Tenzing found him lying in the rubble. A little blood was running down his face but it was only a superficial wound from the flying glass. 'Bless all gods,' Tenzing muttered and helped him up.

Ross fought to stay upright. 'Christalmighty!' Blankly he looked around at the wreckage, then stumbled after Rosemont through the passage into the code room. The safe had vanished, with it the decoder, manuals, phones, leaving a huge hole in the living rock. All electronic equipment was just a mess of twisted metal and wires. Small fires had already started.

'Jesus,' was all Rosemont could say, his voice little more than a croak, his psyche revolted by the nearness to extinction, mind screaming: run, escape this place of your death . . .

'Christ all bloody mighty!'

Helplessly, Rosemont tried to say something more, couldn't, his legs took him into a corner and he was violently sick.

'We'd better—' Ross found it hard to talk, his ears still ringing, a monstrous ache in his head, adrenalin pumping, trying to dominate his own wish to run. 'Tenzing, are – are you finished?'

'Two minutes, sahib.' The man rushed off.

'Gueng?'

'Yes sahib. Two minutes also.' He hurried away.

Ross went to the other corner and retched. Then he felt better. He found the flask and took a long swig, wiped his mouth on the sleeve of his battle dress, went over and shook Rosemont who was leaning against the wall. 'Here.' He gave it to him. 'You all right?'

'Yes. Sure.' Rosemont still felt queasy, but now his mind was working. His mouth tasted foul and he spat the foulness into the rubble. Small fires burned, throwing crazy shadows on the walls and roof. He took a careful sip. After a moment he said, 'Nothing on God's earth like Scotch.' Another sip and he handed the flask back. 'We'd better get the hell out of here.'

With the flashlight he made a quick search of the wreckage, found the twisted remains of the all-important decoder, and picked his way carefully into the next cave and laid the remains near the charge at the base of the corner computers. 'What I don't understand,' he said helplessly, 'is why the whole goddam place didn't go up and blow us all to hell anyway – with all our explosives scattered around.'

'I – before I came back with the rope and sent Gueng off to Tenzing, I told Gueng to remove the explosives and the detonators for safety.'

'You always think of everything?'

Ross smiled weakly. 'All part of the service,' he said. 'Communications room?'

It was mined quickly. Rosemont glanced at his watch. 'Eight minutes to blast-off. We'll forget the generator room.'

'Good. Tenzing, you lead.'

They went up the escape staircase. The iron hatch creaked as it opened. Once in the cave Ross took the lead. Cautiously he peered out at the night and all around. The moon was still high. Three or four hundred yards away the lead truck was grinding up the last incline. 'Which way, Vien?' he asked and Rosemont felt a glow.

301

'Up,' he said, hiding the warmth. 'We climb. If there're troops after us, we forget the coast and head for Tabriz. If no troops we circle and go back the way we came.'

Tenzing led. He was like a mountain goat but he picked the easiest path, knowing the two men were still very shaky. Here the slope was steep but not too difficult with little snow to impede them. They had barely started when the ground shook beneath them, the sound of the first explosion almost totally muffled. In quick succession there were other small quakes.

One to go, Rosemont thought, glad of the cold which was clearing his head. The last explosion – the communications room – where they had used all their remaining explosive was much bigger and really shuddered the earth. Below and to their right, part of the mountain gave way, smoke billowing out of the resulting crater.

'Christ,' Ross muttered.

'Probably an air vent.'

'Sahib. Look down there!'

The lead truck had stopped at the entrance to the cave. Men were jumping out of it, others staring up at the mountainside, illuminated by the lights of the following trucks. The men all had rifles.

Ross and the others slid deeper into the shadows. 'We'll climb up to that ridge,' Rosemont said softly, pointing above and to their left. 'We'll be out of their sight and covered. Then we head for Tabriz, almost due east. Okay?'

'Tenzing, on you go!'

'Yes, sahib.'

They made the ridge and hurried over it to climb again, working their way eastward, not talking, conserving their energy for there were many, many miles to go. The terrain was rough and the snow harried them. Soon their gloves were torn, hands and legs bruised, calves aching but, no longer encumbered by heavy packs, they made good progress and their spirits were high.

They came to one of the paths that crisscrossed the mountains. Whenever the path forked, their choice was always to keep to the heights. There were villages in the valley, very few up this high. 'Better we stay up here,' Rosemont said, 'and . . . and hope we don't run into anyone.'

'You think they'll all be hostile?'

'Sure. It's not only anti-Shah country here but anti-Khomeini, anti-everyone.' Rosemont was breathing heavily. 'It's village against village most of the time and good bandit country.' He waved Tenzing onward, thankful for the moonlight and that he was with the three of them.

Tenzing kept up the pace but it was a mountaineer's pace, measured and unhurried and constant and punishing. After an hour Gueng took over the lead then Ross, Rosemont, and then Tenzing again. Three minutes' rest an hour, then on again.

The moon sank lower in the sky. They were well away now, the going easier, lower down the mountainside. The path meandered but it led generally eastward towards a curiously shaped cleft in the range. Rosemont had recognised it. 'Down in that valley's a side road that goes to Tabriz. It's little more than a track in winter but you can get through okay. Let's go on till dawn, then rest up and make a plan. Okay?'

Now they were down the tree line and into the beginnings of the pine forest, going much slower and feeling the tiredness.

Tenzing still led. Snow muffled their footsteps and the good clean air pleased him greatly. Abruptly he sensed danger and stopped. Ross was just behind him and he stopped also. Everyone waited motionless. Then Ross went forward carefully. Tenzing was peering into the dark ahead, the moon casting strange shadows. Slowly both men used their peripheral vision. Nothing. No sign or smell. They waited. Some snow fell from one of the trees. No one moved. Then a night bird left a branch ahead and to the right and flew noisily away. Tenzing pointed in that direction, motioned Ross to wait, slid his kukri out and went forward alone, melting into the night.

After a few yards Tenzing saw a man crouched behind a tree fifty yards ahead and his excitement picked up. Closer he could see that the man was oblivious of him. Closer. Then his peripheral vision saw a shadow move to his left, another to his right and he knew. 'Ambush!' he shouted at the top of his lungs and dived for cover.

The first wave of bullets passed near him but missed. Part of the second punctured his left lung, ripped a hole out of his back, slamming him against a fallen tree. More guns opened up on the opposite side of the pathway, the crossfire racking Ross and the others, who had scrambled behind tree trunks and into gullies.

For a moment Tenzing lay there helplessly. He could hear the firing but it seemed far away though he knew that it must be near. With a last mighty effort he dragged himself to his feet and charged the guns that had killed him. He saw some of their attackers turn back on him and heard bullets pass him, some tugging at his cowl. One went through his shoulder but he did not feel it, pleased that he was dying as men in the

303

regiment were supposed to die. Going forward. Fearlessly. I am truly without fear. I am Hindu and I go to meet Shiva contentedly, and when I am reborn I pray Brahama, Vishnu, Shiva that I will be born again Gurkha.

As he reached the ambush, his kukri hacked off someone's arm, his legs gave out, a monstrous, peerless light went off in his head and he strode into death without pain.

'Hold all fire,' Ross called out, getting his bearings, pulling the strings of battle back into his hands. He pegged two groups of guns against them, but there was no way that he could get at either. The ambush had been well chosen and the crossfire deadly. He had seen Tenzing hit. It had taken all of his willpower not to go to his aid but first there was this battle to win and the others to protect. The shots were echoing and re-echoing off the mountainside. He had wriggled out of his pack, found the grenades, made sure his carbine was fully automatic, not knowing how to lead the way out of the trap. Then he had seen Tenzing reel to his feet with a battle cry and charge up the slope, creating the diversion Ross needed. At once he ordered Rosemont, 'Cover me,' and to Gueng, 'Go!' pointing towards the same group Tenzing was attacking.

Immediately Gueng jumped out of his gully and rushed them, their attention diverted by Tenzing. When he saw his comrade go down, his rage burst, he let the lever on his grenade fly off, hurled it into their midst and hit the snow. The instant the grenade exploded he was up, his carbine spraying the screams, stopping most of them. He saw one man rushing away, another desperately crawling off into the underbrush. One slash of the kukri took off part of the crawler's head. A short burst cut the other to pieces and again Gueng whirled into cover, not know where the next danger would come from. Another grenade exploding took his attention to the other side of the path.

Ross had crawled forward out of safety. Bullets straddled him but Rosemont opened up with short bursts, drawing fire, giving Ross the help he needed, and he made the next tree safely, found a deep trough in the snow and fell into it. For a second he waited, collecting his breath, then scrambled along the hard, frozen snow towards the firing. Now he was out of sight of the attackers and he made good time. Then he heard the other grenade go off and the screaming, and he prayed that Gueng and Tenzing were all right.

The enemy firing was getting closer, and when he judged that he was in position, he pulled the pin out of the first grenade and with his carbine in his left hand went over the top. The instant he was in the open he saw the men, but not where he had expected them. There were five, barely twenty yards away. Their rifles turned on him but his reactions were just a little faster and he was on the ground behind a tree, the lever off and counting before the first barrage ripped into it. On the fourth second he reached around the tree and lobbed the grenade at them, buried his head under his arms. The explosion lifted him off the ground, blew the trunk of a nearer tree to pieces, burying him under branches and snow from its limbs.

Down by the path Rosemont had emptied his magazine into where he thought the attackers would be. Cursing in his anxiety, he slapped in a new magazine and fired another burst.

Across the path on the other slope, Gueng was huddled behind a rock waiting for someone to move. Then, near the exploded tree, he saw one man running away, bent double. He aimed and the man died, the shot echoing. Now silence.

Rosemont felt his heart racing. He could wait no longer. 'Cover me, Gueng,' he shouted and leaped to his feet and rushed for the tree. A flicker of firing to his right, bullets hissed past, then Gueng opened up from the other slope. A bubbling scream and the firing ceased. Rosemont ran onward until he was straddling the ambush point, his carbine levelled. Three men were in pieces, the last barely alive, their rifles bent and twisted. All wore rough tribal clothes. As he watched, the last man choked and died. He turned away and rushed for the other tree, pulling branches away, fighting his way through the snow to Ross.

On the other slope Gueng waited and watched to kill anything that moved. There was a slight stir amid the carnage behind the rocks where his grenade had ripped the three men apart. He waited, hardly breathing, but it was only a rodent feeding. Soon they will clean the ground and make it whole again, he thought, awed by the cycle of the gods. His eyes ranged slowly. He saw Tenzing crumpled to one side of the rock, his kukri still locked in his grasp. Before I leave I will take it, Gueng thought; his family will cherish it and his son will wear it with equal honour. Tenzing Sheng'khan lived and died like a man and will be reborn as the gods decide. Karma.

Another movement. Ahead in the forest. He concentrated.

The other side of the path Rosemont was pulling at the branches, fighting them away, his arms aching. At last he reached Ross and his heart almost stopped. Ross was crumpled on the ground, his arms over his head, his carbine nearby. Blood stained the snow and the back of the white coveralls. Rosemont knelt and turned him over and almost cried out with relief that Ross was still breathing. For a moment his eyes were blank, then they focused. He sat up and winced. 'Tenzing? And Gueng?'

'Tenzing got clobbered, Gueng's the other side covering us. He's okay.'

'Thank God. Poor Tenzing.'

'Test your arms and legs.'

Gingerly Ross moved his limbs. Everything worked. 'My head hurts like hell, but I'm okay.' He looked around and saw the crumpled attackers. 'Who are they?'

'Tribesmen. Bandits maybe.' Rosemont studied the way ahead. Nothing moved. The night was fine. 'We'd better get the hell out of here before more of the bastards jump us. You think you can go on?'

'Yes. Give me a couple of seconds.' Ross wiped some snow over his face. The cold helped. 'Thanks, eh? You know. Thanks.'

Rosemont smiled back. 'All part of the service,' he said wryly. His eyes went to the tribesmen. Keeping well down he went over to them and searched where he could. He found nothing. 'Probably locals – or just bandits. These bastards can be real cruel if they catch you alive.'

Ross nodded and another spasm of pain soared. 'I'm okay now, I think. We'd better move – the firing must have been heard for miles and this's no place to hang around.'

Rosemont had seen the pain. 'Wait some more.'

'No. I'll feel better moving.' Ross gathered his strength, then called out in Gurkhali, 'Gueng, we'll go on.' He started to get up, stopped as an abrupt keening for danger answered him. 'Get down!' he gasped and pulled Rosemont with him.

A single rifle bullet came out of the night and chose Rosemont and buried itself in his chest, mortally wounding him. Then there was firing from the other slope and a scream and silence once more.

In time, Gueng joined Ross. 'Sahib, I think that was the last. For the moment.'

'Yes.' They waited with Vien Rosemont until he died, then did what they had to do for him and for Tenzing. And then they went on.

The map shows Iran and surrounding regions including USSR, Caspian Sea, AFGHANISTAN, PAKISTAN, IRAQ, KUWAIT, SAUDI ARABIA, BAHRAIN, QATAR, UAE, Gulf of Oman, Persian Gulf, and the Strait of Hormuz. Cities and locations marked include Khvoy, Tabriz, Mount Sabalan, Bandar-e Pahlavi, Qazvin, Tehran, Sadzevar, Meshed, Baghdad, Dez Dam, Abadan, Bandar-e Delam, Kowiss, Kharg Island, Zagros, Jellet, Lengeh, Siri, Al Shargaz. The label ISFAHAN appears in a box with a helicopter illustration.

Isfahan Military Air Base: 5:40 A.M. To the east the dark night was beginning to lighten with the dawn. The base was quiet now, no one about except for armed Islamic Guards who, with the people of Isfahan in their thousands and led by mullahs had stormed the base yesterday and now possessed it, all army and air force officers and men confined to their barracks under guard – or free, openly declared now for Khomeini and the revolution.

The sentry, Relazi, was eighteen and very proud of his green armband and to be on guard outside the shed that contained the traitor General Valik and his family who had been caught yesterday, skulking in the officers' mess with his CIA foreign pilot. God is Great, he thought. Tomorrow they will be cast into hell with all foul People of the Left Hand.

For generations the Relazis had been cobblers in one tiny stall of Isfahan's Old Bazaar. Yes, he thought, I was a bazaari until a week ago when our mullah called me and all the Faithful to God's battle, gave me God's armband and this gun and showed me how to use it. How wonderful are the ways of God!

He was sheltered in the lee of the hut, out of the snow, but the damp cold was going through him even though he was wearing all the clothes he possessed in the world – sweatshirt, a coarse shirt over it, a coat and trousers bought secondhand, an old sweater and ancient army coat that once had belonged to his father. His feet felt numb. 'As God wants,' he said out loud and felt better. 'I'll be relieved soon and then I'll eat again – by God, soldiers lived like veritable pashas, at least two meals every day, one with rice, imagine that, and pay every week . . . pay from Satan but pay even so.' He coughed badly, his breath wheezing, shifted the U.S. army carbine to his other shoulder, found the stub of the cigarette he had been saving and lit it.

By the Prophet, he thought gleefully, who would have imagined that we could take the base so easily, so few of us killed and sent to Paradise before we had overwhelmed the soldiers on the gate and swarmed into the camp – our brothers on the base blocking the runways with trucks, and others seizing the aircraft and helicopters to prevent escape of the Shah traitors. Rushing the bullets of the enemy, the Name of God on our lips. 'Join us, brothers,' we shouted, 'join God's revolution, help do God's work! Come to Paradise . . . don't go to hell . . .'

The young man trembled and began to mouth the words imprinted on him by a dozen mullahs reading from the Koran, then translating: 'there to live for ever with all sinners and the accursed People of the Left Hand, tasting neither refreshment nor any drink but boiling water or molten metal and decaying filth. And when the fires of hell have burned away the skin, they will grow new ones so that their suffering be never ending . . .'

He closed his eyes with the intensity of his prayers: Let me die with one of God's names on my lips, and so guarantee that I will go straight to the Garden of Paradise with all the People of the Right Hand, to be there for ever, never to feel hunger again, never to watch brothers and sisters of the villages with bloated bellies whimper into death, never to cry out in the night at the awfulness of life but to be in Paradise: 'there to lie on silken couches adorned with robes of green silk, attended by fresh blooming youths bearing goblets and ewers and cups of flowing wine, with such fruits that please us best and the flesh of such birds as we shall long for. And ours shall be the houris with large dark eyes like pearls hidden in their shells, for ever young, for ever virgin, amid trees clad with fruit, and in extended shade and by flowing waters, never growing old, for ev –'

The rifle butt pulverised his nose and caved in the front of his skull, permanently blinding him and ending for ever his normality but not

308

killing him before he tumbled unconscious into the snow. His assailant was a soldier, of an age with him, and this man hastily picked up the carbine – used it to break the lock of the flimsy door and shove it open.

'Hurry,' the assailant whispered, sweating with fear. In a moment General Valik poked his head out cautiously. The man grabbed his arm, 'Come on, hurry, by God,' he snarled.

'May God bless you . . .' Valik said, his teeth chattering, then darted back and came out again with two huge bundles of rials that the man stuffed into his battle dress and vanished as silently as he had arrived. Valik hesitated a moment, his heart driving. He saw the carbine in the snow and picked it up, loaded it, and slung it over his shoulder, then grabbed up the attaché case, blessing God that the revolutionaries had been too hasty in their search to discover its false bottom before they were shoved in here to await the coming of the Tribunals.

'Follow me,' he whispered urgently to his family. 'But in the Name of God make no noise. Follow me carefully.' He pulled his coat closer around him and led the way through the snow. His wife, Annoush, his eight-year-old son, Jalal, and his daughter Setarem, six, hesitated in the doorway. All wore ski clothes – Annoush a mink over hers that the Islamic Guards had taunted her about as an open representation of the wages of sin. 'Keep it with you,' they had said contemptuously, 'that alone damns you!' In the night she had been happy for its warmth, huddled on the dirt floor in the unheated shed, wrapping the children in it. 'Come along, my darlings,' she whispered, trying to keep her terror from them.

The sentry's body blocked their way as he lay in the snow, moaning softly.

'Mama, why does he sleep in the snow?' the little girl asked in a whisper.

'Never mind, my darling. Let's hurry. Not a sound now!'

Silently she stepped over him. The little girl could not quite make it and had to tread on him, and she stumbled, sprawling in the snow. But she did not cry out, just scrambled to her feet helped by her brother. Together, hand in hand, they hurried onward.

Valik guided them carefully. When they reached the hangar where the 212 was still parked, he breathed a little easier.

This area was well away from the main camp, the other side of the enormous runway. Making sure there were no guards nearby he ran out to the chopper and peered into the cabin. To his enormous relief no guards were asleep inside. He tried the door. It was not locked. He slid it open as quietly as he could, and beckoned the others. Silently they joined him. He helped them up and got in after them, sliding the door to, locking it from the inside. Quickly he made the children comfortable on some blankets under the jump seats, cautioning them not to make their presence known whatever happened. Then he sat beside his wife, wrapped a blanket around his shoulders, for he was very cold, and held her hand. The tears wet her cheeks.

'Be patient, don't cry. It won't be long now,' he whispered, gentling her. 'We won't have to wait long. Insha'Allah.'

'Insha'Allah,' she echoed brokenly, 'but the whole world's gone mad . . . thrown into a filthy outhouse like criminals . . . what's going to happen to us . . .'

'With the Help of God we've got this far, so why not all the way to Kuwait?'

They had arrived here yesterday just before noon. The flight from the pickup outside Tehran had been without incident, all airwaves silent. His trusted chauffeur of fifteen years had driven his car back to Tehran, with orders to tell no one that they had 'gone to their house on the Caspian'. In this escape we trust no one, Valik had told his wife while they were waiting for the chopper to arrive. She had said of course, but we should have brought Sharazad, that would have helped her and Tom Lochart and guaranteed he would take us onward.

'No, she'd never have left, why should she?' Valik had said. 'With or without Sharazad, he is not to be trusted – he's alien and not one of us.'

'It would have been wiser to have brought her.'

'No,' he had said, knowing what would have to be done with Lochart.

All the way from Tehran to Isfahan he had sat in the front with Lochart. They had stayed low, avoiding towns and airfields. When Lochart had called Isfahan Military Base Control they were obviously expected. The tower had given them directions where to land with an order not to call again and to observe radio silence. Air Force Brigadier General Mohammed Seladi, Valik's uncle, who had arranged for them to land and to refuel, met them at the helipad. The general had greeted them sombrely. As it was near lunchtime he said they should eat on the base before going on.

'But, Mohammed Excellency, we've enough food here on the aircraft,' Valik had told him.

'I must insist,' Seladi had said nervously, 'I must insist, Excellency. You should pay your respects to the commandant. It is necessary, and, er, we must talk.'

It was during this time that the Green Bands and the mob had burst through the gates, swarmed over the station, arrested them all, and had taken Lochart to another part of the base. Sons of dogs, Valik thought angrily, may they all burn in hell! I knew at the time we should have just refuelled and gone on at once. Seladi's a blundering fool. It's all his fault . . .

In an upper storey of a barrack a quarter of a mile away, Tom Lochart was sleeping fitfully. Suddenly he was awakened by a scuffle outside in the corridor, the door burst open, and he was half blinded by a flashlight.

'Quick,' a voice said in American English and the two men helped him stand. At once the two half-seen figures turned and ran off. A split second to collect himself then Lochart rushed in pursuit, along the corridor, down three flights of stairs and into the open. There he stopped with the others, his breathing heavy. He just had time to see that both men were officers, a captain and a major, before they were off again in the semi-darkness, running hard. Dawn brightened the eastern sky. Snow fell lightly, helping to hide them and muffling their footsteps.

Ahead was a guardhouse with a wood fire outside, a few sleepy inattentive revolutionaries huddled around it. The three men diverted and ran down between a line of barracks, diverted again into an alleyway as a truck filled with chanting guards came around a corner, then rushed into the open along the boundary road for the far hangar and the 212. In the lee of the hangar they stopped to catch their breath.

'Listen, pilot,' the major said, panting, 'when I give the word, we run for the chopper and take off. Ready?'

'What about the others?' Lochart asked, a stitch in his side and hardly able to talk. 'What about General Valik and his fam –'

'Forget them. Ali,' the major jerked his thumb at the other man, 'Ali goes in front with you and I'm in the back. How long will it take to get airborne once you start up?'

'Minimum.'

'Make it less,' the major said. 'Come on!'

They rushed for the 212, Lochart and Ali, the captain, heading for the cockpit. At that moment Lochart saw a car without headlights charging along the boundary road towards them and his heart seemed to stop. 'Look!'

'In God's Name hurry, pilot!'

Lochart redoubled his efforts, jumped into the pilot's seat, shoved in the circuit breakers, switched on, and began to crank her up. At the same moment the major reached the sliding door and tore it open. He almost fainted when the carbine was shoved in his face by Valik.

'Oh, it's you, Major! Praise be to God . . .'

'Praise be to God you're here and made your escape, Excellency,' the major gasped, forced his panic away, and clambered in, the engines already winding the blades but nowhere near airspeed yet. 'Praise be to God you made your escape . . . but where's the soldier?'

'He just took the money and fled.'

'Did he bring the guns?'

'No, this is all h –'

'Son of a dog!' the major said furiously, then shouted at Lochart, 'In the Name of God hurryyyyyyy!' He whirled and looked at the approaching car. It was closing fast. He grabbed the carbine from Valik, knelt in the doorway, aimed at the driver and squeezed the trigger. The burst was high – as behind him Annoush and the children cried out in terror – the car hurtled off the road taking evading action and swung behind a row of sheds, came into view for an instant to dart around the hangar and disappear again.

Lochart had his headset on and was watching the needles climbing, willing them to hurry. 'Come on, goddammit,' he muttered, hands and feet ready on the controls, the scream of the jets growing, the captain beside him praying openly. He could not hear Annoush sobbing in the back or the petrified children who had scrambled out of their hiding place to bury themselves in her skirts, or Valik and the major raging at him to hurry.

Needles climbing. Still climbing. Still climbing. Almost in the Green. Now! His left hand started to raise the collective lever but the car whirled around the hangar and came at them head on to stop fifteen yards away. Five men jumped out of it – one rushed directly at the cockpit and pointed an automatic rifle at him, the others went for the cabin door. He was almost airborne but knew he was a dead man if he went the extra inches and he saw the man angrily motion him to stop. He obeyed, then swung around to look into the back. The other men were clambering in. They were all officers, Valik and the major were embracing them and being embraced, then he heard, 'Take off, for crissake!' in his headset and felt a shove in the ribs. It was Ali, the captain, beside him.

'Take off!' Ali said again, his English American-accented, and gave a thumbs-up to the man outside still aiming at them. The man rushed for the door, got in and slammed the door closed. 'Hurry, goddammit, look over there!' He pointed at the other side of the runway. More cars

312

were heading their way. Sparks of machine gun fire from someone leaning out of a window. In seconds Lochart was airborne, all senses concentrating on escape.

Behind him some of the officers cheered, hung on as the chopper took evading action, and sorted themselves into seats. Most were colonels. Some were shaken, particularly General Seladi who sat between Valik and the major. 'I wasn't sure it was you, General Excellency,' the major was saying, 'so I fired high just as a warning. Praise be to God the plan worked so well.'

'But you were going to take off. You were going to leave us! You w –'

'Oh, no, Excellency Uncle,' Valik interrupted smoothly, 'it was the British pilot, he was panicking and didn't want to wait! They've no balls, Britishers! Never mind him,' he added, 'we're armed, we've food, and we're safe! Praise be to God! And more praise that I had time to plan.' Yes, he thought, if it hadn't been for me and my money we'd all be dead – money to bribe the man who released us and you, and the major and captain to release Lochart whom I need just a little longer.

'If we'd been left we'd've been shot!' General Seladi was enraged, his face purple. 'God curse that pilot to hell! Why did you waste time releasing him? Ali can fly a 212!'

'Yes. But Lochart has more experience and we need him to get through the maze.'

Valik smiled encouragingly at Annoush who sat across the aisle facing him, the little girl trembling in her arms, his son sitting on the floor dozing, his head in her lap. Weakly she smiled back, shifting the weight of the child to ease the aches that pervaded her. He reached over and touched her, then settled more comfortably in his seat and closed his eyes, very tired but most content. You're a very clever man, he told himself. In his most secret heart he knew then that without his stratagem of pretending to McIver that SAVAK was going to arrest him – and particularly his family – neither McIver nor Lochart would have helped them to escape. You measured them perfectly as you have Gavallan.

Fools! he thought contemptuously.

And as for you, Seladi, my stupid and rapacious uncle who bartered safe refuelling at Isfahan – which you failed to provide – in return for a safe passage out for yourself and eleven of your friends, you're worse. You're a traitor. If I hadn't had an informant of long-standing in the general staff HQ I would never have heard of the generals' great betrayal in time to escape and we'd've been caught like flies in a honey-pot in Tehran. Loyalists may still prevail, the battle's not lost yet, but meanwhile my family and I will watch events from England, St. Moritz, or New York.

He let himself go into the exciting, wonderful power of the jets that were carrying them to safety, to a house in London, a country house in Surrey, another in California, and to Swiss and Bahamian bank accounts. Ah, yes, he told himself happily, and that reminds me about our blocked S-G joint account in the Bahamas, another $4 million to enrich us – and easy now to pry from Gavallan's grubby paws. More than enough to keep me and my family safe whatever happens here – until we can return. Khomeini won't live for ever even if he wins – God curse him! Soon we'll be able to return home, soon Iran will be normal again, meanwhile we have everything we need.

His ears heard Seladi still muttering about Lochart and almost being left behind. 'Calm yourself, Excellency,' he said, and took his arm, gentling him, and thought, You and your running dogs still have a value, a temporary value. Perhaps as hostages, perhaps as bait – who knows? None are family except you and you betrayed us. 'Calm yourself, my revered uncle, with the help of God the pilot will get what he deserves.'

Yes. Lochart should not have panicked. He should have waited for my order. Disgusting to panic.

Valik closed his eyes and slept, very satisfied with himself.

At the Iran-Toda Refinery, Bandar-e Delam: 12:04 P.M. Scragger was whistling tonelessly, hand-pumping fuel into his main tanks from big barrels that were lined up in a small Japanese half-trunk beside the freshly washed 206, sparkling in the sun. Nearby was a young Green Band who squatted in the shade, leaning on his M16, half asleep.

The noonday sun was warm and the light breeze made the day pleasant and took away the constant humidity, here on the coast. Scragger was dressed lightly, white shirt with captain's epaulet, summer-weight black trousers and shoes, the inevitable dark glasses and peaked cap.

Now the tanks were brimming. 'That's it, me son,' he said to the Japanese assigned to assist him.

'*Hai, Anjin-san*' – Yes, Mr. Pilot – the man said. Like all employees at the refinery he wore white, spotless overalls and gloves, with Iran-Toda Industry emblazoned on the back, then the same thing in Farsi politely above, with the equivalent in Japanese characters beneath it.

'*Hai*, it is,' Scragger said, using one of the words that he had picked

315

up from Kasigi en route from Lengeh yesterday. He pointed. 'Next our long-range tanks, and then we'll fill the spares.' For the journey that de Plessey had grandly authorised on Sunday night – to celebrate their victory over the saboteurs – Scragger had taken out the backseat and lashed in place two 40-gallon drums, 'just in case, Mr. Kasigi. I've connected them to the main tanks. We can use a hand pump and can even refuel in the air, if we have to – if you do the pumping. Now we won't have to land for fuel. You can never tell with weather in the Gulf, there's always sudden storms or squalls, fog, winds can play tricks. Our best bet's to stay a little out to sea.'

'And Jaws?'

Scragger had laughed with him. 'The old hammerhead of Kharg? With any luck we might see him – if we get that far and don't get diverted.'

'Still no callback from Kish radar?'

'No, but it doesn't matter. They've cleared us to Bandar Delam. You're sure you can refuel me at your plant?'

'Yes, we've storage tanks, Captain. Helipads, hangar and repair shop. Those were the first things we built – we had a contract with Guerney.'

'Yes, yes, I knew about that, but they've quit, haven't they?'

'Yes, they did, a week or so ago. Perhaps your company would take over the contract? Perhaps you could be put in charge – there's work for three 212s and perhaps two 206s constantly, while we're building.'

Scragger had chuckled. 'That'd make old Andy the Gav happy as a cat in a barrel of fish sticks and Dirty Dunc fart dust!'

'Please?'

Scragger had tried to explain the joke about McIver. But when he was through Kasigi had not laughed, just said, 'Oh now I understand.'

They're a rum lot, Scragger thought.

When he finished refuelling he did another ground check – engine, rotors, airframe – though he did not expect to leave today. De Plessey had asked him to wait for Kasigi, to fly him where he needed to go, and to bring him back to Lengeh on Thursday. The 206 checked out perfectly. Satisfied he glanced at his watch, then he pointed at his stomach and rubbed it. 'Grub time, *hai?*'

'*Hai!*' His helper smiled and motioned to the small truck nearby, then pointed at the main, four-storey office building two-hundred-odd yards away where the executive offices were.

Scragger shook his head. 'I'll walk,' he said and waggled his two fingers to parody walking so the young man half bowed and got into the truck and drove off. He stood there for a moment, watching and being watched by the guard. Now that the truck had left and the tanks were closed, he could smell the sea and the rotting debris of the nearby shore. It was near low tide – there was only one tide a day in the Gulf, as in the Red Sea, because it was shallow and landlocked but for the narrow Strait of Hormuz.

He liked the sea smell. He had grown up in Sydney, always within sight of the sea. After the war he had settled there again. At least, he reminded himself, I was there between jobs and the missus and the kids stayed there and still stay there, more or less. His son and two daughters were married now with children of their own. Whenever he was on home leave, perhaps once a year, he saw them. They had a friendly, distant relationship.

In the early years his wife and children had come to the Gulf to settle. Within a month they had gone home to Sydney. 'We'll be at Bondi, Scrag,' she had said. 'No more foreign places for us, lad.' During one of his two-year stints in Kuwait she had met another man. When Scragger had returned the next time, she said, 'I think we'll divorce, lad. It's best for the kids – and thee and me,' and so they did. Her new husband lived a few years, then died. Scragger and she drifted back into their pattern of friendliness – not that we ever left off, he thought. She's a good sort and the kids're happy and I'm flying. He still sent her money monthly. She always said she didn't need it. 'Then put it into savings against a rainy day, Nell,' he always told her. So far, touch wood, they've not had rainy days, she and the kids and their kids.

The nearest wood was the butt of the rifle the revolutionary had in his lap. The man was staring at him malevolently from the shade. Shitty bastard, you're not going to spoil my day. He beamed at him, then turned his back, stretched, and looked around.

This's a great site for a refinery, he told himself, close enough to Abadan, to the main pipelines joining the north and south oil fields – great idea to try to save all that gas being burned off, billions of tons of it all over the world. Criminal waste, when you think of it.

The refinery was on a promontory, with its own dredged wharfing set up that stretched out into the Gulf for four hundred yards, that Kasigi had told him would eventually be able to handle two supertankers at the same time of whatever size could be built. Around the helipads were acres of complex cracking plants and buildings, all seemingly inter-connected with miles of steel and plastic pipes of all sizes, mazes of them, with huge cocks and valves, pumping stations, and everywhere cranes and earthmovers and vast piles of all manner of construction

317

materials, mountains of concrete and sand, reinforcing steel mesh scattered around – along with neat dumps the size of football fields, of crates and containers protected with plastic tarpaulins – and half-finished roads, foundations, wharves, and excavations. But almost nothing moving, neither man nor machines.

When they had landed a welcoming committee of twenty or thirty Japanese had been at the helipad, hastily assembled, along with a hundred-odd Iranian strikers and armed Islamic Guards, some wearing IPLO armbands, the first Scragger had ever seen. After much shouting and threatening and examining their papers and the inbound Kish radar clearance, the spokesman had said the two of them could stay but no one could leave or the chopper take off without the komiteh's permission.

En route to the office building, Chief Engineer Watanabe, who could speak English, had explained that the strike komiteh had been, for all intents and purposes, in possession for almost two months. In that time almost no progress had been made and all work had ceased. 'They won't even allow us to maintain our equipment.' He was a hard-faced, tough, grizzle-haired man in his sixties with very strong working hands. He lit another cigarette from his half-smoked one.

'And your radio?'

'Six days ago they locked the radio room, forbidding its use and took away the key. Phones of course have been out for weeks and the telex for a week or more. We've still about a thousand Japanese personnel here – dependants of course were never permitted – food supplies are very short, we've had no mail for six weeks. We can't move out, we can't work. We're almost prisoners and can do nothing without very great troubles indeed. However, at least we are alive to protect what we have done and wait patiently to be allowed to continue. We are very indeed honoured to see you, Kasigi-san, and you, Captain.'

Scragger had left them to their business, feeling the tension between the two men, however much they tried to hide it. In the evening he had eaten lightly, as always, allowed himself one ice-cold Japanese beer, 'Bugger me, it's not as good as Fosters', then had done his eleven minutes of Canadian Air Force exercises and had gone to bed.

Just before midnight while he was still reading, there had been a soft knock. Kasigi had come in excitedly, apologising for disturbing him but he felt Scragger should know at once that they had just heard a broadcast from a Khomeini spokesman in Tehran saying that all the armed services had declared for him, Prime Minister Bakhtiar had resigned, that now Iran was totally free of the Shah's yoke, that by Khomeini's personal

318

order, all fighting should cease, all strikes should stop, oil production should commence again, all bazaars and shops should open, all men should hand in their weapons and return to work, and above everything, all should give thanks to God for granting them victory.

Kasigi had beamed. 'Now we can start again. Thank all gods, eh? Now things will be normal again.'

When Kasigi had left, Scragger had lain there, the light on, his mind racing over the possibilities of what would happen now. Stone the crows, he had thought, how fast everything's been. I'd've bet heavy odds the Shah'd never be shoved out, heavier odds that Khomeini'd never be allowed back, and then my bundle on a military coup.

He had turned off the light. 'Just goes to show, Scrag, old chap. You know eff all.'

In the morning he had awakened early, accepted Japanese green tea in place of the breakfast tea he usually drank – Indian, very strong and always with condensed milk – and gone to check, clean and refuel, and now, everything tidy, he was very hungry. He nodded briefly to the guard who paid no attention to him and strolled off towards the four-storey office building.

Kasigi was standing at one of the windows on the top floor where the executive offices were. He was in the boardroom, a spacious corner office with a huge table and seats for twenty and had been watching the 206 and Scragger absently, his mind in turmoil, hard put to contain his rage. Since early this morning he had been going through cost projections, reports, accounts receivable, work projections, and they all added up to the same result: at least another billion dollars and another year of time to start production. This was only the second time he had visited the refinery which was not in his sphere of responsibility though he was a director and member of the Chairman's Executive Committee that was their conglomerate's highest echelon of decision-making.

Behind him Chief Engineer Watanabe sat alone at the vast table, outwardly patient, chain-smoking as always. He had been in charge for the last two years, deputy Chief since the project began in '71 – a man of great experience. The previous chief engineer had died here, on-site, of a heart attack.

No wonder, Kasigi thought angrily. Two years ago – perhaps four – it must have been quite clear to him our absolute maximum budget of $3.5 billion would be inadequate, that overruns were already vast and delivery dates totally unrealistic.

'Why didn't Chief Engineer Kasusaka inform us? Why didn't he make a special report?'

'He did, Kasigi-san,' Watanabe said politely. 'But by direction of the Head Agreements of the joint venture here, all reports have to go through our court-appointed partners. It's an Iranian pattern – it's always supposed to be a joint venture, fifty-fifty, with shared responsibilities, but gradually the Iranians manage to manoeuvre meetings and contracts and clauses, usually using the court or Shah as an excuse, till they have de facto control and then . . .'

He shrugged. 'You've no idea how clever they are – worse than a Chinese merchant, much worse. They agree to buy the whole animal but renege and take only the steak and leave you with the rest of the carcass on your hands.' He put out the half-smoked cigarette and lit another. 'There was a meeting of the whole board of partners with Gyokotomo-sama – Yoshi Gyokotomo himself, chairman of the Syndicate – here in this office, just before Chief Engineer Kasusaka-san died. I was present. Kasusaka-san cautioned everyone that Iranian bureaucratic delays and harassments – squeeze is the correct word – would put back production dates and cause a vast increase in cost overruns. I was present, I heard him with my own ears, but he was overridden by the Iranian partners who told the chairman everything would be rearranged, that Kasusaka-san didn't understand Iran or the way they did things in Iran.' Watanabe studied the end of his cigarette. 'Kasusaka-san even said the same in private to Gyokotomo-sama, begging him to beware, and gave him a written detailed report.'

Kasigi's face closed. 'Were you present at this meeting?'

'No – but he told me what he had said, that Gyokotomo-sama accepted the report and said that he himself would take it up to the highest level, in Tehran and at home in Japan. But nothing happened, Kasigi-san. Nothing.'

'Where is the copy of the report?'

'There isn't one. The next day, before he left for Tehran, Gyokotomo ordered them destroyed.' Again the older man shrugged. 'Chief Engineer Kasusaka's job, and mine, was and is to get the refinery built, whatever the problems, and not to interfere with the working of the Syndicate.' Watanabe lit a fresh cigarette from the half-smoked cigarette, inhaled deeply, stubbed the other out delicately, wanting to smash it and the ashtray and the desk and the building and the plant to smithereens – along with this interloper Kasigi who dared to question him, who knew nothing, had never worked in Iran, and had his position in the company because he was kinsman to the Todas. 'Unlike Chief Engineer Kasusaka,' he added oh so gently, 'over the years I have kept copies of my monthly reports.'

'*So ka?*' Kasigi said, trying to sound matter-of-fact.

'Yes,' Watanabe said. And copies of these copies in a very safe place, he thought grimly in his most secret heart, taking a thick file from his briefcase and putting it on the desk, just in case you'll try to make me responsible for the failures. 'You may read them if you wish.'

'Thank you.' With an effort Kasigi resisted the temptation to grab the file at once.

Watanabe rubbed his face tiredly. He had been up most of the night preparing for this meeting. 'Once we're back to normal, work will progress quickly. We are eighty percent complete. I'm confident we can complete with the right planning – it's all in my reports, including the matter of the Kasusaka meeting with the partners, and then with Gyokotomo-sama.'

'What do you suggest as an overall solution to Iran-Toda?'

'There isn't one until we're back to normal.'

'We are now. You heard the broadcast.'

'I heard it, Kasigi-san, but normal for me means when the Bazargan government's in full control.'

'That will happen within days. Your solution?'

'The solution is simple: get fresh partners who cooperate, arrange the financing we need and within a year, less than a year, we'll be producing.'

'Can the partners be changed?'

Watanabe's voice became as thin as his lips. 'The old ones were all court-appointed, or approved, therefore Shah men, therefore suspect and "enemies of the people". We haven't seen one since Khomeini returned, or heard from one. We've heard rumours they've all fled but . . .' Watanabe shrugged his great shoulders. 'I've no way of checking with no telex, no phones, no transport. I doubt if the new "partners" will be different in attitude.'

Kasigi nodded and glanced back out of the window, seeing nothing. Easy to blame Iranians and dead men and secret meetings and destroyed reports. Never had Chairman Yoshi Gyokotomo mentioned any meeting with Kasusaka or any written report. Why should Gyokotomo bury such a vital report? Ridiculous because he and his company are equally at risk as ours. Why? If Watanabe's telling the truth and his own reports could prove it, why?

Then, for an instant that Watanabe noticed, Kasigi's face fell to pieces as the answer came to him: because the immense overrun and management failure of the Iran-Toda complex, added to the disastrous slump in world shipping, will break Toda Shipping Industries, will break Hiro Toda personally and lay us open to a takeover! Takeover by whom? Of course by Yoshi Gyokotomo. Of course by that jumped-up peasant family who has hated us who are highborn, samurai-descended from ancient tim –

Then again Kasigi felt as though his brain was going to explode:

Of course by Yoshi Gyokotomo but aided and abetted of course by our arch rivals, Mitsuwari Industries! Oh Gyokotomo'll lose a fortune but they can sustain their portion of the loss while they grease the correct palms suggesting that they will jointly absorb Toda's losses, dismember it, and with the benevolence of MITI put it under proper management. With the Todas will go their kinsmen: the Kasigis and the Kayamas. I might as well be dead.

Oh ko!

And now I am the one who has to bring back the terrible news. Watanabe's reports will prove nothing, for of course Gyokotomo will deny everything, damning me for trying to accuse him and will shout from the rooftops that the Watanabe reports prove conclusively Hiro Toda's mismanagement for years. So I'm in trouble either way. Perhaps it was Hiro Toda's plan to put me in the middle of this mess! Perhaps he wants to replace me with one of his brothers or neph –

At that moment there was a knock and the door burst open. Watanabe's distraught young assistant came in hurriedly, apologising profusely for disturbing them. 'Oh, so sorry, Watanabe-san, oh yes, so sorr –'

'What is it?' Watanabe said, bringing him up short.

'A komiteh is arriving in strength, Watanabe-san, Kasigi-sama! Look!' The white-faced young man pointed at the other windows that fronted the building.

Kasigi was there first. In front of the main door was a truck filled with revolutionaries, other trucks and cars following. Men jumped out of them, began to collect in haphazard groups.

Scragger was approaching and they saw him stop, then go on again towards the main door, but he was waved away as a big Mercedes drove up. Out of its back came a heavy-set man in black robes and a black turban with a white beard, accompanied by another much younger man, moustached, dressed in light clothes with an open-neck shirt. Both wore glasses. Watanabe sucked in his breath.

'Who are they?' Kasigi asked.

'I don't know, but an ayatollah means trouble. Mullahs wear white turbans, ayatollahs wear black.' Surrounded by half a dozen guards the two men strode into the building. 'Bring them up here, Takeo, ceremoniously.' The young man rushed off at once. 'We've only had one visit by an ayatollah, last year, just after the Abadan fire. He called a meeting of all our Iranian staff, harangued them for three minutes, then in the name of Khomeini ordered them to strike.' His face settled into a mask. 'That was the beginning of our trouble here – we expatriates have carried on as best we could ever since.'

'What now?' Kasigi asked.

Watanabe shrugged, strode over to a bureau and lifted up a framed photo of Khomeini that Kasigi had not noticed and hung it on the wall. 'Just for politeness,' he said with a sardonic smile. 'Shall we sit down? They expect formality from us – please take the head of the table.'

'No, Watanabe-san. Please, you are in charge, I am only a visitor.'

'As you wish.' Watanabe took his usual seat, and faced the door. Kasigi broke the silence. 'What was that about the Abadan fire?'

'Ah, sorry,' Watanabe said apologetically, actually disgusted that Kasigi did not know about that most important event. 'It was last August, during their holy month of Ramadan when no Believer may take food or drink from sunup to sunset and tempers are normally thin, at that time there was a small amount of national protest against the Shah, mostly in Tehran and Qom, but nothing serious then and the clashes easily contained by police and SAVAK. On August 15th arsonists set fire to a movie house, the Rex Cinema in Abadan. All the doors "happened" to be locked or jammed, firemen and police "happened" to be slow arriving and in the panic almost five hundred died, mostly women and children.'

'How terrible!'

'Yes. The whole nation was outraged. Instantly SAVAK was blamed, and therefore the Shah, the Shah blamed leftists and swore the police and SAVAK had nothing to do with it. Of course he set up an inquiry which went on for weeks. Unfortunately it left the question of responsibility unresolved.' Watanabe was listening for the sound of footsteps. 'That was the spark that united the warring opposing factions under Khomeini and tore the Pahlavis from their throne.'

After a pause Kasigi said, 'Who do you think set fire to the cinema?'

'Who wanted to destroy the Pahlavis? So easy to cry SAVAK!' Watanabe heard the lift stop. 'What're five hundred women and children to a fanatic – of any persuasion?'

The door was opened by the assistant Takeo. The ayatollah and the civilian strode in importantly, six armed men crowding after them. Watanabe and Kasigi got up politely and bowed.

'Welcome,' Watanabe said in Japanese though he could speak very good Farsi. 'I am Naga Watanabe, in charge here, this is Mr. Kasigi from our head office in Japan. Whom do I have the pleasure of addressing, please?'

Takeo, who could speak perfect Farsi, began to interpret but the civilian, who had already sat down, cut him short. '*Vous parlez français?*' he said rudely to Watanabe.

'*Iye*' – No – Watanabe said in Japanese.

'*Bien sûr, M'sieur,*' Kasigi said hesitantly, his French mediocre. '*Je parle un peu, mais je parle Anglais mieux, et M'sieur Watanabe aussi.*' I speak a little French but I speak English better and Mr. Watanabe also.

'Very well,' the man said curtly, his English Parisian-accented. 'Then we will speak English. I am Muzadeh, deputy minister for the Abadan area for Prime Minister Bazargan an –'

'But Bazargan doesn't make the law, the Imam does,' the ayatollah interrupted him sharply. 'The Imam appointed Bazargan temporary prime minister until, with the Help of God, our Islamic state is formed.' He was in his late sixties, a round-faced man, his eyebrows as white as his beard, his black robe meticulous. 'Under the Imam's leadership,' he added pointedly.

'Yes, of course,' Muzadeh said, then went on as though there had been no interruption, 'and I inform you officially that the Iran-Toda is now under our direct control. There will be a meeting in three days to organise controls and future operations. All previous Shah-inspired, therefore illegal, contracts are voided. I will appoint a new controlling board, myself as chairman, workers' representatives, one Japanese worker and yourself. You w –'

'And myself, and a mullah from Bandar-e Delam,' the ayatollah said, glaring at him.

Muzadeh angrily switched to Farsi, 'We can discuss the makeup of the committee later.' There was an edge to his voice. 'The important thing is to have the workers represented.'

'The important thing is to do the work of God.'

'In this the work of the People and the work of God is the same.'

'Not if the "work of the People" is a covert name for the work of Satan!'

All six of the Iranian guards shifted uneasily. Unconsciously they had regrouped into four and two. In the silence their eyes went from man to man seated at the table. One of the men quietly eased off a safety catch.

'You were saying?' Watanabe said quickly and almost added, Banzai, with relief, as he saw everyone turn their attention back to him. 'You wish to form a new committee?'

'Yes.' With an effort Muzadeh tore his gaze off the ayatollah and continued, 'You will have all books ready for our perusal and you will be held responsible for any – any problems whatsoever, past or future or crimes against Iran, past or future.'

'We've been joint partners with the government of Iran since the beg –'

'With the Shah, not with the Iranian people,' Muzadeh cut in. Behind him the guards, youths, some teenagers, some hardly bearded, began muttering.

'True, Mr. Muzadeh,' Watanabe said, unafraid. He had been through the same sort of confrontation many times in the past few months. 'But we are Japanese. Iran-Toda is being built by Japanese technicians with maximum help from Iranian trainees and workers, it's paid for totally by Japanese money.'

'That has noth –'

'Yes, we know,' the ayatollah said loudly but agreeably, overriding the other, 'we know that and you're welcome in Iran. We know Japanese are not vile Americans or insidious British, and though you're not Muslim, unhappily for yourselves, your eyes not yet open to Allah, we welcome you. But now, now with the Help of God we have possessed our country back, now we must make . . . make new arrangements for future operations. Our people will stay on here, asking questions. Please cooperate with them – you have nothing to fear. Remember, we want the plant finished and operating as much as you. My name is Ishmael Ahwazi, and I am ayatollah of this area.' He got up with an abruptness that made some of the men jump. 'We will return on the fourth day from now!'

Muzadeh said in Farsi hotly, 'There are other orders for these foreign –'

But the ayatollah had already left. Contemptuously Muzadeh got up and stalked out, his men following.

When they were quite alone Kasigi allowed himself to take a handkerchief out and mop his brow. Young Takeo was shock still. Watanabe searched his pockets for his cigarettes but the pack was empty. He crushed the box. Takeo came to life and hurried to a drawer and found a fresh pack, opened it and offered it.

'Thank you, Takeo.' Watanabe sat and accepted a light. 'You can go now.' He looked at Kasigi. 'So,' he said, 'now it begins again.'

'Yes,' Kasigi said, the implications of a new komiteh committed to successful completion possessing him. 'That's the best news we could have. That will be very welcome in Japan.' In fact, he thought with growing excitement, this news will take the curse off Watanabe's reports and perhaps somehow we – Hiro Toda and I – together we can neutralise Gyokotomo. And if, even better, Hiro retired in place of his brother that would be perfect!

'What?' he asked, seeing Watanabe looking at him.

'I didn't mean work begins again, Kasigi-san,' the chief engineer said sharply. 'The new komiteh won't be any better than the other – in fact it will be worse. With the partners the inevitable pishkesh opened doors and you knew where you were. But with these fanatics, these amateurs?' Irritably Watanabe ran his hand through his hair. All gods and spirits give me the strength not to curse this fool for his continual stupidity! he thought. Be wise, calm yourself, he's only an ape, not as well born as you who are a direct descendant of the lords of the north.

'The ayatollah lied, then?' Kasigi's happiness vanished.

'No. That poor fool believed what he said but nothing will happen. Police and SAVAK, whatever new name it will have, still control Abadan and this area – the locals are mostly Arab, Sunnis, not Shi'ite Iranians. I meant the killing begins again.' Watanabe explained the clash the two men had had in Farsi. 'Now it's going to be much worse with every faction manoeuvring for power.'

'These barbarians won't obey Khomeini? Won't disarm?'

'I'm saying the leftists like Muzadeh will carry on the war, aided and abetted by the Soviets who are desperate to possess Iran, have always wanted Iran, will always want Iran – not for the oil but for the Strait of Hormuz. For with their foot on the strait they possess the Western world – and Japan. As far as I'm concerned the West, America and the rest of the world, can rot, but we *must* go to war if the strait is prohibited to our ships.'

'I agree. Of course I agree.' Kasigi was equally irritable. 'We all know that. Of course it means war – while we depend on oil.'

'Yes.' Watanabe smiled grimly. 'Ten years, no more.'

'Yes.' Both men were aware of the enormous national effort in research projects, overt and covert, to develop the alternate source of energy that would make the Japanese self-sufficient – *The* National Project. The source: the sun and the sea. 'Ten years, yes, for ten years only.' Kasigi was confident. 'If we have ten years of peace and free access to the U.S. market – then we'll have our alternate and then we'll own the world. But meanwhile,' he added, his anger returning, 'for the next ten years we have to kowtow to barbarians and bandits of every kind!'

'Didn't Khrushchev say the Soviets didn't have to do anything about Iran because "Iran's a rotten apple that'll drop into our hands"?' Watanabe was enraged. 'I guarantee those dung eaters are shaking the tree with all their might.'

'We beat them once,' Kasigi said darkly, remembering the Japanese-Russian naval war of 1904 that his grandfather had served in. 'We can do it again. That man – Muzadeh? Perhaps he's just a progressive and anti mullah – they're not all fanatical Khomeinites.'

'I agree, Kasigi-san. But some're equally fanatic for their god Lenin-Marx and equally stupid. But I'd bet long odds Muzadeh is one of those so-called intellectuals, an ex-French university student whose tuition was paid for by Shah grants, who was adopted, trained, and fawned on by left-wing teachers in France. I spent two years in the Sorbonne, doing a postgraduate degree. I know these intellectuals, these *cretins* and some of the teachers – they tried to induct me. Once wh –'

A short sharp burst of gunfire outside stopped him. For a moment both men were still, then they rushed for the window. Four storeys down the ayatollah and Muzadeh were on the front steps. Below them in the forecourt one man was threatening them with an automatic rifle, standing alone in the middle of a semicircle of other armed men, the rest were scattered nearer to the trucks, some of them shouting and all hostile. Scragger was on the outskirts and as they watched they saw him ease into a better defensive position. The ayatollah raised his arms and exhorted them all. Watanabe could not hear what the man was saying. Carefully he opened a window and peered down.

'He's saying, "In the Name of God give up your weapons, the Imam has ordered it – you've all heard his broadcast and message – I say again, obey him and give up your weapons!" '

There was more angry shouting and countershouting, men shaking their fists at one another. In the confusion they saw Scragger slip away and vanish behind a building. Watanabe leaned further out, straining to hear better. 'The man covering them with the gun . . . I can't see if he's wearing a green armband or not . . . ah, he isn't so he must be fedayeen or Tudeh . . .'

Now in the forecourt there was a great silence. Imperceptibly men began easing for a better position, all weapons armed, everyone eyeing his neighbour, all nerves jagged. The man covering the two of them raised his gun and bellowed at the ayatollah, 'Order your men to put down their guns!'

Muzadeh stepped forward, not wanting a confrontation here, knowing he was outnumbered. 'Stop it, Hassan! You will st –'

'We didn't fight and our brothers didn't die to give our guns and power to mullahs!'

'The government has power! The government!' Muzadeh raised his voice even more. 'Everyone will keep their guns now but hand them into my office as I represent the new government and th –'

'You don't,' the ayatollah shouted. 'First in the Name of God, all non-Islamic Guards will put their guns on the ground and go in peace, second the government is subject to the Revolutionary Komiteh under the direct guidance of the Imam, and this man Muzadeh is not yet confirmed so has no authority at all! Obey or you will be disarmed!'

'I am the government here!'

'You are not!'

'Allah-u Akbarrr!' someone shouted and pulled his trigger and Hassan, the youth in the centre of them all, took the burst in his back and pirouetted in his death dance. At once other guns went off and men dived for cover or turned on their neighbour. The battle was short and vicious. Many died, but the men of Muzadeh were heavily outnumbered. The Green Bands were ruthless. Some of them had seized Muzadeh and now had him on his knees in the dirt, begging for mercy.

On the steps was the ayatollah. A spray of bullets had caught him in the chest and stomach and now he lay in a man's arms, blood marring his robes. A trickle of blood seeped from his mouth into his beard. 'God is Great . . . God is Great . . .' he muttered, then let out a dribbling groan as pain took him.

'Master,' the man holding him said, tears running down his cheeks, 'tell God we tried to protect you, tell the Prophet.'

'God . . . is . . . Great . . .' he murmured.

'What about this Muzadeh?' someone else asked. 'What shall we do with him?'

'Do God's work. Kill him . . . kill him as you must kill all enemies of Islam. There is no other God but God . . .'

The order was obeyed instantly. Cruelly. The ayatollah died smiling, the Name of God on his lips. Others wept openly – envying him Paradise.

At Kowiss Air Force Base: 2:32 P.M. Manuela Starke was in the bungalow kitchen making chili. Country music filled the small room from a battery cassette player on the windowsill. On the butane stove was a big stewpot filled with stock and some of the makings, and as it came to the boil she turned the gas to simmer and glanced at her wrist watch to gauge the time. Just right, she thought. We'll eat around seven and candles will make the table pretty.

There were more onions and other things to chop and the goat meat to grind, so she continued happily, absently humming or doing a little dance step in time with the music. The kitchen was small and difficult to work in, unlike the huge, high-beamed kitchen in the lovely, old, sprawling Spanish hacienda in Lubbock that her family had had for almost a century, where she and her brother and sister had grown up. But she did not mind being cramped or cooking without the proper utensils. She was glad for something to do to take her mind off the question of when she would see her husband again.

It was Saturday that Conroe had left to go to Bandar-e Delam with

329

the mullah, she thought, trying to reassure herself. Today's Tuesday, that's only three days and today's not even over yet. Last night he was on the HF, 'Hi, honey, everything's fine here – no need to worry. Sorry, got to go – airtime's restricted for the moment, love you and see you soon,' his voice so grand and confident but, even so, she was achingly sure she had heard a nervousness that had filled her mind and permeated her dreams. You're just imagining it. He'll be back soon – leave dreams to the night and work on your daydream that all is very fine. Concentrate on cooking!

She had brought the packets of chili powder with her from London, with extra spices and paprika and cayenne pepper and ginger, fresh garlic and dried chili peppers and dried beans and little else but some night things and toilet paper in the one tote bag that she had been allowed to carry aboard the 747. Chili makings because Starke adored Mexican food and particularly chili, and they both agreed that apart from curry, it was the only way to make goat meat palatable. No need to bring clothes or anything else with her because she still had some in their apartment in Tehran. The only other gift she had brought was a small jar of Marmite that she knew Genny and Duncan McIver loved on the hot buttered toast made from the bread Genny would bake – when she could get the flour and the yeast.

Today Manuela had baked bread. The three loaves were in their baking dishes, cooling on the counter under muslin to keep the few flies off. Damn all flies, she thought. Flies destroy the summer, even in Lubbock . . . Ah Lubbock, wonder how the kids are.

BillyJoe and Conroe Junior and Sarita. Seven and five and three. Ah, my beauties, she thought happily. I'm so glad I sent you home to my daddy and our ten thousand acres to roam on, Granddaddy Starke nearby: 'But wear your snake boots, y'hear now!' in that lovely rough so tender drawl of his.

'Texas for ever,' she said out loud and laughed at herself, her nimble fingers busy chopping and grinding and spooning, tasting the brew from time to time, adding a little more salt or garlic. Out of the window she saw Freddy Ayre crossing the little square to go up to their radio tower. With him was Pavoud, their chief clerk. He's a nice man, she thought. We're lucky to have loyal staff. Beyond them she could see the main runway and most of the base, snow covered, the afternoon sky overcast, hiding the mountain tops. A few of their pilots and mechanics were absently kicking a football, Marc Dubois – who had flown the mullah back from Bandar-e Delam – among them.

Nothing else was going on here, just servicing aircraft, checking spares, painting – no flying since Sunday and the attack on the base. And the mutiny. Sunday evening three mutineers, one airman and two sergeants from the tank regiment, had been court-martialled and, at dawn, shot. All day yesterday and today the base had been quiet. Once, yesterday, they had seen two fighters rush into the sky but no other flights which was strange as this was a training base and usually very busy. Nothing seemed to move. Just a few trucks, no tanks or parades – or visitors this side. In the night some firing and shouting that had soon died down again.

Critically she peered at herself in the mirror that hung on a hook over the sink that was filled with dirty pans and dishes and measuring spoons and cups. She moved her face this way and that and studied her figure, what she could see of it. 'You're fine now, honey,' she said to her reflection, 'but you better haul ass and go ajogging and quit with the bread and the chili and wine and tostadas, burritos, tacos, and muchchas and refried beans and Ma's pancakes dripping with home-grown honey, fried eggs, crisp bacon, and pan fries . . .'

The brew began to spit, distracting her. She turned the flame down a fraction, tasted the thickening reddish stew, still fiery from not enough cooking. 'Man alive,' she said with relish, 'that's going to make Conroe happier'n a pig in wallah . . .' Her face changed. It would, she thought, if he was here. Never mind, the boys will like it just fine.

She began the washing up, but she could not divert her thoughts from Bandar-e Delam. She felt the tears welling. 'Oh shit! Get hold of yourself!'

'CASEVAC!' The faint shout outside startled her and she looked out of the window. The football had stopped. All the men were staring at Ayre who was running down the outside stairs of the tower, calling to them. She saw them crowd around him, then scatter. Ayre headed for her bungalow. Hastily she took off her apron, tidying her hair, brushed away her tears, and met him at the doorway.

'What is it, Freddy?'

He beamed. 'Just thought I'd tell you their tower just got me on the blower and told me to ready a 212 for an immediate CASEVAC to Isfahan – they've got approval from IranOil.'

'Isn't that kinda far?'

'Oh, no. It's just two hundred miles, a couple of hours – there's plenty of light. Marc'll overnight there and come back tomorrow.' Again Ayre smiled. 'Good to have something to do. Curiously, they asked for Marc to do it.'

'Why him?'

'I don't know. Maybe because he's French and they're the ones who helped Khomeini. Well, got to go. Your chili smells great. Marc's peed off he's missing it.' He walked off, heading for the office, tall and handsome.

She stood at the doorway. Mechanics were wheeling out a 212 from the hangar and Marc Dubois, zipping up his winter flight overalls, waved gaily as he hurried over to watch the flight check. Then she saw the procession of four cars approaching along the boundary road. So did Freddy Ayre. He frowned and went into the office. 'Have you got the clearance ready, Mr. Pavoud?'

'Yes, Excellency.' Pavoud handed it to him.

Ayre did not notice the tension in the man, nor that his hands were shaking. 'Thanks. You'd better come too in case it's all in Farsi.'

'But, Excell —'

'Come on!' Buttoning his flight jacket against the breeze, Ayre hurried out. Pavoud wiped his sweating palms. The other Iranians watched him, equally anxious.

'As God wants,' one of them said, blessing God it was Pavoud, not him.

At the 212 the ground check continued. Ayre arrived as the cars arrived. His smile vanished. The cars were crammed with armed men, Green Bands, and they fanned out around the chopper, a few uniformed airmen among them.

The mullah Hussain Kowissi got out of the front seat of the lead car, his turban very white and his dark robes new, his boots old and well used. Over his shoulder was his AK47. Clearly he was in command. Other men opened the back doors of the first car and half pulled Colonel Peshadi out, then his wife. Peshadi shouted at them, cursing them, and they backed off a little. He straightened his uniform greatcoat and braided, peaked cap. His wife wore a heavy winter coat and gloves and a little hat and shoulder bag. Her face was white and drawn but, like her husband, she held her head high and proudly. She reached back into the car for a small tote bag but one of the Green Bands grabbed it, and after a slight hesitation handed it to her.

Ayre tried to keep the shock off his face. 'What's going on, sir?'

'We're . . . we're being sent to Isfahan under guard! Under guard! My base . . . my base was betrayed and is in the hands of mutineers!' The colonel did not keep the fury off his face as he whirled on Hussain, in Farsi: 'I say again, what has my wife to do with this? EH?' he added with a roar. One of the nervous Green Bands nearby shoved a rifle into his back. Without looking around the colonel smashed the rifle away. 'Son of a whore dog!'

'Stop!' Hussain said in Farsi. 'It is orders from Isfahan. I've shown you the orders that you and your wife are to be sent at once t –'

'Orders? A dung filthy piece of paper scrawled in an illegible illiterate handwriting and signed by an ayatollah I've never heard of?'

Hussain walked over to him. 'Get aboard, both of you,' he warned, 'or I'll have you dragged there!'

'When the aircraft is ready!' Contemptuously the colonel took out a cigarette. 'Give me a light,' he ordered the man nearest to him, and when the man hesitated, he snarled, 'Are you deaf? A light!'

The man smiled wryly and found some matches, and all those around nodded approval, even the mullah, admiring courage in the face of death – courage in the face of hell, for surely this man was a Shah man and headed for hell. Of course hell! Didn't you hear him shout, Long live the Shah, only hours ago when, in the night, we invaded and took possession of the camp and his fine house, helped by all the base's soldiers and airmen and some of the officers, the rest of the officers now in cells? God is Great! It was the Will of God, God's miracle that the generals caved in like the walls of shit the mullahs told us they were. The Imam was right again, God protect him.

Hussain went over to Ayre who was rigid, appalled by what was going on, trying to understand, Marc Dubois beside him, equally shocked, the ground check stopped. 'Salaam,' the mullah said trying to be polite. 'You have nothing to fear. The Imam has ordered everything back to normal.'

'Normal?' Ayre echoed angrily. 'That's Colonel Peshadi, tank commander, hero of your expeditionary force sent to Oman to help put down a Marxist-supported rebellion and invasion from South Yemen!' That had been in '73 when the Shah was asked for help by Oman's sultan. 'Hasn't Colonel Peshadi got the Zolfarazan, your highest medal given only for gallantry in battle?'

'Yes. But now Colonel Peshadi is needed to answer questions concerning crimes against the Iranian people and against the laws of God! Salaam, Captain Dubois, I'm glad that you're going to fly us.'

'I was asked to fly a CASEVAC. This isn't a CASEVAC,' Dubois said.

'It's a casualty evacuation – the colonel and his wife are to be evacuated to Command Headquarters in Isfahan.' Hussain added with a sardonic smile, 'Perhaps they are casualties.'

Ayre said, 'Sorry, our aircraft are under licence to IranOil. We can't do what you ask.'

333

The mullah turned and shouted, 'Excellency Esvandiary!'

Kuram Esvandiary, or 'Hotshot' as he was nicknamed, was in his early thirties, popular with the expats, very efficient, and S-G trained – he had had two years of training at S-G HQ at Aberdeen on a Shah grant. He came from the back and, for a moment, not one of the S-G men recognised their station manager. Normally he was a meticulous dresser and clean-shaven, but now he had three or four days' growth of heavy beard, and wore rough clothes with a green armband, slouch hat, an M16 slung over his shoulder. 'The trip's sanctioned, here,' he said, giving Ayre the usual forms, 'I've signed them and they're stamped.'

'But, Hotshot, surely you realise this isn't a legitimate CASEVAC?'

'My name's Esvandiary – Mr. Esvandiary,' he said without a smile and Ayre flushed. 'And it's a legitimate order from IranOil who employ you under contract here in Iran.' His face hardened. 'If you refuse a legitimate order in good flying conditions, you're breaking your contract. If you do that without cause then we've the right to seize all assets, aircraft, hangars, spares, houses, equipment and order you out of Iran at once.'

'You can't do that.'

'I'm IranOil's chief representative here now,' Esvandiary said curtly. 'IranOil's owned by the government. The Revolutionary Komiteh under the leadership of the Iman Khomeini, peace be upon him, is the government. Read your IranOil contract – also the contract between S-G and Iran Helicopters. Are you flying the charter or refusing to?'

Ayre held on to his temper. 'What about . . . what about Prime Minister Bakhtiar and the gov –'

'Bakhtiar?' Esvandiary and the mullah stared at him. 'Haven't you heard yet? He's resigned and fled, the generals capitulated yesterday morning, the Imam and the Revolutionary Komiteh are Iran's government now.'

Ayre and Dubois and those expats nearby gaped at him. The mullah said something in Farsi they did not understand. His men laughed.

'Capitulated?' was all Ayre could say.

'It was the Will of God the generals came to their senses,' Hussain said, his eyes glittering. 'They were arrested, the whole General Staff. All of them. As all enemies of Islam will be arrested now. We got Nassiri too – you've heard of him?' the mullah asked witheringly. Nassiri was the hated head of SAVAK whom the Shah had arrested a few weeks ago and who was in jail awaiting trial. 'Nassiri was found guilty of crimes against humanity and shot – along with three other generals, Rahimi, martial law governor of Tehran, Naji, governor general of Isfahan, Paratrooper Commander Khosrowdad. You're wasting time. Are you flying or not?'

Ayre was barely able to think. If what they say is true, then Peshadi and his wife are as good as dead. It's all so fast, all so impossible. 'We . . . of course we will fly a . . . legal charter. Just exactly what is it you want?'

'To transport His Excellency mullah Hussain Kowissi to Isfahan at once – with his personnel. At once,' Esvandiary interrupted impatiently, 'with the prisoner and his wife.'

'They're . . . Colonel and Mrs. Peshadi're not on the manifest.'

Even more impatiently Esvandiary ripped the paper out of his hands, wrote on it. 'Now they are!' He motioned past Ayre and Dubois to where Manuela was standing in the background, her hair carefully tucked into a hat, wearing overalls. He had noticed her the moment he had arrived – enticing as always, unsettling as always. 'I should arrest her for illegal trespass,' he said, his voice raw. 'She has no right on this base – there are no married quarters, nor are any allowed by base and S-G rules.'

Over by the 212, Colonel Peshadi angrily shouted out in English, 'Are you flying today or not? We're getting cold. Hurry it up, Ayre – I want to spend as little time as possible with these vermin!'

Esvandiary and the mullah flushed. Ayre called back, feeling better for the man's bravery, 'Yes, sir. Sorry. Okay, Marc?'

'Yes.' To Esvandiary, Dubois said, 'Where's my military clearance?'

'Attached to the manifest. Also for your return trip tomorrow.' Esvandiary added in Farsi to the mullah: 'I suggest you board, Excellency.'

The mullah walked off. Guards motioned Peshadi and his wife aboard. Head high, they went up the steps without faltering. Armed men piled in after them and the mullah took the front left seat beside Dubois.

'Wait a minute,' Ayre began, now over the shock. 'We're not flying armed men. It's against the rules – yours and ours!'

Esvandiary shouted an order, jerked a thumb at Manuela. At once four armed men surrounded her. Others moved much closer to Ayre. 'Now, give Dubois a thumbs-up!'

Grimly aware of the danger, Ayre obeyed. Dubois acknowledged and started up. Quickly he was airborne. 'Now into the office,' Esvandiary said above the howl of the engines. He called the men off Manuela and ordered them back into the cars. 'Leave one car here and four guards – I have more orders for these foreigners. You,' he added toughly to Pavoud, 'you get an up-to-date on all aircraft here, all spares, all transport, as well as the quantity of gasoline, also numbers of personnel, foreign and Iranians, their names, jobs, passport numbers, residence permits, work permits, flying licences. Understand?'

'Yes, yes, Excellency Esvandiary. Yes, cert –'

'And I want to see all passports and permits tomorrow. Get busy!'

The man left hurriedly. Esvandiary was bowed through the front door. He led the way into Starke's office and took the main chair and sat behind the desk, Ayre following him. 'Sit down.'

'Thanks, you're so kind,' Ayre said witheringly, taking the chair opposite him. The two men were of an age and they watched each other.

The Iranian took out a cigarette and lit it. 'This will be my office from now on,' he said. 'Now that at long last Iran is back in Iranian hands we can begin to make the necessary changes. For the next two weeks you will operate under my personal guidance until I am sure the new way is understood. I am the top IranOil authority for Kowiss and I'll issue all flight permits, no one takes off without written approval and always with an armed guard an –'

'It's against air law and Iranian law and it's forbidden. Apart from that it's bloody dangerous. Finish!'

There was a big silence. Then Esvandiary nodded. 'You will carry guards who will have guns – but no ammunition.' He smiled. 'There, you see, we can compromise. We can be reasonable, oh, yes. You'll see, the new era will be good for you too.'

'I hope it is. For you too.'

'Meaning?'

'Meaning every revolution I've ever read about always begins by feeding off itself, friends quickly become enemies and even quicker die.'

'Not with us.' Esvandiary was totally confident. 'It won't be that way with us. Ours was a real people's revolution – of all the people. Everyone wanted the Shah out – and his foreign masters.'

'I hope you're right.' You poor bastard, Ayre thought, once having liked him. If your leaders can judge, condemn and shoot four top generals – all good men except for Nassiri – in less than twenty-four hours, can arrest and abuse fine patriots like Peshadi and his wife, God help you. 'Are you finished with me for the present?'

'Almost.' A shaft of anger went through Esvandiary. Through the windows he noticed Manuela walking back to the bungalow with some of the pilots, and his lust increased his rage. 'It would be good to learn manners and that Iran is an Asian, an Oriental country, a world power and never, never again to be exploited by British, Americans, or even Soviets. Never again.' He slouched in his chair and put his feet on the desk as he had seen Starke and Ayre do a hundred times, the soles of his feet towards Ayre, always an insult in this part of the world. 'British were worse than the Americans. They've caused us national shame for a hundred and fifty years, treating our ancient Peacock Throne and country as their private fief, using the defence of India as an excuse. They've dictated to our rulers, occupied us three times, forced unequal treaties on us, bribed our leaders to grant them concessions. For a hundred and fifty years British and Russians have partitioned my country, the British helped those other hyenas to steal our northern provinces, our Caucasus, and helped put Reza Khan on the throne. They occupied us, with the Soviets, in your world war and only our own supreme efforts broke the chain and threw them out.' Abruptly the man's face contorted and he screamed, 'Didn't they?'

Ayre had not moved, nor had his eyes flickered. 'Hotshot, and I'll never call you that again,' he said quietly, 'I don't want lectures, just to do the job. If we can't work out a satisfactory method, then that's something else. We'll have to see. If you want this office, jolly good. If you want to act up a storm, jolly good – within reason – you've a right to celebrate. You've won, you've the guns, you've the power and now you're responsible. And you're right, it is your country. So let's leave it at that. Eh?'

Esvandiary stared at him, his head aching with the suppressed hatred of years that need never be suppressed again. And though he knew it was not Ayre's fault, he was equally certain that a moment ago he would have sprayed him and them with bullets if they had not obeyed and flown the mullah and the traitor Peshadi to the judgment and the hell he deserves. I've not forgotten the soldier Peshadi had murdered – the one who wanted to open the gate to us – or the others murdered two days ago when Peshadi beat us off and hundreds died, my brother and two of my best friends among them. And all the other hundreds, thousands, perhaps tens of thousands who've died all over Iran . . . I've not forgotten them, not one.

A dribble of saliva was running down his chin and he wiped it away with the back of his hand and got his control back, remembering the importance of his mission. 'All right, Freddy.' He said 'Freddy' involuntarily. 'All right, and that's . . . that's the last time I'll call you that. All right, we'll leave it at that.'

He got up, very tired now but proud of the way he had dominated

337

them and very confident he could make these foreigners work and behave until they were expelled. Very soon now, he thought. I'll have no difficulty putting the partners' long-term plan into effect here. I agree with Valik. We've plenty of Iranian pilots and we need no foreigners here. I can run this operation – as a partner – praise God that Valik was always a secret Khomeini supporter! Soon I'll have a big house in Tehran and my two sons will go to university there, so will my darling little Fatmeh, though perhaps she should also go to the Sorbonne for a year or two.

'I'll return at 9 a.m.' He did not close the door behind him.

'Bloody hell,' Ayre muttered. A fly began battering itself against a window-pane. He did not notice it or the noise it made. At a sudden thought he went into the outer office. Pavoud and the others were at the windows, watching the aliens leave. 'Pavoud!'

'Yes . . . yes, Excellency?'

Ayre noticed the man's face had a greyish tinge and he looked much older than usual. 'Did you know about the generals, that they've given in?' he asked, feeling sorry for him.

'No, Excellency,' Pavoud lied easily, used to lying. He was locked in his own mind, trying to remember, petrified that he might have slipped up in the past three years and given himself away to Esvandiary, never for a moment dreaming that the man could have been a secret Islamic Guard. 'We'd . . . we'd heard rumours about their capitulation – but you know how rumours circulate.'

'Yes – yes, I suppose you're right.'

'I . . . do you mind if I sit down, please?' Pavoud groped for a chair, feeling very old. He had been sleeping badly this last week and the two-mile bicycle ride here this morning from the little four-room house in Kowiss he shared with his brother's family – five adults and six children – had been more tiring than usual. Of course he and all the people of Kowiss had heard about the generals meekly giving up – the first news coming from the mosque, spread by the mullah Hussain who said he had got it by secret radio from Khomeini Headquarters in Tehran so it must be true.

At once their Tudeh leader had called a meeting, all of them astounded at the generals' cowardice: 'It just shows how foul the influence of the Americans who betrayed them and so bewitched them that they've castrated themselves and committed suicide, for of course they've all got to die whether we do it or that madman Khomeini!'

Everyone filled with resolve, at the same time frightened of the coming battle against the zealots and the mullahs, the opiate of the people, and Pavoud himself was wet with relief when the leader said they were ordered not to take to the streets yet but to stay hidden and wait, wait until the order came for the general uprising. 'Comrade Pavoud, it's vital you keep on the best of terms with the foreign pilots at the air base. We will need them and their helicopters – or will need to inhibit their use to the enemies of the people. Our orders are to lie low and wait, to have patience. When we finally get the order to take to the streets against Khomeini, our comrades to the north will come over the border in legions . . .'

He saw Ayre watching him. 'I'm all right, Captain, just worried by all this, and the . . . the new era.'

'Just do what Esvandiary asks.' Ayre thought a moment. 'I'm going to the tower to let HQ know what's happened. Are you sure you're all right?'

'Yes, yes, thank you.'

Ayre frowned, then went along the corridor and up the stairs. The astonishing change in Esvandiary who for years had been affable, friendly, and never a glimmer of anti-British, had rocked him. For the first time in Iran he felt their future was doomed.

To his surprise the tower room was empty. Since Sunday's mutiny there had been a permanent guard – Major Changiz had shrugged, blood on his uniform, 'I'm sure you'll understand, "national emergency". We had many loyal men killed here today and we haven't found all traitors – yet. Until further orders you will transmit only during daylight hours, then absolute minimum. All flights are cancelled until further notice.'

'All right, Major. By the way, where's our radio op, Massil?'

'Ah, yes, the Palestinian. He's being interrogated.'

'May I ask what for?'

'PLO affiliation and terrorist activities.'

Yesterday he had been informed that Massil had confessed and been shot – without a chance to hear the evidence or question it or to see him. Poor bastard, Ayre thought, closing the tower door now and switching on the equipment. Massil was always loyal to us and grateful for the job, so overqualified – radio engineering degree from Cairo University, top of the class but nowhere to practise and stateless. Bloody hell! We take our passports for granted – what'd it be like to be without one and to be, say, Palestinian? Must be hairy not to know what's going to happen at every border, with every immigration man, policeman, bureaucrat, or employer a potential inquisitor.

Thank God in Heaven I'm born British and that not even the Queen of England can take that away though the bloody Labour Government's changing our overseas heritage. Well the pox on them for every Aussie, Canuck, Kiwi, Springbok, Kenyan, China hand, and a hundred other Britishers who will soon have to have a bloody visa to go home! 'Arseholes,' he muttered. 'Don't they realise those're sons and daughters of men who made the empire and died for it in many cases?'

He waited for the HF and other radios to warm up. The hum pleased him, red and green lights flickering, and he no longer felt locked off from the world. Hope Angela and young Fredrick are okay. Bloody, having no mail or phones and a dead telex. Well, maybe soon everything will be working again.

He reached for the sending switch, hoping that McIver or someone would be listening out. Then he noticed that, by habit, along with the UHF, HF, he had switched on their radar. He leaned over to turn it off. At that moment a small blip appeared on the outer rim – the twenty-mile line – to the northwest, almost obscured among the heavy scatter of the mountains. Startled, he studied it. Experience told him quickly that it was a helicopter. He made sure that he was tuned into all receiving frequencies and when he looked back he saw the blip vanish. He waited. It did not reappear. Either she's down, shot down or sneaking under the radar net, he thought. Which?

The seconds ticked by. No change, just the revolving, heavy white line of the sweep, in its wake a bird's-eye view of the surrounding terrain. Still no sign of the blip.

His fingers snapped on the UHF sending switch, and he brought the mike closer, hesitated, then changed his mind and switched it off. No need to alert the operators in the base tower, if there're any on duty there, he thought. He frowned at the screen. With a soft, red grease pencil he marked the possible track inbound at eighty knots. Minutes passed. He could have switched to a closer range scan but he did not in case the blip was not inbound but, highly irregularly, sneaking across their area.

Now she should be five or six miles out, he thought. He picked up the binoculars and started to scan the sky, north through west to south. His ears heard light footsteps on the last few stairs. His heart quickening, he snapped the radar off. The screen began dying as the door opened.

'Captain Ayre?' the airman asked, uniform neat, strong good Persian face, clean shaven, in his late twenties, a standard U.S. Army carbine in his hands.

'Yes, yes that's me.'

'I'm Sergeant Wazari, your new air traffic controller.' The man leaned his carbine against a wall, put out his hand, and Ayre shook it. 'Hi, I'm USAAF trained, three years, and a military controller. I even did six months at Van Nuys Airport.' His eyes had taken in all the equipment. 'Nice setup.'

'Yes, er, yes, thank you.' Ayre fumbled with the binoculars and set them down. 'What, er, happens at Van Nuys Airport?'

'It's a nothing little airstrip in San Fernando Valley in Los Angeles but the third busiest airport in the States and a mother to end all mothers!' Wazari beamed. 'The traffic's amateur, most of the jokers're learners who still don't know their ass from a propeller, you've maybe twenty in the system at any one time, eight on final, all wanting to make like Richthofen.' He laughed. 'Great place to learn traffic controlling but after six months you're ape.'

Ayre forced a smile, willing himself not to search the sky. 'This place's pretty quiet. Even normally. We've, er, we've no flights out as you know – you've nothing to do here, I'm afraid.'

'Sure. I just wanted to take a quick look as we begin bright and early tomorrow.' He reached into his uniform pocket and took out a list and gave it to Ayre. 'You've three flights scheduled for the local rigs starting eight a.m. okay?' Without thinking he picked up a rag and wiped the inbound track off the radar screen, tidying the desk alongside. The red grease pencil went into its holder with the others.

Ayre looked back at the list. 'Are these authorised by Esvandiary?'

'Who's he?'

Ayre told him.

The sergeant laughed. 'Well, Captain, Major Changiz personally ordered these so you can bet your ass they're confirmed.'

'He's . . . he wasn't arrested with the colonel?'

'Hell no, Captain. The mullah, Hussain Kowissi, appointed Major Changiz temp base commander, pending confirm from Tehran.' Unerringly his fingers switched channels to the Main Base Frequency. 'Hello, Main Base, this's Wazari at S-G. Do we need tomorrow's flights countersigned by IranOil's Esvandiary?'

'Negative,' came back over the loudspeaker, again American-accented. 'Everything okay over there?'

'Yep. The outbound went off without incident. I'm with Captain Ayre now.' The sergeant scanned the sky as he talked.

'Good. Captain Ayre, this's the senior traffic controller. Any flights authorised by Major Changiz are automatically approved by IranOil.'

'Can I have that in writing please?'

'Sergeant Wazari'll have it for you in duplicate at 8 a.m., okay?'

'Thanks – thank you.'

'Thanks, Main Base,' Wazari said, beginning to sign off, then his eyes fixed. 'Hold it, Main Base, we've got a bird inbound! Chopper, two seventy degrees . . .'

'Where? Where . . . I see him! How the hell did he get in under the radar? You switched on?'

'Negative.' The sergeant trained the binoculars. 'Bell 212, registration . . . can't see it – she's head on to us.' He clicked on the UHF. 'This is Kowiss Military Control! Inbound chopper, what is your registration, where are you bound and what was your point of departure?'

Silence but for the crackle of static. The same call repeated by Main Base. No reply.

'That sonofabitch's in dead trouble,' Wazari muttered. Again he trained the binoculars.

Ayre had the second set and his heart was thumping. As the chopper joined the landing pattern, he read the registration: EP-HBX.

'Echo Peter Hotel Boston X-ray!' the sergeant said simultaneously.

'HBX,' Main Base agreed. Again they tried radio contact. No reply. 'He's in your regular landing pattern. Is he a local? Captain Ayre, is he one of yours?'

'No, sir, not one of mine, not based here.' Ayre added carefully, 'HBX could be an S-G registration however.'

'Based where?'

'I don't know.'

'Sergeant, as soon as that joker lands, arrest him and all passengers, send them over here to HQ under guard, then give me a quick report who why and where from.'

'Yessir.'

Thoughtfully Wazari selected a red grease pencil and traced the same line on the radar screen that Ayre had drawn and he had wiped out. He stared at it a moment, knowing Ayre was watching him intently. But he said nothing, just wiped the glass clean again and put his attention back to the 212.

In silence the two men in the tower watched her make a normal circuit then break off correctly and head for them. But she made no attempt to land, just stayed at the correct height and made a much smaller circuit, waggling from side to side.

'Radio's out – he wants a Green,' Ayre said, and reached for a signal light. 'Okay?'

'Sure, give him one – but his ass's still in a wringer.'

Ayre checked that the powerful, narrow-beamed signal light was set

342

for Green, permission to land. He aimed it at the chopper and switched on. The chopper acknowledged by waggling from side to side and started the approach. Wazari picked up his carbine and went out. Again Ayre trained his binoculars but still could not recognise the pilot or the man beside him, both muffled in winter gear and goggled. Then he rushed down the stairs.

Other S-G personnel, pilots and mechanics, had gathered to watch. From the direction of the main base, a car was speeding their way along the boundary road. Manuela stood in the doorway of the bungalow. The landing pads were in front of the office building. Crouched in the lee were the four Green Bands who had stayed behind, Wazari now with them. Ayre noticed that one was very young, barely a teenager, fiddling with his machine gun. In his excitement, cocking it, the youth dropped it on the tarmac, the gun pointing directly at Ayre. But it did not go off. As he watched, the youth picked it up by the barrel, banged the butt down to knock the snow off, carelessly shoved more snow away from the trigger guard. Some grenades hung from his belt – by the pins. Hastily Ayre joined some of the mechanics taking cover.

'Bloody nit!' one of them said queasily. 'He'll blow himself to hell and us along with him. You all right, Cap'n? We heard Hotshot's got his knickers in a twist.'

'Yes, yes, he has. HBX, where's she from, Benson?'

'Bandar-e Delam,' Benson replied. He was a ruddy-faced, rotund Englishman. 'Fifty quid it's Duke.'

As the 212 put her skids down and cut her engines, Wazari led the rush, some of the guards shouting, 'Allah-u Akbarrr!' They surrounded her, all guns levelled.

'Bloody twits,' Ayre said nervously, 'they're like Keystone Cops.'

He still couldn't see the pilot clearly, so he walked out of cover, praying that it was Starke. The cabin doors slid back. Armed men jumped down, careless of the rotors that still circled, shouting greetings, telling the others to put down their guns. In the pandemonium, someone excitedly fired a welcoming burst into the air. Momentarily everyone began to scatter then, with more shouts, regrouped around the doors as the car arrived and more men rushed to join the others. Hands helped a mullah down. He was badly wounded. Then a stretcher. Then more wounded and Ayre saw Wazari running for him.

'You got medics here?' he said urgently.

'Yes.' Ayre turned and cupped his hands around his mouth. 'Benson, get Doc and the medic on the double,' then to the sergeant, hurrying back with him, 'What the hell's going on?'

'They're from Bandar-e Delam – there was a counter-revolution there, goddam fedayeen . . .'

Ayre saw the pilot's door open and Starke get out, and he didn't hear the rest of what Wazari said and hurried forward. 'Hello, Duke, old chap.' Deliberately he kept his face set and his voice flat, though so happy and excited inside that he felt he would burst. 'Where've you been?'

Starke grinned, used to the English understatement. 'Fishing, old chap,' he said. All at once Manuela came charging through the crowd and was in his arms, hugging him. He lifted her easily and whirled her. 'Why, honey,' he drawled, 'Ah guess ya like me after all!'

She was half crying and half laughing and she hung on. 'Oh, Conroe, when I saw you I liked to die . . .'

'We damn near did, honey,' Starke said involuntarily, but she had not heard him and he hugged her once for luck and put her down. 'Just set there for a bitty while I get things organised. Come on, Freddy.'

He led the way through the crush. The wounded mullah was on the ground, leaning against a skid, semiconscious. The man on the stretcher was already dead. 'Put the mullah on his stretcher,' Starke ordered in Farsi. The Green Bands he had brought in the 212 obeyed at once. Wazari, the only one in uniform here, and the others from the base were astonished – none of them aware of Zataki, the Sunni revolutionary leader who had taken command of Bandar-e Delam, who now leaned against the helicopter, watching carefully, camouflaged by the S-G flight jacket he wore.

'Let me have a look, Duke,' the doctor said, out of breath from hurrying, a stethoscope around his neck, 'so happy to have you back.' Dr. Nutt was in his fifties, too heavy, with sparse hair and a drinker's nose. He knelt beside the mullah and began examining his chest that was wet with blood. 'We'd better get him to the infirmary, quick as poss. And the rest.'

Starke told two of those nearby to pick up the stretcher and follow the doctor. Again he was obeyed without question by men he had brought with him – the other Green Bands stared at him. Now there were nine of them, including Wazari and the four who had stayed.

'You're under arrest,' Wazari said.

Starke looked at him. 'What for?'

Wazari hesitated. 'Orders from the brass, Captain, I just work here.'

'So do I. I'll be here if they want to talk to me, Sergeant.' Starke smiled reassuringly at Manuela who had gone white. 'You go back to the house, honey. Nothing to worry about.' He turned away and went closer to the side door to look inside.

'Sorry, Captain, but you're under arrest. Get in the car. You're to go to the base pronto.'

When Starke turned he was looking into the nozzle of the gun. Two Green Bands jumped him from behind, grabbed his arms, pinioning him. Ayre lunged forward but one of the Green Bands shoved a gun in his stomach, stopping him. The two men started dragging Starke towards the car. Others came to help as he struggled, cursing them. Manuela watched panic-stricken.

Then there was a bellow of rage and Zataki burst through the cordon, dragged the carbine from Sergeant Wazari and swung it at his head, butt first. Only Wazari's great reflexes, boxing trained, moved his head away just in time and backed him out reach. Before he could say anything Zataki shouted, 'What's this dog doing with a gun? Haven't you fools heard that the Imam ordered all servicemen disarmed?'

Wazari began hotly, 'Listen, I'm authorised t—' He stopped in panic. Now there was a pistol at his throat.

'You're not even authorised to shit till the local komiteh clears you,' Zataki said. He was neater than before, clean shaven now, his features well made. 'Have you been cleared by the komiteh?'

'No . . . no bu –'

'Then by God and the Prophet you're suspect!' Zataki kept the gun hard against Wazari's throat, then waved his other hand. 'Let the pilot go and put your arms down, or by God and the Prophet I'll kill you all!' The moment he had grabbed Wazari's gun, his men had circled the others and now had them covered from behind. Nervously, the two men pinioning Starke let him go.

'Why should we obey you?' one of them said sullenly. 'Eh? Who are you to give us orders?'

'I'm Colonel Zataki, member of the Revolutionary Komiteh of Bandar-e Delam, thanks be to God. The American helped save us from a fedayeen counterattack and brought the mullah and others who need medical help here.' Suddenly his rage broke. He shoved Wazari and the sergeant sprawled helplessly on the ground. 'Leave the pilot alone! Didn't you hear?' He aimed and pulled the trigger and the bullet tore through the neck of the sheepskin vest of one of the men beside Starke. Manuela almost fainted and they all scattered. 'Next time I'll put it between your eyes! You,' he snarled at Wazari, 'you're under arrest. I think you're a traitor so we'll find out. The rest of you go with God, tell your komiteh I would be pleased to see them – here.'

He waved them away. The men started muttering among themselves, and in the lull Ayre slipped over to Manuela and put his arm around her. 'Hang in there,' he whispered. 'It's all right now.' He saw Starke motion them away. He nodded. 'Come on, Duke says to leave.'

'No . . . please, Freddy, I'm . . . I'm okay, promise.' She forced a smile and continued praying that the man with the pistol would dominate the others and all this would end. Please God, let it end.

They all watched in silence while Zataki waited, the pistol loose in his hand, the sergeant on the ground near his feet, those opposing him glaring at him, Starke standing in the middle of them, not at all sure that Zataki would win. Zataki checked the magazine. 'Go with God, all of you,' he said again, harder this time, getting angrier. 'Are you all still deaffff?'

Reluctantly they left. The sergeant got up, pasty-faced, and straightened his uniform. Ayre watched Wazari bravely trying to hide his terror.

'You stand there and stay there till I say to move.' Zataki glanced at Starke who was watching Manuela, 'Pilot, we should finish the unloading. Then my men must eat.'

'Yes. And thank you.'

'Nothing. These people did not know – they are not to be blamed.' Again he looked at Manuela, dark eyes piercing. 'Your woman, pilot?' he asked.

'My wife,' Starke replied.

'My wife is dead, killed in the Abadan fire with my two sons. It was the Will of God.'

'Sometimes the Will of God is unendurable.'

'The Will of God is the Will of God. We should finish the unloading.'

'Yes.' Starke climbed into the cabin, the danger only over for the moment as Zataki was as volatile as nitroglycerin. Two more wounded were still strapped in their seats as were two stretcher cases. He knelt beside one of them. 'How you doing, old buddy?' he said softly in English.

Jon Tyrer opened his eyes and winced, a bloody bandage around his head. 'Okay . . . yeah, okay. What . . . what happened?'

'Can you see?'

Tyrer seemed surprised. He peered up at Starke, then rubbed his eyes and forehead. To Starke's relief, he said, 'Sure, it's . . . you're a bit soft focus and my head aches like hell but I can see you okay. Course I can see you, Duke. What the hell happened?'

'During the fedayeen counterattack at dawn this morning you were caught in some crossfire, a bullet creased the side of your head, and when you got up you started running around in circles like a headless chicken crying out, "I can't see . . . I can't see". Then you collapsed and you've been out ever since.'

'Ever since? Goddam!' The American peered out of the cabin door. 'Where the hell are we?'

'Kowiss – I thought I'd better get you and the rest here fast.'

Tyrer was still astonished. 'I remember nothing. Nothing. Fedayeen? For crissake, Duke, I don't even remember being brought aboard.'

'Hang in there, old buddy. I'll explain later.' He turned and called out, 'Freddy, get someone to carry Jon Tyrer to the doc,' adding, in Farsi, to Zataki who watched from the doorway, 'Excellency Zataki, please ask men to carry your men to the infirmary.' He paused a moment. 'My second-in command, Captain Ayre, will make arrangements for feeding everyone. Would you like to eat with me – in my house?'

Zataki smiled strangely and shook his head. 'Thank you, pilot,' he said in English. 'I will eat with my men. This evening we should talk, you and I.'

'Whenever you wish.' Starke jumped out of the cabin. Men began carrying away all the wounded. He pointed at his bungalow. 'That's my house, you are welcome there, Excellency.'

Zataki thanked him and went away, shoving Sergeant Wazari in front of him.

Ayre and Manuela joined Starke. She took his hand. 'When he pulled the trigger, I thought . . .' she smiled weakly, switched to Farsi. 'Ah, beloved, how good the day has become now that you are safe and beside me.'

'And thee beside me.' Starke smiled at her.

'What happened? At Bandar-e Delam?' she asked in English.

'There was a goddam battle between Zataki and his men and about fifty leftists at the base – yesterday Zataki took over our base in the name of Khomeini and the revolution – I had a bit of a run-in with him when I first got there but now he's kind a okay, though he's psycho, dangerous as a rattler. Anyway at dawn the leftist fedayeen rushed the airport in trucks and on foot. Zataki was asleep with the rest of his men, no sentries out, nothing – you heard the generals capitulated and Khomeini's now warlord?'

'Yes, we've just heard actually.'

'The first I knew of the attack was all hell let loose, bullets every-

347

where, coming through the walls of the trailers. Me, you know me, I ducked for cover and scrambled out of the trailer . . . You cold, honey?'

'No, no, darlin'. Let's go home – I could use a drink too . . . oh, my God . . .'

'What is it?'

But she was already running for the house. 'The chili – I left the chili on the stove!'

'Jesus Christ!' Ayre muttered, 'I thought we were about to be shot or something.'

Starke was beaming. 'We got chili?'

'Yes. Bandar-e Delam?'

'Not much to tell, Freddy.' They started walking for the house. 'I evacuated the trailer – I think the attackers figured Zataki and his men would be sleeping in them but Zataki had everyone bedded down in hangars guarding the choppers – Freddy, they're goddam paranoid about choppers, that we're gonna fly away in them, or use them to fly out SAVAK, generals, or enemies of the revolution. Anyway, old Rudi and me, we had our heads down in the back of a spare mud tank, then some of these new bastards – you couldn't tell one from another except Zataki's guys were shouting "Allah-u Akbar" as they died – some of the fedayeen opened up with a Sten gun on the hangars just as Jon Tyrer was evacuating his trailer. I saw him go down and I got as mad as a sonofabitch – now don't you tell Manuela – and got a gun away from one of them and started my own little war to go get Jon. Rudi . . .' Starke started smiling, 'that one's a sonofabitch! Rudi got himself a gun too and we were like Butch Cassidy and the Sundance Kid . . .'

'God Almighty, you must've been crazy!'

Starke nodded. 'We were, but we got Jon out of the line of fire and then Zataki and three of his guys broke out of a hangar and charged the main group, firing like the Wild Bunch. But hell, they ran out of ammo. Poor bastards just stood there and you've never seen anyone nakeder.' He shrugged. 'Rudi and I thought what the hell, shooting a sitting duck's not fair and Zataki's been okay once the mullah – Hussain – had left, and we'd, er, come to an agreement. So we let off a burst over the attackers' heads and that gave Zataki and the others time to get to cover.' Again he shrugged. 'That's about it,' he said. They were near the bungalow now. He sniffed the air. 'We really got chili, Freddy?'

'Yes – unless it's burned. That's all that happened?'

'Sure, except when the shooting stopped I thought we'd best head for Kowiss and Doc Nutt. The mullah looked rough and I was scared for Jon. Zataki said, Sure, why not, I need to go to Isfahan – so here we are.

The radio went out en route – I could hear you but couldn't transmit. No sweat.'

Ayre watched him sniff the air again, knowing that a psychopath like Zataki would never give Starke the authority he had given him – or protect him – for so little assistance.

The Texan opened the bungalow door. At once the grand, spicy smell surrounded him, transporting him home to Texas, God's country, and a thousand meals. Manuela had a drink poured for him, the way he liked it. But he did not drink it, just went into the kitchen area and picked up the big wooden spoon and tasted the brew. Manuela watched, hardly breathing. A second taste.

'How 'bout that?' he said happily. The chili was the best he had ever had.

The map shows Iran and surrounding countries, including USSR, Caspian Sea, Afghanistan, Pakistan, Iraq, Kuwait, Saudi Arabia, Bahrain, Qatar, UAE, and the Persian Gulf. Cities and locations marked include Khvoy, Tabriz, Bandar-e Pahlavi, Qazvin, Tehran, Sadzevar, Meshed, Baghdad, Isfahan, Dez Dam, Abadan, Bandar-e Delam, Kowiss, Kharg Island, Zagros, Jellet, Lengeh, Siri, Al Shargaz, Strait of Hormuz, Gulf of Oman.

DEZ DAM

IRAN

At the Dez Dam: 4:31 P.M. Lochart's 212 was parked just outside the shed that doubled as a hangar near a well-kept landing pad that was beside the cobbled forecourt of the house. He was standing on the copter's upperworks, checking the rotor column with its multitude of couplings, lock pins – and danger points – but he found nothing untoward. Carefully he clambered down and wiped his hands clean of grease.

'Okay?' Ali Abbasi asked, stretched out in the sun. He was the young and very good-looking Iranian helicopter pilot who had helped release Lochart from detention at Isfahan Air Base just before dawn, and had sat up front in the cockpit with him all the way here. 'Everything okay?'

'Sure,' Lochart said. 'She's clean and all set to go.' It was a nice day, cloudless and warm. When the sun went down in an hour or so the temperature would drop twenty or more degrees but that wouldn't matter. He knew that he would be warm because generals always looked after themselves – and those necessary to them for their survival. At the moment I'm necessary to Valik and to General Seladi, but only for the moment, he thought.

Muted laughter came from the house and more from those sunning or swimming in the clear blue waters of the lake below. The house seemed incongruous in such desolation – a modern, spacious, four-bedroom bungalow with separate servants' quarters. It was set on a slight rise overlooking the lake and the dam, the only habitation in this whole area. Surrounding the lake and the dam was a barren wilderness – small, rock hills jutting from a high plateau devoid of any vegetation. The only ways here were to backpack in, or to come by air, by helicopter or light airplane into the very short, narrow, dirt airstrip that had been hacked out of the uneven terrain.

Doubt if even a light twin could get in here, Lochart had thought when he first saw it. Have to be a single engine. And no way to go around again – once you commit you're committed. But it's a great hideaway, no doubt about that – just great.

Ali got up and stretched.

They had arrived here this morning, their flight uneventful. On orders and directions from General Seladi, quietly varied by Captain Ali, Lochart had hugged the ground, weaving through the passes, avoiding all towns and villages. Their radio had been open all the time. The only report they had heard was a venomous broadcast from Isfahan, repeated several times, about a 212 full of traitors that was escaping southward and should be intercepted and shot down. 'They didn't give our names – or our registration,' Ali had said excitedly. 'They must've forgotten to write it down.'

'What the hell difference does that make?' Lochart had said. 'We must be the only 212 in the sky.'

'Never mind. Stay at max a hundred feet and now turn west.'

Lochart had been astonished, expecting to head for Bandar-e Delam that lay almost due south. 'Where we heading?'

'Forget compass bearings, I'll guide you from here on in.'

'Where're we heading?'

'Baghdad.' Ali had laughed.

No one had told him their destination until they were ready to land, and by that time, a little over 200 miles from Isfahan, flying very low all the way with adverse winds, at maximum consumption and far beyond their expected maximum duration – on empty too long – Ali was openly praying.

'If we put down in the godforsaken wilderness we'll never walk out, what about fuel?'

351

'There's plenty there when we arrive . . . God be praised!' Ali had said excitedly as they came over the rise to see the lake and the dam. 'God be praised!'

Lochart had echoed his thanks and had landed quickly. Beside the helipad was a subterranean five-thousand-gallon tank, and the shed hangar. In the shed hangar were some tools and cylinders of air for tyres, and racks of water skis and boating equipment.

'Let's put her away,' Ali said. Together they wheeled the 212 into the shed where she fitted snugly, putting chocks on her wheels. As Lochart adjusted the rotor tie-down he noticed three hang gliders in a rack overhead. They were dust-covered and in tatters now.

'Whose are those?'

'This used to be the private weekend place of the General of the Imperial Air Force, Hassayn Aryani. They were his.'

Lochart whistled. Aryani was the legendary head of the air force who, according to rumour, also had been like captain of the Praetorian Guard in Roman times to the Shah, his confidant and married to one of his sisters. He had been killed hang gliding two years ago. 'Was this where he was killed?'

'Yes.' Ali pointed to the other side of the lake. 'They say he got into still-air turbulence and went into those cliffs.'

Lochart studied him. ' "They say"? You don't believe that?'

'No. I'm sure he was assassinated. In the air force most of us are sure.'

'You mean his hang glider was sabotaged?'

Ali shrugged. 'I don't know. Perhaps, perhaps not, but he was much too careful and clever a pilot and flier to get into turbulence. Aryani would never've flown on a bad day.' He went out into the sun. Below they could hear the voices and laughter of some of the others, and Valik's children playing down by the lake. 'He used a speedboat to take off. He'd wear short water skis, then hold on to a long rope attached to the speedboat that'd go charging down the lake and when he was fast enough he'd drop his skis and go airborne and soar up five hundred, a thousand feet, then cast off and spiral down and land within inches of the raft down there.'

'He was that good?'

'Yeah, he was that good. He was too good, that's why he was murdered.'

'By whom?'

'I don't know. If I did, then he or they would have died long ago.'

Lochart saw the adoration. 'You knew him, then?'

'I was his aide, one of his aides, for a year. He was easily the most wonderful man I have ever known – the best general, the best pilot, best sportsman, skier – everything. If he had been alive now the Shah would never have been trapped by foreigners or snared by our arch-enemy Carter, the Shah'd never have left. Iran would never have been allowed to slide into the abyss, and the generals would never have been allowed to betray us.' Ali Abbasi's face twisted with anger. 'It's impossible to conceive that we could be so betrayed with him alive.'

'Then who killed him? Khomeini's followers?'

'No, not three years ago. He was a famous nationalist, Shi'ite, though a modern. Who? Tudeh, fedayeen or any fanatic of the right, left, or centre who wanted Iran weakened.' Ali looked at him, dark eyes in a chiselled face. 'There are even those who say people in high places feared his growing power and popularity.'

Lochart blinked. 'You mean the Shah might have ordered his death?'

'No. No, of course not, but he was a threat to those who misguided the Shah. He was *farmandeh*, a commander of the people. He was a threat, all over: to British interests, because he supported Prime Minister Mossadegh who nationalised Anglo-Iranian Oil, he supported the Shah and OPEC when they quadrupled the cost of oil. He was pro-Israel though not anti-Arab, so a threat to the PLO and Yasser Arafat. He could have been considered a threat to American interests – to any or all of the Seven Sisters because he didn't give a good goddam for them or anyone. Anyone. For above all he was a patriot.' Ali's eyes had a strange look to them. 'Assassination is an ancient art in Iran. Wasn't ibn-al-Sabbah one of us?' His mouth smiled, his eyes didn't. 'We're different here.'

'Sorry – ibn-al-Sabbah?'

'The Old Man of the Mountains, Hassan ibn-al-Sabbah, the Ismai'li religious leader who invented the Assassins in the eleventh century, and their cult of political assassination.'

'Oh, sure, sorry I wasn't thinking. Wasn't he supposed to be a friend of Omar Khayyám?'

'Some legends say so.' Ali's face was etched. 'Aryani was murdered, by whom, no one knows. Yet.' Together they pulled the shed door closed.

'What now?' Lochart asked.

'Now we wait. Then we'll go on.' Into exile, Ali thought. Never mind, it will only be temporary and at least I know where I'm going, not like the Shah, poor man, who's an outcast. I can go to the States.

Only he and his parents knew that he had a U.S. passport. Goddam,

353

he thought, how clever of Dad: 'You never know, my son, what God has in store,' his father had said gravely. 'I advise you to apply for a passport while you can. Dynasties never last, only family. Shahs come and go, Shahs feed off each other, and the two Pahlavis together are only fifty-four-year Highnesses – Imperial Majesties! What was Reza Khan before he crowned himself King of Kings? A soldier-adventurer, the son of illiterate villagers from Mazandaran near the Caspian.'

'But surely, Father, Reza Khan was a special man. Without him and Mohammed Reza Shah, we'd still be slaves of the British.'

'The Pahlavis were of use to us, my son, yes. In many ways. But Reza Shah failed, he failed himself and failed us by stupidly believing the Germans would win the war and tried to support the Axis – and so gave the occupying British an excuse to depose him and exile him.'

'But, Father, Mohammed Shah can't fail! He's stronger than his father ever was. Our armed forces are the envy of the world. We've more airplanes than Britain, more tanks than Germany, more money than Croesus, America's our ally, we're the biggest military power and policeman of the Middle and Near East, and the leaders of the outside kowtow to him – even Brezhnev.'

'Yes. But we do not yet know what is the Will of God. Get the passport.'

'But a U.S. passport could be very dangerous, you know how it's said almost everything goes through SAVAK to the Shah! What if he heard, or General Aryani heard? That'd ruin me in the air force.'

'Why should it – for of course you would tell them proudly you just got the passport, and kept it secret, against the day you could put it to use for the good of the Pahlavis. Eh?'

'Of course!'

'Open your eyes to the ways of the world, my son – the promises of kings have no value, they can plead expedience. If this Shah or the next, or even your great general has to choose between your life and something of more value to them, which would they choose? Put no trust in princes, or generals, or politicians, they will sell you, your family, and your heritage for a pinch of salt to put on a plate of rice they won't even bother to taste . . .'

And oh how true! Carter sold us out and his generals, then the Shah and his generals, and our generals did the same to us. But how could they be so stupid to assassinate themselves? he asked himself, shuddering at the thought of how close he had been to death in Isfahan. They must have all gone mad!

'It's cold in the shade,' Lochart said.

354

'Yes, yes, it is.' Ali looked back at him and shook off his anxiety. Generals are all the same. My father was right. Even these two bastards Valik or Seladi, they'd have sold us all if need be, still will.

They need me because I'm the only one who can fly them – apart from this poor fool who doesn't know he's in dead trouble.

'Get rid of this Lochart,' Seladi had said. 'Why take him to safety? He would have left us at Isfahan, why not leave him here? Dead. We can't leave him alive, he knows us all and he'd betray us all.'

'No, Excellency Uncle,' Valik had said. 'He's more use as a gift to the Kuwaits, or Iraqis, they can jail him or extradite him. It was he who stole an Iranian helicopter and agreed for money to fly us out. Didn't he?'

'Yes. Even so, he can still give our names to the revolutionaries.'

'By that time we will all be safe and our families safe.'

'I say dispose of him – he would have sacrificed us. Dispose of him and we will go to Baghdad, not Kuwait.'

'Please, Excellency, reconsider. Lochart is the more experienced pilot . . .'

Ali glanced at his watch. Just thirty minutes to takeoff. He saw Lochart glance at the house where Valik, Seladi were. I wonder who won, Valik or Seladi? Is it the inside of a Kuwaiti or Iraqi jail for this poor joker, or a bullet in the head? I wonder if they'll bury him after they shoot him or just leave him to the vultures.

'What's the matter?' Lochart asked.

'Nothing. Nothing, Captain, just thinking how lucky we were to escape Isfahan.'

'Yes, I still owe you a life.' Lochart was certain that if Ali and the major hadn't released him he would have ended up before a komiteh kangaroo court. And if he was caught now? The same. He had not allowed his mind to think about Sharazad or Tehran or to make a plan. That comes later, he told himself again. Once you see how this turns out and where you end up.

Where're they planning to go? Kuwait? Or maybe just a quick stab over the border into Iraq? Iraq's usually hostile to Iranians so that might be dicey for them. Kuwait's an easy flight from here and most Kuwaitis are Sunni, not Shi'ite, and therefore anti-Khomeini. Against that, to get there, you have to sneak through a lot of sensitive airspace, Iranian and Iraqi, both nervous, jumpy, and trigger-happy. Within fifty miles there must be twenty Iranian air bases, fighter operational, with planes gassed up and dozens of petrified pilots anxious to prove loyalty to the new regime.

And what about your promise to McIver not to fly them the last leg?

Because of Isfahan you're marked now – there's no way the revs will have forgotten your name or the registration of the airplane. Did you see anyone write your name down? No, I don't think so. Even so, you'd better get out while you can, you're implicated in an escape, men were killed at Isfahan – whichever way you stack it you're marked.

What about Sharazad? I can't leave her.

You may have to. She's safe in Tehran.

What if they come looking for you and Sharazad answers the door and they take her away in place of you?

'I could use a cold drink,' he said, his mouth suddenly dry. 'You think they have a Coke or something?'

'I'll go see.' They both looked up as Valik's children came bounding up the path from the lake, Annoush close behind them.

'Ah,' she said to them with her happy smile, but dark shadows around her eyes, 'it is a wonderful day, isn't it? We're so lucky.'

'Yes,' both said and wondered how such a woman could marry such a man. She was very good to look at and as beautiful a mother as could be.

'Captain Abbasi, where's my husband?'

'In the house, Highness, with the others,' Ali said. 'May I escort you, I was just going there?'

'Would you find him for me, please, and ask him to join me?'

Ali did not wish to leave her alone with Lochart for she had been present when Valik and Seladi had told him of their plans, asking his advice about their destination – though not about Lochart's elimination, that had come later. 'I wouldn't want to disturb the general by myself, Highness, perhaps we could go together.'

'You will please find him for me.' She was as imperious as the general, though kindly and without insult.

Ali shrugged. Insha'Allah, he thought, and went off. When they were quite alone, her two children running around the shed, playing hide and seek, Annoush touched Lochart gently. 'I haven't thanked you for our lives, Tommy.'

Lochart was startled. This was the first time she had ever called him by his first name – he had always been 'Captain Lochart' or, 'my cousin-in-law' or, 'His Excellency, the husband of Sharazad.' 'I was glad to help.'

'I know that you and dear old Mac did it for the children and me – don't look so surprised, my dear, I know my husband's strengths and . . . and his weaknesses – what wife doesn't?' Tears brimmed her eyes. 'I

356

know what this means for you too – you've jeopardised your life, Sharazad's, your future in Iran, perhaps your company.'

'Not Sharazad's. No, she's perfectly safe. Her father, Excellency Bakravan, will keep her safe until she can get out. Of course she's safe.' He saw Annoush's brown eyes and read behind her eyes and his soul twisted.

'I pray that with all my heart, Tommy, and beg God to grant that wish.' She dabbed her tears away. 'I've never been so sad in all my life. I never knew I could be so sad – sad to be running away, sad for that poor soldier dying in the snow, sad for all our families and friends who have to stay, sad because no one's safe in Iran any more. I'm so afraid most of our circle will be persecuted by the mullahs, we've always been – what shall I say? Too modern and . . . too progressive. No one's safe here any more – not even Khomeini himself.'

Lochart heard himself say, 'Insha' Allah,' but he wasn't listening to her, suddenly petrified that he would never see Sharazad again, never be able to get back into Iran or her able to get out. 'It will be normal again soon, travel permitted and everything okay. Of course it will. In a few months, it's got to be. Of course it will be normal soon.'

'I hope so, Tommy, for I love your Sharazad and would hate not being able to see her and the little one.'

'Eh?' He gaped at her.

'Oh, but of course you wouldn't know,' she said, then brushed the last of her tears away. 'It was too soon for you to know. Sharazad told me she's sure she's carrying her firstborn.'

'But . . . but, well she . . .' He stopped helplessly, aghast, at the same time ecstatic. 'She can't be!'

'Oh, she wasn't sure yet, Tommy, but she felt she was. Sometimes a woman can tell – you feel so different, so very different and so wonderful, so fulfilled,' she added, her voice now joyous.

Lochart was trying to get his mind working, completely aware that it would be impossible for her to understand the turmoil she was creating in him. God in heaven, he thought, Sharazad?

'There are still a few days to be certain,' she was saying. 'I think it's three or four. Let me think. Yes, including today, Tuesday, four more days to be certain. That would make it the day after, after seeing her father,' she said delicately. 'You were to see him this Holy Day, Friday, the 16th, by your counting, weren't you?'

'Yes,' Lochart said. As if I could forget. 'You knew about that?'

'Of course.' Annoush was astonished by his question. 'Such an extraordinary request from you, and such an important decision would have to be known by all of us. Oh, wouldn't it be wonderful if she is with child – didn't you tell Excellency Bakravan you wanted children? I so hope she has been blessed by God for that will surely pass the days and nights happily for her until we can get her out. Kuwait's not far. I'm only sorry she didn't come with us – that would have made everything perfect.'

'Kuwait?'

'Yes, but we won't stop there – we'll go on to London.' Again the torment showed. 'I don't want to leave our home and friends and . . . I don't . . .'

Behind her, Lochart saw the door of the house open. Valik and Seladi came out, Ali with them. He noticed the three of them wore sidearms now. Must have had a cache of weapons here, he thought absently as Ali saluted and hurried down the path towards the lake. Bursting with glee the two children charged from the back of the shed into Valik's arms. He swung the little girl into the air and set her down.

'Yes, Annoush?' he asked his wife.

'You wanted me and the children to be here exactly at this time.'

'Yes. Please get Setarem and Jalal ready. We'll be leaving soon.' At once the children ran off into the house. 'Captain, is the chopper ready?'

'Yes. Yes, it is.'

Valik glanced back at his wife. 'Please get ready, my dear.'

She smiled and did not move. 'I just have to fetch my coat. I'm ready to leave.' The rest of the officers were approaching now. Several carried automatic weapons.

Lochart tore his mind off Sharazad and Holy Day and four days more and broke the silence. 'What's the plan?'

Valik said, 'Baghdad. We'll take off in a few minutes.'

'I thought we were going to Kuwait,' Annoush said.

'We've decided to go to Baghdad. General Seladi thinks it'll be safer than to head south.' Valik kept watching Lochart. 'I want to be airborne in ten minutes.'

'I'd advise you to wait until 2 or 3 in the morning and th –'

Seladi interrupted coldly, 'We could be trapped here. Soldiers could ambush us – there's an air base nearby, they could send out a patrol. You don't understand military matters. We leave for Baghdad at once.'

'Kuwait's better and safer, but in both places the chopper'll be impounded without an Iranian clearance,' Lochart said.

'Perhaps, perhaps not,' Valik said calmly. 'Baksheesh and a few connections will make all the difference.' You, interloper into my family, he thought benignly, you along with the gift of the 212 will be a sop to satisfy even the Iraqis, for we certainly agree you have flown it illegally – even the clearance you obtained from Tehran was illegal. The Iraqis will understand and they won't harm us. Most of them hate and fear Khomeini and his version of Islam. With you, the 212 and a little extra on the side, why should they give me trouble?

He saw Lochart watching him. 'Yes?'

'I think Baghdad's a bad choice.'

General Seladi said curtly, 'We will leave now.'

Lochart flushed at the rudeness. Some of the others shifted nervously. 'No doubt you'll leave when the aircraft is ready and the pilot ready. Have you flown in these mountains?'

'No . . . no I haven't but the 212 has the ceiling and Baghdad's where we will go. Now!'

'Then I wish you luck. I still advise Kuwait and waiting, but you do what you want, because I'm not flying you.'

There was an even bigger silence. Seladi went red in the face. 'You will prepare to leave. Now.'

Lochart said to Valik, 'On the way to Isfahan I told you I wouldn't be flying the last leg. I'm not flying you onward. Ali can do that – he's fully qualified.'

'But you're as wanted as any of us now,' Valik said, astonished at his stupidity. 'Of course you will fly the last leg.'

'No, no I won't. I'll backpack out of here – of course you can't waste time landing me somewhere. Ali can fly you – he's been based in this area and knows the radar. Just leave me a rifle and I'll head for Bandar-e Delam. Okay?'

The others stared from Lochart to Seladi and Valik. Waiting.

Valik thought through this new problem. So did Seladi. Both men came to the same conclusion: Insha'Allah! Lochart had chosen to stay and therefore Lochart had chosen the consequences. 'Very well,' Valik said calmly. 'Ali will fly us.' He smiled and then because he respected Lochart as a pilot, he added quickly, 'As we're a very democratic people, I suggest we put it to a vote – Iraq or Kuwait?'

'Kuwait,' Annoush said at once, and the others echoed her before Seladi could interrupt.

Good, Valik thought, I allowed myself to be overruled because Seladi claimed to know the chief of police in Baghdad and said that safe passage for me and my family and him would be no more than twenty thousand dollars in U.S. notes which would be immeasurably cheaper than Kuwait – how much the others will have to pay will be up

359

to them; I hope they have money with them or the means to get enough quickly. 'Of course you agree, Excellency Uncle? Kuwait. Thank you, Captain. Perhaps you'll tell Ali he'll be flying us – he's down by the lake.'

'Sure. I'll just get my gear. You'll leave me a rifle?'

'Of course.'

Lochart went to the shed and disappeared inside.

Seladi said, 'Some of you get the chopper out and we'll be off.' They went to obey him. Lochart came out, put his flight bag and hold-all beside the door and walked down the path towards the lake. Seladi watched him go, then impatiently walked over to the 212.

Valik saw his wife watching him. 'Yes, Annoush?'

'What's planned for Captain Lochart?' she asked softly though they could not be overheard.

'He's . . . you heard him. He refuses to fly us and wants to stay. He'll walk out.'

'I know how your mind works, my dear. Are you going to have him killed?' There was a nice smile on her face. 'Murdered?'

'Murder would be the wrong word.' His mouth smiled. 'I'm sure you'd agree Lochart represents a great danger now. He knows us all, all our names – all our families will suffer when he's caught and tortured and sentenced. It's the Will of God. He made the choice. Seladi wanted it done anyway – a military decision – I said no, that he should fly us onward.'

'To be a sacrifice in Kuwait, or Baghdad?'

'Seladi gave orders to Ali, I didn't. Lochart's marked, poor man. It's tragic, but necessary. You agree, don't you?'

'No, my dear, I'm sorry but I don't. So if he's hurt, or touched here, there will be many who live to regret it.' Annoush's smile did not change. 'You as well, my dear.'

His face flushed. Behind him men pulled the 212 into the open and now they were loading her. He dropped his voice. 'Didn't you hear me, Annoush, he's a threat! He's not one of us, Jared barely tolerates him and I promise you he's a great danger to us, to those we've left behind – your family as well as mine.'

'Didn't you hear me, husband? I promise you I know only too well the dangers, but if he's killed here – murdered – you will be killed too.'

'Don't be ridiculous!'

'Sometime you will sleep and you will not awaken. It will be the Will of God.' The smile never changed nor the gentleness of her voice.

Valik hesitated, then his face closed and he hurried down the path.

360

The children barrelled out of the house towards her and she said kindly, 'Wait here, my darlings, I'll be back in a moment.'

Esplanaded over the lake on stilts was an open-sided barbecue area and bar under a neat overhang, with a few steps that went down into the water for skiers, or for the motorboat that was tied up in its shelter nearby.

Lochart was on the water's edge, his hands up.

Ali had the automatic levelled. His orders from Seladi had been clear: go to the lake and wait. We will either call you back or send the pilot to find you. If the pilot comes looking for you, kill him and return at once.

He had hated the order – bombarding or attacking revolutionaries or mutineers from a chopper gunship was not murder as this was murder. His face was ashen, he had never killed before and he asked God's pardon, but an order was an order. 'Sorry,' he said, hardly able to talk, and began to pull the trigger.

At that instant Lochart's legs seemed to collapse and he twisted over the side into the water. Automatically, Ali followed the movement, aimed for the centre of the back as though at target practice, knowing he could never miss at this range. Fire!

'Stop!'

The fraction of a second he had hesitated was enough time for his brain to hear the order and obey it thankfully. With shuddering relief, he felt his finger release the pressure on the trigger. Valik rushed up to him and both of them peered into the water, murky here in the shade and quite deep. They waited. Lochart did not appear.

'Perhaps he's under the floor – or under the raft,' Ali said, wiping the sweat off his face and hands, and thanking God that the pilot's blood was not on his soul.

'Yes.' Valik was also sweating, but mostly with fear. He had never seen that look on his wife's face before, the smile that promised a death in the night. It's her vile ancestors, he thought. She's Qajar, her lineage Qajars who could happily blind or murder rivals to the throne – or children of rivals – didn't only one Qajar Shah in their 146-year dynasty relinquish his throne through natural death? Valik looked around, saw her standing up at the head of the path, then turned back to Ali. 'Give me your gun.'

Shakily Valik put the gun down on the rough wooden planking, and called out: 'Lochart, I've left you a gun. This was all a mistake. The captain was mistaken.'

'But General –'

'Go up to the chopper,' Valik ordered loudly. 'Seladi's a fool – he

361

should never have given you orders to kill this poor man. We leave at once and we go to Kuwait – not Baghdad. Ali, go and start the aircraft!'

Ali left. As he passed Annoush he eyed her curiously, then hurried onward. She walked down and joined Valik.

'You saw?' he asked.

'Yes.'

They waited. No sound there, no tide to lap the pilings. It was beautiful and calm, the surface of the lake glassy and windless. 'I . . . pray he's hiding somewhere,' she said, a great void in her soul, but now time to heal the breach. 'I'm glad his blood's not on our hands. Seladi's a monster.'

'We'd better go back.' They were quite hidden from the chopper and the house. He took out his automatic and fired it once into the ground nearby. 'For Seladi. I, er, think I hit Lochart when . . . when he surfaced. Eh?'

She took his arm. 'You're a wise and good man.' They walked back up the rise, arm in arm. 'Without you, your cleverness and courage, we would never have escaped Isfahan. But exile? Wh –'

'Temporary exile,' he said jovially, filled with relief that the vile moment between them had passed. 'Then we'll come home again.'

'That would be wonderful,' she said, forcing herself to believe it. I've got to or I'll go mad. I've got to for the children! 'I'm glad you chose Kuwait – I never liked Baghdad, and those Iraqis, ugh!' Her eyes still had shadows in them. 'What Lochart said about waiting till after dark was wrong?'

'There's an air base within a few miles. We could have been seen on radar, Annoush, or by spotters in the hills. Seladi's right in that – the base will send a patrol after us.' They topped the rise. The children were waiting for them in the cabin doorway, everyone else aboard. They quickened their pace. 'Kuwait's much safer. I'd already decided to overrule that pompous fool Seladi – he's never to be trusted.'

In minutes they were airborne, heading northward over the rim of these hills, skirting the crags, hugging the ground to avoid the nearby danger from the air base. Ali Abbasi was a good pilot and knew the area well. Once over the rim and down into the valley he turned west and scurried through a pass to avoid the outer perimeter of the airfield, the Iraqi border some fifty miles farther ahead. Snow covered the heights of the mountains far above them and parts of the slopes, though the floor of some valleys were green, here and there, among the rocky wilderness. They thundered over an unexpected and unknown village, then curled almost due south, again following the water course, paralleling the border that was far to their right. The whole flight would take barely two hours, depending on the winds, and the winds were favourable.

Those in the cabin near the windows happily watched the land rushing past, the two children given the best position, the major holding Jalal, Valik his daughter, beside Annoush. Everyone was content, a few praying silently. Sunset was not far off and would be good, red-tinged clouds – 'red sky at night, shepherds' delight,' Annoush crooned to Setarem in English – and, up front, the engines sounded good with all needles in the Green.

Ali was glad to be flying, glad that he had not killed Lochart who had stood there in front of him, saying nothing, not begging for his life or saying prayers, just standing there with his hands up, waiting. I'm sure he's safe under the pilings, thanks be to God . . .

He took a quick glance at the map, refreshing his memory. But he did not really need to, he had spent many good years here, flying the passes. Soon he would come down out of the mountains into the marsh plains of the Tigris and Euphrates, staying at ground level, skirting Dezful, then Ahwaz and Khorramshahr, then stab across the Shatt-al-Arab waterway and the border, into Kuwait and freedom.

Ahead was the ridge with the dominating peak that he had been expecting and he swung upward out of the valley to swoop down into the next, the joy of flying possessing him. Then 'HBC, climb to a thousand feet and reduce speed!' filled his headphones and brain. He had been airborne barely six minutes.

The order had been in Farsi and it was repeated in English and then in Farsi and again in English, and all the while he kept her low, desperately trying to get his head working.

'Chopper HBC, you're illegal, climb out of the valley and reduce speed.'

Ali Abbasi peered upward, searching the sky, but he saw no airplane. The valley floor was tearing past. Ahead was another rim and then there'd be a succession of rims and valleys that led down to the plains. Westward the Iraqi border was forty-odd miles away – twenty minutes.

'Chopper HBC, for the last time, you're illegal, climb out of the valley and reduce speed!'

His brain shouted, You've three choices: obey and die, try to escape, or put down and wait the night and try at first light – if you survive their rockets or bullets.

Ahead of him to the left he saw trees and the land falling away, the sides of the valley steepening into a ravine, so he cast himself into it,

363

committing them to escape. Now his mind was working well. He pulled off his headset, put himself into the hands of God and felt the better for it. He slowed as he came nearer the end of the ravine, skirted some trees and ducked into another small valley, reduced speed even more, following the stream bed cautiously. More trees and outcrops and he sneaked around them.

Stay low and slow and save petrol and ease your way south, he thought with growing confidence. Go nearer the border when you can and take your time. They'll never catch you if you use your wits. It'll be dark soon – you can lose them in the dark and you know enough about instrument flying to get to Kuwait. But how did they spot us? It was almost as though they were waiting. Could they have had us on radar going into the Dez Dam – Watch ittttt!

The trees were heavier here and he slewed around a scattering of them on the mountainside, went closer to the rocks, and climbed for the ridge and the next valley. Over it safely and down into the protection of the rocks, eyes searching ahead and above and always for a good spot to put down if an engine failed. He was concentrating and confident and doing his job well. All the instruments were in the safety range. Minutes passed and though he searched the sky diligently he saw nothing. At the head of the next valley he put the chopper into a 360 and carefully scanned the sky. Nothing overhead.

Safe! Lost him! Insha'Allah! He took a deep breath and, very satisfied, turned southward again. Over the next ridge. And the next and there ahead were the plains. The two fighters were waiting. They were F14s.

At Tehran Airport – S-G's Office: 5:48 P.M. '. . . you are not permitted to land!' came over the HF, heavily mixed with static – Gavallan, McIver and Robert Armstrong grouped around it, listening intently, the vista through the windows dull and brooding, night near.

The breezy voice of John Hogg from the incoming 125 came back again: 'Tehran Control, this is EchoTangoLimaLima, as per yesterday, we have clearance from Kish to land an –'

'ETLL, you are not permitted to land!' The traffic controller's voice was raw and frightened and McIver cursed under his breath. 'I say again: negative, all civilian air traffic is grounded and all incoming flights cancelled until further orders of the Imam . . .' Behind his voice they could hear other voices chattering in Farsi, a number of mikes open on this frequency. 'Return to your point of departure!'

'I say again, we have clearance to land from Kish radar who passed us to Isfahan air traffic controller who confirmed our clearance. Long live Ayatollah Khomeini and the victory of Islam – I am forty miles south of checkpoint Varamin, expecting runway 29 left. Please confirm your ILS is functioning. Do you have other traffic in your system?'

For a moment Farsi voices dominated the tower, then, 'Negative traffic, ETLL, negative ILS but you are not per—' The American English stopped abruptly and an angry, heavily accented voice took over: 'Not landings! Komiteh give orders Tehran! Kish not Tehran – Isfahan not Tehran – we give orders Tehran. If landings you arrested.'

John Hogg's happy voice replied at once, 'EchoTangoLimaLima. Understand you don't want us to land, Tehran Tower, and wish to reject our clearances which I believe is an error according to air traffic regulations – Standby One please.' Then at once on their private S-G frequency, mixed with static, came his terse voice, 'HQ advise!'

Immediately McIver switched channels and said into the mike, '360, Standby One,' meaning circle and wait for a reply. He glanced up at Gavallan who was grim-faced. Robert Armstrong was whistling tonelessly.

'We better wave him off – if he lands they could throw the book at him and impound her,' McIver said.

'With official clearances?' Gavallan said. 'You told the tower we've the British ambassador's letter approved by Bazargan's office –'

'But not by Bazargan himself, sir,' Robert Armstrong said, 'and even then, for all practical purposes, those buggers in the tower are the law in the tower for the moment. I'd suggest the—' He stopped and pointed, his face even grimmer. 'Look there!' Two trucks and a radio control car, with its tall aerial waving, were racing along the boundary road. As they watched the trucks drove directly on to runway 29 left, parked in the middle of it. Armed Green Bands jumped out taking up defensive positions. The control car continued to head their way.

'Shit!' McIver muttered.

'Mac, do you think they'll be monitoring our frequency?'

'Safer to assume so, Andy.'

Gavallan took the mike. 'Abort. B repeat B.'

'EchoTangoLimaLima!' Then, on the tower frequency, kind and friendly: 'Tehran Tower: we agree your request to cancel our clearance and formally apply for clearance to land at tomorrow noon to deliver urgent repeat urgent spares required by IranOil, outgoing crew for overdue leave, with immediate turnaround.'

McIver grunted. 'Johnny always was fast on his feet.' Then to Armstrong, 'We'll put y –'

'Standby One, EchoTangoLimaLima,' from the tower over-rode him.

'We'll put you on her passenger list when we can, Mr. Armstrong. Sorry, no joy today. What about your papers?'

Armstrong took his eyes off the approaching car. 'I, er, I'd prefer to be a specialist consultant for S-G, going on leave, if you don't mind. Unpaid, of course.' He stared back at Gavallan. 'What's "B repeat B"?'

'Try again tomorrow, same time.'

'And if they grant ETLL's request?'

'Then it's tomorrow – you'll be a specialist consultant.'

'Thanks. Let's hope it's tomorrow.' Armstrong looked at the approaching car, and added quickly, 'Will you be in about ten tonight, Mr. Gavallan? Perhaps I could drop by – just to chat, nothing important.'

'Certainly. I'll expect you. We've met before, haven't we?'

'Yes. If I'm not there by ten-fifteen I've been delayed and can't come – you know how it is – and I'll check in the morning.' Armstrong began to leave. 'Thanks.'

'All right. Where did we meet?'

'Hong Kong.' Robert Armstrong nodded politely and walked out, tall and gaunt. They saw him go through the office and take the door that led to the hangar and the back door to the S-G car park where he had left his nondescript car – McIver's car was parked in front.

'Almost as though he's been here before,' McIver said thoughtfully.

'Hong Kong? Don't remember him at all. Do you?'

'No.' McIver frowned. 'I'll ask Gen, she has a good memory for names.'

'I'm not sure I like or trust Robert bloody Armstrong, whatever Talbot says.'

At noon they had gone to see Talbot to find out the who and the why of Armstrong. All George Talbot would say was, 'Oh, he's rather decent really, and we'd, er, we'd appreciate your giving him a lift, and er, not asking too many questions. You'll stay for lunch, of course? We've still some rather good Dover sole, fresh frozen, plenty of caviar or smoked salmon if you wish, a couple of La Doucette '76 on ice – or bangers and mash with the house claret which I'd highly recommend if you prefer. Chocolate pudding or sherry trifle, and we've still half of a fairly decent Stilton. The whole world may be on fire, but at least we can watch it burn like gentlemen. How about a pink gin before lunch?'

Lunch had been very good. Talbot had said that Bakhtiar's leaving the field for Bazargan and Khomeini might avert most trouble. 'Now

367

that there's no chance of a coup, things should get back to normal, eventually.'

'When do you think's "eventually"?'

'When "they", whoever "they" are, run out of ammunition. But, my dear old boy, whatever I think really doesn't matter. It's what Khomeini thinks that matters, and only God knows what Khomeini thinks.'

Gavallan remembered the shrill cackle of laughter that Talbot had let out at his own joke and smiled.

'What?' McIver asked.

'I was just remembering Talbot at lunch.'

The car was still a hundred yards away. 'Talbot's hiding a mountain of secrets. What do you think Armstrong wants to "chat" about?'

'Probably to divert us some more – after all, Mac, we did go to the embassy to enquire about him. Curious! Usually I don't forget . . . Hong Kong? Seem to associate him with the races at Happy Valley. It'll come back to me. I'll say one thing for him, he's punctual. I told him five o'clock and he was here – even though he seemed to come out of the woodwork.' Gavallan's eyes twinkled under his heavy eyebrows, then went back to the incoming car that was drawing up outside. 'Sure as God made Scotland he didn't want to meet our friendly komiteh. I wonder why?'

The komiteh consisted of two armed youths, a mullah – not the same as yesterday – and Sabolir, the perspiring senior immigration official, still very nervous.

'Good evening, Excellencies,' McIver said, his nostrils rebelling against their invading smell of stale sweat. 'Would you care for tea?'

'No, no, thank you,' Sabolir said. He was still very much on his guard, though he tried to hide it under a mask of arrogance. He sat down in the best chair. 'We have new regulations for you.'

'Oh?' McIver had had dealings with him over a couple of years, and had provided an occasional case of whisky, fill-ups of petrol, and, from time to time, free air travel – and accommodation – for him and his family on several summer vacations to Caspian resorts: 'We booked rooms for some of our executives and they can't use the space, dear Mr. Sabolir. It's a pity to waste the space, isn't it?' Once he had arranged a week's trip for two to Dubai. The girl had been young and very beautiful, and at Sabolir's blunt suggestion was put on the S-G books as an 'Iranian expert'. 'What can we do for you?'

To their surprise Sabolir took out Gavallan's passport and the previous clearance paper and put them on the desk. 'Here are your passport and papers, er, approved,' he said, his voice automatically oily with officialdom. 'The Imam has ordered normal operations to begin at once. The, er, the Islamic State of Iran is back to normal and the airport will reopen in, er, three days, for normal, pre-agreed traffic. You are to come back to normal now.'

'We begin training the Iranian Air Force again?' McIver asked, hard put to keep the glee out of his voice, for this was a very big contract and very profitable.

Sabolir hesitated. 'Yes, I presume y –'

'No,' the mullah said firmly in good English. 'No – not until the Imam or the Revolutionary Komiteh agrees. I will see that you have a firm answer. I do not think this part of your operation will begin yet. Meanwhile your normal business – spares to your bases and their contract flights to assist IranOil resume oil production, or Iran-Timber and so on – provided the flights are approved in advance, may begin the day after tomorrow.'

'Excellent,' Gavallan said, and McIver echoed him.

'Replacement flight crews and oil rig crews, in and out – if approved in advance and provided their papers are in order,' the mullah continued, 'will resume the day after tomorrow. Oil production is to be a priority. An Islamic Guard will accompany every internal flight.'

'If requested in advance, and the man is on time for the flight. But not armed,' McIver said politely, preparing for the inevitable clash.

'Armed Islamic Guards will be carried for your protection to prevent hijacking by enemies of the state!' the mullah said sharply.

'We will be very pleased to cooperate, Excellency,' Gavallan interrupted calmly, 'very pleased indeed, but I'm sure you won't wish to endanger life or jeopardise the Islamic state. I formally ask you to ask the Imam to agree to no guns whatever – clearly you have immediate access to his presence. Meanwhile all our aircraft are grounded until I have clearance, or clearance from my government.'

'You will not ground flights and you will become normal!' The mullah was very angry.

'Perhaps a compromise pending the Imam's agreement: your guards have their guns but the captain holds the ammunition during the flight. Agreed?'

The mullah hesitated.

Gavallan hardened. 'The Imam ordered ALL weapons handed in, didn't he?'

'Yes. Very well, I agree.'

'Thank you. Mac, prepare the paper for His Excellency to sign and that takes care of it for all our lads. Now, we'll need new flight papers, Excellency, the only ones we've got are the old, er, useless ones from the previous regime. Will you give us the necessary authority? You yourself, Excellency? Clearly you are a man of importance and you know what's going on.' He watched as the mullah seemed to grow in stature with the flattery. The man was in his thirties, his beard was greasy and his clothes threadbare. From his accent Gavallan had pegged him an ex-British student, one of the thousands of Iranians that the Shah had sent abroad on grants for Western education. 'You will of course give us new papers at once, to make us legal with the new era?'

'We, er, we will sign new documents for each of our aircraft, yes.' The mullah took some papers from his battered briefcase and put on a pair of old glasses, the lenses thick and one of them cracked. The paper he sought was at the bottom. 'You have in your trust thirteen Iranian 212s, seven 206s, and four Alouettes in various places, all Iranian registry and owned by Iran Helicopter Company – that's correct?'

Gavallan shook his head. 'Not exactly. At the moment they're still actually owned by S-G Helicopters of Aberdeen. Iran Helicopter Company, our joint venture with our Iranian partners, doesn't own the aircraft until they're paid for.'

The mullah frowned, then brought the paper closer to his eyes. 'But the contract giving ownership to Iran Helicopter, which is an Iranian company, is signed, isn't it?'

'Yes, but it's subject to payments which are . . . are in arrears.'

'The Imam has said all debts will be paid so they will be paid.'

'Of course, but meanwhile ownership passes on actual payment,' Gavallan continued carefully, while hoping against hope the tower would grant Johnny Hogg's clever request for a landing tomorrow. I wonder if this mealy-mouthed bugger could order a clearance? he asked himself. If Khomeini's ordered everything back to normal, it'll go back to normal and I can safely return to London. With any luck I could close the ExTex contract that covers the new X63's lease payments by the weekend. 'For months we've been making payments on behalf of IHC on all these aircraft, with interest, banking charges and so on out of our own funds and w –'

'Islam forbids usury and the paying of interest,' the mullah said with a total finality that rocked Gavallan and McIver. 'Banks may not charge interest. None. It is usury.'

Gavallan glanced at McIver, then uneasily turned his full attention to the mullah. 'If banks cannot charge interest, how will business operate internally and externally?'

'According to Islamic law. Only Islamic law. The Koran forbids usury.' The mullah added distastefully, 'What foreign banks do is evil – it's because of them Iran had many troubles. Banks are evil institutions and will not be tolerated. As to Iran Helicopter Company, the Islamic Revolutionary Komiteh has ordered all joint ventures suspended, pending review.' The mullah waved the papers. 'All these aircraft are Iranian, Iranian registry, Iranian!' Again he peered at the paper. 'Here in Tehran you have three 212s, four 206s, and one 47G4 here at the airport, haven't you?'

'They're spread around,' McIver told him carefully, 'here, Doshan Tappeh and Galeg Morghi.'

'But they're all here, in Tehran?'

McIver had been gauging him while Gavallan had been talking, also trying to read upside down what the papers contained. The one in the mullah's hand listed all their airplanes with their registration numbers and was a copy of the manifest that was kept permanently in the tower, that S-G was obliged to keep permanently up to date. His stomach twisted nastily when he glimpsed EP-HBC ringed in red – Lochart's 212 – also EP-HFC, Pettikin's 206.

'We've one 212 on loan to Bandar-e Delam,' he said, deciding to play it safe, inwardly cursing Valik and hoping that Tom Lochart was either at Bandar-e Delam or safely on the way home. 'The rest're here.'

'On loan – that would be EP – EP-HBC?' the mullah said, very pleased with himself. 'Now, wh—' The traffic controller's voice interrupted him: 'EchoTangoLimaLima, request refused. Call Isfahan on 118.3 – good day.'

'Quite right – good.' The mullah nodded, satisfied.

Gavallan and McIver cursed inwardly even more, and Sabolir, who had been silently watching and listening to the byplay, understanding very clearly how the two men were trying to manipulate the mullah, chortled to himself, carefully avoiding anyone's eyes, staring at the floor for safety. Once, a moment ago, when the mullah's attention was elsewhere, he had deftly caught McIver's eye and half smiled at him, encouragingly, pretending friendship, petrified McIver would misconstrue all those previous favours which were only repayment for his smoothing the way of inbound spares and outbound crews. On the radio this morning, a spokesman for the 'Islamic Revolutionary Komiteh' had urged all loyal citizens to denounce anyone who had committed crimes 'against Islam'.

During today three of his colleagues had been arrested which had sent a shudder of horror through the whole airport. Islamic Guards gave no specific reasons, just dragged the men away and put them into Qasr Jail – the loathed SAVAK prison – where, it was rumoured, half a hundred 'enemies of Islam' had been shot today after summary trials. One of those arrested was one of his own men who had accepted the ten thousand rials and the three cans of petrol from McIver's storeroom yesterday – the man had kept one, and the other two he himself had correctly taken home last night as was his due. Oh, God, let them not search my house.

Over the HF was Johnny Hogg, his voice still breezy: 'EchoTango-LimaLima, thank you. Up the revolution and good day.' Then on their own channel, tersely: 'HQ confirm!'

McIver reached over and switched to their channel. 'Standby One!' he ordered, deeply conscious of the mullah. 'Do you thi –'

'Ah. You talk direct with the aircraft – a private channel?'

'Company channel, Excellency. It's normal practice.'

'Normal. Yes. So EP-HBC is at Bandar-e Delam?' the mullah said and read from the paper: ' "Delivering spares." Is that right?'

'Yes,' McIver said, praying.

'When is this aircraft due to return?'

McIver could feel the weight of the mullah's attention on him. 'I don't know. I haven't been able to raise Bandar-e Delam. As soon as I can, I'll tell you. Now, Excellency, about clearances for our various flights, do you th –'

'EP-HFC. EP-HFC is in Tabriz?'

'She's at the small Forsha airstrip,' McIver said, not feeling very good at all, praying that the madness at the Qazvin roadblock had gone unreported and would be forgotten. Again he wondered where Erikki was – he was supposed to have met them at the apartment at three o'clock to come out to the airport but had never appeared.

'Forsha airstrip?'

He saw the mullah staring at him and concentrated with an effort. 'EP-HFC went to Tabriz on Saturday to deliver spares and pick up a crew change. She returned last night. She'll be on the new manifest tomorrow.'

The mullah was suddenly grim. 'But any incoming or outgoing aircraft must be instantly reported. We have no record of any inward clearance yesterday.'

'Captain Pettikin couldn't raise Tehran ATC yesterday. The military were in charge, I believe. He tried calling all the way inbound.' McIver added quickly, 'If we're to resume operations, who will authorise our IranOil flights? Mr. Darius as usual?'

'Er, yes, I would think so. But why wasn't its arrival reported today?'

Gavallan said with a forced brightness, 'I'm very impressed with your efficiency, Excellency. It's a pity the military air traffic controllers on duty yesterday don't share it. I can see the new Islamic Republic will far surpass any Western operation. It will be a pleasure to serve our new employers. Up the new! May we know your name?'

'I, I'm Mohammed Tehrani,' the man said, diverted again.

'Then Excellency Tehrani, may I ask that you give us the benefit of your authority? If my EchoTangoLimaLima could have your permission to land tomorrow, we could immeasurably improve our efficiency to parallel your own. I can then make sure our company gives the Ayatollah Khomeini and his personal assistants – like yourself – the service he and they have a right to expect. The spares ETLL will carry will put back two more 212s into operation and I can return to London to increase our support for the Great Revolution. Of course, you agree?'

'It's not possible. The komiteh w –'

'I'm sure the komiteh would take your advice. Oh, I notice you've had the misfortune to break your glasses. Terrible. I can hardly see without mine. Perhaps I could have the 125 bring a new pair for you tomorrow from Al Shargaz?'

The mullah was unsettled. His eyes were very bad. The wish for new glasses, good glasses almost overpowered him. Oh, it would be an unbelievable treasure, a gift from God. Surely God has put this thought into the foreigner's head. 'I don't think . . . I don't know. The komiteh couldn't do what you ask so quickly.'

'I know it's difficult, but if you'd intercede for us with your komiteh, surely they'd listen. It would help us immeasurably and we'd be in your debt,' Gavallan added, using the time-honoured phrase that in any language meant, what do you want in exchange? He saw McIver switch to the tower frequency, offer the mike. 'You press the button to talk, Excellency, if you would honour us with your assistance . . .'

The mullah Tehrani hesitated, not knowing what to do. As he looked at the mike, McIver glanced at Sabolir, pointedly.

Sabolir understood at once, his reflexes perfect. 'Of course whatever you decide, Excellency Tehrani, your komiteh will agree,' he said, his voice unctuous. 'But tomorrow, tomorrow I understand you are ordered to visit the other airfields, to make sure where and how many civilian helicopters are in your area which is all Tehran? Yes?'

'Those are orders, yes,' the mullah agreed. 'I and some members of my komiteh have to visit the other airfields tomorrow.'

Sabolir sighed heavily, pretending disappointment, and McIver had difficulty not laughing so overplayed was the performance. 'Unfortunately it would not be possible for you to visit them all by car or foot and still be back to supervise, personally, the arrival and immediate turnaround of this single aircraft that has, through no fault of its own, been turned away because of arrogant traffic controllers in Kish and Isfahan who dared not to consult you first.'

'True, true,' the mullah agreed. 'They were at fault!'

'Would 7 a.m. suit you, Excellency Tehrani?' McIver said at once. 'We'd be glad to help our airport komiteh. I'll give you my best pilot and you'll be back in plenty of time to, er, to supervise the turnaround. How many men would come with you?'

'Six . . .' the mullah said absently, overwhelmed with the idea of being able to complete his orders – God's work – so conveniently and luxuriously, like a veritable ayatollah. 'This . . . this could be done?'

'Of course!' McIver said. 'Seven a.m. here. Captain, er, Chief Captain Nathaniel Lane will have a 212 ready. Seven including yourself, and up to seven wives. You of course would fly in the cockpit with the pilot. Consider it arranged.'

The mullah had only flown twice in his life – to England and university and home again, packed into a special, student charter Iran Air flight. He beamed and reached for the mike: 'Seven a.m.'

McIver and Gavallan did not betray their relief at their victory. Nor did Sabolir.

Sabolir was content that the mullah was entrapped. As God wants! Now if I'm falsely accused, now I have an ally, he told himself. This fool, this son of a dog false mullah, hasn't he accepted a bribe – clearly not pishkesh – two in fact, some new glasses and wasteful, unauthorised air travel? Hasn't he deliberately allowed himself to become the dupe of these glib and ever devious English who still think they can seduce us with trinkets and steal our heritage for a few rials?

Listen to the fool, giving the foreigners what they want!

He glanced at McIver. Pointedly. And caught his eye. Then once more looked back at the floor. Now you arrogant Western son of a dog, he thought, what valuable favour should you do for me in return for my assistance?

* * *

374

At the French Club: 7:10 P.M. Gavallan accepted the glass of red wine from the uniformed French waiter, McIver the white.

Both touched glasses and drank gratefully, tired after their journey from the airport. They were sitting in the lounge with other guests, mostly Europeans, men and women, overlooking the snow-covered gardens and tennis courts, the chairs comfortable and modern, the bar extensive – many other rooms for banquets, dancing, dining, cards, sauna in other parts of this fine building that was in the best part of Tehran. The French Club was the only ex-pat club still functioning – the American Services Club, with its huge complex of entertainment facilities, sportsfield and baseball pitch, as well as the British, Pars-American, German clubs, and most others had been closed, their bars and stocks of liquor smashed.

'My God, that's good,' McIver said, the ice-cold, cleansing wine taking away the dross. 'Don't tell Gen we stopped by.'

'No need to, Mac. She'll know.'

McIver nodded. 'You're right, never mind. I managed to book here tonight for dinner – costs an arm and a leg but worth it. Used to be standing room only at this time of night . . .' He looked around at a burst of laughter from some Frenchmen in a far corner. 'For a moment it sounded like Jean-Luc, seems years since we had his pre-Christmas party here – wonder if we'll ever have another.'

'Sure you will,' Gavallan said to encourage him, concerned that the fire seemed to be out of his old friend. 'Don't let that mullah get to you.'

'He gave me the creeps – so did Armstrong come to think of it. And Talbot. But you're right, Andy, I shouldn't let it get me down. We're in better shape than we were two days ago . . .' More laughter distracted him and he began thinking of all the great times he had had here with Genny and Pettikin and Lochart – won't think about him now – and all the other pilots and their many friends, British, American, Iranian. All gone, most gone. It used to be: 'Gen, let's go over to the French Club, the tennis finals are this afternoon' . . . Or: 'Valik's cocktail party's on from 8 p.m. at the Iranian Officers Club' . . . Or: 'There's a polo match, baseball match, swimming party, skiing party' . . . Or: 'Sorry, can't this weekend we're going to the ambassador's do on the Caspian' . . . Or: 'I'd love to, Genny can't, she's shopping for carpets in Isfahan . . .'

'It used to be we had so much to do here, Andy, the social life was the best ever, no doubt about that,' he said. 'Now it's hard just trying to keep in touch with our ops.'

Gavallan nodded. 'Mac,' he said kindly, 'straight answer to a straight question: Do you want to quit Iran and let someone else take over?'

McIver stared at him blankly. 'Good God, whatever gave you that idea? No, absolutely no! You mean you think because I was a bit down that . . . Good God, no,' he said, but his mind was suddenly jerked into asking the same question, unthinkable a few days ago: are you losing it, your will, your grip, your need to continue – is it time to quit? I don't know, he thought, achingly chilled by the truth but his face smiled. 'Everything's fine, Andy. Nothing we can't deal with.'

'Good. Sorry, I hope you didn't mind me asking. I think I was encouraged by the mullah – except when he was talking about "our Iranian aircraft".'

'The truth is that Valik and the partners've been acting like our aircraft were theirs ever since we signed that contract.'

'Thank God it's a British contract, enforceable under British law.' Gavallan glanced over McIver's shoulder and his eyes widened slightly. The girl coming into the room was in her late twenties, dark-haired, dark-eyed, and stunning. McIver followed his glance, brightened, and got up. 'Hello, Sayada,' he said, beckoning her. 'May I introduce Andrew Gavallan? Andy, this's Sayada Bertolin, a friend of Jean-Luc. Would you like to join us?'

'Thanks, Mac, but no, sorry I can't, I'm just about to play squash with a friend. You're looking well. Pleased to meet you, Mr. Gavallan.' She put out her hand and Gavallan shook it. 'Sorry, got to dash, give my love to Genny.'

They sat down again. 'Same again, waiter, please,' Gavallan said. 'Mac, between you and me, that bird's made me feel positively weak!'

McIver laughed. 'Usually it's the reverse! She's certainly very popular, works in the Kuwaiti embassy, she's Lebanese and Jean-Luc's smitten.'

'My word, I don't blame him . . .' Gavallan's smile faded. Robert Armstrong was coming through the far doorway with a tall, strong-faced Iranian in his fifties. He saw Gavallan, nodded briefly then continued with his conversation and led the way out and up the stairs where there were other lounges and rooms. 'Wonder what the devil that man's g—' Gavallan stopped as recollection flooded his mind. 'Robert Armstrong, chief superintendent CID Kowloon, that's who he is . . . or was!'

'CID? You're sure?'

'Yes, CID or Special Branch . . . wait a minute . . . he, yes, that's

376

right, he was a friend of Ian's, come to think of it, that's where I met him, at the Great House on the Peak, not at the races, though I might have seen him there too with Ian. If I remember rightly it was the night Quillan Gornt came as a very unwelcome guest . . . can't remember exactly, but I think it was Ian and Penelope's anniversary party, just before I left Hong Kong . . . my God that's almost sixteen years ago, no wonder I didn't remember him.'

'I had the feeling he remembered you the instant we met at the airport yesterday.'

'So did I.' They finished their drinks and left, both of them curiously unsettled.

Tehran University: 7:32 P.M. The rally of over a thousand leftist students in the forecourt quadrangle was noisy and dangerous, too many factions, too many zealots, and too many of them armed. It was cold and damp, not yet dark though already there were a few lights and torches in the twilight.

Rakoczy was at the back of the crowd, melded into it, haphazardly dressed like the others, looking like them though now his cover had been changed and he was no longer Smith or Fedor Rakoczy, the Russian Muslim, the Islamic-Marxist sympathiser, but here in Tehran had reverted to Dimitri Yazernov, Soviet representative on the Tudeh Central Committee – a post he had had from time to time over the past few years. He stood in a corner of the quadrangle with five of the Tudeh student leaders, out of the sharpening wind, his assault rifle over his shoulder, armed and ready, and he was waiting for the first gun to go off. 'Any moment now,' he said softly.

'Dimitri, who do I take out first?' one of the leaders asked nervously.

'The mujhadin – that motherless bastard, the one over there,' he said patiently, pointing at the black-bearded man, much older than the others. 'Take your time, Farmad, and follow my lead. He's professional and PLO.'

The others stared at him astonished. 'Why him if he's PLO?' Farmad asked. He was squat, almost misshapen, with a large head and small intelligent eyes. 'The PLO have been our great friends over the years, giving us training and support and arms.'

'Because now the PLO will support Khomeini,' he explained patiently. 'Hasn't Khomeini invited Arafat here next week? Hasn't he given the PLO the Israeli mission headquarters as its permanent headquarters? The PLO can supply all the technicians that Bazargan and Khomeini need to replace the Israelis and the Americans –

377

especially in the oil fields. You don't want Khomeini strong, do you?'

'No, but the PLO have been v –'

'Iran isn't Palestine. Palestinians should stay in Palestine. You won the revolution. Why give strangers your victory?'

'But the PLO have been our allies,' Farmad persisted, and Rakoczy was glad that he had found the flaw before some measure of power was passed over to this man.

'Allies who have become enemies have no value. Remember the aim.'

'I agree with Comrade Dimitri,' another said, an edge to his voice, his eyes cold and very hard. 'We don't want PLO giving orders here. If you don't want to take him out, Farmad, I will. All of them and all the Green Band dogs too!'

'The PLO're not to be trusted,' Rakoczy said, continuing the same lesson, planting the same seeds. 'Look how they vacillate and change positions even on their home ground, one moment saying they're Marxist, the next Muslim, the next flirting with the arch-traitor Sadat then attacking him. We have documents to prove it,' he added, the disinformation fitting in perfectly, 'and documents that prove they plan to assassinate King Hussein, and take over Jordan and make a separate peace with Israel and America. They've had secret meetings with the CIA and Israel already. They're not truly anti-Israel . . .'

Ah, Israel, he was thinking as he let his mouth continue the well-thought-out lesson, how important you are to Mother Russia, set there so nicely in the cauldron, a perpetual irritant guaranteed to enrage all Muslims for ever, particularly the oh, so oil rich sheikdoms, guaranteed to set all Muslims against all Christians, our prime enemy, your American, British and French allies – meanwhile to curb their power and keep them and the West off balance while we consume vital prizes – Iran this year, Afghanistan also, Nicaragua next year, then Panama and others, always to the same plan: possession of the Strait of Hormuz, Panama, Constantinople and the treasure chest of South Africa. Ah, Israel, you're a trump card for us to play in the world Monopoly game. But never to discard or sell! We'll not forsake you! Oh we'll let you lose many battles but never the war, we'll allow you to starve but not to die, we'll permit your banking compatriots to finance us and therefore their own destruction, we'll suffer you to bleed America to death, we'll strengthen your enemies – but not too much – and assist you to be raped. But don't worry, we'll never let you disappear. Oh, no! Never. You're far too valuable.

378

'PLOs are arrogant and full of themselves,' a tall student said darkly, 'and never polite and never conscious of Iran's importance in the world and know nothing of our ancient history.'

'True! They're peasants and they've parasited themselves throughout the Middle East and our Gulf, taking the best jobs.'

'Yes,' another agreed. 'They're worse than the Jews . . .'

Rakoczy laughed to himself. He enjoyed his job very much, enjoyed working with university students – always a fertile field – enjoyed being a teacher. But that's what I am, he thought contentedly, a professor of terrorism, of power and the seizing of power. Perhaps I'm more like a farmer: I plant the seed, nurture it, guard it and harvest it, working all hours and all seasons as a farmer must. Some years are good and some bad but every year a little further forward, a little more experienced, a little wiser about the land, ever more patient – spring summer autumn winter – always the same farm, Iran, always with the same aim: at best for Iran to become Russian soil, at worst a Russian satellite to protect the sacred motherland of Russia. With our foot on the Strait of Hormuz . . .

Ah, he thought, an unearthly, consuming religious glow pervading him, if I could give Iran to Mother Russia my life will not have been lived in vain.

The West deserves to lose, particularly the Americans. They're such fools, so egocentric, but most of all so stupid. It's inconceivable this Carter doesn't see the value of Hormuz in general and Iran in particular and what a catastrophe to the West their loss will be. But there it is; for all practical purposes he's given us Iran.

Rakoczy remembered the shock wave of disbelief that had soared to the very top when their innermost contacts in Washington had whispered that Carter was going to forsake the Shah. Ah, what an ally Carter has been to us. If I believed in God I'd pray: God is Great, God is Great, protect our best ally, President Peanut, and let him win a second term! With him in for a second term we'll own America and so rule the world! God is Great, God is . . .

Abruptly he felt chilled. He had been pretending to be Muslim for so long that sometimes his cover overcame his real self, and he began to question and have doubts.

Am I still Igor Mzytryk, Captain KGB, married to my darling Delaurah, my oh so beautiful Armenian, who's waiting in Tbilisi for me to come home? Is she at home, she who oh so secretly believes in God – the God of the Christians that is the same as the God of the Muslims and of the Jews?

God. God who has a thousand names. Is there a God?

There is no god, he told himself like a litany, and put that thought back into its compartment and concentrated on the riot to be.

Around them tension was growing nicely among the massed students, angry cries raging back and forth: 'We didn't spill our blood for mullahs to take all the power! Unite, brothers and sisters! Unite under the Tudeh banners . . .'

'Down with the Tudeh! Unite for the holy Islamic-Marxist cause, we mujhadin spilled our blood and we are the martyrs of Imam Ali, Lord of the Martyrs and Lenin . . .'

'Down with the mullahs and Khomeini, arch-traitor to Iran . . .'

Vast cheers greeted this shout and others took it up, then gradually again the dominating voice was: 'Unite, brothers and sisters, unite to the real leaders of the revolution, the Tudeh, unite to protect the –'

Rakoczy watched the crowd critically. It was still in pieces, formless, not yet a mob that could be directed and used as a weapon. Some bystranders, Islamics, watched and listened with varying degrees of contempt or rage. The few moderates shook their heads and walked away, leaving the stage to the vast majority who were deeply committed and anti-Khomeini.

Around them the buildings were tall, and brick, the university built by Reza Shah in the thirties. Five years ago Rakoczy had spent a few terms here pretending to be an Azerbaijani though the Tudeh knew him as Dimitri Yazernov and that he had been sent – continuing continuing a pattern – to organise university cells. Since its beginning the university was always a place of dissension, anti-Shah, although Mohammed Shah, more than any monarch in Persia's history, had lavishly supported education. The Tehran students had been the vanguard of the rebellion, long before Khomeini had become the coalescing core.

Without Khomeini, we'd never have succeeded, he thought. Khomeini was the flame around which we could all cluster and unite to tip the Shah off the throne and the U.S. out. He's not senile or a bigot as many say but a ruthless leader with a dangerously clear plan, a dangerously great charisma, and dangerously huge power among the Shi'ites – so now it's time he joined the God that never was.

Rakoczy laughed suddenly.

'What is it?' Farmad asked.

'I was just thinking what Khomeini and all the mullahs will say when they discover there's no god and never was a god – there's no heaven, no hell, no houris and it's all a myth.'

380

The others laughed too. One didn't. Ibrahim Kyabi. There was no laughter left in him, just the wish for revenge. When he had gone home yesterday afternoon he had discovered his house in turmoil, his mother prostrate in tears, his brothers and sisters in anguish. The news had just arrived that his engineer father had been murdered by Islamic Guards outside his IranOil HQ at Ahwaz and that his body had been left to the vultures.

'For what?' he had screamed.

'For – for crimes against Islam,' his uncle, Dewar Kyabi, who had brought home the terrible news, said through his own tears. 'That's what they told us – his murderers. They were from Abadan, fanatics, illiterates mostly, and they told us that he was an American quisling, that for years he had cooperated with the enemies of Islam, allowing and helping them to steal our oil, the –'

'Lies, all lies,' Ibrahim had shouted at him. 'Father was anti-Shah, a patriot – a Believer! Who were those dogs? Who? I will burn them and their fathers. What were their names?'

'It was the Will of God, Ibrahim, that they did it. Insha' Allah! Oh, my poor brother! The Will of God . . .'

'There is no God!'

The others had stared at him, shocked. This was the first time Ibrahim had articulated a thought that had been building for many years, nurtured by student friends returning from overseas, friends at university, fed by some of the teachers who had never said this openly, merely encouraging them to question anything and everything.

'Insha' Allah is for fools,' he had said, 'a curse of superstition for fools to hide under!'

'You mustn't say that, my son!' his mother had cried out, frightened. 'Go to the mosque, beg God's forgiveness – that your father is dead is the Will of God, nothing more. Go to the mosque.'

'I will,' he had said, but in his heart he knew his life had changed – no God could have allowed this to happen. 'Who were those men, Uncle? Describe them.'

'They were just ordinary, Ibrahim, as I already told you, younger than you, most of them – there was no leader or mullah with them, though there was one in the foreigners' helicopter that came from Bandar-e Delam. But my poor brother died cursing Khomeini; if only he hadn't come back by the foreigners' helicopters, if only . . . but then, Insha' Allah, they were waiting for him anyway.'

'There was a mullah in the helicopter?'

'Yes, yes, there was.'

'You will go to the mosque, Ibrahim?' his mother had asked him again.

'Yes,' he had said, the first lie he had ever told her. It had taken him no time to find the university Tudeh leaders and Dimitri Yazernov, to swear allegiance, to get a machine gun, and, most of all, to ask them to find the name of the mullah in the helicopter of Bandar-e Delam. And now he stood there waiting, wanting vengeance, his soul crying out against the outrage committed against his father in the name of the false god. 'Dimitri, let's begin!' he said, his fury whipped by the shouting of the crowd.

'We must wait, Ibrahim,' Rakoczy said gently, very pleased to have the youth with them. 'Don't forget the mob is a means to an end – remember the plan!' When he had told it to them an hour ago they had been stunned.

'Raid the American embassy?'

'Yes,' he had said calmly, 'a quick raid, in and out, tomorrow or the next day. Tonight the rally will become a mob. The embassy's hardly a mile and a half away. It will be easy to send the mob rampaging that way as an experiment. What more perfect cover could we have for a raid than a riot? We let the enemy mujhadin and fedayeen go against Islamics and kill each other off while we take the initiative. Tonight we plant more seeds. Tomorrow or the next day we'll raid the U.S. embassy.'

'But it's impossible, Dimitri, impossible!'

'It's easy. Just a raid, not an attempt at a takeover, that will come later. A raid will be unexpected, it's simple to execute. You can easily grab the embassy for an hour, hold the ambassador and everyone captive for an hour or so while you sack it. Americans do not have the will to resist. That's the key to them! Here are the plans of the buildings and the numbers of marines and I will be there to help. Your coup will be immense – it will hit world headlines and totally embarrass Bazargan and Khomeini, and even more the Americans. Don't forget who the real enemy is and that now you have to act fast to grab the initiative from Khomeini . . .'

It had been easy to convince them. It will be easy to create the diversion, he thought. And it'll be easy to go straight to the CIA basement office and radio room, blow the safe, and empty it of all documents and cipher books, then up the back stairs to the second landing, turn left, into the third room on the left, the ambassador's bedroom, to the safe behind the oil painting hanging over the bed, blow that and empty it similarly. Sudden, swift, and violent – if there's any opposition.

'Dimitri! Look!'

Rakoczy spun around. Coming down the road were hundreds of youths – Green Bands and mullahs at the head. At once Rakoczy roared, 'Death to Khomeini!' and fired a burst into the air. The suddenness of the shots whipped everyone into a frenzy, there were shouts and counter shouts, simultaneously other guns went off all over the quadrangle and everyone began to scatter, trampling over one another in their haste, the screams beginning.

Before he could stop him, he saw Ibrahim aim at the oncoming Green Bands and fire. Some men in the front rank went down, a howl of rage burst from them and guns opened up in their direction. He dived to the ground, cursing. The torrent of bullets missed him but got Farmad and others nearby but not Ibrahim and the remaining three Tudeh leaders. He shouted at them and they all hugged the cement as panic-stricken students opened up with carbines and pistols.

Many were wounded before the big mujhadin Rakoczy had marked for execution rallied his men around him and led a charge at the Islamics and drove them back. At once others came to his aid and the retreat became a rout, a roar went through the students, and the rally became a mob.

Rakoczy grabbed Ibrahim who was just about to charge off mindlessly.

'Follow me!' he ordered, half shoved Ibrahim and the others farther into the lee of the building, then, when he was sure they were with him, took to his heels in a frantic, chest-hurting retreat.

At a junction of paths in the snow-covered gardens, he stopped a moment to catch his breath. The wind was chill and night on them now.

'What about Farmad?' Ibrahim gasped. 'He was wounded!'

'No,' he said, 'he was dying. Come on!'

Again he led the rush unerringly through the garden, along the street near the Scientific Faculty, across the car park into the next, and he did not stop till the sound of the riot was distant. There was a stitch in his side and his breathing came in great pants, tearing at him. When he could speak, he said, 'Don't worry about anything. Go back to your homes or your dormitories. Get everyone ready for the raid, tomorrow or the next day – the committee will give the order.' He hurried away into the gathering night.

* * *

383

At Lochart's Apartment: 7:30 P.M. Sharazad was lying in a foam bath, her head propped on a waterproof pillow, eyes closed, her hair tied up in a towel. 'Oh, Azadeh, darling,' she said drowsily, perspiration beading her forehead, 'I'm so happy.'

Azadeh was also in the bath and she lay with her head at the other end, enjoying the heat and the intimacy and the sweet perfumed water and the luxury – her long hair also up in a pure white towel – the bath large and deep and comfortable for two. But there were still dark rings under her eyes, and she could not shake off the terrors of yesterday at the roadblock or in the helicopter. Outside the curtains, night had come. Gunfire echoed in the distance. Neither paid it any attention.

'I wish Erikki would come back,' Azadeh said.

'He won't be long, there's lots of time, darling. Dinner's not till nine, so we've almost two hours to get ready.' Sharazad opened her eyes and put her hand on Azadeh's slender thighs, enjoying the touch of her. 'Don't worry, darling Azadeh, he'll be back soon, your redheaded giant! And don't forget I'm spending the night with my parents so you two can run naked together all night long! Enjoy our bath, be happy, and swoon when he returns.' They laughed together. 'Everything's wonderful now, you're safe, we're all safe, Iran's safe – with the Help of God the Imam has conquered and Iran's safe and free.'

'I wish I could believe it, I wish I could believe it as you do,' Azadeh said. 'I can't explain how terrible those people near the roadblock were – it was as though I was being choked by their hate. Why should they hate us – hate me and Erikki? What had we done to them? Nothing at all and yet they hated us.'

'Don't think about them, my dear one.' Sharazad stifled a yawn. 'Leftists are all mad, claiming to be Muslim and at the same time Marxist. They're anti-God and therefore cursed. The villagers? Villagers are uneducated as you know too well, and most of them simple. Don't worry – that's past, now everything is going to be better, you'll see.'

'I hope, oh how I hope you're right. I don't want it better but just as it was, normal, like it's always been, normal again.'

'Oh, it will be.' Sharazad felt so contented, the water so silky and so warm and womblike. Ah, she thought, only three more days to be sure and then Tommy tells Father that oh, yes, of course he wants sons and daughters, and then, the next day, the great day, I should know for certain though I'm certain now. Haven't I always been so regular? Then I can give Tommy my gift of God and he'll be so proud. 'The Imam does the work of God. How can it be otherwise than good?'

'I don't know, Sharazad, but never in our history have mullahs been worthy of trust – just parasites on the backs of the villagers.'

'Ah, but now it's different,' Sharazad told her, not really wanting to discuss such serious matters. 'Now we have a real leader. Now he's in control of Iran for the first time ever. Isn't he the most pious of men, the most learned of Islam and the law? Doesn't he do God's work? Hasn't he achieved the impossible, throwing out the Shah and his nasty corruption, stopping the generals from making a coup with the Americans? Father says we're safer now than we've ever been.'

'Are we?' Azadeh remembered Rakoczy in the chopper and what he had said about Khomeini and stepping backwards in history, and she knew he had spoken the truth, a lot of truth, and she had clawed at him, hating him, wanting him dead, for of course he was one of those who would use the simple-minded mullahs to enslave everyone else. 'You want to be ruled by Islamic laws of the Prophet's time, almost fifteen hundred years ago – enforced chador, the loss of our hard-won rights of voting, working and being equal?'

'I don't want to vote, or work, or be equal – how can a woman equal a man? I just want to be a good wife to my Tommy, and in Iran I prefer the chador on the streets.' Delicately Sharazad covered another yawn, drowsed by the warmth. 'Insha' Allah, Azadeh, darling. Of course everything will be as before but Father says more wonderful because now we possess ourselves, our land, our oil, and everything in our land. There'll be no nasty foreign generals or politicians to disgrace us and with the evil Shah gone, we'll all live happily ever after, you with your Erikki, me with my Tommy, and lots and lots of children. How else could it be? God is with the Imam and the Imam is with us! We're so lucky.' She smiled at her and put her arm around her friend's legs affectionately. 'I'm so glad you're staying with me, Azadeh. It seems such a long time since you were in Tehran.'

'Yes.' They had been friends for many years. First in Switzerland where they had met at school, up in the High Country, though Sharazad had only stayed one term, unhappy to be away from her family and Iran, then later at the university in Tehran. And now, for a little over a year, because both had married foreigners in the same company, they had become even closer, closer than sisters, helping each other adapt to foreign idiosyncrasies:

'Sometimes I just don't understand my Tommy at all, Azadeh,' Sharazad had said tearfully in the beginning. 'He enjoys being alone, I mean quite alone, just him and me, the house empty, not even one servant – he even told me he likes to be alone by himself, just reading,

385

no family around or children, no conversation or friends, Oh, sometimes it's just awful.'

'Erikki's just the same,' Azadeh had said. 'Foreigners aren't like us – they're very strange. I want to spend days with friends and children and family, but Erikki doesn't. It's good that Erikki and Tommy work during the days – you're luckier, Tommy's off for two weeks at a time when you can be normal. Another thing, you know, Sharazad, it took me months to get used to sleeping in a bed an –'

'I never could! Oh, so high off the floor, so easy to fall off, always a huge dip on his side, so you're always uncomfortable and you wake up with an ache in your back. A bed's so awful compared with soft quilts on beautiful carpets on the floor, so comfortable and civilised.'

'Yes. But Erikki won't use quilts and carpets, he insists on a bed. He just won't try it any more – sometimes it's such a relief when he's away.'

'Oh, we sleep correctly now, Azadeh. I stopped the nonsense of a Western bed after the first month.'

'How did you do it?'

'Oh, I'd sigh all night long and keep my poor darling awake – then I'd sleep during the day to be fresh again to sigh all night long.' Sharazad had laughed delightedly. 'Seven nights and my darling collapsed, slept like a baby for the next three nights correctly, and now he always sleeps like a civilised person should – he even does so when he's at Zagros! Why don't you try it? I guarantee you'll be successful, darling, particularly if you also complain just a tiny bit that the bed has caused a backache and of course you would still adore to make love but please be a little careful.'

Azadeh had laughed. 'My Erikki's cleverer than your Tommy – when Erikki tried the quilts on our carpet *he* sighed all night and turned and turned and kept me awake – I was so exhausted after three nights I quite liked the bed. When I visit my family I sleep civilised, though when Erikki's at the palace we use a bed. You know, darling, another problem: I love my Erikki but sometimes he's so rude I almost die. He keeps saying "yes" and "no" when I ask him something – how can you have a conversation after yes or no?'

She smiled to herself now. Yes, it's very difficult living with him, but living without him now is unthinkable – all his love and good humour and size and strength and always doing what I want but only just a little too easily so I have little chance to sharpen my wiles. 'We're both very lucky, Sharazad, aren't we?'

'Oh, yes, darling. Can you stay for a week or two – even if Erikki has to go back, you stay, please?'

'I'd like to. When Erikki gets back . . . perhaps I'll ask him.'

Sharazad shifted in the bath, moving the bubbles over her breasts, blowing them off her hands. 'Mac said they'd come here from the airport if they were delayed. Genny's coming straight from the apartment but not before nine – I also asked Paula to join us, the Italian girl, but not for Nogger, for Charlie.' She chuckled. 'Charlie almost swoons when she just looks at him!'

'Charlie Pettikin? Oh, but that's wonderful. Oh, that's very good. Then we should help him – we owe him so much! Let's help him snare the sexy Italian!'

'Wonderful! Let's plan how to give Paula to him.'

'As a mistress or wife?'

'Mistress. Well, let me think! How old is she? She must be at least twenty-seven. Do you think she'd make him a good wife? He should have a wife. All the girls Tommy and I have shown him discreetly, he just smiles and shrugs – I even brought my third cousin who was fifteen thinking that would tempt him, but nothing. Oh good, now we have something to plan. We've plenty of time to plan and dress and get ready – and I've some lovely dresses for you to choose from.'

'It feels so strange, Sharazad, not to have anything – anything. Money, papers . . .' For an instant Azadeh was back in the Range Rover near the roadblock, and there before her was the fat-faced mujhadin who had stolen their papers, his machine gun blazing as Erikki rammed him against the other car, crushing him like a cockroach, blood and filth squeezed from his mouth. 'Having nothing,' she said, forcing the bad away, 'not even a lipstick.'

'Never mind, I've lots of everything. And Tommy'll be so pleased to have you and Erikki here. He doesn't like me to be alone either. Poor darling, don't worry. You're safe now.'

I don't feel safe at all, Azadeh told herself, hating the fear that was so alien to her whole upbringing – that even now seemed to take away the warmth of the water. I haven't felt safe since we left Rakoczy on the ground and even that had only lasted a moment, the ecstasy of escaping that devil – me, Erikki, and Charlie unhurt. Even the joy of finding a car with petrol in it at the little airstrip didn't take my fear away. I hate being afraid.

She ducked down a little in the tub, then reached up and turned on the hot-water tap, swirling the hot currents.

'That feels so good,' Sharazad murmured, the foam heavy, and the water sensuous. 'I'm so pleased you wanted to stay.'

Last evening, by the time Azadeh, Erikki and Charlie had reached

McIver's apartment it was after dark. They had found Gavallan there, so no room for them – Azadeh had been too frightened to want to stay in her father's apartment, even with Erikki – so she had asked Sharazad if they could move in with her until Lochart returned. Sharazad had delightedly agreed at once, glad for the company. Everything had begun to be fine and then, during dinner, there was gunfire nearby, making her jump.

'No need to worry, Azadeh,' McIver had said. 'Just a few hotheads letting off steam, celebrating probably. Didn't you hear Khomeini's order to lay down all arms?' Everyone agreeing and Sharazad saying, 'The Imam will be obeyed,' always referring to Khomeini as 'the Imam', almost associating him with the Twelve Imams of Shi'ism – the direct descendants of Mohammed the Prophet, near divinity – surely a sacrilege: 'But what the Imam's accomplished is almost a miracle, isn't it?' Sharazad had said with her beguiling innocence. 'Surely our freedom's a gift of God?'

Then so warm and toasty in bed with Erikki, but him strange and brooding and not the Erikki she had known. 'What's wrong, what's wrong?'

'Nothing, Azadeh, nothing. Tomorrow I'll make a plan. There was no time tonight to talk to Mac or Gavallan. Tomorrow we'll make a plan, now sleep, my darling.'

Twice in the night she had awakened from violent dreams, trembling and terrified, crying out for Erikki.

'It's all right, Azadeh, I'm here. It was only a dream, you're quite safe now.'

'No, no, we're not. I don't feel safe, Erikki – what's happening to me? Let's go back to Tabriz, or let's go away, go away from these awful people.'

And in the morning Erikki had left her to join McIver and Gavallan, and she had slept some more but gathered little strength from the sleep. Passing the rest of the morning day-dreaming or hearing Sharazad's news about going to Galeg Morghi, or listening to the hourly crop of rumours from her servants: many more generals shot, many new arrests, the prisons burst open by mobs. Western hotels set on fire or shot up. Rumours of Bazargan taking the reins of government, mujhadin in open rebellion in the south, Kurds rebelling in the north, Azerbaijan declaring independence, the nomad tribes of the Kash'kai and Bakhtiari throwing off the yoke of Tehran; everyone laying down their arms or no one laying down their arms. Rumours that Prime Minister Bakhtiar had been captured and shot or escaped to the hills or to Turkey, to America; President Carter preparing an invasion or Carter recognising Khomeini's government; Soviet troops massing on the border ready to invade or Brezhnev coming to Tehran to congratulate Khomeini; the Shah landing in Kurdistan supported by American troops or the Shah dead in exile.

Then going to lunch with Sharazad's parents at the Bakravan house near the bazaar, but only after Sharazad had insisted she wear the chador, hating the chador and everything it stood for. More rumours at the huge, family house, but benign there, no fear and absolute confidence. Abundance as always, just as in her own home in Tabriz, servants smiling and safe and thanks be to God for victory, Jared Bakravan had told them jovially, and now with the bazaar going to open and all foreign banks closed, business will be marvellous as it was before the ungodly laws the Shah instituted.

After lunch they had returned to Sharazad's apartment. By foot. Wrapped in the chador. Never a problem for them and every man deferential. The bazaar was crowded, with pitifully little for sale though every merchant foretold abundance ready to be trucked, trained, or flown in – ports clogged with hundreds of ships, laden with merchandise. On the street, thousands walked this way and that, Khomeini's name on every lip, chanting 'Allah-u Akbarrr,' almost all men and boys armed – none of the old people. In some areas Green Bands, in place of police, haphazardly and amateurishly directed traffic, or stood around truculently. In other areas police as always. Two tanks rumbled past driven by soldiers, masses of guards and civilians on them, waving to the cheering pedestrians.

Even so, everyone was tense under the patina of joy, particularly the women enveloped in their shrouds. Once, they had turned a corner and seen ahead a group of youths surrounding a dark-haired woman dressed in Western clothes, jeering at her, abusing her, shouting insults and making obscene signs, several of them exposing themselves, waggling their penises at her. The woman was in her thirties, dressed neatly, a short coat over her skirt, long legs and long hair under a little hat. Then she was joined by a man who shoved through the crowd to her. At once he began shouting that they were English and to leave them alone, but the men paid no attention to him, jostling him, concentrating on the woman. She was petrified.

There was no way for Sharazad and Azadeh to walk around the crowd that grew quickly, hemming them in, so they were forced to watch. Then a mullah arrived and told the crowd to leave, harangued the two foreigners to obey Islamic customs. By the time they got home

389

they were tired and both felt soiled. They had taken off their clothes and collapsed on the quilt bed.

'I'm glad I went out today,' Azadeh had said wearily, deeply concerned. 'But we women better organise a protest before it's too late. We better march through the streets, without chador or veils, to make our point with the mullahs: that we're not chattel, we have rights, and wearing the chador's up to us – not to them.'

'Yes, let's! After all, we helped win the victory too!' Sharazad had yawned, half asleep. 'Oh, I'm so tired.'

The nap had helped.

Idly Azadeh was watching the bubbles of foam crackling, the water hotter now, the sweet-smelling vapour very pleasing. Then she sat up for a moment, smoothing the foam on her breasts and shoulders. 'It's curious, Sharazad, but I was glad to wear chador today – those men were so awful.'

'Men on the street are always awful, darling Azadeh.' Sharazad opened her eyes and watched her, golden skin glistening, nipples proud. 'You're so beautiful, Azadeh darling.'

'Ah, thank you – but you're the beautiful one.' Azadeh rested her hand on her friend's stomach and patted her. 'Little mother, eh?'

'Oh, I do so hope so.' Sharazad sighed, closed her eyes and gave herself back to the heat. 'I can hardly imagine myself a mother. Three more days and then I'll know. When are you and Erikki going to have children?'

'In a year or two.' Azadeh kept her voice calm as she told the same lie she had told so many times already. But she was deeply afraid that she was barren, for she had used no contraceptives since she was married and had wished, with all her heart, to have Erikki's child from the beginning. Always the same nightmare welling up: that the abortion had taken away any chance of children as much as the German doctor had tried to reassure her. How could I have been so stupid?

So easy. I was in love. I was just seventeen and I was in love, oh, how deeply in love. Not like with Erikki, for whom I will give my life gladly. With Erikki it is true and for ever and kind and passionate and safe. With my Johnny Brighteyes it was dreamlike.

Ah, I wonder where you are now, what you're doing, you so tall and fair with your blue-grey eyes and oh, so British. Who did you marry? How many hearts did you break like you broke mine, my darling?

That summer he was at school in Rougemont – the next village to where she was at finishing school – ostensibly to learn French. It was after Sharazad had left. She had met him at the Sonnenhof, basking in the sun, overlooking all the beauty of Gstaad in its bowl of mountains. He was nineteen then, she three days seventeen, and all that summer long they had wandered the High Country – so beautiful, so beautiful – up in the mountains and the forests, swimming in streams, playing, loving, ever more adventurous, up above the clouds.

More clouds than I care to think of, she told herself dreamily, my head in the clouds that summer, knowing about men and life, but not knowing. Then in the fall him saying, 'Sorry, but I must go now, go back to university but I'll be back for Christmas.' Never coming back. And long before Christmas finding out. All the anguish and terror where there should have been only happiness. Petrified that the school would find out, for then her parents would have to be informed. Against the law to have an abortion in Switzerland without parents' consent – so going over the border to Germany where the act was possible, somehow finding the kindly doctor who had assured her and reassured her. Having no pain, no trouble, none – just a little difficulty borrowing the money. Still loving Johnny. Then the next year, school finished, everything secret, coming home to Tabriz. Stepmother finding out somehow – I'm sure Najoud, my step-sister, betrayed me, wasn't it she who lent me the money? Then Father knowing.

Kept like a spiked butterfly for a year. Then forgiveness, a peace – a form of peace. Begging for university in Tehran. 'I agree, providing you swear by God, no affairs, absolute obedience and you marry only whom I choose,' the Khan had said.

Top of her class. Then begging for the Teaching Corps, any excuse to get out of the palace. 'I agree, but only on our lands. We've more than enough villages for you to look after,' he had said.

Many men of Tabriz wanting to marry her but her father refusing them, ashamed of her. Then Erikki.

'And when this foreigner, this . . . this impoverished, vulgar, ill-mannered, spirit-worshipping monster who can't speak a word of Farsi or Turkish, who knows nothing of our customs or history or how to act in civilised society, whose only talent is that he can drink enormous quantities of vodka and fly a helicopter – when he finds out you're not virgin, that you're soiled, spoiled, and perhaps ruined inside for ever?'

'I've already told him, Father,' she had said through her tears. 'Also that without your permission I cannot marry.'

Then the miracle of the attack on the palace and Father almost killed – Erikki like an avenging warrior from the ancient storybooks. Permission to marry, another miracle. Erikki understanding, another miracle. But as yet no child. Old Dr. Nutt says I'm perfect and normal and to be patient. With the Help of God soon I will have a son, and this time there will be only happiness, like with Sharazad, so beautiful with her lovely face and breasts and flanks, hair like silk and skin like silk.

She felt the smoothness of her friend beneath her fingers and it pleased her greatly. Absently she began to caress her, letting herself drift in the warmth and tenderness. We're blessed to be women, she thought, able to bathe together and sleep together, to kiss and touch and love without guilt. 'Ah Sharazad,' she murmured, surrendering too, 'how I love your touch.'

In the Old City: 7:52 P.M. The man hurried across the snow-covered square near the ancient Mehrid mosque and went through the main gate of the roofed bazaar, out of the freezing cold into the warm, crowded, familiar semi-darkness. He was in his fifties, corpulent, panting in his haste, his astrakhan hat askew, his clothes expensive. A heavily laden donkey blocked his way in the narrow alley and he cursed, stood back to let the animal and its owner squeeze past, then hurried on again, turned left into a passage, then into the street of the clothes sellers.

Take your time, he told himself over and over, his chest hurting and his limbs hurting. You're safe now, slow down. But his terror overcame his mind and, still in panic, he scuttled on to vanish in the vast labyrinth. In his wake, a few minutes behind him, a group of armed Green Bands followed. They did not hurry.

Ahead, the narrow street of the rice shops was blocked with bigger crowds than usual, all vying for the small amount on sale. He stopped for a moment and wiped his brow, then went on again. The bazaar was like a honeycomb, teeming with life, with hundreds of dirt lanes, alleys and passages, lined on both sides with dimly lit open-fronted shops – some two storeyed – and booths and cubbyholes, some barely more than niches scooped out of the walls, for goods or services of all kinds – from foodstuffs to foreign watches, from butchers to bullion, from moneylenders to munitions dealers – all waiting for a customer even though there was not much to sell or to do. Above the noise and clatter and bargaining the high vaulted ceiling had skylights for ventilation and to let light in during the day. The air was heavy with the special smell of the bazaar – smells of smoke and rancid cooking fat, rotting fruit and roasting meat, food, species and urine and dung and dust and petrol, honey and dates and offal, all mixed with the smells of bodies and the sweat of the multitude who were born, lived, and died here.

People of all ages and all kinds crammed the byways – Tehranis,

Turkomans, Kurds, Kash'kai, Armenians and Arabs, Lebanese and Levantines – but the man paid no attention to them or to the constant entreaties to stop and buy, he just shoved and twisted his way through the crowds, darted across his own street of gold-smiths, down that of the spice sellers, the jewellery makers, onward ever deeper into the maze, his hair under his astrakhan hat matted with sweat, his face florid. Two shopkeepers who noticed him laughed, one to another: 'By God, I've never seen old Paknouri waddle so fast before – that old dog must be on his way to collect a ten-rial debt.'

'More likely Miser Paknouri's got a succulent tribes-boy waiting on a carpet, the lad's bum winking in the air!'

Their banter died quickly as the armed Green Bands passed. When they were safely out of sight, someone muttered, 'What do those young motherless dogs want here?'

'They're looking for someone. It must be that. May their fathers burn! Didn't you hear they've been arresting folk all today?'

'Arresting people? What are they doing with them?'

'Putting them in jail. They've possession of jails now – didn't you hear they broke down the door of Qasr Jail and set everyone free and locked up the jailers and now run it. They've set up their own firing squads and courts, I heard, and shot lots of generals and police. And there's a riot going on right now – at the university.'

'God protect us! My son Farmad's at a rally there, the young fool! I told him not to go tonight.'

Jared Bakravan, Sharazad's father, was in his upper-storey, private inner room over the open-fronted shop in the Street of the Money-lenders that had been in his family for five generations and was in one of the best positions. His speciality was banking and financing. He was seated on thick pile carpets, drinking tea with his old friend, Ali Kia, who had managed to be appointed an official in the Bazargan government. Bakravan's eldest son, Meshang, sat just behind him, listening and learning – a good-looking, clean-shaven man in his thirties, inclined to comfortable corpulence. Ali Kia was clean-shaven also, with glasses, Bakravan white-bearded and heavy. Both were in their sixties and had known each other most of their lives.

'And how will the loan be repaid, over what time period?' Bakravan asked,

'Out of oil revenues, as always,' Kia said patiently, 'just as the Shah would have done, the time period over five years, at the usual one percent per month. My friend Mehdi, Mehdi Bazargan, says Parliament will guarantee the loan the moment it meets.' He smiled and added, exaggerating slightly, 'As I'm not only in Mehdi's cabinet but also in his inner cabinet as well, I can personally watch over the legislation. Of course you know how important the loan is, and equally important to the bazaar.'

'Of course.' Bakravan tugged at his beard to prevent himself guffawing. Poor Ali, he thought, just as pompous as ever! 'It's certainly not my place to mention it, old friend, but some of the bazaaris have asked me what about the millions in bullion already advanced to support the revolution? Advanced to the fund for Ayatollah Khomeini – may God protect him,' he added politely, in his heart thinking may God remove him from us quickly now that we've won, before he and his rapacious, blinkered, parasitical mullahs do too much damage. As for you, Ali, old friend, bender of the truth, exaggerater of your own importance, you may be my oldest friend, but if you think I'd trust you further than a camel can cast dung . . . As if any one of us would trust any Iranian outside of immediate family – and then only with caution.

'Of course I know the Ayatollah never saw, needed, or touched a single rial,' he said, meaning it, 'but even so, we bazaaris advanced huge amounts of cash, bullion and foreign exchange on his behalf, financing his campaign – of course for the Glory of God and our beloved Iran.'

'Yes, we know. And God will bless you for it. So does the Ayatollah. Of course these loans will be repaid immediately we have the money – the very second! The Tehran bazaari loans are the first in line to be repaid of all internal debts – we, in government, realise how important your help has been. But Jared, Excellency, old friend, before we can do anything we must get oil production going and to do this we must have some cash. The immediate five million U.S. we need will be like a grain of rice in a barrel now that all foreign banks will be curbed, controlled and *most* cast out. The Pr –'

'Iran does not need any foreign banks. We bazaaris could do everything necessary – if we were asked. Everything. If we search diligently for the glory of Iran, perhaps, perhaps we might discover we have *all* the skills and connections in our midst.' Bakravan sipped his tea with studied elegance. 'My son Meshang has a degree from the Harvard Business School.' The lie bothered none of them. 'With the help of brilliant students like him . . .' He left the thought hanging.

Ali Kia picked it up immediately. 'Surely you wouldn't consider lending his services to my Ministry of Finance and Banking? Surely he's far too important to you and your colleagues? Of course, he must be!'

'Yes, yes, he is. But our beloved country's needs should take precedence over our personal wishes – if of course the government wanted to use his unique talents.'

'I will mention it to Mehdi in the morning. Yes, at my daily morning meeting with my old friend and colleague,' Ali Kia said, wondering briefly when he would be allowed to have his first audience – long overdue – since he had been appointed deputy minister of finance. 'I may tell him also you agree to the loan?'

'I will consult my colleagues at once. It would, of course, be their decision, not mine,' Bakravan added with open sadness that fooled neither of them. 'But I will press your case, old friend.'

'Thank you.' Again Kia smiled. 'We in government, and the Ayatollah, will appreciate the help of the bazaaris.'

'We're always ready to help. As you know, we always have,' the older man said smoothly, remembering the massive financial support given by the bazaar to the mullahs, to Khomeini over the years – or to any political figure of integrity, like Ali Kia, who had opposed either of the Shahs.

God curse the Pahlavis, Bakravan thought, they're the cause of all our trouble. Curse them for all the trouble they've caused with their insistent, too hasty demand for modernisation, for their insane disregard of our advice and influence, for inviting foreigners in, as many as 50,000 Americans alone just a year ago, letting them take all the best jobs and all the banking business. The Shah spurned our help, broke our monopoly, strangled us, and tore away our historic heritage. Everywhere, all over Iran.

But we had our revenge. We gambled our remaining influence and treasure on Khomeini's implacable hatred and his hold over the unwashed and illiterate masses. And we won. And now, with foreign banks gone, foreigners gone, we'll be richer and with more influence than ever before. This loan will be easy to arrange but Ali Kia and his government can sweat a little. We're the only ones who can raise the money. The payment offered is not high enough yet, not nearly enough to compensate for the closing of the bazaar all those months. Now what should it be? he asked himself, highly satisfied with their negotiations. Perhaps the percentage shou –

The door burst open and Emir Paknouri rushed into the room. 'Jared, they're going to arrest me!' he cried out, tears now running down his face.

'Who? Who's going to arrest you and for what?' Bakravan spluttered, the customary calm of his house obliterated, the faces of frightened assistants, clerks, teaboys, and managers now crowding the doorway.

'For . . . for crimes against Islam!' Paknouri wept openly.

'There must be some mistake! It's impossible!'

'Yes, it's impossible but they . . . they came to my house with my name . . . half an hour ago we –'

'Who? Give me their names and I'll destroy their fathers! Who came?'

'I told you! Guards, Revolutionary Guards, Green Bands, yes, them of course,' Paknouri said and rushed on, oblivious of the sudden hush. Ali Kia blanched and someone muttered, God protect us! 'Half an hour or so ago, with my name on a piece of paper . . . my name, Emir Paknouri, chief of the league of goldsmiths who gave millions of rials . . . they came to my house accusing me, but the servants . . . and my wife was there and I . . . by God and the Prophet, Jared,' he cried out as he fell to his knees, 'I've committed no crimes – I'm an Elder of the Bazaar, I've given millions and—' Suddenly he stopped, seeing Ali Kia. 'Kia, Ali Kia, Excellency, you know only too well what I did to help the revolution!'

'Of course.' Kia was white-faced, his heart thumping. 'There has to be a mistake.' He knew Paknouri as a highly influential bazaari. Well respected, Sharazad's first husband, and one of his long-time sponsors. 'There must be a mistake!'

'Of course there's a mistake!' Bakravan put his arm around the poor man and tried to calm him. 'Fresh tea at once!' he ordered.

'A whisky. Please, do you have a whisky?' Paknouri mumbled. 'I'll have tea afterwards, do you have whisky?'

'Not here, my poor friend, but of course there's vodka.' It came at once. Paknouri downed it and choked a little. He refused another. In a minute or two he became a little calmer and began again to tell what had happened. The first he had known that something was wrong were loud voices in the hallway of his palatial house just outside the bazaar – he had been upstairs with his wife, preparing for dinner. 'The leader of the Guards – there were five of them – the leader was waving this piece of paper and demanding to see me. Of course the servants wouldn't dare disturb me or let such an ape in, so my chief servant said he'd see if I was in and came upstairs. He told us the paper was signed by someone called Uwari, on behalf of the Revolutionary Komiteh – in the Name of God, who're they? Who's this man Uwari? Have you ever heard of such a man, Jared?'

'It's a common enough name,' Bakravan said, following the Iranian custom of always having a ready answer to something you don't know. 'Have you, Excellency Ali?'

'As you say, it's a common name. Did this man mention anyone else, Excellency Paknouri?'

'He may have. God protect us! But who are they – this Revolutionary Komiteh? Ali Kia, surely you'd know?'

'Many names have been mentioned,' Kia said importantly, hiding his instant unease every time 'Revolutionary Komiteh' was uttered. Like everyone else in government or outside it, he thought disgustedly, I don't have any real information about its actual makeup or when or where it meets, only that it seemed to come into being the moment Khomeini returned to Iran, barely two weeks ago and, since yesterday when Bakhtiar fled into hiding, it's been acting like it was a law unto itself, ruling in Khomeini's name and with his authority, precipitously appointing new judges, most with no legal training whatsoever, authorising arrests, revolutionary courts, and immediate executions, totally outside normal law and jurisprudence – and against our Constitution! May all their houses burn down and they go to the hell they deserve!

'Only this morning my friend Mehdi . . .' he began confidentially, then stopped, pretending to notice the staff still crowding the doorway for the first time, waved an imperious hand dismissing them. When the door was reluctantly closed, he dropped his voice, passing on the rumour as though it was private knowledge, 'only this morning, with, er, with our blessing, he went to the Ayatollah and threatened to resign unless the Revolutionary Komiteh stopped bypassing him and his authority and so put them in their place for all time.'

'Praise be to God!' Paknouri said, very relieved. 'We didn't win the revolution to let more lawlessness take the place of SAVAK, foreign domination and the Shah!'

'Of course not! Praise be to God that now the government is in the best of hands. But please, Excellency Paknouri, please continue with your harrowing story.'

'There's not much more to tell you, Ali,' Paknouri said, calmer and braver now, surrounded by such powerful friends. 'I, er, I went down to see these intruders at once and told them it was all a fatuous mistake, but this boneheaded, illiterate piece of dog turd just waved the paper in my face, said I was arrested, and that I was to go with them. I told them to wait – I told them to wait and went to fetch some papers but my wife . . . my wife told me not to trust them, that perhaps they were Tudeh or mujhadin in disguise, or fedayeen. I agreed with her and decided it would be best to come here to consult with you and the others.' He put the real facts out of his mind, that he had fled the moment he had heard the leader call out in the name of the Revolutionary Komiteh, and Uwari personally, that Paknouri the Miser submit to God for crimes against God.

'My poor friend,' Bakravan said. 'My poor friend, how you must have suffered! Never mind, you're safe now. Stay here tonight. Ali, directly after first prayer tomorrow, go to the prime minister's office and make sure this matter is dealt with and those fools are punished. We all know Emir Paknouri's a patriot, that he and all the goldsmiths supported the revolution and are essential to this loan.' Wearily he closed his ears to all the platitudes that Ali Kia was uttering now.

He studied Paknouri, seeing his still-pallid face and sweat-matted hair. Poor fellow, what a shock they must have given him. What a shame, with all his riches and good name – connected as he is through cousin Valik's wife Annoush to the Qajars – that all my work for Sharazad came to nought. What a shame he didn't sire children with her and so cement our families together, even one child, for then certainly there would never have been a divorce and my troubles wouldn't have been compounded with this Lochart foreigner. However much this foreigner tries to learn our ways he never will. And how expensive it is to keep him to uphold the family's reputation! I must talk to cousin Valik and again ask him to arrange for Lochart to have extra monies – Valik and his greed-filled IHC partners can well afford to do that for me from the millions they earn, most of it in foreign currency now! What would it cost them? Nothing! The cost would be passed on to Gavallan and S-G. The partners owe me a thousand favours, I who for years have advised them how to gain so much control and wealth with so little effort!

'Pay Lochart yourself, Jared, Excellency,' Valik had said to him rudely the last time he'd asked him. 'Surely that's your own charge. You share everything we gain – and what's such a tiny amount to my favourite cousin and the richest bazaari in Tehran?'

'But it should be a partnership charge. We can use him when we have 100 percent control. With the new plan for the future of IHC, the partnership will be richer than ever an –'

'I will at once consult the other partners. Of course, it is their decision not mine . . .'

Liar, the old man thought, sipping tea, but then, I would have said the same. He stifled a yawn, tired now and hungry. A nap before dinner would do me good. 'So sorry, Excellencies, so sorry but I have urgent business to attend to. Paknouri, old friend, I'm glad everything is resolved. Stay here tonight, Meshang will arrange quilts and cushions, and don't worry! Ali, my friend, walk with me to the bazaar gate – do you have transport?' he asked thinly, knowing that the first perk of a deputy minister would be a car and chauffeur and unlimited petrol.

'Yes, thank you, the PM insisted I arrange it, insisted – the importance of our department, I suppose.'

'As God wants!' Bakravan said.

Well satisfied, they all went out of the room, down the narrow stairs and into the small passageway that led to the open-fronted shop. Their smiles vanished and bile filled their mouths.

Waiting there were the same five Green Bands, lolling on the desks and chairs, all armed with U.S. Army carbines, all in their early twenties, unshaven or bearded, their clothes poor and soiled, some with holed shoes, some sockless. The leader picked his teeth silently, the rest were smoking, carelessly dropping their ash on Bakravan's priceless Kash'kai carpets. One of these youths coughed badly as he smoked, his breath wheezing.

Bakravan felt his knees weakening. All of his staff stood frozen against one of the walls. Everyone. Even his favourite teaboy. Out in the street it was very quiet, no one about – even the owners of the money lending shops across the alley seemed to have vanished.

'Salaam, agha, the Blessing of God on you,' he said politely, his voice sounding strange. 'What can I do for you?'

The leader paid no attention to him, just kept his eyes boring into Paknouri, his face handsome but scarred by the parasite disease, carried by sandflies and almost endemic in Iran. He was in his early twenties, dark eyes and hair and work-scarred hands that toyed with the carbine. His name was Yusuf Senvar – Yusuf the bricklayer.

The silence grew and Paknouri could stand the strain no longer. 'It's all a mistake,' he screamed. 'You're making a mistake!'

'You thought you'd escape the Vengeance of God by running away?' Yusuf's voice was soft, almost kind – though with a coarse village accent that Bakravan could not place.

'What Vengeance of God?' Paknouri screamed. 'I've done nothing wrong, nothing.'

'Nothing? Haven't you worked for and with foreigners for years, helping them to carry off the wealth of our nation?'

'Of course not to do that but to create jobs and help the econ –'

'Nothing? Haven't you served the Satan Shah for years?'

Again Paknouri shouted, 'No, I was in opposition, everyone knows I . . . I was in oppo –'

'But you still served him and did his bidding?'

Paknouri's face was twisted and almost out of control. His mouth worked but he could not get the words out. Then he croaked, 'Everyone served him – of course everyone served him, he was the Shah, but we worked for the revolution – the Shah was the Shah, of course everyone served him while he was in power . . .'

'The Imam didn't,' Yusuf said, his voice suddenly raw. 'Imam Khomeini never served the Shah. In the Name of God, did he?' Slowly he looked from face to face. No one answered him.

In the silence, Bakravan watched the man reach into his torn pocket and find a piece of paper and peer at it and he knew that he was the only one here who could stop this nightmare.

'By Order of the Revolutionary Komiteh,' Yusuf began, 'and Ali'allah Uwari: Miser Paknouri, you are called to judgment. Submit yo –'

'No, Excellency,' Bakravan said firmly but politely, his heart pounding in his ears. 'This is the bazaar. Since the beginning of time you know the bazaar has its own laws, its own leaders. Emir Paknouri is one of them, he cannot be arrested or taken away against his will. He cannot be touched – that is bazaari law from the beginning of time.' He stared back at the young man, fearlessly, knowing that the Shah, even SAVAK had never dared to challenge their laws or right of sanctuary.

'Is bazaari law greater than God's law, Moneylender Bakravan?'

He felt a wave of ice go through him. 'No – no, of course not.'

'Good. I obey God's law and do God's work.'

'But you may not arres –'

'I obey God's law and do only God's work.' The man's eyes were brown and guileless under his black brows. He gestured at his carbine. 'I do not need this gun – none of us need guns to do God's work. I pray with all my heart to be a martyr for God, for then I'll go straight to Paradise *without the need to be judged, my sins forgiven me.* If it's tonight, then I will die blessing him who kills me because I know I will die doing God's work.'

'God is Great,' one of the men said, the others echoed him.

'Yes, God is Great. But you, Moneylender Bakravan, did you pray five times today as the Prophet ordered?'

'Of course, of course,' Bakravan heard himself say, knowing his lie to be sinless because of *taqiyah* – concealment – the Prophet's permission to any Muslim to lie about Islam if he feels his life threatened.

'Good. Be silent and be patient, I come back to you later.' Another chill racked him as he saw the man turn his attention back to Paknouri.

400

'By order of the Revolutionary Komiteh and Ali'allah Uwari: Miser Paknouri, submit yourself to God for crimes against God.'

Paknouri's mouth struggled. 'I . . . I . . . you cannot . . . there . . .' His voice trailed away. A little foam seeped from the corners of his lips. They all watched him, the Green Bands without emotion, the others with horror.

Ali Kia cleared his throat. 'Now listen, perhaps it would be better to leave this until tomorrow,' he began, trying to keep his voice important. 'Emir Paknouri's clearly upset by the mista –'

'Who're you?' The leader's eyes bored into him as they had into Paknouri and Bakravan. 'Eh?'

'I'm Deputy Minister Ali Kia,' Ali replied, keeping his courage under the strength of the eyes, 'of the Department of Finance, member of Prime Minister Bazargan's Cabinet and I suggest you wait u –'

'In the Name of God: you, your Department of Finance, your Cabinet, your Bazargan has nothing to do with me or us. We obey the mullah Uwari, who obeys the Komiteh, who obeys the Imam, who obeys God.' The man scratched absently and turned his attention back to Paknouri. 'In the street!' he ordered, his voice still gentle. 'Or we'll drag you.'

Paknouri collapsed with a groan and lay inert. The others watched helplessly, someone muttered, 'The Will of God,' and the little teaboy began sobbing.

'Be quiet, boy,' Yusuf said without anger. 'Is he dead?'

One of the men went over and squatted over Paknouri. 'No. As God wants.'

'As God wants. Hassan, pick him up, put his head in the water trough and if he doesn't wake up, we'll carry him.'

'No,' Bakravan interrupted bravely, 'no, he'll stay here, he's sick an –'

'Are you deaf, old man?' An edge had crept into Yusuf's voice. Fear stalked the room. The little boy crammed his fist into his mouth to prevent himself from crying out. Yusuf kept his eyes on Bakravan as the man called Hassan, broad-shouldered and strong, lifted Paknouri easily and went out of the shop and up the alley. 'As God wants,' he said, eyes on Bakravan. 'Eh?'

'Where . . . please, where will you be taking him?'

'To jail, of course. Where else should he go?'

'Which . . . which jail, please?'

One of the other men laughed. 'What does it matter what jail?'

For Jared Bakravan and the others, the room was now stifling and

401

cell-like even though the air had not changed and the open front on to the alley was as it had ever been.

'I would like to know, Excellency,' Bakravan said, his voice thick, trying to mask his hatred. 'Please.'

'Evin.' This had been the most infamous of Tehran's prisons. Yusuf sensed another wave of fear. They must all be guilty to be so afraid, he thought. He glanced behind him at his younger brother. 'Give me the paper.'

His brother was barely fifteen, grubby and coughing badly. He took out half a dozen pieces of paper and shuffled through them. He found the one he sought. 'Here it is, Yusuf.'

The leader peered at it. 'Are you sure it's the right one?'

'Yes.' The youth pointed a stubby finger at the name. Slowly he spelled out the characters. 'J-a-r-e-d B-a-k-r-a-v-a-n.'

Someone muttered, 'God protect us!' and in the vast silence Yusuf took the paper and held it out to Bakravan. The others watched, frozen.

Hardly breathing, the old man took it, his fingers trembling. For a moment he could not focus his eyes. Then he saw the words: 'Jared Bakravan of the Tehran bazaar, by order of the Revolutionary Komiteh and Ali'allah Uwari, you are summoned to the Revolutionary Tribunal at Evin Prison tomorrow immediately after first prayer to answer questions.' The paper was signed, Ali'allah, the writing illiterate.

'What questions?' he asked dully.

'As God wills.' The leader shouldered his carbine and got up. 'Until dawn. Bring the paper with you and don't be late.' At that moment he noticed the silver tray and cut glasses and half-empty bottle of vodka that was on a low table almost hidden by a curtain in the dark hallway, glinting in some candlelight. 'By God and the Prophet,' he said angrily, 'have you forgotten the laws of God?'

The shop people scattered out of his way as he upended the bottle, emptying the contents on the dirt floor, and hurled the bottle away. Some of the liquid ran on to one of the carpets. Instinctively the teaboy fell on his knees and began to mop it up.

'Leave it alone!'

Petrified, the boy scuttled away. With his foot, Yusuf carelessly diverted most of the flow. 'Let the stain remind you of the laws of God, old man,' he said. 'If it stains.' For a moment he studied the carpet. 'What colours! Beautiful! Beautiful!' He sighed and scratched, then turned on Bakravan and Kia. 'If you were to take all the wealth of all of us *pasadan* here, and add it to that of all our families, and our fathers' families, still we could not afford even a corner of such a carpet.' Yusuf smiled crookedly. 'But then, if I was as rich as you, Moneylender Bakravan – do you know usury is also against the laws of God? – even if I was so rich, still I wouldn't buy such a carpet. I have no need of such treasure. I have nothing, we have nothing, we need nothing. Only God.'

He stalked out.

Near the U.S. Embassy: 8:15 P.M. Erikki had been waiting for almost four hours. From where he sat in the first-floor window of his friend Christian Tollonen's apartment, he could see the high walls surrounding the floodlit U.S. compound down the road, uniformed marines near the huge iron gates stamping their feet against the cold, and the big embassy building beyond. Traffic was still heavy, snarled here and there, everyone honking and trying to get ahead, pedestrians as impatient and self-centered as usual. No traffic lights working. No police. Not that they'd make any difference, he thought, Tehranis don't give a damn for traffic regulations, never have, never will. Like those madmen on the road down through the mountains who killed themselves. Like Tabrizis. Or Qazvinis.

His great fist bunched at the thought of Qazvin. At the Finnish embassy this morning there had been reports of Qazvin in a state of revolt, that Azerbaijan nationalists in Tabriz had rebelled again and fighting was going on against forces loyal to the Khomeini government and that the whole oil-rich and vastly strategic border province had again declared its independence of Tehran, independence it had fought for over the centuries, always aided and abetted by Russia, Iran's permanent enemy and gobbler of her territory. Rakoczy and others like him must be swarming all over Azerbaijan.

'Of course the Soviets are after us,' Abdollah Gorgon Khan had said angrily, during the quarrel, just before he and Azadeh had left for Tehran. 'Of course your Rakoczy and his men are here in strength. We walk the thinnest tightrope in the whole world because we're their key to the Gulf and the key to Hormuz, the jugular of the West. If it hadn't been for us Gorgons, our tribal connections and some of our Kurdish allies, we'd be a Soviet province now – joined to the other half of Azerbaijan that the Soviets stole from us years ago, helped as always by the insidious British – oh, how I hate the British, even more than Americans who are just stupid and ill-mannered barbarians. It's the truth, isn't it?'

'They're not like that, not the ones I've met. And S-G's treated me fairly.'

'So far. But they'll betray you – the British betray everyone who's not British and even then they'll betray them if it suits them.'

'Insha'Allah.'

Abdollah Gorgon Khan had laughed without humour. 'Insha-Allah! And Insha'Allah the Soviet army retreated over the border and then we smashed their quislings, and stamped out their "Democratic Azerbaijan Republic" and the "Kurdish People's Republic". But I admire the Soviets, they play only to win and change the rules to suit themselves. The real winner of your world war was Stalin. He was the colossus. Didn't he dominate everything at Potsdam, Yalta and Tehran – didn't he outmanoeuvre Churchill and Roosevelt? Didn't Roosevelt even stay with him in Tehran in the Soviet embassy? How we Iranians laughed! The Great President gave Stalin the future when he had the power to stuff him behind his own borders. What a genius! Beside him your ally Hitler was a craven bungler! As God wills, eh?'

'Finland sided with Hitler only to fight Stalin and get back our lands.'

'But you lost, you chose the wrong side and lost. Even a fool could see Hitler would lose – how could Reza Shah have been so foolish? Ah, Captain, I never understood why Stalin let you Finns live. If I'd been him I would have laid waste Finland as a lesson – as he decimated a dozen other lands. Why did he let you all live? Because you stood up to him in your Winter War?'

'I don't know. Perhaps. I agree the Soviets will never give up.'

'Never, Captain. But neither will we. We Azerbaijanis will always outmaneouvre them and keep them at bay. As in '46.'

But then the West was strong, there was the Truman Doctrine towards the Soviets of hands off or else, Erikki thought grimly. And now? Now Carter's at the helm? What helm?

Heavily, he leaned forward and refilled his glass, impatient to get back to Azadeh. It was cold in the apartment and he still wore his overcoat – the central heating was off and the windows draughty. But the room was large and pleasant and masculine with old easy chairs, the walls decorated with small but good Persian carpets and bronze. Books, magazines and journals were scattered everywhere, on tables and chairs and bookshelves – Finnish, Russian, Iranian – a pair of girl's shoes carelessly on one of the shelves. He sipped the vodka, loving the warmth it gave him, then looked out of the window once more at the embassy. For a moment he wondered if it would be worth emigrating to the U.S. with Azadeh. 'The bastions are falling,' he muttered out loud. 'Iran no longer safe, Europe so vulnerable, Finland on the sword's edge . . .'

His attention focused below. Now the traffic was totally blocked by swarms of youths collecting on both roads – the U.S. embassy complex was on the corner of Tahkt-e-Jamshid and the main road called Roosevelt. Used to be called Roosevelt, he reminded himself idly. What's the road called now? Khomeini Street? Street of the Revolution?

The front door of the apartment opened. 'Hey, Erikki,' the young Finn said with a grin. Christian Tollonen wore a Russian-style fur hat and fur-lined-trench coat that he had bought in Leningrad on a drunken weekend with other university friends. 'What's new?'

'Four hours I've been waiting.'

'Three hours and twenty-two minutes and half a bottle of my best contraband Russian Moskava money can buy anywhere, and we agreed three or four hours.' Christian Tollonen was in his early thirties, a bachelor, fair and grey-eyed, deputy cultural attaché at the Finnish embassy. They had been friends since he came to Iran, some years ago. 'Pour me one, by God, I need it – there's another demonstration simmering, and I had a hell of a time getting through.' He kept his trench coat on and went to the window.

The two sections of crowds had joined now, the people milling about in front of the embassy complex. All gates had been closed. Uneasily Erikki noticed that there were no mullahs among the youths. They could hear shouting.

'Death to America, death to Carter,' Christian interpreted – he could speak fluent Farsi because his father too had been a diplomat here and he had spent five years of his youth at school in Tehran. 'Just the usual shit, down with Carter and American imperialism.'

'No Allah-u Akbar,' Erikki said. For a moment his mind took him back to the roadblock, and ice swept into his stomach. 'No mullahs.'

'No. I didn't see one anywhere around.' In the street the tempo picked up with different factions swirling around the iron gates. 'Most of them are university students. They thought I was Russian and they told me there'd been a pitched battle at the university, leftists versus the Green Bands – with perhaps twenty or thirty killed or wounded and it was still going on.' While they watched, fifty or sixty youths began rattling the gates. 'They're spoiling for a fight.'

'And no police to stop them.' Erikki handed him the glass.

'What would we do without vodka?'

405

Erikki laughed. 'Drink brandy. Do you have everything?'

'No – but a start.' Christian sat in one of the armchairs near the low table opposite Erikki and opened his briefcase. 'Here's a copy of your marriage and birth certificates – thank God we had copies. New passports for both of you – I managed to get someone in Bazargan's office to stamp yours with a temporary residence permit good for three months.'

'You're a magician!'

'They promised they'd issue you a new Iranian pilot's licence but when, they wouldn't say. With your S-G ID and the photocopy of your British licence they said you were legal enough. Now, Azadeh's passport's temporary.' He opened it and showed him the photograph. 'It's not standard – I took a Polaroid of the photo you gave me – but it'll pass until we can get a proper one. Get her to sign it as soon as you see her. Has she been out of the country since you were married?'

'No, why?'

'If she travels out on a Finnish passport – well, I don't know how it will affect her Iranian status. The authorities have always been touchy, particularly about their own nationals. Khomeini seems even more xenophobic so his regime's bound to be tougher. It might look to them as though she'd renounced her nationality. I don't think they'll let her back.'

A muted burst of shouting from the massed youths in the street diverted them for a moment. Hundreds were waving clenched fists and somewhere someone had a loudspeaker and was haranguing them. 'The way I feel right now, as long as I can get her out, I don't care,' Erikki said.

The younger man glanced at him. After a moment he said, 'Perhaps she should be aware of the danger, Erikki. There's no way I can get her replacement papers or any Iranian passport, but it'd be very risky for her to leave without them. Why don't you ask her father to arrange them for her? He could get them for her easily. He owns most of Tabriz, eh?'

Bleakly Erikki nodded. 'Yes, but we had another row just before we left. He still disapproves of our marriage.'

After a pause Christian said, 'Perhaps it's because you don't have a child yet, you know how Iranians are.'

'Plenty of time for children,' Erikki said, sick at heart. We'll have children in good time, he thought. There's no hurry and old Dr. Nutt says she's fine. Shit! If I tell her what Christian said about her Iranian papers she'll never leave; if I don't tell her and she's refused re-entry she'll never forgive me, and anyway she'd never leave without her father's permission. 'To get her new papers means we'll have to go back and, well, I don't want to go back.'

'Why, Erikki? Usually you can't wait to get to Tabriz.'

'Rakoczy.' Erikki had told him everything that had happened – except the killing of the mujhadin at the roadblock and Rakoczy killing others during the rescue. Some details are best untold, he thought grimly.

Christian Tollonen sipped his vodka. 'What's the real problem?'

'Rakoczy.' Erikki held his gaze steady.

Christian shrugged. Two refills emptied the bottle. 'Prosit!'

'Prosit! Thanks for the papers and passports.'

Shouting outside distracted them again. The crowd was well disciplined though it was becoming noisier. In the American courtyard more floodlights were on now, and they could see faces clearly in the embassy windows. 'Just as well they've their own generators.'

'Yes – and their own heating units, gasoline pumps, PX, everything.' Christian went over to the sideboard and brought out a fresh bottle. 'That and their special status in Iran – no visas necessary, not being subject to Iranian laws – has caused a lot of the hatred.'

'By God, it's cold in here, Christian. Don't you have any wood?'

'Not a damned bit. The damned heat's been off ever since I moved in here – three months, that's almost all winter.'

'Perhaps that's just as well.' Erikki motioned at the pair of shoes. 'You have heat enough. Eh?'

Christian grinned. 'Sometimes. I will admit Tehran is one of the – used to be one of the great places on earth for all sorts of pleasures. But now, now, old friend . . .' a shadow went over his face. 'Now I think Iran won't be the paradise those poor bastards out there believe they've won, but a hell on earth for most of them. Particularly the women.' He sipped his vodka. There was an eddy of excitement beside the compound wall as a youth, with his U.S. Army rifle slung, climbed on the shoulders of others and tried unsuccessfully to reach the top. 'I wonder what I'd do if that was my wall and those bastards started coming over at me in strength.'

'You'd blow their heads off – which'd be quite legal. Wouldn't it?'

Christian laughed suddenly. 'Only if you got away with it.' He looked back at Erikki. 'What about you? What's your plan?'

'I don't have one. Not until I talk to McIver – there was no chance this morning. He and Gavallan were both busy trying to track down the

Iranian partners, then they had meetings at the British embassy with someone called – I think they said Talbot . . .'

Christian masked his sudden interest. 'George Talbot?'

'Yes, that's right. D'you know him?'

'Yes, he's second secretary.' Christian did not add: Talbot's also covert chief of British Intelligence in Iran, has been for years, and is one very important operator. 'I didn't know he was still in Tehran – I thought he'd left a couple of days ago. What do McIver and Andrew Gavallan want with him?'

Erikki shrugged and turned away, absently watching more youths trying to scale the wall, most of his mind concerned with what to do about Azadeh's papers. 'They said something about wanting to know more about a friend of his they'd met at the airport yesterday – someone called Armstrong, Robert Armstrong.'

Christian Tollonen almost dropped his glass. 'Armstrong?' he asked, forcing calm, very glad that Erikki had his back towards him.

'Yes.' Erikki turned to him. 'Mean anything to you?'

'It's a common enough name,' the younger man said, pleased to hear that his voice was matter of fact. Robert Armstrong, MI 6, ex-Special Branch, who had been in Iran on contract for a number of years – supposedly on loan from the British government – supposedly chief adviser to Iran's highly classified Department of Inner intelligence; a man rarely seen in public and known only to very few, most of whom would be in the intelligence community.

Like me, he thought and wondered what Erikki would say if he knew that he was an Iranian intelligence expert, that he knew a lot about Rakoczy and many other foreign agents, that his prime job was to try to know everything about Iran but to do nothing and never to interfere with any of the combatants, internal or external, just to wait and watch and learn and remember. What's Armstrong still doing here?

He got up to cover his disquiet, pretending to want to see the crowd better. 'Did they find out what they wanted to know?' he asked.

Again Erikki shrugged. 'I don't know. I never caught up with them. I was . . .' He stopped and studied the other man. 'Is it important?'

'No – no, not at all. You hungry? Are you and Azadeh free for dinner?'

'Sorry, not tonight.' Erikki glanced at his watch. 'I'd better be getting back. Thanks again for the help.'

'Nothing. You were saying about McIver and your Gavallan? They have a plan to change operations here?'

'I don't think so. I was supposed to meet them at 3 p.m. to go to the airport but seeing you and getting the passports was more important to me.' Erikki stood up and put out his hand, towering over him. 'Thanks again.'

'Nothing.' Christian shook hands warmly. 'See you tomorrow.'

Now in the street the shouting had ceased and there was an ominous silence. Both men ran for the window. All attention turned towards the main road once called Roosevelt. Then they heard the growing, 'Allahhhh-uuuu Akbarrrr!'

Erikki muttered, 'Is there a back way out of the building?'

'No. No, there isn't'.

The new oncoming horde had mullahs and Green Bands in their front ranks, most of them armed like the following mass of the young men. All were shouting in unison, God is Great, God is Great, totally outnumbering the student demonstration in front of the embassy, though the men there were equally armed.

At once the leftists poured into well-chosen defensive positions in doorways and among the traffic. Men, women and children trapped in cars and trucks began to scatter. The Islamics approached fast. As the front ranks flowed along the sidewalks and through the stalled vehicles and approached the floodlit walls, the tempo of their shouting increased, their pace quickened, and everyone readied. Then, astonishingly, the students began to retreat. Silently. The Green Bands hesitated, nonplussed.

The retreat was peaceful and so the horde became peaceful. Soon the protesters had moved away and now none of them threatened the embassy. Mullahs and Green Bands began directing traffic. Those bystanders who had fled or abandoned their vehicles breathed again, thanked God for His intercession and swarmed back. At once the hooting and cursing opened up in a growing frenzy as cars and trucks and pedestrians fought for space. The great iron gates of the embassy did not open, though a side door did.

Christian's throat felt dry. 'I'd've bet my life there was going to be a pitched battle.'

Erikki was equally astonished. 'It's almost as though they'd expected the Green Bands and knew where they were coming from and when. It was almost as though it was a rehearsal for some—' He stopped and went closer to the window, his face suddenly flushed. 'Look! Down there in that doorway, that's Rakoczy.'

'Where? Wh – oh, you mean the man in the flight jacket talking to the short guy?' Christian squinted into the darkness below. The two men were half in shadow, then they shook hands and came into the light. It was Rakoczy all right. 'Are you sure that . . .'

But Erikki had already pulled the front door open and was halfway down the stairs. Christian had a fleeting glimpse of him as he pulled the great pukoh knife from his belt holster and slipped it into his sleeve, haft in his palm. 'Erikki, don't be a fool,' he shouted but Erikki had already vanished. Christian rushed back to the window and was just in time to see Erikki run out of the doorway below, shove through the crowds in pursuit, Rakoczy nowhere to be seen.

But Erikki had him in view. Rakoczy was half a hundred yards away and he just caught sight of him turning south into Roosevelt to disappear. When Erikki got to the corner, he saw the Soviet ahead, walking quickly but not too quickly, many pedestrians between them, the traffic slow and very noisy. Making a detour around a tangle of trucks, Rakoczy stepped out into the road, waited for a hooting, battered old Volkswagen to squeeze past and glanced around. He saw Erikki. It would have been almost impossible to miss him – almost a foot taller than almost everyone else. Without hesitation Rakoczy took to his heels, weaving through the crowds, and cut down a side street, running fast. Erikki saw him go and raced after him. Pedestrians cursed both of them, one old man sent flying into the filthy dirt as Rakoczy shoved past into another turning.

The side street was narrow, refuse strewn everywhere, no stalls or shops open now and no streetlights, a few weary pedestrians trudging homewards with multitudes of doorways and archways leading to hovels and staircases of more hovels – the whole area smelling of urine and waste and offal and rotting vegetables.

Rakoczy was a little more than forty yards ahead. He turned into a smaller alley, crashing through the street stalls where families were sleeping – howls of rage in his wake – changed direction and fled into a passageway and into another, cut across it into an alley, quite lost now, into another, down this and into another. Aghast, he stopped, seeing that this was a cul-de-sac. His hand went for his automatic, then he noticed a passageway just ahead and rushed for it.

The walls were so close he could touch both of them as he charged down it, his chest heaving, going ever deeper into the curling, twisting warren. Ahead an old woman was emptying night soil into the festering joub and he sent her sprawling as others cowered against the walls to get out of his way. Now Erikki was only twenty yards behind, his rage feeding his strength, and he jumped over the old woman who was still sprawled, half in and half out of the joub, and redoubled his efforts, closing the gap. Just around the corner his adversary stopped, pulled an ancient street stall into the way, and, before Erikki could avoid it, he crashed into it and went down half stunned. With a bellow of rage he groped to his feet, swayed dizzily for a moment, climbed over the wreckage, then rushed onward again, the knife now openly in his hand, and turned the corner.

But the passageway ahead was empty. Erikki skidded to a stop. His breath was coming in great, aching gasps and he was bathed in sweat. It was hard to see though his night vision was very good. Then he noticed the small archway. Carefully he went through it, knife ready. The passage led to an open courtyard strewn with rubble and the rusty skeleton of a ravaged car. Many doorways and openings led off this dingy space, some with doors, some leading to rickety stairways and upper storeys. It was silent – the silence ominous. He could feel eyes watching him. Rats scuttled out of some refuse and vanished under a pile of rubble.

To one side was another archway. Above it was an ancient inscription in Farsi that he could not read. Through the archway the darkness seemed deeper. The pitted vaulted entrance stopped at an open doorway. The door was wooden and girt with bands of ancient iron and half off its hinges. Beyond, there seemed to be a room. As he went closer he saw a candle guttering.

'What do you want?'

The man's voice came out of the darkness at him, the hair on Erikki's neck twisted. The voice was in English – not Rakoczy's – the accent foreign, a gruff eeriness to it.

'Who – who're you?' he asked uneasily, his senses searching the darkness, wondering if it was Rakoczy pretending to be someone else.

'What do you want?'

'I – I want – I'm following a man,' he said, not knowing where to talk to, his voice echoing eerily from the unseen, high-vaulted roof above.

'The man you seek is not here. Go away.'

'Who're you?'

'It doesn't matter. Go away.'

The candle flame was just a tiny speck of light in the darkness, making the darkness seem more strong. 'Did you see anyone come this way – come running this way?'

The man laughed softly and said something in Farsi. At once rustling and some muted laughter surrounded Erikki and he whirled, his knife protectively weaving in front of him. 'Who are you?'

411

The rustling continued. All around him. Somewhere water dripped into a cistern. The air smelled dank and rancid. Sound of distant firing. Another rustle. Again he whirled, feeling someone close by but seeing no one, only the archway and the dim night beyond. The sweat was running down his face. Cautiously he went to the doorway and put his back against a wall, sure now that Rakoczy was here. The silence grew heavier.

'Why don't you answer?' he said. 'Did you see anyone?'

Again a soft chuckle. 'Go away.' Then silence.

'Why're you afraid? Who are you?'

'Who I am is nothing to you, and there's no fear here, except yours.' The voice was as gentle as before. Then the man added something in Farsi and another ripple of amusement surrounded him.

'Why do you speak English to me?'

'I speak English to you because no Iranian or reader of the language of the Book would come here by day or by night. Only a fool would come here.'

Erikki's peripheral vision saw something or someone go between him and the candle. At once his knife came on guard. 'Rakoczy?'

'Is that the name of the man you seek?'

'Yes – yes that's him. He's here, isn't he?'

'No.'

'I don't believe you, whoever you are!'

Silence, then a deep sigh. 'As God wants,' and a soft order in Farsi that Erikki did not understand.

Matches flickered all around him. Candles caught, and small oil lamps. Erikki gasped. There were ragged bundles against the walls and columns of the high-domed cavern. Hundreds of them. Men and women. The diseased, festering remains of men and women lying on straw or beds of rags. Eyes in ravaged faces staring at him. Stumps of limbs. One old crone was almost beside his feet and he leapt away in panic to the centre of the doorway.

'We are all lepers here,' the man said. He was propped against a nearby column, a helpless mound of rags. Another rag half covered the sockets of his eyes. Almost nothing was left of his face except his lips. Feebly he waved the stump of an arm. 'We're all lepers here – unclean. This is a house of lepers. Do you see this man among us?'

'No – no. I'm – I'm sorry,' Erikki said shakily.

'Sorry?' The man's voice was heavy with irony. 'Yes. We are all sorry. Insha'Allah! Insha'Allah.'

Erikki wanted desperately to turn and flee but his legs would not

412

move. Someone coughed, a hacking, frightful cough. Then his mouth said, 'Who – who are you?'

'Once I was a teacher of English – now I am unclean, one of the living dead. As God wants. Go away. Bless God for His mercy.'

Numbed, Erikki saw the man motion with the remains of his arms. Obediently, around the cavern the lights began to go out, eyes still watching him.

Outside in the night air, he had to make a grim effort to stop himself from running away in terror, feeling filthy, wanting to cast off his clothes at once and bathe and soap and bathe and soap and bathe again.

'Stop it,' he muttered, his skin crawling, 'there's nothing to be afraid of.'

Wednesday
February 14, 1979

At Evin Jail: 6:29 A.M. The jail was like any other modern jail – in good days or bad – grey, brooding, high-walled, and hideous.

Today the false dawn was strange, the glow below the horizon curiously red. No overcast or even clouds in the sky – the first time for weeks – and though it was still cold it promised to be a rare day. No smog. The air crisp and clean for a change. A kind wind took away the smoke from the still burning wrecks of cars and barricades from last night's clashes between the now legal Green Bands and the now illegal loyalists, leftists, combined with suspect police and armed forces, as well as the smoke from countless cooking and heating fires of the Tehrani millions.

The few pedestrians who passed the prison walls and the huge door that was wrecked and broken off its hinges, and the Green Band guards who lolled there, averted their eyes and quickened their pace. Traffic was light. Another truck filled with Guards and prisoners ground its gears, stopped briefly at the main gate to be inspected. The temporary barricade opened and closed again. Inside the walls was a sudden volley of rifle fire. Outside the Green Bands yawned and stretched.

With the arrival of the sun the call of the muezzins from the minarets began – their voices mostly carried by loudspeakers, the voices on cassette. And wherever the call was heard, the Faithful stopped what they were doing, faced Mecca, knelt for first prayer.

Jared Bakravan had stopped the car just up the road. Now, with his chauffeur and the others, he knelt and prayed. He had spent much of the night trying to reach his most important friends and allies. The news of Paknouri's unlawful arrest and his own unlawful summons had swept through the bazaar. Everyone was instantly enraged, but no one came forward to marshal the thousands to stage a protest or strike or to close the bazaar. He had had plenty of advice: to protest to Khomeini personally, to Prime Minister Bazargan personally, not to appear at the court, to appear but to refuse to answer any questions, to appear and to answer some questions, to appear and answer all questions. 'As God wants,' but no one had volunteered to go with him, not even his great friend and one of the most important lawyers in Tehran who swore it was more important for him to be seeing the High Court judges on his behalf. No one volunteered, except his wife and son and three daughters who prayed on their own prayer mats behind him.

He finished praying and got up shakily. At once the chauffeur began to collect the prayer mats. Jared shivered. This morning he had dressed carefully and wore a heavy coat and suit and astrakhan hat but no jewellery. 'I . . . will walk from here,' he said.

'No, Jared,' his tearful wife began, hardly noticing the distant gunfire. 'Surely it is better to arrive as a leader should arrive. Aren't you the most important bazaari in Tehran? It wouldn't fit your position to walk.'

'Yes, yes, you're right.' He sat in the back of the car. It was a big blue Mercedes, new and well kept. His wife, a plump matron, her expensive coiffure hidden under a chador that also covered her long brown mink, got in beside him and held on to his arm, her makeup streaked by her tears. His son, Meshang, was equally tearful. And his daughters, Sharazad among them, all had chadors. 'Yes . . . yes, you're right. God curse these revolutionaries!'

'Don't worry, Father,' Sharazad said. 'God will protect you – the Revolutionary Guards are only following the Imam's orders and the Imam only follows God's orders.' She sounded so confident but looked so dejected that Bakravan forget to tell her not to refer to Khomeini as Imam.

'Yes,' he told her, 'of course it's all a mistake.'

'Ali Kia swore on the Koran Prime Minister Bazargan would stop all

418

this nonsense,' his wife said. 'He swore he would see him last night. Orders are probably already at the . . . already there.'

Last night he had told Ali Kia that without Paknouri there could be no loan, that if he himself was troubled the bazaar would revolt and all funds stopped to the government, to Khomeini, to the mosques, and to Ali Kia personally. 'Ali won't fail,' he said grimly. 'He daren't. I know too much about them all.'

The car stopped outside the main gate. Idly the Green Bands stared at it. Jared Bakravan summoned his courage. 'I won't be long.'

'God protect you. We'll wait here for you – we'll wait here.' His wife kissed him and so did the others and there were more tears and then he was standing in front of the Green Bands. 'Salaam,' he said. 'I'm – I'm a witness at the court of Mullah Ali'allah Uwari.'

The leader of the Guards took the paper, glanced at it upside down, gave it to one of the others who could read. 'He's from the bazaar,' the other youth said. 'Jared Bakravan.'

The leader shrugged. 'Show him where to go.' The other man led the way through the broken doorway. Bakravan followed, and as the barricade closed behind him much of his confidence vanished. It was sombre and dank in this small open dirt area between the walls and the main building complex. The air stank. Eastward, hundreds of men were crammed together, sitting or lying down, huddled miserably against the cold. Many wore uniforms – officers. Westward, the space was empty. Ahead was a tall iron-barred gate and it swung open to admit him. In the waiting room were dozens of other men, weary frightened men, sitting in rows on benches or standing or just sitting on the floor, some uniformed officers, and he noticed one full colonel. Some of the others he recognised, important businessmen, court favourites, administrators, deputies – but none he knew intimately. A few recognised him. There was a sudden hush.

'Hurry up,' the Guard said irritably. He was a pockmarked youth and he shoved through to the desk, to the harassed clerk who sat there. 'Here's another for Excellency Mullah Uwari.'

The clerk accepted the paper and waved at Bakravan. 'Take a seat – you'll be called when you're needed.'

'Salaam, Excellency,' Bakravan said, shocked at the man's rudeness. 'When will that be? I was to be here just after fir –'

'As God wants. You'll be called when you're needed,' the man said waving him away.

'But I'm Jared Bakravan of the baz –'

'I can read, agha!' the man said more rudely. 'When you're wanted you'll be called! Iran's an Islamic state now, one law for all, not one for the rich another for the people.'

Bakravan was jostled by others being shoved towards the clerk. Weak with rage, he made his way towards the wall. To one side a man was using a latrine bucket that was already overfull, urine spilling on to the floor. Eyes watched Bakravan. A few muttered, 'God's peace on you.' The room smelled vile. His heart was pounding. Someone made a space for him on a bench and, thankfully, he sat down. 'The Blessing of God upon thee, Excellencies.'

'And on thee, agha,' one of them said. 'You're accused?'

'No, no, I'm called as a witness,' he said shocked.

'The Excellency is a witness in front of Mullah Uwari?'

'Yes, yes, I am, Excellency. Who is he?'

'A judge, a revolutionary judge,' the man muttered. He was in his fifties, small, his face more lined than Bakravan's, his hair tufted. He twitched nervously. 'No one here seems to know what's happening, or why they're called, or who this Uwari is, only that he's appointed by the Ayatollah and judges in his name.'

Bakravan looked into the man's eyes and saw the terror and felt even more unnerved. 'The Excellency is also a witness?'

'Yes, yes I am, though why they should call me who was just a manager in the post office I don't know.'

'The post office is very important – they probably need your advice. Do you think we'll be kept waiting long?'

'Insha'Allah. I was called yesterday after fourth prayer and I've been waiting ever since. They kept me here all night. We have to wait until we're called. That's the only toilet,' the man said, pointing at the bucket. 'The worst night I've ever had, terrible. During the night they . . . there was a great deal of firing; the rumour is three more generals and a dozen SAVAK officials were executed.'

'Fifty or sixty,' the man on the other side of him said, coming out of his stupor. 'The number must be nearer sixty. The whole prison's crammed like bedbugs in a village mattress. All the cells're packed. Two days ago the Green Bands broke down the gates, overpowered the guards, and stuffed them in the dungeons, let most prisoners out and then started filling up the cells with locals' – he dropped his voice more – 'all the cells are crammed, much more than in the Shah's time, God curse him for not . . . Every hour the Green Bands're bringing in more people, fedayeen and mujhadin and Tudeh all mixed up with us innocents, the Faithful . . .' He dropped his voice further, the whites of his eyes showing, 'and good people who should never be touched and

. . . when the mob broke the prison open they found electric probes and whips and . . . and torture beds and . . .' Foam collected at the corner of his mouth. '. . . they say the . . . the new jailers are using them and . . . and once you're here, Excellency, they keep you here.' Tears began to well in his little eyes set in a pudgy face. 'The food's terrible, the prison terrible, and . . . and I've got stomach ulcers and that son of a dog of a clerk, he . . . he won't understand I have to have special foods . . .'

There was a commotion on the far side and the door crashed open. Half a dozen Green Bands came into the room and began shoving a passage clear with their rifles. Behind them, other Guards surrounded an air force officer who walked proudly, his head high, his arms tied behind him, his uniform dishevelled, epaulets half torn off. Bakravan gasped. It was Colonel Peshadi, commander of Kowiss Air Base – also a cousin.

Others recognised the colonel for much had been made of the victorious Iranian expedition a few years ago to Dhofar in southern Oman, the successful smashing of the almost lethal Marxist attack by South Yemenis against Oman, and also of Peshadi's personal bravery leading Iranian tanks in a key battle. 'Isn't that the hero of Dhofar?' someone said incredulously.

'Yes that's him . . .'

'God protect us! If they arrest him . . .'

Impatiently one of the Guards pushed Peshadi in the back, trying to force him to hurry up. At once the colonel lashed out at him, though badly hampered by his manacles. 'Son of a dog,' he shouted, his rage bursting, 'I'm going as fast as I can. May your father burn!' The Green Band cursed him back, then shoved the butt of his rifle in the colonel's stomach. The colonel lost his balance and fell – at his mercy. But he still cursed his captors. And he cursed them as they pulled him to his feet, two on each arm, and frog-marched him outside into the western space between the walls. And there he cursed them, and Khomeini, and false mullahs, in all the names of God, then shouted, 'Long live the Shah there is no other God but G—' Bullets silenced him.

In the waiting room there was a ghastly silence. Someone whimpered. An old man began to vomit. Others began whispering, many started to pray, and Bakravan was sure all this was a nightmare, his tired brain rejecting reality. The fetid air was cold but he seemed to be in an oven and suffocating. Am I dying? he asked himself helplessly and pulled the neck of his shirt open. Then someone touched him and he opened his eyes. For a moment he could not focus them nor fathom where he was. He was lying on the floor, the small man anxiously bending over him. 'Are you all right?'

'Yes, yes, I think so,' he said weakly.

'You fainted, Excellency. Are you sure you're all right?'

Hands helped him sit again. Dully he thanked them. His body seemed very heavy, his senses blunted, eyes leaden.

'Listen,' the man with ulcers was whispering, 'this's like the French Revolution, the guillotine and the terror, but how can it happen with Ayatollah Khomeini in charge, that's what I don't understand?'

'He doesn't know,' the small man said, equally fearfully. 'He can't know, isn't he a man of God, pious and the most learned of all ayatollahs . . . ?'

Tiredness surged through him and he leaned against the wall, letting himself drift away.

Later a rough hand shook him awake. 'Bakravan, you're wanted. Come on!'

'Yes, yes,' he mumbled, and groped to his feet, finding it hard to talk, recognising Yusuf, the leader of the Green Bands who had come to the bazaar last night. He stumbled after him, through the others, out of the room and into the corridor, up steps and along another heatless corridor lined with cells, peepholes in the door, past guards and others who eyed him strangely, someone crying nearby. 'Where – where are you taking me?'

'Save your strength, you'll need it.'

Yusuf stopped at a door, opened it, and shoved him through. The room was small, claustrophobic, crammed with men. In the centre was a wooden table with a mullah and four young men seated on either side of him, some papers and a large Koran on the table, a small barred window high up in the wall, a shaft of sunlight against the blue of the sky. Green Bands leaned against the walls.

'Jared Bakravan, the bazaari, the moneylender,' Yusuf said.

The mullah looked up from the list he had been studying. 'Ah, Bakravan. Salaam.'

'Salaam, Excellency,' Bakravan said shakily. The mullah was fortyish, with black eyes and black beard, white turban and threadbare black robes. The men beside him were in their twenties, unshaven or bearded, and poorly dressed, guns propped behind them. 'How–how can I – I help you?' he asked, trying to be calm.

'I am Ali' allah Uwari, appointed by the Revolutionary Komiteh as a judge, and these men are also judges. This court is ruled by the Word of God and the Holy Book.' The mullah's voice was harsh and his accent Qazvini. 'You know this Paknouri, known as Miser Paknouri?'

'Yes, but may I say, Excellency, according to our Constitution and to ancient bazaar law th –'

'Better you answer the question,' one of the youths interrupted, 'we've no time to waste on speeches! Do you know him or don't you?'

'Yes, yes, of cour –'

'Excellency Uwari,' Yusuf interrupted from the doorway. 'Please, who do you want next?'

'Paknouri, then . . .' the mullah squinted at the list of names. 'Then Police Sergeant Jufrudi.'

One of the others sitting at the tables said, 'That dog was judged by our other revolutionary court last night and shot this morning.'

'As God wills.' The mullah drew a line through the name. All the names above had lines through them. 'Then bring Hassan Turlak – from cell 573.'

Bakravan almost cried out. Turlak was a highly respected journalist and writer, half Iranian – half Afghani, a courageous and zealous critic of the Shah's regime who had even spent some years in jail because of his opposition.

The unshaven young man beside the mullah irritably scratched at the skin blemishes on his face. 'Who's Turlak, Excellency?'

The mullah read from the list. 'Newspaper reporter.'

'It's a waste of time seeing him – of course he's guilty,' another said. 'Wasn't he the one who claimed the Word could be changed, that the words of the Prophet weren't correct for today? He's guilty, of course he's guilty.'

'As God wills.' The mullah turned his attention to Bakravan. 'Paknouri. Did he ever practise usury?'

Bakravan dragged his mind off Turlak. ' No, never, and he w –'

'Did he lend money at interest?'

Bakravan's stomach churned. He saw the cold black eyes and tried hard to get his brain working. 'Yes, but in a modern society int –'.

'Isn't it written clearly in the Holy Koran that lending money at interest is usury and against the laws of God?'

'Yes. Usury in against the laws of God but in modern soc –'

'The holy Koran is blemishless. The Word is clear and for ever. Usury is usury. The Law is the Law.' The mullah's eyes flattened. 'Do you uphold the Law?'

'Yes, yes, Excellency, of course, of course I do.'

'Do you practise the Five Pillars of Islam?' These were obligatory to

423

all Muslims: the saying of the Shahada; ritual prayer five times a day; the voluntary giving of Zakat, a year tax, a tenth part; fasting from dawn to dusk during the holy month of Ramadan; and last, making the Hajj, the ritual journey to Mecca once in a lifetime.

'Yes, yes, I do, except – except the last. I – I haven't yet made the pilgrimage to Mecca – not yet.'

'Why not?' the young man with spots on his face asked. 'You have more money than a dung heap has flies. With your money you could go in any air machine, any! Why not?'

'It's – It's my health,' Bakravan said, keeping his eyes down and praying the lie sounded convincing. 'My – my heart is weak.'

'When were you last in the mosque?' the mullah said.

'On Friday, last Friday, at the mosque in the bazaar,' he said. It was true that he was there, though not to pray but to have a business conference.

'This Paknouri, he practises the Five Pillars as a true Believer?' one of the youths asked.

'I – I believe so.'

'It's well known he didn't, well known he was a Shah supporter. Eh?'

'He was a patriot, a patriot who financially supported the revolution and supported Ayatollah Khomeini, the Blessings of God upon him, financially supported the mullahs over the years an –'

'But he spoke American and worked for Americans and the Shah, helping them exploit and steal our wealth from the soil, didn't he?'

'He, he was a patriot who worked with the foreigners for the good of Iran.'

'When the Satan Shah illegally formed a party, Paknouri joined it, served the Shah as a deputy in the Majlis, didn't he?' the mullah asked.

'He was a deputy, yes,' Bakravan replied. 'But he worked for the rev –'

'And as a deputy he voted for the Shah's so-called White Revolution that took away land from the mosques, decreed equality of women, implanted civil courts and state education against the dictates of the Holy Koran . . .'

Of course he voted for it, Bakravan wanted to scream, the sweat trickling down his face and back. Of course we all voted for it! Didn't the people vote for it overwhelmingly and even many ayatollahs and mullahs? Didn't the Shah control the government, the police, the gendarmerie, SAVAK, the armed forces and own most of the land? The Shah was ultimate power! Curse the Shah, he thought, beside himself with rage, curse him and his White Revolution of '63 that started the rot, sent the mullahs mad, and continues to plague us, all his 'modern reforms' that were directly responsible for the rise of the then obscure Ayatollah Khomeini to prominence. Didn't we bazaaris warns the Shah's advisers a thousand times! As if any of the reforms mattered. As if any of the reforms w –

'Yes or no?'

He was started out of his reverie and cursed himself. Concentrate! he thought in panic. This vile son of a leprous dog is trying to trap you! What did he ask? Be careful – for your own life be careful! Ah, yes, the White Revolution! 'Emir Pak –'

'In the Name of God, yes or no!' the mullah overrode him harshly.

'He – yes – yes, he voted for the, the White Revolution when he was a deputy in the Majlis. Yes, yes he did.'

The mullah sighed and the youths shifted in their seat. One yawned, and scratched his groin, absently playing with himself.

'You are a deputy?'

'No – no I resigned when Ayatollah Khomeini ordered it. Th –'

'You mean when Imam Khomeini, the *Imam* ordered it?'

'Yes, yes,' Bakravan said flustered. 'I resigned, the, er, the moment the Imam ordered it, I – I resigned at once,' he said, and did not add, We all resigned at Paknouri's suggestion when it was safe and certain the Shah had decided to leave and to pass over power to the moderate and rational Prime Minister Bakhtiar, but not for power to be usurped by Khomeini, he wanted to shriek, that was never the plan! God curse the Americans who sold us out, the generals who sold us out, the Shah who's responsible! 'Everyone knows – knows how I supported the Imam, may he live for ever.'

'Yes, the Blessings of God on him,' the mullah echoed with the others. 'But you, Jared Bakravan of the bazaar. Have you ever practised usury?'

'Never,' Bakravan said at once, believing it, though fear racked him. I've loaned money all my life but the interest's always been fair and reasonable, never usury, he thought, never. And all the times I acted as adviser to various people and ministers, arranging loans, private and public, transferring funds out of Iran, private and public, making money, a great deal of money, that was good business and not against the law. 'I opposed the – I opposed the White Revolution and the Shah, wherever I could – it was well known that I opp –'

'The Shah committed crimes against God, against Islam, against the Holy Koran, against the Imam – God protect him – against the Shi'a faith. All those who helped him are equally guilty.' The mullah's eyes

425

were relentless. 'What crimes have you committed against God and the Word of God?'

'None,' he cried out, almost at the limit. 'In God's Name I swear, none!'

The door swung open. Yusuf came into the room with Paknouri. Bakravan almost fainted again. Paknouri's hands were manacled behind him. Muck and urine stained his trousers and vomit was on the front of his coat. His head was twitching uncontrollably, his hair matted and filthy, his mind gone. When he saw Bakravan, his face twisted into a grimace. 'Ah, Jared, Jared, old friend and colleague, Excellency, have you come to join us all in hell?' He shrieked with laughter for a moment. 'It's not like I imagined, the devils haven't arrived yet, nor the boiling oil or flames but there's no air and just stink and you press against others and you can't lie down or sit so you stand and then the screaming begins again and the firing and, all the time you're as an egg, packed like a caviar egg but but but—' The half-incoherent raving stopped as he saw the mullah. Terror swamped him. 'Are you . . . are you God?'

'Paknouri,' the mullah said gently, 'you are charged with crimes against God. This witness against you says y –'

'Yes, yes, I've crimed against God, I'm guilty,' Paknouri screamed. 'Why else am I in hell?' He fell on his knees in a flood of tears, raving. 'There is no God but God is no God there is no God and Mohammed is His prophet of no God and . . .' Abruptly he stopped. His face was even more twisted when he looked up. 'I'm God – you're Satan!'

One of the youths broke the silence. 'He's a blasphemer. He's possessed by Satan. He declared himself guilty. As God wants.'

All the others nodded agreement. The mullah said, 'As God wants.' He motioned to a Green Band who pulled Paknouri to his feet and took him out and looked at Bakravan who stared after his friend, horrified how fast – just overnight – he had been destroyed. 'Now, Bakravan, you w –'

'I've got this Turlak waiting outside,' Yusuf said, interrupting him.

'Good,' the mullah said. Then he turned his eyes back on to Bakravan and Bakravan knew he was as lost as his friend Paknouri was lost and that the sentence would be the same. The blood was rushing in his ears. He saw the lips of the mullah moving, then they stopped and everyone was looking at him. 'Please?' he asked numbly. 'I – I'm sorry, I didn't hear what you – what you said.'

'You can leave. For the moment. Do God's work.' Impatiently the mullah glanced at one of the Green Bands, a tallish, ugly man. 'Ahmed, take him out!' Then to Yusuf, 'After Turlak, Police Captain Mo-hammed Dezi, cell 917 . . .'

Bakravan felt a tug on his arm and turned and went out. In the corridor he almost fell, but Ahmed caught him and, strangely kind, propped him against the wall.

'Catch your breath, Excellency,' he said.

'I'm – I'm free to go?'

'I'm certainly as surprised as you, agha,' the man said. 'Before God and the Prophet I'm as surprised as you, you're the first to be let go today, witness or accused.'

'I – is there – is there any water?'

'Not here. There's plenty outside. Best you leave.' Ahmed dropped his voice even more. 'Best to leave, eh? Lean on my arm.'

Thankfully, Bakravan held on to him, hardly breathing. Slowly they went back the way he had come. He hardly noticed the other guards and prisoners and witnesses. In the corridor that led to the waiting room, Ahmed shouldered the way through a side door, out into the western space. The firing squad was there, three men tied to posts in front of them. One post was empty. Bakravan's bowels and bladder emptied of their own volition.

'Hurry up, Ahmed!' the man in charge said irritably.

'As God wants,' Ahmed said. Happily, he half-carried Bakravan to the empty post that was next to Paknouri who was raving, lost in his own hell. 'So you're not to escape after all. That's right, we all heard your lies, lies before God. We all know you, know your ways, know your lack of Godliness, how you even tried to buy your way to heaven with gifts to the Imam, God protect him. Where did you get all that money if not through usury and theft?'

The volley was not accurate. The man in charge leisurely used a revolver to silence one of the condemned, then Bakravan. 'I wouldn't have recognised him,' the man said shortly. 'It shows how foul and what liars newspapers are.'

'This isn't Hassan Turlak,' Ahmed said, 'he comes next.'

The man stared at him. 'Then who's this one?'

'A bazaari,' Ahmed said. 'Bazaaris are usurers and godless. I know. For years I worked there for Farazan, collecting night soil like my father before me, until I became a bricklayer with Yusuf. But this one . . .' He belched. 'He was the richest usurer. I don't remember much about him except how rich he was, but I remember everything about his women; he never curbed or taught his women who never wore chador, flaunting themselves. I remember everything about his devil daughter

427

who'd visit the Street of the Moneylenders from time to time, half naked, skin like fresh cream, her hair flowing, breasts moving, buttocks inviting – the one called Sharazad who looks like the promised houri must look. I remember everything about her and how I cursed her for putting evil in my head, maddening me, how we all did – for tempting us.' He scratched his scrotum, feeling himself hardening. God curse her and all women who disobey God's law and create evil thoughts in us against the Word of God. Oh, God, let me penetrate her or make me a martyr and go straight to heaven and do it there. 'He was guilty of every crime,' he said, turning away.

'But – but was he condemned?' the man in charge of the firing squad called out after him.

'God condemned him, of course He did. The post was waiting and you told me to hurry. It was the Will of God. God is Great, God is Great. Now I will fetch Turlak, the blasphemer.' Ahmed shrugged. 'It was the Will of God.'

IRAN

BANDAR-E
DELAM

USSR
Khvoy
Tabriz
Mount
Sabalan
Caspian Sea
Bandar-e Pahlavi
Qazvin
Tehran
Sadzevar
Meshed
AFGHANISTAN
Baghdad
Dez Dam
Isfahan
IRAQ
Abadan
KUWAIT
Kharg
Island
Kowiss
PAKISTAN
Zagros
SAUDI ARABIA
Jellet
Lengeh
Persian Gulf
Siri
Strait of Hormuz
BAHRAIN
QATAR
Al Shargaz
Gulf of Oman
UAE

CHAPTER

28

Near Bandar-e Delam: 11:58 A.M. It was the time of noon prayer and the ancient, rickety, overladen bus stopped on the shoulder of the road. Obediently, following the lead of a mullah who was also a passenger, all Muslims disembarked, spread their prayer mats and now were committing their souls to God. Except for the Indian Hindu family who were afraid of losing their seats, most of the other non-Muslim passengers had also disembarked – Tom Lochart among them – glad for the opportunity to stretch their legs or to relieve themselves. Christian Armenians, Oriental Jews, a nomadic Kash'kai couple who, though Muslim, were precluded by ancient custom from the need of the noonday prayer, or their women from the veil or chador, two Japanese, some Christian Arabs – all of them aware of the lone European.

The day was warm, hazy, and humid from the nearby waters of the Gulf. Tom Lochart leaned tiredly against the bonnet that was steaming, the engine overheated, head aching, joints aching, muscles aching from his forced march out from the Dez Dam – now almost two

429

hundred miles to the north – and the cramped, bone-grinding, noisy discomfort of the bus. All the way from Ahwaz where he had managed to talk himself past Green Bands and on to the bus, he had been squeezed into a seat with barely enough room for two, let alone three men, one of them a young Green Band who cradled his M14 along with his child for his pregnant wife who stood in the narrow corridor crammed against thirty others in space for fifteen. Every seat was equally packed with men, women and children of all ages. The air fetid, voices babbling in a multitude of tongues. Overhead and underfoot, bags and bundles and cases, crates packed with vegetables or half-dead chickens, a small undernourished hobbled goat or two – the luggage racks outside on the roof equally laden.

But I'm damned lucky to be here, he thought, his misery returning, half listening to the lilting chant of the Shahada.

Yesterday, near sunset, when he had heard the 212 take off from Dez, he had come out from under the little wharf, blessing God for his escape. The water had been very cold and he was trembling, but he had picked up the automatic, checked the action and then gone up to the house. It was open. There was food and drink in the refrigerator that still hummed nicely, powered by a generator. It was warm inside the house. He took off his clothes and dried them over a heater, cursing Valik and Seladi and consigning them to hell. 'Sonsofbitches! What the hell'd I do to them but save their goddam necks?'

The warmth and the luxury of the house were tempting. His tiredness ached him. Last night at Isfahan had been almost sleepless. I could sleep and leave at dawn, he thought. I've a compass and I know the way more or less: skirt the airfield Ali Abbasi mentioned, then head due east to pick up the main Kermanshah–Ahwaz–Abandan road. Should be no trouble to get a bus or hitch a ride. Or I could go now – the moon'll light my way and then I won't be trapped here if the air base has sent a patrol – Ali was just as nervous about that as Seladi and we could easily have been spotted. Easily. But either way, when you get stopped, what's your story?

He thought about that while he fixed himself a brandy and soda and some food. Valik and the others had opened two half-kilo tins of the best beluga grey caviar and had left them carelessly on the sitting room table, still partially full. He ate it with relish.

The forced march over the mountains had been bad but not as bad as he had expected. Just after dawn he had come down to the main Kermanshah–Ahwaz–Abadan road. Almost at once he had been given a ride by some Korean construction workers evacuating the steel mill they were building under contract at Kermanshah – it was almost custom that expats helped expats on the road. They were heading for Abadan Airport where they had been told transport to fly them back to Korea would be waiting for them. 'Much fighting at Kermanshah,' they had told him in halting English. 'Everyone guns. Iranians killing each other. All mad, barbarians – worse than Japanese.' They had dropped him off at the Ahwaz bus terminal. Miraculously he had managed to talk his way on to the next bus that went past Bandar-e Delam.

Yes. But now what? Gloomily he remembered how, after throwing the empty caviar tins into the garbage, on reflection he had retrieved them and buried them, then gone back and wiped the glass that he had used and even the door handle. You need your head examined, as if they'd check for fingerprints! Yes, but at the time I thought it best not to leave traces I'd been there.

You're crazy! You're on the flight clearance at Tehran, there's your unauthorised pickup of Valik and his family, the breakout from Isfahan, and flying 'enemies of the State and helping them escape' to account for – whether it's from SAVAK or Khomeini! And how does S-G or McIver account for a missing Iranian helicopter that ends up in Kuwait or Baghdad or where the hell ever that's bound to be reported?

What a goddam mess!

Yes. Then there's Sharazad . . .

'Don't worry, agha,' broke into his thoughts, 'we're all in God's hands.'

It was the mullah and he was smiling up at him. He was a youngish man, bearded, and he had joined the bus at Ahwaz with his wife and three children. Over his shoulder was a rifle. 'The driver says you speak Farsi and that you're from Canada and a person of the Book?'

'Yes, yes, I am, agha,' Lochart replied, collecting his wits. He saw that prayer had finished and now everyone crowded the bus doorway.

'Then you too will go to heaven as the Prophet promised if you are found worthy, though not to our part.' The mullah smiled shyly. 'Iran will be the first real Islamic state in the world since the time of the Prophet.' Again the shy smile. 'You're – you're the first person of the Book that I've met or spoken to. You learned to speak Farsi at school.'

'I went to school, Excellency, but mostly I had private teachers.' Lochart picked up his flight bag that he had taken off with him for safety and moved to join the queue. His own seat was already taken. Beside the road several passengers were relieving themselves or defecating, men, women and children.

'And the Excellency works in the oil business?' The mullah moved into line beside him, and at once people stepped aside to let him take preference. Inside the bus passengers were already quarrelling, a few shouting to the driver to hurry.

'Yes, for your great IranOil,' Lochart said, very conscious that those nearby were listening also, jostling to get closer to hear better. Not long to go now, he thought, the airport can't be more than a few miles ahead. Just before noon he had caught a glimpse of a 212 heading in from the Gulf. She was too far away to see if she was civilian or military but she was heading in the general direction of the airport. It'll be great to see Rudi and the others, to sleep and . . .

'The driver says you were on a holiday near Kermanshah?'

'In Luristan, south of Kermanshah.' Lochart concentrated. He retold the story he had decided upon, the same that he had told the ticket seller at Ahwaz, and the Green Bands, who also wanted to know who he was and why he was in Ahwaz. 'I was on a hiking holiday north of Luristan, in the mountains, and got trapped there in a village by a snowfall – for a week. You are going to Shiraz?' This was the final destination of the bus.

'Shiraz is where my mosque is and the place of my birth. Come, we will sit together.' The mullah took the nearest seat beside an old man, put one of his children on his knee, cradled his gun, and left Lochart just enough room on the aisle. Reluctantly Lochart obeyed, not wanting to sit beside a talkative and inquisitive mullah, but at the same time thankful for a place. The bus was filling up quickly. People shoved past, trying to get space or to move further back. 'Your country Canada borders the Great Satan, does it not?'

'Canada and America have common borders,' Lochart said, his bile rising. 'The vast majority of Americans are people of the Book.'

'Ah, yes, but many are Jews and Zionists, and Jews and Zionists and Christians are against Islam, the enemy of Islam, and therefore against God. Isn't it true that Jews and Zionists rule the Great Satan?'

'If you mean America, no, agha, no it is not.'

'But if the Imam says it, it is so.' The mullah was quite confident and gentle and quoted from the Koran, ' "For God is angry with them, and in torment shall they abide for ever." ' Then he added, 'If the Im –'

There was a flurry in the back of the bus, and they turned to see one of the Iranians angrily tug the turbaned Indian out of his seat to take his place. The Indian forced a smile and stayed standing. By custom it was always the first one seated who had the right to stay seated unharmed. The torrent of voices began again and now another

432

man, jammed in the aisle, began cursing all foreigners loudly. He was roughly dressed, armed, and stood alongside the two Japanese who were crammed into a seat with a ragged old Kurd and glared down at them.

'Why should foreigner Infidels sit while we stand? With the Help of God, we're no longer lackeys of Infidels!' the man said even more angrily and jerked his thumb at them. 'Move!'

Neither Japanese moved. One of them took off his glasses and smiled at the man. The man hesitated, began to bluster but thought better of it, then turned and shouted at the driver to hurry up. Just before the Japanese put back his glasses he caught Lochart's eye, nodded and smiled.

Lochart smiled back. At Ahwaz, while they were all pushing their way on to the bus, one of the Japanese had said to Lochart in passable English, 'Follow us, sir, at rush hour Tokyo buses and trains are much worse.' With a great display of politeness the two quickly cleared a path, found him a seat and places at the back for themselves. During the noon stop they had chatted briefly, telling him they were engineers coming back from leave, heading for Iran-Toda.

'Ah,' the mullah said happily, seeing the driver squeeze back into his seat, 'now we continue, thanks be to God.'

With a great flourish the driver started the engine and the bus lumbered on its way. 'Next stop Bandar-e Delam,' he called out. 'God willing.'

'God willing.' The mullah was very content. Once more he turned his attention to Lochart and shouted above the noise, 'Agha, you were saying about the Great Satan?'

Lochart had his eyes closed and he pretended not to hear.

The mullah touched him. 'You were saying, agha, about the Great Satan?'

'I was saying nothing, agha.'

'What? I didn't hear you.'

Lochart kept his face polite, knowing the danger he was in, and said louder, 'I was saying nothing, agha. Travelling is tiring, isn't it?' He closed his eyes again. 'I think I will sleep a little.'

'Why say nothing?' a young man standing alongside in the aisle shouted down at him over the grinding engine. 'America is responsible for all our troubles. If it wasn't for America, there'd be peace in the whole world!'

Grimly Lochart kept his eyes closed and tried to shut his ears, knowing he was near snapping – half of him wishing he had the automatic in his pocket, the other half thankful it was in his bag. He felt the mullah shake him.

'Before you sleep, agha, don't you agree the world would be much better without the American evil?'

Lochart fought down his anger and just kept his eyes closed. Another shake, much rougher, this time from the aisle, and the man shouted in his ear, 'Answer His Excellency!'

He was suddenly sick to death of all the anti-American propaganda and lies continually fed to them. White with rage, he opened his eyes and shoved the man's hand away and exploded in English. 'Well, I'll tell you, mullah, you'd better thank God America exists because without it there'd be goddam nothing in the world and we'd all be in a goddam Gulag or under the goddam ground, you, me, this jerk and even Khomeini!'

'What?'

He saw the mullah gaping at him – and realised he had been speaking English. Taking a tight rein to his mouth, he said in Farsi, knowing there was no way he could explain logically, 'I was quoting the Holy Bible in English,' he said, making it up. 'I was quoting Abraham when he was very angry. Didn't Abraham say: "Evil stalks the earth in many guises – it is the duty of the Believer to . . . to guard against evil, any evil – all evil!" Isn't it?'

The mullah was looking at him strangely and quoted from the Koran: ' "And God said to Abraham, I will make you a leader to mankind, and Abraham said, of my offspring also! God said, My convenant embraceth not the evil doers." '

'I agree,' Lochart said. 'And now I must think about God – the One God, the God of Abraham and Moses and Jesus and Mohammed, whose Name be praised!' Lochart closed his eyes. His heart was pounding. Any moment he expected the angry youth's rifle butt in his face or the mullah to shout for the bus to stop. He expected no mercy. But the moment passed and they left him to his supposed prayers.

The mullah sighed, lack of space pressing him against this Infidel. I wonder how an Infidel prays, he was thinking. What does he say to God – even a person of the Book? How pitiful they are!

At Bandar-e Delam Airport: 12:32 P.M. The Iranian Air Force car swung past the sleepy guards on the gate, its green Khomeini flag fluttering, and pulled up in a swirl of dust outside Rudi's office trailer. Two smartly uniformed officers got out. With them were three Green Bands.

Rudi Lutz went out to meet the officers – a major and a captain. When he recognised the captain, his face lit up, 'Hello, Hushang. I've been wondering how you were do –'

The older officer interrupted him angrily. 'I'm Major Qazani, Air Force Intelligence. What's an Iranian chopper under your control doing trying to leave Iranian airspace, repeatedly disobeying instructions from an intercept, and totally disregarding orders from ground control?'

Rudi stared at them blankly. 'There's only one of my choppers airborne, and she's on a CASEVAC requested by Abadan radar control.'

'What's her registration?'

'EP-HXX. What's this all about?'

'That's what I want to know.' Major Qazani walked past him into the trailer and sat down. His Green Bands waited. 'Come on!' the major said irritably. 'Sit down, Captain Lutz.'

Rudi hesitated, then sat at his desk. A few bullet holes in the wall let in light behind him. The Green Bands and the other officer came in and shut the door.

'What's HXX? A 206 or 212?' the major asked.

'It's a 206. What's th –'

'How many 212s have you here?'

'Two. HXX and HGC. Abadan radar cleared HXX on a CASEVAC yesterday to Kowiss with wounded from the fedayeen attack at dawn yester –'

'Yes, we heard about that. And that you helped the Guards blow them to the hell they deserve, for which many thanks. Is EP-HBC an S-G 212 registration?'

Rudi hesitated. 'I don't know offhand, Major. I don't have records here of all our 212s, but I could find out – if I can raise our base in Kowiss. Radio's been out for a day. Now, please, I'll help all I can, but what's this about?'

Major Qazani lit a cigarette, offered one to Rudi who shook his head. 'It's about a 212, EP-HBC, we believe an S-G-operated 212, with an unknown number of persons aboard that went over the Iraqi border just before sunset last night – with no clearances, disregarding, as I've said, disregarding explicit radio orders to land.'

'I don't know anything about it.' Rudi's mind was racing. Got to be someone making an escape, he thought. 'She's not our bird. We can't even start engines without Abadan Control's okay. That's SOP.'

'How would you explain HBC then?'

'She could be a Guerney aircraft taking some of their personnel away, or Bell, or any one of the other chopper companies. It's been hard, sometimes impossible, to file a flight plan recently. You know, how, er, how fluid radar's been the last few weeks.'

'Fluid's not a good word,' Captain Hushang Abbasi said. He was a lithe, very handsome man with a clipped moustache and dark glasses, and wore wings on his uniform. All of last year he had been based at Kharg where he and Rudi had got to know each other. 'And if she was an S-G aircraft?'

'Then there'll be a correct explanation.' Rudi was glad that Hushang had weathered the revolution – particularly as he had always been an outspoken critic of mullahs meddling in government. 'You're sure she was illegal?'

'I'm sure legal airplanes have clearances, legal airplanes obey air regulations, and legal airplanes don't take evading action and rush for the border,' Hushang said. 'And I'm almost sure I saw the S-G emblem on my first pass, Rudi.'

Rudi's eyes narrowed. Hushang was a very good pilot. 'You were flying the intercept?'

'I led the flight that scrambled.'

The silence grew in the trailer. 'Do you mind if I open a window, Major? The smoke – it gives me a headache.'

The major said irritably, 'If HBC is an S-G chopper someone's going to have more than a headache.'

Rudi opened the window. HBC sounds like one of our registrations. What the hell's going wrong? We seem to be under a spell the last few days – first it was that psychopath Zataki and the murder of our mechanic, then poor old Kyabi, then the God-cursed leftist fedayeen dawn attack yesterday, damn nearly killing us and wounding Jon Tyrer – Christ, I hope Jon's all right – and now more trouble!

He sat down again, feeling very weary. 'Best I can do is to ask.'

'How far north do you operate?' the major asked.

'Normally? Ahwaz. Dezful'd be about our extreme ra—' The base phone intercom rang. He picked it up and missed the look between the two officers. 'Hello?'

It was Fowler Joines, his chief mechanic. 'You okay?'

'Yes. Thanks. No sweat.'

'Shout if you need help, old sport, and we'll all come running.' The phone clicked off.

He turned back to the major feeling better. Since he had stood up to Zataki, all of his men and pilots had treated him like he was Laird

Gavallan himself. And since yesterday when the fedayeen were beaten off, even the komiteh Green Bands had been deferential – all except Base Manager Yemeni who was still trying to give him a hard time. 'Dezful's extreme range – one way. Once we flew . . .' He stopped. He had been going to say, Once we flew our area manager to Kermanshah. But then the memory of the brutal and senseless way Boss Kyabi had been murdered welled up and again he was sickened.

He saw the major and Hushang staring at him. 'Sorry, I was going to say, Major, once we flew a charter to Kermanshah. With refuelling, as you know, we're mobile.'

'Yes, Captain Lutz, yes, we know.' The major stubbed out his cigarette and lit another. 'Prime Minister Bazargan, with of course the prior approval of Ayatollah Khomeini,' he added cautiously, not trusting Abbasi or the Green Bands who also might secretly understand English, 'has issued strict orders about all aircraft in Iran, particularly choppers. We'll call Kowiss now.'

They went into the radio room. At once Yemeni protested that he could not approve the call without permission of the local komiteh, of which he had appointed himself a member as the only one who could read or write. One of the Green Bands went to fetch them but the major overrode Yemeni and got his way. Kowiss did not answer their calls.

'As God wants. It'll be better after dark, agha,' radio operator Jahan said in Farsi.

'Yes, thank you,' the major said.

'What is it you need, agha?' Yemeni said rudely, hating the encroachment, the Shah uniforms almost whipping him into a frenzy. 'I will get it for you!'

'I don't need you for anything, son of a dog,' the major shouted angrily, everyone jumped, and Yemeni was paralysed. 'If you give me trouble I'll haul you in front of our Tribunal for interfering with the work of the prime minister and Khomeini himself! Get out!'

Yemeni fled. The Green Bands laughed and one of them said, 'Shall I beat his head in for you, agha?'

'No, no, thank you. He's no more important than a fly eating a camel's turd.' Major Qazani puffed his cigarette, surrounded with smoke, and glanced at Rudi thoughtfully. The news of how this German had saved Zataki, the most important Revolutionary Guard commander in this area, had flooded their air base.

He got up and went to the window. Beyond he could see his car and the green Khomeini flag and the Green Bands lolling around. Scum, he thought. Sons of dogs, all of them. We didn't get rid of American restraints and influence and help sack the Shah to give over control of our lives and beautiful planes to lice-covered mullahs, however brave some of them may be. 'You wait here, Hushang. I'll leave two Guards with you,' he said. 'Wait here and make the call with him. I'll send the car back for you.'

'Yes, sir.'

The major looked at Rudi, his eyes hard. In English he said: 'I want to know if HBC's an S-G chopper, where it was based, how it got to this area, and who was aboard.' He gave the necessary orders and left in a swirl of dust.

Hushang sent the guards to tell the others what was going on. Now the two of them were alone. 'So,' he said, and smiled and held out his hand. 'I'm pleased to see you, Rudi.'

'Me too.' They shook hands warmly. 'I wondered how you, er, how you fared.'

Hushang laughed. 'You mean if I'd been liquidated? Oh, don't believe all those stories, Rudi. No. Everything's great. When I left Kharg I spent a little time in Doshan Tappeh, then came down to Abadan Air Base.'

Rudi waited. 'And then?'

'And then?' Hushang thought a moment. 'And then, when His Im – when the Shah left Iran, our base commander paraded us, everyone, and told us he considered our oath of allegiance cancelled. All of us in the forces swore allegiance to the Shah personally but when he left, our oaths seemed repudiated somehow. Our commander asked us all to choose what we wanted to do, officers and men, to stay or to leave – but, he said finally, "on this base the transfer of power to the new legal government will be orderly". We were given twelve hours to decide.' Hushang frowned. 'A few left – they were mostly senior officers. What would you have done, Rudi?'

'Stayed. Of course, *Heimat ist immer Heimat.*'

'What?'

'Your homeland is always your homeland.'

'Ah, yes. Yes, that's what I thought.' A shadow went over Hushang. 'After we had all chosen, our commander called in Ayatollah Ahwazi, our chief ayatollah, and formally made the transfer of power. Then he shot himself. He left a note saying, "All my life I have served Mohammed Reza Shah, as my father served Reza Shah, his father. I cannot serve mullahs or politicians, or live with the stench of betrayal that pervades the land." '

Rudi hesitated. 'He meant the Americans?'

438

'The major thinks he meant the generals. Some of us think he meant . . . the betrayal of Islam.'

'By Khomeini?' Rudi saw Hushang looking at him, brown eyes guileless, chiselled face, and for a second Rudi had the uneasy feeling that this was no longer his friend, but someone wearing the same face. Someone who might be ready to trap him. Trap him into what?

'To think that would be treason. Wouldn't it,' Hushang said. It was a statement, not a question, and another shaft of caution went through Rudi. 'I'm frightened for Iran, Rudi. We're so exposed, so valuable, to either superpower, and hated and envied by so many nearby.'

'Ah, but your forces are the biggest and best equipped around – you're the power in the Gulf.' He went to the small built-in-refrigerator. 'How about splitting an ice-cold bottle of beer?'

'No thanks.'

Usually they would share one with relish. 'You on a diet?' Rudi asked.

The other shook his head, smiled strangely. 'No. I've quit. It's my gift to the new regime.'

'Then we'll have tea, like old times,' Rudi said without missing a beat, went into the kitchen, and put on the kettle. But he was thinking, Hushang really has changed. But then, if you were him, you'd've changed too, his world's upside down – like West Germany and East Germany but not as bad as that. 'How's Ali?' he asked. Ali was Hushang's adored elder brother, a helicopter pilot, whom Rudi had never met but Hushang was always talking about, laughing about his legendary adventures and conquests in Tehran, Paris and Rome in the old days – the good old days, he thought emphatically.

'Ali the Great's fine too,' Hushang said with a delighted smile. Just before the Shah had left they had secretly discussed their options and had agreed, whatever happened, they would stay: 'We're still the elite force, we'll still have leaves in Europe!' He beamed, so proud of him, not envious of his successes but wishing he could be a tenth as successful. 'But he'll have to slow down now – at least he will in Iran.'

The kettle began boiling. Rudi made the tea. 'Mind if I ask you about HBC?' He glanced through the doorway into the other room. His friend was watching him. 'That all right?'

'What do you want to know?'

'What happened?'

After a pause Hushang said, 'I was leader of the duty flight. We were scrambled and told to intercept a helicopter that had been spotted sneaking through our area. It turned out to be a civilian, ducking in and

439

out of the valleys around Dezful. She wouldn't answer radio calls in Farsi or in English. We waited, tailing her. Once she was out in the open I buzzed her, that's when I thought I recognised the S-G emblem. But she completely disregarded me, just turned from the border and poured on the coals. My wingman buzzed her but she took more evading action.'

Hushang's eyes narrowed as he remembered the excitement that had possessed him, hunter and hunted, never having hunted before, his ears filled with the sweet scream of his jets, with static and with orders: 'Arm missiles!' Hands and fingers obeying.

Pressing the trigger, the rocket missing first time as the chopper pirouetted, darting this way and that, nimble as a dragonfly, his wingman also firing and missing by a fraction – the missiles not heat-seekers. Another miss. Now she was over the border. Over the border and safe but not safe from me, from justice, so going in with cannons blazing, impression of faces at the windows, seeing her dissolve into a ball of fire and when I came out of the G-wrenching turn to look again she had vanished. Only a puff of smoke remained. And the pleasure.

'I plastered her,' he said. 'Blew her out of the sky.'

Rudi turned away to hide his shock. He had presumed HBC had escaped – whoever was flying. 'There were no . . . no survivors?'

'No, Rudi. She exploded,' Hushang said, wanting to keep his voice calm. And professional. 'It was . . . it was my first kill – I never thought it would be so difficult.'

Not much of a contest, Rudi thought, enraged and disgusted. Missiles and cannons against nothing, but I suppose orders are orders and HBC was in the wrong whoever flew her, whoever was aboard. She should have stopped – I would have stopped. Would I? If I'd been the fighter pilot and this was Germany and the chopper was fleeing towards the enemy-controlled border with God knows what aboard and I was on orders to . . . Wait a minute, did Hushang do it in Iraqi airspace? Well, I'm not going to ask him. As sure as God doesn't speak to Khomeini, Hushang wouldn't tell me if he did – I wouldn't.

Gloomily he filled the teapot from the kettle and was reminded of the other one from his childhood, then glanced out of the window. An old bus was stopping on the road outside the airport perimeter. He saw the tall man get out. For a moment he did not recognise him. Then, with a whoop of delight, he did, and said on the run, 'Excuse me a moment . . .'

They met at the gate, Green Bands watching curiously. 'Tom! *Wie geht's?'* How are you? 'What the hell're you doing here? Why didn't you tell us you were coming? How's Zagros and Jean-Luc?' He was so happy he did not notice Lochart's fatigue, or the state of his clothes – dusty, torn, and travel stained.

'Lot to tell, Rudi,' Lochart said. 'Lot to tell, but I'm bushed. I badly need some tea . . . and some sleep. Okay?'

'Of course.' Rudi beamed at him. 'Of course. Come on, and I'll open my last, secret bottle of whisky I even pretend to myself I haven't got and we'll h—' All at once he noticed the state of his friend and his smile left him. 'What the hell's happened to you? You look like you've been dragged through a bush backward.' He saw Lochart glance impercept- ibly at the guards who stood nearby, listening.

'Nothing, Rudi, nothing at all. First a wash, eh!' he said.

'Sure – yes, of course. You, er, you can use my trailer.' Very perturbed he walked alongside Lochart, heading into the airport. He had never seen him so old and so slow. *He looks shaken up, almost – almost as though he's had an emergency and pranged badly . . .*

Down by the hangar he saw Yemeni peering at them out of the office windows. Fowler Joines and the other mechanic had stopped work and were beginning to stroll over. Then, down at the far end of the encampment, he saw Hushang come out on to the step of his trailer and Rudi's head seemed to explode. 'Oh, Christ,' he gasped. 'Not HBC?'

Lochart jerked to a stop, all colour out of his face. 'How the hell you know about her?'

'But he said HBC was plastered – blown out of the skies! How'd you get out? How?'

'Plastered?' Lochart was in shock. 'Jesus, who–who said that?'

Reflexes helped Rudi, and without being obvious he turned his back on Hushang. 'The Iranian officer in the doorway – don't look, for Christ's sake – he flew the intercept, F14 – he blew her out of the sky!' He put a glassy smile on his face, grabbed Lochart by the arm, and again trying not to be obvious, steered him towards the nearest trailer. 'You can bed down in Jon Tyrer's place,' he said with forced joviality, and the moment he had closed the door behind them, he whispered in a rush, 'Hushang said he shot down HBC near the Iraqi border at sunset yesterday! Totalled her. How'd you get out? Who was aboard? Quick, tell me what happened. Quick!'

'I – I didn't fly the last leg, I wasn't in her,' Lochart said, trying to get his mind working and also keeping his voice down, for the walls of the trailer were very thin. 'They left me at Dez Dam. I backpac –'

441

'Dez Dam? What the hell you doing there? Who left you?'

Lochart hesitated. Everything was happening so fast. 'I don't know if I should . . . should say beca –'

'For Christ's sake, they're on to HBC, we've got to do something fast. Who was flying her, who was aboard?'

'All Iranians evacuating Iran – all air force from Isfahan – General Seladi, eight colonels and majors from Isfahan – I don't know their names – and General Valik, his wife and . . .' Lochart could hardly bring himself to say it, 'and his two children.'

Rudi was appalled. He had heard about Annoush and the two kids and he had met Valik several times. 'That's terrible, terrible. What the hell'm I going to say?'

'What? About what?'

The words tumbled out. 'Major Qazani and Hushang, they arrived barely half an hour ago – the major's just gone but I've been ordered to find out if HBC's S-G, where she was based, and who was aboard. I've been ordered to call Kowiss and find out and Hushang's going to be listening in and he's no fool, no fool, and he was sure he saw the S-G decal before he blew her to pieces. Kowiss'll have to say she was our bird, that they'll call Tehran and that's the end.'

Lochart sat on one of the built-in bunks. Numb. 'I warned them – I warned them to wait for nightfall! What the hell am I going to do?'

'Run for it. Maybe y—' A knock on the door and they froze.

'Skipper, it's me, Fowler. I brought you some tea, thought Tom could use some.'

'Thanks, just a moment, Fowler,' he said, then dropped his voice, 'Tom, what's your story – do you have one?'

'Best I could do was I'm just coming back from a hiking holiday in Luristan, south of Kermanshah. I got caught in a village by a snowfall for about a week and eventually just hiked out.'

'That's good. Where's your base?'

Lochart shrugged. 'Zagros.'

'Good. Anyone ask for your ID yet?'

'Yes. The ticket seller at Ahwaz and some Green Bands.'

'*Scheisse!*' Rudi bleakly opened the door.

Fowler Joines brought the tea tray in. 'How you doing, Tom?' he said with his toothless beam.

'Good to see you, Fowler. Still cursing?'

'Not as bad as Effer Jordon. How is my old mate?'

Tiredness enveloped Lochart and he leaned back against the wall. Zagros and Effer Jordon, Rodrigues, Jean-Luc, Scot Gavallan, and the

442

others seemed so far away. 'Still wearing his hat,' he said with a great effort, accepted the tea gratefully, and swallowed it. Hot, thick, heavy, with sweet condensed milk – the greatest pick-me-up in the world. What did Rudi say? Run for it? I can't, he thought as sleep took him. Not without Sharazad . . .

Rudi finished telling Fowler Lochart's cover story. 'Spread the word.'

The mechanic blinked. 'A hiking holiday? Tom Lochart? On his bleeding tod? With you know who in bleeding Tehran? Are you looped, Rudi, old cock?'

Rudi looked at him.

'Just as you say, old sport.' Fowler turned to talk to Lochart but he was already asleep, his face sagged with exhaustion. 'Cor! He's . . .' His shrewd blue eyes, set deep in the gnarled face, looked back at Rudi. 'I'll spread the word like it was bleeding Genesis itself.' He left.

Just before the door closed Rudi caught a glimpse of Hushang waiting by the trailer and he was sorry he had left him alone so long. He glanced at Lochart. Poor old Tom. What the hell was he doing in Isfahan? God in heaven what a mess! What the hell do I do now? Carefully he took the cup out of Lochart's hands, but the Canadian awoke startled.

For a moment Lochart did not know whether he was awake or in a dream. His heart was pounding, he had a blinding headache, and he was back at the dam at the water's edge, Rudi standing against the light just like Ali, Lochart not knowing whether to dive at him or risk the water, wanting to shout, Don't shoot don't shoot . . .

'Christ, I thought you were Ali,' he gasped. 'Sorry, I'm all right now. No sweat.'

'Ali?'

'The pilot, HBC's pilot, Ali Abbasi, he was going to kill me.' Half asleep Lochart told him what had happened. Then he noticed Rudi had gone chalky. 'What's the matter?'

Rudi jerked his thumb outside. 'That's his brother – Hushang Abbasi – he's the one who totalled HBC . . .'

443

Tehran: 4:17 P.M. Both men were staring anxiously at the telex machine in the S-G penthouse office. 'Come on for God's sake!' McIver muttered and glanced again at his watch. The 125 was due at 5.30. 'We'll have to leave soon, Andy, you never know about traffic.'

Gavallan was rocking absently in a creaky old chair. 'Yes, but Genny's not here yet. Soon as she arrives we'll leave. If worst comes to worst I can call Aberdeen from Al Shargaz.'

'*If* Johnny Hogg makes it through Kish and Isfahan airspace, and the clearance holds in Tehran.'

'He'll arrive this time, I've a good feeling our mullah Tehrani wants the new glasses. Hope to God Johnny's got them for him.'

'So do I.'

This was the first day the komiteh had allowed any foreigners back into the building. Most of the morning had been spent cleaning up and restarting their generator that had, of course, run out of fuel. Almost at once the telex machine had chattered into life: 'Urgent! Please confirm your telex is working and inform Mr. McIver I have an Avisyard telex

444

for the boss. Is he still in Tehran?' The telex was from Elizabeth Chen in Aberdeen. 'Avisyard' was a company code, used rarely, meaning a top classified message for McIver's eyes only and to operate the machine himself. It took him four tries to get the Aberdeen callback.

'So long as we haven't lost a bird,' Gavallan said with an inward prayer.

'I was thinking that too.' McIver eased his shoulders. 'Any idea what could merit an Avisyard?'

'No.' Gavallan hid his sadness, thinking about the real Avisyard, Castle Avisyard, where he had spent so many happy years with Kathy, who had suggested the code. Don't think about Kathy now, he told himself. Not now.

'I hate bloody telex machines – they're always going wrong,' McIver was saying, his stomach churning, mostly because of the row that he had had last night with Genny, insisting that she go on the 125 today, also because there was still no news from Lochart. Added to that, again none of the Iranian office staff had reported for work, only the pilots who had come in this morning. McIver had sent them all away except Pettikin whom he had put on standby. Nogger Lane had wandered in around noon, reporting that his flight with the mullah Tehrani, six Green Bands and five women went well. 'I think our friendly mullah wants another ride tomorrow. He expects you 5.15 sharp at the airport.'

'All right. Nogger, you relieve Charlie.'

'Come on, Mac, old chap, I've worked hard all morning, above and beyond the call, and Paula's still in town.'

'How well I know, "old chap", and the way things look she'll be here for the week!' McIver had told him. 'You relieve Charlie, you get your hot little tail into a chair, bring our aircraft ledgers up to date, and one more bloody word out of you I'll post you to bloody Nigeria!'

They had waited, grimly conscious that telexes had to go part of the way through phone lines. 'Bloody lot of wire between here and Aberdeen,' McIver muttered.

Gavallan said, 'Soon as Genny arrives we'll leave. I'll make sure she's all right in Al Shargaz before I go home. You're quite right to insist.'

'I know, you know, and the whole of Iran knows but she bloody doesn't!'

'Women,' Gavallan said diplomatically. 'Anything else I can do?'

'Don't think so. Squeezing our two remaining partners helped a lot.' Gavallan had tracked them down, Mohammed Siamaki and Turiz Bakhtiar – a common surname in Iran for those from the rich and

445

powerful and multitudinous Bakhtiar tribe of which the ex-prime minister was one of the chiefs. Gavallan had extracted five million rials in cash – a little over sixty thousand, a pittance against what the partners owed – with promises for more every week, in return for a promise, and a handwritten note, to reimburse them personally 'outside the country, should it be necessary, and passage on the 125 should it be necessary'.

'All right, but where's Valik – how do I get hold of him?' Gavallan had asked, pretending to know nothing about his escape.

'We already told you: he's on vacation with his family,' Siamaki had said, rude and arrogant as always. 'He'll contact you in London or Aberdeen – there's the overdue matter of our funds in the Bahamas.'

'Our joint funds, dear partner, and there's the matter of almost four million dollars owing on work already completed, apart from our aircraft lease payments overdue, long overdue.'

'If the banks were open you'd have the money. It's not our fault the Shah's pestilential allies ruined him and ruined Iran. We are not to blame for any of the catastrophes, none. As to the monies owed, haven't we paid in the past?'

'Yes. Usually six months late, but I agree, dear friend, eventually we have extracted our share. But if all joint ventures are suspended as the mullah Tehrani told me, how do we operate from now on?'

'*Some* joint ventures, not all – your information is exaggerated and incorrect, Gavallan. We are on notice to get back to normal as soon as possible – crews can leave once their replacements are safely here. Oil fields must be returned to full production. There will be no problems. But to forestall any trouble, once more we have bailed out the partnership. Tomorrow my illustrious cousin, Finance Minister Ali Kia joins the board a –'

'Hold on a minute! I have prior approval of any change in the board!'

'You used to have that power, but the board voted to change that byelaw. If you wish to go against the board you can bring it up at the next meeting in London – but under the circumstances the change is necessary and reasonable. Minister Kia has assured us we'll be exempt. Of course Minister Kia's fees and percentage will come out of your share . . .'

Gavallan tried not to watch the telex machine but he found it difficult, trying to think a way out of the trap. 'One moment everything seems okay, the next it's rotten again.'

'Yes. Yes, Andy, I agree. Talbot was today's clincher.'

This morning, early, they had met Talbot briefly. 'Oh, yes, old boy,

446

joint ventures are definitely persona non grata now, so sorry,' he had told them dryly. 'The "On High" have decreed that *all* joint ventures are suspended, pending instructions, though what instructions and from whom, they didn't impart. Or who the "On High" are. We presume the Olympian decree is from the dear old Rev. Komiteh, whoever they are! On the other side of the coin, old chap, the Ayatollah and Prime Minister Bazargan have both said all foreign debts will be honoured. Of course Khomeini overrides Bazargan and issues counter-instructions, Bazargan issues instructions which the Revolutionary Komiteh overrules, the local komitehs are vigilantes who're taking their own version of law as gospel, and not one rotten little urchin has yet handed in a weapon. The jails are filling up nicely, heads rolling – and apart from the tumbrils it all has a jolly old tediously familiar ring, old boy, and rather suggests we should all retire to Margate for the duration.'

'You're serious?'

'Our advice to evacuate all unessential personnel still stands the moment the airport opens which is God knows when but promised for Saturday – we've got BA to cooperate with chartered 747s. As to the illustrious Ali Kia, he's a minor official, very minor indeed, with no power and a good weather friend to all sides. By the way we've just heard that the U.S. ambassador in Kabul was abducted by anti-communist, Shi'ite fundamentalist mujhadin who tried to exchange him for other mujhadin held by the pro-Soviet government. In the following shoot-out he was killed. Things are heating up rather nicely . . .'

The telex clicked on, their attention zeroed, but the machine did not function. Both of them cursed.

'Soon as I get to Al Shargaz I can phone the office and find out what's the problem . . .' Gavallan glanced at the door as it opened. To their surprise it was Erikki – he and Azadeh had been due to meet them at the airport. Erikki was smiling his usual smile but there was no light behind it.

'Hello, boss, hi, Mac.'

'Hi, Erikki. What's up?' McIver looked at him keenly.

'Slight change of plan. We're, er, well, Azadeh and I are going back to Tabriz first.'

Yesterday evening Gavallan had suggested that Erikki and Azadeh take immediate leave. 'We'll find a replacement. How about coming with me tomorrow? Perhaps we could get Azadeh replacement papers in London . . .'

447

'Why the change, Erikki?' he asked. 'Azadeh's had second thoughts about leaving Iran without Iranian papers?'

'No. An hour ago we got a message – I got a message from her father. Here, read it for yourself.' Erikki gave it to Gavallan, who shared it with McIver. The handwritten note said: 'From Abdollah Khan to Captain Yokkonen: I require my daughter to come back here at once and ask you to grant her permission.' It was signed, Abdollah Khan. The message was repeated in Farsi on the other side.

'You're sure it's his handwriting?' Gavallan asked.

'Azadeh's sure, and she also knew the messenger.' Erikki added, 'The messenger told us nothing else, only that there's lots of fighting going on there.'

'By road's out of the question.' McIver turned to Gavallan. 'Maybe our mullah Tehrani'd give Erikki a clearance? According to Nogger, he was like a dog-eating wallah after his joyride this morning. We could fit Charlie's 206 with long-range tanks. Erikki could take her, maybe with Nogger or one of the others to bring her right back?'

Gavallan said, 'Erikki, you know the risk you're taking?'

'Yes.' Erikki had not yet told them about the killings.

'You've thought it through – everything? Rakoczy, the road-block, Azadeh herself? We could send Azadeh back alone and you could get on the 125 and we'd put her on Saturday's flight.'

'Come on, boss, you'd never do that and neither will I – I couldn't leave her.'

'Of course, but it had to be said. All right. Erikki, you take care of the long-range tanks, we'll try for the clearance. I'd suggest you both come back to Tehran as quickly as possible and take the 125 on Saturday. Both of you. It might be wise for you to transfer and do a tour somewhere else – Australia, Singapore perhaps – or Aberdeen, but that might be too cold for Azadeh, you let me know.' Gavallan cheerfully stuck out his hand. 'Happy Tabriz, eh?'

'Thanks.' Erikki hesitated. 'Any news of Tom Lochart?'

'No, not yet – still can't raise Kowiss or Bandar-e Delam. Why? Sharazad's getting anxious?'

'More than that. Her father's in Evin Jail an –'

'JesusChrist,' McIver exploded, Gavallan equally shocked, knowing the rumours of arrests and firing squads. 'What for?'

'For questioning – by a komiteh – no one knows what for or how long he'll be held.'

Gavallan said uneasily, 'Well, if it's only for questioning . . . what happened, Erikki?'

448

'Sharazad came home half an hour or so ago in tears. When she went back last night after dinner to her parents' house all hell had broken loose. Apparently some Green Bands went into the bazaar, grabbed Emir Paknouri – you remember, her ex-husband – for "crimes against Islam" and ordered Bakravan to appear at dawn for questioning – for what reason no one knows.' Erikki took a breath. 'They went with him to the prison this morning, she, her mother, sisters and brother. They got there just after dawn and waited and waited and would be still waiting if they hadn't been told to clear off around 2 p.m. by Green Bands on guard there.'

There was a stunned silence.

Erikki broke it. 'Mac, try Kowiss. Get them to contact Bandar-e Delam – Tom should know about Sharazad's father.' He noticed the look between the two men. 'What's going on with Tom?'

'He's on a charter to Bandar-e Delam.'

'Yes, you told me that. Mac's told me that and so has Sharazad. Tom told her he'd be back in a few days.' Erikki waited. Gavallan just looked back at him. 'Well,' Erikki said, 'you must have good reasons.'

'I think so,' Gavallan said. Both he and McIver were convinced that Tom Lochart would not willingly have gone on to Kuwait, whatever bribe Valik offered him – both equally afraid that he had been forced.

'All right – you're the boss. Well, I'll be off. Sorry for bringing bad news but I thought you'd better know.' Erikki forced a smile. 'Sharazad wasn't in good shape. See you in Al Shargaz!'

'Sooner the better, Erikki.'

'McIver said, 'If you bump into Gen – don't mention about Sharazad's father, eh?'

'Of course.' Erikki began to leave.

After Erikki had left, McIver said, 'Bakravan's a pretty important bazaari to summarily arrest.'

'I agree.' After a pause Gavallan said, 'Hope to God Erikki's not going into a trap. That message bit's very smelly, very sm –'

The telex chattering made them both jump. They read the telex, line by line, as it came through. Gavallan began cursing and continued to curse until the machine stopped. 'God curse Imperial Helicopters to hell!' He ripped the telex out, Mac sent their call sign back and 'Standby One'. Gavallan reread it.

Again it was from Liz Chen: 'Dear Boss, we've tried you every hour on the hour since we heard from Johnny Hogg you stayed in Tehran. Sorry to bring bad tidings but early Monday morning Imperial Air and Imperial Helicopters jointly announced "new financial arrangements

449

to revitalise their competitive position in the North Sea''. I have been allowed to write off 17.1 million sterling of taxpayers' money and have capitalised another 48 million of their 68 million debt by issuing paper to the head company in lieu of the debt. We've just heard secretly that 18 of our 19 North Sea contracts due to be renewed by various companies have been awarded to IH *under real cost*. Thurston Dell of ExTex urgently needs to talk to you. Our ops in Nigeria urgently need 3 repeat 3 212s – can you provide from Iran redundancies? Presume you will go to Al Shargaz or Dubai with John Hogg today. Please advise! Mac – if Himself has already left, please advise. Love to Genny.'

'We're buggered!' Gavallan said. 'It's highway bloody robbery with taxpayers' money.'

'Then, then take them to court,' McIver said nervously, shocked at Gavallan's colour. 'Unfair competition!'

'I can't, for God's sake,' then even louder and more angry, 'unless the government screams there's bugger all I can do! Without having to service their legitimate debt they can bid way under even our cost! *Dew neh loh moh* on Callaghan and all his pinkos!'

'Come on, Andy, they're not all pinkos!'

'I know that, for God's sake,' Gavallan roared, 'but it sounds right!' Then his good nature overcame his fury and he laughed though his heart was still working hard. 'Bloody government,' he added sourly, 'they don't know their arse from a hole in the ground.'

McIver could feel his own hands shaking. 'Christ, Andy, I thought you were going to bust a blood vessel.' He was well aware of the implications of the telex. All his own nest egg was in S-G stocks and shares. 'Eighteen contracts out of nineteen, that dents our whole North Sea ops!'

'It dents us everywhere. With those amounts of write-offs IH can undercut us worldwide. And Thurston wanting me to call urgently? That's got to mean ExTex'll back out, the very least renegotiate, because of a new "adjusted" IH bid and I've signed the contract for our X63s.' Gavallan took out his handkerchief and mopped his brow. Then he saw Nogger Lane gaping from the doorway. 'What the hell do you want?'

'Er, er, nothing, sir, I thought the place was on fire.' Nogger Lane hurriedly closed the door.

'Andy,' McIver said softly when it was safe, 'Struan's. Won't they pick up the slack for you?'

'Struan's could, not easily this year, though – Linbar won't.' Gavallan kept his voice down equally. 'When he hears about all this he'll dance a bloody jig. The timing couldn't be more perfect for him.' He smiled wryly, thinking about Ian Dunross's call and his warnings. He had not told McIver about them – McIver was not part of Struan's though an old friend of Ian's too. Where the devil does Ian get his information?

He smoothed out the telex. This was the culmination of a number of problems with Imperial Helicopters. Six months ago IH had deliberately headhunted one of his senior executives who had taken with him many S-G secrets. Only last month Gavallan had lost a very important North Sea Board of Trade tender to IH – after a year of work and huge investment. The Board of Trade specifications were to develop electronic equipment for a helicopter air sea rescue operation in all weather conditions, day or night, so that choppers could safely go out a hundred miles over the North Sea, hover, pick eight men out of the sea and return safely – in zero zero conditions and gale-force winds – fast. In winter months, even with a sea survival suit, about an hour was maximum life expectancy and endurance in those seas.

With Ian Dunross's private enthusiasm: 'Don't forget, Andy, such knowledge and equipment would also fit perfectly into our projected China Seas endeavours,' Gavallan had committed half a million pounds and a year of work developing the electronics and guidance systems with an electronics company. Then, on the great day, the official test pilot had found he couldn't work the equipment, even though six of S-G's line pilots, including Tom Lochart and Rudi Lutz, later had had no trouble. Even so, S-G could not get the necessary certification in time. 'The unfairness of the whole rotten business,' he had written McIver, 'is that IH's got the contract using a Guerney 661 with non-certified Danish equipment aboard. We get the runaround and they get dispensations. It's a bastard – by the way, of course I can't prove it, but I'd bet real money the test pilot was got at – he's been sent "on a long rest". Oh, we'll get the money back and the contract in a year or so because our equipment's better, safer and British built. Meanwhile Imperial's operating at safety levels, I think, that can be improved.'

That's what really counts, he thought, rereading the telex, safety – safety first and safety last. 'Mac, would you send Liz a reply for me: "Leaving for Al Shargaz now and will phone on arrival. Telex Thurston and ask what deal he would offer if I double the number of X63s presently on order." '

'Eh?'

'Well, it costs nothing to ask. IH's bound to hear about our problems here and I'm not going to let those buggers start giving us the finger – better to keep them off balance. In any event we could use two X63s here to service all the Guerney contracts – if things were different. Finish the telex, "see you soon".'

'Okay.'

Gavallan sat back in the easy chair and let his mind drift, collecting his strength. I'm going to have to be very strong. And very clever. This is the one that can bury me and S-G and give Linbar everything he needs – this and Iran together. Yes, and it was stupid to lose your temper like that. What you need is Kathy's Shrieking Tree . . . Ah, Kathy, Kathy.

The Shrieking Tree was an old clan custom, a special tree chosen by the oldest of the clan, somewhere nearby, that you could go out to, alone, when the deevil – as old Granny Dunross, Kathy's grandmother, called it – 'when the deevil was upon you and there you could curse and rant and rave and curse some more until there were no more curses left. Then there would always be peace in the home and never a need to really curse a husband or wife or lover or child. Aye, just a wee tree, for a tree can bear all the curses even the deevil himself invented.'

The first time he had used Kathy's Shrieking Tree was in Hong Kong. There it was a jacaranda in the garden of the Great House, the residence of the taipan of Struan's. Kathy's brother, Ian, was taipan then. He knew the date exactly: it was Wednesday, 21 August, 1963, the night she told him.

Poor Kathy, my Kathy, he thought, loving her still – Kathy, born under an ill-set star. Swept off your feet by one of the Few – John Selkirk, Flight Lieutenant, DFC, RAF – married at once, not yet eighteen, widowed at once not yet three months older, him torched out of the skies and vanished. Rotten war years and more tragedy, two beloved brothers killed in action – one your twin. Meeting you in Hong Kong in '46, at once in love with you, hoping with all my heart that I could make up for some of the unluck. I know Melinda and Scot did – they've turned out wonderfully, so grand. And then, in '63, before your thirty-eighth birthday, the multiple sclerosis.

Going home to Scotland as you'd always wanted – me to put Ian's plans into effect, you to regain your health. But that part not to be. Watching you die. Watching the sweet smile you used to cover the hell inside, so brave and gentle and wise and loving, but going, plateau by plateau. So slowly, yet so fast, so inexorably. By '68 in a wheelchair, mind still crystal, voice clear, the rest a shell, out of control and shaking. Then it was '70.

That Christmas they were at Castle Avisyard. And on the second day of the New Year when the others had gone and Melinda and Scot were skiing in Switzerland, she had said, 'Andy, my darling, I cannot endure another year another month or another day.'

'Yes,' he said simply.

'Sorry, but I'll need help. I need to go and I . . . I'm ever so sorry that it's been so long . . . but I need to go now, Andy. I have to do it myself but I'll need help. Yes?'

'Yes, my darling.'

They had spent a day and a night talking, talking about good things and good times and what he should do for Melinda and Scot, and that she wanted him to marry again, and she told how wonderful life had been with him and they laughed, one with another, and his tears did not spill till later. He held her palsied hand with the sleeping pills and held her shaking head against his chest, helped her with the glass of water – a little whisky in it for luck – and never let her go until the shaking had stopped.

The doctor had said kindly, 'I don't blame her – if I'd been her I would have done it years ago, poor lady.'

Going then to the Shrieking Tree. But shrieking no words, nothing – only tears.

'Andy?'

'Yes, Kathy?'

Gavallan looked up and he saw it was Genny, McIver by the door, both of them watching him. 'Oh, hello, Genny, sorry, I was a million miles away.' He got up. 'It – I think it was the Avisyard that set me thinking.'

Genny's eyes widened. 'Oh, an Avisyard telex? Not a bird down?'

'No, no, thank God, just Imperial Helicopters up to their old tricks.'

'Oh, thank God too,' Genny said, openly relieved. She was dressed in a heavy coat and nice hat. Her large suitcase was in the outer office where Nogger Lane and Charlie Pettikin waited. 'Well, Andy,' she said, 'unless you override Mr. McIver, I suppose we should go. I'm as ready as I'll ever be.'

'Come on, Gen, there's no n—' McIver stopped as she imperiously held up her hand.

'Andy,' she said sweetly, 'please tell Mr. McIver that battle is joined.'

'Gen! Will y –'

'Joined, by God!' Imperiously she waved Nogger Lane away from her suitcase, picked it up, staggered a little under its weight, and swept out with an even more imperious, 'I can carry my own suitcase, thank you very much.'

There was a big hole in the air behind her. McIver sighed. Nogger Lane had a hard time keeping the laughter off his face. Gavallan and Charlie Pettikin thought it best to be noncommittal.

'Well, er, no need for you to drive out with us, Charlie,' Gavallan said gruffly.

'I'd still like to, if it's all right,' Pettikin said, not really wanting to but McIver had asked him privately for support with Genny. 'That's a cute hat, Genny,' he had told her just after a delightful breakfast with Paula. Genny had smiled sweetly: 'Don't you try to butter me up, Charlie Pettikin, or I'll give you what for too. I've had men generally – in fact I'm very pissed off indeed . . .'

Gavallan put on his parka. He picked up the telex and stuck it into his pocket. 'Actually, Charlie,' he said and some of his concern showed now, 'if you don't mind I'd rather you didn't – I've got some unfinished stuff to chat with Mac about.'

'Sure, of course.' Pettikin stuck out his hand and hid the beam. Not going out to the airport would give him a few bonus hours alone with Paula. Paula the Fair, he had thought of her since breakfast even though she was brunette. To McIver he said, 'I'll see you at home.'

'Why not wait here – I want to raise all the bases as soon as it's dark and we can go back together. I'd like you to hold the fort. Nogger, you can quit.' Nogger Lane beamed and Pettikin cursed silently.

In the car McIver drove, Gavallan was beside him, Genny in the back. 'Mac, let's talk about Iran.'

They went through their options. Each time they came back to the same gloomy conclusion: they had to hope the situation came back to normal, the banks reopened, they got the money owing to them, that their joint venture was exempt and they weren't nailed. 'You just have to keep going, Mac. While we can operate, you'll have to continue, whatever the problems.'

McIver was equally grave. 'I know. But how do I operate without money – and what about the lease payments?'

'Somehow I'll get you operating money. I'll bring cash from London in a week. I can carry the lease payment on your aircraft and spares for another few months; I may even be able to do the same with the X63s if I can reschedule payments, but, well, I hadn't planned on losing so many contracts to IH – may be I can get some of them back. Whichever way, it'll be dicey for a while but not to worry. Hope to God Johnny gets in; just have to get home now, there's so much to do . . .'

McIver narrowly avoided a head-on collision with a car that charged out of a side street, almost went into the joub, and came back on to the roadway again. 'Bloody twit! You all right, Gen?' He glanced into the rear mirror and winced, seeing her stony face.

Gavallan felt the icy blast too, started to say something to her but thought better of it. Wonder if I could get hold of Ian – perhaps he could guide me out of the abyss – and thinking of that reminded him of David MacStruan's tragic death. So many of them, the Struans, MacStruans, Dunrosses, their enemies the Gornts, Rothwells, Brocks of ancient days, had died violent deaths or vanished – lost at sea – or died in strange accidents. So far Ian's survived. But how much longer? Not many more times. 'I think I'm up to my eighth, Andy,' Dunross had said the last time they met.

'What now?'

'Nothing much. Car bomb went off in Beirut just after I'd passed by. Nothing to worry about, I've said it before, there's no pattern. I just happen to have a charmed life.'

'Like Macao?'

Dunross was an enthusiastic racer and had driven in many of the Macao Grand Prix. In '65 – the race still amateur then – he had won the race but the right front tyre of his E Type blew out at the winning post and shoved him into the barricade and sent him tumbling down the track, other cars taking evading action, one careening into him. They had cut him out of the wreckage, everything intact, unhurt but for his left foot missing.

'Like Macao, Andy,' Dunross had said with his strange smile. 'Just an accident. Both times.' The other time his engine had exploded but he had been unscathed. Whispers had it that his engine had been tampered with – the finger pointed at his enemy Quillan Gornt, but not publicly.

Quillan's dead and Ian's alive, Gavallan thought. So am I. So's Linbar; that bastard will go on for ever . . . Christ Almighty, I'm getting morbid and stupid – got to stop it. Mac's worried enough as it is. Got to figure a way out of the vice. 'In an emergency, Mac, I'll send messages through Talbot, you do the same. I'll be back in a few days without fail and by then I'll have answers – meanwhile I'll base the 125 until further notice – Johnny can be a courier for us. That's the best I can do for today . . .'

Genny who had not uttered a word and had politely refused to be drawn into the conversation though she listened attentively, was also more than a little worried. It's obvious there's no future for us here, and

455

I'd be quite very glad to leave – provided Duncan comes too. Even so, we can't just meekly run away with our tails between our legs and let all of Duncan's work and life's nest egg be stolen, that'd kill him as certainly as any bullet. Ugh! I do wish he'd do what he's told – he should have retired last year when the Shah was still in power. Men! Bloody stupid, the whole lot of them! Christ Almighty! What fools men are!

Traffic was very slow now. Twice they had to divert because of barricades erected across the roads – both of them guarded by armed men, not Green Bands, who angrily waved them away. Bodies here and there among the piled refuse, burned-out cars and one tank. Dogs scavenging. Once there was sudden firing nearby and they took a side street, avoiding a pitched battle between what factions they never found out. A stray bazooka shell plastered a nearby building but without danger to them. McIver eased his way around the burned hulk of a bus, more than ever glad that he had insisted that Genny evacuate Iran. Again he glanced at her in the rearview mirror and saw the white face under the hat and his heart went out to her. She's damn good, he thought proudly, so much guts. Damn good, but so bloody-minded. Hate that bloody hat. Hats don't suit her. Why the hell won't she do what she's told without arguing? Poor old Gen, I'll be so relieved when she's not in danger.

Near the airport, traffic almost came to a standstill, hundreds of cars crammed with people, many Europeans, men, women, and children, going there on the rumour that the airport had been reopened – enraged Green Bands turning everyone away, crude signs scrawled in Farsi and misspelled English nailed to trees and to walls: AIRPRT FORBIDUN NOW. AIRPRT OPEN MUNDAY – IF TICKUT ANE EXIT PURMIT.

It took them half an hour to talk their way through the barrier. It was Genny who finally managed it. Like most of the wives who had to shop and to deal with servants and day-to-day living, she could speak some Farsi – and though she had not said a word all the way, she leaned forward and spoke to the Green Bands pleasantly. At once they were waved through.

'My God, Gen, that was wonderful,' McIver said. 'What did you tell that bastard?'

'Andy,' she said smugly, 'please tell Mr. McIver I told them he was a suspected smallpox carrier who was being sent out of the country.'

More Green Bands were on the gate that led to the freighting area and their office, but this time it was easier and clearly they were expected. The 125 was already on the runway, surrounded by armed

Green Bands and trucks. Two motorcycle Green Bands motioned them to follow and roared off on to the tarmac, leading the way.

'Why are you late?' the mullah Tehrani said irritably, coming down the 125's steps, two armed revs following. Both Gavallan and McIver noticed he was wearing new glasses. They caught a glimpse of John Hogg inside the cabin, one of the revs at the head of the steps with a levelled submachine gun. 'The aircraft must take off instantly. Why are you late?'

'So sorry, Excellency, the traffic – Insha'Allah! So sorry,' McIver said carefully. 'I understand from Captain Lane your work for the Ayatollah, may he live for ever, was satisfactory?'

'There was not enough time to complete all my work. As God wants. It is, er, it is necessary to go tomorrow. You will arrange it please. For 9 a.m.'

'With pleasure. Here is the passenger crew manifest.' McIver gave him the paper. Gavallan, Genny, and Armstrong were on it, Armstrong as going on leave.

Tehrani read the paper easily now, openly ecstatic with his glasses. 'Where is this Armstrong?'

'Oh, I presumed he was aboard.'

'There's no one aboard but the crew,' the mullah said irritably, the vast pleasure of being able to see overcoming his nervousness at having allowed the 125 to land. But he was glad he had, the glasses were a gift of God and the second pair promised by the pilot next week a protection against breakage and the third pair just for reading . . . Oh, God is Great. God is Great, all thanks to God for putting the thought into the pilot's head and for letting me see so well. 'The aircraft must leave at once.'

'It's not like Mr. Armstrong to be late, Excellency,' Gavallan said with a frown. Neither he nor McIver had heard from him since yesterday – nor had he come to the flat last night. This morning Talbot had shrugged, saying that Armstrong had been delayed, but not to worry, he would be at the airport on time. 'Perhaps he's waiting in the office,' Gavallan said.

'There is no one there who should not be there. The aircraft will leave now. It will not wait. Aboard, please! The aircraft will leave now.'

'Perfect,' Gavallan said. 'As God wants. By the way we'd like clearance for the 125 to come back Saturday and clearance for a 206 to go to Tabriz tomorrow.' With great formality he handed him the papers, neatly filled out.

'The, er, the 125 may return but not flights to Tabriz. Perhaps Saturday.'

'But, Excellency, don't y –'

'No,' the mullah said, conscious of the others watching him. He ordered the truck blocking the runway out of the way and looked at Genny as she got out of the car and nodded approvingly. Gavallan and McIver were surprised to notice that now she had tucked her hair into the scarf part of her hat so none of her hair was showing and, with her long coat, almost gave the impression of being in chador. 'Please to get aboard.'

'Thank you, Excellency,' she said in adequate Farsi that she had been rehearsing with the help of a dictionary all morning, with the necessary perfect amount of seriousness, 'but with your permission I will stay. My husband is not as healthy in the head as he should be, temporarily, but you – being a man of such intelligence – you would understand that though a wife cannot go against her husband's wishes, it is written that even the Prophet Himself had to be looked after.'

'True, true,' the mullah said and looked at McIver thoughtfully. McIver stared back perplexed, without understanding. 'Stay if you wish.'

'Thank you,' Genny said, with great deference. 'Then I stay. Thank you, Excellency, for your agreement and your wisdom.' She hid her glee at her cleverness and said in English, 'Duncan, the mullah Tehrani agrees that I should stay.' She saw his eyes cross and added hastily, 'I'll wait in the car.'

He was there before her. 'You bloody get aboard that kite,' he said, 'or I'll bloody put you aboard.'

'Don't be silly, Duncan, dear!' She was so solicitous. 'And don't shout, it's so bad for your blood pressure.' She saw Gavallan coming over and some of her confidence vanished. Around her was rotten snow and rotten sky and sour youths gaping at her. 'You know I really do love this place,' she said brightly, 'how could I leave?'

'You – you're bloody leaving an—' McIver was so angry he could hardly talk and for a second Genny was afraid she had gone too far.

'I'll leave if you leave, Duncan. Right now. I'm not repeat not going without you and if you try to force me I'll throw such a tantrum that it'll blow the 125 and the whole airport to kingdom come! Andy, explain to this – this person! Oh, I know you can both drag me aboard but if you do you'll both lose total face and I know you both too well! Andy!'

Gavallan laughed. 'Mac, you've had it!'

In spite of his rage, McIver laughed too, and the mullah watching and listening, shook his head with disbelief at the antics of Infidels.

'Gen, you . . . you've been planning this all along,' McIver spluttered.

'Who me?' She was all innocence. 'Perish the thought!'

'All right, Gen,' McIver said, his jaw still jutting, 'all right, you win, but you haven't just lost face, you've lost tail as well.'

'Aboard!' the mullah said.

'What about Armstrong?' McIver said.

'He knows the rules and the time.' Gavallan gave Genny a hug and shook hands with McIver. 'See you soon and take care.' He went aboard, the jet took off, and during the long drive back to the office neither Genny nor Duncan McIver noticed the time passing. Both were preoccupied. Genny sat in the front, her hand resting lightly on his knee. She was very tired but very satisfied. 'You're a good woman, Gen,' he had said the moment that they were alone, 'but you're not forgiven.'

'Yes, Duncan,' she had said meekly, as a good woman does – from time to time.

'You're not bloody forgiven at all.'

'Yes, Duncan.'

'And don't yes Duncan me!' He drove on for a while then he said gruffly, 'I'd rather have you safe in Al Shargaz but I'm glad you're here.'

She said nothing, wisely. Just smiled. And put her hand on his knee. Both of them at peace now.

It was another foul drive, with many detours, more shootings, and more bodies and dogs and angry crowds, and garbage, the streets not cleaned for months now, the jobs long since clogged. Night came swiftly and the cold increased. Odd cars and some army trucks screamed by, careless of road safety, packed with men. 'Are you tired, Duncan? Would you like me to drive?'

'No, I'm fine, thanks,' he said, feeling very tired, and very glad when at length they turned into their street, dark and ominous like all the rest, the only light coming from their penthouse office. He would have preferred to leave the car on the street but he was sure by the time he came back the petrol would have been siphoned out even though there was a lock on the tank – if the car itself was even still there. He drove into their garage, locked the car, locked the garage, and they climbed the stairs.

Charlie Pettikin met them on the landing, his face pasty. 'Hi, Mac.

Thank God y—' Then he saw Genny and he stopped. 'Oh, Genny! What, what happened? Didn't the 125 get in?'

'She came in,' McIver said. 'What the hell's happened, Charlie?'

Pettikin closed the office door after them, glanced at Genny who said wearily, 'All right, I'm going to the loo.'

Christ Almighty, she thought, it's all so bloody stupid – will they never learn? Duncan'll tell me as soon as we're alone so I'll hear it anyway and I'd much rather have it from source. Tiredly she plodded for the door.

'No, Gen,' McIver said and she stopped, startled. 'You chose to stay so . . .' He shrugged and she noticed one thing different in him and did not know if it was good or if it was bad. 'Let's have it, Charlie.'

'Rudi came in on the HF less than half an hour ago,' Pettikin said in a rush. 'HBC's been shot down, blown out of the skies, no survivors b –'

Both Genny and McIver went white. 'Oh, my God!' She groped for a chair.

'I don't understand what's going on,' Pettikin said helplessly. 'It's all crazy, like a dream, but Tom Lochart hasn't been clobbered, he's at Bandar-e Delam with Rudi. H –'

McIver came back to life. 'Tom's safe?' he burst out. 'He got out?'

'You don't get out of a chopper if she was "blown out of the sky". Nothing makes any sense unless it's a cover-up. Tom was flying spares, no passengers, but this officer said she was full of people, and Rudi said, "Tell Mr. McIver that Captain Lochart's back off leave." I even talked to him!'

McIver gaped at him. 'You talked to him? He's safe? You're sure? Off what leave, for God's sake?'

'I don't know but I did talk to him. He came on the blower.'

'Wait a minute, Charlie. How'd Rudi reach us? Is he at Kowiss?'

'No, he said he was calling from Abadan Air Traffic Control.'

McIver muttered an obscenity, so relieved about Lochart and at the same time appalled about Valik and his family. Full of people? Should've been only four! There were fifty questions he wanted answered at once and knew there was no way out of the trap that he and Tom were in. He had told no one of Lochart's real mission or his own dilemma authorising it, other than Gavallan. 'Let's have it from the beginning, Charlie, exactly.' McIver glanced at Genny who was frozen. 'You all right, Gen?'

'Yes, yes. I – I'll make a cuppa.' Her voice seemed very small to both of them and she went over to the kitchenette.

460

Shakily Pettikin sat on the edge of the desk. 'As exactly as I can remember, Rudi said, "I've got an officer from the Iranian Air Force here and have to know officially . . ." 'Then this other voice came over the loudspeaker. "This is Major Qazani, Air Force Intelligence! I require answers at once. Is HBC an S-G 212 or isn't it?" To give myself time I said, "Hang on a minute I'll get the file." I waited, hoping for a lead from Rudi but there wasn't one so I figured it was all right. "Yes, EP-HBC's one of our 212s." At once Rudi blew his stack and cursed as I've never heard him before and said something like, "By God, that's terrible because HBC tried to escape into Iraq and the Iranian Air Force rightly shot the ship down, blew her and all aboard to the hell she deserved – who the hell was flying her and who the hell was aboard?" '

Pettikin wiped away a dribble of sweat. 'I think I swore myself, fell apart a bit, can't remember exactly, Mac, then said something like, "That's terrible! Hold on – I'll get the flight book," hoping the hell my voice sounded more or less okay. I got it and saw Nogger's name crossed off, with "reported sick" alongside, then Tom Lochart's and your signature authorising the charter.' He looked up at McIver helplessly. 'Clearly Rudi didn't want me to say Tom so I just said, "According to our flight book she's not checked out to anyone . . ." '

McIver went red. 'But if you s –'

'It was the best I could do at the time, for God's sake. I said, "She's not checked out to anyone." Rudi began cursing again but I thought his voice sounded different now, more relieved. "What the hell're you talking about?" he said.

' "I'm just telling you, Captain Lutz, according to the records here, HBC's still hangared at Doshan Tappeh. If she's gone she must've been hijacked," I said, hoping my voice sounded convincing. Mac, I was groping and I still don't understand what the problem is. Then this other voice said, "This matter will be taken up through channels at once. I require your flight clearance book at once." I told him okay, where should I send it? That threw him a little because of course there's no way we can get it to him at once. Eventually he said to keep our records safely and we'd get instructions later. Then Tom came on and said something like:

' "Captain Pettikin, please give my apologies to Mr. McIver that I'm late off leave but I was trapped by a snowfall in a village just south of Kermanshah. Soon as I can I'll head for home." ' Pettikin exhaled, glanced at Genny then back at McIver. 'That's it. That's all. What d'you think?'

'About Tom? I don't know.' McIver went over to the window heavily and both Pettikin and Genny saw the weight on him. Snow was on the sill and the wind had picked up a little. Sporadic gunfire sounded from the distance, rifle and automatic, but none of them noticed it.

'Genny?'

'I – it doesn't make any, any sense, Charlie, any sense at all about Tommy.' Weakly she poured the boiling water into the teapot, the cups already laid out, glad to have had something to do with her hands, feeling helpless and wanting to cry, wanting to shout at the injustice of everything, knowing that Tom and Duncan were trapped – her Duncan had signed the flight plan – knowing she could not mention anything about Annoush or the children or Valik – *if* they were aboard, they must be aboard, but then who was flying if it wasn't Tommy? 'The hijack . . . well, obviously Tommy's on the clearance here and so is Duncan. The authorities in Tehran still have the clearance. The clearance has Duncan's name on it so a hijack isn't . . . it doesn't make much sense.'

'I can see that now but at the time the story sounded good.' Pettikin felt awful. He picked up the clearance book. 'Mac, how about if we lose this, get rid of it?'

'Tehran Control's still got the original, Charlie. Tom refuelled, there'll be a record.'

'In normal times, sure. Now? With all this mess going on?'

'Perhaps.'

'May be we could retrieve the original?'

'Come on, for God's sake, not a hope till hell freezes.'

Genny started pouring the tea into the three cups. The silence tightened. In misery Pettikin said, 'I still don't see how if Tom started off from Doshan Tappeh and then . . . unless she was hijacked en route, or when he was refuelling.' Irritably he ran his fingers through his hair. 'It's got to be a hijack. Where did he refuel? Kowiss? Maybe they could help?'

McIver did not answer, just stared out at the night. Pettikin waited, then leafed through the clearance book, found the right duplicate, and looked at the back. 'Isfahan?' he said surprised. 'Why Isfahan?'

Again McIver did not answer.

Genny added condensed milk to the tea and gave one cup to Pettikin. 'I think you did very well, Charlie,' she said, not knowing what else to say. Then she took the other cup to McIver.

'Thanks, Gen.'

She saw the tears and her own tears spilled. He put an arm around

462

her, thinking about Annoush and the Christmas party he and Genny had given for all the kids of their friends, such a short time ago – little Setarem and Jalal, the stars of all the games, such wonderful kids, now cinders of meat for scavengers.

'It's good about Tommy, dear, isn't it?' she said through her own tears, Pettikin forgotten. Embarrassed, Pettikin went out and shut the door behind him and neither of them noticed his going. 'It's good about Tommy,' she said again. 'That's one good thing.'

'Yes, Gen, that's one good thing.'

'What can we do?'

'Wait. We wait and see. We hope to God they didn't buy it but . . . somehow I know they were aboard.' Tenderly he brushed away her tears. 'But come Saturday, Gen, when the 125 goes you're on it,' he told her gently. 'I promise only until we sort this all out – but this time you must go.'

She nodded. He drank his tea. It tasted very good. He smiled down at her. 'You make a damn good cuppa, Gen,' he said, but that did not take away her fear or her misery – or her fury at all the killing and uselessness and tragedy and the blatant usurping of their livelihood, or the age that it was putting on her husband. The worry's killing him. It's killing him, she thought with growing rage. Then all at once the answer came to her.

She looked around to make sure Pettikin wasn't there. 'Duncan,' she whispered, 'if you don't want those bastards to steal our future, why don't we leave and take everything with us?'

'Eh?'

'Planes, spares and personnel.'

'We can't do that, Gen, I've already told you fifty times.'

'Oh, yes, we can if we want to and if we have a plan.' She said it with such utter confidence it swept him. 'There's Andy to help. Andy can make the plan, we can't. You can carry it out, he can't. They don't want us here, so be it, we'll leave – but with our planes and our spares and our self-respect. We'll have to be very secretive but we can do it. We can do it, I know we can.'

BOOK TWO

BOOK TWO

Saturday
February 17, 1979

At Kowiss: 6:38 A.M. The mullah Hussain was sitting cross-legged on the thin mattress checking the action of the AK47. With a practised movement he snapped the new magazine into place 'Good,' he said.

'Will there be more fighting today?' his wife asked. She was across the room, standing beside a wood-burning stove that was heating a pan of water for the first coffee of the day. Her black chador rustled as she moved, masking that she was heavily with child again.

'As God wants.'

She echoed him, trying to hide her fear, afraid of what would become of them when her husband had obtained the martyrdom he sought so relentlessly, wanting in her most secret heart to scream from the minarets that it was too much to bear that God required such sacrifice of her and their children. Seven years of marriage and three live children and four dead children and the deep poverty of all those years – so great a contrast to her previous life with her own family who had owned a butcher's stall in the bazaar, always enough to eat and laughter and going out without chador, picnics and even going to the

469

cinema – had etched lines on her once attractive face. As God wants but it's not fair, not fair! We'll starve – who will want to support the family of a dead mullah?

Their eldest son, Ali, a little boy of six, squatted beside the door of this one-room hut that was beside the mosque, attentively following his father's every movement – his two little brothers, three and two years old, asleep on their straw mattress on the dirt floor, wrapped in an old army blanket. They were curled up like kittens. In the room was a rough wooden table and two benches, a few pots and pans, the big mattress and a small one on old carpets. An oil lamp for light. The joub outside was for washing and for waste. No decorations on the white-washed, dried-mud walls. A tap for water that sometimes worked. Flies and insects. And in a niche, facing Mecca, the place of honour, the well-used Koran.

It was just after dawn, the day chill and overcast, and Hussain had already called for morning prayer in the mosque and had wiped the dirt off the gun and oiled it carefully, cleaned the barrel of spent cordite, and refilled the magazine. Now it's as good as ever, he thought contentedly, ready to do more of God's work and there's plenty of use for such a gun – the AK47 so much better than the M14, simpler, more rugged, and just as accurate at close quarters. Stupid Americans, stupid as ever to make an infantry gun that was complex and accurate at a thousand yards when most fighting was done at nearer to three hundred and you could drag the AK47 in the mud all day and it would still do what it was supposed to do: kill. Death to all enemies of God!

Already there had been clashes between Green Bands and the Marxist-Islamics and other leftists in Kowiss, and more at Gach Saran, a nearby oil refinery town to the northwest. Yesterday, after dark, he had led Green Bands against one of the secret Tudeh safe houses – the meeting betrayed by one of the members in return for the hope of mercy. There would be none. The battle was sudden, short and bloody. Eleven men killed, he hoped some of the leaders. So far the Tudeh had not yet come out into the open in strength, but a mass demonstration by them had been called for tomorrow afternoon in support of the Tudeh demonstration in Tehran, even though Khomeini had expressly warned against it. The confrontation was already planned. Both sides knew it. Many will die, he thought grimly. Death to all enemies of Islam!

'Here,' she said, giving him the hot, sweet black coffee nectar, the one luxury he allowed himself except on Fridays – Holy days – and other special days and all the Holy month of Ramadan when he gave up coffee gladly.

'Thank you, Fatima,' he said politely. When he had been appointed mullah, his father and mother had found her for him and his mentor, Ayatollah Isfahani, had told him to marry so he had obeyed.

He drank the coffee, enjoying it very much, and gave her back the little cup. Marriage had not distracted him from his path, though from time to time he enjoyed sleeping against her, her buttocks large and warm in the chill of winter, sometimes turning her, joining, and then sleeping again, but never really at peace. I will only be at peace in Paradise, only then, he thought, his excitement growing, so soon now. God be thanked that I was named after Imam Hussain, Lord of the Martyrs. Imam Ali's second son, he of the Great Martyrdom, thirteen centuries ago at the Battle of Karbala.

We will never forget him, he thought, his ecstasy growing, reliving the pain of Ashura, the 10th day of Muharram – only a few weeks ago – the anniversary of that martyrdom, the Shi'as' most holy day of mourning. His back still bore the weals. That day he had been in Qom again, as last year and the year before that, taking part in the Ashura processions, the cleansing processions, with tens of thousands of other Iranians – whipping themselves to remind themselves of the divine martyrdom, scourging themselves with whips and chains, mortifying themselves with hooks.

It had taken him many weeks to recover, to be able to stand without pain. As God wants, he told himself proudly. Pain is nothing, this world is nothing. I stood against Peshadi at the air base and took over the air base and subdued it and brought him to Isfahan in bonds as I had been ordered. And now, today, first I will go again to the base to investigate the foreigners and curb them and this Sunni Zataki who thinks he's Genghis Khan, and this afternoon again I will lead the Faithful against the atheist Tudeh, doing God's work in obedience to the Imam who obeys only God. I pray that today I will gain admittance to Paradise, there to recline on couches lined with brocade, and the fruit of the two gardens shall be within easy reach, the so familiar words of the Koran etched on his brain.

'We've no food,' his wife said, interrupting his thought pattern.

'There will be food at the mosque today,' he said, and his son Ali became even more attentive – momentarily distracted from scratching the fly sores and other insect bites. 'From now on you and the children will not be hungry. We will be giving out daily meals of horisht and rice to the needy as we have done throughout history.' He smiled at Ali, reached over, and tousled his head. 'God knows we are among the needy.' Since Khomeini had returned, the mosques had begun again this ancient role of giving daily meals of plain but nourishing food, the food donated as part of Zakat – the voluntary alms tax that all Muslims were subject to – or bought with money from Zakat that was now again the sole prerogative of the mosques. Hussain heaped more curses on the Shah who had cancelled the yearly subsidy to mullahs and mosques two years ago causing them such poverty and anguish.

'Join the people waiting at the mosque,' he told her. 'When they are all fed, take enough for you and the children. Daily you will do this.'

'Thank you.'

'Thank God.'

'I do, oh, yes I do.'

He pulled on his boots and shouldered the gun.

'Can I come too, Father?' Ali asked in his thin, piping voice. 'I want to do God's work too.'

'Of course, come along.'

She closed the door after them and sat down on a bench, her stomach rumbling from hunger, feeling sick and weak, too tired to wave the flies away that settled on her face. She was eight months with child. The midwife had told her that this time would be harder than before because the baby was in a wrong position. She began to weep, remembering the tearing, screaming agony of the last birth and the one before and all of them. 'Don't worry,' the old midwife had said, complacently, 'you're in the Hands of God. A little fresh camel dung spread on your stomach will take the pains away. It's a woman's duty to bear children and you're young.'

Young? I'm twenty-two years old, and old, old old. I know it, and know why, and I've a brain and have eyes and can even write my own name and know we can have better, as the Imam knows once foreigners are expelled and the evil of foreign ways torn out. The Imam, God protect him, is wise and good and talks to God, obeys only god, and God knows that women are not chattels to be abused and cast back into the days of the Prophet as some fanatics want. The Imam will protect us from extremists, and won't allow them to repeal the Shah's Family Act that gave us the vote and protection against summary divorce – he won't allow our votes and rights and our freedoms to be taken away or our rights to choose if we want to wear chador or not, never when he sees how strongly we are against it. Not when he sees our staunch resolve. Throughout the land.

Fatima dried her tears and felt happier at the thought of the planned demonstrations in three days, and some of the pain left her. Yes, we

472

women'll demonstrate through the streets of Kowiss, proudly supporting our sisters in the great cities of Tehran and Qom and Isfahan, except I shall of course wear chador by choice, because of Hussain. Oh, how wonderful to be able to show our solidarity both as women and for the revolution.

The news of the planned marches in Tehran had rushed throughout Iran, by what means no one was sure. But all women knew. Everywhere women decided to follow suit, and all women approved – even those who did not dare to say so.

At the Air Base: 10:20 A.M. Starke was in the S-G tower watching the 125 come in with full flaps to touch down and turn on full reverse thrust. Zataki and Esvandiary were also there with two Green Bands – Zataki clean shaven now.

'Turn right at the end of the runway, EchoTangoLimaLima,' Sergeant Wazari, the young USAF-trained air traffic controller, said throatily. He had on rough civilian clothes in place of his neat uniform. His face was badly bruised, nose mashed, three teeth missing, and his ears swollen from the public beating Zataki had given him. Now he could not breathe through his nose. 'Park in front of main base tower.'

'Roger,' Johnny Hogg's voice came back over the loudspeaker. 'I repeat we are cleared to pick up three passengers, to deliver urgently required spares, with immediate turnaround and departure for Al Shargaz. Please confirm.'

Wazari turned to Zataki, his fear open. 'Excellency, please excuse me but what should I say?'

'You say nothing, vermin.' Zataki picked up his stubby machine gun. To Starke he said, 'Tell your pilot to park, to stop his engines, then to put everyone in the aircraft on to the tarmac. The aircraft will be searched and if cleared by me, it may go onwards and if it is not cleared it will not go onwards. You come with me, and you too,' he added to Esvandiary. He went out.

Starke did as he was ordered and turned to follow, but for a second he and the young sergeant were alone. Wazari caught him by the arm and whispered pathetically, 'For the love of God, help me get aboard her, Captain, I'll do anything, anything . . .'

'I can't – it's impossible,' Starke said, sorry for him. Two days ago Zataki had paraded everyone and beaten the man senseless for crimes against the revolution, brought him around, made him eat filth, and beaten him senseless again. Only Manuela and the very sick had been allowed to stay away. 'Impossible!'

'Please . . . I beg you, Zataki's mad, he'll k—' Wazari turned away in panic as a Green Band reappeared in the doorway. Starke walked past him, down the stairs and out on to the tarmac, masking his disquiet. Freddy Ayre was at the wheel of a waiting jeep. Manuela was in it, along with one of his British pilots, and Jon Tyrer, a bandage around his eyes. Manuela wore loose pants, long coat, and her hair was tied up under a pilot's hat.

'Follow us, Freddy,' Starke said and got in beside Zataki in the back of the waiting car. Esvandiary let in the clutch and sped off to intercept the 125 that was now turning off the main runway, an accompanying swarm of trucks of Green Bands and two motor-cyclists weaving around dangerously. 'Crazy!' Starke muttered.

Zataki laughed, his teeth white. 'Enthusiasts, pilot, not crazy.'

'As God wants.'

Zataki glanced at him, no longer bantering: 'You speak our language, you've read the Koran, and you know our ways. It is time you said the Shahada before two witnesses and became Muslim. I would be honoured to be a witness.'

'I, too,' Esvandiary said at once, also wanting to help save a soul though not for the same reasons: IranOil would need expert pilots to get full production going while replacement Iranians were trained and a Muslim Starke could be one. 'I too would be honoured to be a witness.'

'Thank you,' Starke told them in Farsi. Over the years the thought had occurred to him. Once, when Iran was calm and all he had to do was fly as many missions as he could and look after his men and laugh with Manuela and the children – was that only half a year ago? – he had said to her, 'You know, Manuela, there's so much in Islam that's great.'

'Were you thinkin' of four wives, darlin'?' she had said sweetly and instantly he was on guard.

'C'me on, Manuela, I was serious. There's a lot in Islam.'

'For men, not for women. Doesn't the Koran say: "And the Faithful" – all men by the way – "will lie on silken couches and there will be the houris whom neither man nor djinn hath touched" – Conroe, honey, I never could work that out, why should they be perpetual virgins? Does that do somethin' for a man? And do women get the same deal, youth and as many horny young men as they want?'

'Would you listen, for crissake! I meant that if you lived in the desert, the deep Saudi or Sahara desert – remember the time we were in Kuwait and we went out, just you and me, we went out into the desert, the stars as big as oysters and the quiet so vast, the night so clean and limitless, us insignificant, you remember how touched we were by the Infinite?

Remember how I said, I can understand how, if you were nomad and born into a tent, you could be possessed by Islam.'

'And remember, darlin', how I said we weren't born in no goddam tent.'

He smiled, remembering how he had caught her and kissed her under the stars and they had taken each other, their fill of each other, under the stars. Later he had said, 'I meant the pure teaching of Mohammed, I meant how with so much space, so terrifying in its vastness, that you need a safe haven and that Islam could be such a haven, maybe the only one, his original teaching, not narrow, twisted interpretations of fanatics.'

'Why, sure, darlin',' she had said in her most honeyed voice, 'but we don't live in no desert, never will, and you're Conroe "Duke" Starke, helicopter pilot, and the very moment you start afiguring on those four wives I'm off, me and the kids, and even Texas won't be big enough to escape the roasting you'll get from Manuela Rosita Santa de Cuellar Perez, honey sugar baby lamb . . .'

He saw Zataki staring at him and inhaled the raw smell of petrol and snow and winter. 'Perhaps I will one day,' he told Zataki and Esvandiary. 'Perhaps I will – but in God's time, not mine.'

'May God hurry the time. You're wasted as an Infidel.'

But now all of Starke's concentration was on the 125 that was coming into its parking slot, and on Manuela who must leave today. Difficult for her, goddam difficult, but she has to go.

This morning, early, McIver in Tehran had told Starke by HF they had permission for the 125 to stop off at Kowiss, provided it was also approved in Kowiss, that she would be bringing spares, and there'd be space for three passengers outbound. At length Major Changiz and Esvandiary had agreed but only after Starke had irritably told them in front of Zataki, 'You know our crew changes are long overdue. One of our 212's waiting for spares, and two of the 206s are ready for their 1,500-hour checks. If I can't have fresh crews and spares, I can't operate, and you'll be responsible for not obeying Ayatollah Khomeini – not me.'

The car stopped beside the 125, the engines whining down. The door was not yet open and he could see John Hogg peering out of the cockpit window. Trucks and guns ringed her, excitable Green Bands milling around.

Zataki tried to make himself heard, then, exasperated, fired a burst into the air. 'Get away from the airplane,' he ordered. 'By God and the Prophet only my men will search it! Get away!' Sullenly the other Green

Bands moved back a little. 'Pilot, tell him to open the door quickly, and get everyone out quickly before I change my agreement!'

Starke gave the thumbs-up to Hogg. In a moment the door was opened by the second pilot. The steps came down. At once Zataki leaped up them and stood at the top, machine gun ready. 'Excellency, you don't need that,' Starke told him. 'Everybody out, quick as you can, okay?'

There were eight passengers – four of them pilots, three engineers and Genny McIver. 'My God, Genny! I didn't expect to see you.'

'Hello, Duke. Duncan thought it best and . . . well, never mind. Is Manuela going to co—' She saw her and went over to her. They embraced and Starke noticed the age on Genny.

He followed Zataki into the empty, low-ceilinged aircraft. Extra seats had been lashed in. At the back, near the toilet, were several crates. 'Spares and the spare engine you needed,' Johnny Hogg called out from the pilot's seat, handing him the manifest. 'Hello, Duke!'

Zataki took the manifest and jerked a thumb at Hogg. 'Out!'

'If you don't mind, I'm responsible for the aircraft, sorry,' Hogg said. 'Last time. Out.'

Starke said, 'Get out of your seat a moment, Johnny. He just wants to see if there are any guns. Excellency, it would be safer if the pilot was allowed to stay in place. I will vouch for him.'

'Out!'

Reluctantly, John Hogg eased himself out of the small cockpit. Zataki made sure nothing was in the side pockets, then waved him back into the seat and studied the cabin. 'Those are the spares you need?'

'Yes,' Starke said, and politely made room on the landing where Zataki shouted for some of his men to carry the crates on to the tarmac. The men did this carelessly, banging the sides of the doorway and the steps, making the pilots wince. Then Zataki searched the aircraft carefully, finding nothing that irritated him. Except the wine on ice and the liquor in the cabinet.

'No more liquor into Iran. None! Confiscated!' He had the bottles smashed on the tarmac and ordered the crates opened. One jet engine and many other spares. Everything on the manifest. Starke watched from the cabin doorway trying to make himself inconspicuous.

Zataki said, 'Who are these passengers?' The second officer gave him the list of names. It was headed in English and Farsi: 'Temporarily redundant pilots and engineers, all overdue leave and replacement.' He began to scrutinise it, and them.

476

'Duke,' Johnny Hogg said cautiously from the cockpit, 'I've some money for you and a letter from McIver. Is it safe?'

'For the moment.'

'Two envelopes in my inside uniform pocket, hanging up. The letter's private, Mac said.'

Starke found them and stuffed them into his inner parka pocket. 'What's going on in Tehran?' he asked out of the side of his mouth.

'The airport's a madhouse, thousands trying to get on the three or four planes they've allowed in so far,' Hogg said rapidly, 'with at least six jumbos stacked in a holding pattern aimlessly waiting for permission to land. I, er, I just jumped the queue, peeled in without a real clearance, and said, Oh, so sorry, I thought I was cleared, picked up my lot, and scarpered. Hardly had time to chat with McIver – he was surrounded by trigger-happy revs and an odd mullah or two – but he seems okay. Pettikin, Nogger and the others seemed okay. I'm based at Al Shargaz for at least a week to shuttle back and forth as I can.' Al Shargaz was not far from Dubai where S-G had its HQ that side of the Gulf. 'We've permission from Tehran ATC to bring in spares and crew to match those we intend to take out – looks like they're going to keep us more or less one for one and up to strength – with flights scheduled Saturdays and Wednesdays.' He stopped for breath. 'Mac says for you to find excuses for me to come here from time to time – I'm to be kind of a courier for him and Andy Gavallan till normality re –'

'Watch it,' Starke said, behind his hand, seeing Zataki glance up at the airplane. He had been watching him inspect the passengers and their documents. Then he saw Zataki beckon him and he went down the stairs. 'Yes, Excellency?'

'This man has no exit permit.'

The man was Roberts, one of the fitters, middle-aged, very experienced. Anxiety etched his already lined face. 'I told him I couldn't get one, Cap'n Starke, we couldn't get one, the immigration offices're still all closed. There was no problem at Tehran.'

Starke glanced at the document. It was only four days past expiration. 'Perhaps you could let it go this time, Excellency. It's true that the off –'

'No correct exit permit, no exit. He stays!'

Roberts went white. 'But Tehran passed me and I've got to be in Lon –'

Zataki grabbed him by the parka and jerked him out of the line to send him sprawling. Enraged, Roberts scrambled to his feet, 'By God, I'm cleared an—' He stopped. One of the Green Bands had a rifle in his chest, another was behind him, both now ready to pull the triggers.

Starke said, 'Wait in the jeep, Roberts. Goddammit, wait by the jeep!'

One of the Green Bands roughly shoved the mechanic towards it as Starke tried to cover his own worry. Jon Tyrer and Manuela did not have up-to-date exit papers either.

'No exit permits, no exit!' Zataki repeated venomously and took the next man's papers.

Genny, next in line, was very frightened, hating Zataki and the violence and the smell of the fear surrounding her, sorry for Roberts who needed to be back in England as one of his children was very ill, polio suspected, and no mail or phones and the telex sporadic. She watched Zataki slowly going through the pilot's papers next to her. Rotten bastard! she thought. I've got to get on that plane, got to. Oh, how I wish we were all leaving. Poor Duncan, he simply won't look after himself, won't bother to eat properly and he's bound to get his ulcers back. 'My exit permit's not current,' she said, trying to sound timid, and let some tears glisten her eyes.

'Nor mine,' Manuela said in a small voice.

Zataki looked at them. He hesitated. 'Women are not responsible, men are responsible. You two women may leave. This time. Go aboard.'

'Can Mr. Roberts come too?' Genny asked, pointing to the mechanic. 'He's rea –'

'Get aboard!' Zataki shouted in one of his sudden, maniacal rages, blood in his face. The two women fled up the stairs, everyone else in momentary panic, and even his own Green Bands shifted nervously.

'Excellency, you were right,' Starke said in Farsi, forcing himself to be outwardly calm. 'Women should not argue.' He waited and everyone waited, hardly breathing, the dark eyes boring into him. But he kept his gaze level. Zataki nodded and, sullenly, continued examining the papers in his hand.

Yesterday Zataki had come back from Isfahan and Esvandiary had authorised a flight tomorrow afternoon to carry him back to Bandar-e Delam again. The sooner the better, Starke thought grimly.

And yet he felt sorry for Zataki. Last night he had found him leaning against a helicopter, his hands pressed to his temples, in great pain. 'What is it, agha?'

'My head. I – it's my head.'

He had persuaded him to see Dr. Nutt and taken him privately to the doctor's bungalow.

'Just give me aspirin, or codeine, Doctor, whatever you have,' Zataki said.

'Perhaps you'd let me examine you and th –'

'No examine!' Zataki had shouted. 'I know what's wrong with me. SAVAK is wrong with me, prison is wrong with me . . .' And later, when the codeine had taken away some of the pain, Zataki had told Starke that about a year and a half ago he had been arrested, accused of anti-Shah propaganda. At the time he was working as a journalist for one of the Abadan newspapers. He had been jailed for eight months and then, just after the Abadan fire, released. He had not told Starke what they had done to him. 'As God wants, pilot,' he had said bitterly. 'But since that day, I bless God every day for one more day of life to stamp out more SAVAKs and Shah men, his lackey police and lackey soldiers and any and all who assisted his evil – once I supported him, didn't he pay for my education, here and in England? But he was to blame for SAVAK! He was to blame! That part of my vengeance is just for me – I still haven't started on my revenge for my wife and sons murdered in the Abadan fire.'

Starke had held his peace. The how or why or who of the arson that had caused almost five hundred deaths had never come to light.

He watched Zataki work slowly and laboriously down the line of would-be passengers – how many more with incomplete or not current papers Starke did not know, everyone tense, a brooding pall over them. Soon it would be Tyrer's turn and Tyrer *must* go. Doc Nutt had said to be safe Tyrer should be examined at Al Shargaz or Dubai as soon as possible where there were marvellous hospital facilities. 'I'm sure he's all right, but it's best for him to rest his eyes for the time being. And listen, Duke, for the love of God, keep out of Zataki's way and warn the others to do the same. He's ripe to explode and God only knows what'll happen then.'

'What's the matter with him?'

'Medically, I don't know. Psychologically he's dangerous, very dangerous. I'd say manic depressive, certainly paranoic, probably caused directly by his prison experiences. Did he tell you what they did to him?'

'No. No, he didn't.'

'If it was up to me, I'd recommend he be under sedatives and absolutely nowhere near firearms.'

Great, Starke thought helplessly, how the hell do I get that organised? At least Genny and Manuela're aboard and soon they'll be in Al Shargaz which's a paradise comp –

A warning shout distracted him. Beyond the 125, coming from behind the main tower exit was the mullah Hussain with more Green Bands and they looked very hostile.

At once Zataki forgot the passengers, unslipped his machine gun, and, carrying it loosely in one hand, moved between Hussain and the airplane. Two of his men moved alongside him, and the others moved nearer the airplane into defensive positions, covering him.

'Stone the bloody crows,' someone muttered, 'what's up now?'

'Get ready to duck,' Ayre said.

'Capt'n,' Roberts whispered brokenly, 'I've got to get on that plane, I've got to, my little girl's sicker than anything, can you do something with that bastard?'

'I'll try.'

Zataki was watching Hussain, Hating him. Two days ago he had gone to Isfahan, invited there to consult with their secret komiteh. All eleven members had been ayatollahs and mullahs, and there, for the first time, he had found the real face of the revolution he had fought so hard to achieve and suffered so much for: 'Heretics will be stamped into oblivion. We'll have only Revolutionary Courts. Justice will be quick and final with no appeal . . .' The mullahs were so sure of themselves, so sure of their divine right to rule and to administer justice as they alone interpreted the Koran and Sharia. Carefully Zataki had kept his horror and his thoughts to himself, but he knew that he was again betrayed.

'What do you want, mullah?' he said, the word a curse word.

'First I want you to understand you have no power here – what you do in Abadan is up to the ayatollahs of Abadan – but here you have no power on this base, over these men, or this airplane.' Surrounding Hussain were a dozen armed, hard-faced youths, all Green Bands.

'No power, eh?' Contemptuously Zataki turned his back and shouted in English, 'The airplane will take off at once! All passengers get aboard!' Angrily he motioned at the pilot, waving him away, then faced Hussain again. 'Well? What's second?' he said as, behind him, the passengers hurried to obey and because the Green Bands were concentrating on Zataki and Hussain, Starke ordered Roberts to get aboard, then motioned Ayre to help cover the escape of the mechanic. Together they helped Tyrer out of the jeep.

Zataki toyed with his gun, all his attention on Hussain. 'Well? What's second?' he asked again.

Hussain was nonplussed, his men equally aware of the guns trained on them. The jets came to life. He saw the passengers hurrying aboard,

Starke and Ayre helping a man with bandages over his eyes up the steps, then the two pilots beside the jeep again, the jet engines building, and the instant the last man was inside the steps came up and the airplane taxied away.

'Well, agha, what's next?'

'Next . . . next the komiteh of Kowiss orders you and your men to leave Kowiss.'

Scornfully Zataki shouted to his men above the roar of the engines, his feet planted in the concrete, ready to fight if need be and die if need be, the superheated air from the fans passing him as the airplane moved towards the runway. 'You hear, we are ordered to leave by the komiteh of Kowiss!'

His men began laughing, and one of Hussain's Green Bands, a beardless teenager on the far edge of the group, raised his carbine and died at once, almost cut in half by the accurate burst of gunfire from Zataki's men that neatly culled him. The silence was broken only by the distant jets. Momentarily Hussain was bewildered by the suddenness and by the pool of blood that flowed out on to the concrete.

'As God wants,' Zataki said. 'What do you want, mullah?'

It was then that Zataki noticed the petrified little boy peering out at him, hiding behind the mullah's robes, clutching them for protection, looking so much like his own son, his eldest, that for a moment he was taken back to the happy days before *the* fire when all seemed right and there was some form of a future – the Shah's White Revolution wonderful, the land reforms, curbing the mullahs, universal education, and other things – the good days when I was a father but never again. Never. The electrodes and pincers destroyed that possibility.

A violent stab of pain in his loins soared into his head at the remembrance and he wanted to scream. But he did not, just shoved the torment back, as usual, and concentrated on the killing at hand. He could see the implacability on the mullah's face and he readied. Killing with the machine gun pleased him greatly. The hot staccato, the gun alive in short stabbing bursts, acrid smell of cordite, the blood of the enemies of God and Iran flowing. Mullahs are enemy, and most of all Khomeini who commits sacrilege by allowing his photograph to be worshipped, and his followers to call him Imam, and puts mullahs between us and God – against all the Prophet's teachings. 'Hurry up,' he bellowed, 'I'm losing patience!'

'I – I want that man,' Hussain said, pointing.

Zataki glanced around. The mullah was pointing at Starke. 'The pilot? Why? What for?' he asked, perplexed.

481

'For questioning. I want to question him.'

'What about?'

'About the escape of the officers from Isfahan.'

'What should he know about them? He was with me in Bandar-e Delam hundreds of miles away when that happened, helping the revolution against the enemies of God!' Zataki added venomously. 'Enemies of God are everywhere, everywhere! Sacrilege is everywhere, idol worship practised everywhere – isn't it?'

'Yes, yes, enemies abound, and sacrilege is sacrilege. But he's a helicopter pilot, an Infidel was the pilot of the escape helicopter, he could know something. I want to question him.'

'Not while I'm here.'

'Why? Why not? Why won't y –'

'You won't, not while I'm here, by God! Not while I'm here. Later – or tomorrow or the next day, as God wills, but not now.'

Zataki had gauged Hussain and saw in his face and eyes that he had conceded and was no longer a threat. Carefully he looked from face to face of the Green Bands surrounding the mullah but no longer detected any danger – the quick and sudden death of one, he thought without guilt, as usual controls the others. 'You will want to go back to your mosque now, it is almost time for prayer.' He turned his back and walked to the jeep, knowing his men would be guarding him, beckoned Starke and Ayre and got into the front seat, machine gun ready but not as overt as before. One by one his men retreated to their cars. They drove off.

Hussain was ashen. His Green Bands waited. One of them lit a cigarette, all of them conscious of the body at their feet. And the blood that still seeped.

'Why did you let them go, Father?' the little boy asked in his piping voice.

'I didn't, my son. We have more important things to do immediately, then we will return.'

482

USSR

Caspian Sea

USSR

Khvoy

Tabriz Mount
Sabalan

Bandar-e Pahlavi

Sadzevar

Meshed

Qazvin

Tehran

IRAN

AFGHANISTAN

Baghdad

Dez Dam

Isfahan

IRAQ

Abadan

Bandar-e Delam

Kowiss

PAKISTAN

KUWAIT

Kharg
Island

Jellet

SAUDI ARABIA

ZAGROS

Lengeh

Persian Gulf

Strait of Hormuz

CHAPTER

31

BAHRAIN

Siri

QATAR

Al Shargaz

Gulf of Oman

UAE

At Zagros Three: 12:05 P.M. Scot Gavallan was staring down the barrel of a cocked Sten gun. He had just landed the 212 after the first trip of the day to Rig Rosa delivering another full load of steel pipe and cement, and the moment he had cut the engines, armed Green Bands had rushed out of the hangar to surround him.

Hating the fear that possessed him, he tore his gaze off the gun and looked at the black malevolent eyes. 'What's – what d'you want?' he croaked, then said it in halting Farsi, '*Cheh karbareh?*'

A flood of angry incomprehensible words came from the man with the gun.

He pulled off his headset. '*Man zaban-e shoma ra khoob nami danam, agha!*' he shouted over the whine of the engines – I don't speak your language, Excellency – biting back the obscenity he wanted to add. More angry words and the man motioned him out of the cockpit. Then he saw Nasiri, the Iran Oil base manager, dishevelled and bruised, being frog-marched out of the office towards the 212 by more of the

Revolutionary Guards. He leaned out of the window a little. 'What the hell's going on?'

'They – they want you out of the chopper, Captain,' Nasiri called back. 'They – please hurry!'

'Wait till I shut down!' Nervously Scot finished the procedure. The barrel of the Sten gun had not moved, nor had the enmity around him lessened. The rotors were slowing fast now, and when it was correct to leave, he unbuckled and got out. At once he was half shoved out of the way. Excited, shouting men pulled the cockpit door open further, peered in, while others hauled the main cabin door open and scrambled aboard. 'What the hell happened to you, agha?' he asked Nasiri, seeing the extent of the bruises.

'The – the new komiteh made an error,' Nasiri said, trying to maintain his dignity, 'thinking I was a . . . a Shah supporter and not a man of the revolution and the Imam.'

'Who the hell're these men – they aren't from Yazdek.'

But before Nasiri could answer, the Green Band with the Sten gun elbowed through the pack. 'In office! NOW!' the man said in bad English, then reached out and grabbed Scot by the flight jacket sleeve to hurry him up. Automatically Scot jerked his arm away. A gun went into his ribs. 'All right, for crissake,' he muttered and stalked off towards the office, his face grim.

In the office Nitchak Khan, kalandar of the village, and the old mullah stood alongside the desk, their backs to the wall beside the open window. Both were set-faced. He greeted them and they nodded back, ill at ease. Behind him, many Green Bands crowded into the room after Nasiri.

'*Cheh karbareh*, kalandar?' Scot asked. What's happening?

'These men are . . . claim to be our new komiteh,' Nitchak Khan replied with difficulty. 'They are sent from Sharpur to take over our . . . our village and our . . . airfield.'

Scot was perplexed. What the village leader had said didn't make any sense. Though Sharpur was the nearest town and had nominal jurisdiction over the area, custom had always left the Kash'kai tribesmen of the mountains to govern themselves – so long as they acknowledged the suzerainty of the Shah and Tehran, obeyed the laws and remained disarmed and peaceful. 'But you always govern –'

'Quiet!' the leader of the Green Bands said, waving his Sten gun, and Scot saw Nitchak Khan flush. The leader was bearded, in his thirties, poorly dressed, with dark eyes that had something bad about them. He dragged Nasiri to the front of the group and rattled off more Farsi.

'I – I am to interpret, Captain,' Nasiri said nervously. 'The leader, Ali-sadr, says you are to answer the following questions. I've answered most but he wants . . .' Ali-sadr cursed him and began the questioning, reading from a prepared list, Nasiri translating.

'Are you in command here?'

'Yes, temporarily.'

'What is your nationality?'

'British. Now what the h –'

'Any Americans here?'

'Not to my knowledge,' Scot said at once and kept his face bland, hoping Nasiri who knew that Rodrigues, the mechanic, was American with a false English ID, had not been asked that question. Nasiri translated without hesitation. One of the other Green Bands was writing down his answers.

'How many pilots are here?'

'At the moment I'm the only one.'

'Where are the others, who are they, and what is their nationality?'

'Our senior pilot, Captain Lochart, Canadian, is in Tehran – he's on a charter out of Tehran, I think, expected back any day. The other, second in command, Captain Sessonne, French, had to go on an urgent charter for IranOil today to Tehran.'

The leader looked up, his eyes hard. 'What so urgent?'

'Rig Rosa's ready to log a new well.' He waited while Nasiri explained what this meant and that the oil drillers needed the urgent help of Schlumberger experts, now based in Tehran. This morning Jean-Luc had called their local ATC at Shiraz on the off chance for clearance to go to Tehran. To his astonishment and delight Shiraz ATC gave an immediate approval. 'The Imam has decreed that oil production will begin,' they had said, 'so it will begin.'

Jean-Luc had been airborne within minutes. Scot Gavallan smiled to himself knowing the real reason why Jean-Luc did three cartwheels into the 206's cockpit was that now he could sneak an overdue visit to Sayada. Scot had met her once. 'Has she got a sister?' he had said hopefully.

The leader listened impatiently to Nasiri, then cut in again and Nasiri flinched. 'He, Ali-sadr, he says in future all flights will be cleared by him, or this man—' Nasiri pointed at the youthful Green Band who had been writing down Scot's answers. 'In future all flights will have one of their men aboard. In future no takeoffs without advance permission. In about one hour you will take him and his men to all the rigs in the area.'

485

'Explain to him that it's not possible to do that because we have to deliver more pipe and cement to Rig Rosa. Otherwise when Jean-Luc comes back tomorrow they won't be ready in time.'

Nasiri began to explain. The leader interrupted him rudely, and got up. 'Tell the Infidel pilot to be ready in about an hour and then . . . even better, tell him to come with us to the village where I can watch him. You come too. And tell him to be very obedient, for though the Imam wants oil production started quickly, all persons in Iran are subject to Islamic law if they're Iranian or not. We don't need foreigners here.' The man glanced at Nitchak Khan. 'Now we will return to our village,' he said and strode out. Nitchak Khan flushed. He and the mullah followed.

'Captain, we are to go with him,' Nasiri said, 'to the village.'

'What for?'

'Well, you're the only pilot here and you know the countryside,' Nasiri said readily, wondering what the real reason was. He was very afraid. There had been no warning of any impending changes, nor were they even aware in the village that the road was open from the last snowfall. But this morning the truck with twelve Green Bands had arrived in the village. At once the leader of the komiteh had produced the piece of paper signed by the Sharpur Revolutionary Komiteh giving them jurisdiction over Yazdek and 'all IranOil production and facilities and helicopters in that area'. When, at Nitchak Khan's request, Nasiri had said he would radio IranOil to protest, one of the men had started beating him. The leader had stopped the man but had not apologised, nor had he shown Nitchak Khan the respect due to him as kalandar of this branch of the Kash'kai. More fear rushed through Nasiri and he wished he was back in Sharpur with his wife and family. God curse all komitehs and fanatics and foreigners and the Great American Satan who caused all our problems. 'We'd . . . we'd better go,' he said.

They went outside. The others were already well down the track that led to the village. As Scot passed the hangar, he saw his six mechanics collected under the watchful gaze of an armed guard. The guard was smoking and a twinge went through him. Signs in Farsi and English were everywhere: NO SMOKING – DANGER! To one side their second 212 was in its final stages of the 1,500-hour check, but without the two 206s that made up their present complement of airplanes the hangar seemed empty and forlorn. 'Agha,' he said to Nasiri, nodding back at their own guards, 'tell them I've got to make arrangements about the chopper and order that bugger not to smoke in the hangar.'

Nasiri did as he was asked. 'They said all right, but to hurry up.' The guard who was smoking lazily flicked his cigarette on to the concrete. One of the mechanics hastily ground it out. Nasiri would have stayed but the guards motioned him onwards. Reluctantly he left.

'Tank up FBC and ground-check her,' Scot said carefully, not sure if any of the guards understood English. 'In an hour I'm to take our komiteh for a state visit to the sites. It seems we've a new komiteh from Sharpur now.'

'Oh, shit,' someone muttered.

'What about the gear for Rig Rosa?' Effer Jordon asked. Beside him was Rod Rodrigues. Scot could see his anxiety.

'That'll have to wait. Just tank FBC, Effer, and everyone check her out. Rod,' he said to encourage the older man, 'now that we're getting back to normal, you'll soon get your home leave in London, *capito?*'

'Sure, thanks, Scot.'

The guard beside Scot motioned him to go on. '*Baleh, agha*' – yes, all right, Excellency, Scot said, then added to Rodrigues, 'Rod, do a careful ground check for me.'

'Sure.'

Scot walked off, his guards following. Jordon called out anxiously, 'What's going on, and where're you going?'

'I'm going for a stroll,' he said sarcastically. 'How the hell would I know? I've been flying all morning.' He trudged off feeling tired and helpless and inadequate, wishing that Lochart or Jean-Luc were there in his place. Bloody komiteh bastards! Bunch of bloody thugs.

Nasiri was a hundred yards ahead, walking quickly, the others already vanished around the bend in the track that meandered through the trees. It was just below freezing and the snow crunched underfoot, and though Scot felt warm in his flight gear, walking was awkward in his flying boots and he clomped along moodily wanting to catch Nasiri but unable to. Snow was banked beside the path and heavy on the trees, clear skies above. Half a mile ahead, down the curling pathway was the village.

Yazdek was on a small plateau, nicely protected from the high winds. The huts and houses were made of wood, stone, and mud bricks and grouped around the square in front of the small mosque. Unlike most villages it was prosperous, plenty of wood for warmth in winter, plenty of game nearby, with communal flocks of sheep and goats, a few camels and thirty horses and brood mares that were their pride. Nitchak Khan's home was a two-storey, tile-roofed dwelling of four rooms, beside the mosque and bigger than all the others.

Next door was the schoolhouse, the most modern building. Tom Lochart had designed the simple structure and had persuaded McIver to finance it last year. Up to a few months ago the school had been run by a young man in the Shah's Teaching Corps – the village was almost totally illiterate. When the Shah left, the young man had vanished. From time to time Tom Lochart and others from the base had given talks there – more question-and-answer sessions – partially for good relations and partially for something to do when there was no flying. The sessions were well attended by adults as well as by children, encouraged to do so by Nitchak Khan and his wife.

As he came down the rise, Scot saw the others go into the school-house. The truck that had brought the Green Bands was parked outside. Villagers were collected in groups, silently watching. Men, women, and children, none of them armed. Kash'kai women wore neither veils nor chador but multi-coloured robes.

Scot went up the stairs into the school. The last time he was here, just a few weeks ago, he had given a talk on the Hong Kong he knew when his father still worked there and he would visit from English boarding school during the holidays. It had been hard to explain what Hong Kong was like, with its teeming streets, typhoons, chopsticks and character writing, and foods and freebooting capitalism, the immensity of China overall. I'm glad we came back to Scotland, he thought. Glad the Old Man started S-G that I'm going to run one day.

'You are to sit down, Captain,' Nasiri said. 'There.' He indicated a chair at the back of the low-ceilinged, crowded room. Ali-sadr and four other Green Bands were seated at the table where the teacher would normally sit. Nitchak Khan and the mullah sat in front of them. Villagers stood around.

'What's going on?'

'It's a . . . a meeting.'

Scot saw the fear pervading Nasiri and wondered what he would do if the Green Bands started to beat him. I should've been a black belt or boxer, he thought wearily, trying to understand the Farsi that poured out of the leader.

'What's he saying, agha?' he whispered to Nasiri.

'I . . . he's . . . he's saying . . . he's telling Nitchak Khan how the village will be run in future. Please, I will explain later.' Nasiri moved away.

In time the tirade stopped. Everyone looked at Nitchak Khan. He got up slowly. His face was grave and his words few. Even Scot understood. 'Yazdek is Kash'kai. Yazdek will remain Kash'kai.' He turned his back on the table and began to leave, the mullah following.

At an angry command of the leader, two Green Bands barred his way. Contemptuously, Nitchak Khan brushed them aside, then others grabbed him, tension in the room soared, and Scot saw one villager slip out of the room unnoticed. Those Green Bands holding Nitchak Khan turned him around to face Ali-sadr and the other four who were on their feet, enraged, and shouting. No one had touched the old man who was the mullah. He held up his hand and began to speak, but the leader shouted him down and a sigh went through the villagers. Nitchak Khan did not struggle against the men pinioning him, just looked back at Ali-sadr, and Scot felt the hatred like a physical blow.

The leader harangued all the villagers, then pointed an accusing finger at Nitchak Khan and once more ordered him to obey and once more Nitchak Khan said quietly, 'Yazdek is Kash'kai. Yazdek will remain Kash'kai.'

Ali-sadr sat down. So did the four others. Again Ali-sadr pointed and said a few words. A gasp went through the villagers. The four men beside him nodded their agreement. Ali-sadr said one word. It cut through the silence like a scythe. 'Death!' He got up and walked out, villagers and Green Bands frog-marching Nitchak Khan after him, Scot forgotten. Scot ducked down to one side, trying to make himself scarce. Soon he was alone.

Outside, the Green Bands dragged Nitchak Khan to the wall of the mosque and stood him there. The square was empty now of villagers. As the other villagers came out of the schoolhouse into the square, they too hurried off. Except the mullah. Slowly he walked over to Nitchak Khan and stood beside him, facing the Green Bands who, twenty yards away, readied their guns. On Ali-sadr's orders, two of them pulled the old man away. Nitchak Khan waited by the wall silently, proudly, then he spat in the dirt.

The single rifle shot came out of nowhere. Ali-sadr was dead before he slumped to the ground. The silence was sudden and vast, and the Green Bands whirled in panic, then froze as a voice shouted, 'Allah-u Akbarr, put down your guns!'

No one moved, then one of the firing squad jerked his gun around at Nitchak Khan but died before he could pull the trigger.

'God is Great, put down your guns!'

One of the Green Bands let his gun clatter to the ground. Another followed suit, another rushed for the truck but died before he got ten yards. Now all other guns were on the ground. And all who stood stayed motionless.

Then the door of Nitchak Khan's house opened and his wife came out with the levelled carbine, a young man following, also with a carbine. She was fierce in her pride, ten years younger than her husband, the jingling of her earrings and chains and the swish of her long tan and red robes the only sound in the square.

Nitchak Khan's narrow eyes in his high-cheekboned face narrowed even more, and the deep lines at the corners crinkled. But he said nothing to her, just looked at the eight Green Bands who remained. Mercilessly. They stared back at him, then one of them grabbed for his gun, and she shot him in the stomach and he screamed, writhing on the snow. She left him to howl for a moment. A second shot and the screaming stopped.

Now there were seven.

Nitchak Khan smiled silently. Now, out of the houses and huts, the grown men and women of the village came into the square. All were armed. He turned his attention back to the seven. 'Get in the truck, lie down, and put your hands behind you.' Sullenly the men obeyed. He ordered four of the villagers to guard them, then he turned to the young man who had come out of his house. 'There's one more at the airfield, my son. Take someone with you and deal with him. Bring his body back but cover your faces with scarves so the Infidels won't recognise you.'

'As God wants.' The young man pointed at the schoolhouse. The door was still open, but no sign of Scot. 'The Infidel,' he said softly. 'He's not of our village.' Then he went off quickly.

The village waited. Nitchak Khan scratched his beard thoughtfully. Then his eyes went to Nasiri who cowered beside the schoolhouse stairs.

Nasiri's face drained. 'I – I saw–saw nothing, nothing, Nitchak Khan,' he croaked, and got up and stepped around the bodies. 'I've always – for the two years I've been here I've always done everything I could for the village. I – I saw nothing,' he said louder, abjectly, then his terror crested and he took to his heels out of the square. And died. A dozen had fired at him.

'It's true the only witness to these men's evil should be God.' Nitchak Khan sighed. He had liked Nasiri. But he was not one of their people. His wife came up beside him and he smiled at her. She took out a

490

cigarette and gave it to him and lit it for him, then put the cigarettes and matches back in her pocket. He puffed thoughtfully. Some dogs barked among the houses and a child cried, quickly to be hushed.

'There will be a small avalanche to break the road where it was swept away before, to keep all others out until the thaw,' he said at length. 'We will put the bodies into the truck, and pour petrol over it and them and let it fall off the road into the Ravine of the Broken Camels. It seems that the komiteh decided we could govern ourselves as always and that we should be left in peace as always, then they went away and took Nasiri's body with them. They shot Nasiri here in the square, as all saw, when he tried to escape justice. Unfortunately, they had an accident going back. It is a very dangerous road as all know. Probably they took Nasiri's body to prove they had done their duty and cleansed our mountains of a known Shah supporter and shot him as he tried to escape. Certainly he was a Shah supporter when the Shah had power and before the Shah ran away.' The villagers nodded agreeably and waited. All wanted to know the answer to the final question: what about the last witness? What about the Infidel still in the schoolhouse?

Nitchak Khan scratched his beard. It always helped him to make difficult decisions.

'More Green Bands will come soon, drawn by the magnet of the flying machines, made by foreigners and flown by foreigners for the benefit of foreigners because of the oil that is gathered from our earth for the benefit of enemy Tehranis and enemy tax collectors and more foreigners. If there were no wells there would be no foreigners, therefore there would be no Green Bands. The land is rich in oil elsewhere, easy to gather, elsewhere. Ours is not. Our few wells are not important and the eleven bases difficult of access and dangerous – did they not have to explode the mountaintop to save one from avalanche only a few days ago?'

There was general agreement. He puffed the cigarette leisurely. The people watched him confidently – he was kalandar, their chief who had ruled wisely for eighteen years in good times and bad. 'If there were no flying machines there would be no wells. So if these foreigners departed,' he continued in the same gruff, unhurried voice, 'I doubt if other strangers would venture here to repair and reopen the eleven bases, for surely the bases would quickly fall into disrepair, perhaps even be looted by bandits and damaged. So we would be left in peace. Without our benevolence no one can operate in our mountains. We Kash'kai seek to live in peace – we will be free and ruled by our own ways and own customs. Therefore the foreigners must go, of their own free will. And go quickly. So must the wells. And everything foreign.' Carefully he stubbed his cigarette into the snow. 'Let us begin: Burn the school.'

He was obeyed at once. A little petrol and the tinder dry wood soon made it into a conflagration. Everyone waited. But the Infidel did not appear, nor when they searched the rubble did they find any remains.

Near Tabriz: 11:49 A.M. Erikki Yokkonen was climbing the 206
through the high pass that led at length to the city, Nogger Lane
beside him with Azadeh in the back. She wore a bulky flight jacket over
her ski clothes, but in the carryall beside her was a chador: 'Just for
safety,' she had said. On her head was a third headset that Erikki had
rigged for her.

'Tabriz One, do you read?' he said again. They waited. Still no
answer and well within range. 'Could be abandoned, could be a trap,
like with Charlie.'

'Best take a jolly good look before we land,' Nogger said uneasily, his
eyes scanning the sky and the land.

The sky was clear. It was well below freezing, the mountains heavy
with snow. They had refuelled without incident at an IranOil depot just
outside Bandar-e Pahlavi – already renamed – by arrangement with
Tehran ATC. 'Khomeini's got everything by the short and curlies, with
ATC helpful and the airport opened up again,' Erikki had said, trying
to shove away the depression that sat heavily on all of them.

493

Azadeh was still badly shaken by the news of Emir Paknouri's execution for crimes against Islam and by the even more terrible news about Sharazad's father. 'That's murder,' she had burst out, horrified, when she had heard. 'What crimes could he commit, he who has supported Khomeini and mullahs for generations?'

None of them had had any answers. The family had been told to collect the body and now were in deep and abject mourning, Sharazad demented with grief – the house closed even to Azadeh and Erikki. Azadeh had not wanted to leave Tehran but a second message had arrived from her father to Erikki, repeating the first: 'Captain, I require my daughter in Tabriz urgently.'

And now they were almost home.

Once it was home, Erikki thought. Now I'm not so sure.

Near Qazvin he had flown over the place where his Range Rover had run out of petrol and Pettikin and Rakoczy had rescued Azadeh and him from the mob. The Range Rover was no longer there. Then over the miserable village where the roadblock had been, and he had escaped to crush the fat-faced mujhadin who had stolen their papers. Madness to come back, he thought.

'Mac's right,' Azadeh had pleaded with him. 'Go to Al Shargaz. Let Nogger fly me to Tabriz and fly me back to get on the next shuttle. I'll join you in Al Shargaz whatever my father says.'

'I'll take you home and bring you back,' he had said. 'Finish.'

They had taken off from Doshan Tappeh just after dawn. The base was almost empty, with many buildings and hangars now burned-out shells, wrecked Iranian Air Force airplanes, trucks, and one fire-gutted tank with the Immortals emblem on its side. No one cleaning up the mess. No guards. Scavengers taking away anything burnable – still hardly any fuel oil for sale, or food, but many daily and nightly clashes between Green Bands and leftists.

The S-G hangar and repair shop were hardly damaged. Many bullet holes in the walls but nothing had been looted yet and it was operating, more or less, with a few mechanics and office staff about their normal work. Some back salary from the money McIver had squeezed from Valik and the other partners had been the magnet. He had given some cash to Erikki to pay the staff at Tabriz One: 'Start praying, Erikki! Today I've an appointment at the Ministry to iron out our finances and the money we're owed,' he had told them just before they took off, 'and to renew all our out-of-date licences. Talbot at the embassy fixed it for me – he thinks there's a better than good chance Bazargan and Khomeini can get control

494

now and disarm the leftists. We've just got to keep our bottle, keep our cool.'

Easy for him, Erikki thought.

Now they crested the pass. He banked and came down fast. 'There's the base!' Both pilots concentrated. The wind sock was the only thing that moved. No transport parked anywhere. No smoke from any of the cabins. 'There should be smoke.' He circled tightly at 700 feet. No one came out to greet them. 'I'll take a closer look.'

They whirled in quickly and out again. Still nothing moved so they went back up to a thousand feet. Erikki thought a moment. 'Azadeh, I could set her down in the forecourt of the palace just outside the walls.'

At once Azadeh shook her head: 'No, Erikki, you know how nervous his guards are and how, how sensitive he is about anyone arriving unasked.'

'But we're asked, at least you are. Ordered is the real word. We could go over there, circle and take a look, and if it seems all right, we could land.'

'We could land well away and walk in t –'

'No walking. Not without guns.' He had been unable to obtain one in Tehran. Every damned hooligan has as many as he wants, he thought irritably. Have to get one. Don't feel safe any more. 'We'll go and look and then I'll decide.' He switched to the Tabriz Tower frequency and called. No answer. He called again, then banked and went for the city. As they passed over their village of Abu Mard, Erikki pointed downward and Azadeh saw the little schoolhouse where she had spent so many happy hours, the glades nearby and there, just by the stream, was where she had first seen Erikki and thought him a giant of the forest and had fallen in love, miracle of miracles, to be rescued by him from a life of torment. She reached forward and touched him through the small window.

'You all right? Warm enough?' He smiled at her.

'Oh, yes, Erikki. The village was so lucky for us, wasn't it?' She kept her hand on his shoulder. The contact pleased both of them.

Soon they could see the airport and the railway that went north to Soviet Azerbaijan a few miles away, then on to Moscow, southeast it curled back to Tehran, three hundred and fifty miles away. The city was large. Now they could pick out the citadel and the Blue Mosque and polluting steel factories, the huts and hovels and houses of the 600,000 inhabitants.

'Look over there!' Part of the railway station was smouldering, smoke billowing. More fires near the citadel and no answer from

Tabriz Tower and no activity on the airfield apron, though some small, feeder airplanes were parked there. A lot of activity at the military base, trucks and cars coming and going, but as far as they could see, no firing or battles or crowds in the streets, the whole area near the mosque curiously empty. 'Don't want to go too low,' he said, 'don't want to tempt some trigger-happy crackpot.'

'You like Tabriz, Erikki?' Nogger asked, to cover his disquiet. He had never been here before.

'It's a grand city, old and wise and open and free – the most cosmopolitan in Iran. I've had some grand times here, the food and drink of all the world cheap and available – caviar and Russian vodka and Scottish smoked salmon and once a week, in the good times, Air France brought fresh French breads and cheeses. Turkish goods and Caucasian, British, American, Japanese – anything and everything. It's famous for its carpets, Nogger, and the beauty of its girls . . .' He felt Azadeh pinch his earlobe and he laughed. 'It's true, Azadeh, aren't you Tabrizi? It's a fine city, Nogger. They speak a dialect of Farsi which is more Turkish than anything else. For centuries it's been a big trading centre, part Iranian, part Russian, part Turkish, part Kurd, part Armenian, and always rebellious and independent and always wanted by the tsars and now the Soviets . . .'

Here and there knots of people stared up at them. 'Nogger, see any guns?'

'Plenty, but no one's firing at us. Yet.'

Cautiously Erikki skirted the city and headed eastward. There the land climbed into close foothills and there was the walled palace of the Gorgons on a crest with the road leading up to it. No traffic on the road. Many acres of land within the high walls: orchards, a carpet factory, garages for twenty cars, sheds for wintering herds of sheep, huts and outhouses for a hundred-odd servants and guards, and the sprawling main cupolaed building of fifty rooms and small mosque and tiny minaret. A number of cars were parked near the main entrance. He circled at 700 feet.

'That's some pad,' Nogger Lane said, awed.

'It was built for my great-grandfather by Prince Zergeyev on orders of the Romanov tsars, Nogger, as a pishkesh,' Azadeh said absently, watching the grounds below. 'That was in 1890 when the tsars had already stolen our Caucasian provinces and once more were trying to split Azerbaijan from Iran and wanted the help of the Gorgon Khans. But our line has always been loyal to Iran though they have sought to maintain a balance.' She was watching the palace below. People were coming out of the main house and some of the outhouses – servants and armed guards. 'The mosque was built in 1907 to celebrate the signing of the new Russian-British accord on their partitioning of us, and spheres of infl – oh, look, Erikki, isn't that Najoud and Fazulia and Zadi . . . and, oh, look, Erikki, isn't that my brother Hakim – what's Hakim doing there?'

'Where? Oh, I see him. No, I don't th –'

'Perhaps . . . perhaps Abdollah Khan's forgiven him,' she said excitedly. 'Oh wouldn't that be wonderful!'

Erikki peered at the people below. He had only met her brother once, at their wedding, but he had liked him very much. Abdollah Khan had released Hakim from banishment for this day only, then sent him back to Khvoy in the northern part of Azerbaijan near the Turkish border where he had extensive mining interests. 'All Hakim has ever wanted was to go to Paris to study the piano,' Azadeh had told him. 'But my father wouldn't listen to him, just cursed him and banished him for plotting . . .'

'It's not Hakim,' Erikki said, his eyes much better than hers.

'Oh!' Azadeh squinted against the wind. 'Oh.' She was so disappointed. 'Yes, yes, you're right, Erikki.'

'There's Abdollah Khan!' There was no mistaking the imposing, corpulent man with the long beard, coming out of the main door to stand on the steps, two armed guards behind him. With him were two other men. All were dressed in heavy overcoats against the cold. 'Who're they?'

'Strangers,' she said, trying to get over her disappointment. 'They haven't guns and there's no mullah, so they're not Green Bands.'

'They're Europeans,' Nogger said. 'You have any binoculars, Erikki?'

'No.' Erikki stopped circling and came down to five hundred feet and hovered, watching Abdollah Khan intently. He saw him point at the chopper and then talk with the other men, then go back to watching the chopper again. More of her sisters and family, some wearing chador, and servants had collected, bundled against the cold. Down another hundred feet. Erikki slipped off his dark glasses and headset and slid the side window back, gasped as the freezing air hit him, stuck his head out so they could see him clearly and waved. All eyes on the ground went to Abdollah Khan. After a pause the Khan waved back. Without pleasure.

'Azadeh! Take your headset off and do what I did.'

She obeyed at once. Some of her sisters waved back excitedly, chattering among themselves. Abdollah Khan did not acknowledge her, just waited. *Matyeryebyets*, Erikki thought, then leaned out of the cockpit and pointed at the wide space beyond the mosaic, frozen pool in the courtyard, obviously asking permission to land. Abdollah Khan nodded and pointed there, spoke briefly to his guards, then turned on his heel and went back into the house. The other men followed. One guard stayed. He walked down the steps towards the touchdown point, checking the action of his assault rifle.

'Nothing like a friendly reception committee,' Nogger muttered.

'No need to worry, Nogger,' Azadeh said with a nervous laugh. 'I'll get out first, Erikki, safer for me to be first.'

They landed at once, Azadeh opened her door and went to greet her sisters and her stepmother, her father's third wife and younger than her. His first wife, the Khananam, was of an age with him but now she was bedridden and never left her room. His second wife, Azadeh's mother, had died many years ago.

The guard intercepted Azadeh. Politely. Erikki breathed easier. It was too far away to hear what was said – in any event, neither he nor Nogger spoke Farsi or Turkish. The guard motioned at the chopper. She nodded then turned and beckoned them. Erikki and Nogger completed the shutdown, watching the guard who watched them seriously.

'You hate guns as much as I do, Erikki?' Nogger said.

'More. But at least that man knows how to use one – it's the amateurs that scare me.' Erikki slipped out the circuit breakers and pocketed the ignition key.

They went to join Azadeh and her sisters but the guard stood in the way. Azadeh called out, 'He says we are to go to the Reception Room at once and wait there. Please follow me.'

Nogger was last. One of the pretty sisters caught his eye and he smiled to himself and went up the stairs two at a time.

The Reception Room was vast and cold and draughty and smelled of damp, with heavy Victorian furniture and many carpets and lounging cushions and old-fashioned water heaters. Azadeh tidied her hair at one of the mirrors. Her ski clothes were elegant and fashionable. Abdollah Khan had never required any of his wives or daughters or household to wear chador, did not approve of chador. Then why was Najoud wearing one today? she asked herself, her nervousness increasing. A servant brought tea. They waited half an hour, then another guard arrived and spoke to her. She took a deep breath. 'Nogger, you're to wait here,' she said. 'Erikki, you and I are to go with this guard.'

Erikki followed her, tense but confident that the armed peace he had worked out with Abdollah Khan would hold. The touch of his pukoh knife reassured him. The guard opened a door at the end of the corridor and motioned them forward.

Abdollah Khan was leaning against some cushions, reclining on a carpet facing the door, guards behind him, the room rich, Victorian and formal – and somehow decadent and soiled. The two men they had seen on the steps were seated cross-legged beside him. One was European, a big, well-preserved man in his late sixties with heavy shoulders and Slavic eyes set in a friendly face. The other was younger, in his thirties, his features Asiatic and the colour of his skin yellowish. Both wore heavy winter suits. Erikki's caution soared and he waited beside the doorway as Azadeh went to her father, knelt in front of him, kissed his pudgy, jewelled hands, and blessed him. Impassively her father waved her to one side and kept his dark, dark eyes on Erikki who greeted him politely from the door but stayed near it. Hiding her shame and fear, Azadeh knelt again on the carpet, and faced him. Erikki saw both the strangers flick their eyes over her appreciatively, and his temperature went up a notch. The silence intensified.

Beside the Khan was a plate of halvah, small squares of the honey-rich Turkish delicacies that he adored, and he ate some of them, light dancing off his rings. 'So,' he said harshly, 'it seems you kill indiscriminately like a mad dog.'

Erikki's eyes narrowed and he said nothing.

'Well?'

'If I kill it's not like a mad dog. Whom am I supposed to have killed?'

'One old man in a crowd outside Qazvin with a blow from your elbow, his chest crushed in. There are witnesses. Next, three men in a car and one outside it – he an important fighter for freedom. There are more witnesses. Farther down the road five dead and more wounded in the wake of the helicopter rescue. More witnesses.' Another silence. Azadeh had not moved though the blood had left her face. 'Well?'

'If there are any witnesses you will know also that we were peacefully trying to get to Tehran, we were unarmed, we were set upon by a mob and if it hadn't been for Charlie Pettikin and Rakoczy, we'd probably be—' Erikki stopped momentarily, noticing the sudden glance between the two strangers. Then, even more warily, he continued, 'We'd probably be dead. We were unarmed – Rakoczy wasn't – we were fired on first.'

Abdollah Khan had also noticed the change in the men beside him. Thoughtfully, he glanced back at Erikki. 'Rakoczy? The same with the

Islamic-Marxist mullah and men who attacked your base? The Soviet Muslim?'

'Yes.' Erikki looked at the two strangers, hard-eyed. 'The KGB agent, who claimed he came from Georgia, from Tbilisi.'

Abdollah Khan smiled thinly. 'KGB? How do you know that?'

'I've seen enough of them to know.' The two strangers stared back blandly; the older wore a friendly smile and Erikki was chilled by it.

'This Rakoczy, how did he get into the helicopter?' the Khan said.

'He captured Charlie Pettikin at my base last Sunday – Pettikin's one of our pilots and he'd come to Tabriz to pick us up, Azadeh and me. I'd been asked by my embassy to check with them about my passport – that was the day most governments, mine too, had ordered non-essential expats out of Iran,' he said, the exaggeration easy. 'On Monday, the day we left here, Rakoczy forced Pettikin to fly him to Tehran.' He told briefly what had happened. 'But for him noticing the Finnish flag on the roof we'd be dead.'

The man with Asiatic features laughed softly. 'That would have been a great loss, Captain Yokkonen,' he said in Russian.

The older man with the Slavic eyes said, in faultless English, 'This Rakoczy, where is he now?'

'I don't know. Somewhere in Tehran. May I ask who you are?' Erikki was playing for time and expected no answer. He was trying to decide if Rakoczy was friend or enemy to these two, obviously Soviet, obviously KGB or GRU – the secret police of the armed forces.

'Please, what was his first name?' the older man asked pleasantly.

'Fedor, like the Hungarian revolutionary.' Erikki saw no further reaction and could have gone on but was far too wise to volunteer anything to KGB or GRU. Azadeh was kneeling on the carpet, stiff-backed, motionless, her hands at rest in her lap, her lips red against the whiteness of her face. Suddenly he was very afraid for her.

'You admit killing those men?' the Khan said and ate another sweetmeat.

'I admit I killed men a year or so ago saving your life, Highness, an –'

'And yours!' Abdollah Khan said angrily. 'The assassins would have killed you too – it was the Will of God we both lived.'

'I didn't start that fight or seek it either.' Erikki tried to choose his words wisely, feeling unwise and unsafe and inadequate. 'If I killed those others it was not of my choosing but only to protect your daughter and my wife. Our lives were in danger.'

'Ah, you consider it your right to kill at any time you consider your life to be in danger?'

Erikki saw the flush in the Khan's face, and the two Soviets watching him, and he thought of his own heritage and his grandfather's stories of the olden days in the North Lands, when giants walked the earth and trolls and ghouls were not myth, long long ago when the earth was clean and evil was known as evil, and good as good, and evil could not wear the mask.

'If Azadeh's life is threatened – or mine – I will kill anyone,' he said evenly. The three men felt ice go through them. Azadeh was appalled at the threat, and the guards, who spoke neither Russian nor English, shifted uneasily, feeling the violence.

The vein in the centre of Abdollah's Khan's forehead knotted. 'You will go with this man,' he said darkly. 'You will go with this man and do his bidding.'

Erikki looked at the man with the Asiatic features. 'What do you want with me?'

'Just your skills as a pilot, and the 212,' the man said, not unfriendly, speaking Russian.

'Sorry, the 212's on a fifteen-hundred-hours check and I work for S-G and Iran-Timber.'

'The 212 is complete, already ground-tested by your mechanics, and Iran-Timber has released you to . . . to me.'

'To do what?'

'To fly,' the man said irritably. 'Are you hard of hearing?'

'No, but it seems you are.'

Air hissed out of the man's mouth. The older man smiled strangely. Abdollah Khan turned on Azadeh, and she almost jumped with fright. 'You will go to the Khananam and pay your respects!'

'Yes . . . yes . . . Father,' she stuttered and jumped up. Erikki moved half a step but the guards were ready, one had him covered and she said, near tears, 'No, Erikki, it's . . . I . . . must go . . .' She fled before he could stop her.

The man with the Asiatic face broke the silence. 'You've nothing to fear. We just need your skills.'

Erikki Yokkonen did not answer him, sure that he was at bay, that both he and Azadeh were at bay and lost, and knowing that if there were no guards here he would have attacked now, without hesitation, killed Abdollah Khan now and probably the other two. The three men knew it.

'Why did you send for my wife, Highness?' he said in the same quiet voice, knowing the answer now. 'You sent two messages.'

Abdollah Khan said with a sneer, 'She's of no value to me, but she is to my friends: to bring you back and to make you behave. And by God and the Prophet, you will behave. You will do what this man wants.'

One of the guards moved his snub-nosed machine gun a fraction and the noise he made echoed in the room. The Soviet with the Asiatic features got up. 'First your knife. Please.'

'You can come and take it. If you wish it seriously.'

The man hesitated. Abruptly Abdollah Khan laughed. The laugh was cruel, and it edged all of them. 'You will leave him his knife. That will make your life more interesting.' Then to Erikki, 'It would be wise to be obedient and to behave.'

'It would be wise to let us go in peace.'

'Would you like to watch your co-pilot hung up by his thumbs now?' Erikki's eyes flattened even more. The older Soviet leaned over to whisper to the Khan whose gaze never left Erikki. His hands played with his jewelled dagger. When the man had finished, he nodded. 'Erikki, you will tell your co-pilot that he is to be obedient too, while he is in Tabriz. We will send him to the base, but your small helicopter will remain here. For the moment.' He motioned the man with the Asiatic features to leave.

'My name is Cimtarga, Captain.' The man was not nearly as tall as Erikki but strongly built with wide shoulders. 'First we g –'

'Cimtarga's the name of a mountain, east of Samarkand. What's your real name? And rank?'

The man shrugged. 'My ancestors rode with Timour Tamburlaine, the Mongol, he who enjoyed erecting mountains of skulls. First we go to your base. We will go by car.' He walked past him and opened the door, but Erikki did not move, still looked at the Khan.

'I will see my wife tonight.'

'You will see her when—' Abdollah Khan stopped as again the older man leaned forward and whispered. Again the Khan nodded. 'Good. Yes, Captain, you will see her tonight, and every second night. Providing.' He let the word hang. Erikki turned on his heel and walked out.

As the door closed after them, tension left the room. The older man chuckled. 'Highness, you were perfect, perfect as usual.'

Abdollah Khan eased his left shoulder, the ache in the arthritic joint annoying him. 'He'll be obedient, Petr,' he said, 'but only as long as my disobedient and ungrateful daughter is within my reach.'

'Daughters are always difficult,' Petr Oleg Mzytryk answered. He came from north of the border, from Tbilisi – Tiflis.

'Not so, Petr. The others obey and give me no trouble but this one – she infuriates me beyond words.'

'Then send her away once the Finn has done what's required. Send them both away.' The Slavic eyes crinkled in the good face and he added lightly, 'If I were thirty years younger and she was free I would petition to take her off your hands.'

'If you'd asked before that madman appeared, you could have had her with my blessing,' Abdollah Khan said sourly, though he had noted the underlying hope, hid his surprise, and put it aside for later consideration. 'I regret giving her to him – I thought she'd drive him mad too – regret my oath before God to leave him alive – it was a moment of weakness.'

'Perhaps not. It's good to be magnanimous, occasionally. He did save your life.'

'Insha'Allah! That was God's doing – he was just an instrument.'

'Of course,' Mzytryk said soothingly. 'Of course.'

'That man's a devil, an atheist devil who stinks of bloodlust. If it hadn't been for my guards – you saw for yourself – we would be fighting for our lives.'

'No, not so long as she's in your power to be dealt with . . . improperly.' Petr smiled strangely.

'God willing, they'll both be soon in hell,' the Khan said, still infuriated that he had had to keep Erikki alive to assist Petr Oleg Mzytryk, when he could have given him to the leftist mujhadin and thus be rid of him for ever. The mullah Mahmud, one of the Tabriz leaders of the Islamic-Marxist mujhadin faction that had attacked the base, had come to him two days ago and told him what happened at the roadblock. 'Here are their papers as proof,' the mullah had said truculently, 'both of the foreigner who must be CIA and of the lady, your daughter. The moment he returns to Tabriz we will stand him before our komiteh, sentence him, take him to Qazvin and put him to death.'

'By the Prophet you won't, not until I give you approval,' he had said imperiously, taking their papers. 'That mad dog foreigner is married to my daughter, is not CIA, is under my protection until I cancel it, and if you touch so much as one foul red hair or interfere with him or the base until I approve it, I'll withdraw all my secret support and nothing will stop the Green Bands from stamping out the leftists of Tabriz! He'll be given to you in my time, not yours.' Sullenly the mullah had gone away and Abdollah had at once added Mahmud to his list of imperatives. When he had examined the papers carefully and found Azadeh's passport and ID and other permits he had been delighted, for these gave him an added hold over her, and her husband.

Yes, he thought, looking up at the Soviet, she will do whatever I require of her now. Anything. 'As God wants, but she may be a widow very soon.'

'Let's hope not too soon!' Mzytryk's laugh was good and infectious. 'Not until her husband's finished his assignment.'

Abdollah Khan was warmed by the man's presence and wise counsel and pleased that Mzytryk would do what was required of him. But I'll still have to be a better puppeteer than ever before, he thought, if I'm to survive, and Azerbaijan to survive.

All over the province and in Tabriz the situation now was very delicate, with insurrections of various kinds and factions fighting factions, with tens of thousands of Soviet soldiers poised just over the border. And tanks. And nothing between them and the Gulf to hinder them. Except me, he thought. And once they possessed Azerbaijan – with Tehran indefensible as history's proved time and time again – then Iran will fall into their hands like the rotten apple Khrushchev forecast. With Iran the Gulf, the world's oil, and Hormuz.

He wanted to howl with rage. God curse the Shah who wouldn't listen, wouldn't wait, hadn't the sense to crush a minor mullah-inspired rebellion not twenty years ago and send Ayatollah Khomeini into hell as I advised and so put into jeopardy our absolute, unstoppable, inevitable stranglehold over the entire world outside of Russia, Tsarist or Soviet – our real enemy.

We were so close: the U.S. was eating out of our hands, fawning and pressing on us their most advanced weapons, begging us to police the Gulf and so dominate the vile Arabs, absorb their oil, make vassals of them and their flyblown, foul Sunni sheikdoms from Saudi to Oman. We could have overrun Kuwait in a day, Iraq in a week, the Saudi and Emirate sheiks would have fled back to their deserts screaming for mercy! We could get whatever technology we wanted, whatever ships, airplanes, tanks, arms for the asking, even the Bomb, by God! – our German-built reactors would have made them for us!

So close to doing God's will, we Shi'as of Iran, with our superior intelligence, our ancient history, our oil, and our command of the strait that must eventually bring all the People of the Left Hand to their knees. So close to gaining Jerusalem and Mecca, control of Mecca – Holy of Holies.

So close to being First on Earth, as is our right, but now, now all in

504

jeopardy and we have to start again, and again outmanoeuvre the Satanic barbarians from the North and all because of one man.

Insha'Allah, he thought, and that took some of his anger away. Even so, if Mzytryk had not been in the room he would have ranted and raved and beaten someone, anyone. But the man was here and had to be dealt with, the problems of Azerbaijan arranged, so he controlled his anger and pondered his next move. His fingers picked up the last of the halvah and popped it into his mouth.

'You'd like to marry Azadeh, Petr?'

'You'd like me, older than you, as a son-in-law?' the man said with a deprecating laugh.

'If it was the Will of God,' he replied with the right amount of sincerity and smiled to himself for he had seen the sudden light in his friend's eyes, quickly covered. So, he thought, the first time you see her you want her. Now if I really gave her to you when the monster's disposed of, what would that do for me? Many things! You're eligible, you're powerful, politically it would be wise, and you'd beat sense into her and deal with her as she should be dealt with, not like the Finn who fawns on her. You'd be an instrument of revenge on her. There are many advantages . . .

Three years ago Petr Oleg Mzytryk had taken over the immense dacha and lands that had belonged to his father – also an old friend of the Gorgons – near Tbilisi where, for generations, the Gorgons also had had very important business connections. Since then Abdollah Khan had got to know him intimately, staying at the dacha on frequent business trips. He had found Petr Oleg like all Russians, secretive, volunteering little. But, unlike most, helpful and friendly – and more powerful than any Soviet he knew, a widower with a married daughter, a son in the navy, grandchildren – and rare habits. He lived alone in the huge dacha except for servants and a strangely beautiful, strangely venomous Russian-Eurasian woman called Vertinskya, in her late 30s, whom he had brought out twice in three years, almost like a unique private treasure. She seemed to be part slave, part prisoner, part drinking companion, part whore, part tormentor and part wildcat. 'Why don't you kill her and have done with her, Petr?' he had said when a raging violent quarrel had erupted and Mzytryk had physically whipped her out of the room, the woman spitting and cursing and fighting till servants hauled her away.

'Not . . . not yet,' Mzytryk had said, his hands trembling, 'she's far . . . far too valuable.'

'Ah, yes . . . yes, now I understand,' Abdollah Khan had said,

'Ah, yes . . . yes, now I understand,' Abdollah Khan had said, equally aroused, having almost the same feeling about Azadeh – the reluctance to cast away such an object until she was truly cowed, truly humble and crawling – and he remembered how he had envied Mzytryk that Vertinskya was mistress and not daughter so the final act of revenge could be consummated.

God curse Azadeh, he thought. Curse her who could be the twin of the mother who gave me so much pleasure, who reminds me constantly of my loss, she and her evil brother, both patterns of the mother in face and manner but not in quality, she who was like a houri from the Garden of God. I thought both of our children loved and honoured me, but no, once Napthala had gone to Paradise their true natures came to pass. I know Azadeh was plotting with her brother to murder me – haven't I the proof? Oh, God, I wish I could beat her like Petr does his nemesis, but I can't, I can't. Every time I raise my hand against her I see my Beloved, God curse Azadeh to hell . . .

'Be calm,' Mzytryk said gently.

'What?'

'You were looking so upset, my friend. Don't worry, everything will be all right. You will find a way to exorcise her.'

Abdollah Khan nodded heavily. 'You know me too well.' That's true, he thought, ordering tea for himself and vodka for Mzytryk, the only man he had ever felt at ease with.

I wonder who you really are, he thought, watching him. In years gone by, in your father's time at the dacha when we met, you used to say you were on leave, but you'd never say on leave from what, nor could I ever find out, however much I tried. At first I presumed it was the Soviet army for once when you were drunk you told me you'd been a tank commander during World War II at Sebastopol, and all the way to Berlin. But then I changed my mind and thought it more likely you and your father were KGB or GRU, for no one in the whole USSR retires to such a dacha with such lands in Georgia, the best part of the empire, without very particular knowledge and influence. You say you're retired now – retired from what?

Experimenting to find out the extent of Mzytryk's power in the early days, Abdollah Khan had mentioned that a clandestine communist Tudeh cell in Tabriz was plotting to assassinate him and he would like the cell stamped out. It was only partially true, the real reason being that a son of a man he hated secretly and could not attack openly was part of the group. Within the week all their heads were stuck on spikes near the mosque with a sign, THUS WILL ALL ENEMIES OF GOD PERISH,

506

and he had wept cold tears at the funeral and laughed in privacy. That Petr Mzytryk had the power to eliminate one of their own cells was power indeed – and also, Abdollah knew, a measure of his own importance to them.

He looked at him. 'How long will you need the Finn?'

'A few weeks.'

'What if the Green Bands prevent him flying or intercept him?'

The Soviet shrugged. 'Let's hope he will have finished the assignment. I doubt if there would be any survivors – either him or Cimtarga – if they're found this side of the border.'

'Good. Now, back to where we were before we were interrupted: you agreed there'll be no massive support for the Tudeh here, so long as the Americans stay out and Khomeini doesn't start a pogrom against them?'

'Azerbaijan has always been within our frame of interest. We've always said it should be an independent state – there's more than enough wealth, power, minerals and oil to sustain it and . . .' Mzytryk smiled, 'and enlightened leadership. You could lift the flag, Abdollah. I'm sure you'd get all the support you need to be president – with our immediate recognition.'

And then I'd be assassinated the next day while the tanks roll over the borders, the Khan told himself without venom. Oh, no, my fine friend, the Gulf is too much temptation even for you. 'It's a wonderful idea,' he said earnestly, 'but I would need time – meanwhile I can count also on the communist Tudeh being turned on the insurrectionists?'

Petr Mzytryk's smile remained the same but his eyes changed. 'It would be curious for the Tudeh to attack their stepbrothers. Islamic-Marxism is advocated by many Muslim intellectuals – I hear even you support them.'

'I agree there should be a balance in Azerbaijan. But who ordered leftists to attack the airfield? Who ordered them to attack and burn our railway station? Who ordered the blowing up of the oil pipeline? Obviously no one sensible. I hear it was the mullah Mahmud of the Hajsra mosque.' He watched Petr carefully. 'One of yours.'

'I've never heard of him.'

'Ah,' Abdollah Khan said with pretended joviality, disbelieving him. 'I'm glad, Petr, because he's a false mullah, not even a real Islamic-Marxist, a rabble-rouser – he's the one who invaded Yokkonen's base. Unfortunately he has as many as five hundred fighters supporting him, equally ill-disciplined. And money from somewhere. And helpers like Fedor Rakoczy. What does Rakoczy mean to you?'

'Not much,' Petr said at once, his smile the same and voice the same, far too clever to avoid the question. 'He's a pipeline engineer from Ashara, on the border, one of our Muslim nationals who is believed to have joined the mujhadin as a Freedom Fighter, strictly without permission or approval.'

Petr kept his face bland but inside he was swearing obscenely, wanting to shout, My son, my son, have you betrayed us? You were sent to spy, to infiltrate the mujhadin and report back, that's all! And this time you were sent to try to recruit the Finn, then to go to Tehran and organise university students, not to ally yourself to a mad dog mullah nor to attack airfields or kill scum beside a road. Have you gone mad? You stupid fool, what if you'd been wounded and caught? How many times have I told you they – and we – can break anyone in time and empty him or her of their secrets? Stupid to take such risks! The Finn's temporarily important but not important enough to disobey orders, to risk your future, your brother's future – and mine!

If the son's suspect, so is the father. If the father's suspect so is the family. How many times have I told you that the KGB works by the Book, destroys those who won't obey the Book, who think for themselves, take risks, and exceed instructions.

'This Rakoczy's unimportant,' he said smoothly. Be calm, he ordered himself, beginning the litany: There's nothing to worry about. You know too many secrets to be touched. So does my son. He's good, they must be wrong about him. He's been tested many times, by you and by other experts. You're safe. You're strong, you've your health, and you could beat and bed that little beauty Azadeh and still rape Vertinskya the same day. 'What's important is that you are the focus of Azerbaijan, my friend,' he said in the same soothing voice. 'You will get all the support you need and your views on the Islamic-Marxists will reach the right source. The balance you require, you will have.'

'Good. I will count on it,' the Khan said.

'Meanwhile,' Mzytryk said, coming back to the main reason for his sudden trip here. 'What about the British captain? Can you help us?'

The day before yesterday a top secret, priority-coded telex from Centre had arrived at his home near Tbilisi telling him that the CIA's covert radar listening post on Sabalan's north face had been blown up by saboteurs just before friendly local teams sent to remove all cipher books, cipher machine, and computers had arrived. 'See Ivanovitch personally at once,' the telex had continued, using Abdollah Khan's undercover name. 'Tell him that the saboteurs were British – a captain and two Gurkhas – and an American CIA agent Rosemont (code name

Abu Kurd), guided by one of our mercenaries who was murdered by them before he could lead them into an ambush. One soldier and the CIA agent were killed during their escape and the two survivors are believed to be heading towards Ivanovitch's sector – arrange his cooperation. Section 16/a. Acknowledge.' The Section 16 command meant; this person or persons are priority enemies who are to be intercepted, detained and brought back for interrogation by whatever means necessary. The added 'a' meant: if this cannot be done, eliminate them without fail.

Mzytryk sipped the vodka, waiting. 'We would appreciate your help.'

'You've always got my help,' Abdollah said. 'But to find two expert saboteurs in Azerbaijan who are certain to be disguised by now is almost an impossibility. They're bound to have safe houses to go to – there's a British consulate in Tabriz, and dozens of routes out of the mountains that would bypass us.' He got up and went to the window and stared out of it. From here he could see the 206 parked in the forecourt under guard. The day was still cloudless. 'If I'd been leading that operation I'd pretend to head for Tabriz, but then I'd double back and go out by the Caspian. How did they go in?'

'Caspian. But they were tracked this way. Two bodies were found in the snow, and tracks of the two others headed this way.'

The failure of the Sabalan venture had sent a tremor of rage up the line. That there was so much CIA top secret equipment so near at hand had been a magnet for covert acquisition and infiltration for many years. In the last two weeks information that some of the radar posts had been evacuated but not destroyed in the retreat and panic they had helped foster, had had the hawks ready to move in immediately, in strength. Mzytryk, senior counsellor in this area, had advised caution, to use locals rather than Soviet teams so as not to antagonise Abdollah Khan – his exclusive contact and prize agent – nor risk an international incident.

'It's totally unwise to risk a confrontation,' he had said, keeping to the Book – and his private plan. 'What do we gain by immediate action – if we've not been fed disinformation and Sabalan's not one great booby trap which is probable? A few cipher books that we may or may not already have. As to the advanced computers – our whole Operation Zatopek has that well in hand.'

This was a highly controversial and innovative KGB covert operation – named after the Czech long-distance runner – set up in '65. With an initial budget of ten million dollars of terribly scarce foreign currency, Operation Zatopek was to acquire a continuing supply of

509

the most advanced and best Western technology *by simple purchase through a network of bogus companies* and not by the conventional and very expensive method of theft and espionage.

'The money is nothing compared to the gains,' his top secret initial report to Centre had said when he had first returned from the Far East in '64. 'There are tens of thousands of corrupt businessmen and fellow travellers who will sell us the best and the most up to date for a profit. A huge profit to any individual would be a pittance to us – because we will save billions in research and development which we can spend on our navy, air force, and army. And, just as important, we save years of sweat, toil, and failure. At almost no cost we maintain parity with anything their minds can conceive. A few dollars under their rotten little tables will get us all their treasures.'

Petr Mzytryk felt a glow when he remembered how his plan had been accepted – though naturally and rightly taken over by his superiors as their idea, as he had taken it from one of his own deep-cover agents in Hong Kong, a French national called Jacques de Ville in the big conglomerate of Struan's who had opened his eyes: 'It's not against U.S. law to ship technology to France or West Germany or a dozen other countries, and not against these countries' laws for a company to ship it on to other countries, where there are no laws against shipping goods to the Soviet Union. Business is business, Gregor, and money makes the world go around. Through Struan's alone we could supply you tons of equipment the U.S. has forbidden you. We service China – why not you? Gregor, you seafarers don't understand business . . .'

Mzytryk smiled to himself. In those days he had been known as Gregor Suslev, captain of a small Soviet freighter that plied from Vladivostok to Hong Kong, his cover for his top secret job of deputy controller for Asia for the KGB's First Directorate.

Over the years since '64, when I first proposed the scheme, he thought so proudly, with a total outlay so far of eighty-five million dollars, Operation Zatopek has saved Mother Russia billions and provided a constant, ever-growing flow of NASA, Japanese, and European-developed gadgetry, electronic marvels, hardware, software, plans, robots, chips, micros, medicines, and all manner of magic to duplicate and manufacture at our leisure – with equipment developed by the same enemy, and bought and paid for with loans they provide that we'll never repay. What fools they are!

He almost laughed out loud. Even more important, Zatopek gives me a free hand to continue to operate and manoeuvre as I choose in this area, to play the Great Game the stupid British let slip from their grasp.

He watched Abdollah Khan standing at the window, waiting patiently for him to decide on the favour he wanted in return for catching the saboteurs. Come on, Bad Fats, he thought grimly, using his secret nickname for him, we both know you can catch those *matyeryebyets* if you want to – if they're still in Azerbaijan.

'I'll do what I can,' Abdollah Khan said, still with his back to him, and Mzytryk did not hide his smile. 'If I intercept them, what then, Petr?'

'Tell Cimtarga. He will make all arrangements.'

'Very well.' Abdollah Khan nodded to himself and came and sat down again. 'That's settled, then.'

'Thank you,' Petr said, very satisfied. Such finality from Abdollah Khan promised quick success.

'This mullah we were discussing, Mahmud,' the Khan said, 'he's very dangerous. Also his band of cut-throats. I think they're a threat to everyone. The Tudeh should be directed to deal with him. Covertly, of course.'

Mzytryk wondered how much Abdollah knew about their secret support for Mahmud, one of their best and most fanatic converts. 'The Tudeh must be guarded, and their friends too.' He saw the immediate flash of irritation, so he compromised and added at once, 'Perhaps this man could be moved and replaced – a general split and fratricide would only help the enemy.'

'The mullah's a false mullah and not a true believer in anything.'

'Then he should go. Quickly.' Petr Mzytryk smiled, Abdollah Khan didn't.

'Very quickly, Petr. Permanently. And his group broken.'

The price was steep, but the Section 16/a gave him authority enough. 'Why not quickly and permanently, since you say it's necessary? I agree to, er, pass on your recommendation.' Mzytryk smiled and now Abdollah Khan smiled, also satisfied.

'I'm glad we agree, Petr. Become a Muslim for your eternal soul.'

Petr Mzytryk laughed. 'In time. Meanwhile, become a communist for your earthly pleasure.'

The Khan laughed, leaned forward, and refilled Petr's glass. 'I can't persuade you to stay for a few days?'

'No, but thanks. After we've eaten, I think I'll start back for home.' The smile broadened. 'There's a lot for me to do.'

The Khan was very content. So now I can forget the troublesome mullah and his band and another tooth's been drawn. But I wonder what you would do, Petr, if you knew your saboteur captain and his saboteur soldier were at the other side of my estate, waiting for safe passage out? But out to where? To Tehran or to you? I haven't yet decided.

Oh, I knew you'd come to beg my help, why else did I keep them safe, why else did I meet them secretly in Tabriz two days ago and bring them here secretly if not for you? Perhaps. Pity Vien Rosemont got killed, he was useful. Even so, the information and warning contained in the code he gave the captain for me is more than useful. He'll be difficult to replace.

Yes, and also true that if you receive a favour you must return a favour. The Infidel Erikki is only one. He rang a bell and when the servant appeared, he said, 'Tell my daughter Azadeh she will join us for food.'

At Tehran: 4:17 P.M. Jean-Luc Sessonne banged the brass knocker on the door of McIver's apartment. Beside him was Sayada Bertolin. Now that they were off the street and alone, he cupped her breasts through her coat and kissed her. 'I promise we won't be long, then back to bed!'

She laughed. 'Good.'

'You booked dinner at the French Club?'

'Of course. We'll have plenty of time!'

'Yes, *chérie*.' He wore an elegant, heavy raincoat over his flying uniform and his flight from Zagros had been uneasy, no one answering his frequent radio calls though the airwaves were filled with excitable Farsi which he did not speak or understand.

He had kept at regulation height and made a standard approach to Tehran's International Airport. Still no answer to his calls. The wind sock was full and showed a strong crosswind. Four jumbos were on the apron near the terminal along with a number of other jets, one a burned-out wreck. He saw some were loading, surrounded by too many men, women and children with no order to them, the fore and aft steps

513

to the cabins dangerously overcrowded, discarded suitcases and luggage scattered everywhere. No police or traffic wardens that he could see, nor at the other side of the terminal building where all approach roads were clogged with standstill traffic that was jammed nose to tail. The car park was solid but more cars were trying to squeeze in, the sidewalks packed with laden people.

Jean-Luc thanked God that he was flying and not walking and he landed at the nearby airfield of Galeg Morghi without trouble, bedded the 206 in the S-G hangar, and organised an immediate ride into town with the help of a ten-dollar bill. First stop at the Schlumberger office and a dawn date fixed to fly back to Zagros. Then to her apartment. Sayada had been at home. As always the first time after being so long apart was immediate, impatient, rough, selfish and mutually explosive.

He had met her at a Christmas party in Tehran a year and two months and three days ago. He remembered the evening exactly. The room was crowded and the moment he arrived, he saw her as though the room was empty. She was alone, sipping a drink, her dress sheer and white.

'*Vous parlez français, madame?*' he had asked, stunned by her beauty.

'Sorry, *m'sieur*, only a few words. I would prefer English.'

'Then in English: I am overjoyed to meet you but I have a dilemma.'

'Oh? What?'

'I wish to make love to you immediately.'

'Eh?'

'You are the manifestation of a dream . . .' It would sound so much better in French but never mind, he had thought. 'I've been looking for you for ever and I need to make love to you, you are so desirable.'

'But . . . but my . . . husband is over there. I'm married.'

'That is a condition, *madame*, not an impediment.'

She had laughed and he had known she was his. Only one thing more would make everything perfect. 'Do you cook?'

'Yes,' she had said with such confidence that he knew she would be superb, that in bed she would be divine, and that what she lacked he would teach her. How lucky she is to have met me, he thought happily, and banged on the door again.

Their months together had flown by. Her husband rarely visited Tehran. He was a Lebanese banker in Beirut, of French extraction, 'and therefore civilised,' Jean-Luc had said with total confidence, 'so of course he would approve of our liaison, *chérie*, should he ever find out. He is quite old compared to you, of course he would approve.'

'I'm not so sure, *chéri*, and he's only fifty and you're f –'

514

'Divine,' he had said, helping her. 'Like you.' For him it was true. He had never known such skin and silky hair and long limbs and a sinuous passion that was a gift of heaven. '*Mon Dieu*,' he had gasped one night, kept lingering on the summit by her magic, 'I die in your arms.' Later she had kissed him and brought him a hot towel and slid back into bed. This was on a holiday in Istanbul in the fall of last year, and the utter sensuality of that city had surrounded them.

For her the affair was exciting, but not an affair to end all affairs. She had discussed Jean-Luc with her husband the night of the party. 'Ah,' he had said, amused, 'so that was why you wanted me to meet him!'

'Yes. I thought him interesting – even though French and totally self-centred as always – but he excited me, yes, yes, he did.'

'Well, you'll be here in Tehran for two years, I can't be here more than a few days a month – too dangerous – and it would be a shame for you to be alone, every night. Wouldn't it?'

'Ah, then I have your permission?'

'Where is his wife?'

'In France. He's in Iran for two months, then has one month with her.'

'Perhaps it would be a very good idea, this liaison – good for your soul, good for your body, and good for our work. More importantly, it would divert attention.'

'Yes, that occurred to me too. I told him I did not speak French and he has many advantages – he's a member of the French Club!'

'Ah! Then I agree. Good, Sayada. Tell him I'm a banker of French origin, which is partially true – wasn't my great-great-grandfather a foot soldier with Napoleon on his Middle East drive towards India? Tell your Frenchman we're Lebanese for many generations, not just a few years.'

'Yes, you are wise as always.'

'Get him to make you a member of the French Club. That would be perfect! A great deal of power there. Somehow the Iran–Israel *entente* must be broken, somehow the Shah must be curbed, somehow we have to split Israel from Iran oil or the arch-fiend Begin will be tempted to invade Lebanon to cast our fighters out. With Iranian oil he'll succeed and that will be the end of another civilisation. I'm tired of moving.'

'Yes, yes, I agree . . .'

Sayada was very proud. So much accomplished in the year, unbelievable how much! Next week Leader Yasser Arafat was invited to Tehran for a triumphal meeting with Khomeini as a thank you for his help to the revolution; oil exports to Israel were finished, the fanatically

515

anti-Israel Khomeini installed – and the pro-Israel Shah expelled into ignominy. So much progress since she had first met Jean-Luc. Inconceivable progress! And she knew that she had helped her husband who was highly placed in the PLO, by acting as a special courier taking messages and cassettes to and from Istanbul, to and from the French Club in Tehran – oh, how much intrigue to persuade the Iraqis to allow Khomeini to leave for the safe harbour of France where he would no longer be muzzled – to and from all sorts of places escorted by my handsome lover. Oh, yes, she thought contentedly, Jean-Luc's friends and contacts have been so useful. One day soon we will get back to Gaza and regain our lands and houses and shops and vineyards . . .

McIver's door swung open. It was Charlie Pettikin. 'Good God, Jean-Luc, what the hell're you doing here? Hi, Sayada, you look more beautiful than ever, come on in!' He shook hands with Jean-Luc and gave her a friendly kiss on both cheeks and felt the warmth of her.

Her long, heavy coat and hood hid most of her. She knew the dangers of Tehran and dressed accordingly: 'It saves so much bother, Jean-Luc; I agree it's stupid and archaic but I don't want to be spat on, or have some rotten thug wave his penis at me or masturbate as I pass by – it's not and never will be France. I agree it's unbelievable that now in Tehran I have to wear some form of chador to be safe, yet a month ago I didn't. Whatever you say, *chérie*, the old Tehran's gone for ever . . .'

Pity in some ways, she thought, going into the apartment. It had had the best of the West and best of the East – and the worst. But now, now I pity Iranians, particularly the women. Why is it Muslims, particularly Shi'as, are so narrow-minded and won't let their women dress in a modern way? Is it because they're so repressed and sex besotted? Or is it because they're frightened they'd be shown up? Why can't they be open-minded like us Palestinians, or Egyptians, Shargazi, Dubaians, or Indonesians, Pakistanis, or so many others? It must be impotence. Well nothing's going to keep me from joining the Women's Protest March. How dare Khomeini try to betray us women who went to the barricades for him!

It was cold inside the apartment, the electric fire still down to half power, so she kept her coat on, just opened it to be more comfortable, and sat on one of the sofas. Her dress was warm and Parisian and slit to the thigh. Both men noticed. She had been here many times and thought the apartment drab and uncomfortable though she liked Genny very much. 'Where's Genny?'

'She went to Al Shargaz this morning on the 125.'

'Then Mac's gone?' Jean-Luc said.

'No, just her, Mac's out at the –'

'I don't believe it!' Jean-Luc said. 'She swore she'd never leave without old Dirty Duncan!'

Pettikin laughed. 'I didn't believe it either but she went like a lamb.' Time enough to tell Jean-Luc the real reason why she went, he thought.

'Things've been bad here?'

'Yes, and getting worse. Lots more executions.' Pettikin thought it better not to mention Sharazad's father in front of Sayada. No point in worrying her. 'How about tea? I've just made some. You hear about Qasr Jail today?'

'What about it?'

'A mob stormed it,' Pettikin said, going into the kitchen for extra cups. 'They broke down the door and released everyone, strung up a few SAVAKs and police, and now the rumour is Green Bands have set up shop with kangaroo courts and they're filling the cells with whom the hell ever and emptying them as quickly in front of firing squads.'

Sayada would have said that the prison had been liberated and that now enemies of the revolution, enemies of Palestine, were getting their just punishment. But she held her peace and listened attentively as Pettikin continued: 'Mac went to the airport with Genny early, then to the Ministry, then here. He'll be back soon. How was the traffic at the airport, Jean-Luc?'

'Jammed for miles.'

'The Old Man's stationed the 125 at Al Shargaz for a couple of weeks to get all our people out – if necessary – or bring in fresh crews.'

'Good. Scot Gavallan's overdue for leave and also a couple of our mechanics – can the 125 get clearance to stop at Shiraz?'

'We're trying next week. Khomeini and Bazargan want full oil production back, so we think they'll cooperate.'

'You'll be able to bring in new crews, Charlie?' Sayada asked, wondering if a British 125 should be allowed to operate so freely. Damn British, always conniving!

'That's the plan, Sayada.' Pettikin poured more boiling water into the teapot and did not notice the grimace on Jean-Luc's face. 'We've been more or less ordered by the British embassy to evacuate all non-essential personnel – we got out a few redundancies, and Genny, and then Johnny Hogg went to pick up Manuela Starke at Kowiss.'

'Manuela's at Kowiss?' Sayada was as surprised as Jean-Luc.

Pettikin told him how she had arrived and McIver had sent her down

517

there. 'So much going on it's difficult to keep tabs on everything. What're you doing here and how're things at Zagros? You'll stay for dinner – I'm cooking tonight.'

Jean-Luc hid his horror. 'Sorry, *mon vieux*, tonight is impossible. As to Zagros, at Zagros things are perfect, as always; after all it is the French sector. I'm here to fetch Schlumberger – I return at dawn tomorrow and will have to bring them back in two days – how can I resist the extra flying?' He smiled at Sayada and she smiled back. 'In fact, Charlie, I'm long overdue a weekend – where's Tom Lochart, when's he coming back to Zagros?'

Pettikin's stomach twisted. Since they had had the call three days ago from Rudi Lutz at Abadan Tower reporting that HBC had been shot down trying to sneak over the border and that Tom Lochart was back off leave, they had had no further information other than one formal call relayed through Kowiss that Lochart had started back for Tehran by road. No official inquiries, yet, about the hijack.

I wish to God Tom was back, Pettikin thought. If Sayada wasn't here I'd tell Jean-Luc about it, he's a bigger friend of Tom's than I am, but I don't know about Sayada. After all, she's not family, she works for Kuwaitis and this HBC business could be called treason.

Absently he poured a cup and handed it to Sayada, another to Jean-Luc, hot, black, with sugar and goat's milk which neither of them liked but accepted out of politeness. 'Tom's done what he had to do,' he said carefully, making it sound light. 'He started back from Bandar-e Delam day before yesterday by road. God knows how long he'll take but he should've been here last night. Easy. Let's hope he arrives today.'

'That would be perfect,' Jean-Luc said. 'Then he could take the Schlumberger team back to Zagros and I'd take a few days' leave.'

'You've just had leave. And you're in command.'

'Well, at the very least he can come back with me, take over the base, and I'll return here Sunday.' Jean-Luc beamed at Sayada. '*Voilà*, it's all fixed.' Without noticing it, he took a sip of tea and almost choked. '*Mon Dieu*, Charlie, I love you like a brother but this is *merde*.'

Sayada laughed and Pettikin envied him. Still, he thought, his heart picking up a beat, Paula's Alitalia flight's due back any day . . . what wouldn't I give to have her eyes light up for me like Sayada's do for M'sieur Seduction himself.

Better go easy, Charlie Pettikin. You could make a damn fool of yourself. She's twenty-nine, you're fifty-six, and you've only chatted her up a couple of times. Yes. But she excites me more than I've been excited in years and now I can understand Tom Lochart, going overboard for Sharazad.

The warning buzzer went on the High Frequency transmitter-receiver on the sideboard. He got up and turned up the volume. 'HQ Tehran, go ahead!'

'This is Captain Ayre in Kowiss for Captain McIver. Urgent.' The voice was mixed with static and low.

'This is Captain Pettikin, Captain McIver's not here at the moment. You're two by five.' This was a measure, one to five, of the signal strength. 'Can I help?'

'Standby One.'

Jean-Luc grunted. 'What's with Freddy and you? Captain Ayre and Captain Pettikin?'

'It's just a code,' Pettikin said absently staring at the set, and Sayada's attention increased. 'It just sort of developed and means someone's there or listening in who shouldn't. A hostile. Replying with the same formality means you got the message.'

'That's very clever,' Sayada said. 'Do you have lots of codes, Charlie?'

'No, but I'm beginning to wish we had. It's a bugger not knowing what's going on really – no face-to-face contact, no mail, phones and the telex ropey with so many trigger-happy nutters muscling us all. Why don't they turn in their guns and let's all live happily ever after?'

The HF was humming nicely. Outside the windows, the day was overcast and dull, the clouds promising more snow, the late afternoon light making all the city roofs drab and even the mountains beyond. They waited impatiently.

'This is Captain Ayre at Kowiss . . .' Again the voice was eroded by static and they had to concentrate to hear clearly. '. . . first I relay a message received from Zagros Three a few minutes ago from Captain Gavallan.' Jean-Luc stiffened. 'The message said exactly: "Pan pan pan" ' – the international aviation distress signal just below Mayday – ' "I've just been told by the local komiteh we are no longer persona grata in Zagros and to evacuate the area with all expatriates from all our rigs within 48 hours, or else. Request immediate advice on procedure." End of message. Did you copy?'

'Yes,' Pettikin said hastily, jotting some notes.

'That's all he said except, he sounded chocker.'

'I'll inform Captain McIver and call you back as soon as possible.' Jean-Luc leaned forward and Pettikin let him take the mike.

'This's Jean-Luc, Freddy, please call Scot and tell him I'll be back as

519

planned tomorrow before noon. Good to talk to you, thanks, here's Charlie again.' He handed the mike back, all of his *bonhomie* vanished.

'Will do, Captain Sessonne. Nice to talk to you. Next: the 125 picked up our outgoings along with Mrs. Starke, including Captain Jon Tyrer who'd been wounded in an aborted leftist counter-attack at Bandar-e Delam . . .'

'What attack?' Jean-Luc muttered.

'First I've heard of it.' Pettikin was just as concerned.

'. . . and, according to plan, will bring back replacement crews in a few days. Next: Captain Starke.' They all heard the hesitation and underlying anxiety and the curious stilted delivery as though this information was being read: 'Captain Starke has been taken into Kowiss for questioning by a komiteh . . .' Both men gasped. '. . . to ascertain facts about a mass helicopter escape of pro-Shah air force officers from Isfahan on the 13th, last Tuesday, believed to have been piloted by a European. Next: air operations continue to improve under close supervision of the new management. Mr. Esvandiary is now our IranOil area manager and wants us to take over all Guerney contracts. To do this would require three more 212s and one 206. Please advise. We need spares for HBN, HKJ and HGX and money for overdue wages. That's all for now.'

Pettikin kept scribbling, his brain hardly working. 'I've, er, I've noted everything and will inform Captain McIver as soon as he returns. You said, er, you said "an attack on Bandar-e Delam". Please give the details.'

The airwaves were silent but for static. They waited. Then again Ayre's voice, not stilted now: 'I've no information other than there was an anti-Ayatollah Khomeini attack that Captains Starke and Lutz helped put down. Afterwards Captain Starke brought the wounded here for treatment. Of our personnel only Tyrer was creased. That is all.'

Pettikin felt a bead of sweat on his face and he wiped it off. 'What . . . what happened to Tyrer?'

Silence. Then: 'A slight head wound. Dr. Nutt said he'd be okay.'

Jean-Luc said, 'Charlie, ask him what was that about Isfahan.'

As though in dreamtime, Pettikin saw his fingers click on the sender switch. 'What was that about Isfahan?'

They waited in the silence. Then: 'I have no information other than what I gave you.'

'Someone's telling him what to say,' Jean-Luc muttered.

Pettikin pressed the sending button, changed his mind. So many questions to ask that Ayre clearly could not answer. 'Thank you, Captain,' he said, glad that his voice sounded firmer. 'Please ask Hotshot to put his request for the extra choppers in writing, with suggested contract time and payment schedule. Put it on our 125 when they bring your replacements. Keep . . . keep us informed about Captain Starke. McIver'll get back to you as soon as possible.'

'Wilco. Out.'

Now only static. Pettikin fiddled with the switches. The two men looked at each other, oblivious of Sayada who sat quietly on the sofa, missing nothing. ' "Close supervision"? That sounds bad, Jean-Luc.'

'Yes. Probably means they have to fly with armed Green Bands.' Jean-Luc swore, all his thinking on Zagros and how young Scot Gavallan would cope without his leadership. '*Merde!* When I left this morning everything was five by five with Shiraz ATC as helpful as a Swiss hotelier off-season. *Merde!*'

Pettikin was suddenly reminded of Rakoczy and how close he had come to disaster. For a second he considered telling Jean-Luc, then decided against it. Old news! 'Maybe we should contact Shiraz ATC for help?'

'Mac might have an idea. *Mon Dieu*, doesn't sound too good either for Duke – these komitehs're breeding like lice. Bazargan and Khomeini better deal with them quickly before the two of them're bitten to death.' Jean-Luc got up, very concerned, and stretched, then saw Sayada curled up on the sofa, her untouched cup of tea on the small table beside her, smiling at him.

At once his *bonhomie* returned. There's nothing more I can do for young Scot at the moment, or for Duke, but there is for Sayada. 'Sorry, *chérie*,' he said with a beam. 'You see, without me there are always problems at Zagros. Charlie, we'll leave now – I've got to check the apartment but we'll return before dinner. Say 8 p.m.; by then Mac should be back, eh?'

'Yes. Won't you have a drink? Sorry, we've no wine. Whisky?' He offered it halfheartedly as this was their last three-quarters of a bottle.

'No thanks, *mon vieux*.' Jean-Luc got into his coat, noticed in the mirror that he was looking as dashing as ever, and thought of the cases of wine and the tins of cheese he had had the wisdom to tell his wife to stock in their apartment. '*A bientôt*, I'll bring you some wine.'

'Charlie,' Sayada said, watching both of them carefully as she had done since the HF came to life, 'what did Scotty mean about the helicopter escape?'

Pettikin shrugged. 'All sorts of rumours about all sorts of escapes, by

521

land, sea and air. Always "Europeans" supposed to be involved,' he said, hoping he sounded convincing. 'We're blamed for everything.'

And why not, you are responsible, Sayada Bertolin thought without malice. Politically, she was delighted to see them both sweating. Personally, she wasn't. She liked both of them and most of the pilots, particularly Jean-Luc who pleased her immensely and amused her constantly. I'm lucky to be Palestinian, she told herself, and Coptic Christian – of ancient lineage. That gives me strengths they don't have, an awareness of a heritage back to Biblical times, an understanding of life they could never reach, along with the capacity to dissociate politics from friendship and the bedchamber – as long as it is necessary and prudent. Haven't we had thirty centuries of survival training? Hasn't Gaza been settled for 3,000 years?

'There's a rumour Bakhtiar's slipped out of the country and fled to Paris.'

'I don't believe that, Charlie,' Sayada said. 'But there's another that I do,' she added, noticing he had not answered her question about the Isfahan helicopter. 'It seems your General Valik and his family fled to join the other IHC partners in London. Between them they're supposed to have salted away millions of dollars.'

'Partners?' Jean-Luc said contemptuously. 'Robbers, all of them, whether here or London, every year worse than before.'

'They're not all bad,' Pettikin said.

Jean-Luc said, 'Those *crétins* steal the sweat of our brow, Sayada. I'm astounded Old Man Gavallan lets them get away with it.'

'Come off it, Jean-Luc,' Pettikin said. 'He fights them every inch of the way.'

'Every inch of our way, old friend. We do the flying, he doesn't. As for Valik . . .' Jean-Luc shrugged with Gallic extravagance. 'If I was an Iranian of wealth, I would have gone months ago with all I could collect. It's been clear for months that the Shah was out of control. Now it's the French Revolution and the Terror all over again but without our style, sense, civilised heritage, or manners.' He shook his head disgustedly. 'What a waste! When you think of all the centuries of teaching and wealth we French've put in trying to help these people crawl out of the Dark Ages and what have they learned? Not even how to make a decent loaf of bread!'

Sayada laughed and, on tiptoe, kissed him. 'Ah, Jean-Luc, I love you and your confidence. Now, *mon vieux*, we should go, you've lots to accomplish!'

After they had left, Pettikin went to the window and stared out at the rooftops. There was the inevitable sporadic gunfire and some smoke near Jaleh. Not a big fire but enough. A stiff breeze scattered the smoke. Clouds reached down the mountains. The cold from the windows was strong, ice and snow on the sills. In the street below were many Green Bands. Walking or in trucks. Then from minarets everywhere muezzins began calling to afternoon prayer. Their calls seemed to surround him.

Suddenly he was filled with dread.

At the Ministry of Aviation: 5:04 P.M. Duncan McIver was sitting wearily on a wooden chair in a corner of the crowded antechamber of the deputy minister. He was cold and hungry and very irritable. His watch told him he had been waiting almost three hours.

Scattered around the room were a dozen other men, Iranians, some French, American, British, and one Kuwaiti wearing a galabia – a long-flowing Arabian robe – and headband. A few moments ago the Europeans had politely stopped chatting as, in response to the muezzins' calls that still came through the tall windows, the Muslims had knelt, faced Mecca, and prayed the afternoon prayer. It was short and quickly over and once more the desultory conversation picked up – never wise to discuss anything important in a government office, particularly now. The room was draughty, the air chilly. They all still wore their overcoats, were equally weary, a few stoic, most seething, for all, like McIver, had long overdue appointments.

'Insha'Allah,' he muttered but that didn't help him.

With any luck Gen's already at Al Shargaz, he thought. I'm damned glad she's safely out, and damned glad she came up with the reason herself: 'I'm the one who can talk to Andy. You can't put anything into writing.'

'That's true,' he had said, in spite of his misgivings, reluctantly adding, 'Maybe Andy can make a plan that we could carry out – might carry out. Hope to God we don't have to. Too bloody dangerous. Too many lads and too many planes spread out. Too bloody dangerous. Gen, you forget we're not at war though we're in the middle of one.'

'Yes, Duncan, but we've nothing to lose.'

'We've people to lose, as well as birds.'

'We're only going to see if it's feasible, aren't we, Duncan?'

Old Gen's certainly the best go-between we could have – if we really needed one. She's right, much too dangerous to put in a letter: 'Andy, the only way we can safely extract ourselves from this mess is to see if we can come up with a plan to pull out all our planes – and spares – that're presently under Iranian registry and technically owned by an Iranian company called IHC . . .'

Christ! Isn't that a conspiracy to defraud!

Leaving is not the answer. We've got to stay and work and get our money when the banks open. Somehow I've got to get the partners to help – or maybe this minister can give us a hand. If he'll help, whatever it costs, we could wait out the storm here. Any government's got to have help to get their oil up, they've got to have choppers and we'll get our money . . .

He looked up as the inner door opened and a bureaucrat beckoned one of the others into the inner room. By name. There never seemed to be a logic to the manner of being called. Even in the Shah's time it was never first come, first served. Then it was only influence. Or money.

Talbot of the British embassy had arranged the appointment for him with the deputy prime minister and had given him a letter of introduction. 'Sorry, old boy, even I can't get into the PM, but his deputy Antazam's a good sort, speaks good English – not one of these rev twits. He'll fix you up.'

McIver had got back from the airport just before lunch and had parked as near as he could to the government offices. When he had presented the letter in English and Farsi to the guard on the main door in plenty of time, the man had sent him with another guard down the street to another building and more inquiries and then, from there, down another street to this building and from office to office until he arrived here, an hour late and fuming.

'Ah, don't worry, agha, you're in plenty of time,' the friendly reception clerk said to his relief in good English, and handed back the envelope containing the introduction. 'This is the right office. Please go through the door and take a seat in the anteroom. Minister Kia will see you as soon as possible.'

'I don't want to see him,' he had almost exploded. 'My appointment's with Deputy Prime Minister Antazam!'

'Ah, Deputy Minister Antazam, yes, agha, but he's no longer in Prime Minister Bazargan's government. Insha'Allah,' the young man said pleasantly. 'Minister Kia deals with everything to do with, er, foreigners, finances and airplanes.'

'But I must insist th—' McIver stopped as the name registered and he remembered what Talbot had said and how remaining IHC partners had implanted this man on the board with an enormous retainer and no guarantees of assistance. 'Agha Minister Ali Kia?'

'Yes, agha. Minister Ali Kia will see you as soon as possible.' The receptionist was a pleasant, well-dressed young man in a suit and white shirt and blue tie, just like in the old days. McIver had had the foresight to enclose a pishkesh of 5,000 rials in the envelope with the introduction, just like in the old days. The money had vanished.

Perhaps things are really getting back to normal, McIver thought, went into the other room and took a chair in the corner and began to wait. In his pocket was another wad of rials and he wondered if he should refill the envelope with the appropriate amount. Why not, he thought, we're in Iran, minor officials need minor money, high officials, high money – sorry, pishkesh. Making sure no one observed him, he put some high denomination notes into the envelope, then added a few more for safety. Maybe this bugger can really help us – the partners used to have the court buttoned up, perhaps they've done the same to Bazargan.

From time to time harassed bureaucrats hurried importantly through the anteroom into the inner room, papers in their hands, and came out again. Occasionally, one of the men waiting would be politely ushered in. Without exception they were inside for just a few minutes and emerged taut-faced or red-faced, furious, and obviously empty-handed. Those who still waited felt more and more frustrated. Time passed very slowly.

'Agha McIver!' The inner door was open now, a bureaucrat beckoning him.

Ali Kia was seated behind a very large desk with no papers on it. He wore a smile but his eyes were hard and small and McIver instinctively disliked him.

'Ah, Minister, how kind of you to see me,' McIver said, forcing *bonhomie*, offering his hand. Ali Kia smiled politely and shook hands limply.

'Please sit down, Mr. McIver. Thank you for coming to see me. You have an introduction I believe?' His English was good, Oxford-accented, where he had gone to university just before World War Two on a Shah grant, staying for the duration. He waved a tired hand at the bureaucrat beside the door. The man left.

'Yes, it, er, it was to Deputy Minister Antazam, but I understand it should have been directed to you.' McIver handed him the envelope. Kia took out the introduction, noticed the amount of the notes exactly, tossed the envelope carelessly on to the desk to indicate more should be forthcoming, read the handwritten note with care, then put it down in front of him.

'Mr. Talbot is an honoured friend of Iran though a representative of a hostile government,' Kia said, his voice smooth. 'What particular help can I give the friend of such an honoured person?'

'There're three things, Minister. But perhaps I may be allowed to say how happy we are at S-G that you've considered giving us the benefit of your valuable experience by joining our board.'

'My cousin was most insistent. I doubt I can help, but, as God wants.'

'As God wants.' McIver had been watching him carefully, trying to read him, and could not explain the immediate dislike he took great pains to hide. 'First, there's a rumour that all joint ventures are suspended, pending a decision of the Revolutionary Komiteh.'

'Pending a decision of the government,' Kia corrected him curtly. 'So?'

'How will that affect our joint company, IHC?'

'I doubt if it will affect it at all, Mr. McIver. Iran needs helicopter service for oil production. Guerney Aviation has fled. It would seem the future looks better than ever for our company.'

McIver said carefully, 'But we haven't been paid for work done in Iran for many months. We've been carrying all lease payments for the aircraft from Aberdeen and we're heavily overcommitted here in air-craft for the amount of work we have on the books.'

'Tomorrow the banks . . . the Central Bank is due to open. By order of the PM – and the Ayatollah, of course. A proportion of the money owed will, I'm sure, be forthcoming.'

'Would you conjecture how much we can expect, Minister?' McIver's hope quickened.

'More than enough to . . . to keep our operation going. I've already arranged for you to take out crews once their replacements are here.' Ali Kia took a thin file from a drawer and gave him a paper. It was an order directed to Immigration at Tehran, Abadan, and Shiraz airports to allow out accredited IHC pilots and engineering crews, one for one, against incoming crew. The order was badly typed but legible, in Farsi and English, and signed on behalf of the komiteh responsible for IranOil by and dated yesterday. McIver had never heard of him.

'Thank you. May I also have your approval for the 125 to make at least three trips a week for the next few weeks – of course only until your international airports are back to normal – to bring in crews, spares, and equipment, replacement parts, and so on, and,' he added matter-of-factly, 'to take out redundancies.'

'It might be possible to approve that,' Kia said.

McIver handed him the set of papers. 'I took the liberty of putting it into writing – to save you the bother, Minister – with copies addressed to Air Traffic Control at Kish, Kowiss, Shiraz, Abadan, and Tehran.'

Kia read the top copy carefully. It was in Farsi and English, simple, direct, and with the correct formality. His fingers trembled. To sign them would far exceed his authority but now that the deputy prime minister was in disgrace, as well as his own superior – both supposedly dismissed by this still mysterious Revolutionary Komiteh – and with mounting chaos in the government, he knew he had to take the risk. The absolute need for him, his family, and his friends to have ready access to a private airplane, particularly a jet, made the risk worthwhile.

I can always say my superior told me to sign it, he thought, keeping his nervousness away from his face and eyes. The 125 is a gift from God – just in case lies are spread about me. Damn Jared Bakravan! My friendship with that bazaari dog almost embroiled me in his treason against the state; I've never lent money in my life, or engaged in plots with foreigners, or supported the Shah.

To keep McIver off balance he tossed the papers beside the introduction almost angrily. 'It might be possible for this to be approved. There would be a landing fee of $500 per landing. Was that everything, Mr. McIver?' he asked, knowing it was not. Devious British dog! Do you think you can fool me?

'Just one thing, Excellency.' McIver handed him the last paper. 'We've three aircraft that're in desperate need of servicing and repair. I need the exit permit signed so I can send them to Al Shargaz.' He held his breath.

'No need to send valuable airplanes out, Mr. McIver; repair them here.'

'Oh, I would if I could, Excellency, but there's no way I can do that. We don't have the spares or the engineers – and every day that one of our choppers're not working costs the partners a fortune. A fortune,' he repeated.

'Of course you can repair them here, Mr. McIver, just bring the spares and the engineers from Al Shargaz.'

'Apart from the cost of the aircraft there're the crews to support and pay for. It's all very expensive; perhaps I should mention that's the Iranian partners' cost – that's part of their agreement . . . to supply all the necessary exit permits.' McIver continued to wheedle. 'We need to get every available piece of equipment ready to service all the new Guerney contracts if the Ay – if, er, the government's decree to get oil production to normal is to be obeyed. Without equipment . . .' he left the word hanging and again held his breath, praying he'd chosen the right bait.

Kia frowned. Anything that cost the Iranian partnership money came partially out of his own pocket now. 'How soon could they be repaired and brought back?'

'If I can get them out within a couple of days, two weeks, maybe more, maybe less.'

Again Kia hesitated. The Guerney contracts, added to existing IHC contracts, helicopters, equipment, fixtures and fittings were worth millions of which he now had a sixth share – for no investment, he chortled deep inside. Particularly if everything was provided, without cost, by these foreigners! Exit permits for three helicopters? He glanced at his watch. It was Cartier and bejewelled – a pishkesh from a banker who, two weeks ago, had needed a private half an hour access to a working telex. In a few minutes he had an appointment with the chairman of Air Traffic Control and could easily embroil him in this decision.

'Very well,' he said, delighted to be so powerful, an official on the rise, to be able to assist the implementation of government oil policy, and save the partnership money at the same time. 'Very well, but the exit permits will only be valid for two weeks, the licence will be –' he thought a moment – 'will be $5,000 U.S. per aircraft in cash prior to exit, and they must be back in two weeks.'

'I, I can't get that money in cash in time. I could give you a note, or cheques payable on a Swiss bank – for $2,000 per aircraft.'

They haggled for a moment and settled on $3,100. 'Thank you, Agha McIver,' Ali Kai said politely. 'Please leave downcast lest you encourage those rascals waiting outside.'

When McIver was once more in his car he took out the papers and stared at the signatures and official stamps. 'It's almost too good to be true,' he muttered out loud. The 125's legal now, Kia says the suspension won't apply to us, we've exit permits for three 212s that're needed in Nigeria – $9,000-odd against their value of 3 million's more than fair! I never thought I'd get away with it! 'McIver,' he said happily, 'you deserve a Scotch! A very large Scotch!'

In the Northern Suburbs: 6:50 P.M. Tom Lochart got out of the battered old cab and gave the man a twenty-dollar note. His raincoat and flight uniform were crumpled and he was very tired and unshaven and dirty and felt soiled, but his happiness at being outside his own apartment building and near Sharazad at long last took away all of it. A few flakes of snow were falling but he hardly noticed them as he

528

hurried inside and up the staircase – no need to try the lift, it had not worked for months.

The car that he had borrowed from one of the pilots at Bandar-e Delam had run out of petrol yesterday, halfway to Tehran, the petrol gauge defective. He had left it at a garage and fought on to the next bus and then another and then, after breakdowns and delays and diversions, had reached the main terminal in Tehran two hours ago. Nowhere to wash, no running water, the toilets just the usual festering, clogged, flyblown holes in the ground.

No cabs at the cab rank or on the streets. No buses running anywhere near his home. Too far to walk. Then a cab appeared and he stopped it and even though it was almost full, following custom, he pulled open a door and forced his way in, beseeching the other passengers to allow him to share their transport. A reasonable compromise was reached. They would be honoured if he would stay and he would be honoured to pay for all of them, and be last, and to pay the driver in cash. American cash. It was his last bill.

He got out his keys and turned the lock but the door was bolted from the inside, so he pressed the bell, waiting impatiently for the maid to open the door – Sharazad would never have opened it herself. His fingers drummed a happy beat, his heart filled with love for her. His excitement grew as he heard the maid's footsteps approach, the bolts being pulled back, the door inched open. A strange chadored face stared at him. 'What do you want, agha?' Her voice was as coarse as her Farsi.

His excitement vanished and left a sickening hole. 'Who're you?' he said, as rudely. The woman started to close the door, but he put his foot out and shoved it open. 'What're you doing in my house? I'm Excellency Lochart and this is my house! Where's Her Highness, my wife? Eh?'

The woman glowered at him, then padded away across his hallway towards his living-room door and opened it. Lochart saw strangers there, men and women – and guns leaning against his wall. 'What the hell's going on?' he muttered in English and strode into his living-room. Two men and four women stared up at him from his carpets, crosslegged or leaning against his cushions, in the middle of a meal in front of his fireplace, a fire burning merrily, eating off his plates that were spread carelessly, their shoes off, their feet dirty. One man older than the other, in his late thirties, had his hand on an automatic that was stuck in his belt.

Blinding rage soared through Lochart, the presence of these aliens a

529

rape and a sacrilege. 'Who're you? Where's my wife? By God, you get out of m—' He stopped. The gun was pointing at him.

'Who're you, agha?'

With a supreme effort Lochart dominated his fury, his chest hurting him. 'I'm – I'm – this is – is my house – I'm the owner.'

'Ah, the owner! You're the owner?' the man, called Teymour, interrupted with a short laugh. 'The foreigner, the husband of the Bakravan woman? Yo –' the automatic cocked as Lochart readied a lunge at him. 'Don't! I can shoot quickly and very accurately. Search him,' he told the other man who was on his feet instantly. Expertly this man ran his hands over him, pulled the flight bag out of his hands and looked through it.

'No guns. Flight manuals, compass – you're the pilot Lochart?'

'Yes,' Lochart said, his heart pumping.

'Sit down over there! Now!'

Lochart sat in the chair, far away from the fire. The man put the gun on the carpet beside him and took out a paper. 'Give it to him.' The other man did as he was told. The paper was in Farsi. They all watched him carefully. It took Lochart a little time to decipher the writing: 'Confiscation Order. For crimes against the Islamic State, all property of Jared Bakravan is confiscated except his family house and his shop in the bazaar.' It was signed on behalf of a komiteh by a name he could not read and dated two days ago.

'This's – this's ridiculous,' Lochart began helplessly. 'His – his Excellency Bakravan was a huge supporter of the Ayatollah Khomeini. Huge. There must be some mistake!'

'There isn't. He was jailed, found guilty of usury, and shot.'

Lochart gaped at him. 'There . . . there's got to be a mistake!'

'There's none, agha. None,' Teymour said, his voice not unkind, watching Lochart carefully, seeing the danger in him. 'We know you're Canadian, a pilot, that you've been away, that you're married to one of the traitor's daughters and not responsible for his crimes, or hers if she's committed any.' His hand went to the gun, seeing Lochart flush. 'I said "if", agha, control your anger.' He waited and did not pick up the dull, well-kept Luger, though completely ready. 'We're not untrained rabble, we're freedom fighters, professionals, and we've been given these quarters to guard for VIPs who arrive later. We know you're not a hostile, so be calm. Of course this must be a shock to you – we understand, of course we understand, but we have the right to take what is ours.'

'Right? What right do y –'

'Right of conquest, agha – has it ever been different? You British should know that more than any.' His voice stayed level. The women watched with cold, hard eyes. 'Calm yourself. None of your possessions have been touched. Yet.' He waved his hand. 'See for yourself.'

'Where is my wife?'

'I don't know, agha. There was no one here when we arrived. We arrived this morning.'

Lochart was nearly demented with worry. If her father's been found guilty will the family suffer? Everyone? Wait a minute! Everything confiscated . . . except the family house, wasn't that what the paper said? She's got to be there . . . Christ, that's miles away and I've no car . . .

He was trying to get his mind working. 'You said, you said nothing's been touched – "yet". You mean it will be touched soon?'

'A wise man protects his own possessions. It would be wise to take your possessions to a safe place. Everything of Bakravan stays here, but your possessions?' He shrugged. 'Of course you may take them, we're not thieves.'

'And my wife's possessions?'

'Hers too. Of course. Personal things. I told you we aren't thieves.'

'How – how long do I have?'

'Until 5 p.m. tomorrow.'

'That's not enough time. Perhaps the day after?'

'Until 5 p.m. tomorrow. Would you like some food?'

'No, no, thank you.'

'Then goodbye, agha, but first please give me your keys.'

Lochart flushed in spite of his resolve. He took them out and the other man who was nearby accepted them. 'You said VIPs. What VIPs?'

'VIPs, agha. This place belonged to an enemy of the state; now it is the property of the state for whomever it chooses. Sorry, but of course you understand.'

Lochart looked at him, then at the other man and back again. His weariness weighed him down. And his helplessness. 'I, er, before I leave I want to change and – and shave. Okay?'

After a pause Teymour said, 'Yes. Hassan, go with him.'

Lochart walked out, hating him and them and everything that was happening, the man Hassan following him. Along the corridor and into his own room. Nothing had been touched though all the cupboards were open, and the drawers, and there was a smell of tobacco smoke but no sign of a hasty departure or of violence. The bed had been used.

531

Get yourself together and make a plan. I can't. All right, then shave and shower and change and go to Mac, he's not far away, and you can walk there and he'll help you, he'll lend you money and a car and you'll find her at her family house – and don't think of Jared, just don't.

Near the University: 8:10 P.M. Rakoczy moved the oil lamp nearer to the bundle of papers, diaries, files and documents he had stolen from the upstairs safe in the U.S. embassy, continuing to sort them out. He was alone in a small tenement room – one of a warren of similar rooms, mostly for students, that had been rented for him by Farmad, the student Tudeh leader who had been killed the night of the riot. The room was dingy, without heat, just a bed and rickety table and chair and one tiny window. The panes were cracked and half covered with cardboard.

He laughed out loud. So much achieved and at so little cost. Such good planning. Our covering riot perfectly staged outside the embassy gates – then sudden firing from the opposite rooftops, creating panic, quickly breaking down the gates and rushing the compound – our only opposition marines armed with shotguns and even then ordered not to fire – just enough time before Khomeini supporters could arrive to subdue the riot, kill us, or capture us. Covered by the pandemonium, rushing around the back of the building, smashing the side door, then up the back stairs alone while my cadre outside created more diversions, firing into the air, shouting, careful not to kill anyone but lots of noise and screaming. One landing and then the next, then running along the corridor shouting at the Americans, two frightened old women and a young man, 'Get on the floor, lie down, or you'll all be killed!'

Frantically they obeyed and all the others – I don't blame them, the attack so sudden and they unprepared, unarmed, and carefully panicked. Into the bedroom. Empty but for a paralysed Iranian servant, arms over his head, half under the bed. Blowing the safe quickly, everything into the carryall, then out again and down the stairs three at a time, then away into the milling crowds. Ibrahim Kyabi and the others covering me, retreating perfectly, every objective achieved.

Source's got to be impressed, he thought again, my promotion to major's got to be assured, and Father'll be so proud of me. 'By God and the Prophet of God,' he said involuntarily as another surge of ecstasy swept him – not noticing what he had said. 'I've never felt so fulfilled.'

Happily he went back to his work. So far the safe had revealed no treasures, but lots of documents about CIA involvement in Iran, some private ambassador rubber stamps, one cipher that could be special, private accounts, some jewellery of little value, a few ancient coins. Never mind, he thought. There's lots to go through yet, diaries and personal papers.

Time passed for him easily. Soon Ibrahim Kyabi would be here to discuss the Women's March. He wanted to know how to disrupt it to further Tudeh objectives and to damage Khomeini and Shi'ism. Khomeini's the real danger, he thought, the only danger. That strange old man, him and his granite inflexibility. The quicker he's brought before the No God the better.

A current of freezing air came through the broken panes. It did not disturb him. He was warm for he wore his heavy leather jacket and sweater and shirt and underwear and good socks and strong shoes: 'Always have good socks and shoes in case you've got to run,' his teachers had said; 'always be prepared to run . . .'

He remembered, amused, running away from Erikki Yokkonen, leading him into the maze and losing him near the Deathhouse of the Lepers. I'm sure I'm going to have to kill him one day, he thought. And his hellcat wife. What about Azadeh? What about the daughter of the Abdollah Khan, Abdollah the Cruel who though valuable as a double agent is becoming too arrogant, too independent and too important for our safety? Yes, but now I'd like both husband and wife back in Tabriz, doing what we require of them. And as for me, I'd like to be on leave again, once more home again, safe again, Igor Mzytryk, captain KGB again, safe at home with Delaurah, my arms around her, in our fine bed with the finest linens from Ireland, her green eyes sparkling, skin like cream, and so so beautiful. Only seven more weeks and our firstborn arrives. Oh, I hope it's a son . . .

With half an ear – as always most of his hearing tuned to detect danger – he heard the muezzins calling for evening prayer. He began clearing the little table. Very soon now Ibrahim Kyabi would be here and there was no need for the young man to know what did not concern him. Everything went quickly into the carryall. He lifted the floorboard and put the carryall into the hollow beneath that also contained a loaded, spare automatic, carefully wrapped in oilcloth, and half a dozen British fragmentary grenades. A little dirt scuffed into the cracks and now no sign of a hiding place. He doused the oil lamp until the wick was just alight and pulled the curtains back. A little snow had collected on the inside of the sill. Contentedly he began to wait. Half an hour passed. Not like Kyabi to be late.

Then he heard footsteps. His automatic covered the door. The code

533

of the knock was flawless, even so when he unlocked the door he slid into ambush in the comparative safety of the wall and swung the door open, ready to blast the hostile if it was a hostile. But it was Ibrahim Kyabi, bundled up and pleased to be here. 'Sorry, Dimitri,' he said, stamping his feet, a little snow in his curling black hair, 'but buses are almost non-existent.'

Rakoczy relocked the door. 'Punctuality's important. You wanted to know who the mullah was in the Bandar-e Delam helicopter when your father was murdered, poor man – I've got his name for you.' He saw the youth's eyes light up and hid a smile. 'His name's Hussain Kowissi and he's the mullah of Kowiss. Do you know it?'

'No, no, I've never been there. Hussain Kowissi? Good, thank you.'

'I checked him out for you. He appears to be a fanatic anti-communist, fanatic for Khomeini, but in reality, he's secretly CIA.'

'What?'

'Yes,' Rakoczy said, the disinformation perfectly justified. 'He spent a number of years in the U.S., sent there by the Shah, speaks fluent English, and was secretly turned by them when he was a student. His anti-Americanism's as false as his fanaticism.'

'How d'you do it, Dimitri? How do you know so much so fast – without phones, or telex, or anything?'

'You forget every bus contains some of our people, every taxi, truck, village, post office. Don't forget,' he added, believing it, 'don't forget the Masses are on our side. We are the Masses.'

'Yes.'

He saw the young man's zeal and he knew Ibrahim was the correct instrument. And ready. 'The mullah Hussain ordered the Green Bands to shoot your father, accusing him of being a plant and dupe of foreigners.'

All colour left Kyabi's face. 'Then – then I want him. He's mine.'

'He should be left to professionals. I'll arrange at –'

'No. Please. I must have revenge.'

Rakoczy pretended to think about that, hiding his content. Hussain Kowissi had been marked for extinction for some time. 'In a few days I'll arrange weapons, a car and a team to go with you.'

'Thank you. But all I need will be this.' Kyabi pulled out a pocket knife, his fingers shaking. 'This, and an hour or two, and some barbed wire and I'll show him the extent of a son's revenge.'

'Good. Now the Women's March. It's definitely scheduled in three days. Wh—' He stopped aghast, abruptly leaped for the side wall, pulled a half-seen knot. A section of the wall swung open to give access to the unlit rickety fire exit staircase. 'Come on,' he ordered and raced down it to freedom, Kyabi blindly following in a panic run. At that moment without warning the door burst open, almost torn off its hinges, and the two men who had shouldered it open almost fell into the room, others on their heels. All were Iranian, all wore Green Bands and they charged in pursuit, guns out.

Down the stairs three at a time, hunted and hunters, stumbling and almost falling, scrambling up and rushing out into the street and the night, into the crowds and then Rakoczy went straight into the ambush and into their arms. Ibrahim Kyabi did not hesitate, just changed direction and fled across the street and into the crowded alley and was swallowed up in the darkness.

In an old parked car across the street from the side exit, Robert Armstrong had seen their men go in and Rakoczy caught and Kyabi escape. Rakoczy had been quickly bundled into a waiting van before many people in the street knew what was happening. Two of the Green Bands strode over towards Armstrong, both better dressed than usual. Both had holsters on their belts for their Mausers. People moved out of their way uneasily, watching without watching, wanting no trouble. The two men got into the car and Armstrong let in the clutch and eased away, the remaining Green Bands mixing with the pedestrians.

In moments Robert Armstrong was part of the rush-hour traffic. The two men slid off their green armbands and pocketed them. 'Sorry we lost that young bastard, Robert,' the older of the two said in fluent English, American-accented. He was a clean-shaven man in his fifties – Colonel Hashemi Fazir, deputy chief of Inner Intelligence, U.S. trained and SAVAK before the separate secret service department was formed.

'Not to worry, Hashemi,' Armstrong said.

The younger man in the backseat said, 'We've got Kyabi on film at the embassy riot, agha. And at the university.' He was in his twenties, with a luxuriant moustache and his lips twisted cruelly. 'We'll pick him up tomorrow.'

'Now that he's on the run, I wouldn't if I were you, Lieutenant,' Armstrong said, driving carefully. 'Since he's pegged, just tail him – he'll lead you to bigger fish. He led you to Dimitri Yazernov.'

The others laughed. 'Yes, yes, he did.'

'And Yazernov'll lead us to all sorts of interesting people and places.' Hashemi lit a cigarette, offered them. 'Robert?'

'Thanks.' Armstrong took a puff and grimaced. 'My God, Hashemi, these are awful, they'll really kill you.'

'As God wants.' Then Hashemi quoted in Farsi. ' "Wash me in wine

535

when I die,/At my funeral use a text concerning wine,/Would you wish to find me on the Day of Doom,/Look for me in the dust at the wineshop's door." '

'Cigarettes, not wine'll kill you,' Armstrong said dryly, the lilt of the Persian words beautiful.

'The colonel was quoting from the *Rubáiyát of Omar Khayyám*,' the young man in the back said helpfully in English. 'It means th –'

'He knows what it means, Mohammed,' Hashemi interrupted. 'Mr. Armstrong speaks perfect Farsi – you've a lot to learn.' He puffed his cigarette for a while, watching the traffic. 'Pull over for a moment, will you, Robert?'

When the car stopped Hashemi said, 'Mohammed, go back to the HQ and wait for me there. Make sure no one – no one – gets at Yazernov before me. Tell the team just to make sure everything's ready. I want to start at midnight.'

'Yes, Colonel.' The younger man left them.

Hashemi watched him vanish into the crowds. 'I could use a large whisky and soda. Drive on for a while, Robert.'

'Sure.' Armstrong let in the clutch, glanced at him, hearing an undercurrent. 'Problem?'

'Many.' Hashemi studied the traffic and the pedestrians, his face set. 'I don't know how long we'll be allowed to operate, how long we're safe, or who to trust.'

'What else's new?' Armstrong smiled mirthlessly. 'That's an occupational hazard,' he said – the lesson well learned from eleven years as adviser to Inner Intelligence, and twenty years before that in the Hong Kong police.

'You want to be present when Yazernov's interrogated, Robert?'

'Yes, if I'm not in the way.'

'What does MI6 want with him?'

'I'm just an ex-CID, Special Branch, on private contract to help you fellows set up the equivalent service, remember?'

'I remember very well. Two five-year contracts, the last happily extended until next year when you retire with a pension.'

'Fat chance,' Armstrong said disgustedly. 'Khomeini and the government'll pay my pension? Fat chance.' It was very much on his mind that now all his Iranian service was wasted, and along with the devaluation of the Hong Kong dollar since he retired in '66, his real retirement would be scratchy. 'My pension's had it.'

The dark eyes hardened. 'Robert, what does MI6 want with this bastard?'

Armstrong frowned. Something was very wrong tonight. The youth Kyabi should not have escaped the net and Hashemi's as nervous as a rookie agent on his first drop behind the lines. 'Far as I know they don't. I'm interested in him. Me,' he said casually.

'Why?'

Such a long story, Armstrong thought. Should I tell you that Dimitri Yazernov's a cover for Fedor Rakoczy, the Russian Islamic-Marxist you've been trying to catch for months? Should I tell you the real reason I was told to help you grab him tonight is that, quite by chance, MI6's just discovered through a Czech defector his real name is Igor Mzytryk, son of Petr Oleg Mzytryk who back in my Hong Kong days used to be known as Gregor Suslev, master spy, we thought long since dead.

No, we don't want Yazernov but we do want – I want – the father who's supposed to live just north of the border somewhere, within reach, oh God, let him be alive and within reach for we would dearly like to debrief that sod by any means possible – ex intelligence chief, Far East, senior lecturer in espionage at Vladivostok University, senior party member and God knows what since.

'I think – we think – Yazernov's more important than Tudeh liaison with students. He's a dead ringer for your Kurdish dissident, Ali bin Hassan Karakose.'

'You mean he's the same man?'

'Yes.'

'Impossible.'

Armstrong shrugged. He had thrown him a bone; if he didn't want to gnaw it that was his problem. The traffic was snarled again, everyone hooting and cursing. The big man shut his ears to the noise, stubbed out the local Iranian cigarette.

Hashemi frowned, watching him. 'What's your interest in Karakose and the Kurds – if what you say's true?'

'Kurds straddle all the borders. Soviet, Iraqi, Turkish and Iranian,' he said easily. 'The whole Kurdish national movement's very sensitive and easy for the Soviets to exploit – with heavy international implications throughout Asia Minor. Of course we're interested.'

The colonel stared out of the window, lost in thought, snow falling lightly. A cyclist squeezed passed, carelessly banging the side of the car. To Armstrong's surprise – usually Hashemi was well tempered – he furiously wound down his window and cursed the youth and all his generations. Grimly he stubbed his cigarette out. 'Drop me here, Robert. We'll begin with Yazernov at midnight. You're welcome.' He started to open the door.

'Hang on, old son,' Armstrong said. 'We've been friends a long time. What the hell's up?'

The colonel hesitated. Then he pulled the door to. 'SAVAK's been outlawed by the government, so have all intelligence departments, including us, and ordered disbanded at once.'

'Yes, but the prime minister's office has already told you to continue, undercover. You've nothing to fear, Hashemi. You're not tainted. You've been told to smash the Tudeh, the fedayeen, and the Islamic-Marxists . . . you showed me the order. Wasn't tonight's operation following this line?'

'Yes. Yes, it was.' Again Hashemi paused, his face set and his voice thick. 'Yes, it was – but! What do you know about the Islamic Revolutionary Komiteh?'

'Only that it's supposed to consist of men personally selected by Khomeini,' Armstrong began honestly. 'Its powers are loose, we don't know the who, how many, where or when they meet or even if Khomeini presides or what.'

'I now know for a fact that, with Khomeini's approval, in future ultimate power is to be invested in this komiteh, that Bazargan is only a momentary figurehead until the komiteh issues the new Islamic Constitution which will put us back to the time of the Prophet.'

'Bloody hell!' Armstrong muttered. 'No elected government?'

'None.' Hashemi was beside himself with rage. 'Not as we know the term.'

'Perhaps the Constitution'll be rejected, Hashemi. The people'll have to vote it in, not everyone's a fanatic support –'

'By God and the Prophet, don't fool yourself, Robert!' the colonel said harshly. 'The vast majority are fundamentalist, that's all they've got to hang on to. Our bourgeois, rich, and middle classes are Tehranis, Tabrizis, Abadanis, Isfahanis, all Shah-sponsored, a handful compared to the other thirty-six million of us, most of whom can't even read or write. Of course whatever Khomeini approves will be voted in! And we both know what his vision of Islam, the Koran, and Sharia is.'

'How soon will . . . how soon will they have the Constitution ready?'

'Do you understand so little about us, after all this time?' Hashemi said irritably. 'The moment we seize power we use it before it slips away. The new Constitution went into effect the moment that poor bastard Bakhtiar was betrayed by Carter, betrayed by the generals, and forced to flee. As to Bazargan, pious, honest, fair, and democratically inclined, Khomeini appointed, legal prime minister pending elections, the poor bastard's just a dupe for anything and everything that goes wrong between now and then.'

'You mean he'll be the scapegoat – be put on trial?'

'Trial? What trial? Haven't I told you what the komiteh considers a trial? If they charge him, he's shot. Insha'Allah! Lastly, and it's why I can't think straight and I'm so angry I need to get drunk, I heard this afternoon, very privately, I heard that SAVAK's been secretly reorganised, it's going to be rechristened SAVAMA – and Abrim Pahmudi's been made director!'

'Christ Almighty!' Armstrong felt as though he'd been smashed in the stomach. Abrim Pahmudi was one of three lifelong friends of the Shah who had been to school with him in Iran and later in Switzerland, who had risen to become high in the Imperial SAVAK, and, it was rumoured, after the Shah's family, his most-sought-after counsellor – who right now was supposed to be in hiding, waiting an opportunity to negotiate with the Bazargan government on the Shah's behalf a constitutional monarchy and the Shah's abdication in favour of his son Reza. 'Christ Almighty! That explains a lot.'

'Yes,' Hashemi said bitterly. 'For years that bastard's been part of almost every crucial military or political meeting, every head of state conference, every secret agreement, and in the last days part of every important meeting with the U.S. ambassador, U.S. generals, every important decision of the Shah, of our generals, and present every time a coup d'état was discussed – and turned down.' He was so angry that tears ran down his cheeks. 'We're all betrayed. The Shah, the revolution, the people, you, me, everyone! How many times have we reported to him over the years together, and me dozens of other times? With lists, names, bank accounts, liaisons, secrets that only we could find out and know. Everything – everything in writing but one copy only – wasn't that the rule? We're all betrayed.'

Armstrong felt chilled. Of course Pahmudi knew all about his involvement with Inner Intelligence. Pahmudi had to know everything of value about George Talbot, about Masterson, his CIA opposite number, Lavenov, his Soviet opposite number, all our short and long contingency planning, operations to neutralise the CIA's top secret radar sites with men like young Captain Ross, invasion planning.

'Bloody hell,' he muttered, at the same time furious that their own sources had not forewarned them. Pahmudi, suave, intelligent, trilingual, and discreet. Never once over the years had there been the slightest suspicion against him. Never. How could he have escaped cleanly, even from the Shah who was constantly having his top associates checked and double-checked and rechecked? With every right, he thought. Five assassination attempts against him, bullets in his body and face, wasn't he ruler of a people known for violence towards and from their rulers?

Christ! Where will it all end?

In the Same Traffic: 9:15 P.M. McIver was inching along, well to the south, heading for the bazaar area where Jared Bakravan's family house was, Tom Lochart beside him.

'It'll all work out,' McIver said, sick with worry.

'Sure, Mac. No sweat.'

'Yes, not to worry.' When McIver had got back home to his apartment from Ali Kia and the Ministry, elated, Tom Lochart was there, arrived just moments before. His even greater joy at finding Tom Lochart safe was dashed at once by the look of him and by the news Pettikin gave him about Freddy Ayre's relayed radio call from Scot Gavallan at Zagros, and about Starke being taken by the Kowiss komiteh for questioning about 'the Isfahan escape'.

'It's all my goddam fault, Mac, all of it,' Tom Lochart had said.

'No, not your fault, Tom. We were both trapped – anyway I okayed the flight, not that it helped Valik. Were they all aboard; how the hell did you get out? Tell us what happened, then I'll call Freddy – you'd like a drink?'

'No, no, thanks. Listen, Mac, I've got to find Sharazad. She wasn't home, I'm hoping she's at her folks' house and I've got t –'

'She's there, I know she's there, Tom. Erikki told me just before he left this morning for Tabriz. Did you hear about her father?'

'Yes, I have, awful, bloody awful! You're sure she's there?'

'Yes.' McIver walked heavily over to the sideboard and fixed himself a drink as he continued. 'She hasn't been at your flat since you left and she was fine until . . . Erikki and Azadeh saw her the day before yesterday. Yesterday they . . .'

'Did Erikki say how she was?'

'He said she was as well as could be expected – you know how close Iranian families are. We don't know anything about her dad other than what Erikki told us – that he had been ordered to the jail as a witness, and the next thing the family was told to pick up his body, he'd been shot for "crimes against Islam". Erikki said they picked up the, er, the body and, well, yesterday they were in mourning. Sorry, but there you are.' He took a deep swallow of the lovely, peat-tasting drink and felt a little better. 'She's safe at home – first tell us what happened to you, then I'll call Freddy and we'll go and find Sharazad.'

Quickly Lochart did so. They listened, appalled. 'When Rudi told me that this Iranian Air Force officer, Abbasi, was the one who shot down HBC I almost went mad. I, I kinda collapsed and the next thing I remember was the next day. Abbasi and the others had gone by then and it was all SOP. Mac, Charlie's idea about a "hijack" – that's not going to stand up – no way!'

'We know that, Tom,' McIver had said. 'First finish your story.'

'I couldn't get a clearance to fly back so I borrowed a car, just got back a couple of hours ago and went straight to the apartment. The bastard of it is it's been confiscated by Green Bands, along with all Mr. Bakravan's property, except the shop in the bazaar and his family home.' Lochart told them what had happened, adding, 'I'm – I'm a waif in the storm. I've nothing now, we've nothing, Sharazad and I.' He laughed and it was a bad laugh and McIver could see that he was dying inside. 'It's true it was Jared's building, the apartment and everything in it though . . . though part of Sharazad's, er, dowry . . . Let's go, huh, Mac?'

'First let me call Freddy. Th –'

'Oh, of course, sure, sorry. I'm so worried I can't think straight.'

McIver finished his drink and went to the HF. He stared at it. 'Tom,' he said sadly, 'what do you want to do about Zagros?'

Tom Lochart hesitated. 'I could take Sharazad there with me.'

'Too dangerous, laddie. Sorry, but there it is.' McIver saw Lochart look into himself and measure himself, and sighed, feeling very old.

'If Sharazad's okay I'll go back with Jean-Luc tomorrow morning and we'll sort out Zagros, and she goes on the next shuttle to Al Shargaz,' Lochart said. 'Depending on what we find at Zagros . . . if we have to close down, Insha'Allah, we'll ferry all our riggers to Shiraz to go out by regular flights – their company'll tell them where they're to go – and we'll move everything to Kowiss, airplanes, spares and personnel. Okay?'

'Yes. Meanwhile I'll get on to the Ministry first thing tomorrow and see if I can straighten it out.' McIver clicked on the sender. 'Kowiss, this is HQ. Do you read?'

Almost instantly: 'HQ this is Kowiss, Captain Ayre, go ahead please, Captain McIver.'

'First, about Zagros Three: tell Captain Gavallan that Captains Lochart and Sessonne will be back tomorrow around noon with instructions. Meanwhile prepare plans to obey the komiteh.' Rotten bloody sods, he thought, then went on for the benefit of those who were listening in: 'The Zagros IranOil base manager should remind the komiteh that the Ayatollah and the government have specifically ordered oil production back to normal. Closing down Zagros will severely interfere with orderly production in that area. Inform Captain Gavallan I will take this up at once with Minister Kia personally who, an hour ago, confirmed this to me, and gave me written approvals to take out and replace crew by our own 125 until . . .'

'Christ, Mac, that's great news,' came over the airwaves involuntarily.

'Yes . . . by our own 125 until regular service resumes. Crew replacements and replacement aircraft to service all the extra work and Guerney contracts the government are asking us to service, so I cannot understand the actions of the local komiteh. Got it, Captain Ayre?'

'Yessir. Message received five by five.'

'Has Captain Starke returned yet?'

A long silence, then: 'Negative, HQ.'

McIver's voice became even colder. 'Call me at once when he does. Captain Ayre, just between you and me and to go no further: if he has any problems whatsoever and isn't safe back at base by dawn, I will ground all our aircraft throughout Iran, close down all our operations, and order one hundred percent of all our personnel out of Iran.'

'Good, Mac,' Pettikin said softly.

McIver was too concentrated to hear him. 'Did you get that, Kowiss?'

Silence, then: 'Affirmative.'

'As far as you're concerned,' McIver added, developing his sudden thought, 'inform Major Changiz and Hotshot from me, I'm ordering you right now to cease all operations including all CASEVACs until Starke's back on the base. Got that?'

Silence, then: 'Affirmative. The message will be relayed at once.'

'Good. But only the information that applies to your base. The rest's private until dawn.' He smiled grimly, then added, 'I'll be making an inspection trip as soon as the 125 returns so make sure all manifests are up to date. Anything else?'

'No sir. Not for the present. We'll look forward to seeing you and we'll listen out as usual.'

'HQ over and out.'

Pettikin said, 'That should do it, Mac, that'll put a hornet up their arses.'

'Maybe, maybe not. We can't stop CASEVACs – apart from humanitarian reasons that makes us illegal and they can steal everything.' McIver finished his drink, glanced at his watch. 'Come on, Tom, we won't wait for Jean-Luc, let's go and find Sharazad.'

The traffic had lessened a little now but was still inching along, snow griming the windshield. The road was slippery and banked with dirty snow.

'Turn right at the next corner,' Lochart said.

'Okay, Tom.' They drove in silence again. McIver turned the corner. 'Tom, did you sign for the fuel at Isfahan?'

'No, no, I didn't.'

'Anyone interview you, ask for your name, that sort of thing? Green Bands? Anyone?'

Lochart pulled his mind off Sharazad. 'No, not that I remember. I was just "Captain" and part of the scenery. Far as I remember I wasn't introduced to anyone. Valik and . . . and Annoush and the kids, they went off for lunch as soon as we landed with the other general – Christ, I can't remember his name – ah, yes, Seladi, that was it. Everyone called me "Captain" – I was just a piece of the scenery. Matter of fact I stayed with the chopper at the hangar all the time we were there, watching the refuelling and checking her out – they even brought me some food on a tray and I ate sitting in the cabin. I stayed there all the time until those goddam Green Bands fell on me and dragged me off and locked me in the room. I had no warning, Mac. They just enveloped the base, they must've been helped lavishly from inside, had to be. The bastards that grabbed me were all hopped up, shouting I was CIA, American – they kept on about that, but they were more concerned about subduing the base than about me. Take the left fork, Mac. It's not far now.'

McIver drove on uneasily, the area very run down and passersby glaring at them. 'Maybe we could get away with it – pretend HBC was hijacked from Doshan Tappeh by someone unknown. Maybe they won't follow it up from Isfahan.'

'Then why did they grab Duke Starke?'

'Routine.' McIver sighed heavily. 'I know it's a long shot but it might work. Maybe the "American CIA" will stick and that's all. Grow a moustache, or beard, just in case.'

Lochart shook his head. 'That's no help. I'm on the first clearance. We both are . . . that's the kicker.'

'When you took off from Doshan Tappeh, who saw you off?'

Lochart thought a moment. 'No one. I think it was Nogger who supervised the fuelling the day before. Th –'

'That's right, I remember now, he was bitching, said I was giving him too much work with young Paula in town. Were there any Iranian staff, guards there? Did you pay anyone baksheesh?'

'No, there was no one. But they could have me on their automatic recorders . . .' Lochart peered out of the side window. His excitement picked up and he pointed. 'There's the turning, not far now.'

McIver steered into the narrow street, just room for two cars to pass. Snow banked the sides up to the high walls – doors and doorways either side. McIver had never been here before and was surprised that Bakravan, so rich, would live in an area so clearly poor. Was rich, he reminded himself with an involuntary shiver, and now very dead for crimes against the state – and what constitutes a crime against the state? Again he shivered.

'There's the door, there on the left.'

They stopped beside the snowbank heavy with refuse. The nonde-script doorway was cut into the high, mildewed wall. The door was iron-banded, the iron rusty. 'Come on in, Mac.'

'I'll wait for a moment, then if all's well I'll leave. I'm pooped.' There's only one solution, McIver thought, and he reached out and stopped Lochart. 'Tom, we've permission to fly out three 212s. You take one. Tomorrow. The hell with Zagros, Jean-Luc can cope with that. I don't know about Sharazad, if they'll let her go or not, but you'd better get out, fast as you can. It's the only thing to do, get out while you can. We'll put her on the next 125 flight – the very next one.'

'And you, what about you, Mac?'

'Me? Nothing to worry about. You get out – if they'll let her go, take her too. Jean-Luc can handle Zagros – looks like we'll have to close down there anyway. All right?'

Lochart looked at him. 'Let me think about that one, Mac. But thanks.' He got out. 'I'll be by just after dawn – don't let Jean-Luc go without me. We can decide then, okay?'

'Yes.' McIver watched his friend use the old-fashioned knocker. The sound was loud. Both men waited, Lochart nauseous with anxiety, preparing for the family surrounding him, the tears and the welcome and the questions, having to be polite when all he wanted was to take her off to their own rooms and hold her and feel safe and all the nightmare gone. Waiting in front of the door. Then knocking again, louder. Waiting. McIver switching off to save petrol, the silence making the waiting worse. Snow flakes on the windshield building up. People passing like wraiths, everyone suspicious and hostile.

Muffled footsteps approached and the grilled peephole opened a fraction. The eyes that peered at Lochart were cold and hard and he did not recognise the little part of the face he could see.

'It's me, Excellency Lochart,' he began in Farsi, trying to sound normal. 'My wife, the Lady Sharazad is here.'

The eyes peered closer to see if he was alone or accompanied, examining the car behind him and McIver in the driving seat. 'Please wait, agha.'

The peephole closed. Again waiting, stamping his feet against the cold. Waiting, then impatiently using the knocker again, wanting to smash the door down, knowing he couldn't. More footsteps. The peephole opened again. Different eyes and face. 'What's your name, agha?'

Lochart wanted to shriek at the man but he did not. 'My name is Agha Pilot Thomas Lochart, husband of Sharazad. Open the door. It is cold and I'm tired and I have come for my wife.'

Silently the peephole closed. A moment of agonised waiting, then to his relief he heard the bolts being pulled back. The door swung open. The servant held an oil lamp on high. Beyond him was the high-walled courtyard, an exquisite fountain in the centre, trees and plants winter protected. On the far side was another door, iron studded. This door was open and he saw her silhouetted against the lamplight; he rushed forward and she was in his arms, weeping and moaning.

The door on the street slammed closed and the bolts shoved home. 'Wait!' Lochart called out to the servant, remembering McIver. Then he heard the car start up and drive off.

'What is it, agha?' the servant asked.

'Nothing,' he said and helped Sharazad into the house and into the warmth. When he saw her in the light, his happiness vanished and his stomach filled with ice. Her face was puffy and dirty, her hair limp and dirty, eyes sightless, her clothes were crumpled.

'Jesus Christ . . .' he muttered but she paid no attention, just clung to him demented, moaning a mixture of Farsi and English, tears running down her cheeks. 'Sharazad, it's all right, all right now . . .' he said, trying to gentle her. But she just continued with her monotonous gibberish.

'Sharazad, Sharazad, my darling, I'm back now . . . it's all right . . .' He stopped. It was almost as though he hadn't said anything and, suddenly, he was petrified that her mind had gone. He started to shake her gently but that had no effect either. Then he noticed the old servant standing by the staircase, waiting for orders. 'Where's – where's Her Highness Bakravan?' he asked, Sharazad's arms tight around his neck.

'She's in her rooms, agha.'

'Please tell her I'm here and . . . and that I'd like to see her.'

'Oh, she'll see no one now, agha. No one. As God wants. She hasn't seen anyone since the day.' Tears glistened in the old eyes. 'Your Excellency has been away, perhaps you won't know that His Ex –'

'I heard. Yes, I heard.'

'Insha'Allah, agha, Insha'Allah, but what crimes could the Master commit? Insha'Allah that he should be chosen Insh –'

'Insha'Allah. Please tell Her Highness . . . Sharazad, stop it! Come on, darling,' he said in English, her moans maddening him, 'stop it!' Then in Farsi to the servant, 'Please ask Her Highness to see me.'

'Oh, yes, I'll ask her, agha, but Her Highness won't open the door nor answer me nor see you but I'll go at once and do your bidding.' He began to leave.

'Wait, where is everyone?'

'Who, agha?'

'The family? Where's the rest of the family?'

'Ah, the family. Her Highness is in her rooms, the Lady Sharazad is here.'

Again Lochart felt his rage scourged by her moaning. 'I mean where's Excellency Meshang and his wife and children and my sisters-in-law and their husbands?'

'Where else would they be but in their homes, agha?'

'Then tell Excellency Meshang I'm here,' he said. Meshang, the eldest son, and his family were the only ones semi-permanently in residence here.

'Certainly, agha. As God wants, I'll go to the bazaar myself.'

'He's at the bazaar?'

The old man nodded. 'Of course, agha, tonight he is, he and his family. Now he is the Master and has to run the business. As God wants, agha, he is head of the house of Bakravan now. I'll go at once.'

'No, send someone else.' The bazaar was close by and it would be no imposition. 'Is there anyone . . . Sharazad, Sharazad, stop it!' he said roughly but she did not seem to have heard him. 'Is there hot water in the house?'

'There should be, agha. The furnace is very good but it's not on.'

'You've no fuel?'

'Oh, there should be fuel, agha. Would you like me to make sure?'

'Yes, put the furnace on and bring us some food, and tea.'

'Certainly, agha. What is it His Excellency's pleasure to have?'

Lochart held on to his sanity with difficulty, her whimperings setting him even more on edge. 'Anything – no, rice and horisht, chicken horisht,' he said, correcting himself, naming a common and easy dish, 'chicken horisht.'

'If you wish it, agha, but the cook prides himself on his chicken horisht and it will take him hours to make it to your satisfaction.' Politely the old man waited, eyes going from Lochart to the girl and back again.

'Then . . . then, oh, for the love of God, just fruit. Fruit and tea, whatever fruit you have . . .' Lochart could stand it no longer and he lifted Sharazad into his arms and went up the staircase and along the corridors to the rooms they usually used in this three-storey, flat-roofed house that was palatial, rich, and meandering. He opened the door and kicked it closed.

'Sharazad, listen to me . . . Sharazad, listen! For Christsake listen!'

But she just leaned against him, gibbering and moaning. He carried her into the stuffy inner room, windows tight shut and shutters closed, and forced her to sit on the unmade bed, then rushed into the bathroom that was modern – most of the plumbing modern – except the toilet.

No hot water. The cold water ran and it did not seem too brackish. He found some towels and soaked one and went back again, his chest hurting, knowing he was out of his depth. She had not moved. He tried to wash her face but she resisted and began to blubber, making herself even more ugly. Saliva seeped out of the sides of her mouth.

'Sharazad . . . Sharazad my darling, for the love of God, my darling . . .' he lifted her and held her closer but nothing touched her. Only the moans remained constant, pushing him nearer and nearer his limit. 'Get hold of yourself,' he said helplessly out loud, and got up, but her hands caught his clothes and tried to drag him back.

'Oh God give me strength . . .' He saw his hand smash her across the face. For a moment the moaning stopped, she stared at him incredulously, then her eyes went blank again, the gibberish started once more, and she clawed at his clothes. 'God help me,' he said brokenly, then began to smack her face, harder and harder, open-handed, desperately trying to be hard but not too hard and then shoved her face downwards on the bed and belted her hard on the buttocks, hit her till his palm ached and hand ached and all at once he heard screams that were real screams and not gibberish, 'Tommyyyy . . . stop, oh, please Tommy please stopppppp . . . Tommy, you're hurting me what have I done? I swear I've not thought about anyone oh God Tommy please stoppp . . .'

He stopped. Sweat was in his eyes, his clothes wringing, and he stumbled panting off the bed. She was writhing in pain, her buttocks scarlet and face scarlet, but her tears were real tears now and her eyes her own now and her brain her own.

'Oh, Tommyyyyy, you hurt me, you hurt me,' she sobbed as a whipped child would sob, 'Whyyyyy? Whyyy? I swear I love you . . . I've never done anything . . . anything to . . . to hurt you and make you . . . make you hurt me . . .' Racked with pain and shame that she had enraged him, not understanding why but only that she must help him out of his rage, she crawled off the bed and fell at his feet, begging his forgiveness through her tears.

Her tears stopped as her mind flooded with reality and she looked up at him. 'Oh, Tommy,' she said brokenly, 'Father's dead . . . murdered . . . murdered by Green Bands . . . murdered . . .'

'Yes . . . yes, my darling, I know, oh I know . . . I'm so sorry . . .'

He lifted her up and his tears mixed with hers and he held her tight and gave her of his strength and made her whole as she gave him of her strength and made him whole. Then they slept fitfully – waking sometimes, but sleeping again peacefully, gathering life, the flame of the oil lamp casting kind shadows. Just before midnight he awoke. Her eyes were watching him. Tentatively she moved to kiss him but a shaft of pain stopped her.

'Oh, you all right?' His arms at once around her.

'Oh, be careful . . . sorry, yes . . . it's . . .' Painfully she tried to look at her back, then found she was in soiled clothes. She grimaced. 'Ugh, these clothes, please excuse me, my darling . . .' She stood awkwardly and tore them off. Painfully she picked up the damp towel and cleaned her face and brushed her hair. Then, when she went closer to the light, he saw that one of her eyes was already slightly black and her buttocks badly bruised. 'Please forgive me . . . what did I . . . I do to offend you?'

'Nothing, nothing,' he said appalled, and told her how he had found her.

She stared at him blankly. 'But . . . you say that I . . . I don't remember any of that only . . . only being . . . only being beaten.'

'I'm so sorry but it was the only way I could . . . I'm so sorry.'

'Oh I'm not, not now, my darling.' Trying to recollect she came back and carefully lay on the bed on her stomach. 'But for you . . . As God wants but if I was as you say . . . strange, and I remember nothing, nothing from the time I . . .' Her voice broke a little then she continued, trying to be firm, 'but for you, perhaps I would have been mad for ever.' She squirmed closer and kissed him. 'I love you, Beloved,' she said in Farsi.

'I love you, Beloved,' he told her, possessed.

After a moment she said in a strange voice, 'Tommy, I think what sent me mad . . . I saw Father . . . saw him yesterday, the day before . . . I can't remember . . . was that he looked so small dead, so tiny, dead, with all those holes in him, in his face and head – I never remembered him so small but they had made him small, they'd taken away his . . .'

'Don't,' he said, gently, seeing the tears brimming. 'It's Insha'Allah. Don't think about it.'

'Certainly, husband, if you say so,' she said at once, formally, in Farsi. 'Of course it's as God wants, yes, but it's important for me to tell you, to remove the shame from me, you finding me like this . . . I would like to tell you one day.'

'Then tell me now, Sharazad, and we can put it behind us for ever,' he told her, equally formally. 'Please tell me now.'

'It was that they had made the biggest man in my world – after you – had made him insignificant. For no reason. He was always against the Shah when he could be and a great supporter of this mullah Khomeini.' She said it calmly and he heard the word 'mullah' and not Ayatollah or Imam or *farmandeh* and a warning rushed through him. 'They murdered my father for no reason without trial and outside the law and made him small, they took away everything that he had as a man, a father, as a beloved father. As God wants I should say and I will try. But I cannot believe it is what God wants. It may be what Khomeini wants. I don't know. We women will soon find out.'

'What? What do you mean?'

'In three days we women march in protest – all the women of Tehran.'

'Against what?'

'Against Khomeini and mullahs who are against women's rights – when he sees us marching without chador he will not do what is wrong.'

Lochart was half listening, remembering her a few days ago – was it only a few days ago that all this nightmare began? – Sharazad so content with herself and wearing chador, so happy to be just wife and not a modern like Azadeh. He saw her eyes and read her resolve and knew that she had committed herself. 'I don't want you to take part in this protest.'

'Yes, of course, husband, but every woman in Tehran will march and I am sure you would not wish me shamed before the memory of my father – against the representatives of his murderers, would you?'

'It's a waste of time,' Lochart said, knowing he was going to lose but

549

impelled onwards. 'I'm afraid, my love, a protest march of every woman in Iran or all Islam will not touch Khomeini a little bit. Women in his Islamic state will have nothing not granted in the Koran, nothing. Nor will anyone else. He's inflexible – isn't that his strength?'

'Of course you are right – but we will march in protest and then God will open his eyes and make all clear to him. It's as God wants, not as Khomeini wants – in Iran we have historic ways of dealing with such men.'

His arms were around her. Marching is not the answer, he thought. Oh, Sharazad, there's so much to decide, to say, to tell, now not the time. But there's Zagros and a 212 to ferry out. But that leaves Mac alone to carry the can, if there's a can to carry. What if I took him too? I couldn't, unless by force. 'Sharazad, I might have a ferry to do. To take a 212 to Nigeria. Would you come too?'

'Of course, Tommy. How long would we be gone?'

He hesitated. 'A few weeks – perhaps longer.' He felt her change in his arms, imperceptibly.

'When would you want to leave?'

'Very soon. Perhaps tomorrow.'

She moved out of his embrace without moving. 'I wouldn't be able to leave Mother, not for a while. She's . . . she's torn apart with grief, Tommy, and . . . and if I went I'd be afraid for her. And then there's poor Meshang – he has to run the business, he has to be helped – there's so much to do and to look after.'

'Do you know about the confiscation order?'

'What order?'

He told her. Tears filled her eyes again and she sat up, her pain for the moment forgotten. She stared at the oil flame and at the shadows it cast. 'Then we've no home, nothing. As God wants,' she said dully. Then almost at once in a different voice, 'No, not as God wants! As Green Bands want. Now we have to join together to save the family otherwise they will have beaten Father – we cannot allow them to murder him and then beat him as well, that would be terrible.'

'Yes, I agree, but this ferry'd solve our problems for a few weeks . . .'

'You're right, Tommy, as always, yes, yes it would if we needed to leave but this is our home just as much if not more, oh how happy we'll be here! In the morning I will get servants and bring everything of ours from the apartment – pah! what are a few carpets and trinkets when we have this house and ourselves. I will arrange everything – oh, we will be happy here.'

'But if y –'

550

'This theft makes it even more important for us to be here, to resist, to protest – it makes the march, oh, so much more important.' She put a finger on his lips as she saw him start to speak. 'If you must do this ferry – and of course you must do your work – then go, my darling, but hurry back quickly. In a few weeks Tehran will be normal and kind again and I know that is what God wants.'

Oh, yes, she thought confidently, her happiness overcoming the pain, but then it will be my second month and Tommy will be so proud of me and meanwhile it will be wonderful to live here, surrounded by family, Father avenged, the house filled with laughter again. 'Everyone will help us,' she said, lying back in his arms, so tired but so happy. 'Oh, Tommy, I'm so glad you're home, we're home, it will be so wonderful, Tommy.' Her words became slower as waves of sleep washed over her. 'We'll all help Meshang . . . and those abroad will come back, Aunt Annoush and the children . . . they'll help . . . and Uncle Valik will guide Meshang . . .'

Lochart did not have the heart to tell her.

Sunday
February 18, 1979

CHAPTER

34

At the Khan's Palace, Tabriz: 3:13 A.M. In the darkness of the small room Captain Ross opened the leather cover of his watch and peered at the luminous figures. 'All set, Gueng?' he whispered in Gurkhali.

'Yes, sahib,' Gueng whispered, glad that the waiting was over.

Carefully and quietly both men got off their pallets that lay on old, smelly carpets on the hard-packed, earthen floor. They were fully dressed and Ross picked his way across to the window and peered out. Their guard was slumped down beside the door, fast asleep, his rifle in his lap. Two hundred yards away beyond the snow-covered orchards and outbuildings was the four-storey palace of the Gorgon Khan. The night was dark and cold with some clouds, a nimbus around the moon that came through brightly from time to time.

More snow, he thought, then eased the door open. Both men stood there, searching the darkness with all their senses. No lights anywhere. Noiselessly Ross moved over to the guard and shook him but the man did not wake from the drugged sleep that was good for at least two hours. It had been easy to give him the drug in a piece of chocolate, kept

555

for just that purpose in their survival kit – some of the chocolate drugged, some poisoned. Once more he concentrated on the night, waiting patiently for the moon to go behind a cloud. Absently he scratched at the bite of a bedbug. He was armed with his kukri, and one grenade: 'If we're stopped, Gueng, we're only going for a stroll,' he had told him earlier. 'Better to leave our weapons here. Why have kukris and one grenade? It's an old Gurkha custom – an offence against our regiment to be unarmed.'

'I think I would like to take all our weapons now and slip back into the mountains and make our way south, sahib.'

'If this doesn't work, we'll have to but it's a rotten gamble,' Ross had said. 'It's a rotten gamble. We'll be trapped in the open – those hunters're still searching and they won't give up till we're caught. Don't forget we only just made it to the safe house. It was only the clothes that saved us.' After the ambush where Vien Rosemont and Tenzing had been killed, he and Gueng had stripped some of their attackers and put tribesmen's robes over their uniforms. He had considered dumping their uniforms entirely but thought that unwise. 'If we're caught we're caught and that's the end of it.'

Gueng had grinned. 'Therefore better you become a good Hindu now. Then if we get killed, it's not an end but a beginning.'

'How do I do that, Gueng? Become a Hindu?' He smiled wryly, remembering the perplexed look on Gueng's face and the vast shrug. Then they had tidied the bodies of Vien Rosemont and Tenzing and left them together in the snow according to the custom of the High Lands: 'This body has no more value to the spirit and, because of the immutability of rebirth, it is bequeathed to the animals and to the birds that are other spirits struggling in their own Karma towards Nirvana – the place of Heavenly Peace.'

The next morning they had spotted those who followed relentlessly. When they came down out of the hills into the outskirts of Tabriz, their pursuers were barely half a mile behind. Only their camouflage had saved them, allowing them to be lost in the crowds, many tribesmen as tall as he and with blue eyes, many as well armed. More luck was with them and he had found the back door of the filthy little garage the first time, used Vien Rosemont's name, and the man there had hidden them. That night Abdollah Khan had come with his guards, very hostile and suspicious. 'Who told you to ask for me?'

'Vien Rosemont. He also told us about this place.'

'Who is this Rosemont? Where is he now?'

Ross had told him what had happened at the ambush and noticed something new behind the man's eyes now, even though he remained hostile.

'How do I know you're telling me the truth? Who are you?'

'Before Vien died he asked me to give you a message – he was delirious and his dying bad, but he made me repeat it three times to make sure. He said: "Tell Abdollah Khan that Peter's after the Gorgon's head and Peter's son is worse than Peter. The son plays with curds and whey and so does the father who'll try to use a Medusa to catch the Gorgon." ' He saw the older man's eyes light up at once but not happily. 'So it means something to you?'

'Yes. It means you know Vien. So Vien's dead. As God wants, but that's a pity. Vien was good, very good, and a great patriot. Who are you? What was your mission? What were you doing in our mountains?'

Again he hesitated, remembering that Armstrong had told him at his briefing not to trust this man too far. Yet Rosemont whom he had trusted had said in his dying, 'You can trust that old bastard with your life. I have, half a dozen times, and he's never failed me. Go to him, he'll get you out . . .'

Abdollah Khan was smiling, his mouth cruel like his eyes. 'You can trust me – I think you have to.'

'Yes.' But not very far at all, he added silently, loathing the word, the word that costs millions their lives, more millions their freedom and every adult on earth peace of mind at some time or another. 'It was to neutralise Sabalan,' he said and told him what had happened there.

'God be praised! I will pass word to Wesson and Talbot.'

'Who?'

'Ah, doesn't matter. I'll get you south. Come with me, it's not safe here – the hue and cry's out, with a reward, for "two British saboteurs, two enemies of Islam". Who are you?'

'Ross. Captain Ross and this is Sergeant Gueng. Who were the men chasing us? Iranians – or Soviets? Or Soviet led?'

'Soviet's don't operate openly in my Azerbaijan – not yet.' The Khan's lips twisted into a strange smile. 'I have a station wagon outside. Get into it quickly and lie down in the back. I'll hide you and when it's safe, get you both back to Tehran – but you have to obey my orders. Explicitly.'

That was two days ago, but then the coming of the Soviet strangers and the arrival of the helicopter had made everything different. He saw the moon go behind a cloud and he tapped Gueng on the shoulder. The small man vanished into the orchard. When the all-clear signal came out of the night, he followed. They leapfrogged each other, moving very well until they were beside the corner of the north wing of the great house. No guards or guard dogs yet though Gueng had seen some Doberman pinschers chained up.

It was an easy climb up a balustrade to the first-floor balcony. Gueng led. He hurried down half its length, passed the corridor of shuttered windows to the staircase that climbed to the next balcony. At the top he waited, getting his bearings. Ross came alongside. Gueng pointed at the second set of windows and took out his kukri but Ross shook his head and motioned to a side door that he had noticed, deep in shadow. He tried the handle. The door squeaked loudly. Some night birds skeetered out of the orchard, calling to one another. Both men concentrated on where the birds had come from, expecting to see a patrol. None appeared. Another moment to make sure, then Ross led the way inside, adrenalin heightening his tension.

The corridor was long, many doors on either side, some windows to the south. Outside the second door he stopped, warily tried the handle. This door opened silently and he went in quickly, Gueng following, his kukri out and grenade ready. The room seemed to be an anteroom – carpets, lounging pillows, old-fashioned Victorian furniture and sofas. Two doors led off it. Praying it was the correct choice, Ross opened the door nearest the corner of the building and went in. The curtains were drawn but a crack of moonlight to one side showed them the bed clearly and the man he sought and a woman asleep there under the thick quilt. It was the right man but he had not expected a woman. Gueng eased the door closed. Without hesitation they went to either side of the bed, Ross taking the man and Gueng the woman. Simultaneously they clapped the bunched handkerchiefs over the mouths of the sleepers, holding them down with just enough pressure under their noses to keep them from crying out.

'We're friends, pilot, don't cry out,' Ross whispered, close to Erikki's ear, not knowing his name or who the woman was, only recognising him as the pilot. He saw the blank fright of the sudden awakening transformed into blinding rage as sleep vanished and the great hands came up to rip him apart. He avoided their grasp, increasing the pressure just under Erikki's nose, holding him down easily. 'I'm going to release you, don't cry out, pilot. We're friends, we're British. British soldiers. Just nod if you're awake and you understand.' He waited, then felt more than saw the huge man nod, watching his eyes. The eyes shouted danger. 'Keep her gagged, Gueng, until we're all set this side,' he said softly in Gurkhali, then to Erikki, 'Pilot, don't be afraid, we're friends.'

He released the pressure and leaped out of the way as Erikki lunged at him, then squirmed in the bed to get at Gueng but stopped rigid. Moonlight glinted off the curved kukri held near her throat. Azadeh's eyes were wide open and she was petrified.

'Don't! Leave her alone . . .' Erikki said hoarsely in Russian, seeing only Gueng's Oriental eyes, thinking it must be one of Cimtarga's men, still confused and in panic. He was heavy with sleep, his head aching from hours of flying, mostly on instruments in bad conditions. 'What do you want?'

'Speak English. You're English, aren't you?'

'No, no, I'm Finnish.' Erikki peered at Ross, little more than a silhouette in the shaft of moonlight. 'What the hell do you want?'

'Sorry to wake you like this, pilot,' Ross said hastily, coming a little closer, keeping his voice down, 'sorry, but I had to talk to you secretly. It's very important –'

'Tell this bastard to let my wife go! Now!'

'Wife? Oh, yes . . . yes, of course, sorry. She . . . she won't scream? Please tell her not to scream.' He watched the huge man turn towards the woman who lay motionless under the heavy quilt, her mouth still covered, the kukri unwavering. He saw him reach out warily and touch her, eyes on the kukri. His voice was gentle and encouraging but he did not speak English or Farsi but another language. In panic Ross thought it was Russian and he was further disoriented, expecting a British S-G pilot, without a bed partner, not a Finn with a Russian wife, and he was petrified he had led Gueng into a trap. The big man's eyes came back on him and more danger was there.

'Tell him to let my wife go,' Erikki said in English, finding it hard to concentrate. 'She won't scream.'

'What did you say to her? Was it Russian?'

'Yes, it was Russian and I said, "This bastard's going to release you in a second. Don't shout out. Don't shout out, just move behind me. Don't move quickly, just behind me. Don't do anything unless I go for the other bastard, then fight for your life." '

'You're Russian?'

'I told you, Finnish, and I tire quickly of men with knives in the night, British, Russian, or even Finnish.'

'You're a pilot with S-G helicopters?'

'Yes, hurry up and let her go whoever you are or I'll start something.'

Ross was not yet over his own panic. 'Is she Russian?'

'My wife's Iranian, she speaks Russian and so do I,' Erikki said icily, moving slightly to get out of the narrow beam of moonlight into

559

shadows. 'Move into the light, I can't see you, and for the last time tell this little bastard to release my wife, tell me what you want, and then get out.'

'Sorry about all this. Gueng, let her go now.'

Gueng did not move. Nor did the curved blade. In Gurkhali he said, 'Yes, sahib, but first take the knife from under the man's pillow.'

In Gurkhali Ross replied, 'If he goes for it, brother, even touches it, kill her, I'll get him.' Then in English he said pleasantly, 'Pilot, you have a knife under your pillow. Please don't touch it, sorry, but if you do until this is all okay . . . please be patient. Let her go, Gueng,' he said, his attention never leaving the man. With the side of his eyes he saw the vague shape of a face, long hair tousled and half covering her, then she moved behind the great shoulders, bunching her long-sleeved, winter nightclothes closer. Ross had his back to the light and he saw little of her, only the hatred in her half-seen eyes, even from the shadows. 'Sorry to arrive like a thief in the night. Apologies,' he said to her. She did not answer. He repeated the apology in Farsi. She still did not answer. 'Please apologise to your wife for me.'

'She speaks English. What the hell do you want?' Erikki felt a little better now that she was safe, still very aware how close the other man with the curved knife was.

'We're sort of prisoners of the Khan, pilot, and I came to warn you and to ask your help.'

'Warn me about what?'

'I helped one of your captains a few days ago – Charles Pettikin.' He saw the name register at once so he relaxed a little. Quickly he told Erikki about Doshan Tappeh and the SAVAK attack and how they had escaped, describing Pettikin accurately so there could be no mistake.

'Charlie told us about you,' Erikki said, astonished, no longer afraid, 'but not that he'd dropped you off near Bandar-e Pahlavi – only that some British paratroopers had saved him from a SAVAK who'd have blown his head off.'

'I asked him to forget my name. I, er, we were on a job.'

'Lucky for Charlie you, we—' Ross saw the woman whisper in her husband's ear, distracting him. The man nodded and turned his eyes back again. 'You can see me, I can't see you, move into the light – as to Abdollah, if you were his prisoners, you'd be chained up, or in a dungeon, not loose in the palace.'

'I was told the Khan would help us if we had trouble and he said he'd hide us until he could get us back to Tehran. Meanwhile he put us in a hut, out of sight, across the estate. There's a permanent guard on us.'

'Hide you from what?'

'We were on a, er, classified job, and being hunted an –'

'What classified job? I still can't see you, move into the light.'

Ross moved but not enough. 'We had to blow some secret American radar stuff to prevent it being pinched by Soviets or their supporters. I rec –'

'Sabalan?'

'How the hell did you know that?'

'I'm being forced to fly a Soviet and some leftists to ransack radar sites near the border, then take the stuff down to Astara on the coast. One of them was wrecked on the north face – they got nothing out of that one and so far the rest haven't produced anything worthwhile – as far as I know. Go on – warn me about what?'

'You're being forced?'

'My wife's hostage to the Khan and the Soviets – for my cooperation and good behaviour,' Erikki said simply.

'Christ!' Ross's mind was working overtime. 'I, er, I recognised the S-G decal when you were circling and came to warn you Soviets were here, they came here early this morning, and they're planning to kidnap you with the friendly help of the Khan – it seems he's playing both ends against the middle, double agent.' He saw Erikki's astonishment. 'Our people should know that quickly.'

'Kidnap me to do what?'

'I don't know exactly. I sent Gueng on a recce after your chopper arrived – he slipped out of a back window. Tell them, Gueng.'

'It was after they had eaten lunch, sahib, the Khan and the Soviet, and they were beside the Soviet's car when he was leaving – I was in the undergrowth near and could hear well. They were talking English. The Soviet said, Thanks for the information and the offer. The Khan said, Then we have an agreement? Everything, Patar? The Soviet said, Yes I'll recommend everything you want. I'll see the pilot never bothers you again. When he's finished here he'll be brought north . . .' Gueng stopped as the air hissed out of Azadeh's mouth. 'Yes, memsahib?'

'Nothing.'

Gueng concentrated, wanting to get it perfect for them: 'The Soviet said: I'll see that the pilot never bothers you again. When he's finished here he'll be brought north, permanently. Then . . .' He thought a moment. 'Ah, yes! Then he said, the mullah won't trouble you again and in return you'll catch the British saboteurs for me? Alive, I'd like them alive if possible. The Khan said, Yes, I'll catch them, Patar, Do y –'

'Petr,' Azadeh said, her hand on Erikki's shoulder. 'His name was Petr Mzytryk.'

'Christ!' Ross muttered as it fell into place.

'What?' Erikki said.

'I'll tell you later. Finish, Gueng.'

'Yes, sahib. The Khan said, I'll catch them, Patar, alive if I can. What's my favour if they're alive? The Soviet laughed. Anything, within reason, and mine? The Khan said, I'll bring *her* with me on my next visit. Sahib, that was all. Then the Soviet got into his car and left.'

Azadeh shuddered.

'What?' Erikki said.

'He means me,' she said, her voice small.

Ross said, 'I don't follow.'

Erikki hesitated, the tightness in his head greater than before. She had told him about being summoned for lunch by her father, and about Petr Mzytryk inviting her to Tbilisi – 'and your husband, of course, if he's free, I would love to show you our countryside . . .' and how attentive the Soviet had been. 'It's . . . it's personal. Not important,' he said. 'It seems you've done me a big favour. How can I help?' He smiled tiredly and stuck out his hand. 'My name's Yokkonen, Erikki Yokkonen and this is my wife, Az –'

'Sahib!' Gueng hissed warningly.

Ross jerked to a stop. Now he saw Erikki's other hand was under the pillow. 'Don't move a muscle,' he said, kukri suddenly out of its scabbard. Erikki recognised the tone and obeyed. Cautiously Ross moved the pillow aside but the hand was not near the knife. He picked the knife up. The blade glinted in the shaft of moonlight. He thought a moment, then handed it back to Erikki, haft first. 'Sorry, but it's better to be safe.' He shook the outstretched hand that had never wavered and felt the enormous strength. He smiled at him and turned slightly, the light now on his face for the first time. 'My name's Ross, Captain John Ross, and this's Gueng . . .'

Azadeh gasped and jerked upright. They all looked at her and now Ross saw her clearly for the first time. It was Azadeh, his Azadeh of ten years ago, Azadeh Gorden as he had known her then, Azadeh Gorden of the High Country staring up at him, more beautiful than ever, eyes bigger than ever, still heaven sent. 'My God, Azadeh, I didn't see your face . . .'

'Nor I yours, Johnny.'

'Azadeh . . . good God,' Ross stammered. He was beaming and so

562

was she, and then he heard Erikki and looked down and saw him staring up at him, the great knife in his fist, and a shaft of fear rushed through him and through her.

'You're "Johnny Brighteyes"?' Erikki said it flat.

'Yes, yes, I'm . . . I had the privilege of knowing your wife years ago, many years ago . . . Good Lord, Azadeh, how wonderful to see you!'

'And you . . .' Her hand had not left Erikki's shoulder.

Erikki could feel her hand and it was burning him but he did not move, mesmerised by the man in front of him. She had told him about John Ross and about their summer and the result of the summer, that the man had not known about the almost child, nor had she ever tried to find him to tell him, nor did she want him ever to know. 'The fault was mine, Erikki, not his,' she had told him simply. 'I was in love, I was just a few days seventeen and he nineteen – Johnny Brighteyes I called him; I had never seen a man with such blue eyes before. We were deeply in love but it was only a summer love, not like ours which is for ever, mine is, and yes, I will marry you if Father will allow it, oh yes, please God, but only if you can live happily with knowing that once upon a time, long long ago, I was growing up. You must promise me, swear to me you can be happy as a man and a husband for perhaps one day we will meet him – I will be happy to meet him and will smile at him but my soul will be yours, my body yours, my life yours, and all that I have . . .'

He had sworn as she had wished, truly and with all his soul, happily brushing aside her concern. He was modern and understanding and Finnish – wasn't Finland always progressive, hadn't Finland been the second country on earth after New Zealand to give women the vote? There was no worry in him. None. He was only sad for her that she had not been careful, for she had told him of her father's anger – an anger he could understand.

And now here was the man, fine and strong and young, far nearer her size than he, nearer her age than he. Jealousy ripped him apart.

Ross was trying to collect his wits, her presence possessing him. He pulled his eyes off her and the memory of her and looked back at Erikki. He read his eyes clearly. 'A long time ago I knew your wife, in Switzerland at . . . I was at school there for a short time.'

'Yes, I know,' Erikki said. 'Azadeh told me about you. I'm . . . I'm . . . it's a . . . it's a sudden meeting for all of us.' He got out of bed, towering over Ross, the knife still in his hand, all of them aware of the knife. Gueng on the other side of the bed still had his kukri out. 'So. Again, Captain, again thanks for the warning.'

'You said you're being forced to fly the Soviets?'

563

'Azadeh's hostage, for my good behaviour,' Erikki said simply.

Thoughtfully Ross nodded. 'Not much you can do about that if the Khan's hostile. Christ, that's a mess! My thought was that as you were threatened too, you'd want to escape too and that you'd give us a ride in the chopper.'

'If I could I would, yes . . . yes, of course. But I've twenty guards on me all the time I'm flying and Azadeh . . . my wife and I are watched very closely when we're here. There's another Soviet called Cimtarga who's like my shadow, and Abdollah Khan's . . . very careful.' He had not yet decided what to do about this man Ross. He glanced at Azadeh and saw that her smile was true, her touch on his shoulder true, and that clearly this man meant nothing more than an old friend to her now. But this did not take away his almost blinding urge to run amok. He made himself smile at her. 'We must be careful, Azadeh.'

'Very.' She had felt the surge under her hand when he had said 'Johnny Brighteyes' and knew that, of the three of them, only she could control this added danger. At the same time, Erikki's jealousy that he sought so hard to hide excited her, as did the open admiration of her long-lost love. Oh, yes, she thought, Johnny Brighteyes, you are more wonderful than ever, slimmer than ever, stronger than ever – more exciting, with your curved knife and unshaven face and filthy clothes and man smell – how could I not have recognised you? 'A moment ago when I corrected this man's "Patar" to "Petr" it meant something to you, Johnny. What?'

'It was a code message I had to give the Khan,' Ross said, achingly aware she still bewitched him. ' "Tell Abdollah Khan that Peter" – that could be Gueng's Patar or Petr, the Soviet – "that Peter's after the Gorgon's head and Peter's son is worse than Peter. The son plays with curds and whey and so does the father, who'll try to use a Medusa to catch the Gorgon." '

Azadeh said, 'That's easy. Erikki?'

'Yes,' Erikki said, distracted. 'But why "curds and whey"?'

'Perhaps this,' she said, her excitement rising. 'Tell Abdollah Khan that Petr Mzytryk, KGB, is after his head, that Mzytryk's son – let's presume also KGB – is worse than his father. The son plays at curds and whey – perhaps that means the son is involved with the Kurds and their rebellion that threatens Abdollah Khan's power base in Azerbaijan, that the KGB, the father, and the son are also involved – and that Petr Mzytryk will use a Medusa to catch the Gorgon.' She thought a moment. 'Could that be another pun and mean "use a woman", perhaps even an evil woman to catch my father?'

Ross was shocked. 'The Khan's . . . My God, the Khan's your father?'

'Yes, I'm afraid so. Gorgon's my family name,' Azadeh said. 'Not Gorden. But the principal of the school at Château d'Or told me the first day I could hardly have a name like Gorgon – I would get teased to death – so I was to be just Azadeh Gorden. It was fun for me, and the principal thought it better for me that I was just plain Azadeh Gorden and not the daughter of a Khan.'

Erikki broke the silence. 'If the message's correct, the Khan won't trust that *matyeryebyets* at all.'

'Yes, Erikki. But my father trusts no one. No one at all. If Father's playing both sides as Johnny thinks – there's no telling what he'll do. Johnny, who gave you the message to give to him?'

'A CIA agent who said I could trust your father with my life.'

Erikki said witheringly, 'I always knew the CIA were . . . were crazy.'

'This one was all right,' Ross said more sharply than he meant. He saw Erikki flush and her smile vanish.

Another silence. More jagged. The moonlight in the room faded as the moon went behind a bank of cloud. It was uneasy in the gloom. Gueng who had watched and listened felt the increased disquiet and he silently called on all gods to extricate them from Medusa, the pagan devil with snakes for hair that the missionaries had taught about in his first school in Nepal. Then his special sense felt the approaching danger, he hissed a warning and went to the window and peered out. Two armed guards with a Doberman pinscher on a leash were coming up the staircase opposite.

The others were equally rigid now. They heard the guards pad along the terrace, the dog sniffing and straining on the leash. Then go towards the outside door. Again it creaked open. The men came into the building.

Muffled voices outside the door of the bedroom and the sound of the dog snuffling. Then near the door of the anteroom. Gueng and Ross moved into ambush, kukris ready. In time the guards moved down the corridor, out of the building and down the staircase again. Azadeh shifted nervously. 'They don't come here normally. Ever.'

Ross whispered back hastily, 'Maybe they saw us coming up here. We'd better leave. If you hear firing, you don't know us. If we're still free tomorrow night, could we come here, say just after midnight? We could perhaps make a plan?'

565

'Yes,' Erikki said. 'But make it earlier. Cimtarga warned me we might have to leave before dawn. Make it around 11 p.m. We'd better have several plans ready – to get out is going to be very difficult, very.'

'How long will you be working for them – before you're finished?'

'I don't know. Perhaps three or four days.'

'Good. If we don't make contact with you – forget us. Okay?'

'God protect you, Johnny,' Azadeh told him anxiously; 'don't trust my father, you mustn't let him . . . mustn't let him or them take you.'

Ross smiled and it lit up the room, even for Erikki. 'No problem – good luck to all of us.' He waved a devil-may-care salute and opened the door. In a few seconds he and Gueng were gone as quietly as they had arrived. Erikki watched out of the window and saw them only as shadows going down the steps, noting how cleverly and silently the two men used the night, envying Ross his careless elegance of manner and movement.

Azadeh was standing alongside him, a head smaller, her arm around his waist, also watching. After a moment, his arm went around her shoulders. They waited, expecting shouting and firing, but the night remained undisturbed. The moon came out from the clouds again. No movement anywhere. He glanced at his watch. It was 4.23.

He looked at the sky, no sign of any dawn yet. At dawn he had to leave, not to the north face of Sabalan but to other radar sites further west. Cimtarga had told him that the CIA still operated certain sites nearer the Turkish border but that today the Khomeini government had ordered them closed, evacuated, and left intact. 'They'll never do that,' Erikki had said. 'Never.'

'Perhaps, perhaps not.' Cimtarga had laughed. 'The moment we get orders, you and I will just fly there with my "tribesmen" and hurry them up . . .'

Matyer! And *matyer* Johnny Brighteyes arriving to complicate our lives. Even so, thank all gods for the warning he brought. What's Abdollah planning for Azadeh? I should kill that old swine and have done with it. Yes, but I can't, I swore by the Ancient Gods an oath that may not be broken, not to touch her father – as he himself swore by the One God not to hinder us though he'll find a way to break that oath. Can I do the same? No. An oath is an oath. Like the one you swore to her that you could live happily with her, knowing about him – *him* – didn't you? His mind blackened and he was glad of the darkness.

566

So the KGB plan to kidnap me. If it's a real plan I'm done for. Azadeh? What's that devil Abdollah planning for her now? And now this Johnny arrives to harass us all – I never thought he'd be so good-looking and tough and no man to mix with, him with that sodding great knife, killing knife . . .

'Come back to bed, Erikki,' she said. 'It's very cold, isn't it?'

He nodded and followed and got in his side, greatly troubled. When they were back under the great quilt, she snuggled against him. Not enough to provoke a reaction but just enough to appear normal and untouched. 'How extraordinary to find it was him, Erikki! John Ross – in the street I certainly wouldn't have recognised him. Oh, that was such a long time ago, I'd forgotten all about him. I'm so pleased you married me, Erikki,' she said, her voice calm and loving, sure that his mind was grinding her long-lost love to dust. 'I feel so safe with you – if it hadn't been for you I would have died of fright.' She said it as though expecting an answer. But I don't expect one, my darling, she thought contentedly and sighed.

He heard her sigh and wondered what it meant, feeling her warmth against him, loathing the rage that possessed him. Was it because she's sorry she had smiled at her lover as she did? Or is she furious with me – she must have seen my jealousy. Or is she saddened that I have forgotten my oath, or is she hating me because I hate that man? I swear I'll exorcise him from her . . .

Ah, Johnny Brighteyes, she was thinking, what ecstasy I enjoyed in your arms, even the first time when it was supposed to hurt, but it never did. Just a pain that became a burning that became a melting that tore away life and gave life back to me again, better than before, oh how so much better than before! And then Erikki . . .

It was much warmer now under the quilt. Her hand went across his loins. She felt him move slightly and she hid her smile, sure that her warmth was reaching him now, so easy to warm him further. But unwise. Very unwise, for then she knew he would only take her with Johnny in the forefront of his mind, taking her to spite Johnny and not to love her – perhaps even thinking that in her acquiescence she was feeling guilty and was trying to make up for her guilt. Oh, no, my love, I'm not a foolish child, you're the guilty one, not me. And though you'd be stronger than usual and more rough, which would normally, increase my pleasure, this time it would not, for, like it or not, I would resist even more than you, aware of my other love. So, my darling, it is ten thousand times better to wait. Until the dawn. By then, my darling, if I'm lucky you will have persuaded yourself that you are wrong to hate him and be jealous and you will be my Erikki again. And if you haven't? Then I will begin again – there are ten thousand ways to heal my man. 'I love you, Erikki,' she said and kissed the cloth that covered his chest, turned over, and settled her back against him and went into sleep, smiling.

At Kowiss Air Base: 8:11 A.M. Freddy Ayre bunched his fists. 'No, by God! You heard McIver's orders: If Starke's not back by dawn all flights are grounded. It's past eight o'clock and Starke's not back so all fl –'

'You will obey *my* flight orders!' Esvandiary, the IranOil manager, shouted at him, his voice echoing around the S-G base. 'I've ordered you to deliver a new mud tank and pipe under Guerney's contract to Rig Si –'

'No flying until Captain Starke's back!' Ayre snarled. They were on the flight line near the three 212s that Esvandiary had scheduled for today's operations, the three pilots geared and ready since dawn, the rest of the expats watching in varying degrees of nervousness or anger. Around them were a truckload of hostile Green Bands and servicemen from the base who had just arrived with Esvandiary. Four of Zataki's men squatted near the choppers but none of them had moved since the quarrel had erupted though all of them were watching closely. 'All flights are grounded!' Ayre repeated.

Furiously Esvandiary called out in Farsi, 'These foreigners refuse to obey legitimate orders of IranOil.' A mutter of anger went through his supporters, guns covered the expats, and he stabbed a finger at Ayre. 'They need an example!'

Without warning rough hands grabbed Ayre, and the beating began. One of the pilots, Sandor Petrofi, rushed forward to intervene but he was shoved back, slipped and was kicked back to the others who were helpless under the guns.

'Stop it!' Pop Kelly, the tall captain, shouted out, his face chalky. 'Leave him alone, we'll fly the missions!'

'Good.' Esvandiary told his men to stop. They dragged Ayre to his feet. 'Get all flights under way. At once!'

When the flights were airborne he dismissed the expats roughly. 'There'll be no more mutinies against the Islamic state. By God, all orders of IranOil will – will – be obeyed instantly.' Very satisfied with himself that he had put down the mutiny as he had promised the camp commandant, he strode into the main office, down the corridor into Starke's office that he had commandeered, and stood at the window surveying his domain.

He saw two choppers, well away now, the third was hovering twenty feet over the mud tank a hundred yards away, waiting for the ground crew to link its skyhook into the big steel ring that topped the hawsers. In front of the office Ayre, surrounded by other expats, was being succoured by Doc Nutt. Rotten bastard to give me so much trouble, Esvandiary thought, and glanced at his watch, admiring it. It was a gold Rolex that he had bought on the black market this morning as befitted his increased stature, the money pishkesh from a bazaari who wanted his son to join IranOil.

'Do you need anything, Excellency?' Pavoud asked unctuously from the doorway. 'May I add my congratulations for the way that you handled the foreigners. For years they've all needed a good beating to put them in their places, how wise you were.'

'Yes. From now on the base *will* run smoothly. The moment there's a problem, whoever's in charge will be made an example of. Praise God that son of a dog Zataki leaves in an hour with his thugs for Abadan.'

'That's one flight that will leave on time, Excellency.' Both men laughed.

'Yes. Bring me some tea, Pavoud.' Deliberately Esvandiary left out the normal politeness and noted the man's humility increase. He stared out of the window again. Doc Nutt was dabbing a cut over Ayre's eye. I enjoyed watching Freddy being beaten, he thought. Yes, yes, I did.

In the chill wind Doc Nutt had wrapped a spare parka around Ayre. 'You'd better come over to the surgery, laddie,' he said.

'I'm all right,' Ayre said, hurting all over. 'Don't think . . . don't think anything's damaged.'

'Bastards,' someone said. 'Freddy, we'd better figure how we're going to get to hell out of here.'

'It's me on the first plane out . . . I'm not going to risk an –'

They all looked up as the jet engines of the chopper hovering over the mud tank picked up tempo. Getting such a heavy load airborne was tricky – particularly in this wind – but no problem for a professional like Sandor. The hook went in first time and the moment the ground crew had their hands clear, he increased power, the engines screamed at a higher pitch, taking the strain, then chopper and load eased into the sky. The guard in the front seat beside Sandor waved excitedly – as did the one in the cabin.

'You're doing fine, Captain . . . no sweat,' came into Sandor's headphones from Wazari in their tower, Sandor estimating the distance, gaining height, his hands and feet perfectly coordinated – seeing only Esvandiary at the office window, still maddened by Ayre's savage beating by many armed men on the orders of a coward. It had torn him back in time to others he had been forced to witness as a child, in Budapest, during the Hungarian revolution.

'You're okay, HFD, but kinda close.' Wazari's voice cautioned him. 'You're kinda close, ease south . . .'

Sandor increased power, moving towards the tower that topped the office building. 'Is the load okay?' he asked. 'Feels strange.'

'Looks fine, no sweat, but ease south as you climb. Everything five by five . . . ease south, do you read me?'

'You're sure, for crissake? She feels sluggish as all hello . . .' The needle climbed through a hundred feet. Sandor's face closed and his hand snapped the stick right, at the same time he gave her hard right rudder. At once the chopper reeled sickeningly, the guard in the seat beside him was thrown off balance, he bashed against the door, then grabbed Sandor, trying to steady himself and tangled with the controls. Again Sandor overcorrected, cursing the guard as though the petrified man was a real hazard.

For a moment it seemed as though the gathering swing would take the chopper out of the sky, then Sandor shoved the frantic guard away. 'Mayday – load's shifted,' he shouted, his ears shut to Wazari, eyes concentrating below, oblivious of everything except the need for revenge. 'Load's shifted!'

571

His hand pulled the Emergency Load Release, the hook freed, the steel tank plummeted out of the sky directly on to the office. The ton and a half of steel smashed through the roof, pulverising rafters and walls and glass and metal and desks, obliterating the whole corner, and came to rest upended against the remains of the inner wall.

A moment of appalled silence took the whole camp, then the screaming engines filled the sky as, released suddenly from its load, the chopper had careened upwards out of control. Sandor's reflexes fought the controls, his mind not caring whether he dominated them or not, whether he landed or not, just knowing that he had had vengeance on one brute. Beside him the guard was vomiting and his earphones were filled with 'Jesuschrist . . . Jesuschrist . . .' from the tower.

'Christ, look outttttt!' someone shouted as the chopper whirled down at them. Everyone scattered but Sandor's reflexes cut engines and went for the impossible emergency landing. The skids hacked into the snow of the grass verge, did not buckle, and the chopper skeetered forward to come to rest unharmed forty yards away.

Ayre was the first at the cockpit. He jerked the door open. Sandor was sheet white, numb, staring ahead. 'Load shifted . . .' he croaked.

'Yes,' was all Ayre could say, knowing it to be a lie, then others joined them and they helped Sandor, his limbs momentarily uncontrollable, out of the cockpit. Behind him, near the building, Ayre saw Green Bands gaping at the wreckage, then Pavoud and the other clerk tottered out of the front door in shock, the window and corner where Esvandiary had been standing was rubble. Doc Nutt pushed through the crowd and hurried towards the ruins as Wazari came down the emergency steps outside the tower that were twisted precariously, half off the side of the building. Christ, Ayre thought, Wazari must've seen everything. He knelt beside his friend. 'You all right, Sandy?'

'No,' Sandor said shakily. 'I think I went crazy. I couldn't stop.'

Wazari was shoving through the people towards the cockpit, still panicked from seeing the tank hurtling down on him, knowing the pilot had deliberately disregarded his instructions. 'You crazy, goddammit?' he exploded at Sandor over the wind-down scream of the engines.

Ayre's temper snapped. 'Goddammit, the load shifted! We all saw it and so did you!'

'You're goddam right I saw it and so did you.' Wazari's eyes were frantically darting this way and that, watching for Green Bands, but none were near – then he saw Zataki approaching from one of the bungalows. His dread escalated. He was still badly bruised from the beating Zataki had given him, his nose mashed, his mouth still aching where three teeth had been knocked out, and he knew he would admit anything to prevent another beating. He knelt beside Sandor, half pulling Ayre with him. 'Listen,' he whispered desperately, 'you swear by God you'll help me? You promise, huh?'

'I said I'd do what I could!' Angrily Ayre jerked his arm away, the pain of bending very bad. He stood upright and found he was looking into Zataki's face. The suddenness chilled him – and the eyes. Everyone else had backed away from them.

'Pilot, you did that to kill Esvandiary. Eh?'

Sandor stared up at him from the snow. 'The load shifted, Colonel.'

Zataki put his eyes on Ayre who remembered what Doc Nutt had said about the man, his own head aching, his groin, and pain everywhere. 'The, er, the operation's difficult, it was the wind. The load shifted. An act of God, Excellency . . .'

Wazari went back a pace as Zataki turned on him. 'It's true, Excellency,' he said at once. 'The winds aloft're gust—' He cried out as Zataki's fist rammed into his stomach and he doubled up in agony, then Zataki grabbed him and shoved him against the chopper. 'Now tell me the truth, vermin!'

'It's the truth,' Wazari whimpered, barely able to talk through his nausea. 'It's the truth! It was Insha'Allah!' He saw Zataki's fist ready again and he cried out in a jumble of Farsi and English, 'If you hit me I'll say anything you want, anything, I can't stand another beating and I'll swear to anything you want, anything, but the load shifted – by God, the load shifted, I swear by God the load shifted . . .'

Zataki stared at him. 'God will put you into the fiery vats for all eternity if you've sworn a lie by His Name,' he said. 'You swear it was God's will alone? That load shifted? You swear it was an act of God?'

'Yes, yes, I swear it!' Wazari was trembling, helpless in his grasp. He tried to keep his eyes guileless, knowing that his only chance for life lay with Ayre, proving his value to him. 'I swear by God and the Prophet it was an accident, an . . . an act of God. Insha'Allah . . .'

'As God wants.' Zataki nodded, absolved, and released him. Wazari slid to the snow, retching, and all the others were thanking God or joss or heaven or karma that, for the moment, this crisis had passed. Zataki jerked a thumb at the wreckage. 'Get what remains of Esvandiary out of there.'

'Yes . . . yes, at once,' Ayre said.

'Unless the captain returns, you will fly me and my men to Bandar-e Delam.' Zataki walked off. His Green Bands went with him.

'Christ!' someone muttered, all of them almost sick with relief. They helped Sandor to stand and Wazari. 'You okay, Sergeant?' Ayre asked.

'No, goddammit, no, I'm not!' Wazari spat out some vomit. When he saw the Green Bands had gone with Zataki his face twisted with hatred. 'That bastard! I hope he fries!'

Ayre pulled Wazari aside and dropped his voice. 'I won't forget I said I'd try to help you. When Zataki leaves you'll be okay. I won't forget.'

'Nor me,' Sandor said weakly. 'Thanks, Sergeant.'

'You owe me your goddam life,' the younger man said and spat again, his knees weak and chest hurting. 'You could've killed me too with that goddam tank!'

'Sorry.' Sandor stuck out his hand.

Wazari looked at the hand, then up into his face. 'I'll shake hands with you when I'm safe out of this goddam country.' He limped off.

'Freddy!' Dr. Nutt was at the wreckage with a couple of mechanics, lifting off rafters and mess, beckoning him. Green Bands stood around watching. 'Give us a hand here, will you?'

All of them went to help, none of them wishing to be the first one to see Esvandiary.

They found him crumpled in a pocket under one side of the tank. Dr. Nutt squeezed down beside him, examining him awkwardly. 'He's alive,' he cried out, and Sandor's stomach turned over. Quickly they all helped get the last of the splintered rafters and the remains of Starke's desk out of the way and gently eased the man out. 'I think he's all right,' Dr. Nutt said, hoarsely. 'Get him over to the infirmary – nasty bonk on the head but limbs seem okay and nothing crushed. Someone get a stretcher.' People rushed to do his bidding, the pall off them now, all of them hating Hotshot but all of them hoping he'd be all right. Unnoticed, Sandor went behind the building, so relieved he could have wept, and was very sick.

When he came back only Ayre and Nutt were waiting. 'Sandy, you'd better come along too, let me give you the once-over-lightly,' Nutt said. 'Bloody casualty ward, that's what we've got now.'

'You're sure Hotshot'll be okay?'

'Pretty sure.' The doctor's eyes were watery and pale blue and a little bloodshot. 'What went wrong, Sandy?' he asked quietly.

'Don't know, Doc. All I wanted was to get that bastard an' at the time dumping the tank seemed the perfect way to do it.'

'You know that would have been murder?'

Uneasily Ayre said, 'Doc, don't you think it'd be better to leave it?'

'No, no, I don't.' Nutt's voice hardened. 'Sandy, you know that was a deliberate attempt at murder.'

'Yes.' Sandor looked back at him. 'Yes, I understand that and I'm sorry.'

'You're sorry he's not dead?'

'Swear to God, Doc, I thank God he's alive. I still think he's become vile and evil and everything I detest and I can't forgive him for . . . for ordering Freddy's beating but that's no excuse for what I did. Doing what I did was crazy, and no excuse, and I really thank God he's alive.'

'Sandy,' Nutt said, his voice even quieter, 'you'd better not fly for a day or two. You were pushed beyond the limit – nothing to worry about, laddie, so long as you understand. Just take it easy for a day or so. You'll get the shakes tonight but don't worry. You too, Freddy. Of course this's all between the three of us and the load shifted. I saw it shift.' He brushed the threads of hair over his bald pate that the wind toyed with. 'Life's strange, very strange, but just between us three, God was with you today, Sandy, if there is such a thing.' He walked off, crumpled like an old sack of potatoes.

Ayre watched him. 'Doc's right, you know, we were bloody lucky, so near to disaster, so n –'

There was a shout and they looked up. One of the pilots near the main gate shouted again and pointed. Their hearts leaped. Starke was coming down the road from the direction of the town. He was alone. As far as they could see he was unhurt, walking tall. They waved excitedly and he waved back, the word flashed throughout the camp and Ayre was already running to meet him, oblivious of his pain. Maybe there's a God in heaven after all, he was thinking happily.

At Lengeh 2:15 P.M. Scragger was sunbathing on the big raft that was moored a hundred yards offshore, a small rubber dinghy attached to it. The raft was made with planks lashed to empty oil drums. In the dinghy was fishing equipment and the walkie-talkie, and below it hung a strong wire cage with the dozen fish that he and Willi Neurchtreiter had already caught for dinner – the Gulf being abundant with shrimp, Spanish mackerel, tuna, sea bass, rock cod, and dozens of other species.

Willi, another pilot, was swimming lazily in the warm shallow water nearby. On the shore was their base – half a dozen trailers, cookhouse, dormitories for the Iranian staff, office trailer with attached radio tower and antenna, hangars with space for a dozen 212s and 206s.

The present complement was five pilots, including himself, seven mechanics, fifteen Iranian staff, day labourers, cooks and houseboys, and the IranOil manager Kormani, presently sick. Of the other pilots two were British, the last, Ed Vossi, American.

On the base now were three 212s – with just enough work for one at the moment – and two 206 Jet Rangers with hardly any work at all.

Apart from the French Consortium with their Siri contracts from Georges de Plessey, all other contracts had been cancelled or held up pending the end of the troubles. There were still rumours of bad trouble at the big naval base of Bandar-e Abbas eastward and of fighting all along the coast. Two days ago trouble had spilled over to the base for the first time. Now they had a permanent komiteh of Green Bands, police, and one mullah: 'To protect the base against leftists, Excellency Captain.'

'But, Excellency Mullah, old sport, we don't need protection.'

'As God wants, but our vital Siri Island oil installations were attacked and hurt by those sons of dogs. Our helicopters are vital to us and will not be hurt. But don't be concerned, nothing will be changed by us – we understand your nervousness about flying with guns so none of us will be armed though one of us will fly with you every time – for your protection.'

Scragger and the others had been reassured by the presence on the komiteh of their local police sergeant, Qeshemi, with whom they had always had good relations. The troubles of Tehran, Qom and Abadan had hardly touched them here on the Strait of Hormuz. Strikes had been minimal and orderly. De Plessey was paying EPF's bills, so everything had been fine, except for the lack of work.

Idly Scragger glanced shoreward. The base was tidy and he could see men about their tasks, cleaning, repairing, a few of the komiteh idly sitting around in the shade. Ed Vossi was near the duty 206 doing his ground check.

'Just not enough work,' Scragger muttered. It had been the same for months and he knew only too well how costly and disastrous that could be. It was the lack of steady charters and the need to get modern equipment that had persuaded him to sell his Sheik Aviation to Andrew Gavallan so many years ago.

But I've no regrets, he thought. Andy's a beaut, he's been straight with me, I've a little piece of the company, and I can fly so long's I'm fit. But Iran's terrible for Andy now – not even getting paid for work done or for current work, excepting here, and that's a pittance. It must be four or five months the banks've been closed, so he's been carrying Iran ops out of his own swag bag. Something's got to go. With only Siri working, that's not enough to half pay our way.

Three days ago, when Scragger had brought Kasigi back from the Iran-Toda plant near Bandar-e Delam, Kasigi had asked de Plessey if he could charter a 206 to go to Al Shargaz or Dubai. 'I need to be in immediate telephone-telex touch with my head office in Japan to confirm arrangements I've made with you for your spot price, and about uplifting future supplies.' De Plessey had agreed immediately. Scragger had decided to do the charter himself and was glad he had. While he was in Al Shargaz he had met up with Johnny Hogg and Manuela. And Genny.

In private she had brought him up to date, particularly about Lochart.

'Gawd Almighty!' he had said, shocked how rapidly their ops were falling apart and the revolution was embroiling them personally. 'Poor old Tom.'

'Tom was due from Bandar-e Delam the day before I left but he never arrived so we still don't know what really happened – at least I don't,' she said. 'Scrag, God knows when we can talk privately again but there's something else: just between us?'

'Cross my heart and cut my throat!'

'I don't think the government's ever going to get back to normal. I wanted to ask you: even if it does, could the partners – with or without official help – or IranOil, force us out and keep our planes and equipment?'

'Why should they do that? They've got to have choppers . . . but, if they wanted to, sure, too right they could,' he had said and whistled, for that possibility had never occurred to him before. 'Bloody hell, if they decided they didn't need us, Genny, that'd be dead easy, dead easy. They could get other pilots, Iranian or mercenaries – isn't that what we are? Sure they could order us out and keep our equipment. And if we lost everything here, that'd gut S-G.'

'That's what Duncan thought. Could we *leave with our planes and spares* – if they tried to do that?'

He had laughed. 'It'd be a bonza heist and that's what it'd be. But it couldn't be done, Genny. If we tried and they caught us, they'd throw the book at us. There's no way we could do it – not without Iran CAA approval.'

'Say this was Sheik Aviation?'

'It'd make no difference, Genny.'

'You'd just let them steal your life's work, Scrag? Scrag Scragger, DFC and Bar, AFC and Bar? I don't believe it.'

'Nor do I,' he said at once, 'though what I'd do God only knows.'

He saw the nice face looking at him, dark glasses perched on her head, anxiety behind the eyes, knowing her concern was not only for McIver and all that he had built, not only for their own stock and pension that, like his, was tied to S-G – but also for Andy Gavallan and all the others. 'What'd I do?' he said slowly. 'Well, we've almost as much in spares in Iran as birds. We'd have to start getting them out, though how to do it without making the locals suspicious I don't know. We couldn't get 'em all out, but we could dent the amount. Then we'd all have to leave at the same time – everyone, all choppers – from Tehran, Kowiss, Zagros, Bandar-e Delam, and here. We'd . . .' He thought a moment. 'We'd have to make for here, Al Shargaz . . . But, Genny, we'd all have different distances to go and some'd have to refuel once, maybe twice, and even if we got to Al Shargaz they'd still impound us without proper clearances.' He studied her. 'Andy believes that's what the partners're going to do?'

'No, no, he doesn't, not yet, nor does Duncan, not for certain. But it is a possibility and Iran's getting worse every day – that's why I'm here, to ask Andy. You . . . you can't put that in a letter or telex.'

'You phoned Andy?'

'Yes, and said as much as I dared – Duncan said to be careful – and Andy told me he'd try to check in London and when he arrives in a couple of days he'd decide what we should plan to do.'

She pushed her glasses back on her nose. 'We should be prepared, shouldn't we, Scrag?'

'I wondered why you'd left the Dunc. He sent you?'

'Of course. Andy'll be here in a couple of days.'

Scragger's mind was buzzing. If we do a bunk, someone's bound to get hurt. What'd I do about Kish, Lavan, and Lengeh Radar who could scramble twenty fighters in minutes to catch us before we went into friendly skies if we took off without clearance? 'Dunc thinks they're going to do us proper?'

'No,' she had said. 'He doesn't – but I do.'

'In that case, Genny, just between us, we'd better make a plan.'

He remembered how her face had lit up, and thought again what a lucky man Duncan McIver was even though he was as ornery and opinionated as a man could be.

His eyes were watching the sea when he heard the 206 wind up and saw it neatly airborne. Ed's a bonza pilot, he thought.

'Hey, Scrag!'

'Yes, Willi?'

'You swim and I'll watch.' Willi climbed into the raft.

'Good on you, mate.' Along with abundant edible fish there were also predators, sharks and stingrays, and others – with occasional poisonous jellyfish – but few here in these shallows, and provided you kept your eyes open you could see their shadows a long way off with plenty of time to make the raft. Scragger touched wood, as always, before he dived into the six feet of water that was lukewarm.

Willi Neurchtreiter was also naked. He was a short stocky man of 48 with brown hair and more than five thousand hours in helicopters, ten years with the German Army and eight with S-G – working Nigeria, the North Sea, Uganda, and here. His peaked cap was on the raft and he put it on and his sunglasses, squinted at the 206 that was heading out into the Gulf, then watched Scragger. In moments the sun had dried him. He enjoyed the sun and swimming and being at Lengeh.

So different from home, he thought. Home was in Kiel in northern Germany on the Baltic where the climate was harsh and mostly cold. His wife and three children had gone home last year because of the children's educational needs, and he had elected to do two months here and one in Kiel, and had got a transfer back to the North Sea to be closer. Next month, after his leave, he would not return to Lengeh.

Shit on the North Sea with its foul moods and constant danger, on the crummy quarters and the vast boredom of two weeks' flying off a rig a hundred miles offshore to earn one week at home in Kiel and barely enough money to pay the mortage and schooling and stay ahead with a little to spare for holidays. But you'll be near the kids and Hilda and Ma and Pa, your homeland is always your homeland. Yes, it is, and with any luck, some day soon, all Germans will mix freely with all Germans, Ma can visit her family in Schwerin whenever she wants – and Schwerin and all our other Schwerins won't be occupied any more. Oh, God, let me live to see that day.

'Scrag, a shadow's coming in.'

Scragger had seen it almost at the same time, and he swam back to the raft and got aboard. The shadow came in fast. It was a shark. 'Stone the crows,' he gasped. 'Look at her size!'

The shark slowed, then leisurely began to circle, its large dorsal fin cutting the calm surface. Dull grey, lethal and unhurried. Both men watched silently, awed. Then Scragger chuckled. 'How about it, Willi?'

'Yes, by God, Harry, he's not Jaws but he's the biggest beetch I've ever seen so I think we get him, by God!' Gleefully, he got the fishing tackle that was in the dinghy. 'What about bait? What you think for bait?'

'The sea bass, the big one!'

Laughing, Willi reached down into the cage and pulled out the squirming fish and baited the steel shark hook. There was blood on his hands now and he washed them off in the water, watching the prey.

Then he got up, checked the short length of chain attached to the hook, knotted it carefully to the heavy nylon fishing line that was on the reel of the rod. 'Here you are, Scrag.'

'No, cobber. You spotted her first!'

Excitedly Willi wiped the sea salt off his forehead with the back of his hand, settled his cap jauntily, and looked at the shark that still circled twenty yards away. With great care he threw the bait directly into its path, gently tightened the line. The shark passed the bait and continued circling. Both men cursed. Willi reeled in. The sea bass danced and kicked spasmodically, dying fast. A thin trail of blood was in its wake. Again Willi cast perfectly. Again nothing happened.

'God damn,' Willi said. This time he left the bait where it was, watching it settle lower until it lay on the bottom, keeping just enough tension on the line. The shark came around, passed over it, almost touching it with its belly, and continued circling.

'Maybe he's not hungry.'

'Those sons of beetches're always hungry! Maybe he knows we're waiting for him – or he's going to trick us. Scrag, get a smaller fish and throw it just where the bait is as he comes around.'

Scragger chose a rock cod. He threw it deftly. The fish fell into the water ten yards ahead of the shark, sensed the danger, and fled for the sandy bottom. The shark paid no attention to it, nor to the sea bass so close by, just flicked its tail and circled. 'Let the bait stay where it is,' Scragger said. 'That bugger can't have not got its scent.'

Now they could see the yellow eyes and the three small pilot fish hovering over its head, the thin line of the vast mouth under the blunt nose, the sleek skin and power of the great tail. Another circuit. A little closer this time. 'Betcha he's nearer eight feet than six, Willi.'

'That sonofabitch's watching us, Scrag,' Willi said uneasily, his excitement gone now, a hollowness in its place.

Scragger frowned, having the same feeling. He looked away from the eyes to the dinghy. No weapons there of any value, just a small sheath knife, a light aluminium three-pronged fishing spear and some oars. Even so, he tugged on the painter to bring the dinghy closer, knelt down, and reached for the knife and fishing spear. Wish I had a gun, he thought.

A sudden cry from Willi made him jump back and he just had time to see the shark coming straight for him at full speed. It smashed against the side of the rubber dinghy, its ugly head now out of the water, jaws gaping as it lunged at him, crashing against the oil drums, making the bow of the dinghy rear up out of the water. Then it was gone, both men aghast.

581

'By God Harry . . .' Willi shouted and pointed. The shark was charging towards the bait. They saw it take it and the hook into its mouth and swim away, the line singing off the reel. Willi held his breath, tightened the line, then with both hands on the rod, he struck hard. 'Gotttt heemmm!' he shouted, taking the strain, the reel shrieking as the line rushed out, the hook deeply embedded now.

'Bloody bastard near did me,' Scragger said, his heart racing, watching the taut line. 'Don't let the bugger cheat you.'

Willi put more strain on the line and began to fight him, the line taut.

'Watch him, Willi, he'll turn and come back fast . . .' But the shark did not, just slowed and fought the line and hook in a frenzy, boiling the water around it, half in and out of the water, rolling over and turning. But the hook held and the line was strong enough and Willi gave the fish just enough leeway, allowing it to swim off a way, then once more began to reel in. Minutes passed. The strain of fighting such a fish without a harness or chair, unable to use his legs to help him, was overwhelming. But Willi held on. Abruptly the shark stopped fighting, beginning to circle again. Slower.

'Good on you, Willi, you got him, Willi.'

'Scrag, if he comes in fast see if you can keep the line from fouling, and when I get him near enough, jab him with the harpoon.' Willi felt the pain in his back and hands but now he was exhilarated, waiting for the next move. It came quickly.

The shark swirled and headed for them. Frantically Willi reeled in to take up the slack lest the shark turn again and snap the line, but it kept barrelling and went directly under the raft. Miraculously the line did not foul and when the shark came out on the other side to charge off towards deeper water, Willi let him take line with him and gradually got the tension back. Once more the shark tried to shake off the hook in a paroxysm of rage, churning the water white, and once more Willi held him. But his muscles were weakening, he knew he would not be able to hold him alone and swore silently. 'Give me a hand, Scrag.'

'Okay, mate.'

Together the two men held the rod now, Willi working the reel, pulling the shark in, playing him, closer and closer. The shark was slowing. 'He's tiring, Willi.' Inch by inch they pulled him in. Now the shark was thirty yards out from the raft just making headway, its great tail waving slowly back and forth, almost wallowing in the water. To breathe, a shark must have forward motion. If it stops it drowns.

Patiently they fought it, its huge weight hurting them. Now they could see its great size, the yellow eyes, jaws tight shut, the pilot fish. Twenty-five yards, twenty, eighteen, seventeen . . .

Then it happened. The shark came to life and tore away from them for fifty yards at incredible speed, line screeching off the reel, then turned ninety degrees at full speed and was going away but Willi somehow got tension back on the line, forcing the fish to circle, but he could not bring it nearer. Another circuit, Willi using all his strength on the reel to no avail. On the next circuit he gained a little. Another inch. Another, then both men lurched and nearly fell overboard as the line came free. 'Lost heem by God Harry . . .'

Both were panting and aching and bitterly disappointed. There was no sign of the shark now. 'God-cursed line,' Willie said, reeling in, swearing in two languages. But it wasn't the line. It was the chain. The links nearest the hook were smashed. 'That bugger must've just chewed through it!' Scragger said, awed.

'He was playing with us, Scrag,' Willi said disgustedly. 'He could have bust it any time he wanted. He was giving us the finger.' They searched the water all around but there was no sign of it. 'He could be on the bottom, waiting,' he said thoughtfully.

'More likely he's two miles away, mad as a rabid dingo.'

'I betcha he's mad, Scrag. That hook'll do him no good at all.' Both men searched the sea. Nothing. Then they noticed the rubber dinghy was listing by the bow and half submerged. Scragger bent down and carefully examined it, his eyes on the sea and under the raft.

'Look,' he said. There was a great rip in one of the air chambers. 'The bugger must've done it when he came charging in.' The air was escaping fast. 'No problems. We can make the shore in time. Let's go.'

Willi looked at the raft, then at the sea. 'You go, Scrag. Me I wait for the wood dinghy with someone up front with a machine gun.'

'There's no problem, for God's sake. C'me on.'

'Scrag,' Willi said sweetly, 'I love you like a brother but I'm not moving. That beetch frightened me to death.' He sat down in the centre of the raft and put his arms around his knees. 'That motherless beetch's lurking somewhere, bottoming. You want to go, okay, but me, I know the Book says when in doubt, duck. Order up the other boat on the walkie-talkie.'

'I'll bring her myself.' The dinghy squelched as Scragger stepped carefully into it, nearly capsized, and he scrambled back on the raft cursing, quicker than he wanted to. 'What the hell're you laughing about?'

'You got out of there like you got jellyfish on your bum.' Willi was still laughing. 'Scrag, why don't you swim home?'

'Get stuffed.' Scragger looked at the shore, heart pounding. Today it seemed far away when most days it was so close.

'You swim and you're crazy,' Willi said, seriously now. 'Don't do it.'

Scragger paid no attention to him. You know something? he was thinking. You're scared fartless. That bugger was a small one and you hooked him and he got away and now he's miles out in the Gulf. Yes, but where?

He put a tentative toe in the water. Something below caught his eyes. He knelt on the side of the raft and pulled the cage. It was empty. The whole side was torn off. 'Stone the crows!'

'I'll call up the boat,' Willi said, reaching for the walkie-talkie. 'With a machine gun.'

'No need for that, Willi,' Scragger said with a show of bravado. 'Race you to the shore.'

'Not on your Nelly! Scrag, for God's sake don't . . .' Willi was appalled as Scragger dived over the side. He saw him surface and strike out strongly, then all at once turn back and scramble back on to the raft, spluttering and choking with laughter.

'Fooled you, huh? You're right, me son, anyone who swims ashore's crazy! Call up the boat, I'm fishing for more dinner.'

When the boat came, one of the mechanics was on the tiller with two excited Green Bands in the bow, others watching from the beach. They were halfway back to shore when the shark appeared out of nowhere and began circling. The Green Bands started firing and, in their excitement, one fell overboard. Scragger managed to grab his gun and opened up on the shark that raced for the petrified man now standing in the shallow water. The bullets went into the shark's head and into the eyes and though the shark was dead it did not believe it, just rolled over thrashing, its jaws working and tail working, then went driving ahead for its prey. But without the guidance of scent or eyesight it missed the man and went on up the sloping bottom until it beached itself and thrashed around, half in and half out of the water.

'Scrag,' Willi said, when he could talk, 'you've the luck of the devil. If you'd swum in he'd've got you. You've the luck of the devil.'

USSR

Caspian Sea

USSR

Khvoy

Tabriz Mount
Sabalan Bandar-e Pahlavi

Qazvin

Sadzevar

Meshed

Tehran

IRAN

AFGHANISTAN

Baghdad

Dez Dam

Isfahan

IRAQ

Abadan

Bandar-e Delam

Kowiss

PAKISTAN

KUWAIT

Kharg
Island

ZAGROS

SAUDI ARABIA

Jellet

Persian Gulf

Lengeh

Strait of Hormuz

CHAPTER

37

BAHRAIN

QATAR

Siri

Al Shargaz

Gulf of Oman

UAE

At Rig Rosa – Zagros: 3:05 P.M. Tom Lochart got out of the 206 stiffly and shook hands with Mimmo Sera, the 'company man' who greeted him warmly. With Lochart was the Schlumberger expert, Jesper Almqvist, a tall young Swede in his late twenties. He carried his special case with the necessary down-hole tools – all his other equipment already here, on site. '*Buon'giorno*, Jesper, good to see you. She's waiting for you.'

'Okay, Mr. Sera, I'll go to work.' The young man walked off towards the rig. He had logged most of the wells in the field.

'Come inside for a moment, Tom.' Sera led the way through the snow to the office trailer. Inside it was warm and a pot of coffee was on the big-bellied, iron, wood-burning furnace near the far wall. 'Coffee?'

'Thanks, I'm bushed, the trip from Tehran was boring.'

Sera handed him a cup. 'What the hell's going on?'

'Thanks. I don't know exactly – I just dropped off Jean-Luc at the base, had a brief word with Scot, then thought it best to bring Jesper at once and come see you myself. Haven't seen Nitchak Khan yet; I'll do that soon as I get back but Scot was quite clear: Nitchak Khan told him the komiteh had given us forty-eight hours to leave. McI –'

'But why? *Mamma mia*, if you leave we'll have to close down the whole field completely.'

'I know. My God, the coffee's good! Nitchak's always been reasonable in the past – you heard this komiteh shot Nasiri and burned the schoolhouse?'

'Yes, terrible. He was a fine fellow, though pro-Shah.'

'So were we all – when the Shah was in power,' Lochart said, thinking of Sharazad and Jared Bakravan and Emir Paknouri and HBC – always back to HBC, and Sharazad. At dawn he had left her, hating to leave her. She was still deep in sleep. He had thought about waking her but there was little to say. Zagros was his responsibility – and she looked so exhausted, the bruise on her face vivid. His note said: 'Back in a couple of days. Any problem see Mac or Charlie. All my love.' He looked back at Sera. 'McIver's got an appointment this morning with a top official in the government, so with any luck he can straighten everything out. He said he'd get a message to us soon as he got back. Your radio's working?'

Sera shrugged. 'The usual: from time to time.'

'If I hear anything I'll get word to you, either tonight or first thing. I hope it's all a storm in a bucket of shit. But if we have to clear out, McIver told me temporarily to base out of Kowiss. There's no way in hell we can service you from there. What do you think?'

'If you're forced out, we'll have to evacuate. You'll have to ferry us to Shiraz. We've company HQ there; they can put us up or fly us out until we're allowed back. *Madonna*, there would be eleven bases to close, double shifts.'

'We could use both 212s, no sweat.'

'Plenty of sweat, Tom.' Sera was very worried. 'There's no way to close down and get the men out in forty-eight hours. No way at all.'

'Maybe it won't be necessary. Let's hope, huh?' Lochart got up.

'If we have to evacuate, most of the crew'll cheer – we haven't had a replacement in weeks and they're all overdue leave.' Sera got up and glanced out of the window. They could just see the afternoon sun glinting off the crest over Rig Bellissima. 'You heard what a fine job Scot did, with Pietro?'

'Yes. The lads call him Bomber Pietro now. Sorry about Mario Guineppa.'

'*Che sara sara!* Doctors're all *stronzo* – he had a medical last month or so. It was perfect. *Stronzo!*' The Italian looked at him keenly. 'What's up, Tom?'

'Nothing.'

'How was Tehran?'

'Not good.'

'Did Scot tell you anything I don't know?'

'A reason for the komiteh's order? No. No, he didn't. Maybe I can get something out of Nitchak Khan.' Lochart shook hands and went off. Once he was airborne, he thought of the story Scot had told him, Jean-Luc and Jesper about what happened in the village after the komiteh had sentenced Nitchak Khan to death:

'The moment they marched Nitchak Khan out of the school-house and I was alone, I slipped out the back window and sneaked into the forest as quietly as I could. A couple of minutes later I heard a lot of firing and rushed back to base as fast as possible – must admit I was scared fartless. It took me quite a time, bloody snow's in ten-foot drifts in places. Not long after I got back old Nitchak Khan and the mullah and some of the villagers came up here – my God, I was so relieved! I thought for certain Nitchak and the mullah'd been shot and I guess they were just as relieved because they stared at me pop-eyed, thinking me dead too.'

'Why?' Tom had asked.

'Nitchak said that just before the komiteh left they fired the school-house, supposedly with me still in it. He said they had ordered all foreigners out of the Zagros. Everyone – particularly us with our choppers, out by tomorrow night.'

Lochart was watching the land below, the base not far off, the village nearby. The afternoon sun was sliding off it, going behind the mountains. There was plenty of daylight left but no longer the sun to warm them. Just before he had left with Jesper for Rig Rosa and no one was near, Scot had told him really what happened. 'I saw it all, Tom. I didn't run off when I said I did. I haven't dared tell anyone but I was watching out of the schoolhouse window, frightened to bloody death and saw it all. Everything happened so fast. My God, you should've seen old Nitchak's wife with the rifle, talk about a tigress. And tough! She shot a Green Band in the belly, then left him to scream a bit and . . . banggg! stopped it. I'll bet she was the one who shot the first bastard, the leader, whoever the hell he was. Never seen such a woman, never'd believe she could be like that.'

'What about Nasiri?'

'Nasiri never had a chance. He just ran off and they shot him. I'm

587

sure they shot him just because he was a witness and not a villager. That got my wits working, and my legs, and I sneaked out of the window like I said, and when Nitchak came up here I pretended to believe his story. But I swear to God, Tom, all those komiteh bastards were dead before I left the village, so Nitchak must've ordered the schoolhouse burned.'

'Nitchak Khan wouldn't do that, not with you in it. Someone must've seen you sneak out.'

'I hope to Christ you're wrong because then I'm a living threat to the village – the only witness.'

Lochart landed and walked down to the village. He went alone. Nitchak Khan and the mullah were waiting for him in the coffee-house as arranged. And many villagers, no women. The coffeehouse was the meeting house, a one-room but made from logs and mud wattle with a sloping roof and crude chimney, the rafters black from years of the wood fire's smoke. Rough carpets to sit on.

'Salaam, Kalandar, peace be upon you,' Lochart said, using the honorific title to imply that Nitchak Khan was also leader of the base.

'Peace be upon you, Kalandar of the Flying Men,' the old man said politely. Lochart heard the slap and saw there was none of the friendliness of olden times within the eyes. 'Please sit here in comfort. Your journey was beneficent?'

'As God wants. I missed my home here in the Zagros, and my friends of the Zagros. You are blessed by God, Kalandar.' Lochart sat on the uncomfortable carpet and exchanged the interminable pleasantries, waiting for Nitchak Khan to allow him to come to the point. The room was claustrophobic and smelled rancid, the air heavy with body odours and goat smells and sheep smells. The other men watched silently.

'What brings Your Excellency to our village?' Nitchak Khan said and a current of expectancy went through the closeness.

'I was shocked to hear that strangers came to our village and had the impertinence to lay evil hands on you.'

'As God wants.' Nitchak's eyes narrowed slightly. 'Strangers came to *our* village but they went away leaving *our* village as it has always been. *Your* camp, unfortunately, is not to be the same.'

'But why, Kalandar? We have been good for the village and employ many of your peo –'

'It is not for me to question *our* government or these komitehs of *our* government or *our* Commander of the People, the Ayatollah himself. The young flier saw and heard, so there is nothing more to be said.'

Lochart perceived the trap. 'The young flier heard and saw only what happened in the schoolhouse, Kalandar. I ask that we, as old but

588

known guests . . .' he chose the word carefully, 'that we be allowed time to seek a change in a ruling that appears to go against the interests of the Zagros.'

'The Zagros extends a thousand miles and crosses Kash'kai lands into Bakhtiari and the lands of a hundred other tribes. Yazdek is Yazdek,' Nitchak rasped, then quoted from the *Rubáiyát*, ' "Resign your body to fate and put up with pain, because what the Pen has written for you, it will not unwrite." '

'True, but did not Omar Khayyám also write: "The good and evil that are in man's heart, The joy and sorrow that are our fortune and destiny, Do not impugn them to the wheel of heaven because, in the light of reason, The wheel is a thousand more times more helpless than you." '

A rustle went through the villagers. The old mullah nodded, pleased, and said nothing. Nitchak Khan's eyes smiled though his mouth did not and Lochart knew the meeting would be better now. He blessed Sharazad who had opened his ears and eyes and senses to the *Rubáiyát* that, in Farsi, was beyond elegance.

Everyone waited. Nitchak Khan scratched his beard, reached into his pocket, and found a pack of cigarettes. Lochart casually brought out the pishkesh, a gold-plated Dunhill lighter he had bought from Effer Jordon for just this purpose: 'Effer, I'll goddam kill you if it doesn't work first time!' He caressed the flint. The wick ignited and he breathed again. His hand was very steady as he leaned forward and held the light for the old man.

Nitchak Khan hesitated, then puffed and took a deep drag of smoke. 'Thank you.' His eyes narrowed as Lochart put the lighter on the carpet in front of him.

'Perhaps you would accept this gift from all of us in your camp who are grateful for your guidance and protection. After all, didn't you break down the gates and take possession of the base in the name of the people? Didn't you win the toboggan race, beating the best of us, through the quality of your courage?'

Another rustle in the room, everyone waited filled with delight as the contest stiffened, though all knew the Infidel had said only what was true. The silence grew, then the Khan reached over and picked up the lighter and looked at it closely. His gnarled thumb clicked up the lid as he had seen others in the camp do. With hardly any motion it lit the very first time and everyone was as pleased as he with the quality of the pishkesh.

'What guidance does His Excellency need?'

'Nothing in particular, not really, Excellency Kalandar,' Lochart said deprecatingly, continuing the game according to Persian rules.

'But there must be something that might make His Excellency's lot better?' The old man stubbed his cigarette into the earth.

At length Lochart allowed himself to be persuaded. 'Well, since Your Excellency has the magnanimity to ask, if Your Excellency would intercede for us with the komiteh to give us a little more time, I would be very grateful. Your Excellency, who knows these mountains like the inside of his own eating bowl, knows we cannot obey the orders of strangers who obviously don't know we cannot clear the rigs of personnel, nor safeguard the rigs – the Zagros property of the illustrious Yazdek branch of the Kash'kai – nor take away our machines and spares by tomorrow sunset.'

'True, strangers know nothing,' Nitchak Khan said agreeably. Yes, he thought, strangers know nothing and those sons of dogs who dared to try to implant their filthy stranger's ways were quickly punished by God. 'Perhaps the komiteh would grant an extra day.'

'That would be more than I would dare ask. But you, Kalandar, it would hardly be enough to show them how little they know about your Zagros. Perhaps they need to be taught a lesson. They should be told at least two weeks – after all, you are kalandar of Yazdek and of all eleven rigs, and the whole Zagros knows of Nitchak Khan.'

Nitchak Khan was very proud and so were the villagers, pleasantly swept along with the Infidel's logic. He took out his cigarettes and his lighter. It lit the first time. 'Two weeks,' he said and everyone was very satisfied, including Lochart. Then he added, to give himself time to consider if two weeks was too long, 'I will send a messenger and ask for two weeks.'

Lochart got up and thanked the Khan profusely. Two weeks would give McIver time. Outside, the air tasted like wine and he filled his lungs gratefully, pleased with the way he had handled the delicate negotiation. 'Salaam, Nitchak Khan, peace be upon you.'

'And upon you.'

Across the square was the mosque and beside it the ruined schoolhouse. The other side of the mosque was Nitchak Khan's two-storeyed house and, at the door, his wife and two of his children with some other village women also colourfully dressed.

'Why was the schoolhouse burned, Kalandar?'

'One of the komiteh was heard to say, "Thus should perish everything foreign. Thus will perish the base and all that it contains – we need no foreigners here, want no foreigners here." '

Lochart was saddened. That's what most of you believe, if not all of you, he thought. And yet lots of us try to be part of Iran, speak the language, want to be accepted but never will be. Then why do we stay, why do we try? Perhaps for the same reason Alexander the Great stayed, why he and ten thousand of his officers married Iranian women in one vast ceremony – because there's a magic to them and to Iran that is indefinable, totally obsessive, that consumes as I am consumed.

A burst of laughter came from the women surrounding Nitchak Khan's wife at something she had said.

'It's better when wives are happy, eh? That's God's gift to men, eh?' the Khan said jovially, and Lochart nodded, thinking how fantastically lucky Nitchak Khan had been and what a gift of God his wife was – like Sharazad was to him and, thinking of her, once more the horror of last night welled up, his terror of almost losing her, her madness and unhappiness, then hitting her and seeing the bruises when all he wanted was her happiness in this world and the next, if there was a next.

'And lucky for me, God made her such a fine shot, eh?'

'Yes,' Lochart said before he could stop himself. His stomach heaved and he cursed himself for letting his attention wander. He saw the shrewd eyes watching him and added hastily, 'Shot? Your wife's a fine shot? Please excuse me, Excellency, I didn't hear you clearly. You mean with a rifle?'

The old man said nothing, just studied him, then nodded thoughtfully. Lochart kept his gaze steady and looked back across the square, wondering if it had been a deliberate trap. 'I've heard that many Kash'kai women can use a rifle. It would seem that, er, that God has blessed you in many ways, Kalandar.'

After a moment Nitchak Khan said, 'I will send word to you tomorrow, how much time the komiteh agrees. Peace be upon you.'

Going back to the base Lochart asked himself, Was it a trap I fell into? If the remark was involuntary, made from pride in her, then perhaps, perhaps we're safe and Scot's safe. In any event we've time – perhaps we have, but perhaps Scot hasn't.

The sun had gone from this part of the plateau and the temperature had quickly fallen below freezing again. The cold helped to clear his head but did not eliminate his anxiety or overcome his weariness.

A week, two weeks, or a few days, you've not much time, he thought. In Tehran McIver had told him about getting export licences for three 212s to go to Al Shargaz for repairs. 'Tom, I'll send one of yours, one from here, and one from Kowiss – thence to Nigeria, but for God's sake keep that part to yourself. Here're the exit papers dated for Wednesday next, I think you should go yourself and get out while you can. You get out and stay at Al Shargaz – there's plenty of pilots there to take the 212 onwards.'

He came up out of the trees and saw the base, Scot and Jean-Luc waiting for him beside a 212.

I'll send Scot on the ferry whatever happens, Lochart thought, and having made the decision, some of his concern left him. The main decision's do we start the evacuation or not? To decide that, you have to decide how far to trust Nitchak Khan. Not very far at all.

CHAPTER

38

At Inner Intelligence HQ: 6:42 P.M. It was barely twenty-three hours since Rakoczy had been captured, but he was already broken and babbling the third level – the truth. The first two levels were cover stories of partial truths rehearsed and rerehearsed by all career agents until they were deeply embedded into the subconscious in the hope that these partial truths would deflect questioners from probing deeper, or make them believe they already had all the truth. Unfortunately for Rakoczy, his interrogators were expert and anxious to probe ever deeper. Their problem was to keep the torment from killing him first. His problem was how to die quickly.

When he had been caught yesterday evening, he had at once tried to get his teeth into the point of his collar where the poison vial was sewn – a trained reflex action. But his captors had forestalled him, held his head backward while they chloroformed him, then carefully stripped him, probed his mouth for a false tooth of poison and his anus for a capsule.

He had expected beating and psychedelic drugs: 'If they use those on you, Captain Mzytryk, you're finished,' his teachers had said. 'Nothing much to do but to try to die before giving secrets away. Better to die before they break you. Never forget we'll avenge you. Our reach can span fifty years and we'll get those who betrayed you.'

But he had not expected the level of agony to which they had taken him so fast, or the unspeakable things they had done to him, electrodes inside him, in his ears nose mouth stomach rectum, on his testicles and eyeballs – with drug injections to put him to sleep, to wake him up, minutes only between sleep wake sleep wake, disoriented, upside down, inside out.

'For Christ's sake, Hashemi,' Robert Armstrong had said, sickened, long long ago in the beginning, 'why don't you just give him the truth drugs, you've got them, no need for all this shit.'

Colonel Hashemi Fazir had shrugged. 'A little cruelty is good for the soul. By Allah, you've seen the files, you've seen what the KGB's done to some of our citizens who weren't even spies.'

'That's no excuse.'

'We need his information quickly, by God. We need to reach the third level you're always harping about. I've no time for your twisted ethics, Robert. If you don't want to stay, leave.'

Armstrong had stayed. He had muffled his ears against the screams, loathing the brutality. No need for that, not nowadays, he had said to himself, knowing he would have died long since.

He watched the two men through the one-sided mirror as they worked Rakoczy over again in the small, well-equipped chamber, sorry for him in an oblique way – after all, Rakoczy was a professional like him, a brave man who had held out against them extraordinarily.

Abruptly the screams stopped and Rakoczy was against inert. Hashemi spoke into the mike that fed into the earphones of the man below. 'Is he dead? I told you stupid sons of dogs to be careful!'

One of the two men was a doctor. The headset he wore cut out all sound except instructions from the interrogators. Irritably he lifted Rakoczy's eyelids and peered at his eyes, then, with his stethoscope, listened to his heartbeat.

'He's alive, Colonel. He's . . . there's still a way to go yet.'

'Give him five minutes, then wake him up. And don't kill him until I say so.' Angrily Hashemi clicked off the mike and cursed the man. 'Don't want him dead when we're so close to cleaning him out.' He glanced at Armstrong, eyes glittering. 'He's the best we've ever had, ever, eh? By God, Robert, he's a gold mine.'

Rakoczy had babbled out his two covers long since and then his real name, KGB number, where he was educated, born, married, lived, his known superiors in Tbilisi, their involvement in Iran, the Tudeh, the mujhadin, how and where they supported the Kurdish independence movement, who his contacts were.

'Who's the top KGB Azerbaijani?'

'I . . . no more please . . . pleasestoppppp it's Abdollah Khan of Tabriz . . . him, only him of importance and he . . . he was . . . is to to to be the first President when Azer . . . Azerbaijan be . . . becomes independent but now he's too big and inde . . . independent so . . . so now he's a Section 16/a . . .'

'You're not telling us all the truth – teach him a lesson!'

'Oh I amIamIampleaseeeeee . . .'

Then reviving him and him babbling again, about Ibrahim Kyabi, Ibrahim's father, the mullah Kowissi, who the Tudeh student leaders were, about his own wife, about his father and where he lived in Tbilisi, and about his grandfather who was in the tsar's secret police before being a founding member of the Cheka, then OGPU, NKVD, and finally the KGB – founded in '54 by Khrushchev after Beria had been shot as a Western spy.

'You believe Beria was a spy for us, Mzytryk?'

'Yes . . . yes . . . yes he was, the KGB had proof oh yes . . . please stoppppp . . . please stopppppp I'll tell you anyththinggggg . . .'

'How could they have proof to that lie?'

'Yes it was a lie but we were to believe it we were . . . we had to had to had to . . . please stopppppp I begggggg you . . .'

'Stop hurting him, you devils.' Armstrong's voice came in on cue. 'No need to hurt him if he's cooperating – how many times do I have to tell you! So long as he tells the truth don't touch him. Give him a glass of water. Now, Mzytryk, tell us all you know about Gregor Suslev.'

'He's . . . he's a spy I think.'

'You're not telling us the truth!' Hashemi roared at him, on cue. 'Teach him a lesson!'

'No . . . no . . . noplease stopppppppppohGodplease stoppppp he's he's Petr Oleg Mzytryk my father my father . . . Suslev was his . . . his cover name in the in the Far East based out of Vlad . . . Vladivostok and and and another cover's Brodnin . . . and and and he lives in in Tbilisi and he's commissar and senior ad . . . adviser Iranian affairs and con controller of Abdollah Abdollah Khan . . .'

'You're lying again. How could you know such secrets? Teach him a les –'

'Please no I swearrrrrr I'm not lying I . . . read his secret dossier and I

595

know it's true . . . Brodnin was last and then he . . . Allah helppppp meeeeee . . .' Again he fainted again. Again they revived him.

'How does Abdollah Khan contact his controller?'

'He . . . my . . . they meet when whenever . . . some . . . sometimes at the . . . at the dacha sometimes at Tabriz . . .'

'Where in Tabriz?'

'At . . . at the Khan's palace . . .'

'How do they arrange a meeting?'

'By code . . . coded telex from Tehran . . . from HQ . . .'

'What code?'

'The . . . G16 . . . G16 . . .'

'What's Abdollah Khan's code name?'

'Ivanovitch.'

'And his controller's?' Armstrong was careful not to agitate the helpless man by reminding him he betrayed his father.

'Ali . . . Ali Khoy . . .'

'Who were Brodnin's contacts?'

'I . . . I don't . . . I don't rememb remember . . .'

'Help him remember!'

'Pleaseplease oh God oh Godddddd wait let me think I can't remember it was it was . . . wait he told me there were there were three . . . it was something like like like one of them was a colour a colour . . . wait, yes, Grey yes Grey that was it . . . and and an another was . . . and another was Broad something . . . Broad something . . . I think . . . you it was Julan Broad something . . .'

'Who else?' Armstrong asked. 'The third?'

'I . . . I can't remem . . . no waittttttt let me thinkkkk . . . there was there was anoth . . . told me there were he told me about . . . about four . . . one . . . one was . . . Ted . . . Ever . . . Ever something . . . Everly . . . and and another there were . . . if . . . I . . . pleaseeee if I think let me think and it was it was Peter . . . no Percy . . . Percy Smedley yes Smedey Tailler or Smidley . . .'

The colour left Armstrong's face.

'. . . that was all that was all that he that he told me . . .'

'Tell us all you know about Roger Crosse!'

No answer.

Through the mirror they saw the man writhing on the operating table, heaving against the wires as more pain was fed into him and, mixed with the moans, the words poured out again: 'He he . . . stopppppppppppppp he was head no assistant head of MI6 and almost our top English secret agent for for for . . . twenty or more years for us and . . . and Brodnin Brod my father found . . . found out he was a double . . . triple agent and ordered him Section 16/a . . . Cross cheated us for years cheated cheated cheated . . .'

'Who tipped Brodnin about Crosse?'

'Idontknow I swearIdontknow I can't know everything everything only what was in his dossier and and what he told me . . .'

'Who was Roger Crosse's controller?'

'I don't know, don't know, how could I know I only know what I read secretly in my father's doss . . . you've got to believe mmmmmmeeeeeee . . .'

'Tell me everything in the dossier,' Hashemi said, as vitally interested now as Armstrong.

They listened, sifting the words from the screams. At times the almost incoherent mixture of Russian and Farsi as Rakoczy continued to bring forth more names and addresses and covers and ranks in answer to their questions, his memory prompted by new levels of pain, until he was spent and repeating and now confused, himself confused and no longer of value. Then mixed with the gibberish . . . 'Pah . . . mud . . . Pah . . . mudi . . .'

'What about Pahmudi?' Hashemi said abruptly.

'I . . . he's . . . helppp meeee . . .'

'What about Pahmudi? Is he a Soviet agent?'

Now only gibberish and weeping and confusion.

'Better give him a rest, Hashemi. His memory's too good to blow – we can get what Pahmudi means tomorrow and go back over the stuff.' Armstrong was equally drained, secretly marvelling at the knowledge Rakoczy had provided. 'I advise a rest period, let him sleep for five hours, then we could begin again.'

In the chamber the two men were waiting for instructions. The doctor glanced at his watch. He had been at it for six hours without a break, his back ached and so did his head. But he was a long-term SAVAK specialist and very pleased that he had brought Rakoczy to the level of truth without drugs. Atheist son of a burnt father! he thought disgustedly.

'Let him sleep for four hours, then we begin again,' came over the loudspeaker.

'Yes Colonel. Very good.' He peered at the eyes under the lids, then said carefully to his assistant who was a deaf-mute but could lip-read. 'Leave him as he is – that'll save time when we come back. He'll need a wake-up injection.' The man nodded and, when the door was opened from the outside, both men left.

In the room behind the mirror the air was smoky and dry.

'What about Pahmudi?'

'He has to be connected with Mzytryk, Petr Oleg.' Armstrong was sifting all Rakoczy's information, awed.

Hashemi took his eyes off the man lying on the table and switched off the cassette recorder, pressed the rewind button. In a half-opened drawer were seven other cassettes.

'Can I have copies?' Armstrong asked.

'Why not?' Hashemi's eyes were red-rimmed and the stubble of his heavy beard showed darkly even though he had shaved only a few hours ago. 'What was so important about Petr Oleg's cover "Brodnin", and those names, Grey, Julan Broad something, Ted Ever something, and Percy Smedley or Smidley Tailler?'

Armstrong got up to ease the pain in his shoulders, also to give himself a little time to think. 'Brodnin was a Soviet businessman, KGB, but a double agent for us – never a suspicion he was duping us. Julan Broad something has got to mean Julian Broadhurst. We've never had anything on him, never a whisper, nothing. He's a leading light of the Fabian Society, a highly respected member of the Labour party, in or out of the cabinet at his whim, adviser and confidant of prime ministers.' He added disgustedly, 'Patriot.'

'So now you have him. Traitor. So put him on a table for a few hours, milk him dry, then drown him in the Thames. Grey?'

'Lord Grey, firebrand of the left, ex-trades unionist, rabid leader of the anti-China anti-Hong Kong lobby, politely anti-communist, sent up to the Lords a few years ago to create more trouble. We did an investigation on him a few years ago but he came up clean as a whistle – nothing except his politics.' My God, Armstrong was thinking, if they're both spies and traitors – and we could prove it – that would rip Labour apart, let alone the explosion Percy'd cause the Tories. But how to prove it and stay alive? 'We've had nothing on him ever.'

'So now you have him too. Traitor. Clean him out and shoot him. Ted Ever something?'

'Everly – golden boy of the TUC being groomed for high office. Impeccable centrist politics. Never a smell of pink let alone communist.'

'Now you have him. Rack him. Smedley or Smidley-Tailler?'

Robert Armstrong offered his cigarettes. Percy Smedley-Taylor: landed gentry, rich, Trinity College – an apolitical deviate who manages to keep his aberrations out of the press when he's caught – well-known ballet critic, publisher of erudite magazines, with impeccable, untouchable connections into the highest and most delicate sources of English power. Christ Almighty, if he's a Soviet spy . . . It's impossible! Don't be bloody silly, you've done too many years, know too many secrets to be surprised about anyone. 'Doesn't mean beans, but I'll check him out, Hashemi,' he said, not wanting to share the knowledge until he had thought through what he should do.

The cassette clicked off as the rewind finished. Hashemi took it out, put it with the others in the lower drawer and locked the drawer carefully. 'Then deal with them in our fashion: send an emissary to them, Robert, to them and their lousy high-blown friends. They'll soon give you plenty of pishkesh to compensate for your loss of pension.' Hashemi laughed mirthlessly, inserting a new cassette. 'But don't go yourself or you'll end up in a back alley with a knife in your back or poison in your beer – these high-blown bastards are all the same.' He was very tired but his elation at all the marvellous knowledge Rakoczy had given them pushed away the need for sleep. 'We've already got enough from him to dynamite the Tudeh, control the Kurds, stop the insurrection in Azerbaijan, make Tehran safe, Kowiss safe – and cement Khomeini into power,' he said almost to himself.

'Is that what you want? What about Abrim Pahmudi?'

Hashemi's face darkened. 'Allah let me deal with him properly! Rakoczy's given me a golden key perhaps even to him.' He looked at Armstrong. 'Gold for you too, eh? This Suslev – Petr Oleg – who murdered the great Roger Crosse? Eh?'

'Yes. You too. Now you know who's your top enemy.'

'What's Mzytryk, this Suslev, to you?'

'I had a run-in with him years ago in Hong Kong.' Armstrong sipped some cold coffee, baiting the hook. 'He could provide you – and me – with more gold than his son. He could peg Abrim Pahmudi, and if him, Christ only knows who else – perhaps the Rev Komiteh? I'd give a lot to debrief Suslev. How can we do that?'

Hashemi tore his concentration off Pahmudi and put it back on the personal danger he himself and his family were in. 'In return you will arrange me a British passport, safe passage out, and a substantial pension – if I need it?'

Armstrong put out his hand. 'Done,' he said. The two men shook hands, neither believing the gesture had any value other than as a politeness, both knowing they would deliver if they could, but only so long as it was then to their own advantage.

'If we get him, Robert, I control the briefing and I ask what I want first.'

'Of course, you're the boss.' Armstrong's eyes veiled his excitement. 'Could you get him?'

'Perhaps I could persuade Abdollah Khan to arrange a meeting this side of the border. Rakoczy's given us enough on him to make even him squirm though I'd have to be careful – he's one of our best agents too!'

'Barter the knowledge of the Section 16/a – I bet he doesn't know they've betrayed him.'

Hashemi nodded. 'If we get Petr Oleg over the border, no need to bring him here. We could clean him out in our place in Tabriz.'

'I didn't know you had a place there.'

'Lots of things you don't know about Iran, Robert.' Hashemi stubbed out his cigarette. How much time have I got? he asked himself nervously, totally unused to feeling like the hunted and not the hunter. 'On second thoughts, give me the passport tomorrow.'

'How soon could you "persuade" Abdollah Khan?'

'We'd still have to be careful – that bastard's all-powerful in Azerbaijan.' They both glanced at Rakoczy as he stirred momentarily, moaned, then went back into nightmare again. 'Have to be very careful.'

'When?'

'Tomorrow. Soon as we've finished with Rakoczy we'll visit Abdollah. You provide the plane – or chopper. You're very friendly with IHC, aren't you?'

Armstrong smiled. 'You know everything, don't you?'

'Only about Tehran things, Islamic things, Iranian things.' Hashemi wondered what McIver and the other oil support foreigners would do if they knew that Deputy Minister Ali Kia, newly appointed to the ATC board, had, some days ago, recommended immediate nationalisation of all foreign oil-based companies, all Iran-registered airplanes, airplane companies and the expulsion of all foreign pilots and personnel. 'How are you going to service the oil fields, Excellency Minister?' he had asked when he had been told.

'We don't need foreigners. Our own pilots will service our own fields – haven't we hundreds of pilots who need to prove their loyalty? I presume you have secret files on all foreign pilots, executives, and so on. The, er, the Komiteh require them.'

'I don't think we have anything, Excellency. Those files were SAVAK-instigated,' Hashemi had said smoothly. 'I presume you know those terrible people have an extensive file on your Excellency?'

'What file? Me? SAVAK? You must be mistaken . . .'

'Perhaps. I've never read it, Excellency, but I was told of its existence.

I was told it goes back over twenty years. Probably it contains nothing but lies . . .'

He had left a badly shaken Deputy Kia with the promise that he would try to obtain the file secretly and give it to him and had laughed all the way back to Inner Intelligence HQ. The file on Ali Kia – that he had a copy of – really did go back twenty years and contained unshakable proof of all sorts of smelly business deals, usury, pro-Shah voting and informing, together with highly ingenious – photographed – sexual practices that would send conservative fundamentalists into a frenzy.

'What's the joke?' Armstrong asked.

'Life, Robert. A couple of weeks ago I had at my disposal a whole air force if need be, now I must ask you to arrange the charter. You arrange the charter, I'll arrange the clearance.' He smiled. 'You'll give me the British passport, very bloody valid, as Talbot might say, prior to takeoff. Agreed?'

'Agreed.' Armstrong stifled a yawn. 'While we're waiting, can I hear the last cassette?'

'Why not?' Hashemi reached for his key, stopped at the knock on the door. Tiredly he got up and opened it. His fatigue vanished. Four men were outside. One of his own men, white-faced, and three Green Bands. Armed. He knew the oldest of them. 'Salaam, General,' he said politely, his heart grinding. 'Peace be upon you.'

'Salaam, Colonel. Peace be upon you.' General Janan was hard-faced with a thin line for a mouth. SAVAK. He looked at Armstrong coldly, then took out a paper, offered it to Hashemi. 'You are to hand over the prisoner Yazernov to me at once.'

Hashemi took the paper, thanking God he had risked everything to capture Rakoczy and ram him through to the third level fast. 'To Colonel Hashemi Fazir, Inner Intelligence. Immediate. Immediate. By authority of the Revolutionary Komiteh: The Department of Inner Intelligence is disbanded and all personnel absorbed into this organisation at once under the command of General Janan. You are suspended from all duties pending further orders. You will hand over to General Janan the prisoner Yazernov and all interrogation tapes at once. (signed) Abrim Pahmudi, Director, SAVAMA.'

'The spy's still on the second level and you'll have to wait. It's dangerous to remove him an –'

'He's no longer your responsibility.' The general motioned to one of his men who went out, beckoned to others in the corridor, then walked down the steps and into the chamber below, the doctor, white-faced and very nervous, now with them. When the Green Bands saw the naked man on the table and the instruments and the way he was wired, their eyes glittered. The doctor began to unwire him.

In the interrogation room above, Hashemi looked back at the general. 'I formally tell you it's dangerous to move him. You're responsible.'

'Insha'Allah. Just give me the tapes.'

Hashemi shrugged and unlocked the top drawer and gave him the dozen, almost useless tapes from the first and second level.

'And the others! Now!'

'There aren't any.'

'Open the drawer!'

Again Hashemi shrugged, selected a key, and used it carefully. If turned correctly, the key set the magnetiser into operation and wiped the tapes. Only he and Armstrong knew the secret – and about the secret installation of duplicate cassette recorders: 'You never know, Hashemi, when you might be betrayed or by whom,' Armstrong had told him years ago when, together, they had installed the devices. 'You might want to wipe tapes, then use the secret ones to barter for your freedom. You can never be too careful in this game.'

Hashemi slid the drawer open, praying that both devices were operating. Insha'Allah, he thought, and gave over the eight cassettes. 'They're empty I tell you.'

'If they are, accept my apologies, if they're not . . . Insha'Allah!' The general looked at Armstrong, his eyes granite. 'Better you leave Iran quickly. I give you a day and a night for past services.'

At the Bakravan House, near the Bazaar: 8:57 P.M. Sharazad was lying on her stomach on the bed, being massaged, and she groaned with pleasure as the old woman caressed oil into her bruises and into her skin. 'Oh, be careful, Jari . . .'

'Yes, yes, my princess,' Jari crooned, her hands softly strong, easing the pain away. She had been nursemaid and servant to Sharazad ever since her birth, and had given her suck when her own baby, born a week earlier, had died. For two years she suckled Sharazad and then, because Jari was a quiet and gentle woman, now widowed, she had been given full charge of her. When Sharazad married Emir Paknouri she accompanied her into his house and then, the marriage finished, happily they had returned home. Stupid to marry such a flower to one who prefers boys, however much money he has, Jari had always thought but never said out loud. Never never never. Dangerous to go against the head of the house – any head of a family – even more so with a moneygrubbing miser like Jared Bakravan, she thought, not sorry he was dead.

When Sharazad had married the second time, Jari had not gone to stay in the apartment. But that did not matter, for Sharazad spent days here when the Infidel was away. All the household called him that and tolerated him because of her happiness that only women understood.

'Eeeee, what devils men are,' she said and hid her smile, understanding very well. They had all heard the screams last night and the sobbing, and though they all knew a husband was entitled to beat his wife and that God had allowed the Infidel's blows to shake their mistress out of her fit, she herself had heard the different cries, just before dawn this morning, the cries of her and him in the Garden of God.

Never had she been there herself. Others had told her about being transported, so had Sharazad, but the few times her own husband had lain with her had been for his pleasure and not hers. Her share had been pain and six children before she was twenty, four dying in infancy. Then him dying to release her from the childbirth death that she knew, for her, would otherwise have been inevitable. As God wants! Oh, yes, she told herself so contentedly, God rescued me and made him die and now, surely, he burns in hell, for he was a foul blasphemer who barely prayed once a day. God also gave me Sharazad!

She looked down on the beautiful, satin body and long, dark-dark hair. Eeeee, she told herself, how blessed to be so young, so moist, so resilient, so ready to do God's work at long last.

'Turn over, Princess, an –'

'No, Jari, it hurts so.'

'Yes, but I must knead your stomach muscles and condition them.' Jari chuckled. 'They must be very strong soon.'

At once, Sharazad turned and looked up at her, pain forgotten. 'Oh, Jari, are you sure?'

'Only God is sure, Princess. But have you ever been late before? Isn't your time overdue – and a son long overdue?'

The two women laughed together, then Sharazad lay back and gave herself to the hands and to the future and to the happy time she would have when she told him: Tommy, I'm honoured to tell . . . no, that's no good. Tommy, God has blessed us . . . no, that's no good either though it's true. If only he was Muslim and Iranian it'd be so much easier. Oh, God, and Prophet of God, make Tommy Muslim and so save him from hell, make my son strong and let him grow up to have sons and daughters and them sons . . . oh, how blessed we are by God . . .

She let herself drift. The night was calm, still a little snow falling and not much gunfire. Soon they would have their evening meal and then she would play backgammon with her cousin Karim or with Zarah, her brother Meshang's wife, then to sleep contentedly, the day well spent.

This morning when Jari had awakened her the sun was up, and though she had wept a little from the pain, oil and massage soon took the most of it away. Then the ritual washing and first prayer of the day, kneeling in front of the little shrine in a corner of the bedroom and its *sajadeh*, the small square of lovely wrought tapestry with its bowl of sacred sand from Cabella and, beyond that, the string of prayer beads and her copy of the Koran, beautifully decorated. A quick breakfast of tea, fresh bread still hot from the kiln oven, butter and honey and milk, a boiled egg as always – rarely a shortage even during the bad troubles – then quickly to the bazaar, veiled and chadored, to see Meshang, her adored brother.

'Oh Meshang, my darling, you look so tired. Did you hear about our apartment?'

'Yes, yes, I did,' he said heavily, dark shadows around his eyes. The four days since their father had gone to Evin Jail had aged him. 'Sons of dogs, all of them! But they're not our people. I heard they're PLO acting on instructions of this Revolutionary Komiteh.' He shuddered. 'As God wants.'

'As God wants, yes. But my husband said a man called Teymour, the leader, this man said we had until afternoon prayer today to take our things away.'

'Yes, I know. Your husband left a message for me before he left this morning for Zagros. I've sent Ali and Hassan and some of the other servants, told them to pretend they were movers and to collect everything they could.'

'Oh, thank you, Meshang, how clever you are.' She was greatly relieved. It would have been unthinkable for her to have gone herself. Her eyes filled with tears. 'I know it's the will of God but I feel so empty without Father.'

'Yes, yes, it's the same for me . . . Insha'Allah.' There was nothing more he could do. He had done everything correctly, overseeing the washing of the body, binding it with the best muslin, and then the burial. Now the first part of mourning was over. On the fortieth day would be another ceremony at the cemetery when once more they would weep and rend their clothes and all would be inconsolable. But then, as now, each would once more take up the weight of living, there was the shahada to say five times a day, the Five Pillars of Islam to obey to ensure you went to heaven and not to hell – your only important reason for life. I will certainly go to Paradise, he thought with total confidence.

They sat silently in the small room over the shop that such a short time ago was the private domain of Jared Bakravan. Was it only four days since Father was negotiating with Ali Kia for the new loan – that we still somehow have to provide – and Paknouri burst in and all our troubles began? Son of a dog! It's all his fault. He led the Green Bands here. Yes, and he's been a curse for years. If it hadn't been for his weakness, Sharazad would have had five or six children by now and we wouldn't be saddled with the Infidel who makes us the butt of a thousand bazaari sneers.

He saw the bruise around her left eye and did not comment. This morning he had thanked God and agreed with his wife that the beating had brought her out of her fit. 'No harm to a good beating from time to time, Zarah,' he had said with relish, and thought, All women need a good beating now and then with their constant nagging and nattering and crying and bickering, and jealousies and interference and all this ungodly talk of voting and marches and protests. Against what? Against the laws of God!

I'll never understand women. Still, even the Prophet, whose Name be Praised, he, the most perfect man that ever lived, even he had problems with women and ten more wives after Khadija, his first, had died after having given him six children – how sad that no sons survived him, only his daughter Fatima. Even after all this experience with women it's written that even the Prophet, even he, would have to take himself aside for peace from time to time.

Why can't women be content to stay in the home, be obedient, keep quiet and not meddle?

So much to do. So many threads to pick up and to find, secrets to unlock, accounts and promissory notes and debts to uncover, and so little time. All our property stolen, villages, the estate on the Caspian, houses and apartments and buildings all over Tehran – all the ones the devils know about! Devils! The Revolutionary Komiteh and mullahs and Green Bands are devils on earth. How am I going to deal with them all? But I must, somehow. I must, then next year I will make the pilgrimage to Mecca.

'As God wants,' he said and felt a little better. And it's as God wants that I am put in charge long before I expected it, even though I'm as well trained as any son could be to take over an empire, even the Bakravan empire.

It's also as God wants that I already know where most of the secrets are, whispered to me by Father over the last few years when he discovered I was to be trusted, cleverer than he had ever expected. Didn't I suggest the numbered Swiss bank accounts nearly seven years ago, and explain about U.S. Treasury bills, real-estate investment in America, and most of all about the Seven Sisters. We made millions, all of it safe from these sons of dogs, thanks be to God! Safe in Switzerland in gold, land, blue chips, dollars, Deutschmarks, yen, and Swiss francs . . .

He saw Sharazad looking at him, waiting. 'The servants will do everything before sunset, Sharazad, don't worry,' he said, loving her though wanting her to leave so that he could continue his work. But it was time to gather in other strings: 'This husband of yours, he agreed to become a Muslim, didn't he?'

'How kind of you to remember, dear Meshang. My husband agreed to consider it,' she said defensively. 'I've been teaching him whenever I can.'

'Good. When he returns please tell him to come to see me.'

'Yes, of course,' she said at once. Meshang was head of the family now, and, as such, was to be obeyed without question.

'The year and a day is overdue, is it not?'

Sharazad's face lit up. 'I'm honoured to tell you, darling Meshang, that perhaps God has blessed us, I am overdue one or two days.'

'God be praised. Now that is worth celebrating! Father would have been so pleased.' He patted her hand. 'Good. Now, what about him – your husband? This would be the perfect time to divorce, wouldn't it?'

'No! Oh, how could you say such a thing?' she burst out before she could stop herself. 'Oh, absolutely not, oh, no, that would be terrible, I would die, it would be terr –'

'Be quiet, Sharazad! Think!' Meshang was astonished by her bad manners. 'He's not Iranian, not Muslim, he has no money, no future, he's hardly worthy to be part of the Bakravans, wouldn't you agree?'

'Yes, yes, of course I . . . I agree to everything you say but if I may add . . .' she said hastily, keeping her eyes lowered to cover her shock, cursing herself for not being aware how much Meshang was opposed to her Tommy, that therefore he was enemy, to be guarded against. How could I have been so naive and so stupid? 'I agree there may be problems, my darling, and agree with everything you say . . .' she heard herself tell him in her most honeyed voice, her mind working with the speed of light, analysing, discarding, trying to make a plan – for now and for the future – for without Meshang's benevolence, life would

606

be very difficult. 'You're the wisest man I know . . . but perhaps I may be allowed to say that God put him into my path, Father agreed to my marriage, so until God takes him out of my path and guides m –'

'But now I am head of the family and everything's changed – the Ayatollah's changed everything,' he said curtly. He had never liked Lochart, resented him as an Infidel, the cause of all their present and past troubles, despised him as an interloper and an unwarranted expense, but because he had had no power to interfere and because of their father's tacit agreement he had always kept it hidden. 'Don't worry your pretty little head, but the revolution's changed everything. We live in a different world, and in the light of this I must consider your future and the future of your son.'

'You're perfectly right, Meshang, and I bless you for thinking of me and my child, how wonderful you are and how fortunate that you're here to take care of us,' she said, back in control now. She continued to flatter, cajole, being penitent for her lack of manners, using all of her guile, allowing him no opening and turning their conversation to other things. Then at the perfect time she said, 'I know you must be very busy.' She got up, smiling. 'Will you and Zarah be home for dinner? Cousin Karim's coming if he can get away from the base, won't that be fun? I haven't seen him since . . .' she stopped herself in time. 'For at least a week, but most important, Meshang, cook is making your favourite horisht, just the way you like it.'

'Oh? He is? Oh, well, yes, yes, we will – but tell him not to use too much garlic – now concerning your husb –'

'Oh that reminds me, darling Meshang,' she said, playing her last card – for the moment. 'I heard that Zarah now has your permission to go on the Women's March, the day after tomorrow, how sensitive of you.' She saw the sudden flush and laughed to herself, knowing that Zarah was as adamant about going as he was adamant against it. His fury soared. She listened patiently, her eyes guileless, nodding in agreement from time to perfect time.

'My husband agrees with you totally, darling Meshang,' she said with suitable fervour. 'Yes, totally, dearest brother, and I'll certainly remind Zarah, if she asks me, about your feelings . . .' Not that this will make the slightest difference to her, or to me, because on this protest march we *will* go. She kissed him lightly. 'Good-bye, my darling, try not to work too hard. I'll make sure about the horisht.'

Then she had gone at once to Zarah and had warned her that Meshang was still furious about the march: 'Ridiculous! All our friends will be there, Sharazad. Does he want us shamed before our friends?'

607

Together they had made a plan. By this time it was late afternoon and she had rushed home to command horisht, 'just as the Master likes it and if you use too much garlic and it's not perfect I'll . . . I'll get Old Ashabageh the Soothsayer to put the evil eye on you! Go to the market and buy the melon he adores!'

'But, mistress, there haven't been any melons for s –'

'Get one!' she had screeched and stamped her foot. 'Of course you can get one!'

Then supervising Jari tidying away all her clothes and Tommy's clothes, shedding a tear now and then, not for the loss of their apartment that he had wanted and enjoyed more than she, but only from happiness to be home again. A rest, last prayer, and then a bath and now the massage.

'There, Princess,' Jari said, her arms tired. 'Now you should dress for dinner. What would you like to wear?'

Wearing the dress that would please Meshang the most, the multi-coloured woollen skirt and blouse he admired. Then once more checking on the horisht and the polo – the golden-crusted, mouth-watering Iranian way of cooking rice – and the other Meshang speciality, the melon, sweet smelling and juicy and perfectly sculptured.

Waiting for her cousin Karim Peshadi to arrive – loving him, remembering their lovely times growing up, their families always intermingled, summers on their Caspian estates, swimming and sailing and, in the winter, skiing near Tehran, nothing but parties and dances and laughter, Karim tall like his father, the colonel commandant at Kowiss, and as fine. Always associating Karim with that first September evening she had seen the strange tall foreigner with the blue-grey eyes – eyes that had glowed with the heavenly fire the ancient poets wrote about, the instant he had seen her . . .

'Highness, His Excellency your cousin Captain Karim Peshadi requests permission to see you.'

Joyfully running to greet him. He was staring out of a window in the smaller of the reception rooms, the walls all small mirrors and windows set into an artistic Persian design, the only furniture the usual low, continuous sofa around the walls, a few inches off the close-sheared carpet, soft-padded and upholstered with the finest Persian fabric – like the backrest that was attached to the walls.

'Darling Karim, how wonder—' She stopped. This was the first time she had seen him since the day, a week ago, when they had gone together to the riot of Doshan Tappeh, and now she was looking at a stranger – stretched skin over the high cheekbones, the dreadful pallor, dark rings around his eyes, stubbled beard, untidy clothes when usually he was impeccably dressed and groomed. 'Oh, Karim, what is it?'

His lips moved but no sound came out. He tried again. 'Father's dead, shot for crimes against Islam, I'm suspect and suspended and may be arrested any moment,' he said bitterly. 'Most of our friends are suspect. Colonel Jabani's vanished, accused of treason – you remember him, the one who led the people against the Immortals and had most of his hand blown off . . .'

Numbed, she sat listening, watching him.

'. . . but there's worse to come, darling Sharazad. Uncle . . . Uncle Valik and Annoush and little Jalal and Setarem are all dead, killed trying to escape to Iraq in a civilian 212 . . .'

Her heart seemed to stop and doom began.

'. . . they were intercepted and shot down near the Iraqi border. I was at HQ today, waiting to answer our komiteh's questions when the telex came in from our base at Abadan – those komiteh sons of dogs can't read so they asked me to read it out, not knowing I had any connection with Valik, that we were related. The telex was marked secret and it said the traitors General Valik and a General Seladi had been identified in the 212's wreckage from identity cards, along with others and . . . and a woman and two children . . . and asked us to check out the chopper, supposedly one of Tom's company that'd been hijacked, EP-HBC . . .'

She fainted.

When she came to, Jari was patting her forehead with a cold towel, other servants anxiously grouped around, Karim, white-faced and apologetic in the background. Blankly she stared at him. Then what he had said flooded back, what Erikki had said flooded back, and Tommy's strangeness. And once again the three mixed, another wave of terror started to engulf her. 'Has . . . has Excellency Meshang arrived yet?' she asked weakly.

'No, no, Princess. Let me help you to bed, you'll feel bett –'

'I'm . . . no, thank you, Jari, I'm . . . I'm fine. Please leave us alone.'

'But, Prin –'

'Leave us alone!'

They obeyed. Karim was filled with anguish. 'Please excuse me, darling Sharazad, I shouldn't have worried you with all these problems, but I'm . . . I only discovered about . . . about Father this morning, I'm so sorry, Sharazad, it's not a woman's place to worry about wh –'

'Karim, listen to me, I beg you,' she interrupted with growing desperation. 'Whatever you do, don't mention about Uncle Valik,

609

don't mention to Meshang about him and . . . and the others, not yet, please, not yet! Don't mention about Valik!'

'But why?'

'Because . . . because . . .' Oh God oh God what do I do? she was thinking, wanting to cry out, I'm sure Tommy was flying HBC, oh God let me be wrong but I'm sure that's what Erikki said when I asked him how long Tommy'd be away. Didn't Erikki say: 'Don't worry, Tommy's charter's to Bandar-e Delam – HBC with spares – that shouldn't take but a day or two.' Isn't Bandar-e Delam beside Abadan that's beside the border? Didn't Uncle Valik come to see Tommy late at night, much too late unless the matter was very urgent, and then, after he'd left, wasn't Tommy changed, in misery, staring into the fire? 'Family must look after family,' wasn't that what he muttered? Oh God help me . . .

'What is it, Sharazad, what is it?'

I daren't tell you, Karim, even though I'd trust you with my life, I've got to protect Tommy . . . if Meshang finds out about Tommy that'll be the end of us, the end of everything! He'll denounce him, he won't risk any more trouble . . . or crimes against God! I can't oppose the family, Meshang will make me divorce. God help me, what shall I do? Without Tommy I'll . . . I'll die, I know I will, I'll . . . what was it Tommy said about taking a helicopter on a ferry? A ferry to Al Shargaz? Was it there or to Nigeria? I daren't tell you, Karim, I daren't . . .

But when her eyes saw the enormity of his concern, her mouth opened and she blurted out everything that she had not dared to tell.

'But it's impossible,' he stuttered, 'impossible, the telex said there were no survivors, impossible he should be flying it.'

'Yes, but he was he was, I'm sure of it, I'm sure of it. Oh, Karim, what am I going to do? Please help me, please, I beg you, please help meeeeee!' The tears were running down her cheeks and he held her, trying to comfort her. 'Please don't tell Meshang, please help me, if my Tommy . . . I'd die . . .'

'But Meshang's bound to find out! He's got to know.'

'Please help me. There must be something you can do, there must be som –'

The door opened and Meshang hurried in, Zarah with him. 'Sharazad, my dear, Jari said you fainted, what happened, are you all right? Karim, how are you?' Meshang stopped, astonished at Karim's ill-kempt appearance and pallor. 'What on earth's happened?'

In the silence Sharazad put her hand to her mouth, petrified she would blurt everything out again. She saw Karim hesitating. The silence worsened, then she heard him say in a rush, 'I've terrible news. First . . . first about my . . . my father. He's been shot, shot for . . . for crimes against Islam . . .'

Meshang burst out, 'That's not possible! The hero of Dhofar? You must be mistaken!'

'Excellency Jared Bakravan wasn't possible but he's dead and Father's dead like him, and there's other news, all bad . . .'

Helplessly Sharazad began to cry, Zarah put her arms around her, and Karim's heart went out to her and he buried Valik and his wife and children for others to bring forth.

'Insha' Allah,' he said, loathing the catchall excuse that he could no longer accept for blasphemous crimes committed by men in the Name of God that such men would never know. The Ayatollah's truly a gift from God. We need only to follow him to cleanse Islam of these foul blasphemers, he thought. God will punish them after death as we, the living, must punish them into death.

'My news is all bad, I'm suspect, most of my friends, the air force's being put on trial. Foolishly I told Sharazad . . . I wanted you to know, Meshang, but foolishly I told her and that was the reason she . . . she fainted. Please excuse me, I'm so sorry, I won't stay, I can't, I've got to . . . got to get back. I just came to tell you about . . . I had to tell someone.'

At McIver's Office: 10:20 P.M. McIver was alone in the penthouse offices, sitting in his creaking chair, feet comfortably on his desk, reading – the light good and the room warm thanks to their generator. Telex was on, and the HF. It was late but there was no point in going home yet where it was cold and damp and no Genny. He looked up. Footsteps were hurrying up the outside stairs. The knock was nervous. 'Who is it?'

'Captain McIver? It's me, Captain Peshadi, Karim Peshadi.'

Astonished, McIver unlocked the door, knowing the young man quite well, both as a helicopter student and favoured cousin of Sharazad. He stuck out his hand, covering his further surprise at the youth's appearance. 'Come in, Karim, what can I do for you? I was terribly sorry to hear about your father's arrest.'

'He was shot two days ago.'

'Oh, Christ.'

'Yes. Sorry, none of this is going to be pleasant.' Hurriedly Karim closed the door and dropped his voice. 'Sorry, but I've got to hurry, I'm

611

already hours overdue but I've just come from Sharazad – I went to your apartment but Captain Pettikin said you were here. Tonight I read a secret telex from our base in Abadan.' He told him what it said.

McIver was appalled and tried to cover it. 'Did you tell Captain Pettikin?'

'No, no, I thought I should tell only you.'

'Far as we know HBC was hijacked. None of our pilots were invol –'

'I'm not here officially, I just came to tell you because Tom's not here. I didn't know what else to do. I saw Sharazad tonight and found out, also quite by chance, about Tom.' He repeated what Sharazad had told him. 'How could Tom be alive and them all dead?'

McIver felt the hurt in his chest begin again. 'She's mistaken.'

'In the Name of God, tell me the truth! You must know! Tom must've told you, you can trust me,' the young man exploded, beside himself with worry. 'You've got to trust me. Perhaps I can help. Tom's in terrible danger, so's Sharazad and all our families! You've got to trust me! How did Tom get out?'

McIver felt the knot tightening around them all – Lochart, Pettikin, him. Don't lose your wits, he ordered himself, be careful. You daren't admit anything. Don't admit anything. 'Far as I know Tom was nowhere near HBC.'

'Liar!' the young man said enraged and spilled out what he had concluded all the way here, walking, fighting on a bus, walking again, snow falling and cold and desperate – the komeiteh still to appear before. 'You must've signed the clearance, you or Pettikin, and Tom's name's got to be on the clearance – I know you all too well, you and your hammering into us about flying by the book, signing forms, always have a form signed. You did, didn't you? Didn't you?' he shouted.

'I think you'd better go, Captain,' McIver said curtly.

'You're as involved as Tom, don't you see? You're in trouble as mu –'

'I think you'd better leave it. I know you're overwrought and it's terrible about your father,' he said kindly. 'I'm truly, terribly sorry.'

Now there was no sound but the gentle hum of the HF and the generator that was above on the roof. McIver waited. Karim waited. Then the young man half nodded. 'You're right,' he said crestfallen, 'why should you trust me? Trust's gone away from us. Our world's become hell on earth and all because of the Shah. We trusted him but he failed us, gave us false allies, muzzled our generals, ran away and left us in the pit, shamed, left us to false mullahs. I swear by God you can trust

612

me but what difference does that make to you or anyone? Trust's gone from us.' His face twisted. 'Perhaps God's gone from us.' The HF in the other room crackled gently, static from an electrical storm somewhere. 'Can you get Zagros? Sharazad said Tom went back this morning.'

'I tried earlier but can't raise them,' McIver said truthfully. 'This time of the year it's almost impossible but I heard they arrived safely. Our base in Kowiss relayed a report just after noon.'

'You'd . . . you'd better tell Tom, tell him what I told you. Tell him to get out.' Karim's voice was dulled. 'You're all blessed, you can all go home.' Then his despair burst and tears spilled down his cheeks.

'Oh, laddie . . .' Compassionately McIver put an arm around his shoulders and gentled him, the youth of an age with his own son safe in England, safely born English, safe on the ground, a doctor and nothing to do with flying, safe . . . God in heaven, who the hell is ever safe?

In a little while he felt the heaving of the youth's chest lessen. To save Karim's face, he backed off and turned and looked at the kitchenette and said, matter of fact, 'I was just going to have some tea, will you join me?'

'I'll . . . just have some water and then, then I'll go, thank you.'

At once McIver went to fetch some. Poor lad, he was thinking, how terrible about his father – such a wonderful fellow, tough, hard-line but straight and loyal and never a fiddle on the side. Terrible. God Almighty, if they'll shoot him, they'll shoot anyone. We'll all be dead soon, one way or another. 'Here,' he said, sickened, giving Karim the glass.

The youth accepted it, embarrassed that he had lost control in front of a foreigner. 'Thank you. Good night.' He saw McIver staring at him strangely. 'What is it?'

'Just a sudden idea, Karim. Could you get access to Doshan Tappeh Tower?'

'I don't know. Why?'

'If you could, without anyone knowing what you wanted, maybe you could get HBC's clearance – it's got to be in the takeoff book, if they were using one that day. Then we could see, couldn't we, who was flying her. Eh?'

'Yes, but what good would that do?' Karim watched the pale eyes set in the craggy face. 'They'd have the automatic tape recorders on.'

'Maybe, maybe not. There'd been fighting there – maybe they were not so efficient. Far as we know, whoever took HBC didn't have verbal clearance to or from the tower. He just took off. Maybe in all the excitement they didn't even record any clearance.' McIver's hope grew as he developed his thought. 'Only the book'd tell, the takeoff clearance book. Wouldn't it?'

Karim tried to see where McIver was leading him. 'And what if it says Tom Lochart?'

'I don't see how it could, because then it'd have my signature on it, and then it'd, er, it'd have to be a forgery.' McIver loathed the falsehoods, his hastily made-up story sounding weaker every minute. 'The only clearance I signed was for Nogger Lane to take some spares to Bandar-e Delam but cancelled it and him before he could go. The spares were unimportant and what with one thing and another, by that time HBC'd been hijacked.'

'The clearance's the only proof?'

'Only God knows that for certain. If the clearance says Tom Lochart and it's signed by me, it's a forgery. A forgery like that could cause lots of troubles. As such it shouldn't exist. Should it?'

Slowly Karim shook his head, his mind already taking him to the tower, past the guards – would there be guards? – finding the book and the right page and seeing . . . seeing the Green Band in the doorway but killing him, taking the book and hurrying away, as silently and secretly as he had entered, going to the Ayatollah, telling him about the monstrous crime committed against his father, the Ayatollah wise and listening and not like the dogs who abused the Word, at once ordering revenge in the Name of the One God. Then going to Meshang and telling him the family was saved, but more important, knowing the Sharazad he loved to distraction and wanted to distraction but never possible in this life – first cousin and against Koranic law – was also saved.

'The clearance shouldn't exist,' he said, very tired now. He got up. 'I'll try. Yes, I'll try. What happened to Tom?'

Behind McIver the telex began to chatter. Both jumped. McIver put his attention back on Karim. 'When you see him ask him, that's the right thing to do. Isn't it? You ask Tom.'

'Salaam.'

They shook hands and he left and McIver relocked the door. The telex was from Genny in Al Shargaz: 'Hello number one child. Talked at length with Chinaboy who arrives tomorrow night, Monday, and will be on the 125 to Tehran, Tuesday. He says imperative you meet him for conference at airport. All arrangements made here for repairs on the 212s and fast turnaround. Acknowledge. Talked to kids in England and all's well. I'm having a wonderful time here, whooping it up and on the town, glad you're not here, why aren't you? MacAllister.'

MacAllister was her maiden name and she used it only when she was very pissed off with him. 'Good old Gen,' he said aloud, the thought of her making him feel better. Glad she's safe and out of this mess. Glad she called the kids, that'll make her happy. Good old Gen. He reread the telex. What the hell's imperative with Andy? I'll know soon enough. At least we're in touch through Al Shargaz. He sat at the secretary chair and began to type out the acknowledgment.

At dusk he had got a telex from HQ in Aberdeen, but it had arrived garbled. Only the signature was legible: Gavallan. At once he had telexed for a repeat and had been waiting ever since. Tonight radio reception was also bad. There were rumours of big snowstorms in the mountains and the BBC World Service, fading badly and worse than usual, told of huge storms across all of Europe and the East Coast of America, terrible floods in Brazil. News had been generally rotten: strikes continuing in Britain, heavy fighting inside Vietnam between Chinese and Vietnamese armies, a Rhodesian airliner coming in to land shot down by guerrillas, Carter expected to order gasoline rationing, Soviets testing a fifteen hundred mile cruise missile, and in Iran, 'Chairman Yasser Arafat met Ayatollah Khomeini in a tumultuous welcome, the two leaders embraced publicly, and the PLO took over Israeli Mission Headquarters in Tehran. Four more generals were reported shot. Heavy fighting continued in Azerbaijan between pro- and anti-Khomeini forces, Prime Minister Bazargan ordered the U.S. to close two radar listening posts on the Iran-Soviet border, and arranged a meeting with the Soviet ambassador and Ayatollah Khomeini in the next few days to discuss outstanding differences . . .'

Depressed, McIver had turned the set off, the strain of trying to sift the news from the static had given him a worse headache. He had had one all day. It had started after his meeting this morning with Minister Ali Kia. Kia had accepted the notes on a Swiss bank, 'licence fees' for the three 212 departures, and also for six landing and takeoffs for the 125 and had promised to find out about the Zagros expulsions: 'Tell the Zagros komiteh meanwhile their order is overruled by this department pending investigation.'

Fat lot of good that'll do when you're looking down the barrel of a gun! he thought. Wonder how Erikki and Nogger are doing now? This afternoon a telex relayed by Tabriz ATC from Iran-Timber had come in: 'Captains Yokkonen and Lane are required here for emergency work for three days. Usual terms for the charter. Thanks.' It was signed as usual by the area manager and a normal request. Better for Nogger than sitting on his butt, McIver had thought. Wonder what Azadeh's father wanted her for?

Promptly at 7.30 p.m. Kowiss had come through but transmission was barely two by five, just enough to be partially audible, and heterodyning badly. Freddy Ayre reported that Starke had returned unharmed.

'Thank God for that!'

'Say ag . . . I'm read . . . g you one by five, Cap . . . ver.'

'I say again,' he said slowly and carefully. 'Tell Starke I'm very glad he's back. He's okay?'

'. . . tain Starke . . . swered ques . . . iteh . . . oryly.'

'Say again, Kowiss.'

'I say again, Capt . . . arke answ . . . uestions of the . . . iteh sa . . .'

'You're one by five. Try again at nine a.m.; even better I'll be here late and I'll try around eleven.'

'Understand yo . . . ry later . . . ound . . . leven tonight?'

'Yes. Around eleven tonight.'

'Capt . . . hart and Jean-Luc arriv . . . Zagro . . . ree safely . . .'

The rest of the transmission was incomprehensible. Then he had settled back to wait. While he waited he slept a little and read a little and now, sitting at the telex machine, again he glanced at his watch: 10.30.

'Soon as this's done, I'll call Kowiss,' he said out loud. Carefully he finished the telex to his wife adding for Manuela's sake that everything was fine at Kowiss – it is, he thought, so long as Starke's back and he's okay, and the lads okay.

He fed the hole-punched tape into the cogged sender, typed the number for Al Shargaz, waited interminably for the answer-back, then pressed the transmit button. The tape chattered through the cogs. Another long wait but the Al Shargaz accept code came up.

'Good.' He got up and stretched. In the desk drawer were his pills and he took the second of the day. 'God-cursed blood pressure,' he muttered. His pressure was 160 over 115 at his last medical. The pills brought it down to a comfortable 135 over 85: 'But listen, Mac, that doesn't mean you can swill the whisky, wine, eggs and cream – your cholesterol's up too . . .'

'What bloody whisky and cream, for Christ's sake, Doc? This's Iran . . .'

He remembered how foul-tempered he had been and when Genny said, 'How was it?' 'Great,' he had said, 'better than last time and don't bloody nag!' The hell with it! Nothing I can do that I'm not doing but I

616

certainly could use a large whisky and soda and ice and then another one. Normally there would be a bottle in the safe and ice and soda in the little refrigerator. Now there was none. Supplies zero. He made a cup of tea. What about Karim and HBC? I'll think about that later: 11:00 p.m.

'Kowiss, this is Tehran, do you read?' Patiently he called and recalled and then stopped. In a quarter of an hour he tried again. No contact. 'Got to be the storm,' he said, out of patience now. 'To hell with it, I'll try from home.'

He put on his heavy coat and went up the spiral staircase to the roof to check the level of generator fuel. The night was very black and quiet, hardly any gunfire and what there was was deadened by the snow. No lights anywhere that he could see. Snow still fell gently, almost five inches since dawn. He brushed it off his face and shone the flashlight on the gauge. The level of fuel was all right but somehow they'd have to get another supply in the next few days. Bloody nuisance. What about HBC? If Karim could get the book and the book could be destroyed, there'd be no evidence, would there? Yes, but what about Isfahan, refuelling at Isfahan?

Lost in thought, he went back, locked up, and, using the flash to light his way, started down the five flights of stairs. He did not hear the telex chatter into life behind him.

In the garage he went to his car and unlocked it. His heart leaped as he saw a tall figure approaching. SAVAK and HBC jumped into his head; he almost dropped the flash but the man was Armstrong, dark raincoat and hat.

'Sorry, Captain McIver, I didn't mean to startle you.'

'Well, you bloody did,' he said furiously, heart still pounding. 'Why the hell didn't you announce yourself or come up to the office instead of hiding in the bloody shadows like a bloody villain?'

'You might have had more visitors – I saw one come out so I thought I'd just wait. Sorry. Please put the flash down.'

Angrily McIver did as he was asked – since Gavallan had pinpointed Armstrong, he had searched his own memory but had no recollection of ever meeting him. 'Special Branch and CID' did nothing to ease his dislike. 'Where the hell've you been? We expected you at the airport but you didn't show.'

'Yes, sorry about that. When does the 125 come back to Tehran?'

'Tuesday, God willing. Why?'

'Approximately when?'

'Noon, why?'

'Excellent. That would be perfect. I need to go to Tabriz; could I and a friend charter her?'

'No way. I could never get a clearance and who's the friend?'

'I'll guarantee the clearance. Sorry, Captain, but it's very important.'

'I heard there's heavy fighting in Tabriz: it was on the news tonight. Sorry, couldn't authorise that, it'd be an unnecessary risk to air crew.'

'Mr. Talbot will be glad to add his request for assistance,' Armstrong said in the same quiet, patient voice.

'No. Sorry.' McIver turned away but was stopped at the sudden venom.

'Before you go shall I ask you about HBC and Lochart and your partner Valik and his wife and two children?'

McIver was shock-still. He could see the chiselled face and the hard mouth and eyes that glittered in the reflected light from the flash. 'I – I don't know what you mean.'

Armstrong reached into his pocket and pulled out a piece of paper and held it up to McIver's face. McIver directed the circle of light on to it. The paper was a photocopy of an entrance in a clearance book. The writing was neat. 'EP-HBC cleared at 0620 for an IHC charter to Bandar-e Delam, delivery of spares, pilot Captain T. Lochart, flight authorised by Captain McIver.' The lower half of the paper was a photocopy of the actual clearance, signed by him with Captain N. Lane crossed out 'sick', and Capt T. Lochart substituted. 'A present, with my compliments.'

'Where did you get it?'

'When the 125 gets into Tehran airspace, radio Captain Hogg that he's got an immediate charter to Tabriz. You'll have the clearance in good time.'

'No. I'll not se –'

'If you don't arrange everything happily, and keep it all rather quiet – just between us,' Armstrong said with such finality that McIver was quite frightened, 'the originals of these go to SAVAK – renamed SAVAMA.'

'That's blackmail!'

'It's barter.' Armstrong shoved the paper into his hand, began to leave.

'Wait! Where – where are the originals?'

'Not in their hands, for the moment.'

'If – if I do what you say, I get them back all right?'

'You must be joking! Of course you get nothing.'

'That's not fair – that's not bloody fair!'

Armstrong came back and stood over him, his face a mask. 'Of course it's not fair. If you get these back you're out of the vice, aren't you? All of you. So long as these exist, you will do what's required of you, won't you?'

'You're a bloody bastard!'

'And you're a fool who should look after his blood pressure.'

McIver gasped. 'How d'you know about that?'

'You'd be astounded what I know about you and Genevere MacAllister and Andrew Gavallan and the Noble House and lots of other things that I haven't begun to use yet.' Armstrong's voice became rougher, his tiredness and anxiety taking away his control. 'Don't you bloody understand there's the very strong probability of Soviet tanks and aircraft permanently stationed this side of Hormuz and Iran a bloody Soviet province? I'm tired of playing silly buggers with you ostriches – just do what I ask without arguing and if you don't I'll shop the bloody lot of you.'

Tuesday
February 20, 1979

Tabriz: 5:12 A.M. In the small hut on the edge of the Khan's estate, Ross was suddenly awake. He lay motionless, keeping his breathing regular but all of his senses concentrated. Seemingly nothing untoward, just the usual insects and closeness of the room. Through the window he could see that the night was dark, the sky mostly overcast. Across the room on the other pallet, Gueng slept curled up, breathing normally. Because of the cold, both men had gone to bed with their clothes on. Noiselessly, Ross went to the window and searched the darkness. Still nothing. Then, close to his ear, Gueng whispered, 'What is it, sahib?'

'I don't know. Probably nothing.'

Gueng nudged him and pointed. There was no guard in the seat outside on the veranda.

'Perhaps he's just gone to take a leak.' There had always been at least one guard. By day or night. Last night there had been two so Ross had made a mock dummy in his bed and left Gueng to divert them and had slipped out of the back window and gone to see Erikki and Azadeh alone. Coming back he had almost stumbled into a patrol but they had been sleepy and unattentive so he had passed them by.

'Take a look out the back window,' Ross whispered.

Again they watched and waited. Dawn in about an hour, Ross thought.

'Sahib, perhaps it was just a spirit of the mountain,' Gueng said softly. In the Land Atop the World it was a superstition that by night, spirits visited the beds of sleeping men and women and children, for good purposes or ill, and that dreams were the stories they whispered.

The little man kept his eyes and ears feeling out the darkness. 'I think perhaps we'd better pay attention to the spirits.' He went back to his bed and pulled on his boots, put the talisman he had kept under his pillow back into his uniform pocket, then put on the tribesman robes and turban. Nimbly he checked his grenades and carbine and settled the rough backpack that contained ammunition, grenades, water and a little food. No need to check his kukri, that was never out of reach, always oiled and cleaned nightly – just before sleep.

Now Ross was equally ready. But ready for what? he asked himself. It's hardly five minutes since you awoke and here you are, kukri loose in the scabbard, safety catch off and for what? If Abdollah meant you harm, he would've already taken away your weapons – or tried to take them.

Yesterday afternoon they had heard the 206 take off and shortly afterwards Abdollah Khan had visited them. 'Ah, Captain, sorry for the delay but the hue and cry is worse than ever. Our Soviet friends have put a very large price on your heads,' he had said jovially. 'Enough even to tempt me, perhaps.'

'Let's hope not, sir. How long will we have to wait?'

'A few days, no more. It seems the Soviets want you very much. I've had another deputation from them asking me to help capture you, the first was before you arrived. But don't worry, I know where the future of Iran lies.'

Last night Erikki had confirmed about the reward: 'Today I was near Sabalan, cleaning out another radar site. Some of the workers thought I was Russian – lots of Russian speakers among the border people – and said they hoped they'd be the ones to catch the tall British saboteur and his helper. The reward's five horses and five camels and fifty sheep. That's a fortune, and if they know about you that far north you can bet they're looking here.'

'Were Soviets supervising you?'

'Only Cimtarga, but even then he didn't seem to be in charge. Just of

624

me and the aircraft. The Russian speakers kept asking me when we were coming over the border in strength.'

'My God – did they have anything to base that on?'

'I doubt it, just more rumours. People here feed on them. I said, "Never", but this man scoffed and said he knew we had "leagues" of tanks and armies waiting, that he'd seen them. I can't speak Farsi so I don't know if he was another KGB plant disguised as a tribesman.'

'The "stuff" you're carrying? Is it anything important?'

'I don't know. Some computers and lots of black boxes and papers – they keep me away from it but none of it's dismantled by experts, just pulled out of walls, wires cut, and hanging loose and stacked carelessly. The only thing the workers're interested in is stores, cigarettes particularly.'

They had talked about escaping. Impossible to make plans. Too many imponderables. 'I don't know how long they want me to keep flying,' Erikki had said. 'This bastard Cimtarga told me Prime Minister Bazargan has ordered the Yanks out of two sites, far to the east, near Turkey, the last they've got here, ordered them to evacuate at once and to leave the equipment intact. We're supposed to fly up there tomorrow.'

'Did you use the 206 today?'

'No. That was Nogger Lane, one of our captains. He came here with us – to take the 206 back to Tehran. Our base manager told me they've co-opted Nogger to recce some places where fighting's going on. When McIver doesn't hear from us he'll go into shock and send out a search party. That might give us another chance. What about you?'

'We might sneak off. I'm getting very nervous in that rotten little hut. If we evacuate, we might head for your base and hide out in the forest. If we can, we'll contact you – but don't expect us. All right?'

'Yes – but don't trust anyone at the base – except our two mechanics, Dibble and Arberry.'

'Anything I can do for you?'

'Could you leave me a grenade?'

'Of course, have you ever used one?'

'No, but I know how they work.'

'Good. Here. Pull the pin and count to three – not four – and heave it. Do you need a gun?'

'No, no thanks. I've my knife – but the grenade might come in handy.'

'Remember they can be rather messy. I'd better be going. Good luck.'

Ross had been looking at Azadeh when he had said it, seeing how beautiful she was, so very aware that their time was already written among the stars or on the wind or in the chimes of the bells that were as much a part of the summer High Country as the peaks themselves. Wondering why she never replied to his letters, then the school telling him she had gone. Gone home. Gone. On their last day she had said, 'All this that has come to pass may not come to pass again, my Johnny Brighteyes.'

'I know. If it doesn't, I can die happy because I know what love is. Truly. I love you, Azadeh.'

Last kiss. Then down to his train and waving goodbye, waving until she was lost. Lost for ever. Perhaps we both knew that it was forever, he thought, waiting here in the darkness of the little hut, trying to decide what to do, to wait more, to sleep or to flee. Maybe it's as the Khan said and we're safe here – for the moment. No reason to mistrust him completely. Vien Rosemont was no fool and he said to trust h –

'Sahib!'

He had heard the stealthy footsteps at the same instant. Both men moved into ambush, one covering the other, both of them glad that the time for action had arrived. The door opened quietly. It was a ghoulish spirit of the mountain standing there peering into the greater darkness of the hut – a shape and vague face. To his astonishment he recognised Azadeh, the chador blending her with the night, her face puffy from crying.

'Johnny?' she whispered anxiously.

For a moment Ross did not move, gun still levelled and expecting enemies. 'Azadeh, here, beside the door,' he whispered back, trying to adjust.

'Quick, follow me, you're both in danger! Hurry!' At once she ran off into the night.

He saw Gueng shake his head uneasily and he hesitated. Then he decided, 'We go.' He slid out of the doorway and ran after her, the moonlight small, Gueng following, flanking, automatically covering him. She was waiting beside some trees. Before he reached her, she beckoned him to follow, unerringly led the way through the orchard and around some farm buildings. The snow muffled their way but left tracks and he was very aware of them. He was ten paces behind her, watching the terrain carefully, wondering what danger and why had she been crying and where's Erikki?

Clouds were toying with the moon, hiding it mostly. Whenever it came clear, she would stop and motion him to stop and to wait, then she would move on again, using cover well, and he wondered where she had learned woodsmanship then remembered Erikki and his great knife and Finns and Finland – land of lakes and forests and mountains and trolls and hunting. Concentrate, fool, time enough to let your mind wander later, not now when you're endangering everyone! Concentrate!

His eyes searched, expecting trouble, wanting it to begin. Soon they were near the perimeter wall. The wall was ten feet high and made of hewn stone, with a wide, empty swathe between it and the trees. Again she motioned him to stop in cover and walked forward into the open, seeking a special place. Finding it without trouble, she beckoned him. Before he was beside her she was already climbing, her feet fitting easily into the notches and cracks with sufficient hand holds, some natural, some cleverly embedded to make the climb easy. The moon came into a bare patch of sky and he felt naked and climbed more quickly. When he reached the top she was already halfway down the other side. He slithered over and found some footholds, ducked down to wait for Gueng. His anxiety mounted until he saw the shadow darting over the ground, reaching the wall safely.

The climb down was more difficult and he slipped and fell the last six feet, cursed and looked around to get his bearings. She was already across the boundary road and heading for a rocky outcrop on the steep mountainside two hundred yards away. Below and to the left he could see part of Tabriz, fires on the far side of the city near the airport. Now he could hear distant guns.

Gueng landed neatly beside him, grinned and motioned him onward. When he reached the outcrop she had vanished.

'Johnny! Here!'

He saw the small crack in the rock and went forward. Just enough room to squeeze through. He waited until Gueng came up, and then went through the rock into darkness. Her hand came out and guided him to one side. She beckoned Gueng and did the same for him, then moved a heavy leather curtain across the crack. Ross reached into his pack for his flash but before he could pull it out the match flamed. Her hand was cupped around it. She was kneeling and lit the candle that was in a niche. Quickly he looked around. The curtain over the entrance seemed lightproof, the cave spacious, warm and dry, some blankets, old carpets on the ground, a few drinking and eating utensils – some books and toys on a natural shelf. Ah, a child's hideout, he thought and looked back at her. She had stayed kneeling by the candle, her back to him, and now, as she pulled the chador away from her head, she became Azadeh again.

'Here.' He offered her some water from his water bottle. She accepted it gratefully but avoided his eyes. He glanced at Gueng and read his mind. 'Azadeh, do you mind if we put the light out – now that we see where we are – then we can pull the curtain back and keep watch and hear better. I've a flash if we need it.'

'Oh, oh, yes . . . yes, of course.' She turned back to the candle. 'I . . . oh, just a minute, sorry . . .' There was a mirror on the shelf he had not noticed. She picked it up and peered at herself, hated what she saw, the streaks of sweat and puffy eyes. Hastily she brushed away some smudges, picked up the comb and tidied herself as best she could. A final check in the mirror and she blew out the candle. 'Sorry,' she said.

Gueng moved the curtain away and went through the rock and stood there listening. More gunfire from the city. A few buildings burning beyond the single runway of the airfield below and to the right. No lights there and very few on in the city itself. A few car headlights in the streets. The palace still dark and silent and he could sense no danger. He came back and told Ross what he had seen, speaking Gurkhali, and added, 'Better I stay outside, safer, there's not much time, sahib.'

'Yes.' Ross had heard disquiet in his voice but did not comment. He knew the reason. 'You all right, Azadeh?' he asked softly.

'Yes. Yes I am now. It's better in the dark – sorry I looked such a mess. Yes, I'm better now.'

'What's this all about – and where's your husband?' He used the word deliberately and heard her move in the darkness.

'Just after you left last night, Cimtarga and a guard came and told Erikki he had to dress at once and leave – this man Cimtarga said he was sorry but there'd been a change of plan and he wanted to leave at once. And I, I was summoned to see my father. At once. Before I went into his room I overheard him giving orders for you both to be captured and disarmed, just after dawn.' There was a catch to her voice. 'He was planning to send for you both to discuss your departure tomorrow, but you would be led into ambush near the farmhouses and bound up and put into a truck and sent north at once.'

'Where north?'

'Tbilisi.' Nervously she hurried onward: 'I didn't know what to do, there was no way to warn you – I'm watched as closely as you and kept away from the others. When I saw my father, he said Erikki wouldn't be back for a few days, that today he, my father, he was going on a business trip to Tbilisi and that . . . that I would be going with him. He . . . he said we would be away two or three days and by that time Erikki would be finished and then we would go back to Tehran.' She was almost in tears. 'I'm so frightened. I'm so frightened something's happened to Erikki.'

'Erikki will be all right,' he said, not understanding about Tbilisi, trying to decide about the Khan. Always back to Vien: 'Trust Abdollah with your life and don't believe the lies about him.' And yet here was Azadeh saying the opposite. He looked across at her, unable to see her, hating the darkness, wanting to see her face, her eyes, thinking that perhaps he could read something from them. Wish to Christ she'd told me all this the other side of the bloody wall or at the hut, he thought, his nervousness increasing. Christ, the guard! 'Azadeh, the guard, do you know what happened to him?'

'Oh, yes I . . . I bribed him, Johnny, I bribed him to be away for half an hour. It was the only way I could get . . . it was the only way.'

'God Almighty,' he muttered. 'Can you trust him?'

'Oh, yes. Ali is . . . he's been with Father for years. I've known him since I was seven and I gave him a pishkesh of some jewellery, enough for him and his family for years. But, Johnny, about Erikki . . . I'm so worried.'

'No need to worry, Azadeh. Didn't Erikki say they might send him near to Turkey?' he said encouraging her, anxious to get her back safely. 'I can't thank you enough for warning us. Come on, first we'd better get you an –'

'Oh, no, I can't,' she burst out. 'Don't you understand? Father'll take me north and I'll never get away, never – my father hates me and he'll leave me with Mzytryk, I know he will, I know he will.'

'But what about Erikki?' he said shocked. 'You can't just run away!'

'Oh, yes, I have to, Johnny, I have to. I daren't wait, I daren't go to Tbilisi, it's much safer for Erikki that I run away now. Much safer.'

'What're you talking about? You can't run away just like that! That's madness! Say Erikki comes back tonight and finds you gone? Wh –'

'I left him a note – we made an arrangement that in an emergency I'd leave a note in a secret place in our room. We had no way of telling what Father would do while he was away. Erikki'll know. There's something else. Father's going to the airport today, around noon. He has to meet a plane, someone from Tehran, I don't know who or what about but I thought perhaps you could . . . you could persuade them to take us back to Tehran or we could sneak aboard or you . . . you could force them to take us.'

'You're crazy,' he said angrily. 'This's all crazy, Azadeh. It's madness to run off and leave Erikki – how do you know it's not just as your father says, for God's sake? You say the Khan hates you – my God, if you run off like this, whether he does or doesn't he'll blow a gasket. Either way you put Erikki into more danger.'

'How can you be so blind? Don't you see? So long as I'm here Erikki has no chance, none. If I'm not here he has to think only of himself. If he knows I'm in Tbilisi he'll go there and be lost for ever. Don't you see? I'm the bait. In the Name of God, Johnny, open your eyes! Please help me!'

He heard her crying now, softly but still crying, and this only increased his fury. Christ Almighty, we can't take her along. There's no way I could do that. That'd be murder – if what she says about the Khan's true the dragnet'll be out for us in a couple of hours and we'll be lucky if we see sunset – the dragnet's already out for God's sake, think clearly! Bloody nonsense about running away! 'You have to go back. It's better,' he said.

The crying stopped. 'Insha'Allah,' she said in a different voice. 'Whatever you say, Johnny. It's better you leave quickly. You've not much time. Which way will you go?'

'I – I don't know.' He was glad for the darkness that hid his face from her. My God, why must it be Azadeh? 'Come on, I'll see you safely back.'

'There's no need. I'll . . . I'll stay here for a while.'

He heard the falsehood and his nerves jangled even more. 'You're going to go back. You've got to.'

'No,' she said defiantly. 'I can never go back. I'm staying here. He won't find me, I've hidden here before. Once I was here two days. I'm safe here. Don't worry about me. I'll be all right. You go on. That's what you've got to do.'

Exasperated, he managed to control his urge to drag her to her feet, and instead sat back against the wall of the cave. I can't leave her, can't carry her back against her will, can't take her. Can't leave her, can't take her. Oh you can take her with you but for how long and then, when she's captured, she's mixed up with saboteurs and Christ only knows what else they'd accuse her of and they stone women for that. 'When we're found missing – if you are too – the Khan'll know you tipped us off. If you stay here, eventually you'll be found and anyway the Khan'll know you gave us the tip and that'll make it worse than ever for you, and worse for your husband. You must go back.'

'No, Johnny. I'm in the Hands of God and not afraid.'

'For God's sake, Azadeh, use your head!'

'I am. I'm in God's hands, you know that. Didn't we talk about that

630

in our High Country a dozen times? I'm not afraid. Just leave me a grenade like the one you gave to Erikki. I'm safe in God's hands. Please go now.'

In the other time they had talked about God often. On a Swiss mountaintop it was easy and ordinary and nothing to be shy about – not with your beloved who knew the Koran and could read Arabic and felt very close to the Infinite and believed in Islam absolutely. Here in the darkness of the small cave it was not the same. Nothing was the same.

'Insha'Allah it is,' he said and decided. 'We'll go back, you and I, and I'll send Gueng on.' He got up.

'Wait.' He heard her get up too and felt her breath and nearness. Her hand touched his arm. 'No, my darling,' she said, her voice as it used to be. 'No, my darling, that would destroy my Erikki – and you and your soldier. Don't you see, I'm the lodestone to destroy Erikki. Remove the lodestone and he has a chance. Outside my father's walls, you too have a chance. When you see Erikki, tell him . . . tell him.'

What should I tell him? he was asking himself. In the darkness he took her hand in his and, feeling its warmth, was back in time again in the darkness together in the great bed, a vast summer storm lashing the windows, the two of them counting the seconds between the lightning flashes and the thunder that bounced off the sides of the high valley – sometimes only one or two seconds, oh, Johnny it must be almost overhead, Insha'Allah if it hits us, never mind we're together – holding hands together just like this. But not like this, he thought sadly. He put her hand to his lips and kissed it. 'You can tell him yourself,' he said. 'We'll give it a go – together. Ready?'

'You mean go on – together?'

'Yes.'

After a pause she said, 'First ask Gueng.'

'He does what I say.'

'Yes, of course. But please ask him. Another favour. Please?'

He went to the neck of the cleft. Gueng was leaning against the rocks outside. Before he could say anything Gueng said softly in Gurkhali, 'No danger yet, sahib. Outside.'

'Ah, you heard?'

'Yes, sahib.'

'What do you think?'

Gueng smiled. 'What I think, sahib, has no weight, affects nothing. Karma is karma. I do what you say.'

*　　*　　*

631

At Tabriz Airport: 12:40 P.M. Abdollah Khan stood beside his bullet-proof Rolls on the snowcovered concrete apron near the airport terminal. He was flushed with rage, watching the 125 turn on to final, praying it would crash. Yesterday a telex relayed through police HQ had been brought by his nephew, Colonel Mazardi, the chief of police. 'Please meet jet G-ELTT, ETA 1240 tomorrow Tuesday. (signed) Colonel Hashemi Fazir.' The name had sent an immediate shudder through him and everyone else who had access to the message. Inner Intelligence had always been above the law and Colonel Hashemi Fazir its grand inquisitor, a man whose ruthlessness was legend even in Iran where ruthlessness was expected and admired.

'What does he want here, Highness?' Mazardi had asked, very afraid.

'To discuss Azerbaijan,' he had said, hiding his dread and seething at the curtness of the telex, completely thrown by this unexpected and unwanted arrival. 'Of course to ask how he can assist me – he's been a secret friend for years,' he added, lying automatically.

'I'll order an honour guard and welcoming komiteh and ma –'

'Don't be a fool! Colonel Fazir likes secrecy. Do nothing, don't go near the airport, just make sure the streets are quiet and . . . ah, yes, increase pressure on the Tudeh. In fact, implement Khomeini's orders to crush them. Burn their headquarters tonight and arrest their known leaders.' That will be a perfect pishkesh should I need one, he had thought, delighted with his cleverness. Isn't Fazir fanatically anti-Tudeh? God be thanked that Petr Oleg gave his approval.

Then he had sent Mazardi away and cursed everyone near him and sent them away too. Now what does that son of a dog Fazir want with me?

Over the years they had met several times and had exchanged information to their mutual advantage. But Colonel Hashemi Fazir was one of those who believed that Iran's only protection lay in absolute centralised government, ruled from Tehran, and that tribal chieftains were archaic and a danger to the state – and also Fazir was a Tehrani with the power to uncover too many secrets, secrets that could be used against him. God curse all Tehranis and send them to hell. And Azadeh, and her God-cursed husband!

Azadeh! Did I truly sire that demon? It's not possible! Someone must have . . . God forgive me that I suspect my Beloved Napthala! Azadeh's Satan-possessed. But she won't escape, oh no, I swear I'll take her to Tbilisi and I'll let Petr use her . . .

Blood began roaring in his ears again and the clawing started in his chest again, a grasping pain. Stop it, he told himself desperately, calm

632

yourself. Put her aside, you'll get your revenge later. Stop it or you'll kill yourself! Stop it and put her aside and think of Fazir, you'll need all your cunning to deal with him. She can't escape.

When, just after dawn, petrified guards had rushed in to tell him the two prisoners had vanished and, almost at the same time she was also discovered missing, his violence had known no bounds. At once he had sent men to search her hiding place in the rocks that he had known about for years and ordered them not to come back without her or the saboteurs. He had had the nose of the night guard cut off, the rest of the guards flogged and shoved into jail, charged with conspiracy, her maids whipped. At length he had stormed off to the airport, leaving a pall of terror over the whole palace.

God curse them all, he thought, making a great effort to calm himself, his eyes never leaving the jet. The sky was patchy blue with ominous clouds and a bad wind that swept the snow-covered runway. He wore an astrakhan hat and fur-collared winter coat and fur lined boots, the cold misting his glasses. In his pocket was a small revolver. Behind him, the small terminal building was empty but for his men who had secured it and the access road beyond. Above, on the roof, he had put a sniper into ambush with instructions to shoot Fazir if he took out a white handkerchief and blew his nose. I've done all I can, he thought, now it is up to God. Crash, you son of a burnt father!

But the 125 made a perfect touchdown, snow flaring from her wheels in a vast spray. His dread increased. And the sound of his own heartbeat. 'As God wants,' he muttered and got into the back of the car, partitioned from the chauffeur and Ahmed, his most trusted counsellor and bodyguard, by the movable, bulletproof glass. 'Intercept it,' he ordered and checked the revolver, leaving the safety off.

The 125 came off the far end of the runway into the feeder area, turned into the wind and stopped. It was bleak here, just snowdrifts and empty space. The big black Rolls pulled up alongside, and the door of the jet swung open. He saw Hashemi Fazir standing there, beckoning him, 'Salaam! Peace be upon you, Highness, come aboard.'

Abdollah Khan opened the window and called back, 'Salaam, peace be upon you, Excellency, join me here.' You must think me a fool to put my head in such a trap, he thought. 'Ahmed, go aboard, go armed and pretend you don't speak English.'

Ahmed Dursak was a Muslim Turkoman, very strong, very quick with a knife or gun. He got out, the submachine gun loose in one hand and ran nimbly up the steps, the wind pulling at his long coat. 'Salaam, Excellency Colonel,' he said in Farsi, standing outside on the top step.

'My Master begs you to please join him in the car – cabins of small jets make him disquieted. In the car you can talk in private and in peace, totally alone if you wish. He asks if you will honour his poor house and stay with him during your stay here.'

Hashemi was shocked that Abdollah had had the effrontery – and confidence – to send the emissary armed. Going to the car did not suit him either, too easy to be bugged, or booby-trapped. 'Tell His Highness I sometimes have car sickness and I beg him to come here. Here we can speak in private, be alone also and it would be a favour to me. Of course you should search the cabin in case a foul alien sneaked aboard.'

'My Master would prefer, Excellency, that you –'

Hashemi came closer to him and now his lips were a thin line and his voice as tight. 'Search the airplane! Now! And do it quickly, Ahmed Dursak, three times murderer – one a woman called Najmeh – and do what I order or you will not last one more week on this earth.'

'Then all the sooner I will be in Paradise because serving the Khan I do God's work,' Ahmed Dursak said, 'but I will search as you wish.' He stepped through the doorway and saw the two pilots in the cockpit. In the cabin was Armstrong. His eyes narrowed but he said nothing, just went past politely and opened the lavatory door making sure it was empty. There was nowhere else that anyone could hide. 'Should what you suggest be possible, Excellency, the pilots will leave?'

Earlier Hashemi had asked the captain, John Hogg, if he would oblige, should it become necessary.

'Sorry, sir,' Hogg had said, 'but I don't like that idea at all.'

'It would only be a few minutes. You can take the ignition key with you – and the circuit breakers,' Robert Armstrong had said. 'I will personally guarantee no one gets into the cockpit or touches anything.'

'I still don't like that idea, sir.'

'I know,' Armstrong had said. 'But Captain McIver told you you were to do what we asked. Within reason. And this's within reason.'

Hashemi saw the arrogance in Ahmed's face and he wanted to smash it off. That comes later, he promised himself. 'The pilots will wait in the car.'

'And the Infidel?'

'This Infidel speaks better Farsi than you, louse, and if you're wise, louse, you'll be polite to him and call him Excellency for I can assure you and your dog Turkoman ancestors he has as long a memory as me and can be more cruel than you can imagine.'

Ahmed's mouth smiled. 'And his Excellency, the Infidel, he waits on the runway also?'

'He stays here. The pilots wait *in* the car. Should His Highness want one guard with him – to make sure no assassins wait in ambush – he is of course welcome. If this arrangement does not suit him, then perhaps we should meet in police headquarters. Now take your foul manners away.'

Ahmed thanked him politely and strode back and told the Khan what had been said, adding, 'I think that dog's turd must be very sure of himself to be so rude.' And in the airplane Hashemi was saying in English, 'Robert, that son of a dog must be very sure of himself to have such arrogant servants.'

'You'd really haul the Khan of all the Gorgons down to police HQ?'

'I could try.' Hashemi lit another cigarette. 'I don't think I'd succeed. His nephew Mazardi's still chief of police and police here still hold most of their power – Green Bands and komitehs aren't dominant. Yet.'

'Because of Abdollah?'

'Of course Abdollah. For months, on his orders, the Tabrizi police covertly supported Khomeini. The only difference from Shah days to Khomeini days is that Shah pictures have been replaced with Khomeini pictures, Shah emblems taken off all uniforms, and now Abdollah's grasp is tighter than ever.' A chill draught came through the half open door. 'Azerbaijanis are a treacherous breed, and cruel – the Qajar shahs came from Tabriz – so did Shah Abbas, who built Isfahan and tried to insure his longevity by murdering his eldest son and blinding another . . .'

Hashemi Fazir was watching the car out of the window, willing Abdollah Khan to concede. He was feeling better now and more confident that he would see Holy Day this week than he had been on Sunday evening when General Janan had burst into his HQ with orders for the dissolution of Inner Intelligence and had taken possession of the cassettes and Rakoczy. All that night he had been at his wits' end, then at dawn yesterday when he had left his house he had found men tailing him and, during the morning, his wife and children were jostled on the streets. It had taken him until early afternoon to lose those who followed him. By that time one of his secret Group Four leaders was waiting at a safe house and that evening when General Janan got out of his bulletproof limousine to go into his home, a nearby parked car filled with plastic explosive blew him and two of his most trusted assistants to pieces, totally wrecking his house, obliterating his wife and three children and seven servants – and his elderly, bedridden father. Men shouting leftist mujhadin slogans were heard running away. In their wake they left crudely written pamphlets: 'Death to SAVAK now SAVAMA.'

In the early hours of this morning, half an hour after Abrim Pahmudi had discreetly left the bed of his very secret mistress, cruel men had paid her a visit. More leftist slogans were heard and the same message daubed on her walls, using her blood and vomit and faeces for paint. At nine this morning he had gone by appointment to give his condolences to Abrim Pahmudi for both tragedies – of course Inner Intelligence had informed him of them. As a pishkesh he brought part of Rakoczy's testimony as though it was information that had come into his hands from another source – just enough to be of value. 'I'm sure, Excellency, if I were allowed to resume my work I could gather much more. And if my department was to be honoured with your confidence and allowed to operate as before – but to report solely to you and no other power – I could prevent such foul deeds and perhaps smash these terrorist dogs off the earth.'

While he was there an aide had rushed in, distraught, to say that more terrorists had assassinated one of the most important ayatollahs in Tehran – another car bomb – and the Revolutionary Komiteh required Pahmudi's immediate presence. At once Pahmudi had got up but before he left he rescinded his previous order. 'I agree, Excellency Colonel. For thirty days. You have thirty days to prove your value.'

'Thank you, Excellency, your confidence overwhelms me, you may be sure of my loyalty. May I have Rakoczy back, please?'

'That dog, General Janan, allowed him to escape.'

Then he had gone to the airport and joined Robert Armstrong at the 125, and, once airborne, had laughed and laughed. It was the first time that a car bomb with a remote detonator had been used in Iran. 'By God, Robert,' he had said jovially, 'it's totally efficient. From a hundred yards away you wait until you're sure it's him, then you just touch the switch on the sender that's no bigger than a pack of cigarettes and . . . boom! another enemy gone for ever – and his father!' He wiped the tears out of his eyes, his laughter infectious. 'That's what really got to Pahmudi. Yes, and without Group Four it would've been me and my family.'

Group Four had grown out of a suggestion of Armstrong's that he had taken and elaborated: small teams of very select bands of men and women, highly trained in the most modern anti-terrorist tactics, very highly paid and carefully protected – all non-Iranian, none of whom knew any of the other cells – and all known and loyal only to Hashemi.

Their anonymity meant that some could be used against the others if necessary, individually they were expendable and easily replaceable – in the Middle and Near East there was too much poverty, too many betrayed causes, too much hatred, too many beliefs, too many homeless not to provide a ready ocean of men, and women, desperate for such a job.

Over the years his Group Four team had prospered, its coups secret, the vast majority secret even from Armstrong. He looked at him and smiled. 'Without them I'd be dead.'

'Me too, probably – I was very bloody frightened when that bugger Janan said, "I give you a day and a night for past services." That bugger would never've let me get out.'

'True.' A few thousand feet below them the land was deep in snow and the jet already high over the mountains, the journey to Tabriz little more than half an hour.

'What about Rakoczy? You believe what Pahmudi said about him escaping?'

'Of course not, Robert. Rakoczy was a trade, a pishkesh. When Pahmudi found the tapes empty and the state Rakoczy was in he had no value – other than as payment for past favour – he couldn't possibly know the connection with your Petr Oleg Mzytryk. Or could he?'

'Not likely – I'd say impossible.'

'It's probable he's in Soviet HQ – if he's not already dead. Soviets'd want to know what he gave away . . . could he tell them anything?'

'I doubt it – he was on the brink.' Armstrong shook his head. 'Doubt it. What'll you do now that you're Mr. Big again? Feed Pahmudi more info within the thirty days – if he's alive in thirty days.'

Hashemi smiled thinly and did not reply. I'm not your Mr. Big yet, he thought, or even safe until Pahmudi's in hell – with many others. I may still have to use your passport. Armstrong had given it to him before takeoff. He had checked it very carefully.

Then he had closed his eyes and settled back, enjoying the luxury and convenience of the private jet that was already over Qazvin, just a quarter of an hour out of Tabriz. But he did not nap. He spent the time considering what to do about SAVAMA, Pahmudi and Abdollah Khan, and what to do about Robert Armstrong who knew too much.

Through the cabin window, he continued to watch the Rolls, big, immaculate, and possessed by so few on earth. By God and the Prophet, what riches, he thought, awed at this proof of the Khan's position and power. What power to flaunt such a possession so

637

fearlessly in the faces of the komitehs, and mine. Abdollah Khan won't be easy to bend.

He knew that here in the airplane they were dangerously exposed – easy targets if Abdollah ordered his men to fire on them – but he had dismissed that possibility, certain that even Abdollah Khan would not dare such an open murder of three Infidels and one jet, and him. But just in case the Khan arranged an 'accident', two Group Four teams were already en route by road, one for Abdollah personally, the other for his family, to be stopped only by codeword from him personally. He smiled. Once Robert Armstrong had told him that a Chinese punishment for an important person in olden days was 'death – *and all his generations*'.

'I like that, Robert,' he had said. 'That has style.'

He saw the front side door of the car open. Ahmed got out, carrying the submachine gun oddly, then walked to the back door and opened it for Abdollah.

'You win the first round, Hashemi,' Armstrong said and went forward as agreed. 'All right, Captain. We'll be as quick as we can.'

Reluctantly the two pilots squeezed out of the little cockpit, pulled on their parkas, and hurried out into the cold and down the steps. They saluted the Khan politely. He motioned them into the back of the car, began to climb the gangway, Ahmed following him.

'Salaam, Highness, peace be upon you,' Hashemi said warmly, greeting him at the door, a concession that Abdollah noted at once.

'And upon you, Excellency Colonel.' They shook hands. Abdollah walked past him into the cabin, his eyes on Armstrong, and sat in the chair nearest the exit.

'Salaam, Highness,' Armstrong said. 'Peace be upon you.'

'This is a colleague of mine,' Hashemi said, sitting opposite the Khan. 'An Englishman, Robert Armstrong.'

'Ah, yes, the Excellency who speaks Farsi better than my Ahmed and is famous for his memory – and cruelty.' Behind him Ahmed had closed the heavy curtain over the outside door and stood with his back to the cockpit, on guard, gun ready but not impolitely so. 'Eh?'

Armstrong smiled. 'That was a pleasantry of the colonel, Highness.'

'I don't agree. Even in Tabriz we've heard of the Special Branch expert, twelve years in service of the Shah, and running dog of his running dogs,' Abdollah said scornfully in Farsi. The smile vanished from Armstrong's face, and both he and Hashemi tensed at the blatant bad manners. 'I've read your record.' He turned his black eyes on Hashemi, completely sure that his plan would work: Ahmed would kill them at his signal, boobytrap the airplane, send the pilots back aboard and into a hasty takeoff and fiery death – nothing to do with him, as God wants, and he, himself, after such a wonderful discussion where he had promised 'complete support for the central government', would be filled with sadness.

'So, Excellency,' he said, 'we meet again. What can I do for you – I know your time is, unfortunately, short with us.'

'Perhaps, Highness, it is what I can do for you? Per –'

'Come to the point, Colonel,' the Khan said harshly, now in English, totally sure of himself. 'You and I know each other, we can dispense with flattery and compliments and get to the point. I'm busy. If you'd had the courtesy to come to my car, alone, I would have been more comfortable, we could have spoken in private, leisurely. Now come to the point!'

'I want to talk to you about your controller, Colonel General Petr Oleg Mzytryk,' Hashemi said as harshly, but suddenly petrified that he'd been trapped and that Abdollah was a secret Pahmudi supporter, 'and about your long-term KGB connection through Mzytryk, code name Ali Khoy.'

'Controller? What controller? Who's this man?' Abdollah Khan heard himself say, but his head was shrieking, You can't know that, impossible, not possible. And through the torrent of his own heartbeat he saw the colonel's mouth open and say other things that made everything worse, much worse, and worst of all it tore his plan to shreds. If the colonel spoke such secrets so openly in front of this foreigner and Ahmed, the secrets would be recorded elsewhere in a safe place to be read by the Revolutionary Komiteh and his enemies in case of an 'accident'.

'Your controller,' Hashemi slammed at him, seeing the change, and pressed home his advantage. 'Petr Oleg, whose dacha is beside Lake Tzvenghid in the Place of Hidden Valleys, east of Tbilisi, code name Ali Khoy, yours is Iv –'

'Wait,' Abdollah said throatily, his face livid – not even Ahmed knew that, must not know that. 'I – give me some water.'

Armstrong began to get up but froze as Ahmed's gun covered him. 'Please sit, Excellency. I will get it. Fasten your belt, both of you.'

'There's no n –'

'Do it,' Ahmed snarled and waved the gun, aghast at the Khan's change in face and tactic, and quite prepared to put the other plan into operation himself. 'Fasten them!'

They obeyed. Ahmed was near the water fountain and he filled a plastic cup and gave it to the Khan. Hashemi and Armstrong watched unbalanced. Neither had expected such an immediate capitulation from the Khan. The man seemed to have shrunk before their eyes, his pallor and breathing bad.

The Khan finished the water and looked at Hashemi, his small eyes bloodshot behind his glasses. He took them off and polished them absently, trying to regain his strength. Everything seemed to be taking more time than normal. 'Wait for me beside the car, Ahmed.'

Uneasily, Ahmed obeyed. Armstrong unsnapped his belt and closed the curtain again. For a moment the Khan felt better, the chill air that came in momentarily helping to clear his head. 'Now, what do you want?'

'Your code name's Ivanovitch. You've been a KGB spy and helper since January 1944. In that time y –'

'All lies. What do you want?'

'I want to meet Petr Oleg Mzytryk. I want to question him seriously. In secret.'

The Khan heard the words and considered them. If this son of a dog knew Petr's code name and his own code name and about Hidden Valley and January '44 when he went secretly to Moscow to join the KGB, he would know other more punishable matters. That he himself was playing both sides for the good of his Azerbaijan would make little difference to the assassins of the Right or of the Left. 'In return for what?'

'Freedom to manoeuvre in Azerbaijan – so long as you do what is good for Iran – and a firm working relationship with me. I will give you information that will put the Tudeh, the leftists, *and* the Kurds into your hands – and give you evidence how the Soviets are thwarting you. For example, you're declared Section 16/a.'

The Khan gaped at him. His ears began roaring. 'I don't believe it!'

'Immediate. Petr Oleg Mzytryk signed the order,' Hashemi said.

'Pr . . . proof, I . . . I want proof,' he choked out.

'Entice him this side of the border, alive, and I'll give you proof – at least he will.'

'You're . . . you're lying.'

'Haven't you planned to go to Tbilisi today or tomorrow, at his invitation? You would never have returned. The story would be that supposedly you had fled Iran. You'd be denounced, your possessions confiscated and family disgraced – and fed to the mullahs.' Now that Hashemi knew he had Abdollah in his grasp, the only thing that worried him was the state of the man's health. His head now had a slight twitch to it, the normally swarthy face was pallid with a strange reddishness around the eyes and temples, the vein in his forehead prominent. 'You'd better not go north, and double your guards. I could barter Petr Oleg – even better I could allow you to rescue him and . . . well, there are many solutions if I had possession of him.'

'What . . . what do you want with him?'

'Information.'

'I would . . . I would be party to it?'

Hashemi smiled. 'Why not? Then it's agreed?'

The Khan's mouth moved soundlessly. Then he said, 'I will try.'

'No,' the colonel said roughly, judging the time for the *coup de grâce* had come. 'No. You have four days. I will return Saturday. At noon Saturday I will be at your palace to take delivery. Or if you prefer, you can deliver him secretly to this address.' He put the piece of paper on the table between them. 'Or, third, if you give me the time and place he comes over the border I will take care of everything.' He unsnapped his seat belt and stood up. 'Four days, Ivanovitch.'

Abdollah's rage almost burst his eardrums. He tried to get up but failed. Armstrong helped him to stand and Hashemi went to the curtain but before he opened it, he took his automatic out of his shoulder holster. 'Tell Ahmed not to trouble us.'

Weakly the Khan stood in the open doorway and did as he was ordered. Ahmed was at the foot of the steps, his gun levelled. The wind had changed direction, now blowing towards the far end of the runway and had picked up considerably.

'Didn't you hear His Highness?' the colonel called down. 'Everything's all right but he needs help.' He kept his voice reassuring. 'He should perhaps see his doctor as soon as possible.'

Ahmed was flustered, not knowing what to do. There was his Master, clearly worse than before, but here were the men who caused it – who were to be killed.

'Help me into the car, Ahmed,' the Khan said with a curse and that settled everything. At once he obeyed. Armstrong took his other side and together they went down the stairs. Hastily the pilots got out and hurried into the airplane as Armstrong helped the sick man into the back seat. Abdollah settled himself with difficulty, Armstrong feeling more naked than he had ever been, him out in the open alone, Hashemi standing up there safely in the cabin door. The jet's engines fired up.

'Salaam, Highness,' he said. 'I hope you're all right.'

'Better you leave our land quickly,' the Khan said, then to the driver, 'Go back to the palace.'

Armstrong watched the car hurrying away, then turned. He saw Hashemi's strange smile, the half concealed automatic in his hand, and for a moment thought the man was going to shoot him.

'Hurry up, Robert!'

He ran up the steps, his legs chilled. The co-pilot had already stabbed the Steps Retract button. The steps came up, the door closed, and they were moving. In the warmth and closeness he came to life again. 'It's cold out there,' he said.

Hashemi paid no attention to him. 'Quick as you can, Captain, take off,' he ordered, standing behind the pilots.

'I'll have to taxi back, sir. I daren't take off this way with this wind up our tails.'

Hashemi cursed and peered through the cockpit windows. The other end of the runway looked a million miles away, the wind whisking snow off the drifts. To use the proper exit ramp would take them close to the terminal parking area. They would have to cross it and use the opposite ramp to the takeoff point. Over towards the terminal the Rolls was speeding along. He could see armed men collecting to meet it. 'Taxi back along the runway and do a short field takeoff.'

'That's highly irregular without tower clearance,' John Hogg said.

'Would you prefer a bullet in your head or a SAVAK jail? Those men there are hostiles. Do it!'

Hogg could see the guns. He clicked on his transmit button. 'Echo-TangoLimaLima requesting permission to backtrack,' he said, not expecting any answer – after they had cleared Tehran airspace there had been none all the way here, and no contact with this tower. He swung the jet back on to the runway, skidding, and opened the throttle some more, keeping to the left side, paralleling their landing tracks. 'Tower, this is EchoTangoLimaLima, backtracking.' Gordon Jones, the co-pilot was checking everything, setting up for their Tehran inbound. The wind was tugging at them, their wheels uncertain. Over at the terminal he saw the Rolls stop and men surround it.

'Quick as you can – turn around, there's plenty of runway,' Hashemi said.

'Soon as I can, sir,' John Hogg said politely, but he was thinking, bloody twit, Colonel whoever you are, I'm more than a little anxious to be up in the Wild Blue myself but I've got to get a run at it. He had seen the hostility of the men in the car and, at Tehran, McIver's nervousness. But Tehran Tower had cleared him instantly, given him priority as though he was carrying Khomeini himself. Bloody hell, what we do for England and a pint of beer! His hands and feet were feeling the snow and the ice and the slipperiness of the surface. He eased off the throttles a little.

'Look!' the co-pilot said. A jet helicopter was crossing the airspace, low down a mile or so ahead. '212, isn't she?'

'Yes. Doesn't look like she's inbound here,' Hogg said, his eyes sweeping constantly. At the terminal another car had joined the men near the Rolls; ahead to the left was a glint of light; now the 212 had gone behind a hill; to the right was a flock of birds; all needles safe in the Green; more men near the Rolls and someone on the roof of the terminal building; fuel fine; snow not too deep, sheet ice underneath; watch the drift ahead; go right a little; radio's correctly tuned; wind's still up our tail; thunder clouds building up to the north; back a hair on the left engine!

Hogg corrected the lurching swing, the airplane over responsive on the icy surface. 'Perhaps you'd better go back to your seat, colonel,' he said.

'Get airborne as fast as possible.' Hashemi went back. Armstrong was peering out of the windows towards the terminal. 'What're they doing there, Robert? Any problem?' he asked.

'Not yet. Congratulations – you handled Abdollah brilliantly.'

'If he delivers.' Now that it was over, Hashemi felt a little sick. Too close to death that time, he thought. He fastened his seat belt, then undid it, took the automatic from his side pocket, put the safety on, and slipped it into the shoulder holster. His fingers touched the British passport in his inner pocket. Perhaps I won't need it after all, he thought. Good. I'd hate having to disgrace myself by using it. He lit a cigarette.

'Do you think he'll last till Saturday? I thought he was going to have a fit.'

'He's been that fat and that foul for years.'

Armstrong heard the violent undercurrent. Hashemi Fazir was always dangerous, always on the edge, his fanatic patriotism mixed with his contempt for most Iranians. 'You handled him wonderfully,' he said and looked out of the window again. The Rolls and the other car and the men surrounding them were quite far and half hidden by the snow dunes, but he could see many guns among them and from time to time someone would point in their direction. Come on, for God's sake, he thought, let's get aloft.

'Colonel,' Hogg's voice came over the intercom, 'could you come forward, please?'

Hashemi unlocked his belt and went to the cockpit.

'There, sir,' Hogg said pointing off to the right, past the end of the runway, to a clump of pines in front of the forest. 'What do you make of that?' The tiny fleck of light began winking again. 'It says SOS.'

'Robert,' Hashemi called out, 'look ahead and to the right.'

The four men concentrated. Again the light repeated the SOS. 'No mistaking it, sir,' Hogg said. 'I could signal them back.' He pointed to the heavy-duty signal flash that was for emergency use to give a Green or a Red light in case their radios failed.

Hashemi called back into the cabin. 'What do you think, Robert?' 'It's SOS all right!'

The 125 was hurrying down the runway towards the signal. They waited, then saw three tiny figures come out from the trees, two men and a woman in chador. And they saw their guns.

'It's a trap,' Hashemi said at once, 'don't go any closer, turn around!'

'I can't,' Hogg said, 'haven't got enough runway.' He eased the throttles a little more open. The jet was taxiing very fast, paralleling their landing tracks. They could see the figures waving their guns.

Armstrong called out, 'Let's get to hell out of here!'

'Soon as I can, sir. Colonel, perhaps you'd better get back to your seat, this might be kind of bumpy,' Hogg said, his voice nerveless, then dismissed them both from his mind. 'Gordon, keep your eye on those buggers out there and on the terminal.'

'Sure. No sweat.'

The captain turned momentarily to check the other end of the runway, judged they were not quite far enough yet, but eased back on the throttle and touched the brakes. The skid began so he loosed them, keeping the jet as straight as he could, the wind shifting. The figures near the trees were larger now.

'They look a ropey lot, tribesmen, I'd say. Two automatic carbines.' Gordon Jones squinted at the Terminal. 'Rolls's gone but a car heading our way along the ramp.'

Pulling off the throttles now. Still too fast to turn.

'Christ, I think . . . I think one of the tribesmen fired a gun,' Jones said, his voice picking up.

'Here we go,' Hogg said into the intercom mike, braked, felt her slide, held it, then began his right turn on to the width of the runway, their momentum skidding them and the wind still hostile.

In the cabin Armstrong and Hashemi were hanging on grimly, peering out of the windows. They could see one of the figures running towards them, brandishing his gun. Armstrong muttered, 'We're bloody sitting ducks.' He felt the jet sliding in the turn, no traction, and he cursed.

In the cockpit Hogg was whistling tonelessly. The jet surged over their landing tracks, still skidding, the far side of the runway banked by solid, heavy dunes. He did not dare to gun her yet and waited, mouth dry, willing her to come around faster and into the wind. But she didn't, just continued to slide, wheels useless, brakes dangerous, engines growling, the subsurface ice.

Inexorably the snow dunes came closer and closer. He could see the jagged ice edges that would tear their thin skin asunder. Nothing to do but wait. Then a gust took her tail section and buffeted it around and now, though she was still sliding, she faced into the wind. Delicately he gunned both engines, felt the slide slowing, and at once began inching the throttles forward until he had some forward speed, more open and faster, and more control and now complete control and he shoved the throttles hard against the gate. The 125 surged ahead, his wheels left the surface, he touched the undercart retract, and they were soaring.

'You may smoke if you wish,' he said laconically into the intercom, totally pleased with himself.

On the airfield, not far from the trees, Ross had stopped running and waving, his chest hurting him. 'Bloody bastard,' he shouted at the airplane. 'Haven't you any bloody eyes?'

Bitterly disappointed, he started walking back to the others who had obediently waited on the edge of the forest. Over all of them was a deep gloom. So near, he thought. Through his binoculars he had seen the Khan arrive, then go aboard, then, later, Armstrong come down the steps with the Khan, helping him. 'Oh, let me look, Johnny,' Azadeh had said anxiously and refocused the lenses to suit her eyes. 'Oh, dear, Father looks sick – I hope he's all right,' she had said. 'The doctor's always telling him to diet and take his life easier.'

'He's doing just fine, Azadeh,' he had said, trying to keep the sarcasm out of his voice. But she had heard it and flushed and she said, 'Oh so sorry, I didn't mean . . . I know he's . . .'

'I meant nothing,' he had said and refocused on Armstrong, ecstatic that it was Armstrong, devising a plan how to get aboard. So easy. An S-G airplane – easy to see the decal – and Armstrong. We're safe! But now we're not safe, we're in a mess, he told himself even more bitterly, trudging back in the snow, feeling filthy and wanting a bath and helpless with rage. They've got to have seen the SOS. Were their heads in their arses? Why the hell didn't th –

He heard Gueng's keening danger signal and he whirled. A car was a

645

few hundred yards away, heading their way. He ran back and pointed into the forest, 'That way!'

Earlier he had made a plan. First the airport, then, if that didn't work, they would head for Erikki's base. The base was about four miles away, southeast of Tabriz. Covered by the trees, he paused and looked back. The car stopped at the end of the runway and men got out, started after them, but found the going too heavy through the drifts. They climbed back into the car and headed away. 'They won't catch us now,' Ross said. He led the way deeper into the forest, of necessity keeping to the crude path.

On the edge of this clump of forest were frozen fields that in the summer would be abundant with crops, most of it belonging to a few landowners, in spite of the Shah's land reforms. Beyond the fields were the outlying slums of Tabriz. They could see the minarets of the Blue Mosque and smoke from many fires pulled away by the wind. 'Can we skirt the city, Azadeh?'

'Yes,' she said, 'but it's . . . it's quite a long way.'

They heard her underlying concern. So far she had moved quickly and without complaint. But she was still a hazard. They wore their tribesmen's clothes over their uniforms. Their scrubby boots would pass. So would their weapons. And her chador. He looked at her, still not used to the ugliness that it made of her. She felt his glance and tried to smile. She understood. Both about the chador and about being a burden.

'Let's go through the town,' she said. 'We can stay in the side streets. I have some . . . some money and we can buy food. Johnny, you could pretend to be Caucasian from, say, from Astara, I could pretend to be your wife. Gueng, you speak Gurkhali or a foreign tongue and be rough and arrogant like the Turkomen from the north – you'd pass for one of them – they were descended from the Mongols, many Iranians are. Or perhaps I could buy some green scarves and make you Green Bands . . . That's the best I can do.'

'That's good, Azadeh. Perhaps we'd better not stay bunched up. Gueng, you tail us.'

Azadeh said, 'In the streets Iranian wives follow their husbands. I . . . I will stay a pace behind you, Johnny.'

'It's a good plan, memsahib,' Gueng said. 'Very good. You guide us.'

Her smile thanked him. Soon they were in the markets and the streets and alleys of the slums. Once a man shoved into Gueng carelessly. Without hesitation Gueng slammed his fist into the man's throat, sending him sprawling into the joub senseless, cursing him loudly in a dialect of Ghurkali. There was a moment's silence in the crowd, then noise picked up again and those nearby kept their eyes down and passed onward, a few surreptitiously making a sign against the evil eye that all those who came from the north, the descendants of the hordes who knew not the One God, were known to possess.

Azadeh bought food from street vendors, fresh bread from the kilns, charcoaled lamb kebab and bean and vegetable horisht, heavy with rice. They sat on rough benches and gorged, then went on again. No one paid any attention to them. Occasionally someone would ask him to buy something but Azadeh would intervene and protect him well, coarsening her voice and talking the local Turkish dialect. When the muezzins called for afternoon prayer, she stopped, afraid. Around them, men and women searched for a piece of carpet or material or newspaper or cardboard or box to kneel on and began to pray. Ross hesitated, then following her pleading look, pretended to pray also and the moment passed. In the whole street only four or five remained standing, Gueng among them, leaning against a wall. No one bothered those who stood. Tabrizi came from many races, many religions.

They continued onward, making their way southeast and now were in the outlying suburbs, shantytowns filled with refuse and mangy, half-starved dogs, the joub the only sewer. Soon the hovels would end, the fields and orchards would begin, then the forest and the main Tehran road that curled upward to the pass that would lead them to Tabriz One. What he would do when they got there, Ross did not know, but Azadeh had said that she knew of several caves nearby where they could hide until a helicopter landed.

They went through the last of the slums, out on to the crude, snow-banked track. The snow of the surface was stained from mule and donkey droppings, pitted and treacherous, and they joined others who trudged along, some leading burdened donkeys, others bent over under the weight of their loads, others relieving themselves, men and women and children – a handful of snow with the left hand, then on again – a polyglot of people, tribesmen, nomads, townspeople – only their poverty in common, and their pride.

Azadeh was feeling very tired, the strain of crossing the city heavy on her. She had been afraid she would make a mistake, afraid they would be spotted, frantic with worry over Erikki and worried how they would get to the base and what then? Insha'Allah, she told herself, over and over. God will look after you and after him and after Johnny.

When they came near the junction of the track and the Tehran road they saw Green Bands and armed men standing beside a makeshift roadblock, peering into vehicles and watching the people filing past. There was no way to avoid them.

'Azadeh, you go first,' Ross whispered. 'Wait for us up the road – if we get stopped, don't interfere, just go on – head for the base. We'll split up, safer.' He smiled at her. 'Don't worry.' She nodded, her fear making her face more pale, and walked off. She was carrying his rucksack. Coming out of the town she had insisted: 'Look at all the other women, Johnny. If I don't carry something, I'll stand out terribly.'

The two men waited, then went to the side of the track and urinated into the snowbank. People plodded by. Some noticed them. A few cursed them as Infidels. One or two wondered about them – unknowingly, they were relieving themselves towards Mecca, an act no Muslim would ever do.

'Once she's through, you next, Gueng. I'll follow in ten minutes.'

'Better you next,' Gueng whispered back. 'I'm a Turkoman.'

'All right, but if I'm stopped – do not interfere. Sneak by in the fracas and get her to safety. Don't fail me!'

The little man grinned, his teeth very white. 'Don't you fail, sahib. You have much yet to do before you're a Lord of the Mountain.' Gueng looked past him towards the roadblock, a hundred yards away. He saw that Azadeh was in line now. One of the Green Bands said something to her, but she kept her eyes averted, replied, and the man waved her through. 'Don't wait for me on the road, sahib. I may cross the fields. Don't worry about me – I'll track you.' He pushed through the pedestrians and joined the stream going back towards the town. After a hundred yards or so, he sat on an upturned crate and unlaced his boot as though it were hurting him. His socks were in shreds but that did not matter. The soles of his feet were like iron. Taking his time, he relaced his boots, enjoying being a Turkoman.

At the roadblock Ross joined the line of those leaving Tabriz. He noticed police standing around with the Green Bands, watching the people. The people were irritable, hating any authority as always and any infringement of their right to go where and how and when they pleased. Many were openly angry and a few almost came to blows. 'You,' a Green Band said to him, 'where are your papers?'

Angrily Ross spat on the ground. 'Papers? My house is burned, my wife burned, and my child burned by leftist dogs. I have nothing left but this gun and some ammunition. God's will – but why don't you go and burn Satanists and do the work of God instead of stopping honest men?'

'We're honest!' the man said angrily. 'We're doing the Work of God. Where do you come from?'

'Astara. Astara on the coast.' He let the anger come out. 'Astara. And you?'

The next man in line and the one behind him began cursing and telling the Green Band to hurry up and not cause them to wait around in the cold. A policeman was edging over towards them, so Ross decided to chance it and he shoved past with another curse, the man behind followed, and the next and now they were out in the open. The Green Band sullenly shouted an obscenity after them, then went back to watching others file through.

It took Ross a little while to breathe easier. He tried not to hurry and his eyes searched ahead. No sign of Azadeh. Cars and trucks were passing now, grinding up the incline or coming down too fast, people scattering from time to time with the inevitable stream of curses. The man who had been behind him at the roadblock came up alongside, pedestrians thinning out now, turning off into the side paths that led to hovels beside the road or to villages within the forest. He was a middle-aged man with a lined, very strong face, poorly dressed, his rifle well serviced. 'That Green Band son of a dog,' he said with a thick accent. 'You're right, agha, they should be doing God's work, the Imam's work, not Abdollah Khan's.'

Ross was instantly on guard. 'Who?'

'I come from Astara and from your accent I know you don't come from Astara, agha. Astaris never piss towards Mecca or with their backs to Mecca – we're all good Muslims in Astara. From your description you must be the saboteur the Khan's put a price on.' The man's voice was easy, curiously friendly, the old Enfield rifle over his shoulder.

Ross said nothing, just grunted, not changing his pace.

'Yes, the Khan's put a good price on your head. Many horses, a herd of sheep, ten or more camels. A Shah's ransom to ordinary folk. The ransom's better for alive than dead – more horses and sheep and camels then, enough to live for ever. But where's the woman Azadeh, his daughter, the daughter that you kidnapped, you and another man?'

Ross gaped at him and the man chuckled. 'You must be very tired to give yourself away so easily.' Abruptly the face hardened, his hand went into the pocket of his old jacket, pulled out a revolver and shoved it into Ross's side. 'Walk ahead of me a pace, don't run or do anything or I shall just shoot you in the spine. Now where's the woman – there's a reward for her too.'

At that moment a truck coming down from the pass careened around the bend ahead, lurched to the wrong side of the road, and charged them, hooting loudly. People scattered. Ross's reflexes were faster and he sidestepped, shoved his shoulder into the man's side and sent him reeling into the truck's path. The truck's front wheels went over the man and the back wheels. The truck skidded to a stop a hundred feet below.

'God protect us, did you see that?' someone said. 'He lurched into the truck.'

Ross dragged the body out of the road. The revolver had vanished into the snow.

'Ah, is the sacrifice of God your father, agha?' an old woman said.

'No . . . no,' Ross said with difficulty, everything so fast, in panic. 'I . . . he's a stranger. I've never seen him before.'

'By the Prophet, how careless walkers are! Have they no eyes? Is he dead?' the truck driver called out, coming back up the hill. He was a rough, bearded, swarthy man. 'God witness that he moved into my path as all could see! You,' he said to Ross, 'you were beside him, you must have seen it.'

'Yes . . . yes, it is as you say. I was behind him.'

'As God wants.' The trucker went off happily, everything correct and finished. 'His Excellency saw it. Insha'Allah!'

Ross pushed away through the few who had bothered to stop and walked up the hill, not fast, not slow, trying to get himself together, not daring to look back. Around the bend in the road, he quickened his pace, wondering if it was right to react so quickly – almost without thought. But the man would have sold her and sold them. Put him away, karma is karma. Another bend and still no Azadeh. His anxiety increased.

Here the road was twisting, the grade steep. He passed a few hovels half hidden in the forest verge. Mangy dogs were scavenging. The few that came near him he cursed away, rabies usually rampant among them. Another bend, sweat pouring off him, and there she was squatting beside the road, resting like any of a dozen other old crones. She saw him at the same moment, shook her head cautioning him, got up, and started off up the road again. He fell into place twenty yards behind her. Then there was firing below them. With everyone else, they stopped and looked back. They could see nothing. The roadblock was far behind, around many corners, half a mile or more away. In a moment the firing ceased. No one said anything, just began climbing more hurriedly.

The road was not good. They walked on for a mile or so, stepping aside for traffic. Occasionally a bus groaned past but always over-loaded and none would stop. These days you could wait a day or two even at a correct stop before there was space. Trucks sometimes would stop. For payment.

Later one chugged past him and as it came alongside Azadeh, it slowed to her pace. 'Why walk when those who are tired can ride with the help of Cyrus the trucker – and God,' the driver called out, leering at her, nudging his companion, a dark-bearded man of his own age. They had been watching her for some time, watching the sway of her hips that not even a chador could hide. 'Why should a flower of God walk when she could be warm in a truck or on a man's carpet?'

She looked up at him and gave him a gutter curse and called back to Ross, 'Husband, this leprous son of a dog dared to insult me and made lewd remarks against the laws of God . . .' Ross was already alongside her, and the driver found himself looking into the barrel of a gun. 'Excellency . . . I was asking if . . . if you and she would . . . would like to ride,' the driver said in panic. 'There's room in the back . . . if his Excellency would honour my vehicle . . .'

The truck was half-filled with scrap iron, but it would be better than walking. 'On your head, driver, where do you go?'

'To Qazvin, Excellency, Qazvin. Would you honour us?'

The truck did not stop but it was easy for Ross to help her climb up over the tailgate. Together they ducked down out of the wind. Her legs were shaking and she was chilled and very nervous. He reached out and put his arms around her and held her.

'Oh, Johnny, if you hadn't been there . . .'

'Don't worry, don't worry.' He gave her of his warmth. Qazvin, Qazvin? Isn't that halfway to Tehran? Of course it is! We'll stick with the truck until Qazvin, he told himself, gathering strength. Then we can get another ride, or find a bus, or steal a car, that's what we'll do.

'The turnoff to the base is two or three miles ahead,' she said, shivering in his arms. 'To the right.'

Base? Ah, yes, the base. And Erikki. But more important, what about Gueng? What about Gueng? Get your mind working. What are you going to do?

'What's the . . . what's the land like there, open and flat or a ravine or what?' he asked.

'It's fairly flat. Our village is soon, Abu Mard. We pass our village, then shortly afterwards, the land flattens into a kind of a wooded plateau where our own road is. Then the main road climbs again up to the pass.'

Ahead he could see the road curling away, occasionally coming into view as it wound precariously along the mountainside. 'We'll get off the other side of the village, before the flat, circle through the forest, and get to the base. That possible?'

'Yes. I know the country very well. I . . . I taught in the village school and used to take the children for . . . for walks. I know the paths.' Again she trembled.

'Keep down out of the wind. You'll soon be warm.'

The old truck was labouring on the incline not much faster than walking but better than walking. He kept his arm around her and in time she stopped trembling. Over their tailgate, he noticed a car overtaking them fast, gears shrieking, followed by a mottled green half truck. The driver of the car kept his hand on the horn. There was nowhere for their truck to pull over, so the car swung over to the wrong side of the road and charged ahead. Hope you bloody kill yourself, he thought, angered by the noise and the incredible stupidity. Idly he had noticed that it had been filled with armed men. So was the following half truck though all these men stood in the back, hanging on to metal stanchions, the tailgate down and banging wildly. As it roared past, he caught a glimpse of a body slumped under their feet. At first he thought it was the old man. But it wasn't. It was Gueng. No mistaking the remains of the uniform. Or the kukri one of the men had stuck in his belt.

'What is it, Johnny?'

He found himself beside her, not feeling her or anything, only that he had failed the second of his men. His eyes were filled with tears.

'What is it, what's the matter?'

'Nothing. It's just the wind.' He brushed the tears away, then knelt and looked ahead. Curling away, the road disappeared and appeared again. So did the car and half truck. He could see the village now. Beyond it the road climbed again, then flattened, just as she had said. The car and half truck went through the village full tilt. In his pocket were his small but very powerful binoculars. Steadying himself against the rocking of the truck, he focused on the car. Once the car came up on to the flat it speeded up, then turned right on to the side road to the base and disappeared. When the half truck reached the intersection it stopped, blocking most of the road outward bound. Half a dozen of the men jumped down, spread out across the road and stood facing Tabriz. Then, the half truck turned right and vanished after the car.

Their truck slowed as the driver shifted noisily into bottom gear. Just ahead was a short, steeper grade, a path nearby, no pedestrians on this section of road. 'Where does that go, Azadeh?'

She got on to her knees and looked where he pointed. 'Towards Abu Mard, our village,' she said. 'It wanders this way and that but that's where it ends.'

'Get ready to jump out – there's another roadblock ahead.'

At the right moment he slipped over the side, helped her down, and they scrambled into hiding. The truck did not stop nor the driver look around. Soon it was well away. Hand in hand, they fled into the trees.

At Zagros Three: 4:05 P.M. Lochart leaned against the cockpit of the
212 waiting to go again to Rig Rosa with another load of pipe – sky
cloudless, the mountains so clean and sharp he felt he could almost
reach out and touch them. He was watching Rodrigues, his mechanic,
who knelt in the snow and peered into a belly inspection panel. 'It's an
afternoon for skiing or tobogganing, Rod, not grinding away.'

'It's a day to get the hell outta here, Tom.'

'Maybe we won't have to,' Lochart said. Since Sunday when he had
his confrontation with Nitchak Khan he had heard nothing more from
him or anyone in the village. 'Maybe the komiteh will change their
minds or Mac'll get the order cancelled. Crazy for us to be shoved out
when they need all the oil they can get and Rosa's new well's a bonanza
– Jesper Almqvist said he figured it'd pump 18,000 barrels a day when it
was put on stream. That's almost $360,000 a day, Rod.'

'Mullahs don't give a shit for oil or anything but Allah, the Koran or
Paradise, you said it a million times.' Rodrigues wiped an oil streak
away. 'We should've all gone with Jesper to Shiraz – then out. We're

654

not wanted. Nasiri got his head blown off, right? For what? He was one nice guy. Never hurt no one. We've been told to get out – what the hell're we waiting for?'

'Maybe the komiteh changed its mind. We've eleven rigs to service.'

'The rigs are down to minimums, crews all itchy to get the hell out and anyway they've had no replacements for weeks.' Rodrigues got up, knocked the snow off his knees, and began wiping the oil off his hands. 'Crazy to stay where you're not wanted. Young Scot's acting mighty strange – so are you, come to think of it.'

'Bull,' Lochart said. He had told no one what Scot said had really happened in the village square. His anxiety returned – for Scot, the base, Sharazad, HBC, and always back to Sharazad again.

'Bull nothing,' Rodrigues was saying, 'you've been itchy as hell since you got back from Tehran. You wanna stay in Iran, Tom, okay, that's different – you're married to Iran. Me, I want out.'

Lochart took his mind off Sharazad. He saw the fear in his friend's face. 'What's the problem, Rod?'

The heavyset man pulled his belt over the beginnings of his paunch, and closed his parka again. 'I'm nervous as all hell about my false IDs, Tom. Shit, soon's I open my mouth, they gotta know I'm not a Brit. All my permits're outta date. So it's the same with some of the other guys, but I'm the only American here, I gave a talk in the school on the States, and goddam mullahs and Khomeini say I'm Satan – me a goddam good Catholic for crissake! I'm not sleeping nights.'

'Why the hell didn't you say so before? No need for you to stay, Rod. The 212's due out tomorrow. How about going with Scot? Once you get to Al Shargaz you can transfer to Nigeria, Kenya, or where the hell ever.'

For a moment Rodrigues said nothing, his face bleak. 'I'd like that, Tom. Sure, if you can okay it, that'd be one helluva load off my back.'

'It's done. We've got to send a mechanic – why not you, you're senior.'

'Thanks. Yeah, thanks, Tom.' Rodrigues beamed. 'I'll just tighten the foot pedal, and then you're as good as new.'

Down by the supply helipad Lochart saw that the load of pipe was ready for pickup. Two Iranian labourers were waiting to guide the skyhook into the ringbolt. He began to get into the cockpit, stopped on seeing two men striding up the village path a hundred yards away. Nitchak Khan, and another man carrying a carbine. Even from this distance it was easy to see the green armband.

Lochart went to meet them, preparing his mind to think and speak

Farsi. 'Salaam, kalandar, salaam, agha,' he said to the other man, also bearded but much younger.

'Salaam,' Nitchak said. 'You have been granted until the fifth sunset.'

Lochart tried to hide his shock. Today was Tuesday, the fifth day would be Sunday. 'But Excellency, th –'

'Until the fifth sunset,' the Green Band said without politeness. 'You may not work or fly on Holy Day – better you give thanks to God – and on the fifth sunset from tonight if all foreigners and their planes have not left, the base will be fired.'

Lochart just looked at him. Behind the man was the cookhouse and he saw Jean-Luc come out, then walk over towards them. 'Four working days will be very difficult, agha, and I don't th –'

'Insha' Allah.'

'If we go, all the rigs will have to stop. Only we can supply them and their men. That will hurt Iran, that w –'

'Islam does not *need* oil. Foreigners *need* oil. Five sunsets. Be it on your own heads if you stay.'

Nitchak Khan looked sideways at the man. Then to Lochart he said, 'Agha, I wish to go with this man to see the kalandar of the Italian foreigners. I would like to go now, please.'

'It is my honour, kalandar,' Lochart said, and he was thinking, Mimmo Sera's been in the mountains for years, he'll know what to do. 'I've a load of pipe to deliver to Rig Rosa, we can go at once.'

'Pipe?' the youth said rudely. 'No need for pipe. We go straight. No pipe.'

'IranOil says pipe and the pipe goes or you don't,' Lochart said angrily. 'Ayatollah Khomeini ordered oil production to come back to normal – why does the komiteh disobey him?'

Sullenly the youth looked at the Khan, who said quietly, 'As God wills. The Ayatollah is the Ayatollah, komitehs obey only him. Let us go, agha.'

Lochart took his eyes off the youth. 'All right. We will go at once.'

'Salaam, kalandar,' Jean-Luc said joining them. 'Tom, what's the answer?' he asked in English.

'Sunset Sunday. We have to be out by then and can't fly Friday.'

Jean-Luc swallowed a curse. 'No negotiations?'

'None. Unless you want to argue with this mother.'

Insolently the youth with the gun stared back at Jean-Luc. 'Tell this son of a dog he smells vilely.'

Lochart had caught a faint whiff of garlic. 'He says your cooking

656

smells great, Jean-Luc. Listen, they want to go to see Mimmo Sera – I'll be back as quick as I can, then we'll decide what to do. Kalandar, we will go now,' he said in Farsi and opened the cabin door.

'Lookit!' Rodrigues said suddenly and pointed northwards high into the mountains. Smoke was billowing in the sky. 'That Maria?'

'Might be Bellissima,' Jean-Luc said.

Nitchak Khan was squinting into the distance. 'That is near where we should go. Yes?'

'Not far off course, kalandar.'

The old man appeared very worried. 'Perhaps it would be better to take the pipe on your next flight, pilot. For days now we heard that leftists were infiltrating the hills, wanting to sabotage and create trouble. Last night one of my shepherds had his throat cut and genitals hacked off – I have men out searching for the murderers.' Grim-faced he got into the cabin. The Green Band followed.

'Rod,' Lochart said, 'get the 206 out. Jean-Luc, stand by on the HF – I'll radio you.'

'*Oui. Pas de problème.*' Jean-Luc looked back at the smoke.

Lochart left the load of pipe at the base and hurried northward. It was Bellissima and it was on fire. From quite far out he could see flames spouting thirty feet from one of the trailers that, tinder dry in the moistureless air, was now almost gutted. Off to one side near the drilling rig was another fire, near the dynamite shed and a body lay in the snow. Above the base, the snowcap of the mountain, re-formed by Pietro's explosion and the resultant avalanche, was benign.

As he got closer he noticed half a dozen figures running down the winding path that led at length into the valley – all of them armed. Without hesitation he banked and went after them, seeing them ahead now, directly ahead, cursing that he wasn't a gunship – no problem to blast them all. Six men, bearded, in nondescript tribesman clothes. Then he saw one man stop and aim and the familiar sparks from the muzzle of the gun and he peeled away, taking evading action, and when he was around again, higher and safer, the figures had disappeared.

He looked back into the cabin. Nitchak Khan and the Green Band were staring down out of the side windows, noses pressed against them. He shouted but could not make himself heard, so he banged the side of the cabin to attract their attention and beckoned Nitchak Khan. The old man came forward, holding on, ill at ease flying.

'Did you see them?' he shouted.

'Yes – yes,' Nitchak Khan shouted back. 'Not mountain people – they're the terrorists.'

657

Lochart went back to flying. 'Jean-Luc, do you read?'

'Loud and clear, Tom, go ahead.'

He told him what he had seen and to stay on the radio, then concentrated on the landing – in over the immensity of the ravine as usual, updraughts bad and stiff wind today. This was the first time he had been to Bellissima since he had come back from Tehran. With the death of Guineppa, Bellissima was down to a minimum, one shift only. As he touched down he saw Pietro, now senior in Guineppa's place, leave the fire near the rig and hurry towards them.

'Tom! We need help,' he shouted into the pilot's window, almost in tears. 'Gianni's dead and a couple hurt in the fire . . .'

'Okay. No sweat.' Lochart began shutdown. 'Nitchak's in the back with a Green Band – don't worry, okay?' He twisted in his seat again and pointed at the door. The old man nodded. 'What the hell happened, Pietro?' he asked, his fingers finding the switches.

'Don't know . . . I don't know, *amico*.' Pietro put his head close to the cockpit window. 'We were having lunch when this *stronzo* bottle with gasoline and a burning rag came through the *stronzo* window and we were on fire . . .' He looked back as flames caught a half-full oil drum and leaped into the sky, choking black smoke billowing. The four men fighting the fire backed off. '*Si*, we were on fire quickly in the dining room and when we rushed out there were these men, tribesmen, banditos . . . *Mamma mia*, they started shooting so we scattered and took cover. Then later Gianni saw them starting a fire in the generator room, near where the dynamites are and . . . and he just ran out to warn them but one of them shot him. *Mamma Mia*, no reason to shoot him! *Bastardi, stronzo bastardi . . .*'

Quickly Lochart and the others climbed out of the airplane. The only sound was that of the wind and the flames and the single fire pump – Pietro had cut the generators and pumps and done an emergency closedown of the whole rig. The roof of the trailer collapsed and sparks and embers soared, many falling on nearby roofs, but these were heavy with snow and no danger to them. The fire was still out of control near the rig, fed by waste oil and oil fumes, and highly dangerous. The men sprayed foam, but flames still reached towards the dynamite shed, licking a corrugated iron wall.

'How much is in there, Pietro?'

'Too much.'

'Let's get it out.'

'*Mamma mia* . . .' Pietro followed Lochart, their hands over their faces against the flames, and forced the door open – no time to find the key. The dynamite was in neat boxes. A dozen of them. Lochart picked up a box and went out, felt the blast of heat, and then he was clear. One of the other men took the box from him and hurried it to safety while Lochart returned for another.

Near the helicopter Nitchak Khan and the Green Band stood in the lee of the wind out of danger. 'As God wants.'

'As God wants,' the Green Band echoed. 'What shall we do now?'

'There are terrorists to consider. And the dead man.'

The young man looked across the snow at the figure lying like a broken doll. 'If he hadn't come to our hills he would not be dead. It's his fault he's dead – no one else's.'

'True.' Nitchak Khan watched the fire and the men fighting it and by the time Lochart and Pietro had cleared the shed of dynamite, the others had the fire contained.

Lochart leaned against a trailer wall to catch his breath. 'Pietro, we've only got till Sunday sunset. Then it's get out or else.'

Pietro's face closed. He glanced at the Green Band and Nitchak Khan. 'Five days? That saves me a decision, Tom. We evacuate to Shiraz – via Rig Rosa or direct.' Pietro gestured at the fire with his clenched left fist, his other hand on the bicep. 'For the moment Bellissima is ruined. I'll need Almqvist to plug the wells. *Mamma mia*, that's a lot of men to transport. What a waste! I'm glad old Guineppa's not here to see the foulness of the day. Best I come to see Mimmo.'

'At once, with those who're hurt. What about Gianni?'

Pietro glanced at the body. 'We'll leave him until last, my poor blood brother,' he said sadly. 'He won't rot.'

At Rig Rosa: Mimmo Sera was sitting opposite Nitchak Khan and the Green Band in the mess hall, Lochart, Pietro and the three senior riggers also at the table. For half an hour Mimmo, who spoke good Farsi, had tried to persuade the komiteh Green Band to extend the time, or to allow him to leave skeleton crews while he and Lochart went with him to see the chief of IranOil in Shiraz.

'In the Name of God, enough!' the Green Band said irritably.

'But Excellency, without the helicopters we'll have to shut down the whole field and start evacuating at once. Surely, Excellency, because the Ayatollah, bless him, and your Prime Minister Bazargan want oil production back to normal we should consult IranOil in Sh –'

'Enough! Kalandar,' the Green Band added to Nitchak Khan, 'if these mosquito brains disobey, it's on your head, you're finished,

Yazdek is finished and all your people! If one foreigner or one flying machine remains on the fifth sunset and you haven't fired the base, we will! Then we will burn the village, by hand or by air force. You,' the Green Band snarled at Lochart, 'start up the airplane. We go back. Now!' He stormed out.

They all stared after him dismayed. Lochart felt sad for all those who had found the oil and developed the field and put so much energy, money, talent, gamble, and risk into it. Scandalous, he thought, but we've no option. Nothing else to do. We evacuate. I cancel Scot leaving and use all airplanes and do the job. We work like hell for five days and forget Tehran and Sharazad and that today's the day of the Protest March she's forbidden.

'Kalandar,' he said. 'Without your benevolence, and assistance, we must leave.'

Nitchak Khan saw all the eyes turn to him. 'I have to choose between the base and my village,' he said gravely. 'That is no choice. I will try to find the terrorists and bring them to justice. Meanwhile, best that you take no chances. These hills are full of hiding places.'

With great dignity he got up and walked out, quite sure that now he would not have to burn the base, though, if God wanted, he knew he would do it without a moment's hesitation, whether it be full or empty.

He allowed himself the shadow of a smile. His plan had worked impeccably. All the foreigners had accepted Hassan the Goatherd as a genuine Green Band whose pretended arrogance and temper was marvellous to see; the foreigners had swallowed his fabrication about 'terrorists' murdering a shepherd and he had seen their fear; these same 'terrorists' had mutilated the oil rig, the most difficult to reach of all eleven and, in the black hours tonight, these same 'terrorists' would fire part of the Rig Rosa and then would vanish for ever – back into the village life stream from which they came. And by dawn tomorrow, he thought with satisfaction, terror will be widespread, all foreigners will be falling over themselves to leave, their evacuation is assured, and peace will come to Yazdek.

Fools to play games where only we know the rules! But there is still the problem of the young pilot. Was he a witness, or wasn't he? The elders have advised an 'accident' to be safe. Yesterday would have been perfect when the young man was hunting alone. So easy to slip and fall on your gun. Yes. But my wife advised against an 'accident'.

'Why?'

'Because the schoolhouse was a marvellous thing,' she had said. 'Wasn't it the first we have ever had? Without the pilots it would never have been. But now we know and can easily build another of our own; because the pilots have been good for us, without them we would not know much that we know now, nor would we have such a rich village; because I think that young man told the truth. I commend that you should let him go, don't forget how that young man made us laugh with his fairy stories about this place called Kong in the land called China, where there are a thousand times a thousand times a thousand times a thousand people, where all their hair is black, all eyes black, and they eat with pieces of wood.'

He remembered how he had laughed with her. How could there be so many people in one land, all the same? 'There is still the danger he lied.'

'Then test him,' she had said. 'There's still time.'

Yes, he thought, there are four days to uncover the truth – five including Holy Day.

Tehran: 5:16 P.M. Now the Women's March was over.

It had begun that morning with the same air of expectancy that had enveloped Tehran for two days – when for the first time in history, women by themselves as a group were about to take to the streets in protest, to show their solidarity against any encroachment of their hard earned rights by the new rulers, even by the Imam himself.

'*The proper dress for a woman is the* hijab *that requires them to cover their hair and arms and legs and* zinaat – *their enticing parts.*'

'I chose to wear the chador as a protest against the Shah, Meshang,' Zarah, his wife, had screeched at him. 'I chose it! I did! I'll never wear a veil or chador or scarf against my will, never never never . . .'

'*Co-education introduced by the Satan Shah a few years ago will cease as in practice it has turned many of our schools into houses of prostitution.*'

'Lies, all lies! Ridiculous!' Sharazad had told Lochart. 'The truth must be shouted from the rooftops. It's not the Imam saying these things, it's the zealots surrounding him . . .'

662

'*The Satan Shah's heinous Marriage Protection Act is disapproved.*'

'Surely that's a mistake, Hussain,' the mullah's wife had said carefully. 'The Imam can't be saying that. It protects us against rejection by a husband, against polygamy, and grants us the right of divorce, gives us the vote and protects a wife's property . . .'

'*In our Islamic nation everyone will be governed only by the Koran and the Sharia. Women should not work, they must return to the home, stay in the home, to do their blessed, God-ordained duty to bear and bring up children and look after their Masters.*'

'By the Prophet, Erikki, as much as I wish to have your children and be the best wife to you,' Azadeh had said, 'I swear I cannot sit idly by and watch my less fortunate sisters be forced back into the Dark Ages without any freedom, or right. It's the fanatics, the zealots, not Khomeini who are trying to do this. I will march wherever I am . . .'

All over Iran women had prepared sympathy marches – in Qom, Isfahan, Meshed, Abadan, Tabriz, even small towns like Kowiss – but never in the villages. All over Iran there had been arguments and quarrels between most fathers and their daughters, most husbands and their wives, most brothers and their sisters, the same fights, pleadings, cursing, demands, promises, beggings, forbidding and, God protect us, even rebellions – covert and overt. And all over Iran was the same secret resolve of the women.

'I'm glad my Tommy's not here, that makes it so much easier,' Sharazad had told her reflection in the mirror this morning, the march due to begin at noon. 'I'm glad he's away because whatever he said, eventually I'd disobey him.' A tremor of excitement, pleasing and at the same time painful.

She was checking her makeup in the mirror a last time, just to make sure that the bruise around her left eye was well covered with powder. It hardly showed at all now. She smiled at herself, pleased with what she saw. Her hair was curled and flowing and she wore a warm green sweater and green skirt and nylons and Russian suede boots, and when she went out she had decided to wear a matching fur-lined coat and hat. Isn't green the colour of Islam? she thought happily, all her soreness forgotten.

Behind her the bed was littered with ski clothes and outer clothes that she had considered and discarded. After all, women have never protested as a group before so we should certainly look our best. What a pity it's not spring, then I could wear my light yellow silk dress and yellow hat and . . .

A sudden sadness took her. Her father had given her that dress for her birthday present last year, and the lovely pearl choker necklace. Poor dear Father! she thought, her anger welling. God curse the evil men who murdered him. God cast them into the pit for ever! God protect Meshang and all the family and my Tommy and let not zealots take away our freedoms.

Now there were tears in her eyes and she brushed them away. Insha'Allah, she thought. Father's in Paradise where the Faithful belong so there's no real reason to mourn. No. Only the wish to see justice done to the foul murderers. Murder! Uncle Valik. HBC. Annoush and the children. HBC! How I hate those letters! What's happened to Karim? She had heard nothing since Sunday and did not know if he was denounced, dead or free, or anything more about the telex – nothing to do but pray.

So she did. Again. And swept those problems out of her mind on to the shoulders of God and felt cleansed. As she put on her little fur-lined hat, the door opened and Jari hurried in also dressed in her best. 'It's time, Princess, her Highness Zarah has arrived, oh, how pretty you look!'

Filled with excitement, Sharazad picked up her coat and ran down the corridor, skirts flying, down the stairs to greet Zarah who waited for her in the hallway. 'Oh, you look beautiful, Zarah darling,' she said embracing her. 'Oh I thought Meshang'd stop you at the last minute!'

'He never had a chance,' Zarah said with a laugh, a cute fur hat jauntily on her head, 'I started on him yesterday at breakfast and continued all day and all night and this morning about the new sable coat that was absolutely necessary, that I absolutely must have or I would die of shame in front of my friends. He fled to the bazaar to escape and forgot all about the march. Come along, we mustn't be late, I've a taxi waiting. It's stopped snowing, the day promises to be fair, though it's chilly.'

There were already three other women in the taxi, friends and cousins, two proudly wearing jeans and high heels and ski jackets, hair free, one with a ski hat, and they were all as excited as if they were going to a barbecue picnic in the old days. None of them noticed the muttering disapproval of the taxidriver, or cared about him. 'To the university,' Zarah ordered, and then they all chatted together like so many birds. When they were still two streets away from the university gates where the march was to assemble, the taxi had to stop, the crush was so huge.

Where a few hundred had been expected, there were thousands and more arriving every minute from all points of the compass. Young old, highborn lowborn, literate illiterate, peasant patrician, rich poor – jeans, skirts, pants, boots, shoes, rags, furs – and over all the same fervour, even from those who had come wearing chador. Some of the more militant were already making speeches and a few were shouting slogans:

'No chador by force . . .

'Unity, struggle, victory . . .

'Women unite, we refuse to be forced into purdah or chador . . .'

'I was at Doshan Tappeh against the Immortals – we didn't fight and suffer to give ourselves over to despotism . . .'

'Death to despotism by any name . . .'

'Yesssssss! Hooray for women,' Sharazad shouted, 'down with enforcing the chador and veils and scarves!' Like the others she was caught up in the excitement. Zarah paid the man and gave him a good tip, turned back joyfully, linking arms with Sharazad and Jari, and none of them heard the taxidriver call out, 'Whores, all of you,' as he drove away.

The crowds were milling around, not knowing what to do, most of them overwhelmed by the enormous numbers and variety of women and costumes and ages – even a few men joining them enthusiastically. 'We're protesting, Zarah, we're really here, aren't we?'

'Oh, yes, Sharazad! And there're so many of us . . .'

Shouting in the noise, listening to a well-dressed woman, a well-known Tehrani lawyer and activist and champion of women's rights, Namjeh Lengehi – a few groups of men, students and teachers, for and against, along with a few mullahs, all against, also listening: 'Some mullahs say we women can't be judges, should not be educated and must wear chador. For three generations we have been unveiled, for three generations we have had the right of education and for one generation the right to vote. God is Great . . .'

'God is Great,' a thousand echoed her.

'Some of us are more fortunate than others, some better educated than others, some even better educated than some men. Some of these know modern law better, even Koranic law better than some men – why shouldn't those women be judges? Why?'

'No reason! Those women for judges,' Zarah called out with a hundred others, drowning the mullahs and their supporters who shouted, 'Sacrilege!'

When she could make herself heard, Namjeh Lengehi continued; 'We supported the Ayatollah with all our hearts . . .' More cheers interrupted her, a great outpouring of affection. 'We bless him for what he

665

did and we fought as best we could, side by side with men, shared their suffering and the prisons and helped with the revolution and threw out the despot and now we are free, Iran is free from his yoke and from foreign yoke. But that does not give anyone, mullahs, even the Ayatollah, the right to turn back the clock . . .'

Huge cries of, 'No! No! No despots. Votes for women! No to despotism under any cover! Lengehi for the Majlis! Lengehi for minister of education!'

'Oh, Zarah, isn't this wonderful?' Sharazad said. 'Have you ever voted?'

'No, darling, of course not. But that doesn't mean I don't want the right to if I wanted to. A hundred times I told Meshang that of course I'd ask him who to vote for, but I still want to go into the booth myself, by myself, if I choose to!'

'You're right!' Sharazad turned and shouted, 'Up the revolution. God is Great! God is Great! Lengehi for the High Court! Women for judges! We insist on our rights . . .'

Teymour, the PLO-trained Iranian who had taken over Sharazad's apartment and had been sent to monitor the march and identify the militants, recognised her from photographs he had seen there. His anger increased. 'Women to obey God's law,' he shouted. 'No women judges! Women to God's work!' But he was drowned by the thousands and no one paid any attention to him.

No one knew how the march began. They just seemed to set off and soon they massed the avenues, wall to wall, stopping all traffic, surging happily along, an irresistible force. Those at the stalls and at the windows and balconies of houses adjoining stared at the marchers open-mouthed.

Most men were shocked. 'Look at that one, the young whore with the green coat that flaps open in front to show her cleft, look, look there! God curse her for tempting me . . .'

'Look at that one with the pants like an outer skin.'

'Where! Ah, I see her, the blue pants! God protect us! You can see every ripple of her *zinaat*! She's inviting it! Like the one she's linking arms with – the green coat! Harlot! Hey, harlot down there, you just want a cock – that's what you all want . . .'

Men watched and seethed. Lust followed the march.

Women watched and wondered. More and more forgot their shopping or their stalls and joined their sisters, aunts, mothers, grandmothers, fearlessly removing their head scarves and veils and chador – wasn't this the capital, weren't they Tehranis, the elite of Iran, no longer villagers? It was different here, not like back in the village where they would never have dared to shout slogans and pull away veils and scarves and chadors. 'Women unite, God is Great, God is Great! Victory, unity, struggle. Equality for women! The vote! No to despotism, any despotism . . .'

Ahead of the marchers, behind them, around them, on highways and in the side streets, groups of men began forming. Those for and those against. Arguments became more and more violent – Koranic law demanded that Muslims resist any attempt against Islam. A few scuffles began. One man pulled a knife and died, another man's knife in his back. A few guns and woundings. Many clashes. Scattered riots between liberals and fundamentalists, between leftists and Green Bands. A few heads broken, another man dead and, here and there, children caught in the crossfire, some dead, others cowering behind parked cars.

Ibrahim Kyabi, the student Tudeh leader who had escaped the ambush the night Rakoczy had been caught, ran into the street and picked up one of the petrified children while his friends gave him covering fire. He made the safety of the corner. Once he was sure the little girl was unhurt, he shouted to his friends, 'Follow me,' knowing they were outnumbered here and took to his heels. There were six of them and they ran into the alleys and side streets. Soon they were safe and heading for Roosevelt Avenue. The Tudeh had been ordered to avoid open clashes with Green Bands, to march with the women, too infiltrate the ranks and to proselytise. He was glad to be active again after being in hiding.

Within half an hour of Rakoczy's being captured, he had reported the betrayal to his controller at Tudeh HQ. The man had told him not to go home, to shave off his beard and keep out of sight in a safe house near the University: 'Do nothing until the Women's Protest on Tuesday. Join that with your cell as planned, then leave for Kowiss the next day – that should keep you safe for a while.'

'What about Dimitri Yazernov?' – the only name he knew Rakoczy by.

'Don't worry, we'll get him away from the scum. Tell me again what the men looked like.'

Ibrahim had told them the little he had remembered about the Green Bands and the ambush. And then he had asked, 'How many men will come with me to Kowiss?'

'You and two others should be enough for one rotten mullah.'

Yes, he thought again, more than enough – soon my father will be avenged. His hands tightened on the M16 that had been stolen a week ago from Doshan Tappeh's armoury. 'Freedom!' he shouted, and hurried into Roosevelt to join the front ranks of the protest, his friends spreading out.

A hundred yards farther back, an open truck filled with youths trundled along slowly, surrounded by the thousands, waving and shouting encouragement. These were airmen out of uniform. Among them was Karim Peshadi. For hours he had been searching the marchers for Sharazad but had not seen her. He and the others were stationed at Doshan Tappeh where order and discipline were almost nonexistent, komitehs holding sway, issuing orders and counterorders, others coming from the High Command subservient to Prime Minister Bazargan, others from the Revolutionary Komiteh – and others over the radio where, from time to time Ayatollah Khomeini would speak and set the law.

As all other pilots and officers throughout the land, Karim had been ordered before a komiteh to be cross-questioned on his record, his political beliefs and his pre-revolutionary connections. His record was good, and he could truthfully swear he supported Islam, Khomeini and the Revolution. But the spectre of his father hung over him and he had carefully buried his desire for revenge in his most secret heart. So far he had been untouched.

The night before last he had tried to sneak into the Doshan Tappeh Tower to find the HBC clearance book but had been turned back. Tonight he was going to try again – he had sworn himself not to fail. I mustn't fail, he thought, Sharazad depends on me . . . oh, Sharazad, thou who gives my life meaning even though thou art forbidden.

Anxiously he hunted for her among the marchers, knowing she was somewhere here. Last night he and a group of his friends heard a violently incendiary broadcast by an ayatollah fundamentalist, opposing the women's protest and demanding there be counter-protests by 'Believers'. He had become gravely concerned for Sharazad, his sisters, and relations whom he knew would also be marching. His friends were equally concerned for theirs. So this morning they had taken the truck and had joined the protest. With guns.

'Equality for women,' he shouted. 'Democracy for ever! Islam for ever! Democracy and law and Islam for ev—' The words died.

Ahead of the march men had formed a thick barrier across the road now, barring progress. The women to the forefront saw their anger and raised fists. Instinctively the women in the first half dozen ranks tried to slow but could not. The swell of the thousands pushed them inexorably forward.

'Why're those men so angry?' Sharazad asked, her happiness evaporating, the crush increasing.

'They're just misguided, villagers mostly,' Namjeh Lengehi said bravely. 'They want us as slaves, slaves, don't be afraid! God is Great . . .'

'Link arms,' Zarah shouted, 'they can't stop us! Allahhh-u Akbarrr . . .'

Among the men blocking the road was the man who had, at Evin Jail, led Jared Bakravan to slaughter. He had recognised Sharazad in the vanguard. 'God is Great,' he muttered in ecstasy, his words drowned by the shouting, 'God made me an instrument to send the evil bazaari to hell and now God has given into my hands the harlot daughter.' His eyes gloated over her, seeing her naked on the couch, spread, breasts proud, her eyes filled with lust, mouth moist, lips moist, hearing her begging him, 'Take me, take me, quick, for you no money, let me have it, all of it, quick, quick, fill me, stretch me, for you anything, quick quick . . . oh, Satan, help me suck God out of his organ . . .'

He jerked out his knife, loins throbbing, manhood proud, and hurled himself at her, 'God is Greatttt . . .' His rush was sudden and he went across the space separating him from the women, knocked down half a dozen, reaching for her, but slipped and fell in his excitement, his knife flailing. Those he wounded were screaming and he fought to his feet and groped for her, seeing only her, her eyes wide, terror-stricken, knife in his fist ready to gut her, now only three paces away, two paces, one . . . his head filled with her perfume, the stench of the Devil Incarnate. The death blow began but never touched her and he knew Satan had sent an evil djinn his way – there was a monstrous burning in his chest, his eyes became sightless, and he died with the Name of God on his lips.

Sharazad stared down at the crumpled figure, Ibrahim beside her now, the gun in his hand, shouts and more screams and a roar of rage from a thousand women pressing behind them.

Another shot, another man fell screaming. 'Forward for God!' Lengehi cried over her own fear, her shout taken up by Ibrahim who tugged at Sharazad: 'Don't be afraid, forward for women . . .'

She saw his confidence and for a moment mistook him for her cousin Karim so similar in height and build and face, then her terror and hatred at what had happened burst and she shouted, 'Forward for my father . . . Down with zealots and Green Bands . . . down with murderers!' She grabbed Zarah. 'Come on! Forward!' and she linked arms with her and with Ibrahim, her saviour, so like Karim they could be brothers, and they started off again. More men were running to the front in support, the truck with the airmen among them.

Another knife wielder came at them screaming.

'God is Great . . .' Sharazad shouted, the horde with her, and before he was neutralised the screaming youth had slashed Namjeh Lengehi's arm. Inexorably, the front ranks pressed forward, both sides roaring 'God is Great,' both sides equally sure they were right. Then the opposition crumpled.

'Let them march,' a man shouted. 'Our women are there too, some of them, there's too many of them . . . too many . . .' Those men in the way backed off, others stood aside and now the way was clear. A roar of triumph from the marchers: 'Allahhh-u Akbarrr . . . God is with us, sisters!'

'Forward,' Sharazad shouted again and the march continued again. Those who were wounded were carried or helped to the side, the others streaming onward. Now the protest became orderly again. No more opposition barred their way though many men watched sullenly from the side lines, Teymour and others photographing the militants.

'It's a success,' Namjeh Lengehi said weakly, still walking in the front rank, a scarf staunching the flow of blood from her arm. 'We're a success – even the Ayatollah will know of our resolution. Now we can go home to our husbands and families. We've done what we wanted and now we can go home.'

'No,' Sharazad said, her face pale and dirt stained, not yet over her fright. 'We must march tomorrow and tomorrow and tomorrow until the Imam agrees publicly to no enforced chador and to our rights.'

'Yes,' Ibrahim said, 'if you stop now the mullahs will crush you!'

'You're right, agha, oh how can I thank you for saving us?'

'Yes,' Zarah said, still shaken. 'We will march tomorrow or those . . . those madmen will destroy us!'

The march proceeded without more trouble and this was the pattern in the cities, initial trouble then the peaceful protest continued.

But in the villages and small towns the march was stopped before it began and far to the south, in Kowiss, there was silence in the town square except for the sound of the lash and the screams. When the march had formed the mullah Hussain had been there. 'This protest is forbidden. All women not dressed according to the *hijab* are liable to sentencing for public nakedness against the dictates of the Koran.' Only half a dozen women among two hundred were dressed in overcoats and western dress.

'Where does it say in the Koran we disobey God if we don't wear chador?' one woman shouted. She was the bank manager's wife, and had been to Tehran University. Her dress was modest, she wore a skirt and her hair was free.

' "Oh, Prophet, say to thy wives and daughters and believing women, that they draw their veils closer to them . . ." Iran is an Islamic State . . . the first in history. The Imam has decreed *hijab*. It is *hijab*. Go and dress properly at once!'

'But Believers in other lands aren't required chador, nor do their leaders or husbands force them into it.'

' "Men are managers of the affairs of women, for that God has preferred in bounty one of them over another . . . righteous women are therefore obedient . . . Those that you fear may be rebellious, admonish; banish them to their couches and beat them. If they then obey you, look not for any way against them." Go and cover your hair!'

'I will not. For more than forty years Iranian women have been unveiled an –'

'Forty lashes will curb your disobedience! God is Great!' Hussain motioned to one of his acolytes. Others grabbed the woman and pinioned her. The whip soon ripped through the material on her back to the jeers of the men who watched. When it was over, the senseless woman was carried away. By other women. The rest went back to their homes. In silence.

There Hussain looked at his wife, her stomach huge with child. 'How dare you join a protest of harlots and loose women?'

'It . . . it was an error,' she said, petrified. 'It was a great error.'

'Yes. You will have no food, only water for two days to remind you. If you weren't with child you would have had the same, in the square.'

'Thank you for being merciful, God bless you and keep you. Thank you . . .'

At Tehran Airport: 6:40 P.M. With Andrew Gavallan beside him, McIver drove out of the freight area on to the feeder road heading for their 125, ETLL, that was parked on the freight apron a quarter of a mile away. She had been back from Tabriz for about an hour and was refuelled and ready for the return flight across the Gulf. When she had landed, Armstrong had thanked them profusely for allowing them the use of the airplane. So had Colonel Hashemi Fazir.

'Captain Hogg says the 125 returns on Saturday, Mr. Gavallan,' Hashemi had said politely. 'I wonder if you'd be kind enough to give us a ride to Tabriz. Just one way this time, no need to wait, we can make our own way back.'

671

'Of course, Colonel,' Gavallan had said pleasantly, not feeling pleasant about either of the men. When he had arrived from Al Shargaz this morning McIver had told him at once, in private, why it was necessary to cooperate. 'I'll deal with that right smartly with Talbot, Mac,' he had said, furious at the blackmail. 'CID or Special Branch notwithstanding!'

They all held their hands over their ears as a giant USAAF transport taxied past on its way to the distant takeoff point – one of the many U.S. government charters arranged to evacuate remaining American service and embassy personnel except for a skeleton staff. Superheated air from the jets tore up snow and washed over them. When Gavallan could make himself heard, he said, 'Talbot left a message for you, Mr. Armstrong, and asked if you'd see him as soon as possible.' He saw the glance between the two men and wondered what it meant.

'Did he say where, sir?'

'No, just to see him as soon as possible.' Gavallan was distracted by a big black limo hurrying towards them, the official Khomeini flag on the bumper. Two hard-faced men got out and saluted Hashemi deferentially, held the door open for him.

'Until Saturday – thank you again, Mr. Gavallan.' Hashemi got into the back.

'How do we contact you, Colonel – in case there's a change in plan?'

'Through Robert. He can get a message to me. Is there anything I can do for you? Here at the airport?'

McIver said quickly, 'About refuelling – thanks for arranging it – if you could see we get the same rapid service every time I'd appreciate it. And also our clearances serviced.'

'I'll take care of it. You *will* have priority for Saturday's flight. If there's anything else, please ask Robert. Come on, Robert!'

Robert Armstrong said, 'Thanks again, Mr. Gavallan, see you Saturday, if not before.'

When Talbot had come by earlier to find out Armstrong's arrival time back from Tabriz, Gavallan had taken him aside and almost howled with rage over the blackmail. 'Bless my soul,' Talbot had said, shocked. 'What a ghastly accusation, terribly un-British, Andrew, if I may say so! I understand Robert went to a considerable amount of trouble to try to extricate you, your company, Duncan, and Lochart – good man that, lovely wife, sad about her father – from a disaster that can raise its ugly head at any moment. Couldn't it?' He smiled sweetly. 'I understand Robert *asked*, only asked for a modest favour, easy to provide, no skin off the old nose, Andrew.'

'He's Special Branch, ex CID Hong Kong, isn't he?'

Talbot's smile had never lost its sweetness. 'I wouldn't know. But he does seem to want to do you a favour. Rather nice of him. Isn't it?'

'Does he have the clearance book?'

'I wouldn't know anything about that sort of thing.'

'Who's this Colonel Fazir anyway?'

Talbot had lit a cigarette. 'Just a friend. Good man to have as a friend.'

'I can see that. He arranged refuelling and immediate priority clearance as though he was God all bloody mighty.'

'Oh, he's not, by no means not. Near it, but not God. God's English,' Talbot had chuckled. 'And a woman. No masculine intelligence could balls up the world so satisfactorily. A word to the wise, old chap: I hear, following the advice of your fellow board member, Ali Kia, *they* intend nationalising all foreign aircraft companies, particularly yours, if ever they can get the piece of paper together.'

Gavallan was shocked. 'Who're "*they*"?'

'Does it matter?'

After Talbot had driven off, Gavallan had stalked back into the office that was well staffed today. Not back to normal yet but getting there – radio op, telex op, office manager, stores men and some secretaries, no women present today as all had requested permission to go on the protest march. 'Mac, let's take a walk.'

McIver glanced up from a pile of reports. 'Sure,' he said, seeing the gravity.

They had had no time to talk privately yet, impossible in or near the office, the walls all thin and ears wide open everywhere. From the moment Gavallan had arrived hours ago, the two of them had been busy going through the cash ledgers, contracts still in service, contracts held up or cancelled, and the current status of each base – all of them reporting, guardedly, minimum work and maximum harassment – the only good piece of news McIver's permission to export the three 212s and even that was not sure. Yet.

The two men went out on to the freight apron. A JAL jumbo roared into the sky. 'They say there're still a thousand Japanese techs kicking their heels at Iran-Toda,' McIver said absently.

'Their consortium's taking a hell of a beating. Today's *Financial Times* said their override's already half a billion dollars, no way they can get finished this year and no way to pull out – that and the world shipping glut must be hurting Toda badly.' Gavallan saw there was no one near. 'At least our capital investment's mobile, Mac, most of it.'

McIver looked up at him, seeing the craggy face, grey bushy eyebrows, brown eyes. 'That's the reason for "imperative conference"?'

'One of them.' Gavallan told him what Talbot had said. ' "Nationalised"! That means we lose the lot – unless we do something about it. Genny's right, you know. We've got to do it ourselves.'

'I don't think it's possible. Did she tell you that?'

'Of course, but I think we can. Try this on for size: say today's Day One. All non-essential personnel begin to quit Iran for reassignment or on leave; we get out all the spares we can – either by our 125 or on regular airlines when they start up again – as obsolete, redundant, for repair or as personal baggage. Zagros Three retreats to Kowiss, Tabriz closes "temporarily" and Erikki's 212 goes to Al Shargaz, then to Nigeria along with Tom Lochart from Zagros, and one 212 from Kowiss. You close HQ in Tehran and relocate at Al Shargaz to run operations and control our three remaining bases of Lengeh, Kowiss and Bandar-e Delam "pending return to normality" from there – we're all still under our government orders to evacuate all nonessential personnel.'

'Right, but th –'

'Let me finish, laddie. Say we can do the prep and planning and all that in thirty days. Day Thirty-one's D-day. At an exact time on D-day – or D plus One or Two depending on weather or Christ knows what – we radio a code word from Al Shargaz. Simultaneously all remaining pilots and choppers take off, head across the Gulf for Al Shargaz. There we remove the rotors, stow the choppers into 747 freighters I've chartered from somewhere, they'll fly to Aberdeen and Bob's your bloody uncle,' Gavallan ended with a beam.

McIver stared at him blankly. 'You're crazy! You're stark raving bonkers, Chinaboy. It's got so many holes in it . . . you're bonkers.'

'Name one hole.'

'I can give you fifty, firs –'

'One at a time, laddie, and remember your bloody pressure. How is it by the way – Genny asked me to ask?'

'Fine, and don't you bloody start. First, the same takeoff time: choppers from the different bases'll take vastly different times because of the distances they have to go. Kowiss'll have to refuel – can't make it in one hop, even across the Gulf.'

'I know that. We make separate subplans for each of the three bases. Each base commander makes his own plan how to get out – we're responsible for them on arrival. Scrag can zip across the Gulf easy, so can Rudi from Bandar-e De –'

'He can't. Neither Rudi from Bandar-e Delam nor Starke from Kowiss can make it in one hop all along the Gulf to Al Shargaz – even if they can get across the Gulf in the first place. They'll have to go through Kuwait, Saudi and Emirate airspace and God only knows if they'd impound us, jail, or fine us – Al Shargaz too, no reason why they should be any different.' McIver shook his head. 'The Sheikdoms can't do anything without proper Iranian clearances – rightly they're all scared fartless Khomeini's revolution'll spread to them, they've all got big Shi'a minorities, they're no match for Iranian navy army and air force if he decides to get mean.'

'One point at a time,' Gavallan said calmly. 'You're right about Rudi and Starke's planes, Mac. But say they have permission to fly through all those territories?'

'Eh?'

'I telexed all Gulf ATC's individually for permission and I've got telex confirms that S-G choppers in transit can go through.'

'Yes, but –'

'But one point at a time, laddie. Next, say all our planes were back on British registry – they are British, they *are* our planes, we're paying for them, we own them whatever the partners try to pull. On British registry they're not subject to Iran or anything to do with them. Right?'

'Once they're out, yes, but you won't get Iran Civil Aviation Authority to agree to the transfer, therefore you can't get them back to British.'

'Say I could get them on to British registry regardless.'

'How in the hell would you do that?'

'Ask. You ask, laddie, you ask the registry lads in London to do it. In fact I did before I left London. "Things are kind of ropey in Iran," says I. "Totally snafu, old boy, yes," says they. "I'd like you to put my birds back on British registry, temporarily," says I, "I may bring them out until the situation normalises – of course, the powers that be in Iran'd approve but I can't get a bloody piece of paper signed there at the moment, you know how it is." "Certainly, old boy," says they, "same with our bloody government – any bloody government. Well, they are your kites, no doubt about that, it's tiny bit irregular but I imagine it might be all right. Are you going to the Old Boys' beer-up?" '

McIver had stopped walking and stared at him in wonder. 'They agreed?'

'Not yet, laddie. Next?'

'I've got a hundred "nexts" but!' Irritably McIver started walking again, too cold to stand still.

'But?'

'But if I give them one at a time, you'll give me an answer – and a *possible* solution but they still won't all add up.'

'I agree with Genny, we have to do it ourselves.'

'Maybe, but it has to be feasible. Another thing: we've permission to take three 212s out, maybe we could get out the rest.'

'The three aren't out yet, Mac. The partners, let alone ICAA, won't let us out of their grasp. Look at Guerney – all their choppers are impounded. Forty-eight, including all their 212s – maybe 30 million dollars rotting, they can't even service them.' They glanced at the runway. An RAF Hercules was landing. Gavallan watched it. 'Talbot told me by the end of the week all British army, navy and air force technicians and training personnel'll be out and at the embassy they'll be down to three, including him. It seems that in the fracas at the U.S. embassy – someone sneaked in under cover of it, blew open safes, grabbed ciphers . . .'

'They still had secret stuff there?' McIver was appalled.

'Seems so. Anyway, Talbot said the infiltration caused every diplomatic sphincter in Christendom – and Sovietdom – and Arabdom – to palpitate. All embassies are closing. The Arabs are the most fractured of all – not one of the oil sheiks wants Khomeinism across the Gulf and they're anxious, willing and able to spend petro dollars to prevent it. Talbot said: "Fifty pounds against a bent hat pin that Iraq privately now has an open chequebook, the Kurds likewise, and anyone else who's Arab, pro-Sunni and anti-Khomeini. The whole Gulf's poised to explode." '

'But meanwhile th –'

'Meanwhile, he's not so bullish as he was a few days ago and not so sure that Khomeini's going to quietly retire to Qom. "It's jolly old Iran for the Iranians, old boy, so long as they're Khomeini and mullahs," he said. "It's in with Khomeinism if the leftists don't assassinate him first and out with the old. That means us." ' Gavallan banged his gloved hands together to keep the circulation going. 'I'm bloody frozen. Mac, it's clear from the books we're in dead trouble here. We've got to look after ourselves.'

'It's a hell of a risk. I think we'd lose some birds.'

'Only if luck's against us.'

'You're asking a lot from luck, Andy. Remember those two mechanics in Nigeria who've been jailed for fourteen years just for servicing a 125 that was flown out illegally?'

'That was Nigeria, the mechanics stayed behind. We'd leave no one.'

'If just one expat gets left behind, he'll be grabbed, tossed into jail and become a hostage for all of us and all the birds – unless you're prepared to let him take the flak. If you're not, they'll use him to force us back and when we come back they'll be plenty bloody irritated. What about all our Iranian employees?'

Doggedly Gavallan said, 'If luck's against us it'll be a disaster whatever we do. I think we should come up with a proper plan with all the final details, *in case*. That'll take weeks – and we'd better keep the planning super secret, just between us.'

McIver shook his head. 'We'll have to consult Rudi, Scragger, Lochart and Starke, if you want to be serious.'

'Just as you say.' Gavallan's back was aching and he stretched. 'Once it's properly planned . . . We don't have to press the final tit until then.'

They walked for a while in silence, snow crunching loudly. Now they were almost at the end of the apron. 'We'd be asking a hell of a lot from the lads,' McIver said.

Gavallan did not appear to have heard him. 'We can't just leave fifteen years of work, can't toss away all our savings, yours, Scrag's, and everything,' he said. 'Our Iran's gone. Most of the fellows we've worked with over the years have fled, are in hiding, dead – or against us if they like it or not. Work's at a minimum. We've got nine choppers working out of twenty-six here. We're not being paid for the little we do, or any back money. I think that's all a write-off.'

Doggedly McIver said, 'It's not as bad as you think. The partn –'

'Mac, you've got to understand I can't write off the money we're owed *plus our birds and spares* and stay in business. I can't. Our thirteen 212s are worth 13 million U.S., nine 206s another one point three odd million, three Aouettes another million and a half, and 3 million of spares – 20 million give or take a few dollars. I can't write that off. Ian warned me Struan's need help this year, there's no spare cash – Linbar's made some bad decisions and . . . well you know what I think of him and he of me. But he's still taipan. I can't write off Iran, can't get out of the new contracts for the X63s, can't battle Imperial who're presently clobbering us in the North Sea with their unfair bloody bookkeeping with taxpayers' money. Can't be done.'

'You'd be asking a hell of a lot from the lads, Chinaboy.'

'And from you, Mac, don't forget you. It'd be a team effort, not just for me, for them too – because it's that or go under.'

'Most of our lads can get jobs with no problem. The market's desperate for trained chopper pilots who're oilers.'

'So what? Bet you all of them'd rather be with us, we look after them,

677

pay top dollar, we've the best safety record – S-G's the best chopper company on earth, and they know it! You and I know we're part of the Noble House, by God, and that means something too.' Gavallan's eyes suddenly lit up with his irrepressible twinkle. 'It'd be a great caper if we pulled it off. I'd love to shove Linbar's nose in it. When the time comes we'll ask the lads. Meanwhile all systems go, eh, laddie?'

'All right,' McIver said without enthusiasm. 'For the planning.'

Gavallan looked at him. 'I know you too well, Mac. Soon you'll be raring to go and I'll be the one saying, Hold it, what about so-and-so . . .'

But McIver wasn't listening. His mind was trying to formulate a plan, despite the impossibility of it – except for the British registry. Could that make the difference?

'Andy, about the plan. We'd better have a code name.'

'Genny says we should call it "Whirlwind" – that's what we're mixed up in.'

BOOK THREE

Thursday
February 22, 1979

Northwest of Tabriz: 11:20 A.M. From where he sat on the cabin steps of his parked 212 high up on the mountainside, Erikki could see deep into Soviet Russia. Far below the river Aras flowed eastward towards the Caspian, twisting through gorges and marking much of the Iran – USSR border. To his left he could see into Turkey, to soaring Mount Ararat, 15,500 feet, and the 212 was parked not far from the cave mouth where the secret American listening post was.

Was, he thought with grim amusement. When he had landed here yesterday afternoon – the altimeter reading 8,562 feet – the motley bunch of leftist fedayeen fighters he had brought with him had stormed the cave, but the cave was empty of Americans and when Cimtarga inspected it he found all the important equipment destroyed and no cipher books. Much evidence of a hasty departure, but nothing of real value to be scavenged. 'We'll clean it out anyway,' Cimtarga had said to his men, 'clean it out like the others.' To Erikki he had added, 'Can you land there?' He pointed far above where the complex of radar masts stood. 'I want to dismantle them.'

'I don't know,' Erikki had said. The grenade Ross had given him was still taped in his left armpit – Cimtarga and his captors had not searched him – and his pukoh knife was still in its back scabbard. 'I'll go and look.'

'*We'll* look, Captain. We'll look together,' Cimtarga had said with a laugh. 'Then you won't be tempted to leave us.'

He had flown him up there. The masts were secured to deep beds of concrete on the northern face of the mountain, a small flat area in front of them. 'If the weather's like today it'd be okay, but not if the wind picks up. I could hover and winch you down.' He had smiled wolfishly.

Cimtarga had laughed. 'Thanks, but no. I don't want an early death.'

'For a Soviet, particularly a KGB Soviet, you're not a bad man.'

'Neither are you – for a Finn.'

Since Sunday, when Erikki had begun flying for Cimtarga, he had come to like him – not that you can like or trust any KGB, he thought. But the man had been polite and fair, had given him a correct share of all food. Last night he had split a bottle of vodka with him and had given him the best place to sleep. They had slept in a village twenty kilometres south on carpets on a dirt floor. Cimtarga had said that though this was all mostly Kurdish territory the village was secretly fedayeen and safe. 'Then why keep the guard on me?'

'It's safe for us, Captain – not safe for you.'

The night before last at the Khan's palace when Cimtarga and guards had come for him just after Ross had left, he had been driven to the air base and, in darkness and against IATC regulations, had flown to the village in the mountains north of Khvoy. There, in the dawn, they had collected a full load of armed men and had flown to the first of the two American radar posts. It was destroyed and empty of personnel like this one. 'Someone must have tipped them we would be coming,' Cimtarga said disgustedly. '*Matyeryebyets* spies!'

Later Cimtarga told him locals whispered that the Americans had evacuated the night before last, whisked away by helicopters, unmarked and very big. 'It would have been good to catch them spying. Very good. Rumour says the bastards can see a thousand miles into us.'

'You're lucky they weren't here, you might have had a battle and that would have created an international incident.'

Cimtarga had laughed. 'Nothing to do with us – nothing. It was the Kurds again, more of their rotten work – bunch of thugs, eh? They'd've been blamed. Rotten *yezdvas*, eh? Eventually the bodies would have been found – on Kurdish land. That'd be proof enough for Carter and his CIA.'

Erikki shifted on the plane's steps, his seat chilled by the metal, depressed and weary. Last night he had slept badly again – nightmares about Azadeh. He hadn't slept well since Ross had appeared.

You're a fool, he thought for the thousandth time. I know, but that doesn't help. Nothing seems to help. Maybe the flying's getting to you. You've been putting in too many hours in bad conditions, too much night flying. Then there's Nogger to worry about – and Rakoczy to brood about and the killings. And Ross. And most of all Azadeh. Is she safe?

He had tried to make his peace with her about her Johnny Brighteyes the next morning. 'I admit I was jealous. Stupid to be jealous. I swore by the ancient gods of my forefathers that I could live with your memory of him – I can and I will,' he had said, but saying the words had not cleansed him. 'I just didn't think he'd be so . . . so much a man and so . . . so dangerous. That kukri would be a match for my knife.'

'Never, my darling. Never. I'm so glad you're you and I'm me and we're together. How can we get out of here?'

'Not all of us, not together at the same time,' he had told her honestly. 'The soldiers'd be better to get out while they can. With Nogger, and them, and while you're here – I don't know, Azadeh. I don't know how we can escape yet. We'll have to wait. Maybe we could get into Turkey . . .'

He looked eastwards into Turkey now, so close and so far with Azadeh still in Tabriz – thirty minutes by air to her. But when? If we got into Turkey and if my chopper wasn't impounded, and if I could refuel we could fly to Al Shargaz, skirting the border. If if if! Gods of my ancestors, help me!

Over vodka last night Cimtarga had been as taciturn as ever, but he had drunk well and they had shared the bottle glass to glass to the last drop. 'I've another for tomorrow night, Captain.'

'Good. When will you be through with me?'

'It'll take two to three days to finish here, then back to Tabriz.'

'Then?'

'Then I'll know better.'

But for the vodka Erikki would have cursed him. He got up and watched the Iranians piling the equipment for loading. Most of it seemed to be very ordinary. As he strolled over the broken terrain, his boots crunching the snow, his guard went with him. Never a chance to escape. In all five days he had never had a single chance. 'We enjoy your company,' Cimtarga had said once, reading his mind, his Oriental eyes crinkling.

Above, he could see some men working on the radar masts, dismantling them. Waste of time, he thought. Even I know there's nothing special about them. 'That's unimportant, Captain,' Cimtarga had said. 'My Master enjoys bulk. He said get everything. More is better than less. Why should you worry – you're paid by the hour.' Again the laugh, not taunting.

Feeling his neck muscles taut, Erikki stretched and touched his toes and, in that position, let his arms and head hang freely, then waggled his head in as big a semicircle as he could, letting the weight of his head stretch the tendons and ligaments and muscles and smooth out the kinks, forcing nothing, just using the weight. 'What're you doing?' Cimtarga asked, coming up to him.

'It's great for neck ache.' He put his dark glasses back on – without them the reflected light from the snow was uncomfortable. 'If you do it twice a day you'll never get neck ache.'

'Ah, you get neck aches too? Me, I'm always getting them – have to go to a chiropractor at least three times a year. That helps?'

'Guaranteed. A waitress told me about it – carrying trays all day gives them plenty of neck and backache, like pilots; it's a way of life. Try it and you'll see.' Cimtarga bent over as Erikki had done and moved his head. 'No, you're doing it wrong. Let your head and arms and shoulders hang freely, you're too stiff.'

Cimtarga did as he was told and felt his neck crack and the joints ease and when he raised himself again, he said, 'That's wonderful, Captain. I owe you a favour.'

'It's a return for the vodka.'

'It's worth more than a bottle of vod –'

Erikki stared at him blankly as blood spurted out of Cimtarga's chest in the wake of the bullet that pierced him from behind, then came a thraaakkk followed by others as tribesmen poured out of ambush from the rocks and trees, shrieking battle cries and 'Allah-u Akbarrr', firing as they came. The attack was brief and violent and Erikki saw Cimtarga's men going down all over the plateau, quickly overwhelmed. His own guard, one of the few who was carrying a weapon, had opened up at the first bullet but was hit at once, and now a bearded tribesman stood over him and gleefully finished him with the rifle butt. Others charged into the cave. More firing, then silence again.

Two men rushed him and he put his hands up, feeling naked and foolish, his heart thundering. One of these turned Cimtarga over and shot him again. The other bypassed Erikki and went to the cabin of the 212 to make sure no one was hiding there. Now the man who had shot

686

Cimtarga stood in front of Erikki, breathing hard. He was small and olive-skinned and bearded, dark eyes and hair and wore rough garments and stank.

'Put your hands down,' he said in heavily accented English. 'I am Sheik Bayazid, chief here. We need you and helicopter.'

'What do you want with me?'

Around them the tribesmen were finishing off the wounded and stripping the dead of anything of value. 'CASEVAC.' Bayazid smiled thinly at the look on Erikki's face. 'Many of us work the oil and rigs. Who is this dog?' He motioned at Cimtarga with his foot.

'He called himself Cimtarga. He was a Soviet. I think also KGB.'

'Of course Soviet,' the man said roughly. 'Of course KGB – all Soviets in Iran KGB. Papers, please.' Erikki gave him his ID. The tribesman read it and nodded half to himself. And, to Erikki's further surprise, handed it back. 'Why you flying Soviet dog?' He listened silently, his face darkening as Erikki told him how Abdollah Khan had entrapped him. 'Abdollah Khan no man to offend. The reach of Abdollah the Cruel very wide, even in the lands of the Kurds.'

'You're Kurds?'

'Kurds,' Bayazid said, the lie convenient. He knelt and searched Cimtarga. No papers, a little money that he pocketed, nothing else. Except the holstered automatic and ammunition which he also took. 'Have you full fuel?'

'Three-quarter full.'

'I want go twenty miles south. I direct you. Then pick up CASEVAC, then go Rezaiyeh, to hospital there.'

'Why not Tabriz – it's much closer.'

'Rezaiyeh in Kurdistan. Kurds are safe there, sometimes. Tabriz belong to our enemies: Iranians, Shah or Khomeini no difference. Go Rezaiyeh.'

'All right. The Overseas Hospital would be best. I've been before and they've a helipad. They're used to CASEVACs. We can refuel there – they've chopper fuel, at least they had in . . . the old days.'

Bayazid hesitated. 'Good. Yes. We go at once.'

'And after Rezaiyeh – what then?'

'And then, if serve us safely, perhaps you released to take your wife from the Gorgon Khan.' Sheik Bayazid turned away and shouted for his men to hurry up and board the airplane. 'Start up, please.'

'What about him?' Erikki pointed at Cimtarga. 'And the others?'

'The beasts and birds soon make here clean.'

It took them little time to board and leave, Erikki filled with hope

687

now. No problem to find the site of the small village. The CASEVAC was an old woman. 'She is our chieftain,' Bayazid said.

'I didn't know women could be chieftains.'

'Why not, if wise enough, strong enough, clever enough, and from correct family? We Sunni Muslims – not leftists or heretic Shi'a cattle who put mullahs between man and God. God is God. We leave at once.'

'Does she speak English?'

'No.'

'She looks very ill. She may not last the journey.'

'As God wants.'

But she did last the hour's journey and Erikki landed on the helipad. The Overseas Hospital had been built, staffed and sponsored by foreign oil companies. He had flown low all the way, avoiding Tabriz and military airfields. Bayazid had sat up front with him, six armed guards in the back with their high chieftain. She lay on the stretcher, awake but motionless. In great pain but without complaining.

A doctor and orderlies were at the helipad seconds after touchdown. The doctor wore a white coat with a large red cross on the sleeve over heavy sweaters, and he was in his thirties, American, dark rings around bloodshot eyes. He knelt beside the stretcher as the others waited in silence. She groaned a little when he touched her abdomen even though his hands were healing hands. In a moment he spoke to her gently in halting Turkish. A small smile went over her and she nodded and thanked him. He motioned to the orderlies and they lifted the stretcher out of the cabin and carried her away. At Bayazid's order, two of his men went with her.

The doctor said to Bayazid in halting dialect, 'Excellency, I need name and age and . . .' he searched for the word, 'history, medical history.'

'Speak English.'

'Good, thank you, agha. I'm Doctor Newbegg. I'm afraid she's near the end, agha, her pulse is almost zero. She's old and I'd say she was hemorrhaging – bleeding – internally. Did she have a fall recently?'

'Speak slower, please. Fall? Yes, yes, two days ago. She slip in snows and fell against a rock, on her side against a rock.'

'I think she's bleeding inside. I'll do what we can but . . . sorry, I can't promise good news.'

'Insha' Allah.'

'You're Kurds?'

'Kurds.' More firing, closer now. They all looked off to where the sound came from. 'Who?'

688

'I don't know, just more of the same, I'm afraid,' the doctor said uneasily. 'Green Bands against leftists, leftists against Green Bands, against Kurds – many factions – and all're armed.' He rubbed his eyes. 'I'll do what I can for the old lady – perhaps you'd better come with me, agha, you can give me the details as we go.' He hurried off.

'Doc, do you still have fuel here?' Erikki called after him.

The doctor stopped and looked at him blankly. 'Fuel? Oh, chopper fuel? I don't know. Gas tank's in back.' He went up the stairs to the main entrance, his white coat-tail flapping.

'Captain,' Bayazid said, 'you will wait till I return. Here.'

'But the fuel? I ca –'

'Wait here. Here.' Bayazid rushed after the doctor. Two of his men went with him. Two stayed with Erikki.

While Erikki waited, he checked everything. Tanks almost empty. From time to time cars and lorries arrived with wounded to be met by doctors and medics. Many eyed the chopper curiously but none approached. The guards made sure of that.

During the flight here Bayazid had said: 'For centuries we Kurds try for independent. We a separate people, separate language, separate customs. Now perhaps 6 million Kurds in Azerbaijan, Kurdistan, over Soviet border, this side of Iraq, and Turkey.' He had almost spat the word. 'For centuries we fight them all, together or singly. We hold the mountains. We are good fighters. Salah-al-din – he was Kurd. You know of him?' Salah-al-din – Saladin – was the chivalrous Muslim opponent of Richard the Lionheart during the crusades of the twelfth century, who made himself Sultan of Egypt and Syria and captured the Kingdom of Jerusalem in A.D. 1187 after smashing the allied might of the Crusaders.

'Yes, I know of him.'

'Today other Salah-al-dins among us. One day we recapture again all the Holy places – after Khomeini, betrayer of Islam, is stamped into joub.'

Erikki had asked, 'You ambushed Cimtarga and the others and wiped them out just for the CASEVAC?'

'Of course. They enemy. Yours and ours.' Bayazid had smiled his twisted smile. 'Nothing happens in our mountains without us knowing. Our chieftain sick – you nearby. We see the Americans leave, see scavengers arrive, and you were recognised.'

'Oh? How?'

'Redhead of the Knife? The Infidel who kills assassins like lice, then given a Gorgon whelp as reward! CASEVAC pilot?' The dark, almost

689

sloe eyes were amused. 'Oh, yes, Captain, know you well. Many of us work timber as well as oil – a man must work. Even so, it's good you not Soviet or Iranian.'

'After the CASEVAC will you and your men help me against Gorgon Khan?'

Bayazid had laughed. 'Your blood feud is your blood feud, not ours. Abdollah Khan is for us, at the moment. We not go against him. What you do is up to God.'

It was cold in the hospital forecourt, a slight wind increasing the chill factor. Erikki was walking up and down to keep his circulation going. I've got to get back to Tabriz. I've got to get back and then somehow I'll take Azadeh and we'll leave for ever.

Firing nearby startled him and the guards. Outside the hospital gates, the traffic slowed, horns sounding irritably, then quickly snarled. People began running past. More firing and those trapped in their vehicles got out and took cover or fled. Inside the gates the expanse was wide, the 212 parked on the helipad to one side. Wild firing now, much closer. Some glass windows on the top floor of the hospital blew out. The two guards were hugging the snow behind the plane's undercarriage, Erikki fuming that his airplane was so exposed and not knowing where to run or what to do, no time to take off, and not enough fuel to go anywhere. A few ricochets, and he ducked down as the small battle built outside the walls. Then it died as quickly as it had begun. People picked themselves up out of cover, horns began sounding, and soon the traffic was as normal and as spiteful as ever.

'Insha' Allah,' one of the tribesmen said, then cocked his rifle and came on guard. A small petrol truck was approaching from behind the hospital, driven by a young Iranian with a broad smile. Erikki went to meet it.

'Hi, Cap,' the driver said happily, his accent heavily New York. 'I'm to gas you up. Your fearless leader, Sheik Bayazid fixed it.' He greeted the tribesmen in Turkish dialect. At once they relaxed and greeted him back. 'Cap, we'll fill her brimming. You got any temp tanks, or special tanks?'

'No. Just the regular. I'm Erikki Yokkonen.'

'Sure. Red the Knife.' The youth grinned. 'You're kinda a legend in these parts. I gassed you once, maybe a year ago.' He stuck out his hand. 'I'm "Gasoline" Ali – Ali Reza that is.'

They shook hands and, while they talked, the youth began the refuel. 'You went to American school?' Erikki asked.

'Hell, no. I was sort of adopted by the hospital, years ago, long

690

before this one was built, when I was a kid. In the old days the hospital worked out of one of the Golden Ghettos on the east side of town – you know, Cap, U.S. Personnel Only, an ExTex depot.' The youth smiled, screwed the tank cap back carefully, and started to fill the next. 'The first doc who took me in was Abe Weiss. Great guy, just great. He put me on the payroll, taught me about soap and socks and spoons and toilets – hell, all sorts of gizmos un-Iranian for street rats like me, with no folks, no home, no name and no nothing. He used to call me his hobby. He even gave me my name. Then, one day, he left.'

Erikki saw the pain in the youth's eyes, quickly hidden. 'He passed me on to Doc Templeton, and he did the same. At times it's kinda hard to figure where I'm at. Kurd but not, Yank but not – Iranian but not, Jew but not, Muslim but not Muslim.' He shrugged. 'Kinda mixed up, Cap. The world, everything. Huh?'

'Yes.' Erikki glanced towards the hospital. Bayazid was coming down the steps with his two fighters beside orderlies carrying a stretcher. The old woman was covered now, head to foot.

'We leave soon as fuel,' Bayazid said shortly.

'Sorry,' Erikki said.

'Insha'Allah.' They watched the orderlies put the stretcher into the cabin. Bayazid thanked them and they left. Soon the refuel was complete.

'Thanks, Mr. Reza.' Erikki stuck out his hand. 'Thanks.'

The youth stared at him. 'No one's ever called me mister before, Cap, never.' He pummelled Erikki's hand. 'Thanks – any time you want gas, you got it.'

Bayazid climbed in beside Erikki, fastened his belt, and put on the headset, the engines building. 'Now we go to village from whence we came.'

'What then?' Erikki asked.

'I consult new chieftain,' Bayazid said, but he was thinking, this man and the helicopter will bring a big ransom, perhaps from the Khan, perhaps from the Soviets, or even from his own people. My people need every rial we can get.

Near Tabriz One – in the Village of Abu Mard: 6:16 P.M. Azadeh picked up the bowl of rice and the bowl of horisht, thanked the headman's wife, and walked across the dirty, refuse-fouled snow to the hut that was set a little apart. Her face was pinched, her cough not good. She knocked, then went through the low doorway. 'Hello, Johnny. How do you feel? Any better?'

'I'm fine,' he said. But he wasn't.

The first night they had spent in a cave not far away, huddled together, shivering from the cold. 'We can't stay here, Azadeh,' he had said in the dawn. 'We'll freeze to death. We'll have to try the base.' They had gone through the snows and watched from hiding. They saw the two mechanics and even Nogger Lane from time to time – and the 206 – but all over the base were armed men. Dayati, the base manager, had moved into Azadeh and Erikki's cabin – he, his wife and children. 'Sons and daughters of dogs,' Azadeh hissed, seeing the wife wearing a pair of her boots. 'Perhaps we could sneak into the mechanics' huts. They'll hide us.'

'They're escorted everywhere; I'll bet they've even guards at night. But who are the guards, Green Bands, the Khan's men, or who?'

'I don't recognise any of them, Johnny.'

'They're after us,' he said, feeling very low, the death of Gueng preying on him. Both Gueng and Tenzing had been with him since the beginning. And there was Rosemont. And now Azadeh. 'Another night in the open and you'll have had it, we'll have had it.'

'Our village, Johnny. Abu Mard. It's been in our family for more than a century. They're loyal, I know they are. We'd be safe there for a day or two.'

'With a price on my head? And you? They'd send word to your father.'

'I'd ask them not to. I'd say Soviets were trying to kidnap me and you were helping me. That's true. I'd say that we needed to hide until my husband comes back – he's always been very popular, Johnny, his CASEVACs saved many lives over the years.'

He looked at her, a dozen reasons against. 'The village's on the road, almost right on the road an –'

'Yes, of course, you're quite right and we'll do whatever you say, but it sprawls away into the forest. We could hide there – no one'd expect that.'

He saw her tiredness. 'How do you feel? How strong do you feel?'

'Not strong, but fine.'

'We could hike out, go down the road a few miles – we'd have to skirt the roadblock, it's a lot less dangerous than the village. Eh?'

'I'd . . . I'd rather not. I could try.' She hesitated, then said, 'I'd rather not, not today. You go on. I'll wait. Erikki may come back today.'

'And if he doesn't?'

'I don't know. You go on.'

692

He looked back at the base. A nest of vipers. Suicide to go there. From where they were on a rise, he could see as far as the main road. Men still manned the roadblock – he presumed Green Bands and police – a line of traffic backed up and waiting to leave the area. No one'll give us a ride now, he thought, not unless it's for the reward. 'You go to the village. I'll wait in the forest.'

'Without you they'll return me to my father – I know them, Johnny.'

'Perhaps they'll betray you anyway.'

'As God wants. But we could get some food and warmth, perhaps even a night's rest. In the dawn we could sneak away. Perhaps we could get a car or truck from them – the kalandar has an old Ford.' She stifled a sneeze. Armed men were not far away. More than likely there were patrols out in the forest – coming here they had had to detour to avoid one. The village's madness, he thought. To get around the roadblock'll take hours in daylight, and by night – we can't stay outside another night.

'Let's go to the village,' he said.

So they had gone yesterday and Mostafa, the kalandar, had listened to her story and kept his eyes away from Ross. News of their arrival had gone from mouth to mouth and in moments all the village knew and this news was added to the other, about the reward for the saboteur and kidnapper of the Khan's daughter. The kalandar had given Ross a disused, one-room hut with dirt floor and old mildewed carpets. The hut was well away from the road, on the far edge of the village, and he noticed the steel hard eyes and matted hair and stubbled beard – his carbine and kukri and ammunition-heavy knapsack. Azadeh he invited into his home. It was a two-room hovel. No electricity or running water. The joub was the toilet.

At dusk last night, hot food and a bottle of water had been brought to Ross by an old woman.

'Thank you,' he said, his head aching and the fever already with him. 'Where is Her Highness?' The woman shrugged. She was heavily lined, pockmarked, with brown stubs of teeth. 'Please ask her to receive me.'

Later he was sent for. In the headman's room, watched by the headman, his wife, some of his brood, and a few elders, he greeted Azadeh carefully – as a stranger might a highborn. She wore chador of course and knelt on carpets facing the door. Her face had a yellowish, unhealthy pallor, but he thought it might be from the light of the spluttering oil lamp. 'Salaam, Highness, your health is good?'

'Salaam, agha, yes, thank you, and yours?'

693

'There is a little fever I think.' He saw her eyes flick up from the carpet momentarily. 'I have medicine. Do you need any?'

'No. No, thank you.'

With so many eyes and ears what he wanted to say was impossible. 'Perhaps I may greet you tomorrow,' he said. 'Peace be upon you, Highness.'

'And upon you.'

It had taken him a long time to sleep. And her. With the dawn the village awoke, fires were stoked, goats milked, vegetable horisht set to stew – little to nourish it but a morsel of chicken, in some huts a piece of goat or sheep, the meat old, tough and rancid. Bowls of rice but never enough. Food twice a day in good times, morning and before last light. Azadeh had money and she paid for their food. This did not go unnoticed. She asked that a whole chicken be put into tonight's horisht to be shared by the whole household, and she paid for it. This, too, did not go unnoticed.

Before last light she had said, 'Now I will take food to him.'

'But, Highness, it's not right for you to serve him,' the kalandar's wife said. 'I'll carry the bowls. We can go together if you wish.'

'No, it's better if I go alone beca –'

'God protect us, Highness. Alone? To a man not your husband? Oh no, that would be unseemly, that would be very unseemly. Come, I will take it.'

'Good, thank you. As God wants. Thank you. Last night he mentioned fever. It might be plague. I know how Infidels carry vile diseases that we are not used to. I only wished to save you probable agony. Thank you for sparing me.'

Last night everyone in the room had seen the sheen of sweat on the Infidel's face. Everyone knew how vile Infidels were, most of them Satan worshippers and sorcerers. Almost everyone secretly believed that Azadeh had been bewitched, first by the Giant of the Knife, and now again by the saboteur. Silently the headman's wife had handed Azadeh the bowls and she had walked across the snow.

Now she watched him in the semidarkness of the room that had as window a hole in the adobe wall, no glass, just sacking covering most of it. The air was heavy with the smell of urine and waste from the joub outside.

'Eat, eat while it's hot. I can't stay long.'

'You okay?' He had been lying under the single blanket, fully dressed, dozing, but now he sat crosslegged and alert. The fever had abated somewhat with the help of drugs from his survival kit but his stomach was upset. 'You don't look so good.'

She smiled. 'Neither do you. I'm fine. Eat.'

He was very hungry. The soup was thin but he knew that was better for his stomach. Another spasm started building but he held on and it went away. 'You think we could sneak off?' he said between mouthfuls, trying to eat slowly.

'You could, I can't.'

While he had been dozing all day gathering his strength, he had tried to make a plan. Once he had started to walk out of the village. A hundred eyes were on him, everyone watching. He went to the edge of the village then came back. But he had seen the old truck. 'What about the truck?'

'I asked the headman. He said it was out of order. Whether he was lying or not I don't know.'

'We can't stay here much longer. A patrol's bound to come here. Or your father will hear about us or be told. Our only hope is to run.'

'Or to hijack the 106 with Nogger.'

He looked at her. 'With all those men there?'

'One of the children told me that they went back to Tabriz today.'

'You're sure?'

'Not sure, Johnny.' A wave of anxiety went over her. 'But there's no reason for the child to lie. I, I used to teach here before I was married – I was the only teacher they had ever had and I know they liked me. The child said there's only one or two left there.' Another chill swirled up and made her weak. So many lies, so many problems the last few weeks, she thought. Is it only weeks? So much terror since Rakoczy and the mullah burst in on Erikki and me after our sauna. Everything so hopeless now. Erikki, where are you? she wanted to scream, where are you?

He finished the soup and the rice and picked at the last grain, weighing the odds, trying to plan. She was kneeling opposite him and she saw his matted hair and filth, his exhaustion and gravity. 'Poor Johnny,' she murmured and touched him. 'I haven't brought you much luck, have I?'

'Don't be silly. Not your fault – none of this is.' He shook his head. 'None of it. Listen, this's what we'll do: we'll stay here tonight, tomorrow after first light we'll walk out. We'll try the base – if that doesn't work then we'll hike out. You try to get the headman to help us by keeping his mouth shut, his wife too. The rest of the villagers should behave if he orders it, at least to give us a start. Promise them a big reward when things are normal again, and here . . .' He reached into his pack into the secret place, found the gold rupees, ten of them. 'Give him five, keep the other five for emergency.'

'But . . . but what about you?' she said, wide-eyed and filled with hope at so much potential pishkesh.

'I've ten more,' he said, the lie coming easily. 'Emergency funds, courtesy of Her Majesty's Government.'

'Oh, Johnny, I think we've a chance now – this is so much money to them.'

They both glanced at the window as a wind picked up and rustled the sacking that covered it. She got up and adjusted it as best she could. Not all the opening could be covered. 'Never mind,' he said. 'Come and sit down.' She obeyed, closer than before. 'Here. Just in case.' He handed her the grenade. 'Just hold the lever down, pull the pin out, count three, and throw. Three, not four.'

She nodded and pulled up her chador and carefully put the grenade into one of her ski jacket pockets. Her tight ski pants were tucked into her boots. 'Thanks. Now I feel better. Safer.' Involuntarily, she touched him and wished she hadn't for she felt the fire. 'I'd . . . I'd better go. I'll bring you food at first light. Then we'll leave.'

He got up and opened the door for her. Outside it was dark. Neither saw the figure scuttle away from the window, but both felt eyes feeding on them from every side.

'What about Gueng, Johnny? Do you think he'll find us?'

'He'll be watching, wherever he is.' He felt a spasm coming. ''Night, sweet dreams.'

'Sweet dreams.'

They had always said it to each other in the olden times. Their eyes touched and their hearts and both of them were warmed and at the same time filled with foreboding. Then she turned, the darkness of her chador making her at once almost invisible. He saw the door of the headman's hut open and she went in and then the door closed. He heard a truck grinding up the road not far off, then a honking car that went past and soon faded away. A spasm came and it was too much so he squatted. The pain was big but little came out and he was thankful that Azadeh had gone. His left hand groped for some snow and he cleansed himself. Eyes were still watching him, all around. Bastards, he thought, then went back into the hut and sat on the crude straw mattress.

In the darkness he oiled the kukri. No need to sharpen it. He had done that earlier. Lights glinted off the blade. He slept with it out of its scabbard.

At the Palace of the Khan: 11:19 P.M. The doctor held the Khan's wrist and checked his pulse again. 'You must have plenty of rest, Highness,' he said worriedly, 'and one of these pills every three hours.'

'Every three hours . . . yes,' Abdollah Khan said, his voice small and breathing bad. He was propped on cushions in the bed that was made up on deep carpets. Beside the bed was Najoud, his eldest daughter, thirty-five, and Aysha, his third wife, seventeen. Both women were white-faced. Two guards stood at the door and Ahmed knelt beside the doctor. 'Now . . . leave me.'

'I'll come back at dawn with the ambulance an –'

'No ambulance! I stay here!' The Khan's face reddened, another pain went through his chest. They watched him, hardly breathing. When he could speak he said throatily, 'I stay . . . here.'

'But Highness, you've already had one heart attack, God be thanked just a mild one,' the doctor said, his voice quavering. 'There's no telling when you could have . . . I've no equipment here; you should have immediate treatment and observation.'

'What . . . whatever you need, bring it here. Ahmed, see to it!'

'Yes Highness.' Ahmed looked at the doctor.

The doctor put his stethoscope and blood pressure equipment into his old-fashioned bag. At the door he slipped his shoes on and went out. Najoud and Ahmed followed him. Aysha hesitated. She was tiny and had been married two years and had a son and a daughter. The Khan's face had an untoward pallor and his breath rasped heavily. She knelt closer and took his hand but he pulled it away angrily, rubbing his chest, cursing her. Her fear increased.

Outside in the hall, the doctor stopped. His face was old and lined, older than his age, his hair white. 'Highness,' he said to Najoud, 'better he should be in hospital. Tabriz is not good enough. Tehran would be much better. He should be in Tehran though the trip there might . . . Tehran is better than here. His blood pressure's too high, it's been too high for years but, well, as God wants.'

'Whatever you need we'll bring here,' Ahmed said.

Angrily the doctor said, 'Fool, I can't bring an operating theatre and dispensary and aseptic surroundings!'

'He's going to die?' Najoud said, her eyes wide.

'In God's time, only in God's time. His pressure's much too high . . . I'm not a magician and we're so short of supplies. Have you any idea what caused the attack – was there a quarrel or anything?'

'No, no quarrel, but it was surely Azadeh. It was her again, that half-sister of mine.' Najoud began wringing her hands. 'It was her, running off with a saboteur yesterday morning, it wa –'

'What saboteur?' the doctor asked astonished.

'The saboteur everyone is looking for, the enemy of Iran. But I'm sure he didn't kidnap her, I'm sure she ran off with him – how could he kidnap her from inside the palace? She's the one who caused His Highness such rage – we've all been in terror since yesterday morning . . .'

Stupid hag! Ahmed thought. The insane, roaring outburst was because of the men from Tehran, Hashemi Fazir and the Farsi-speaking Infidel, and what they demanded of my Master and what my Master had to agree to. Such a little thing, giving over to them a Soviet, a pretended friend who was an enemy, surely no cause to explode? Clever of my Master to set everything into motion: the day after tomorrow the burnt offering comes back over the border into the web and the two enemies from Tehran come back into the web. Soon my Master will decide and then I will act. Meanwhile, Azadeh and the saboteur are safely bottled in the village, at my Master's will – word sent to him by the headman the first moment. Few men on earth are as clever as Abdollah Khan and only God will decide when he should die, not this dog of a doctor. 'Let us go on,' he said. 'Please excuse me, Highness, but we should fetch a nurse and drugs and some equipment. Doctor, we should hurry.'

The door at the far end of the corridor opened. Aysha was even paler. 'Ahmed, His Highness wants you for a moment.'

When they were alone, Najoud caught the doctor by the sleeve and whispered, 'How bad is His Highness? You must tell me the truth. I've got to know.'

The doctor lifted his hands helplessly. 'I don't know, I don't know. I've been expecting worse than this for . . . for a year or more. The attack was mild. The next could be massive or mild, in an hour or a year, I don't know.'

Najoud had been in a panic ever since the Khan had collapsed a couple of hours before. If the Khan died, then Hakim, Azadeh's brother, was his legitimate heir – Najoud's own two brothers had died in infancy. Aysha's son was barely a year old. The Khan had no living brothers, so his heir should be Hakim. But Hakim was in disgrace and disinherited so there would have to be a regency. Her husband, Mahmud, was senior of the sons-in-law. He would be regent, unless the Khan ordered otherwise.

Why should he order otherwise? she thought, her stomach once more

698

a bottomless pit. The Khan knows I can guide my husband and make us all strong. Aysha's son – shaw, a sickly child, as sickly as the mother. As God wants, but infants die. He's not a threat, but Hakim – Hakim is.

She remembered going to the Khan when Azadeh had returned from school in Switzerland: 'Father, I bring you bad tidings but you must know the truth. I overheard Hakim and Azadeh. Highness, she told him she'd been with child but with the help of a doctor had cast it out.'

'*What?*'

'Yes . . . yes, I heard her say it.'

'*Azadeh could not . . . Azadeh would not, could not do that!*'

'Question her – I beg you do not say from where you heard it – ask her before God, question her, have a doctor examine her, but wait, that's not all. Against your wishes, Hakim's still determined to become a pianist and he told her he was going to run away, asking Azadeh to come with him to Paris "then you can marry your lover", he said, but she said, Azadeh said, "Father will bring you back, he'll force us back. He'll never permit us to go without his prior permission, never." Then Hakim said, "I *will* go. I'm not going to stay here and waste my life. I'm going!" Again she said, "Father will never permit it, never." "Then better he's dead," Hakim said and she said, "I agree." '

'*I – I don't – believe it!*'

Najoud remembered the face gone purple, and how terrified she had been. 'Before God,' she had said, 'I heard them say it, Highness, before God. Then they said we must plan, we m—' She had quailed as he shouted at her, telling her to tell it exactly.

'Exactly he said, Hakim said, "a little poison in his halvah, or in a drink, we can bribe a servant, perhaps we could bribe one of his guards to kill him or we could leave the gates open at night for assassins – there are a hundred ways for any one of a thousand enemies to do it for us, everyone hates him. We must think and be patient . . ." '

It had been easy for her to weave her spell, deeper and deeper into the fabrication so that soon she was believing it as she believed it now. Except for the protestation 'Before God' it would be the truth.

God will forgive me, she told herself confidently as she always told herself. God will forgive me. Azadeh and Hakim have always hated us, the rest of the family, wanted us dead, outcast, to take all our heritage unto themselves, they and their witch of a mother who cast an evil spell over Father to turn his face from us for so many years. Eight years he was under the spell – Azadeh this and Azadeh that, Hakim this and Hakim that. Eight years he dismissed us and our mother, his first wife, took no notice of me, carelessly married me to this clod, Mahmud, this foul-smelling, now impotent, vile snoring clod, and so ruined my life. I hope my husband dies, eaten by worms, but not before he becomes Khan so my son will become Khan after him.

Father must get rid of Hakim before he dies. God keep him alive to do that – he must do it before he dies – and Azadeh must be humbled, cast out, destroyed too – even better, caught in her adultery with the saboteur, oh yes, then my revenge would be complete.

Friday
February 23, 1979

Near Tabriz One, at the Village of Abu Mard: 6:17 A.M. In the dawn, the face of another Mahmud, the Islamic-Marxist mullah, was contorted with rage. 'Have you lain with this man?' he shouted. 'Before God have you lain with him?'

Azadeh was on her knees in front of him, panic-stricken. 'You've no right to burst into th –'

'Have you lain with this man?'

'I . . . I am faithful to my . . . my husband,' she gasped. It was only seconds ago that she and Ross had been sitting on the carpets in the hut, hastily eating the meal she had brought him, happy together, ready for immediate departure. The headman had gratefully and humbly accepted his pishkesh – four gold rupees to him and one she had secretly given to his wife – telling them to sneak out of the village by the forest side the moment they had finished eating, blessing her – then the door had burst open, aliens had rushed them, overpowering him and dragging them both into the open, shoving her at Mahmud's feet and battering Ross into submission. 'I'm faithful, I swear it. I'm faithf –'

703

'Faithful? Why aren't you wearing chador?' he had shouted down at her, most of the village collected around them now, silent and afraid. Half a dozen armed men leaned on their weapons, two stood over Ross who was face downward in the snow, unconscious, blood trickling from his forehead.

'I was . . . I was wearing chador but I . . . I took it off while I was eat –'

'You took off your chador in a hut with the door closed eating with a stranger? What else had you taken off?'

'Nothing, nothing,' she said in more panic, pulling her unzipped parka closer about her, 'I was just eating and he's not a stranger but an old friend of mi . . . old friend of my husband,' she corrected herself hastily but the slip had not gone unnoticed. 'Abdollah Khan is my father and you have no r –'

'Old friend? If you're not guilty you've nothing to fear! Before God, have you lain with him? Swear it!'

'Kalandar, send for my father, send for him!' The kalandar did not move. All eyes were grinding into her. Helplessly she saw the blood on the snow, her Johnny groaned, coming around. 'I swear by God I'm faithful to my husband!' she screamed. The cry went over them all and into Ross's mind and seared him awake.

'Answer the question, woman! Is it yes or no! In the Name of God, have you lain with him?' The mullah was standing over her like a diseased crow, the villagers waiting, everyone waiting, the trees and the wind waiting – even God.

Insha'Allah.

Her fear left her. In its place was hate. She stared back at this man Mahmud as she got up. 'In the Name of God, I am and have always been faithful to my husband,' she pronounced, 'In the Name of God, yes, I loved this man, years upon years ago.'

Her words made many that were there shudder and Ross was appalled that she had admitted it.

'Harlot! Loose woman! You openly admit yourself guilty. You will be punished accord –'

'No,' Ross shouted over him. He dragged himself on to his knees and though the two mujhadin had guns at his head, he ignored them. 'It was not the fault of Her Highness. I – I'm to blame, only me, only me!'

'You'll be punished, Infidel, never fear,' Mahmud said, then turned to the villagers. 'You all heard the harlot admit fornication, you all heard the Infidel admit fornication. For her there is but one punishment – for the Infidel – what should happen to the Infidel?'

The villagers waited. The mullah was not their mullah, nor of their village, nor a real mullah but an Islamic-Marxist. He had come uninvited. No one knew why he had come here, only that he had appeared suddenly like the wrath of God with leftists – also not of their village. Not true Shi'as, only madmen. Hadn't the Imam said fifty times all such men were madmen who only paid lip service to God, secretly worshipping the Satan Marx-Lenin.

'Well? Should he share her punishment?'

No one answered him. The mullah and his men were armed.

Azadeh felt all eyes boring into her but she could no longer move or say anything. She stood there, knees trembling, the voices distant, even Ross's shouting, 'You've no jurisdiction over me – or her. You defile God's name . . .' as one of the men standing over him gave him a brutal shove to send him sprawling then put a booted foot on his neck pinioning him. 'Castrate him and be done with it,' the man said and another said, 'No, it was the woman who tempted him – didn't I see her lift her chador to him last night in the hut. Look at her now, tempting us all. Isn't the punishment for him a hundred lashes?'

Another said, 'He put his hands on her, take off his hands.'

'Good,' Mahmud said. 'First his hands, then the lash. Tie him up!'

Azadeh tried to cry out against this evil but no sound came out, the blood roaring in her ears now, her stomach heaving, her mind unhinged as they dragged her Johnny to his feet, fighting, kicking, to tie him spread-eagled between the rafters that jutted from the hut – remembering the time she and Hakim were children and he, filled with bravado, had picked up a stone and thrown it at a cat, and the cat squealed as it rolled over and got up, now injured, and tried to crawl away, squealing all the time until a guard shot it, but now . . . now she knew no one would shoot her. She lurched at Mahmud with a scream, her nails out, but her strength failed her and she fainted.

Mahmud looked down at her, 'Put her against that wall,' he said to some of his men, 'then bring her her chador.' He turned and looked at the villagers. 'Who is the butcher here? Who is the butcher of the village?' No one replied. His voice roughened. 'Kalandar, who is your butcher?'

Quickly the headman pointed to a man in the crowd, a small man with rough clothes. 'Abrim, Abrim is our butcher.'

'Go and get your sharpest knife,' Mahmud told him. 'The rest of you collect stones.'

Abrim went to do his bidding. As God wants, the others muttered to each other. 'Have you ever seen a stoning?' someone asked. A very old woman said, 'I saw one once. It was in Tabriz when I was a little girl.' Her voice quavered. 'The adulteress was the wife of a bazaari, yes, I remember she was the wife of a bazaari. Her lover was a bazaari too and they hacked off his head in front of the mosque, then the men stoned her. Women could throw stones too if they wanted but they didn't, I didn't see any woman do it. It took a long time, the stoning, and for years I heard the screams.'

'Adultery is a great evil and must be punished, whoever the sinner, even *her*. The Koran says a hundred lashes for the man . . . the mullah is the lawgiver, not us,' the kalandar said.

'But he's not a true mullah and the Imam has warned against their evil!'

'The mullah is the mullah, the law, the law,' the kalandar said darkly, secretly wanting the Khan humbled and this woman who had taught new, disturbing thoughts to their children destroyed. 'Collect the stones.'

Mahmud stood in the snow, ignoring the cold and the villagers and the saboteur who cursed and moaned and, frenzied, tried to fight out of his bonds, and the woman inert at the wall.

This morning, before dawn, coming to take over the base, he had heard about the saboteur and *her* being in the village. She of the sauna, he had thought, his anger gathering, she who had flaunted herself, the highborn whelp of the cursed Khan who pretends to be our patron but who has betrayed us and betrayed me, already engineering an assassination attempt on me last night, a burst of machine-gun fire outside the mosque after last prayer that killed many but not me. The Khan tried to have me murdered, me who is protected by the Sacred Word that Islam together with Marx-Lenin is the only way to help the world rise up.

He looked at her, seeing the long legs encased in blue ski pants, hair uncovered and flowing, breasts bulging against the blue and white ski jacket. Harlot, he thought, loathing her for tempting him. One of his men threw the chador over her. She moaned a little but did not come out of her stupor.

'I'm ready,' the butcher said, fingering his knife.

'First the right hand,' Mahmud said to his men. 'Bind him above the wrists.'

They bound strips of sacking ripped from the window tightly, villagers pressing forward to see better, and Ross used all his energy to stop his terror from bursting the dam, saw only the pockmarked face above the carving knife, the bedraggled moustache and beard, the eyes blank, the man's thumb testing the blade absently. Then his eyes focused. He saw Azadeh come out of her spell and he remembered.

'The grenade!' he shrieked. 'Azadeh, the grenade!'

She heard him clearly and fumbled for it in her side pocket as he shrieked again and again, further startling the butcher, dragging everyone's attention to himself. The butcher came forward cursing him, took hold of his right hand firmly, fascinated by it, moved it a little this way and that, the knife poised, deciding where to slice through the sinews of the joint, giving Azadeh just enough time to pick herself up and hurtle across the small space to shove him in the back, sending him flying and the knife into the snow, then to turn on Mahmud, pull the pin out, and stand there trembling, the lever held in her small hand.

'Get away from him,' she screamed. 'Get away!'

Mahmud did not move. Everyone else scattered, trampling some, rushing for safety across the square, cursing and shouting.

'Quick, over here, Azadeh,' Ross called out. '*Azadeh!*' She heard him through her mist and obeyed, backing towards him, watching Mahmud, flecks of foam at the corner of her mouth. Then Ross saw Mahmud turn and stalk off towards one of his men out of range and he groaned, knowing what would happen now. 'Quick, pick up the knife and cut me loose,' he said to distract her. 'Don't let go of the lever – I'll watch them for you.' Behind her he saw the mullah take the rifle from one of his men, cock it and turn towards them. Now she had the butcher's knife and she reached for the bonds on his right hand and he knew the bullet would kill or wound her, the lever would fly off, four seconds of waiting, and then oblivion for both of them – but quick and clean and no obscenity. 'I've always loved you, Azadeh,' he whispered and smiled and she looked up startled, and smiled back.

The rifle shot rang out, his heart stopped, then another and another, but they did not come from Mahmud but from the forest and now Mahmud was screaming and twisting in the snow. Then a voice followed the shots: 'Allah-u-Akbar! Death to all enemies of God! Death to all leftists, death to all enemies of the Imam!'

With a bellow of rage one of the mujhadin charged the forest and died. At once the rest fled, falling over themselves in their panic-stricken rush to hide. Within seconds the village square was empty but for the babbling howls of Mahmud, his turban no longer on his head. In the forest the leader of the four-man Tudeh assassination team who had tracked him since dawn silenced him with a burst of machine gun fire, then the four of them retreated as silently as they had arrived.

Blankly Ross and Azadeh looked at the emptiness of the village. 'It can't be . . . can't be . . .' she muttered, still deranged.

'Don't let go of the lever,' he said hoarsely. 'Don't let go of the lever. Quick, finish cutting me loose . . . quick!'

The knife was very sharp. Her hands were trembling and slow and she cut him once but not badly. The moment he was free he grabbed the grenade, his hands tingling and hurting, but held the lever, began to breathe again. He staggered into the hut, found his kukri that had been mixed up in the blanket in the initial struggle, stuck it in its scabbard and picked up his carbine. At the doorway he stopped. 'Azadeh, quick, get your chador and the pack and follow me.' She stared at him. 'Quick!'

She obeyed like an automaton, and he led her out of the village into the forest, grenade in his right hand, gun in the left. After a faltering run of a quarter of an hour, he stopped and listened. No one was following them. Azadeh was panting behind him. He saw she had the pack but had forgotten the chador. Her pale blue ski clothes showed clearly against the snow and trees. He hurried on again. She stumbled after him, beyond talking. Another hundred yards and still no trouble.

No place to stop yet. He went on, slower now, a violent ache in his side, near vomiting, grenade still ready, Azadeh flagging even more. He found the path that led to the back of the base. Still no pursuit. Near the rise, at the back of Erikki's cabin, he stopped, waiting for Azadeh, then his stomach heaved, he staggered and went down on his knees and vomited. Weakly, he got up and went up the rise to better cover. When Azadeh joined him she was labouring badly, her breath coming in great gulping pants. She slumped into the snow beside him, retching.

Down by the hangar he could see the 206, one of the mechanics washing it down. Good, he thought, perhaps it's being readied for a flight. Three armed revolutionaries were huddled on a nearby veranda under the overhang of a trailer in the lee of the small wind, smoking. No sign of life over the rest of the base, though chimney smoke came from Erikki's cabin and the one shared by the mechanics, and the cook house. He could see as far as the road. The roadblock was still there, men guarding it, some trucks and cars held up.

His eyes went back to the men on the veranda and he thought of Gueng and how his body had been tossed like a sack of old bones into the filth of the half truck under their feet, perhaps these men, perhaps not. For a moment his head ached with the strength of his rage. He glanced back at Azadeh. She was over her spasm, still more or less in shock, not really seeing him, a dribble of saliva on her chin and a streak of vomit. With his sleeve he wiped her face. 'We're fine now, rest a while then we'll go on.' She nodded and sank back on her arms, once more in her own private world. He returned his concentration to the base.

Ten minutes passed. Little change. Above, the cloud cover was a dirty blanket, snow heavy. Two of the armed men went into the office and he could see them from time to time through the windows. The third man paid little attention to the 206. No other movement. Then a cook came out of the cookhouse, urinated on the snow, and went back inside again. More time. Now one of the guards walked out of the office and trudged across the snow to the mechanics' trailer, an M16 slung over his shoulder. He opened the door and went inside. In a moment he came out again. With him was a tall European in flight gear and another man. Ross recognised the pilot Nogger Lane and the other mechanic. The mechanic said something to Lane, then waved and went back inside his trailer again. The guard and the pilot walked off towards the 206.

Everyone pegged, Ross thought, his heart fluttering. Awkwardly he checked his carbine, the grenade in his right hand inhibiting him, then put the last two spare magazines and the last grenade from his haversack into his side pocket. Suddenly fear swept into him and he wanted to run, oh, God help me, to run away, to hide, to weep, to be safe at home, away anywhere . . .

'Azadeh, I'm going down there now,' he forced himself to say. 'Get ready to rush for the chopper when I wave or shout. Ready?' He saw her look at him and nod and mouth yes, but he wasn't sure if he had reached her. He said it again and smiled encouragingly. 'Don't worry.' She nodded mutely.

Then he loosened his kukri and went over the rise like a wild beast after food.

He slid behind Erikki's cabin, covered by the sauna. Sounds of children and a woman's voice inside. Dry mouth, grenade warm in his hand. Slinking from cover to cover, huge drums or piles of pipe and saws and logging spares, always closer to the office trailer. Peering around to see the guard and the pilot nearing the hangar, the man on the veranda idly watching them. The office door opened, another guard came out, and beside him a new man, older, bigger, clean-shaven, possibly European, wearing better quality clothes and armed with a Sten gun. On the thick leather belt around his waist was a scabbard kukri.

Ross released the lever. It flew off. 'One, two, three,' and he stepped out of cover, hurled the grenade at the men on the veranda forty yards away and ducked behind the tank again, already readying another.

They had seen him. For a moment they were shock-still, then as they dropped for cover the grenade exploded, blowing most of the veranda and overhang away, killing one of them, stunning another, and maiming the third. Instantly Ross rushed into the open, carbine levelled, the new grenade held tightly in his right hand, index finger on the trigger. There was no movement on the veranda, but down by the hangar door the mechanic and pilot dropped to the snow and put their arms over their heads in panic, the guard rushed for the hangar and for an instant was in the clear. Ross fired and missed, charged the hangar, noticed a back door, and diverted for it. He eased it open and leaped inside. The enemy was across the empty space, behind an engine, his gun trained on the other door. Ross blew his head off, the firing echoing off the corrugated iron walls, then ran for the other door. Through it he could see the mechanic and Nogger Lane hugging the snow near the 206. Still in cover, he called to them. 'Quick! How many more hostiles're here?' No answer. 'For Christ sake, answer me!'

Nogger Lane looked up, his face white. 'Don't shoot, we're civilians, English – don't shoot!'

'How many more hostiles are here?'

'There . . . there were five . . . five . . . this one here and the rest in . . . in the office . . . I think in the office . . .'

Ross ran to the back door, dropped to the floor, and peered out at ground level. No movement. The office was fifty yards away – the only cover a detour around the truck. He sprang to his feet and charged for it. Bullets howled off the metal and then stopped. He had seen the automatic fire coming from a broken office window.

Beyond the truck was a little dead ground, and in the dead ground was a ditch that led within range. If they stay in cover they're mine. If they come out and they should, knowing I'm alone, the odds are theirs.

He slithered forward on his belly for the kill. Everything quiet, wind, birds, enemy. Everything waiting. In the ditch now. Progress slow. Getting near. Voices and a door creaking. Silence again. Another yard. Another. Now! He got his knees ready, dug his toes into the snow, eased the lever off the grenade, counted three, lurched to his feet, slipped but just managed to keep his balance, and hurled the grenade through the broken window, past the man standing there, gun pointing at him, and hit the snow again. The explosion stopped the burst of gunfire, almost blew out his own eardrums and once again he was on his feet charging the trailer, firing as he went. He jumped over a corpse and went on in still firing. Suddenly his gun stopped and his stomach turned over, until he could jerk out the empty mag and slam in the new. He killed the machine gunner and stopped.

Silence. Then a scream nearby. Cautiously he kicked the broken door away and went on to the veranda. The screamer was legless, demented, but still alive. Around his waist was the leather belt and kukri that had been Gueng's. Fury blinded Ross and he tore it out of the scabbard. 'You got that at the roadblock?' he shouted in Farsi.

'Help me help me help me . . .' A paroxysm of some foreign language then '. . . whoareyou who . . . help meeee . . .' The man continued screaming and mixed with it was, '. . . helpmehelpmeee yes I killed the saboteur . . . helpme . . .'

With a bloodcurdling scream Ross hacked downward and when his eyes cleared he was staring into the face of the head that he held up in his left hand. Revolted, he dropped it and turned away. For a moment he did not know where he was, then his mind cleared, his nostrils were filled with the stench of blood and cordite, he found himself in the remains of the trailer and looked around.

The base was frozen, but men were running towards it from the roadblock. Near the chopper Lane and the mechanic were still motionless in the snow. He rushed for them, hugging cover.

Nogger Lane and the mechanic Arberry saw him coming and were panic- stricken – the stubble-bearded, matted-haired, wild-eyed maniac tribesman mujhadin or fedayeen who spoke perfect English, whose hands and sleeves were bloodstained from the head that only moments ago they had seen him hack off with a single stroke and a crazed scream, the bloody short sword-knife still in his hand, another in a scabbard, carbine in the other. They scrambled to their knees, hands up. 'Don't kill us – we're friends, civilians, don't kill u –'

'Shut up! Get ready to take off. Quick!'

Nogger Lane was dumbfounded. 'What?'

'For Christ sake, hurry,' Ross said angrily, infuriated by the look on their faces, completely oblivious of what he looked like. 'You,' he pointed at the mechanic with Gueng's kukri. 'You, see that rise there?'

'Yes . . . yes, sir,' Arberry croaked.

'Go up there as fast as you can, there's a lady there, bring her down . . .' He stopped, seeing Azadeh come out of the forest edge and start running down the little hill towards them. 'Forget that, go and get the other mechanic, hurry for Christ's sake, the bastards from the road-block'll be here any minute. Go on, hurry!' Arberry ran off, petrified but more petrified of the men he could see coming down the road. Ross whirled on Nogger Lane. 'I told you to get started.'

711

'Yes . . . Yessir . . . that . . . that woman . . . that's not Azadeh, Erikki's Azadeh is it?'

'Yes – I told you to start up!'

Nogger Lane never got a 206 into takeoff mode quicker, nor did the mechanics ever move faster. Azadeh still had a hundred yards to go and already the hostiles were too close. So Ross ducked under the whirling blades and got between her and them and emptied the magazine at them. Their heads went down and they scattered, and he threw the empty in their direction with a screaming curse. A few heads came up. Another burst and another, conserving ammunition, kept them down, Azadeh close now but slowing. Somehow she made a last effort and passed him, reeling drunkenly for the back seat to be half pulled in by the mechanics. Ross fired another short burst retreating, groped into the front seat and they were airborne and away.

USSR

Caspian Sea

USSR

Khvoy

Tabriz
Mount
Sabalan

Bandar-e Pahlavi

Qazvin

Sadzevar

Meshed

Tehran

IRAN

AFGHANISTAN

Baghdad

Isfahan

Dez Dam

IRAQ

Abadan

Bandar-e Delam

KOWISS

PAKISTAN

KUWAIT

Kharg
Island

SAUDI ARABIA

Jellet

Zagros

Persian Gulf

Lengeh

Strait of Hormuz

CHAPTER

44

BAHRAIN

Siri

QATAR

Al Shargaz

Gulf of Oman

UAE

Kowiss Air Force Base: 5:20 P.M. Starke picked up the card he had been dealt and looked at it. The ace of spades. He grunted, superstitious like most pilots, but just slid it importantly into his hand. The five of them were in his bungalow playing draw poker: Freddy Ayre, Doc Nutt, Pop Kelly, and Tom Lochart who had arrived late yesterday from Zagros Three with another load of spares, continuing the evacuation but too late to fly back. Because of the order forbidding flying today, Holy Day, he was grounded here until dawn tomorrow. There was a wood fire in the grate, the afternoon cold. In front of all of them were piles of rials, the biggest in front of Kelly, the smallest Doc Nutt's.

'How many cards, Pop?' Ayre asked.

'One,' Kelly said without hesitation, discarded, and put the four he was keeping face downward on the table in front of him. He was a tall, thinnish man with a crumpled face, thin fair hair, ex-RAF, and in his early forties. 'Pop' was his nickname because he had seven children and another en route.

Ayre dealt the one card with a flourish. Kelly just stared at it for a

713

moment, then, without looking at it, slowly mixed it with the others, then very carefully and elaborately, picked up the hand, sneaked a look at the merest sliver of the top right corner, card by card, and sighed happily.

'Bullshit!' Ayre said and they all laughed. Except Lochart who stared moodily at his cards. Starke frowned, worried about him but very glad that he was here today. There was Gavallan's secret letter that John Hogg had brought on the 125 to discuss.

'A thousand rials for openers,' Doc Nutt said and everyone looked at him. Normally he would bet a hundred rials at the most.

Absently Lochart studied his hand, not interested in the game, his mind on Zagros – and Sharazad. The BBC last night had reported major clashes during the Women's Protest marches in Tehran, Isfahan and Meshed with more marches scheduled for today and tomorrow. 'Too rich for me,' he said and threw in his cards.

'See you, Doc, and up a couple of thousand,' Starke said and Doc Nutt's confidence vanished. Nutt had drawn two cards, Starke one, Ayre three.

Kelly looked at his straight, 4–5–6–7–8. 'Your two thousand, Duke, and up three!'

'Fold,' Ayre said instantly, throwing away two pairs, kings and tens.

'Fold,' Doc Nutt said with a sigh of relief, shocked with himself for being so rash initially and threw in the three queens he had been dealt, sure that Starke had filled a straight, flush or full house.

'Your three, Pop, and up thirty – thousand,' Starke said sweetly, feeling very good inside. He had split a pair of sixes to keep four hearts, going for a flush. The ace of spades had made it a very busted flush but a winning hand if he could bluff Kelly to back off.

All eyes were on Kelly. The room was silent. Even Lochart was suddenly interested.

Starke waited patiently, guarding his face and hands, uneasy about the air of confidence surrounding Kelly and wondering what he would do if Kelly raised him again, knowing what Manuela'd say if she found out he was preparing to put a week's pay on a busted flush.

She'd bust a girdle for starters, he thought and smiled.

Kelly was sweating. He had seen Starke's sudden smile. He had caught him bluffing once but that was weeks ago and not for thirty thousand, only four. I can't afford to lose a week's pay, still, the bugger could be bluffing. Something tells me old Duke's bluffing, and I could use an extra week's wages. Kelly rechecked his cards to make sure that his straight was a straight – of course it's a bloody straight for God's sake and Duke's bluffing! He felt his mouth begin to say, 'I'll see your thirty thousand,' but he stopped it and said instead, 'Up yours, Duke,' threw his cards in and everyone laughed. Except Starke. He picked up the pot, slid his cards into the deck, and shuffled them to make sure they could not be seen.

'I'll bet you were bluffing, Duke,' Lochart said and grinned.

'Me? Me with a straight flush?' Starke said innocently amid jeers. He glanced at his watch. 'I've got to do the rounds. Let's quit, continue after dinner, huh? Tom, you wanta come along?'

'Sure.' Lochart put on his parka and followed Starke outside. This was the best time of day for them in normal times – just before sundown, flying done, all the choppers washed and refuelled ready for tomorrow, a drink to look forward to, time to read a little, write a few letters, listen to some music, eat, call home, then bed.

The base checked out fine. 'Let's stroll, Tom,' Starke said. 'When're you going back to Tehran?'

'How about tonight?'

'Bad, huh?'

'Worse. I know Sharazad was on the Women's March even though I told her not to, then there's all the rest.'

Last night Lochart had told him about her father, and all about the loss of HBC. Starke had been appalled, still was, and once more blessed his luck that he had not known when he had been taken by Hussain and his Green Bands for questioning.

'Mac'll have got hold of Sharazad by now, Tom. He'll make sure she's okay.' When Lochart had arrived, they had got on to McIver on the HF, reception good for a change, and had asked him to see that she was safe. In a few minutes they would again have their one daily allowable radio link with Tehran HQ – 'You're restricted but only until we're back to normal when you can call all you want – any day now,' Major Changiz, the base commander, had said. And though they were monitored by the main tower across at the air force base, the link kept their sanity and gave an appearance of normality.

Starke said, 'After Zagros Three's cleaned out Sunday and you're all here, why not take the 206, Monday, first thing? I'll fix it with Mac.'

'Thanks, that'd be dandy.' Now that his own base was closed down, Lochart was nominally under Starke's command.

'Have you thought of getting the hell out, taking the 212 instead of Scot? Once he's out of the Zagros he should be okay. Or even better, both of you going? I'll talk to Mac.'

'Thanks but no, Sharazad can't leave her family just now.'

They walked on awhile. Night was coming fast, cold but crisp, the air smelling heavily of petrol from the huge refinery nearby that was still almost totally shut down and mostly dark, except for the tall stacks burning off oil vapour. On the base, lights were already on in most of their bungalows, hangars, and cookhouse – they had their own backup generators in case base power went out. Major Changiz had told Starke there was no chance the base generator system would be interfered with now: 'The revolution is completely over, Captain, the Imam is in charge.'

'And the leftists?'

'The Imam has ordered them eliminated, unless they conform to our Islamic state,' Major Changiz had said, his voice hard and ominous. 'Leftists, Kurds, Baha'is, aliens – any enemy. The Imam knows what to do.'

Imam. It was the same at Starke's questioning in front of Hussain's komiteh. Almost as though he was semidivine. Hussain had been the chief judge and prosecutor and the room, part of the mosque, crowded with hostile men of all ages, all Green Bands, five judges – no bystanders. 'What do you know of the escape of the enemies of Islam from Isfahan by helicopter?'

'Nothing.'

At once one of the other four judges, all young men, rough and hardly literate said, 'He's guilty of crimes against God and crimes against Iran as an exploiter for American Satanists. Guilty.'

'No,' Hussain said. 'This is a court of law, Koranic law. He is here to answer questions, not yet for crimes, not yet. He is not accused of any crime. Captain, tell us everything you have heard about the Isfahan crime.'

The air in the room had been fetid. Starke saw not a friendly face, yet all knew who he was, all knew about the battle against the fedayeen at Bandar-e Delam. His fear was a dull ache, knowing he was on his own now, at their mercy.

He took a breath and chose his words carefully. 'In the Name of God the Compassionate, the Merciful,' he said, starting as all the suras of the Koran begin, and an astonished stir went through the room. 'I know nothing myself, I have witnessed nothing to do with it or been part of it. I was in Bandar-e Delam at the time. To my knowledge none of my people have had anything to do with it. I only know what Zataki of Abadan told me when he returned from Isfahan. Exactly he said: "We heard that Tuesday some Shah supporters, all officers, fled south

716

in a helicopter piloted by an American. God curse all Satanists." That's all he said. That's all I know.'

'You're a Satanist,' one of the other judges interrupted triumphantly, 'you're American. You're guilty.'

'I am a person of the Book and I've already proved I'm no Satanist. If it wasn't for me many here would be dead.'

'If we'd died at the base we'd be in Paradise now,' a Green Band at the back of the room said angrily. 'We were doing the Work of God. It was nothing to do with you, Infidel.'

Shouts of agreement. Suddenly Starke let out a bellow of rage. 'By God and the Prophet of God,' he shouted, 'I'm a person of the Book, and the Prophet gave us special privileges and protections!' He was shaking with rage now, his fear vanished, hating this kangaroo court and their blindness and stupidity and ignorance and bigotry. 'The Koran says: "Oh, People of the Book, overstep not the bounds of truth in your religion; neither follow the desires of those who have already gone astray and caused many others to stray from the evenness of the path." I haven't,' he ended harshly, bunching his fists, 'and may God curse him who says otherwise.'

Astonished, they all stared at him, even Hussain.

One of the judges broke the silence. 'You . . . you quote the Koran? You read Arabic as well as speak Farsi?'

'No. No, I don't but th –'

'Then you had a teacher, a mullah?'

'No. No, I rea –'

'Then you're a sorcerer!' another shouted. 'How can you know the Koran if you had no teacher nor read Arabic, the holy language of the Koran?'

'I read it in English, my own language.'

Even greater astonishment and disbelief until Hussain spoke. 'What he says is true. The Koran is translated into many foreign languages.'

More astonishment. A young man peered at him myopically through cracked, thick-lensed glasses, his face pitted. 'If it is translated into other languages, Excellency, then why isn't it in Farsi for us to read – if we could read?'

Hussain said, 'The language of the Holy Koran is Arabic. To know the Holy Koran properly the Believer must read Arabic. Mullahs of all countries learn Arabic for this reason. The Prophet, whose Name be praised, was Arab. God spoke to him in that language for others to write down. To know the Holy Book truly it must be read as it was written.' Hussain turned his black eyes on Starke. 'A translation is always less than the original. Isn't it?'

Starke saw the curious expression. 'Yes,' he said, his intuition telling him to agree. 'Yes, yes, it is. I would like to be able to read the original.'

Another silence. The young man with glasses said, 'If you know the Koran so well that you can quote from it to us like a mullah, why aren't you Muslim, why aren't you a Believer?'

A rustle went through the room. Starke hesitated, almost in panic, not knowing how to answer but sure that the wrong answer would hang him. The silence grew then he heard himself say, 'Because God has not yet taken away the skin over my ears nor, not yet, opened my spirit,' then added involuntarily, 'I do not resist and I wait. I wait patiently.'

The mood in the room changed. Now the silence was kind. Compassionate. Hussain said softly, 'Go to the Imam and your waiting will be ended. The Imam would open your spirit to the glory of God. The Imam would open your spirit. I *know*, I've sat at the Imam's feet. I've heard the Imam preaching the Word, giving the Law, spreading the Calm of God.' A sigh went through the room and now all concentrated on the mullah, watched his eyes and the light therein, heard the newness to his voice and the growing ecstasy therein – even Starke who felt chilled and at the same time elated. 'Hasn't the Imam come to open the spirit of the world? Hasn't the Imam appeared among us to cleanse Islam of Evil and to spread Islam throughout the world, to carry the message of God . . . as has been promised? The Imam *is*.'

The word hung in the room. They all understood. So did Starke. *Mahdi!* he thought, hiding his shock. Hussain's implying Khomeini's in reality the Mahdi, the legendary twelfth Imam who vanished centuries ago and Shi'as believe is just hidden from human sight – the Immortal One, promised by God to reappear some day to rule over a perfected world.

He saw them all staring at the mullah. Many nodding, tears running down the faces of others, all rapt and satisfied and not a disbeliever among them. Good God, he thought, dumbfounded, if Iranians give Khomeini that mantle there'll be no end to his power, there'll be twenty, thirty million men, women and kids desperate to do his bidding, who'll rush happily to death at his merest whim – and why not? *Mahdi* would guarantee them a place in Heaven, guarantee it!

Someone said, 'God is Great', others echoed it and they talked, one with another, Hussain leading them, Starke forgotten. At length they noticed him and they let him go, saying, 'See the Imam, see and believe . . .'

Walking back to camp his feet had been strangely light, and he remembered now how the air had never tasted better, never had he been so full of the joy of life. Perhaps that's because I was so close to death, he thought. I was a dead man and somehow I was given back life. Why? And Tom, why did he escape Isfahan. Dez Dam, even HBC herself? Is there a reason? Or was it just luck?

And now in the dusk he watched Lochart, gravely concerned for him. Terrible about HBC, terrible about Sharazad's father, terrible that Tom and Sharazad are in a cauldron of no escape. Soon they'll both have to choose: exile together, probably never to return here – or to part, probably for ever.

'Tom, there's something special. Very secret, just between us. Johnny Hogg brought a letter from Andy Gavallan.' They were safely away from the base, strolling along the boundary road, skirting the eight-strand barbed-wire fence, and no fear of anyone overhearing. Even so he kept his voice down. 'Basically Andy's mighty downbeat on our future here and says he's considering evacuating to cut his losses.'

'No need for that,' Lochart said quickly, a sudden bite in his voice. 'Things'll get back to normal – they have to. Andy's got to sweat it out – we're sweating it out, so can he.'

'He's sweating it out plenty, Tom. It's simple economics, you know that as well as any. We're not being paid for work done months ago, we've not enough work now for the birds and pilots here that he's paying out of Aberdeen, Iran's in a shambles, and we're getting a hard time all over.'

'You mean because Zagros Three's been closed down there'll be a huge write-off on the books? Not my goddam fault th –'

'Slow down, Tom. Andy's heard on the grapevine all foreign airplane companies, joint ventures or what the hell ever, particularly choppers, are going to be nationalised mighty damned soon.'

Lochart was filled with a sudden hope. Wouldn't this give me a perfect excuse to stay? If they steal – nationalise – our birds they'll still need trained pilots, I can speak Farsi, I could train Iranians which's got to be their end plan and – and what about HBC? Back to HBC, he thought helplessly, always back to HBC. 'How does he know, Duke?'

'The way Andy put it was an "impeccable" source. What he's asking us – you, Scrag, Rudi and me – is if he and Mac can come up with a workable plan, would we and however many pilots it takes, fly all our birds into the wild blue across the Gulf?'

Lochart gaped at him. 'Jesus, you mean just take off, no clearance no nothing?'

719

'Sure – but keep your voice down.'

'He's crazy! How could we coordinate Lengeh, Bandar-e Delam, Kowiss and Tehran – everyone'd have to go at the same time and the distances won't add up.'

'Somehow they're gonna have to, Tom. Andy said it's that or close up.'

'I don't believe it! The company's operating all over the world.'

'He says if we lose Iran we're through.'

'Easy for him,' Lochart said bitterly. 'It's just money. Easy to twist our arm when you're nice and safe and all you risk's money. He's saying if he just pulls personnel and leaves everything else, S-G's going belly up?'

'Yes. That's what he's saying.'

'I don't believe it.'

Starke shrugged. Their ears caught the faint banshee wail and they turned and looked past their base to the far side of their part of the field. In the falling light they could just see Freddy Ayre with his bagpipes where, by common consent, he was allowed to practise. 'Goddam,' Starke said sourly, 'that noise drives me crazy.'

Lochart ignored him. 'Surely you're not going along with a goddam hijack, because that's what it'll be! No way would I go along with that.' He saw Starke shrug. 'What do the others say?'

'They don't know yet and won't be asked yet. As I said this's between us at the moment.' Starke glanced at his watch. 'Almost time to call Mac.' He saw a tremor go through Lochart. The lament of the bagpipes drifted on the wind. 'How anyone can claim that's music, goddamned if I know,' he said. 'Andy's idea's worth considering, Tom. As an end plan.'

Lochart did not answer him, feeling bad, the twilight bad, everything bad. Even the air smelled bad, polluted by the nearby refinery, and he wished he was back in Zagros, up near the stars where the air and the earth were not polluted, all of him desperate to be in Tehran where it was even more polluted – but she was there.

'Count me out,' he said.

'Think about it, Tom.'

'I have, I'm out, it's crazy, the whole idea. Soon as you think it out you'll see it's a mad dog scheme.'

'Sure, old buddy.' Starke wondered when his friend would realise that he, Lochart, of all of them, was counted in – one way or another.

At the Hotel International, Al Shargaz: 6:42 P.M. 'Could you do it, Scrag?' Gavallan said, sunset near.

'It'd be easy for me to sneak my five birds and men out of Lengeh, Andy,' Scragger said. 'It'd have to be the right sort of day and we'd have to slide under Kish radar but we could do it – if the lads wanted to be part of the caper. But with all our spares too? No way, not possible.'

'Would you do it, if it was possible?' Gavallan asked. He had arrived on today's flight from London, all his business news from Aberdeen rotten – Imperial Air putting on the pressure, under-cutting him in the North Sea, the oil companies squeezing him, Linbar calling a special board meeting to investigate S-G's 'possible' mismanagement. 'Would you, Scrag?'

'Just me on my tod and everyone else safe and out? Like a shot.'

'Would your lads do it?'

Scragger thought for a moment and sipped his beer. They were sitting at a table on one of the immaculate terraces surrounding the swimming pool of this, the newest of hotels in the tiny sheikdom, other

721

guests scattered around but none near, the air balmy and in the 70's with just enough breeze to tremble the palm fronds and promise a perfect evening. 'Ed Vossi would.' He grinned. 'He's got enough Aussie larceny and Yankee get up and go. Don't think Willi Nerchtreiter would. It'd be tough for him to break so many regs when it's not his tail and he's not threatened. What does Duke Starke say? And Tom Lochart and Rudi?'

'I don't know yet. I sent a letter to Duke via Johnny Hogg Wednesday.'

'That's kind of dangerous, isn't it?'

'Yes and no. Johnny Hogg's a safe courier, but it's a big problem to have safe communications. Tom Lochart'll soon be in Kowiss – you heard about Zagros?'

'Too right! They're all bonkers up in the mountains. What about old Rudi?'

'Don't know how to get to him safely yet. Maybe Mac'll have an idea. I'm on the 125 in the morning to Tehran and we're to talk at the airport. Then I'll come right back and I'm booked on the night flight to London.'

'You're pushing it a bit, aren't you, old son?'

'I've a few problems, Scrag.' Gavallan stared into his glass, absently swirling the whisky around the ice cubes. Other guests were going past. Three were girls, bikinied, golden skins, long black hair, towels casually around their shoulders. Scragger noticed them, sighed, then turned his attention back to Gavallan.

'Andy, I may have to take Kasigi back to Iran-Toda in a day or two – old George's been touching his toes since Kasigi agreed to pay him $2 over spot. Kasigi thinks it'll go to $20 a barrel by Christmas.'

Gavallan's worry increased. 'If it does it'll send a shock wave through every industrialised nation – inflation's going to soar again. I suppose if anyone'd know it'd be them.' Earlier, the moment Scragger had mentioned Kasigi and Toda he had reacted instantly, Struan's supplied crews and based many of the ships Toda built and were old associates. 'Years ago I knew this Kasigi's boss, man called Hiro Toda. Did he ever mention it?'

'No, no, he never did. You knew him where? In Japan?'

'No, Hong Kong. Toda was doing business with Struan's – the company I used to work for – in those days it was Toda Shipping, shipbuilders mostly, not the huge conglomerate they are today.' Gavallan's face hardened. 'My family were Shanghai China traders from way back, our company got more or less wiped out in the first

722

world war, then we joined up with Struan's. My old man was at Nanking in '31 when the Japs raped it, and he got caught in Shanghai just after Pearl Harbor and never made it out of POW camp.' He watched the reflections of his glass, his gloom increasing. 'We lost a lot of good chums in Shanghai and Nanking. I can never forgive them for what they did in China, never will, but then we have to move on, don't we? Have to bury the hatchet some day though you'd best keep your eyes on the tooth marks.'

'It's the same for me.' Scragger shrugged. 'Kasigi seems okay.'

'Where is he now?'

'Kuwait. He's back tomorrow and I'm to take him to Lengeh for consultations in the morning.'

'If you go to Iran-Toda, you think you might be able to get over to see Rudi? Maybe sound him out?'

'Too right. That's a good idea, Andy.'

'When you see Kasigi mention I know his chairman.'

'Sure, sure I will. I could ask him if h—' He stopped, glanced over Gavallan's shoulder. 'Look, Andy, now there's a sight for sore eyes!'

Gavallan looked around, westward. The sunset was unearthly – reds and purples and browns and golds painting the distant clouds, the sun almost three quarters under the horizon, blooding the waters of the Gulf, the touch of wind flickering the candles on the starched table-cloths already laid for dinner on the dining terrace. 'You're right, Scrag,' he said at once. 'It's the wrong time to be serious, it can wait. There's no sight in the world like a sunset.'

'Eh?' Scragger was staring at him blankly. 'For God's sake, I didn't mean the sunset – I meant the sheila.'

Gavallan sighed. The sheila was Paula Giancani, just out of the pool below them, her bikini briefer than brief, the beads of water on her olive skin glistening and bejewelled by the sunset, now drying her legs and arms and back and now her legs again, putting on a gossamer swim-ming wrap, totally and joyously aware there was not a man within sight who did not appreciate her performance – or a woman who was not envious. 'You're a horny bastard, Scrag.'

Scragger laughed and thickened his accent. 'It's me one joy in life, old cock! Cor', that Paula's one for the book.'

Gavallan studied her. 'Well, Italian girls generally have something extra special about them, but that young lady . . . she's not a stunner like Sharazad, and doesn't have Azadeh's exotic mystery, but I agree, Paula's something else.'

Along with everyone else, they watched her walk though the tables, lust following, envy following, until she had vanished into the vast hotel lobby. They were all having dinner later, Paula, Genny, Manuela, Scragger, Gavallan, Sandor Petrofi, and John Hogg. Paula's Alitalia jumbo was again at Dubai, a few miles down the highway, waiting for clearance to go to Tehran for another load of Italian nationals, and Genny McIver had met her by chance shopping.

Scragger sighed. 'Andy old chap, I'd certainly like to give her one, no doubt about it!'

'Wouldn't do you a bit of good, Scrag.' Gavallan chuckled and ordered another whisky and soda from a crisply dressed, smiling Pakistani waiter who came instantly, some of the other guests already elegantly and expensively dressed for a lovely evening, latest Paris fashions, much décolletage, starched white dinner jackets – along with the expensive casual. Gavallan wore well-cut tan tropicals, Scragger regulation uniform, short-sleeved white shirt with epaulets and bars, black trousers and shoes. 'Beer, Scrag?'

'No, thanks, mate. I'll nurse this and get ready for Pulsating Paula.'

'Dreamer!' Gavallan turned back to the sunset, feeling better, put back together by his old friend. The sun was almost under the horizon, never more beautiful, reminding him of sunsets in China in the old days, sweeping him back to Hong Kong and Kathy and Ian, laughter in the Great House on the Peak, all the family fine and strong, their own house on a promontory at Shek-o – when they were young and together, Melinda and Scot still children, amahs padding about, sampans and junks and ships of all sizes far below in the sunset on a safe sea.

The tip of the sun went under the sea. With great solemnity, Gavallan quietly clapped his hands.

'What's that for, Andy?'

'Um? Oh, sorry, Scrag. In the old days we use to applaud the sun, Kathy and I, the very second after it disappeared. To thank the sun for being there and for the unique performance and for being alive to be able to enjoy it – the last time ever you'd see that particular sunset. Like tonight. You'll never see that one again.' Gavallan sipped his whisky, watching the afterglow. 'The first person who introduced me to the idea was a wonderful fellow, we became good friends – still are. Great man, his wife's crackerjack too. I'll tell you about them some time.' He turned his back to the west and leaned forward, 'Lengeh. You think it's possible?'

'Oh, yes – if it was just us at Lengeh. We'd still have to plan very careful, Kish radar's more itchy than ever, but we could slip under her on the right day. Big problem's that our Italian ground crew and staff, along with our presently friendly but zealous komiteh and our new unfriendly IranOil joker, would know within minutes we'd done a bunk, they'd have to with all birds up and away. At once they'd holler to IATC and they'd radio an allpoints alert to Dubai, Abu Dhabi, here – in fact from Oman through Saudi and Kuwait up to Baghdad – telling them to impound us on arrival. Even if we all got here . . . well, the old sheik's a great guy, liberal and a friend, but hell, he couldn't go against Iran ATC when they were right – even if they were wrong. He couldn't pick a fight with Iran, he's got a good percentage of Shi'as among his Sunnis, not as bad as some on the Gulf, worse'n others.'

Gavallan got up and walked to the edge of the terrace and looked down at the old city – once a great pearling port, pirate stronghold, and slave market, trading centre and, like Sohar in Oman, called the Port of China. Since ancient times the Gulf was the golden sealink between the Mediterranean – then centre of the world – and Asia. Seafaring Phoenician traders, who came from Oman originally, dominated this incredibly wealthy trade route, landing the goods of Asia and India at Shatt-al-Arab thence by short caravan routes to their markets, eventually to carve their own seaborn Mediterranean empire, founding city-states like Carthage to threaten even Rome herself.

The old walled city was beautiful in the dying light, flat roofs, unspoiled and protected from modern buildings, the sheik's fort dominating it. Over the years Gavallan had come to know the old sheik and to admire him. The sheikdom was surrounded by the Emirates but was an independent, sovereign enclave barely twenty miles deep with seven miles of coastline. But inland and out to sea for a hundred miles up to Iranian waters, within easy drilling, was a pool of oil many billion barrels thick. So Al Shargaz had the old city and a separate new city with a dozen modern hotels and skyscrapers, and an airport that could just handle a jumbo. In riches nothing to compare with the Emirates, or Saudi or Kuwait but enough for abundance in everything, if chosen wisely. The sheik was as wise as his Phoenician ancestors were worldly-wise, as fiercely independent, and though he himself could not read or write, his sons were graduates from the best universities on earth. He and his family and his tribe owned everything, his word was law, he was Sunni, not a fundamentalist, and tolerant with his foreign subjects and guests, provided they behaved.

'He also detests Khomeini and all fundamentalists, Scrag.'

'Yes. But he still daren't pick a fight with Khomeini – that won't help us.'

'It won't hurt us.' Gavallan felt cleansed by the sunset. 'I plan to hire a couple of jumbo freighters, get them here, and when our choppers arrive we strip rotors, stuff their bellies full and blast off. Speed's the key – and planning.'

Scragger whistled. 'You really mean to do it?'

'I really mean to see if we *can* do it, Scrag, and what the odds are. This's the big one, if we lose all our Iranian choppers, equipment and spares, we close. No insurance covers us and we're still liable to pay what we owe. You're a partner, you can see the figures tonight. I brought them for you – and for Mac.'

Scragger thought about his stake in the company, all the stake he had, and about Nell and his kids and their kids back in Sydney, and the station of Baldoon that had been the family sheep and cattle station for a century but was lost in the great drought, that he had had his eyes on for years and years and years to repossess for them.

'No need for me t'look at figures, Andy. If you say it's that bad, it's that bad.' He was watching the patterns of the sky. 'Tell you what, I'll take care of Lengeh if you can figure a plan and if the others're in. After dinner maybe we could talk logistics for an hour, and finish up over breakfast. Kasigi won't be back from Kuwait until 9 a.m. We'll figure her out.'

'Thanks, Scrag.' Gavallan clapped him on the shoulder, towering over him. 'I'm damned glad you were here, damned glad you've been with us all these years. For the first time I think we've a chance and I'm not dreaming.'

'One condition, old sport,' Scragger added.

Gavallan was instantly on guard. 'I can't square your medical if it's not up to scratch. There's no way th –'

'Do you mind?' Scragger was pained. 'It's nothing to do with Dirty Duncan and my medical – that's going to be good till I'm seventy-three. No, the condition is at dinner you sit next to Pulsating Paula, Genny on her other side, Manuela beside me, and that horny Hungarian Sandor way down the other end along with Johnny Hogg.'

'Done!'

'Bonza! Now don't you worry, mate. I've been sodded about by enough generals in five wars to've learned something. Time to change for dinner. Lengeh was getting boring and no doubt about it.' He walked off, thin, straight and spritely.

Gavallan gave over his credit card to the smiling Pakistani waiter.

'No need for that, sahib, please just sign the bill,' the man said. Then added softly, 'If I might suggest, Effendi, when you pay, don't use American Express, it is the most expensive for the management.'

Bemused, Gavallan left a tip and walked off.

On the other side of the terrace two men watched him leave. Both were well dressed and in their forties, one American, the other Middle Eastern. Both wore tiny hearing aids. The man who was Middle Eastern was toying with an old-fashioned fountain pen, and as Gavallan passed a well-dressed Arab and a very attractive young European girl in deep conversation, his curiousity peaked, the man with the fountain pen pointed it at them and steadied it. At once both men could hear the voices in their earphones: 'My dear, five hundred dollars U.S. is much more than market price,' the man was saying.

'It depends what market forces concern you, my dear,' she replied, her middle-European accent pleasing, and they saw her smile gently. 'The fee includes the very best silk underwear you wish to rip to pieces and the probe you require inserted at your moment of truth. Expertise is expertise and special services require special handling and if your schedule only permits between 6 and 8 tomorrow evening –'

The voices vanished as the man turned the cap and put the pen on the tabletop with a wry smile. He was handsome and olive-skinned an importer-exporter of fine carpets like generations of his forebears, American educated, his name Aaron ben Aaron – his main occupation major, Israeli Special Intelligence. 'I'd never have figured Abdu bin Talak as kinky,' he said dryly.

The other man grunted. 'They're all kinky. I wouldn't have figured the girl for a hooker.'

Aaron's long fingers toyed with the pen, reluctant to let it go. 'Great gadget, Glenn, saves so much time. Wish I'd had one years ago.'

'KGB've got a new model out this year, good for a hundred yards' range.' Glenn Wesson sipped his bourbon on the rocks. He was American, a longtime oil trader. Real profession, career CIA. 'It's not as small as this but effective.'

'Can you get us some?'

'Easier for you to do it, get your guys to ask Washington.' They saw Gavallan disappear into the lobby. 'Interesting.'

'What'd'you think?' Aaron asked.

'That we could throw a British chopper company to the Khomeini wolves anytime we want – along with all their pilots. That'd make Talbot bust a gut and Robert Armstrong and all MI6 which isn't a bad idea.' Wesson laughed softly. 'Talbot needs a good shafting from time to time. What's the problem with S-G, you think they're an MI6 cover operation?'

'We're not sure what they're up to, Glenn. We suspect just the reverse, that's why I thought you should listen in. Too many coincidences. On the surface they're legit – yet they've a French pilot Sessone, who's sleeping with, and sponsoring, a well-connected PLO courier, Sayada Bertolin; they've a Finn, Erikki Yokkonen closely associated with Abdollah Khan who's certainly a double agent leaning more to the KGB than our side and openly, violently anti-Jew; Yokkonen's very close to the Finnish Intelligence man, Christian Tollonen, who's suspect by definition, Yokkonen's family connections in Finland would position him to be a perfect deep-cover Soviet asset and we just got a buzz that he's up in the Sabalan with his 212, helping Soviets dismantle your covert radar sites all over.'

'Jesus. You sure?'

'No – I said a buzz. But we're checking it out. Next, the Canadian Lochart: Lochart's married into a known anti-Zionist bazaari family, PLO agents are living in his apartment right now, h –'

'Yes, but we heard the pad was commandeered and don't forget he tried to help those pro-Shah, pro-Israel officers escape.'

'Yes, but they got shot out of the skies, they're all dead and curiously he isn't. Valik and General Seladi would certainly have been in or near any cabinet-in-exile – we lost another two very important assets. Lochart's suspect, his wife and her family're pro-Khomeini which means anti-us.' Aaron smiled sardonically. 'Aren't we the great Satan after you? Next: the American Starke helps put down a fedayeen attack at Bandar-e Delam, gets very friendly with another rabid anti-Shah, anti-Israel zealot Zataki wh –'

'Who?'

'An anti-Shah fighter, intellectual, Sunni Muslim who organised Abadan oil-field strikes, blew up three police stations and now is heading up the Abadan Revolutionary Komiteh and not long for this earth. Drink?'

'Sure, thanks. Same. You mentioned Sayada Bertolin – we've had her tabbed too. You think she could be turned?'

'I wouldn't trust her. Best thing to do with her is just watch and see who she leads to. We're after her controller – can't peg him yet.' Aaron ordered for Wesson and a vodka for himself. 'Back to S-G. So Zataki's enemy. Starke speaks Farsi, like Lochart. Both keep bad company. Next Sandor Petrofi: Hungarian dissident with family still in Hungary, another potential KGB mole or at least a KGB tool. Rudi Lutz, German with close family over the Iron Curtain, always suspect, Neurchtreiter in Lengeh the same.' He nodded to where Scragger had been. 'The old man's just a trained killer, a mercenary to point at us, you, anyone with the same result. Gavallan? You should get your London people to tab him – don't forget he chose all the others, don't forget he's British – quite possibly his whole operation's a KGB cover an –'

'No way,' Wesson said, suddenly irritated. Goddam – he thought, why're these guys so paranoid – even old Aaron who's the best there is. 'It's all too pat. No way.'

'Why not? He could be fooling you. The British are past masters at it – like Philby, Maclean, Blake, and all the rest.'

'Like Crosse.' Wesson's lips went into a thin line. 'In that you're right, old buddy.'

'Who?'

'Roger Crosse – ten-odd years back, Mister Spymaster, but buried and covered up with all the skill Limeys have – from the Old Boys' club, the foulest traitors of them all.'

'Who was Crosse?'

'Armstrong's ex-boss and friend from Hong Kong Special Branch in the old days. Officially a minor deputy director of MI6 but really top of their cream operation, Special Intelligence, traitor, terminated by the KGB at his own request just before we were going to nail the bastard.'

'You proved it? That they terminated him?'

'Sure. Poison dart from close range, SOP, that's what sent him onwards. We had him cornered, no way he could get away like the others. We had him nailed, triple agent. At that time we'd a plant inside the Soviet Embassy in London – guy called Brodnin. He gave us Crosse then disappeared, poor bastard, someone must've fingered him.'

'God-cursed British, they breed spies like lice.'

'Not true, they've some great catchers too – we've all got traitors.'

'We don't.'

'Don't bet on it, Aaron,' Wesson said sourly. 'There're traitors all over – with all the leaks in Tehran before and since the Shah left, there's got to be another high-up traitor our side.'

'Talbot or Armstrong?'

Wesson winced. 'If it's either of them we should just quit.'

'That's what the enemy wants you to do, quit and get to hell out of the Middle East. We can't, so we think differently,' Aaron said, eyes dark and cold, face set, watching him carefully. 'Talking of that, why should our old friend Colonel Hashemi Fazir get away with murdering the new SAVAMA hatchet man, General Janan?'

Wesson blanched, 'Janan's dead? You're sure?'

'Car bomb, Monday night.' Aaron's eyes narrowed. 'Why so sorry? Was he one of yours?'

'Could have been. We, er, we were negotiating.' Wesson hesitated, then sighed. 'But Hashemi's still alive? I thought he was on the Rev Komiteh's urgent condemned list.'

'He was, not now. I heard this morning his name's off, his rank's confirmed, Inner Intelligence's reinstated – supposedly all approved by on high.'

Aaron sipped his drink. 'If he's back in favour, after all he did for the Shah and us, he's got to have a very high protector.'

'Who?' Wesson saw the other shrug, eyes ranging the terraces. His smile vanished. 'That could mean he's been working for the Ayatollah all the time.'

'Perhaps.' Aaron toyed with the fountain pen again. 'Another curiosity. Tuesday Hashemi was seen getting on the S-G 125 at Tehran Airport with Armstrong; they went to Tabriz and were back in three hours odd.'

'I'll be goddammed!'

'What's that all add up to?'

'Jesus, I don't know – but I think we better find out.' Wesson dropped his voice further. 'One thing's certain, for Hashemi to get back in favour he's got to know where some very important bodies are buried, huh? Such information would be highly valuable . . . highly valuable, say to the Shah.'

'Shah?' Aaron started to smile, stopped as he saw Wesson's expression. 'You don't seriously figure the Shah's got a chance to come back?'

'Stranger things've happened, old buddy,' Wesson said confidently and finished his drink. Why is it these guys don't understand what's going on in the world, he was thinking. It's time they smartened up, stopped being so one-track about Israel, the PLO, and the whole Middle East, and gave us room to manoeuvre. 'Sure the Shah's gotta chance, though his son's a better bet – soon's Khomeini's dead and buried it'll be civil war, the army'll take over and they'll need a figurehead. Reza'd be a great constitutional monarch.'

Aaron been Aaron kept the disbelief off his face with difficulty, astounded that Wesson could still be so naive. After all the years you've been in Iran and the Gulf, he thought, how can you still misunderstand the explosive forces ripping Iran apart? If he had been a different man he would have cursed Wesson for the stupidity he represented, the hundreds of alarm signals disregarded, the hills of secret intelligence reports gathered with so much blood and cast aside unread, their years of pleading with politicians and generals and Intelligence – American and Iranian – warning of the gathering conflagration.

All to no avail. For years and years. The Will of God, he thought. God does not want it to be easy for us. Easy? In all history it's never once been easy for us. Never never never.

He saw Wesson watching him. 'What?'

'You wait and see. Khomeini's an old man, he won't last the year. He's old and time's with us – you wait and see.'

'I will.' Aaron put aside his inclination to argue violently. 'Meanwhile, the problem in hand: S-G could be a front for enemy cells. When you think about it, chopper pilots specialising in oil support'd be valuable assets for all kinds of sabotage if the going gets worse.'

'Sure. But Gavallan wants out of Iran. You heard him.'

'Maybe he knew we were listening, or it's a ploy he's pulling.'

'Come on, Aaron. I think he's kosher, and the rest of it's coincidence.' Wesson sighed. 'Okay, I'll put a tab on him, and he won't shit without you knowing, but hell, old buddy, you guys see enemies under the bed, on the ceiling and under the carpet.'

'Why not? They're plenty around – known, unknown, active, or passive.' Aaron was methodically watching around him, checking on newcomers, expecting enemies, aware of the multitude of enemy agents in Al Shargaz and the Gulf. And we know about enemies, here, outside in the old city and in the new city, up the road to Oman and down the road to Dubai and Baghdad and Damascus, to Moscow and Paris and London, across the sea to New York, south to both the Capes and north to the Arctic Circle, wherever there're people who're not Jews. Only a Jew not automatically suspect and even then, these days, you've got to be careful.

There're many among the Chosen who don't want Zion, don't want to go to war or pay for war, don't want to understand Israel hangs in the balance with the Shah, our only ally in the Middle East and sole OPEC supplier of oil for our tanks and planes, cast aside, don't want to know our backs are to the Wailing Wall and we've to fight and die to protect our God-given land of Israel we repossessed with God's help at such cost!

He looked up at Wesson, liking him, forgiving him his faults, admiring him as a professional but sorry for him: he wasn't a Jew and therefore suspect. 'I'm glad I was born a Jew, Glenn. It makes life so much easier.'

'How?'

'You know where you stand.'

At Disco Tex, Hotel Shargaz: 11:52 P.M. Americans, British and French dominated the room – some Japanese and other Asians. Europeans in the majority, many, many more men than women, their ages ranging between twenty-five and forty-five – the Gulf expat work force had to be young, strong, preferably unmarried, to survive the hard, celibate life. A few drunks, some noisy. Ugly and not so ugly, overweight and not so overweight, most of them lean, frustrated, and volcanic. A few Shargazi and others of the Gulf, but only the rich, the Westernised, the sophisticated, and men. Most of these sat on the upper level drinking soft drinks and ogling, and the few who danced on the small floor below danced with European women: secretaries, embassy personnel, airline staff, nurses, or other hotel staff – partners at a premium. No Shargazi or Arabian women were here.

Paula danced with Sandor Petrofi, Genny with Scragger, and Johnny Hogg was cheek to cheek with the girl who had been deep in conversation on the terrace, swaying at half tempo. 'How long're you staying, Alexandra?' he murmured.

'Next week, only until next week. Then I must join my husband in Rio.'

'Oh, but you're so young to be married! You're all alone till then?'

'Yes, alone, Johnny. It's sad, no?'

He did not reply, just held her a little tighter and blessed his luck that he had picked up the book she had dropped in the lobby. The strobe lights dazzled him for a moment, then he noticed Gavallan on the upper level, standing at the rail, grave and lost in thought, and again felt sorry for him. Earlier he had reluctantly arranged tomorrow's night flight to London for him, trying to persuade him to rest over a day. 'I know how jet lag plays hell with you, sir.'

'No problem, Johnny, thanks. Our takeoff for Tehran's still at 10 a.m.'

'Yes, sir. Our clearance's still priority – and the charter onward to Tabriz.'

'Let's hope that goes smoothly, just there and straight back.'

John Hogg felt the girl's loins against him. 'Will you have dinner tomorrow? I should be back sixish.'

'Perhaps – but not before nine.'

'Perfect.'

Gavallan was looking down on the dancers, hardly seeing them, then turned and went down the stairs and outside on to the ground-floor terrace. The night was lovely, moon huge, no clouds. Around were acres of delicately floodlit, beautifully kept gardens within the encircling walls, some of the sprinklers on.

The Shargaz was the biggest hotel in the sheikdom, one side the sea, the other the desert, its tower eighteen storeys, with five restaurants, three bars, cocktail lounge, coffee shop, the disco, two swimming pools, saunas, steam rooms, tennis courts, health centre, shopping mall with a dozen boutiques and antiques, an Aaron carpet shop, hairdressing salons, video library, bakery, electronics, telex office, typing pool, with, like all the modern European hotels, all rooms and suites air-conditioned, bathrooms and bidets en suite, twenty-four-hour room service – mostly smiling Pakistanis – same-day cleaners, instant pressing, a colour TV in every room, in-house movies, stock market channel, and satellite distant dialling to every capital in the world.

True, Gavallan thought, but still a ghetto. And though the rulers of Al Shargaz and Dubai and Sharjah are liberal and tolerant so expats can drink in the hotels, can even buy liquor, though God help you if you resell any to a Muslim, our women can drive and shop and walk about, that's no guarantee it'll last. A few hundred yards away, Shargazi are living as they've lived for centuries, a few miles away over the border liquor's forbidden, a woman can't drive or be on the street alone and has to cover her hair and arms and shoulders and wear loose pants and over there in the real desert, people exist on a stratum of life that's pitiless.

A few years ago he had taken a Range Rover and a guide and, together with McIver and Genny and his new wife Maureen, had gone out into the desert to spend the night in one of the oases on the edge of Rub-al-Khali, the Empty Quarter. It had been a perfect spring day. Within minutes of their passing the airport, the road became a track that quickly petered out and they were grinding over the stony expanse under the bowl of sky. Picnic lunch, then on again, sometimes sandy, sometimes rocky, detouring in the wilderness where it never rained and nothing grew. Nothing. On again. When they stopped and turned the engine off, the silence came at them like a physical presence, the sun bore down, and space enveloped them.

That night was blue black, stars enormous, tents fine and carpets soft, and even greater silence, greater space, so much space inconceivable. 'I hate it, Andy,' Maureen had whispered. 'It frightens me to death.'

733

'Me too. Don't know why but it does.' Around the palm trees of the oasis, the desert went to every horizon, taunting and unearthly. 'The immensity seems to suck the life out of you. Imagine what it's like in summer!'

She trembled. 'It makes me feel less than a grain of sand. It's crushing me – somehow it's taken my balance away. Och, ay, laddie, once is enough for me. It's me for Scotland – London at a pinch – and never again.'

And she had never come back. Like Scrag's Nell, he thought. Don't blame them. It's tough enough in the Gulf for men, but for women . . . He glanced around. Genny was coming out of the French windows, fanning herself, looking much younger than in Tehran. 'Hello, Andy. You're the wise one, it's so stuffy in there, and the smoke, ugh!'

'Never was much of a dancer.'

'The only time I get to dance is when Duncan's not with me. He's such a stick in the mud.' She hesitated. 'On tomorrow's flight, do you think I co –'

'No,' he said kindly. 'Not yet. In a week or so – let the dust settle.'

She nodded, not hiding her disappointment. 'What did Scrag say?'

'Yes – if the others are in and it's feasible. We had a good talk and we're having breakfast.' Gavallan put his arm around her and gave her a hug. 'Don't worry about Mac, I'll make sure he's all right.'

'I've another bottle of whisky for him, you don't mind, do you?'

'I'll put it in my briefcase – we're on notice by IATC not to have any booze as aircraft stores – no problem, I'll hand carry it.'

'Then perhaps you'd better not, not this time.' She found his gravity unsettling, so unusual in him. Poor Andy, anyone can see he's beside himself with worry.

'Andy, can I make a suggestion?'

'Of course, Genny.'

'Use this colonel and Roberts, no Armstrong, the VIPs you've got to ferry to Tabriz. Why not ask them to route you back through Kowiss, say you need to pick up some engines for repair, eh? Then you can talk to Duke directly.'

'Very good idea – go to the top of the class.'

She reached up and gave him a sisterly kiss. 'You're not bad yourself. Well, it's me back to the fray – haven't been so popular since the war.' She laughed and so did he. ' 'Night, Andy.'

Gavallan went back to his hotel that was just down the road. He did not notice the men tailing him, nor that his room had been searched, his papers read, nor that now the room was bugged and the phone tapped.

At Tehran International Airport: 11:58 A.M. The cabin door of the 125
closed behind Robert Armstrong and Colonel Hashemi Fazir. From
the cockpit John Hogg gave Gavallan and McIver who stood on the
tarmac beside his car a thumbs-up and taxied away, outward bound for
Tabriz. Gavallan had just arrived from Al Shargaz and this was the first
moment he and McIver had been alone.

'What's up, Mac?' he said, the chill wind tugging at their winter
clothes and billowing the snow around them.

'Trouble, Andy.'

'I know that. Tell it to me quickly.'

McIver leaned closer. 'I've just heard we've barely a week before
we're grounded pending nationalisation.'

'What?' Gavallan was suddenly numb. 'Talbot told you?'

'No, Armstrong, a few minutes ago when the colonel was in the loo
and we were alone.' McIver's face twisted, so worried that he was
stumbling over the words. 'The bastard told me with his smooth, put-
on politeness, "I wouldn't bet on more than ten days if I were you – a

735

week'd be safe – and don't forget, Mr. McIver, a closed mouth catches no flies." '

'My God, does he know we are planning something?' A gust speckled them with powdered snow.

'I don't know. I just don't know, Andy.'

'What about HBC? Did he mention her?'

'No. When I asked about the papers, all he said was, They're safe.'

'Did he say when we're to meet today?'

McIver shook his head. ' "If I'm back in time I'll be in touch." Bastard.' He jerked his car door open.

In turmoil Gavallan brushed off the excess snow and slid into the warmth. The windows were fogged up. McIver switched the defrost and fan to maximum, heat already at maximum, then pushed the music cassette home, jacked the sound up, turned it down again, cursing.

'What else's up, Mac?'

'Just about everything,' McIver blurted out. 'Erikki's been kidnapped by Soviets or the KGB and he's somewhere up near the Turkish border with his 212, doing Christ knows what – Nogger thinks he's being forced to help them clean out secret U.S. radar sites. Nogger, Azadeh, two of our mechanics and a British captain barely escaped from Tabriz with their lives, they got back yesterday and they're at my place at the moment – at least they were when I left this morning. My God, Andy, you should have seen the state they were in when they arrived. The captain was the same one who saved Charlie at Doshan Tapeh, who Charlie dropped off at Bandar-e Pahlavi . . .'

'He what?'

'It was a secret op. He's a captain in the Gurkhas . . . name's Ross, John Ross, he and Azadeh were both pretty incoherent, Nogger too was pretty excited and at least they're safe now back home,' McIver's voice became brittle. 'Sorry to tell you we've lost a mechanic at Zagros, Effer Jordon, he was shot an –'

'Jesus Christ! Old Effer dead?'

'Yes . . . yes I'm afraid so and your son was nicked . . . not badly,' McIver added hastily as Gavallan blanched. 'Scot's all right, he's okay an –'

'How badly?'

'Bullet through the fleshy part of the right shoulder. No bones touched, just a flesh wound – Jean-Luc said they've penicillin, a medic, the wound's clean. Scot won't be able to ferry the 212 out tomorrow to Al Shargaz so I asked Jean-Luc to do it and take Scot with him, then come back to Tehran on the next 125 flight and we'll get him back to Kowiss.'

'You're sure? That Scot was just nicked?'

'Yes, Andy. Sure.'

'What the hell happened?'

'I don't know exactly. I got a relayed message from Starke this morning who'd just picked it up from Jean-Luc. It seems that terrorists are operating in the Zagros, I suppose the same bunch that attacked Bellissima and Rosa, they must've been hiding in ambush in the forests around our base. Effer Jordon and Scot were loading spares into the 212 just after dawn this morning and got sprayed. Poor old Effer got most of the bullets and Scot just one . . .' Again McIver added hurriedly, seeing Gavallan's face, 'Jean-Luc assured me Scot's all right, Andy, honest to God!'

'I wasn't thinking just about Scot,' Gavallan said heavily. 'Effer's been with us damn nearly since we started – hasn't he got three kids?'

'Yes, yes he has. Terrible.' McIver let in the clutch and eased the car through the snow back towards the office. 'They're all still at school, I think.'

'I'll do something about them soon as I get back. Go on about Zagros.'

'Nothing much more. Tom wasn't there – he had to stay overnight at Kowiss Friday. Jean-Luc said they didn't see any of the attackers, no one did, the shots just came out of the forest – the base's in chaos anyway what with our birds working overtime, bringing men from all the outlying rigs and ferrying them in batches to Shiraz, everyone pitching in to clear out before the deadline tomorrow at sunset.'

'Will they make it?'

'More or less. We'll get out all our oilers and our chaps, most of our valuable spares and all choppers to Kowiss. The rig support equipment'll have to be left but that's not our responsibility. God knows what'll happen to the base and rigs without servicing.'

'It'll all go back to wilderness.'

'I agree, bloody stupid waste! Bloody stupid! I asked Colonel Fazir if there was anything he could do. The bastard just smiled his thin rotten smile and said it was hard enough to find out what the hell was going on at the office next door in Tehran, let alone so far south. I asked him what about the komiteh at the airport – could they help? He said no, that komitehs have almost no liaison with anyone else, even in Tehran. To quote him: "Up in the Zagros among the half-civilised nomads and tribemen, unless you've guns, or you're Iranian, preferably an ayatollah, you'd best do what they say." ' McIver coughed and blew his nose irritably. 'The bastard wasn't laughing at us, Andy. Even so, he wasn't unhappy either.'

Gavallan was in dismay, so many questions to ask and to be answered, everything in jeopardy, here and at home. A week to doomsday? Thank God that Scot . . . poor old Effer . . . Christ Almighty, Scot shot! Gloomily he looked out of the windshield and saw they were nearing the freight area. 'Stop the car for a minute, Mac, better to talk in private, eh?'

'Sorry, yes, I'm not thinking too clearly.'

'You're all right? I mean your health?'

'Oh, that's fine, if I get rid of this cough . . . It's just that . . . it's just that I'm afraid.' McIver said it flat but the admission spiked through Gavallan. 'I'm out of control, I've already lost one man, there's HBC still hanging over us, old Erikki's in danger, we're all in danger, S-G and everything we've worked for.' He fiddled with the wheel. 'Gen's fine?'

'Yes, yes, she is,' Gavallan said patiently. This was the second time he had answered that question. McIver had asked him the moment he had come down the steps of the 125. 'Genny's fine, Mac,' he said, repeating what he had said earlier, 'I've mail from her, she's talked to both Hamish and Sarah, both families're fine and young Angus has his first tooth. Everyone's well at home, all in good shape and I've a bottle of Loch Vay in my briefcase from her. She tried to talk her way past Johnny Hogg on to the 125 – to stowaway in the loo – even after I'd said no, so sorry.' For the first time he saw a glimmer of a smile on McIver.

'Gen's bloody-minded, no doubt about it. Glad she's there and not here, very glad, curious though how you miss 'em.' McIver stared ahead. 'Thanks, Andy.'

'Nothing.' Gavallan thought a moment. 'Why get Jean-Luc to take the 212? Why not Tom Lochart? Wouldn't it be better to have him out?'

'Of course but he won't leave Iran without Sharazad . . . there's another problem.' The music on the tape went out and he turned it over and started it again. 'I can't track her down. Tom was worried about her, asked me to go to her home near the bazaar which I did. Couldn't get an answer, didn't seem to be anyone there, Tom's sure she was on the Women's Protest March.'

'Christ! We heard about the riots and arrests on the BBC – and attacks by nutters on some of the women. You think she's in jail?'

'I hope to God she isn't – you heard about her father? Oh, of course,

I told you myself last time you were here, didn't I?' McIver wiped the windshield absently. 'What would you like to do – wait here until the bird comes back?'

'No. Let's go into Tehran – do we have time?' Gavallan glanced at his watch. It read 12:25.

'Oh, yes. We've got a load of "redundant" stores to put aboard. We'll have time if we leave now.'

'Good. I'd like to see Azadeh and Nogger – and this man Ross – and particularly Talbot. We could go past the Bakravan house on the off chance. Eh?'

'Good idea. I'm glad you're here, Andy, very glad.' He eased in the clutch, the wheels skidding.

'So'm I, Mac. Actually I've never been so down either.'

McIver coughed and cleared his throat. 'Home news is lousy?'

'Yes.' Idly Gavallan wiped away the condensation from his side window with the back of his glove. 'There's a special board meeting of Struan's Monday. I'll have to come up with answers about Iran. Damned nuisance!'

'Will Linbar be there?'

'Yes. That bugger's going to ruin the Noble House before he's through. Stupid to expand into South America when China's on the threshold of opening up.'

McIver frowned at the new edge to Gavallan's voice but said nothing. For many years he had known of their rivalry and hatred, the circumstances of David MacStruan's death and everyone's surprise in Hong Kong that Linbar had achieved the top job. He still had many friends in the Colony who sent him clippings or the latest piece of gossip or rumour – the lifeblood of Hong Kong – about the Noble House and their rivals. But he never discussed them with his old friend.

'Sorry, Mac,' Gavallan had said gruffly, 'don't want to discuss those sort of things, or what goes on with Ian, Quillan, Linbar or anyone else connected with Struan's. Officially I'm no longer with the Noble House. Let's leave it at that.'

Fair enough, McIver had thought at the time and had continued to hold his peace. He glanced across at Gavallan. The years have been kind to Andy, he told himself, he's still as grand a looking man as ever – even with all the troubles. 'Not to worry, Andy. Nothing you can't do.'

'I wish I believed that right now, Mac. Seven days presents an enormous problem, doesn't it?'

'That's the understatement of the y—' McIver noticed his fuel gauge was on empty and he exploded: 'Someone must've siphoned my tank while she was parked.' He stopped and got out a moment and came back and slammed the door. 'Bloody bastard broke the sodding lock. I'll have to fill up – fortunately we've still got a few five gallon drums left and the underground tank's still half full of chopper fuel for emergencies.' He lapsed into silence, his mind beset with Jordon and Zagros and HBC and seven days. Who do we lose next? Silently he began to curse and then he heard Genny's voice saying, We can do it if we want to, I know we can, I know we can . . .

Gavallan was thinking about his son. I won't rest easily until I see him with my own eyes. Tomorrow with any luck. If Scot's not back before my plane to London, I'll cancel and go Sunday. And somehow I've got to see Talbot – maybe he can give me some help. My God, only seven days . . .

It took McIver no time to refuel, then he swung out of the airport into the traffic. A big USAF jet transport came low overhead in the landing pattern. 'They're servicing about five jumbos a day, still with military controllers and "supervising" Green Bands, everyone giving orders, countermanding them and no one listening anyway,' McIver said. 'BA's promised me three seats on every one of their flights for our nationals – with baggage. They hope to get a jumbo in every other day.'

'What'd they want in return?'

'The crown jewels!' McIver said, trying to lighten their depression but the joke sounded flat. 'No, nothing, Andy. The BA manager, Bill Shoesmith is a great chap and doing a great job.' He swung around the wreck of a bus that was on its side half across the road as though it were neatly parked. 'The women are marching again today – rumour has it they're going to go on and on until Khomeini relents.'

'If they stick together he'll have to.'

'I don't know what to think these days.' McIver drove on a while then jerked a thumb out of the windows at the pedestrians walking this way and that. 'They seem to know all's well in the world. The mosques are packed, marches in support of Khomeini are multitudes, Green Bands're fighting the leftists fearlessly who fight back equally fearlessly.' He coughed wheezily. 'Our employees, well, they just give me the usual Persian flattery and politeness and you never know what they're really thinking. Except you're sure they want us O-U-T!' He swerved on to the pavement to avoid a head-on collision with an oncoming car that was on the wrong side of the road, horn blaring, going much too fast for the snow conditions – then drove on again. 'Bloody twit,' he said. 'If it wasn't for the fact I love old Lulu, I'd swop her for a beat up half-track and have at the bloody lot of them!' He glanced at Gavallan and smiled. 'Andy, I'm so glad you're here. Thanks. I feel better now. Sorry.'

'No problem,' Gavallan said calmly but inside he was churning. 'What about Whirlwind?' he asked, not able to bottle it up any longer.

'Well, whether it's seven days or seventy . . .' McIver swerved to avoid another accident neatly, returned the obscene gesture, and drove on again. 'Let's pretend we're all agreed, and we could push the button if we wanted on D-day, in seven days – no, Armstrong said best not to count on more than a week so let's make it six, six days from today, Friday next – a Friday'd be best anyway, right?'

'Because it's their Holy Day, yes, my thought too.'

'Then adapting what we've come up with – Charlie and me: Phase One: From today on we send out every expat and spare we can, every way we can, by the 125, by truck out to Iraq or Turkey, or as baggage and excess baggage by BA. Somehow I'll get Bill Shoesmith to increase our seat reservations and get priority of freight space. We've already got two of our 212s out "for repair" and the Zagros one's due off tomorrow. We've five birds left here in Tehran, one 212, two 206s and two Alouettes. We send the 212 and the Alouettes to Kowiss ostensibly to service Hotshot's request for choppers though why he wants them, God only knows – Duke says his birds are not all employed as it is. Anyway, we leave our 206s here as camouflage.'

'Leave them?'

'There's no way we get all our choppers out, Andy, whatever our lead time. Now, D minus Two, next Wednesday, the last of our headquarter staff – Charlie, Nogger, our remaining pilots and mechanics and me – we get on the 125 Wednesday and flit the coop to Al Shargaz, unless of course we can get some of them out beforehand by BA. Don't forget we're supposed to be up to strength, one in for one out. Next we th –'

'What about papers, exit permits?'

'I'll try to get blanks from Ali Kia – I'll need some blank Swiss cheques, he understands pishkesh but he's also a member of the board, very clever, hot and hungry but not anxious to risk his skin. If we can't, then we'll just pishkesh our way on to the 125. Our excuse to the partners, Kia or whomever, when they discover we've gone is that you've called an urgent conference at Al Shargaz – it's a lame excuse but that's beside the point. That ends Phase One. If we're prevented from going then that ends Whirlwind because we'd be used as hostages for the return of all birds and I know you won't agree to expend us. Phase Two: we set up sh –'

'What about all your household things? And all those of the chaps who have apartments or houses in Tehran?'

'The company'll have to pay fair compensation – that should be part of Whirlwind's profit and loss. Agreed?'

'What'll that add up to, Mac?'

'Not a lot. We've no option but to pay compensation.'

'Yes, yes, I agree.'

'Phase Two: We set up shop at Al Shargaz by which time several things have happened. You've arranged for the 747 jumbo freighters to arrive at Al Shargaz the afternoon of D minus One. By then, Starke somehow has secretly cached enough 40 gallon drums on the shore to carry them across the Gulf. Someone else's cached more fuel on some godforsaken island off Saudi or the Emirates for Starke if he needs them, and for Rudi and his lads from Bandar-e Delam who definitely will. Scrag has no fuel problems. Meanwhile, you've arranged British registry for all birds we plan to "export", and you've got permission to fly through Kuwait, Saudi and Emirate airspace. I'm in charge of Whirlwind's actual operation. At dawn on D-day you say to me, go or no-go. If it's no-go, that's final. If it's go, I can abort the go order if I think it's prudent, then that becomes final too. Agreed?'

'With two provisos, Mac: you consult with me before you abort, as I'll consult with you before go or no-go, and second, if we can't make D-day we try again D plus one and D plus two.'

'All right.' McIver took a deep breath. 'Phase Three: at dawn on D-day, or D plus One or D plus Two – three days is the maximum I think we could sweat out – we radio a code message which says "Go!" The three bases acknowledge and at once all escaping birds get airborne and head for Al Shargaz. There's likely to be a four-hour difference between Scrag's arrivals and the last ones, probably Duke's – if everything goes well. The moment the birds land anywhere outside Iran we replace the Iranian registry numbers with British ones and that makes us partially legal. The moment they land at Al Shargaz the 747s are loaded, and then take off into the wild blue with everyone aboard.' McIver exhaled. 'Simple.'

Gavallan did not reply at once, sifting the plan, seeing the holes – the vast expanse of dangers. 'It's good, Mac.'

'It isn't, Andy, it isn't good at all.'

'I saw Scrag yesterday and we had a long talk. He says Whirlwind's possible for him and he's in if it's a go. He said he'd sound out the others over the weekend and let me know, but he was sure on the right day he could get his birds and lads out.'

McIver nodded but said nothing more, just drove on, the roads icy and dangerous, twisting through the narrow streets to avoid the main highways he knew would be congested. 'We're not far from the bazaar now.'

'Scrag said he might be able to get into Bandar-e Delam in the next few days and see Rudi and sound him out – letters're too risky. By the way, he gave me a note for you.'

'What's it say, Andy?'

Gavallan reached into the back for his briefcase. He found the envelope and put on reading glasses. 'It's addressed: D. D. Captain McIver Esq.'

'I'll give him what for one day with his bloody "Dirty Duncan",' McIver said. 'Read it out.'

Gavallan opened the envelope, pulled out the paper with another attached to it and grunted. 'The letter just says: "Get stuffed." Clipped to it's a medical report . . .' he peered at it. '. . . signed by Dr. G. Gernin, Australian Consulate, Al Shargaz. The old bastard's ringed cholesterol normal, blood pressure 130/85, sugar normal . . . everything's bloody normal and there's a PS in Scrag's writing: 'I'm going to buzz you on me f'ing seventy-third birthday, old cock!" '

'I hope he does, the bugger, but he won't, time's not on his side. He'll m –' McIver braked cautiously. The street led out on to the square in front of the bazaar mosque but the exit was blocked by shouting men, many waving guns. There was no way to turn aside or detour, so McIver slowed and stopped. 'It's the women again,' he said catching sight of the surging demonstration beyond, cries and countercries growing in violence. Traffic on both sides of the street piled up with great suddenness, horns blaring angrily. There were no pavements, just the usual muck-filled joubs and banked snow, a few street stalls and pedestrians.

They were hemmed in on all sides. Bystanders began to join those ahead, pressing into the roadway around the cars and trucks. Among them were urchins and youths, and one made a rude sign at Gavallan through his side window, another of them kicked the mudguard, then another and they all ran off laughing.

'Rotten little bastards.' McIver could see them in the rear mirror, other youths collecting around them. More men pushed past, more hostile looks and a couple banged the sides carelessly with their firearms. Ahead the main part of the marching women, 'Allah-u Akbarrrrr . . .' dominating, were passing the junction.

A sudden crash startled them as a stone slammed against the car,

743

narrowly missing the window, then the whole car began to rock as urchins and youths swarmed around it, jumping on and off the bumpers, making more obscene gestures. McIver's rage exploded and he tore the door open, sending a couple of the youths sprawling, then jumped out and ripped into the pack that scattered at once. Gavallan got out equally fast, to charge those trying to overturn the car at the rear. He belted one and sent him flying. Most of the others retreated, slipping and shouting, amid curses from pedestrians, but two of the bigger youths rushed Gavallan from behind. He saw them coming and smashed one in the chest, slammed the other against a truck, stunning him, and the truck driver laughed and thumped the side of his cabin. McIver was breathing hard. On his side the youths were out of range, shouting obscenities.

'Look out, Mac!'

McIver ducked. The stone narrowly missed his head and smashed into the side of a truck, and the youths, ten or twelve of them, surged forward. There was nowhere for McIver to go so he stood his ground by the bonnet and Gavallan put his back to the car, also at bay. One of the youths darted at Gavallan with a piece of wood raised as a club while three others came at him from the side. He twisted away but the club caught the edge of his shoulder and he gasped, lunged at the youth, hit him in the face off balance, slipped and sprawled in the snow. The rest came in for the kill. Suddenly he was not on the snow surrounded by hacking feet but being helped up. An armed Green Band was helping him, the youths cowering against the wall under the levelled gun of another, an elderly mullah nearby shouting at them in rage, pedestrians encircling them all. Blankly he saw McIver was also more or less unhurt near the front of the car, then the mullah came back to him and spoke to him in Farsi.

'*Nam zaban-e shoma ra khoob namu danan, agha*' – sorry, I don't speak your language, Excellency – Gavallan croaked, his chest hurting him. The mullah, an old man with white beard and white turban and black robes turned and shouted above the din at the watchers and people in other cars.

Reluctantly a driver nearby got out and came over and greeted the mullah deferentially, listened to him, then spoke to Gavallan in good though stilted English: 'The mullah informs you that the youths were wrong to attack you, agha, and have broken the law, and that clearly you were not breaking a law or provoking them.'

Again he listened to the mullah a moment, then once more turned to Gavallan and McIver. 'He wishes you to know that the Islamic Republic is obedient to the immutable laws of God. The youths broke the law which forbids attacking unarmed strangers peacefully going about their business.' The man, bearded, middle-aged, his clothes threadbare, turned back to the mullah who now loudly addressed the crowd and the youths and there was widespread approval and agreement. 'You are to witness that the law is upheld, the guilty punished and justice done at once. The punishment is fifty lashes, but first the youths will beg your forgiveness and the forgiveness of all others here.'

In the midst of the uproar from the nearby demonstration, the terrified youths were shoved and kicked in front of McIver and Gavallan where they went down on their knees and abjectly begged forgiveness. Then they were herded back against the wall and thrashed with mule scourges readily offered by the interested and jeering crowd. The mullah, the two Green Bands and others selected by the mullah enforced the law. Pitilessly.

'My God,' Gavallan muttered, sickened.

The driver-translator said sharply, 'This is Islam. Islam has one law for all people, one punishment for each crime, and justice immediate. The law is God's law, untouchable, everlasting, not like in your corrupt West where laws can be twisted and justice twisted and delayed for the benefit of lawyers who fatten on the twistings and corruptions and vilenesses or misfortunes of others . . .' Screams of some of the youths interrupted him. 'Those sons of dogs have no pride,' the man said contemptuously, going back to his car.

When the punishment was over, the mullah gently admonished those youths who were still conscious, then dismissed them and went forward with his Green Bands. The crowd drifted away leaving McIver and Gavallan beside the car. Their attackers were now pathetic bundles of inert, bloodstained rags or moaning youths trying to drag themselves to their feet. Gavallan went forward to help one of them, but the youth scrambled away petrified so he stopped, then came back. The bumpers were dented, there were deep scores in the paintwork from stones the youths had used maliciously. McIver looked older than before. 'Can't say they didn't deserve it, I suppose,' Gavallan said.

'We'd've been trampled and very bloody hurt if the mullah hadn't come along,' McIver said throatily, so glad that Genny had not been here. She'd have been punished by every lash they got, he thought, his chest and back aching from the blows. He pulled his eyes off his car, eased his shoulders painfully. Then he noticed the man who had translated for them in a nearby car still in the traffic jam and trudged painfully across the snow to him.

'Thanks, thanks for helping us, agha,' he said to him, shouting through the window and above the noise. The car was old and bent and four other men were crammed into the other seats.

The man rolled down the window. 'The mullah asked for a translator, I was helping *him*, not you,' he said, his lips curling. 'If you had not come to Iran, those young fools would not have been tempted by your disgusting display of material wealth.'

'Sorry, I just wanted to th –'

'And if it wasn't for your equally disgusting films and television that glorify your godless street gangs and rebellious classrooms that the Shah imported at the behest of his Masters to corrupt our youth – my own son and own pupils included – those poor fools would be all correctly law abiding. Better for you to leave before you too are caught breaking the law.' He rolled down the window and, angrily, jabbed the horn.

At Lochart's Apartment: 2:37 P.M. Her knuckles rapped a short code on the penthouse door. She was wearing a veil and dirt-stained chador. A series of knocks answered her. Again she tapped four rapid and one slow. At once the door swung open a crack, Teymour was there with a gun in her face and she laughed. 'Don't you trust anyone any more, my darling?' she said in Arabic, Palestinian dialect.

'No, Sayada, not even you,' he replied and when he was sure she truly was Sayada Bertolin and alone, he opened the door wider, and she pulled away her veil and scarf and went into his arms. He kicked the door shut and relocked it. 'Not even you.' Then they kissed hungrily. 'You're late.'

'On time. You're early.' Again she laughed and broke away and handed him the bag. 'About half's there, I'll bring the rest tomorrow.'

'Where did you leave the rest?'

'In the locker at the French Club.' Sayada Bertolin put her chador aside and was transformed. She wore a padded ski jacket and warm cashmere turtleneck sweater and tartan skirt and thick socks and high fur boots and everything couturier. 'Where are the others?' she asked.

His eyes smiled. 'I sent them out.'

'Ah, love in the afternoon. When do they return?'

'Sunset.'

'Perfect. First a shower – the water's still hot?'

'Oh yes, and central heating's on, and the electric blanket. Such luxury! Lochart and his wife knew how to live, this's a veritable pasha's – what's the French word? – ah yes, *garçonnière*.'

Her laugh warmed him. 'You've no idea what a pishkesh a hot shower is, my darling, so much nicer than a bath – let alone the rest.' She sat on a chair to slip off her boots. 'But it was old lecher Jared Bakravan, not Lochart, who knew how to live – originally this apartment was for a mistress.'

'You?' he asked without malice.

'No, my darling, he required them young, very young. I'm mistress to no one, not even my husband. Sharazad told me. Old Jared knew how to live, a pity he didn't have more luck in his dying.'

'He had served his purpose.'

'That was no way for such a man. Stupid!'

'He was a notorious usurer and Shah supporter, even though he gave to Khomeini lavishly. He had offended the laws of God an –'

'The laws of zealots, my darling, zealots – as you and I break all sorts of laws, eh?' She got up and kissed him lightly, walked down the corridor on the lovely carpets and went into Sharazad and Lochart's bedroom, across it into the luxurious mirrored bathroom and turned on the shower, and stood there waiting for the water to heat up. 'I always loved this apartment.'

He leaned against the doorway. 'My superiors thank you for suggesting it. How was the march?'

'Awful. Iranians are such animals, hurling abuse and filth at us, waving their penises at us, all because we want to be a little equal, want to dress as we want, to try to be beautiful for such a little time, we're young such a little time.' Again she put her hand under the water, testing it. 'Your Khomeini will have to relent.'

He laughed. 'Never – and only some are animals, Sayada, the rest know no better. Where's your civilised Palestinian tolerance?'

'Your men here have put it all into a squatting hole, Teymour. If you were a woman you'd understand.' She tried the water again and felt the heat beginning. 'It's time I went back to Beirut – I never feel clean here. I haven't felt clean in months.'

'I'll be glad to get back too. The war here is over, but not in Palestine, Lebanon or Jordan – they need trained fighters there. There are Jews to kill, the curse of Zion to cast out, and Holy places to recapture.'

'I'm glad you'll be back in Beirut,' she said, her eyes inviting. 'I've been told to go home too in a couple of weeks which suits me perfectly – then I can still be a marcher. The protest planned for Thursday is going to be the biggest ever!'

'I don't understand why you bother, Iran's not your problem and all your marches and protest meetings will achieve nothing.'

'You're wrong – Khomeini's not a fool – I take part in the marches for the same reason I work for the PLO – for our home, for equality, equality for the women of Palestine as . . . and yes, and for women everywhere.' Her brown eyes were suddenly fiery and he had never seen her more beautiful. 'Women are on the march, my darling, and by God of the Copts, the One God, and by your Marxist-Lenin you secretly admire, the day of man's dominance is over!'

'I agree,' he said at once and laughed.

Abruptly she laughed with him. 'You're a chauvinist – you who know differently.' The temperature of the water was perfect. She took off her ski jacket. 'Let's shower together.'

'Good, tell me about the papers.'

'Afterwards.' She undressed without shame and so did he, both aroused but patient for they were confident lovers – lovers of three years, in Lebanon and Palestine and here in Tehran – and he soaped her and she soaped him and they toyed, one with another, their playing gradually more intimate and more sensuous and more erotic until she cried out and cried out again, and then, the instant he was within they melded perfectly, ever more urgent now, one with another, imploding together – then later at peace together lying in the bed, the electric blanket warming them.

'What's the time?' she said sleepily with a great sigh.

'Time for love.'

Quietly she reached over and he jerked, unprepared, and retreated protesting, then caught her hand and held her closely. 'Not yet, not even you, my love!' she said, content in his arms.

'Five minutes.'

'Not for five hours, Teymour.'

'One hour . . .'

'Two hours,' she said smiling. 'In two you'll be ready again but by then I won't be here – you'll have to bed one of your soldier whores.' She stifled a yawn, then stretched as a cat would stretch. 'Oh Teymour, you're a wonderful lover, wonderful.' Then her ears caught a sound. 'Is that the shower?'

'Yes. I left it running. What luxury, eh?'

'Yes, yes, it is, but a waste.'

She slid out of bed and closed the bathroom door, used the bidet, then went into the shower and sang to herself as she washed her hair, then wrapped a fine towel around herself, dried her hair with an electric dryer and when she came back she expected to find him contentedly asleep. But he wasn't. He was lying in bed with his throat cut. The blanket that half covered him was soaked with blood, his severed genitals were neatly on the pillow beside him and two men stood there watching her. Both were armed, their revolvers fitted with silencers. Through the open bedroom door she saw another man by the front door, on guard.

'Where're the rest of the papers?' one of the men said in curiously accented English, the revolver pointed at her.

'At . . . at the French Club.'

'Where at the French Club?'

'In a locker.' She had been too many years in the PLO undercover, and too versed in life to panic. Her heartbeat was slow and she was trying to decide what to do before she died. There was a knife in her handbag but she had left the handbag on the bedside table and now it was on the bed, the contents spilled out, and there was no knife. No weapon near at hand to help her. Nothing but time – at sunset the others came back. It was nowhere near sunset. 'In the ladies section,' she added.

'Which locker?'

'I don't know – there are no numbers and it's the custom to give whatever you want kept safely to the woman attendant, you sign your name in the book which she initials and she will give whatever it is back to you when you ask for it – but only to you.'

The man glanced at the other one who nodded briefly. Both men were dark-haired and dark-eyed, moustached, and she could not place the accent. They could be Iranian, Arab or Jew – and from anywhere, from Egypt to Syria or south to Yemen. 'Get dressed. If you try anything you will not go to hell painlessly like this man – we did not wake him first. Clear?'

'Yes.' Sayada went back and began to dress. She did not try to hide. The man stood at the doorway and watched carefully, not her body but her hands. They're professionals, she thought, sickened.

'Where did you get the papers?'

'From someone called Ali. I've never seen him befo –'

'Stop!' The word cut like a razor though it was softly said. 'The next time you lie to us I will slice off that beautiful nipple and make you eat it, Sayada Bertolin. One lie, to experiment, is forgiven. Never again. Go on.'

Fear now gushed through her. 'The man's name was Abdollah bin Ali Siba, and this morning he went with me to the old tenement near the university. He led the way to the apartment and we searched where we had been told an fo –'

'Who told you?'

'The "Voice". The voice on the phone – I only know him as a voice. From . . . from time to time, he calls me with special instructions.'

'How do you recognise him?'

'Of course by his voice, and there is always a code.' She pulled her sweater over her head and now she was dressed, except for her boots. The automatic with the silencer had never wavered. 'The code is that he always mentions the previous day in some way or another in the first few minutes, whatever the day is.'

'Go on.'

'We searched under the floorboards and found the material, letters, files and some books. I put them into my bag and went to the French Club and . . . and then, because the strap on the bag broke, I left half and came here.'

'Where did you meet the man, Dimitri Yazernov?'

'I never have, I was just told to go there with Abdollah and to make sure that no one was watching, to find the papers and to give them to Teymour.'

'Why Teymour?'

'I did not ask. I never ask.'

'Wise. What does – what did Teymour do?'

'I don't know, exactly, other than he's . . . he was an Iranian, trained as a Freedom Fighter by the PLO,' she said.

'Which branch?'

'I don't know.' Beyond the man she could see into the bedroom but she kept her eyes away from the bed and on this man who knew too much. From the questioning they could be agents of SAVAMA, KGB, CIA, MI6, Israel, Jordan, Syria, Iraq, even one of the PLO extremist groups who did not acknowledge Arafat as leader – all of whom would like possession of the contents of the U.S. ambassador's safe.

'When does the Frenchman, your lover, return?'

'I don't know,' she said at once, allowing her surprise to show.

'Where is he now?'

'At his base in the Zagros. It's called Zagros Three.'

'Where is the pilot Lochart?'

'I think also at Zagros.'

'When does he return here?'

'You mean here? This apartment? I don't think he'll ever return here.'

'To Tehran?'

Her eyes strayed to the bedroom as much as she tried to resist and she

750

saw Teymour. Her stomach revolted, she groped for the toilet and was violently sick. The man watched without emotion, satisfied that one of her barriers was broken. He was used to bodies reacting of their own volition to terror. Even so, his gun covered her and he watched carefully in case of a trick.

When the spasm had passed, she cleaned her mouth with a little water, trying to dominate her nausea, cursing Teymour for being so stupid as to send the others away. Stupid! she wanted to shriek, stupid when you're surrounded by enemies on the right, or the left or in the centre – did it ever bother me before to make love when others were around so long as the door was closed?

She leaned back against the basin, facing her enemies.

'First we go to the French Club,' he said. 'You will get the rest of the material and give it to me. Clear?'

'Yes.'

'From now on you will work for us. Secretly. You will work for us. Agreed?'

'Do I have a choice?'

'Yes. You can die. Badly.' The man's lips thinned even more and his eyes became reptilian. 'After you have died, a child by the name of Yassar Bialik will receive attention.'

All colour left her face.

'Ah, good! Then you remember your little son who lives with your uncle's family, in Beirut's Street of the Flower Merchants?' The man stared at her, then, 'Well, do you?'

'Yes, yes of course,' she said, barely able to talk. Impossible for them to know about my darling Yassar, even my husband doesn't kn –

'What happened to the boy's father?'

'He . . . he was killed . . . he was . . . killed.'

'Where?'

'In . . . the Golan heights.'

'Sad to lose a young husband just a few months married,' the man said thinly. 'How old were you then?'

'Sev . . . seventeen.'

'Your memory does not fail you. Good. Now you choose to work for us, you and your son and uncle and his family are safe. If you do not obey us perfectly, or if you try to betray us, or commit suicide, the boy Yassar will cease to be a man and cease to see. Clear?'

Helplessly she nodded, her face ashen.

'If we die, others will make sure we are avenged. Do not doubt it. Now, what's your choice?'

751

'I will serve you,' and make my son safe and be avenged but how, how, *how*?

'Good, on the eyes and balls and cock of your son you will serve us?'

'Yes. Pl . . . please, who . . . who do I serve?'

Both men smiled. Without humour. 'Never ask again or try to find out. We will tell you when it is necessary, if it is necessary. Clear?'

'Yes.'

The man with the gun unscrewed the silencer and put it and the gun into his pocket. 'We want to know immediately when either the Frenchman or Lochart return – you will make it your duty to find out – also how many helicopters they have here in Tehran and where. Clear?'

'Yes. How do I get in touch with you, please?'

'You will be given a phone number.' The eyes flattened even more. 'For yourself alone. Clear?'

'Yes.'

'Where does Armstrong live? Robert Armstrong?'

'I don't know.' Warning signals rushed through her. Rumour had it that Armstrong was a trained assassin employed by MI6.

'Who is Telbot?'

'Talbot? He's an official in the British Embassy.'

'What official? What's his job?'

'I don't know, just an official.'

'Are either of them your lovers?'

'No. They . . . they go to the French Club sometimes. Acquaintances.'

'You will become Armstrong's mistress. Clear?'

'I . . . I will try.'

'You have two weeks. Where is Lochart's wife?'

'I . . . I think at the Bakravan family house near the bazaar.'

'You will make sure. And get a key to the front door.' The man saw her eyes flicker and hid his amusement. If that goes against your scruples, he thought, never mind. 'Get your coat, we go at once.'

Her knees were weak as she went across the bedroom, heading for the front door.

'Wait!' The man stuffed the contents back into her handbag and then, as an afterthought, carelessly wrapped that which was on the pillow in one of her paper tissues and put that also into the handbag. 'To remind you to obey.'

'No, please.' Her tears flooded. 'I can't . . . not that.'

The man shoved the handbag into her hands. 'Then get rid of it.'

In misery she staggered back to the bathroom and threw it into the squatter and was very sick again, more than before.

'Hurry up!'

When she could make her legs work she faced him. 'When the others . . . when they come back and find . . . if I'm not here they . . . they will know that . . . that I'm part of those who . . . who did this and . . .'

'Of course. Do you think we're fools? Do you think we're alone? The moment the four of them return they're dead and this place conflagrated.'

At McIver's Apartment: 4:20 P.M. Ross said, 'I don't know, Mr. Gavallan, I don't remember much after I left Azadeh on the hill and went into the base, more or less up to the time we got here.' He was wearing one of Pettikin's uniform shirts and a black sweater and black trousers and black shoes and was shaved and neat, but his faced showed his utter exhaustion. 'But before that, everything happened as . . . as I told you.'

'Terrible,' Gavallan said. 'But thank God for you, Captain. But for you the others'd be dead. Without you they'd all be lost. Let's have a drink, it's so damned cold. We've some whisky.' He motioned to Pettikin. 'Charlie?'

Pettikin went to the sideboard. 'Sure, Andy.'

'I won't, thanks, Mr. McIver,' Ross said.

'I'm afraid I will and the sun's not over the yardarm,' McIver said.

'So will I,' Gavallan said. The two of them had arrived not long ago, still shaken from their almost disaster, and worried because at Sharazad's house they had used the iron door knocker again and again but to no avail. Then they had come here. Ross, dozing on the sofa, had almost leaped out of sleep when the front door opened, kukri threateningly in his hand.

'Sorry,' he had said shakily, sheathing the weapon.

'That's all right,' Gavallan had pretended, not over his fright. 'I'm Andrew Gavallan. Hi, Charlie! Where's Azadeh?'

'She's still asleep in the spare bedroom,' Pettikin answered.

'Sorry to make you jump,' Gavallan had said. 'What happened, Captain, at Tabriz?'

So Ross had told them, disjointedly, jumping back and forth until he had finished. Exploding out of heavy sleep had creased him. His head ached, everything ached, but he was glad to be telling what had happened, reconstructing everything, gradually filling in the blank parts, putting the pieces into place. Except Azadeh. No, I can't put her in place yet.

This morning when he had come out of a malevolent wake-sleep dream he had been terrified, everything mixed up, jet engines and guns and stones and explosions and cold, and staring at his hands to make sure what was dream and what was real. Then he had seen a man peering at him and had cried out, 'Where's Azadeh?'

'She's still asleep, Captain Ross, she's in the spare room down the hall,' Pettikin had told him, calming him. 'Remember me? Charlie Pettikin – Doshan Tappeh?'

Searching his memory. Things coming back slowly, hideous things. Big blanks, very big. Doshan Tappeh? What about Doshan Tappeh? Going there to hitch a chopper ride and . . . 'Ah yes, Captain, how are you? Good to . . . to see you. She's asleep?'

'Yes, like a baby.'

'Best thing, best thing for her to sleep,' he had said, his brain still not working easily.

'First a cuppa. Then a bath and shave and I'll fix you up with some clothes and shaving gear. You're about my size. You hungry? We've eggs and some bread, the bread's a bit stale.'

'Oh, thanks, no, no I'm not hungry – you're very kind.'

'I owe you one – no, at least ten, I'm damned pleased to see you. Listen, much as I'd like to know what happened . . . well, McIver's gone to the airport to pick up our boss, Andy Gavallan. They'll be back shortly, you'll have to tell them so I can find out then – so no questions till then, you must be exhausted.'

'Thanks, yes it's . . . it's still all a bit . . . I can remember leaving Azadeh on the hill, then almost nothing, just flashes, dreamlike, until I woke a moment ago. How long have I been asleep?'

'You've been out for about sixteen hours. We, that's Nogger and our two mecs, half-carried you both in here and then you both passed out. We put you and Azadeh to bed like babies – Mac and I. We undressed you, washed part of the muck off, carried you to bed – not too gently by the way – but you never woke up, either of you.'

'She's all right? Azadeh?'

'Oh, yes. I checked her a couple of times but she's still flat out. What did . . . sorry, no questions! First a shave and bath. 'Fraid the water's barely warm but I've put the electric heater in the bathroom, it's not too bad . . .'

Now Ross was watching Pettikin who was handing the whisky to McIver and to Gavallan. 'Sure you won't, Captain?'

'No, no thanks.' Without noticing it he felt his right wrist and rubbed it. His energy level was ebbing fast. Gavallan saw the man's tiredness and knew there was not much time. 'About Erikki. You can't remember anything else to give us an idea where he might be?'

'Not any more than I've told you. Azadeh may be able to help – the Soviet's name was something like Certaga, the man Erikki was forced to work with up by the border – as I said they were using her as a threat and there was some complication about her father and a trip they were going to make together – sorry, I can't remember exactly. The other man, the one who was friends with Abdollah Khan was called Mzytryk, Petr Oleg.' That reminded Ross about Vien Rosemont's code message for the Khan, but he decided that was none of Gavallan's business, nor about all the killing, nor about shoving the old man in front of the truck on the hill, nor that one day he would go back to the village and hack off the head of the butcher and the kalandar who, but for the grace of God or the spirits of the High Land, would have stoned her and mutilated him. He would do that after the debriefing when he saw Armstrong, or Talbot, or the American colonel, but before that he would ask them who had betrayed the operation at Mecca. Someone had. For a moment the thought of Rosemont and Tenzing and Gueng blinded him. When the mist cleared, he saw the clock on the mantelpiece. 'I have to go to a building near the British Embassy. Is that far from here?'

'No, we could take you if you like.' Gavallan glanced at McIver. 'Mac, let's go now . . . perhaps I can catch Talbot. We'll still have time to come back to see Azadeh, and Nogger if he's here.'

'Good idea.'

'Could that be now? Sorry, but I'm afraid I'll pass out again if I don't get with it.'

Gavallan got up and put on his heavy coat.

Pettikin said to Ross, 'I'll lend you a coat and some gloves.' He saw his eyes stray down the corridor. 'Would you like me to wake Azadeh?'

'No, thanks. I'll . . . I'll just look in.'

'It's the second door on the left.'

They watched him go along the corridor, his walk noiseless and catlike, open the door silently and stand there a moment and close it again. He collected his assault rifle and the two kukris, his and Gueng's. He thought a moment, then put his on the mantelpiece.

'In case I don't get back,' he said, 'tell her this's a gift, a gift for Erikki. For Erikki and her.'

At the Palace of the Khan: 5:19 P.M. The kalandar of Abu Mard was on his knees and petrified. 'No, no, Highness, I swear it was the mullah Mahmud who told us –'

'He's not a real mullah, you son of a dog, everyone knows that! By God, you . . . you were going to stone my daughter?' the Khan shrieked, his face mottled, his breath coming in great pants. '*You* decided? *You* decided you were going to stone *my* daughter?'

'It was him, Highness,' the kalandar whispered, 'it was the mullah who decided after questioning her and her admitting adultery with the saboteur . . .'

'You son of a dog! You aided and abetted that false mullah . . . Liar! Ahmed told me what happened!' The Khan propped himself on his bed pillows, a guard behind him, Ahmed and other guards close to the kalandar in front of him, Najoud, his eldest daughter, and Aysha, his young wife, seated to one side trying to hide their terror at his rage and petrified that he would turn on them. Kneeling beside the door still in his travel-stained clothes and filled with dread was Hakim, Azadeh's

756

brother, who had just arrived and had been rushed here under guard in response to the Khan's summons, and who had listened with equal rage to Ahmed relating what had happened at the village.

'You son of a dog,' the Khan shouted again, his mouth salivating. 'You let . . . you let the dog of a saboteur escape . . . you let him drag my daughter off with him . . . you harbour the saboteur and then . . . then you dare to judge one of my–MY – family and would stone . . . without seeking my–MY – approval?'

'It was the mullah . . .' the kalandar cried out, repeating it again and again.

'*Shut him up!*'

Ahmed hit him hard on one of his ears, momentarily stunning him. Then dragged him roughly back on to his knees and hissed, 'Say one more word and I'll cut your tongue out.'

The Khan was trying to catch his breath. 'Aysha, give me . . . give me one of those . . . those pills . . .' She scurried over, still on her knees, opened the bottle and put a pill into his mouth and wiped it for him. The Khan kept the pill under his tongue as the doctor had told him and in a moment the spasm passed, the thundering in his ears lessened and the room stopped weaving. His bloodshot eyes went back on to the old man who was whimpering and shaking uncontrollably. 'You son of a dog! So you dare to bite the hand that owns you – you, your butcher and your festering village? Ibrim,' the Khan said to one of the guards, 'take him back to Abu Mard and stone him, have the villagers stone him, *stone him*, then cut off the hands of the butcher.'

Ibrim and another guard pulled the howling man to his feet, smashed him into silence and opened the door, stopped as Hakim said harshly, 'Then burn the village!'

The Khan looked at him, his eyes narrowed. 'Yes, then burn the village,' he echoed and kept his eyes on Hakim who looked back at him, trying to be brave. The door closed and now the quiet heightened, broken only by Abdollah's breathing. 'Najoud, Aysha, leave!' he said.

Najoud hesitated, wanting to stay, wanting to hear sentence pronounced on Hakim, gloating that Azadeh had been caught in her adultery and was therefore due punishment whenever she was recaptured. Good, good, good. With Azadeh they both perish, Hakim and the Redhead of the Knife. 'I will be within instant call, Highness,' she said.

'You can go back to your quarters. Aysha – you wait at the end of the corridor.' Both women left. Ahmed closed the door contentedly, everything going as planned. The other two guards waited in silence.

The Khan shifted painfully, motioning to them. 'Wait outside. Ahmed, you stay.' When they had gone and there were just the three of them in the big, cold room he changed his gaze back to Hakim. 'Burn the village, you said. A good idea. But that doesn't excuse your treachery, or your sister's.'

'Nothing excuses treachery against a father, Highness. But neither Azadeh or I have betrayed you or plotted against you.'

'Liar! You heard Ahmed! She admitted fornicating with the saboteur, she admitted it.'

'She admitted "loving" him, Highness, years and years ago. She swore before God she had never committed adultery or betrayed her husband. Never! In front of those dogs and sons of dogs and worse, that mullah of the Left Hand, what should the daughter of a Khan say? Didn't she try to protect your name in front of that godless mob of shit?'

'Still twisting words, still protecting the whore she became?'

Hakim's face went ashen. 'Azadeh fell in love as Mother fell in love. If she's a whore, then you whored my mother!'

Blood surged back into the Khan's face. '*How dare you say such a thing!*'

'It's true. You lay with her before you were married. Because she loved you she let you secretly into her bedroom and so risked death. She risked death because she loved you and you begged her. Didn't our *mother* persuade her father to accept you, and persuade your father to allow *you* to marry her, instead of your older brother who wanted her as a second wife for himself?' Hakim's voice broke, remembering her in her dying, him seven, Azadeh six, not understanding very much, only that she was in terrible pain from something called 'tumour' and outside, in the courtyard, their father Abdollah beset with grief. 'Didn't she always stand up for you against your father and your older brother and then, when your brother was killed and you became heir, didn't she heal the breach with your father?'

'You can't . . . can't know such things, you were . . . you were too young!'

'Old Nanny Fatemeh told us, she told us before she died, she told us everything she could remember . . .'

The Khan was hardly listening, remembering too, remembering his brother's hunting accident he had so deftly engineered – old Nanny might have known about that too and if she did then Hakim knows and Azadeh knows, all the more reason to silence them. Remembering, too, all the magic times he had had with Napthala the Fair, before and after

758

marriage and during all the days until the beginning of the pain. They had been married not even one year when Hakim was born, two when Azadeh appeared, Napthala just sixteen then, tiny, physically a pattern of Aysha but a thousand times more beautiful, her long hair like spun gold. Five more heavenly years, no more children but that never mattered, hadn't he a son at long last, strong and upright – where his three sons from his first wife had all been born sickly, soon to die, his four daughters ugly and squabbling. Wasn't his wife still only twenty-two, in good health, as strong and as wonderful as the two children she had already birthed? Plenty of time for more sons.

Then the pain beginning. And the agony. No help from all the doctors in Tehran.

Insha'Allah, they said.

No relief except drugs, ever more strong as she wasted away. God grant her the peace of Paradise and let me find her there. He was watching Hakim, seeing the pattern of Azadeh who was a pattern of the mother, listening to him running on. 'Azadeh only fell in love, Highness. If she loved that man, can't you forgive her? Wasn't she only sixteen and banished to school in Switzerland as later I was banished to Khvoy?'

'Because you were both treacherous, ungrateful, and poisonous!' the Khan shouted, his ears beginning to thunder again. 'Get out! You're to . . . to stay away from all others, under guard, until I send for you. Ahmed, see to it, then come back here.'

Hakim got up, near tears, knowing what was going to happen and powerless to prevent it. He stumbled out. Ahmed gave the necessary orders to the guards and came back into the room. Now the Khan's eyes were closed, his face very grey, his breathing more laboured than before. Please God do not let him die yet, Ahmed prayed.

The Khan opened his eyes and focused. 'I have to decide about him, Ahmed. Quickly.'

'Yes, Highness,' his counsellor began, choosing his words carefully, 'you have but two sons, Hakim and the babe. If Hakim were to die or,' he smiled strangely, 'happened to become sightless and crippled, then Mahmud, husband of her Highness Najoud will be regent unt –'

'That fool? Our lands and power would be lost within a year!' Patches of redness flared in the Khan's face and he was finding it increasingly difficult to think clearly. 'Give me another pill.'

Ahmed obeyed and gave him water to drink, gentling him. 'You're in God's hands, you will recover, don't worry.'

'Don't worry,' the Khan muttered, pain in his chest. 'The Will of

God the mullah died in time . . . strange. Petr Oleg kept his bargain . . . though he . . . the mullah died too fast . . . too fast.'

'Yes, Highness.'

In time the spasm again passed. 'Wh . . . what's your advice . . . about Hakim?'

Ahmed pretended to think a moment. 'Your son Hakim is a good Muslim, he could be trained, he has managed your affairs in Khvoy well and has not fled as perhaps he could have done. He is not a violent man – except to protect his sister, eh? But that's very important, for therein lies his key.' He came closer and said softly, 'Decree him your heir, High –'

'Never!'

'Providing he swears by God to guard his young brother as he would his sister, providing further his sister returns at once of her own will to Tabriz. In truth, Highness, you have no real evidence against them, only hearsay. Entrust me to find out the truth of him and of her – and to report secretly to you.'

The Khan was concentrating, listening carefully though the effort was taxing him. 'Ah, the brother's the bait to snare the sister – as she was the bait to snare the husband?'

'As they're both bait for the other! Yes, Highness, of course you thought of it before me. In return for giving the brother your favour, she must swear before God to stay here to help him.'

'She'll do that, oh, yes, she'll do that!'

'Then they'll both be within your reach and you can toy with them at your pleasure, giving and withholding at your whim, whether they're guilty or not.'

'They're guilty.'

'If they're guilty, and I will know quickly if you give me complete authority to investigate, then it's God's will that they will die slowly, that you decree Fazulia's husband to be Khan after you, not much better than Mahmud. If they're not guilty, then let Hakim remain heir, providing she stays. And if it were to happen, again at God's will, that she is a widow, she'd even betroth him whom you choose, Highness, to keep Hakim your heir – even a Soviet, should he escape the trap, no?'

For the first time today, the Khan smiled. This morning when Armstrong and Colonel Hashemi Fazir had arrived to take possession of Petr Oleg Mzytryk, they had pretended to be suitably concerned about the Khan's health as he had pretended outwardly to be sicker than he had felt at that time. He had kept his voice wan and hesitant and very low so they both had had to lean forward to hear him. 'Petr Oleg is coming here today. I was going to meet him but I asked him to come here because of my . . . because I'm sick. I sent him word to come here and he should be at the border at sunset. At Julfa. If you go at once you'll be in plenty of time . . . he sneaks over the border in a small Soviet helicopter gunship and lands near a side road off the Julfa-Tabriz road where his car is waiting for him . . . no chance to miss the turning, it's the only one . . . a few kilometres north of the city . . . it's the only side road, desolate country, soon little more than a track. How you . . . how you take him is your affair and . . . and as I cannot be present, you will give me a tape of the . . . the investigation?'

'Yes, Highness,' Hashemi had said. 'How would you advise us to take him?'

'Choke the road both sides of the turnoff with a couple of old, heavily laden farm trucks . . . firewood or crates of fish . . . the road's narrow and twisting and potholed and heavy with traffic, so an ambush should be easy. But . . . but be careful, there're always Tudeh cars to run interference for him, he's a wise man and fearless . . . there's a poison capsule in his lapel.'

'Which one?'

'I don't know . . . I don't know. He will land near sunset. You can't miss the turnoff, it's the only one.'

Abdollah Khan sighed, lost in his thoughts. Many times he had been picked up by the same helicopter to go to the dacha at Tbilisi. Many good times there, the food lavish, the women young and accommodating, full lipped and hungry to please – then, if he was lucky, Vertinskya, the hellcat, for further entertainment.

He saw Ahmed watching him. 'I hope Petr escapes the trap. Yes, it would be good for him to . . . to have her.' Tiredness swamped him. 'I'll sleep now. Send my guard back and after I've eaten tonight, assemble my "devoted" family here and we will do as you suggest.' His smile was cynical. 'It's wise to have no illusions.'

'Yes, Highness.' Ahmed got to his feet. The Khan envied him his lithe and powerful body.

'Wait, there was something . . . something else.' The Khan thought a moment, the process strangely tiring. 'Ah yes, where's Redhead of the Knife?'

'With Cimtarga, up near the border, Highness. Cimtarga said they might be away for a few days. They left Tuesday night.'

'Tuesday? What's today?'

'Saturday, Highness,' Ahmed replied, hiding his concern.

'Ah yes, Saturday.' Another wave of tiredness. His face felt strange and he lifted his hand to rub it but found the effort too much. 'Ahmed, find out where he is. If anything happens . . . if I have another attack and I'm . . . well, see that . . . that I'm taken to Tehran, to the International Hospital, at once. At once. Understand?'

'Yes, Highness.'

'Find out where he is and . . . and for the next few days keep him close by . . . overrule Cimtarga. Keep He of the Knife close by.'

'Yes, Highness.'

When the guard came back into the room, the Khan closed his eyes and felt himself sinking into the depths. 'There is no other God but God . . .' he muttered, very afraid.

Near the North Border, East of Julfa: 6:05 P.M. It was near sunset and Erikki's 212 was under a crude, hastily constructed lean-to, the roof already a foot deep in snow from the storm last night, and he knew much more exposure in sub zero weather would ruin her. 'Can't you give me blankets or straw or something to keep her warm?' he had asked Sheik Bayazid the moment they had arrived back from Rezaiyeh with the body of the old woman, the Chieftain, two days ago. 'The chopper needs warmth.'

'We do not have enough for the living.'

'If she freezes she won't work,' he had said, fretting that the Sheik would not allow him to leave at once for Tabriz, barely sixty miles away – worried sick about Azadeh and wondering what had happened to Ross and Gueng. 'If she won't work, how are we going to get out of these mountains?'

Grudgingly, the Sheik had ordered his people to construct the lean-to and had given him some goat and sheep skins that he had used where he thought they would do the most good. Just after dawn yesterday he had tried to leave. To his total dismay Bayazid had told him that he and the 212 were to be ransomed.

'You can be patient, Captain, free to walk our village with a calm guard, to tinker with your airplane,' Bayazid had said curtly, 'or you can be impatient and angry and you will be bound up and tethered as a wild beast. I seek no trouble, Captain, want none, or argument. We seek ransom from Abdollah Khan.'

'But I've told you he hates me and won't help me to be rans –'

'If he says no, we seek ransom elsewhere. From your company in Tehran, or your government – perhaps your Soviet employers. Meanwhile, you stay here as guest, eating as we eat, sleeping as we sleep, sharing equally. Or bound and tethered and hungry. Either way you stay until ransom is paid.'

'But that might take months an –'

'Insha'Allah!'

All day yesterday and half the night Erikki had tried to think of a way out of the trap. They had taken his grenade but left him his knife. But his guards were watchful and constant. In these deep snows, it would be almost impossible for him in flying boots and without winter gear to get down to the valley below, and even then he was in hostile country. Tabriz was barely thirty minutes away by 212, but by foot?

'More snow tonight, Captain.'

Erikki looked around. Bayazid was a pace away and he had not heard him approach. 'Yes, and a few more days in this weather and my bird, my airplane, won't fly – the battery'll be dead and most of the instruments wrecked. I have to start her up to charge the battery and warm her pots, have to. Who's going to ransom a wrecked 212 out of these hills?'

Bayazid thought a moment. 'For how long must engines turn?'

'Ten minutes a day – absolute minimum.'

'All right. Just after full dark, each day you may do it but first you ask me. We help you drag her – why is it "she", not an "it" or a "he"?'

Erikki frowned. 'I don't know. Ships are always "she" – this is a ship of the sky.' He shrugged.

'Very well. We help you drag her into open and you start her up and while her engines running there will be five guns within five feet should you be tempted.'

Erikki laughed. 'Then I won't be tempted.'

'Good.' Bayazid smiled. He was a handsome man though his teeth were bad.

'When do you send word to the Khan?'

'It already gone. In these snows it takes a day to get down to road, even on horseback, but not long to reach Tabriz. If the Khan replies favourably, at once, perhaps we hear tomorrow, perhaps day after, depending on the snows.'

'Perhaps never. How long will you wait?'

'Are all people from Far North so impatient?'

Erikki's chin jutted. 'The ancient gods were very impatient when they were held against their will – they passed it on to us. It's bad to be held against your will, very bad.'

'We are a poor people, at war. We must take what the One God gives us. To be ransomed is an ancient custom.' He smiled thinly. 'We

763

learned from Saladin to be chivalrous with our captives, unlike many Christians. Christians are not known for their chivalry. We are treat –'
His ears were sharper than Erikki's and so were his eyes. 'There, down in the valley!'

Now Erikki heard the engine also. It took him a moment to pick out the low-flying, camouflaged helicopter approaching from the north. 'A Kajychokiv 16. Close-support Soviet army gunship . . . what's she doing?'

'Heading for Julfa.' The Sheik spat on the ground. 'Those sons of dogs come and go as they please.'

'Do many sneak in now?'

'Not many – but one is too many.'

Near the Julfa Turnoff: 6:15 P.M. The winding side road through the forest was snow heavy and not ploughed. A few cart and truck tracks and those made by the old, four-wheel drive Chevy that was parked under some pines near the open space, a few yards off the main road. Through their binoculars Armstrong and Hashemi could see two men in warm coats and gloves sitting in the front seat, the windows open, listening intently.

'He hasn't much time,' Armstrong muttered.

'Perhaps he's not coming after all.' They had been watching for half an hour from a slight rise among the trees overlooking the landing area. Their car and the rest of Hashemi's men were parked discreetly on the main road below and behind them. It was very quiet, little wind. Some birds went overhead, cawing plaintively.

'Hallelujah!' Armstrong whispered, his excitement picking up. One man had opened the side door and got out. Now he was looking into the northern sky. The driver started the engine. Then, over it, they heard the incoming chopper, saw her slip over the rise and fall into the valley, hugging the tree tops, her piston engine throttled back nicely. She made a perfect landing in a billowing cloud of snow. They could see the pilot and another man beside him. The passenger, a small man, got out and went to meet the other. Armstrong cursed.

'You recognise him, Robert?'

'No. That's not Suslev – Petr Oleg Mzytryk. I'm certain.' Armstrong was bitterly disappointed.

'Facial surgery?'

'No, nothing like that. He was a big bugger, heavyset, tall as I am.' They watched as he met the other, then handed over something.

'Was that a letter? What did he give him, Robert?'

'Looked like a package, could be a letter.' Armstrong muttered another curse, concentrating on their lips.

'What're they saying?' Hashemi knew Armstrong could lip read.

'I don't know – it's not Farsi, or English.'

Hashemi swore and refocused his already perfectly focused binoculars. 'It looked like a letter to me.' The man spoke a few more words then went back to the chopper. At once the pilot put on power and swirled away. The other man then trudged back to the Chevy. 'Now what?' Hashemi said exasperated.

Armstrong watched the man walking towards the car. 'Two options: intercept the car as planned and find out what "it" is, providing we could neutralise those two bastards before they destroyed "it" but that'd blow that we know the arrival point for Mister Big – or just tail them, presuming it's a message for the Khan giving a new date.' He was over his disappointment that Mzytryk had avoided the trap. You must have the luck in our game, he reminded himself. Never mind, next time we'll get him and he'll lead us to our traitor, to the fourth man and fifth and sixth man and I'll piss on their graves and Suslev's – or whatever Petr Oleg Mzytryk calls himself – if the luck's with me. 'We needn't even tail them – he'll go straight to the Khan.'

'Why?'

'Because he's a vital pivot in Azerbaijan, either for the Soviets or against them, so they'd want to find out firsthand just how bad his heart is – and who he's chosen as regent till the babe comes of age, or more likely is levitated. Doesn't the power go with the title, along with the lands and the wealth?'

'And the secret, numbered Swiss bank accounts – all the more reason to come at once.'

'Yes, but don't forget something serious might have happened in Tbilisi to make for the delay – Soviets're just as pissed off and anxious as we are about Iran.' They saw the man climb back into the Chevy and begin talking volubly. The driver let in the clutch and turned back for the main road. 'Let's get back to our car.'

The way back down the rise was fairly easy going, traffic heavy on the Julfa-Tabriz road below, a few headlamps already on and no way for their prey to escape the ambush if they decided to stage it. 'Hashemi, another possibility's that Mzytryk could have found out in the nick that he's been betrayed by his son, and he's sent a warning to the Khan whose cover would also have been blown. Don't forget we still haven't found out what happened to Rakoczy since your late departed friend General Janan let him go.'

765

'That dog'd never do it on his own,' Hashemi said with a twisted smile, remembering his vast joy when he had touched the transmit button and had seen the resultant car bomb explosion obliterate that enemy, along with his house, his future and his past. 'That would be ordered by Abrim Pahmudi.'

'Why?'

Hashemi veiled his eyes and glanced at Armstrong but read no hidden guile therein. You know too many secrets, Robert, know about the Rakoczy tapes, and worst of all about my Group Four and that I assisted Janan into hell – where the Khan will soon join him, as Talbot's due too in a couple of days, and you, my old friend, at my leisure. Should I tell you Pahmudi has ordered Talbot punished for his crimes against Iran? Should I tell you I'm happy to oblige? For years I've wanted Talbot removed but've never dared to go against him alone. Now Pahmudi is to blame, may God burn him, and another irritant will be out of my way. Ah yes, and Pahmudi himself this coming week – but you, Robert, you're the chosen assassin for that, probably to perish. Pahmudi's not worth one of my real assassins.

He chortled to himself, trudging down the hill, not feeling the cold, not worried about Mzytryk's nonappearance. I've more important worries, he was thinking. At all costs I've got to protect my Group Four assassins – my guarantee for an earthly paradise with power over even Khomeini himself.

'Pahmudi's the only one who could have ordered Rakoczy's release,' he said. 'Soon I'll find out why and where he is. He's either in the Soviet embassy, a Soviet safe house or in a SAVAMA interrogation dungeon.'

'Or safely out of the country by now.'

'Then he's safely dead – the KGB don't tolerate traitors.' Hashemi smiled sardonically. 'What's your bet?'

For a moment Armstrong did not answer, thrown by the question that was unusual for Hashemi who disapproved of gambling, as he did. Now. The last time he had bet was in Hong Kong in '63 with bribe money that had been put into his desk drawer when he was a Superintendent, CID. Forty thousand Hong Kong dollars – about seven thousand U.S. then. Against all his principles, he had taken the *heung yau*, the Fragrant Grease as it was called there, out of the drawer and, at the races that afternoon, had bet it all on the nose of a horse called Pilot Fish, all in one insane attempt to recoup his gambling losses – horses and the stock market.

This was the first bribe money he had ever taken in eighteen years in the force though it was always readily available in abundance. That afternoon he had won heavily and had replaced the money before the police sergeant giver had noticed it had been touched – with more than enough left over for his debts. Even so he had been disgusted with himself and appalled at his stupidity. He had never bet again, nor touched *heung yau* again though the opportunity was always there. 'You're a bloody fool, Robert,' some of his peers would say, 'no harm in a little dolly money for retirement.'

Retirement? What retirement? Christ, twenty years a copper in Hong Kong on the straight and narrow, eleven years here, equally so, helping these bloodthirsty twits, and it's all up the bloody spout. Thank God I've only me to worry about, no wife now or kids or close relations, just me. If I get bloody Suslev who'll lead me to one of our high-up murdering bloody traitors, it'll all have been worth it.

'Like you, I'm not a betting man, Hashemi, but if I was . . .' He stopped and offered his packet of cigarettes and they lit up gratefully. The smoke mixed with the cold air and showed clear in the falling light. 'If I was, I'd say it was odds on that Rakoczy was your Pahmudi's pishkesh to some Soviet VIP, just to play it safe.'

Hashemi laughed. 'You're becoming more Iranian every day. I'll have to be more careful.' They were almost to the car now and his assistant got out to open the rear door for him. 'We'll go straight to the Khan, Robert.'

'What about the Chevvy?'

'We'll leave others to tail it, I want to get to the Khan first.' The colonel's face darkened. 'Just to make sure that traitor's more on our side than theirs.'

At Kowiss Airbase: 6:35 P.M. Starke stared at Gavallan in total shock. 'Whirlwind in six days?'

' 'Fraid so, Duke.' Gavallan unzipped his parka and put his hat on the hall stand. 'Wanted to tell you myself – sorry but there it is.' The two men were in Starke's bungalow and he had stationed Freddy Ayre outside to make sure they were not overheard. 'I heard this morning all our birds are going to be grounded, pending nationalisation. We've six safe days to plan and execute Whirlwind – if we do it. That makes it next Friday. On Saturday we're on borrowed time.'

'Jesus.' Absently Starke unzipped his flight jacket and clomped over to the sideboard, his flying boots leaving a little trail of snow and water droplets on the carpet. At the back of the bottom drawer was his last bottle of beer. He nipped the top off, poured half into a glass and gave it to Gavallan. 'Health,' he said, drinking from the bottle, and sat on the sofa.

'Health.'

'Who's in, Andy?'

'Scrag. Don't know yet about the rest of his lads but I'll know tomorrow. Mac's come up with a schedule and an overall, three-phase plan that's full of holes but possible. Let's say it's possible. What about you and your lads?'

'What's Mac's plan?'

Gavallan told him.

'You're right, Andy. It's full of holes.'

'If you were to do a bunk, how'd you plan it from here – you've got the longest distances and the most difficulty?'

Starke went over to the flight map on the wall and pointed at a line that went from Kowiss to a cross a few miles out in the Gulf, indicating a rig. 'This rig's called Flotsam, one of our regulars,' he said and Gavallan noticed how tight his voice had become. 'It takes us about twenty minutes to reach the coast and another ten to get to the rig. I'd cache fuel on the shore near that bearing. I think it could be done without causing too much suspicion, it's just sand dunes and no huts within miles and a lot of us used to picnic there. An "emergency" landing to safety-check flotation gear before going out to sea shouldn't get radar too itchy though they get worse every day. We'd have to cache two 40-gallon drums per chopper to get us across the Gulf and we'd have to refuel in flight by hand.'

It was almost dusk. Windows looked out on the runway and beyond it to the Air Force base. The 125 was parked on the apron, waiting for the fuel truck to arrive. Officious, nervous Green Bands surrounded her. With priority clearance onward to Al Shargaz, refuelling was not really necessary but Gavallan had told John Hogg to request it anyway to give him more time with Starke. The other two passengers, Arberry and Dibble, being sent on leave after their escape from Tabriz – and crammed between a full load of crates of spares hastily packed and marked in English and Farsi: 'For Immediate Repair and return to Tehran' – were not allowed to land, even to stretch their legs. Nor the pilots, except to ground check and to supervise the fuelling when the truck arrived.

'You'd head for Kuwait?' Gavallan asked, breaking the silence.

'Sure. Kuwait'd be our best bet, Andy. We'd have to refuel in Kuwait, then work our way down the coast to Al Shargaz. If it was up to me I guess I'd park more fuel against an emergency.' Starke pinpointed a tiny speck of an Island off Saudi. 'Here'd be good – best to stay offshore Saudi, no telling what they'd do.' Queasily he stared at all the distances. 'The island's called Jellet, the Toad, which's what it looks like. No huts, no nothing but great fishing. Manuela and I went out there once or twice when I was stationed at Bahrain. I'd park fuel there.'

He took off his flight cap and wiped the droplets off his forehead then put his cap back on again, his face more etched and tired than usual, all flights more harassed than usual, cancelled then reordered and cancelled again, Esvandiary more foul than usual, everyone edgy and irritable, no mail or contact with home for weeks. Most of his people, including himself, overdue leave and replacement. Then there's the added problems of the incoming Zagros Three personnel and airplanes and what to do with old Effer Jordon's body when it arrives tomorrow. That had been Starke's first question when he had met Gavallan at the 125 steps.

'I've got that in hand, Duke,' Gavallan had said heavily, the wind ten knots and chill. 'I've got ATC's permission for the 125 to come back tomorrow to pick up the coffin. I'll ship it back to England on the first available flight. Terrible. I'll see his wife as soon as I get back and do what I can.'

'Lousy luck – thank God young Scot's okay, huh?'

'Yes, but lousy that anyone got hurt, lousy.' What if it was Scot's corpse and Scot's coffin? Gavallan was thinking again, the question never ending. What if it had been Scot, could you still compartmentalise the murder so easily? No, of course not. All you can do is bless your joss this time and do the best you can – just do the best you can. 'Curiously, Tehran ATC and the airport komiteh were as shocked as we were, and very helpful. Let's go and chat – I've not much time. Here's mail for some of the lads and one from Manuela, she's fine, Duke. She said not to worry. Kids're fine and want to stay in Texas. Your folks're fine too – she asked me to tell you first thing when I caught up with you . . .'

Then Gavallan had delivered the bombshell of six days and now Starke's mind was in a fog. 'With Zagros's birds here, I'll have three 212s, one Alouette and three 206s plus a load of spares. Nine pilots, including Tom Lochart and Jean-Luc, and twelve mechanics. That's way too many for a caper like Whirlwind, Andy.'

'I know.' Gavallan looked out of the window. The fuelling truck was lumbering alongside the 125 and he saw Johnny Hogg come down the steps. 'How long will she take to refuel?'

'If Johnny doesn't hurry them up, three quarters of an hour, easy.'

'Not much time to make a plan,' Gavallan said. He looked back at the map. 'But then there'd never be enough. Is there a rig near that bearing that's empty – still closed down?'

'Dozens. There're dozens that're still as the strikers left them months ago – doors welded closed, crazy, huh? Why?'

'Scrag said one of them might be an ideal spot to park gasoline and refuel.'

Starke frowned. 'Not in our area, Andy. He's got some big platforms – ours're little bitty ones mostly. We've none that could take more than one chopper at a time and we sure as hell wouldn't want to wait around. What'd old Scrag say?'

Gavallan told him.

'You think he'll get to go see Rudi?'

'He said in the next few days. I can't wait that long now. Could you find an excuse to get down to Bandar-e Delam?'

Starke's eyes narrowed. 'Sure. Maybe we could send a couple of our birds there an' say we're redeploying them – even better, tell Hotshot we're putting 'em on loan for a week. We can still get occasional clearances – so long as that sonofabitch's out the way.'

'We can't operate any longer in Iran. Poor old Jordon should never have happened, and I'm damned sorry I didn't order an evacuation weeks ago. Damned sorry.'

'He wasn't your fault, Andy.'

'In a way he was. In any event we have to pull out. With or without our planes. We have to try to salvage what we can – without risking personnel.'

'Any caper's going to be goddam risky, Andy.' Starke's voice was gentle.

'I know. I'd like you to ask your lads if they'd be part of Whirlwind.'

'There's no way we could get out all our choppers. No way.'

'I know, so I propose we concentrate on our 212s only.' Gavallan saw Starke look at him with more interest. 'Mac agreed. Could you fly your three out?'

Starke thought a moment. 'Two's max that I could handle – we'd need two pilots, with say one mechanic per chopper for emergencies and some hands to handle the spare drums or in-flight refuel – that'd be minimum. It'd be tricky but if we got lucky . . .' He whistled tonelessly, 'Maybe we could send the other 212 to Rudi at Bandar-e Delam? Sure, why the hell not? I'd tell Hotshot she's on loan for ten days. You could send me a confirm telex asking for the transfer. But hell, Andy, we'd still have three pilots here an –'

The interbase phone rang. 'Goddam,' he said irritably, getting up and going over to it. 'I'm so used to having the phones out, every time

771

one rings I jump like a scalded cat expecting Armageddon. Hello, this's Starke. Yeah?'

Gavallan watched Starke, tall, lean and so strong. Wish I were as strong, he thought.

'Ah, thanks,' Starke was saying. 'Okay . . . sure, thanks, Sergeant. Who? . . . Sure, put him on.' Gavallan noticed the change in the voice and his attention increased. ' 'Evening . . . No, we can't, not now . . . NO! We can't! Not now, we're busy.' He put the phone down with a muttered sonofabitch. 'Hotshot, wanting to see us. Asshole! "I want you both over in my office at once!" ' He sipped some beer and felt better. 'It was also Wazari in the tower reporting the last of our birds has just touched down.'

'Who?'

'Pop Kelly, he's been on the Flotsam run, ferrying a few oilers from rig to rig – they're way down in strength, except in fat-ass komitehs who're more concerned with prayer meetings and kangaroo courts than pumping oil.' He shivered. 'I tell you, Andy, the komitehs are Satan sponsored.' Gavallan noted the word but said nothing as Starke continued, 'They're the pits.'

'Yes. Azadeh nearly got killed – by stoning.'

'What?'

Gavallan told him about the village and her escape from the village. 'We still don't know where the hell old Erikki is – I saw her before I left and she was . . . glazed is about the only word, still not over the shock.'

Starke's face became even grimmer. With an effort he shook off his anger. 'Say we can get the 212s out, what about the guys? We've still three pilots and maybe ten mecs to get out before the caper, what about them? And what about all the spares? We'd be leaving three 206s and the Alouette . . . and what about all our household bits and pieces, our bank accounts, apartments in Tehran, and all the kids' stuff – hell, not just ours but all the other guys', the ones we got out in the exodus? If we shove off, everything'll be lost. Everything.'

'The company'll reimburse everyone. I can't do the bric-a-brac but we'll pay bank accounts and cover the rest. Most're minimal as most of you keep your funds in England and draw on them as you need them. For the last few months – certainly since the banks went on strike – we've been crediting all pay and allowances in Aberdeen. We'll pay to replace furniture and personal stuff. Seems to me we can't get most of it out anyway – ports are still clogged, practically no truckers, railways aren't working, air freight almost non-existent. Everyone'll be reimbursed.'

Starke nodded slowly. He finished his beer to the dregs. 'Even if we get the 212s out, you're going to take a bath.'

Gavallan said patiently, 'No. Add it up for yourself. Each 212's worth a million U.S., each 206 a hundred and fifty thousand, an Alouette five hundred thousand. We've twelve 212s in Iran. If we could get them out we'd be okay, still in business and I could absorb Iran's losses. Just. Business's booming and twelve 212s would keep us going. Any spares we could get out'd be an extra bonus – again we could concentrate on 212 spares only. With our 212s we're in business.'

He tried to maintain his confidence, but it was waning. So many hurdles to jump, mountains to scale, gorges to cross. Yes, but don't forget that a journey of ten thousand leagues begins with one step. Be a little Chinese, he told himself. Remember your childhood in Shanghai and old Nanny Ah Soong and how she taught you about joss – part luck, part karma: 'Joss is joss, young Master, good or bad. Sometimes you can pray for good joss and get it, sometimes not. But *ayeeyah*, don't trust the gods too far – gods are like people. They sleep, go out to lunch, get drunk, forget what they're supposed to do, lie, and promise, and lie again. Pray all you want but don't depend on gods – only yourself and your family and even with them depend on yourself. Remember gods don't like people, young Master, because people remind them of themselves . . .'

'Of course we'll get the lads out, every last one. Meanwhile, would you ask for volunteers to fly out your two birds if, *if* I push the button on Whirlwind?'

Starke glanced back at the map. Then he said, 'Sure. It'll be me and either Freddy or Pop Kelly – the other guy can take the 212 to Rudi and join him in his plan, they've not so far to go.' He smiled wryly. 'Okay?'

'Thanks,' Gavallan said, feeling very good inside. 'Thanks. Did you mention Whirlwind to Tom Lochart when he was here?'

'Sure. He said to count him out, Andy.'

'Oh.' The good feeling vanished. 'Then that's it. If he stays we can't go forward.'

'He's a "go", Andy, whether he likes it or not,' Starke said compassionately. 'He's committed – with or without Sharazad. That's the tough part, with or without. He can't escape HBC, Valik and Isfahan.'

After a moment Gavallan said, 'I suppose you're right. Unfair, isn't it?'

'Yes. Tom's all right, he'll understand eventually. I'm not so sure about Sharazad.'

'Mac and I tried to see her in Tehran. We went to her house and

773

knocked for ten minutes. No answer. Mac went yesterday too. Maybe they're just not answering the door.'

'Not like Iranians.' Starke took off his flight jacket and hung it up in the small hall. 'Soon as Tom gets back here tomorrow, I'll send him to Tehran if there's enough daylight left – latest, Monday morning. I was going to clear it with Mac tonight on our regular call.'

'Good idea.' Gavallan went on to the next problem. 'Damned if I know what to do about Erikki either. I saw Talbot and he said he'd see what he could do, then I went to the Finnish embassy and saw a First Secretary called Tollonen and told him too. He seemed very concerned – and just as helpless. "That's rather a wild country and the border's as fluid as the rebellion, insurrection or fighting that's going on there. If the KGB's involved . . ." he left it hanging, Duke, just like that, "if the KGB's involved . . ." '

'What about Azadeh, can't her daddy, the Khan, help?'

'Seems they all had a huge row. She was very shaken. I asked her to forget her Iranian papers and get on the 125 and wait for Erikki in Al Shargaz, but that went down like a lead balloon. She won't move till Erikki reappears. I pointed out the Khan's a law unto himself – he can reach into Tehran and kidnap her back too easily if he wants. She said, "Insha'Allah". '

'Erikki'll be okay. I'd bet on that.' Starke was confident. 'His ancient gods'll guard him.'

'Hope so.' Gavallan had kept his parka on. Even so he was still feeling cold. Out of the window he could see the fuelling still continuing. 'How about a cuppa before I leave.'

'Sure.' Starke went to the kitchen. Above the sink was a mirror and over the butane stove opposite, was an old, worn needlepoint mounted in a frame that a friend in Falls Church had given to Manuela as a wedding present: 'Screw Home Cooking'. He smiled, remembering how they had laughed when they had got it, then noticed the reflection of Gavallan in the mirror brooding at the map. I must be crazy, he thought, zeroing back to six days and two choppers. How the hell're we gonna clean out the base and still keep ourselves in one piece 'cause Andy's right that one way or another we're finished here. I must be crazy to volunteer. But what the hell? You can't ask one of your guys to volunteer if you don't do it yourself. Yeah, bu –

There was a knock on the front door and it opened immediately. Freddy Ayre said softly, 'Hotshot's heading this way with a Green Band.'

'Come on in, Freddy, and shut the door,' Starke said. They waited in silence. An imperious knock. He opened the door, saw the arrogant sneer on Esvandiary, instantly recognising the young Green Band as one of the mullah Hussain's men and also a member of the komiteh at his questioning. 'Salaam,' he said politely.

'Salaam, agha,' the Green Band said with a shy smile, thick cracked glasses and threadbare clothes and M16.

Abruptly Starke's mind went into overload and he heard himself say, 'Mr. Gavallan, I think you know Hotshot.'

'My name's Esvandiary – Mr. Esvandiary!' the man said angrily. 'How many times do you have to be told? Gavallan, it would help your operation greatly to get rid of this man before we throw him out as an undesirable!'

Gavallan flushed at the rudeness. 'Now just a minute, Captain Starke's the best capt –'

'You're Hotshot, you're also a sonofabitch,' Starke exploded, bunching his fists, suddenly so dangerous that Ayre and Gavallan were aghast, Esvandiary backed off a foot, and the young Green Band gaped. 'You've always been Hotshot and I'd call you Esvandiary or whatever goddam name you want but for what you did to *Captain* Ayre. You're a sonofabitch with no balls and need pasting and before you're very much older you're gonna get it!'

'I'll have you before the komiteh tom –'

'You're a yellow bellied eater of camel dung, so go blow it outta your ass.' Contemptuously Starke turned to the Green Band who was still gaping at him, and without missing a beat, switched to Farsi, his voice now polite and deferential. 'Excellency, I told this dog,' he jerked his thumb rudely at Esvandiary, 'that he is an eater of camel dung, with no courage, who needs *men* with guns to protect him while he orders other *men* to beat and threaten unarmed peaceful members of my tribe against the law, who will not . . .'

Choked with rage, Esvandiary tried to interrupt but Starke overrode him, '. . . who will not stand against me as a man – with knife or sword or gun or fist – according to custom among the Bedouin to avoid a family blood feud, and according to my custom also.'

'Blood feud? You've gone mad! In the Name of God, what blood feud? Blood feuds're against the law . . .' Esvandiary shouted and continued the tirade, Gavallan and Ayre watching helplessly, not understanding Farsi and completely thrown by Starke's outburst. But the young Green Band closed his ears to Esvandiary, then held up his hand, still awed by Starke and his knowledge and not a little envious. 'Please, Excellency Esvandiary,' he said, his eyes magnified by

775

the thickness of the old cracked lenses, and when there was quiet he said to Starke, 'You claim the ancient right of blood feud against this man?'

Starke could feel his heart pumping, and he heard himself say firmly, 'Yes,' knowing it was a dangerous gamble but he had to take it, 'Yes.'

'How can an Infidel claim such a right?' Esvandiary said furiously. 'This is not the Saudi desert, our laws forbid blo –'

'I claim that right!'

'As God wants,' the Green Band said and looked at Esvandiary. 'Perhaps this man is not an Infidel, not truly. This man can claim what he likes, Excellency.'

'Are you mad? Of course he's an Infidel and don't you know blood feuds're against the law? You fool, it's against the law, it's ag –'

'You're not a mullah!' the youth said, angry now. 'You're not a mullah to say what is the law and what isn't! Shut your mouth! I'm no illiterate peasant, I can read and write and I'm a member of the komiteh to keep the peace here and now you threaten the peace.' He glared at Esvandiary who once more backed off. 'I will ask the komiteh and mullah Hussain,' he said to Starke. 'There is little chance that they would agree but . . . as God wants. I agree the law is the law and that a man does not need other men with guns to beat unarmed innocents against the law – or even to punish the evil, however evil, only the strength of God. I leave you to God.' He turned to go.

'A moment, agha,' Starke said. He reached over and took a spare parka that hung on a hook beside the still-open door. 'Here,' he said, offering the coat, 'please accept this small gift.'

'I could not possibly do that,' the youth said, eyes wide and filled with longing.

'Please, Excellency, it is so insignificant that it hardly bears noticing.'

Esvandiary began to say something but stopped as the youth looked over at him, then again turned his attention to Starke. 'I could not possibly accept it – it is so rich and I could not possibly accept it from His Excellency.'

'Please,' Starke said patiently, continuing the formality, then at length held the coat up for the youth to slip on.

'Well, if you insist . . .' the youth said, pretending reluctance. He gave Ayre the M16 while he slipped into the coat, the others not knowing quite what was going on, except Esvandiary who watched and waited, swearing revenge. 'It is wonderful,' the youth said, zipping it up, feeling warm for the first time in many months. Never in all his life had he had such a coat. 'Thank you, agha.' He saw the look on Esvandiary's face and his disgust for him increased – wasn't he just accepting pishkesh as was his right? 'I shall try to persuade the komiteh to grant the right His Excellency asks,' he said, then contentedly went off into the gloaming.

At once Starke whirled on Esvandiary. 'Now what the hell did you want?'

'Many pilots' licences and resident permits're out of date an –'

'No British or American pilots' licence's out of date – only Iranian and they're automatic if the others are okay! Of course they're out of date! Haven't your offices been closed for months – pull your head out of your ass!'

Esvandiary went beet red and the moment he started to reply, Starke turned his back on him and looked directly at Gavallan for the first time. 'It's clearly impossible to operate here any longer, Mr. Gavallan – you've seen it for yourself now, we're harassed, Freddy here was beaten, we're overruled, and there's no way we can work with this sort of crap. I think you should close down the base for a couple of months. At once!' he added.

Gavallan suddenly understood. 'I agree,' he said and grabbed the initiative. Starke sighed with relief, pushed past and sat down with pretended sullenness, heart racing in his chest. 'I'm closing the base at once. We'll send all our choppers and personnel elsewhere. Freddy, get five men overdue leave and put them aboard the 125 right now with their luggage, *right now* an –'

'You can't close down the base,' Esvandiary snarled. 'Nor can y –'

'It's closed, by God,' Gavallan said, working himself into a towering rage. 'They're my aircraft and my personnel and we're not going to suffer all this harassment and beating. Freddy, who's overdue leave?'

Blankly Ayre began to give names and Esvandiary was in shock. To close down the base did not suit him at all. Wasn't Minister Ali Kia visiting here on Thursday and wasn't he then going to offer him an extraordinary pishkesh? If the base was closed that would ruin all his plans.

'You can't take our helicopters out of this area without my approval,' he shouted. 'They're Iranian property!'

'They're the property of the joint venture when they're paid for,' Gavallan shouted back, more than a little imposing in rage. 'I'm going to complain to higher authority you're interfering with the Imam's direct order to get production back to normal. You are! Y –'

'You're forbidden to close down. I'll have the komiteh put Starke in jail for mutiny if y –'

'Balderdash! Starke, I'm ordering you to close the base down.

777

Hotshot, you seem to forget we're well connected. I'll complain directly to Minister Ali Kia. He's adviser to our Board now and he'll deal with you and IranOil!'

Esvandiary blanched. 'Minister Kia's on . . . on the . . . on the board?'

'Yes, yes, he is.' For a split second Gavallan was nonplussed. He had used Kia's name as the only one he knew in the present government and was astonished at the impact it had had on Esvandiary. But hardly missing a beat, he pressed home his advantage. 'My close friend Ali Kia will deal with all this! And with you. You're a traitor to Iran! Freddy, get five men aboard the 125 right now! And Starke, send every aircraft we have to Bandar-e Delam at first light – at first light!'

'Yessir!'

'Wait,' Esvandiary said, seeing his whole plan in ruins. 'There's no need to close the base, Mr. Gavallan. There may have been misunderstandings, mostly due to Petrofi and that man Zataki. I wasn't responsible for that beating, it wasn't me!' He forced his voice to be reasonable but inside he wanted to shout with rage and see them all in jail, flogged and screaming for mercy they would never get. 'No reason to close the base down, Mr. Gavallan. Flying can stay normal!'

'It's closed,' Gavallan said imperiously and glanced at Starke for guidance. 'Much as I'm against it.'

'Yessir. You're right.' Starke was very deferential. 'Of course you can close the base. We can redeploy the choppers or mothball them. Bandar-e Delam needs an immediate 212 for . . . for the Iran-Toda contract. Perhaps we could send 'em one of ours and close down the rest.'

Esvandiary said quickly, 'Mr. Gavallan, work is getting more normal every day. The revolution is successful and over, the Imam in charge. The komitehs . . . the komitehs'll soon disappear. There'll be all the Guerney contracts to service, double the number of 212s needed. As to overdue licence renewals – insha'Allah! We will wait thirty days. No need to close operations.' No need to be hasty, Mr. Gavallan, you've been on this base a long time, you've a big investment here an –'

'I know what our investment is,' Gavallan snapped with real anger, hating the unctuous undercurrent. 'Very well, Captain Starke, I'll take your advice and by God you'd better be right. Put two men on the 125 tonight, their replacements will be back next week. Send the 212 to Bandar-e Delam tomorrow – how long is she to be on loan?'

'Six days, sir, back next Sunday.'

Gavallan said to Esvandiary, 'She'll come back, pending an improved situation here.'

'The 212 is ours . . . the 212 is this base's equipment, Mr. Gavallan,' Esvandiary corrected himself quickly. 'We carry it on our manifests. It will have to come back. As to personnel, the rule is that incoming pilots and mechanics arrive first to replace those going on leave an –'

'Then we're going to bend the rules – Mr. Esvandiary – or I close the base now,' Gavallan said curtly and held on to his hope. 'Starke, put two men on the plane tonight, all but a skeleton staff on the Thursday flight and we'll send her back with full replacements on Friday, pending the situation coming back to normal.'

Starke saw Esvandiary's rage returning so he said quickly, 'We're not allowed to fly on Holy Day, sir. The full crew should come first thing Saturday morning.' He glanced at Esvandiary. 'Don't you agree?'

For a moment Esvandiary thought he was going to explode, his pent up rage almost overcoming his resolve. 'If you . . . if you apologise – for the foul names and your foul manners.'

There was a big silence, the door still open, the room chill but Starke felt the sweat on his back as he weighed his answer. They had achieved so much – if Whirlwind was to come to pass – but Esvandiary was no fool and a quick acquiescence would make him suspicious, as a refusal might jeopardise their gains. 'I apologise for nothing – but I will call you Mr. Esvandiary in future,' he said.

Without a word Esvandiary turned on his heel and stormed off. Starke closed the door, his shirt under his sweater sticking to him.

'What the hell was all that about, Duke?' Ayre said angrily. 'Are you bonkers?'

'Just a moment, Freddy,' Gavallan said. 'Duke, will Hotshot go along with it?'

'I . . . I don't know.' Starke sat down, his knees trembling. 'Jesus.'

'If he does . . . if he does . . . Duke, you were brilliant! It was a brilliant idea, brilliant.'

'You caught the ball, Andy, you made the touchdown.'

'If it is a touchdown.' Gavallan wiped the sweat off his own brow. He began to explain to Ayre, stopped as the phone rang.

'Hello? This's Starke . . . Sure, hang on . . . Andy, it's the tower. McIver's on the HF for you. Wazari asks if you want to go over right away or call him back – McIver says to tell you he's gotten a message from a guy called Avisyard.'

In the control room, Gavallan touched the send switch, almost sick with worry, Wazari watching him, another English-speaking Green Band as attentive. 'Yes, Captain McIver?'

'Evening, Mr. Gavallan, glad I caught you.' McIver's voice was heavy with static and noncommittal. 'How do you read?'

'Three by five, Captain McIver, go ahead.'

'I've just got a telex from Liz Chen. It says: Please forward to Mr. Gavallan the following telex, dated 25 Feb, just arrived: "Your request is approved, (signed) Masson Avisyard." A copy has gone to Al Shargaz. Message ends.'

For a moment Gavallan did not believe his ears. 'Approved?'

'Yes. I repeat: "Your request is approved." Telex's signed Masson Avisyard. What should I reply?'

Gavallan was hard put to keep the glow off his face. Masson was the name of his friend in the Aviation Registration Office in London and the request was to put all their Iranian-based helicopters temporarily back on to British registry. 'Just acknowledge it, Captain McIver.'

'We can proceed with planning.'

'Yes. I agree. I'm off in a couple of minutes, is there anything else?'

'Not for the moment – just routine. I'll bring Captain Starke up to date tonight at our regular time. Very glad about Masson, happy landings.'

'Thanks, Mac, and you.' Gavallan clicked off the switch and handed the mike back to young Wazari. He had noticed the bad bruising, broken nose and that some of his teeth were missing. But he said nothing. What was there to say, 'Thank you, Sergeant.'

Wazari motioned out of the windows at the apron below where the refuelling crew had started winding in the long hoses. 'She's all gassed, s . . .' he just stopped the automatic sir. 'We've, er, we've no runway lights operating so you'd best be aboard soon as possible.'

'Thank you.' Gavallan felt almost lightheaded as he walked for the stairs. The interbase HF crackled into life. 'This's the base commander. Put Mr. Gavallan on.'

At once Wazari clicked the send switch, 'Yessir.' Nervously he handed the mike to Gavallan whose caution had soared. 'He's Maj – sorry, he's now Colonel Changiz.'

'Yes, Colonel? Andrew Gavallan.'

'Aliens are forbidden to use the HF for code messages – who is Masson Avisyard?'

'A design engineer,' Gavallan said. It was the first thought that came into his head. Watch yourself, this bastard's clever. 'I certainly wasn't tr –'

'What was your "request" and who is . . .' there was a slight pause and muffled voice '. . . is Liz Chen?'

'Liz Chen is my secretary, Colonel. My request was to . . .' To what? he wanted to shout, then all at once the answer came to him. '. . . to confine seating to configuration six rows of two seats either side of a gangway of a new chopper, er, the X63. The manufacturers want a different configuration but our engineers believe that this six by four would enhance safety and make for speedy exit in case of emergency. It would also save money and m –'

'Yes, very well,' the colonel interrupted him testily. 'I repeat, the HF is not to be used except with prior approval until the emergency is over and certainly not for code. Your refuelling is completed, you're cleared for immediate take off. Tomorrow's landing to pick up the body of the Zagros casualty is not approved. EchoTangoLimaLima may land Monday between 1100 and 1200, subject to confirm by HQ that will be sent to Kish radar. Good night.'

'But we already have Tehran's formal approval, sir. My pilot gave it to your landing chief the moment he arrived.'

The colonel's voice hardened even more: 'The Monday clearance is subject to confirmation by Iran Air Force HQ. *Iran Air Force HQ*. This is an Iran Air Force base, you are subject to Iran Air Force regulation and discipline and will abide by Iran Air Force regulations and discipline. Do you understand?'

After a pause, Gavallan said, 'Yes, sir, I understand, but we're a civilian oper –'

'You're in Iran, on an Iran Air Force Base and therefore subject to Iran Air Force regulations and discipline.' The channel went dead. Nervously Wazari tidied his already meticulous desk.

Sunday
February 25, 1979

Zagros – Rig Bellissima: 11:05 A.M. In the biting cold Tom Lochart watched Jesper Almqvist, the down-hole expert, handle the big plug that now was suspended by a wire over the exposed drilling hole. All around was the wreckage of the rig and trailers from the terrorist firebomb attack, already half buried in new snow.

'Lower away,' the young Swede shouted. At once his assistant in the small, self-contained cabin started the winch. Awkwardly fighting the wind, Jesper guided the plug down into the well's metal casing. The plug consisted of an explosive charge over two metal half cups fixed around a rubber sealing ring. Lochart could see how tired both men were. This was the fourteenth well they had capped over the last three days, still five more to go, the sunset deadline only seven hours away, each well a two to three hour job in good conditions – once they were on site.

'Sonofabitching conditions,' Lochart muttered, equally weary. Too many flying hours since the Green Band of the komiteh had decreed the deadline, too many problems: scrambling to close down the whole field

785

with its eleven sites, rushing to Shiraz to fetch Jesper, airlifting crews to Shiraz from dawn to dusk, spares to Kowiss – deciding what to take and what to leave, impossible to do everything at such short notice. Then the death of Jordon and Scot being clipped.

'That's it, hold her there!' Jesper shouted, then hurried back through the snow to the cabin. Lochart watched him check the depth then stab a button. There was a muffled explosion. A puff of smoke came out of the drill hole. At once his assistant winched in the remains of the wire as Jesper went back, fought the pipe rams closed over the drill hole, and it was done – 'the explosive charge blows the two cups together,' Jesper had explained earlier; 'this forces the rubber seal against the steel casing and she's capped, the seal good for a couple of years. When you want to open her, we come back and with another special tool drill out the plug and she's as good as new. Maybe.'

He wiped his face with his sleeve. 'Let's get the hell out, Tom!' He trudged back to the cabin, turned the main electric switch off, stuffed all the computer printouts into a briefcase, closed and locked the door.

'What about all the gear?'

'It stays. The cabin's okay. Let's get aboard, I'm frozen to hell.' Jesper headed for the 206 that was parked on the helipad. 'Soon as I get back to Shiraz I'll see IranOil and get 'em to get us permission to come back and pick the cabin up, along with the others. Eleven cabins're one hell of an investment to leave lying around and not working. Weatherwise they're good for a year, locked up. They're designed to take a lot of weather beating, though not vandalising.' He motioned to the wreckage around them. 'Stupid!'

'Yes.'

'Stupid! Tom, you should've seen the IranOil execs when I told them you've been ordered out and Mr. Sera was closing down the field.' Jesper grinned, fair hair, blue eyes. 'They screamed like slitted pigs and swore there were no komiteh orders to stop production.'

'I still don't see why they didn't come back with you and overrule the bastards here.'

'I invited them and they said next week. This's Iran, they'll never come.' He looked back at the site. 'That well alone's worth sixteen thousand barrels a day.' He got into the left seat beside Lochart, his assistant, a taciturn Breton, clambered into the back and pulled the door closed. Lochart started up, heat to maximum.

'Next Rig Maria, okay?'

Jesper thought a moment. 'Better leave her till last. Rig Rosa's more important.' He stifled another yawn. 'We've two producers to cap there and the one still drilling. Poor bastards haven't had time to tip out about seven thousand feet of pipe so we'll have to plug her with it all in. Sonofabeetching waste.' He clipped his seat belt on and huddled closer to the heat fan.

'What happens then?'

'Routine.' The young man laughed. 'When you want to open her up, we core the plug, then start fishing the pipe out piece by piece. Slow, tedious and expensive.' Another huge yawn. He closed his eyes and was almost instantly asleep.

Mimmo Sera met the 206 at Rig Rosa. A 212 was also on the pad, engine idling, Jean-Luc at the controls, men loading luggage and getting aboard. '*Buon'giorno*, Tom.'

'Hi, Mimmo. How's it go?' Lochart waved a greeting to Jean-Luc.

'These are the last of my men except for a roustabout to help Jesper.' Mimmo Sera was bleary with fatigue. 'There was no time to tip pipe out of Three.'

'No problem – we'll cap her as is.'

'*Si*.' A tired smile. 'Think of all the money you'll make tipping it out.'

Jesper laughed. '7,860 feet at – maybe we'll make you a special price.'

Goodnaturedly the older man made an expressive Italian gesture.

Lochart said, 'I'll leave you two to it. When do you want me to come back for you?'

Jesper looked at his watch. It was near noon. 'Come for us at four thirty. Okay?'

'Four thirty on the dot. Sunset's at six thirty-seven.' Lochart went over to the 212.

Jean-Luc was muffled against the could but still managed to look elegant. 'I'll take this batch direct to Shiraz – they're the last – except for Mimmo and your crew.'

'Good. How's it below?'

'Chaos.' Jean-Luc swore with great passion. 'I smell disaster, more disaster.'

'You expect disaster all the time – except when you're bedding. Not to worry, Jean-Luc.'

'Of course to worry.' Jean-Luc watched the loading for a moment – almost completed now, suitcase, kitbags, two dogs, two cats with a full load of men waiting impatiently – then turned back, lowered his voice, and said seriously, 'Tom, the sooner we're out of Iran the better.'

'No. Zagros's just an isolated case. Anyway, I'm still hoping Iran works out.' HBC swirled up into the front of Lochart's brain, and

Sharazad, and Whirlwind. He had told no one here about Whirlwind and his talk with Starke: 'I'll leave that to you, Duke,' he had said just before he left. 'You can put the case better than me – I'm totally against it.'

'Sure. That's your privilege. Mac approved your trip to Tehran Monday.'

'Thanks. Has he seen Sharazad yet?'

'No, Tom, not yet.'

Where the hell is she? he thought, another twinge going through him. 'I'll see you at the base, Jean-Luc. Have a safe trip.'

'Make sure Scot and Rodrigues are ready when I get back. I'll have to do a quick turn around if I'm to get to Al Sharagaz tonight.' The cabin door slammed shut, Jean-Luc glanced around, and got the thumbs-up. He acknowledged, then turned back again. 'I'm off – make sure Scot slips aboard quietly, eh? I don't want to get shot out of the skies – I still say Scot was their target, no one else.'

Lochart nodded bleakly, headed for his 206. He had been en route back from Kowiss when the dawn disaster had happened yesterday. Jean-Luc was getting up at the time and, by chance, had been looking out of his window. 'The two of them, Jordon and Scot, were very close together, carrying spares between them, loading HTW,' he had told Lochart as soon as he had landed. 'I didn't see the first shots, just heard them, but I saw Jordon stagger and cry out, hit in the head, and Scot look off towards the trees at the back of the hangar. Then Scot bent down and tried to help Jordon – I've seen enough men shot to know poor Effer was dead before he touched the snow. Then there were more shots, three or four, but it wasn't a machine gun, more like a M16 on automatic. This time Scot got one in the shoulder and it spun him around and he fell into the snow beside Jordon, half covered by him – Jordon between him and the trees. Then the bullets started pumping again . . . at Scot, Tom, I'm sure of it.'

'How can you be sure, Jean-Luc?'

'I'm certain. Effer was directly in the line of fire, directly, and took them all – the attackers weren't spraying the base, just aiming at Scot. I grabbed my Verey pistol and charged out, saw no one, but fired anyway in the general direction of the trees. When I got to Scot, he had the shakes and Jordon was a mess, hit perhaps eight times. We got Scot to the medic – he's all right, Tom, shoulder wound, I watched him patched myself, wound's clean and the bullet went right through.'

Lochart had gone at once to see Scot in the trailer room they called the infirmary. Kevin O'Sweeney the medic, said, 'He's okay, Captain.'

'Yes,' Scot echoed, his face white and still in shock. 'Really okay, Tom.'

'Let me talk to Scot a moment, Kevin.' When they were alone he said quietly, 'What happened while I was away, Scot? You see Nitchak Khan? Anyone from the village?'

'No. No one.'

'And you told no one about what happened in the square?'

'No, no, not at all. Why, what's all this about, Tom?'

'Jean-Luc thinks you were the target, not Jordon or the base, just you.'

'Oh Christ! Old Effer bought it because of me?'

Lochart remembered how distraught Scot had been. The base had been filled with gloom, everyone still working frantically, boxing spares, loading the two 212s, the 206 and the Alouette for today, last day at Zagros. The only bright spot yesterday was dinner – barbecued haunch of fresh wild goat that Jean-Luc had cooked with plenty of delicious Iranian rice and horisht.

'Great barbecue, Jean-Luc,' he had said.

'Without French garlic and my skill this would taste like old English mutton, ugh!'

'The cook buy it in the village?'

'No, it was a gift. Young Darius – the one who speaks English – he brought us the whole carcass on Friday as a gift from Nitchak's wife.'

Abruptly the meat in Lochart's mouth tasted foul. 'His wife?'

'*Oui.* Young Darius said she'd shot it that morning. *Mon Dieu*, I didn't know she was a hunter, did you? What's the matter, Tom?'

'It was a gift to whom?'

Jean-Luc frowned. 'To me and to the base . . . actually Darius said, "This is from the kalandaran for the base and to give thanks for France's help to the Imam, may God protect him." Why?'

'Nothing,' Lochart had said but later he had taken Scot aside. 'Were you there when Darius delivered the goat?'

'Yes, yes, I was. I happened to be in the office and just thanked him an—' The colour had left Scot's face. 'Now that I think of it, Darius said as he was leaving, "It's fortunate that the kalandaran is a great shot, isn't it?" I think . . . I think I said, "Yes, fantastic." That'd be a dead giveaway, wouldn't it?'

'Yes – if you add it to my slip which now, now I think's got to be a deliberate trap. I was trapped too, so now Nitchak's got to know there're two of us who could be witnesses against the village.'

789

Last night and all today Lochart had been wondering what to do, how to get Scot and himself out and he still had no solution.

Absently he climbed into the 206, waited until Jean-Luc was clear and took off. Now he was flying over the Ravine of the Broken Camels. The road that led to the village was still buried under tons of snow the avalanche had brought. They'll never dig that out, he thought. On the rolling plateau he could see herds of goats and sheep with their shepherds. Ahead was Yazdek village. He skirted it. The schoolhouse was a scar in the earth, black amid the whiteness. Some villagers were in the square and they looked up briefly then went about their business. I won't be sorry to leave, he thought. Not with Jordon murdered here. Zagros Three'll never be the same.

The base was in chaos, men milling about – the last of those brought from other rigs and due to go to Shiraz, thence out of Iran. Cursing, exhausted mechanics were still packing spares, piling boxes and luggage for transshipment to Kowiss. Before he could get out of the cockpit, the refuelling tender arrived with Freddy Ayre jauntily sitting on the bonnet. Yesterday, at Starke's suggestion, Lochart had brought Ayre and another pilot Claus Schwartenegger, to substitute for Scot. 'I'll take her now, Tom,' Ayre said. 'You go and eat.'

'Thanks, Freddy. How's it go?'

'Ropey. Claus's taken another load of spares to Kowiss and he'll be back in good time for the last one. Come sunset I'll take the Alouette, she's loaded to the gills and a bit more. What'd you want to fly out?'

'The 212 – I'll have Jordon aboard. Claus can take the 206. You're off to Shiraz?'

'Yes. We've still got ten bods to get there – I was, er, thinking of taking five passengers instead of four for two trips. Eh?'

'If they're small enough – no luggage – and so long as I don't see you. Okay?'

Ayre laughed, the cold making his bruises more livid. 'They're all so anxious I don't think they care much about luggage – one of the guys from Rig Maria said they heard shooting nearby.'

'One of the villagers hunting, probably.' The spectre of the huntress with her high-powered rifle or for that matter any of the Kash'kai – all expert marksmen – filled him with dread. We're so goddam helpless, he thought, but kept it off his face. 'Have a safe trip, Freddy.' He went to the cookhouse and got some hot horisht.

'Agha,' the cook said nervously, the other four helpers crowding around. 'We're due two months' pay – what's going to happen to our pay and to us?'

'I've already told you, Ali. We'll take you back to Shiraz where you came from. This afternoon. We pay you off there and as soon as I can I'll send you the month's severance pay we owe you. You keep in touch through IranOil as usual. When we come back you get your jobs back.'

'Thank you, agha.' The cook had been with them for a year. He was a thin, pale man with stomach ulcers. 'I don't want to stay among these barbarians,' he said nervously. 'When this afternoon?'

'Before sunset. At four o'clock you start cleaning up and get everything neat and tidy.'

'But agha, what's the point of that? The moment we leave, the lice-covered Yazdeks will come and steal everything.'

'I know,' Lochart said wearily. 'But you will leave everything neat and tidy and I will lock the door and maybe they won't.'

'As God wants, agha. But they will.'

Lochart finished his meal and went to the office. Scot Gavallan was there, face drawn, arm painfully in a sling. The door opened. Rod Rodrigues came in, dark rings around his eyes, his face pasty. 'Hi, Tom, you haven't forgotten, huh?' he asked anxiously. 'I'm not on the manifest.'

'No problem. Scot, Rod's going with HJX. He's going with you and Jean-Luc to Al Shargaz.'

'Great, but I'm fine, Tom. I think I'd rather go to Kowiss. Old Doc Nutt's th –'

'For Christ's sake, you're out to Al Shargaz and that's the end of it!'

Scot flushed at the anger. 'Yes. All right, Tom.' He walked out.

Rodrigues broke the silence. 'Tom, what you want we send with HJX?'

'How the hell do I know, for Ch—' Lochart stopped. 'Sorry, I'm getting tired. Sorry.'

'No sweat, Tom, so're we all. Maybe we send her empty, huh?'

With an effort Lochart put away his fatigue. 'No, put the spare engine aboard – and any other 212 spares to make up the load.'

'Sure. That'd be good. Maybe y—' The door opened and Scot came back in quickly. 'Nitchak Khan! Look out the window!' Twenty or more men were coming up the track from the village. All were armed. Others were already spreading out over the base, Nitchak Khan heading for the office trailer. Lochart went to the back window, jerked it open. 'Scot, go to my hut, keep away from the windows, don't let 'em see you and don't move until I come get you. Hurry!'

Awkwardly Scot climbed out and rushed off. Lochart pulled the window closed.

The door opened. Lochart got up. 'Salaam, kalandar.'

'Salaam. Strangers have been seen in the forests nearby. The terrorists must be back so I have come to protect you.' Nitchak Khan's eyes were hard. 'As God wants, but I would regret it if there were more deaths before you leave. We will be here until sunset.' He left.

'What'd he say?' Rodrigues asked, not understanding Farsi.

Lochart told him and saw him tremble. 'No problem, Rod,' he said, covering his own fear. There was no way they could take off or land without being over forest, low, slow, and in sitting-duck range. Terrorists? Bullshit! Nitchak knows about Scot, knows about me, and I'll bet my life he's got marksmen planted all around, and if he's here till sunset there's no way to sneak off, he'll know which chopper we're on. Insha'Allah. Insha'Allah, but meanwhile what the hell're you going to do?

'Nitchak Khan knows the countryside,' he said easily, not wanting to panic Rod, enough fear on the base already without adding to it. 'He'll protect us, Rod – if they're there. Is the spare engine crated?'

'Huh? Sure, Tom, sure, she's crated.'

'You take care of the loading. I'll see you later. No sweat.'

For a long time Lochart stared at the wall. When it was time to return to Rig Rosa, Lochart went to find Nitchak Khan. 'You will want to see that Rig Rosa's been closed down properly, kalandar, isn't it on your land?' he said, and though the old man was reluctant, to his great relief he managed to persuade him with flattery to accompany him. With the Khan aboard, Lochart knew he would be safe for the time being.

So far so good, he thought. I'll have to be the last away. Until we're well away, Scot and I, I have to be very clever. Too much to lose now: Scot, the lads, Sharazad, everything.

At Rig Rosa: 5:00 P.M. Jesper was driving their unit truck fast along the path through the pines that led to the last well to be capped. Beside him was Mimmo Sera, the roustabout and his assistant were in the back, and he was humming to himself, mostly to keep awake. The plateau was large, almost half a mile between wells, the countryside beautiful and wild. 'We're overdue,' Mimmo said wearily, looking at the lowering sun. '*Stronzo!*'

'We'll give it a go,' Jesper said. In the side pocket was the last of the energy-giving chocolate bars. The two men shared it. 'This looks a lot like Sweden,' Jesper said, skidding a bend, the speed exhilarating him.

'Never been to Sweden. There she is,' Mimmo said. The well was in a clearing, already on stream and producing about twelve thousand barrels daily, the whole field immensely rich. Over the well was a giant column of valves and pipes, called the Christmas Tree, that connected it to the main pipeline. 'This was the first we drilled here,' he said absently. 'Before your time.'

When Jesper switched the engine off the silence was eerie, no pumps needed here to bring the oil to the surface – abundant gas pressure trapped in the oil dome thousands of feet below did that for them and would do so for years yet. 'We've no time to cap it properly, Mr. Sera – unless you want to overstay our welcome.'

The older man shook his head, pulled his woollen cap down over his ears. 'How long will the valves hold?'

Jesper shrugged. 'Should be as long as you want – but unattended or inspected from time to time? Don't know. Indefinitely – unless we get a gas surge – or one of the valves or seals're faulty.'

'*Stronzo!*'

'*Stronzo,*' Jesper said agreeably, motioned to his assistant and the roustabout and went forward. 'We'll just shut it down, no capping.' The snow crunched underfoot. Wind rustled the treetops and then they heard the incoming engine of the chopper back from the base. 'Let's get with it.'

They were hidden from the helipad and main buildings of Rosa, half a mile away. Irritably, Mimmo lit a cigarette and leaned against the bonnet and watched the three men work diligently, fighting the valves, some stuck, then fetching the huge wrench to unglue them, then the bullet ricocheted off the Christmas Tree and the following crackkkk echoed through the forest. All of them froze. They waited. Nothing.

'You see where it came from?' Jesper muttered. No one answered him. Again they waited. Nothing. 'Let's finish,' he said and again put his weight on to the wrench. The others came forward to help. At once there was another shot and the bullet went through the windshield of the truck, tore a hole in the cabin wall, and ripped a computer screen and some electrical gear apart before going out the other side. Silence.

No movement anywhere. Just wind and a little snow falling, disturbed by the wind. Sound of the chopper jets shrieking now in the landing flare.

Mimmo Sera shouted out in Farsi, 'We just shut down the well, Excellencies, to make it safe. We shut it down and then we leave.' Again they waited. No answer. Again, 'We only make the well safe! Safe for Iran – not for us! For Iran and the Imam – it's your oil not ours!'

Waiting again and never a sound but the sounds of the forest.

Branches crackling. Somewhere far off an animal cried out. '*Mamma mia*,' Mimmo said, his voice hoarse from shouting, then walked over and picked up the wrench and the bullet sang past his face so close he felt its wake. His shock was sudden and vast. The wrench slipped from his gloves. 'Everyone in the truck. We leave.'

He backed away and got into the front seat. The others followed. Except Jesper. He retrieved the wrench and when he saw the havoc the errant bullet had caused in *his* cabin, to *his* equipment, his face closed, his anger exploded and he hurled the wrench impotently at the forest with a curse and stood there a moment, feet slightly apart, knowing he was an easy target but suddenly not caring. '*Forbannades shitdjau-lerrrrrr!*'

'Get in the car,' Mimmo called out.

'*Forbannades shitdjauler*,' Jesper muttered, the Swedish obscenity pleasing him, then got into the driver's seat. The truck went back the way it had come and when it was out of sight a fusillade of bullets from both sides of the forest slammed into the Christmas Tree, denting or scoring parts of the metal, screaming away into the snow or sky. Then silence. Then someone laughed and called out, 'Allahhhh-u Akbarrr . . .'

The cry echoed. Then died away.

At Zagros Three: 6:38 P.M. The sun touched the horizon. Last of the spares and luggage being put aboard. All four choppers were lined up, two 212s, the 206 and the Alouette, pilots ready, Jean-Luc stomping up and down – departures delayed by Nitchak Khan who had, earlier, arbitrarily ordered all aircraft to leave together which had made it impossible for Jean-Luc to make Al Shargaz tonight, only Shiraz, there to overnight as night flying was forbidden in Iranian skies.

'Explain to him again, Tom,' Jean-Luc said angrily.

'He's already told you no, told me no, so it's no and it's too goddam late anyway! You all set, Freddy?'

'Yes,' Ayre called out irritably. 'We've been waiting an hour or more!'

Grimly Lochart headed for Nitchak Khan who had heard the anger and irritation and saw with secret delight the discomfiture of the strangers. Standing beside Nitchak Khan was the Green Band Lochart presumed was from the komiteh, and a few villagers. The rest had drifted away during the afternoon. Into the forest, he thought, his mouth dry. 'Kalandar, we are almost ready.'

'As God wants.'

Lochart called out, 'Freddy, last load, now!' He took off his peaked cap and the others did likewise as Ayre, Rodrigues and two mechanics carried the makeshift coffin out of the hangar across the snow and carefully loaded it into Jean-Luc's 212. When it was done, Lochart stepped aside. 'Shiraz party board.' He shook hands with Mimmo, Jesper, the roustabout, and Jesper's assistant as they climbed aboard, settling themselves amid the luggage, spares and coffin. Uneasily Mimmo Sera and his Italian roustabout crossed themselves, then locked their seat belts.

Jean-Luc climbed into the pilot's seat, Rodrigues beside him. Lochart turned back to the rest of the men. 'All aboard!'

Watched carefully by Nitchak Khan and the Green Band, the remainder went aboard, Ayre flying the Alouette, Claus Schwartenegger the 206, all seats full, tanks fulls, cargo belly full, external skid carriers lashed with spare rotor blades. Lochart's 212 was crammed and over maximum: 'By the time we get to Kowiss we'll've used a lot of fuel so we'll be legal – anyway it's downhill all the way,' he had told all pilots when he had briefed them earlier.

Now he stood alone on the snow of Zagros Three, everyone else belted in and doors closed. 'Start up!' he ordered, his tension mounting. He had told Nitchak Khan he had decided to act as Take Off Master.

Nitchak Khan and the Green Band came up to Lochart. 'The young pilot, the one who was wounded, where is he?'

'Who? Oh, Scot? If he's not here, he's in Shiraz, kalandar,' Lochart said and saw anger rush into the old man's face and the Green Band's mouth drop open. 'Why?'

'That's not possible!' the Green Band said.

'I didn't see him board so he must have gone on an earlier flight . . .' Lochart had to raise his voice over the growing scream of the jets, all engines now up to speed, '. . . on an earlier flight when we were at Rig Rosa and Maria, kalandar. Why?'

'That's not possible, kalandar,' the Green Band repeated, frightened, as the old man turned on him. 'I was watching carefully!'

Lochart ducked under the whirling blades and went to the pilot's window of Jean-Luc's 212, taking out a thick white envelope. 'Here, Jean-Luc, *bonne chance*,' he said and gave it to him. 'Take off!' For an instant he saw the glimmer of a smile before he hurried to safety, Jean-Luc shoved on maximum power for a quick take off and she lifted and trundled away, the wash from the blades ripping at his clothes and those of the villagers, the jets drowning out what Nitchak Khan was shouting.

Simultaneously – also by prearrangement – Ayre and Schwartenegger gunned their engines, easing away from each other before lumbering in a slow laboured climb for the trees. Lochart held on to his hope and then the furious Green Band caught him by the sleeve and pulled him around.

'You lied,' the man was shouting, 'you lied to the kalandar – the young pilot did not leave earlier! I would have seen him, I watched carefully – tell the kalandar you lied!'

Abruptly Lochart ripped his sleeve away from the young man, knowing that every second meant a few more feet of altitude, a few more yards to safety. 'Why should I lie? If the young pilot's not in Shiraz then he's still here! Search the camp, search my airplane – come on, first let us search my airplane!' He stalked off towards his 212 and stood at the open door, from the corner of his eyes seeing Jean-Luc's 212 now over the tree line, Ayre so overloaded barely making it, and the 206 still climbing. 'In all the names of God, let's search,' he said, willing their attention on to him and away from the escaping choppers, willing them not to search his airplane but the camp itself. 'How can a man hide here? Impossible. What about the office or the trailers, perhaps he's hiding . . .'

The Green Band pulled the gun off his shoulder and aimed at him. 'Tell the kalandar you lied or you die!'

With hardly any effort, Nitchak Khan angrily ripped the gun out of the youth's hands and threw it into the snow. 'I'm the law in Zagros – not you! Go back to the village!' Filled with fear the Green Band obeyed instantly.

The villagers waited and watched. Nitchak Khan's face was graven and his small eyes went from chopper to chopper. They were away now, but not yet out of range of those he had posted around the base – to fire only on his signal, only his. One of the smaller choppers was banking, still climbing as fast as possible, coming around in a big circle. To watch us, Nitchak Khan thought, to watch what happens next. As God wants.

'Dangerous to shoot down the sky machines,' his wife had said. 'That will bring wrath down upon us.'

'Terrorists will do that – we will not. The young pilot saw us, and the Farsi-speaking kalandar pilot knows. They must not escape. Terrorists have no mercy, they care nothing for law and order, and how can their existence be disproved? Aren't these mountains ancient havens for brigands? Haven't we chased these terrorists to the limit of our power? What could we do to prevent the tragedy – nothing.'

And now before him was the last of the Infidels, his main enemy, the one who had cheated him and lied and whisked the other devil away. At least this one will not escape, he thought. The barest tip of the sun was just above the horizon. As he watched, it vanished. 'Peace be with you, Pilot.'

'And with you, kalandar, God watch you,' Lochart said thinly. 'That envelope I gave to my French pilot. You saw me give it to him?'

'Yes, yes, I saw it.'

'That was a letter addressed to the Revolutionary Komiteh in Shiraz, with a copy to the Iranian kalandar in Dubai across the Great Sea, signed by the young pilot, witnessed by me, telling exactly what occurred in the village square, what was done by whom, to whom, who was shot, the number of men bound in the Green Band truck before it went into the Ravine of the Broken Camels, the manner of Nasiri's murder, your terr –'

'Lies, all lies! By the Prophet what is this word murder? Murder? That is for bandits. The man died – as God wants,' the old man said sullenly, aware of the villagers gaping at Lochart. 'He was a known supporter of the Satanic Shah who surely you will meet in hell soon.'

'Perhaps, perhaps not. Perhaps my loyal servant who was murdered here by cowardly sons of dogs has already told the One God and the One God knows who is telling the truth!'

'He was not Muslim, he did not serve Islam an –'

'But he was a Christian and Christians serve the One God and my tribesman was murdered by cowards from ambush, sons of dogs with no courage who shot from ambush – surely eaters of shit and men of the Left Hand and accursed! It's true he was murdered like the other Christian at the rig. By God and the Prophet of God, their deaths will be avenged!'

Nitchak Khan shrugged. 'Terrorists,' he blustered, very afraid, 'terrorists did that, of course it was terrorists! As to the letter it's all lies, lies, the pilot was liar, we all know what happened in the village. It's all lies what he said.'

'All the more reason that the letter should not be delivered.' Lochart was choosing his words very carefully. 'Therefore please protect me from the "terrorists" as I fly away. Only I can prevent the letter being delivered.' His heart was beating heavily as he saw the old man take out a cigarette, weighing the pros and cons, and light the cigarette with Jordon's lighter and he wondered again how he could have vengeance for Jordon's murder, still an unresolved part of the plan that so far had worked perfectly: his taking the too vigilant Nitchak Khan away, Scot

Gavallan sneaking into the makeshift coffin to be carried aboard Jean-Luc's 212, Jordon's shrouded body already put into the long crate that once housed tail rotors to be loaded into his 212, then the letter and the three choppers flying off together, all perfectly as planned.

And now it was time to finish. Ayre in the Alouette circled overhead in station, well out of range. 'Salaam, kalandar, God's justice be with you,' he said and headed for his cockpit.

'I have no control over terrorists!' And when Lochart did not stop, Nitchak Khan shouted louder, 'Why would you stop delivery of the lies, eh?'

Lochart got into the cockpit, wanting to be away, hating this place now and the old man. 'Because, before God, I deplore lies.'

'Before God, you would stop the delivery of these lies?'

'Before God I will see that letter burned. God's justice be with you, kalandar, and with Yazdek.' He pressed the starter. The first jet fired up. Above him the blades began to turn. More switches. Now the second engine caught and all the time he was watching the old man. Rot in hell, old man, he thought, Jordon's blood's on your head, and Gianni's, I'm sure of it though I'll never prove it. Perhaps mine too.

Waiting. Now all needles in the Green. Lift-off.

Nitchak Khan watched the chopper shudder into the air, hesitate, then turn slowly and begin to leave. So easy to raise my hand, he thought, and so soon the Infidel and that howling monster become a funeral pyre falling out of the sky, and as to the letter, lies, all lies.

Two men dead? All know that it's their own fault they're dead. Did we invite them here? No, they came to exploit our land. If they had not come here they would still be alive and waiting for the hell that inevitably is their due.

His eyes never left the air machine. There was plenty of time yet. He smoked slowly, enjoying the cigarette greatly, enjoying the knowledge that he could terminate such a great machine just by raising his hand. But he did not. He remembered the advice of the kalandaran and lit another cigarette from the stub and smoked that, waiting patiently. Soon the hateful sound of the engines was distant, fading quickly, and then, overhead, he saw the smaller air machine break off circling and also head south and west.

When all Infidel sound had quite gone he judged that peace had once more come to his Zagros. 'Fire the base,' he said to the others. Soon the flames were high. Without regret he cast the lighter into the flames and, contentedly, he strolled home.

Near Bandar-e Delam Air Base: 9:16 A.M. In torrential rain the Subaru station wagon with the Iran-Toda insignia on the doors hurried along the road, windshield wipers full speed, the road potholed and water-logged in parts, the driver Iranian. Scragger sat uneasily beside him, his seat belt tight, and in the back a Japanese radio mechanic hung on as best he could. Ahead through the heavy rain splats, Scragger saw an old bus hogging most of the road and, not far away, oncoming traffic.

'Minoru, tell him to slow down. Again,' he said. 'He's witless.'

The young Japanese leaned forward and spoke sharply in Farsi, and the driver nodded benignly and paid no attention, jabbed his palm on the horn, and kept it there as he swerved out almost on to the other shoulder, overtaking the bus, accelerated when he should have braked, skidded, recovered, and just made the narrowing gap between the bus and the oncoming car, all three vehicles with their horns shrieking.

Scragger muttered another curse. Beaming, the driver, a young bearded man, took his attention off the road and said something in Farsi, bouncing through a large pothole in a shower of water. Minoru interpreted: 'He says with the Help of God we'll be at the airfield in a few minutes, Captain Scragger.'

'With the Help of God we'll be there in one piece and not fifty.' Scragger would have preferred to drive but it had not been allowed, nor were any Iran-Toda personnel allowed to drive themselves. 'We've found it to be good policy, Captain Scragger, the roads and the rules and Iranians being what they are,' Watanabe, the engineer in charge, had said. 'But Mohammed is one of our best drivers and very reliable. See you this evening.'

To Scragger's relief he saw the airfield ahead. Green Bands guarded the gate. The driver paid them no attention, just barrelled through and pulled up in a shower of water outside the two-storey office building. 'Allah-u Akbar,' he said proudly.

Scragger exhaled. 'Allah-u Akbar it is,' he said, unlocked his seat belt, readying his umbrella as he looked around, his first time here. Big apron and small tower, some windows smashed, others boarded up, the two-storey office building derelict with more broken windows, S-G company trailers, good hangars now closed against the storm, with bullet holes all over and in the walls of the trailers. He whistled, remembering being told about the fight here between the Green Bands and the mujhadin. Must've been a lot worse than Duke let on, he thought.

Two Royal Iran Air twin jet passenger airplanes were parked haphazardly – the 'Royal' now crudely slashed out with black paint – tyres flat, cockpit windows smashed, and left to rot. 'Bloody sacrilege,' he muttered, seeing the rain pouring into the cockpits.

'Minoru, me son, tell Mohammed here not to move a muscle till we're ready to leave, okay?'

Minoru did as he was asked, then followed Scragger out into the rain. Scragger stood beside the car, not knowing where to go. Then one of the trailer doors opened.

'*Mein Gott*, Scrag! I thought it was you – what the hell're you doing here?' It was Rudi Lutz, beaming. Then he saw Starke join Rudi and his heart picked up.

'Hi, me sons!' He shook hands warmly with both of them, all three talking together for a moment. 'Well, Duke, this's a pleasant surprise!'

'What the hell're you doing here, Scrag?'

'First things first, me son. This's Minoru Fuyama, radio mec with Iran-Toda. My UHF was acting up on the way in – I'm on a beaut charter from Lengeh. Minoru's pulled the box and it's in the car, can you replace her?'

'No problem. Come along, Mr. Fuyama.' Rudi went next door to find Fowler Joines to make the arrangements.

'I'm damn glad to see you, Scrag – lots to talk about,' Starke said.

'Like weather problems and whirlwinds?'

'Yes, yes, I'd say the weather's been on my mind a lot.' Starke seemed older, his eyes ranging the base, the downpour even heavier than before, the day warm and tacky.

'I saw Manuela at Al Shargaz, she's same as usual, pretty as a picture – anxious, but okay.'

Rudi rejoined them, splashing through the rain, and led the way back into his office trailer. 'You won't be flying in this mess, Scrag. Would you like a beer?'

'No thanks, mate, but I'd love a cuppa.' Scragger said it automatically though his thirst for a cool beer was monumental. But ever since his first medical with Dr. Nutt just after he had sold Sheik Aviation to Gavallan, and Dr. Nutt had said, 'Scrag, unless you quit smoking and cut down on the beer you'll be grounded in a couple of years,' he had been extra careful. Too bloody right, he thought. No fags, no booze, no food, and plenty of sheilas. 'You still have supplies, Rudi? At Lengeh it's getting rough 'cept for de Plessey and his wine.'

'I got some off a tanker that's tied up down at the port,' Rudi called back from the small kitchen, putting on the kettle. 'CASEVAC, seaman with his head and face smashed up. The captain said he'd had a fall but it looked more like a bad fight. Not surprising really, the ship's been stuck at anchor for three months. *Mein Gott*, Scrag, did you see the pileup in the port when you came in? Must be a hundred ships waiting to unload, or to take on oil.'

'Same at Kharg and all along the coast, Rudi, everywhere's clogged. Wharfs sky high with crates, bales, an' Gawd knows what, all left rotting in the sun or rain. Enough of that, what're you doing here, Duke?'

'I ferried a 212 from Kowiss yesterday. But for the weather I'd've left at dawn – glad I didn't now.'

Scragger heard the caution in the voice and looked around. No one listening that he could see. 'Problem?' He saw Starke shake his head. Rudi turned on the music cassette. Wagner. Scragger hated Wagner. 'What's up?'

'Just cautious – these damn walls are too thin – and I caught one of the staff eavesdropping. I think most of them are spies. Then we've a new base manager, Numir, Nasty Numir we call him. He's off today, otherwise you'd be explaining why you're here in triplicate.' Rudi made his voice lower. 'There are whirlwinds to talk about, Scrag. But what are you doing here, why didn't you call us?'

'Came into Iran-Toda yesterday on a charter for a guy called Kasigi who's the big buyer of Siri crude and a bigwig with Iran-Toda – old Georges de Plessey arranged it. I'm here for today, leave tomorrow early. Andy asked me to see you to sound you out and this was as soon as I could make it. I couldn't raise you on the UHF coming in – could've been the storm, I just snuck in in time. Couldn't get permission to fly over here, so I pulled a wire off the pot just in case and "urgently needed a repair." Duke, Andy told you what we talked about in Al Shargaz?'

'Yes, yes, he did. And you better know there's a new twist. Andy's been told we're being grounded pending nationalisation and we've only five days – five safe days only. If we're to do it, at the latest it should be Friday.'

'Jesus H. Christ!' Scragger felt his chest tighten. 'Duke, there's no way I can get ready by Friday.'

'Andy says we take out 212s only.'

'Eh?'

Starke explained what had happened at Kowiss and what, hopefully, would happen 'if Andy pushes the go.'

'Come off it – not if, when. Andy has to. The question is, do we stick our necks out?'

Starke laughed. 'You already have. I said I'm in if everyone else is – with two 212s it's possible for me, and now that . . . well, now that our birds're back on British registry once we're out, that makes it legit.'

'The hell it does,' Rudi said. 'It's just not legal. I told you last night and Pop Kelly agreed. Scrag, how're –'

'Pop's here?'

'Sure,' Starke said. 'He came down with me.' He explained why, then added, 'Hotshot approved the "loan", we got two guys out on the 125 and the rest scheduled for Thursday but I'm not so sure about that. Colonel Changiz said in future all personnel movements're to be approved by him, not just by Hotshot.'

'How're you getting back?'

'I'll take a 206.' Starke looked out of the window at the rain. 'Goddam front!'

'She'll be through by tonight, Duke,' Scragger said confidently.

Rudi said, 'How're you going to get your men out, Scrag? *Hein?*'

'If it's just my two 212s, that makes it much easier. Much.' Scragger

802

saw Rudi quaff some of his ice cold beer, the beads on the can glistening, and his thirst increased. 'Friday'd be a good day for a caper because Iranians'll be at prayer meetings or whatever.'

'I'm not so sure, Scrag,' Rudi said. 'Friday they still man the radar – they'll have to know something's up with my four birds charging across the Gulf, let alone your three and Duke's two. Abadan's itchy as all hell about choppers – particularly after HBC.'

'There been any more inquiries about her, Rudi?'

'Yes. Last week Abbasi came by, he's the pilot who blew her out of the sky. Same questions, nothing more.'

'Does he know his brother was HBC's pilot?'

'Not yet, Scrag.'

'Tom Lochart was bloody lucky. Bloody lucky.'

'We've all been "bloody lucky". So far,' Starke said. 'Except Erikki.' He brought Scragger up to date with the little they knew.

'Christ, what next? How're we going to do Whirlwind with him still in Iran?'

'We can't, Scrag – that's what I think,' Rudi said. 'We can't leave him.'

'That's right but maybe . . .' Starke drank some coffee, his own anxiety making him feel a little bilious. 'Maybe Andy won't push the button. Meanwhile we hope to God Erikki gets away, or is let go before Friday. Then Andy can. Shit, if it was up to me, just me, goddamned if I'd risk Whirlwind.'

'Nor me.' Rudi was equally queasy.

'If they were all your planes and your company and your future, bet you would. Know I would.' Scragger beamed. 'Me, I'm for Whirlwind. I got to be for it, sport, no bloody company'll employ me at my age so I bloody have to keep Dirty Dunc and Andy and Gav in biz if I'm to keep flying.' The kettle began singing. He got up. 'I'll make it, Rudi. What about you? You in or out?'

'Me, I'm in if you two are, and if it's a possible – but I like it not a bit and I'm telling you straight I'll only lead my four out if *I* really think we've a chance. We talked to the other pilots last night, Scrag. Marc Dubois and Pop Kelly said they'd have a go. Block and Forsyth said thanks but no thanks so we've three pilots for four 212s. I've asked Andy to send me a volunteer.' Rudi mirrored his disquiet. 'But *scheissen mit reissen*! I'll have four to get airborne somehow, all at the same time, when we're supposed to have start-up clearance – with Green Bands all over the base, our radio op Jahan no idiot, and then there's Nasty Numir . . .' His eyebrows soared.

'You've no problem, old cock,' Scragger said airily. 'Tell 'em you're going to do a flyby victory salute for Khomeini over Abadan!'

'Up yours, Scrag!' The music ended and Rudi turned the tape over. Then his face hardened. 'But I agree with you that Andy *will* push the button and the when's Friday. Me, I say if one of us aborts we all abort – agreed?'

Scragger broke the silence. 'If Andy says go, I go. I have to.'

Bandar-e Delam Port: 3:17 P.M. Scragger's station wagon turned off a main road in the sprawling, noisy town into a lesser road, cut down it then turned into a square in front of a mosque, Mohammed driving as usual, his finger on the horn almost constantly. The rain had lessened appreciably but the day was still miserable. In the backseat Minoru dozed, cradling the replacement radio. Scragger was absently staring ahead, so much to think about, plans, codes and what about Erikki? Poor old bugger! But if anyone can make it he will. Swear to God old Erikki'll make it somehow. Say he doesn't or Andy doesn't push go, what you going to do for a job? I'll worry about that next week.

He did not see the police car come charging out of a side turning, skid on the slippery surface and smash into the back of them. There was no way that Mohammed could have avoided the accident, and the speed of the police car, added to his own, hurtled them broadside across the road into a street stall and the crowds, killing one old woman, decapitating another and injuring many as the wheels fell into the joub, the momentum rolling the car over to smash it against the high walls with a howling screech of metal.

Instinctively Scragger had put his hands over his face but the final crash bashed his head against the side, stunning him momentarily, the seat belt saving him from real damage. The driver had gone through the windshield and now was half in and half out of the car, badly injured. In the back, the seat had protected Minoru and he was the first to recover, the radio still protectively in his lap. Amid the screams and pandemonium he fought his door open and scrambled out, covered by the mêlée of pedestrians, and injured, unnoticed as a passenger, Japanese from Iran-Toda normal in the streets here.

At that moment the occupants of the police car that now was swivelled half across the road – its front crumpled – ran over. The police shoved their way up to the station wagon, took one look at the driver then pulled the side door open and hauled Scragger out.

Angry shouts of 'Amerikan!' and more screams and noise, Scragger still half stunned. 'Tha . . . thanks, I'm . . . I'm okay . . .' but they held him firmly, shouting at him.

'For Christ's sake . . .' he gasped, 'I wasn't driving . . . what the hell happ—' Around him was a tumult of Farsi and panic and anger and one of the police snapped handcuffs on him and then they dragged him roughly to the other car, pushed him into the back seat and got in, still cursing him. The driver started up.

On the other side of the road, Minoru was futilely trying to push through the crowd to help Scragger. He stopped, crestfallen, as the car hurtled away down the street.

Near Doshan Tappeh: 3:30 P.M. McIver was driving along the empty perimeter road outside the barbed wire fence of the military airfield. The bumpers were badly scored and there were many more dents than before. One headlight was cracked and roughly taped, the red glass of one tail light missing, but the engine still sounded sweet and her snow tyres were firm on the surface. Snow banked the roadway. No sun came through the overcast that was barely twelve hundred feet and obscured all but the foothills of the northern mountains. It was cold and he was late.

On the inside of his windshield was a big green permit and, seeing it, the motley group of Green Band and air force guards stationed near the gate waved him through, then crowded back around the open fire to warm themselves. He headed for the S-G hangar. Before he could reach it, Tom Lochart came out of a side door to intercept him.

'Hi, Mac,' he said, getting in quickly. He was wearing flight gear and carried his flight bag and had just flown in from Kowiss. 'How's Sharazad?'

806

'Sorry to take so long, traffic was terrible.'

'Have you seen her?'

'No, not yet. Sorry.' He saw Lochart's immediate tension. 'I went again early this morning. A servant answered the door but didn't seem to understand me – I'll get you there as soon as I can.' He let in the clutch and turned for the gate. 'How was Zagros?'

'Rotten, I'll fill you in on that in a second,' Lochart said hurriedly. 'Before we can leave we've got to report to the base commander.'

'Oh? Why?' McIver put on the brake.

'They didn't say. They left a message with the clerk that when you came in today to report to the base commander. Any problems?'

'Not that I know of.' McIver let in the clutch and swung around. Now what, he thought, holding down his anxiety.

'Could it be HBC?'

'Let's hope not.'

'What happened to Lulu? You have a prang?'

'No, just some street vandals,' McIver said, his mind on HBC.

'Every day it gets rougher. Any news of Erikki?'

'Nothing. He's just vanished. Azadeh's pretty upset – sits by the phone all day in the office.'

'She's still staying with you?'

'No, she went back to her own apartment on Saturday. My place, well, my place's a bit cramped.' McIver was heading for the buildings the other side of the runway, driving carefully through the debris from the recent battle that was still scattered about, burnt out trucks, a tank half on its side, hangars and buildings bullet marked. 'Tell me about Zagros.' He listened without comment until Lochart had finished. 'What a bastard!'

'Yes, but Nitchak Khan didn't give the signal to shoot me down – or us down. Not a goddam thing we could have done about it. If he had he'd've gotten away with it. Goddam hard to break the "terrorist story". I think he'd've gotten away with it, Mac. Anyway, when we got to Kowiss, Duke and Andy had had a fracas with Hotshot.' Lochart told him about that, 'but the ruse seems to be working, yesterday Duke and Pop ferried the 212 to Rudi and this morning EchoTangoLima-Lima came in for Jordon's body.'

'Terrible. Feel very responsible for old Effer.'

'Guess we all do.' Ahead they could see the HQ building with sentries outside it. 'We all turned out and put the coffin aboard, young Freddy played a lament on the pipes, not much else we could do. Curiously Colonel Changiz sent an air force honour guard and gave us a proper coffin. Iranians're strange, so strange. They seemed genuinely sorry.' Lochart was talking automatically, sick with anxiety at the delays – having to wait at Kowiss, then flying here and ATC harassing him, then no transport and waiting interminably for McIver to arrive and now another delay. What's happened to Sharazad?

They were near the office building that housed the base commander's suite and officers' mess where they both had spent many good times in the past. Doshan Tappeh had been an elite base – the Shah had kept some of his private jet fleet and his Fokker Friendship here. Now the walls of the two-storey building were scored by bullets and broken here and there by shell fire, most windows out, a few boarded up. Outside a few Green Bands and slovenly airmen lolled around as sentries.

'Peace be with you! Excellency McIver and Lochart to see the Camp Commandant,' Lochart said in Farsi. One of the Green Bands waved them into the building. 'Where is the office, please?'

'Inside.'

They walked up the steps towards the main door, the air heavy with the smell of fire and cordite and drains. Just as they reached the top step, the main door slammed open and a mullah with some Green Bands hurried out, dragging two young air force officers between them, their hands bound and uniforms torn and filthy. Lochart gasped, recognising one of them. 'Karim!' he burst out and now McIver recognised the youth also – Karim Peshadi, Sharazad's adored cousin, the man he had asked to try to retrieve HBC's clearance from the tower.

'In the Name of God tell them I'm not a spy or traitor,' Karim shouted, in English. 'Tom, tell them!'

'Excellency,' Lochart said in Farsi to the mullah, 'surely there's some mistake. This man is Pilot Captain Peshadi, a loyal helper of the Ayatollah, a supp –'

'Who're you, Excellency?' asked the mullah, dark eyed, short, stocky. 'American?'

'My name is Lochart, Excellency, Canadian, a pilot for IranOil, and this is the leader of our company across the airfield, Captain McIver, an –'

'How do you know this traitor?'

'Excellency, I'm sure there's a mistake, he can't possibly be a traitor, I know him because he is a cousin of my wife and the so –'

'Your wife is Iranian?'

'Yes, Excell –'

'You are Muslim?'

'No, Excellen –'

'Better then she divorces and so saves her soul from pollution. As God wants. There's no mistake about these traitors – mind your own business, Excellency.' The mullah motioned to the Green Bands. At once they went on down the steps, half carrying, half dragging the two young officers who shouted and protested their innocence, then he turned back for the main door.

'Excellency,' Lochart called out urgently, catching up with him. 'Please, in the Name of the One God, I know that young man to be loyal to the Imam, a good Muslim, a patriot of Iran, I know for a fact that he was one of those who went against the Immortals here at Doshan Tappeh and helped the revolu –'

'Stop!' The mullah's eyes hardened even more. 'This is not your affair, foreigner. No longer do foreigners or foreign laws or a foreign-dominated Shah rule us. You are not Iranian, nor a judge, nor a lawgiver. Those men were tried and judged.'

'I beg your patience, Excellency, there must be some mistake, there mu—' Lochart whirled as a volley of rifle shots exploded nearby. The sentries below were staring across the road at some barracks and buildings. From his position atop the steps he could not see what they saw. Then the Green Bands reappeared from behind one of the barracks, shouldering their arms. They trooped back up the steps. The mullah motioned them back inside.

'The law is the law,' the mullah said, watching Lochart. 'Heresy must be removed. Since you know his family you can tell them to beg forgiveness of God for harbouring such a son.'

'What was he supposed to have been guilty of?'

'Not "supposed", Excellency,' the mullah said, an angry edge creeping into his voice. 'Karim Peshadi openly admitted stealing a truck and leaving the base without permission, openly admitted joining forbidden demonstrations, openly declared against our forthcoming absolute Islamic state, openly opposed the abolition of the anti-Islamic Marriage Act, openly advocated acts contrary to Islamic law, was caught in suspected acts of sabotage, openly decried the total absoluteness of the Koran, openly defied the Imam's right to be *faquira* – he who is above the law and final arbiter of the law.' He pulled his robes closer about him against the cold. 'Peace be with you.' He went back into the building.

For a moment Lochart could not speak. Then he explained to McIver what had been said. ' "Suspected acts of sabotage," Tom? Was he caught in the tower?'

'What does it matter?' Lochart said bitterly. 'Karim's dead – for crimes against God.'

809

'No, laddie,' McIver said kindly, 'not against God, against their version of truth spoken in the name of the God they will never know.' He squared his shoulders and led the way inside the building. At length they found the base commander's office and were ushered in.

Behind the desk was a major. The mullah sat beside him. Above them, the only decoration in the small untidy room was a big photograph of Khomeini. 'I'm Major Detami, McIver,' the man said crisply in English. 'This is the mullah Tehrani.' Then he glanced at Lochart and switched to Farsi. 'As His Excellency Tehrani does not speak English, you will interpret for me. Your name, please.'

'Lochart, Captain Lochart.'

'Please sit down, both of you. His Excellency says you are married to an Iranian. What was her maiden name?'

Lochart's eyes hardened. 'My private life is my private life, Excellency.'

'Not for a foreign helicopter pilot in the middle of our Islamic revolution against foreigner domination,' the major said angrily, 'nor one who knows traitors to the State. Do you have something to hide, Captain?'

'No, no of course not.'

'Then please answer the question.'

'Are you police? By what authority do y –'

The mullah said, 'I am a member of the Doshan Tappeh komiteh – you prefer to be summoned officially? Now? This minute?'

'I prefer not to be questioned about my private life.'

'If you have nothing to hide you can answer the question. Please choose.'

'Bakravan.' Lochart saw the name register on both men. His stomach became even more queasy.

'Jared Bakravan – the bazaari moneylender? One of his daughters?'

'Yes.'

'Her name, please.'

Lochart held on to his blinding rage, compounded by Karim's murder. It *is* murder, he wanted to shout, whatever you say. 'Her Excellency, Sharazad.'

McIver had been watching intently. 'What's all this about, Tom?'

'Nothing. Nothing. I'll tell you later.'

The major made a note on a piece of paper. 'What is your relationship to the traitor Karim Peshadi?'

'I've known him for about two years, he was one of my student pilots. He's my wife's first cousin – was my wife's first cousin – and I

810

can only repeat, it's inconceivable that he would be a traitor to Iran or Islam.'

The major made another note on the pad, the pen scratching loudly. 'Where are you staying, Captain?'

'I . . . I'm not sure. I was staying at the Bakravan house near the bazaar. Our . . . our apartment was commandeered.'

The silence gathered in the room, making it claustrophobic. The major finished writing then picked up a page of notes and looked directly at McIver. 'First, no foreign helicopters may be moved in or out of Tehran airspace without Air Force HQ clearance.'

Lochart translated and McIver nodded noncommittally. This was nothing new, except that the komiteh at Tehran International Airport had just issued official written instructions on behalf of the all-powerful Revolutionary Komiteh that the komiteh alone could authorise and grant such clearances. McIver had got permission to send out his remaining 212 and one of his Alouettes to Kowiss 'on temporary loan' just in time, he thought grimly, concentrating on the major, but wondering what the sharp Farsi exchange with Lochart had been all about.

'Second: we require a complete list of all helicopters under your present control, where they are in Iran, their engine numbers and the amount and type of spares you are carrying per helicopter.'

Lochart saw McIver's eyes widen, his own mind locked into Sharazad and why they wanted to know where he lived and her relationship with Karim, hardly listening to the words as he translated back and forth. 'Captain McIver says: "Very well. It will take me a little time, because of communications, but I will get it for you as soon as possible." '

'I would like it tomorrow.'

'If I can get it by then, Excellency, rest assured you will have it. You will have it as soon as possible.'

'Third: all your helicopters in the Tehran area will be assembled here starting tomorrow, and from now on will operate only out of here.'

'I will certainly inform my superiors in IranOil of your request, Major. Instantly.'

The major's face hardened. 'The Air Force is the arbiter of this.'

'Of course. I will inform my superiors at once. Was that all, Major?'

The mullah said, 'About the helicopter,' he referred to a note on the desk in front of him. 'HBC. We w –'

'HBC!' McIver allowed his panic to explode into a righteous anger that Lochart had a hard time keeping up with: 'Security's the responsibility of the Air Force on the base and how they could have been so lax to allow HBC to be hijacked I don't know! Time and again I've complained about laxness, sentries never appearing, no guards at night. A million dollars of theft! Irreplaceable! I am instituting a claim against the Air Force for negligence an —'

'It wasn't our fault,' the major began angrily but McIver paid no attention and continued the offensive, allowing him no opening, nor did Lochart who turned McIver's tirade into apt Iranian words and phrases for an even more slashing attack on Air Force perfidy.

'. . . unbelievable negligence — I might even say deliberate treachery and collusion by other officers — to allow some unknown American to get into our hangar under the very noses of our supposed guardians, to be given clearance to fly off by our supposed protectors and then allowed to do damage to the great Iranian State! Unforgivable! Of course it was treachery and preplanned by "persons unknown holding officer rank" and I must ins —'

'How dare you imply th —'

'Of course it must have been with Air Force officer collusion — who controls the base? Who controls the airwaves, who sits in the tower? We hold the Air Force responsible and I'm registering the complaint to the highest level of IranOil demanding restitution and . . . and next week, next week I will apply for redress to the illustrious Revolutionary Komiteh and the Imam himself, may God protect him! Now, Excellency, if you will excuse us we will go about our business. Peace be with you!'

McIver went for the door, Lochart following, both men overloaded with adrenalin, McIver feeling terrible, his chest aching.

'Wait!' the mullah ordered.

'Yes, Excellency?'

'How do you explain that the traitor Valik — who "happens" to be a partner of your company and kinsman of the usurer and Shah supporter, Bakravan — arrived in Isfahan in this helicopter to pick up other traitors, one of whom was General Seladi, another kinsman of Jared Bakravan — father-in-law to one of your senior pilots?'

Lochart's mouth was very dry as he spoke the doom-filled words but McIver did not hesitate and came back to the attack. 'I did not appoint General Valik to our board, he was appointed by high-up Iranians according to your then current law — we did not seek Iranian partners, it was Iranian law that we had to have them, they were forced upon us. Nothing to do with me. As to the rest, Insha'Allah — the Will of God!'

Heart thundering, he opened the door and stalked off, Lochart finished translating. 'Salaam.' He followed.

'You've not heard the last of this,' the major shouted after him.

Near the University: 6:07 P.M. They were lying side by side on soft carpets in front of the wood fire that burned merrily in the pleasant room. Sharazad and Ibrahim Kyabi. They were not touching, just watching the fire, listening to the good, modern music from the cassette player, lost in thought, each too aware of the other.

'Thou, gift of the Universe,' he murmured, 'thou of the ruby lips and breath like wine, thou, tongue of Heaven . . .'

'Oh Ibrahim,' she laughed. 'What is this "tongue of Heaven"?'

He raised himself on to an elbow and looked down at her, blessing fate that had allowed him to save her from the insane zealot at the Women's March, the same fate that would soon guide him to Kowiss to revenge his father's murder. 'I was quoting the *Rubáiyát*,' he said, smiling at her.

'I don't believe a word of it! I think you made it up.' She returned his smile, then shielded her eyes from the glow of his stare and looked again at the embers.

After the first Protest March, now six days ago, long into that evening they had talked together, discussing the revolution and finding common cause in the murder of her father and his father, both of them children of loneliness now, their mothers not understanding, only weeping and Insha'Allah and never the need for revenge. Their lives turned upside down like their country, Ibrahim no longer a Believer – only in the strength and purpose of the People – her belief shaken, questioning for the first time, wondering how God could permit such evil and all the other evils that had come to pass, the corruption of the land and its spirit, 'I agree, Ibrahim, you're right. We haven't rid ourselves of one despot to acquire another, you're right, the despotism of the mullahs daily becomes more clear,' she had said. 'But why does Khomeini oppose the rights that the Shah gave to us, reasonable rights?'

'They're your inalienable rights as a human being, not the Shah's to give, or anyone – like your body's your own, not a field to be ploughed.'

'But why is the Imam opposed?'

'He's not an Imam, Sharazad, just an ayatollah, a man and a fanatic. It's because he's doing what priests have always done throughout history: he's using his version of religion to drug the people into senselessness, to keep them dependent, uneducated, to secure mullahs into power. Doesn't he want only mullahs responsible for education? Doesn't he claim mullahs alone understand "the law", study "the law", have the knowledge of "the law"? As if they alone have *all* knowledge!'

'I never thought of it like that, I accepted so much, so very much. But you're right, Ibrahim, you make everything so clear to me. You're right, mullahs believe only what's in the Koran – as if what was correct for the days of the Prophet, peace be upon him, should apply today! I refuse to be a chattel without the vote and the right to choose . . .'

Finding so many common grounds of thought, he a modern, university trained, she wanting to be modern but unsure of her way. Sharing secrets and longings, understanding each other instantly, using the same nuances, belonging to the same heritage – he so very much like Karim in speech and looks they could be brothers.

That night she had slept blissfully and the next morning slipped out early to meet him again, drinking coffee in a little café, she chadored for safety and secrecy, laughing so much together, for no reason or every reason, serious sometimes. Both aware of the currents, no need to speak them. Then the second Protest March, bigger than the first, better and with little opposition.

'When do you have to be back, Sharazad?'

'I, I told Mother I would be late, that I'd visit a friend on the other side of the city.'

'I'll take you there now, quickly, and you can leave quickly and then, if you like we could talk some more, or even better I've a friend who has an apartment and some wonderful records . . .'

That was five days ago. Sometimes his friend, another Tudeh student leader, would be here, sometimes other students, young men and women, not all of them communist but new ideas, free exchange, heady ideas of life, and love and living free. Occasionally they were alone. Heavenly days, marching and talking and laughing and listening to records and peace-filled nights at home near the bazaar.

Yesterday victory. Khomeini had relented, publicly, saying that women were not forced to wear chador, provided they covered their hair and dressed modestly. Last night celebrating, dancing with joy in the apartment, all of them young, embracing and then going home again. But last night her sleep had been all about him and her together. Erotic. Lying there half asleep this morning, afraid yet so excited.

The cassette ended. It was one of the Carpenters, slow, romantic. He turned it and now the other side, even better. Dare I? She asked herself, dreamily, feeling his eyes on her. Through a crack in the curtains she could see that the sky was darkening. 'It's almost time to go,' she said, not moving, a throb in her voice.

'Jari can wait,' he said tenderly. Jari, her maid, was party to their secret visits. 'Better no one knows,' he had said on the second day. 'Even her.'

'She has to know, Ibrahim, or I can never get out alone, never see you. I've nothing to hide but I am married and it's . . .' No need to articulate "dangerous". Every moment they were alone screamed danger.

So he had shrugged and petitioned fate to protect her, as he did now. 'Jari can wait.'

'Yes, yes, she can, but first we've got to do some errands and my dear brother Meshang won't – tonight I have to have dinner with him and Zarah.'

Ibrahim was startled. 'What's he want? He doesn't suspect you?'

'Oh, no, it's just family, just that.' Languorously she looked at him. 'What about your business in Kowiss? Will you wait another day or will you go tomorrow?'

'It's not urgent,' he said carelessly. He had delayed and delayed even though his Tudeh controller had said that every extra day he stayed in Tehran was dangerous: 'Have you forgotten what happened to Comrade Yazernov? We hear Inner Intelligence was involved! They must have spotted you going into the building with him, or coming out of it.'

'I've shaved off my beard, I've not gone home and I'm avoiding the university. By the way, comrade, it's better we don't meet for a day or two – I think I'm being followed.' He smiled to himself, remembering the alacrity with which the other man, an old-time Tudeh supporter, had vanished around the street corner.

'Why the smile, my darling?'

'Nothing. I love you, Sharazad,' he said simply and cupped her breast as he kissed her.

She kissed him back but not completely. His passion grew, and hers, and though she tried to hold back she felt herself going over the brink, his hands caressing her, fire in their wake.

'I love you, Sharazad . . . love me.'

She did not wish to pull away from the heat, or his hands, or the pressure of his limbs, or the thunder of her heart. But she did, not knowing why. 'Not now, my darling,' she murmured and gained a breathing space and then, when the thunder lessened, she looked up at him, searching his eyes. She saw disappointment but no anger. 'I'm . . . not ready, not for love, not now . . .'

'Love happens. You're safe, Sharazad, your love will be safe with me.'

'I know, oh yes, I know that. I . . .' She frowned, not understanding herself only that now was wrong. 'I have to be sure of what I'm doing. Now I'm not.'

He debated with himself, then leaned down and kissed her, not forcing the kiss on her – quite confident that soon they would be lovers. Tomorrow. Or the next day. 'You're wise as always,' he said. 'Tomorrow we will have the apartment to ourselves. I promise. Let's meet as usual, coffee at the usual place.' He got up, and helped her up. She held on to him and kissed him and thanked him and he unlocked the front door. Silently she wrapped the chador around her, gave him another kiss and left, perfume in her wake. Then that too vanished.

With the door relocked he went back and put on his shoes. Thoughtfully he picked up his M16 that stood in the corner of the room, checked the action and the magazine. Away from her spell he had no illusions about the danger or the realities of his life – and early death. His excitement quickened.

Death, he thought. Martyrdom. Giving my life for a just cause, freely embracing death, welcoming it. Oh, I will, I will. I can't lead an army like the Lord of the Martyrs, but I can revolt against Satanists calling themselves mullahs and extract revenge on the mullah Hussain of Kowiss for murdering my father in the name of false gods, and for desecrating the revolution of the People!

He felt his ecstasy growing. Like the other. Stronger than the other.

I love her with all my soul but I should go tomorrow. I don't need a team with me, alone it would be safer. I can easily catch a bus. I should go tomorrow. I should but I can't, not yet. After we've made love . . .

Al Shargaz Airport: 6:17 P.M. Almost eight hundred miles away, southeast, across the Gulf, Gavallan was standing at the heliport watching the 212 coming in to land. The evening was balmy, the sun on the horizon. Now he could see Jean-Luc at the controls with one of the other pilots beside him, not Scot as he had thought and expected. His anxiety increased. He waved and then, as the skids touched, impatiently went forward to the cabin door. It swung open. He saw Scot unbuckling one-handed, his other arm in a sling, his face stretched and pale but in one piece. 'Oh, my son,' he said, heart pounding with relief, wanting to rush forward and hug him but standing back and waiting until Scot had walked down the steps and was there on the tarmac beside him.

'Oh, laddie, I was so worried . . .'

'Not to worry, Dad. I'm fine, just fine.' Scot held his good arm tightly around his father's shoulders, the reassuring contact so necessary to both of them, oblivious of the others. 'Christ, I'm so happy to see you. I thought you were due in London today.'

'I was. I'm on the red-eye in an hour.' Now I can return, now that you're here and safe. 'I'll be there first thing.' He brushed a tear away, pretending it was dust and pointed at a car nearby. Genny was at the wheel. 'Don't want to fuss you but Genny'll take you to the hospital right away, just X-ray, Scot, it's all arranged. No fuss, promise – you've a room booked next door to mine at the hotel. All right?'

'All right, Dad. I, er, I . . . I could use an aspirin. I admit I feel lousy – the ride was bumpy to hell. I, er, I . . . you're on the red-eye? When're you back?'

'Soon as I can. In a day or so. I'll call you tomorrow, all right?'

Scot hesitated, his face twisting. 'Could you . . . perhaps . . . perhaps you could come with me – I can fill you in about Zagros, would you have time?'

'Of course. It was bad?'

'No and yes. We all got out – except Jordon but he was shot because of me, Dad, he was . . .' Tears filled Scot's eyes though his voice stayed controlled and firm. 'Can't do anything about it . . . can't.' He wiped the tears away and mumbled a curse and hung on with his good hand. 'Can't do anything . . . don't don't know how to . . .'

'Not your fault, Scot,' Gavallan said, torn by his son's despair, frightened for him. 'Come along, we'll . . . let's get you started.' He called out to Jean-Luc, 'I'm taking Scot off for X-rays, be back right away.'

Tehran – At McIver's Apartment: 6:35 P.M. In candlelight, Charlie Pettikin and Paula were sitting at the dining table, clinking wine-filled glasses with Sayada Bertolin, a large bottle of Chianti open, plates with two big salamis, one partially eaten, a huge slice of dolce latte cheese as yet untouched, and two fresh French baguettes that Sayada had brought from the French Club, one mostly gone: 'There may be a war on,' she said with forced gaiety when she had arrived uninvited, half an hour ago, 'but whatever happens, the French must have proper bread.'

'*Vive la France*, and *viva l'Italia*,' Pettikin had said, reluctantly inviting her in, not wanting to share Paula with anyone. Since Paula had terminated any interest in Nogger Lane, he had rushed into the breach, hoping against hope. 'Paula came in on this afternoon's flight, smuggled in all the swag at the risk of her life and – and doesn't she look superisssssima?'

Paula laughed. 'It's the dolce latte, Sayada; Charlie told me it was his favourite.'

'Isn't it the best cheese on earth? Isn't everything Italian the best on earth?'

Paula brought out the corkscrew and handed it to him, her green-flecked eyes sending more shivers down his spine. 'For you, *caro!*'

'*Magnifico!* Are all young ladies of Alitalia as thoughtful, brave, beautiful, efficient, tender, sweet smelling, loving and, er, cinematic?'

'Of course.'

'Join the feast, Sayada,' he had said. When she came closer into the light he saw her properly, noticing the strangeness to her. 'You all right?'

'Oh, yes, it's, it's nothing.' Sayada was glad for the candlelight to hide behind. 'I, er, thanks I won't stay, I . . . I just miss Jean-Luc, wanted to find out when he's back, I thought you could use the baguettes.'

'Delighted you arrived – we haven't had a decent loaf for weeks, thanks, but stay anyway. Mac's gone to Doshan Tappeh to pick up Tom. Tom'll know about Jean-Luc – they should be back any moment.'

'How's Zagros?'

'We've had to close it down.' As he busied himself getting glasses and setting up the table, Paula helping and doing most of it, he told them the why, and about the terrorist attack on Rig Bellissima, Gianni's being killed, then later, Jordon, and Scot Gavallan being wounded. 'Bloody business, but there you are.'

'Terrible,' Paula said. 'That explains why we're routed back through Shiraz with instructions to keep fifty seats open. Must be for our nationals from the Zagros.'

'What rotten luck,' Sayada said, wondering if she should pass that information on. To *them* – and *him*. The Voice had called yesterday, early, asking what time she had left Teymour on Saturday. 'About five, perhaps five fifteen, why?'

'The cursed building caught fire just after dark – somewhere on the third floor, trapping the two above. The whole building's gutted, many people killed and there's no sign of Teymour or the others. Of course the fire department was too late . . .'

No problem to find real tears and to let her agony pour out. Later in the day the Voice had called again: 'Did you give Teymour the papers?'

'Yes . . . yes, yes I did.'

There had been a muffled curse. 'Be at the French Club tomorrow afternoon. I will leave instructions in your box.' But there was no message so she had wheedled the loaves from the kitchen and had come here – nowhere else to go and still very frightened.

'So sad,' Paula was saying.

'Yes, but enough of that,' Pettikin said, cursing himself for telling them – none of their problem, he thought. 'Let's eat, drink and be merry.'

'For tomorrow we die?' Sayada said.

'No.' Pettikin raised his glass, beamed at Paula. 'For tomorrow we live. Health!' He touched glasses with her, then Sayada, and he thought what a smashing pair they make but Paula's far and away the most . . .

Sayada was thinking: Charlie's in love with this siren harpy who'll consume him at her whim and spew out the remains with hardly a belch, but why do *they* – my new masters whoever they are – why do *they* want to know about Jean-Luc and Tom and want me to be Armstrong's mistress and how do they know about my son, God curse *them*.

Paula was thinking: I hate this shit-roll of a city where everyone's so gloomy and doom-ridden and downbeat like this poor woman who's obviously got the usual man-trouble, when there's Rome and sunshine and Italy and the sweet life to become drunk with, wine and laughter and love to be enjoyed, children to bear with a husband to cherish but only so long as the devil behaves – why are all men rotten and why do I like this man Charlie who is too old and yet not, too poor and yet not, too masculine and yet . . .

'*Alora*,' she said, the wine making her lips more juicy, 'Charlie, *amore*, we must meet in Rome. Tehran is so . . . so depression, *scusa*, depressing.'

'Not when you're around,' he said.

Sayada saw them smiling at each other, and envied them. 'I think I'll come back later,' she said, getting up. Before Pettikin could say anything, a key turned in the lock and McIver came in.

'Oh, hello,' he said, trying to throw off his weariness. 'Hi, Paula, hi, Sayada – this is a pleasant surprise.' Then he noticed the table. 'What's this, Christmas?' He took off his heavy coat and gloves.

'Paula brought it – and Sayada the bread. Where's Tom?' Pettikin asked, immediately sensing something was wrong.

'I dropped him off at Bakravan's, near the bazaar.'

'How is she?' Sayada asked. 'I haven't seen her since . . . since the day of the march, the first march.'

'Don't know, lassie, I just dropped him off and came on.' McIver accepted a glass of wine, returned Pettikin's look levelly. 'Traffic was rotten. Took me an hour to get here. Health! Paula, you're a sight for sore eyes. You staying tonight?'

'If that's all right? I'm off early in the morning, no need for transport, *caro*, one of the crew dropped me off and will pick me up. Genny said I could use the spare room – she thought it might need a spring clean but it looks fine.' Paula got up and both men, unknowingly, were instantly magnetised by the sensuousness of her movements. Sayada cursed her, envying her, wondering what it was, certainly not the uniform that was quite severe though beautifully tailored, knowing that she herself was far more beautiful, far better dressed – but not in the same race. Cow!

Paula reached into her handbag and found the two letters and gave them to McIver. 'One from Genny and one from Andy.'

'Thanks, thanks very much,' McIver said.

'I was just going, Mac,' Sayada said. 'Just wanted to ask when Jean-Luc'll be back.'

'Probably on Wednesday – he's ferrying a 212 to Al Shargaz. He should be there today and back Wednesday.' McIver glanced at the letters. 'No need to go, Sayada . . . excuse me a second.'

He sat down in the easy chair by the electric fire that was at half power, switched on a nearby lamp. The light took away much of the romance of the room. Gavallan's letter read: 'Hi, Mac, this in a hurry, courtesy of the fairest of them all! I'm waiting for Scot. Then red-eyeing it to London tonight if he's all right, but I'll be back in two days, three at the most. Finessed Duke out of Kowiss down to Rudi in case Scrag's delayed – he should be back Tuesday. Kowiss is very dicey – had a big run in with Hotshot – so's Zagros. Have just talked to Masson from here and that's fact. So I'm pushing the button for planning. It's pushed. See you Wednesday. Give Paula a hug for me and Genny says don't you bloody dare!'

He stared at the letter, then sat back a moment, half listening to a story Paula was telling about their incoming flight to Tehran. So the button's pushed. Don't delude yourself, Andy, I knew you'd push it from the first moment – that's why I said, all right, provided I can abort Whirlwind if I think it's too risky and my decision's final. I think you must push the button all the way – you've no alternative if you want S-G to survive.

The wine tasted very good. He finished the glass, then opened Genny's letter. It was just news about home and the kids, all of them

820

healthy and in place, but he knew her too well not to read the underlying concern: 'Don't worry, Duncan, and don't sweat out winds, any winds. And don't think I plan on a rose-covered cottage in England. It's us for the casbah and me for a yashmak and I'm practising belly-dancing so you'd better hurry. Luv Gen.'

McIver smiled to himself, got up and poured himself some wine, calmer now. 'Here's to women, bless 'em.' He touched glasses with Pettikin. 'Smashing wine, Paula. Andy sends you a hug . . .' At once she smiled and reached over and touched him and he felt the current rush up his arm. What the hell is it about her, he asked himself, unsettled, and quickly said to Sayada, 'He'd send one to you too if he knew you were here.' A candle on the mantelpiece was guttering. 'I'll get it. Any messages?'

'One from Talbot. He's doing all he can to find Erikki. Duke's delayed at Bandar-e Delam by a storm but he should be back at Kowiss tomorrow.'

'And Azadeh?'

'She's better today. Paula and I walked her home. She's okay, Mac. You better have something to eat, there's bugger all for dinner.'

Sayada said, 'How about dining at the French Club? The food's still passable.'

'I'd love to,' Paula said brightly and Pettikin cursed. 'What a wonderful idea, Sayada! Charlie?'

'Wonderful. Mac?'

'Sure, if it's my treat and you don't mind an early night.' McIver held his glass up to the light, admiring the colour of the wine. 'Charlie, I want you to take the 212 to Kowiss bright and early, Nogger'll take the Alouette – you can help Duke out for a couple of days. I'll send Shoesmith in a 206 to bring you back Saturday. All right?'

'Sure,' Pettikin said, wondering why the change of plan that had been for McIver, Nogger and him to get aboard the Wednesday flight, two other pilots to go to Kowiss tomorrow. Why? Must be Andy's letter. Whirlwind? Is Mac aborting?

In the Slums of Jaleh: 6:50 P.M. The old car stopped in the alleyway. A man got out of the side door and looked around. The alley was deserted, high walls, a joub to one side that long ago was buried under snow and refuse. Across from where the car had stopped, dimly seen in the reflection from the headlights, was a broken-down square. The man tapped on the roof. The headlights were doused. The driver got out and went to help the other man who had opened the boot. Together they carried the body, wrapped and bound in a dark blanket, across the square.

'Wait a moment,' the driver said in Russian. He took out his flashlight and switched it on briefly. The circle of light found the opening in the far wall they sought.

'Good,' the other said and they went through it, then once more stopped to get their bearings. Now they were in a cemetery, old, almost derelict. The light went from gravestone to gravestone – some of the writing Russian, some in Roman letters – to find the open grave, newly dug. A shovel stood upright in the mound of earth.

They went and stood on the lip. The taller man, the driver, said, 'Ready?'

'Yes.' They let the body fall into the hole. The driver shone the light on to it. 'Straighten him up.'

'He won't give a shit,' the other man said and took up the shovel. He was broad-shouldered and strong and he began to fill the grave. The driver lit a cigarette, irritably threw the match into the grave. 'Maybe you should say a prayer for him.'

The other laughed. 'Marx-Lenin wouldn't approve – nor old Stalin.'

'That mother fornicator – may he rot!'

'Look what he did for Mother Russia! He made us an empire, the biggest in the world, he screwed the British, outsmarted the Americans, built the biggest and best army, navy, airforce and made the KGB all powerful.'

'For damn near every rouble we've got and twenty million lives. Russian lives.'

'Expendables! Scum, fools, the dregs, plenty more where they came from.' The man was sweating now and he gave the shovel to the other. 'What the hell's the matter with you anyway – you've been pissed off all day.'

'Tired, I'm just tired. Sorry.'

'Everyone's tired. You need a few days off. Apply for Al Shargaz – I had a great three days, didn't want to come back. I've applied for a transfer there – we've quite an operation now, growing every day, the Israelis have stepped up their ops too – so've the CIA. What's happened since I was away?'

'Azerbaijan's warming up nicely. There's a rumour old Abdollah Khan's dying or dead.'

'The Section 16/a?'

'No, heart attack. Everything else's normal. You really had a good time?'

The other laughed. 'There's an Intourist secretary who's very accommodating.' He scratched his scrotum at the thought. 'Who is this poor sod anyway?'

'His name wasn't listed,' the driver said.

'Never is. So who was he?'

'Agent called Yazernov, Dimitri Yazernov.'

'Means nothing to me. To you?'

'He was an agent from Disinformation on the university detail, I worked with him for a short time, a year back. Smartass, university type, full of ideological bullshit. It seems he was caught by Inner Intelligence and interrogated seriously.'

'Bastards! They killed him, eh?'

'No.' The taller man stopped shovelling a moment and looked around. No chance of them being overheard and while he did not believe in ghosts or God or anything but the Party and the KGB – the spearhead of the Party – he did not like this place. He lowered his voice. 'When he was sprung, almost a week ago, he was in bad shape, unconscious, should never've been moved, not in his state. SAVAMA got him away from Inner Intelligence – the director thinks SAVAMA worked him over too before handing him back.' He leaned on the shovel a moment. 'SAVAMA gave him to us with the report that they thought he'd been cleaned out through the third level. The director said to find out who he was fast, if he had other secret clearances, or was an internal spy or a plant from higher up, and what the hell he'd told them – who the hell he was. He's not carried on our files as anything other than an agent on the university detail.' He wiped the sweat off his forehead and began shovelling again. 'I heard the team waited and waited for him to regain consciousness, then today gave up waiting and tried to wake him up.'

'A mistake? Someone gave him too much?'

'Who knows – the poor sod's dead.'

'That's the one thing that scares me,' the other said with a shiver. 'Getting fed too much. Nothing you can do about it. He never woke up? Never said anything?'

'No. Not a damned thing. The shit's that he was caught at all. It was his own fault – the mother was working on his own.'

The other cursed. 'How'd he get away with that?'

'Buggered if I know. I remember him as one of those who think they know it all and sneer at the book. Smart? Bullshit! These bastards cause more trouble than they're worth.' The taller man worked strongly and steadily. When he was tired the other took a turn.

Soon the grave was filled. The man patted the earth flat, his breathing heavy. 'If this mother got himself caught, why're we taking all this trouble then?'

'If the body can't be repatriated, a comrade's entitled to be buried properly, that's in the book. This's a Russian cemetery, isn't it?'

'Sure, of course it is, but damned if I'd like to be buried here.' The man wiped the dirt off his hands then turned and relieved himself on the nearest gravestone.

The taller man was working a gravestone loose. 'Give me a hand.' Together they lifted the stone and replanted it at the head of the grave they had just filled.

Damn the young bastard for dying, he thought, cursing him. Not my fault he died. He should've withstood the dose. Sodding doctors! They're supposed to know! We had no option, the bastard was sinking anyway and there were too many questions to be answered, like what was so important about him that that arch bastard Hashemi Fazir did the interrogation himself, along with that sonofabitch Armstrong? Those two high flying professionals don't waste their time on small fry. And why did Yazernov say 'Fedor . . .' just before he croaked? What's the significance of that?

'Let's go home,' the other man said. 'This place's foul and it stinks, it stinks worse than normal.' He took the shovel and trudged off into the night.

Just then the writing on the stone caught the driver's eye but it was too dark to read. He switched on the light momentarily. The writing said, Count Alexi Pokenov, Plenipotentiary to Shah Nasiru'd Din, 1830–1862.

Yazernov'd like that, he thought, his smile twisted.

At the Bakravan House, near the Bazaar: 7:15 P.M. The outer door in the wall swung open. 'Salaam, Highness.' The servant watched Sharazad as she swept past happily, followed by Jari, into the forecourt and pulled the chador off and was now shaking her hair and puffing it with her fingertips more comfortably. 'The . . . your husband's back, Highness; he came back just after sunset.'

For a moment Sharazad was frozen in the light of the oil lamps that flickered in the snow-covered courtyard leading to the front door.

Then it's over, she was thinking. Over before it began. It almost began today. I was ready and yet not . . . and now, now I'm saved from . . . from my lust or love, was that what I was trying to decide? I don't know, I don't know but . . . but tomorrow I'll see him a last time, I have to see him once more, have to, just . . . just once more . . . just to say goodbye . . .

Tears filled her eyes and she ran into the house and into the rooms and salons and up the stairs and into their suite and into his arms. 'Oh Tommyyyyyy you've been away such a long time!'

'Oh I've missed you, where have you . . . don't cry, my darling, there's no need to cry . . .'

His arms were around her and she caught the faint, familiar oil-gasoline smell that came from his flight clothes hanging on a peg. Not giving him a second, she stood on tiptoe, kissed him, and said in a rush, 'I've such wonderful news, I'm with child, oh yes it's true and I've seen a doctor and tomorrow I'll get the result of the test but I *know*!' Her smile was vast and true. 'Oh Tommy,' she continued in the same rush, feeling his arms tighten even more. 'Will you marry me, please please please?'

'But we are mar –'

'Say it, oh please, please say it!' She looked up and saw he was still pale and smiling only a very little but that was enough for the moment, and she heard him say, Of course I'll marry you. 'No, say it properly, I marry you Sharazad Bakravan. I marry you I marry you I marry you,' then hearing him say it and that made everything perfect. 'Perfect,' she burst out and hugged him back, then pushed away and ran over to the mirror to repair her makeup. She caught sight of Lochart in the mirror, his face so severe, unsettled. 'What is it?'

'You're sure, sure about the child?'

She laughed. 'Oh I'm sure, but the doctor needs proof, husbands need proof. Isn't it wonderful?'

'Yes . . . yes it is.' He put his hands on her shoulders. 'I love you!'

In her head she heard the other I love you that had been said with such passion and longing, and she thought how strange that though her husband's love was sure and proven, Ibrahim's was not – yet I believe his was without reservation whereas, even after her wonderful news, her husband frowned at her.

'The year and a day have gone, Tommy, the year and a day you wanted,' she said gently and got up from the dressing table, put her hands around his neck, smiling up at him, knowing that it was up to her to help him: 'Foreigners aren't like us, Princess,' Jari had said, 'their reactions are different, training different, but don't worry, just be your own delightful self and he will be clay in your hands . . .' Tommy'll be the best father ever, she promised herself, irrepressibly happy that she had not melted this afternoon, that she had made her announcement, and now they would live happily ever after. 'We will, Tommy, won't we?'

825

'What?'

'Live happily ever after.'

For a moment her joy obliterated his misery about Karim Peshadi and worry about what to do and how to do it. He caught her up in his arms and sat in the deep chair, cradling her. 'Oh, yes. Oh yes, we will. There's so much to talk ab—' Jari's knock on the door interrupted him.

'Come in, Jari.'

'Please excuse me, Excellency, but His Excellency Meshang and her Highness have arrived and are waiting to have the pleasure of seeing you both when convenient.'

'Tell His Excellency we'll be there as soon as we've changed.' Lochart did not notice Jari's relief as Sharazad nodded and beamed at her.

'I'll run your bath, Highness,' Jari said and went into the bathroom. 'Isn't it wonderful about Her Highness, Excellency? Oh, many congratulations, Excellency, many congratulations . . .'

'Thank you, Jari,' Lochart said not listening to her, thinking about the child to be, and Sharazad, lost in worry and happiness. So complicated now, so difficult.

'Not difficult,' Meshang said after dinner.

Conversation had been boring with Meshang dominating it as he always did now that he was head of the household, Sharazad and Zarah hardly talking, Lochart saying little – no point in mentioning Zagros as Meshang had always been totally uninterested in his opinions or what he did. Twice he had almost blurted out about Karim – no reason to tell them yet, he had thought, hiding his despair. Why be the bearer of bad tidings?

'You don't find life in Tehran difficult now?' he said. Meshang had been moaning about all the new regulations implanted on the bazaar.

'Life is always difficult,' Meshang said, 'but if you're Iranian, a trained bazaari, with care and understanding, with hard work and logic; even the Revolutionary Komiteh can be curbed – we've always curbed tax collectors and overlords, shahs, commissars, or Yankee and British pashas.'

'I'm glad to hear it, very glad.'

'And I'm very glad you're back, I've been wanting to talk to you,' Meshang said. 'My sister has told you about the child to be?'

'Yes, yes she has. Isn't it wonderful?'

'Yes, yes it is. God be praised. What are your plans?'

'How do you mean?'

'Where are you going to live? How are you going to pay for everything now?'

The silence was vast. 'We'll manage,' Lochart began. 'I int –'

'I don't see how you can, logically. I've been going through last year's bills an—' Meshang stopped as Zarah got up.

'I don't think this is a good time to talk about bills,' she said, her face suddenly white, Sharazad's equally so.

'Well, I do,' Meshang said harshly. 'How's my sister going to survive? Sit down, Zarah, and listen! Sit down! And when I say you will not go on a protest march or anything else in future you will obey or I'll whip you! *Sit down!*' Zarah obeyed, shocked at his bad manners and violence. Sharazad was stunned, her world collapsing. She saw her brother turn on Lochart. 'Now, Captain, your bills for the last year, the bills paid by my father, not counting the ones still owing and due, are substantially more than your salary. Is that true?'

Sharazad's face was burning with shame and anger and before Lochart could answer she said quickly in her most honeyed voice, 'Darling Meshang, you're quite right to be concerned about us but the apar –'

'Kindly keep quiet! I have to ask your husband, not you, it's his problem, not yours. Well, Cap –'

'But darling Mesh –'

'Keep quiet! Well, Captain, is it true or isn't it?'

'Yes, it's true,' Lochart replied, desperately seeking a way out of the abyss. 'But you'll remember His Excellency gave me the apartment, in fact the building, and the other rents paid the bills and the rest was for an allowance to give to Sharazad for which I was eternally grateful. As to the future, I'll take care of Sharazad, of course I will.'

'With what? I've read your divorce settlement and it's clear that with the payments you make to your previous wife and child there's little chance you can keep my sister out of penury.'

Lochart was choked with rage. Sharazad shifted in her chair and Lochart saw her fear and dominated his urge to smash Meshang into the table. 'It's all right, Sharazad. Your brother has the right to ask. That's fair, he has the right.' He read the smugness under the etched handsome face and knew that the fight was joined. 'We'll manage, Meshang, I'll manage. Our apartment, it won't be commandeered for ever, or we can take another. We'll m –'

'There is no apartment, or building. It burned down on Saturday. It's all gone, everything.'

They gaped at him, Sharazad the most shocked. 'Oh, Meshang, you're sure? Why didn't you tell me? Wh –'

'Is your property so abundant you don't check it from time to time? It's gone, all of it!'

'Oh Christ!' Lochart muttered.

'Better you don't blaspheme,' Meshang said, finding it hard not to gloat openly. 'So there's no apartment, no building, nothing left. Insha'Allah. Now, now how do you intend to pay your bills?'

'Insurance!' Lochart burst out. 'There's got to be in –'

A bellow of laughter drowned him, Sharazad knocked over a glass of water that no one noticed. 'You think insurance will be paid?' Meshang jeered. 'Now? Even if there was any? You've taken leave of your senses, there is no insurance, there never was. So, Captain: many debts, no money, no capital, no building – not that it was even legally yours, merely a face-saving way my father arranged to provide you with the means to look after Sharazad.' He picked up a piece of halvah and popped it into his mouth. 'So what do you propose?'

'I'll manage.'

'How, please tell me – and Sharazad, of course, she has the right, the legal right to know. How?'

Sharazad muttered, 'I've jewellery, Tommy, I can sell that.'

Cruelly Meshang left the words hanging in the air over the table, delighted that Lochart was at bay, humiliated, stripped naked. Filthy Infidel! If it wasn't for the Locharts in our world, the rapacious foreigners, exploiters of Iran, we'd be free of Khomeini and his mullahs, my father would still be alive, and Sharazad married properly. 'Well?'

'What do you suggest?' Lochart said, no way out of the trap.

'What do *you* suggest?'

'I don't know.'

'Meanwhile you've no house, very substantial bills and soon you'll be jobless – I doubt if your company will be allowed to operate here very much longer, quite correctly foreign companies are persona non grata,' Meshang was delighted that he had remembered the Latin phrase, 'no longer needed, wanted, or necessary.'

'If that happens I'll resign and apply to fly choppers for Iranian companies. They'll need pilots immediately. I can speak Farsi, I'm an expert pilot and trainer. Khomeini . . . the Imam wants oil production brought back to normal immediately, so of course they'll need trained pilots.'

Meshang laughed to himself. Yesterday Minister Ali Kia had come to the bazaar, correctly humble and anxious to please, bringing an exquisite pishkesh – wasn't his annual 'consulting fee' due for renewal soon! – and had told him of his plans to acquire all partnership airplanes and freeze all bank accounts. 'We'll have no problem to get all the mercenaries we need to fly *our* helicopters, Excellency Meshang,' Kia had said. 'They'll flock to us at half their normal salaries.'

Yes, they will, but not you, temporary husband of my sister, not even for a tenth salary. 'I suggest you be more practical.' Meshang examined his beautifully manicured nails that this afternoon had fondled the fourteen-year-old Ali Kia had given him: 'the first of many, Excellency!' Lovely white Circassian skin, the temporary marriage for this afternoon that he had gladly extended for the week so easily arranged. 'The present rulers of Iran are xenophobic, particularly about Americans.'

'I'm Canadian.'

'I doubt if that matters. It's logical to presume you won't be permitted to stay.' He looked sharply at Sharazad, 'Or to return.'

'Surmise,' Lochart said through his teeth, seeing the look on her face.

'Captain, my late father's charity can no longer be supported – times are hard. I want to know how you intend to support my sister and her forthcoming child, where you intend to live and how.'

Abruptly Lochart got up, startling everyone else. 'You've made your point, clearly, Excellency Meshang. I'll answer you tomorrow.'

'I want an answer now.'

Lochart's face closed. 'First I'll talk to my wife and then I'll talk to you tomorrow. Come on, Sharazad.' He stalked out. In tears she stumbled after him and closed the door.

Meshang smiled sardonically, picked up another sweet and began to eat it.

Zarah exhaled, enraged. 'What in the name of G –'

He reached over and smashed her open-handed around the face. 'Shut up!' he shouted. It was not the first time he had hit her but never before with such violence. 'Shut up or I'll divorce you! I'll divorce you, you hear? I'm going to take another wife anyway – someone young, not dry and an old nagging hag like you. Don't you understand Sharazad's in danger, we're all in danger because of that man? Go beg God's forgiveness for your foul manners! Get out!' She fled. He hurled a cup after her.

In the Northern Suburbs: 9:14 P.M. Azadeh drove the small, badly dented car fast along the street that was lined with fine houses and apartment buildings – most of them dark, a few vandalised – headlights carelessly on full, dazzling the oncoming traffic, her horn blaring. She braked, skidded as she cut dangerously across the traffic, narrowly avoiding an accident, and headed into the garage of one of the buildings with a screech of rubber.

The garage was dark. In the side pocket was a flash. She turned it on, got out, and locked the car. Her coat was well cut and warm, skirt and boots and fur mitts and hat, her hair flowing. On the other side of the garage was a staircase and a switch for the lights. When she tried it, the nearest bulb sparked and died. She went up the stairs heavily. Four apartments on each landing. The apartment that her father had loaned to her and Erikki was on the third landing, facing the street. Today was Monday. She had been here since Saturday. 'It's not risky, Mac,' she had said when she announced she was going and he had tried to persuade her to remain in his apartment, 'but if my father wants me back in Tabriz, staying here with you won't help me at all. In the apartment I've a phone, I'm only half a mile away and can walk it easily, I've clothes there and a servant. I'll check every day and come into the office, and wait, that's all I can do.'

She had not said that she preferred to be away from him and Charlie Pettikin. I like them both dearly, she thought, but they're rather old and pedantic and nothing like Erikki. Or Johnny. Ah, Johnny, what to do about you, dare I see you again?

The third landing was dark but she had the flash and found her key, put it in the lock, felt eyes on her and whirled in fright. The swarthy, unshaven lout had his pants open and he waved his stiff penis at her. 'I've been waiting for you, princess of all whores, and God curse me if it's not ready for you front or back or sideways . . .' He came forward mouthing obscenities and she backed against the door in momentary terror, grabbed the key, turned it and flung the door open.

The Doberman guard dog was there. The man froze. An ominous growl, then the dog charged. In panic the man screamed and tried to beat the dog off, then took to his heels down the steps, the dog growling and snarling and ripping at his legs and back, tearing his clothes, and Azadeh shouted after him, 'Now show it to me!'

'Oh, Highness, I didn't hear you knock, what's going on?' the old man-servant called out, rushing from the kitchen area.

Angrily she wiped the perspiration off her face and told him. 'God curse you, Ali, I've told you twenty times to meet me downstairs with the dog. I'm on time, I'm always on time. Have you no brains?'

The old man apologised but a rough voice behind her cut him short. 'Go and get the dog!' She looked around. Her stomach twisted.

'Good evening, Highness.' It was Ahmed Dursak, tall, bearded, chilling, standing in the doorway of the living-room. Insha'Allah, she thought. The waiting is over and now it begins again. 'Good evening, Ahmed.'

'Highness, please excuse me, I didn't realise about people in Tehran or I would have waited downstairs myself. Ali, get the dog!'

Afraid and still mumbling apologies, the servant scuttled down the stairs. Ahmed closed the door and watched Azadeh use the heel fork to take off her boots, slip her small feet into curved Turkish slippers. She went past him into the comfortable, Western-style living room and sat down, her heart thumping. A fire flickered in the grate. Priceless carpets, others used as wall hangings. Beside her was a small table. On the table was the kukri that Ross had left her. 'You have news of my father and my husband?'

'His Highness the Khan is ill, very ill an –'

'What illness?' Azadeh asked, at once genuinely concerned.

'A heart attack.'

'God protect him – when did this happen?'

'On Thursday last.' He read her thought. 'That was the day you and . . . and the saboteur were in the village of Abu Mard. Wasn't it?'

'I suppose so. The last few days have been very confused,' she said icily. 'How is my father?'

'The attack on Thursday was mild, thanks be to God. Just before midnight Saturday he had another. Much worse.' He watched her.

'How much worse? Please don't play with me! Tell me everything at once!'

'Ah so sorry, Highness, I did not mean to toy with you.' He kept his voice polite and his eyes off her legs, admiring her fire and pride and wanting to toy with her very much. 'The doctor called it a stroke and now the left side of His Highness is partially paralysed; he can still talk – with some difficulty – but his mind is as strong as ever. The doctor said he would recover much quicker in Tehran but the journey is not possible yet.'

'He will recover?' she asked.

'I don't know, Highness. As God wants. To me he seems very sick. The doctor, I don't think much of him, all he said was His Highness's chances would be better if he was here in Tehran.'

'Then bring him here as soon as possible.'

'I will, Highness, never fear. Meanwhile I have a message for you.

The Khan, your father, says, "I wish to see you. At once. I do not know how long I will live but certain arrangements must be made and confirmed. Your brother Hakim is with me now and –" '

'God protect him,' Azadeh burst out. 'Is my father reconciled with Hakim?'

'His Highness has made him his heir. But pl –'

'Oh that's wonderful, wonderful, God be praised! But h –'

'Please be patient and let me finish his message: "Your brother Hakim is with me now and I have made him my heir, subject to certain conditions, from you and from him." ' Ahmed hesitated and Azadeh wanted to rush into the gap, her happiness brimming and her caution brimming. Her pride stopped her.

' "It is therefore necessary that you return with Ahmed at once." That is the end of the message, Highness.'

The front door opened. Ali relocked it and unleashed the dog. At once the dog loped into the living room and put his head in Azadeh's lap. 'Well done, Reza,' she said petting him, welcoming the moment to collect her wits. 'Sit. Go on, sit! Sit!' Happily the dog obeyed, then lay at her feet, watching the door and watching Ahmed who stood near the other sofa. Absently her hand played with the hilt of the kukri, its touch giving her reassurance. Obliquely Ahmed was conscious of it and its implications. 'Before God you have told me the truth?'

'Yes, Highness. Before God.'

'Then we will go at once.' She got up. 'You came by car?'

'Yes, Highness. I brought a limousine and chauffeur. But there's a little more news – good and bad. A ransom note came to His Highness on Sunday. His Excellency your husband is in the hands of bandits, tribesmen . . .' She tried to maintain her composure, her knees suddenly weak. '. . . somewhere near the Soviet border. Both him and his helicopter. It seems that these . . . these bandits claim to be Kurds but the Khan doubts it. They surprised the Soviet Cimtarga and his men and killed them all, capturing His Excellency and the helicopter, early Thursday they claimed. Then they flew to Rezaiyeh where he was seen and appeared unharmed before flying off again.'

'Praise be to God,' was all her pride allowed herself. 'Is my husband ransomed?'

'The ransom note arrived late on Saturday, through intermediaries. As soon as His Highness regained consciousness yesterday he gave me the message for you and sent me here to fetch you.'

She heard the 'fetch' and knew its seriousness but Ahmed made nothing of it openly and reached into his pocket. 'His Highness Hakim gave me this for you.' He handed her the sealed envelope. She ripped it open, startling the dog. The note was in Hakim's handwriting: 'My darling, His Highness has made me his heir and reinstated both of us, subject to conditions, wonderful conditions easy to agree. Hurry back, he's very ill and he will not deal with the ransom until he sees you. Salaam.'

Swamped with happiness she hurried out, packed a bag in almost no time, scribbled a note for McIver, telling Ali to deliver it tomorrow. As an after-thought she picked up the kukri and walked out, cradling it. Ahmed said nothing, just followed her.

Tuesday
February 27, 1979

USSR

Khvoy

Tabriz · Mount
Sabalan

Caspian Sea

Bandar-e Pahlavi

USSR

Sadzevar

Qazvin ·

Meshed

· Tehran

IRAN

BANDAR-E
DELAM

AFGHANISTAN

· Baghdad

· Isfahan

Dez Dam

IRAQ

Abadan

Kowiss

KUWAIT

Kharg
Island

PAKISTAN

· Zagros

SAUDI ARABIA

· Jellet

Lengeh

Persian Gulf

CHAPTER

52

BAHRAIN

Siri

Strait of Hormuz

QATAR

· Al Shargaz

Gulf of Oman

UAE

Bandar-e Delam: 8:15 A.M. Kasigi was hurrying after the grim-faced police officer through the drab crowded corridors of the hospital – the radio mechanic, Minoru, a few paces behind him. Sick and wounded men and women and children were on stretchers or chairs or standing or simply lying on the floor, waiting for someone to help them, the very sick mixed with the lightly sick, a few relieving themselves, a few eating and drinking provisions brought by their visiting relatives who abounded – and all who could, complained loudly. Harassed nurses and doctors went in and out of rooms, all women dressed in chador except a few British, Queen Alexandra nurses whose severe headdress was almost the equivalent and acceptable.

Eventually the policeman found the door he sought and pushed his way into the crowded ward. Beds lined both sides with another row in the middle all occupied by men patients – their visiting families chattering or complaining, children playing, and over in one corner, an old woman cooking on a portable stove.

Scragger had one wrist and one ankle handcuffed to an old iron bedstead. He was lying on a straw mattress in his clothes and shoes, a bandage around his head, unshaven and dirty. When he saw Kasigi and Minoru behind the policeman his eyes lit up. 'Hello, mates,' he said, his voice raw.

'How are you, Captain?' Kasigi said, appalled by the handcuffs.

'If I could get free I'd be fine.'

Irritably the policeman interrupted loudly in Farsi for the benefit of the watchers, 'This is the man you wanted to see?'

'Yes, Excellency,' Minoru said for Kasigi.

'So now you've seen him. You can report to your government or whomever you wish that clearly he's been given treatment. He will be tried by the traffic komiteh.' Pompously he turned to go.

'But the captain pilot wasn't the driver,' Kasigi said patiently in English, Minoru translating for him, having said it for most of the night and since dawn this morning to various policemen of various ranks, always getting varying degrees of the same answer: 'If the foreigner wasn't in Iran the accident would never have happened, of course he's responsible.'

'It doesn't matter he wasn't the driver, he's still responsible!' the policeman said angrily, his voice echoing off the walls. 'How many times must you be told? He was in charge of the car. He ordered it. If he hadn't ordered it the accident would never have happened, people were killed and injured, of course he's responsible!'

'But, I repeat, my assistant here was an eyewitness and will give evidence that the accident was caused by the other car.'

'Lies in front of the komiteh will be dealt with seriously,' the man said darkly, one of those who had been in the police car.

'Not lies, agha. There are other witnesses,' Kasigi said, not that he had any, his voice sharpening. 'I insist this man be released. He's an employee of my government which has invested billions of dollars in our Iran-Toda petro-chemical plant, to the benefit of Iran and particularly all people in Bandar-e Delam. Unless he is released at once, at once, I will order all Japanese out and cease all work!' His biliousness increased, for he did not have the authority, nor would he issue such orders. 'Everything will stop!'

'By the Prophet, we're no longer subject to foreign blackmail,' the man blustered and turned away. 'You'll have to discuss this with the komiteh!'

'Unless he's released at once, all work ceases and there'll be no more jobs. None!' As Minoru translated, Kasigi noticed a difference in the silence and the mood of those around. And even in the police officer himself, nastily aware that all eyes were on him and sensing the sudden hostility. One youth nearby wearing a green band on his grimy pyjamas said thickly, 'You want to jeopardise our jobs, eh? Who're you? How do we know you're not a Shah man? Have you been cleared by the komiteh?'

'Of course I have! By the One God I've been for the Imam for years!' the man replied angrily but a wave of fear went through him. 'I helped the revolution, everyone knows. You,' he pointed at Kasigi, silently cursing him for causing all this trouble, 'you follow me!' He pushed a way through the onlookers.

'I'll be back, Captain Scragger, don't worry.' Kasigi and Minoru rushed off in pursuit.

The police officer led the way down a flight of stairs and along a corridor and down other stairs, all of them crowded. Kasigi's nervousness increased as they descended deeper into the hospital. Now the man opened a door with a notice in Farsi on it.

Kasigi broke out in a cold sweat. They were in the morgue. Marble slabs with bodies covered with grimy sheets. Many of them. Odour of chemicals and dried blood and offal and excrement. 'Here!' the police officer said and tore back a sheet. Beneath it was the headless corpse of a woman. Her head was obscenely near the trunk, eyes open. 'Your car caused her death, what about her and her family?' Kasigi heard the 'your' and a freezing current went through him. 'And here!' he ripped away another sheet. A badly mashed woman, unrecognisable. 'Well?'

'We're . . . we're deeply sorry of course . . . of course we're deeply sorry that anyone was hurt, deeply sorry, but that is karma, Insha'Allah, not our fault or the fault of the pilot upstairs.' Kasigi was hard put to hold his nausea down. 'Deeply sorry.'

Minoru translated, the police officer leaning insolently against the slab. Then he replied and the young Japanese's eyes widened. 'He says, he says the bail, the fine to release Mr. Scragger immediately is one million rials. At once. What the komiteh decide is nothing to do with him.'

One million rials was about twelve thousand dollars. 'That's not possible, but we could certainly pay one hundred thousand rials within the hour.'

'A million,' the man shouted. He grabbed the woman's head by the hair and held it up to Kasigi who had to force himself to stand erect. 'What about her children who are now condemned for ever to be motherless? Don't they deserve compensation? Eh?'

'There's . . . there's not that amount of cash in . . . in the whole plant, so sorry.'

The policeman swore and continued to haggle but then the door opened. Orderlies with a trolley and another body came in, eyeing them curiously. Abruptly the policeman said, 'Very well. We will go to your office at once.'

They went and got the last amount Kasigi had offered, two hundred and fifty thousand rials – about three thousand dollars – but no receipt, only a verbal agreement that Scragger could leave. Not trusting the man, Kasigi gave him half in the office and put the rest into an envelope that he put in his pocket. They returned to the hospital. There he waited in the car while Minoru and the man went inside. The waiting seemed interminable, but finally Minoru and Scragger came down the steps with the policeman. Kasigi got out and gave the policeman the envelope. The man cursed all foreigners and went away truculently.

'So,' Kasigi said and smiled at Scragger. They shook hands, Scragger thanking him profusely, apologising for all the trouble, both men cursing fate, blessing it, getting into the car quickly. The Iranian chauffeur swerved out into the traffic, swore loudly at an overtaking car that had the right of way and almost collided with him, jabbing the horn.

'Tell him to slow down, Minoru,' Kasigi said. Minoru obeyed and the driver nodded and smiled and obeyed. The slowdown lasted a few seconds.

'Are you all right, Captain?'

'Oh yes. Headache's a beaut but okay. The worst was wanting to pee.'

'What?'

'The bastards kept me handcuffed to the bed and wouldn't let me get to the loo. I just couldn't just do it in my pants, or in the bed, and it wasn't till early this morning a nurse brought me a bottle. Christ, I thought my bladder was bust.' Scragger rubbed the tiredness out of his eyes. 'No problem, old sport. I owe you one. Plus the ransom! How much was it?'

'Nothing, nothing to you. We have a fund for these hazards.'

'It's no problem. Andy Gavallan'll pay – oh that reminds me, he said he knew your boss some years ago, Toda, Hiro Toda.'

'*Ah so desu ka*?' Kasigi was genuinely surprised. 'Gavallan has choppers in Japan?'

'Oh no. It was when he was a China Trader, out of Hong Kong, when he was working for Struan's.' The name sent a warning bolt through Kasigi that he kept bottled. 'You ever heard of them?'

'Yes, a fine company. Toda's do, or did business with Struan's,'

840

Kasigi said matter of fact, but he docketed the information for future consideration – wasn't it Linbar Struan who unilaterally cancelled five shipping leasing contracts two years ago that almost broke us? Perhaps Gavallan could be an instrument to recoup, one way or another. 'Sorry you had such a bad time.'

'Not your fault, cobber. But Andy'd want to pay the ransom. What'd they stick us for?'

'It was very modest. Please, let it be a gift – you saved my ship.'

After a pause Scragger said, 'Then I owe you two, old sport.'

'We selected the driver – it was our fault.'

'Where is he, where's Mohammed?'

'So sorry, he's dead.'

Scragger swore. 'It wasn't his fault, it wasn't at all.'

'Yes, yes I know. We have given his family compensation and we will do the same for the victims.' Kasigi was trying to read how shaken Scragger was, wanting to know very much when he would be fit to fly and greatly irritated with the day's delay. It was imperative to get back to Al Shargaz as soon as possible, thence home to Japan. His work here was finished. Chief Engineer Watanabe was now totally on his side, the copies of his private reports would cement his own corporate position and enormously help him – and Hiro Toda – to reopen the possibility of persuading the government to declare Iran-Toda a National Project.

Not possibility, certainty! he thought, more confident than he had ever been. We'll be saved from bankruptcy, we'll bury our enemies, the Mitsuwari and Gyokotomo, and gain nothing but face ourselves – and profit, vast profit! Oh yes. And the added piece of good fortune, Kasigi allowed himself a cynical smile, the explosively important copy of dead Chief Engineer Kasusaka's private report to Gyokotomo, dated and signed, that Watanabe had miraculously 'found' in a forgotten file while I was in Al Shargaz! I'll have to be very careful how I use it, oh, very careful indeed, it makes it all the more important that I get home as soon as possible.

The streets and alleys were clogged with traffic. Above, the sky was still overcast but the storm had passed through and he knew the weather was flyable. Ah, I wish I had my own airplane, he thought. Say a Lear jet. The reward for all my work here should be substantial.

He let himself drift happily, enjoying his sense of achievement and power. 'It looks like we will be able to begin construction very soon now, Captain.'

'Oh?'

'Yes. The head of the new komiteh assured us of their cooperation. It seems he knows one of your pilots, a Captain Starke – his name's Zataki.'

Scragger glanced at him sharply. 'He's the one Duke, Duke Starke, saved from the leftists and flew to Kowiss. If I were you, cobber, I'd, er, watch him.' He told Kasigi how volatile the man was. 'He's a right madman.'

'He didn't give that appearance, not at all. Curious – Iranians are very . . . very curious. But more important, how are you feeling?'

'I'm bonza now.' Scragger exaggerated blithely. Yesterday and all night had been very bad, all the cursing and shouting and being handcuffed, not being able to make anyone understand, surrounded by hostility, eyes everywhere. Lost. And afraid. The pain increasing. Time agonisingly slow, hope fading, sure that Minoru was injured or dead along with the driver so that no one would know where he was or what had happened.

'Nothing that a good cup of tea won't cure. If you'd like to leave at once, I'm okay. Just a quick bath and shave and cuppa and some grub and we'll be on our merry way.'

'Excellent. Then we'll leave the moment you're ready – Minoru has installed the radio and checked it.'

All the way to the refinery and during the flight back to Lengeh, Kasigi was in very good spirits. Near Kharg they thought they spotted the huge hammerhead shark Scragger had once mentioned. They kept low and close inshore, the clouds still low and heavy, nimbus here and there with an occasional flash of lightning menacing them but not badly, only a little bumpy now and then. Radar surveillance and clearances were efficient and immediate which increased Scragger's foreboding. Two days to Whirlwind, not counting today, was in the forefront of his mind. Losing a day makes it all the more hairy, he thought anxiously. What's happened since I was away?

Well past Kharg he landed to refuel and take a break. His stomach still ached nastily and he noticed a little blood in his urine. Nothing to worry about, he told himself. Sure to be a little haemorrhage after an accident like that. Shit in a bucket but I was lucky!

They were on a sandbank, finishing a packed lunch – cold rice and pieces of fish and pickles. Scragger had a big hunk of Iranian bread he had scrounged from the spotless cookhouse and lots of cold yakatori chicken and soya sauce that he enjoyed very much. Kasigi was sipping Japanese beer that Scragger had refused: 'Thanks, but drinking and driving don't mix.'

Kasigi ate sparingly, Scragger hungrily and quickly. 'Good grub,' he said. 'Soon as you're ready we'd better get on.'

'I'm finished.' Soon they were airborne again. 'Will there be time to get me on to Al Shargaz or Dubai today?'

'Not if we go to Lengeh.' Scragger adjusted his headset slightly. 'Tell you what, when we get into Kish Traffic Control I'll ask if I can divert to Bahrain. You could pick up an international or local flight there. We'll need to refuel at Lavan but they'll approve that if they agree. As I said, I owe you a couple.'

'You owe us nothing.' Kasigi smiled to himself. 'At the komiteh meeting yesterday, this man Zataki asked how soon we'd have our chopper fleet up to strength. I promised immediate action. As you know, Guerney no longer services us. What I'd like is three of your 212s and two 206s for the next three months, a year-long contract to be negotiated then, depending on our needs, renewable annually – with you in charge. Would that be possible?'

Scragger hesitated, not knowing how to reply. Normally such an offer would send glad tiding bells ringing all the way to Aberdeen, Gavallan would be on the phone personally, and everyone would be in for a huge bonus. But with Whirlwind scheduled, Guerney out of the picture and no one else available, there was no way to help Kasigi. 'When, er, when would you need the birds to start?' he asked to give himself time to think.

'Immediately,' Kasigi continued blithely, watching a tanker below. 'I guaranteed Zataki and the komiteh that if they cooperated we'd start up at once. Tomorrow or the next day at the latest. Perhaps you could ask your head office temporarily to divert some of the 212s stationed at Bandar-e Delam and not being used to capacity. Yes?'

'I'll certainly ask, as soon as we land.'

'For a week or so we'll need a temporary airlink with Kuwait to pick up and replace crews from Japan – Zataki said their komiteh'd arrange with the Abadan Airport komiteh today to open it for us, certainly by the end of the week . . .'

Scragger was only half listening to the confident plans of this man who had befriended him, without whom he would still be handcuffed to the bed. His choice was simple: you tell him about Whirlwind or you leave him in the shit. But if you tell him you betray a bigger trust, a long-term trust. Kasigi might let Whirlwind slip. He's bound to tell de Plessey. The question is how far can I trust him – and de Plessey?

Greatly unsettled he glanced out of his window and rechecked his position. 'Sorry to interrupt but I've got to report in.' He pressed the send button: 'Kish radar, this is HotelSierraTango, do you read?'

'HST, Kish radar, we read you four by five, go ahead.'

'HST on charter from Iran-Toda in bound to homebase in Lengeh, approaching Lavan at 1,000, one passenger aboard. Request permission to refuel at Lavan and divert to Bahrain to drop my passenger who has urgent business on behalf of Iran.'

'Request refused, maintain 1,000 and present heading.'

'My passenger is Japanese, head of Iran-Toda, and urgently needs to consult his Japanese government on behalf of the Iran government's wish to resume immediate operations. Request special consideration in this instance.'

'Request refused. No trans-Gulf flights are authorised without a twenty-four-hour notice. Turn to 095 degrees for direct Lengeh, report abeam Kish, not overhead Kish. Do you copy?'

Scragger glanced at Kasigi who could also hear the exchange. 'Sorry, mate.' He eased on to the new heading. 'HST copies. Request clearance for Al Shargaz at dawn tomorrow with one passenger.'

'Standby one.' Static cracked in their earphones. To starboard the sea bridge of tankers continued, inbound and outbound, from or to the Gulf terminals of Saudi, the Emirates, Abu Dhabi, Bahrain, Kuwait, and Iraq. None were loading at Kharg or Abadan where normally a dozen would be serviced with another dozen waiting. Now there were only the swarms of ships waiting, some over two months. The sky was still overcast and nasty. 'HST, this is Kish. In this instance your request is approved to go from Lengeh to Al Shargaz, tomorrow Wednesday 28th, noon departure. Until further notice all, repeat, all trans-Gulf flights will require a 24-hour notice, and all, repeat, all engine starts require clearance. Do you copy?'

Scragger swore, then acknowledged.

'What is it?' Kasigi asked.

'We've never had to get clearance to start engines before. The bastards are really getting touchy.' Scragger was thinking about Friday and his two 212s to start up and Kish too nosy and too efficient. 'Crummy lot!'

'Yes. Will you be able to head up our chopper requirements?'

'There're lots of better guys than me.'

'Ah, so sorry, but it would be important to me. I would know that the operation would be in good hands.'

Again Scragger hesitated. 'Thanks, if I could I would, sure, sure I would.'

'Then it's settled. I'll formally apply to your Mr. Gavallan.' Kasigi glanced at Scragger. Something's changed, he thought. What? Now that I think of it, the pilot didn't react with the amount of enthusiasm I would have forecast when I announced the deal – he certainly would understand the value of the contract he's being offered. What's he hiding? 'Could you contact Bandar-e Delam through your base at Kowiss to ask them about supplying us with at least one 212 tomorrow?' he asked, beginning to probe.

'Yes, yes, of course . . . soon as we arrive.'

Ah, Kasigi thought, having watched and listened very carefully, I was right, something's very definitely different now. The friendliness's gone. Why? I've certainly not said anything to offend him. It can't be the deal – that's too good for any chopper company. His health? 'Are you feeling all right?'

'Oh fine, old sport, I'm fine.'

Ah, the smile was real that time and the voice as usual. Then it has to be something to do with the choppers. 'If I don't have your help, it will make things very difficult for me.'

'Yes, I know. Me, I'd like to help you all I can.'

Ah, the smile vanished and the voice became serious again. Why? And why the 'me, I'd like to help' as though he would help but is forbidden to help by someone else. Gavallan? Could it be he knows that Gavallan, because of Struan's, wouldn't help us?

For a long time Kasigi considered all manner of permutations but could not come up with a satisfactory answer. Then he fell back on the one, almost infallible, ploy to use with a foreigner such as this one.

'My friend,' he said, using his most sincere voice, 'I know something's the matter, please tell me what it is.' Seeing Scragger's face become even more solemn, he added the *coup de grâce*. 'You can tell me, you can trust me, I really am your friend.'

'Yes . . . yes, I know that, mate.'

Kasigi watched Scragger's face and waited, watched the fish wriggling on the hook that was held by a line so thin and so strong that stretched back to a broken rotor blade, a handshake, shared danger aboard the *Rikumaru*, shared war service, and common reverence for dead comrades. So many of us dead, so young. Yes, he thought with a sudden anger, but if we'd had a tenth of their airplanes, their armaments and their ships and a twentieth part of their oil and raw materials we would have been invincible and the Emperor would never have had to terminate the war as *he* did. We'd have been invincible – but for the bomb, the two bombs. All gods torment for all eternity those who invented the bomb that broke *his* will that took preference over ours. 'What is it?'

'I, er, can't tell you, just yet – sorry.'

Danger signals went through Kasigi. 'Why, my friend? I assure you you can trust me,' he said soothingly.

'Yes . . . yes, but it's not just up to me. In Al Shargaz, tomorrow, bear with me, will you?'

'If it's that important, I should know now, shouldn't I?' Again Kasigi waited. He knew the value of waiting and of silence at a time like this. No need to remind the other man of the 'I owe you two.' Yet.

Scragger was remembering. At Bandar-e Delam, Kasigi saved my bloody neck and no doubt about that. Aboard his ship at Siri he proved he's got balls and today he's proved a good friend, he needn't've gone to all that trouble so fast, tomorrow or the next day wouldn't have mattered to him.

His eyes were scanning the instruments and the outside and he saw no dangers within or without, Kish coming up soon to starboard and he glanced across at Kasigi. Kasigi was staring ahead, his strong, good-looking face set, frowning slightly. Shit, old sport, if you don't perform Zataki's likely to go berserk! But you can't perform. You can't, old sport, and it's so hard to see you just sitting there, not reminding me what I owe you. 'Kish, this is HST abeam Kish, steady at 1,000.'

'Kish. Maintain 1,000. You have traffic due east at 10,000.'

'I have them in sight.' They were two fighters. He pointed for Kasigi who had not seen them. 'They're F14s, probably out of Bandar-e Abbas,' he said. Kasigi did not reply, just nodded, and this made Scragger feel worse. The minutes passed. Droning onward.

Then Scragger decided, hating having to do it. 'Sorry,' he said gruffly, 'but you'll have to wait until Al Shargaz. Andy Gavallan can help, I can't.'

'He can help? In what way? What's the trouble?'

After a pause Scragger said, 'If anyone can help, he can. Let's leave it at that, cobber.'

Kasigi heard the finality but dismissed it and let the matter rest for a moment, his mind abuzz with fresh danger signals. That Scragger had not fallen into his trap and told him the secret made him respect the man more. But that doesn't forgive him, he thought, his fury building. He's told me enough to forewarn me, now it's up to me to find out the rest. So Gavallan's the key? To what?

Kasigi felt his head about to burst. Haven't I promised that madman Zataki we would be in business at once? How dare these men jeopardise our whole project – our *national* project. Without choppers we can't start! It's tantamount to treason against Japan! What is it they're planning?

With a great effort he kept his face bland. 'I'll certainly see Gavallan as soon as possible, and let's hope you'll head up our new operation, eh?'

'Whatever Andy Gavallan says, it's up to him.'

Don't be too sure, Kasigi was thinking, because whatever happens I will have choppers, at once – yours, Guerneys', I don't care whose. But by my samurai ancestors, the Iran-Toda will not be put to further risk! It will not! *Nor will I!*

Tabriz – at the Khan's Palace: 10:50 A.M. Azadeh followed Ahmed into the Western-style room and over to the fourposter bed, and now that she was again within the walls she felt her skin crawling with fear. Sitting near the bed was a nurse in a starched white uniform, a book half open in her lap, watching them curiously through her glasses. Musty brocade curtains covered the windows against draughts. Lights were dimmed. And the stench of an old man hung in the air.

The Khan's eyes were closed, his face pasty and breathing strangled, his arm connected to a saline drip that stood beside the bed. Half asleep in a chair nearby was Aysha, curled up and tiny, her hair dishevelled and her face tear-stained. Azadeh smiled at her tentatively, sorry for her, then said to the nurse in a voice not her own, 'How is His Highness, please?'

'Fair. But he mustn't have an excitement, or be disturbed,' the nurse said softly in hesitant Turkish. Azadeh looked at her and saw that she was European, in her fifties, dyed brown hair, a red cross on her sleeve.

'Oh, you're English, or French?'

848

'Scots,' the woman replied in English with obvious relief, her accent slight. She kept her voice down, watching the Khan. 'I'm Sister Bain from the Tabriz Hospital and the patient is doing as well as can be expected – considering he will no' do as he's told. And who might you be, please?'

'I'm his daughter, Azadeh. I've just arrived from Tehran – he sent for me. We've . . . we travelled all night.'

'Ah, yes,' she said, surprised that someone so beautiful could have been created by a man so ugly. 'If I might suggest, lassie, it would be better to leave him sleeping. As soon as he wakes I'll tell him you're here and send for you. Better he sleeps.'

Ahmed said irritably, 'Please, where's His Highness's guard?'

'There's no need for armed men in a sickroom. I sent him away.'

'There will always be a guard here unless the Khan orders him out or I order him out.' Angrily Ahmed turned and left.

Azadeh said, 'It's just a custom, Sister.'

'Aye, very well. But that's another custom we can do without.'

Azadeh looked back at her father, hardly recognising him, trying to stop the terror that possessed her. Even like that, she thought, even like that he can still destroy us, Hakim and me – he still has his running dog Ahmed. 'Please, really, how is he?'

The lines on the nurse's face creased even more. 'We're doing all we can.'

'Would it be better for him to be in Tehran?'

'Aye, if he has another stroke, yes it would.' Sister Bain took his pulse as she talked. 'But I wouldna' recommend moving him, not at all, not yet.' She made a notation on a chart and then glanced at Aysha. 'You could tell the lady there's no need to stay, she should get some proper rest too, poor child.'

'Sorry, I may not interfere. Sorry, but that's a custom too. Is . . . is it likely he'll have another stroke?'

'You never know, lassie, that's up to God. We hope for the best.'

They looked around as the door opened. Hakim stood there beaming. Azadeh's eyes lit up and she said to the nurse, 'Please call me the instant His Highness awakes,' then hurried across the room, out into the corridor, closed the door, and hugged him. 'Oh, Hakim, my darling, it's been such a long time,' she said breathlessly. 'Oh, is it really true?'

'Yes, yes, it is but how did . . .' Hakim stopped, hearing footsteps. Ahmed and a guard turned into the corridor and came up to them. 'I'm glad you're back, Ahmed,' he said politely. 'His Highness will be happy too.'

'Thank you, Highness. Has anything happened in my absence?'

'No, except that Colonel Fazir came this morning to see Father.'

Ahmed was chilled. 'Was he allowed in?'

'No. You left instructions no one was to be admitted without His Highness's personal permission, he was asleep at the time and he's been asleep most of the day – I check every hour and the nurse says he's unchanged.'

'Good. Thank you. Did the colonel leave a message?'

'Only that he was going to Julfa today as arranged with his "associate". Does that mean anything to you?'

'No, Highness,' Ahmed lied blandly. He glanced from one to the other but before he could say anything, Hakim said, 'We'll be in the Blue Salon, please summon us the moment my father awakens.'

Ahmed watched them go arm in arm down the corridor, the young man tall and handsome, the sister willowy and desirable. Traitors? Not much time to get the proof, he thought. He went back into the sickroom and saw the pallor of the Khan, his nostrils rebelling against the smell. He squatted on his haunches, careless of the disapproving nurse and began his vigil.

What did that son of a dog Fazir want? he asked himself. Saturday evening when Hashemi Fazir and Armstrong had come back from Julfa without Mzytryk, Fazir had angrily demanded to see the Khan. Ahmed had been present when the Khan had seen them, declared himself as mystified as they that Mzytryk was not with the helicopter. 'Come back tomorrow – if the man brings me a letter you can see it,' the Khan had said.

'Thank you but we will wait – the Chevy can't be far behind us.'

So they had waited, the Khan seething but unable to do anything, Hashemi's men spread around the palace in ambush. An hour later the Chevy had arrived. He himself had admitted the chauffeur while Hashemi and the Farsi-speaking Infidel hid in the room next door. 'I have a private message for His Highness,' the Soviet had said.

In the sickroom the Soviet said, 'Highness, I'm to give it to you when you're alone.'

'Give it to me now. Ahmed is my most trusted counsellor. Give it to me!' Reluctantly the man obeyed and Ahmed remembered the sudden flush that had rushed into the Khan's face the moment he began to read it.

'There is an answer?' the Soviet had said truculently.

Choked with rage the Khan had shaken his head and dismissed the man and had handed Ahmed the letter. It read: 'My friend, I was shocked to hear about your illness and would be with you now but I have to stay here on urgent matters. I have bad news for you: it may be that you and your spy ring are betrayed to Inner Intelligence or SAVAMA – did you know that turncoat Abrim Pahmudi now heads this new version of SAVAK? If you're betrayed to Pahmudi, be prepared to defect at once or you'll quickly see the inside of a torture chamber. I have alerted our people to help you if necessary. If it appears safe, I will arrive Tuesday at dusk. Good luck.'

The Khan had had no option but to show the message to the two men. 'Is it true? About Pahmudi?'

'Yes. He's an old friend of yours, isn't he?' Fazir had said, taunting him.'

'No . . . no he is not. Get out!'

'Certainly. Highness. Meanwhile this palace is under surveillance. There's no need to defect. Please do nothing to interfere with Mzytryk's arrival on Tuesday, do nothing to encourage any more revolt in Azerbaijan. As to Pahmudi and SAVAMA, they can do nothing here without my approval. I'm the law in Tabriz now. Obey and I'll protect you, disobey and you'll be his pishkesh.'

Then the two men had left, and the Khan had exploded with rage, more angry than Ahmed had ever seen him. The paroxysm became worse and worse then suddenly it ceased, the Khan was lying on the floor and he was looking down on him, expecting to see him dead but he was not. Just a waxen pallor and twitching, breathing choked.

'As God wants,' Ahmed muttered, not wanting to relive that night.

In the Blue Salon: 11.15 A.M. When they were quite alone, Hakim swung Azadeh off her feet. 'Oh, it's wonderful wonderful wonderful to see you again . . .' she began but he whispered, 'Keep your voice down, Azadeh, there are ears everywhere and someone's sure to misinterpret everything and lie again.'

'Najoud? May she be cursed for ever an –'

'Shushhhh, darling, she can't hurt us now. I'm the heir, officially.'

'Oh, tell me what happened, tell me everything!'

They sat on the long cushion sofa and Hakim could hardly get the words out fast enough. 'First about Erikki: the ransom is ten million rials, for him and the 212 an –'

'Father can bargain that down and pay, he can certainly pay, then find them and have them torn apart.'

'Yes, yes of course he can and he told me in front of Ahmed as soon as you're back he'll start and it's true he's made me his heir provided I swear by God to cherish little Hassan as I would cherish you – of course I did that happily at once – and said that you would also swear by God to do the same, that we would both swear to remain in Tabriz, me to learn how to follow him and you to be here to help me and oh we're going to be so happy!'

'That's all we have to do?' she asked incredulously.

'Yes, yes, that's all – he made me his heir in front of all the family – they looked as though they would die but that doesn't matter, Father named the conditions in front of them, I agreed at once, of course, as you will – why shouldn't we?'

'Of course, of course – anything! God is watching over us!' Again she embraced him, burying her face into his shoulder so that the tears of joy would be dried away. All the way back from Tehran, the journey rotten and Ahmed uncommunicative, she had been terrified what the 'conditions' would be. But now? 'It's unbelievable, Hakim, it's like magic! Of course we'll cherish little Hassan and you'll pass the Khanate on to him or his successors if that's Father's wish. God protect us and protect him and Erikki, and Erikki can fly as much as he likes – why shouldn't he? Oh it's going to be wonderful.' She dried her eyes. 'Oh I must look awful.'

'You look wonderful. Now tell me what happened to you – I know only that you were caught in the village with . . . with the British saboteur and then somehow escaped.'

'It was another miracle, only with the help of God, Hakim, but at the time terrible, that vile mullah – I can't remember how we got out only what Johnny . . . what Johnny told me. My Johnny Brighteyes, Hakim.'

His eyes widened. 'Johnny from Switzerland?'

'Yes. Yes it was him. He was the British officer.'

'But how . . . It seems impossible.'

'He saved my life, Hakim, and oh, there's so much to tell.'

'When Father heard about the village he . . . you know the mullah was shot by Green Bands, don't you?'

'I don't remember it but Johnny told me.'

'When Father heard about the village he had Ahmed drag the kalandar here, questioned him, then sent him back, had him stoned, the hands of the butcher cut off and then the village burned. Burning the village was my idea – those dogs!'

Azadeh was greatly shocked. The whole village was too terrible a vengeance.

But Hakim allowed nothing to interrupt his euphoria. 'Azadeh,

Father's taken off the guard and I can go where I like – I even took a car and went into Tabriz today alone. Everyone treats me as heir, all the family, even Najoud though I know she's gnashing her teeth and has to be guarded against. It's . . . it's not what I expected.' He told her how he had been almost dragged from Khvoy, expecting to be killed, or mutilated. 'Don't you remember when I was banished, he cursed me and swore Shah Abbas knew how to deal with traitorous sons?'

She trembled, recollecting that nightmare, the curses and rage and so unfair, both of them innocent. 'What made him change? Why should he change towards you, towards us?'

'The Will of God. God's opened his eyes. He has to know he's near death and must make provisions . . . he's, he's the Khan. Perhaps he's frightened and wants to make amends. We were guilty of nothing against him. What does the reason matter? I don't care. We're free of the yoke at long last, free.'

In the Sickroom: 11:16 P.M. The Khan's eyes opened. Without moving his head he looked to his limits. Ahmed, Aysha and the guard. No nurse. Then he centred on Ahmed who was sitting on the floor. 'You brought her?' He stammered the words with difficulty.

'Yes, Highness. A few minutes ago.'

The nurse came into his field of vision. 'How do you feel, Excellency?' she said in English as he had ordered her, telling her her Turkish was vile.

'S'ame.'

'Let me make you more comfortable.' With great tenderness and care – and strength – she lifted him and straightened the pillows and bed. 'Do you need a bottle, Excellency?'

The Khan thought about that. 'Yes.'

She administered it and he felt befouled that it was done by an Infidel woman but since she had arrived he had learned she was tremendously efficient, very wise and very good, the best in Tabriz, Ahmed had seen to that – so superior to Aysha who had proved to be totally useless. He saw Aysha smile at him tentatively, big eyes, frightened eyes. I wonder if I'll ever thrust it in again, up to its hilt, stiff as bone, like the first time, her tears and writhing improving the act, momentarily . . .

'Excellency?'

He accepted the pill and the sip of water and was glad for the cool of her hands that guided the glass. Then he saw Ahmed again and he smiled at him, glad his confidant was back. 'Good jour'ney?'

'Yes, Highness.'

853

'Will'ingly? Or with for'ce?'

Ahmed smiled. 'It was as you planned, Highness. Willingly. Just as you planned.'

'I dinna think you should talk so much, Excellency,' the nurse said. 'Go aw'ay.'

She patted his shoulder kindly. 'Would you like some food, perhaps a little horisht?'

'Halvah.'

'The doctor said sweets were not good for you.'

'Halvah!'

Sister Bain sighed. The doctor had forbidden them and then added, 'But if he insists you can give him them, as many as he wants, what does it matter now? Insha'Allah.' She found them and popped one into his mouth and wiped the saliva away, and he chewed it with relish, nutty but smooth and oh so sweet.

'Your daughter's arrived from Tehran, Excellency,' she said. 'She asked me to tell her the moment you awoke.'

Abdollah Khan was finding talking very strange. He would try and say the sentences, but his mouth did not open when it was supposed to open and the words stayed in his mind for a long time and then, when a simple form of what he wanted to say came out, the words were not well formed though they should have been. But why? I'm not doing anything differently than before. Before what? I don't remember, only a massive blackness and blood roaring and possessed by red-hot needles and not being able to breathe.

I can breathe now and hear perfectly and see perfectly and my mind's working perfectly and filled with plans as good as ever. It's just getting it all out. 'Ho'w?'

'What, Excellency?'

Again the waiting. 'How ta'lk bett'r?'

'Ah,' she said, understanding at once, her experience of strokes great. 'Dinna worry, you'll find it just a wee bit difficult at first. As you get better, you'll regain all your control. You must rest as much as you can, that's very important. Rest and medicine, and patience, and you'll be as good as ever. All right?'

'Yes.'

'Would you like me to send for your daughter? She was very anxious to see you, such a pretty girl.'

Waiting. 'Late'r. See late'r. Go 'way, everyone . . . not Ahm'd.'

Sister Bain hesitated, then again patted his hand kindly. 'I'll give you ten minutes – if you promise to rest afterwards. All right?'

'Y'es.'

When they were alone Ahmed went closer to the bed. 'Yes, Highness?'

'Wh'at time?'

Ahmed glanced at his wristwatch. It was gold and ornate and he admired it very much. 'It's almost one thirty on Tuesday.'

'Pe'tr?'

'I don't know, Highness.' Ahmed told him what Hakim had related. 'If Petr comes today to Julfa, Fazir will be waiting for him.'

'Insh'Allah. Az'deh?'

'She was genuinely worried about your health and agreed to come here at once. A moment ago I saw her together with your son. I'm sure she will agree to anything to protect him – as he will to protect her.' Ahmed was trying to say everything clearly and concisely, not wanting to tire him. 'What do you want me to do?'

'Ev'thing.' Everything I've discussed with you and a little more, the Khan thought with relish, his excitement picking up: now that Azadeh's back cut the throat of the ransom messenger so the tribesmen in fury will do the same to the pilot; find out if those whelps're traitors by whatever means you want, and if they are take out Hakim's eyes and send her north to Petr. If they're not, cut up Najoud slowly and keep them close confined here, until the pilot's dead by whatever means, then send her north. And Pahmudi! Now I'm putting a price on his head that would tempt even Satan. Ahmed, offer it first to Fazir and tell him I want vengeance, I want Pahmudi racked, poisoned, cut up, mutilated, castrated . . .

His heart began creaking, palpitating, and he lifted his hand to rub his chest but his hand did not move. Not an inch. Even now as he looked down at it lying on the counterpane, willing it to move, there was no motion. Nothing. Nor feeling. Neither in his hand nor in his arm. Fear gushed through him.

Don't be afraid, the nurse said, he reminded himself desperately, sound of waves roaring in his ears. You've had a stroke, that's all, not a bad one, the doctor said and he said many people have strokes. Old Komargi had one a year or so ago and he's still alive and active and claims he can still bed his young wife. With modern treatment . . . you're a good Muslim and you'll go to Paradise so there's nothing to fear, nothing to fear, nothing to fear . . . nothing to fear if I die I go to Paradise . . .

I don't want to die, he shrieked. I don't want to die, he shrieked again but it was only in his head and no sound came out.

855

'What is it, Highness?'

He saw Ahmed's anxiety and that calmed him a little. God be thanked for Ahmed, I can trust Ahmed, he thought, sweat pouring out of him. Now what do I want him to do? 'Family, all he're later. First Aza'deh, H'kim Naj'oud – under's'd?'

'Yes Highness. To confirm the succession?'

'Y'es.'

'I have your permission to question Her Highness?'

He nodded, his eyelids leaden, waiting for the pain in his chest to lessen. While he waited he moved his legs, feeling pins and needles in his feet. But nothing moved, not the first time, only the second and only then with an effort. Terror rushed back into him. In panic he changed his mind: 'Pay ran'som quick'ly, get pil'ot here, Erikki here, me to Teh'ran. Under'stand?' He saw Ahmed nod. 'Quickly!' he mouthed and motioned him to go but his left hand still did not move. Terrified he tried his right hand and it worked, not easily, but it moved. Part of his panic subsided. 'Pay ran'som no'w – kee'p secr't. Get nur'se.'

At the Julfa Turnoff: 6:25 P.M. Hashemi Fazir and Armstrong were once more in ambush under the snow-laden trees. Below the Chevy waited, lights off, windows open, two men in the front seat, just as before. Down the slope behind them both sides of the Julfa–Tabriz road were primed for the intercept with half a hundred paramilitary poised. The sun had vanished over the mountains and now the sky was blackening perceptibly.

'He's not got much more time,' Hashemi muttered again.

'He arrived at dusk last time. It's not dusk yet.'

'Piss on him and his ancestors – I'm chilled to the bone.'

'Not long now, Hashemi, old chap!' If it was up to him, Armstrong knew he would wait for ever to catch Mzytryk, alias Suslev, alias Brodnin. Just as he had said he would wait in Tabriz after the debacle on Saturday and their confrontation with the Khan: 'Leave me the men, Hashemi, I'll lead the ambush Tuesday. You go back to Tehran, I know you've a million things to do, I'll wait here and get him and bring him to you.'

'No, I'll leave at once and be back early Tuesday. You can stay here.'

'Here' was a safe house, an apartment overlooking the Blue Mosque, warm and meandering and stocked with whisky. 'You really meant what you said to Abdollah Khan, Hashemi, that now you're the law here and SAVAMA and Pahmudi are powerless without your support?'

'Yes, oh yes.'

'Pahmudi really got under Abdollah's skin – that must've blown his mind. What's that all about?'

'Pahmudi had Abdollah banned from Tehran.'

'Christ! Why?'

'Old enmity, goes back years, before our time. Ever since Abdollah became Khan in '53, he truculently advised various prime ministers and Court officials to be cautious over political reforms and so-called modernisations. Pahmudi, the well-bred, European-trained intellectual, despised him, was always against him, always blocking him from private access to the Shah. Unfortunately for the Shah, Pahmudi had the Shah's ear.'

'To betray him in the end.'

'Oh, yes, Robert, perhaps even from the beginning. The first time Abdollah Khan and Pahmudi clashed openly was in '63 over the Shah's proposed reforms, giving the women the vote, giving the voting franchise to non Muslims and allowing non Muslims to be elected to the Majlis. Of course Abdollah, along with every thinking Iranian, knew this would bring an immediate outcry from all religious leaders, particularly Khomeini who was just getting into his stride then.'

'Almost unbelievable that no one could get to the Shah,' Armstrong had said, 'to warm him.'

'Many did, but no one with enough influence. Most of us agreed with Khomeini, openly or secretly. I did. Abdollah lost round after round with Pahmudi. Against all our advice the Shah changed the calendar from the Islamic one as sacred to Muslims as B.C. and A.D. are to Christians and tried to force a phony counting back to Cyrus the Great . . . of course that blew the minds of all Muslims and after near revolution it was withdrawn.' Hashemi finished his drink and poured another. 'Then, publicly, Pahmudi told Abdollah to piss off, literally – I have it all documented – taunted him that he was stupid, behind the times, living in the Dark Ages, "is it any wonder coming from Azerbaijan," and to stay out of Tehran until he was summoned or he would be arrested. Worse he jeered at him at a major function and had thinly veiled cartoons published in the press.'

'I never took Pahmudi for that much of a fool,' Armstrong said to encourage him to continue, wondering if he would make a slip and reveal something of value.

'Thank God he is – and that's why his days are numbered.'

Armstrong remembered the strange confidence that had pervaded Hashemi and how unsettled he had been. The feeling had stayed with him all during the waiting for Hashemi to return to Tabriz, unwise to wander the streets that were still filled with rival mobs trying to possess them. During the day the police and loyalist army maintained the peace in the name of the Ayatollah – at night, it was much more difficult if not impossible to stop small groups of fanatics bent on violence from terrorising parts of the city. 'We can still stamp them out, easily, if that old devil Abdollah will help us,' Hashemi had said angrily.

'Abdollah Khan still has so much power, even like that, half dead?'

'Oh, yes, he's still hereditary chief of a vast tribe – his wealth, hidden and real, would rival a Shah's, not Mohammed Reza Shah but certainly his father's.'

'He's going to die soon. What then?'

'His heir'll have the same power – presuming that poor sonofabitch Hakim stays alive to use it. Did I tell you he's made him heir?'

'No. What's strange about that?'

'Hakim is his eldest son who's been banished to Khvoy for years in disgrace. He's been brought back and reinstated.'

'Why? Why was he banished?'

'The usual – he was caught plotting to send his father on – as Abdollah did his father.'

'You're sure?'

'No, but curiously Abdollah's father died at your Mzytryk's dacha in Tbilisi.' Hashemi smiled sardonically at the effect of his information. 'Of apoplexy.'

'How long have you known?'

'Long enough. We'll ask your Mzytryk if it's true when we catch him. We will catch him, though it'd certainly be easier with Abdollah alive.' Hashemi became grimmer. 'I hope he stays alive long enough to order support for us to stop the war. Then he can rot. I hate that vile old man for double-dealing and double-crossing and using us all for his own purposes, that's why I taunted him with Pahmudi. Sure I hate him, even so I'd never deliver him to Pahmudi, he's too much of a patriot in his own vile way. Well, I'm off to Tehran, Robert, you know where to find me. You'd like company for your bed?'

'Just hot and cold running water.'

'You should experiment a little, try a boy for a change. Oh, for the love of God don't be so embarrassed. There're so many times you disappoint me, I don't know why I'm so patient with you.'

'Thanks.'

'You English're all so depraved and twisted about sex, too many of you overt or covert homosexuals which the rest of you find disgusting and sinful and vile in the extreme, against the laws of God – which it isn't. And yet in Arabia where connection between men is historically normal and ordinary – because by law it's hands off a woman unless you're married to her or else – homosexuality as you understand it is unknown. So a man prefers sodomy, so what? That doesn't interfere with his masculinity here. Give yourself a new experience – life is short, Robert. Meanwhile, she'll be here to use if you wish. Don't insult me by paying her.'

'She' had been Caucasian, Christian, attractive, and he had partaken of her without need or passion, for politeness, and had thanked her and let her sleep in the bed and stay the next day, to clean and cook and entertain him and then, before he awoke this morning, she had vanished.

Now Armstrong looked up into the western sky. It was much darker than before, the light going fast. They waited another half an hour.

'The pilot won't be able to see to land now, Robert. Let's leave.'

'The Chevy hasn't moved yet.' Armstrong took out his automatic and checked the action. 'I'll leave when the Chevy leaves. Okay?'

The thickset Iranian stared at him, his face hard. 'There'll be a car below, parked facing Tabriz. It'll take you to our safe house. Wait for me there – I'm going back to Tehran now, there are some important things that cannot wait, more important than this son of a dog – I think he knows we're on to him.'

'When will you be back here?'

'Tomorrow – there's still the problem of the Khan.' He stomped off into the darkness, cursing.

Armstrong watched him go, glad to be alone. Hashemi was becoming more and more difficult, more dangerous than usual, ready to explode, nerves too taut, too taut for a Head of Inner Intelligence with so much power and a private band of trained assassins in secret. Robert, it's time to begin a bail-out. I can't, I can't, not yet. Come on, Mzytryk, there's plenty of moonlight to land with, for God's sake.

Just after ten o'clock the Chevy's lights came on. The two men wound up the windows and drove away into the night. Carefully Armstrong lit a cigarette, his gloved hand cupping the tiny flame against the wind. The smoke pleased him greatly. When he had finished he threw the stub into the snow and stubbed it out. Then he too left.

Near the Iran-Soviet Border: 11:05 P.M. Erikki was pretending to sleep in the small, crude hut, his chin stubbled. A wick, floating in oil in an old chipped clay cup, was guttering and cast strange shadows. Embers in the rough stone fireplace glowed in the draughts. His eyes opened and he looked around. No one else was in the hut. Noiselessly he slid

859

from under the blankets and animal skins. He was fully dressed. He put on his boots, made sure his knife was under his belt and went to the door, opened it softly.

For a moment he stood there, listening, head slightly on one side. Layers of high clouds misted the moon and the wind moved the lightest of the pine branches. The village was quiet under its coverlet of snow. No guards that he could see. No movement near the lean-to where the 212 was parked. Moving as a hunter would move, he skirted the huts and headed for the lean-to.

The 212 was bedded down, skins and blankets where they were most needed, all the doors closed. Through a side window of the cabin he could see two tribesmen rolled up in blankets sprawled full length on the seats snoring. Rifles beside them. He eased forward slightly. The guard in the cockpit was cradling his gun, wide awake. He had not yet seen Erikki. Quiet footsteps approaching, the smell of goat and sheep and stale tobacco preceding them.

'What is it, pilot?' the young Sheik Bayazid asked softly.

'I don't know.'

Now the guard heard them and he peered out of the cockpit window, greeted his leader and asked what was the matter. Bayazid replied, 'Nothing,' waved him back on guard and searched the night thoughtfully. In the few days the stranger had been in the village he had come to like him and respect him, as a man and as a hunter. Today he had taken him into the forest, to test him, and then as a further test and for his own pleasure he had given him a rifle. Erikki's first shot killed a distant, difficult mountain goat as cleanly as he could have done. Giving the rifle was exciting, wondering what the stranger would do, if he would, foolishly, try to turn it on him or even more foolishly take off into the trees when they could hunt him with great enjoyment. But the Redhead of the Knife had just hunted and kept his thoughts to himself, though they could all sense the violence simmering.

'You felt something – danger?' he asked.

'I don't know.' Erikki looked out at the night and all around. No sounds other than the wind, a few night animals hunting, nothing untoward. Even so he was unsettled. 'Still no news?'

'No, nothing more.' This afternoon one of the messengers had returned. 'The Khan is very sick, near death,' the man had said. 'But he promises an answer soon.'

Bayazid had reported all this faithfully to Erikki. 'Pilot, be patient,' he said, not wanting trouble.

'What's the Khan sick with?'

'Sick – the messenger said they'd been told he was sick, very sick. Sick!'

'If he dies, what then?'

'His heir will pay – or not pay. Insha'Allah.' The Sheik eased the weight of his assault rifle on his shoulder. 'Come into the lee, it's cold.' From the edge of the hut now they could see down into the valley. Calm and quiet, a few specks of headlamps from time to time on the road far, far below.

Barely thirty minutes from the palace and Azadeh, Erikki was thinking, and no way to escape.

Every time he started engines to recharge his batteries and circulate the oil, five guns were pointing at him. At odd times he would stroll to the edge of the village or, like tonight, he would get up, ready to run and chance it on foot but never an opportunity, guards too alert. During the hunting today he had been sorely tempted to try to break out, useless of course, knowing they were just playing with him.

'It's nothing, pilot, go back to sleep,' Bayazid said. 'Perhaps there'll be good news tomorrow. As God wants.'

Erikki said nothing, his eyes raking the darkness, unable to be rid of his foreboding. Perhaps Azadeh's in danger or perhaps . . . or perhaps it's nothing and I'm just going mad with the waiting and the worry and what's going on? Did Ross and the soldier make a break for it and what about Petr *matyeryebyets* Mzytryk and Abdollah? 'As God wants, yes, I agree, but I want to leave. The time has come.'

The younger man smiled, showing his broken teeth. 'Then I will have to tie you up.'

Erikki smiled back, as mirthlessly. 'I'll wait tomorrow and tomorrow night, then the next dawn I leave.'

'No.'

'It will be better for you and better for me. We can go to the palace with your tribesman, I can lan –'

'No. We wait.'

'I can land in the courtyard, and I'll talk to him and you'll get the ransom and th –'

'No. We wait. We wait here. It's not safe there.'

'Either we leave together or I leave alone.'

The Sheik shrugged. 'You have been warned, Pilot.'

At the Palace of the Khan: 11:38 P.M. Ahmed drove Najoud and her husband Mahmud down the corridor before him like cattle. Both were tousled and still in their nightclothes, both petrified, Najoud in tears,

861

two guards behind them. Ahmed still had his knife out. Half an hour ago he had rushed into their quarters with the guards, dragged them out of their carpet beds, saying the Khan at long last knew they'd lied about Hakim and Azadeh plotting against him, because tonight one of the servants admitted he had overheard the same conversation and nothing wrong had been said.

'Lies,' Najoud gasped, pressed against the carpet bed, half blinded by the flashlight that one of the guards directed at her face, the other guard holding a gun at Mahmud's head, 'all lies . . .'

Ahmed slid out his knife, needle sharp, and poised it under her left eye. 'Not lies, Highness! You perjured yourself to the Khan, *before God*, so I am here at the Khan's orders to take out your sight.' He touched her skin with the point and she cried out, 'No please I beg you I beg you please don't . . . wait wait . . .'

'You admit lying?'

'No. I never lied. Let me see my father he'd never order this without seeing me fir –'

'You'll never *see* him again! Why should he *see* you? You lied before and you'll lie again!'

'I . . . I never lied never lied . . .'

His lips twisted into a smile. For all these years he had known she had lied. It had mattered nothing to him. But now it did. 'You lied, *in the Name of God*.' The point pricked the skin. The panic-stricken woman tried to scream but he held his other hand over her mouth and he was tempted to press the extra half inch, then out and in again the other side and out and all finished, finished for ever. 'Liar!'

'Mercy,' she croaked, 'mercy, in the Name of God . . .'

He relaxed his grip but not the point of the knife. 'I cannot grant you mercy. Beg the mercy of God, the Khan has sentenced you!'

'Wait . . . wait,' she said frantically, sensing his muscles tensing for the probe, 'please . . . let me go to the Khan . . . let me ask his mercy I'm his daugh –'

'You admit you lied?'

She hesitated, eyes fluttering with panic along with her heart. At once the knife point went in a fraction and she gasped out, 'I admit . . . I admit I exagg –'

'In God's Name did you lie or didn't you?' Ahmed snarled.

'Yes . . . yes . . . yes I did . . . please let me see my father . . . please.' The tears were pouring out and he hesitated, pretending to be unsure of himself, then glared at her husband who lay on the carpet nearby quivering with terror. 'You're guilty too!'

'I knew nothing about this, nothing,' Mahmud stuttered, 'nothing at all, I've never lied to the Khan never never I knew nothing . . .'

Ahmed shoved them both ahead of him. Guards opened the door of the sickroom. Azadeh and Hakim and Aysha were there, summoned at a moment's notice, in nightclothes, all frightened, the nurse equally, the Khan awake and brooding, his eyes bloodshot. Najoud went down on her knees and blurted out that she had exaggerated about Hakim and Azadeh and when Ahmed came closer she suddenly broke, 'I lied I lied I lied please forgive me Father please forgive me . . . forgive me . . . mercy . . . mercy . . .' in a mumbling gibberish. Mahmud was moaning and crying, saying he knew nothing about this or he would have spoken up, of course he would have, before God, of course he would, both of them begging for mercy – everyone knowing there would be none.

The Khan cleared his throat noisily. Silence. All eyes on him. His mouth worked but no sound came out. Both the nurse and Ahmed came closer. 'Ah'med stay an'd Hakim, Aza'deh . . . res't go – *them* un'der gu'ard.'

'Highness,' the nurse said gently, 'can it no' wait until tomorrow? You've tired yourself very much. Please, please make it tomorrow.'

The Khan just shook his head. 'N'ow.'

The nurse was very tired. 'I dinna accept any responsibility, Excellency Ahmed. Please make it as short as possible.' Exasperated, she walked out. Two guards pulled Najoud and Mahmud to their feet and dragged them away. Aysha followed shakily. For a moment the Khan closed his eyes, gathering his strength. Now only his heavy, throttled breathing broke the silence. Ahmed and Hakim and Azadeh waited. Twenty minutes passed. The Khan opened his eyes. For him the time had been only seconds. 'My so'n, trus't Ahmed as fir'st confid'ant.'

'Yes, Father.'

'Swea'r by G'd, bo'th of you.'

He listened carefully as they both chorused, 'I swear by God I will trust Ahmed as first confidant.' Earlier they had both sworn before all the family the same thing and everything else he required of them: to cherish and guard little Hassan; for Hakim to make Hassan his heir; for the two of them to stay in Tabriz, Azadeh to stay at least two years in Iran without leaving: 'This way, Highness,' Ahmed had explained earlier, 'no alien outside influence, like that of her husband, could spirit her away before she's sent north, whether guilty or innocent.'

That's wise, the Khan thought, disgusted with Hakim – and Azadeh – that they had allowed Najoud's perjury to be buried for so many years and to let it go unpunished for so many years – loathing Najoud and Mahmud for being so weak. No courage, no strength. Well, Hakim'll learn and she'll learn. If only I had more time . . .

'Aza'deh.'

'Yes, Father?'

'Naj'oud. Wh'at punish'ment?'

She hesitated, frightened again, knowing how his mind worked, feeling the trap close on her. 'Banishment. Banish her and her husband and family.'

Fool, you'll never breed a Khan of the Gorgons, he thought but he was too tired to say it so he just nodded and motioned her to leave. Before she left, Azadeh went to the bed and bent and kissed her father's hand. 'Be merciful, please be merciful, Father.' She forced a smile, touched him again, and then she left.

He watched her close the door. 'Hak'im?'

Hakim also had detected the trap and was petrified of displeasing his father, wanting vengeance but not the malevolent sentence the Khan would pronounce. 'Internal banishment for ever, penniless,' he said. 'Let them earn their own bread in future and expel them from the tribe.'

A little better, thought Abdollah. Normally that would be a terrible punishment. But not if you're a Khan and them a perpetual hazard. Again he moved his hand in dismissal. Like Azadeh, Hakim kissed his father's hand and wished a good night's sleep.

When they were alone, Abdollah said, 'Ah'med?'

'Tomorrow banish them to the wastelands north of Meshed, penniless, with guards. In a year and a day when they're sure they've escaped with their lives, when they've got some business going or house or hut, burn it and put them to death – and their three children.'

He smiled. 'G'ood, do i't.'

'Yes, Highness.' Ahmed smiled back at him, very satisfied.

'Now sl'eep.'

'Sleep well, Highness.' Ahmed saw the eyelids close and the face fall apart. In seconds the sick man was snoring badly.

Ahmed knew he had to be most careful now. Quietly he opened the door. Hakim and Azadeh were waiting in the corridor with the nurse. Worriedly, the nurse went past him, took the Khan's pulse, peering at him closely.

'Is he all right?' Azadeh asked from the doorway.

'Who can say, lassie? He's tired himself, tired himself badly. Best you all leave now.'

Nervously, Hakim turned to Ahmed, 'What did he decide?'

'Banished to the lands north of Meshed at first light tomorrow, penniless and expelled from the tribe. He will tell you himself tomorrow, Highness.'

'As God wants.' Azadeh was greatly relieved that worse had not been ordered. Hakim was glowing that his advice had been taken. 'My sister and I, we, er, we don't know how to thank you for helping us, Ahmed, and, well, for bringing the truth out at long last.'

'Thank you, Highness, but I only obeyed the Khan. When the time comes I will serve you as I serve His Highness, he made me swear it. Good night.' Ahmed smiled to himself and closed the door and went back to the bed. 'How is he?'

'No' so good, agha.' Her back was aching and she was sick with tiredness. 'I must have a replacement tomorrow. We should have two nurses and a sister in charge. Sorry, but I canna continue alone.'

'Whatever you want you will have, provided you stay. His Highness appreciates your care of him. If you like I will watch him for an hour or two. There's a sofa in the next room and I can call you in case anything happens.'

'Oh, that's very kind of you, I'm sure. Thank you, I could use a wee rest, but call me if he wakes, and anyway in two hours.'

He saw her into the next room, told the guard to relieve him in three hours and dismissed him, then began a vigil. Half an hour later he quietly peered in at her. She was deeply asleep. He came back into the sickroom and locked the door, took a deep breath, tousled his hair and rushed for the bed, shaking the Khan roughly. 'Highness,' he hissed as though in panic, 'wake up, wake up!'

The Khan clawed his way out of leaden sleep, not knowing where he was or what had happened or if he was nightmaring again. 'Wh'at . . . wh'at . . .' Then his eyes focused and he saw Ahmed, seemingly terrified which was unheard of. His spirit shuddered. 'Wh'a –'

'Quick, you've got to get up, Pahmudi's downstairs, Abrim Pahmudi with SAVAMA torturers, they've come for you,' Ahmed panted; 'someone opened the door to them, you're betrayed, a traitor betrayed you to him, Hashemi Fazir's given you to Pahmudi and SAVAMA as a pishkesh, quick, get up, they've overpowered all the guards and they're coming to take you away . . .' He saw the Khan's gaping horror, the bulging eyes, and he rushed on. 'There're too many to stop. Quick, you've got to escape . . .'

Deftly he unclipped the saline drip and tore the bedclothes back, started to help the mouthing, frantic man to get up, abruptly shoved him back and stared at the door. 'Too late,' he gasped, 'listen, here they come, here they come, Pahmudi at the head, here they come!'

Chest heaving, the Khan thought he could hear their footsteps, could see Pahmudi, could see his thin gloating face and the instruments of torture in the corridor outside, knowing there would be no mercy and they would keep him alive to howl his life away. Demented he shouted at Ahmed, Quick, help me. I can get to the window, we can climb down if you help me! In the Name of God, Ahmeddddddd . . . but he could not make the words come out. Again he tried but still his mouth did not coordinate with his brain, his neck muscles stretched with effort, the veins overloaded.

It seemed for ever he was screaming and shouting at Ahmed who just stood watching the door, not helping him, footsteps coming closer and closer. 'He'lp,' he managed to gasp, fighting to get out of bed, the sheets and coverlet weighing him down, restricting him, drowning him, chest pains growing and growing, monstrous now like the noise.

'There's no escape, they're here, I've got to let them in!'

At the limit of his terror he saw Ahmed start for the door. With the remains of his strength he shouted at him to stop but all that happened was a strangled croak. Then he felt something twist in his brain and something else snap. A spark leaped across the wires of his mind and chain-reacted the core. Pain ceased, sound ceased. He saw Ahmed's smile. His ears heard the quiet of the corridor and silence of the palace and he knew that he was truly betrayed. With a last, all-embracing effort, he lunged for Ahmed, the fires in his head lighting his way down into the funnel, red and warm and liquid, and there, at the nadir, he blew out all the fire and possessed the darkness.

Ahmed made sure the Khan was dead, glad that he had not had to use the pillow to smother him. Hastily he reconnected the saline drip, checked that there were no telltale leaks, partially straightened the bed, and then, with great care examined the room. Nothing to give him away that he could see. His breathing was heavy, his head throbbing, and his exhilaration immense. A second check, then he walked over to the door, quietly unlocked it, noiselessly returned to the bed. The Khan was lying sightlessly against the pillows, blood haemorrhaged from his nose and mouth.

'Highness!' he bellowed. 'Highness . . .' then leaned forward and grabbed him for a moment, released him and rushed across the room, tore open the door. 'Nurse!' he shouted and rushed into the next room, grabbed the woman out of her deep sleep and half carried, half dragged her back to the Khan.

'Oh my God,' she muttered, weak with relief that it had not happened while she was alone, perhaps to be blamed by this knife-wielding, violent bodyguard or these mad people, screaming and raving. Sickly awake now, she wiped her brow and pushed her hair into shape, feeling naked without her headdress. Quickly she did what she had to and closed his eyes, her ears hearing Ahmed moaning and grief-stricken. 'Nothing anyone could do, agha,' she was saying. 'It could have happened any time. He was in a great deal of pain, his time had come, better this way, better than living as a vegetable.'

'Yes . . . yes, I suppose so.' Ahmed's tears were real. Tears of relief. 'Insha' Allah, Insha' Allah.'

'What happened?'

'I . . . I was dozing and he just . . . just gasped and started to bleed from his nose and mouth.' Ahmed wiped some of the tears away, letting his voice break. 'I grabbed him as he was falling out of bed and then . . . then I don't know I . . . he just collapsed and . . . and I came running for you.'

'Dinna worry, agha, nothing anyone could do. Sometimes it's sudden and quick, sometimes not. Better to be quick, that's a blessing.' She sighed and straightened her uniform, glad it was over and now she could leave this place. 'He, er, he should be cleaned before the others are summoned.'

'Yes. Please let me help, I wish to help.'

Ahmed helped her sponge away the blood and make him presentable and all the time he was planning: Najoud and Mahmud to be banished before noon, the rest of their punishment a year and a day from now; find out if Fazir caught Petr Oleg; make sure the ransom messenger's throat was cut this afternoon as he had ordered in the Khan's name.

Fool, he said to the corpse, fool to think I'd arrange to pay ransom to bring back the pilot to fly you to Tehran to save your life. Why save a life for a few more days or a month? Dangerous to be sick and helpless with your sickness, minds become deranged, oh, yes, the doctor told me what to expect, losing more of your mind, more vindictive than ever, more dangerous than ever, dangerous enough to perhaps turn on me! But now, now the succession is safe, I can dominate the whelp and with the help of God marry Azadeh. Or send her north – her hole's like any other.

The nurse watched Ahmed from time to time, his deft strong hands and their gentleness, for the first time glad of his presence and not afraid of him, now watching him combing the beard. People are so strange, she thought. He must have loved this evil old man very much.

Wednesday
February 28, 1979

Tehran: 6:55 A.M. McIver continued sorting through the files and papers he had taken from the big office safe, putting only those that were vital into his briefcase. He had been at it since 5:30 this morning and now his head ached, his back ached, and the briefcase was almost full. So much more I should be taking, he thought, working as fast as he could. In an hour, perhaps less, his Iranian staff would arrive and he would have to stop.

Bloody people, he thought irritably, never here when we wanted them but now for the last few days, can't get rid of them, like bloody limpets: 'Oh, no, Excellency, please allow me to lock up for you, I beg you for the privilege . . .' or 'Oh no, Excellency, I'll open the office for you, I insist that is not the job for your Excellency.' Maybe I'm getting paranoid but it's just as though they're spies, ordered in to watch us, the partners more nosy than ever. Almost as though someone's on to us.

And yet, so far – touch wood – everything's working like a well-tuned jet: us out by noon today or a little after; already Rudi's poised for Friday with all of his extra bods and a whole load of spares already out of Bandar-e Delam by road to Abadan where a BA Trident snuck in, cleared by Duke's friend Zataki to evacuate British oilers; at Kowiss, by now Duke should have cached the extra fuel, all his lads still cleared to leave tomorrow on the 125 – touch more wood – already three truck loads of spares out to Bushire for trans-shipment to Al Shargaz; Hotshot, Colonel Changiz and that damned mullah, Hussain, still behaving themselves, fifty times touch wood; at Lengeh Scrag'll be having no problems, plenty of coastal ships available for his spares and nothing more to do but wait for D – no, not D-day – W-day.

Only bad spot, Azadeh. And Erikki. Why the devil didn't she tell me before leaving on a wild-goose chase after poor old Erikki? My God, she escapes Tabriz with the skin of her skin and then goes and puts her pretty little head back in it. Women! They're all crazy. Ransom? Balls! I'll bet it's another trap set by her father, the rotten old bastard. At the same time, it's just as Tom Lochart said: 'She would have gone anyway, Mac, and would you have told her about Whirlwind?'

His stomach began churning. Even if the rest of us get out there's still the problem of Erikki and Azadeh. Then there's poor old Tom and Sharazad. How the hell can we get those four to safety? Must come up with something. We've two more days, perhaps by th –

He whirled, startled, not having heard the door open. His chief clerk, Gorani, stood in the doorway, tall and balding, a devout Shi'ite, a good man who had been with them for many years. 'Salaam, agha.'

'Salaam. You're early.' McIver saw the man's open surprise at all the mess – normally McIver was meticulously tidy – and felt as though he'd been caught with his hand in the chocolate box.

'As God wants, agha. The Imam's ordered normality and everyone to work hard for the success of the revolution. Can I help?'

'Well, er, no, no, thank you. I, er, I'm just in a hurry. I've lots to do today, I'm off to the embassy.' McIver knew his voice was running away from him but he was unable to stop it. 'I've, er, appointments all day and must be at the airport by noon. I have to do some homework for the Doshan Tappeh komiteh. I won't come back to the office from the airport so you can close early, take the afternoon off – in fact you can take the day off.'

'Oh, thank you, agha, but the office should remain open until the us –'

'No, we'll close for the day when I leave. I'll go straight home and be there if I'm needed. Please come back in ten minutes, I want to send some telexes.'

'Yes, agha, certainly, agha.' The man left.

McIver hated the twistings of the truth. What's going to happen to Gorani? he asked himself again, to him and all the rest of our people all over Iran, some of them fine, them and their families?

Unsettled, he finished as best he could. There were a hundred thousand rials in the cashbox. He left notes, relocked the safe, and sent some inconsequential telexes. The main one he had sent at 5:30 this morning to Al Shargaz with a copy to Aberdeen in case Gavallan had been delayed: 'Air freighting the five crates of parts to Al Shargaz for repairs as planned.' Translated, the code meant that Nogger, Pettikin and he, and the last two mechanics he had not been able to get out of Tehran, were readying to board the 125 today, as planned, and it was still all systems go.

'Which crates are these, agha?' Somehow Gorani had found the copies of the telex.

'They're from Kowiss, they'll go on the 125 next week.'

'Oh very well. I'll check it for you. Before you go, could you please tell me when does our 212 return? The one we loaned to Kowiss.'

'Next week, why?'

'Excellency Minister and Board Director Ali Kia wanted to know, agha.'

McIver was instantly chilled. 'Oh? Why?'

'He probably has a charter for it, agha. His assistant came here last night, after you had left, and he asked me. Minister Kia also wanted a progress report today of our three 212s sent out for repairs. I, er, I said I would have it today – he is coming this morning, so I can't close the office.'

They had never discussed the three aircraft, or the peculiarly great number of spares they had been sending out by truck, car, or as personal baggage – no aircraft space for freight. It was more than possible that Gorani would know the 212s did not need repair. He shrugged and hoped for the best. 'They'll be ready as planned. Leave a note on the door.'

'Oh, but that would be very impolite. I will relay that message. He said he would return before noon prayer and particularly asked for an appointment with you. He has a very private message from Minister Kia.'

'Well, I'm going to the embassy.' McIver debated a moment. 'I'll be back as soon as I can.' Irritably he picked up the briefcase and hurried down the stairs, cursing Ali Kia and then adding a curse for Ali Baba too.

Ali Baba – so named because he reminded McIver of the Forty

Thieves – was the wheedling half of their live-in couple who had been with them for two years but had vanished at the beginning of the troubles. Yesterday at dawn Ali Baba came back, beaming and acting as though he had just been away for the weekend instead of almost five months, happily insisting he take his old room back: 'Oh, most definitely, agha, the home has to be most clean and prepared for the return of Her Highness; next week my wife will be here to do that but meanwhile I bring you tea-toast in a most instant as you ever liked. May I be sacrificed for you but I bargained mightily today for fresh bread and milk from the market at the oh so reasonable best price for me only, but the robbers charge five times last year's, so said, but please give me the money now, and as most soon as the Bank is opened you can pay me my mucroscupic back salary . . .'

Bloody Ali Baba, the revolution hasn't changed him a bit. 'Mucroscupic?' It's still one loaf for us and five for him, but never mind, it was fine to have tea and toast in bed – but not the day before we sneak out. How the hell are Charlie and I going to get our luggage out without him smelling the proverbial rat?

In the garage he unlocked his car. 'Lulu, old girl,' he said, 'sorry, there's bugger all I can do about it, it's time for the Big Parting. Don't quite know how I'm going to do it, but I'm not leaving you as a burnt offering or for some bloody Iranian to rape.'

Talbot was waiting for him in a spacious, elegant office. 'My dear Mr. McIver, you're bright and early, I heard all the adventures of young Ross – my word we were all very lucky, don't you think?'

'Yes, yes we were. How is he?'

'Getting over it. Good man, did a hell of a good job. I'm seeing him for lunch and we're getting him out on today's BA flight – just in case he's been spotted, can't be too careful. Any news of Erikki? We've had some inquiries from the Finnish embassy asking for help.'

McIver told him about Azadeh's note. 'Bloody ridiculous.'

Talbot steepled his fingers. 'Ransom doesn't sound too good. There's, er, there's a rumour the Khan's very sick indeed. Stroke.'

McIver frowned. 'Would that help or hurt Azadeh and Erikki?'

'I don't know. If he does pop off, well, it'll certainly change the balance of power in Azerbaijan for a while, which will certainly encourage our misguided friends north of the border to agitate more than usual, which'll cause Carter and his powers-that-be to fart more dust.'

'What the devil's he doing now?'

'Nothing, old boy, sweet Fanny Adams – that's the trouble. He scattered his peanuts and scarpered.'

'Anything more on us being nationalised – Armstrong said it's imminent.'

'It might well be you'll lose positive control of your aircraft imminently,' Talbot said with studied care and McIver's attention zeroed. 'It, er, might be more of a personal acquisition by interested parties.'

'You mean Ali Kia and the partners?'

Talbot shrugged. 'Ours not to reason why, eh?'

'This is official?'

'My dear chap, good Lord, no!' Talbot was quite shocked. 'Just a personal observation, off the record. What can I do for you?'

'Off the record, on Andy Gavallan's instructions, all right?'

'Let's have it on the record.'

McIver saw the slightly pink humourless face and got up, relieved. 'No way, Mr. Talbot. It was Andy's idea to keep you in the picture, not mine.'

Talbot sighed with practised eloquence. 'Verywell, off the record.'

McIver sat. 'We're, er, we're transferring our HQ to Al Shargaz today.'

'Very wise. So?'

'We're going today. All remaining expat personnel. On our 125.'

'Very wise. So?'

'We're er, we're closing down all operations in Iran. On Friday.'

Talbot sighed wearily. 'Without personnel I'd say that's axiomatic. So?'

McIver was finding it very hard to say what he wanted to say. 'We, er, we're taking our aircraft out on Friday – this Friday.'

'Bless my soul,' Talbot said in open admiration. 'Congratulations! How on earth did you twist that rotter Kia's arm to get the permits? You must've promised him a life membership at the Royal Box at Ascot!'

'Er, no, no, we didn't. We decided not to apply for exit permits, waste of time.' McIver got up. 'Well, see you soo –'

Talbot's smile almost fell off his face. 'No permits?'

'No. You know yourself our birds're going to be nicked, nationalised, taken over. Whatever you want to call it, there's no way we could get exit permits so we're just going.' McIver added airily, 'Friday we flit the coop.'

'Oh, my word!' Talbot was shaking his head vigorously, his fingers toying with a file on his desk. 'Bless my soul, very very un-bloody-wise.'

'There isn't any alternative. Well, Mr. Talbot, that's all, have a nice day. Andy wanted to forewarn you so you could . . . so you could do whatever you want to do.'

'What the hell is that?' Talbot exploded.

'How the hell do I know?' McIver was equally exasperated. 'You're supposed to protect your nationals.'

'But y –'

'I'm just not going to be put out of business and that's the end of it!'

Talbot's fingers drummed nervously. 'I think I need a cup of tea.' He clicked on the intercom. 'Celia, two cups of the best and I think you better insert a modest amount of Nelson's Blood into the brew.'

'Yes, Mr. Talbot,' the adenoidal voice said and sneezed.

'Bless you,' Talbot said automatically. His fingers stopped drumming and he smiled sweetly at McIver. 'I'm awfully glad you didn't tell me anything about anything, old boy.'

'So'm I.'

'Rest assured, should I ever hear you're in pokey doing – what's the expression? Ah, yes, "doing porridge" – I shall be glad to visit you on behalf of Her Majesty's Government and attempt to extricate you from the errors of your ways.' Talbot's eyebrows went off his forehead. 'Grand larceny! Bless my soul, but jolly good luck, old boy.'

In Azadeh's Apartment: 8:10 A.M. The old maidservant carried the heavy silver breakfast tray along the corridor – four boiled eggs, toast and butter and marmalade, two exquisite coffee cups, steaming coffee-pot, and the finest Egyptian cotton napkins. She put the tray down and knocked.

'Come in.'

'Good morning, Highness. Salaam.'

'Salaam,' Sharazad said dully. She was propped against the many pillows of the carpet bed, her face puffy from tears. The bathroom door was ajar, sound of water running. 'You can put it here, on the bed.'

'Yes, Highness.' The old woman obeyed. With a sidelong glance at the bathroom, she left silently.

'Breakfast, Tommy,' Sharazad called out, trying to sound bright. No answer. She half shrugged to herself, sniffed a little, more tears not far away, then looked up as Lochart came back into the bedroom. He was shaved and dressed in winter flying gear – boots, trousers, shirt and heavy sweater. 'Coffee?' she asked with a tentative smile, hating his set face and the air of disapproval that he wore.

'In a minute,' he said without enthusiasm. 'Thank you.'

'I . . . I ordered everything just as you like it.'

'Looks good – don't wait for me.' He went over to the bureau and began to tie his tie.

'It really was wonderful of Azadeh to lend us the apartment while she's away, wasn't it? So much nicer than home.'

Lochart looked at her in the mirror. 'You didn't say that at the time.'

'Oh, Tommy, of course you're right but please don't let's quarrel.'

'I'm not. I've said it all and so have you.' I've had that, he thought, anguished, knowing she was as miserable as he was but unable to do anything about it. When Meshang had challenged him in front of her and Zarah, two nights ago, the nightmare had begun that continued even now, tearing them apart, bringing him to the edge of madness. Two days and nights of broken tears and him saying over and over, 'No need to worry, we'll manage somehow, Sharazad,' and then discussing the future. What future? he asked his reflection, once more wanting to explode.

'Here's your coffee, darling Tommy.'

Glumly he took it, sat on a chair facing her, not looking at her. The coffee was hot and excellent but it did not take away the foul taste in his mouth, so he left it almost untouched and got up and went for his flight jacket. Thank God I've today's ferry to Kowiss, he thought. Goddamn everything!

'When do I see you, darling, when do you come back?'

He watched himself shrug, hating himself, wanting to take her in his arms and tell her the depth of his love but he had been through that agony four times in the last two days and she was still as relentless and inflexible as her brother: 'Leave Iran? Leave home for ever?' she had cried out. 'Oh, I can't, I can't!'

'But it won't be for ever, Sharazad. We'll spend some time in Al Shargaz then go to England, you'll love England and Scotland and Aberd –'

'But Meshang says the –'

'Screw Meshang!' he had shouted and saw the fear in her and that only served to whip his anger into a frenzy. 'Meshang's not God Almighty, for Christ's sake! What the goddam hell does he know?' and she had sobbed like a terrified child, cowering away from him. 'Oh, Sharazad, I'm sorry . . .' Taking her into his arms, almost crooning his love to her, she safe in his arms.

'Tommy, listen, my darling, you were right and I was wrong, it was my fault, but I know what to do, tomorrow I'll go and see Meshang, I'll persuade him to give us an allowance and . . . what's the matter?'

'You haven't heard a goddamned word I've said.'

'Oh, but I have, yes indeed, I listened very carefully, please don't be angry again, you're right of course to be angry but I list –'

Flaring back: 'Didn't you hear what Meshang said? We've no money – the money's finished, the building's finished, he has total control over the family money, total, and unless you obey him and not me you'll get nothing more. But that's not important, I can make enough for us! I can! The point is we have to leave Tehran. Leave for . . . for a little while.'

'But I haven't any papers, I haven't, Tommy, and can't get any yet and Meshang's right when he says if I leave without papers they'll never let me back, never, never.'

More tears and more arguing, not being able to get through to her, more tears, then going to bed, trying to sleep, no sleep for either of them. 'You can stay here, Tommy. Why can't you stay here, Tommy?'

'Oh, for Christ's sake, Sharazad, Meshang made that very clear. I'm not wanted and foreigners are out. We'll go somewhere else. Nigeria, or Aberdeen, somewhere else. Pack a suitcase. You'll get on the 125 and we'll meet at Al Shargaz – you've a Canadian passport. You're Canadian!'

'But I can't leave without papers,' she wailed and sobbed and the same arguments, over and over, and more tears.

Then, yesterday morning, hating himself, he had put aside his pride and had gone to the bazaar to reason with Meshang, to get him to relent – all that he was going to say painstakingly worked out. But he had come up against a wall as high as the sky. And worse.

'My father held a controlling interest in the IHC partnership, which of course I inherit.'

'Oh, that's wonderful, that makes all the difference, Meshang.'

'It makes no difference at all. The point is how do you intend to pay your debts, pay your ex-wife, and pay for my sister and her child without a very great infusion of charity?'

'A job's not charity, Meshang, it's not charity. It could be mightily profitable for both of us. I'm not suggesting a partnership, anything like that, I'd work for you. You don't know the helicopter business, I do, inside out. I could run the new partnership for you, make it instantly profitable. I know pilots and how to operate. I know all of Iran, most of the fields. That would solve everything for both of us. I'd work like hell to protect the family interests, we'd stay in Tehran, Sharazad could have the baby here an –'

'The Islamic state will require Iranian pilots only, Minister Kia assures me. One hundred percent.'

Sudden understanding. His universe ripped asunder. 'Ah, now I get it, no exceptions, eh, particularly me?'

He had seen Meshang shrug disdainfully. 'I'm busy. To be blunt, you cannot stay in Iran. You've no future in Iran. Out of Iran Sharazad has no future of any value with you and she will never permanently exile herself – which will happen if she goes without my permission and without proper papers. Therefore you must divorce.'

'No.'

'Send Sharazad back from the Khan's apartment this afternoon – more charity by the way – and leave Tehran immediately. Your marriage wasn't Muslim so it's unimportant – the Canadian civil ceremony will be annulled.'

'Sharazad will never agree.'

'Oh? Be at my house at 6 p.m. and we will make final this matter. After you've left I'll settle your Iranian debts – I cannot have bad debts hanging over our good name. 6 p.m. sharp. Good morning.'

Not remembering how he got back to the apartment but telling her and more tears and then to the Bakravan house that evening and Meshang repeating what he had said, infuriated with Sharazad's abject begging: 'Don't be ridiculous, Sharazad! Stop howling, this is for your own good, your son's good, and the family's good. If you leave on a Canadian passport without proper Iranian papers you'll never be allowed back. Live in Aberdeen? God protect you, you'd die of cold in a month and so would your son . . . Nanny Jari won't go with you, not that he could pay for her; she's not mad, she won't leave Iran and her family for ever. You'll never see us again, think of that . . . think of your son . . .' over and over until Sharazad was reduced to incoherence and Lochart to pulp.

'Tommy.'

This brought him out of his reverie. 'Yes?' he asked, hearing the old tone in her voice.

'Thou, art thou leaving me for ever?' she said in Farsi.

'I can't stay in Iran,' he said, at peace now, the 'thou' helping so very much. 'When we're closed down there's no job for me here, I've no money, and even if the place hadn't burned down . . . well, I was never one for handouts.' His eyes were without guile. 'Meshang's right about a lot of things: there wouldn't be much of a life with me and you're right to stay, certainly without papers it'd be dangerous to leave and you've to think of the child, I know that. There's also . . . no, let me finish,' he said kindly, stopping her. 'There's also HBC.' This reminded him about her cousin, Karim. Another horror yet to arrive. Poor Sharazad . . .

'Thou, art thou leaving me for ever?'

'I'm leaving today for Kowiss. I'll be there a few days then I'll go to Al Shargaz. I'll wait there, I'll wait a month. This will give you time to think it through, what you want. A letter or telex care of Al Shargaz Airport will find me. If you want to join me, the Canadian embassy'll arrange it at once, priority, I've already fixed that . . . and of course I'll keep in touch.'

'Through Mac?'

'Through him or somehow.'

'Thou, art thou divorcing me?'

'No, never. If you want that or . . . let me put it another way, if you think it's necessary to protect our child, or for whatever reason, then whatever you want I will do.'

The silence grew and she watched him, a strange look in her huge dark eyes, somehow older than before and yet so much younger and more frail, the translucent nightgown enhancing the sheen of her golden skin, her hair flowing around her shoulders and breasts.

Lochart was consumed with helplessness, dying inside, wanting to stay, knowing there was no longer any reason to stay. It's all been said and now it's up to her. If I was her I wouldn't hesitate, I'd divorce, I'd never have married in the first place. 'Thou,' he said in Farsi, 'fare thee well, beloved.'

'And thee, beloved.'

He picked up his jacket and left. In a moment she heard the front door close. For a long time she stared after him, then, thoughtfully, poured some coffee and sipped it, hot and strong and sweet and life-giving.

As God wants, she told herself, at peace now. Either he will come back or he will not come back. Either Meshang will relent or he will not relent. Either way I must be strong and eat for two and think good thoughts while I build my son.

She decapitated the first of the eggs. It was perfectly cooked and tasted delicious.

At McIver's Apartment: 11:50 A.M. Pettikin came into the living room carrying a suitcase and was surprised to see the servant, Ali Baba, tentatively polishing the sideboard. 'I didn't hear you come back. I thought I'd given you the day off,' he said irritably, putting down the suitcase.

'Oh, yes, agha, but there is most much to do, the place she is filth-filled and the kitchen . . .' His lush brown eyebrows rose to heaven.

'Yes, yes, that's true but you can start in tomorrow.' Pettikin saw him looking at the suitcase and swore. Directly after breakfast he had sent Ali Baba off for the day with instructions to be back at midnight, which normally would mean that he would not come back until the next morning. 'Now off you go.'

'Yes, agha, you are going on holiday or on the leaves?'

'No, I'm, er, I'm going to stay with one of the pilots for a few days, so make sure my room's cleaned tomorrow. Oh, yes, and you better give me your key, I've misplaced mine.' Pettikin held out his hand, cursing himself for not thinking of it before. With curious reluctance, Ali Baba gave it to him. 'Captain McIver wants the place to himself, he has work to do and doesn't want to be disturbed. See you soon, good-bye.'

'But agha . . .'

'Good-bye!' He made sure Ali Baba had his coat, opened the door, half shoved him out, and closed it again. Nervously he glanced again at his watch. Almost noon and still no McIver and they were supposed to be at the airport by now. He went into the bedroom, reached into the cupboard for the other suitcase, also packed, then came back and put it beside the other one, near the front door.

Two small cases and a carryall, he thought. Not much to show for all the years in Iran. Never mind, I prefer to travel light and perhaps this time I can get lucky and make more money or start a business on the side and then there's Paula. How in the hell can I afford to get married again? Married? Are you mad? An affair's about all you could manage. Yes, but Goddam, I'd like to marry her an –

The phone rang and he almost jumped out of himself, so unused to its ringing. He picked it up, his heart pounding. 'Hello?'

'Charlie? It's me, Mac, thank God the bloody thing's working, tried it on the off chance. I've been delayed.'

'You've a problem?'

'Don't know, Charlie, but I've got to go and see Ali Kia – bastard's sent his bloody assistant and a Green Band to fetch me.'

'What the hell does Kia want?' Outside, all over the city, muezzins began calling the Faithful to noon prayer, distracting him.

'Don't know. The appointment's in half an hour. You'd better go on out to the airport and I'll get there as soon as I can. Get Johnny Hogg to delay.'

'Okay, Mac. What about your gear, is it in the office?'

'I snuck it out early this morning while Ali Baba was snoring and it's in Lulu's boot. Charlie, there's one of Genny's needle-points in the kitchen, "Down with cornbeef pie". Stick it in your suitcase for me, will you? She'd have my guts for garters if I forgot that. If I've time I'll come back and make sure everything's okay.'

'Do I shut the gas off, or electricity?'

'Christ, I don't know. Leave it, okay?'

'All right. You sure you don't want me to wait?' he asked, the metallic, loudspeaker voices of muezzins adding to his disquiet. 'I don't mind waiting. Might be better, Mac.'

'No, you go on out. I'll be there right smartly. 'Bye.'

''Bye.' Pettikin frowned, then, having a dialling tone, he dialled their office at the airport. To his astonishment the connection went through.

'Iran Helicopters, hello?'

He recognised the voice of their freight manager. 'Morning, Adwani, this's Captain Pettikin. Has the 125 come in yet?'

'Ah, Captain, yes it's in the pattern and should be landing any minute.'

'Is Captain Lane there?'

'Yes, just a moment please . . .'

Pettikin waited, wondering about Kia.

'Hello, Charlie, Nogger here – you've friends in high places?'

'No, the phone just started working. Can you talk privately?'

'No. Not possible. What's cooking?'

'I'm still at the flat. Mac's been delayed – he's got to go and see Ali Kia. I'm on my way to the airport now and he'll come directly from Kia's office. Are you ready to load?'

'Yes, Charlie, we're sending the engines for repair and reconditioning as Captain McIver ordered. Everything as ordered.'

'Good, are the two mecs there?'

'Yes. But those spares are also ready for shipping.'

'Good. No problem that you can see?'

'Not yet, old chum.'

'See you.' Pettikin hung up. He looked around the apartment a last time, now curiously saddened. Good times and bad times but the best when Paula was staying. Out of the window he noticed distant smoke over Jaleh and now as the muezzins' voices died away, the usual sporadic gunfire. 'The hell with all of them,' he muttered. He got up and went out with his luggage and locked the door carefully. As he drove out of the garage he saw Ali Baba duck back into a doorway across the road. With him were two other men he had never seen before. What the hell's that bugger up to, he thought uneasily.

At the Ministry of Transport: 1:07 P.M. The huge room was freezing in spite of a log fire, and Minister Ali Kia wore a heavy, expensive Astrakhan overcoat with a hat to match, and he was angry. 'I repeat, I need transport to Kowiss tomorrow and I require you to accompany me.'

'Can't tomorrow, sorry,' McIver said, keeping his nervousness off his face with difficulty. 'I'd be glad to join you next week. Say Monday an –'

'I'm astonished that after all the "co-operation" I've given you it's necessary even to argue! Tomorrow, Captain, or . . . or I shall cancel all clearances for our 125 – in fact, I'll hold it on the ground today, impound it today pending investigations!'

McIver was standing in front of the vast desk, Kia sitting behind it in a big carved chair that dwarfed him. 'Could you make it today, Excellency? We've an Alouette to ferry to Kowiss. Captain Lochart's leav –'

'Tomorrow. Not today.' Kia flushed even more. 'As ranking board director you are ordered: you *will* come with me, we *will* leave at ten o'clock. Do you understand?'

McIver nodded bleakly, trying to figure a way out of the trap. The pieces of a tentative plan fell into place. 'Where do you want to meet?'

'Where's the helicopter?'

'Doshan Tappeh. We'll need a clearance. Unfortunately there's a Major Delami there, along with a mullah, and both're rather difficult, so I don't see how we can do it.'

Kia's face darkened even more. 'The PM's given new orders about mullahs and interference with the legal government and the Imam agrees wholeheartedly. They both better behave. I will see you at 10 tomorrow an –'

At that moment there was a large explosion outside. They rushed to the window but could see only a cloud of smoke billowing into the cold sky from around the bend in the road. 'Sounded like another car bomb,' McIver said queasily. Over the last few days there had been a number of assassination attempts and car bomb attacks by left-wing extremists, mostly on high-ranking ayatollahs in the government.

'Filthy terrorists, may God burn their fathers, and them!' Kia was clearly frightened, which pleased McIver.

'The price of fame, Minister,' he said, his voice heavy with concern. 'Those in high places, important people like you, are obvious targets.'

'Yes . . . yes . . . we know, we know. Filthy terrorists . . .'

McIver smiled all the way back to his car. So Kia wants to go to

Kowiss. I'll see he bloody gets to Kowiss and Whirlwind continues as planned.

Around the corner, the main road ahead was partially blocked with debris, a car still on fire, others smouldering, and a hole in the roadbed where the parked car bomb had exploded, blowing out the front of a restaurant and the shuttered foreign bank beside it, glass from them and other shop windows scattered everywhere. Many injured, dead or dying. Agony and panic and the stink of burning rubber.

Traffic was jammed both ways. There was nothing to do but wait. After half an hour an ambulance arrived, some Green Bands and a mullah began directing traffic. In time McIver was waved forward, cursed forward. Easing past the wreckage, all traffic enraged and blaring, he did not notice the headless body of Talbot half buried under the restaurant debris, nor recognise Ross dressed in civvies, lying unconscious nearby, half against the wall, his coat ripped, blood seeping from his nose and ears.

Al Shargaz Airport Foyer – Across the Gulf: 2:05 P.M. Scot Gavallan was among the crowd waiting outside the Customs and Immigration area, his right arm in a sling. From the loudspeaker came air traffic announcements in Arabic and English, and the big arrival and departure board clattered, fixing schedules and boarding gates, the whole terminal thriving. He saw his father come through the green door, his face lit up, and he went forward to intercept him. 'Hi, Dad!'

'Oh, Scot, laddie!' Gavallan said so happily and hugged him back but carefully, because of his shoulder. 'How are you?'

'I'm fine, Dad, really. I told you, I'm fine now.'

'Yes, I can see that.' Since Gavallan had left on Monday he had spoken to his son by phone many times. But talking on the phone's not the same, he thought. 'I – I was so worried . . .' Gavallan had not wanted to leave at all, but the English doctor at the hospital had assured him Scot was all right and there were urgent business problems in England and the postponed board meeting to deal with. 'The X-ray showed no bone damage, Mr. Gavallan. The bullet's gone through part of the muscle, the wound nasty but repairable.' To Scot the doctor had said: 'It'll ache a lot and you won't be flying for two months or more. As to the tears . . . no need to worry either. It's just a fairly normal reaction to a gunshot wound. The flight from Zagros didn't help – you escaped in a coffin, you say? That's enough to give you the heebie-jeebies, let alone being shot. It would me. We'll keep you overnight.'

'Is that necessary, Doctor? I'm . . . I'm feeling much better . . .' Scot had got up, his knees had given way on him and he would have fallen if Gavallan had not been ready.

'First we have to fix you up. A good sleep and he'll be as right as rain, Mr. Gavallan, promise you.' The doctor gave Scot a sedative and Gavallan had stayed with him reassuring him about Jordon's death. 'If anyone's responsible, it's me, Scot. If I'd ordered an evacuation before the Shah left, Jordon'd still be alive.'

'No, that's not right, Dad . . . the bullets were meant for me . . .'

Gavallan had waited until he was asleep. By this time he had missed his connection but just caught the midnight flight and was in London in good time.

'What the hell's going to happen in Iran?' Linbar had asked without preamble.

'What about the others?' Gavallan had said tightly. Only one other director was in the room, Paul Choy, nicknamed 'Profitable', who had flown in from Hong Kong. Gavallan respected him greatly for his business acumen – the only cloud between them Choy's close involvement at David MacStruan's accidental death and Linbar's subsequent succession. 'We should wait for them, don't you think?'

'No one else is coming,' Linbar rapped. 'I cancelled them and don't need them. I'm taipan and can do whatever I like. Wh –'

'Not with S-G Helicopters, you can't.' Tightly Gavallan looked across at Choy. 'I propose we postpone.'

'Sure we can,' Profitable Choy said easily, 'but hell, Andy, I came in special and the three of us can constitute a quorum, if we want to vote it.'

'I vote it,' Linbar said. 'What the hell're you afraid of?'

'Nothing. Bu –'

'Good. Then we've a quorum. Now what about Iran?'

Gavallan held on to his temper. 'Friday's D-day, weather permitting. Whirlwind's set up as best we can.'

'I'm sure of that, Andy.' Profitable Choy's smile was friendly. 'Linbar says you plan only to try to get 212s out?' He was a good-looking, immensely wealthy man in his late thirties, a director of Struan's and many of its subsidiary boards for a number of years, who had major interests outside of Struan's, in shipping, pharmaceutical manufacturing in Hong Kong and Japan and in the Chinese Stock Exchange. 'What about our 206s and Alouettes?'

'We have to leave them – can't possibly fly them out. No way.' A silence followed his explanation.

Profitable Choy said, 'What's the final Whirlwind plan?'

'Friday at 7 a.m., weather permitting, I radio the code that Whirlwind's a go. All flights get airborne. We'll have four 212s positioned at Bandar-e Delam under Rudi, they'll head for Bahrain, refuel, then on to Al Shargaz; our two 212s at Kowiss have to refuel on the coast then head for Kuwait for more fuel, then to Jellet – that's a small island off Saudi where we've cached fuel – then on to Bahrain and Al Shargaz. The three at Lengeh under Scragger shouldn't have any problem, they just head for Al Shargaz direct – Erikki gets out through Turkey. As soon as they arrive we start stripping them for loading into the 747s I've already chartered and get out as fast as possible.'

'What odds're you giving on not losing a man or a chopper?' Profitable Choy asked, his eyes suddenly hard. He was a famous gambler and racehorse owner and a steward of Hong Kong's Jockey Club. Rumour had it he was also a member of Macao's gambling syndicate.

'I'm not a betting man. But the chances are good – otherwise I wouldn't even contemplate it. McIver's already managed to get three 212s out, that's a saving of better than three million. If we get all our 212s out and most of the spares, S-G'll be in good shape.'

'Rotten shape,' Linbar said curtly.

'Better shape than Struan's will be this year.'

Linbar flushed. 'You should have been prepared for this catastrophe, you and bloody McIver. Any fool could see the Shah was on his last legs.'

'Enough of this, Linbar,' Gavallan snapped. 'I didn't come back to quarrel, just to report, so let's finish and I can get my plane back. What else, Profitable?'

'Andy, even if you get 'em out what about Imperial undercutting you in the North Sea, taking twenty-odd contracts from you – then there's your commitment for the six X63s?'

'A bloody stupid and ill-timed decision,' Linbar said.

Gavallan dragged his eyes off Linbar and concentrated. Choy had the right to ask and he had nothing to hide. 'So long as I've my 212s I can get back to normal; there's a huge amount of work for them. I'll start dealing with Imperial next week – I know I'll get some of the contracts back. The rest of the world's frantic for oil, so ExTex will come around with the new Saudi, Nigerian and Malaysian contracts, and when they get our report on the X63 they'll double their business with us – and so will all the other majors. We'll be able to give them better than ever service, more safety in all weather conditions, at less

886

cost per mile per passenger. The market's great, soon China'll open up an –'

'Pipe dream,' Linbar said. 'You and bloody Dunross have your heads in the clouds.'

'China'll never be any good for us,' Profitable Choy said, his eyes curious. 'I agree with Linbar.'

'I don't.' Gavallan noticed something odd about Choy but his rage took him onwards. 'We'll wait on that one. China has to have oil somewhere, in abundance. To finalise, I'm in good shape, great shape, last year profits were up fifty percent and this year we're the same if not better. Next week I'll b –'

Linbar interrupted. 'Next week you'll be out of business.'

'This weekend will tell it one way or another.' Gavallan's chin came out. 'I propose we reconvene on Monday next. That'll give me time to get back.'

'Paul and I return to Hong Kong on Sunday. We'll reconvene there.'

'That's not possible for me an –'

'Then we will have to get on without you.' Linbar's temper broke. 'If Whirlwind fails you're finished, S-G helicopters will be liquidated, a new company, North Sea Helicopters, already formed by the way, will acquire the assets, and I doubt if we'll pay half a cent on the dollar.'

Gavallan flushed. 'That's bloody robbery!'

'Just the price of failure! By God if S-G goes down you're finished and none too soon for me. And if you can't afford to buy your own plane ticket to board meetings you won't be missed.'

Gavallan was beside himself with suppressed rage, but he held on. Then at a sudden thought, he looked across at Profitable Choy. 'If Whirlwind's a success, will you help me finance a Struan buy-out?'

Before Choy could answer Linbar bellowed, 'Our controlling interest's not for sale.'

'Maybe it should be, Linbar,' Profitable Choy said thoughtfully. 'That way maybe you ease out of the hole you're in. Why not unload an irritant – you two guys hack all the time and for what? Why not call it a day, huh?'

Linbar said tightly, 'Would you finance the buy-out?'

'Maybe. Yeah, maybe, but only if you agreed, Linbar, only then. This's a family matter.'

'I'll never agree, Profitable.' Linbar's face twisted and he glared at Gavallan. 'I want to see you rot – you and bloody Dunross!'

Gavallan got up. 'I'll see you at the next meeting of the Inner Office. We'll see what they say.'

'They'll do what I tell them to do. I'm taipan. By the way, I'm making Profitable a member.'

'You can't, it's against Dirk's rules.' Dirk Struan, founder of the company, had set down that members of the Inner Office could only be family, however loosely connected, and Christian. 'You swore by God to uphold them.'

'The hell with Dirk's rules,' Linbar slammed back at him; 'you're not party to all of them or to Dirk's legacy, only a taipan is, by God, and what I swore to uphold's my own business. You think you're so goddamned clever, you're not! Profitable's become Episcopalian, last year he was divorced, and soon he's going to marry into the family, one of my nieces, with my blessing – he'll be more family than you!' He laughed uproariously.

Gavallan did not. Nor did Profitable Choy. They watched each other, the die cast now. 'I didn't know you were divorced,' Gavallan said. 'I should congratulate you on . . . on your new life and appointment.'

'Yeah, thanks,' was all his enemy said.

Scot bent down to pick up his father's suitcase, other passengers bustling past, but Gavallan said, 'No, thanks, Scot, I can manage.' He picked it up. 'I could use a shower and a couple of hours' sleep. Hate flying at night.'

'Genny's got the car outside.' Scot had noticed his father's tiredness from the first moment. 'You had a rough time back home?'

'No, no, not at all. So glad you're okay. What's new here?'

'Everything's terrific, Dad, going according to plan. Like clockwork.'

In Tehran's Northern Suburbs: 2:35 P.M. Jean-Luc, debonair as always in his tailored flying gear and custom-made boots, got out of the taxi. As promised, he took out the hundred-dollar bill and carefully tore it in half. '*Voilà!*'

The driver examined his half of the note closely. 'Only one hour, agha? In God's name, agha, no more?'

'One hour and a half, as we agreed, then straight back to the airport. I'll have some luggage.'

'Insha'Allah.' The driver looked around nervously. 'I can't wait here – too many eyes. One hour and half hour. I around corner, there!' He pointed ahead, then drove off.

Jean-Luc went up the stairs and unlocked the door of Apartment 4a that overlooked the tree-lined road and faced south. This was *his* pad, though his wife, Marie-Christine, had found it and arranged it for him and stayed here on her rare visits. One bedroom with a big, low double-bed, well-equipped kitchen, living room with a deep sofa, good hi-fi and record player: 'To beguile your lady friends, *chéri*, so long as you don't import one into France!'

'Me, *chérie*? Me, I'm a lover not an importer!'

He smiled to himself, glad to be home and only a little irritated that he had to leave so much – the hi-fi was the best, the records wonderful, the sofa seductive, the bed, oh so resilient, the wine so painstakingly smuggled in, and then there were his kitchen utensils. '*Espèce de con*,' he said out loud and went into the bedroom and tried the phone. It wasn't working.

He took a suitcase out of the neat wall bureau and started packing, quickly and efficiently, for he had given it much thought. First his favourite knives and omelette pan, then six bottles of the very best wines, the remaining forty-odd bottles would stay for the new tenant, a temporary tenant in case he ever came back, who was renting the whole place from him from tomorrow – with payment in good French francs, monthly in advance into Switzerland, with another good cash deposit for breakages, also in advance.

The deal had been simmering since before he went on Christmas leave. While everyone else wore blinkers, he chortled, I was ahead of the game. But then of course I have an extreme advantage over the others. I'm French.

Happily he continued packing. The new owner was also French, an elderly friend in the embassy who for weeks had desperately needed an immediate, well-equipped *garçonnière* for his teenage Georgian-Cir-cassian mistress who was swearing to leave him unless he delivered: 'Jean-Luc, my dearest friend, let me rent it for a year, six months, three – I tell you emphatically, soon the only Europeans resident here will be diplomats. Tell no one else, but I have it on the highest authority from our inside contact with Khomeini in Neauphle-le-Château! Frankly we know everything that's going on – aren't many of his closest associates French speaking and French university trained? Please, I beg you, I simply have to satisfy the light of my life.'

My poor old friend, Jean-Luc thought sadly. Thank God I'll never have to kowtow to any woman – how lucky Marie-Christine is that she's married to me who can wisely guard her fortune!

The last items he packed were his flight instruments and half a dozen pairs of sunglasses. All his clothes he had put away in one locked cupboard. Of course I shall be reimbursed by the company and buy new ones. Who needs old clothes?

Now he was finished, everything neat and tidy. He looked at the clock. It had taken him only twenty-two minutes. Perfect. The La Doucette in the freezer was cool, the freezer still working in spite of the electricity cuts. He opened the bottle and tried it. Perfect. Three minutes later the door knocker sounded. Perfect.

'Sayada, *chérie*, how beautiful you are,' he said warmly and kissed her, but he was thinking, you don't look good at all, tired and weary. 'How are you, *chérie?*'

'I've had a chill, nothing to worry about,' she said. This morning she had seen worry lines and the dark rings in her mirror and knew Jean-Luc would notice. 'Nothing serious and I'm over it now. And you, *chéri?*'

'Today fine, tomorrow?' He shrugged, helped her off with her coat, lifted her easily into his arms and sank into the embrace of the sofa. She was very beautiful and he was saddened to leave her. And Iran. Like Algiers, he thought.

'What're you thinking about, Jean-Luc?'

'In '63, being shoved out of Algiers. Just like Iran in a way. We're being forced out the same way.' He felt her stir in his arms. 'What is it?'

'The world's so awful sometimes.' Sayada had told him nothing about her real life. 'So unfair,' she said, sickened, remembering the '67 war in Gaza and the death of her parents, then fleeing – her story much like his – remembering more the catastrophe of Teymour's murder and *them*. Nausea swept into her as she pictured little Yassar and what they would do to her son if she misbehaved. If only I could find out who *they* are . . .

Jean-Luc was pouring the wine that he had put on the table in front of them. 'Bad to be serious, *chérie*. We've not much time. '*Santé!*'

The wine tasted cool and delicate and of spring. 'How much time? Aren't you staying?'

'I must leave in an hour.'

'For Zagros?'

'No, *chérie*, for the airport, then Kowiss.'

'When will you be back?'

'I won't,' he said and felt her stiffen. But he held her firmly and, in a moment, she relaxed again and he continued – never a reason not to trust her implicitly. 'Between us, Kowiss is temporary, very. We're pulling out of Iran, the whole company – it's obvious we're not wanted, we can't operate freely any more, the company's not being paid. We've been tossed out of the Zagros . . . one of our mechanics was killed by terrorists a few days ago and young Scot Gavallan missed getting killed by a millimetre. So we're pulling out. *C'est fini.*'

'When?'

'Soon. I don't know exactly.'

'I'll . . . I will miss . . . will miss you, Jean-Luc,' she said and nestled closer.

'And I'll miss you, *chérie*,' he said gently, noticing the silent tears now flooding her cheeks. 'How long are you staying in Tehran?'

'I don't know.' She kept the misery out of her voice. 'I'll give you an address in Beirut, they'll know where to find me.'

'You can find me through Aberdeen.'

They sat there on the sofa, she lying in his arms, the clock on the mantelpiece over the fireplace ticking, normally so soft but now so loud, both of them conscious of the time that passed and the ending that had occurred – not of their volition.

'Let's make love,' she murmured, not wanting to but knowing that bed was expected of her.

'No,' he said gallantly, pretending to be strong for both of them, knowing that bed was expected of him, and then they would get dressed and be French and sensible about the ending of their affair. His eyes strayed to the clock. Forty-three minutes left.

'You don't want me?'

'More than ever.' His hand cupped her breast and his lips brushed her neck, her perfume light and pleasing, ready to begin.

'I'm glad,' she murmured in the same sweet voice, 'and so glad that you said no. I want you for hours, my darling, not for a few minutes, not now. It would spoil everything to hurry.'

For a moment he was nonplussed, not expecting that gambit in the game they played. But now that it was said he was glad too. How brave of her to forego such pleasure, he thought, loving her deeply. Much better to remember the great times than to thrash around hurriedly. It certainly saves me a great deal of sweat and effort and I didn't check if there's any hot water. Now we can sit and chat and enjoy the wine, weep a little and be happy. 'Yes, I agree. For me too.' Again his lips brushed her neck. He felt her tremble and for a moment he was tempted to inflame her. But decided not to. Poor darling, why torment her?

'How are you all leaving, my darling?'

'We'll fly out together. Wine?'

'Yes, yes, please, it's so good.' She sipped the wine, dried her cheeks, and chatted with him, probing this extraordinary 'pull out'. Both *they* and *the Voice* will find all this very interesting, perhaps even bring me to discover who *they* are. Until I know I can't protect my son. Oh, God help me to corner *them*.

'I love you so much, *chéri*,' she said.

At Tehran Airport: 6:05 P.M. Johnny Hogg, Pettikin and Nogger stared at McIver blankly. 'You're staying – you're not leaving with us?' Pettikin stuttered.

'No. I told you,' McIver said briskly. 'I've got to accompany Kia to Kowiss tomorrow.' They were beside his car in their car park, away from alien ears, the 125 on the apron, labourers loading the last few crates, the inevitable group of Green Band guards watching. And a mullah.

'The mullah's one we've never seen before,' Nogger said nervously, like all of them trying to hide it.

'Good. Is everyone else ready to board?'

'Yes, Mac, except Jean-Luc.' Pettikin was very unsettled. 'Don't you think you'd better chance leaving Kia?'

'That'd really be crazy, Charlie. Nothing to worry about. You can set up everything at Al Shargaz Airport with Andy. I'll be there tomorrow. I'll get on the 125 tomorrow at Kowiss with the rest of the lads.'

'But for God's sake they're all cleared, you're not,' Nogger said.

'For God's sake, Nogger, none of us're cleared from here, for God's sake.' McIver added with a laugh, 'How the hell will we be sure of our Kowiss lads until they're airborne and out of Iran airspace? Nothing to worry about. First things first, we've got to get this part of the show in the air.' He glanced at the taxi skidding to a stop. Jean-Luc got out, gave the driver the other half of the note and strolled over carrying a suitcase.

'*Alors, mes amis,*' he said with a contented smile. '*Ça marche?*'

McIver sighed. 'Jolly sporting of you to advertise you're going on a holiday, Jean-Luc.'

'What?'

'Never mind.' McIver liked Jean-Luc, for his ability, his cooking, and single-mindedness. When Gavallan had told Jean-Luc about Whirlwind, Jean-Luc had said at once, 'Me, I will certainly fly out one of the Kowiss 212s – providing I can be on the Wednesday flight to Tehran and go into Tehran for a couple of hours.'

'To do what?'

'*Mon Dieu*, you *Anglais!* To say *adieu* to the Imam perhaps?'

McIver grinned at the Frenchman. 'How was Tehran?'

'*Magnifique!*' Jean-Luc grinned back, and thought, I haven't seen Mac so young in years. Who's the lady? '*Et toi, mon vieux?*'

'Good.' Behind him, McIver saw Jones, the co-pilot, come down the steps two at a time, heading for them. Now there were no more crates left on the tarmac and their Iranian ground crew were all strolling back to the office. 'You all set aboard?'

'All set, Captain, except for passengers,' Jones said, matter of fact. 'ATC's getting itchy and says we're overdue. Quick as you can, all right?'

'You're still cleared for a stop at Kowiss?'

'Yes, no problem.'

McIver took a deep breath. 'All right, here we go, just as we planned, except I'll take the papers, Johnny.' Johnny Hogg handed them to him and the three of them, McIver, Hogg and Jones, went ahead, straight to the mullah, hoping to distract him. By prearrangement the two mechanics were already aboard, ostensibly loaders. 'Good day, agha,' McIver said, and ostentatiously handed the mullah the manifest, their position blocking a direct view of the steps. Nogger, Pettikin and Jean-Luc went up them nimbly to vanish inside.

The mullah leafed through the manifest, clearly not accustomed to it. 'Good. Now inspect,' he said, his accent thick.

'No need for that, agha, ev—' McIver stopped. The mullah and the two guards were already going for the steps. 'Soon as you're aboard, start engines, Johnny,' he said softly and followed.

The cabin was piled with crates, the passengers already seated, seat belts fastened. All eyes studiously avoided the mullah. The mullah stared at them. 'Who men?'

McIver said brightly, 'Crews for replacements, agha.' His excitement picked up as the engines began to howl. He motioned haphazardly at Jean-Luc. 'Pilot for Kowiss replacement, agha,' then more hurriedly, 'Tower komiteh wants the aircraft to leave now. Hurry, all right?'

'What in crates?' The mullah looked at the cockpit as Johnny Hogg called out in perfect Farsi, 'Sorry to interrupt, Excellency, as God wants, but the tower orders us to take off at once. With your permission, please?'

'Yes, yes, of course, Excellency pilot.' The mullah smiled. 'Your Farsi is very good, Excellency.'

'Thank you, Excellency, God keep you, and His blessings on the Imam.'

'Thank you, Excellency pilot, God keep you.' The mullah left.

On his way out McIver leaned into the cockpit. 'What was that all about, Johnny? I didn't know you spoke Farsi.'

'I don't,' Hogg told him dryly – and what he had said to the mullah. 'I just learned that phrase, thought it might come in handy.'

McIver smiled. 'Go to the top of the class!' Then he dropped his voice. 'When you get to Kowiss get Duke to arrange with Hotshot, however he can, to pull the lads' ferry forward, early as possible in the morning. I don't want Kia there when they take off – get 'em out early, however he can. Okay?'

'Yes, of course, I'd forgotten that. Very wise.'

'Have a safe flight – see you in Al Shargaz.' From the tarmac he gave them a beaming thumbs up as they taxied away.

The second they were airborne Nogger exploded, with a cheer, 'We did it!' that everyone echoed, except Jean-Luc who crossed himself superstitiously and Pettikin touched wood. '*Merde*,' he called out. 'Save your cheers, Nogger, you may be grounded in Kowiss. Save your cheers for Friday, too much dust to blow across the Gulf between now and then!'

'Right you are, Jean-Luc,' Pettikin said, sitting in the window seat beside him, watching the airport receding. 'Mac was in good humour. Haven't seen him that happy for months and he was pissed off this morning. Curious how people can change.'

'Yes, curious. Me, I would be very pissed off indeed to have such a change of plan.' Jean-Luc was getting himself comfortable and sat back, his mind on Sayada and their parting that had been significant and sweet sorrow. He glanced at Pettikin and saw the heavy frown. 'What?'

'I suddenly wondered how Mac's getting to Kowiss.'

'By chopper, of course. There're two 206s and an Alouette left.'

'Tom ferried the Alouette to Kowiss today, and there aren't any pilots left.'

'So he is going by car, of course. Why?'

'You don't think he'd be crazy enough to fly Kia himself, do you?'

'Are you mad? Of course not, he's not that cr—' Jean-Luc's eyebrows soared. '*Merde*, he's that crazy.'

At Inner Intelligence HQ: 6:30 P.M. Hashemi Fazir stood at the window of his vast office, looking out over the roofs of the city and the minarets, huge mosque domes among the modern, tall high-rise hotels and buildings, the last of the muezzins' sunset calls dying away. A few more city lights on than usual. Distant gunfire. 'Sons of dogs,' he muttered, then, without turning added sharply, 'That's all she said?'

'Yes, Excellency. "In a few days." She said she was "fairly sure" the Frenchman did not know exactly when they were leaving.'

'She should have made sure. Careless. Careless agents are dangerous. Only 212s, eh?'

'Yes, she was sure about that. I agree she's careless and should be punished.'

Hashemi heard the malicious pleasure in the voice but did not let it disturb his good humour, just let his mind wander, deciding what to do about Sayada Bertolin and her information. He was very pleased with himself.

Today had been excellent. One of his secret associates had been appointed number two to Abrim Pahmudi in SAVAMA. At noon a telex from Tabriz had confirmed the death of Abdollah Khan. Immediately he had telexed back to arrange a private appointment tomorrow with Hakim Khan and requisitioned one of SAVAMA's light twin-engined airplanes. Talbot's assist into hell had gone perfectly, and he had found no traces of the men responsible – a Group Four team – when he had inspected the bomb area, for, of course, he had been instantly summoned. Those nearby had seen no one park the car: 'One moment there was God's peace, the next Satan's rage.'

An hour ago Abrim Pahmudi had called personally, ostensibly to congratulate him. But he had avoided the trap and had carefully denied the explosion had anything to do with him – better not to draw attention to the similarity with the first car bomb that blew General Janan to pieces, better to keep Pahmudi guessing and off guard and under pressure. He had hidden his laughter and said gravely, 'As God wants, Excellency, but clearly this was another cursed leftist terrorist attack. Talbot wasn't the target though his convenient demise certainly eliminates that problem. Sorry to tell you but the attack was again against the favoured of the Imam.' Blaming terrorists and claiming the attack was against the ayatollahs and mullahs who frequented the restaurant would frighten them and it nicely led the trail away from Talbot and so would avoid possible British retaliation – certainly from Robert Armstrong if he ever found out – and so squashed several scorpions with one stone.

Hashemi turned and looked at the sharp-faced man, Suliman al Wiali, the Group Four team leader who had planted today's car bomb – the same man who had caught Sayada Bertolin in Teymour's bedroom. 'In a few minutes I'm leaving for Tabriz. I'll be back tomorrow or the next day. A tall Englishman, Robert Armstrong, will be with me. Assign one of your men to follow him, make sure the man knows where

Armstrong lives, then have him finish him off somewhere in the streets, after dark. Don't do it yourself.'

'Yes, Excellency. When?'

Hashemi thought through his plan again and could find no flaw: 'Holy Day.'

'This is the same man you wanted the Sayada woman to fornicate with?'

'Yes. But now I've changed my mind.' Robert's no longer of any value, he thought. More than that, his time has come.

'Do you have any other work for her, Excellency?'

'No. We've broken the Teymour ring.'

'As God wants. May I make a suggestion?'

Hashemi studied him. Suliman was his most efficient, trustworthy and deadly Group Four leader with a cover job as a minor agent for Inner Intelligence reporting directly to him. Suliman claimed that originally he came from Shrift Mountains north of Beirut before his family was murdered and he was driven out by Christian militiamen. Hashemi had inducted him five years ago after bribing him out of a Syrian prison where he had been condemned to death for murder and banditry on both sides of the borders, his sole defence: 'I only killed Jews and Infidels as God ordered, so I do God's work. I am an Avenger.'

'What suggestion?' he asked.

'She's an ordinary PLO courier, not a very good one and in her present state dangerous and a possible threat – easy to be subverted by Jews or CIAs and used against us. Like good farmers we should plant seeds where we can to reap a future crop.' Suliman smiled. 'You're a wise farmer, Excellency. My suggestion is I tell her it's time to go back to Beirut, that we, the two of us who caught her in her harlotry, now want her to work for us there. We let her overhear us talking privately – and we pretend to be part of a cell of Christian militiamen from southern Lebanon, acting under Israeli orders for their CIA masters.' The man laughed quietly, seeing his employer's surprise.

'And then?'

'What would turn a lukewarm anti-Israeli, Palestinian Copt into a permanent, fanatic hellcat bent on vengeance?'

Hashemi looked at him. 'What?'

'Say *some* of these same "Christian militiamen, acting under Israeli orders for their CIA masters", maliciously, openly hurt her child, hurt him badly, the day before she arrived back, then vanished – wouldn't that make her a fiendish enemy of our enemies?'

896

Hashemi lit a cigarette to hide his disgust. 'I agree that her usefulness is over,' he said and saw a flash of irritation.

'What value has her child, and what future?' Suliman said scornfully. 'With such a mother and living with Christian relatives he will remain Christian and go to hell.'

'Israel is our ally. Stay out of Middle Eastern affairs or they will eat you up. It's forbidden!'

'If you say it is forbidden it is forbidden, Master.' Suliman bowed and nodded agreement. 'On the head of my children.'

'Good. You did very well today. Thank you.' He went to the safe and took a bundle of used dollars off the stacks there. He saw Suliman's face light up. 'Here's a bonus for you and your men.'

'Thank you, thank you, Excellency, God protect you! The man Armstrong may be considered dead.' Very gratefully, Suliman bowed again and left.

Now that he was alone Hashemi unlocked a drawer and poured himself a whisky. A thousand dollars is a fortune to Suliman and his three men, but a wise investment, he thought contentedly. Oh yes. Glad I decided about Robert. Robert knows too much, suspects too much – wasn't it he who named my teams? 'Group Four teams must be used for good and not evil, Hashemi,' he had said in that know-all voice of his. 'I just caution you, their power could be heady and backfire on you. Remember the Old Man of the Mountains. Eh?'

Hashemi had laughed to cover his shock that Armstrong had read his most secret heart. 'What has al-Sabbah and his assassins to do with me? We're living in the twentieth century and I'm not a religious fanatic. More important, Robert, I don't have a castle Alamut!'

'There's still hashish – and better.'

'I don't want addicts or assassins, just men I can trust.'

'Assassin' was derived from 'hashashin', he who takes hashish. Legend told that in the eleventh century at Alamut – Hassan ibn al-Sabbah's impregnable fortress in the mountains near Qazvin – he had had secret gardens made just like the Gardens of Paradise described in the Koran, where wine and honey flowed from fountains and beautiful, complaint maidens lay. Here hashish drugged devotees would be secretly introduced and given a foretaste of the promised, eternal and erotic bliss that awaited them in Paradise after death. Then, in a day or two or three, the 'Blessed One' would be brought 'back to earth', to be guaranteed quick passage back – in return for absolute obedience to his will.

From Alamut Hassan ibn al-Sabbah's fanatical band of simple-minded, hashish-taking zealots – the Assassins – terrorised Persia, soon to reach into most of the Middle East. This continued for almost two centuries. Until 1256. Then a grandson of Genghis Khan, Hulugu Khan, came down into Persia and set his hordes against Alamut, tore it stone by stone from its mountain peaks, and stamped the Assassins into the dust.

Hashemi's lips were in a thin line. Ah, Robert, how did you pierce the veil to see my secret plan: to modernise al-Sabbah's idea, so easy to do now that the Shah has gone and the land's in ferment. So easy with psychedelic drugs, hallucinogens and a never-ending pool of simple-minded zealots already imbued with the wish for martyrdom, who just have to be guided and pointed in the right direction – to remove whomever I choose. Like Janan and Talbot. Like you!

But what carrion I have to deal with for the greater glory of my fief. How can people be so cruel? How can they openly enjoy such wanton cruelty, like cutting off that man's genitals, like contemplating hurting a child? Is it just because they're of the Middle East, live in the Middle East, and belong nowhere else? How terrible that they can't learn from us, can't benefit from our ancient civilisation. The Empire of Cyrus and Darius must come to pass again, by God – in that the Shah was right. My assassins will lead the way, even back to Jerusalem.

He sipped his whisky, very pleased with his day's work. It tasted very good. He preferred it without ice.

Thursday
March 1, 1979

In the Village Near the North Border: 5:30 A.M. In the light of false dawn Erikki pulled on his boots. Now on with his flight jacket, the soft, well-worn leather rustling, knife out of the scabbard and into his sleeve. He eased the hut door open. The village was sleeping under its snow coverlet. No guards that he could see. The chopper's lean-to was also quiet but he knew she would still be too well guarded to try. Various times during the day and night he had experimented. Each time the cabin and cockpit guards had just smiled at him, alert and polite. No way he could fight through the three of them and take off. His only chance by foot and he had been planning it ever since he had had the confrontation with Sheik Bayazid the day before yesterday.

His senses reached out into the darkness. The stars were hidden by thin clouds. Now! Surefooted he slid out of the door and along the line of huts, making for the trees, and then he was enmeshed in the net that seemed to appear out of the sky and he was fighting for his life.

Four tribesmen were on the ends of the net used for trapping and for curbing wild goats. Skillfully they wound it around him, tighter and tighter, and though he bellowed with rage and his immense strength ripped some of the ropes asunder, soon he was helplessly thrashing in the snow. For a moment he lay there panting, then again tried to break his bonds, the feeling of impotence making him howl. But the more he fought the ropes, the more they seemed to knot tighter. Finally he stopped fighting and lay back, trying to catch his breath, and looked around. He was surrounded. All the village was awake, dressed and armed. Obviously they had been waiting for him. Never had he seen or felt so much hatred.

It took five men to lift him and half carry, half drag him into the meeting hut and throw him roughly on the dirt floor in front of Sheik Bayazid who sat cross-legged on skins in his place of honour near the fire. The hut was large, smoke-blackened and filled with tribesmen.

'So,' the Sheik said. 'So you dare to disobey me?'

Erikki lay still, gathering his strength. What was there to say?

'In the night one of my men came back from the Khan.' Bayazid was shaking with fury. 'Yesterday afternoon, on Khan's orders, my messenger's throat was cut against all the laws of chivalry! What do you say to that? His throat cut like a dog! Like a dog!'

'I . . . I can't believe the Khan would do that,' Erikki said helplessly. 'I can't believe it.'

'In all the Names of God, his throat was cut. He's dead and we're dishonoured. All of us, me! Disgraced, because of you!'

'The Khan's a devil. I'm sorry but I'm no –'

'We treated with the Khan honourably, and you honourably, you were spoils of war won from Khan's enemies and ours, you married to his daughter, and he's rich with more bags of gold than a goat has hairs. What's ten million rials to him? A piece of goat's shit. Worse, he's taken away our honour. God's death on him!'

A murmur went through those who watched and waited, not understanding the English but hearing the jagged barbs of anger.

Again the hissing venom: 'Insha' Allah! Now we release you as you want, on foot, and then we will hunt you. We will not kill you with bullets, nor will you see the sunset and your head will be a Khan's gift.' The Sheik recalled the punishment in his own tongue and waved his hand. Men surged forward.

'Wait, wait!' Erikki shouted as his fear thrust an idea at him.

'You wish to beg for mercy?' Bayazid said contemptuously. 'I thought you were a man – that's why I didn't order your throat cut while you sleep.'

'Not mercy, vengeance!' Then Erikki roared, 'Vengeance!' There was an astonished silence. 'For you and for me! Don't you deserve vengeance for such dishonour?'

The younger man hesitated. 'What trickery is this?'

'I can help you regain your honour – I alone. Let us sack the palace of the Khan and both be revenged on him.' Erikki prayed to his ancient gods to make his tongue golden.

'Are you mad?'

'The Khan is my enemy more than yours, why else would he disgrace both of us if not to infuriate you against me? I know the palace. I can get you and fifteen armed men into the forecourt in a split second an –'

'Madness,' the Sheik scoffed. 'Should we throw our lives away like hashish-infected fools? The Khan has too many guards.'

'Fifty-three on call within the walls, no more than four or five on duty at any one time. Are your fighters so weak they can't deal with fifty-three? We have surprise on our side. A sudden commando attack from the sky, a relentless charge to average your honour – I could get you in and out the same way in minutes. Abdollah Khan's sick, very sick, guards won't be prepared, nor the household. I know the way in, where he sleeps, everything . . .'

Erikki heard his voice pick up excitement, knowing it could be done: the violent flare over the walls and sudden touchdown, jumping out, leading the way up the steps and in, up the staircase on to the landing, down the corridor, knocking aside Ahmed and whoever stood in the way, into the Khan's room, then stepping aside for Bayazid and his men to do what they wanted, somehow getting to the north wing and Azadeh and saving her, and if she was not there or hurt, then killing and killing, the Khan, guards, these men, everyone.

His plan possessed him now. 'Wouldn't your name last a thousand years because of your daring? Sheik Bayazid, he who dared to humble, to challenge the Khan of all the Gorgons inside his lair for a matter of honour? Wouldn't minstrels sing songs about you for ever at the campfires of all the Kurds? Isn't that what Saladin the Kurd would do?'

He saw the eyes in the firelight glowing differently now, saw Bayazid hesitate, the silence growing, heard him talk softly to his people – then one man laughed and called out something that others echoed and then, with one voice, they roared approval.

Willing hands cut him loose. Men fought viciously for the privilege of being on the raid. Erikki's fingers trembled as he pressed Engine Start. The first of the jets exploded into life.

*   *   *

903

In the Palace of the Khan: 6:35 A.M. Hakim came out of sleep violently. His bodyguard near the door was startled. 'What is it, Highness?'

'Nothing, nothing, Ishtar, I was . . . I was just dreaming.' Now that he was wide awake, Hakim lay back and stretched luxuriously, eager for the new day. 'Bring me coffee. After my bath, breakfast here – and ask my sister to join me.'

'Yes, Highness, at once.'

His bodyguard left him. Again he stretched his taut body. Dawn was murky. The room ornate and vast and draughty and chilly but the bedroom of the Khan. In the huge fireplace a fire burned brightly, fed by the guard through the night, no one else allowed in, the guard chosen by him personally from the fifty-three within the palace, pending a decision about their future. Where to find those to be trusted, he asked himself, then got out of bed, wrapping the warm brocade dressing gown tighter – one of a half a hundred that he had found in the wardrobe – faced Mecca and the open Koran in the ornately tiled niche, knelt and said the first prayer of the day. When he had finished he stayed there, his eyes on the ancient Koran, immense, bejewelled, hand calligraphed and without price, the Gorgon Khan's Koran – *his* Koran. So much to thank God for, he thought, so much still to learn, so much still to do – but a wonderful beginning already made.

Not long after midnight yesterday, before all the assembled family in the house, he had taken the carved emerald and gold ring – symbol of the ancient Khanate – from the index finger of his father's right hand and put it on his own. He had had to fight the ring over a roll of fat and close his nostrils to the stink of death that hung in the room. His excitement had overcome his revulsion, and now he was truly Khan. Then all the family present knelt and kissed his ringed hand, swearing allegiance, Azadeh proudly first, next Aysha trembling and frightened, then the others, Najoud and Mahmud outwardly abject, secretly blessing God for the reprieve.

Then downstairs in the Great Room with Azadeh standing behind him, Ahmed and the bodyguards also swore allegiance – the rest of the far-flung family would come later, along with other tribal leaders, personal and household staff and servants. At once he had given orders for the funeral and then he allowed his eyes to see Najoud. 'So.'

'Highness,' Najoud said unctuously, 'with all our hearts, before God, we congratulate you, and swear to serve you to the limits of our power.'

'Thank you, Najoud,' he had said. 'Thank you. Ahmed, what was the Khan's sentence decreed on my sister and her family before he died?' Tension in the Great Room was sudden.

'Banishment, penniless to the wastelands north of Meshed, Highness, under guard – at once.'

'I regret, Najoud, you and all your family will leave at dawn as decreed.'

He remembered how her face had gone ashen and Mahmud's ashen and she had stammered, 'But, Highness, now you are Khan, your word is our law. I did not expect . . . you're Khan now.'

'But the Khan, our father, gave the order when he was the law, Najoud. It is not correct to overrule him.'

'But you're the law now,' Najoud had said with a sickly smile. 'You do what's right.'

'With God's help I will certainly try, Najoud. I can't overrule my father on his deathbed.'

'But, Highness . . .' Najoud had come closer. 'Please, may . . . may we discuss this in private?'

'Better here before the family, Najoud. What did you want to say?'

She had hesitated and come even closer and he felt Ahmed tense and saw his knife hand ready, and the hair on his neck stiffened. 'Just because Ahmed *says* that the Khan gave such an order doesn't mean that it . . . does it?' Najoud had tried to whisper but her words echoed off the walls.

Breath sighed out of Ahmed's lips. 'May God burn me for ever if I lied.'

'I know you didn't, Ahmed,' Hakim had said sadly. 'Wasn't I there when the Khan decided? I was there, Najoud, so was Her Highness, my sister, I regret th –'

'But you can be merciful!' Najoud had cried out. 'Please, please be merciful!'

'Oh but I am, Najoud. I forgive you. But the punishment was for lying in the Name of God,' he had said gravely, 'not punishment for lying about my sister and me, causing us years of grief, losing us our father's love. Of course we forgive you that, don't we, Azadeh?'

'Yes, yes, that is forgiven.'

'That is forgiven openly. But lying in the Name of God? The Khan made a decree. I cannot go against it.'

Mahmud burst out over her pleadings, 'I knew nothing about this, Highness, nothing, I swear before God, I believed her lies. I divorce her formally for being a traitor to you, I never knew anything about her lies!'

In the Great Room everyone watched them both grovel, some loathing them, some despising them for failing when they had had the power. 'At dawn, Mahmud, you are banished, you and your family,' he had said so sadly, 'penniless, under guard . . . pending my pleasure. As to divorce it is forbidden in my house. If you wish to do that north of Meshed . . . Insha'Allah. You are still banished there, pending my pleasure . . .'

Oh you were perfect, Hakim, he told himself delightedly, for of course everyone knew this was your first test. You were perfect! Never once did you gloat openly or reveal your true purpose, never once did you raise your voice, keeping calm and gentle and grave as though you really were sad with your father's sentence but, rightly, unable to overrule it. And the benign, sweet promise of 'pending my pleasure'? My pleasure's that you're all banished for ever and if I hear one tiny threat of a plot, I will snuff you all out as quickly as an old candle. By God and the Prophet, on whose Name be Praise, I'll make the ghost of my father proud of this Khan of all the Gorgons – may he be in hell for believing such wanton lies of an evil old hag.

So much to thank God for, he thought, mesmerised by the firelight flickering in the Koran's jewels. Didn't all the years of banishment teach you secretiveness, deception and patience? Now you've your power to cement, Azerbaijan to defend, a world to conquer, wives to find, sons to breed and a lineage to begin. May Najoud and her whelps rot!

At dawn he had 'regretfully' gone with Ahmed to witness their departure. Wistfully he had insisted that none of the rest of the family see them off. 'Why increase their sorrow and mine?' There, on his exact instructions, he had watched Ahmed and guards tear through their mountains of bags, removing anything of value until there was but one suitcase each for them and their three children who watched, petrified.

'Your jewellery, woman,' Ahmed had said.

'You've taken everything, everything . . . please, Hakim . . . Highness, please . . .' Najoud sobbed. Her special jewel satchel, secreted in a pocket of her suitcase, had already been added to the pile of valuables. Abruptly Ahmed reached out and ripped off her pendant and tore the neck of her dress open. A dozen necklaces weighed her down, diamonds, rubies, emeralds and sapphires.

'Where did you get these?' Hakim had said, astonished.

'They're . . . they're my . . . my mother's and mine I bought over the ye—' Najoud stopped as Ahmed's knife came out. 'All right . . . all right . . .' Frantically she pulled the necklaces over her head, unfastened the rest and gave them to him. 'Now you have everyth –'

'Your rings!'

'But Highness leave me someth—' She screamed as Ahmed impatiently grabbed a finger to cut it off with the ring still on it, but she pulled away, tore the rings off and also the bracelets secreted up her sleeve, howling with grief, and threw them on the floor. 'Now you've everything . . .'

'Now pick them up and hand them to His Highness, on your knees!' Ahmed hissed and when she did not obey instantly, he grabbed her by the hair and shoved her face on the floor, and now she was grovelling and obeying.

Ah, that was a feast, Hakim thought, reliving every second of their humiliation. After they're dead, God will burn them.

He made another obeisance, put God away until next prayer at noon and jumped up, brimming with energy. A maid was on her knees pouring the coffee, and he saw the fear in her eyes and was very pleased. The moment he became Khan, he had known it was vital to work quickly to take over the reins of power. Yesterday morning he had inspected the palace. The kitchen was not clean enough for him, so he had had the chef beaten senseless and put outside the walls, then promoted the second chef in his place with dire warnings. Four guards were banished for oversleeping, two maids whipped for slovenliness. 'But, Hakim, my darling,' Azadeh had said when they were alone, 'surely there was no need to beat them?'

'In a day or two there won't be,' he had told her. 'Meanwhile the palace *will* change to the way I want it.'

'Of course you know best, my darling. What about the ransom?'

'Ah yes, at once.' He had sent for Ahmed.

'I regret, Highness, the Khan your father ordered the messenger's throat cut yesterday afternoon.'

Both he and Azadeh had been appalled. 'But that's terrible! What can be done now?' she had cried out.

Ahmed said, 'I will try to contact the tribesmen – perhaps, because now the Khan your father is dead they will . . . they will treat with you newly. I will try.'

Sitting there in the Khan's place, Hakim had seen Ahmed's suave confidence and realised the trap he was in. Fear swept up from his bowels. His fingers were toying with the emerald ring on his finger. 'Azadeh, come back in half an hour, please.'

'Of course,' she said obediently and when he was alone with Ahmed, he said, 'What arms do you carry?'

'A knife and an automatic, Highness.'

'Give them to me.' He remembered how his heart had throbbed and there was an unusual dryness in his mouth but this had had to be done and done alone. Ahmed had hesitated then obeyed clearly not pleased to be disarmed. But Hakim had pretended not to notice, just examined the action of the gun and cocked it thoughtfully. 'Now listen carefully, Counsellor: you won't *try* to contact the tribesmen, you will do it very quickly and you will make arrangements to have my sister's husband returned safely – on your head, by God and the Prophet of God!'

'I – of course, Highness.' Ahmed tried to keep the anger off his face.

Lazily Hakim pointed the gun at his head, sighting down it. 'I swore by God to treat you as first counsellor and I will – while you live.' His smile twisted. 'Even if you happen to be crippled, perhaps emasculated, even blinded by your enemies. Do you have enemies, Ahmed Dursak the Turkoman?'

Ahmed laughed, at ease now, pleased with the *man* who had become Khan and not the whelp that he had imagined – so much easier to deal with a man, he thought, his confidence returning. 'Many, Highness, many. Isn't it custom to measure the quality of a man by the importance of his enemies? Insha' Allah! I didn't know you knew how to handle guns.'

'There are many things you don't know about me, Ahmed,' he had said with grim satisfaction, an important victory gained. He had handed him back the knife, but not the automatic. 'I'll keep this as pishkesh. For a year and a day don't come into my presence armed.'

'Then how can I protect you, Highness?'

'With wisdom.' He had allowed a small measure of the violence he had kept pent up for years to show. 'You have to prove yourself. To me. To me alone. What pleased my father won't necessarily please me. This is a new era, with new opportunities, new dangers. Remember, by God, the blood of my father rests easily in my veins.'

The remainder of the day and well into the evening he had received men of importance from Tabriz and Azerbaijan and asked questions of them, about the insurrection and the leftists, the mujhadin and fedayeen and other factions. Bazaaris had arrived and mullahs and two ayatollahs, local army commanders and his cousin, the chief of police, and he had confirmed the man's appointment. All of them had brought suitable pishkesh.

And so they should, he thought, very satisfied, remembering their contempt in the past when his fortune had been zero and his banishment to Khvoy common knowledge. Their contempt will be very costly to every last one.

'Your bath is ready, Highness, and Ahmed's waiting outside.'

'Bring him in, Ishtar. You stay.' He watched the door open. Ahmed was tired and crumpled.

'Salaam, Highness.'

'What about the ransom?'

'Late last night I found the tribesmen. There were two of them. I explained that Abdollah Khan was dead and the new Khan had ordered me to give them half the ransom asked at once as a measure of faith, promising them the remainder when the pilot is safely back. I sent them north in one of our cars with a trusted driver and another car to follow secretly.'

'Do you know who they are, where their village is?'

'They told me they were Kurds, one named Ishmud, the other Alilah, their chief al-Drah and their village was called Broken Tree in the mountains north of Khvoy – I'm sure all lies, Highness, and they're not Kurds though they claim to be. I'd say they were just tribesmen, bandits mostly.'

'Good. Where did you get the money to pay them?'

'The Khan, your father, put twenty million rials into my safekeeping against emergencies.'

'Bring the balance to me before sunset.'

'Yes, Highness.'

'Are you armed?'

Ahmed was startled. 'Only with my knife, Highness.'

'Give it to me,' he said, hiding his pleasure that Ahmed had fallen into the trap he had set for him, accepting the knife, hilt first. 'Didn't I tell you not to come into my presence armed for a year and a day?'

'But as . . . you gave my knife back to me I thought . . . I thought the knife . . .' Ahmed stopped, seeing Hakim standing in front of him, knife held correctly, eyes dark and hard and the pattern of the father. Behind him, the guard Ishtar watched open mouthed. The hackles on Ahmed's neck twisted, 'Please excuse me, Highness, I thought I had your permission,' he said in real fear.

For a moment Hakim Khan just stared at Ahmed, the knife poised in his hand, then he slashed upwards. With great skill only the point of the blade went through Ahmed's coat, touched the skin but only enough to score it then came out again in perfect position for the final blow. But Hakim did not make it, though he wanted to see blood flow and this a good time, but not the perfect time. He still had need of Ahmed.

'I give you back your . . . your body.' He chose the word and all it implied with great deliberation. 'Intact, just-this-once.'

'Yes, Highness, thank you, Highness,' Ahmed muttered, astonished that he was still alive, and went down on his knees. 'I . . . it will never happen again.'

'No, it won't. Stay there. Wait outside, Ishtar.' Hakim Khan sat back on the cushions and toyed with the knife, waiting for the adrenalin to subside, remembering that vengeance was a dish best eaten cold. 'Tell me everything you know about the Soviet, this man called Mzytryk: what holds he had over my father, my father over him.'

Ahmed obeyed. He told him what Hashemi Fazir had said in the 125, what the Khan had told him in secret over the years, about the dacha near Tbilisi that he too had visited, how the Khan contacted Mzytryk, their code words, what Hashemi Fazir had said and threatened, what was in Mzytryk's letter, what he had overheard and what he had witnessed a few days ago.

The air hissed out of Hakim's mouth. 'My father was going to take my sister to . . . he was going to take her to this dacha and give her to Mzytryk?'

'Yes, Highness, he even ordered me to send her north if . . . if he had to leave her for hospital in Tehran.'

'Send for Mzytryk. Urgently. Ahmed, do it now. At once.'

'Yes Highness,' Ahmed said and trembled at the contained violence. 'Best, at the same time, best to remind him of his promises to Abdollah Khan, that you expect them fulfilled.'

'Good, very good. You've told me everything?'

'Everything I can remember now,' Ahmed told him sincerely. 'There must be other things – in time I can tell you all manner of secrets, Khan of all the Gorgons, and I swear again before God to serve you faithfully.' I'll tell you everything, he thought fervently, except the manner of the Khan's death and that now, more than ever, I want Azadeh as wife. Some way I will make you agree – she'll be my only real protection against you, spawn of Satan!

Just Outside Tabriz: 7:20 A.M. Erikki's 212 came over the rise of the forest, inbound at max revs. All the way Erikki had been at treetop level, avoiding roads and airfields and towns and villages, his mind riveted on Azadeh and vengeance against Abdollah Khan, all else forgotten. Now, suddenly ahead, the city was rushing towards them. As suddenly a vast unease washed over him.

'Where's the palace, pilot?' Sheik Bayazid shouted gleefully, 'where is it?'

'Over the ridge, agha,' he said into the boom mike, part of him wanting to add, We'd better rethink this, decide if the attack's wise, the other part shouting This's the only chance you've got, Erikki, you can't change plans, but how in the hell're you going escape with Azadeh from the palace and from this bunch of maniacs? 'Tell your men to fasten their seat belts, to wait until the skids touch down, not to take off their safety catches until they're on the ground and spread out, tell two of them to guard the chopper and protect it with their lives. I'll count down from "ten" for the landing and . . . and I'll lead.'

'Where's the palace, I can't see it.'

'Over the ridge, a minute away – tell them!' The trees were blurring as he went closer to them, his eyes on the col in the mountain ridge, horizon twisting. 'I want a gun,' he said, sick with anticipation.

Bayazid bared his teeth. 'No gun until we possess the palace.'

'Then I won't need one,' he said with a curse. 'I've got to ha –'

'You can trust me, you have to. Where's this palace of the Gorgons?'

'There!' Erikki pointed to the ridge just above them, 'Ten . . . nine . . . eight . . .'

He had decided to come in from the east, partially covered by the forests, city well to his right, the col protecting him. Fifty yards to go. His stomach tightened.

The rocks hurtled at them. He felt more than saw Bayazid cry out and hold up his hands to protect himself against the inevitable crash, then Erikki slid through the col and swung down, straight for the walls. At the exact last moment he cut all power, hauled the chopper up over the wall with inches to spare, flaring into an emergency stop procedure, banked slightly for the forecourt and let her fall out of the air, cushioned the fall perfectly and set down on the tiles to skid forward a few yards with a screech, then stop. His right hand jerked the circuit breakers out, his left unsnapped the seat belt and shoved the door open and he was still easily first on the ground and rushing for the front steps. Behind him Bayazid was now following, the cabin doors open and men pouring out, falling over one another in their excitement, the rotor still turning but the engines dying.

As he reached the front door and swung it open, servants and an astonished guard came running up to see what all the commotion was about. Erikki tore the assault rifle out of his hands, knocked him unconscious. The servants scattered and fled, a few recognising him. For the moment the corridor ahead was clear. 'Come on!' he shouted, then as Bayazid and some of the others joined him, rushed down the hallway and up the staircase towards the landing. A guard poked his head over the banister, levelled his gun but tribesmen peppered him. Erikki jumped over the body and rushed the corridor.

A door opened ahead. Another guard came out, gun blazing. Erikki felt bullets slice through his parka but he was untouched, Bayazid blew the man against the doorjamb, and together they charged past towards the Khan's room. Once there Erikki kicked the door open. Sustained gunfire came at him, missed him and the Sheik but caught the man next to him and spun the man around. The others scattered for cover and the badly hurt tribesman went forward towards the tormentor, taking more bullets and more but firing back even after he was dead.

For a second or two there was a respite, then to Erikki's shock Bayazid pulled the pin out of a grenade and tossed it through the doorway. The explosion was huge. Smoke billowed out into the corridor. At once Bayazid leaped through the opening, gun levelled, Erikki beside him.

The room was wrecked, windows blown out, curtains ripped, the carpet bed torn apart, the remains of the guard crumpled against a wall. In the alcove at the far end of the huge room, half-covered from the main bedroom, the table was upended, a serving-maid moaning, and two inert bodies half buried under tablecloth and smashed dishes. Erikki's heart stopped as he recognised Azadeh. In panic he rushed over and shoved the debris off her – in passing noticed the other person was Hakim – lifted her into his arms, her hair flowing, and carried her into the light. His breathing did not start again until he was sure she was still alive – unconscious, only God knew how damaged, but alive. She wore a long blue cashmere peignoir that hid all of her, but promised everything. The tribesmen pouring into the room were swept by her beauty. Erikki took off his flight jacket and wrapped it around her, oblivious of them. 'Azadeh . . . Azadeh . . .'

'Who this, Pilot?'

Through his fog Erikki saw Bayazid was beside the wreckage. 'That's Hakim, my wife's brother. Is he dead?'

'No.' Bayazid looked around furiously. Nowhere else for the Khan to hide. His men were crowding through the doorway and he cursed them, ordering them to take up defensive positions at either end of the corridor and for others to go outside on to the wide patio and to guard that too. Then he scrambled over to Erikki and Azadeh and looked at her bloodless face and breasts and legs pressing against the cashmere, 'Your wife?'

'Yes.'

'She's not dead, good.'

'Yes, but only God knows if she's hurt. I've got to get a doctor . . .'

'Later, first we ha –'

912

'Now! She may die!'

'As God wants, Pilot,' Bayazid said, then shouted angrily, 'You said you knew everything, where the Khan would be, in the Name of God where is he?'

'These . . . these were his private quarters, agha, private, I've never seen anyone else here, heard of anyone else here, even his wife could only come here by invitation an—' A burst of firing outside stopped Erikki. 'He's got to be here if Azadeh and Hakim are here!'

'Where? Where can he hide?'

In turmoil Erikki looked around, settled Azadeh as best he could then rushed for the windows – they were barred, the Khan could not have escaped this way. From here, a defensible corner abutment of the palace, he could not see the forecourt or the chopper, only the best view of the gardens and orchards southward, past the walls to the city a mile or so distant below. No other guards threatening them yet. As he turned, his peripheral vision caught a movement from the alcove, he saw the automatic, shoved Bayazid out of the way of the bullet that would have killed him and lunged for Hakim who lay in the debris. Before other tribesmen could react he had the young man pinioned, the automatic out of his hand and was shouting at him, trying to get him to understand, 'You're safe, Hakim, it's me, Erikki, we're friends, we came to rescue you and Azadeh from the Khan . . . we came to rescue you!'

'Rescue me . . . rescue me from what?' Hakim was staring at him blankly, still numb, still dazed, blood seeping from a small wound in his head. 'Rescue?'

'From the Khan an—' Erikki saw terror come into the eyes, whirled and caught the butt of Bayazid's assault rifle just in time. 'Wait, agha, wait, it's not his fault, he's dazed . . . wait, he was . . . he was aiming at me not you, he'll help us. Wait!'

'Where's Abdollah Khan?' Bayazid shouted, his men beside him now, guns cocked and ready to kill. 'Hurry and tell me or you're both dead men!'

And when Hakim didn't answer at once, Erikki snarled, 'For God's sake, Hakim, tell him where he is or we're all dead.'

'Abdollah Khan's dead, he's dead . . . he died last night, no . . . the night before last. He died the night before last, near midnight . . .' Hakim said weakly and they stared at him with disbelief, his mind coming back slowly and he still could not understand why he was lying here, head pounding, legs numb, Erikki holding him when Erikki was kidnapped by tribesmen, when he was having breakfast with Azadeh,

913

then guns exploding and diving for cover, guards firing and then the explosion and half the ransom's already been paid.

Abruptly his mind cleared. 'In God's Name,' he gasped. He tried to get up and failed. 'Erikki, in God's Name why did you fight in here, half your ransom's been paid . . . why?'

Erikki got up angrily. 'There's no ransom, the messenger's throat was cut, Abdollah Khan had the man's throat cut!'

'But the ransom – half was paid, Ahmed did it last night!'

'Paid, paid to whom?' Bayazid snarled. 'What lies are these?'

'Not lies, half was paid last night, half paid by the new Khan as . . . as an act of faith for the . . . the mistake about the messenger. Before God, I swear it. Half's paid!'

'Lies,' Bayazid scoffed, and aimed the gun at him. 'Where's the Khan?'

'Not lies! Should I lie before God? I tell you before God! Before God! Send for Ahmed, send for the man Ahmed, he paid them.'

One of the tribesmen shouted something, Hakim blanched and repeated in Turkish: 'In the Name of God, half the ransom's already paid! Abdollah Khan's dead! He's dead and half the ransom was paid.' A murmur of astonishment went through the room. 'Send for Ahmed, he'll tell you the truth. Why are you fighting here, there's no reason to fight!'

Erikki rushed in: 'If Abdollah Khan's dead and half's been paid, agha, the other half promised, your honour's vindicated. Agha, please do as Hakim asks, send for Ahmed – he'll tell you who he paid and how.'

Fear in the room was very high now, Bayazid and his men hating the closeness here, wanting to be in the open, in the mountains, away from these evil people and place, feeling betrayed. But if Abdollah's dead and half's paid . . . 'Pilot, go and get his man Ahmed,' Bayazid said, 'and remember, if you cheat me, you will find your wife noseless.' He ripped the automatic out of Erikki's hand. 'Go and get him!'

'Yes, yes of course.'

'Erikki . . . first help me up,' Hakim said, his voice throaty and weak. Erikki was helplessly trying to make sense of all this as he lifted him easily and pushed through the men crowding near, and settled him on the sofa cushions beside Azadeh. Both saw her pallid face, but both also noticed her regular breathing. 'God be thanked,' Hakim muttered.

Then once more Erikki was half in nightmare, walking out of the room unarmed to the head of the stairs, shouting for Ahmed not to shoot, 'Ahmed, Ahmed, I've got to talk to you, I'm alone . . .'

Now he was downstairs and still alone, still no firing. Again he shouted for Ahmed but his words just echoed off the walls and he wandered into rooms, no one around, everyone vanished and then a gun was in his face, another in his back. Ahmed and a guard, both nervous.

'Ahmed, quick,' he burst out, 'is it true that Abdollah's dead and there's a new Khan and that half the ransom's paid?'

Ahmed just gaped at him.

'For Christ sake is it true?' he snarled.

'Yes, yes that's true. But th –'

'Quick, you've got to tell them!' Relief flooding over him for he had only half believed Hakim. 'Quick, they'll kill him and kill Azadeh – come on!'

'Then the . . . they're not dead?'

'No, of course not, come on!'

'Wait! What exactly did th . . . did His Highness say?'

'What the hell difference do –'

The gun jammed into Erikki's face. '*What did he say exactly?*'

Erikki searched his memory and told him as best he could, then added, 'Now for the love of God, come on!'

For Ahmed time stopped. If he went with the Infidel he would probably die, Hakim Khan would die, his sister would die and the Infidel who was responsible for all this trouble would probably escape with his devil tribesmen. But then, he thought, if I could persuade them to let the Khan live and his sister live, persuade them to leave the palace, I would have proved myself beyond all doubt, both to the Khan and to *her* and I can kill the pilot later. Or I can kill him now and escape easily and live – but only as a fugitive despised by all as one who betrayed his Khan. Insha' Allah!

His face creased into a smile. 'As God wants!' He took out his knife and gave it and his gun to the white-faced guard and walked around Erikki. 'Wait,' Erikki said. 'Tell the guard to send for a doctor. Urgently. Hakim and my wife . . . they may be hurt.'

Ahmed told the man to do it and went along the corridor and into the hall and up the staircase. On the landing tribesmen searched him roughly for arms then escorted him into the Khan's room, crowding after him, shoving him into the vast, empty space – Erikki they held at the door, a knife at his throat – and when Ahmed saw his Khan was truly alive, sitting bleakly on the cushions near Azadeh who was still unconscious, he muttered, 'Praise be to God,' and smiled at him. 'Highness,' he said calmly, 'I've sent for a doctor.' Then he picked out Bayazid.

'I am Ahmed Dursak the Turkoman,' he said proudly, speaking Turkish with great formality. 'In the Name of God: it's true that Abdollah Khan is dead, true that I paid half the ransom – five million rials – last night on the new Khan's behalf to two messengers of the chief al-Drah of the village of Broken Tree as an act of faith because of the unwarranted dishonour to your messenger ordered by the dead Abdollah Khan. Their names were Ishmud and Alilah and I hurried them north in a fine car.' A murmur of astonishment went through the room. There could be no mistake for all knew these false names, code names, given to protect the village and the tribe. 'I told them, on behalf of the new Khan, the second half would be paid the moment the pilot and his air machine were released safely.'

'Where is this new Khan, if he exists?' Bayazid scoffed. 'Let him talk for himself.'

'I am Khan of all the Gorgons,' Hakim said and there was a sudden silence. 'Hakim Khan, eldest son of Abdollah Khan.'

All eyes left him and went to Bayazid who noticed the blank astonishment on Erikki's face. He scowled, unsure. 'Just because you say it doesn't mean th –'

'You call me a liar in my own house?'

'I only say to this man,' Bayazid jerked a thumb at Ahmed, 'just because he says he paid the ransom, half of it, does not mean he paid it and did not then have them ambushed and killed – like my other messenger, by God!'

Ahmed said venomously, 'I told you the truth before God, and say again before God that I sent them north, safely with the money. Give me a knife, you take a knife, and I will show you what a Turkoman does to a man who calls him liar!' The tribesmen were horrified that their leader had put himself into such a bad position. 'You call me a liar and my Khan liar?'

In the silence Azadeh stirred and moaned, distracting them. At once Erikki began to go to her but the knife never wavered, the tribesman muttered a curse and he stopped. Another little moaning sigh that almost drove him mad, then he saw Hakim awkwardly move closer to his sister and hold her hand and this helped him a little.

Hakim was afraid, aching everywhere, knowing he was as defenceless as she was defenceless and needing a doctor urgently, that Ahmed was under siege, Erikki impotent, his own life threatened and his Khanate in ruins. Nonetheless he gathered his courage back. I didn't outfox Abdollah Khan and Najoud and Ahmed to concede victory to these dogs! Implacably he looked up at Bayazid. 'Well? Do you call Ahmed a liar – yes or no?' he said harshly in Turkish so all could understand him and Ahmed loved him for his courage. All eyes now on Bayazid. 'A *man* must answer that question. Do you call him a liar?'

'No,' Bayazid muttered. 'He spoke the truth, I accept it as truth.' Someone said, 'Insha'Allah,' fingers loosened off triggers but nervousness did not leave the room.'

'As God wants,' Hakim said, his relief hidden, and rushed onward, every moment more in command. 'More fighting will achieve nothing. So, half the ransom is already paid and the other half promised when the pilot is released safely. The . . .' He stopped as nausea threatened to overwhelm him but dominated it, easier this time than before. 'The pilot's there and safe and so is his machine. Therefore I will pay the rest at once!'

He saw the greed and promised himself vengeance on all of them. 'Ahmed, over by the table, Najoud's satchel's somewhere there.' He watched Ahmed shove through the tribesmen arrogantly, to begin searching the debris for the soft leather purse he had been showing to Azadeh just before the attack began, happily telling her the jewels were family heirlooms that Najoud had admitted stealing and, in complete contrition, had given him before she left. 'I'm glad you didn't relent, Hakim, very glad,' Azadeh had said. 'You'd never be safe with her and her brood close to you.'

I'll never be safe again, he thought without fear, concentrating on Ahmed. I'm glad I left Ahmed whole, he thought, and glad we had the sense, Azadeh and I, to stay in the alcove under cover of the wall at the first sound of firing. If we'd been here in the room . . . Insha' Allah. His fingers gripped her wrist and the warmth pleased him, her breathing still regular. 'God be praised,' he murmured then noticed the men threatening Erikki. 'You,' he pointed imperiously at them, 'let the pilot go!' Nonplussed the rough, bearded men looked at Bayazid who nodded. At once Erikki went through them to Azadeh, eased his heavy sweater away to give him readier access to the knife in the centre of his back, then knelt, holding her hand, and faced Bayazid, his bulk protecting her and Hakim.

'Highness!' Ahmed gave Hakim Khan the purse. Leisurely he opened it, spilling the jewels into his hands. Emeralds and diamonds and sapphires, necklaces, encrusted golden bracelets, pendants. A great sigh went through the room. Judiciously Hakim chose a ruby necklace worth ten to fifteen million rials, pretending not to notice how all eyes were concentrated and the almost physical smell of greed that permeated the room. Abruptly he discarded the rubies and chose a pendant worth twice as much, three times as much.

'Here,' he said still speaking Turkish, 'here is full payment.' He held up the diamond pendant and offered it to Bayazid who, mesmerised by the fire glittering from the single stone, came forward, his hand out. But before Bayazid could take it, Hakim closed his fist. 'Before God you accept it as full payment?'

'Yes . . . yes, as full payment, before God,' Bayazid muttered, never believing that God would grant him so much wealth – enough to buy herds and guns and grenades and silks and warm clothes. He held out his hand, 'I swear it before God!'

'And you will leave here at once, in peace, before God?'

Bayazid pulled his brain off his riches. 'First we have to get to our village, agha, we need the airplane and the pilot.'

'No, by God, the ransom's for the safe return of the airplane and the pilot, nothing more.' Hakim opened his hand, never taking his eyes off Bayazid who now only saw the stone. 'Before God?'

Bayazid and his men stared at the liquid fire in the rock steady hand. 'What's . . . what's to prevent me taking all of them, everything,' he said sullenly, 'what's to prevent me killing you – killing you and burning the palace and taking her hostage to force the pilot, eh?'

'Nothing. Except honour. Are Kurds without honour?' Hakim's voice rasped and he was thinking, how exciting this is, life the prize and death for failure. 'This is more than full payment.'

'I . . . I accept it before God as payment in full, for the pilot and the . . . and the airplane.' Bayazid tore his eyes off the gem. 'For the pilot and the airplane. But for you, you and the woman . . .' The sweat was trickling down his face. So much wealth there, his mind was shouting, so much, so easy to take, so easy but there is honour in this, oh yes, very much. 'For you and the woman there should be a fair ransom too.'

Outside a car gunned its engine. Men rushed to the broken window. The car was racing for the main gate and as they watched, it hurtled through, heading for the city below.

'Quick,' Bayazid said to Hakim, 'make up your mind.'

'The woman is worthless,' Hakim said, afraid of the lie, aware that he had to bargain or they were still lost. His fingers chose a ruby bracelet and offered it. 'Agreed?'

'To you the woman may be worthless – not to the pilot. The bracelet and the necklace, that one, together with the bracelet with the green stones.'

'Before God that's too much,' Hakim exploded, 'this bracelet's more than enough – that's more than the value of the pilot and the airplane!'

918

'Son of a burnt father! This one, the necklace and that other bracelet, the one with the green stones!'

They haggled back and forth, angrier and angrier, everyone listening intently except Erikki who was still locked in his own private hell, only concerned with Azadeh and where was the doctor and how he could help her and help Hakim. His hand was stroking her hair, his nerves pushed near the breaking point by the enraged voices of the two men as they reached the crescendo, the insults even more violent. Then Hakim judged the moment right and let out a wail that was also part of the game of bargaining. 'You're too good a negotiator for me, by God! You'll beggar me! Here, my final offer!' He put the diamond bracelet and the smaller of the emerald necklaces and the heavy gold bracelet on to the carpet. 'Do we agree?'

It was a fair price now, not as much as Bayazid wanted but far more than he had expected. 'Yes,' he said and scooped up his prize and contentment filled the room. 'You swear by God not to pursue us? Not to attack us?'

'Yes, yes, before God.'

'Good. Pilot, I need you to take us home . . .' Bayazid said in English now and saw the rage soar into Hakim's face and added hastily, 'I ask, not order, agha. Here,' he offered Erikki the gold bracelet, 'I wish to hire your services, this's paym—' He stopped and looked up as one of his men guarding the patio, called out urgently, 'There's a car coming up from the city!'

Bayazid was sweating more now. 'Pilot, I swear by God I'll not harm you.'

'There's not enough gasoline.'

'Then not all the way, halfway, just halfw –'

'There's not enough gasoline.'

'Then take us and drop us in the mountains – just a little way. I ask you – not order,' Bayazid said, then added curiously, 'By the Prophet I treated you fairly and him fairly and . . . have not molested her. I ask you.'

They had all heard the threat under the voice, perhaps a threat, perhaps not, but Erikki knew beyond any doubt that the fragile bubble of 'honour' or 'before God' would vanish with the first bullet, that it was up to him now to try to correct the disaster that the attack had become, chasing a Khan already dead, the ransom already half paid, and now Azadeh lying there, hurt as only God knows, and Hakim almost killed. Set-faced he touched her a last time, glanced at the Khan, nodded, half to himself, then got up, abruptly jerked the Sten gun out

919

of the nearest tribesman's hands. 'I'll accept your word before God and I'll kill you if you cheat. I'll drop you north of the city, in the mountains. Everyone in the chopper. Tell them!'

Bayazid hated the idea of the gun in the hands of this brooding, revenge-seeking monster. Neither of us has forgotten I threw the grenade that perhaps has killed this Houri, he thought. 'Insha' Allah!' Quickly he ordered the retreat. Taking the body of their dead comrade with them, they obeyed. 'Pilot, we will leave together. Thank you, Agha Hakim Khan. God be with you,' he said and backed to the door, weapon held loosely, but ready. 'Come on!'

Erikki raised his hand in farewell to Hakim, consumed with anguish at what he has precipitated. 'Sorry . . .'

'God be with you, Erikki, and come back safely,' Hakim called out and Erikki felt better for that. 'Ahmed, go with him, he can't fly and use a gun at the same time. See that he gets back safely.' Yes, he thought, icily, I've still a score to settle with him for the attack on *my* palace!

'Yes, Highness. Thank you, Pilot.' Ahmed took the gun from Erikki, checked the action and magazine, then smiled crookedly at Bayazid. 'By God and the Prophet, on whose Name be Praise, let no man cheat.' Politely he motioned Erikki to leave, then followed him. Bayazid went last.

At the Foothills to the Palace: 11:05 A.M. The police car was racing up the winding road towards the gates, other cars and an army lorry filled with troops following. Hashemi Fazir and Armstrong were in the back of the lead car which skidded through the gate into the forecourt where an ambulance and other cars were already parked. They got out and followed the guard into the Great Room. Hakim Khan was waiting for them in his place of honour, pale and drawn but regal, guards around him, this part of the palace undamaged.

'Highness, God be praised you were not hurt – we've just heard about the attack. May I introduce myself? I'm Colonel Hashemi Fazir of Inner Intelligence and this is Superintendent Armstrong who has assisted us for years and is an expert in certain areas that could concern you – he speaks Farsi by the way. Would you please tell us what happened?' The two men listened intently as Hakim Khan related his version of the attack – they had already heard the rumoured details – both of them impressed with his bearing.

Hashemi had come prepared. Before leaving Tehran yesterday evening he had meticulously gone through Hakim's files. For years both he and SAVAK had had him under surveillance in Khvoy: 'I know how much he owes and to whom, Robert, what favours and to whom, what he likes to eat and read, how inept he is with gun, piano or a knife, every women he's ever bedded and every boy.'

Armstrong had laughed. 'What about his politics?'

'He has none. Unbelievable – but true. He's Iranian, Azerbaijani and yet he hasn't joined any group, taken any sides, none, not said anything even a little seditious – even against Abdollah Khan – and Khvoy's always been a festering bed of nettles.'

'Religion?'

'Shi'ite, but calm, conscientious, orthodox, neither right nor left. Ever since he was banished, no, that's not quite true, since he was seven when his mother died and he and his sister went to live in the palace, he's been a feather wafted by his father's merest breath, waiting in fear for inevitable disaster. As God wants, but it's a miracle he's Khan, a miracle that that vile son of a dog died before doing him and his sister harm. Strange! One moment his head's on the block, and now he controls untold riches, untold power and I've got to deal with him.'

'That should be easy – if what you say's true.'

'You're suspicious, always suspicious – is that the strength of the English?'

'Just the lesson an old cop's learned over the years.'

Hashemi had smiled to himself and now he did it again, concentrating on the young man, Khan of all the Gorgons, in front of him, watching him closely, studying him for clues. What're your secrets – you've got to have secrets!

'Highness, how long ago did the pilot leave?' Armstrong was asking.

Hakim glanced at his watch. 'About two and a half hours ago.'

'Did he say how much fuel he had with him?'

'No, only that he would take them a little way and drop them.'

Hashemi and Robert Armstrong were standing in front of the raised platform with its rich carpets and cushions, Hakim Khan dressed formally in warm brocades, a string of pearls around his neck with a diamond pendant four times the size of the one he had bartered their lives for. 'Perhaps,' Hashemi said delicately, 'perhaps, Highness, the pilot was really in league with the Kurdish tribesmen, and won't come back.'

'No, and they weren't Kurds though they claimed to be, just bandits, and they'd kidnapped Erikki and forced him to lead them against the Khan, my father.' The young Khan frowned then said firmly, 'The Khan my father should not have had their messenger killed. He should have bartered the ransom down then paid it – and then had them killed for their impertinence.'

Hashemi docketed the clue. 'I will see they are all hunted down.'

'And all my property recovered.'

'Of course. Is there anything, anything at all, I or my department can do for you?' He was watching the young man closely and saw, or thought he saw, a flash of sardonic amusement and it rattled him. At that moment the door opened and Azadeh came in. He had never met her though he had seen her many times. She should be possessed by an Iranian, he thought, not by a rotten foreigner. How could she contain that monster? He did not notice Hakim scrutinising him as intently. Armstrong did, watching the Khan without watching him.

She was dressed in Western clothes, grey green that set off her green-flecked eyes, stockings and soft shoes – her face very pale and made up just enough. Her walk was slow and somewhat painful, but she bowed to her brother with a sweet smile, 'Sorry to interrupt you, Highness, but the doctor asked me to remind you to rest. He's about to leave, would you like to see him again?'

'No, no thank you. You're all right?'

'Oh, yes,' she said and forced a smile. 'He says I'm fine.'

'May I present Colonel Hashemi Fazir and Mr. Armstrong, Super-intendent Armstrong – Her Highness, my sister, Azadeh.'

They greeted her and she greeted them back. 'Superintendent Arm-strong?' she said in English with a little frown, 'I don't remember "Superintendent" but we've met before, haven't we?'

'Yes, Highness, once at the French Club, last year. I was with Mr. Talbot of the British embassy and a friend of your husband's from the Finnish embassy, Christian Tollonen – I believe it was your husband's birthday party.'

'You've a good memory, Superintendent.'

Hakim Khan smiled strangely. 'That's a characteristic of MI6, Azadeh.'

'Just of ex-policemen, Highness,' Armstrong said easily. 'I'm just a consultant to Inner Intelligence,' then to Azadeh: 'Colonel Fazir and I were both so relieved that neither you or the Khan were hurt.'

'Thank you,' she said, her ears and head still aching badly and her back giving her problems. The doctor had said, 'We'll have to wait for a few days, Highness, although we will X-ray you both as soon as possible. Best you go to Tehran, both of you, they have better equipment. With an explosion like that . . . you never know, Highness, best to go, I wouldn't like to be responsible . . .'

Azadeh sighed, 'Please excuse me for interrup—' She stopped abruptly, listening, head slightly on its side. They listened too. Just the wind picking up and a distant car.

'Not yet,' Hakim said kindly.

She tried to smile and murmured, 'As God wants,' then went away.

Hashemi broke the small silence. 'We should leave you too, Highness,' he said deferentially, in Farsi again, 'it was kind of you to see us today. Perhaps we could come back tomorrow?' He saw the young Khan take his eyes off the door and look at him under his dark eyebrows, the handsome face in repose, fingers toying with the jewelled ornamental dagger at his belt. He must be made of ice, he thought, politely waiting to be dismissed.

But instead Hakim Khan dismissed all his guards, except one he stationed at the door, well out of listening range, and beckoned the two men closer. 'Now we will speak English. What is it you really want to ask me?' he said softly.

Hashemi sighed, sure that Hakim Khan already knew, and more than sure now that here he had a worthy adversary, or ally. 'Help on two matters, Highness: your influence in Azerbaijan could immeasurably help us to put down hostile elements in rebellion against the state.'

'What's the second?'

He had heard the touch of impatience and it amused him. 'Second is somewhat delicate. It concerns a Soviet called Oleg Petr Mzytryk, an acquaintance of your father, who for some years, from time to time, visited here – as Abdollah Khan visited his dacha in Tbilisi. Whilst Mzytryk posed as a friend of Abdollah Khan and Azerbaijan, in reality he's a very senior KGB officer and very hostile.'

'Ninety-eight out of every hundred Soviets who come to Iran are KGB, therefore enemy, and the other two GRU, therefore enemy. As Khan, my father would have to deal with all manner of enemies' – again a fleeting sardonic smile that Hashemi noted – 'all manner of friends and all those in between. So?'

'We would very much like to interview him.' Hashemi waited for some reaction but there was none and his admiration for the young man increased. 'Before Abdollah Khan died he had agreed to help us. Through him we heard the man intended secretly to come over the border last Saturday and again on Tuesday, but both times he did not appear.'

'How was he entering?'

Hashemi told him, not sure how much Hakim Khan knew, feeling his way with greater caution. 'We believe the man may contact you – if so, would you please let us know? Privately.'

Hakim Khan decided it was time to put this Tehrani enemy and his British dog lackey in place. Son of a burnt father, am I so naive I don't know what's going on? 'In return for what?' he said bluntly.

Hashemi was equally blunt. 'What do you want?'

'First: all senior SAVAK and police officers in Azerbaijan put on suspension at once, pending review – by me – and all future appointments to be subject to my prior approval.'

Hashemi flushed. Not even Abdollah Khan had ever had this. 'What's second?' he asked dryly.

Hakim Khan laughed. 'Good, very good, agha. Second will wait until tomorrow or the next day, so will third and perhaps fourth. But about your first point, at 10 a.m. tomorrow bring me specific requests how I could help stop all fighting in Azerbaijan – and how you, personally, if you had the power, how you would . . .' he thought for a moment, then added, 'how you would make us safe against enemies from without, and safe from enemies from within.' He turned his attention to Armstrong.

Armstrong had been hoping the exchange would go on for ever, ecstatic that he was having the opportunity to witness this new Khan at first hand going against a hardened adversary like Hashemi. Great balls of fire, if this little bugger can operate so confidently like this on Day Two of becoming Khan after being almost blown to kingdom come a couple of hours ago, Her Majesty's Government better put him high on the 'S' danger list, 'Slowly, slowly catchee monkee'! Now he saw the eyes fix on him. With an effort he kept his face bland, groaning inwardly: Now it's your turn.

'You're an expert in what certain areas that would concern me?'

'Well, Your Highness, I, er, I was in Special Branch and understand a little about Intelligence and, er, counter intelligence. Of course good information, private information's essential to someone in your position. If you wanted, perhaps I could, in conjunction with Colonel Fazir, suggest ways to improve this for you.'

'A good thought, Mr. Armstrong. Please give me your views in writing – as soon as possible.'

'I'd be glad to.' Armstrong decided to gamble. 'Mzytryk could provide you rapidly with a lot of the answers you need, most of the important answers you need on the "within and without" you mentioned, particularly if Colonel Fazir could, er, chat with him in private.' The words hung in the air. Beside him, he saw Hashemi shift his feet nervously. I'll bet my life you know more than you're letting on, Hakim, me lad, and bet my balls you didn't spend all those years just a bloody 'feather'! Christ, I need a cigarette!

The eyes were boring into him and he would have loved to light up and say airily, For Christ's sake, stop all this sodding about and shit or get off the pot . . . Then his mind pictured this Khan of all the Gorgons squatting on a lavatory seat, everything hanging out, and he had to cough to stop his sudden laugh. 'Sorry,' he said, trying to sound meek.

Hakim Khan frowned. 'How would I have access to the information?' he said, and both men knew that he was hooked.

'However you want, Highness,' Hashemi said, 'however you want.'

Another small silence. 'I'll consider what y—' Hakim Khan stopped, listening. Now they all heard the approaching putt-putt of rotors and the sound of the jets. Both men started for the tall windows. 'Wait,' Hakim said. 'One of you please give me a hand.'

Astonished, they helped him stand. 'Thank you,' he said, painfully. 'That's better. It's my back. In the explosion I must have twisted it.' Hashemi took some of his weight and between them he hobbled to the tall windows that overlooked the forecourt.

The 212 was coming in slowly, drifting down to her landing. As she got closer they recognised Erikki and Ahmed in the front seats but Ahmed was slumped down, clearly hurt. A few bullet holes in the airframe, a great chunk of plastic out of a side window. Their concern increased. She settled into a perfect landing. At once the engines began to die. Now they saw the blood staining Erikki's white collar and sleeve.

'Christ . . .' Armstrong muttered.

'Agha,' Hakim Khan said urgently to Hashemi, 'see if you can stop the doctor leaving.' Instantly Hashemi rushed off.

From where they were they could see the front steps. The huge door opened and Azadeh ran out and stood there a moment, a statue, others gathering beside her now, guards and servants and some of the family. Erikki opened his side door and got out awkwardly. Tiredly he went towards her. But his walk was firm and tall and then she was in his arms.

In Kowiss Town: 12:10 P.M. Ibrahim Kyabi waited impatiently in ambush for the mullah Hussain to come out of the mosque into the crowded square. He sat slumped against the fountain opposite the huge door, his arms cradling the canvas bag that camouflaged his cocked M16. His eyes were red-rimmed with tiredness, his whole body aching from his six hundred-odd kilometre journey.

Idly he noticed a tall European among the crowds. The man was following a Green Band, and wore dark clothes, parka, and peaked cap. He watched the two of them bypass the mosque and disappear into the alley beside it. Nearby was the maw of the bazaar. Its darkness and warmth and safety tempted him to leave the cold.

'Insha'Allah,' he muttered automatically, then dully reminded himself to stop using that expression, pulled the old overcoat closer around him, and settled more comfortably against the fountain that, when winter's ice had gone, would once more trickle for passersby to drink or ritually to wash their hands and faces before going to prayers.

'What's this mullah Hussain like?' he had asked the street vendor who was ladling him a portion of the steaming bean horisht out of the cauldron that hung over the charcoal. It was morning then and he had just arrived after interminable delays, fifteen hours overdue. 'What's he like?'

The man was old and toothless and he shrugged. 'A mullah.'

Another customer nearby swore at him. 'May you be sacrificed! Don't listen to him, stranger, the mullah Hussain is a true leader of the people, a man of God, who owns nothing but a gun and ammunition to kill the enemies of God.' Other customers echoed this unshaven youth and told about the taking of the airbase. 'Our mullah's a true follower of the Imam, he'll lead us into Paradise, by God.'

Ibrahim had almost cried out in rage. Hussain and all mullahs deserve death for feeding these poor peasants such nonsense. Paradise? Fine raiments and wine and forty perpetual virgins on silk couches?

I won't think of loving, I won't think of Sharazad, not yet.

His hands caressed the hidden strength of the gun. This took away some of his fatigue and hunger, but none of his utter loneliness.

Sharazad. Now part of a dream. Better this way, much better: he had been waiting for her at the coffee shop when Jari had accosted him and muttered, 'In the Name of God, the husband has returned. That which never began is finished for ever,' then had vanished into the crowds. At once he had left and fetched his gun and walked all the way to the bus station. Now he was waiting, soon to be martyred taking vengeance in the name of the Masses against blind tyranny. So soon now. Soon into blackness or into light, oblivion or understanding, alone or with others; prophets, imams, devils, who?

In ecstasy he closed his eyes. Soon I'll know what happens when we die and where we go. Do we, at long last, find the answer to the great riddle: Was Mohammed the last Prophet of God, or madman? Is the Koran true? Is there God?

In the alley beside the mosque, the Green Band leading Starke stopped and motioned towards a hovel. Starke stepped across the befouled joub and knocked. The door opened. 'Peace be upon you, Excellency Hussain!' he said in Farsi, tense and on guard. 'You sent for me?'

'Salaam, Captain. Yes, yes I did,' the mullah Hussain replied in English and motioned him to enter.

Starke had to stoop to go inside the one-room hut. Two babes were sleeping fitfully on their straw pallets on the dirt floor. A young boy stared back at him, hands clasped around an old rifle and he recognised him as the same child at the fight between Hussain's men and Zataki's men. A well serviced AK47 leaned against a wall. Over by the sink a nervous old woman in a black, stained chador sat on a rickety chair.

'These are my sons and this is my wife,' Hussain said.

'Salaam.' Starke hid his astonishment that she should be so old. Then he looked closer and saw the age was not in years.

'I sent for you for three reasons: first for you to see how a mullah lives. Poverty is one of a mullah's prime duties.'

'And learning, leadership and lawgiving. That apart, agha, I know you're a hundred percent sincere in your beliefs,' and trapped by them, Starke wanted to add, loathing this room with the terrible, never-ending poverty it represented, its stench and the helplessness that he knew need not be, but would exist for all the days of their lives here – and in countless other homes of all religions, all the world over. But not with my family, thank God! Thank God I was born Texan, thank God ten billion trillion times that I know better and my kids won't, *won't by God*, won't have to live in the dirt like these poor little critters. With an effort he stopped himself from brushing their flies away, wanting to curse Hussain for enduring that which need not be endured.

'You said three reasons, agha?'

'The second is: why are all but a few men scheduled to leave today?'

'They're long overdue leave, agha. Work's slow at the base, this's a perfect time.' Starke's anxiety increased. This morning, before he had been summoned here, there had already been three telexes and two calls on the HF from their HQ in Tehran, the last from Siamaki, now the ranking board member, demanding to know where Pettikin, Nogger Lane, and the others were. He had sluffed him off, saying that McIver would call him back the instant he arrived with Minister Kia, very conscious of Wazari's curiosity.

Yesterday had been the first he had heard of Ali Kia's visit. Charlie Pettikin, during his brief stopover outward bound for Al Shargaz, had told him what had happened to McIver and their fears about him. 'Jesus . . .' was all he could mutter.

But yesterday had not been all bad. John Hogg had brought Gavallan's provisional schedule for Whirlwind with codes and times and co-ordinates of refuelling alternates set up on the other side of the Gulf. 'Andy said to tell you they've all been passed on to Scrag at Lengeh and Rudi at Bandar-e Delam and to take into account the problems of all three bases,' Hogg had told him. 'Two 747 freighters are booked for Al Shargaz, dawn Friday. That'll give us plenty of time, Andy says. I'll bring another update when I come for the lads, Duke.

The final button's not to be pressed until 7 a.m. Friday or same time Saturday or Sunday. Then it's no go.'

None of Esvandiary's spies had been around so Starke had managed to squeeze another crate of very valuable 212 avionics aboard the 125. And there was more good luck: All their personnel exit permits were still valid, enough 40-gallon drums of fuel had been cached safely on the shore, and Tom Lochart had come in from Zagros on time, now a Whirlwind pilot. 'Why the change, Tom? Thought you were dead set against it,' he had said, perturbed by Lochart's manner. But his friend had just shrugged and he had left it at that.

Still, the thought of their 212s making a rush for it worried him very much. They had no real plan, just several possibilities. With an effort he concentrated, the room becoming increasingly claustrophobic. 'Sorry, agha, what did you say?'

'When will their replacements be arriving?'

'Saturday, that's when they're scheduled.'

'Esvandiary says you've been sending out many spares.'

'Spares need replacement and checking from time to time, agha.'

Hussain studied him, then nodded thoughtfully. 'What caused the accident that nearly killed Esvandiary?'

'The load shifted. It's a tricky operation.'

Another small silence. 'Who is this man Kia, Ali Kia?'

Starke was not expecting any of these questions, wondering if he was being tested again, and how much the mullah knew. 'I was told he was a minister for Prime Minister Bazargan on a tour of inspection.' Then added, 'Also that he was, or is, a consultant to our joint partnership, IHC, maybe even a director, but I don't know about that.'

'When is he arriving?'

'I'm not sure. Our director, Captain McIver, was ordered to escort him.'

'Ordered?'

'Ordered, so I understand.'

'Why should a Minister be a consultant to a private company?'

'I imagine you'd have to ask him, agha.'

'Yes, I agree,' Hussain's face hardened. 'The Imam has sworn that corruption will cease. We'll go to the base together.' He picked up the AK47 and slung it over his shoulder. 'Salaam,' he said to his family.

Starke and the Green Band followed Hussain along the alley to a side door of the mosque. There the mullah kicked off his shoes, picked them up and went inside. Starke and the Green Band did the same, except that Starke also took off his peaked hat. Along a passageway and

929

through another door and then they were in the mosque itself, a single room under the dome, covered with carpets and no ornaments. Just decorative tiles, here and there, with exquisite inlaid Farsi quotations from the Koran. A lectern with an open Koran, nearby a modern cassette player and loudspeakers, wires carelessly strung, all electric lights bare and dim. From the loudspeakers came the muted singsong of a man reading from the Koran.

Men were praying, others gossiping, some sleeping. Those who saw Hussain smiled at him and he smiled back, leading the way to a columned alcove. There he stopped and put down his shoes and gun, waved the Green Band away. 'Captain, have you thought any more about what we discussed at the questioning?'

'In what way, agha?' Starke's apprehension soared, his stomach queasy.

'About Islam, about the Imam, God's peace upon him, about going to see him?'

'It's not possible for me to see him, even if I wanted to.'

'Perhaps I could arrange it. If you saw the Imam, watched him talk, listened to him, you would find God's peace you seek. And the truth.'

Starke was touched by the mullah's obvious sincerity. 'If I had the chance I'd sure . . . I'd sure take it up, if I could. You said three things, agha?'

'This was the third. Islam. Become Muslim. There is not a moment to lose. Submit to God, accept that there is only One God and that Mohammed is his Prophet, accept it and have life everlasting in Paradise.'

The eyes were dark and penetrating. Starke had experienced them before and found them almost hypnotic. 'I . . . I told you already, agha, perhaps I will, in . . . God's time.' He pulled his eyes away and felt the dominating force lessen. 'If we're going back, we'd better go now. I don't want to miss seeing my guys off.'

It was almost as though he had not spoken. 'Isn't the Imam the Most Holy of men, the most stalwart, the most relentless against oppression? The Imam is, Captain. Open your eyes and spirit to him.'

Starke heard the underlying emphasis through the fervour and once more the seeming sacrilege disquieted him. 'I wait, patiently.' He looked back at the eyes that seemed to be looking through him, through the walls, into infinity. 'If we're going, we'd better go,' he said as gently as he could.

Hussain sighed. The light went out of his eyes. He shouldered his gun and led the way out. At the main door he stepped into his shoes, waited for Starke to do the same. Four more Green Bands joined them. 'We're going to the base,' Hussain told them.

'I parked my car just outside the square,' Starke said, enormously relieved to be in the open again and out of the man's spell. 'It's a station wagon, we can go in that if you like.'

'Good. Where is it?'

Starke pointed and walked off, weaving through the stalls. He was almost a head taller than most of the crowd and now his mind was buzzing with thought and counter thought, sifting what the mullah had said, trying to plan what to do about Whirlwind.

'Goddam,' he muttered, swamped by the danger. I hope Rudi aborts, then I will, whatever Scrag does. Automatically his eyes were scanning as they would in a cockpit, and he noticed a commotion ahead by the fountain. Because of his great height he was the first to see the youth with a gun, the crowds scattering. He stopped, frozen with disbelief, Hussain coming alongside. But there was no mistake, the shrieking berserk youth was charging through the people directly at him. 'Assassin,' he gasped, the men and women in front fleeing in terror, running, tripping, falling out of the youth's path and now the way was clear. Blankly he saw the youth skid to a stop and point the gun directly at him.

'Look out!' But before he could dive for the ground and the cover of a stall, the impact of the first bullet spun him, slamming him back against one of the Green Bands. More bullets, someone nearby screamed, then another gun opened up, deafening him.

It was Hussain. His reflexes had been very good. At once he had realised the assassin attack was against him and the moment of respite that Starke had given him was enough. With one smooth movement he had swung his gun off his shoulder, aimed, and pulled the trigger, his mind shouting, 'There is no other God but . . .'

His fire was coldly accurate and holed Ibrahim Kyabi, thrusting the life out of him, tearing the gun from the dead hands and putting him into the dirt. Numbly the mullah stopped firing and found he was still upright, disbelieving that he was not hit, impossible for the assassin to miss, impossible that he was not martyred and on the path to Paradise. Shakily he looked around in the pandemonium, wounded being helped, others wailing and cursing, one of his Green Bands splayed out, dead, many bystanders hurt. Starke was crumpled on the ground, half under the stalls.

'Praise be to God, Excellency Hussain, you're unhurt,' a Green Band called out.

'As God wants . . . God is Great . . .' Hussain went over to Starke and knelt beside him. He saw blood was dripping from his left sleeve, his face was white. 'Where are you hit?'

'I'm . . . I'm not sure. It's my . . . I think it's my shoulder or chest.' It was the first time Starke had ever been shot. When the bullet had smashed him backwards to the ground, there was no pain but his mind was screaming: I'm dead, the bastard's killed me, I'll never see Manuela, never get home, never see the kids. I'm dead . . . Then he had had a blinding urge to run – to flee from his own death. He had wanted to jump to his feet but the pain tore the strength out of him and now Hussain was kneeling beside him.

'Let me help you,' Hussain said, then to the Green Band, 'Take his other arm.'

He cried out as they turned him and tried to help him up. 'Wait . . . for crissake . . .' When the spasm had passed he found he could not move his left arm at all, but his right worked. With his good right hand he felt himself, moved his legs. No pain there. Everything seemed to be working, except his left arm and shoulder, and his head was bleary. Gritting his teeth he opened his parka and pulled away his shirt. Blood seeped from the hole that was in the centre of his shoulder but it wasn't pumping out, and there was no unbearable discomfort in his breathing, just a stabbing pain if he moved incautiously. 'It's . . . I don't think it's . . . it's in my lungs . . .'

'Son of a burnt father, Pilot,' the Green Band said with a laugh. 'Look, there's another hole in the back of your jacket, it's bleeding too, the bullet must've gone right through you.' He started to probe the hole with a dirty finger and Starke cursed him violently. 'Curse yourself, Infidel,' the man said. 'Curse yourself, not me. Perhaps God in his mercy gave you your life back, though why God would do that . . .' He shrugged and got up, looked at his dead comrade nearby and the other wounded, shrugged again, and sauntered over to Ibrahim Kyabi who lay in the dirt like a bag of old rags, and began to go through his pockets.

The crowd in the square was pressing forward, encroaching on the two of them, so Hussain got up and waved them away. 'God is Great, God is Great,' he shouted. 'Keep back. Help those who are hurt!' When they had space again he knelt beside Starke, 'Didn't I warn you your time was short? God protected you this time to give you another chance.'

But Starke hardly heard him. He had found his handkerchief and was stuffing it against the hole, trying to staunch the blood, feeling the warm trickle down his back, muttering and cursing, now over his black terror, but not the fear that he would still shame himself by running away. 'What the hell was that bastard trying to kill me for?' he muttered. 'Sonofabitch, goddam crazy!'

'He was trying to kill me, not you.'

Starke stared up at him. 'Fedayeen, mujhadin?'

'Or Tudeh. What does it matter, he was an enemy of God. God killed him.'

Another pain knifed into Starke's chest. He muffled a curse, hating all this God talk, not wanting to think about God but only about the kids and Manuela and normality and getting to hell out: I'm sick to death of all this madness and killing in the name of their own narrow version of God. 'Sonsofbitches!' he muttered, his words swallowed in the noise. His shoulder was throbbing, the pain spreading. As best he could he balled the handkerchief, using it as a dressing, and closed his parka, muttering obscenities.

What the hell'm I gonna do now for crissake? Goddammed bastard! How the hell'm I gonna fly now? He shifted his position slightly. Pain dragged another involuntary groan from him and he cursed again, disgusted with himself, wanting to be stoic.

Hussain came out of his reverie, anguished that God had decided to leave him alive when, again, he should have been martyred. Why? Why am I so cursed? And this American, impossible for the spray of bullets not to have killed him also – why was he too left alive? 'We'll go to your base. Can you stand up?'

'I'll . . . sure, just a moment.' Starke readied. 'Okay, careful . . . oh sweet Jesus . . .' Even so he stood, weaving slightly, pain nauseating him. 'Can one of your men drive?'

'Yes.' Hussain called out to the Green Band kneeling beside Kyabi. 'Hurry up!' Obediently the man came back.

'Just these coins in his pockets, Excellency, and this. What's it say?'

Hussain examined it closely. 'It's a current Tehran University identity card.'

The photo showed a handsome youth smiling at the camera. 'Ibrahim Kyabi, 3rd Year, Engineering Section. Birth date 12 March 1955.' Hussain glanced at the back of the card. 'There's a Tehran address on it.'

'Stinking universities,' another young Green Band said. 'Hotbeds of Satan and Western evil.'

'When the Imam reopens them, God grant him peace, mullahs will be in charge. We'll stamp out all Western, anti-Islam ideas for ever. Give the card to the komiteh, Fivouz. They can pass it on to Tehran. Komitehs in Tehran will interrogate his family and friends, and deal with them.' Hussain saw Starke looking at him. 'Yes, Captain?'

Starke had seen the photo. 'I was just thinking, in a few days he'd've been twenty-four. Kind of a waste, isn't it.'

'God punished his evil. Now he is in hellfire.'

North of Kowiss: 4:10 P.M. The 206 was cruising nicely over the Zagros foothills, McIver at the controls, Ali Kia dozing beside him. McIver was feeling very good. Ever since he had decided to fly Kia himself he had been light-headed. It was a perfect solution, the only one. So my medical's not current, so what? We're in a war operation, we have to take risks, and I'm still the best bloody pilot in the company.

He looked across at Kia. 'If you weren't such a horse's arse, I'd hug you for giving me the excuse.' He beamed and clicked on the sender. 'Kowiss, this is HotelTangoX-ray at one thousand, heading 185 degrees inbound from Tehran with Minister Ali Kia aboard.'

'HTX. Maintain heading, report at Outer Marker.'

His flight and refuelling at Isfahan International Airport had been uneventful, except for a few minutes after landing when excited, shouting Green Bands had surrounded the helicopter threateningly, even though he had had clearance to land and refuel. 'Get on the radio and insist the Station Supervisor come at once,' Kia had said to McIver, seething, 'I represent the government!'

McIver had obliged. 'The, er, the tower says if we're not refuelled and away within the hour the komiteh will impound us.' He added sweetly, delighted to pass on the message, 'They, er, said, "foreign pilots and foreign airplanes are not welcome in Isfahan, nor running dogs of Bazargan's foreign-dominated government!" '

'Barbarians, illiterate peasants,' Kia had said disgustedly, but only when they were safely airborne again, McIver enormously relieved that he had been allowed into the civilian airport and had not had to use the airforce base where Lochart had refuelled.

McIver could see the whole Kowiss air base now. On the far side of the field near their IHC complex he saw the company 125 and his heart did a flip. I told Starke to get the lads off early, he thought irritably. 'IHC Control, HTX from Tehran with Minister Kia aboard.'

'IHC control. HTX, land on helipad 2. Wind's 30–35 knots at 135 degrees.'

McIver could see Green Bands on the main gate, some near the helipad with Esvandiary and the Iranian staff. A group of mechanics

934

and pilots was also collecting nearby. My reception committee, he thought, recognising John Hogg, Lochart, Jean-Luc and Ayre. No Starke yet. So I'm illegal. What can they do? I outrank them, but if the ICAA find out they could be plenty bloody mad. He had his speech all ready, in case: 'I apologise but the exigencies of Minister Kia's order necessitated an immediate decision. Of course it won't happen again.' It wouldn't have happened at all if Whirlwind wasn't planned. He leaned over and shook Kia awake. 'We'll be landing in a couple of minutes, agha.'

Kia rubbed the fatigue out of his face, glanced at his watch, then straightened his tie, combed his hair and carefully readjusted his Astrakhan hat. He studied the people below, the neat hangars and all the helicopters neatly lined up – two 212s, three 206s, two Alouettes – *my* helicopters, he thought with a glow. 'Why was the flight so slow?' he said curtly.

'We're on time, Minister. We've had a bit of a headwind.' McIver was concentrating on the landing, needing to make it very good. It was.

Esvandiary swung Kia's door open. 'Excellency Minister, I'm Kuram Esvandiary, chief of IranOil in this area, welcome to Kowiss. Agha Manager Siamaki called to make sure we were prepared for you. Welcome!'

'Thank you.' Ostentatiously Kia said to McIver, 'Pilot, be ready to take off at 10 a.m. tomorrow. I may want to go around some oil sites with Excellency Esvandiary before going back. Don't forget, I have to be in Tehran for my 7 p.m. meeting with the Prime Minister.' He got out and was bustled off to inspect the choppers. Immediately Ayre, Lochart and the others ducked under the blades and came quickly alongside McIver's window. He disregarded their faces and beamed. 'Hello, how're tricks?'

'Let me finish the shutdown for you, Mac,' Ayre said, 'we've as –'

'Thanks, but I'm perfectly capable,' McIver said crisply, then into the mike, 'HTX closing down.' He saw Lochart's face and sighed again. 'So I'm slightly out of whack, Tom. So?'

'It's not that, Mac,' Lochart said in a rush, 'Duke's been shot.' McIver listened appalled as Lochart told him what had happened. 'He's in the infirmary now. Doc Nutt says his lung may be punctured.'

'Christ Almighty! Then put him aboard the 125, go on, Johnny, get g –'

'He can't, Mac,' Lochart overrode him with the same urgency: 'Hotshot's held up her departure till Kia's inspection – yesterday old Duke tried every which way to get her in and out before you

935

arrived but Hotshot's a sonofabitch. And that's not all, I think Tehran's rumbled us.'

'*What?*'

Lochart told him about the telexes and the HF calls. 'Siamaki's been bending Hotshot's ear, getting him worked up. I took Siamaki's last call – Duke had gone to the mullah's – and he was mad as a sonofabitch. I told him the same as Duke and sluffed him off saying you'd call when you got in, but Jesus, Mac, he knows you and Charlie've cleaned out your apartment.'

'Ali Baba! He must've been a plant.' McIver's head was reeling. Then he noticed the little gold St. Christopher that habitually he hung around the magnetic compass when flying. It was a present from Genny, a first present, a war present, just after they'd met, he in the RAF, she a WAAF: 'Just so you don't get lost, me lad,' she had said. 'You don't have much of a nose for north.'

He smiled now and blessed her. 'First I'll see Duke.' He could see Esvandiary and Kia wandering down the line of choppers. 'Tom, you and Jean-Luc see if you can chivvy Kia along, butter the bugger up, flatter the balls off him – I'll join you as quick as I can.' They went off at once. 'Freddy, you spread the word that the moment we get the okay for the 125 to leave, everyone's to board fast and quietly. Is all the baggage aboard?'

'Yes, but what about Siamaki?'

'I'll worry about that bugger, off you go.' McIver hurried away. Johnny Hogg called out after him, 'Mac, a word in your ear as soon as poss.'

The underlying urgency stopped him. 'What, Johnny?'

'Urgent and private from Andy: If this weather worsens he may postpone Whirlwind from tomorrow till Saturday. The wind's changed. It'll be a headwind now instead of a tail –'

'You saying I don't know southeast from northwest?'

'Sorry. Andy also said, as you're here he can't give you the overriding yes or no he promised.'

'That's right. Ask him to give it to Charlie. What else?'

'The rest can wait. I haven't told the others.'

Doc Nutt was in the infirmary with Starke. Starke lay on a cot, arm in a sling, his shoulder heavily bandaged. 'Hello, Mac, you have a good flight?' he said witheringly.

'Don't you start! Hi Doc! Duke, we'll get you out on the 125.'

'No. There's tomorrow.'

'Tomorrow'll take care of tomorrow and meanwhile you're on the

936

124–125! For Christ sake,' McIver said irritably, his relief at having made the flight safely, and at seeing Starke alive peeled away his control, 'don't act like you're Deadeye Dick at the Alamo!'

'He wasn't at the goddam Alamo,' Starke slammed back angrily, 'and who the hell're you to act like Chuck Yeager?'

Doc Nutt said mildly, 'If you both don't slow down, I'll order the two of you bloody enemas.'

Abruptly both men laughed and Starke gasped as pain rocked him. 'For crissake, Doc, don't make me laugh . . .' And McIver said, 'Duke, Kia insisted I accompany him. I couldn't tell him to push off.'

'Sure.' Starke grunted. 'How was it?'

'Grand.'

'What about the wind?'

'It's not a plus for tomorrow,' McIver said carefully. 'It can change back again just as quickly.'

'If it stays this way it's a 30-knot headwind or worse, and we can't make it across the Gulf. There's no way we can carry enough fu –'

'Yes. Doc, what's the poop?'

'Duke should be X-rayed as soon as possible. Shoulder blade's shattered and there's some tendon and muscle damage, wound's clean. There might be a splinter or two in the left lung, he's lost a pint or so but all in all he's been very bloody lucky.'

'I feel okay, Doc, I'm mobile,' Starke said. 'One day won't make that amount of difference. I can still go along tomorrow.'

'Sorry, old top, but you're shook, bullets do that. You may not feel it now but in an hour or two you will, guaranteed.' Doc Nutt was very glad he was leaving with the 125 today. Don't want to cope anymore, he told himself. Don't want to see any more fine young bodies bullet-torn and mutilated. I've had it. Yes, but I'll have to stick it for a few more days, there're going to be others to patch up because Whirlwind's just not going to work. It's not, I feel it in my bones. 'Sorry, but you'd be a hazard on any op, even a little one.'

'Duke,' McIver said, 'it's best you go at once. Tom can take one. Freddy the other – no need for Jean-Luc to stay.'

'And what the hell you figure on doing?'

McIver beamed. 'Me, I'll be a passenger. Meanwhile I'm just bloody Kia's very private bloody pilot.'

In the Tower: 4:50 P.M. 'I repeat, Mr. Siamaki,' McIver said tightly into the mike, 'there's a special conference in Al Shargaz.'

'And I repeat why wasn't I informed at once?' The voice over the loudspeaker was shrill and irritated.

McIver's knuckles were white from the grip on the mike's stem, and he was being watched intently by a Green Band and Wazari whose face was still swollen from the beating Zataki had given him. 'I repeat, Agha Siamaki,' he said, his voice tidy, 'Captains Pettikin and Lane were needed for an urgent conference in Al Shargaz and there was no time to inform you.'

'Why?' I'm here in Tehran. Why wasn't the office informed, where are their exit permits? Where?'

McIver pretended to be slightly exasperated. 'I've already told you, agha, there was no time – phones in Tehran aren't working – and I cleared their exits with the komiteh at the airport, personally with his Excellency the mullah in charge.' The Green Band yawned, bored, non English speaking, and noisily cleared his throat. 'Now if you'll excu –'

'But you and Captain Pettikin have removed your valuables from your apartment. Is that so?'

'Merely a precaution to remove temptation from vile mujhadin and fedayeen burglars and bandits while we're away,' McIver said airily, very conscious of Wazari's attention and sure that the tower at the airbase was monitoring this conversation. 'Now if you'll excuse me, Minister Kia requires my presence!'

'Ah, Minister Kia, ah yes!' Siamaki's irritability softened a little, 'What, er, what time do you both arrive back in Tehran tomorrow?'

'Depending on the winds . . .' McIver's eyes almost crossed as he had a sudden, almost overwhelming desire to blurt out about Whirlwind. I must be going potty, he thought. With an effort he concentrated. 'Depending on Minister Kia, the winds and refuelling, some time in the afternoon.'

'I will be waiting for you, I may even meet you at the airport if we know your ETA, there are cheques to be signed and many rearrangements to be discussed. Please give Minister Kia my best wishes and wish him a pleasant stay in Kowiss. Salaam.' The transmission clicked off. McIver sighed, put the mike down. 'Sergeant, while I'm here I'd like to call Bandar-e Delam and Lengeh.'

'I'll have to ask base,' Wazari said.

'Go ahead.' McIver looked out the window. The weather was deteriorating, the southeaster crackling the wind sock and the stays of the radio mast. Thirty knots, gusting to thirty-five on the counter. Too much, he thought. The upended mud tank that had crashed through the roof was only a few yards away. He could see Hogg and Gordon patiently waiting in the 125 cockpit, the cabin door invitingly open. Through the other window he saw Kia and Esvandiary had finished their inspection and were heading this way, towards the offices directly below. Idly he saw that a connector on the main roof aerial was loose, then noticed the wire almost free. 'Sergeant, you'd better fix that right smartly, you could lose all transmission.'

'Jesus, sure, thanks.' Wazari got up, stopped. Over the loudspeaker came: 'This is Kowiss Tower. Request to call Bandar-e Delam and Lengeh approved.' He acknowledged, switched frequencies, and made the call.

'This's Bandar-e Delam, go ahead Kowiss.' McIver's heart picked up, recognising Rudi Lutz's voice.

Wazari handed the mike to McIver, his eyes outside on the faulty connection. 'Sonofabitch,' he muttered, picked up some tools, opened the door on to the roof, and went out. He was still within easy hearing distance. The Green Band yawned, watching uninterestedly.

'Hello, Captain Lutz, McIver. I'm here overnighting here,' McIver said, matter-of-fact, choosing the words very carefully. 'Had to escort a VIP, Minister Kia, from Tehran. How're things at Bandar-e Delam?'

'We're five by five but if . . .' The voice stopped. McIver had heard the inrush of breath and concern, quickly bottled. He glanced at Wazari who was squatting beside the connector. 'How long . . . how long're you staying, Mac?' Rudi asked.

'I'll be en route tomorrow as planned. Providing the weather holds,' he added carefully.

'Understand. No sweat.'

'No sweat. All systems go for a long and happy year. How about you?'

Another pause. 'Everything five by five. All systems go for a long and happy year and *Vive* the Imam!'

'Quite right. Reason for the call is that HQ Aberdeen urgently wants information about your "updated impress file".' This was code for Whirlwind's preparations. 'Is it ready?'

'Yes, yes, it is. Where should I send it?' Code for: Do we still head for Al Shargaz?

'Gavallan's in Al Shargaz on an inspection trip so send it there – it's important you make a special effort and get it there quickly. I heard in Tehran there was a BA flight going into Abadan tomorrow. Get it on that flight for Al Shargaz tomorrow, all right?'

'Loud and clear. I've been working on the details all day.'

'Excellent. How's your crew change situation?'

'Great. Outgoing crew've gone. Incoming replacements due Saturday, Sunday at the latest. Everything's prepared for their arrival. I'll be on the next crew change.'

'Good, I'm here if you want me. How's your weather?'

A pause. 'Stormy. It's raining now. We've a southeasterly.'

'Same here. No sweat.'

'By the way, Siamaki called Numir, our IranOil manager, a couple of times.'

'What about?' McIver said.

'Just checking on the base, Numir said.'

'Good,' McIver said carefully. 'Glad he's interested in our operations. I'll call tomorrow, everything's routine. Happy landings.'

'You too, thanks for calling.'

McIver signed off cursing Siamaki. Nosy bloody bastard! He looked outside. Wazari still had his back to him, kneeling beside the base of the aerial, near the skylight of the office below, totally concentrated, so he left him to it and made the call to Lengeh.

Scragger was quickly on the other end. 'Hello, sport. Yes, we heard you were on a routine side trip escorting a VIP – Andy called from Al Shargaz. What's the form?'

'Routine. Everything's as planned. HQ Aberdeen needs information of your "updated impress file". Is it ready.'

'Ready as she'll ever be. Where should I send it?'

'Al Shargaz, that's easiest for you. Can you get it over tomorrow?'

'Gotcha, old sport, I'll plan on it. How's your weather?'

'South-easterly, 30 to 35 knots. Johnny said it might lighten tomorrow. You?'

'About the same. Let's hope she dies down. No problem for us.'

'Good. I'll call tomorrow. Happy landings.'

'Same to you. By the way, how's Lulu?'

McIver cursed under his breath, because in the excitement of the change of plan, having to escort Kia, he had totally forgotten his pledge to his car to save her from a fate worse than. He had just left her in one of the hangars as a further indication to the staff there he was returning tomorrow. 'She's fine,' he said. 'How's your medical?'

'Fine. How's yours, old sport?'

'See you soon, Scrag.' Wryly McIver clicked off the sender. Now he was very tired. He stretched and got up, noticed that the Green Band had gone and now Wazari was standing at the doorway from the roof, his face strange. 'What's the matter?'

'I . . . nothing, Captain.' The young man closed the door, chilled, was startled to see the Tower empty but for the two of them. 'Where's the Green Band?'

'I don't know.' Quickly Wazari checked the stairwell, then turned on him and dropped his voice: 'What's going on, Captain?'

McIver's fatigue left him. 'I don't understand.'

'All those calls from that Siamaki, telexes, guys leaving Tehran without permits, all the guys leaving here, spares going out, sneaked out.' He jerked a thumb at the skylight. 'Minister curses all of a sudden!'

'Crews need replacements, spares become redundant. Thanks for your help.' McIver began to walk around him but Wazari stood in his way.

'Something's mighty goddam crazy! You can't tell me th—' He stopped, footsteps approaching from downstairs. 'Listen, Captain,' he whispered urgently, 'I'm on your side, I've a deal with your Captain Ayre, he's gonna help me . . .'

The Green Band came stomping up the stairs into the room, said something in Farsi to Wazari, whose eyes widened.

'What did he say?' McIver asked.

'Esvandiary wants you below.' Wazari smiled sardonically, then went back out on to the roof again and squatted beside the connector, fiddling with it.

In Esvandiary's Office: 5:40 P.M. Tom Lochart was frozen with rage, and so was McIver. 'But our exit permits are valid and we've clearance to send personnel out today, right now!'

'With Minister Kia's approval the permits're held up until the replacements arrive,' Esvandiary said curtly. He sat behind the desk, Kia beside him, Lochart and McIver standing in front of him. On the desk was the pile of permits and passports. It was nearing sunset now. 'Agha Siamaki agrees too.'

'Quite correct.' Kia was amused and pleased at their discomfiture. Damned foreigners. 'No need for all this urgency, Captain. Much better to do things in an orderly fashion, much better.'

'The flight is orderly, Minister Kia,' McIver said tight-lipped. 'We've the permits. I insist the plane leaves as planned.'

'This is Iran, not England,' Esvandiary sneered. 'Even there I doubt if you could insist on anything.' He was very pleased with himself. Minister Kia had been delighted with his pishkesh – the revenue from a future oil well – and had at once offered him a seat on the IHC board.

Then, to his vast amusement, Kia had explained that exit permits should have fees attached to them: Let the foreigners sweat, the minister had added. By Saturday they will be most anxious of their own accord to press on you say three hundred U.S. dollars in cash, per head. 'As the Minister says,' he said importantly. 'We should be orderly. Now I'm busy, good aftern –'

The door swung open and now Starke was in the small office, his face blotchy, his good first bunched, left arm in a sling. 'What the hell's with you, Esvandiary? You can't cancel the permits!'

McIver burst out, 'For God's sake, Duke, you shouldn't be here!'

'The permits're postponed, not cancelled. Postponed!' Esvandiary's face contorted, 'and how many times do I have to tell you ill-mannered people to knock? Knock! This isn't your office, it's mine, I run this base, you don't, and Minister Kia and I are having a meeting that you've all interrupted! Now get out, get out the lot of you!' He turned to Kia as though the two of them were alone and said in Farsi in a new voice, 'Minister, I do apologise for all of this, you see what I have to deal with. I strongly recommend we nationalise all foreign airplanes and use our own p –'

Starke's jaw jutted. He bunched his fist. 'Listen you sonofabitch.'

'GET OUT!' Esvandiary reached into his drawer where there was an automatic. But he never pulled it out. The mullah Hussain came through the door, Green Bands behind him. A sudden silence pervaded the room.

'In the Name of God, what's going on here?' Hussain said in English, cold hard eyes on Esvandiary and Kia. At once Esvandiary got up and began to explain, speaking Farsi, Starke cut in with their side and soon both men were getting louder and louder. Impatiently Hussain held up his hand. 'First you, Agha Esvandiary. Please speak Farsi so my komiteh can understand.' He listened impassively to the long-winded Farsi address, his four Green Bands crowding the door. Then he motioned to Starke. 'Captain?'

Starke was carefully brief and blunt.

Hussain nodded at Kia. 'Now you, Excellency Minister. May I see your authority to override Kowissi authority and exit permits?'

'Override, Excellency mullah? Postpone? Not I,' Kia said easily. 'I'm merely a servant of the Imam, God's peace upon him, and of his personally appointed Prime Minister and his government.'

'Excellency Esvandiary said you approved the postponement.'

'I merely agreed with his wish for an orderly rearrangement of foreign personnel.'

Hussain looked down at the desk. 'Those are the exit permits with passports?'

Esvandiary's mouth went dry. 'Yes, Excellency.'

Hussain scooped them up and handed them to Starke. 'The men and airplane will leave at once.'

'Thank you, Excellency,' Starke said, the strain of standing getting to him.

'Let me help.' McIver took the passports and permits from him. 'Thank you, agha,' he said to Hussain, elated with their victory.

Hussain's eyes were just as cold and hard as ever. 'The Imam has said, "If foreigners want to leave, let them leave, we have no need of them." '

'Er, yes, thank you,' McIver said, not liking to be near this man at all. He went out. Lochart followed.

Starke was saying in Farsi, 'I'm afraid I have to go on the airplane too, Excellency.' He told him what Doc Nutt had said, adding in English, 'I don't want to go but well, that's it. Insha' Allah.'

Hussain nodded absently. 'You won't need an exit permit. Go aboard. I will explain to the komiteh. I will see the airplane leave.' He walked out and went up to the tower to inform Colonel Changiz of his decision.

It took no time at all for the 125 to be filled. Starke was last to the gangway, legs very shaky now. Doc Nutt had given him enough painkillers to get him aboard. 'Thank you, Excellency,' he said to Hussain over the howl of the jets, still afraid of him yet liking him. 'God's peace be with you.'

Over Hussain now hung a strange pall. 'Corruption and lies and cheating are against the laws of God, aren't they?'

'Yes, yes they are.' Starke saw Hussain's indecision. Then the moment passed.

'God's peace be with you, Captain.' Hussain turned and stalked off. The wind freshened slightly.

Weakly Starke climbed the steps, using his good hand, wanting to walk tall. At the top he held on to the handrail and turned back a moment, head throbbing, chest very bad. So much left here, so much, too much, not just choppers and spares and material things – so much more. Goddam, I should be staying, not leaving. Bleakly he waved farewell to those who were left behind and gave them a thumbs-up, achingly aware that he was thankful not to be among them.

*   *   *

943

In the office Esvandiary and Kia watched the 125 taxiing away. God's curse on them, may they all burn for interfering, Esvandiary thought. Then he threw off his fury, concentrating on the vast feast that selected friends who desperately wished to meet Miniŝter Kia, *his* friend and fellow director, had arranged, the entertainment of dancers to follow, then the temporary marriages . . .

The door opened. To his astonishment, Hussain came in, livid with rage, Green Bands crowding after him. Esvandiary got up. 'Yes, Excellency? What can I d—' He stopped as a Green Band roughly pulled him out of the way to allow Hussain to sit behind the desk. Kia sat where he was, perplexed.

Hussain said, 'The Imam, God's peace on him, has ordered komitehs to cast out corruption wherever it is to be found. This is the Kowiss airbase komiteh. You are both accused of corruption.'

Kia and Esvandiary blanched and both started talking, claiming that this was ridiculous and they were falsely accused. Hussain reached over and jerked the gold band of the gold watch on Esvandiary's wrist. 'When did you buy this and with what did you pay?'

'My . . . my savings and —'

'Liar. Pishkesh for two jobs. The komiteh knows. Now, what about your scheme to defraud the state, secretly offering future oil revenues to corrupt officials for future services?'

'Ridiculous, Excellency, lies all lies!' Esvandiary shouted in panic.

Hussain looked at Kia who also had gone pasty grey. 'What officials, Excellency?' Kia asked, keeping his voice calm, sure that his enemies had set him up to be trapped far away from the seat of his influence. Siamaki! It has to be Siamaki!

Hussain motioned to one of the Green Bands who went out and brought in the radio operator, Wazari. 'Tell them, before God, what you told me,' he ordered.

'As I told you earlier, I was on the roof, Excellency,' Wazari said nervously, 'I was checking one of our lines and overheard them through the skylight. I heard him make the offer.' He pointed a blunt finger at Esvandiary, delighted for an opportunity for revenge. If it hadn't been for Esvandiary I'd never have been picked on by the madman Zataki, never been beaten and hurt, never been almost killed. 'They were speaking English and he said, I can arrange to divert oil revenues from new wells, I can keep the wells off the lists and can divert funds to you . . .'

Esvandiary was appalled. He had carefully sent all the Iranian staff out of the office building and further, for safety, talked English. Now he was damned. He heard Wazari finish and Kia begin to speak, quietly, calmly, avoiding all complicity, saying he was only leading this corrupt and evil man on: 'I was asked to visit here for just this purpose, Excellency, sent here by the Imam's government, God protect him, just for this purpose: to root out corruption wherever it existed. May I congratulate you on being so zealous. If you will allow me, the moment I get back to Tehran, I will commend you directly to the Revolutionary Komiteh itself-and of course to the Prime Minister.'

Hussain looked at the Green Bands. 'Is Esvandiary guilty or not guilty?'

'Guilty, Excellency.'

'Is the man Kia guilty or not guilty?'

'Guilty,' Esvandiary shouted before they could answer.

One of the Green Bands shrugged, 'All Tehranis are liars. Guilty,' and the others nodded and echoed him.

Kia said politely, 'Tehrani mullahs and ayatollahs are not liars, Excellencies, the Revolutionary Komiteh are not liars, nor the Imam, God save him, who perhaps could be called Tehrani because he lives there now. I just happen to live there too. I was born in Holy Qom, Excellencies,' he added, blessing the fact for the first time in his life.

One of the Green Bands broke the silence. 'What he says is true, Excellency, isn't it?' He scratched his head, 'about all Tehranis?'

'That not all Tehranis are liars? Yes, that's true.' Hussain looked at Kia, also unsure. 'Before God, are you guilty or not?'

'Of course not guilty, Excellency, before God!' Kia's eyes were guileless. Fool, do you think you can catch me with that? *Taquiyah* gives me the right to protect myself if I consider my life threatened by false mullahs!

'How do you explain you're a government minister, but also a director of this helicopter company?'

'The Minister in charge . . .' Kia stopped, for Esvandiary was blubbering loudly and mouthing accusations. 'I'm sorry, Excellencies, as God wants, but this noise, it's difficult to speak without shouting.'

'Take him outside!' Esvandiary was dragged away. 'Well?'

'The Minister in charge of Civil Aviation Board asked me to join the IHC board as the Government's representative,' Kia said, telling the twisted truth as though he was imparting a state secret; adding other exaggerations equally importantly, 'we're not sure of the loyalty of the directors. Also may I tell you privately, Excellency, that in a few days all foreign airplane companies are being nationalised . . .'

He talked to them intimately, modulating his voice for the most

945

effect, and when he considered the moment perfect, he stopped and sighed, 'Before God I confess I am without corruption like you, Excellency, and though without your great calling, I too have dedicated my life to serving the people.'

'God protect you, Excellency,' the Green Band burst out.

The others agreed and even Hussain had had most of his doubt pushed aside. He was about to probe a little more when they heard a distant muezzin from the airbase calling to evening prayer and he chided himself for being diverted from God. 'Go with God, Excellency,' he said, ending the Tribunal, and got up.

'Thank you, Excellency. May God keep you and all mullahs safe to rescue us and our great Islamic nation from the works of Satan!'

Hussain led the way outside. There, following his lead, they all ritually cleansed themselves, turned towards Mecca, and prayed – Kia, Green Bands, office staff, labourers, kitchen workers – all pleased and content that once more they could each openly testify their personal submission to God and the Prophet of God. Only Esvandiary wept through his abject prayers.

Then Kia came back into the office. In the silence, he sat behind the desk and allowed himself a secret sigh and many secret congratulations. How dare that son of a dog Esvandiary accuse me! Me, Minister Kia! May God burn him and all enemies of the state. Outside there was a burst of firing. Calmly he took out a cigarette and lit it. The sooner I leave this dung heap the better, he thought. A squall shook the building. Drizzle spotted the windows.

Lengeh: 6:50 P.M. The sunset was malevolent, clouds covering most of the sky, heavy and black-tinged. 'It'll be closed in by morning, Scrag,' the American pilot, Ed Vossi said, his dark curly hair tugged by the wind that blew from the Hormuz up the Gulf towards Abadan. 'Goddam wind!'

'We'll be all right, sport. But Rudi, Duke and the others? If she holds or worsens they'll be up shit creek without a paddle.'

'Goddam wind! Why choose today to change direction? Almost as though the gods're laughing at us.' The two men were standing on the promontory overlooking the Gulf beneath their flagpole, the waters grey and, out in the strait, white-topped. Behind them was their base and the airfield, still wet from this morning's passing rain squall. Below and to the right was their beach and the raft they swam from. Since the day of the shark no one had ventured there, staying close in the shallows in case another lay in wait for them. Vossi muttered, 'I'll be goddam glad when this's all over.'

Scragger nodded absently, his thoughts reaching into the weather patterns, trying to read what would happen in the next twelve hours, always difficult in this season when the usually placid Gulf would erupt with sudden and monstrous violence. For three hundred and sixty-three days a year the prevailing wind was from the northwest. Now it wasn't. The base was quiet. Only Vossi, Willi Nurchtreiter, and two mechanics were left. All the other pilots and mechanics and their British office manager had gone two days ago, Tuesday, while he was en route back from Bandar-e Delam with Kasigi.

Willi had got them all out of Al Shargaz by sea: 'We had no trouble, Scrag, by God Harry,' Willi had told him delightedly when he landed. 'Your plan worked. Sending 'em by boat was clever, better than by chopper, and cheaper. The komiteh just shrugged and took over one of the trailers.'

'They're sleeping on base now?'

'Some of them, Scrag. Three or four. I've made sure we feed them plenty of rice and horisht. They're not a bad group. Masoud's trying to keep in their good books too.' Masoud was their IranOil manager.

'Why did you stay, Willi? I know how you feel about this caper, I told you to be on the boat, no need for you.'

'Sure there is, Scrag, by God Harry, but you'll need a proper pilot along with you – you might get lost.'

Good old Willi, Scragger thought. Glad he stayed. And sorry.

Since getting back from Bandar-e Delam on Tuesday, Scragger had found himself greatly unsettled, nothing that he could isolate, just a feeling that elements over which he had no control were waiting to pounce. The pain in his lower stomach had lessened, but from time to time there was still a flick of blood in his urine. Not forewarning Kasigi about the Whirlwind pullout had added to his unease. Hell, he thought, I couldn't have risked that, spilling Whirlwind. I did the best I could, telling Kasigi to go to Gavallan.

Yesterday, Wednesday, Vossi had taken Kasigi across the Gulf. He had given Vossi a private letter to Gavallan explaining what had happened in Bandar-e Delam and his dilemma about Kasigi, leaving it to Gavallan to decide what to do. Also in the letter he had given details of his meeting with Georges de Plessey who was gravely concerned that troubles would again spill over into the Siri complex:

'Damage to pumping and piping at Siri's worse than first thought and I don't think she'll be pumping this month. Kasigi's fit to be tied and he's got three tankers due at Siri for uplifts in the next three weeks according to the deal he worked out with Georges. It's a carve up, Andy. Nothing we can do. There's little chance of avoiding sabotage if

948

terrorists really decide to have at them. Of course I haven't told Georges about anything. Do what you can for Kasigi and see you soonest, Scrag.'

On this morning's route call from Al Shargaz, Gavallan had said only he had received his report and was dealing with it. Otherwise he was noncommittal.

Scragger had not mentioned McIver, nor had Gavallan. He beamed. Bet my life Dirty Dunc flew the 206! Never would've bet old By the Book McIver would have it! Even so, bet my life he was like a pig in shit at the chance and no bloody wonder. I'd've done the same . . .

'Scrag!'

He glanced around. One look at Willi Nurchtreiter's face was enough. 'What's up?'

'I just found out Masoud's given all our passports to the gendarmes – every last one!'

Vossi and Scragger gaped at him. Vossi said, 'What the hell he do that for?' Scragger was more vulgar.

'It was Tuesday, Scrag, when the others left on the boat. Of course a gendarme was there to see them off, count them aboard, and that's when he asked Masoud for our passports. So Masoud gave them to him. If it'd been me I'd've done the same.'

'What the hell did he want them for?'

Willi said patiently, 'To re-sign our residence permits in Khomeini's name, Scrag, he wanted us to be legal – you've asked them enough times, haven't you?' Scragger cursed for a good minute and never used the same word twice.

'For crissake, Scrag, we gotta get 'em back,' Vossi said shakily, 'we gotta get 'em back or Whirlwind's blown.'

'I know that, sport.' Blankly Scragger was sifting possibilities.

Willi said, 'Maybe we could get new ones in Al Shargaz or Dubai – say we'd lost 'em.'

'For crissake, Willi,' Vossi exploded, 'for crissake, they'd put us in the slammer so fast we wouldn't know which way was up! Remember Masterson?' One of their mechanics, a couple of years ago, had forgotten to renew his Al Shargaz permit and had tried to bluff his way through Immigration. Even though the visa was only four days out of date and his passport otherwise valid, immigration had at once marched him into jail where he languished very uncomfortably for six weeks, then to be let out but banished for ever: 'Dammit,' the resident British official had said, 'you're bloody lucky to get off so lightly. You knew the law. We've pointed it out until we're blue in the face . . .'

'Goddammed if I'll leave without mine,' Vossi said. 'I can't. Mine's loaded with goddam visas for all the Gulf states, Nigeria, the UK and hell and gone – it'd take me months to get new ones, months, if ever . . . and what about Al Shargaz, huh? That's one mighty fine place but without a goddam passport and their valid visa, into the slammer!'

'Too right, Ed. Bloody hell and tomorrow's Holy Day when everything's shut tighter'n a gnat's arse. Willi, you remember who the gendarme was? Was he one of the regulars – or a Green Band?'

After a moment Willi said, 'He wasn't a Green Band, Scrag, he was a regular. The old one, the one with grey hair.'

'Qeshemi? The sergeant?'

'Yes, Scrag. Yes it was him.'

Scragger cursed again. 'If old Qeshemi says we've got to wait till Saturday, or Saturday week, that's it.' In this area gendarmes still operated as they had always done as part of the military except that now they had taken off their Shah badges and wore armbands with Khomeini's name scrawled upon them.

'Don't wait supper for me.' Scragger stomped off into the twilight.

At the Lengeh Police Station: 7:32 P.M. The corporal gendarme yawned and shook his head politely, speaking Farsi to the base radio operator, Ali Pash, whom Scragger had brought with him to interpret. Scragger waited patiently, too used to Iranian ways to interrupt them. They had already been at it for half an hour.

'Oh, you wanted to ask about the foreigners' passports? The passports are in the safe, where they should be,' the gendarme was saying. 'Passports are valuable and we have them locked up.'

'Perfectly correct, Excellency, but the captain of the foreigners would like to have them back, please. He says he needs them for a crew change.'

'Of course he may have them back. Are they not his property? Have not he and his men flown many mercy missions over the years for our people? Certainly, Excellency, as soon as the safe is opened.'

'Please may it be opened now? The foreigner would appreciate your kindness very much.' Ali Pash was equally polite and leisurely, waiting for the gendarme to volunteer the information he sought. He was a good looking Tehrani in his late twenties who had been trained at the U.S. Radio School at Isfahan and had been with IHC for three years at Lengeh. 'It would certainly be a kindness.'

'Certainly, but he cannot have them back until the key reappears.'

'Ah, may I dare ask where the key is, Excellency?'

The corporal gendarme waved his hand to the big, old-fashioned safe that dominated this outer office. 'Look, Excellency, you can see for yourself, the key is not on its peg. More than likely the sergeant has it in his safekeeping.'

'How very wise and correct, Excellency. Probably his Excellency the sergeant is at home now?'

'His Excellency will be here in the morning.'

'On Holy Day? May I offer an opinion that we are fortunate our gendarmerie have such a high sense of duty to work so diligently? I imagine he would not be early.'

'The sergeant is the sergeant but the office opens at 7.30 in the morning though of course the police station is open day and night.' The gendarme stubbed out his cigarette. 'Come in the morning.'

'Ah, thank you, Excellency. Would you care for another cigarette while I explain to the captain?'

'Thank you, Excellency. It is rare to have a foreign one, thank you.' The cigarettes were American and highly appreciated but neither mentioned it.

'May I offer you a light, Excellency?' Ali Pash lit his own too and told Scragger what had been said.

'Ask him if the sergeant's at home now, Ali Pash.'

'I did, Captain. He said His Excellency will be here in the morning.' Ali Pash hid his weariness, too polite to tell Scragger he had realised in the first few seconds that this man knew nothing, would do nothing and this whole conversation and visit was a total waste of time. And of course gendarmes would prefer not to be disturbed at night about so insignificant an affair. What does it matter? Have they ever lost a passport? Of course not! What crew change? 'If I may advise you, agha? In the morning.'

Scragger sighed. 'In the morning' could mean tomorrow or the following day. No point in probing further, he thought irritably. 'Thank him for me and say I'll be here bright and early in the morning.'

Ali Pash obeyed. As God wants, the gendarme thought wearily, hungry and worried that another week had gone by and still there was no pay, no pay for months now and the bazaari moneylenders were pressing for their loans to be repaid, and my beloved family near starving. '*Shab be khayr*, agha,' he said to Scragger. 'Good night.'

'*Shab be khayr*, agha.' Scragger waited, knowing their departure would be as politely long-winded as the interview.

Outside in the small road that was the main road of the port town, he felt better. Curious bystanders, all men, surrounded his battered old station wagon, the winged S-G symbol on the door. 'Salaam,' he said breezily and a few greeted him back. Pilots from the base were popular, the base and the oil platforms a main source of very profitable work, their mercy missions in all weather well known, and Scragger easily recognisable: 'That's the chief of the pilots,' one old man whispered knowledgeably to his neighbour, 'he's the one who helped young Abdollah Turik into the hospital at Bandar-e Abbas that only the highborn get into normally. He even went to visit his village just outside Lengeh, even went to his funeral.'

'Turik?'

'Abdollah Turik, my sister's son's son! The young man who fell off the oil platform and was eaten by sharks.'

'Ah yes, I remember, the young man some say was murdered by leftists.'

'Not so loud, not so loud, you never know who's listening. Peace be with you, Pilot, greetings, Pilot!'

Scragger waved to them cheerily and drove off.

'But the base is the other way, Captain. Where do we go?' Ali Pash asked.

'To visit the sergeant, of course.' Scragger whistled through his teeth, disregarding Ali Pash's obvious disapproval.

The sergeant's house was on the corner of a dingy, dirt street still puddled from this morning's squall, just another door in the high walls across the joub. It was getting dark now so Scragger left the headlights on and got out. No sign of life in the whole street. Only a few of the high windows dimly lit.

Sensing Ali Pash's nervousness he said, 'You stay in the car. There's no problem, I've been here before.' He used the iron knocker vigorously, feeling eyes everywhere.

The first time he had been here was a year or so ago when he had brought a huge food hamper, with two butchered sheep, some sacks of rice and cases of fruit as a gift from the base to celebrate 'their' sergeant getting the Shah's Bronze Sepah Medal for bravery in action against pirates and smugglers who were endemic in these waters. The last time, a few weeks ago, he had accompanied a worried gendarme who wanted him to report at once the tragedy at Siri One, picking Abdollah Turik out of the shark-infested water. Neither time had he been invited into the house but had stayed in the little courtyard beyond the tall wooden door, and both times had been in daylight.

The door creaked open. Scragger was not prepared for the sudden flashlight that momentarily blinded him. The circle of light hesitated, then went to the car and centred on Ali Pash who almost leapt out of the car, half-bowed and called out, 'Greetings, Excellency Chief Officer, peace be upon you. I apologise that the foreigner disturbs your privacy and dares to c –'

'Greetings.' Qeshemi overrode him curtly, clicked the light off, turning his attention back to Scragger.

'Salaam, Agha Qeshemi,' Scragger said, his eyes adjusting now. He saw the strong-featured man watching him, his uniform coat unbuttoned and the revolver loose in its holster.

'Salaam, Cap'tin.'

'Sorry to come here, agha, at night,' Scragger said slowly and carefully, knowing Qeshemi's English was as limited as his own Farsi was almost non existent. '*Loftan, gozar nameh. Loftan*' – Please, need passports. Please.

The gendarme sergeant grunted with surprise then waved a hard tough hand towards the town. 'Passports in stat'ion, Cap'tin.'

'Yes. But, sorry, there is no key.' Scragger parodied opening a lock with a key. 'No key,' he repeated.

'Ah. Yes. Understand. Yes, no key. To'morrow. To'morrow you get.'

'Is it possible, tonight? Please. Now?' Scragger felt the scrutiny.

'Why tonight?'

'Er, for a crew change. Men to Shiraz, crew change.'

'When?'

Scragger knew he had to gamble. 'Saturday. If I have key, go station and return at once.'

Qeshemi shook his head. 'To'morrow.' Then he spoke sharply to Ali Pash who at once bowed and thanked him profusely again, apologising for disturbing him. 'His Excellency says you can have them tomorrow. We'd, er, we'd better leave, Captain.'

Scragger forced a smile. '*Mamnoon am, agha,*' – thank you, Excellency. '*Mamnoon am, Agha Qeshemi.*' He would have asked Ali Pash to ask the sergeant if he could have the passports as soon as the station opened but he did not wish to agitate the sergeant unnecessarily. 'I will come after first prayer. *Mamnoon am, agha.*' Scragger put out his hand and Qeshemi shook it. Both men felt the other's strength. Then he got into the car and drove off.

Thoughtfully Qeshemi closed and rebolted the door.

In summertime the small patio with its high walls and trellised vines and small fountain was cool and inviting. Now it was drab. He crossed

953

it and opened the door opposite that led into the main living room and rebolted it. The sound of a child coughing somewhere upstairs. A wood fire took off some of the chill but the whole house was draughty, none of the doors or windows fitting properly. 'Who was it?' his wife called down from upstairs.

'Nothing, nothing important. A foreigner from the airbase. The old one. He wanted their passports.'

'At this time of night? God protect us! Every time there's a knock on the door I expect more trouble – rotten Green Bands or vile leftists!' Qeshemi nodded absently, but said nothing, warming his hands by the fire, hardly listening to her rattle on. 'Why should he come here? Foreigners are so ill-mannered. What would he want passports for at this time of night? Did you give them to him?'

'They're locked in our safe. Normally I bring the key with me as always, but it's lost.' The child coughed again. 'How's little Sousan?'

'She still has a fever. Bring me some hot water, that'll help. Put a little honey in it.' He set the kettle on the fire, sighed, hearing her grumbling, 'Passports at this time of night! Why couldn't they wait till Saturday? So ill mannered and thoughtless. You said the key's lost?'

'Yes. Probably that goathead excuse for a policeman, Lafti, has it and forgot to put it back again. As God wants.'

'Mohammed, what would the foreigner want with passports at this time of night?'

'I don't know. Curious, very curious.'

At Bandar-e Delam Airfield: 7:49 P.M. Rudi Lutz stood on the veranda of his trailer under the eaves, watching the heavy rain. '*Scheiss*,' he muttered. Behind him his door was open and the shaft of light sparkled the heavy raindrops. Soft Mozart came from his tape deck. The door of the next trailer, the office trailer, opened and he saw Pop Kelly come out holding an umbrella over his head and slop through the puddles towards him. Neither noticed the Iranian in the shadows. Somewhere on the base a tomcat was spitting and yowling. 'Hi, Pop. Come on in. You get it?'

'Yes, no problem.' Kelly shook the rain off. Inside the trailer it was warm and comfortable, neat and tidy. The cover was off the built-in, reconnected HF that was on Standby, muted static mixing with the music. A coffee pot percolated on the stove.

'Coffee?'

'Thanks – I'll help myself.' Kelly handed him the paper and went over to the kitchen area. The paper had hastily jotted columns of figures on it, temperatures, wind directions and strengths for every few thousand feet, barometric pressures and tomorrow's forecast. 'Abadan Tower said it was up to date. They claimed it included all today's incoming BA data. Doesn't look too bad, eh?'

'If it's accurate.' The forecast predicted lessening precipitation around midnight and reduced wind strength. Rudi turned up the music and Kelly sat down beside him. He dropped his voice. 'It could be all right for us, but a bitch for Kowiss. We'll still have to refuel in flight to make Bahrain.'

Kelly sipped his coffee with enjoyment, hot, strong, with a spoon of condensed milk. 'What'd you do if you were Andy?'

'With the three bases to worry about I'd . . .' A slight noise outside. Rudi got up and glanced out of the window. Nothing. Then again the sound of the tomcat, closer. 'Damn cats, they give me the creeps.'

'I rather like cats.' Kelly smiled. 'We've three at home: Matthew, Mark and Luke. Two're Siamese, the other's a tabby, Betty says the boys're driving her mad to get "John" to round it off.'

'How is she?' Today's BA flight into Abadan had brought Sandor Petrofi for the fourth 212, along with mail from Gavallan, routed since the troubles through HQ at Aberdeen, their first for many weeks.

'Fine, super in fact – three weeks to the day. The old girl's usually on time. I'll be glad to be home when she pops.' Kelly beamed. 'The doc says he thinks it's going to be a girl at long last.'

'Congratulations! That's wonderful.' Everyone knew that the Kellys had been hoping against hope. 'Seven boys and one girl, that's a lot of mouths to feed.' Rudi thought how hard he found it to keep up with the bills and school fees with only three children and no mortgage on the house – the house left to his wife by her father, God bless the old bastard. 'Lot of mouths, don't know how you do it.'

'Oh we manage, glory be to God.' Kelly looked down at the forecast, frowned. 'You know, if I was Andy I'd press the tit and not postpone.'

'If it was up to me I'd cancel and forget the whole crazy idea.' Rudi kept his voice down and leaned closer. 'I know it'll be rough for Andy, maybe the company'll close, maybe. But we can all get new jobs, even better paying ones, we've families to think of and I hate all this going against the book. How in the hell can we sneak out? Not possible. If we—' Car headlights splashed the window, the approaching sound of the high powered engine growing then stopping outside.

Rudi was the first at the window. He saw Zataki get out of the car with some Green Bands, then Numir, their base manager, came from the office trailer with an umbrella to join him. '*Scheiss*,' Rudi muttered again, turned the music down, quickly checked the trailer for incriminating evidence and put the forecast into his pocket. 'Salaam, Colonel,' he said, opening the door. 'You were looking for me?'

'Salaam, Captain, yes, yes I was.' Zataki came into the room, a U.S. army sub-machine gun over his shoulder. 'Good evening,' he said. 'How many helicopters are here now, Captain?'

Numir began, 'Four 212s an –'

'I asked the captain,' Zataki flared, 'not you. If I want information from you I'll ask! Captain?'

'Four 212s, two 206s, Colonel.'

To their shock, particularly Numir's, Zataki said, 'Good. I want two 212s to report to the Iran-Toda tomorrow at 8 a.m. to work under instructions of Agha Watanabe, the chief there. From tomorrow, you'll report daily. Have you met him?'

'Er, yes, I, er, once they had a CASEVAC and we helped them out.' Rudi tried to collect himself. 'Er, will . . . will they be working on er, Holy Day, Colonel?'

'Yes. So will you.'

Numir said, 'But the Ayatollah said . . .'

'He's not the law. Shut up.' Zataki looked at Rudi. 'Be there at 8 a.m.'

Rudi nodded. 'Er, yes. Can I, er can I offer you coffee, Colonel?'

'Thank you.' Zataki propped his submachine gun against the wall and sat at the built-in table, eyes on Pop Kelly. 'Didn't I see you at Kowiss?'

'Yes, yes you did,' the tall man said. 'That's, er, that's my normal base. I, er, I brought down a 212. I'm Ignatius Kelly.' Weakly he sank back into his chair opposite him, as blown as Rudi, wilting under the searching gaze. 'A night for fishes, isn't it?'

'What?'

'The, er, the rain.'

'Ah yes,' Zataki said. He was glad to be speaking English, improving his, convinced that Iranians who could speak the international language and were educated were going to be sought after, mullahs or no mullahs. Since Kowiss and taking the pills Doctor Nutt had given him, he had felt much better, the blinding headaches lessening. 'Will the rain prevent flying tomorrow?'

'No, not –'

'It depends,' Rudi called out quickly from the kitchen, 'if the front worsens or improves.' He brought the tray with two cups and sugar and condensed milk, still trying to cope with this new disaster. 'Please help yourself, Colonel. About Iran-Toda,' he said carefully, 'all our choppers are on lease, are contracted to IranOil and Agha Numir here's in charge.' Numir nodded, started to say something but thought better of it. 'We've contracts with IranOil.'

The silence thickened. They all watched Zataki. Leisurely he put three heaped teaspoons of sugar into his coffee, stirred and sipped it. 'It's very good, Captain. Yes, very good, and yes I know about IranOil, but I have decided Iran-Toda takes preference over IranOil for the time being and tomorrow you will supply two 212s at 8 a.m. to Iran-Toda.'

Rudi glanced at his base manager who avoided his eyes. 'But . . . well, presuming this is all right with IranOil th –'

'It is all right,' Zataki said to Numir. 'Isn't it, agha?'

'Yes, yes, agha,' meekly, Numir nodded. 'I, I will of course inform Area Headquarters of your . . . your eminent instructions.'

'Good. Then everything is arranged. Good.'

It's not arranged, Rudi wanted to shout out in dismay. 'May I ask how, er, how we'll be paid for the, er, new contract?' he asked, feeling stupid.

Zataki shouldered his gun and got up. 'Iran-Toda will make arrangements. Thank you. Captain, I will be back after first prayer tomorrow. You will fly one helicopter and I will accompany you.'

'Smashing idea, Colonel,' Pop Kelly burst out suddenly, beaming, and Rudi could have killed him. 'No need to come before 8 a.m., that'd be better for us – that's plenty of time to get there by say 8.15. Smashing idea to service Iran-Toda, smashing. We've always wanted that contract, can't thank you enough, Colonel! Fantastic! In fact Rudi we should take all four birds, put the lads into the picture at once, save time, at once, yes sir, I'll set them up for you!' He rushed off.

Rudi stared after him, almost cross-eyed with fury.

Near Al Shargaz Airport: 8:01 P.M. The night was beautiful and balmy, heavy with the smell of flowers, and Gavallan and Pettikin were sitting on the terrace of the Oasis Hotel, on the edge of the airfield on the edge of the desert. They were having a pre-dinner beer, Gavallan smoking a thin cigar and staring into the distance where the sky, purple-black and star-studded, met the darker land. The smoke drifted upwards. Pettikin shifted in his lounging chair. 'Wish to God there was something more I could do.'

'Wish to God old Mac was here, I'd break his bloody neck,' Gavallan said and Pettikin laughed. A few guests were already in the dining room behind them, starched tablecloths, sparkling glasses, high ceiling, its paint peeling. The Oasis was old and dilapidated, Empire baroque, the home of the British Resident when British power was the only power in the Gulf and, until '71 kept down piracy and maintained the peace. Music as ancient as the three-piece combo wafted out of the tall doors – piano, violin, and double bass, two elderly ladies and a white-haired gentleman on the piano.

'My God, isn't that *Chu Chin Chow?*'

'You've got me, Andy.' Pettikin glanced back at them, saw Jean-Luc among the diners, chatting with Nogger Lane, Rodrigues and some of the other mechanics. He sipped his beer, noticed Gavallan's glass was empty. 'Like another?'

'No, thanks.' Gavallan let his eyes drift with the smoke. 'I think I'll go over to the met office, then look in on ours.'

'I'll come with you.'

'Thanks, Charlie, but why don't you stay in case there's a phone call?'

'Sure, just as you like.'

'Don't wait for me to eat, I'll join you for coffee. I'll drop by the hospital to see Duke on my way back.' Gavallan got up, walked through the dining room, greeting those of his men who were there and went into the lobby that had seen better days.

'Mr. Gavallan, excuse me, Effendi, but there's a phone call for you.' The receptionist indicated the phone booth to one side. It had red plush inside, no air-conditioning and no privacy. 'Hello? Gavallan here,' he said.

'Hello boss, Liz Chen . . . just to report we've had a call about the two consignments from Luxembourg and they'll arrive late.' 'Consignment from Luxembourg' was code for the two 747s freighters he had chartered. 'They can't arrive Friday – they'll only guarantee Sunday 4 p.m.'

Gavallan was dismayed. He had been warned by the charterers that they had a very tight schedule between charters and there might be a twenty-four hour delay. He had had great difficulty arranging the airplanes. Obviously none of the regular airlines who serviced the Gulf or Iran could be approached and he had had to be vague about the reason for the charters and their cargo. 'Get back to them at once and try and bring the date forward. It'd be safer if they'd arrive Saturday, much safer. What's next?'

'Imperial Air have offered to take over our position on our new T63s.'

'Tell them to drop dead. Next?'

'ExTex have revised their offer on the new Saudi, Singapore, Nigerian contracts ten percent downward.'

'Accept the offer by telex. Fix a lunch for me with the Brass in New York on Tuesday. Next?'

'I've a checklist of part numbers you wanted.'

'Good. Hang on.' Gavallan took out the secretarial notebook he always carried and found the page he sought. It listed the present Iranian registration call signs of their ten remaining 212s, all beginning with 'EP' standing for Iran, then 'H' for helicopter and the final two letters. 'Ready. Off you go.'

'AB, RV, KI . . .'

As she read out the letters he wrote them alongside the other column. For security he did not put the full new registration, 'G-' denoting Great Britain, 'H' for Helicopter, just jotted the two new letters. He reread the list and they tallied with those already supplied. 'Thanks, they're spot on. I'll call you last thing tonight, Liz. Give Maureen a call and tell her all's well.'

'All right, boss. Sir Ian called half an hour ago to wish you luck.'

'Oh, great!' Gavallan had tried unsuccessfully to reach him all the time he was in Aberdeen. 'Where is he? Did he leave a number?'

'Yes, he's in Tokyo: 73 73 84. He said he'd be there for a while and if you missed him he'd call tomorrow. He also said he'll be back in a couple of weeks and would like to see you.'

'Even better. Did he say what about?'

'Oil for the lamps of China,' his secretary said cryptically.

Gavallan's interest picked up. 'Wonderful. Fix a date at his earliest convenience. I'll call you later, Liz. Got to rush.'

'All right. Just to remind you it's Scot's birthday tomorrow.'

'Godalmighty, I forgot, thanks, Liz. Talk to you later.' He hung up, pleased to hear from Ian Dunross, blessing the Al Shargazi phone system and distance dialling. He dialled. Tokyo was five hours ahead. Just after 1 a.m.

'*Hai?*' the Japanese woman's voice said sleepily.

'Good evening. Sorry to call so late but I had a message to call Sir Ian Dunross. Andrew Gavallan.'

'Ah, yes. Ian is not here for the moment, he will not be back until the morrow, so sorry. Perhaps at ten o'clock. Please, can I have your number, Mr. Gavallan?'

Gavallan gave it to her, disappointed. 'Is there another number I can reach him at, please?'

'Ah, so sorry, no.'

'Please ask him to call me, call any time.' He thanked her again and hung up thoughtfully.

Outside was his rented car and he got in and drove to the main airport entrance.

Overhead a 707 was coming around for final, landing lights on, tail and wing lights winking.

'Evening Mr. Gallavan,' Sibbles, the Met officer said. He was British, a small, thin, dehydrated man, ten years in the Gulf. 'Here you are.' He handed him the long photocopy of the forecast. 'Weather's going to be changeable here for the next few days.' He handed him three other pages. 'Lengeh, Kowiss and Bandar-e Delam.'

'And the bottom line is?'

'They're all about the same, give or take ten or fifteen knots, a few hundred feet of ceiling – sorry, just can't get used to metrics – a hundred metres or so of ceiling. Weather's gradually improving. In the next few days the wind should come back to our standard, friendly north-westerly. From midnight we're forecasting light rain and lots of low clouds and mist over most of the Gulf, wind southeasterly about twenty knots overall with thunderstorms, occasional small turbulences,' he looked up and smiled, 'and whirlwinds.'

Gavallan's stomach heaved even though the word was said matter-of-fact, and Sibbles was not party to the secret. At least, I don't think he is, he thought. That's the second curious coincidence today. The other was the American lunching at a nearby table with a Shargazi whose name he had not caught: 'Good luck for tomorrow,' the man had said with a pleasant smile, full of bonhomie, as he was leaving.

'Sorry?'

'Glen Wesson, Wesson Oil Marketing, you're Andrew Gavallan, right? We heard you and your guys were organising a . . . "a camel race" tomorrow out at the Dez-al oasis, right?'

'Not us, Mr. Wesson. We don't go in much for camels.'

'That a fact? You should try it, yes sir, lotta fun. Good luck anyway.'

Could have been a coincidence. Camel races were a diversion here for expats, a hilarious one, and the Dez-al a favourite place for the Islamic weekend. 'Thanks, Mr. Sibbles, see you tomorrow.' He pocketed the forecasts and went down the stairs into the terminal lobby, heading for their office which was off to one side. Neither a positive yes or a positive no, he was thinking, Saturday safer than tomorrow. You pays your money and you takes your chances. I can't put it off much longer. 'How're you going to decide?' his wife, Maureen, had asked, seeing him off at dawn the day before yesterday, Aberdeen almost socked in and pouring.

'Don't know, lassie. Mac's got a good nose, he'll help.'

And now no Mac! Mac gone bonkers, Mac flying without a medical, Mac conveniently stuck at Kowiss and no way out but Whirlwind; Erikki still God knows where, and poor old Duke fit to be tied that he's off the roster but bloody lucky he came here. Doc Nutt had been right.

X-rays showed several bone splinters had punctured his left lung with another half a dozen threatening an artery. He glanced at the lobby clock. 8:27. Should be out of the anaesthetic by now.

Got to decide soon. In conjunction with Charlie Pettikin I've got to decide soon.

He went through the 'No Admittance Except on Official Business' door, down the corridor, double glazed windows the length of it. On the apron the 707 was being guided into its disembarking slot by a Follow Me car, the sign in English and Farsi. Several Fokkerwolf forty passenger, prop feeders, were parked neatly, a Pan Am jumbo that was part of the evacuation milkrun to Tehran, and half a dozen private jets, their 125 among them. Wish it was Saturday, he thought. No, perhaps I don't.

On the door of their office suite was 'S-G Helicopters, Sheik Aviation.'

'Hello, Scot.'

'Hello, Dad.' Scot grinned. He was alone, Duty Officer, and he sat in front of the HF that was on standby, a book in his lap, his right arm in a sling. 'Nothing new except a message to call Roger Newbury at home. Shall I get him?'

'In a moment, thanks.' Gavallan handed him the met reports. Scot scanned them rapidly. The phone rang. Without stopping reading, he picked it up. 'S-G?' He listened a moment. 'Who? Oh yes. No, he's not here, sorry. Yes, I'll tell him. 'Bye.' He replaced the phone, sighed. 'Johnny Hogg's new bird, Alexandra – "the Hot Tamale" Manuela calls her because she's certain he's going to get his pecker burned.' Gavallan laughed. Scot looked up from the reports. 'Neither one thing or the other. Could be very good, lots of cover. But if the wind picks up could be rotten, Saturday better than Friday.' His blue eyes watched his father who stared out of the window at the apron traffic, passengers disembarking from the jet.

'I agree,' Gavallan said, noncommittally. 'There's someth—' He stopped as the HF came to life: 'Al Shargaz, this is Tehran Head Office, do you read?'

'This is Al Shargaz, Head Office, you're four by five, go ahead,' Scot said.

'Director Siamaki wants to talk to Mr. Gavallan immediately.'

Gavallan shook his head. 'I'm not here,' he whispered.

'Can I take a message, Head Office?' Scot said into the mike. 'It's a little late but I'll get it to him as soon as possible.'

Waiting. Static. Then the arrogant voice Gavallan detested. 'This is

963

Managing Director Siamaki. Tell Gavallan to call me back tonight. I'll be here until 10:30 tonight or anytime after 9 a.m. tomorrow. Without fail. Understand?'

'Five by five, Head Office,' Scot said sweetly. 'Over and out!'

'Bloody twit,' Gavallan muttered. Then more sharply, 'What the devil's he doing in the office at this time of night?'

'Snooping, has to be, and if he plans to "work" on Holy Day . . . that's pretty suspicious, isn't it?'

'Mac said he would clean the safe out of important stuff and throw his key and the spare into the joub. Bet those buggers have duplicates,' Gavallan said testily. 'I'll have to wait until tomorrow for the pleasure of talking with him. Scot, is there any way we can jam him listening to our calls?'

'No, not if we use our company frequencies which's all we've got.'

His father nodded. 'When Johnny comes in, remind him I may want him airborne tomorrow at a moment's notice.' It was part of the Whirlwind plan to use the 125 as a high altitude VHF receiver/transmitter to cover those choppers only equipped with VHF. 'From seven o'clock onwards.'

'Then it's a go for tomorrow?'

'Not yet.' Gavallan picked up the phone and dialled. 'Mr. Newbury please, Mr. Gavallan returning his call.' Roger Newbury was one of the officials at the British Consulate who had been very helpful, easing permits for them. 'Hello, Roger, you wanted me? Sorry, you're not at dinner are you?'

'No, glad you called. Couple of things: first, bit of bad news, we've just heard George Talbot's been killed.'

'Good God, what happened?'

' 'Fraid it's all rather rotten, just an accident. He was in a restaurant where there were some rather high level ayatollahs. A terrorist car bomb blew the place to bits and him with it, yesterday lunchtime.'

'How bloody awful!'

'Yes. There was a Captain Ross with him, he was hurt too. I believe you knew him?'

'Yes, yes, I'd met him. He helped the wife of one of our pilots get out of a mess at Tabriz. A nice young man. How badly was he hurt?'

'We don't know, it's all a bit sketchy but our embassy in Tehran got him to the Kuwait International Hospital yesterday, I'll get a proper report tomorrow and will let you know. Now, you asked if we could find out the whereabouts of your Captain Erikki Yokkonen.' A pause and the rustle of papers and Gavallan held on to his hope. 'We had a

964

telex this evening from our man in Tabriz, just before I left the office: "Please be advised in answer to your query about Captain Erikki Yokkonen, he is believed to have escaped from his kidnappers and is now believed to be with his wife at the palace of Hakim Khan. A further report will be forthcoming tomorrow as soon as this can be checked." '

'You mean Abdollah Khan, Roger.' Excitedly Gavallan covered the mouthpiece and whispered to Scot, 'Erikki's safe!'

'Fantastic,' Scot said, wondering what the bad news had been.

'The telex definitely says Hakim Khan,' Newbury was saying.

'Never mind, thank God he's safe.' And thank God another major hurdle against Whirlwind removed. 'Could you get a message to him for me?'

'I could try. Come in tomorrow. Can't guarantee it'll reach him, the situation in Azerbaijan is quite fluid. We could certainly try.'

'I can't thank you enough, Roger. Very thoughtful of you to let me know. Terribly sorry about Talbot and young Ross. If there's anything I can do to help Ross, please let me know.'

'Yes, yes, I will. By the way, the word's out.' It was said flat.

'Sorry?'

'Let's say, "Turbulences", ' Newbury said delicately.

For a moment Gavallan was silent, then he recovered. 'Oh?'

'Oh. It seems a certain Mr. Kasigi wanted you to service Iran-Toda from yesterday and you told him you wouldn't be able to give him an answer for 30 days. So, er, we added two to two, and with all the rumours got a bullseye, the word's out.'

Gavallan was trying to get cool. 'Not being able to service Iran-Toda's a business decision, Roger, nothing more. Operating anywhere in Iran's bloody difficult now, you know that. I couldn't handle Kasigi's extra business.'

'Really?' Newbury's voice was withering. Then, sharply, 'Well if what we hear is true we'd strongly, very strongly advise against it.'

Gavallan said stubbornly, 'You surely don't advise me to support Iran-Toda when all Iran's falling apart, do you?'

Another pause. A sigh. Then, 'Well, mustn't keep you, Andy. Perhaps we could have lunch. On Saturday.'

'Yes, thank you. I'd, I'd like that.' Gavallan hung up.

'What was the bad?' Scot asked.

Gavallan told him about Talbot and Ross and then about 'turbulences.' 'That's too close to Whirlwind to be funny.'

'What's this about Kasigi?'

'He wanted two 212s from Bandar-e Delam at once to service Iran-Toda – I had to stall.' Their meeting had been brief and blunt: 'Sorry, Mr. Kasigi, it's not possible to service you this week, or the next. I couldn't, er, consider it for thirty days.'

'My chairman would greatly appreciate it. I understand you know him?'

'Yes, yes I did and if I could help I certainly would. Sorry, it's just not possible.'

'But . . . then can you suggest an alternative? I *must* get helicopter support.'

'What about a Japanese company?'

'There isn't one. Is there . . . is there someone else to hold me over?'

'Not to my knowledge. Guerney'll never go back but they might know of someone.' He had given him their phone number and the distraught Japanese had rushed off.

He looked at his son. 'Damned shame but nothing I could do to help him.'

Scot said, 'If the word's out . . .' He eased the sling more comfortably. 'If the word's out then it's out. All the more reason to press the titty.'

'Or to cancel. Think I'll drop by and see Duke. Track me down if anyone calls. Nogger's taking over from you?'

'Yes. Midnight. Jean-Luc's still booked on the dawn flight to Bahrain, Pettikin to Kuwait. I've confirmed their seats.' Scot watched him.

Gavallan did not answer the unsaid question. 'Leave it like that for the moment.' He saw his son smile and nod and his heart was suddenly overflowing with love and concern and pride and fear for him, inter-mixed with his own hopes for a future that depended on his being able to extract all of them from the Iranian morass. He was surprised to hear himself say, 'Would you consider giving up flying, laddie?'

'Eh?'

Gavallan smiled at his son's astonishment. But now that he had said it, he decided to continue. 'It's part of a long term plan. For you and the family. In fact I've two – just between ourselves. Of course both depend on whether we stay in business or not. The first is you give up flying and go out to Hong Kong for a couple of years to learn that end of Struan's, back to Aberdeen for perhaps another year, then back to Hong Kong again where you'd base. The second's that you go for a conversion course on the X63s, spend six months or so in the States, perhaps a year learning that end of the business, then to the North Sea for a season. Then out to Hong Kong.'

'Always back to Hong Kong?'

'Yes. China will open up some time soon for oil exploration and Ian and I want Struan's to be ready with a complete operation, support choppers, rigs, the whole kit and caboodle.' He smiled strangely. Oil for the lamps of China was code for Ian Dunross's secret plan to achieve this, most of which Linbar Struan was not party to. 'Air Struan'll be the new company and its area responsibility and operation'd be China, the China Seas and the whole China basin. Our end plan is that you'd head it.'

'Not much potential there,' Scot said with pretended diffidence. 'Do you think Struans would have a future?' Then he let his smile out.

'Again this is all just between us – Linbar's not been given the facts yet.'

Scot frowned. 'Will he approve me going out there, joining Struan and doing this?'

'He hates me, Scot, not you. He hasn't opposed you seeing his niece, has he?'

'Not yet. No he hasn't, not yet.'

'The timing's right and we have to have a future plan – for the family. You're the right age, I think you could do it.' Gavallan's eyes picked up a light. 'You're half Dunross, you're a direct descendant of Dirk Struan and so you've responsibilities above and beyond yourself. You and your sister inherited your mother's shares, you'd qualify for the Inner Office if you're good enough. That burk Linbar'll have to retire one day – even he can't destroy the Noble House totally. What do you say to my plan?'

'I'd like to think it over, Dad.'

What's there to think over, laddie, he thought. ' 'Night, Scot, I may drop back later.' He gave him a careful pat on his good shoulder and walked out. Scot won't fail me, he told himself proudly.

In the spacious Customs and Immigration hall, passengers were trickling in from Immigration, others waiting for their baggage. The arrival board announced the Gulf Air flight 52 from Muscat, Oman's capital, had arrived on time and was due to leave in fifteen minutes for Abu Dhabi, Bahrain and Kuwait. The newsstand was still open so he wandered over to see what papers were in. He was reaching for the London *Times* when he saw the headline, 'Prime Minister Callaghan Cites Labour's Successes' and changed his mind. What do I need that for, he thought. Then he saw Genny McIver.

She was sitting alone near the boarding gate with a small suitcase beside her. 'Hello, Genny. What're you doing here?'

She smiled sweetly. 'I'm going to Kuwait.'

He smiled sweetly back. 'What the hell for?'

'Because I need a holiday.'

'Don't be ridiculous. The button's not even pushed yet and anyway, there's nothing you can do there, nothing. You'd be in the way. You're much better off waiting here. Genny, for God's sake be reasonable.'

The set smile had not even flickered. 'Are you finished?'

'Yes.'

'I am reasonable, I'm the most reasonable person you know. Duncan McIver isn't. He's the most misguided, misbegotten twit I've ever come across in all my born days and to Kuwait I am going.' It was all said with an Olympian calm.

Wisely he changed tactics. 'Why didn't you tell me you were going instead of sneaking off like this? I'd've been worried to death if you'd been missing.'

'If I'd asked you you'd've shanghaied me. I asked Manuela to tell you later, flight time, hotel and phone number. But I'm glad you're here, Andy. You can see me off. I'd like someone to see me off, hate seeing myself off – oh you know what I mean!'

It was then he saw how frail she seemed. 'You all right, Genny?'

'Oh yes. It's just . . . well I just must be there, have to be, I can't sit here and anyway part of this was my idea, I'm responsible too and I don't want anything – anything – to go wrong.'

'It won't,' he said and both of them touched the wooden seat. Then he slipped his arm through hers. 'It's going to be all right. Listen, one good piece of news.' He told her about Erikki.

'Oh, that's wonderful. Hakim Khan?' Genny searched her memory. 'Wasn't Azadeh's brother, the one who was living in . . . blast, I've forgotten, some place near Turkey, wasn't his name Hakim?'

'Perhaps the telex was right then and it is Hakim "Khan". That should be great for them.'

'Yes. Her father sounded like an awful old man.' She looked up at him. 'Have you decided yet? If it's tomorrow?'

'No, not yet, not finally.'

'What about the weather?'

He told her. 'Not much of a decider, either way,' she said.

'Wish Mac was here. He'd be wise in a situation like this.'

'No wiser than you, Andy.' They looked across at the departure board as the announcer called for passengers on Flight 52. They got up. 'For what it's worth, Andy, all other things being equal, Mac's decided it's tomorrow.'

'Eh? How do you know that?'

'I know Duncan. 'Bye, darling Andy.' She kissed him hurriedly and did not look back.

He waited until she had vanished. Deep in thought he went outside, not noticing Wesson near the newsstand, putting his fountain pen away.

BOOK FOUR

Al Shargaz – The Oasis Hotel: 5:37 A.M. Gavallan stood at his window, already dressed, night still heavy except to the east, dawn due soon now. Threads of mist came in from the coast, half a mile away, to vanish quickly in the desert reaches. Sky eerily cloudless to the east, gradually building to thick cover overall. From where he was he could see most of the airfield. Runway lights were on, a small jet already taxiing out, and the smell of kerosene was on the wind that had veered more southerly. A knock on the door. 'Come in! Ah, 'morning, Jean-Luc, 'morning, Charlie.'

' 'Morning, Andy. If we're to catch our flight it's time to leave,' Pettikin said, his nervousness running the words together. He was due to go to Kuwait, Jean-Luc to Bahrain.

'Where's Rodrigues?'

'He's waiting downstairs.'

'Good, then you'd best be on your way,' Gavallan was pleased that his voice sounded calm. Pettikin beamed, Jean-Luc muttered *Merde*. 'With your approval, Charlie, I propose pushing the button at 7 a.m. as planned – provided none of the bases pull the plug beforehand. If they do we'll try again tomorrow. Agreed?'

'Agreed. No calls yet?'

'Not yet.'

Pettikin could hardly contain his excitement. 'Well, off we go into the wild blue yonder! Come on, Jean-Luc!'

Jean-Luc's eyebrows soared. '*Mon Dieu*, it's Boy Scouts time!' Then he went for the door. 'Great news about Erikki, Andy, but how's he going to get out?'

'I don't know. I'm seeing Newbury at the consulate first thing to try to get a message to him to get out via Turkey. Both of you call me the second you land. I'll be in the office from six. See you later.'

He closed the door after them. Now it was done. Unless one of the bases aborted.

At Lengeh: 5:49 A.M. False dawn's light was barely perceptible through the overcast. Scragger wore a raincoat and trudged through the drizzle and puddles towards the cookhouse that had the only light on in the base. The wind pulled at his peaked flying cap, driving the soft rain into his face.

To his surprise Willi was already in the cookhouse, sitting near the wood stove drinking coffee. ' 'Morning, Scrag, coffee? I've just made it.' He motioned with his head into a corner. Curled up on the floor, fast asleep and near to the warmth, was one of the camp Green Bands. Scragger nodded and took off his raincoat.

'Tea for me, me son. You're up early, where's the cook?'

Willi shrugged and put the kettle back on the stove. 'Late. I thought I'd have an early breakfast. I'm going to have some scrambled. How about if I cook for you too?'

Scragger was suddenly famished. 'You're on! Four eggs for me and two pieces of toast and I'll go easy at lunch. We have any bread, sport?' He watched Willi open the refrigerator. Three loaves, plenty of eggs and butter. 'Good oh! Can't eat eggs without buttered toast. They don't taste right.' He glanced at his watch.

'Wind's veered almost south and up to thirty knots.'

'My nose says she'll lessen.'

'My arse says she'll lessen too but still she's shitty.'

Scragger laughed. 'Have confidence, mate.'

'I'll be much more confident with my passport.'

'Too right, so will I – but the plan still stays.' When he had got back last night from the sergeant, Vossi and Willi had been waiting

976

for him. Well away from prying ears he had told them what had happened.

Willi had said at once, and Vossi agreed, 'We better alert Andy, we may have to abort.'

'No,' Scragger said. 'I figure it this way, sport: if Andy doesn't call for Whirlwind in the morning I've all day to get our passports. If he calls for Whirlwind, it'll be exactly at 7:00. That gives me plenty of time to get to the station at 7:30 and back by 8:00. While I'm away you start the plan rolling.'

'Jesus, Scrag, we been thr –'

'Ed, will you listen? We leave anyway but bypass Al Shargaz where we know we'd have trouble and duck into Bahrain – I know the port officer there. We throw ourselves on his mercy – maybe even have an "emergency" on the beach. Meanwhile we radio Al Shargaz the moment we're clear of Iran skies for someone to meet us and bail us out. It's the best I can think of and at least we're covered, either way.'

And it's still the best I can think of, he told himself, watching Willi at the stove, the butter in the frying pan beginning to sizzle. 'I thought we were having scrambled?'

'This's the way to scramble.' Willi's voice edged.

'Bloody isn't you know,' Scragger said sharply. 'You have to use water or milk an –'

'By God Harry,' Willi snapped, 'if you don't want the . . . Sorry, didn't mean to bite your head, Scrag. Sorry.'

'I'm touchy too, sport. No problem.'

'The, er, this way's the way my mother does them. You put the eggs in without beating them, the whites cook white and then, quick as a wink you put in a little milk and you mix her, then the white's white and the yolk's yellow . . .' Willi found himself not able to stop. He had had a bad night, bad dreams, and bad feelings and now with the dawn he felt no better.

Over in the corner the Green Band stirred, his nose filled with the smell of cooking butter and he yawned, nodded to them sleepily, then settled more comfortably and dozed off again. When the kettle boiled Scragger made himself some tea, glanced at his watch. 5:56. Behind him the door opened and Vossi wandered in, shook the rain off the umbrella.

'Hi Scrag! Hey Willi, coffee and two over easy with a side order of crisp bacon and hash brown for me.'

'Get stuffed!'

They all laughed, their anxiety making them light-headed. Scragger glanced at his watch again. Stop it! Stop it, he ordered himself. You've got to keep calm, then they'll be calm. Easy to see they're both ready to blow.

At Kowiss: 6:24 A.M. McIver and Lochart were in the tower looking out at the rain and overcast. Both were dressed in flight gear, McIver seated in front of the HF, Lochart standing at the window. No lights on – just the reds and greens of the functioning equipment. No sound but the pleasing hum and the not so pleasing whine of the wind that came in the broken windows, rattling the aerial stanchions.

Lochart glanced at the wind counter. Twenty-five knots, gusting to thirty from the south-southeast. Over by the hangar two mechanics were washing down the already clean two 212s, and the 206 McIver had brought from Tehran. Lights on in the cookhouse. Except for a skeleton cookhouse staff, McIver had told the office staff and labourers to take Friday off. After the shock of Esvandiary's summary execution for 'corruption' they had needed no encouragement to leave.

Lochart glanced at the clock. The second hand seemed interminably slow. A truck went by below. Another. Now it was exactly 6:30 a.m. 'Sierra One, this is Lengeh.' It was Scragger reporting in as planned. McIver was greatly relieved. Lochart became grimmer.

'Lengeh, this's Sierra One, you're five by five.' Scot's voice from Al Shargaz was clean and clear. Sierra One was code for the office at Al Shargaz Airport, Gavallan not wanting to draw any more attention to the sheikdom than necessary.

McIver clicked on the HF transmit. 'Sierra One, this is Kowiss.'

'Kowiss, this is Sierra One, you're four by five.'

'Sierra One, this's Bandar-e Delam.' Both heard the tremble in Rudi's voice.

'Bandar-e Delam, this's Sierra One, you're two by five.'

Now only static from the loudspeaker. McIver wiped his palms. 'So far so good.' The coffee in his cup was cold and tasted awful but he finished it.

'Rudi sounded uptight, didn't he?' Lochart said.

'I'm sure I did too. So did Scrag.' McIver studied him, concerned for him; Lochart did not meet his eyes, just went over to the electric kettle and plugged it in. On the desk were four phones, two internal and two outside lines. In spite of his resolve, Lochart tried one of the outside phones, then the other. Both still dead. Dead for days now. Dead like me. No way of being in touch with Sharazad, no post.

'There's a Canadian consul in Al Shargaz,' McIver said gruffly. 'They could get through to Tehran for you from there.'

'Sure.' A gust rattled the temporary boarding over the broken windows. Lochart paid the outside no attention, wondering about Sharazad, praying she would join him. Join me for what? The kettle began to sing. He watched it. Since he had walked out of the apartment, he had blocked the future out of his mind. In the night it had surged back, much as he tried to prevent it.

From the base came the first call of a muezzin. 'Come to prayer, come to progress, prayer is better than sleep . . .'

At Bandar-e Delam: 6:38 A.M. A sodden dawn, rain slight, wind less than yesterday. At the airfield Rudi Lutz, Sandor Petrofi, and Pop Kelly were in Rudi's trailer, no lights on, drinking coffee. Outside on the veranda, Marc Dubois was stationed on guard against eavesdroppers. No lights on elsewhere in the base. Rudi glanced at his watch. 'Hope to God it's today,' Rudi said.

'It's today or never.' Kelly was very grim. 'Make the call, Rudi.'

'A minute yet.'

Through the window Rudi could see the maw of the hangar and their 212s. None of them had long range tanks. Somewhere in the darkness, Fowler Joines and three mechanics were quietly putting the last of the spare fuel aboard, finishing preparations begun cautiously last night while the pilots diverted the camp guards and Numir. Just before going to bed the four of them had individually made their range calculations. They were all within ten nautical miles of each other.

'If the wind holds at this strength, we're all in the goddam sea,' Sandor had said softly, difficult to talk over the music but not safe without it – earlier Fowler Joines had spotted Numir lurking near Rudi's trailer.

'Yes,' Marc Dubois had agreed. 'About ten kilometres out.'

'Maybe we should blow Bahrain and divert to Kuwait, Rudi?'

'No, Sandor, we've got to leave Kuwait open for Kowiss. Six Iranian registered choppers all zeroing in there? They'd have a haemorrhage.'

'Where the hell're the new registration numbers we were promised?' Kelly said, his nervousness growing every moment.

'We're being met. Charlie Pettikin's going to Kuwait, Jean-Luc to Bahrain.'

'*Mon Dieu*, that's our bad luck,' Dubois had said, disgustedly. 'Jean-Luc's always late, always. Those Pied Noirs, they think like Arabs.'

'If Jean-Luc screws up this time,' Sandor had said, 'he'll be goddam 'burger meat. Listen, about the gas, maybe we can get extra from Iran-

Toda. It's gonna look mighty suspicious to be loaded with all that gas, just to go down there.'

'Rudi, make the call. It's time.'

'Okay, okay!' Rudi took a deep breath, picked up the mike. 'Sierra One, this's Bandar-e Delam, do you read? This is . . .'

At Al Shargaz H.Q.: 6:40 A.M. '. . . Bandar-e Delam, do you read?'

Gavallan was sitting in front of the HF, Scot beside him, Nogger Lane leaning against a desk behind them, Manuela in the only other chair. All were rigid, staring at the loudspeaker, all sure the call meant trouble as the Whirlwind plan called for radio silence before 7 a.m. and during the actual escape, except in emergencies. 'Bandar-e Delam, Sierra One,' Scot said throatily. 'You're two by five, go ahead.'

'We don't know how your day is but we've some planned flights this morning and we'd like to bring them forward to now. Do you approve?'

'Standby one,' Scot said.

'Damnation,' Gavallan muttered. 'It's essential all bases leave at the same time.' Then again the airwaves crackled into life.

'Sierra One, this's Lengeh,' Scragger's voice was much louder and clearer and more sharp. 'We've flights too but the later the better. How's your weather?'

'Standby one, Lengeh.' Scot glanced across at Gavallan, waiting.

'Call Kowiss,' Gavallan said and everyone relaxed a little. 'We'll check with them first.'

'Kowiss, this's Sierra One, do you read?' Silence. 'Kowiss, this's Sierra One, do you read?'

'This's Kowiss, go ahead.' McIver's voice sounded strained and was intermittent.

'Did you copy?'

'Yes. Prefer firm forecast as planned.'

'That decides it.' Gavallan took the mike. 'Sierra One, all bases, our weather's changeable. We will have your firm forecast at 0700.'

'We copy,' Scragger said happily.

'We copy,' Rudi's voice was brittle.

'We copy.' McIver sounded relieved.

Again the airwaves were silent. Gavallan said to no one in particular, 'Better stick to the plan. Don't want to alert ATC unnecessarily, or get that bugger Siamaki more difficult than usual. Rudi could have aborted if it was urgent, he still can.' He got up and stretched, then

980

sat down again. Static. They were also listening on the emergency channel, 121.5. The Pan Am jumbo took off, rattling the windows.

Manuela shifted in her seat, feeling she was encroaching even though Gavallan had said, 'Manuela, you listen with us too, you're the only Farsi speaker among us.' The time did not weigh so heavily for her. Her man was safe, a little damaged but safe and her heart was singing with joy for the blessed luck that brought him out of the maelstrom. 'Because that's what it is, honey,' she had told him last night at the hospital.

'Maybe, but without Hussain's help I'd still be in Kowiss.'

If it wasn't for that mullah you would never've been hit, she had thought but did not say it, not wanting to agitate him. 'Can I get you anything, darlin'?'

'A new head!'

'They're bringing a pill in a minute. Doctor said you'll be flying in six weeks, that you've the constitution of a roan buffalo.'

'I feel like a bent chicken.'

She had laughed.

Now she let herself drift comfortably, not having to sweat out the waiting like the others, particularly Genny. Two minutes to go. Static. Gavallan's fingers drumming. A private jet took off and she could see another airplane on final, a jumbo with Alitalia colours. Wonder if that'll be Paula's flight back from Tehran?

The minute hand on the clock touched 12. At 7 a.m. Gavallan took the mike. 'Sierra One to all bases: Our forecast's settled and we expect improving weather but watch out for small whirlwinds. Do you copy?'

'Sierra One, this's Lengeh,' Scragger was breezy. 'We copy and will watch for whirlwinds. Out.'

'Sierra One, this's Bandar-e Delam, we copy, and will watch for whirlwinds. Out.'

Silence. The seconds ticked by. Unconsciously Gavallan bit his lower lip. Waiting, then he clicked the transmit button. 'Kowiss, do you read?'

At Kowiss: 7:04 A.M. McIver and Lochart were staring at the HF. Almost together they checked their watches. Lochart muttered, 'It's an abort for today,' wet with relief. Another day's reprieve, he thought. Maybe today the phones'll come back in, maybe today I can talk to her . . .

'They'd still call, that's part of the plan, they call either way.'

McIver clicked the switch on and off. The lights all checked out. So did the dials. 'To hell with it,' he said and clicked on the sender. 'Sierra

One, this's Kowiss, do you read?' Silence. Again, even more anxiously, 'Sierra One, this's Kowiss, do you read?' Silence.

'What the hell's with them?' Lochart said through his teeth.

'Lengeh, this's Kowiss, do you read?' No answer. Abruptly McIver remembered and jumped to his feet and ran to the window. The main cable to the transmitter/receiver aerial was hanging loose, flapping in the wind. Cursing, McIver tore the door to the roof open and went out into the cold. His fingers were strong but the nuts were too rusted to move and he saw the soldered wire ring was eaten away by rust and had fractured. 'Bloody hell . . .'

'Here.' Lochart was beside him and gave him the pliers.

'Thanks.' McIver began to scrape the rust away. The rain had almost stopped but neither noticed it. A rumble of thunder. Sheet lightning flickered in the Zagros, most of the mountains clouded. As he worked hurriedly he told Lochart how Wazari had spent so much time on the roof yesterday fixing the cable. 'When I came on this morning I made a routine call so I knew she was working and we were loud and clear at 6:30 and again at 6:40. The wind must've pulled the wire between then and now . . .' The pliers slipped and he ripped a finger and cursed more.

'Let me do it?'

'No, it's fine. Couple of seconds.'

Lochart went back into the tower cabin. 7:07. The base still quiet. Over at the airbase some trucks were moving around but no airplanes. Down by the hangar their two mechanics still fiddled with the 212s, according to plan, Freddy Ayre with them. Then he saw Wazari cycling along the inside perimeter road. His heart flipped. 'Mac, there's Wazari, coming from the base.'

'Stop him, tell him anything but stop him.' Lochart rushed off down the stairs. McIver's heart was thundering. 'Come on, for God's sake,' he said and cursed himself again for not checking. Check check and recheck, safety is no accident it has to be planned!

Again the pliers slipped. Again he applied them and now the nuts were moving down the bolt. Now one side was tight. For a second he was tempted to risk it, but his caution overcame his anxiety and he tightened the other side. A tentative pull on the cable. Tight. He hurried back, sweat pouring off him. 7:16.

For a moment he could not catch his breath. 'Come on, McIver, for the love of God!' He took a deep breath and that helped. 'Sierra One, this is Kowiss, do you read?'

Scot's anxious voice came back at once, 'Kowiss, Sierra One, go ahead.'

'Do you have any information on any weather for us?'

At once Gavallan's voice, even more anxious: 'Kowiss, we sent out the following at exactly 0700: our forecast's settled and we expect improving weather but watch out for small whirlwinds. Do you copy?'

McIver exhaled, 'We copy, and will watch for small whirlwinds. Did, did the others copy?'

'Affirmative . . .'

At Al Shargaz H.Q.: '. . . I say again, affirmative.' Gavallan repeated into the mike. 'What happened?'

'No problem,' McIver's voice came back, his signal weak. 'See you soon, out.' Now the airwaves were silent. A sudden cheer erupted in the room, Scot embraced his father and gasped as pain ripped up from his shoulder, but no one noticed in the pandemonium, Manuela was hugging Gavallan, and she said, 'I'm going to phone the hospital, Andy, I'll be back in a second,' and ran off. Nogger was jumping up and down with glee and Gavallan said happily, 'I think all nonpilots deserve a large bottle of beer!'

At Kowiss: McIver switched off the set and slumped back in the chair, collecting himself, feeling strange – light-headed and heavy-handed. 'Never mind that, it's a go!' he said. It was quiet in the tower except for the wind that creaked the door he had left open in his haste. He closed it and saw the rain had stopped, the clouds still gloomy. Then he noticed his finger was still bleeding. Beside the HF was a paper towel and he tore a piece off and wrapped it crudely around the wound. His hands were trembling. On a sudden impulse, he went outside and knelt beside the connecting wire. It took all his strength to pull it loose. Then he double-checked the tower, wiped the sweat off his brow and went down the stairs.

Lochart and Wazari were in Esvandiary's office, Wazari unshaven and grubby, a curious electricity in the air. No time to worry about that, McIver thought, Scrag and Rudi're already airborne. ' 'Morning, Sergeant,' McIver said curtly, aware of Lochart's scrutiny. 'I thought I gave you the day off – we've no traffic of any importance.'

'Yeah, Captain, you did but I, er, I couldn't sleep and . . . I don't feel safe over in the base.' Wazari noticed McIver's flushed face and the crude paper bandage. 'You okay?'

'Yes, I'm all right, just cut my finger on the broken window.' McIver glanced at Lochart who was sweating as much as he was. 'We'd better be going, Tom. Sergeant, we're ground testing the 212s.' He saw Lochart glance at him abruptly.

'Yessir. I'll inform base,' Wazari said.

'No need for that.' Momentarily McIver was at a loss, then the answer came to him. 'For your own sake, if you're going to hang around here, you'd better get ready for Minister Kia.'

The colour went out of the man's face. 'What?'

'He's due shortly for the return flight to Tehran. Weren't you the only witness against him and poor bloody Hotshot?'

'Sure, but I heard them,' Wazari flared, needing to justify himself. 'Kia's a bastard and a liar and so's Hotshot and they had this deal cooking. Have you forgotten Hotshot was the one who ordered Ayre beaten up? They would have killed him, have you forgotten that? Esvandiary and Kia, everything I said was true, it was true.'

'I'm sure it was. I believe you. But he's bound to be plenty bloody aggravated if he sees you, isn't he? So will the office staff, they were all very angry. They'll certainly give you away. Perhaps I can divert Kia,' McIver said as a sop, hoping to keep him on their side, 'perhaps not. If I were you I'd make myself scarce, don't hang around here. Come on, Tom.' McIver turned to go but Wazari stood in his way.

'Don't forget I'm the one who stopped a massacre by saying Sandor's load shifted, but for me he'd be dead, but for me you'd all be up before a komiteh . . . you've got to help me . . .' Tears were streaming down his face now, 'you gotta help me . . .'

'I'll do what I can,' McIver said, sorry for him, and walked out. Outside he had to stop himself from running over to the others, seeing their anxiety, then Lochart caught up with him.

'Whirlwind?' he asked, having to hurry to keep alongside.

'Yes, Andy pressed the button on the dot as planned, Scrag and Rudi copied and are probably already on their way,' McIver said, the words tumbling over one another, not noticing Lochart's sudden despair. Now they reached Ayre and the mechanics. 'Whirlwind!' McIver croaked and to all of them the word sounded like a clarion call.

'Jolly good,' Freddy Ayre kept his voice flat, holding his excitement inside. The others did not. 'Why the delay? What happened?'

'Tell you later, start up, let's get on with it!' McIver headed for the first 212, Ayre the second, the mechanics already jumping into the cabins. At that moment a staff car with Colonel Changiz and some airmen swung into the compound and stopped outside the office building. All the airmen carried guns, all wore green armbands.

'Ah, Captain, you're flying Minister Kia back to Tehran?' Changiz seemed a little flustered, and angry.

'Yes, yes I am, at ten, ten o'clock.'

'I had a message that he wants to bring his departure forward to eight o'clock but you're not to leave until ten as your clearance states, Clear?'

'Yes, but in –'

'I would have phoned but your phones are out again and there's something wrong with your radio. Don't you service your equipment? It was working then went off.' McIver saw the colonel look at the three choppers lined up, begin to go towards them. 'I didn't know you had revenue flights today.'

'Just ground-testing one and the other has to test avionics for tomorrow's crew change at Rig Abu Sal, Colonel,' McIver said hastily and to further divert him, 'What's the problem with Minister Kia?'

'No problem,' he said irritably, then glanced at his watch and changed his mind about inspecting the helicopters. 'Get someone to fix your radio and you come with me. The mullah Hussain wants to see you. We'll be back in good time.'

Lochart got his mouth moving. 'I'd be glad to drive Captain McIver over in a minute, there're a few things here he sho –'

'Hussain wants to see Captain McIver, not you – now! You deal with the radio!' Changiz told his men to wait for him, got into the driving seat and beckoned McIver to sit beside him. Blankly, McIver obeyed. Changiz drove off and his driver wandered towards the office, the other airmen spread out, peered at the choppers. Both 212s were crammed with the last of the important spares, loaded last night. Trying to be nonchalant, the mechanics closed the cabin doors, started polishing.

Ayre and Lochart stared after the departing car. Ayre said, 'Now what?'

'I don't know – we can't leave without him.' Lochart felt nauseous.

At Bandar-e Delam: 7:26 A.M. The four 212s were out of the hangar parked for take off. Fowler Joines and the other three mechanics were pottering in the back of the cabins, waiting impatiently. Unwieldy forty gallon drums of reserve gasoline were lashed in place. Many crates of spares. Suitcases hidden under tarpaulins.

'Com' on, for eff's sweet sake,' Fowler said and wiped the sweat off, the air of the cabin heavy with gasoline.

Through the open cabin door he could see Rudi, Sandor and Pop Kelly still waiting in the hangar, everything ready as planned except for the last pilot, Dubois, ten minutes late and no one knowing if Base Manager Numir or one of the staff of Green Bands had intercepted him. Then he saw Dubois come out of his door and almost had a fit. With Gallic indifference, Dubois was carrying a suitcase, his raincoat over his arm. As he strolled past the office, Numir appeared at the window.

'Let's go,' Rudi croaked and went for his cabin as calmly as he could, clipped on his seat belt and stabbed Engines Start. Sandor did likewise, Pop Kelly a second behind him, their rotors gathering speed. Leisurely, Dubois tossed his suitcase to Fowler, laid his raincoat carefully on a crate, and got into the pilot's seat, at once started up, not bothering with his seat belt or checklist. Fowler was swearing incoherently. Their jets were building nicely and Dubois hummed a little song, adjusted his headset and now, when all was prepared, fastened his seat belt. He did not see Numir rush out of his office.

'Where're you going?' Numir shouted to Rudi through his side window.

'Iran-Toda, it's on the manifest.' Rudi continued with the start-up drill. VHF on, HF on, needles coming into the green.

'But you haven't asked Abadan for "engine start" an –'

'It's Holy Day, agha, you can do that for us.'

Numir shouted angrily, 'That's your job! You're to wait for Zataki. You must wait for the col –'

'Quite right, I want to make sure my chopper's ready the instant he arrives – very important to please him, isn't it?'

'Yes, but why was Dubois carrying a suitcase?'

'Oh, you know Frenchmen,' he said, saying the first thing that came into his head, 'clothes are important, he's sure he's going to be based at Iran-Toda and he's taking a spare uniform.' His gloved thumb hovered over the transmit switch on the column. Don't, he ordered himself, don't be impatient, they all know what to do, don't be impatient.

Then, behind Numir, through the haze, visibility down to a few hundred yards, Rudi saw the Green Band truck lumber through the main gate and stop, its noise covered by their jets. But it wasn't Zataki, just some of their normal Green Band guards and they stood there in a group watching the 212 curiously. Never before had four 212s been started up at once.

In his headphones he heard Dubois, 'Ready, *mon vieux*,' then Pop Kelly, then Sandor, and he clicked the send switch and said into the boom mike, 'Go!' leaned closer to the window and beckoned Numir. 'No need for the others to wait, I'm waiting.'

'But you were ordered to go in a group and your clearances . . .' The base manager's voice was drowned by the mass of engines shoved to full power, emergency take-off procedure, conforming to the plan the pilots had secretly agreed on last night, Dubois going right, Sandor left,

Kelly straight ahead like a covey of snipe scattering. In seconds they were airborne and away, staying very low. Numir's face went purple, 'But you were told th –'

'This's for your safety, agha, we're trying to protect you,' Rudi called out over the jets, beckoning him forward again, all his own needles in the green; 'this way's better, agha, this way we'll do the job and no problem. We've got to protect you and IranOil.' In his earphones he heard Dubois break mandatory silence and say urgently, 'There's a car almost at the gates!'

At that instant Rudi saw it and recognised Zataki in the front seat. Maximum power. 'Agha, I'm just going to take her up a few feet, my torque counter's jumping . . .'

Whatever Numir was screaming was lost in the noise. Zataki was barely a hundred yards away. Rudi felt the rotors biting into the air, then lift off. For a moment it looked as though Numir was going to jump on to a skid but he ducked out of the way, the skid scraping him, and fell, as Rudi got forward momentum and lumbered away, almost bursting with excitement. Ahead the others were in station over the marsh. He waggled his chopper from side to side as he joined them, gave them the thumbs-up and led the rush for the Gulf four miles distant.

Numir was choked with rage as he picked himself up and Zataki's car skidded to a halt beside him. 'By God, what's going on?' Zataki said furiously, jumping out, the choppers already vanished into the haze, the sound of the engines dying away now. 'They were supposed to wait for me!'

'I know, I know, Colonel, I told them but they . . . they just took off an—' Numir screamed as the fist smashed him in the side of the face and felled him. The other Green Bands watched indifferently, used to these outbursts. One of the men pulled Numir to his feet, slapped his face to bring him around.

Zataki was cursing the sky and when the spasm of rage had passed, he said, 'Bring that piece of camel's turd and follow me.' Storming past the open hangar he saw the two 206s parked neatly in the back, spares laid out here and there, a fan drying some new paintwork – all Rudi's painstaking camouflage to give them an extra few minutes. 'I'll make those dogs wish they'd waited,' he muttered, his head aching.

He kicked the door of the office open and stormed over to the radio transmitter and sat down near it. 'Numir, get those men on the loudspeaker!'

'But Jahan our radio operator's not here yet and I do –'

'Do it!'

The terrified man switched on the VHF, his mouth bleeding, and hardly able to talk. 'Base calling Captain Lutz!' He waited, then repeated the order, adding 'urgent!'

In the Airplanes: They were barely ten feet above the marshland and a few hundred yards away when they heard Zataki's angry voice cut in. 'All helicopters are recalled to base, recalled to base! Report in!' Rudi made a slight adjustment to the engine power and to the trim. In the chopper nearest to him he saw Marc Dubois point at his headset and make an obscene gesture. He smiled and did likewise, then noticed the sweat running down his face. 'ALL HELICOPTERS REPORT IN! ALL . . .'

At the Airfield: '. . . HELICOPTERS REPORT IN,' Zataki was shrieking into the mike, 'ALL HELICOPTERS REPORT IN!'

Nothing but static answered him. Suddenly Zataki slammed the mike on to the table. 'Get Abadan Tower! HURRY UP!' he shouted and the terrified Numir, blood trickling into his beard, switched channels, and after the sixth call, this time in Farsi, got the tower. 'Here is Abadan Tower, agha, please go ahead.'

Zataki tore the mike out of his hand. 'This is Colonel Zataki, Abadan Revolutionary Komiteh,' he said in Farsi, 'calling from Bandar-e Delam airfield.'

'Peace be upon you, Colonel,' the voice was very deferential. 'What can we do for you?'

'Four of our helicopters took off without approval, going to Iran-Toda. Recall them, please.'

'Just a moment please.' Muffled voices. Zataki waited, his face mottled. Waiting and waiting, then, 'Are you sure, agha? We do not see them on the radar screen.'

'Of course I'm sure. Recall them!'

More muffled voices and more waiting, Zataki ready to explode, then a voice in Farsi said, 'The four helicopters that left Bandar-e Delam are ordered to return to their base. Please acknowledge you are doing this.' It was transmitted ineptly and repeated. Then the voice added, 'perhaps their radios are not functioning, agha, the blessings of God upon you.'

'Keep calling them! They're low and heading towards Iran-Toda!'

More muffled voices, then more Farsi as before, then a sudden voice cut in in American English, 'Okay, I'll take it! This is Abadan Control. Choppers on a heading of 090 degrees, do you read?'

In Dubois' Cockpit: His compass heading was 091 degrees. Again the crisp voice in his earphones: 'This is Abadan Control, choppers on a heading of 090 degrees one mile from the coast, do you read?' A pause. 'Abadan Control, choppers on a heading of 090 switch to channel 121.9 . . . do you read?' This was the emergency channel that all aircraft were supposed to listen in on automatically. 'Choppers on a heading of 090 degrees one mile from the coast, return to base. Do you read?'

Through the haze Dubois saw that the coast was approaching fast, less than half a mile away, but flying this low he doubted if they could possibly be on radar. He looked left. Rudi pointed at his earphones and then a finger to his lips meaning silence. He gave him the thumbs-up and passed the message to Sandor who was on his right, turned to see Fowler Joines climbing in from the cabin to sit beside him. He motioned to the spare headset hanging above the seat. The voice was more brittle now: 'All choppers outward bound from Bandar-e Delam to Iran-Toda return to base. Do you read?'

Fowler, connected now through the headset, said into their intercom, 'Hope the effer drops dead!'

Then again the voice and their smiles faded: 'Abadan Control to Colonel Zataki. Do you read?'

'Yes, go ahead.'

'We picked up a momentary radar trace, probably nothing, but it could have been a chopper or choppers tightly bunched, heading 090 degrees' – the transmission was weakening slightly – 'this would take them direct . . .'

At the Airfield: '. . . Iran-Toda. Not requesting engine start and not being in radio contact is a serious violation. Please give us their call signs and names of the captains. Iran-Toda's VHF is still inoperative otherwise we would contact them. Suggest you send someone down there to arrest the pilots and bring them before the ATC Abadan at once for contravening air regulations. Do you copy?'

'Yes . . . yes I understand. Thank you. Just a moment.' Zataki shoved the mike into Numir's hands. 'I'm going to Iran-Toda! If they come back before I get them, they're under arrest! Give Traffic Control what they want to know!' He stormed out, leaving three men on base with machine guns.

Numir began, 'Abadan Control, Bandar-e Delam: HVV, HGU, HKL, HXC, all 212s. Captains Rudi Lutz, Marc Dubois . . .'

In Pop Kelly's Cockpit: '. . . Sandor Petrofi, and Ignatius Kelly, all seconded from IranOil by Colonel Zataki's order to Iran-Toda.'

'Thank you, Bandar-e Delam, keep us advised.'

Kelly looked right and gave an enthusiastic thumbs-up to Rudi who acknowledged . . .

In Rudi's Cockpit: . . . and did the same to Dubois who also acknowledged. Then he peered into the haze once more.

The closely bunched choppers were almost over the coastline. Iran-Toda was to their left, about a half a mile away, but Rudi could see none of it through the haze or mist. He accelerated slightly to get ahead, then turned from his heading of due south to due east. This gave them a deliberate direct course over the plant and he increased altitude only enough to clear the buildings. The complex rushed past but he knew that those on the ground would be well aware of their flight because of the howling suddenness of its appearance. Once past, he went down low again and held this same course, now heading inland for a little more than ten miles. Here the land was desolate, no villages nearby. Again, according to their plan, he turned due south for the sea.

At once visibility began to deteriorate. Down here at twenty feet visibility was barely a quarter of a mile with a partial white-out where there was no demarcation between the sky and sea. Ahead, almost directly in their path, sixty-odd miles away, was Kharg Island with its immensely powerful radar and, beyond that, another two hundred and twenty miles, their landfall Bahrain. At least two hours of flying. With this wind more, the thirty-five southeasterly becoming a relative twenty knot headwind.

Down here in the soup it was dangerous. But they thought they should be able to slip under radar if the screens were manned – and should be able to avoid fighter intercept, if any.

Rudi moved the stick from side to side waggling his chopper, then touched his HF transmit button momentarily. 'Delta Four, Delta Four,' he said clearly, their code to Al Shargaz that all four Bandar-e Delam choppers were safe and leaving the coast. He saw Dubois point upwards asking him to go higher. He shook his head, pointed ahead and down, ordering them to stay low and stick to the plan. Obediently they spread out and together they left the land and went into the deepening haze.

*   *   *

At Al Shargaz – S-G's Office: Gavallan was excitedly on the phone to the hospital: 'Give me Captain Starke, please . . . Hello, Duke, it's Andy, I just wanted to tell you we received "Delta Four" from Rudi a minute ago, isn't that marvellous?'

'Wonderful, great! Fantastic! Four out and five to go!'

'Yes, but it's six, don't forget Erikki . . .'

Lengeh: 8:04 A.M. Scragger was still waiting in the outer office of the police station. He sat disconsolately on a wooden bench in front of the gendarme corporal who looked down on him from a tall desk behind a chest-high partition.

Once again Scragger checked his watch. He had arrived at 7:20 in case the office opened early but the corporal had not arrived until 7:45 and waved him politely to the bench and invited him to wait. It was the longest wait he had ever had.

Rudi and the Kowiss lads must be airborne by now, he thought miserably, just like we'd've been if it wasn't for the bloody passports. Another minute then that's it. Daren't wait any longer – daren't, it'll still take us an hour or more to get away and sure to God there'll be a slip up somewhere between the three bases, bound to be some nosy parker who'll start asking questions and set the airwaves afire – apart from that burk, Siamaki. Last night Scragger had been on the HF and had monitored Siamaki's petulant calls to Gavallan at Al Shargaz, also to McIver at Kowiss telling him that he would meet him today at Tehran Airport.

Bloody burk! But I still think I was right not to call Andy and abort. Hell, we've got the easiest shot of all and if I'd put Whirlwind off until tomorrow there'd be something else, either with us or with one of the others, and there'd be no way old Mac could avoid flying back to Tehran today with bloody Kia. Can't risk that, just can't. Easy to hear Mac was as nervous as an old woman out to sea in a bucket.

The door opened and he looked up. Two young gendarmes came in, dragging a bruised young man between them, his clothes ripped and filthy. 'Who's he?' the corporal asked.

'A thief. We caught him stealing, Corporal, the poor fool was stealing rice from the bazaari Ishmael. We caught him during our patrol, just before dawn.'

'As God wants. Put him in the second cell.' Then the corporal shouted at the youth, startling Scragger who did not understand the Farsi, 'Son of a dog! How can you be so stupid to be caught? Don't you know it's no longer a simple beating now! How many times do you all have to be told? It's Islamic law now. Islamic law!'

'I . . . I was hungry . . . my . . .'

The terrified youth moaned as one of the gendarmes shook him roughly. 'Hunger's no excuse, by God. I'm hungry, our families're hungry, we're all hungry, of course we're hungry!' They frog-marched the youth out of the room.

The corporal cursed him again, sorry for him, then glanced at Scragger, nodded briefly, and went back to his work. How stupid for the foreigners to be here on a Holy Day but if the old one wants to wait all day and all night until the sergeant comes tomorrow he can wait all day and all night.

His pen scratched loudly, setting Scragger's teeth on edge. 8:11. Grimly he got up, pretended to thank the corporal who politely pressed him to stay. Then he went for the door and almost bumped into Qeshemi. 'Oh, sorry, mate! Salaam, Agha Qeshemi, salaam.'

'Salaam, agha.' Qeshemi saw Scragger's relief and impatience. Sardonically he motioned him to wait as he went over to the desk, his shrewd eyes reading the corporal clearly. 'Greetings, Achmed, God's peace on you.'

'And on you, Excellency Sergeant Qeshemi.'

'What trouble do we have today – I know what the foreigner wants.'

'There was another Islamic-Marxist meeting near midnight down by the docks. One mujhadin was killed and we've another seven in the cells – it was easy, the ambush went easily, thanks be to God, and Green Bands helped us. What'll we do with them?'

'Obey the new rules,' Qeshemi said patiently. 'Bring the prisoners up before the Revolutionary Komiteh when they get here tomorrow morning. Next?' The corporal told him about the youth. 'Same with him – son of a dog to be caught!' Qeshemi went through the partition gate to the safe, pulled out the key and began to open it.

'Thanks be to God, I thought the key was lost,' the corporal said.

'It was but Lafti found it. I went to his house this morning. He had it in his pocket.' The passports were on the boxes of ammunition. He brought them over to the desk, carefully checked them, signed the permit in the name of Khomeini, checked them again. 'Here, Agha Pilot,' he said, and handed them to Scragger.

'*Mamnoon am, agha, khoda haefez.*' Thank you, Excellency, goodbye.

'*Khoda haefez, agha.*' Sergeant Qeshemi shook the proffered hand, thoughtfully watched him leave. Through the window he saw Scragger drive off quickly. Too quickly. 'Achmed, do we have gasoline in the car?'

'There was yesterday, Excellency.'

At Bandar-e Delam Airport: 8:18 A.M. Now Numir was running frantically from one mechanic's trailer to the next, but they were all empty. He rushed back to his office. Jahan, the radio op, looked at him startled.

'They've gone! Everyone's gone, pilots, mechanics . . . and most of their things are gone too!' Numir stuttered, his face still livid from the blow Zataki had given him. 'Those sons of dogs!'

'But . . . but they've only gone to Iran-Toda. Excell –'

'I tell you they've fled, and they fled with our helicopters!'

'But our two 206s are there in the hangar, I saw them and a fan's even drying the paint. Excellency Rudi wouldn't leave a fan on like tha –'

'By God I tell you they've gone!'

Jahan, a middle-aged man wearing glasses, switched on the HF. 'Captain Rudi, this's base, do you read?'

In Rudi's Cockpit: Both Rudi and his mechanic Faganwitch heard the call clearly. 'Base to captain Rudi, do you read?' Rudi moved the trim a fraction then relaxed again, looking right and left. He saw Kelly motion at his headset, raise two fingers and gesture. He acknowledged. Then his glee faded: 'Tehran, this's Bandar-e Delam, do you read?' All pilots tensed. No answer. 'Kowiss, this's Bandar-e Delam, do you read?' No answer. 'Lengeh, this's Bandar-e Delam, do you read?'

'Bandar-e Delam, this's Lengeh, you're two by five, go ahead.'

At once there was a spate of Farsi from Jahan that Rudi did not understand, then the two operators talked back and forth. After a pause, Jahan said in English: 'Tehran, this is Bandar-e Delam, do you read?' Static. The call repeated. Static. Then, 'Kowiss, do you read?' Then silence again.

'For the moment,' Rudi muttered.

'What was all that about, Captain?' Faganwitch asked.

'We're pegged. It's barely fifty minutes since we took off and we're pegged!' There were fighter bases all around them and ahead was the big, very efficient one at Kharg. He had not doubt whatsoever that if they were intercepted they would be shot down. Correctly, he thought grimly. And though they were safe enough at the moment down here just above the waves, visibility now less than a quarter of a mile, before long the haze would thin out and then they would be helpless. Again Jahan's voice, 'Tehran, this is Bandar-e Delam, do you read?' Static. 'Kowiss, this is Bandar-e Delam, do you read?' No reply.

Rudi cursed to himself. Jahan was a good radio op, persistent, and would keep calling until Kowiss or Tehran reported in. And then? That's their problem, not mine. Mine's to get my four out safely, that's all I have to worry about. I've got to lead my four out safely.

Ten to fifteen feet below were the waves, not yet white-topped but grey and nasty and the wind had not lessened. He looked across at Kelly and waved his hand from left to right, the signal to spread out more and not to try to keep visual contact if visibility got any worse. Kelly acknowledged. He did the same to Dubois who passed the message on to Sandor, on his extreme right, then settled down to squeeze maximum range with minimum fuel, straining his eyes to pierce the white-out ahead. Soon they would be deep in the real sea lanes.

Lengeh, at the Airfield: 8:31 A.M. 'Jesus, Scrag, we thought you'd been arrested,' Vossi burst out, Willi with him, intercepting his car, both of them weak with relief, their three mechanics also crowding around. 'What happened?'

'I've got the passports, so let's get on with it.'

'We gotta problem.' Vossi was white.

Scragger grimaced, still sweating from the waiting and the ride back. 'Now what?'

'Ali Pash's here. He's on the HF. He came in as usual and we tried to send him off but he wouldn't go an –'

Impatiently Willi butted in, 'And for the last five minutes, Scrag, for the last five or ten minutes he's been by God Harry peculiar an –'

'Like he's got a vibrator up his ass, Scrag, never seen him like th—' Vossi stopped. Ali Pash came out on to the veranda of the office radio room and beckoned Scragger urgently.

'Be right there, Ali,' Scragger called out. To Benson, their chief mechanic, Scragger whispered, 'You and your lads all set?'

'Yessir.' Benson was small, wiry and nervous. 'I got your stuff into the wagon just before Ali Pash came along. We scarper?'

'Wait till I get to the office. Ev –'

'We got Delta Four, Scrag.' Willi said, 'nothing from the others.'

'Bonza. Everyone wait till I give the signal.' Scragger took a deep breath and walked off, greeting the Green Bands he passed. 'Salaam, Ali Pash, g'day,' he said, seeing the nervousness and anxiety. 'I thought I gave you the day off.'

'Agha, there someth –'

'Just a sec, me son!' Scragger turned and with pretended irascibility called out, 'Benson, I told you if you and Drew want to go and picnic to go, but you'd better be back by two o'clock or else! And what the hell're you two waiting for? Are you ground-checking or aren't you?'

'Yeah, Scrag, sorry, Scrag!'

He almost laughed seeing them fall over one another, Benson and the American mechanic, Drew, jumping into the old van and driving off, Vossi and Willi heading for their cockpits. Once inside the office he breathed easier, put his briefcase with the passports on his deak. 'Now, what's the problem?'

'You're leaving us, agha,' the young man said to his shock.

'Well, we, er, we're not leaving,' Scragger began, 'we're ground-test –'

'Oh, but you're leaving, you are! There's . . . there's no crew change tomorrow, there's no need for suitcases – I saw Agha Benson with suitcases – and why all the spares sent out and all the pilots and mechanics . . .' The tears began streaming down the young man's cheeks. '. . . it's true.'

'Now listen here, me son, you're upset. Take the day off.'

'But you're leaving like those at Bandar-e Delam, you're leaving today and now what's going to happen to us?'

A burst of Farsi from the HF loudspeaker overrode him. The young man wiped away his tears and touched the transmit, replying in Farsi, then added in English, 'Standby One,' and said miserably, 'That was Agha Jahan again repeating what he radioed ten minutes ago. Their four 212s have vanished, agha. They've gone, agha. They took off at

7.32 to go to Iran-Toda but didn't land there, just went inland.'

Scragger had groped for his chair, trying to appear calm. Again the HF, in English now: 'Tehran, this's Bandar-e Delam, do you read?'

'He calls Tehran every few minutes, and Kowiss but no answer . . .' More tears welled out of the young man's eyes. 'Have Kowiss already gone too, agha? Is Tehran empty of your people? What're we going to do when you've gone?' On the ramp the first of the 212s started up noisily, closely followed by the second. 'Agha,' Ali Pash said uneasily, 'we're supposed to request "Engine Start" from Kish now.'

'No need to bother them on their holiday, it's hardly a flight, just testing,' Scragger said. He switched on the VHF and wiped his chin, feeling somehow dirty and greatly unsettled. He liked Ali Pash and what the young man had said was true. With them gone there was no job, no business and for the Ali Pashes there was only Iran, and only God knew what would happen here. Over the VHF came Willi's voice: 'My torque counter's acting up, Scrag.'

Scragger took the mike. 'Take her over to the cabbage patch and test her.' This was an area some five miles inland, well away from the town where they tested engines and could practise emergency procedures. 'Stay there, Willi, any problem call me, I can always fetch Benson if you need an adjustment. How you doing, Ed?'

'Dandy, real dandy. Scrag, if it's okay, I'd like to practise some engine-outs, my licence renewal's coming up soon – Willi can bird-dog me, huh?'

'Okay. Call me in an hour.' Scragger went to the window, glad to have his back to Ali Pash and away from those sad, accusing eyes. Both choppers took off and headed inland away from the coast. The office seemed to be stuffier than usual. He opened the window. Ali Pash was sitting gloomily by the radio. 'Why not take the day off, lad?'

'I have to reply to Bandar-e Delam. What should I say, agha?'

'What did Jahan ask you?'

'He said Agha Numir wanted to know if I'd noticed anything strange, if anything strange had happened here, spares leaving, airplanes leaving, pilots and mechanics.'

Scragger watched him. 'Seems to me nothing strange's happened here. I'm here, mechanics've gone picnicking, Ed and Willi are off on routine checks. Routine. Right?' He kept his eyes on him, willing him to come over to their side. He had no way of persuading him, nothing to offer him, no pishkesh, except . . . 'You approve of what's happening here, me son?' he asked carefully. 'I mean, what the future holds for you here?'

'Future? My future's with the company. If . . . if you leave then . . . then I have no job, I won't . . . I can't afford to . . . I won't, can't afford anything. I'm the only son . . .'

'If you wanted to leave, well, there'd be your job and a future if you wanted it – outside Iran. Guaranteed.'

The youth gaped at him, suddenly understanding what Scragger was offering. 'But . . . but what is guaranteed, agha? A life in your West, me alone? What of my people, my family, my young bride-to-be?'

'Can't answer that, Ali Pash,' Scragger said, eyes on the clock, conscious of time slipping by, the lights and the hum of the HF, readying to overpower the young man who was taller than he, bigger built, younger by thirty-five years, and then disable the HF and make a run for it. Sorry, me son, but one way or another you're going to cooperate. Casually he moved closer, into a better position. 'Insha'Allah is your way of putting it,' he said kindly, and readied.

Hearing that come from the mouth of this kind, strange old man he respected so much, Ali Pash felt a flood of warmth pervade him.

'This is my home, agha, my land,' Ali Pash said simply. 'The Imam is the Imam and he obeys only God. The future is the future and in God's hands. The past too is the past.'

Before Scragger could stop him, Ali Pash called Bandar-e Delam and now was speaking Farsi into the mike. The two operators talked with one another for a moment or two, then abruptly he signed off. And looked up at Scragger. 'I don't blame you for leaving,' he said. 'Thank you, agha, for . . . for the past.' Then, with great deliberation, he switched the HF off, took out a circuit breaker and pocketed it. 'I told him we . . . we were closing down for the day.'

Scragger exhaled. 'Thanks, me son.'

The door opened. Qeshemi stood there. 'I wish to inspect the base,' he said.

Al Shargaz HQ: Manuela was saying, '. . . and then, Andy, Lengeh's operator, Ali Pash, said to Jahan, "No, nothing's strange here," then added, kinda abruptly, "I'm closing down for the day. I must go to prayers." Numir called him back at once, asking him to wait a few minutes but there was no answer.'

'Abruptly?' Gavallan asked, Scot and Nogger also listening intently. 'What sort of abruptly?'

'Like, like he kinda got fed up, or had a gun to his head – not usual for an Iranian to be that abrupt.' Manuela added uneasily, 'I might be reading something into it that wasn't there, Andy.'

'Does that mean Scrag's still there or not?'

Scot and Nogger grimaced, appalled at the thought. Manuela shifted nervously. 'If he was, wouldn't he have answered himself to let us know? I think I would have. Perhaps h—' The phone rang. Scot picked it up: 'S-G? Oh hello Charlie, hang on.' He passed the phone to his father. 'From Kuwait . . .'

'Hello, Charlie. All's well?'

'Yes, thanks, I'm at Kuwait airport, phoning from Patrick's office at Guerneys'.' Though the two companies were rivals worldwide, they had very friendly relations. 'What's new?'

'Delta Four, nothing else yet. I'll phone the moment Jean-Luc's checked in from Bahrain – he's with Delarne at Gulf Air de France if you want him. Is Genny with you?'

'No, she went back to the hotel but I'm all set the moment Mac and the others arrive.'

Gavallan said quietly, 'Did you tell Patrick, Charlie?' He heard Pettikin's forced laugh.

'Funny thing, Andy, the BA rep here, a couple of other guys and Patrick have this crazy idea we're up to something – like pulling all our birds out. Can you imagine?'

Gavallan sighed. 'Don't jump the gun, Charlie, keep to the plan.' This was to keep quiet until the Kowiss choppers were in the Kuwait system, then to trust Patrick. 'I'll phone when I have anything. 'Bye – oh hang on, I almost forgot. You remember Ross, John Ross?'

'Could I ever forget? Why?'

'I heard he's in Kuwait International Hospital. Check on him when you've squared away, will you?'

'Of course, right away, Andy. What's the matter with him?'

'Don't know. Call me if you have any news. 'Bye.' He replaced the phone. Another deep breath. 'The word's out in Kuwait.'

'Christ, if it's out th—' Scot was interrupted by the phone ringing. 'Hello? Just a moment. It's Mr. Newbury, Dad.'

Gavallan took it. ' 'Morning, Roger, how're tricks?'

'Oh. Well, I, er, wanted to ask you that. How are things going? Off the record of course.'

'Fine, fine,' Gavallan said noncommittally. 'Will you be in your office all day? I'll drop by, but I'll call before I leave here.'

'Yes, please do, I'll be here until noon. It's a long weekend you know. Please phone me the moment you, er, hear anything – off the record. The moment. We're rather concerned and, well, we can discuss it when you arrive. 'Bye.'

'Hang on a moment. Did you get word about young Ross?'

'Yes, yes I did. Sorry but we understand he was badly hurt, not expected to survive. Damn shame but there you are. See you before noon. 'Bye.'

Gavallan put the phone down. They all watched him. 'What's wrong?' Manuela asked.

'Apparently . . . it seems young Ross is badly hurt, not expected to survive.'

Nogger muttered, 'What a bugger! My God, not fair . . .' He had told them all about Ross, how he had saved their lives, and Azadeh's.

Manuela crossed herself and prayed fervently to the Madonna to keep him then begged Her again and again to bring all the men back safe, all of them, without favour, and Azadeh and Sharazad, and let there be peace please please please . . .

'Dad, did Newbury tell you what happened?'

Gavallan shook his head, hardly hearing him. He was thinking about Ross, of an age with Scot, more tough and rugged and indestructible than Scot and now . . . Poor laddie! Maybe he'll pull through . . . oh God, I hope so! What to do? Continue, that's all you can do. Azadeh'll be rocked, poor lassie. Erikki'll be as rocked as Azadeh, he owes her life to him. 'I'll be back in a second,' he said and walked out, heading for their other office where he could phone Newbury in private.

Nogger was standing at the window, looking out at the day and the airfield, not seeing any of it. He was seeing the wild-eyed, maniac killer at Tabriz One holding the severed head aloft, baying like a wolf to the sky, the angel of sudden death who became the giver of life – to him, to Arberry, to Dibble, and most of all to Azadeh. God, if you are God, save him like he saved us . . .

'Tehran, this is Bandar-e Delam, do you read?'

'Five minutes on the dot,' Scot muttered. 'Jahan doesn't miss a bloody second. Didn't Siamaki say he'd be in the office from 0900 onwards?'

'Yes, yes he did.' All their eyes went to the clock. It read 8.54.

At Lengeh Airport: 9:01 A.M. Qeshemi was standing in the hangar looking at the two parked 206s within. Behind him Scragger and Ali Pash watched nervously. A momentary shaft of sun broke the clouds and overcast and sparkled off the 212 that was waiting on the helipad fifty yards away, a battered police car and the driver, Corporal Achmed, beside it. 'Have you flown in one of those, Excellency Pash?' Qeshemi asked.

1000

'The 206? Yes, Sergeant Excellency,' Ali Pash said, giving the sergeant his most pleasing smile. 'The captain sometimes takes me or the other radio operator when we're off duty.' He was very sorry the Devil had moved his feet here today, worse than sorry because now he was inescapably involved in treason – treason to break rules, treason to lie to police, treason not to report curious happenings. 'The captain would take you any time you wished,' he said pleasantly, his whole being concentrated now on extricating himself from the mire the Devil and the captain had put him into.

'Today would be a good day?'

Ali Pash almost broke under the scrutiny. 'Of course, if you ask the captain, of course, agha. You wish me to ask?'

Qeshemi said nothing, just moved out into the open, careless of the Green Bands, half a dozen of them, who watched curiously. To Scragger he said directly in Farsi, 'Where is everyone today, agha?'

Ali Pash acted as interpreter for Scragger, though he twisted the words, making them sound better and more acceptable, explaining that today being Holy Day, with no revenue flights, the Iranian staff had correctly been given the day off, the captain had ordered the 212s to their designated training area of testing, had allowed the remaining mechanics to go picnicking, and that he himself was leaving to go to the Mosque as soon as his Excellency the sergeant had finished whatever he wished to finish.

Scragger was totally frustrated that he did not understand Farsi, and loathed being out of control of the situation but he was, completely. His life and those of his men were in the hands of Ali Pash.

'His Excellency asks, What do you plan for the rest of the day?'

'That's a bloody good question,' Scragger muttered. Then the family motto came into his mind: 'You hang for a lamb, you hang for a sheep, so you might as well take the whole bleeding flock,' – the motto that had been handed down by his ancestor who had been transported for life to Australia in the early 1800s. 'Please tell him, soon as he's finished, I'm going to the cabbage patch as Ed Vossi needs checking out. His licence's due for renewal.'

He watched and waited and Qeshemi asked a question that Ali Pash answered and all the time he was wondering what to do if Qeshemi said, Fine, I'm coming along.

'His Excellency asks if you would be so kind as to loan the police some gasoline?'

'What?'

'He wants some gasoline, Captain. Wants to borrow some gasoline.'

1001

'Oh. Oh certainly, certainly, agha.' For a moment Scragger was filled with hope. Hold it, me son, he thought. The cabbage patch's not so far away and Qeshemi could want the gas to send the car there and still fly with me. 'Come on, Ali Pash, you can give me a hand,' he said, not wanting to leave him alone with Qeshemi and led the way to the pump, beckoning the police car. The wind sock was dancing. He saw that the clouds aloft were building up, nimbus among them, travelling fast, shoved along by a contrary wind. Here below it was still southeasterly though it had veered even more southerly. Good for us but more of a bloody headwind for the others, he thought grimly.

In the Helicopters, Nearing Kish Island: 9:07 A.M. Rudi's four choppers were in sight of each other, closer than before, cruising calmly just over the waves. Visibility varied between two hundred yards to half a mile. All pilots were conserving fuel, seeking maximum range, and again Rudi bent forward to tap his gas gauge. The needle moved slightly, still registering just under half full. 'No problem, Rudi, she's working fine,' Faganwitch said through the intercom. 'We've plenty of time to refuel, right? We're on time and on schedule, right?'

'Oh yes.' Even so Rudi recalculated their range, always coming up with the same answer: enough to reach Bahrain but not enough for the legal amount of fuel in reserve. 'Tehran, this is Bandar-e Delam do you read?' Jahan's voice came in his headphones again, irritating him with its persistence. For a moment he was tempted to turn off but dismissed that as too danger –

'Bandar-e Delam, this is Tehran. We read you four by five, go ahead!'

Now a flood of Farsi. Rudi picked out 'Siamaki' several times but little else as the two radio ops spoke back and forth and then he recognised Siamaki's voice, irritable, arrogant and now very angry. 'Standby One, Bandar-e Delam! Al Shargaz, this is Tehran, do you read?' Now even more angrily. 'Al Shargaz, this is Director Siamaki, do you read?' No answer. The call repeated more angrily, then another spate of Farsi, then Faganwitch cried out, 'AHEAD! Lookout!'

The supertanker, almost a quarter of a mile long, was hurtling at them broadside through the haze, towering over them, dwarfing them, easing her way carefully upstream towards her Iraqi terminal, foghorn droning. Rudi knew he was trapped, no time to climb, no space to break left or right or he would collide with the others so he went into emergency stop procedure. Kelly on his left, banking perilously left, just made it past the stern, Sandor, extreme right, safe around the bow –

Dubois not safe but instantly on to max power, stick right and back into a too steep climbing turn, tighter tighter tighter 50–60–70–80 degrees, bow rushing at him, not going to make it, *'espèce de con . . .'* not going to make it, stick back, G-force sucking him and Fowler down into their seats, the ship's gunwale racing at them, then they roared over the foredeck with millimetres to spare, the appalled deck crew scattering. Once safe, Dubois hauled her around into a 180 to go back for Rudi in the slight hope Rudi had managed to cushion the impact and had escaped into the sea.

Rudi had the stick back, nose up, power off, watching the airspeed tumble, nose a little higher, no time to pray, nose higher, side of the tanker closer and closer, nose higher still, stall warning howling, not going to make it, stall warning shrieking, any moment she'll fall out of the sky, tanker only yards away, seeing rivets, portholes, rust, paint peeling, closing on them but slowing, slowing, but too late, too late but maybe enough to soften the crash, now plummeting, stick forward, full power on momentarily to cushion the dreadful impact and fall and suddenly she was locked in hover five feet above the waves, the mushing blades barely inches from the side of the tanker that slid past gently. Somehow Rudi backed away a yard, then another and hovered.

When his eyes could focus he looked up. On the bridge of the vessel so far above them he could see the officers staring down at them, most of them shaking their fists in rage. A purple-faced man had a loud-speaker now, and he was shouting at them, 'Bloody idiot!' but they could not hear him. The stern passed them by, wake churning, the spray speckling them. The way ahead was clear.

'I'm . . . I'm going to hav'ta take a shit.' Weakly Faganwitch began to crawl back into the cabin.

You can take one for me, Rudi was thinking but he had no energy to say it. His knees were trembling and teeth chattering. 'Careful,' he muttered, then eased the throttle open, gained height and forward speed and soon he was quite safe. No sign of the others. Then he spotted Kelly coming round, looking for him. When Kelly saw him he waggled from side to side so happily, came into station alongside, gave him a thumbs-up. To save the others vital fuel coming back to search for the pieces, Rudi put his lips very close to the boom mike and hissed through his teeth, 'dot-dot-dot-dash, dot-dot-dot-dash, dot-dot-dot-dash,' their privately agreed code for each to head for Bahrain independently, and to let them know he was safe. He heard Sandor acknowledge in the same simulated morse, then Dubois who swooped alongside out of the haze, adding some self generated static, and accelerated away. But Pop Kelly was shaking his head, motioning that he would prefer to stay alongside. He pointed ahead.

Once more in their headsets: 'Al Shargaz, this is Agha Siamaki in Tehran, do you read?' Then more Farsi. 'Al Shargaz . . .'

At Al Shargaz, HQ: '. . . This is Agha Siamaki . . .' Then another splurge of Farsi. Gavallan's fingers drummed on the desk top, outwardly calm, inwardly not. He had not been able to reach Pettikin before he left for the hospital and there was nothing he could do to choke Siamaki and Numir off the air. Scot adjusted the volume slightly, lessening the harangue, pretending with Nogger to be nonchalant. Manuela said throatily, 'He's plenty mad, Andy.'

At Lengeh: 9:26 A.M. Scragger had the nozzle gushing petrol into the police car. It frothed, overflowing, staining him. Muttering a curse he let the lever go, hung the nozzle back on the pump. Two Green Bands were nearby, watching closely. The corporal screwed the tank cap back into place. Qeshemi spoke to Ali Pash a moment. 'His Excellency asks if you could spare him some five gallon cans, Captain? Of course full ones.'

'Sure, why not? How many does he want?'

'He says he could take three in the boot and two inside. Five.'

'Five it is.'

Scragger found the cans and filled them and together they loaded the police car. She's a bloody Molotov cocktail, he thought. Storm clouds were building quickly. A flash of lightning in the mountains. 'Tell him best not to smoke in the car.'

'His Excellency thanks you.'

'Any time.' Thunder came down from the mountains. More lightning. Scragger watched Qeshemi leisurely look around the camp. The two Green Bands were waiting. A few others were squatting in the lee of the wind, watching idly. Now he could stand it no longer. 'Well, agha, I better be off,' he said, pointing at the 212 then into the sky. 'Okay?'

Qeshemi looked at him strangely. 'Okay? What okay, agha?'

'I go now.' Scragger motioned with his hand, pantomiming flying away, and kept his glazed smile. '*Mamnoon am, khoda haefez.*' Thank you, goodbye. He held out his hand to him.

The sergeant stared at the hand then looked up at him, the shrewd hard eyes boring into him. Then the sergeant said, 'Okay. Goodbye, agha,' and firmly shook hands.

The sweat was running down Scragger's face and he forced himself not to wipe it away. '*Mamnoon am. Khoda haefez, agha.*' He nodded at Ali Pash, wanting to make it a good farewell, wanting to shake hands too but not daring to stretch their luck, so he just clapped him on the back in passing. 'See you, me son. Happy days.'

'Good landings, agha.' Ali Pash watched Scragger climb into the cockpit and get airborne and wave as he flew away. He waved back, then saw Qeshemi looking at him. 'If I may be permitted, if you will excuse me, Excellency Sergeant, I will lock up and then go to the Mosque.'

Qeshemi nodded and turned back to the departing 212. How obvious they are, he was thinking, the old pilot and this young fool. So easy to read the minds of men if you're patient and watch for clues. Very dangerous to fly off illegally. Even more dangerous to help foreigners fly off illegally and stay behind. Madness! Men are very strange. As God wants.

One of the Green Bands, a barely bearded youth with an AK47, wandered closer, pointedly looked at the cans of petrol in the back of the car. Qeshemi said nothing, just nodded to him. The youth nodded back, eyes hard, strolled off insolently to join the others.

The sergeant got into the driving seat. Leprous sons of dogs, he thought sardonically, you're not the law in Lengeh yet – thanks be to God. 'Time to go, Achmed, time to go.' As the corporal climbed in beside him Qeshemi saw the helicopter go over the rise and vanish. Still so easy to catch you, old man, he told himself, bemused. So easy to alert the net, our phones are working and we've a direct link with Kish fighter base. Are a few gallons pishkesh enough for your freedom? I haven't decided, yet.

'I'll drop you at the station, Achmed, then I'm off duty till tomorrow. I'll keep the car for the day.'

Qeshemi let in the clutch. Perhaps we should have gone with the foreigners – easy to force them to take us, my family and I, but then that would have meant living the wrong side of our Persian Gulf, living among Arabs. I've never liked Arabs, never trusted them. No, my plan's better. Quietly down the old coast road all today and all tonight, then my cousin's dhow to Pakistan with plenty of spare petrol for pishkesh. Many of our people are there already. I'll make a good life for my wife and my son and little Sousan until, with the help of God, we can come home again. Too much hatred here now, too many years serving the Shah. Good years. As Shahs go he was fine for us, we were always paid.

*   *   *

1005

North of Lengeh: 9:32 A.M. The cabbage patch was ten kilometres northeast of the base, a desolate, barren rocky area in the foothills of mountains and the two helicopters were parked, side by side, engines ticking over. Ed Vossi was standing at Willi's cockpit window. 'I feel like throwing up, Willi.'

'Me too.' Willi shifted his headset slightly, the VHF on but, according to plan, not to be used unless in emergency, only listened to.

'You got something, Willi?' Vossi asked.

'No, just static.'

'Shit. He must be in dead trouble. Another minute then I go look, Willi.'

'We go look together.' Willi watched the lightning in the hills, visibility about a mile with the clouds black and closing in. 'No day for joy riding, Ed.'

'No.'

Then Willi's face lit up like a rocket and he pointed, 'There he is!' Scragger's 212 was approaching at about seven hundred feet, dawdling along. Vossi took to his heels for his cockpit and got in. Now in their headphones: 'How's your torque counter, Willi?'

'Not good, Scrag,' Willi said happily, following their plan in case anyone was listening. 'I asked Ed to take a look at her and he's not sure either – his radio's out.'

'I'll land and we'll have a conference. Scragger to base, do you read?' No answer. 'Scragger to base, we'll be on the ground a while.' No answer.

Willi gave the thumbs up to Vossi. Both opened their throttles, concentrating on Scragger who was coming down in on a leisurely landing approach. At ground level Scragger checked his descent and led the rush for the coast. Now the exhilaration was extreme, Vossi was shouting with glee and even Willi was smiling. 'By God Harry . . .'

Scragger went up over the ridge and down the other side and now he could see the coast and their small van parked on the rocky foreshore just above the waves. His heart missed a beat. A herd of goats with three herdsmen dotted his landing area. Fifty yards up the beach was a car with some people and children playing where never before had they seen anyone. Just out to sea a small powered boat was cruising along. Could be a fishing boat, could be one of the regular patrols against smugglers or escapees, for here, with Oman and the pirate coast so close, historically there had always been great coastal vigilance.

Can't change now, he thought, heart racing. He saw Benson and the other two mechanics spot him, jump into the van and drive towards his landing area. Behind him Willi and Vossi had throttled back to give him time. Without hesitation he went into his landing fast, goats scattering, herdsmen and picnickers transfixed. The moment his skis touched he shouted, 'Come on!'

The mechanics needed no urging. Benson rushed for the cabin door and hurled it open, charged back to help the other two who had unlocked the van's tailgate. Together they pulled out suitcases and satchels and baggage and stumbled over to begin loading – the cabin already stuffed with spares. Scragger looked around and saw that Willi and Vossi had gone into hover, on guard. 'So far so good,' he said out loud, concentrating on the onlookers who were over their astonishment and were coming closer. No real danger yet. Nonetheless he made sure his Verey pistol was ready just in case, and willed the mechanics to hurry, worried that any moment the police car would come hurrying down the road. A second load. Then another, then the last, all three mechanics sweating, and now two clambered into the cabin, slammed the door. Benson fell into the front seat beside him, swore and began to get out. 'I forgot to switch off the van . . .'

'To hell with that, here we go.' Scragger opened up the throttles and got airborne, Benson locking the door, fixing his seatbelt, and they were over the waves out into the haze of the Gulf. He looked left and right. Willi and Vossi were flanking him tightly and he wished he was HF equipped so he could report 'Lima Three,' to Gavallan. Never mind, we'll be there in a jiffy.

Once past the first of the rigs, he began to breathe easier. Hate leaving young Ali Pash like that, he thought, hate leaving Georges de Plessey and his lads, hate leaving the two 206s, hate leaving. Well, I've done me best. I've left recommendations and job promises for when we come back, if we come back, for Ali Pash and the others in the clerk's top drawer with all the money I had left.

He checked his course, heading southwest for Siri as though on their milkrun in case they were on radar. Near Siri he would turn southeast for Al Shargaz and home. All being well, he thought, and touched the rabbit's foot Nell had given him so many years ago for luck. Past another rig to port, Siri Six. The electrical storm was crackling his headphones, then mixed with it loud and clear was: 'Hey, Scragger, you and *les gars*, you're low, *n'est ce pas?*'

It was the voice of François Menange, the manager of the rig they had just passed and he cursed the man's vigilance. To close him down, he clicked on the transmit: 'Mum's the word, François, quiet, eh? Practising. Be quiet, eh?'

Now the voice was laughing. '*Bien sûr*, but you're crazy to practise low on a day like today. *Adieu*.'

Sweat was beginning again. Four more rigs to pass before he could turn into the open sea.

They went through the first squall line, the wind buffeting them, rain loud on the windows, streaking them, plenty of sheet lightning all around. Willi and Vossi were tight on station and he was pleased to be flying with them. Forty times I thought Qeshemi was going to say you comealonga-me and take me down to the pokey. But then he didn't and here we are and in an hour forty-odd minutes we'll be home and Iran only a memory.

At Kowiss Airbase HQ: 9:46 A.M. The mullah Hussain said patiently, 'Tell me more about Minister Kia, Captain.' He sat behind the desk in the base commander's office. A hard-faced Green Band guarded the door.

'I've told you everything I know,' McIver said exhaustedly.

'Then please tell me about Captain Starke.' Polite, insistent and unhurried as though there was all day and all night and all tomorrow.

'I've told you about him too, agha. I've told you about them both for almost a couple of hours. I'm tired and there's nothing more to tell.' McIver got up from his chair and stretched and sat down again. No use trying to leave. He had done that once and the Green Band had silently motioned him back. 'Unless you have something specific I can't think of anything to add.'

He had not been surprised at the mullah probing about Kia and had repeated over and over how a few weeks ago Kia had suddenly been made a director out of nowhere, about his own limited dealings with him in the last few weeks, though not about the cheques on banks in

Switzerland that had greased the way for the 125 and got three 212s out of the cauldron. Damned if I'm going to do a Wazari on Kia, he had told himself.

Kia's understandable, but why Duke Starke? Where Duke went to school, what he eats, how long he's been married, one wife or more, how long with the company, is he Catholic or Protestant – anything and everything and then tell it all again. Insatiable. And always the same quiet, evasive answer to his question, Why?

'Because he interests me, Captain.'

McIver looked out of the window. A speckle of rain. Clouds low. Distant thunder. There'd be updraughts and a few real whirlwinds in the thunderclouds eastwards – great cover for the dash across the Gulf. What's happening with Scrag and Rudi and their lads? rushed back into the forefront of his mind. With an effort he pushed that away for later – and his weariness, and worry – and what the hell he was going to do when this interrogation finished. If it finished. Beware! Concentrate! You'll make a mistake if you're not a hundred percent, then you'll all be lost.

He knew his reserves were badly depleted. Last night he had slept badly and that had not helped. Nor had Lochart's enormous sadness over Sharazad. Difficult for Tom to face the truth, impossible to say it to him: wasn't it bound to fall apart, Tom, old friend? She's Muslim, she's rich, you'll never be, her heritage's bound in steel, yours in gossamer, her family's her lifeblood, yours isn't, she can stay, you can't and the final sword hanging over you, HBC. So sad, he thought. Did it ever have a chance? With the Shah, maybe. With the inflexibility of the new?

What would I do if I was Tom? With an effort he stopped his mind wandering. He could feel the mullah's eyes boring into him. They had hardly wavered once since Changiz had brought him here and had gone away.

Ah yes, Colonel bloody Changiz. In the car coming over here and during the waiting he too had been probing. But his probing was just to establish exactly when and how often their 125 was scheduled for Kowiss, how many Green Bands were stationed their side of the base, when they arrived, how many stayed on the base and did they surround and guard the 125 all the time she was on the ground. The questioning had been casual, nothing asked that could not be more than just interest, but McIver was certain the real reason was to erect an escape route – if necessary. The final cement, the barter: 'Even in a revolution mistakes happen, Captain. Friends are needed in high places more than ever, sad but true.' You scratch my back or I'll claw yours.

The mullah got up, 'I will take you back now.'

'Oh. Very well, thank you.' McIver guardedly studied Hussain. The brown-black eyes under the heavy eyebrows gave nothing away, skin stretched over his high cheek bones, a strange, handsome face masking a spirit of enormous resolution. For good or for bad? McIver asked himself.

In their Radio Tower: 9:58 A.M. Wazari was hunched down near the door to the roof, still waiting. When McIver and Lochart had left him in the office he had been torn between fleeing and staying, then Changiz and the airmen had arrived, almost simultaneously Pavoud with other staff, so he had sneaked up here unseen and ever since had been in hiding. Just before 8 a.m. Kia had driven up in a taxi.

From his vantage point up here he had seen Kia go into a paroxysm of rage because McIver was not waiting beside the 206, ready for take off. The green-banded airmen relayed what Changiz had ordered. Kia had protested loudly. More apologetic shrugs and Kia stormed into the building, loudly proclaiming he would phone Changiz and radio Tehran at once, but Lochart had intercepted Kia at the bottom of the stairs and told him the phones were out, the set malfunctioning and no radio repairer available until tomorrow. 'Sorry, Minister, there's nothing we can do about it – unless you want to go over to HQ yourself,' Wazari had heard Lochart say. 'I'm sure Captain McIver won't be long, the mullah Hussain sent for him.' At once most of the bombast had gone out of Kia and that had pleased him but did not allay his grinding anxiety and he had stayed there in the wind and the cold, forlorn, lost and in misery.

His temporary safety did nothing to cast off his anxieties or fears or suspicions, about Kia today and up before the komiteh again tomor-row – 'you're needed for further questioning' – and why were those bastards Lochart and McIver so nervous, huh? Why did they lie to that sonofabitch turncoat Changiz about a crew change at Rig Abu Sal? No goddam crew change needed there, not unless it was ordered in the night. Why're we down to three pilots and two mecs with a load of work starting Monday – why so many spares shipped out? Oh Christ Jesus get me to hell outta here.

It was so cold and blustery he came back inside, but left the door ajar for a quick retreat. Cautiously he looked out of the windows and through cracks in the boards. If he was careful he could see most of the base without being seen. Ayre, Lochart and the mechanics were over by the 212s. The main gate was well guarded by regular Green Bands. No activity over at the base that he could see. A chill went through him. Rumours of another purge by the komiteh, that now he was high on their list because of his evidence against Esvandiary and Minister Kia: 'By the Prophet, I heard they want to see you tomorrow. You took your life in your hands speaking out like that, don't you know the first rule of survival here for four thousand years has been to keep your tongue silent and your eyes closed on the doings of those above, or very soon, you'll have neither left in your head? Of course those above are corrupt, has it ever been different?'

Wazari moaned, helpless in the maelstrom and near breaking. Ever since Zataki had beaten him so badly, nose smashed – can't seem to breathe any more – four teeth knocked out and an almost perpetual headache, his spirit had left him and so had his courage. He had never been beaten before. So Hotshot and Kia were both guilty, so what, so what? What business was it of yours? And now your stupidity will consume you too.

Tears spilled down the bruises. 'For crissake, for crissake help, help me . . .' Then 'malfunction' jumped into his head and he seized on it. What malfunction? The set was working fine yesterday.

He brushed the tears away. Making no sound, he slid over to the desk and quietly switched on the radio, keeping the volume to absolute minimum. All seemed fine. Dials checked out. Lots of static from an electrical storm but no traffic. Unusual that there should be no traffic on the company frequency, someone somewhere should be sending. Not daring to turn the volume up, he reached into a drawer for a pair of headphones and plugged them in, bypassing the loudspeaker. Now he could have the signal as loud as he pleased. Curious. Still nothing. Carefully he switched out of the company channel to others. Nothing. Over to the VHF. Nothing, anywhere. Back to HF. He could not even pick up a routine, recorded weather report that still came out of Tehran.

He was a good radio operator and well trained and it took him no time to zero in on the fault. A look through the crack in the roof door confirmed the wire hanging free. Sonofabitch, he thought. Why the hell didn't I notice it when I was out there?

Carefully he switched off and crawled out again and when he was at the foot of the mast and saw that the wire had been sheared off but the rust at the end had been newly cleaned off, anger possessed him. Then excitement. Those bastards, he thought. Those hypocritical bastards, McIver and Lochart. They musta been listening and transmitting when I arrived. What the hell're they up to?

The connection was quickly repaired. HF on and instantly Farsi filled his ears on the company frequency: HQ at Tehran talking to Bandar-e Delam, then calling Al Shargaz and Lengeh and him at Kowiss, something about four choppers not going where they were supposed to go. Iran-Toda? Not one of our bases.

'Kowiss, this is Bandar-e Delam, do you read?'

He recognised Jahan's voice from Bandar-e Delam. Automatically his finger went to the transmit switch, then stopped. No need to call back yet, he thought. The company airwaves were full now, Numir and Jahan from Bandar-e Delam and Gelani at Tehran, and Siamaki ranting and raving. 'Sonofabitch,' he muttered after a few minutes, everything falling into place.

In the Helicopters Off Siri: 10:05 A.M. Siri Island itself was a mile ahead, but before Scragger and his team could turn southeast for the international boundary line, there were three more rigs to bypass. Like a bleeding minefield, Scragger thought. So far safe and no more shocks. All needles in the Green and the engines sounding sweet. His mechanic Benson, beside him, was staring at the waves rushing past just below them. Static in their earphones. From time to time, overflying international flights would report their positions to Kish radar, a checkpoint in their area, to be answered at once.

Into the intercom Benson said, 'Kish're spot on, Scrag.'

'We're under their radar. No sweat.'

'I'm sweating. Are you?'

Scragger nodded. Kish was abeam of them, fifteen-odd miles to his right. He looked left and right. Vossi and Willi were alongside and he gave them a thumbs-up and they returned it – Vossi enthusiastically.

'Another twenty minutes and we're over the border,' Scragger said. 'Soon as we are, we'll go up to 700.'

'Good. Weather's improving, Scrag,' Benson said. The cloud cover above had thinned appreciably, visibility about the same. In plenty of time they both saw the outward bound, heavily laden tanker ahead. With Willi, Scragger banked astern of her with plenty to spare but Vossi exuberantly pulled up high over her, then came down into station alongside him.

At once in their headphones: 'This is Kish Control, low flying helicopter on a course 225, report height and destination!'

Scragger weaved from side to side to attract Willi and Vossi and pointed southwest and waved them off, commanding them to stay low and to leave him. He saw their reluctance, but he jabbed his finger

1013

southeast, waved a farewell and pulled up in a climb, leaving them on the surface of the sea. 'Hold on to your balls, Benson,' he said, a weight in his stomach, then began transmitting, moving his boom mike back and forth from his mouth, simulating a bad signal: 'Kish, this is chopper HVX out of Lengeh, inbound Siri Nine with spares, course 225. Thought I saw a capsized dhow but it was negative.' Siri Nine was the farthest rig they normally serviced, just this side of the Iran/Emirate boundary, still under construction and not yet equipped with their own VHF. 'Climbing back to seven hundred.'

'Chopper HVX, you're two by five, your transmission intermittent. Maintain course and report seven hundred feet. Confirm you were informed of mandatory new regulations start engines request at Lengeh.' The operator's American-accented voice was five by five, crisp and professional.

'Sorry, Kish, this is the first day I've been back on duty.' Scragger saw Willi and Vossi vanish into the haze. 'Do I need to request engine start from Siri Nine after I've landed? I'll be there at least an hour.' Scragger wiped a bead of sweat off. Kish would be within their right to order him to land at Kish first to give him a roasting for breaking regulations.

'Affirmative. Standby One.'

In the intercom, Benson said uneasily, 'Now what, Scrag?'

'They'll be having a little conference.'

'What're we going to do?'

Scragger beamed. 'Depends on what they do.' He clicked the sender: 'Kish, HVX at seven hundred.'

'Kish. Maintain course and altitude. Standby One.'

'HVX.' More silence. Scragger was sifting alternates, enjoying the danger. 'This's better than flying a milkrun, now isn't it, me son?'

'To be honest it isn't. If I could get hold of Vossi I'd strangle him.'

Scragger shrugged. 'It's done. We could've been in and out of radar ever since we left. Maybe Qeshemi reported us.' He began whistling tonelesssly. They were well past Siri Island now with rig Siri Nine five kilometres ahead. 'Kish, this's HVX,' Scragger said, still working the mike. 'Leaving seven hundred on approach for Siri Nine.'

'Negative HVX, maintain seven hundred and hold. Your transmission is intermittent and two by five.'

'HVX – Kish, please say again, your transmission is garbled. I say again, am leaving seven hundred on approach for Siri Nine,' Scragger repeated slowly continuing to simulate bad transmission. Again he beamed at Benson. 'Trick I learned in the RAF, me son.'

'HVX, Kish. I say again maintain seven hundred and hold.'

'Kish, it's bumpy and the haze's thickening. Leaving seven hundred now through six hundred. I will report on landing and call requesting engine start. Thanks and g'day!' he added with a prayer.

'HVX, your transmission is intermittent. Abort landing at Siri Nine. Turn to 310 degrees, maintain seven hundred, and report direct to Kish.'

Benson went white. Scragger belched. 'Say again Kish, you're one by five.'

'I say again, abort landing at Siri Nine, turn to 310 degrees and report direct Kish.' The operator's voice was unhurried.

'Roger, Kish, understand we're to land Siri Nine and report Kish next. Going through four hundred for low level approach, thank you and g'day.'

'Kish, this is JAL 664 flight from Delhi,' broke in. 'Overhead at 38,000 inbound Kuwait on 300. Do you read?'

'JAL 664, Kish. Maintain course and altitude. Call Kuwait on 118.8, good day.'

Scragger peered through the haze. He could see the half constructed rig, a work barge moored to one of its legs. Instrument needles all in the Green and – hey, wait a moment, temperature's up, oil pressure's down on Number One engine. Benson had seen it too. He tapped the dial, bent closer. The oil pressure needle went up slightly then fell back again, temperature a few degrees above normal – no time to worry about that now, get ready! The deck crew had heard and seen them and stopped working, clearing away from the well-marked helipad. When he was fifty feet off the rig, Scragger said: 'Kish, HVX landing now. G'day.'

'HVX. Report direct Kish next. Request engine start. I repeat, report direct Kish next,' all said very clearly. 'Do you read?'

But Scragger did not acknowledge, or land. At a few feet he just pulled into a hover, waved to the deck crew who recognised him and presumed it was just a practice or a familiarisation-training run for a new pilot, a constant habit of Scragger's. A last wave, then he got forward motion, dropped neatly over the side and, hugging the sea, turned southwest at full throttle.

At Kowiss Airbase: 10:21 A.M. The mullah Hussain was driving, and he stopped the car outside the office building. McIver got out. 'Thank you,' he said, not knowing what to expect now; Hussain had been silent since they had left the office. Lochart, Ayre and the others were over by the helicopters. Kia stalked out of the office, stopped on seeing the mullah, then came down the steps. 'Good morning, Excellency Hussain, greetings, how pleasant to see you.' He used a ministerial voice for an honoured guest, but not an equal, then to McIver in English, curtly, 'We should leave at once.'

'Er, yes, agha. Just give me a couple of minutes to get organised.' Glad I'm not Kia, he told himself, as he walked off, his stomach churning. 'Hello, Tom.'

'You all right, Mac?'

'Yes.' He added quietly, 'We'll have to play this by nose for the next few minutes. Don't know what the mullah's up too. Have to wait and see what he does about Kia, don't know whether Kia's in the creek or not. Soon as we know we can move.' He dropped his voice even more. 'I can't avoid taking Kia – unless Hussain grabs him. I plan to take him part of the way, just over the hills out of VHF range, pretend an emergency and land. When Kia's out of the cockpit and cooling his heels, I'll take off and skirt this area and meet you at the rendezvous.'

'Don't like that idea, Mac. Better let me do it. You don't know the place and those sand dunes are look alikes for miles. I'd better take him.'

'I've thought about that, but then I'd be flying one of the mecs without a licence. I'd rather put Kia at risk than them. Besides, you might be tempted to keep on going back to Tehran. All the way. Eh?'

'Better that I drop him off and meet you at the rendezvous. Safer.'

McIver shook his head, feeling rotten about putting his friend into a box. 'You'd go on, wouldn't you?'

After a strange pause, Lochart said, 'While I was waiting for you if I could've gotten airborne I'd've put him aboard and gone.' He smiled a twisted smile. 'The airmen said no way, to wait. Better watch them, Mac, some of them speak English. What happened to you?'

'Hussain just questioned me about Kia – and Duke.'

Lochart stared at him. 'Duke? What about?'

'Everything about him. When I asked Hussain why, all he'd say was: "Just because he interests me." ' McIver saw a tremor go through Lochart.

'Mac, I think it's best if I take Kia. You might miss the rendezvous – you can go in tandem with Freddy. I'll get off first and wait for you.'

'Sorry, Tom, can't risk that – you'll keep on going. If I was you I'd do the same and the hell with the risk. But I can't let you go back. To go back now'd be a disaster. It'd be a disaster for you – I'm sure of that, Tom – as well as for the rest of us. That's the truth.'

'Hell with the truth,' Lochart said bitterly. 'All right, but by God, the moment we touch down at Kuwait, I'm on the month's leave I'm owed, or resigned from S-G whichever you want – from the very second.'

'Fair enough but it has to be from Al Shargaz. We'll have to refuel in Kuwait and get out of there as fast as we can – if we're lucky enough to get there and *if* they'll let us fly out.'

'No. Kuwait's the end of the line for me.'

'Please yourself,' McIver said, hardening. 'But I'll make sure you don't get a plane into Tehran, Abadan or anywhere else in Iran.'

'You're a bastard,' Lochart said, sick that McIver had read his intentions so clearly. 'Goddam you to hell!'

'Yes, sorry. From Al Shargaz I'll help all I c—' McIver stopped, seeing Lochart mutter a curse. He turned around. Kia and Hussain were still conversing by the car. 'What's the matter?'

'In the tower.'

McIver looked up. Then he noticed Wazari, half-hidden by one of the boarded windows, beckoning them clearly. No way to pretend they had not seen him. As they watched, Wazari beckoned again and moved back into cover.

'Goddam him,' Lochart was saying, 'I checked the tower just after you'd left to make sure he hadn't slipped up there and he hadn't so I thought he'd made a run for it.' His face flushed with rage. 'Come to think of it, I didn't go right up into the room, so he could've hidden on the roof – sonofabitch must've been there all the time.'

'Christalmighty! Maybe he found the broken wire.' McIver was rocked.

Lochart's face closed. 'You stay here. If he tries to give us any trouble I'll kill him.' He stalked off.

'Wait, I'll come too. Freddy,' he called out, 'we'll be back in a moment.'

As they passed Hussain and Kia, McIver said, 'I'm just going to ask for clearance, Minister. Take off in five minutes?'

Before Kia could answer, the mullah said cryptically, 'Insha'Allah.'

Kia said curtly to McIver, 'Captain, you haven't forgotten I told you I must be in Tehran for an important meeting at 7 p.m? Good,' and turned his back on them, again concentrating on Hussain. 'You were saying, Excellency?'

The two pilots went into the office, seething at Kia's rudeness, bypassed Pavoud and the other staff, and headed for the tower staircase.

The tower was empty. Then they saw the door to the roof ajar and

1017

heard Wazari whisper, 'Over here.' He was just outside, crouched by the wall.

Wazari did not move. 'I know what you're up to. There's no radio malfunction,' he said, hardly able to contain his excitement. 'Four choppers have pushed off from Bandar-e Delam and've vanished. Your managing director Siamaki's screaming like a stuck pig because he can't raise Lengeh, us, or Al Shargaz and Mr. Gavallan there – they're just sitting tight, that's it, isn't it? Huh?'

'What's that got to do with us?' Lochart said tautly.

'Everything, of course everything, because it all fits. Numir at Bandar-e Delam says all expats've gone, there's no one left at Bandar. Siamaki says the same about Tehran, he even told Numir your house-boy, Captain McIver, your houseboy says most of your personal things and a Captain Pettikin's're out of the apartment.'

McIver shrugged and went to switch on the VHF. 'Safety precaution while Pettikin's on leave and I'm away. Been lots of robberies.'

'Don't make a call yet. Please. Listen, for crissake listen, I'm begging you . . . there's no way you can stop the truth. Your 212s and guys have gone from Bandar, Lengeh's silent to they're the same, Tehran's closed down, the same, there's only here left and you're all set.' Wazari's voice was curious and they could not tell yet what was under it. 'I'm not gonna give you away, I want to help you. I want to help. I swear I want to help you.'

'Help us do what?'

'Get away.'

'Why should you do that, even if what you say's true?' Lochart said angrily.

'You were right not to trust me before, Captain, but I swear to God you can trust me now, I'm together now, earlier I wasn't but now I am and you're my only hope to get out. I'm up before the komiteh tomorrow and . . . and look at me, for crissake!' he burst out. 'I'm a mess, and unless I can get a proper doctor I'll be a mess for ever and maybe even a dead man – there's something pressing here, hurts like hell,' Wazari touched the top of his mashed nose. 'Since that bastard Zataki beat me my head's been aching and I've been crazy, sure I have, I know it, but I can still help. I can cover you from here if you'll take me with you, just let me sneak aboard the last chopper – I swear I'll help.' Tears filled his eyes. The two men stared at him.

McIver clicked on the VHF sender. 'Kowiss tower, IHC testing, testing.'

A long pause, then in heavily accented English, 'This is the tower, IHC, you five by five.'

'Thank you. We seem to have cleared the fault. Our 206 charter to Tehran will leave in ten minutes, also our morning flight to rigs Forty, Abu Sal, and Gordy with spares.'

'Okay. Report airborne. Your Bandar-e Delam has been trying to contact you.'

McIver felt the sweat start. 'Thanks, Tower. Good day.' He looked at Lochart, then switched on the HF. At once they heard Jahan's voice in Farsi and Lochart began interpreting: 'Jahan's saying the last sighting of their flight was northeast, inland from the coast . . . that Zataki . . .' For a moment his voice faltered, '. . . that Zataki had ordered the four choppers to service Iran-Toda and should be at Iran-Toda by now and is sure to call or send a message . . .' Then McIver recognised Siamaki. Lochart was sweating. 'Siamaki's saying he'll be off the air for half an hour to an hour but he'll call when he gets back and to keep trying to raise us and Al Shargaz . . . Jahan says okay and he'll wait out and if he has any news he'll call.'

Static for a moment. Then Jahan's voice in English: 'Kowiss, this is Bandar-e Delam, do you read?'

Lochart muttered, 'If the tower's been picking all this up, why aren't we all in the slammer?'

'It's Friday, no reason for them to monitor your company frequency.' Wazari wiped the tears away, back in control now. 'Friday's crew's minimal and trainee – no flying, nothing happening, the komiteh sacked all radar officers and five of the sergeants – sent them to the stockade.' He shuddered then hurried on, 'Maybe one of the guys picked up Bandar-e Delam once or twice. So Bandar've lost contact with some of their choppers, so what, they're foreigners and it happens all the time. But, Captain, if you don't close Bandar and Tehran down, they've gotta . . . someone's gotta get steamed up.' He took out a grubby handkerchief and wiped a trickle of blood from his nose. 'If you switch to your alternate channel you'll be safe enough, the tower don't have that.'

McIver stared at him. 'You're sure?'

'Sure, listen why don't y—' He stopped. Footsteps were approaching. Noiselessly he ducked back on to the roof into hiding. Kia stomped halfway up the stairs.

'What's keeping you, Captain?'

'I'm . . . I'm waiting for clearance to be confirmed, Minister. Sorry, I've been told to wait. Nothing I can do.'

'Of course there is! We can take off and leave! Now! I'm tired of wait –'

'I'm tired too but I don't want my head blown off.' McIver's temper snapped and he flared, 'You'll wait! Wait! Understand? You bloody wait and if your bloody manners don't improve I'll cancel the whole trip and mention a pishkesh or two to the mullah Hussain I happened to forget at the questioning. Now get to hell out of here.'

For a moment they thought Kia was going to explode, but he thought better of it and went away. McIver rubbed his chest, cursing himself for losing his temper. Then he jerked a thumb at the roof and whispered, 'Tom, what about him?'

'We can't leave him behind. He could give us away in a minute.' Lochart looked around. Wazari was at the doorway.

'I swear I'll help,' he whispered desperately. 'Listen, when you take off with Kia, what d'you plan, to dump him, huh?' McIver did not answer, still unsure. 'Jesus, Captain, you gotta trust me. Look, call Bandar-e on the alternate and chew Numir out like you did that bastard'n tell him you ordered all the choppers here. That'll take the heat off for an hour or two.'

McIver glanced at Lochart.

Lochart said excitedly, 'Why not? Hell, that's a good idea, then you take off with Kia and . . . and Freddy can get going. I'll wait here and . . .' the words trailed off.

'Then what, Tom?' McIver said.

Wazari came over and switched to the alternate channel, said quickly to Lochart, 'You stall for a while, Cap, and when Cap McIver's gone and Ayre's out of the area, you tell Numir, you're sure his four choppers've just switched off their HF, no need to use it and they're on VHF. That gives you the excuse to get airborne and wander around, then you rush off to the fuel cache.' He saw their look. 'Jesus, Cap, anyone's gotta know you can't make it in one across the Gulf, no way, so you've gotta have stashed spare fuel somewheres. On shore, or on one of the rigs.'

McIver took a deep breath and pressed the transmit 'Bandar-e Delam, we've been trying to reach you for hours an –'

'Jahan, put Agha Numir on,' McIver said curtly. A moment, then Numir came on but before the IranOil manager could launch into a tirade, McIver cut in with his own. 'Where are my four helicopters? Why haven't they reported in? What's going on down there? And why are you so inefficient that you don't know I ordered my helicopters and personnel here . . .'

*   *   *

1020

At Al Shargaz – S-G's Office: '. . . and why don't you remember that crew replacements are due in Bandar-e Delam after the weekend?' McIver's voice was faint but clear over the loudspeaker, and Gavallan, Scot and Manuela were staring at it, aghast that McIver was still in place at Kowiss – did that mean Lochart, Ayre and the others too?

'But we've been calling you all morning, Captain,' Numir said, his voice fainter. 'You ordered our 'copters to Kowiss? But why? And why wasn't I informed? Our 'copters were supposed to go to Iran-Toda this morning but never landed and have vanished! Agha Siamaki's also been trying to reach you.'

'There's been a fault on our HF. Now listen here, Numir, I ordered *my* choppers to Kowiss. I never approved an Iran-Toda contract, know nothing about an Iran-Toda contract so that's the end to it. Now stop creating a stink about nothing!'

'But they are our helicopters and everyone's left, everyone, mechanics and all pilots an –'

'I ordered them all here pending an investigation. I repeat I am very dissatisfied with your operation. And will so report to IranOil! Now stop calling.'

In the office they were all still in shock. That McIver was still in Kowiss was a disaster. Whirlwind was going badly awry. It was 10:12 and Rudi and his three were overdue Bahrain. '. . . but we don't know their actual headwind, Dad,' Scot had said, 'or how long they'll take to inflight refuel. They could be three quarters to an hour late and still be okay – say an ETA at Bahrain of 11 to 11:15.' But everyone knew that there could not safely be that amount of fuel on board.

Nothing yet from Scrag and his two but that's to be expected – they don't have HF aboard, Gavallan thought. Their flight to Al Shargaz should take about an hour and a half. If they'd left at say 7:30 and did the pick up and got out without incident, say at 7:45, their ETA should be 9:15 whichever way you figure it: 'No need to worry, Manuela, you understand about headwinds,' he had said, 'and we don't actually know when they left.'

So many things to go wrong. My God, this waiting's rotten. Gavallan felt very old, picked up the phone and dialled Bahrain. 'Gulf Air de France? Jean-Luc Sessonne please? Jean-Luc, anything?'

'No, Andy. I've just called the tower and there's nothing in the system. *Pas problème.* Rudi'll be conserving fuel. The tower said they'd call me the instant they see them. Anything about anyone else?'

'We just found out Mac's still in Kowiss.' Gavallan heard the gasp and the obscenities. 'I agree. I'll call you.' He dialled Kuwait. 'Charlie, is Genny with you?

'No, she's at the hotel. Andy, I –'

'We've just heard Mac's still at Kowiss an –'

'Christ Almighty, what's happened?'

'Don't know, he's still transmitting. I'll call back when I've something definite. Don't tell Genny yet. 'Bye.'

Again the nauseating waiting, then the HF came alive: 'Tehran, this is Kowiss, Captain McIver. Go ahead.'

'Kowiss, Tehran, we've been calling all morning. Agha Siamaki has been trying to reach you. He'll be back in about an hour. Please confirm that you ordered the four 212s to Kowiss.'

'Tehran, this is Kowiss. Bandar-e Delam, you copy too.' McIver's voice was slower and clearer but very angry. 'I confirm, I have all my 212s – I repeat all my 212s – under my control. All of them. I will be unavailable to talk to Agha Siamaki as I am cleared to leave here for Tehran with Minister Kia in five minutes but will expect Agha Siamaki to meet the 206 at Tehran International. In a few moments we will be closing down for repairs – on orders from the authorities – and will be operating only on VFR. For your information Captain Ayre will be leaving in five minutes for rig Abu Sal with spares and Captain Lochart will remain on standby to meet my Bandar-e Delam 212s, according to plan. Did you copy, Tehran?'

'Affirmative, Captain McIver, but can you please te –'

McIver cut in over him: 'Did you copy, Numir, or are you more useless than ever?'

'Yes but I must insist that we be infor –'

'I'm tired of all this nonsense. I'm managing director of this operation and as long as we operate in Iran that's the way it is going to be, simple direct and no fuss. Kowiss is closing down to make repairs as ordered by Colonel Changiz and will report as soon as we are on the air again. Remain on this channel but keep it clear for testing. Everything will proceed as planned. Over and out!'

Just then the door opened and Starke came in, an anxious young nurse with him. Manuela was dumbfounded. Gavallan leaped up and helped him to a chair, his chest heavily bandaged. He wore pyjama bottoms and a loose towelling dressing gown. 'I'm okay, Andy,' Starke said. 'How are you, honey?'

'Conroe, are you crazy?'

'No. Andy, tell me what's happening?'

The nurse said, 'We really can't take responsibil –'

Starke said patiently, 'I promise only a couple of hours and I'll be real careful. Manuela, please take her back to the car, would you, honey?' He looked at her with that special look husbands have for wives and wives for husbands when it's not the time to argue. At once she got up and ushered the nurse out and when they had both gone, Starke said, 'Sorry, Andy, couldn't stand it anymore. What's going on?'

At Kowiss: 10:48 A.M. McIver came down the tower steps, feeling sick and empty and not sure he would make it to the 206, let alone put the rest of the plan into effect. You'll make it, he told himself. Get yourself together.

The mullah Hussain was still talking to Kia, leaning against the car, his AK 47 slung over one shoulder. 'We're all set, Minister,' McIver said. 'Of course, if it's all right, Excellency Hussain?'

'Yes, as God wants,' Hussain said, with a strange smile. Politely he put out his hand. 'Goodbye, Minister Kia.'

'Goodbye, Excellency.' Kia turned and walked off briskly for the 206.

Uneasily McIver offered his hand to the mullah. ' 'Bye, Excellency.'

Hussain turned to watch Kia get into the cockpit. Again the strange smile. 'It is written: "The mills of God grind slowly yet they grind exceeding small." Don't they, Captain?'

'Yes. But why do you say that?'

'As a parting gift. You can tell your friend Kia when you land at Tehran.'

'He's not my friend, and why then?'

'You're wise not to have him as a friend. When will you see Captain Starke again?'

'I don't know. Soon I hope.' McIver saw the mullah glance back at Kia, and his disquiet increased. 'Why?'

'I would like to see him soon.'

Hussain unslung the gun and got into the car and, with his Green Bands, drove off.

'Captain?' It was Pavoud. He was shaky and upset.

'Yes, Mr. Pavoud, just a minute. Freddy!' McIver beckoned Ayre who came at a run. 'Yes, Mr. Pavoud?'

'Please, why are the 212s loaded with spares and luggage and all th —'

'A crew change,' McIver said at once and pretended not to notice Ayre's eyes crossing. 'I've four 212s due here from Bandar-e Delam. You'd better get accommodations ready. Four pilots and four mechanics. They're due in about two hours.'

'But we've no manifest or reason to h –'

'Do it!' McIver's tension boiled over again. 'I gave the orders. Me! Me personally! I ordered *my* 212s here! Freddy, what the hell're you waiting for? Get going with your spares.'

'Yessir. And you?'

'I'm taking Kia, Lochart's in charge until I get back. Off you go. No, wait, I'll go with you. Pavoud, what the devil are you waiting for? Captain Lochart will be very bloody irritable if you're not ready in time.' McIver stomped off with Ayre, praying that Pavoud was convinced.

'Mac, what the hell's going on?'

'Wait till we get to the others.' When McIver reached the 212s he turned his back to Pavoud who still stood on the office steps and quickly told them what was going on. 'See you at the coast.'

'You all right, Mac?' Ayre said, very concerned with his colour.

'Of course I am. Take off!'

Off Bahrain: 10:59 A.M. Rudi and Pop Kelly were still in tandem battling the headwind, nursing their engines – their fuel gauges reading empty, red warning lights on. Half an hour ago they had both gone into hover. The mechanics had swung the cabin doors open and leaned out, taking off the tank caps. Then they had uncurled the hoses and stuck the nozzle into the tank neck and come back into the cabin. With the makeshift pumps, laboriously they had pumped the first of the forty gallon drums dry, then the second. Neither of the mechanics had ever refuelled in the air like this. Both had been violently sick when they finished. But the operation was successful.

The haze was still strong, sea swell heavy under the wind, and since the near miss with the tanker all had been routine, grinding along, seeking maximum range, adjusting, always adjusting and praying. Rudi had seen nothing of Dubois or Sandor. One of Rudi's jets coughed but picked up almost at once.

Faganwitch winced. 'How far we got to go?'

'Too far.' Rudi switched on his VHF, breaking their radio silence, 'Pop, switch to HF, listen out,' he said rapidly and switched over. 'Sierra One, this is Delta One, do you read?'

'Loud and clear, Delta One,' Scot's voice came back instantly, 'go ahead.'

'Off Boston' – their code for Bahrain – 'at seven hundred, heading 185, low on fuel. Delta Two is with me, Three and Four on their own.'

'Welcome from Britain to sunny lands, G-HTXX and G-HJZI,

repeat G-HTXX and G-HJZI! Jean-Luc is waiting for you. We've no news yet of Delta Three and Four.'

'HTXX and HJZI!' Immediately Rudi acknowledged with their new British call signs. 'What about Lima Three and Kilo Two?' Lima for Lengeh's three Kilo for Kowiss's two.

'No news yet except that Kilo Two is still in place.' Rudi and Pop Kelly were shocked. Then they heard, 'This is Tehran HQ, Al Shargaz do you read?' quickly followed by Siamaki's voice: 'This is Tehran, who is calling on this channel? Who is Kilo Two and Lima Three? Who is Sierra One?'

Scot's voice cut in loudly, 'No sweat, HTXX, some twit's using our channel. Phone us on landing,' he added to caution against unnecessary talk.

Pop Kelly butted in excitedly, 'Sandbanks ahead, HTXX!'

'I see them. Sierra One, HTXX, we're almost at the coast now . . .'

Again one of Rudi's engines coughed, worse than before but picked up, the rev counter needles spinning drunkenly. Then through the haze he saw the coast, a point of land and some sandbanks and now the beach and knew exactly where he was. 'Pop, you deal with the tower, Sierra One tell Jean-Luc I'm . . .'

At Al Shargaz H.Q.: Gavallan was already dialling Bahrain and over the loudspeaker Rudi continued urgently, '. . . I'm at the northwest point at Abu Sabh beach, to the east . . .' a burst of static, then silence.

Gavallan said into the phone, 'Gulf Air de France? Jean-Luc, please. Jean-Luc, Andy. Rudi and Pop're . . . Standby One . . .' Kelly's voice came in loudly: 'Sierra One, I'm following Delta One down, he's engined out . . .'

'This is Tehran, who is engined out and where? Who's calling on this channel? This is Tehran who is call –'

At The Bahrain Shore: The beach had good white sand, but was almost empty of people right here, many sailing boats and other pleasure craft out to sea, flocks of wind surfers in the fine breeze, the day balmy. Up the shore was the Hotel Starbreak, brilliant white, with palm trees and gardens and multicoloured sunshades dotting the terraces and beaches. Rudi's 212 came out of the haze fast, rotors windmilling, jets coughing and no longer useful. His line of descent gave him little choice but he was thankful that it would be a hard landing and not a sea landing. The beach was rushing towards them and he chose the exact point of landing just past a lonely sunshade slightly up the beach towards the road. He was into the wind now and very close, steadied, then pulled the collective, altering the pitch of the blades to give momentary lift enough to cushion the fall and he skidded forward a few yards on the uneven surface, tipped a fraction but not enough to do any damage and they were safe.

'Bloody hell . . .' Faganwitch said, breathing again, heart working again, sphincter locked.

Rudi began the shut down, the silence eerie, his hands and knees trembling now. On the beach ahead sunbathers and people on the terraces had got up and were looking at them. Then Faganwitch gasped, frightening him. He turned around and gasped too.

She wore dark glasses and little else under the lonely sunshade, topless, as good as bottomless, blonde and beautiful and propped on one elbow watching them. Without hurrying she got up and slipped on the excuse of a bikini top.

'Christalmighty . . .' Faganwitch was speechless.

Rudi waved and called out throatily, 'Sorry, I ran out of fuel.'

She laughed, then Kelly came out of the sky and spoiled it all and they both cursed him as the wash of his rotors tugged at the sunshade and her long hair, blowing her towel away and scattering sand. Now Kelly saw her too, politely backed down wind, nearer the road and, as distracted as the others, promptly landed a foot high.

At Bahrain International Airport: 11:13 A.M. Jean-Luc and the mechanic Rod Rodrigues came out of the building at a run and headed across the tarmac towards a small tanker truck marked GAdeF – Gulf Air de France – that he had arranged to borrow. The airfield was busy, the modern terminal and allied buildings grand and gleaming white. Many jets of many nations loading or unloading, a JAL jumbo just landing.

'*On y va*, let's go,' Jean-Luc said.

'Of course, Sayyid.' The driver turned up the volume of his intercom, and with one smooth movement started the engine, got into gear and was in motion. He was a slim, young Palestinian Christian wearing dark glasses and company overalls. 'Where should we go?'

'You know Abu Sabh beach?'

'Oh, yes, Sayyid.'

'Two of our choppers've landed there out of fuel. Let's go!'

'We are almost there!' The driver did a racing change and increased speed. Over his intercom loudspeaker came: 'Alpha Four?' He picked up the hand mike and continued to drive flamboyantly one-handed. 'This is Alpha Four.'

'Give me Captain Sessonne.'

Jean-Luc recognised the voice of Mathias Delarne, the Gulf Air de France manager for Bahrain – an old friend from French Air Force days and Algeria. 'This's Jean-Luc, old friend,' he said in French.

In French Delarne said quickly, 'The tower called me to say another chopper's just come into the system on your expected heading, Dubois or Petrofi, eh? Tower keep calling her but cannot make contact yet.'

'Just one?' Jean-Luc was abruptly concerned.

'Yes. She's on a correct VFR approach for helipad 16. The problem we discussed, eh?'

'Yes.' Jean-Luc had told his friend what was really happening and the problem of the registrations. 'Mathias, tell the tower from me she's G-HTTE in transit,' he said, giving the third of his four allocated call signs. 'I'll send Rodrigues to deal with Rudi and Kelly. We'll deal with Dubois or Sandor – you and me – bring the spare batch of stuff. Where do we meet?'

'My God, Jean-Luc, after this lot we'll have to join the Foreign Legion. Meet me in front of the office.'

Jean-Luc acknowledged, hung the mike back on its hook. 'Stop here!' The truck stopped instantly. Rodrigues and Jean-Luc almost went through the windscreen. 'Rod, you know what to do.' He jumped out. 'Off you go!'

'Listen I'd rather walk an—' The rest of it was lost as Jean-Luc ran back and the truck rushed off again with a screech of tyres, out through the gate and on to the road that led to the sea.

At Kowiss, In the Tower: 11:17 A.M. Lochart and Wazari were watching McIver's distant 206 climbing up into the Zagros mountains. 'Kowiss, this is HOC,' McIver was saying over the VHF, 'leaving your system now. Good day.'

'HOC, Kowiss. Good day,' Wazari said.

Over the HF loudspeaker, in Farsi: 'Bandar-e Delam, this is Tehran, have you heard from Kowiss yet?'

'Negative. Al Shargaz, this is Bandar-e Delam, do you read?' Static, then the call repeated, now silence again.

Wazari wiped his face. 'You think Cap Ayre'd be at your rendezvous yet?' he asked, desperately anxious to please. It was not hard to sense Lochart's dislike of him, or his distrust. 'Huh?'

Lochart just shrugged, thinking about Tehran and what to do. He had told McIver to send both mechanics with Ayre: 'Just in case I get caught, Mac, or Wazari's discovered or betrays us.'

'Don't do anything stupid, Tom, like going to Tehran in the 212, with or without Wazari.'

'There's no way I could sneak back to Tehran without alerting the whole system and screwing Whirlwind. I'd have to refuel and they'd stop me.'

Is there a way? he asked himself, then saw Wazari watching him. 'What?'

'Is Cap McIver gonna give you a sign or call when he's dumped Kia?' When Lochart just looked at him, Wazari said bleakly, 'Goddammit, don't you see, whatever you want I gotta do, you're my only hope to get out . . .'

Both men whirled, feeling eyes. Pavoud was peering at them through the stair banisters.

'So!' he said softly. 'As God wants. You're both caught in your betrayals.'

Lochart took a step towards him. 'I don't know what's bothering you,' he began, throat parched. 'There's noth –'

'You're caught. You and the Judas! You're all escaping, running off with our helicopters!'

Wazari's face contorted and he hissed, 'Judas, eh? You get your commie ass up here! I know all about you and your Tudeh comrades!'

Pavoud had gone white. 'You're talking nonsense! You're the one who's caught, you're the –'

'You're the Judas, you lousy commie bastard! Corporal Ali Fedagi's my roommate and he's commissar on the base and he's your boss. I know all about you – he tried to get me to join the Party months ago. Get your ass up here!' And when Pavoud hesitated, Wazari warned, 'If you don't I'm calling the komiteh and blowing you, Fedagi, along with Mohammed Berari and a dozen others an' I don't give a shit . . .' His fingers went to the VHF send switch but Pavoud gasped out, 'No,' and came on to the landing and stood there shakily. For a moment nothing happened, then Wazari grabbed the whimpering, petrified man and shoved him down into a corner, picked up a spanner to smash his head in. Lochart caught the blow just in time.

'Why're you stopping me, for crissake?' Wazari was shaking with fear. 'He'll betray us!'

'No need . . . no need for that.' Lochart had difficulty talking for a moment. 'Be patient. Listen, Pavoud, if you keep quiet, we'll keep quiet.'

'I swear by God, of course I'll ke –'

Wazari hissed, 'You can't trust these bastards.'

'I don't,' Lochart said. 'Quick. Write it all down! Quick! All the names you can remember. Quick – and make three copies!' Lochart shoved a pen into the young man's hand. Wazari hesitated then grabbed the pad and began to scribble. Lochart went closer to Pavoud who cringed from him, begging mercy. 'Shut up and listen. Pavoud, I'll make a deal, you say nothing, we'll say nothing.'

'By God, of course I won't say anything, agha, haven't I faithfully served the company, faithfully all these years, haven't I been ev –'

'Liar,' Wazari said, then added to Lochart's shock, 'I've overheard you and the others lying and cheating and slobbering after Manuela Starke, peeping at her in the night.'

'Lies, more lies, don't belie –'

'Shut up, you bastard! Wazari said.

Pavoud obeyed, petrified by the venom, and huddled back into the corner. Lochart tore his eyes off the quaking man and took one of the lists, put it into his pocket. 'You keep one, Sergeant. Here,' he said to Pavoud, shoving the third into his face. The man tried to back away, couldn't, and when the list was thrust into his hand, he moaned and dropped it as though it were on fire. 'If we get stopped I promise you before God this goes to the first Green Band and don't forget we both speak Farsi and I know Hussain! Understand?' Numbly Pavoud nodded. Lochart leaned down and picked the list up and stuffed it into the man's pocket. 'Sit down over there!' He pointed to a seat in the corner, then wiped his sweating hands on his trousers.

Lochart switched on the VHF, picked up the mike.

'Kowiss calling inbound choppers from Bandar-e Delam, do you read?' Lochart waited, then repeated the call. Then, 'Tower, this is base, do you read?'

After a pause a weary, heavily accented voice said, 'Yes, we hearing you.'

'We're expecting four inbound choppers from Bandar-e Delam that're only equipped with VHF. I'm going to get airborne and try to raise them. We'll be off the air until I get back. Okay?'

'Okay.'

Lochart switched off. From the HF came: 'Kowiss, this is Tehran, do you read?'

'What about him?' Lochart asked. Both of them looked at Pavoud who seemed to shrink into his chair.

The stabbing pain behind Wazari's eye was the worst it had ever been. I gonna have to kill Pavoud, that's the only way I can prove I'm on Lochart's side. 'I'll deal with him,' he said and got up.

'No,' Lochart said. 'Pavoud, you're taking the rest of the day off. You walk downstairs, you tell the others you're sick and you're going home. You say nothing else and leave at once. We can see you and hear you from here. If you betray us, by the Lord God, you and every man on this list'll be betrayed too.'

'You swear you . . . you'll . . .' the words started to pour out, 'you swear you'll tell no one, you swear?'

'Get out and go home! And it's on your head not ours! Go on, get out!' They watched him totter away. And when they saw him on his bicycle pedalling slowly down the road towards the town, they both felt a little easier.

'We should have killed him . . . we should have, Cap. I'd've done it.'

'This way's just as safe and . . . well, killing him wouldn't solve anything.' Nor help me with Sharazad, Lochart thought.

Again over the HF, again the nagging: 'Kowiss, this is Bandar-e Delam, do you read?'

'It's not safe to leave those bastards broadcasting, Cap. Tower's gotta pick 'em up, however untrained and inefficient they are.'

Lochart put all his mind on to the problem. 'Sergeant, get on the HF for an instant, pretend you're a radio mec who's pissed off with having his holiday screwed up. Tell 'em in Farsi to shut up, to stay the hell off our channel until we're repaired, that this lunatic Lochart's gone aloft to raise the four choppers on the VHF, perhaps one of them had an emergency and the others are with him on the ground. Okay?'

'Got it!' Wazari did it all, perfectly. When he switched off he held his head in his hands a moment, pain blinding him. Then he looked up at Lochart. 'You trust me now?'

'Yes.'

'I can come with you? Honest?'

'Yes.' Lochart put out his hand. 'Thanks for the help.' He pulled the company HF frequency crystal out, mutilated it and put it back, then pulled out the breaker of the VHF and pocketed it. 'Come on.'

In the office downstairs he stopped a moment. 'I'm going aloft,' he told the three clerks who stared at him strangely. 'I'm going to try to raise the Bandar-e choppers on the VHF.' The three men said nothing, but Lochart felt they knew the secret too. Then he turned to Wazari, 'See you tomorrow, Sergeant.'

'Hope it's okay to quit. My head hurts like hell.'

'See you tomorrow.' Lochart pottered in the office, conscious of the scrutiny, to give Wazari enough time to pretend to saunter off, actually to go around the hangar and sneak aboard: 'Once you're out of the office you're on your own,' Lochart had told him. 'I won't check the cabin, I'll just take off.'

'God help us all, Captain.'

At Bahrain Airport: 11:28 A.M. Jean-Luc and Mathias Delarne were standing beside a station wagon near the helipad, watching the incoming 212, shading their eyes against the sun, still unable to recognise the pilot. Mathias was a short, thickset man, with dark wavy hair, half a face, the other half badly burn-scarred when he had bailed out on fire not far from Algiers.

'It's Dubois,' he said.

'No, you're wrong, it's Sandor.' Jean-Luc waved, motioning him to land crosswind. The moment the skids touched, Mathias rushed under the rotors for the left cockpit door – paying no attention to Sandor who was shouting across at him. He carried a large paintbrush and a can of quick drying airplane paint and he slapped the white paint over the Iran registration letters just below the door's window. Jean-Luc used the stencil they had prepared and black paint and his brush, then carefully peeled the stencil off. Now she was G-HXXI and legal.

Meanwhile Mathias had gone to the tail boom and painted out IHC, ducked under the boom to do the same the other side. Sandor just had time to move his arm out of the way of the door as, enthusiastically, Jean-Luc stencilled the second G-HXXI.

'*Voilà!*' Jean-Luc gave his material back to Mathias who went to the station wagon to stash it under a tarpaulin, while Jean-Luc wrung Sandor's hand and told him about Rudi and Kelly and asked about Dubois.

'Don't know, old buddy,' Sandor said. 'After the pile-up—' he explained about the near miss – 'Rudi waved us off to head here independently. I never saw any of them again. Me, I put her into minimum consumption, stuck to the waves and prayed. I've been on empty, warning lights on, for maybe ten goddam minutes and crapping for twenty. What about the others?'

'Rudi and Kelly landed on Abu Sabh beach – Rod Rodrigues's looking after them – nothing yet on Scrag, Willi, or Vossi, but Mac's still at Kowiss.'

'Jesusss!'

'*Oui*, along with Freddy and Tom Lochart, at least they were, ten or fifteen minutes ago.' Jean-Luc turned to Mathias who came up to them, 'Are you tuned into the tower?'

'Yes, no problem.'

'Mathias Delarne, Sandor – Johnson, our mec.'

They greeted each other and shook hands. 'How was your trip – *merde*, best you don't tell me,' Mathias added, then saw the approaching car. 'Trouble,' he warned.

'Stay in the cockpit, Sandor,' Jean-Luc ordered. 'Johnson, back in the cabin.'

The car was marked 'official' and it stopped broadside to the 212 twenty yards away. Two Bahraini men got out, a uniformed Immigration captain and an officer from the tower, the latter wearing a long-flowing white dishdash and headcloth with a twisted black coil holding it in place. Mathias went to meet them. ' 'Morning, Sayyid Yusuf, Sayyid Bin Ahmed. This is Captain Sessonne.'

' 'Morning,' both said politely and continued to study the 212. 'And the pilot?'

'Captain Petrofi. Mr. Johnson, a mechanic, is in the cabin.' Jean-Luc felt sick. The sun was glistening off the new paint but not the old, and the bottom of the '*I*' had a dribble of black from each corner. He waited for the inevitable remark and then the inevitable question, 'What was her last point of departure?' and then his airy, 'Basra, Iraq' as the nearest possible. But so simple to check there and no need to check, just walk forward five yards and draw a finger through the new paint to find the permanent letters below. Mathias was equally perturbed. Easy for Jean-Luc, he thought, he doesn't live here, doesn't have to work here.

'How long will G-HXXI be staying, Captain?' the Immigration officer asked. He was a clean-shaven man with sad eyes.

Jean-Luc and Mathias groaned inwardly at the accent on the letters. 'She's due to leave for Al Shargaz at once, Sayyid,' Mathias said, 'for Al Shargaz, at once – the very moment she's refuelled. Also the others who, er, ran out of fuel.'

Bin Ahmed, the tower officer, sighed. 'Very bad planning to run out of fuel. I wonder what happened to the legal 30 minutes of reserve.'

'The, er, the headwind I expect, Sayyid.'

'It is strong today, that's certain.' Bin Ahmed looked out into the Gulf, visibility about a mile. 'One 212 here, two on our beach and the fourth . . . the fourth out there.' The dark eyes came back on to Jean-Luc. 'Perhaps he turned back for . . . for his departure point.'

Jean-Luc gave him his best smile. 'I don't know, Sayyid Bin Ahmed,' he answered carefully, wanting to end the cat-and-mouse game, wanting to refuel and backtrack for half an hour to search.

Once more the two men looked at the chopper. Now the rotor stopped. The blades trembled a little in the wind. Casually Bin Ahmed took out a telex. 'We've just received this from Tehran, Mathias, about some missing helicopters,' he said politely. 'From Iran's Air Traffic Control. It says, "Please be on the lookout for some of our helicopters that have been exported illegally from Bandar-e Delam. Please impound them, arrest those aboard, inform our nearest embassy who will arrange for immediate deportation of the criminals and repatriation of our equipment." ' He smiled again and handed it to him. 'Curious, eh?'

'Very,' Mathias said. He read it, glazed, then handed it back.

'Captain Sessonne, have you been to Iran?'

'Yes, yes I have.'

'Terrible, all those deaths, all the unrest, all the killings, Muslim killing Muslim. Persia's always been different, troublesome to others who live in the Gulf. Claiming our Gulf, the Persian Gulf, as though we, this side, did not exist,' Bin Ahmed said, matter-of-fact. 'Didn't the Shah even claim our island was Iranian just because three centuries ago Persians conquered us for a few years, we who have always been independent?'

'Yes, but he, er, he renounced the claim.'

'Ah, yes, yes, that is true – and occupied the oil islands of Tums and Abu Musa. Very hegemonistic are Persian rulers, very strange, whoever they are, wherever they come from. Sacrilege to plant mullahs and ayatollahs between man and God. Eh?'

'They, er, they have their way of life,' Jean-Luc agreed, 'others have theirs.'

Bin Ahmed glanced into the back of the station wagon. Jean-Luc saw part of the handle of a paintbrush sticking out from under the tarpaulin. 'Dangerous times we're having in the Gulf. Very dangerous. Anti-God Soviets, closer every day from the north, more anti-God Marxists south in Yemen arming every day, all eyes on us and our wealth – and Islam. Only Islam stands between them and world dominance.'

Mathias wanted to say, What about France and of course America? Instead he said, 'Islam'll never fail. Nor will the Gulf States if they're vigilant.'

'With the help of God, I agree.' Bin Ahmed nodded and smiled at Jean-Luc. 'Here on our island we must be very vigilant against all those who wish to cause us trouble. Eh?'

Jean-Luc nodded. He was finding it hard not to look at the telex in the man's hand; if Bahrain had one, the same would have gone to every tower this side of the Gulf.

'With the help of God we will succeed.'

The Immigration officer nodded agreeably. 'Captain, I would like to see the pilot's papers, and the mechanic's. And them. Please.'

'Of course, at once.' Jean-Luc walked over to Sandor. 'Tehran's telexed them to be on the lookout for Iran registereds,' he whispered hastily and Sandor went pasty. 'No need for panic, *mon vieux*, just show your passports to the Immigration officer, volunteer nothing, you too Johnson, and don't forget you're G-HXXI out of Basra.'

'But Jesus,' Sandor croaked, 'we'd have to've been stamped outta Iraq, and I got Iranian stamps over most every page.'

'So you were in Iran, so what? Start praying, *mon brave*. Come on.'

The Immigration officer took the American passport. Punctiliously he studied the photograph, compared it to Sandor who weakly took off his sunglasses, then handed it back without leafing through the other pages. 'Thank you,' he said and accepted Johnson's British passport. Again the studious look at the photograph only. Bin Ahmed went a pace nearer the chopper. Johnson had left the cabin door open.

'What's aboard?'

'Spares,' Sandor, Johnson and Jean-Luc said together.

'You'll have to clear customs.'

Mathias said politely, 'Of course he *is* in transit, Sayyid Yusuf, and will take off the moment he's refuelled. Perhaps it would be possible to allow him to sign the transit form, guaranteeing he lands nothing and carries no arms or drugs or ammunition.' He hesitated. 'I would guarantee it too, if it was of value.'

'Your presence is always of value, Sayyid Mathias,' Yusuf said. It was hot on the tarmac and dusty and he pulled out a handkerchief and blew his nose, then went up to Bin Ahmed – still with Johnson's passport in his hand. 'I suppose for a British plane in transit, it would be all right, even for the other two on the beach. Eh?'

The tower man turned his back on the chopper. 'Why not? When those two arrive we'll set them down here, Sayyid Captain Sessonne. You meet them with the fuel truck and we'll clear them for Al Shargaz as soon as they're refuelled.' Again he looked out to sea and his dark eyes showed his concern. 'And the fourth, when she arrives? What about her – I presume she's also British registered?'

'Yes, yes she is,' Jean-Luc heard himself say, giving him the new registration. 'With . . . with your permission, the three will backtrack for half an hour, then go on to Al Shargaz.' It's worth a try, he thought, saluting the two men with Gallic charm as they left, hardly able to grasp the miracle of the reprieve.

Is it because their eyes were blinded or because they did not wish to see? I don't know, I don't know but blessed be the Madonna for looking after us again.

'Jean-Luc, you'd better phone Gavallan about the telex,' Mathias said.

Offshore Al Shargaz: Scragger and Benson were staring at the oil and pressure gauges on number one engine. Warning lights were on, the needle of the temperature gauge at maximum, top of the red, oil pressure needle fading, almost at zero. Now they were flying at seven hundred feet, in good but hazy weather, past the international boundary with Siri and Abu Musa just behind them, and Al Shargaz directly ahead. The tower was three by five in their headsets, guiding traffic.

'I'm going to shut her down, Benson.'

'Yes, don't want her seizing up.'

Sound lessened and the chopper sank a hundred feet but when Scragger had increased power on Number Two and made adjustments she held her altitude. Both men were uneasy without the backup.

'No reason for her to go like that, Scrag, none at all. I did her check myself a few days ago. How we doing?'

'Just fine. Home's not too far ahead.'

Benson was very uneasy. 'Is there anywhere we could land in an emergency? Sand banks? A rig?'

'Sure, sure there are. Lots,' Scragger lied, eyes and ears seeking danger but finding none. 'You hear something?'

'No . . . no, nothing. Bloody hell, I can hear every bloody parched cog.'

Scragger laughed. 'So can I.'

'Shouldn't we call Al Shargaz?'

'Plenty of time, me son. I'm waiting for Vossi or Willi.' They flew onwards and every flicker of turbulence, decibel of pitch change from the engine, or tremble of a needle made the sweat greater.

'How far we got to go, Scrag?' Benson loved engines but hated flying, particularly in choppers. His shirt was clammy and chilled.

Then, in their headsets was Willi's voice: 'Al Shargaz, this's EP-HBB inbound with EP-HGF at seven hundred, course 140 degrees. ETA twelve minutes,' and Scragger groaned and held his breath, Willi had automatically given full Iranian call signs when they all had agreed to see if they could get away with the last three letters only. The very English voice of the controller came back loud and brittle, 'Chopper calling Al Shargaz, we understand you're in transit, inbound on 140 degrees and, er, your transmission was garbled. Please confirm you are, er, G-HYYR and G-HFEE? I say again, GolfHotelYankee Yankee-Romeo and GolfHotelFoxtrot EchoEcho?'

Bursting with excitement, Scragger let out a cheer. 'They're expecting us!'

Willi's voice was hesitant and Scragger's temperature went up twenty points: 'Al Shargaz, this . . . this is G-HY . . . YR . . .' then Vossi excitedly cut in over him, 'Al Shargaz, this is GolfHotelFoxtrotEcho-Echo, and GolfHotelYankee YankeeRomeo reading you loud and clear, we'll be with you in ten minutes and request landing at the north helipad, please inform S-G.'

'Certainly, G-HFEE,' the controller said and Scragger could almost see the man's relief. 'You're cleared for the north helipad and please call S-G on 117.7. Welcome! Welcome to Al Shargaz, maintain course and altitude.'

'Yes sir! Yessir indeedeee, 117.7,' Vossi said. At once Scragger switched to the same channel and again Vossi: 'Sierra One, this is HFEE and HYYR do you read?'

'Loud and wonderfully clear, Welcome all – but – where's Golf-HotelSierraVictor Tango?'

* * *

At Al Shargaz Office: 'He's in back of us, Sierra One,' Vossi was saying.

Gavallan, Scot, Nogger and Starke were listening on the VHF loudspeaker on their company frequency the tower frequency also being monitored, everyone very conscious that any transmission could be overheard, particularly their HF by Siamaki in Tehran and Numir at Bandar-e Delam. 'He's in back of us a few minutes, he, er, he ordered us to go on independently.' Vossi was being pointedly careful. 'We don't, er, we don't know what happened.' Then Scragger cut in and they all heard the beam in his voice, 'This is G-HSVT on your tails, so clear the decks . . .'

The room erupted in a sudden cheer, Gavallan mopped his brow, and muttered 'Thank God,' sick with relief, then jerked his thumb at Nogger. 'Get going, Nogger!'

Gleefully the young man left and almost knocked over Manuela who, set-faced, was approaching from the corridor with a tray of cold drinks. 'Scrag, Willi and Ed are about to land,' he called out on the run, by now at the far end. 'Oh, how wonderful!' she said and hurried into the room. 'Isn't that . . .' She stopped. Scragger was saying, '. . . am on one engine, so I'll request a straight in, best get a fire truck ready just in case.'

Willi's voice at once: 'Ed, do a 180 and join up with Scrag, bring him in. How're you on gas?'

'Plenty. I'm on my way.'

'Scrag, this's Willi. I'll take care of the landing request and straight in. How're you for gas.'

'Plenty. HSVT, eh? That's a lot better than HASVD!' They heard his laugh and Manuela felt better.

For her the strain of this morning, trying to contain her fears, had been awful, hearing the disembodied voices so far away and yet so near, all of them related to persons that she liked or loved, or hated – those of the enemy: 'That's what they are,' she had said fiercely a few minutes ago, near tears because their wonderful friends Marc Dubois and old Fowler were missing missing missing and oh God it could have been Conroe and then maybe . . . 'Jahan's enemy! Siamaki, Numir, they all are, all of them.' Then Gavallan had said gently, 'No, they're not, Manuela, not really, they're just doing their job . . .' But the gentleness had only goaded her, infuriated her, adding to her worry that Starke was here and not in bed at the hospital, the operation only last night, and she had flared: 'It's a game, that's all Whirlwind is to all of you, just a goddam game! You're a buncha gung-ho glory boys and you . . . and you . . .' Then she had run out and gone to the ladies room and wept.

When the storm had passed she gave herself a good talking to for losing her control, reminding herself that men were stupid and infantile and would never change. Then she blew her nose and redid her makeup and fixed her hair and went to get the drinks.

Quietly Manuela put down the tray. No one noticed her.

Starke was on the phone to Ground Control explaining what was necessary, Scot on the VHF. 'We'll take care of everything, Scrag,' Scot said.

'Sierra One. How's tricks?' Scragger asked, 'Your Deltas and Kilos?'

Scot looked at Gavallan. Gavallan leaned forward and said heavily, 'Delta Three are fine, Kilo Two . . . Kilo Two are still in place, more or less.'

Silence on the loudspeakers. On the tower frequency they heard the English controller clearing some inbounds. A bristle of static. Scragger's voice was different now. 'Confirm Delta *Three*.'

'Confirm Delta Three,' Gavallan said, still in shock at the news about Dubois and the Bahrain telex that Jean-Luc had phoned in a few minutes ago, expecting an imminent explosion from their own tower, and from Kuwait. To Jean-Luc he had said, 'Air-sea rescue? We'd better call a Mayday.'

'We're the air-sea rescue, Andy. There isn't any other. Sandor's already taken off to search. As soon as Rudi and Pop are refuelled they'll go too – I've worked out a block search for them – then they'll head direct Al Shargaz like Sandor. We can't hang around here, *mon Dieu*, you can't imagine how close we were to disaster. If he's afloat, they'll find him – there're dozens of sand banks to land on.'

'Won't that stretch their range, Jean-Luc?'

'They'll be okay, Andy. Marc didn't put out a Mayday so it must've been sudden or perhaps his radios failed or more probably he put down somewhere. There're a dozen good possibilities – he could have put down on a rig for fuel, if he went into the sea he could've been picked up – any one of a dozen things – don't forget radio silence was one of the primes. No sweat, *mon chér ami*.'

'Very much sweat.'

'Anything on the others?'

'Not yet . . .'

Not yet, he thought again and a twinge went through him.

'Who's Delta Four?' It was Willi asking.

'Our French friend and Fowler,' Gavallan said matter-of-fact, not knowing who might be listening. 'A full report when you land.'

'Understand.' Static, then, 'Ed, how you doing?'

'Fine and dandy, Willi. Climbing to one thousand and doing fine. Hey, Scrag, what's your heading and altitude?'

'142, at seven hundred and if you'd open your eyes and look two o'clock you'd see me 'cause I can see you.'

Silence for a moment. 'Scrag, you done it again!'

Gavallan got up to stretch and saw Manuela, 'Hello, m'dear.'

She smiled, a little tentatively. 'Here,' she said, offering a bottle, 'you're entitled to a beer, and a "sorry".'

'No sorries, none. You were right.' He gave her a hug and drank gratefully. 'Oh that's good, thank you, Manuela.'

'How about me, darlin'?' Starke said.

'All you'll get from me, Conroe Starke, is water and a thick ear if you weren't plain muscle between the ears.' She opened the bottle of mineral water and gave it to him, but her eyes were smiling and she rested her hand lightly on him, loving him.

'Thank you, honey,' he said, so relieved that she was here and safe and others were safe, though Dubois and Fowler were question marks and many others still to go. His shoulder and chest were aching badly and he was becoming increasingly nauseated, his head throbbing. Doc Nutt had given him a painkiller and told him it was good for a couple of hours: 'It'll hold you till noon, Duke, not much longer and perhaps less. You'd better be a noontime Cinderella or you'll be very bloody uncomfortable indeed . . . I mean bloody as in haemorrhage.' He glanced past Manuela at the clock: 12:04 p.m.

'Conroe, darlin', won't you please come back to bed, please?'

His eyes changed. 'How about in four minutes?' he said softly.

She reddened at his look, then laughed and dug her nails lightly into his neck as a cat would when purring. 'Seriously, darlin', don't you think –'

'I'm serious.

The door opened and Doc Nutt came in. 'Beddy-bye, Duke! Say good night like a good boy!'

'Hi, Doc.' Obediently Starke started to get up, failed the first time, just managed to cover his lapse and stood erect, cursing inside. 'Scot, we got a walkie talkie or a radio with the tower frequencies?'

'Sure, sure we have.' Scot reached into a side drawer and gave him the small portable. 'We'll keep in touch – you've a phone by the bed?'

'Yes. See you later – honey, no I'm fine, you stay in case of the Farsi. Thanks,' then his eyes focused out of the window. 'Hey, look at that!'

For a moment all their cares were forgotten. The London–Bahrain

Concorde was taxiing out, needle sharp, peerless, her nose drooped for takeoff. Cruising speed, 1500 miles per hour at 65,000 feet, the four thousand three hundred miles flight – 3 hours 16 minutes. 'She's gotta be the most beautiful bird alive,' Starke said, as he left.

Manuela sighed, 'I'd just love to go in her once, just once.'

'The only way to travel,' Scot said dryly. 'Heard they're stopping this run next year, aren't they?' Most of his attention was monitoring Willi and Scragger and Vossi talking back and forth, no problem there yet. From his position he could see the truck with Nogger, mechanics, paint and stencils speeding for the helipad near the far end of the runway, a firetruck already standing by.

'They're bloody idiots,' Gavallan said sourly. 'Bloody government doesn't know its arse from a hole in the ground, French the same. They should just write off research and development costs – they're written off already in actuality – then she's a perfectly viable business proposition for certain runs and priceless. LA to Japan's a natural, to Australia, Buenos Aires too . . . anyone see our birds yet?'

'Tower's in a better position, Dad.' Scot eased up the tower frequency. 'Concorde 001 you're next for takeoff. *Bon voyage*,' the controller was saying. 'When airborne call Baghdad on 119.9.'

'Thank you, 119.9.' Concorde was moving proudly, supremely confident that all eyes were on her.

'By God, she's worth looking at.'

'Tower, this is Concorde 001. What's the fire truck for?'

'We've three choppers inbound for the north helipad, one on one engine . . .'

In the Control Tower: '. . . Would you like us to divert them until you're off?' the controller asked. His name was Sinclair and he was English, an ex-RAF officer like many of the controllers employed in the Gulf.

'No, no thanks, just curious.'

Sinclair was a short, stocky balding man, and he sat in a swivel chair at a low desk with a panoramic view. Around his neck hung a pair of high-powered binoculars. He put them to his eyes and focused. Now he could see the three choppers in V formation. Earlier he had positioned the one with the failed engine at the head of the V – he knew it was Scragger but pretended not to know. Around him in the tower was an abundance of first-class radar and communication equipment, telexes, with three Shargazi trainees and a Shargazi controller. The controller was concentrating on his radar screen, positioning the other six airplanes presently in the system.

Without losing the choppers in his binoculars, Sinclair clicked on his sender: 'HSVT, this is the tower, how are you doing?'

'Tower, HSVT.' Scragger's voice was clear and precise. 'No problem. Everything in the green. I see Concorde approaching for takeoff – would you like me to hold or hurry up?'

'HSVT, continue your direct approach at safety maximum. Concorde, go into position and hold.' Sinclair called out to one of the trainees on the Ground Control, 'Mohammed, soon as the chopper lands I turn him over to you, all right?'

'Yes, Sayyid.'

'Are you in contact with the fire truck?'

'No, Sayyid.'

'Then do it quickly! That's your responsibility.' The youth started to apologise. 'Don't worry, you made a mistake, that's over, get on with it!'

Sinclair adjusted the focus a hair. Scragger was fifty feet off, approach perfect. 'Mohammed, tell the fire truck to get with it – come on for God's sake, those buggers should be ready with the foam hoses.' He heard the young controller cursing the fire-fighters, then saw them piling out, readying their hoses. Again he moved the glasses over to Concorde waiting patiently, lined up in the centre of the runway, ready for take-off, nowhere near any danger even if all three choppers blew up. Holding Concorde for thirty seconds against a million to one chance her wake turbulence could cause a freak whirlwind for the wounded chopper was a small price. Whirlwind. Godalmighty!

The rumour that S-G was going to stage an illegal pullout of Iran had been all over the field for two days now. His binoculars went from Concorde back to Scragger's chopper. Her skids touched down. The fire-fighters closed in. No fire. 'Concorde 001, you're cleared for take off,' he said calmly, 'HFEE and HYYR land when convenient, Pan Am 116 you're cleared to land, runway 32, wind twenty knots at 160.'

Behind him a telex chattered. He paused a moment watching Concorde take off, marvelling at her power and angle of climb, then again centred on Scragger, deliberately not noticing the tiny figures ducking under the rotors with stencils and paint. Another man, Nogger Lane, who on Gavallan's instructions had privately given him advance notice of what was going on though long after he already knew – was waving the fire truck away. Scragger was to one side retching, and the other man, he assumed the second pilot, was urinating monstrously. The other two choppers settled into their landings. Painters swarmed over to them. Now what on earth are they doing?

1042

'Good,' he murmured, 'no fire, no fuss, no farting about.'

'Sayyid Sinclair, you should read this telex perhaps.'

'Uh?' Absently he glanced at the youth who was awkwardly trying to use the spare binoculars on the choppers. One look at the telex was enough. 'Mohammed, have you ever used binoculars backward?' he asked.

'Sayyid?' The youth was perplexed.

Sinclair took the glasses from him, unfocused them and gave them back reversed. 'Train them on the choppers and tell me what you see?'

It took the youth a few moments to get the image centred. 'They're so far away I can hardly make the three of them out.'

'Interesting. Here, sit in my chair a moment.' Puffed with pride the youth obeyed. 'Now, call Concorde and ask for a position report.'

The other trainees were filled with envy, all else forgotten. Mohammed's fingers trembled with excitement holding down the transmit. 'Concorde, this . . . this is Bahrain tower, please your position report please.'

'Tower, 001 going through 34,000 for 62,000, Mach 1.3 for Mach 2– 1,500 miles per hour, heading 290, leaving your area now.'

'Thank you, Concorde, good day . . . oh, call Baghdad 119.9, good day!' he said beaming and when the time was correct, Sinclair pointedly picked up the telex and frowned.

'Iranian choppers?' He gave the youth the spare glasses. 'Do you see any Iranian choppers here?'

After examining the three incoming strangers very carefully, the youth shook his head. 'No, Sayyid, those are British, the only others here we know are Shargazi.'

'Quite right.' Sinclair was frowning. He had noticed that Scragger was still slumped on the ground, Lane and some of the others standing around him. Not like Scragger, he thought.

'Mohammed, send a medic and ambulance over to those British choppers on the double.' Then he picked up the phone, dialled. 'Mr. Gavallan, your birds are down safe and sound. When you have a moment could you drop by the tower?' He said it in the peculiarly casual, understated English way that only another Englishman would detect at once meant 'urgently'.

In the S-G Office: Gavallan said into the phone, 'I'll be there right away, Mr. Sinclair. Thanks.'

Scot saw his face. 'More trouble, Dad?'

'I don't know. Call me if anything happens.' At the door, Gavallan

1043

stopped. 'Damn, I forgot about Newbury. Call him and see if he's available this afternoon. I'll go to his house, anywhere – fix whatever you can. If he wants to know what's going on, just say, "Six out of seven so far, one on standby and two to go." ' He hurried away with, ' 'bye, 'bye, Manuela. Scot, try Charlie again and find out where the devil he is.'

'Okay.' Now they were alone, Scot and Manuela. His shoulder was aching and intruding more and more. He had noticed her depression. 'Dubois'll turn up, you'll see,' he said, wanting to sound very confident and mask his own fear they were lost, 'and nothing could kill old Fowler.'

'Oh I do hope so,' she said, her tears near. She had seen her husband stumble and was achingly aware of the extent of his pain. Soon I'm going to have to leave for the hospital and the hell with Farsi. 'It's the waiting.'

'Only a few more hours, Manuela, two more birds and five bods. Then we can celebrate,' Scot added, hoping against hope, and thinking: Then the weight'll be off the Old Man too, he'll smile again and live a thousand years.

My God, give up flying? I love flying and don't want a desk job. Hong Kong for part of the year'd be fine but Linbar? I can't deal with Linbar! The Old Man'll have to deal with him – I'd be lost . . .

The old, nagging question leaped into his mind: what'd I do if the Old Man wasn't around? A chill went through him. Not if, when, it's got to happen someday. It could happen any day. Look at Jordon, Talbot – or Duke or me. A fraction of an inch and you're dead – or you're alive. The will of God? Karma? Joss? I don't know and it doesn't matter! All I'm sure of is since I was hit I'm different, my whole life's different, my certainty that nothing would ever touch me has vanished for ever and all that's left is a God-cursed, icy, stench-ridden certainty of being very mortal. Christ Almighty! Does that always happen? Wonder if Duke feels the same?

He looked at Manuela. She was staring at him. 'Sorry, I wasn't listening,' he said and began to dial Newbury.

'I just said, "Isn't it three birds and eight bods?" You forgot Erikki and Azadeh – nine if you count Sharazad.'

Tehran, At The Bakravan House: 1:14 P.M. Sharazad stood in front of the long mirror in her bathroom, naked, examining the profile of her stomach, seeing if there was an added roundness yet. This morning she had noticed that her nipples seemed more sensitive and her breasts appeared tight. 'No need to worry,' Zarah, Meshang's wife had laughed. 'Soon you'll be like a balloon and in tears, you'll be wailing that you'll never be able to get into your clothes again and oh how ugly you look! Don't worry, you will – get into your clothes – and you won't look ugly.'

Sharazad was very happy today, dawdling, and she frowned at herself and peered closer to see if she had any wrinkles, looking at herself this way and that, trying her hair up and down, bunched or to one side, contended and pleased with what she saw. The bruises were fading. Her body was quite dry from her bath and she powdered herself, stepped into her underclothes.

Jari bustled in. 'Oh, Princess, aren't you ready yet? His Eminence your brother is expected back for lunch any minute and the whole house is frightened he'll be in another of his rages, oh please hurry, we don't want to excite him now do we . . .' Automatically she pulled the plug out of the bath, began tidying, all the time fussing and muttering and chivvying Sharazad along. In moments Sharazad was dressed. Stockings – no panty hose on sale for months now, even on the black market – no need for a bra. Warm blue cashmere dress of Paris cut with matching short sleeved shawl coat. A quick brush and her naturally wavy hair was perfect, the barest touch of lip make up, a line of kohl around her eyes and she was ready.

'But Princess, you know how your brother doesn't like make up!'

'Oh but I'm not going out, and Meshang's not . . .' Sharazad was going to say 'my father' but stopped herself, not wanting to articulate that or to bring back that tragedy from the recesses of her mind. Father's in Paradise, she told herself firmly. His Day of Mourning, the fortieth day since he died, is still twenty five days away and until then, when there will be all the wailing and weeping and rending of garments, we must get on with living.

And loving?

She had not asked Jari what had happened at the coffee shop, the day she had sent her there to tell *him* her husband had returned and that what had never begun was ended. I wonder where he is, if he'll continue to visit me in my dreams?

There was a commotion downstairs and they knew Meshang had arrived. She checked herself a last time, then went to meet him.

After the night of his clash with Lochart, Meshang had moved back into the house with his family. The house was very big, Sharazad still had her rooms and was delighted that Zarah and her three children noised away the crushing silence and gloom that had previously been pervading it. Her mother was a recluse now, in her own wing, even eating there, served only by her own maid, praying and weeping most of the day. Never coming out, never inviting any of them in: 'Leave me alone! Leave me alone!' was all she would whimper through the locked door.

During the hours that Meshang was in the house, Sharazad, Zarah and others in the family were careful to cajole and flatter him. 'Don't worry,' Zarah had told her. 'He'll be to heel soon enough. He thinks I've forgotten he insulted me and hit me and dares to flaunt the young whore that that vile son of a dog Kia tempted him with! Oh, don't worry, darling Sharazad, I'll have my revenge – it was unforgivable bad manners to treat you and . . . your husband like that. Soon we'll be able to travel again . . . Paris, London, even New York . . . I doubt if he'll have the time to go with us and then, ah, and then we'll kick up our heels, wear see-throughs and have fifty suitors each!'

'I don't know about New York – putting oneself in so much danger of Satan,' Sharazad had said. But in her secret heart she trembled with excitement at the thought. I'll go to New York with my son, she promised herself. Tommy will be there. Soon we'll be normal again, the power of the mullahs over Khomeini will be broken, may God open his eyes, their control of the Green Bands eliminated, the Revolutionary Komiteh disbanded, we'll have a true, fairly elected democratic Islamic government with Prime Minister Bazargan its leader under God, women's rights will never be touched again, the Tudeh no longer outlawed but working for all and there will be peace in the land – just as *he* said would happen.

I'm glad I am who I am, Sharazad thought. 'Hello, darling Meshang, how nice you look today but so tired, oh, you mustn't work so hard for all of us. Here, let me pour you some more cool lemon and water, just the way you like it.'

'Thank you.' Meshang was lounging on the carpets, propped against cushions, his shoes off, already eating. A small brazier was ready to barbecue the kebabs, and twenty or thirty dishes of horisht and rice and vegetables and sweetmeats and fruit were within easy reach. Zarah was nearby and she beckoned Sharazad to sit on the carpet beside her.

'How do you feel today?'

'Wonderful, not the least bit sick.'

Meshang's face became sour. 'Zarah was sick all the time, and moping, not like a normal woman. Let's hope you're normal, but you're so thin . . . Insha'Allah.'

Both women put on a smile, hiding their loathing, understanding each other. 'Poor Zarah,' Sharazad said. 'How was your morning, Meshang? It must be terribly difficult for you with so much to do, so many of us to look after.'

'It's difficult because I'm surrounded by fools, dear Sister. If I had efficient staff, trained as I am, it would all be so easy.' And so much easier if you had not beguiled Father, twisted him, failed your first husband and disgraced us with your choice of the second. So much anguish you've caused me, dear sister, you with your consumptive-looking face and body and stupidity – me who has worked all hours to rescue you from yourself. Praise be to God my efforts have borne such fruits!

'It must be terribly hard for you, Meshang, I wouldn't know where to start,' Zarah was saying and she was thinking, Simple to run the business providing you know where the keys are, the bank accounts, the debtors' papers – and all the skeletons. I don't want us to have equality or the vote because we'd easily work you into the joub and take the best jobs.

The rich lamb horisht and crisped golden rice was delicious, fragrantly spiced just as he liked, and he ate with enjoyment. Mustn't eat too much, he told himself. You don't want to get too tired before little Yasmin this afternoon. I never realised how succulent a zinaat could be, or lips so grasping. If she gets with child then I shall marry her and Zarah can rot.

He glanced at his wife. Immediately she stopped eating, smiled at him and gave him a napkin to take the grease and dribbles of soup from his beard. 'Thank you,' he said politely and once more concentrated on his plate. After I've had Yasmin, he was thinking, after her I can sleep an hour and then back to work. I wish that dog Kia was back, we've much to talk about, much to plan. And Sharazad will ha –

'Meshang, dearest, did you hear the rumour the generals have decided to launch their coup,' Zarah asked, 'and that the army's ready to take over?'

'Of course, it's all over the bazaar.' Meshang felt a twinge of anxiety. He had hedged as best he could in case it was true. 'The son of Mohammed the goldsmith swears his cousin who is a telephonist at Army Headquarters overheard one of the generals saying they've waited to give an American task force time to get in range, and it'll be supported by an airborne landing.'

Both women were shocked. 'Parachutists? Then we should leave at once, Meshang,' Zarah said. 'It won't be safe in Tehran, we'd better go to our house in the Caspian and wait for the war to end. When could you leave? I'll start packing immed –'

'What house on the Caspian! We don't have any house on the Caspian!' Meshang said irritably. 'Wasn't it confiscated along with all our other property that we worked generations to acquire? God curse the thieves after all we've done for the revolution and for mullahs over the generations?' He was red in the face. A dribble of horisht went into his beard. 'And now . . .'

'Do forgive me, you're right, dearest Meshang, you're right as usual. Do forgive me, I spoke without thinking. You're right as usual but if it pleases you we could go and stay with my uncle Agha Madri, they have a spare villa on the coast, we could take that and we could leave tomorrow –'

'Tomorrow? Don't be ridiculous! Do you think I won't have enough warning?' Meshang wiped his beard, somewhat mollified by her abject apology, and Sharazad thought how fortunate she had been with her two husbands who had never mistreated her or shouted at her. I wonder how Tommy's getting on at Kowiss or wherever he is. Poor Tommy, as if I could leave my home and family and go into exile for ever.

'Of course we bazaaris will have warning,' Meshang said again. 'We're not empty-headed fools!'

'Yes, yes of course, dear Meshang,' Zarah said soothingly, 'I'm sorry, I only meant I was worried for your safety and wanted to be prepared.' However foul he is, she thought, her insides fluttering, he's our only defence against the mullahs and their equally vile Green Band thugs. 'Do you believe the coup will happen?'

'Insha'Allah,' he said and belched. Either way I'll be prepared, with the help of God. Either way, whoever wins, they'll still need us bazaaris, they always have and always will – we can be as modern as any foreigners, and smarter, some of us can be, certainly me. Son of a dog Paknouri, may he and his fathers be in hell for endangering us!

The Caspian? Her uncle Madri's a good idea, the perfect idea. I would have thought of it myself in a moment. Zarah may be used up and her zinaat as dry as summer's dust but she's a good mother and her counsel – if you forget her foul humour – is always wise. 'Another rumour's that our glorious ex-Prime Minister Bakhtiar is still in hiding in Tehran, under the protection and roof of his old friend and colleague, Prime Minister Bazargan.'

Zarah gasped. 'If the Green Bands catch him there . . .'

'Bazargan's useless. Pity. No one obeys him any more, or even listens to him. The Revolutionary Komiteh would execute both of them if they're caught.'

Sharazad was trembling. 'Jari said there was a rumour in the market this morning that Excellency Bazargan has resigned already.'

'That's not true,' Meshang said shortly, passing on another rumour as though it were private knowledge. 'My friend close to Bazargan told me he offered Khomeini his resignation but the Imam refused it, telling him to stay where he was.' He held out his plate for Zarah to give him some more. 'That's enough horisht, a little more rice.'

She gave him the crisped part and he began to eat again, almost replete. The most interesting rumour today, whispered in enormous secrecy from ear to ear, was that the Imam was near death, either from natural causes or poisoned by communist Tudeh agitators or mujhadin or CIA and, even worse, that Soviet legions were waiting just over the border ready to march into Azerbaijan again, and on to Tehran the moment he was dead.

Nothing but death and disaster ahead if that's true, he thought. No, that won't happen, can't happen. The Americans will never let the Soviets conquer us, they can't allow them to take control of Hormuz – even Carter will see that! No. Let's just hope the first part's true – that the Imam is going to Paradise quickly. 'As God wants,' he said piously, waved the servants away and when they were alone he turned his full attention on to his sister. 'Sharazad, your divorce is all arranged, but for the formalities.'

'Oh,' she said, at once on guard, hating her brother for disturbing her calm, sending her brain into overdrive: I don't want to divorce, Meshang could easily have given us money from all the Swiss accounts and not been so nasty to my Tommy and then we could have gone – don't be silly, you couldn't leave without papers and exile yourself and Tommy left you, it was his decision. Yes, but Tommy said it would be for a month, didn't he, that he'd wait for a month. In a month so many things can happen.

'Your divorce presents no problem. Nor your remarriage.'

She gaped at him, speechless.

'Yes, I've agreed to a dowry, much more than I expected for . . .' He was going to say for a twice divorced woman carrying an Infidel's child, but she was his sister and it was a great match, so he did not. 'The marriage will be next week and he's admired you for years. Excellency Farazan.'

For a moment both women could hardly believe their ears. Sharazad felt a sudden flush, disoriented even more. Keyvan Farazan was from a rich bazaari family, twenty-eight, handsome, recently back from Cambridge University and they had been friends all of her life. 'But . . . but I thought Keyvan's going to be ma –'

1049

'Not Keyvan,' Meshang said, irritated by her stupidity. 'Everyone knows Keyvan's about to be betrothed. Daranoush! Excellency Daranoush Farazan.'

Sharazad was transfixed. Zarah gasped and tried to cover her lapse. Daranoush was the father, recently widowed of his second wife who had died in childbirth like his first, a very wealthy man who owned the monopoly for the collection of waste in the whole bazaar area. 'It's . . . it's not possible,' she muttered.

'Oh yes it is,' Meshang said, almost glowing with pleasure, totally misreading her. 'I never believed it myself when he broached the idea after hearing about your divorce. With his riches and connections, together we become the most powerful conglomerate in the bazaar, togeth –'

Sharazad burst out, 'But he's loathsome and small and old, old and bald and ugly and he likes boys, and everyone knows he's a ped –'

'And everyone knows you're twice divorced, used, you're with child by a foreigner,' Meshang exploded, 'that you go on marches and disobey, your head's filled with Western nonsense and you're stupid!' He knocked over some of the plates in his fury. 'Don't you understand what I've done for you? He's one of the richest men in the bazaar. I persuaded him to accept you – you're redeemed and now yo –'

'But Meshang, ha –'

'Don't you understand, you ungrateful bitch,' he bellowed, 'he's even agreed to adopt your child! By all the Names of God, what more do you want?'

Meshang was almost purple, quivering with rage, his fist bunched, shaking it in Sharazad's face, Zarah staring at her and then him, aghast at his fury as he ranted on.

Sharazad heard nothing, saw nothing, except what Meshang had decreed for her: the rest of her life joined to that little man, the butt of a thousand bazaari jokes who stank perpetually of urine, fertilising her once a year to bear and live and bear again until she died in childbirth or because of it – like his other two wives. Nine children from the first, seven from the second. She was doomed. Nothing she could do. Princess Night Soil until she died.

Nothing.

Nothing except I could die now, not by suicide, for then I'm forbidden Paradise and condemned to hell. Not suicide. Never. Never suicide but death doing God's work, death with God's name on my lips.

What?

Kowiss Base: 1:47 P.M. Colonel Changiz, the mullah Hussain, and some Green Bands jumped out of their car, the Green Bands spread out over the base searching, while the colonel and Hussain hurried into the office building.

In the office the two remaining clerks were in shock at the suddenness of the colonel's arrival, 'Yes . . . yes, Excellency?'

'Where is everyone?' Changiz shouted. 'Eh?'

'God knows we don't know anything, Excellency Colonel except Excellency Captain Ayre is gone with spares to Rig Abu Sal and Excellency Captain McIver with Excellency Minister Kia to Tehran and Excellency Captain Lochart went to search for the incoming 212s an –'

'What incoming 212s?'

'The four 212s Excellency Captain McIver ordered here from Bandar-e Delam with pilots and other personnel and we're getting . . . we're getting ready to . . . receive them.' The clerk, whose name was Ishmael, wilted under the penetrating stare of the mullah. 'As God knows, the captain went alone, to look alone for them as they've no HF and an airborne VHF could perhaps reach them.'

Changiz was greatly relieved. He said to Hussain, 'If the 212s are all coming here, there's been a panic for no reason.' He mopped his brow. 'When are they due?'

'I would imagine soon, Excellency,' Ishmael said.

'How many foreigners are on the base now?'

'I . . . I don't know, Excellency, we've . . . we've been diligently busy trying to make up a manifest an –'

A Green Band ran into the office, 'We can't find any foreigners, Excellency,' he said to Hussain. 'One of the cooks said the last two mechanics went with the big helicopters this morning. Iranian labourers said they heard replacement crews were due on Sunday or Monday.'

'Saturday, Excellencies, tomorrow we were told, Excellencies,' Ishmael interjected. 'But with the incoming four 212s, they've mechanics on board as well as pilots and personnel, Excellency McIver said. Do you need mechanics?'

The Green Band was saying, 'Some of the rooms – it looks as if the Infidels packed hurriedly, but there are three helicopters still in the hangars.'

Changiz turned on Ishmael, 'What're those?'

'One . . . no two 206s and a French one, an Alouette.'

'Where's Chief Clerk Pavoud?'

'He was sick, Excellency Colonel, he left sick just after noon prayers, and went home. Isn't that so, Ali?' he said to the other clerk.

'Yes, yes he was sick and he left saying he would be back tomorrow . . .' the words trailed off.

'Captain McIver ordered the 212s here from Bandar-e Delam?'

'Yes, yes, Excellency, that's what he told Excellency Pavoud, I heard him tell him that exactly, with the pilots and other personnel, wasn't that so, Ali?'

'Yes, before God, that's what happened, Excellency Colonel.'

'All right, that's enough.' To Hussain the colonel said, 'We'll radio Lochart.' To the clerk he said, 'Is Sergeant Wazari in the tower?'

'No, Excellency Colonel, he went back to the base just before Excellency Captain Lochart took off to search for the four 212s that should arr –'

'Enough!' Colonel Changiz thought a moment, then said rudely to the Green Band, 'You! Get my corporal on the double to the tower.'

The youthful Green Band flushed at the tone and glanced at Hussain who said coldly, 'The colonel means, please find Corporal Borgali and bring him to the tower quickly.'

Changiz started blustering, 'I meant no impoliteness of cour –'

'Of course.' Hussain stalked down the corridor towards the staircase that led to the tower. Very much chastened, Changiz followed.

Half an hour before a telex had arrived at the airbase from Tehran ATC asking for an immediate check on all IHC foreign personnel and helicopters at Kowiss: '. . . four 212s have been reported missing from IHC base at Bandar-e Delam by IHC Managing Director Siamaki, who believes they might have been illegally flown out of Iran to one of the Gulf States.'

At once Changiz had been summoned by the duty Green Band who had already taken the telex to Hussain and the komiteh. The komiteh was in session on the base, painstakingly continuing investigations into Islamic reliability of all officers and men, and into crimes committed against God in the name of the Shah. Changiz felt nauseated. The komiteh was pitiless. No one who had been pro-Shah had yet escaped. And though he was commandant, appointed by the komiteh with Hussain's approval, confirmation from the all powerful Revolutionary Komiteh had not yet arrived. Until that happened, Changiz knew he was on trial. And hadn't he taken an oath of allegiance to the Shah personally, like every man in the forces?

In the tower he saw Hussain staring at the equipment. 'Can you work the radios, Colonel?' the mullah asked, his robes old but clean, turban white and freshly washed, but old too.

'No, Excellency, that's why I sent for Borgali.' Corporal Borgali came up the stairs two at a time and stood to attention. 'VHF and HF,' the colonel ordered.

'Yessir.' Borgali switched on. Nothing. A quick check and he found the mutilated crystal and that the VHF circuit break was missing. 'Sorry, sir, this equipment's non-functioning.'

'You mean sabotaged,' Hussain said softly and looked at Changiz.

Changiz was numb. God burn all foreigners, he was thinking in despair. If it's deliberate sabotage . . . then this is proof they've fled and taken our choppers with them. That dog McIver must have known they were going to do it this morning when I was asking about the 125.

Prickles of ice needles went through him. No 125 now, no private escape route, no chance of taking Lochart or one of the other pilots hostage on a trumped-up charge, then secretly bartering the man's escape from jail for a seat for himself – if necessary. His entrails heaved. What if the komiteh finds out my wife and family are already in

Baghdad, not as supposed at Abadan where my poor mother is dying. The nightmare devils were always jeering, shouting the truth. 'What mother? Your mother's been dead for seven or eight years! You've planned to flee, you're guilty of crimes against God and the Imam and the revolution . . .'

'Colonel,' Hussain said in the same chilling voice, 'if the radios are sabotaged does it not follow that Captain Lochart is not searching for the other helicopters, he's not searching but has fled like the other one, and that McIver lied about ordering the other 212s here?'

'Yes . . . yes, Excellency, yes it does an –'

'And then it also follows that they have fled illegally and taken two helicopters from here illegally, apart from the four from Bandar-e Delam?'

'Yes . . . yes, that would be true too.'

'As God wants, but you are responsible.'

'But Excellency surely you must realise that it's not possible to have foreseen a secret, illegal operation like . . .' He saw the eyes and read them and his words faded away.

'So you've been duped?'

'Foreigners are sons of dogs who lie and cheat all the time . . .' Changiz stopped as thought filled his mind. He grabbed the phone, cursed finding it inoperative. In a different voice he said quickly, 'Excellency, a 212 can't fly across the Gulf without refuelling, it's not possible, and McIver's got to refuel too to get to Tehran with Kia – he'll have to refuel too so we can catch them.' To Borgali he said, 'On the double, go back to our tower and find out where the 206 cleared for Tehran with McIver and Minister Kia is scheduled to refuel. Tell the duty officer to alert the base and arrest the pilot, detain the helicopter and send Minister Kia on to Tehran . . . by road.' He looked at Hussain. 'You agree, Excellency?' Hussain nodded. 'Good. Off you go!'

The corporal rushed down the stairs.

It was cold in the tower, the wind blustering. A small rain squall pelted the windows for a moment then passed by. Hussain did not notice it, his eyes on Changiz.

'We'll catch that dog, Excellency. Minister Kia will thank us.'

Hussain did not smile. He had already arranged a reception komiteh for Kia at Tehran Airport, and if Kia could not explain all manner of curiosities in his behaviour, soon the government would be less one corrupt minister. 'Perhaps Kia is part of the plot and he's fleeing Iran with McIver, have you thought of that, Colonel?'

1054

The colonel gaped. 'Minister Kia? Do you think so?'

'Do you?'

'By God, it's . . . it's certainly possible, if you think so,' Changiz replied cautiously, trying as never before to be alert. 'I've never met the man in my life. You'd know better than me, Excellency, about Kia, you questioned him in front of the komiteh.' And exonerated him, he thought with malicious delight. 'When we catch McIver we can use him as a hostage to bring back the rest, we'll catch him, Excellency . . .'

Hussain saw the fear on the colonel's face and he wondered what the man was guilty of, was the colonel also part of the escape plan that had been obvious to him since he had questioned Starke yesterday and McIver this morning?

'And if it was obvious,' he had imagined a religious superior asking, 'why did you keep it secret and why didn't you prevent it?'

'Because of Starke, Eminence. Because I truly believe that somehow that man, though Infidel, is an instrument of God and God-protected. Three times he prevented forces of evil giving me the blessed peace of Paradise. Because of him my eyes have been opened to the truth of God's wish that I must no longer seek martyrdom but must remain on an earthly path to become a relentless scourge for God and the Imam, against enemies of Islam and his enemies.'

'But the others? Why allow them to escape?'

'Islam needs neither foreigners nor their helicopters. Should Iran need helicopters, in Isfahan there are a thousand others.'

Hussain was completely sure he was right, as right as this pro-Shah, American-supporting turncoat colonel was wrong. 'So, Colonel, what about the two 212s, will you catch them too? How?'

Changiz went to the wall map quite sure that though both of them had been duped, he was commandant and responsible if the mullah wanted to make him responsible. But don't forget this is the mullah who made a deal with Colonel Peshadi the night of the first attack on the base, the same one who befriended the American Starke and the odious maniac Zataki from Abadan. And am I not a supporter of the Imam and the revolution? Didn't I correctly give over the base to the soldiers of God?

Insha'Allah. Concentrate on the foreigners. If you can catch them, even one of them, you'll be safe from this mullah and his Green Band thugs.

Several standard flight paths were drawn on the map from Kowiss to various oil sites and to rigs out into the Gulf. 'That dog clerk said spares to Abu Sal,' he muttered. 'Now if I was them, where would I refuel?' His finger stabbed the rigs. 'One of these, Excellency,' he said excitedly. 'That's where they'd refuel.'

'The rigs carry spare fuel?'

'Oh yes, in case of an emergency.'

'And how are you going to catch them?'

'Fighters.'

On Shore at the Rendezvous: 2:07 P.M. The two 212s were parked on the desolate, undulating beach in light rain. Dejectedly Freddy Ayre and Lochart sat in the open door of one of the cabins, their two mechanics and Wazari in the other, all of them tired from handling the big, cumbersome forty-gallon drums of fuel and taking turns pumping the petrol into the tanks. Never had two 212s been refuelled faster, nor full spares heaved aboard into each and secured faster, in case of emergency. Freddy Ayre had arrived here about 11:30, Lochart just after 12:00, half an hour to refuel, and they had been waiting ever since.

'We'll give him another half an hour,' Lochart said.

'Christ, you're acting as though we've all the time in the world.'

'It's stupid for us both to wait, safer for you to go separately – how many times do I have to say it? Take everyone and I'll wait.'

'When Mac arrives we can all g –'

'Goddammit, take the mechanics and Wazari and I'll wait. That's what Mac'd say if he was here and you were waiting for me. For crissake, stop trying to play hero and push off.'

'No. Sorry, but I'm waiting until he arrives or we both leave.'

Lochart shrugged, his spirit as drab as the day. As soon as he had arrived he had worked out McIver's tentative schedule: 'Freddy, Mac was safe out of the Kowiss system by eleven-twenty. Say at the very outside he flies on for another half an hour, then another half an hour, maximum, to fake the emergency, land and get rid of Kia, maximum an hour to get here, absolute max, at the very outside means one-thirty. My bet's he'll be here one to one-fifteen.'

But it was after two and no Mac yet and maybe no Mac at all – there's got to've been a foul up. He studied the clouds, seeking answers in the weather, and refining plans and counterplans. Empty drums were in a neat pile, another five still full. The drums had been brought here during routine runs to the rigs and cached under tarpaulins and camouflaged with sand and seaweed. Out to sea, barely visible, was a rig, high above the water level, perched on stilts.

He had had no trouble getting here from Kowiss. As soon as they were airborne and it was safe, Wazari had crawled forward. 'Best you stay under cover until we're launched into the Gulf,' Lochart had said. But once they had landed, Wazari had become very sick so he had changed his mind and told the others what had happened. Now Wazari had recovered and was accepted. But still considered suspect.

The shore stank of rotting fish and seaweed. Wind, steady at about thirty knots, throbbed the rotor blades, still adverse to their planned escape route to Kuwait. The murky ceiling had lowered, now down to about two hundred feet. But little of this registered on Lochart. More and more his mind was pulled northward to Tehran and Sharazad – while his hearing reached out over the wind and the waves for the sound of the 206. Come on, Mac, he prayed. Come on, don't let me down. Come on Mac, don't let me down . . .

Then he heard her. A few seconds to make sure, and he jumped out of the cabin, mouth slightly open to increase the strength of his hearing and directional ability. Now Ayre came out of his reverie and was beside him, both of them peering into the overcast, listening now, the engine growing louder, out to sea, then passing them by and Lochart cursed. 'He's missed us!'

'VHF?' Ayre asked.

'Too goddam dangerous . . . not yet . . . he'll make another pass, he's too good not to.'

Again waiting, sound of the engines dying, dying, then the level and holding. The engine sound grew. Again the chopper made a pass and missed them and began to die away, then once more turned back. Engine sounds growing and growing, then she came down through the murk half a mile up the beach, spotted them and began her approach. No doubt now that she was theirs, McIver the pilot and alone. They cheered.

In the 206 Cockpit: McIver had had a very hard time finding the rendezvous, mud flats all looking the same, coast line the same, with conditions bad. Then he had remembered the non-working rig just offshore and had eased out to find it and, using that as a marker, had come inland.

When his skids were solid on the ground he muttered, 'Thank God for that,' and exhaled, stomach aching and desperate to urinate, opened the cockpit door at once, and said over their questions, 'Sorry, got to pee. Freddy, shut her down for me, will you?' Lochart, who was closer, said, 'I'll do her, Mac.'

'Thanks.' McIver had unsnapped his seat belt, scrambled out, and hurried under the blades for the nearest dune. When he could speak he glanced around, saw Ayre waiting for him, the others over by the 212s. 'My back teeth've been floating for a hour or more.'

'I know how it feels.'

McIver shook himself, zipped up and noticed Wazari. 'What the hell's he doing here?'

'Tom thought it best to bring him, safer than leaving him and he did help. We'd better get going, Mac. We're all refuelled. What about the 206?'

'We'll have to leave her.' She was not equipped with long-range tanks and it would take too much time to rig a temporary inflight refuelling system. Even then, this adverse wind would gulp fuel and make the voyage not possible. McIver pointed out to sea, 'I thought about parking her on the rig in the hope we could come back and pick her up, but that's a pipe dream. There's not enough space to land her and a 212 at the same time to pick me up. Bloody shame, but there you are.'

'No problem with Kia?'

'No. He was a bit of a pain in the butt an—' He whirled. Behind them Lochart had gunned the 206 and now she was lifting and backing away. 'For God's sake, Tom . . .' he bellowed and ran for the helicopter but Lochart backed faster and hauled her up twenty feet. 'Tommmm!'

Lochart leaned out of the cockpit window. 'Don't wait for me, Mac!' he shouted.

'But you're almost out of fuel . . .'

'There's plenty for the moment – I'll wait till you're gone then I'll refuel. See you in Al Shargaz!'

'What the hell's he playing at?' Ayre said.

'Sharazad,' McIver said, cursing himself for forgetting. 'He must've had fifty plans to take the 206, one way or another.' Then he cupped his hands around his mouth and shouted, 'Tom, you'll screw up Whirlwind for Christ's sake! You've got to come with us!'

'They'll never make me a hostage, Mac! Never! It's on my head, not yours . . . it's my decision, by God. Now push off!'

McIver thought a second, then bellowed, 'Land now, we'll refuel for you, save you trouble.' He saw Lochart shake his head, point at the 212s.

'I'm going back for Sharazad,' Lochart shouted. 'Don't try and stop me or wait me out . . . it's my neck not yours . . . Happy landings.' He waved then moved away to safety down the beach, turned into wind facing them and landed. But the engines were kept up, ready for instant takeoff.

1058

'No way to rush him,' McIver muttered, furious with himself for not being prepared.

'We . . . we could wait till he runs out of fuel,' Ayre said.

'Tom's too smart to be trapped.' Almost in panic McIver glanced at his watch, his mind giddy. 'Bloody fools, me and Tom.' He saw all the others looking at him.

'What're we going to do, Mac?' Ayre said.

McIver forced himself to think clearly: You're the leader. Decide. We're terribly late. Tom's decided after everything I said. That's his privilege. Sorry but that means he's on his own. Now think of the others. Erikki's got to be all right. Rudi and Scragger and their lads're safe – let's presume they're safe – so get into the 212 and begin the next leg.

He wanted to groan aloud, the thought of having to nurse a 212 to Kuwait at low level for the next two and a half hours plus almost crushed him. 'Bloody hell,' he muttered. The others still watched him and waited. 'Tom's going back to get his wife – we'll leave him to it.'

'But if he gets caught, won't that screw Whirlwind?' Ayre asked.

'No. Tom's on his own. You heard what he said. We're leaving for Kuwait as planned. Everyone into Freddy's 212, I'll take Lochart's. Off you all go and we'll stay low and close. Radio silence until we're well across the line.' McIver went for the other 212. Uneasily they looked at one another. They had all noticed his pallor and all knew about his lack of a medical.

Kyle, the short, lithe mechanic went after him. 'Mac, no point in going alone, I'll fly with you.'

'Thanks, but no. Everyone in Freddy's machine! Come on, get with it!'

Ayre said, 'Mac, I'll go and talk to Tom. He must be crazy, I'll persuade him to come to Kuw –'

'You won't. If it was Gen. I'd be just as crazy. Everyone get aboard!' At that moment, the sound of two jet fighters at low level going through the sound barrier drowned the beach. The silence they left behind was vast.

'Jesus.' Wazari shivered. 'Captain, if you'll have me along, I'll fly with you?'

'No, everyone with Freddy, I'd prefer to fly alone.'

'Your non-licence makes no odds to me.' Wazari shrugged. 'Insha'Allah! I'll monitor the radio.' He jerked his thumb skywards: 'Those bastards won't speak English.' He turned for the 212 and got into the left seat.

Ayre said, 'It's a good idea, Mac.'

'All right. We'll stay close and low as planned. Freddy, if one of us runs into trouble the other goes on.' At Ayre's look, 'I mean any trouble.' A last look at Lochart, McIver waved again and went aboard. He was very glad not to be alone. 'Thanks,' he said to Wazari, 'I don't know what'll happen at Kuwait, Sergeant, but I'll help all I can.' He locked his seat-belt and pressed Engine Start on Number One.

'Sure. Thanks. Hell, I got nothing to lose, my head's busting, I've had every aspirin outta the medical packs . . . What happened with Kia?'

McIver adjusted the volume of his headset, pressed Engine Start on Number Two, checking fuel tanks and instruments as he spoke. 'I had to do the emergency a little later than I planned – I landed about a mile from a village – but it went fine, too fine, the bugger fainted and then I couldn't get him out of the cockpit. Somehow he'd entwined himself in his seat and shoulder belts and I couldn't get him free. Didn't have a bloody knife to cut him loose. I tried every way, pushing and pulling, but the catch had stuck so I gave up and waited for him to come around. While I waited I got his luggage out and put it near to the road where he'd find it. When he came to, I had the hell's own job getting him to leave the cockpit.' McIver's fingers went accurately from switch to switch. 'Eventually I pretended we had a fire and jumped out, leaving him. That did it and he somehow got the catch undone and left in a hurry. I'd kept the engines running, bloody dangerous but had to chance it, and once he was clear, I rushed back and took off. Scraped a rock or two but no sweat . . .'

His heart had been pounding, his throat dry at the frantic take off, Kia clawing at the door handle, raving at him, hanging on, one foot on the skid, McIver afraid he would have to land again. Fortunately Kia's nerve failed and he let go and dropped back the few feet they were off the ground, and now McIver was free and away. He had circled once to make sure Kia was all right and the last he saw of Kia, he was shaking his fist and red with rage. Then he had set course for the coast, hugging the undulating trees and rocks. And though he was safe, the pounding in his chest did not lessen. Waves of nausea and heat began to sweep through him.

It's just the strain of the last week or so catching up, he had told himself grimly. Just strain and trying to haul that bugger out of the cockpit, along with worries over Whirlwind and being scared fartless by the mullah's questioning.

1060

For a few more minutes after leaving Kia, he had flown onwards. Difficult to concentrate. Pain increasing. Controls unfamiliar. A spasm of nausea and he almost lost control so decided to land and rest a moment. He was still in the mountain foothills, rocks and clumps of trees and snow, the ceiling low and fairly thin. Through a haze of sickness he chose the first possible plateau and landed. The landing was not good and that, more than anything, frightened him very much. Nearby was a stream, partially frozen, the water frothing as it tumbled down the rocks. The water beckoned him. In bad pain now he shut down, stumbled over to it, lay on the snow and drank deeply. The shock of the cold made him retch and when the spasm had passed he cleansed his mouth and drank sparingly. This and the cold of the air helped him. A handful of snow rubbed into the back of his neck and temples made him feel even better. Gradually the pain lessened, the tingling in his left arm went away. When it had almost gone he groped to his feet and, stumbling a little, made the cockpit, sank back in his seat.

His cockpit was warm and cosy and familiar – enclosing. Automatically he snapped his seat belt. Silence filled his ears and his head. Only the sound of the wind, and the water, no engines or traffic or static, nothing but the softness of the wind and water. Peacefulness. His eyelids were heavier than they had ever been. He closed them. And slept.

His sleep was deep and barely half an hour and very good. When he awoke he was revitalised – no pain, no discomfort, just a little light headed as though he had dreamed the pain. He stretched gloriously. Tiny sounds of metal chinking against metal. He looked around. Seated on a small mountain pony, watching him silently, was a youth, a tribesman. In a saddle sheath was a rifle and another was across his back with a bandolier of cartridges.

The two of them stared at each other, then the youth smiled and the plateau seemed to light up. 'Salaam, agha.'

'Salaam, agha.' McIver smiled back, surprised that he was completely unafraid, somehow put at his ease by the wild beauty of the youth. '*Lotfan befarma'id shoma ki hastid*?' He used one of his few stock phrases: May I ask who you are?

'Agha Mohammed Rud Kahani,' and then some words McIver did not understand and he finished with another smile and, 'Kash'kai.'

'Ah, Kash'kai,' McIver nodded, understanding that the youth was one of the nomadic tribes that spread across the Zagros. He pointed at himself. 'Agha McIver,' and added another stock phrase, '*Mota assef am, man zaban shoma ra khoob nami danam.*' Sorry, I don't speak your language.

'Insha'Allah. America?'

'English. Englishman.' He was watching himself and the other man. Helicopter and horse, pilot and tribesman, gulfs between them but no threat, one to the other. 'Sorry, I must go now,' he said in English, then parodied, flying away with his hands. '*Khoda haefez*,' goodbye, 'Agha Mohammed Kash'kai.'

The youth nodded and raised his hand in salute. '*Khoda haefez, agha,*' then moved his horse to safety and stood there watching him. When the engines were up to power, McIver waved once and left. All the way to the rendezvous he had thought about the youth. No reason for that youth not to shoot me, or perhaps no reason to shoot me. Did I dream him, dream the pain? No, I didn't dream the pain. Did I have a heart attack?

Now, ready to leave for Kuwait, for the first time he faced the question. Disquiet returned and he glanced at Wazari who was staring disconsolately out of the side window at the sea. How dangerous am I now? he asked himself. If I had one attack, even a mild one, I could have another, so am I risking his life as well as my own? I don't think so. I've only high blood pressure and that's under control, I take the two pills a day and no problem. I can't leave a 212 just because Tom's gone mad. I'm tired, but okay and Kuwait's only a couple of hours. I'd be happier not to be flying. My God, I never thought I'd ever feel that. Old Scrag can have the flying, I'm done with it for ever.

His ears were listening to the pitch of the engines. Ready for takeoff now, no real need to check the instruments. Through the rain speckles on his windshield he saw Ayre give him a thumbs-up, also ready. Down the beach he could see Lochart in the 206. Poor old Tom. Bet he's cursing us to hurry, anxious to refuel and rush north to a new destiny. Hope he succeeds – at least he'll have a following wind.

'Okay to switch on the VHF?' Wazari asked, distracting him. 'I'll tune into military frequencies.'

'Good.' McIver smiled at Wazari, pleased to have him for company.

Lots of static in his headphones, then Farsi voices. Wazari listened awhile then said throatily, 'It's the fighters talking to Kowiss. One of them said, "In all the Names of God, how're we going to find two choppers in this pool of dog shit?"'

'They won't, not if I have anything to do with it.' McIver tried to sound confident over a sudden tide of foreboding. He got Ayre's attention, pointed upwards, indicating the fighters and motioned across his throat. Then he pointed a last time out into the Gulf and gave a thumbs-up. A glance at his watch: 2:21 p.m.

'Here we go, Sergeant,' he said and twisted the throttles full open, 'next stop Kuwait. ETA 4.40 p.m., or thereabouts.'

At Kuwait Airport: 2:56 P.M. Genny and Charlie Pettikin were sitting in the open-air restaurant on the upper level of the sparkling, newly opened terminal. It was a grand, sunny day, sheltered from the wind. Bright yellow tablecloths and umbrellas, everyone eating and drinking with enjoyment and gusto. Except for them. Genny had hardly touched her salad, Pettikin had picked at his rice and curry.

'Charlie,' Genny said abruptly, 'I think I'll have a vodka martini after all.'

'Good idea.' Pettikin waved for a waiter and ordered for her. He would have liked to join her but he was expecting to replace or spell either Lochart or Ayre on the next leg down the coast to Jellet Island – at least one refuelling stop, perhaps two, before reaching Al Shargaz – God curse this sodding wind. 'Won't be long now, Genny.'

Oh, for Christ's sake, how many times do you have to say it, Genny wanted to scream, sick of waiting. Stoically she kept up her pretence of calm. 'Not long, Charlie. Any moment now.' Their eyes went seawards. The distant seascape was hazed, visibility poor, but they would know the instant the choppers came into Kuwait radar range. The Imperial Air rep was waiting in the tower.

How long is long? she asked herself, trying to pierce the heat haze, all her energy pouring out, seeking Duncan, sending prayers and hopes and strengths that he might need. The word that Gavallan had passed on this morning had not helped: 'What on earth's he flying Kia for, Andy? Back to Tehran? What does that mean?'

'Don't know, Genny. I'm telling you as he said it. Our interpretation is that Freddy was sent to the fuel rendezvous first. Mac took off with Kia – he's either taking him to the rendezvous or he'll put him off en route. Tom's holding the fort for a time to give the others a breathing space, then he'll head for the RV. We got Mac's initial call at ten-forty-two. Give him till eleven a.m. for him and Freddy to take off. Give them another hour to get to the RV and refuel, add two hours thirty flight time, they should arrive Kuwait around two-thirty at the earliest. Depending on how long they wait at the RV it could be anytime, from two-thirty onwards . . .'

She saw the waiter bringing her drink. On the tray was a mobile phone. 'Phone call for you, Captain Pettikin,' the waiter said as he put the glass in front of her. Pettikin pulled out the antenna, held the phone to his ear. 'Hello? Oh, hello, Andy.' She watched his face, 'No . . . no, not yet . . . Oh? . . .' He listened intently for a long time, just an occasional grunt and nod, nothing showing outwardly, and she wondered what Gavallan was saying that she was not supposed to hear. '. . . Yes, sure . . . no . . . yes, everything's covered as far as we can . . . Yes, yes, she is . . . all right, hang on.' He passed the phone over. 'He wants to say hello.'

'Hello, Andy, what's new?'

'Just reporting in, Genny. Not to worry about Mac and the others – no telling how long they had to wait at the RV.'

'I'm fine, Andy. Don't worry about me. What about the others?'

'Rudi, Pop Kelly and Sandor are en route from Bahrain – they refuelled at Abu Dhabi and we're in contact with them – John Hogg's our relay station – their ETA here's in twenty minutes. Scrag's fine, Ed and Willi no problem, Duke's sleeping and Manuela's here. She wants to say hello . . .' A moment and then Manuela's voice: 'Hi, darlin', how are ya, and don't say great!'

Genny smiled half heartedly. 'Great. Is Duke all right?'

'Sleepin' like a baby, not that babies sleep quiet all the time. Just wanted you to know we're sweating it out too. I'll pass you back to Andy.'

A pause, then: 'Hello, Genny. Johnny Hogg'll be in your area about now and he'll be listening too. We'll keep in touch. Can I speak to Charlie again, please.'

'Of course, but what about Marc Dubois and Fowler?'

A pause. 'Nothing yet. We're hoping they've been picked up – Rudi, Sandor and Pop backtracked and searched as long as they could. No wreckage, there're lots of ships in those waters and platforms. We're sweating them out.'

'Now tell me what Charlie's supposed to know but I'm not.' She scowled into the dead silence on the phone, then heard Gavallan sigh.

'You're one for the book, Genny. All right. I asked Charlie if any telex had arrived from Iran yet, like the one we got here, in Dubai and Bahrain. I'm trying to pull all the strings I can through Newbury and our Kuwaiti embassy in case of a foul-up, though Newbury says not to expect much, Kuwait being so close to Iran and not wanting to offend Khomeini and petrified he'll send or allow a few export fundamentalists to stir up the Kuwaiti Shi'as. I told Charlie that I'm trying to get word to Ross's parents in Nepal and to his regiment. That's the lot.' In a more kindly voice, 'I didn't want to upset you more than necessary. Okay?'

'Yes, thanks. Yes, I'm . . . I'm fine. Thanks, Andy.' She passed the phone back and looked at her glass. Beads of moisture had formed. Some were trickling. Like the tears on my cheeks, she thought and got up, 'Back in a sec.'

Sadly Pettikin watched her go. He listened to Gavallan's final instructions. 'Yes, yes, of course,' he said. 'Don't worry, Andy I'll take care of . . . I'll take care of Ross, and I'll call the very moment we have them on the screen. Bloody awful about Dubois and Fowler, we'll just have to think good thoughts and hope. Great about the others. 'Bye.'

Finding Ross had shattered him. The moment he had got Gavallan's call this morning he had rushed to the hospital. Today being Friday, with minimum staff, there was just one receptionist on duty and he spoke only Arabic. The man smiled and shrugged and said, '*Bokrah*' – tomorrow. But Pettikin had persisted and eventually the man had understood what he wanted and had made a phone call. At length a male nurse arrived and beckoned him. They went along corridors and then through a door and there was Ross naked on a slab.

It was the suddenness, the totality of nakedness, of seeming defilement, and the obliteration of any shred of dignity that had torn Pettikin apart, not the fact of death. This man who had been so fine in life had been left like a carcass. On another slab were sheets. He took one and covered him and that seemed to make it better.

It had taken Pettikin more than an hour to find the ward where Ross had been, to track down an English-speaking nurse and to find his doctor.

'So very sorry, so very sorry, sir,' the doctor, a Lebanese, had said in halting English. 'The young man arrived yesterday in a coma. He had a fractured skull and we suspected brain damage; it was from a terrorist bomb we were told. Both eardrums were broken and he had a number of minor cuts and bruises. We X-rayed him, of course, but apart from binding his skull there was little we could do but wait. He had no internal damage or haemorrhage. He died this morning with the dawn. The dawn was beautiful today, wasn't it? I signed the death certificate – would you like a copy? We've given one to the English embassy – together with his effects.'

'Did he . . . did he recover consciousness before he died?'

'I do not know. He was in intensive care and his nurse . . . let me see.' Laboriously the doctor had consulted his lists and found her name.

'Sivin Tahollah. Ah, yes. Because he was English we assigned her to him.'

She was an old woman, part of the flotsam of the Middle East, knowing no forebears, part of many nations. Her face was ugly and pockmarked but she was not, her voice gentle and calming, her hands warm. 'He was never conscious, Effendi,' she said in English, 'not truly.'

'Did he say anything particularly, anything you could understand, anything at all?'

'Much that I understood, Effendi, and nothing.' The old woman thought a moment. 'Most of what he said was just mind wanderings, the spirit fearing what should not be feared, wanting that which could not be had. He would murmur "azadeh" – azadeh means "born free" in Farsi though it is also a woman's name. Sometimes he would mutter a name like "Erri" or "Ekki" or "Kukri" and then again "azadeh". His spirit was at peace but not quite though he never wept like some do, or cry out, nearing the threshold.'

'Was there anything more – anything?'

She toyed with the watch she wore on her lapel. 'From time to time his wrists seemed to bother him and when I stroked them he became calm again. In the night he spoke a tongue I have never heard before. I speak English, a little French, and many dialects of Arabic, many. But this tongue I have never heard before. He spoke it in a lilting way, mixed with wanderings and "azadeh", sometimes words like . . .' She searched her memory. 'Like "regiment" and "edelweiss" and "highlands" or "high land", and sometimes, ah, yes, words like "gueng" and "tens'ng", sometimes a name like "Roses" or "Rose mountain" – perhaps it was not a name but just a place but it seemed to sadden him.' Her old eyes were rheumy. 'I've seen much of death, Effendi, very much, always different, always the same. But his passing was peaceful and his going over the threshold without hurt. The last moment was just a great sigh – I think he went to Paradise, if Christians go to Paradise, and found his Azadeh . . .'

Tabriz – At the Khan's Palace: 3:40 P.M. Azadeh walked slowly along the corridor towards the Great Room where she was meeting her brother, her back still troubling her from the grenade explosion yesterday. God in heaven, was it only yesterday that the tribesmen and Erikki almost killed us? she thought. It seems more like a thousand days, and a light-year since Father died.

It was another lifetime. Nothing good in that lifetime except Mother and Erikki and Hakim, Erikki and . . . and Johnny. A lifetime of hatreds and killings and terrors and madness, madness living like pariahs, Hakim and I, surrounded by evil, madness at the Qazvin roadblock and that vile, fat-faced mujhadin squashed against the car, oozing like a swatted fly, madness of our rescue by Charlie and the KGB man – what was his name, ah yes, Rakoczy – Rakoczy almost killing all of us, madness at Abu Mard that has changed my life for ever, madness at the base where we'd had so many fine times, Erikki and I, but where Johnny killed so many so fast and so cruelly.

She had told Erikki everything last night – almost everything. 'At the base he . . . he became a killing animal. I don't remember much, just flashes, giving him the grenade in the village, watching him rush the base . . . grenades and machine guns, one of the men wearing a kukri, then Johnny holding up his severed head and howling like a banshee . . . I know now the kukri was Gueng's. Johnny told me in Tehran.'

'Don't say any more now, leave the rest until tomorrow, my darling. Go to sleep, you're safe now.'

'No. I'm afraid to sleep, even now in your arms, even with all the glorious news about Hakim, when I sleep I'm back in the village, back at Abu Mard and the mullah's there, cursed of God, the kalandar's there and the butcher's got his carving knife out.'

'There's no more village or mullah, I've been there. No more kalandar nor butcher. Ahmed told me about the village, part of what had happened there.'

'You went to the village?'

'Yes, this afternoon, when you were resting. I took a car and went there. It's a heap of burned rubble. Just as well,' Erikki had said ominously.

In the corridor Azadeh stopped a moment and held on to the wall until the fit of trembling passed. So much death and killing and horror. Yesterday when she had come out on to the steps of the palace and had seen Erikki in the cockpit, blood streaming down his face and into his stubbled beard, more dripping from his sleeve, Ahmed crumpled beside him, she had died and then, seeing him get out and stand tall and walk to her, her own legs unless, and catch her up into his arms, she had come to life again, all her terrors had poured out with her tears. 'Oh, Erikki, oh, Erikki, I've been so afraid, so afraid . . .'

He had carried her into the Great Room and the doctor was there with Hakim, Robert Armstrong and Colonel Hashemi Fazir. A bullet had torn away part of Erikki's left ear, another had scored his forearm. The doctor had cauterised the wounds and bound them up, injecting him with antitetanus serum and penicillin, more afraid of infection than of loss of blood: 'Insha'Allah, but there's not much I can do, Captain, you're strong, your pulse is good, a plastic surgeon can make your ear look better, your hearing's not touched, praise be to God! Just beware of infection . . .'

'What happened, Erikki?' Hakim had asked.

'I flew them north into the mountains and Ahmed was careless – it wasn't his fault, he got airsick – and before we knew what was happening Bayazid had a gun to his head, another tribesman had one to mine and Bayazid said, "Fly to the village, then you can leave."

1068

' "You swore a holy oath you wouldn't harm me!" I said.

' "I swore I wouldn't harm you and I won't, but my oath was mine, not of my men," Bayazid said, and the man with a gun to my head laughed and shouted, "Obey our Sheik or by God you will be so filled with pain you will beg for death." '

'I should have thought of that,' Hakim said with a curse. 'I should have bound them all with the oath. I should have thought of that.'

'It wouldn't have made any difference. Anyway it was all my fault; I'd brought them here and almost ruined everything. I can't tell you how sorry I am but it was the only way to get back and I thought I'd find Abdollah Khan. I never thought that *matyeryebyets* would use a grenade.'

'We're not hurt, through God's will, Azadeh and I. How could you know Abdollah Khan was dead, or that half your ransom was paid? Go on with what happened,' Hakim had said and Azadeh noticed a strangeness under the voice. Hakim's changed, she thought. I can't understand what's in his mind like I used to. Before he became Khan, really Khan, I could but not now. He's still my darling brother but a stranger. So much has changed, so fast. I've changed. So has Erikki, my God how much! Johnny hasn't changed . . .

In the Great Room, Erikki had continued: 'Flying them away was the only way to get them out of the palace without further trouble or killing. If Bayazid hadn't insisted, I would have offered – no other way'd've been safe for you and Azadeh. I had to gamble that somehow they'd obey the oath. But whatever happened, it was them or me, I knew it and so did they, for of course I was the only one who knew who they were and where they lived and a Khan's vengeance is serious. Whatever I did, drop them off halfway or go to the village, they'd never let me go. How could they – it was the village or me and their One God would vote for their village along with them, whatever they'd agreed or sworn!'

'That's a question only God could answer.'

'My gods, the ancient gods, don't like to be used as an excuse, and they don't like this swearing in their name. They disapprove of it greatly, in fact they forbid it.' Azadeh heard the bitterness and touched him gently. He had held her hand. 'I'm fine now, Azadeh.'

'What happened next, Erikki?' Hakim asked.

'I told Bayazid there wasn't enough gasoline and tried to reason with him and he just said, "As God wants," stuck the gun into Ahmed's shoulder and pulled the trigger. "Go to the village! The next bullet goes into his stomach." Ahmed passed out and Bayazid reached over him for the Sten gun that had slipped to the floor of the cockpit, half under the seat, but he couldn't quite get it. I was strapped in, so was Ahmed, they weren't, so I shifted her around the skies in ways I didn't think a chopper could stand, then let her drop out and made a landing. It was a bad one; I thought I'd broken a skid but later I found it was only bent. As soon as we'd stopped I used the Sten and my knife and killed those who were conscious and hostile, disarmed the unconscious ones, and dumped them out of the cabin. Then, after a time, I came back.'

'Just like that,' Armstrong had said. 'Fourteen men.'

'Five, and Bayazid. The others . . .' Azadeh had her arm on his shoulder and she felt the shrug and the following tremor. 'I left them.'

'Where?' Hashemi Fazir had said. 'Could you describe where, Captain?' Erikki had done so, accurately, and the colonel had sent men to find them.

Erikki put his good hand into his pocket and brought out the ransom jewels and gave them to Hakim Khan. 'Now I think I would like to talk to my wife, if it pleases you. I'll tell you the rest later.' Then she and he had gone to their own rooms and he said nothing more, just held her gently in his great embrace. Her presence soothed away his anguish. Soon to sleep. She slept barely at all, at once back in the village to tear herself in panic from its suffocating grasp. She had stayed quiet for a time in his arms, then moved to a chair and half dozed, content to be with him. He had slept dreamlessly until it was dark, then awoke.

'First a bath and then a shave and then some vodka and then we will talk,' he had said, 'I've never seen you more beautiful nor loved you more and I'm sorry, I was jealous – no, Azadeh, don't say anything yet. Then I want to know everything.'

In the dawn she had finished telling all there was to tell – as much as she would ever tell – and he his story. He had hidden nothing, not his jealousy, or the killing rage and the joy of battle or the tears he had shed on the mountainside, seeing the savagery of the mayhem he had dealt to the tribesmen. 'They . . . they did treat me fairly in their village and ransom is an ancient custom. If it hadn't been for Abdollah murdering their messenger . . . that might have made the difference, perhaps, perhaps not. But that doesn't forgive the killings. I feel I'm a monster, you married a madman, Azadeh. I'm dangerous.'

'No, no, you're not, of course you're not.'

'By all my gods, I've killed twenty or more men in half that number of days and yet I've never killed before except those assassins, those men who charged in here to murder your father before we were married. Outside of Iran I've never killed anyone, never hurt anyone

– I've had plenty of fights with or without pukoh but never serious. Never. If that kalandar and the village had existed, I would have burned him and them without a second thought. I can understand your Johnny at the base; I thank all gods for bringing him to us to protect you and curse him for taking away my peace though I know I'm in his immortal debt. I can't deal with the killings and I can't deal with him. I can't, I can't, not yet.'

'It doesn't matter, not now, Erikki. Now we've time. Now we're safe, you're safe and I'm safe and Hakim's safe, we're safe, my darling. Look at the dawn, isn't it beautiful? Look, Erikki, it's a new day now, so beautiful, a new life. We're safe, Erikki.'

In the Great Room: 3:45 P.M. Hakim Khan was alone except for Hashemi Fazir. Half an hour ago Hashemi had arrived unbidden. He had apologised for the intrusion, handing him a telex. 'I thought you'd better see this at once, Highness.'

The telex read: 'URGENT. To Colonel Fazir, Inner Intelligence, Tabriz: Arrest Erikki Yokkonen, husband of Her Highness, Azadeh Gorgon, for crimes committed against the State, for complicity in air piracy, hijacking, and high treason. Put him in chains and send him at once to my Headquarters here. Director, SAVAMA, Tehran.'

Hakim Khan dismissed his guards. 'I don't understand, Colonel. Please explain.'

'The moment I'd decoded it, I phoned for further details, Highness. It seems last year S-G Helicopters sold a number of helicopters to IHC an –'

'I don't understand.'

'Sorry, to Iran Helicopters Company, an Iranian company Captain Yokkonen's present employer. Amongst them were – are – ten 212s including his. Today the other nine, valued at nine million dollars, were stolen and illegally flown out of Iran by IHC pilots – SAVAMA presumes to one of the Gulf states.'

Hakim Khan said coldly, 'Even if they have, this doesn't affect Erikki. He's done nothing wrong.'

'We don't know that for certain, Highness. SAVAMA says perhaps he knew of the conspiracy – it certainly had to have been planned for some time because three bases are involved – Lengeh, Bandar-e Delam, and Kowiss – as well as their Tehran Head Office. SAVAMA are very, very agitated because it's also been reported that vast quantities of valuable Iranian spares have been whisked away. Even mo –'

'Reported by whom?'

'The IHC managing director, Siamaki. Even more serious, all IHC foreign personnel, pilots and mechanics and office staff, have vanished as well. Everyone, so of course it was a conspiracy. It seems that yesterday there were perhaps twenty of them all over Iran, last week forty, today none. There are no S-G, or more correctly IHC foreigners left in all Iran. Except Captain Yokkonen.'

At once the implication of Erikki's importance leaped into Hakim's mind and he cursed himself for allowing his face to give him away when Hashemi said blithely, 'Ah, yes, of course you see it too! SAVAMA told me that even if the captain is innocent of complicity in the conspiracy, he's the essential means to persuade the ringleaders and criminals, Gavallan and McIver – and certainly the British government must have been party to the treason – to return our airplanes, our spares, to pay an indemnity of very serious proportions, to return to Iran and stand trial for crimes against Islam.'

Hakim Khan shifted uneasily on his cushions, the pain in his back surfacing, and he wanted to shout with rage because all the pain and anguish was unnecessary, and now, hardly able to stand without pain, he might be permanently injured. Put that aside for later, he told himself grimly, and deal with this dangerous son of a dog who sits there patiently like an accomplished salesman of precious carpets who has laid out his wares and now waits for the negotiation to begin. If I want to buy.

To buy Erikki out of the trap I shall have to give this dog a personal pishkesh, of value to him not SAVAMA, God curse them by any name. What? Petr Oleg Mzytryk at least. I could pass him over to Hashemi without a belch if he comes, when he comes. He'll come. Yesterday Ahmed sent for him in my name – I wonder how Ahmed is, did his operation go well? I hope the fool doesn't die; I could use his knowledge for a while more. Fool to be caught off guard, fool! Yes he's a fool but this dog isn't. With the gift of Mzytryk and more help in Azerbaijan, and a promise of future friendship, I can buy Erikki out of the trap. Why should I?

Because Azadeh loves him? Unfortunately she is sister to the Khan of all the Gorgons and this is a khan's problem, not a brother's problem.

Erikki's a hazard to me and to her. He's a dangerous man with blood on his hands. The tribesmen, be they Kurds or not, will seek vengeance – probably. He's always been a bad match though he brought her great joy, still brings her happiness – but no children – and now he cannot stay in Iran. Impossible. No way for him to stay. I couldn't buy him two years of protection and Azadeh's sworn by God to stay here at

1072

least two years – how cunning my father was to give me power over her. If I buy Erikki out of the trap she can't go with him. In two years many estrangements could happen by themselves. But if he's no good for her, why buy him out? Why not let them take Erikki to checkmate a treason? It's treason to steal our property.

'This is too serious a matter to answer at once,' he said.

'There is nothing for you to answer, Highness. Only Captain Yokkonen. I understand he's still here.'

'The doctor ordered him to rest.'

'Perhaps you would send for him, Highness.'

'Of course. But a man of your importance and learning would understand there are rules of honour and hospitality in Azerbaijan, and in my tribe. He is my brother-in-law and even SAVAMA understands family honour.' Both men knew this was just an opening gambit in a delicate negotiation – delicate because neither wanted SAVAMA's wrath on their heads, neither knew yet how far to go, or even if a private deal was wanted. 'I presume many know of this . . . this treason?'

'Only me, here in Tabriz, Highness. At the moment,' Hashemi said at once, conveniently forgetting Armstrong to whom he had suggested this phony telex this morning: 'There's no way that son of a dog, Hakim, can expose it as a hoax, Robert,' he had said, delighted with his own brilliance. 'He's got to barter. We barter the Finn for Mzytryk at no cost to ourselves. That bloodthirsty maniac Finn can fly off into the sunset when we get what we want – until then we bottle him up.'

'Say Hakim Khan won't agree, won't or can't deliver Mzytryk?'

'If he doesn't want to barter, we seize Erikki anyway. Whirlwind's bound to leak soon and I can use Erikki for all sorts of concessions – he's hostage at least for nine million dollars worth of planes . . . or perhaps I barter him to the tribesmen as a peace offering . . . The fact that he's a Finn helps. I could link him closely with Rakoczy and the KGB and cause the Soviets all sorts of mischief, equally the CIA, eh? Even MI6, eh?'

'The CIA's never harmed you. Or MI6.'

'Insha' Allah! Don't interfere in this, Robert. Erikki and the Khan are an internal Iranian matter. On your own head, don't interfere. With the Finn I can get important concessions.' But important only to me, Robert, not to SAVAMA, Hashemi had thought and smiled to himself. Tomorrow or the next day we will return to Tehran and then my assassin follows you into the night and then, poof, you're blown out like a candle. 'He'll deliver him,' he had said calmly.

1073

'If Hakim gives up Erikki, he'll get hell and damnation and no peace from his beloved sister. I think she'd go to the stake for him.'

'She may have to.'

Hashemi remembered the glow of joy he had felt and now it was even better. He could see Hakim Khan's disquiet and was sure he had him trapped. 'I'm sure you'll understand, Highness, but I have to answer this telex quickly.'

Hakim Khan decided on a partial offer. 'Treason and conspiracy should not go unpunished. Anywhere it is to be found. I've sent for the traitor you wanted. Urgently.'

'Ah. How long will it take for Mzytryk to answer?'

'You'd have a better idea of that than me. Wouldn't you?'

Hashemi heard the flatness and cursed himself for making the slip. 'I would be astonished if Your Highness wasn't answered very quickly,' he said with great politeness. 'Very quickly.'

'When?'

'Within twenty-four hours, Highness. Personally or by messenger.' He saw the young Khan shift painfully and tried to decide whether to delay or to press home his advantage, sure the pain was genuine. The doctor had given him a detailed diagnosis of the Khan's possible injuries and those of his sister. To cover every eventuality he had ordered the doctor to give Erikki some heavy sedation tonight, just in case the man tried to escape.

'The twenty-four hours will be up at seven this evening, Colonel.'

'There is so much to do in Tabriz, Highness, following your advice of this morning, that I doubt if I could deal with the telex before then.'

'You destroy the leftist mujhadin headquarters tonight?'

'Yes, Highness,' now that we have your permission, and your guarantee of no repercussions from the Tudeh, Hashemi wanted to add but did not. Don't be stupid. This young man's not as three-faced as the dog Abdollah, may he burn in hell. This one's easier to deal with – providing you have more cards than he has and are not afraid to show your fangs when needed. 'It would be unfortunate if the captain was not available for . . . for questioning this evening.'

Hakim Khan's eyes narrowed at the unnecessary threat. As if I didn't understand, you rude son of a dog. 'I agree.' There was a knock on the door. 'Come in.'

Azadeh opened it. 'Sorry to interrupt, Highness, but you told me to remind you half an hour before it was time to go to the hospital for X-rays. Greetings, peace be with you, Colonel.'

'And God's peace be with you, Highness.' I'm glad such beauty will

1074

be forced into chador soon, Hashemi was thinking. She'd tempt Satan, let alone the unwashed illiterate scum of Iran. He looked back at the Khan. 'I should be going, Highness.'

'Please come back at seven, Colonel. If I've any news before then I'll send for you.'

'Thank you, Highness.'

She closed the door after him. 'How're you feeling, Hakim, darling?'

'Tired. Lots of pain.'

'Me too. Do you have to see the colonel later?'

'Yes. It doesn't matter. How's Erikki?'

'Asleep.' She was joyous. 'We're so lucky, the three of us.'

In Tabriz City: 4:06 P.M. Robert Armstrong checked the action of the small automatic, his face a mask. 'What're you going to do?' Henley asked, not liking the gun at all. He was also English, but much smaller, with a wispy moustache, and he wore glasses and sat behind the desk in the untidy, grubby office under a picture of Queen Elizabeth.

'Best you don't ask that. But don't worry, I'm a copper, remember? This's just in case some villain tries to do me. Can you get the message to Yokkonen?'

'I can't go to the palace uninvited, what the hell'd be my excuse?' Henley's eyebrows soared. 'Do I say to Hakim Khan, "Terribly sorry, old boy, but I want to speak to your brother-in-law about getting a chum out of Iran by private helicopter".' His banter vanished. 'You're quite wrong about the colonel, Robert. There's no proof whatsoever the colonel's responsible for Talbot.'

'If you had you wouldn't admit it,' Armstrong said, angry with himself for exploding when Henley had told him about the 'accident'. Again his voice rasped. 'Why the devil did you wait till today to tell me Talbot was blown up? For God's sake it happened two days ago!'

'I don't decide policy, I just carry messages and anyway we've just heard. Besides you've been difficult to track down. Everyone thought you'd left, last seen boarding a British aircraft bound for Al Shargaz. Damn it, you've been ordered out for almost a week and you're still here, not on any assignment I know of, and whatever you've decided to do, don't, except kindly remove yourself from Iran because if you're caught and they get you to the third level, a lot of people are going to be very bloody peed off.'

'I'll try not to disappoint them.' Armstrong got up and put on his old raincoat with the fur collar. 'See you soon.'

'When?'

'When I bloody choose.' Armstrong's face tightened. 'I'm not under your authority and what I do and when I come and go is not up to you. Just see my report's kept in the safe until you've a diplomatic bag to pass it urgently to London, and keep your bloody mouth shut.'

'You're not usually so rude, or so touchy. What the hell's up, Robert?'

Armstrong stalked out and down the steps and out into the cold of the day. It was overcast and promised to snow again. He went down the crowded street. Passers by and street merchants pretended not to notice him, presumed he was Soviet, and cautiously went about their own business. Though he was watching to see if he was being followed, his mind was sifting ways and means to deal with Hashemi. No time to consult his superiors, and no real wish to. They would have shaken their heads: 'Good God, our old friend Hashemi? Send him onwards on suspicion he levitated Talbot? First we'd need proof . . .'

But there'll never be any proof and they won't believe about Group Four teams or about Hashemi fancying himself as a modern Hassan ibn-al-Sabbah. But I know. Wasn't Hashemi bursting with happiness about assassinating General Jana. Now he's got bigger fish to skewer. Like Pahmudi. Or the whole Rev Komiteh, whoever they are – I wonder if he's pegged them yet? I wonder if he'd go for the Imam himself? No telling. But one way or another he'll pay for old Talbot – after we've got Petr Oleg Mzytryk. Without Hashemi I've no chance of getting him, and through him the sodding traitors we all know are operating up top in Whitehall, Philby's bosses, the fourth, fifth, and sixth man – in a Cabinet, MI5, or MI6. Or all three.

His rage was all possessive, making his head ache. So many good men betrayed. The touch of his automatic pleased him. First Mzytryk, he thought, then Hashemi. All that's left to decide is when and where.

Bahrain – at the International Airport: 4:24 P.M. Jean-Luc was on the phone in Mathias's office. '. . . No, Andy, we've nothing either.' He glanced at Mathias who listened, and gravely made a thumbs down to him.

'Charlie's beside himself,' Gavallan was saying. 'I just got off the phone to him. Damn shame but nothing we can do but wait. Same with Dubois and Fowler.' Jean-Luc could hear the great weariness in Gavallan's voice.

'Dubois will turn up – after all he's French. By the way I told Charlie if . . . when,' he corrected himself hastily, 'when Tom Lochart and Freddy Ayre land, to tell them to refuel at Jellet and not come here, unless there's an emergency. Mathias put the spare fuel on Jellet himself so we know it's there. Andy, you'd better call Charlie and add your authority because Bahrain could be difficult, I don't want to risk another confrontation – their warning was clear whether we're flying on British registry or not. I still don't know how we squeaked Rudi, Sandor and Pop through. I'm certain they'll impound any Iran registers, and the crews – and next time they'll check the paint and papers.'

'All right, I'll tell him at once. Jean-Luc, there's no reason for you to come back to Al Shargaz, why not go direct to London tomorrow, then up to Aberdeen? I'm posting you to the North Sea until we get sorted out, all right?'

'Good idea. I'll report in Aberdeen on Monday,' Jean-Luc said quickly, stealing a free weekend. *Mon Dieu* I've earned it, he thought, and changed the subject to give Gavallan no time to argue. 'Has Rudi arrived yet?'

'Yes, safe and sound. All three of them're bedded down. So're Vossi and Willi too. Scrag's fine. Erikki's out of danger, Duke's mending slowly but surely . . . if it wasn't for Dubois and Fowler, Mac, Tom and their lot . . . Hallelujah! I've got to go, 'bye.'

'*Au revoir.*' Then to Mathias, '*Merde*, I'm posted to the North Sea.'

'*Merde.*'

'What's Alitalia's extension?'

'22134. Why?'

'If I have to invoke the pope himself, I'm on the early flight to Rome tomorrow with the connection to Nice – I need Marie-Christine, the kids, and some decent food. *Espèce de con* on the North Sea!' Worriedly he looked at the clock. '*Espèce de con* on this waiting! Where're our Kowiss birds, eh?'

Kuwait – Offshore: 4:31 P.M. The red fuel warning light came on. McIver and Wazari saw it instantly and both cursed. 'How much we got left, Captain?'

'With this bloody wind, not much.' They were just ten feet off the waves.

'How far we got to go?'

'Not far.' McIver was exhausted and feeling terrible. The wind had freshened to nearly thirty-five knots, and he had been nursing the 212, trying to eke out their fuel, but there was not much he could do at this low level. Visibility was still poor, the overcast thinning rapidly as they neared the coast. He looked out of his window across at Ayre, pointed at his instrument panel, and gave a thumbs down. Ayre nodded. His warning light had not yet come on. Now it did.

'Bloody hell,' Kyle, Ayre's mechanic said. 'We'll be in the open in a few minutes and sitting bloody ducks.'

'Not to worry. If Mac doesn't call Kuwait soon, I'm going to.' Ayre peered upwards, thought he glimpsed the fighters above them, but it was just two seabirds. 'Christ, for a moment . . .'

'Those bastards wouldn't dare follow us this far, would they?'

'I don't know.' Since leaving the coast they had been playing hide-and-seek with the two jet fighters. Abeam Kharg, happily sneaking past in the rain and haze, not varying their height over the waves, he and McIver had been spotted: 'This is Kharg radar control: choppers illegally outward bound on heading 275 degrees, climb to one thousand and hold – climb to one thousand and hold.'

For a moment they were in shock, then McIver waved Ayre to follow him, turned 90 degrees due north away from Kharg, and went even lower to the sea. In a few minutes, his earphones were filled with the Farsi from the fighters to air force control and back again. 'They're being given our coordinates, Captain,' Wazari gasped. 'Orders to arm their rockets . . . now they're reporting they're armed . . .'

'This is Kharg! Choppers illegally on course 270, climb to one thousand and hold. If you do not obey you will be intercepted and shot down; I repeat you will be intercepted and shot down.'

McIver took his hand off the collective to rub his chest, the pain returning, then doggedly held the course as Wazari gave him snatches of what was being said, '. . . the leader's saying follow me down . . . now the wingman says, all rockets armed . . . how're we going to find them in this shit . . . I'm slowing down . . . we don't want to miss them . . . Ground controller says, "Confirm rockets armed, confirm kill" . . . Jesus, they're confirming rockets armed and on collision course with us.'

Then the two jet fighters had come hurtling at them from out of the murk ahead but to the right and fifty feet above them and then they were past and vanished. 'Christ, did they see us?'

'Jesus, Captain, I don't know but those bastards carry heat seekers.'

McIver's heart was racing as he motioned to Ayre and went into hover, just above the waves, to throw the hunters off. 'Tell me what they're saying, Wazari, for Christ's sake!'

'Pilots're cursing . . . reporting they're at two thousand, two hundred knots . . . one's saying there're no holes in the soup and the ceiling's around four hundred . . . difficult to see the surface . . . Controller's saying go ahead to international line and to get between it and the pirates . . . Jesus, pirates? Get between them and Kuwait . . . see if the cloud cover's any thinner . . . stay in ambush at two thousand . . .'

What to do? McIver was asking himself. We could bypass Kuwait and head direct for Jellet. No good – with this wind we'd never make it. Can't turn back. So it's Kuwait and hope we can slither past them.

At the international line the clouds were just enough to hide them. But the fighters were lurking somewhere there in a holding pattern, waiting for a window, or for the clouds to thin, or for their prey to presume they were safe and climb up into regulation approach height. For a quarter of an hour the military channel had been silent. They could hear Kuwait controllers now.

'I'm going to cut one engine to save gas,' McIver said.

'You want me to call Kuwait, Skipper?'

'No, I'll do that. In a minute. You'd better go back into the cabin and prepare to hide. See if you can find some sea overalls, there're some in the locker. Use a sea safety coverall. Dump your uniform over the side and have a Mae West handy.'

Wazari blanched. 'We're going into the sea?'

'No. Just camouflage, in case we're inspected,' McIver lied, not expecting to make the coast. His voice was calm and his head was calm though his limbs were leaden.

'What's the plan when we land, Skipper?'

'We'll have to play that as it happens. Do you have any papers?'

'Only my operator licences, American and Iranian. Both say I'm Iranian Air Force.'

'Stay undercover, I don't know what's going to happen . . . but we'll hope.'

'Skipper, we should climb out of this crap, no need to press our luck,' Wazari said. 'We're over the line, safe now.'

McIver looked aloft. The cloud and haze cover was thinning very fast, now hardly any cover for them at all. The red warning light seemed to fill his horizon. Better climb, eh? Wazari was right, no need to press our luck, he thought. 'We're only safe when we're on the ground,' he said out loud. 'You know that.'

Kuwait Airport Tower: 4:38 P.M. The big room was fully staffed. Some British controllers, some Kuwaiti. The best modern equipment, Telex and phones and efficiency. The door opened and Charlie Pettikin came in. 'You wanted me, sir?' he said anxiously to the duty controller, a rotund, florid-faced Irishman wearing a headset with a thin-tubed boom mike and single tiny earpiece.

'Yes, yes indeed I did, Captain Pettikin,' the man said curtly, and at once Pettikin's anxiety increased. 'My name's Sweeney.' He used his grease pencil as a pointer. On the outer periphery of his radar screen at the twenty-mile line was a small blip of light. 'That's a chopper, possibly two. He, or they have just appeared, haven't reported in yet. 'Tis yourself who's expecting two inbounds, so I'm told, in transit from the UK, is that it now?'

'Yes,' Pettikin said, wanting to cheer that, at long last, one or both were in the system – they had to be from Kowiss on such a course – at the same time achingly aware they were a long way yet from being safe. 'That's correct,' he said with a prayer.

'Perhaps they're not yours at all for, Glory be, that's a deevil of a curious course to use, approaching from the east, if he or they're transiting from the UK.' Pettikin said nothing under Sweeney's scrutiny. 'Supposing he or they belong to yourself, now what would their call signs be?'

Pettikin's discomfort increased. If he gave the new British ones and the choppers reported in on their Iran registrations – as they were legally bound to do – they were all in trouble. The actual call letters had to be seen from the tower when the choppers came in to land – no way that controllers would not see them. But if he gave Sweeney the Iranian registrations . . . that would blow Whirlwind. The bastard's trying to trap you, he thought, a great emptiness inside him. 'I'm sorry,' he said lamely. 'I don't know. Our paper work's not the best. Sorry.'

The phone on the desk purred softly. Sweeney picked it up. 'Ah yes, yes, Commander? . . . Yes . . . no, not at the moment . . . we think it's two . . . yes, yes, I agree . . . no, it's fine now. It goes out from time to time . . . yes, very well.' He hung up, once more concentrating on the screen.

Uneasily Pettikin looked at the screen again. The all important blip did not seem to be moving.

Then Sweeney switched to maximum range and the screen picture reached out far into the Gulf, westward the few miles to the Kuwaiti border with Iraq, northwest to the Iraq–Iran border, both so very close. 'Our long range's been out for a while or we'd've seen them sooner, now she's fine, glory be to God. Lots of fighter bases there,' he said absently, his grease pencil indicating the Iran side of the Shatt-al-Arab border waterway towards Abadan. Then the pencil moved out into the Gulf on a line from Kowiss to Kuwait and poised over a blip. 'These're your choppers, if there are two – if they belong to yourself.' The point moved north a little to two other rapidly moving dots. 'Fighters. Not ours. But in our area.' He looked up and Pettikin was chilled. 'Unbidden and not cleared, so hostiles.'

'What're they doing?' he asked, sure now he was being toyed with.

'That's what we'd all like to know, indeed we would.' Sweeney's voice was not friendly. With his grease pencil he indicated two other blips, outward bound from the Kuwaiti military strip. 'They're ours going to have a look.' He handed Pettikin a spare earpiece, clicked on his sender. 'This is Kuwait: inbound chopper or choppers heading 274 degrees, what is your call sign and altitude?'

Static. The call repeated patiently. Then Pettikin recognised McIver's voice. 'Kuwait this is chopper . . . this is chopper Boston Tango with chopper Hotel Echo in transit for Al Shargaz, going through six hundred for seven hundred.' McIver had given only the last two letters of the Iranian registration, instead of all the letters required on the initial call, including the prefix EP for Iran.

Astonishingly Sweeney accepted the call: 'Choppers Boston Tango and Hotel Echo report at outer marker,' he said, and Pettikin saw that he was distracted, concentrating on the two hostile blips that were now closing on the choppers fast, tracking them with his pencil on the glass. 'They're flat out,' he muttered. 'Ten miles astern.'

McIver's voice in their earphones: 'Kuwait, please confirm outer marker. Request straight in, we're low on fuel.'

'Straight in approved, report outer marker.'

Pettikin heard the inflexibility and suppressed a groan. Sweeney began humming. The senior controller, a Kuwaiti, quietly got up from his desk and came over to stand behind them.

They watched the circling trace leaving a picture of the land and the blips of light in its wake, seeing them not as blips but as two hostile fighters and two slower Kuwaiti interceptors still far away, two choppers helpless between them. Closer. The hostiles were almost merged with the choppers now, then they moved off and away, heading eastwards back across the Gulf. For a moment all three men held their breath. Rockets took time to reach their targets. Seconds passed. Chopper blips remained. Kuwaiti interceptor blips remained, closing on the choppers, then they too turned back for home. Momentarily Sweeney switched into their channel and listened to the Arabic. He glanced up at the senior controller and spoke to him in Arabic. The man said, 'Insha' Allah,' nodded briefly at Pettikin, and went out of the room.

'Our interceptors reported seeing nothing,' Sweeney said to Pettikin, his voice flat. 'Except two choppers. 212s. They saw nothing.' He went back into the regular band, airplanes reporting in and being channelled for takeoff or landing, then he switched the radar to closer range. Now the choppers were separated into two blips, still well out to sea. Their approach seemed interminably slow against the tracks of incoming and outgoing jets.

McIver's voice cut through the other voices, 'Pan-pan-pan! Kuwait, this is chopper BT and HE, pan pan pan, both our warning lights are on, empty, pan pan pan.' The emergency call, one step below Mayday.

Sweeney said, 'Permission to land on Messali Beach helipad directly ahead, near the hotel – we'll alert them and send you fuel. Do you copy?'

'Roger, Kuwait, thank you. I know the hotel. Please inform Captain Pettikin.'

'Wilco, at once.' Sweeney picked up the phone and put their air-sea rescue helicopter on standby, ready for instant takeoff, sent a fire truck to the hotel, then held out his hand for Pettikin's earpiece, glanced at the door, and beckoned him closer. 'Now listen to me,' he hissed, keeping his voice down. ' 'Tis yourself who'll meet them and refuel them, clear them through customs and immigration – if you can – and get them the deevil out of Kuwait within minutes or yourself and they and your high and mighty "important" friends will all be in jail and good riddance! Holy Mother of God, how dare you jeopardise Kuwait with your madcap adventures against those trigger-happy Iran fanatics and make honest men risk their jobs for the likes of you. If one of your choppers was shot down . . . it was only the luck of the deevil himself stopped an international incident.' He reached into his pocket and shoved a piece of paper into Pettikin's hand who was stunned by the venom and suddenness. 'Read it, then flush it.'

Sweeney turned his back and got on the phone again. Weakly, Pettikin went out. When it was safe he glanced at the paper. It was a telex. The telex. From Tehran. Not a photocopy. The original.

Christ Almighty! Did Sweeney intercept it and cover for us? But didn't he say, 'clear them through customs and immigration – if you can.'?

Messali Beach Hotel: The small fuel truck with Genny and Pettikin aboard swung off the coast road and into the vast hotel gardens, sprinklers going. The helipad was well west of the huge car-park area. A fire truck already there and waiting. Genny and Pettikin jumped out, Pettikin with a short-wave walkie-talkie, both of them searching the haze out to sea. 'Mac, do you read?'

They could hear the engines but not see them yet, then: 'Two by five, Charlie . . .' much static . . . 'but I . . . Freddy, you take the helipad, I'll go alongside.' More static.

'There they are!' Genny cried. The 212s came out of the haze about six hundred feet. Oh, God, help them in . . .

'We have you in sight, Mac, fire trucks standing by, no problem.' But Pettikin knew they were in deep trouble, no possibility of changing the lettering with so many people watching. One engine missed and coughed but they did not know which. Another cough.

Ayre's voice, too dry, said, 'Stand by below, I'm coming into the helipad.'

They saw the left 212 detach slightly and start losing altitude, reaching for distance, engine spluttering. The fire fighters readied. McIver doggedly held course, maintaining altitude to give himself the best chance if his own engines cut. 'Shit,' Pettikin muttered involuntarily seeing Ayre coming in fast, too fast, but then he flared maximum and set her down in dead centre, safe. McIver into emergency approach now – for Christ's sake, why's he flying alone and where the hell's Tom Lochart – committed now, no room to manoeuvre, no one breathing, and then the skids touched and at that moment the engines died.

Fire fighters, in radio contact with the airfield, reported, 'Emergency over,' began packing their gear, and now Pettikin was pummelling McIver's hand and he rushed over to Ayre to do the same. Genny stood beside McIver's open cockpit door, beaming at him.

'Hello, Duncan,' she said, holding her hair out of her eyes. 'Good trip?'

'Worst I've ever had, Gen,' he said trying to smile, not quite with it yet. 'In fact I never want to fly again, not fly myself, so help me! I'm still going to check Scrag – but only once a year!'

She laughed and gave him an awkward hug and would have released him but he held on to her, loving her – so relieved to see her and to be on ground again, his passenger safe, his bird safe, that he felt like crying. 'You all right, luvey?'

That made her tears flow. He had not called her that for months, perhaps years. She hugged him even tighter. 'Now look what you've made me do.' She found her handkerchief, let him go, then gave him a little kiss. 'You deserve a whisky and soda. Two large ones!' For the first time she noticed his pallor. 'You all right, luv?'

'Yes. Yes, I think so. I'm a bit shook.' McIver looked over her to Pettikin who was laughing and talking excitedly with Ayre, the truck driver already pumping fuel into the tanks. Beyond them an official-looking car was pulling in from the road. 'What about the others, what's happened?'

'Everyone's safe – except Marc Dubois and Fowler Joines. They're still missing.' She told him what she knew about Starke and Gavallan and Scragger, Rudi and his men. 'One fantastic piece of news is that Newbury, he's a consulate man in Al Shargaz, got a message from Tabriz that Erikki and Azadeh are safe at her father's place, but her father's dead, it seems, and now her brother's Khan.'

'My God, that's wonderful! Then we've done it, we've done it, Gen!'

'Yes, yes, we have – damn this wind,' she pushed a strand of hair out of her eyes, 'and Andy and Charlie and the others think Dubois has a good ch—' She stopped, her happiness evaporating, suddenly realising what was wrong. She whirled and looked at the other 212. 'Tom? Where's Tom Lochart?'

South of Tehran: 5:10 P.M. The deserted oil well and pumping station was in desolate hills about a hundred miles from Tehran. Lochart's 206 was parked beside the fuel pump and he had refuelled manually, almost finished now.

It was a way station for helicopters serving this area, part of the great northern pipeline that, in normal times, housed an Iranian maintenance crew. In a rough hut were a few spare bunks for overnighting if you were caught in one of the sudden storms endemic here. The original British owners of the site had called it 'D' Arcy 1908' to commemorate the Englishman by that name who had first discovered oil in Iran in that year. It belonged to IranOil but they had kept the name, and kept the fuel tanks topped up.

Thank God for that, Lochart thought again, the pumping tiring him. At the RV on the coast, he had lashed two empty fifty gallon drums on the back seat against the possibility that D'Arcy 1908 would be open, and rigged a temporary pump. There was still enough fuel left at the shore to top up on the way out of Iran and Sharazad could work the pump in flight. 'Now we've a chance,' he said out loud, knowing where to land, how to park safely, and how to sneak into Tehran.

He was confident again, making plans and counterplans, what to say to Meshang, what to avoid, what to tell Sharazad and how they would escape. There's got to be a way for her to get her rightful inheritance, enough to give her the security she needs . . .

Petrol overflowed from the brimful tanks and he swore at his carelessness, capped them carefully, wiped the excess away. Now he was finished, the drums in the backseat already filled and the pump in place.

In one of the huts he had found some cans of corned beef and wolfed one of them – impossible to eat and fly, unless with his left hand, and he had been too long in Iran to do that – then picked up the bottle of beer he had set in the snow to chill, and sipped it sparingly. There was water in a barrel. He broke the ice and splashed water on his face to refresh himself but did not dare to drink it. He dried his face. The stubble of his beard rasped and he again swore, wanting to look his best for her. Then he remembered his flight bag and the razors there. One was battery-operated. He found it. 'You can shave in Tehran,' he said to his reflection in the cockpit window, anxious to go on.

A last look around. Snow and rocks and not much else. In the far distance was the Qom–Tehran road. Sky overcast but the ceiling high. Some birds circled far overhead. Scavengers. Vultures of some sort, he thought, buckling his seat belt.

Tehran – At the Bakravan House: 5:15 P.M. The door in the outer wall opened and two heavily chadored and veiled women came out, Sharazad and Jari unrecognisable. Jari closed the door, hastily waddled after Sharazad, who walked away quickly through the crowds. 'Princess, wait . . . there's no hurry . . .'

But Sharazad did not decrease her pace until she had turned the corner. Then she stopped and waited impatiently. 'Jari, I'm leaving you now,' she said giving her no time to interrupt, 'don't go home but meet me at the coffee shop, you know the one, at six-thirty, wait for me if I'm late.'

'But, Princess . . .' Jari could hardly talk, 'but His Excellency Meshang . . . you told him we're going to the doctor's and there's n –'

'At the coffee shop about six-thirty, six-thirty to seven, Jari!' Sharazad hurried off down the street, cut dangerously into the traffic and across the road to avoid her maid who started to come after her, went into an alley, down another, and soon she was free. 'I'm not going to marry that awful man, I'm not I'm not I'm not!' she muttered out loud.

The derision had already begun this afternoon though it was only at lunch that Meshang had announced the great evil. Her best girlfriend had arrived an hour ago to ask if the rumours were true that Sharazad was going to marry into the Farazan family: 'It's all over the bazaar, dearest Sharazad, I came at once to congratulate you.'

'My brother has many plans, now that I am to be divorced,' she had said carelessly. 'I have many suitors.'

'Of course, of course, but the rumour is that the Farazan dowry has already been agreed.'

'Oh? First I've heard of it, what liars people are!'

'I agree, awful. Other vile rumour-mongers claim that the marriage is to take place next week and your . . . and the prospective husband is chortling that he outsmarted Meshang on the dowry.'

'Someone outsmart Meshang? It has to be a lie!'

'I knew the rumours were false! I knew it! How could you marry old Diarrhoea Daranoush, Shah of the Night Soil? How could you?' Her friend had laughed uproariously. 'Poor darling, which way would you turn?'

'What does it matter?' Meshang had screeched at her. 'They're only jealous! The marriage will take place and tonight we will entertain him at dinner.'

Perhaps I will, perhaps I won't, she thought seething. Perhaps the entertainment will not be what they expect.

Again she checked her directions, knees weak. She was going to *his* friend's apartment, not far away now. There she would find the secret key in the niche downstairs and go in and look under the carpet in the bedroom and take up the board as she had seen him do. Then she would take out the pistol and the grenade – God be thanked for the chador to cover them and keep me hidden – then carefully replace the board and the carpet and come home again. Her excitement was almost choking her now. Ibrahim will be so proud of me, going into battle for God, to be martyred for God. Didn't he go south to be martyred doing battle with evil in just the same way? Of course God will forgive his leftist silliness.

How clever of him to show me how to take off the safety catch and to arm the gun and to hold the grenade, to pull the pin, then throw it at the enemies of Islam, shouting 'God is Great, God is Great . . .' Then charging them, shooting them, being lifted into Paradise, this evening if I can, tomorrow at the latest, the whole city rife with rumours that leftists at the university have begun their expected insurrection. We will stamp them out, my son and I, we will, Soldiers of God and the Prophet on whose name be praised, we will!

'God is Great. God is Great . . .' Just pull the pin and count to four and throw it, I remember everything he said exactly.

Kuwait – At the Hotel Messali Helipad: 5:35 P.M. McIver and Pettikin watched the two Immigration and Customs men, the first peering impassively at the airplane papers, the other poking about in the cabin

1086

of the 212. So far their inspections had been perfunctory though time-consuming. They had collected all passport and airplane papers but had just glanced at them and asked McIver his opinion of the current situation in Iran. They had not yet asked directly where the helicopters had come from. Any moment now, McIver and Pettikin thought, waiting queasily.

McIver had considered leaving Wazari in hiding, but had decided against the risk. 'Sorry, Sergeant, you'll have to take your chances.'

'Who's he?' the Immigration man had asked at once, Wazari's complexion giving him away, and his fear.

'A radio-radar operator,' McIver said noncommittally.

The official had turned away and left Wazari standing there, sweating in the heavy, seaproofed plastic coverall, Mae West half done up.

'So, Captain, you think there'll be a coup in Tehran, a military coup?'

'I don't know,' McIver had told him. 'Rumours abound like locusts. The English papers say it's possible, very possible, and also that Iran's caught up in a kind of madness – like the Terror of the French or Russian revolutions, the aftermath. May I get our mechanics to check everything while we wait?'

'Of course.' The man waited while McIver gave the orders, then he said, 'Let's hope the madness doesn't spread across the Gulf, eh? No one wants any trouble this side of the *Islamic Gulf*.' He used the word with great deliberation, all the Gulf states loathing the term, Persian Gulf. 'It is the Islamic Gulf, isn't it?'

'Yes, yes, it is.'

'All maps will have to be changed. The Gulf is the Gulf, Islam is Islam and not just for the Shi'a sect.'

McIver said nothing, his caution increasing, adding to his disquiet. There were many Shi'as in Kuwait and most of the Gulf states. Many. Usually they were the poor. Rulers, the sheiks, were usually Sunni.

'Captain!' the Customs officer in the doorway of the 212 cabin parked on the helipad was beckoning to him. Ayre and Wazari had been told to wait away from the helicopters in the shade until inspections were finished. Mechanics were busy ground-checking. 'Are you carrying arms of any kind?'

'No, sir – apart from the regulation Verey Light pistol.'

'Contraband of any kind?'

'No, sir. Just spares.' All the usual questions, interminably, that would be repeated as soon as they were released to the airport. At length the man thanked him and motioned him away. The Immigration officer had gone back to his car with their passports. The radio-transmitter had been left on and McIver could hear Ground Control clearly. He saw the man scratch his beard thoughtfully, then pick up the mike and talk into it in Arabic. This increased his concern. Genny was sitting in the shade nearby and he went over to her.

'Stiff upper lip,' she whispered. 'How's it going?'

'Wish to God they'd let us get on with it,' McIver said irritably. 'We'll have to endure another hour at the airport and damned if I know what to do.'

'Has Charlie sa –'

'Captain!' The Immigration officer was beckoning him and Pettikin over to the car. 'So you're in transit, is that it?'

'Yes. To Al Shargaz. With your permission, we'll leave at once,' McIver said. 'We'll go to the airport, file our flight plan, and take off as quickly as we can. Is that all right?'

'Where did you say you are in transit to?'

'Al Shargaz via Bahrain for fuel.' McIver was getting sicker by the minute. Any airport official would know they would have to refuel before Bahrain even without this wind, and all airports between here and there were Saudi, so he would have to file a flight plan for a Saudi landing. Bahrain, Abu Dhabi, Al Shargaz had all received the same telex. Kuwait too, and even if it had been intercepted here privately by a well-wisher, for whatever reason, the same would not be true of Saudi airports. Rightly, McIver thought, and saw the man look at the Iran registration letters under the cockpit windows. They had arrived under Iran registration, he would have to file the flight plan and leave under the same letters.

To their astonishment, the man reached into the pocket of his car and brought out a pad of forms. 'I am inst – I will accept your flight plan here and clear you to Bahrain direct and you can leave at once. You can pay me the regulation landing fees and I'll stamp your passports too. There'll be no need to go to the airport.'

'What?'

'I will accept your flight plan now and you can leave direct from here. Please make it out.' He handed the pad to McIver. It was the correct form. 'As soon as you've done it, sign it and bring it back.' Some flies circling in the car were bothering him and he waved them away. Then he picked up the radio mike, pointedly waited until McIver and Pettikin walked off, and talked quietly into it.

Hardly able to believe what had happened, they went to lean against their truck. 'Jesus, Mac, do you think they know and are just letting us go?'

1088

'I don't know what to think. Don't waste time, Charlie.' McIver shoved the pad into his hands and said more irritably than he meant to, 'Just make out the flight plan before he changes his mind: Al Shargaz – if we happen to have an emergency on Jellet, that's our problem. For God's sake do it and let's get airborne as quick as we can.'

'Sure. Right away.'

Genny said, 'You're not flying, are you, Duncan?'

'No, Charlie's going to do that.'

Pettikin thought a moment, then took out a key and his money. 'This's my room key, Genny. Would you get my stuff for me, nothing there of any importance, pay the bill, and catch the next plane – Biddle'll get you a priority.'

'What about your passport and licence?' she asked.

'Always carry them, frightened to death of losing them, and a hundred-dollar note – never know when you'll need some baksheesh.'

'Consider it done.' She pushed her dark glasses back on to the bridge of her nose, smiled at her husband. 'What'll you do, Duncan?'

Without noticing it, McIver exhaled heavily. 'I'll have to go on, Gen. Daren't stay here – doubt if they'd let me. They're desperate not to rock any boat and want to see the last of us. It's obvious, isn't it – who ever heard of being cleared from a beach? We're a bloody embarrassment and a threat to the state, of course we are. That's the truth! Do what Charlie says, Gen. We'll refuel at Jellet – change the registrations there and hope for the best – do you have the stencils, Charlie?'

'Brushes, paint, everything.' Pettikin did not stop filling in the forms. 'What about Wazari?'

'He's crew until someone asks a question. Put him down as radio operator. That's no lie. If they don't challenge him at Bahrain, they certainly will at Al Shargaz. Perhaps Andy can work something out for him.'

'All right. He's crew. That's it, then.'

'Good. Gen, Jellet's easy from here, Bahrain too, and Al Shargaz. Weather's good, moon'll be out, so a night jaunt'll be fine. Do what Charlie says. You'll be there in good time to meet us.'

'If you leave at once, you'll need food and some bottled water,' she said. 'We can get some here. I'll get them, Charlie. Come along, Duncan, you need a drink.'

'Pour it for me at Al Shargaz, Gen.'

'I will. But I'll pour you one now. You're not flying, you need it, and so do I.' She went over to the Immigration officer and got permission to buy sandwiches and make a phone call.

'Back in a second, Charlie.' McIver followed her into the hotel lobby and went straight for the toilet. There he was very sick. It took him some time to recover. When he came out she was getting off the phone.

'Sandwiches any second, your drink's poured, and I've booked you a call to Andy.' She led the way out to a table on the sumptuous bar terrace. Three ice-cold Perriers with sliced lemon, and a double tot of whisky straight, no ice, just the way he liked it. He downed the first Perrier without stopping. 'My God, I needed that . . .' He eyed the whisky but did not touch it. Thoughtfully he sipped the second glass of Perrier, and watched her. When it was half gone he said, 'Gen, I think I'd like you to come along.'

She was startled. Then she said, 'Thank you, Duncan. I'd like that. Yes, yes, I would.'

The lines in his face crinkled. 'You'd've come anyway. Wouldn't you?'

She gave him a little shrug. Her eyes dropped to the whisky. 'You're not flying, Duncan. The whisky would be good for you. It would settle the tum.'

'You noticed, eh?'

'Only that you're very tired. More tired than I've ever seen you, but you've done wonderfully, you've done a smashing job, and you should rest. You've . . . you've been taking your pills and all that rubbish?'

'Oh, yes, though I'll need a refill soon. No problem, but I felt pretty bloody a couple of times.' At her sudden anxiety, 'I'm fine now, Gen. Fine.'

She knew better than to probe. Now that she was invited she could relax a little. Since he had landed she had been watching him very carefully, her concern growing. With the sandwiches she had ordered some aspirins, she had Veganin in her bag and the secret survival kit Dr. Nutt had given her. 'What was it like flying again? Really?'

'From Tehran down to Kowiss was grand, the rest not so good. This last leg wasn't good at all.' The thought of being hunted by the fighters and so near to disaster so many times made him feel bilious again. Don't think about that, he ordered himself, that's over. Whirlwind's almost over, Erikki and Azadeh're safe, but what about Dubois and Fowler, what the hell's happened to them? And Tom? I could bloody strangle Tom, poor bugger.

'You all right, Duncan?'

'Oh yes, I'm fine. Just tired – it's been quite a couple of weeks.'

'What about Tom? What'll you tell Andy?'

'I was just thinking about him. I'll have to tell Andy.'

1090

'That's one hell of a spanner in Whirlwind, isn't it?'

'He's . . . he's on his own, Gen. Maybe he can get Sharazad and sneak out again. If he's caught . . . we'll have to wait and see and hope,' he said. But he was thinking, *when* he's caught. McIver reached over and touched her, glad to be with her, not wanting to worry her more than she was now. Tough on her, all this. I think I'm going to die.

'Please excuse me, sahib, memsahib, your order's been taken out to the helicopter,' the waiter said.

McIver handed him a credit card and the waiter left. 'Which reminds me, what about your hotel bill, and Charlie's? We'll have to take care of them before we leave.'

'Oh, I phoned Mr. Biddle while you were in the loo,' she said, 'and asked him if he'd take care of our bills and ship our bags and everything if I didn't call back in an hour. I've my handbag, passport, and . . . what're you smiling about?'

'Nothing . . . nothing, Gen.'

'It was just in case you asked me. I thought . . .' She watched the bubbles in her glass. Again the tiny shrug and she looked up and smiled so happily. 'I'm ever so glad you asked me, Duncan. Thank you.'

Al Shargaz – on the Outskirts of the City: 6:01 P.M. Gavallan got out of his car and walked briskly up the steps towards the front door of the Moroccan-style villa that was enclosed behind high walls.

'Mr. Gavallan!'

'Oh, hello, Mrs. Newbury!' He changed direction to join the woman who was half hidden, kneeling down, planting some seedlings near the driveway. 'Your garden looks wonderful.'

'Thank you. It's such fun and keeps me fit,' she said. Angela Newbury was tall and in her thirties, her accent patrician. 'Roger's in the gazebo and expecting you.' With the back of her gloved hand she wiped the perspiration off her forehead and left a smudge in it wake. 'How's it going?'

'Great,' he told her, omitting the news about Lochart. 'Nine out of ten so far.'

'Oh, super, oh, that is a relief. Congratulations, we've all been so concerned. Wonderful, but for God's sake don't tell Roger I asked, he'd have a fit. Nobody's supposed to know!'

He returned her smile and walked around the side of the house through the lovely gardens. The gazebo was in a clump of trees and flower beds, with chairs, side tables, portable bar and phone. His joy faded, seeing the look on Roger Newbury's face. 'What's up?'

1091

'You're what's up. Whirlwind's what up. I made it perfectly clear that it was ill advised. How's it going?'

'I've just heard our Kowiss two are safe in Kuwait and cleared on to Bahrain with no trouble, so that makes nine out of ten if we include Erikki's one in Tabriz, Dubois and Fowler're still not accounted for but we're hoping. Now what's the problem, Roger?'

'There's hell to pay all over the Gulf with Tehran screaming bloody murder and all our offices on alert. The Old Man and yours truly, Roger Newbury Esquire, are cordially invited at seven thirty to explain to the Illustrious Foreign Minister why there's a sudden influx of helicopters here, albeit British registered, and how long they intend to stay.' Newbury, a lean man with sandy hair and blue eyes and prominent nose, was clearly very irritated. 'Glad about the nine out of ten, would you like a drink?'

'Thanks. A light Scotch and soda.'

Newbury went to fix it. 'The Old Man and I would be delighted to know what you suggest we say.'

Gavallan thought a moment. 'The choppers are out the moment we can get them aboard the freighters.'

'When's that?' Newbury gave him the drink.

'Thanks. The freighters're promised by 6.00p.m. Sunday. We'll work all night and have them off Monday morning.'

Newbury was shocked. 'Can't you get them out before that?'

'The freighters were ordered for tomorrow but I was let down. Why?'

'Because, old boy, a few minutes ago we had a friendly, very serious high level leak that so long as the choppers weren't here by sunset tomorrow they might not be impounded.'

Now Gavallan was also shocked. 'That's not possible – can't be done.'

'I'm suggesting that you'd be wise to make it possible. Fly them out to Oman or Dubai or wherever.'

'If we do that . . . if we do that we'll be deeper in the mire.'

'I don't think you can get any deeper, old boy. The way the "leak" put it was after sunset tomorrow you'll be in over your eyeballs.' Newbury toyed with his drink, a lemon pressé. Blast all this, he was thinking. While we're obliged to help our important trading interests salvage what they can from the Iran catastrophe we've got to remember the long term as well as the short. We can't put Her Majesty's Government at risk. Apart from that, my weekend's ruined, I should be having a nice tall vodka gimlet with Angela and here I am, sipping slop. 'You'll have to move them.'

1092

'Can you get us a forty-eight-hour reprieve, explain that the freighters are chartered but it's got to be Sunday?'

'Wouldn't dare suggest it, Andy. That would admit culpability.'

'Could you get us a forty-eight hour transit permit to Oman?'

Newbury grimaced. 'I'll ask the Old Man but we couldn't feel them out until tomorrow, too late now, and my immediate reaction's that the request would correctly be turned down. Iran has a considerable goodwill presence there, after all they really did help put down Yemen-backed communist insurgents. I doubt that they'd agree to offend a very good friend however much the present fundamentalist line might displease them.'

Gavallan felt sick. 'I'd better see if I can bring my freighters forward or get alternatives – I'd say I've one chance in fifty.' He finished his drink and got up. 'Sorry about all this.'

Newbury got up too. 'Sorry I can't be more helpful,' he said, genuinely sorry. 'Keep me posted and I'll do the same.'

'Of course. You said you might be able to get a message to Captain Yokkonen in Tabriz?'

'I'll certainly try. What is it?'

'Just from me that he should, er, should leave as soon as possible, by the shortest route. Please sign it GHPLX Gavallan.'

Without comment Newbury wrote it down. 'GHPLX?'

'Yes.' Gavallan felt sure that Erikki would understand this would be his new British registry number. 'He's not aware of, er, of certain developments so if your men could also privately explain the reason for haste I'd be very, very grateful. Thanks for all your help.'

'For your sake, and his, I agree the sooner he leaves the better, with or without his aircraft. There's nothing we can do to help him. Sorry, but that's the truth.' Newbury fiddled with his glass. 'Now he represents a very great danger to you. Doesn't he?'

'I don't think so. He's under the protection of the new Khan, his brother-in-law. He's as safe as he could ever be,' Gavallan said. What would Newbury say if he knew about Tom Lochart? 'Erikki'll be okay. He'll understand. Thanks again.'

Tabriz – At the International Hospital: 6:24 P.M. Hakim Khan walked painfully into the private room, the doctor and a guard following him. He was using crutches now and they made his walking easier, but when he bent or tried to sit, they did not relieve the pain. Only pain killers did that. Azadeh was waiting downstairs, her X-ray better than his, her pain less than his.

'So, Ahmed, how do you feel?'

Ahmed lay in bed, awake, his chest and stomach bandaged. The operation to remove the bullet lodged in his chest had been successful. The one in his stomach had done much damage, he had lost a great deal of blood, and internal bleeding had started again. But the moment he saw Hakim Khan he tried to raise himself.

'Don't move, Ahmed,' Hakim Khan said, his voice kind. 'The doctor says you're mending well.'

'The doctor's a liar, Highness.'

The doctor began to speak but stopped as Hakim said, 'Liar or not, get well, Ahmed.'

1094

'Yes, Highness. With the Help of God. But you, you are all right?'

'If the X-ray doesn't lie, I've just torn ligaments.' He shrugged, 'With the Help of God.'

'Thank you . . . thank you for the private room, Highness. Never have I had . . . such luxury.'

'It's merely a token of my esteem for such loyalty.' Imperiously he dismissed the doctor and the guard. When the door was shut, he went closer. 'You asked to see me, Ahmed?'

'Yes, Highness, please excuse me that I could not . . . could not come to you.' Ahmed's voice was phlegmy, and he spoke with difficulty. 'The Tbilisi man you want . . . *The Soviet* . . . he sent a message for you. It's . . . it's under the drawer . . . he taped it under the drawer there.' With an effort he pointed to the small bureau.

Hakim's excitement picked up. Awkwardly he felt underneath the drawer. The adhesive bandages strapping him made bending difficult. He found the small square of folded paper and it came away easily. 'Who brought it and when?'

'It was today . . . some time today . . . I'm not sure, I think it was this afternoon. I don't know. The man wore a doctor's coat and glasses but he wasn't a doctor. An Azerbaijani, perhaps a Turk, I've never seen him before. He spoke Turkish – all he said was, "This is for Hakim Khan, from a friend in Tbilisi. Understand?" I told him yes and he left as quickly as he arrived. For a long time I thought he was a dream . . .'

The message was scrawled in writing Hakim did not recognise: 'Many, many congratulations on your inheritance, may you live as long and be as productive as your predecessor. Yes, I would like to meet urgently too. But here, not there. Sorry. Whenever you're ready I would be honoured to receive you, with pomp or in privacy, whatever you want. We should be friends, there's much to accomplish and we have many interests in common. Please tell Robert Armstrong and Hashemi Fazir that Yazernov is buried in the Russian Cemetery at Jaleh and he looks forward to seeing them when convenient.' There was no signature.

Greatly disappointed, he went back to the bed and offered the paper to Ahmed. 'What do you make of that?'

Ahmed did not have the strength to take it. 'Sorry, Highness, please hold it so I can read it.' After reading it, he said, 'It's not Mzytryk's writing. I'd . . . I'd recognise his writing but it . . . I believe it genuine. He would have transmitted it to . . . to underlings to bring here.'

'Who's Yazernov and what does it mean?'

'I don't know. It's a code . . . it's a code they'd understand.'

'It is an invitation to a meeting, or a threat. Which?'

'I don't know, Highness. I would guess a meet—' A spasm of pain went through him. He cursed in his own language.

'Is Mzytryk aware that both the last times they were in ambush? Aware that Abdollah Khan had betrayed him?'

'I . . . I don't know, Highness. I told you he was cunning and the Khan your father very . . . very careful in his dealings.' The effort of talking and concentrating was taking much of Ahmed's strength. 'That Mzytryk knows they are in contact with you . . . that both of them are here now means nothing, his spies abound. You're Khan and of course . . . of course you know you're . . . you're spied on by all kinds of men, most of them evil, who report to their superiors – most of them even more evil.' A smile went over his face and Hakim pondered its meaning. 'But then, you know all about hiding your true purpose, Highness. Not once . . . not once did Abdollah Khan suspect how brilliant you are, not once. If . . . if he'd known one hundredth part of who you really are . . . really are, he would have never banished you but made you . . . made you heir and chief counsellor.'

'He would have had me strangled.' Not for a millionth of a second was Hakim Khan tempted to tell Ahmed that he had sent the assassins whom Erikki had killed, or about the poison attempt that had also failed. 'A week ago he would have ordered me mutilated and you would have done it happily.'

Ahmed looked up at him, eyes deep set and filled with death. 'How do you know so much?'

'The Will of God.'

The ebb had begun. Both men knew it. Hakim said, 'Colonel Fazir showed me a telex about Erikki.' He told Ahmed the contents. 'Now I have no Mzytryk to barter with, not immediately. I can give Erikki to Fazir or help him escape. Either way my sister is committed to stay here and cannot go with him. What is your advice?'

'For you it is safer to give the Infidel to the colonel as a pishkesh and pretend to her there's nothing you can do to prevent the . . . the arrest. In truth there isn't if the colonel wants it that way. He of the Knife . . . he will resist and so he will be killed. Then you can promise her secretly to the Tbilisi . . . But never give her to him, then you will control . . . then you may control him . . . but I doubt it.'

'And if He of the Knife "happens" to escape?'

'If the colonel allowed it . . . he will require payment.'

'Which is?'

'Mzytryk. Now or sometime . . . sometime in the future. While He of

1096

the Knife lives, Highness, she will never divorce him – forget the saboteur, he was another lifetime – and when the two years are . . . are over she will go to him, that is if . . . if he allows her to . . . to stay here. I doubt if even Your Highness . . .' Ahmed's eyes closed and a tremor went through him.

'What happened with Bayazid and the bandits? Ahmed . . .'

Ahmed did not hear him. He was seeing the steppes now, the vast plains of his homelands and ancestors, the seas of grass from whence his forebears came forth to ride near the cloak of Genghis Khan, and then that of the grandson Kubla Khan and *his* brother Hulagu Khan who came down into Persia to erect mountains of skulls of those who opposed him. Here in the golden lands since ancient times, Ahmed thought, lands of wine and warmth and wealth and women of great doe-eyed beauty and sensuality, prized since ancient times like Azadeh . . . ah, now I will never take her like she should be taken, dragged off by the hair as spoils of war, shoved across a saddle to be bedded and tamed on the skins of wolves . . .

From a long way off he heard himself say, 'Please, Highness, I would beg a favour, I would like to be buried in my own land and in our own fashion . . .' Then I can live for ever with the spirits of my fathers, he thought, the lovely space beckoning him.

'Ahmed, what happened with Bayazid and the bandits when you landed?'

With an effort Ahmed came back. 'They weren't Kurds, just tribesmen pretending to be Kurds and He of the Knife killed them all, Highness, with very great brutality,' he said with strange formality. 'In his madness he killed them all – with knife and gun and hands and feet and teeth, all except Bayazid who, because of his oath to you, would not come against him.'

'He left him alive?' Hakim was incredulous.

'Yes, God give him peace. He . . . put a gun in my hand and held the Bayazid near the gun and I . . .' The voice trailed away, waves of grass beckoning as far as eyes could see . . .

'You killed him?'

'Oh yes, looking . . . looking into his eyes.' Anger came into Ahmed's voice. 'The son of a . . . dog shot me in the back, twice, without honour, the son of a dog, so he died without honour and without . . . without manhood, the son of a dog.' The bloodless lips smiled and he closed his eyes. He was dying fast now, his words imperceptible. 'I took vengeance.'

Hakim said quickly, 'Ahmed, what haven't you told me that I need to know?'

1097

'Nothing . . .' In a little while his eyes opened and Hakim saw into the pit. 'There is no . . . no other God but God and . . .' A little blood seeped out of the side of his mouth. '. . . I made you Kh . . .' The last of the word died with him.

Hakim was uncomfortable under the frozen stare.

'Doctor!' he called out.

At once the man came in, and the guard. The doctor closed his eyes. 'As God wills. What should we do with the body, Highness?'

'What do you usually do with bodies?' Hakim moved his crutches and walked away, the guard followed. So, Ahmed, he was thinking, so now you're dead and I'm alone, cut from the past and obliged to no one. Made me Khan? Is that what you were going to say? Did you know there were spy holes in that room too?

A smile touched him. Then hardened. Now for Colonel Fazir and Erikki, He of the Knife as you called him.

At the Palace: 6:48 P.M. In the failing light Erikki was carefully repairing one of the bullet holes in the plastic windshield of the 212 with clear tape. It was difficult with his arm in a sling but his hand was strong and the forearm wound shallow – no sign of infection. His ear was heavily taped, part of his hair shaved away for cleanliness, and he was mending fast. His appetite was good. The hours of talk that he had had with Azadeh had given him a measure of peace.

That's all it is, he thought, it's only a measure, not enough to forgive the killings or the danger that I am. So be it. That's what gods made me and that's what I am. Yes, but what about Ross and what about Azadeh? And why does she keep the kukri so close by her: 'It was his gift to you, Erikki, to you and to me.'

'It's unlucky to give a man a knife without taking money, at once, just a token, in return. When I see him I will give him money and accept his gift.'

Once again he pressed Engine Start. Once again the engine caught, choked and died. What about Ross and Azadeh?

He sat back on the edge of the cockpit and looked at the sky. The sky did not answer him. Nor the sunset. The overcast had broken up in the west, the sun was down and the clouds menacing. Calls of the muezzins began. Guards on the gate faced Mecca and prostrated themselves; so did those inside the palace and those working in the fields and carpet factory and sheep pens.

Unconsciously his hand went to his knife. Without wishing to, his eyes checked that the Sten gun was still beside his pilot's seat and armed with a full clip. Hidden in the cabin were other weapons, weapons from the tribesmen. AK47s and M16s. He could not remember taking them or hiding them, had discovered them this morning when he made his inspection for damage and was cleaning the interior.

With the tape over his ear he did not hear the approaching car as soon as he would have done normally, and was startled when it appeared at the gate. The Khan's guards there recognised the occupants and waved the car through to stop in the huge forecourt near the fountain. Again he pressed Engine Start, again the engine caught for a moment, then shuddered the whole airframe as it died.

' 'Evening, Captain,' the two men said, Hashemi Fazir and Armstrong. 'How are you feeling today?' the colonel asked.

' 'Evening. With luck, in a week or so I'll be better than ever,' Erikki said pleasantly but his caution was complete.

'The guards say that Their Highnesses are not back yet – the Khan expects us, we're here at his invitation.'

'They're at the hospital being X-rayed. They left while I was asleep, they shouldn't be long.' Erikki watched them. 'Would you care for a drink? There's vodka, whisky and tea, of course coffee.'

'Thank you, whatever you have,' Hashemi said. 'How's your helicopter?'

'Sick,' he said disgustedly. 'I've been trying to start her for an hour. She's had a miserable week.' Erikki led the way up the marble steps. 'The avionics are messed. I need a mechanic badly. Our base's closed as you know and I tried to phone Tehran but the phones are out again.'

'Perhaps I can get you a mechanic, tomorrow or the next day, from the air base.'

'You could, Colonel?' His smile was sudden and appreciative. 'That'd help a lot. And I could use fuel, a full load. Would that be possible?'

'Could you fly down to the airfield?'

'I wouldn't risk it, even if I could start her – too dangerous. No I wouldn't risk that.' Erikki shook his head. 'The mechanic must come here.' He led the way along a corridor, opened the door to the small salon on the ground floor that Abdollah Khan had set aside for non-Islamic guests. It was called the European Room. The bar was well stocked. By custom, there were always full ice trays in the refrigerator, the ice made from bottled water, with club soda and soft drinks of many kinds – and chocolates and the halvah he had adored. 'I'm having vodka,' Erikki said.

'Same for me, please,' Armstrong said. Hashemi asked for a soft drink, 'I'll have a vodka too, when the sun's down.' Faintly the muezzins were still calling. '*Prosit!*' Erikki clinked glasses with Armstrong, politely did the same with Hashemi and drank the tot in one swallow. He poured himself another. 'Help yourself, Superintendent.' Hearing a car they all glanced out of the window. It was the Rolls.

'Excuse me a minute, I'll tell Hakim Khan you're here.' Erikki walked out and greeted Azadeh and her brother on the steps. 'What did the X-rays show?'

'No sign of bone damage for either of us.' Azadeh was happy, her face carefree. 'How are you, my darling?'

'Fine. It's wonderful about your backs. Wonderful!' His smile at Hakim was genuine. 'I'm so pleased. You've some guests, the colonel and Superintendent Armstrong – I put them in the European Room.' Erikki saw Hakim's tiredness. 'Shall I tell them to come back tomorrow?'

'No, no thank you. Azadeh, would you tell them I'll be fifteen minutes but to make themselves at home. I'll see you later, at dinner.' Hakim watched her touch Erikki and smile and walk off. How lucky they are to love each other so much, and how sad for them. 'Erikki, Ahmed's dead, I didn't want to tell her yet.'

Erikki was filled with sadness. 'My fault he's dead – Bayazid – he never gave him a chance *Matyeryebyets.*'

'God's will. Let's go and talk a moment.' Hakim went down the corridor into the Great room, leaning more and more on the crutches. The guards stayed at the door, out of listening range. Hakim went to a niche, put aside his crutches, faced Mecca, gasped with pain as he knelt and tried to make obeisance. Even forcing himself, he failed again and had to be content with intoning the Shahada. 'Erikki, give me a hand, will you, please?'

Erikki lifted him easily. 'You'd better give that a miss for a few days.'

'Not pray?' Hakim gaped at him.

'I meant . . . perhaps the One God will understand if you say it and don't kneel. You'll make your back worse. Did the doctor say what it was?'

'He thinks it's torn ligaments – I'll go to Tehran as soon as I can with Azadeh and see a specialist.' Hakim accepted his crutches. 'Thanks.' After a moment's consideration he chose a chair instead of his usual lounging cushions and eased himself into it, then ordered tea.

Erikki's mind was on Azadeh. So little time. 'The best back specialist in the world's Guy Beauchamp, in London. He fixed me up in five minutes after doctors said I'd have to lie in traction for three months or

1100

have two joints fused. Don't believe an ordinary doctor about your back, Hakim. The best they can do is pain-killers.'

The door opened. A servant brought in the tea. Hakim dismissed him and the guards. 'See that I'm not disturbed.' The tea was hot, mint-flavoured, sweet and drunk from tiny silver cups. 'Now, we must settle what you're to do. You can't stay here.'

'I agree,' Erikki said, glad that the waiting was over. 'I know I'm . . . I'm an embarrassment to you as Khan.'

'Part of Azadeh's agreement and mine with my father, for us to be redeemed and me to be made heir, were the oaths we swore to remain in Tabriz, in Iran, for two years. So, though you must leave, she may not.'

'She told me about the oaths.'

'Clearly you're in danger, even here. I can't protect you against police or the government. You should leave at once, fly out of the country. After two years when Azadeh can leave, she will leave.'

'I can't fly. Fazir said he could give me a mechanic tomorrow, maybe. And fuel. If I could get hold of McIver in Tehran he could fly someone up here.'

'Did you try?'

'Yes, but the phones are still out. I would have used the HF at our base but the office's totally wrecked – I flew over the base coming back here, it's a mess, no transport, no fuel drums. When I get to Tehran McIver can send a mechanic here to repair the 212. Until she can fly, can she stay where she is?'

'Yes. Of course.' Hakim poured himself some more tea, convinced now that Erikki knew nothing about the escape of the other pilots and helicopters. But that changes nothing, he told himself. 'There aren't any airlines serving Tabriz or I'd arrange one of those for you. Still, I think you should leave at once; you are in very great danger, immediate danger.'

Erikki's eyes narrowed. 'You're sure?'

'Yes?'

'What?'

'I can't tell you. But it's not in my control, it's serious, immediate, does not concern Azadeh at the moment but could, if we're not careful. For her protection this must remain just between us. I'll give you a car, any one you want from the garage. There're about twenty, I believe. What happened to your Range Rover?'

Erikki shrugged, his mind working. 'That's another problem, killing that *matyeryebyets* mujhadin who took my papers, and Azadeh's, then Rakoczy blasting the others.'

'I'd forgotten about Rakoczy.' Hakim pressed onward. 'There's not much time.'

Erikki moved his head around to ease the tension in his muscles and take away the ache. 'How immediate a danger, Hakim?'

Hakim's eyes were level. 'Immediate enough to suggest you wait till dark, then take the car and go – and get out of Iran as quickly as you can,' he added deliberately. 'Immediate enough to know that if you don't, Azadeh will have greater anguish. Immediate enough to know you should not tell her before you leave.'

'You swear it?'

'Before God I swear that is what I believe.'

He saw Erikki frown and he waited patiently. He liked his honesty and simplicity but that meant nothing in the balance. 'Can you leave without telling her?'

'If it's in the night, nearer to dawn so long as she's sleeping. If I leave tonight, pretending to go out, say to go to the base, she'll wait for me and if I don't come back it will be very difficult – for her and for you. The village preys on her. She'll have hysterics. A secret departure would be wiser, just before dawn. She'll be sleeping then – the doctor gave her sedatives. She'll be sleeping and I could leave a note.'

Hakim nodded, satisfied. 'Then it's settled.' He wanted no hurt or trouble for or from Azadeh either.

Erikki had heard the finality and he knew beyond any doubt, now, that if he left her he would lose her for ever.

In the Bathhouse: 7:15 P.M. Azadeh lowered herself into the hot water up to her neck. The bath was beautifully tiled and fifteen yards square and many tiered, shallow at one end with lounging platforms, the hot water piped from the furnace room adjoining. The room was warm and large, a happy place with kind mirrors. Her hair was tied up in a towel and she rested against one of the tilted backrests, her legs stretched out, the water easing her. 'Oh, that's so good, Mina,' she murmured.

Mina was a strong good-looking woman, one of Azadeh's three maidservants. She stood over her in the water, wearing just a loincloth, gently massaging her neck and shoulders. The bath-house was empty but for Azadeh and the maidservants – Hakim had sent the rest of the family to other houses in Tabriz: 'to prepare for a fitting Mourning Day for Abdollah Khan,' had been the excuse, but all were aware that the forty days of waiting was to give him time to inspect the palace at his leisure and reapportion suites as it pleased him. Only the old Khananum was undisturbed, and Aysha and her two infants.

Without disturbing Azadeh's tranquillity, Mina eased her into shallower water and on to another platform where Azadeh lay full length, her head propped comfortably on a pillow, so that she could work on her chest and loins and thighs and legs, preparing for the real oil massage that would come later when the water's heat had become deep-seated.

'Oh, that's so good,' Azadeh said again. She was thinking how much nicer this was than their own sauna – that raw strong heat and then the frightful plunge into the snow, the aftershock tingling and life-giving but not as good as this, the sensuality of the perfumed water and quiet leisure and no aftershocks and oh that is so good . . . but why is the bathhouse a village square and now it's so cold and there's the butcher and the false mullah's shouting, 'First his right hand . . . stone the harlotttt!' She screamed soundlessly and leapt away.

'Oh, did I hurt you, Highness, I'm so sorry!'

'No, no, it wasn't you, Mina, it was nothing, nothing, please go on.' Again the soothing fingers. Her heart slowed. I hope soon I'll be able to sleep without . . . without the village. Last night with Erikki it was already a little better, in his arms it was better, just being near him. Perhaps tonight it will be better still. I wonder how Johnny is. He should be on his way home now, home to Nepal on leave. Now that Erikki's back I'm safe again, just so long as I'm with him, near him. By myself I'm not . . . not safe even with Hakim. I don't feel safe anymore. I just don't feel safe anymore.

The door opened and Aysha came in. Her face was lined with grief, her eyes filled with fear, the black chador making her appear even more emaciated. 'Hello, Aysha dear, what's the matter?'

'I don't know. The world is strange and I've no . . . I'm centreless.'

'Come into the bath,' Azadeh said, sorry for her, she looked so thin and old and frail and defenceless. Difficult to believe she's my father's widow with a son and daughter, and only seventeen. 'Get in, it's so good.'

'No, no, thank you I . . . I just wanted to talk to you.' Aysha looked at Mina then dropped her eyes and waited. Two days ago she would have just sent for Azadeh who would have come at once and bowed and knelt and waited for orders, as now she knelt as petitioner. As God wills, she thought; except for my terror for the future of my children I would shout with happiness – no more of the the foul stench and sleep-shattering snores, no more of the crushing weight and moans and rage and biting and desperation to achieve that which he could but rarely. 'It's your fault, your fault your fault . . .' How could it be my fault?

How many times did I beg him to show me what to do to help, and I tried and tried and tried and yet it was only so rarely and then at once the weight was gone, the snoring would begin, and I was left awake to lie in the sweat and in the stink. Oh, how many times I wanted to die.

'Mina, leave us alone until I call you,' Azadeh said. She was obeyed instantly. 'What's the matter, Aysha dear?'

The girl trembled. 'I'm afraid. I'm afraid for my son, and I came to beg you to protect him.'

Azadeh said gently, 'You've nothing to fear from Hakim Khan and me, nothing. We've sworn by God to cherish you, your son and daughter, you heard us, we did it in front of . . . of your husband, our father, and then again, after his death. You've nothing to fear. Nothing.'

'I've everything to fear,' the girl stammered. 'I'm not safe anymore, nor is my son. Please, Azadeh, couldn't . . . couldn't Hakim Khan . . . I'd sign any paper giving up any rights for him, any paper, I only want to live in peace and for him to grow up and live in peace.'

'Your life is with us, Aysha. Soon you will see how happy we'll all be together,' Azadeh said. The girl's right to be afraid, she thought. Hakim will never surrender the Khanate out of his line if he has sons of his own – he must marry now, I must help find him a fine wife. 'Don't worry, Aysha.'

'Worry? You're safe now, Azadeh, you who just a few days ago lived in terror. Now I'm not safe and I'm in terror.'

Azadeh watched her. There was nothing she could do for her. Aysha's life was settled. She was the widow of a Khan. She would stay in the palace, watched and guarded, living as best she could. Hakim would not dare to let her remarry, could not possibly allow her to give up a son's rights granted by the public will of the dying husband. 'Don't worry,' she said.

'Here.' Aysha pulled out a bulky manila envelope from under her chador. 'This is yours.'

'What is it?' Azadeh's hands were wet and she didn't want to touch it.

The girl opened the envelope and showed her the contents. Azadeh's eyes widened. Her passport, ID, and other papers, Erikki's also, all the things that had been stolen from them by the mujhadin at the roadblock. This was a pishkesh indeed. 'Where did you get them?'

The girl was sure there was no one listening, but still lowered her voice. 'The leftist mullah, the same mullah of the village, he gave them to His Highness, the Khan, to Abdollah Khan two weeks ago, when you were in Tehran . . . the same mullah as at the village.'

Incredulously Azadeh watched her. 'How did he get them?'

Nervously the girl shrugged her thin shoulders. 'The mullah knew all about the roadblock and what happened there. He came here to try to take possession of the . . . of your husband. His Highness . . .' She hesitated, then continued in her halting whispers. 'His Highness told him no, not until he approved it, sent him away, and kept the papers.'

'Do you have other papers, Aysha? Private papers?'

'Not of yours or your husband's.' Again the girl trembled. 'His Highness hated you all so much. He wanted your husband destroyed, then he was going to give you to the Soviet, and your brother was to be . . . neutered. There's so much I know that could help you and him, and so much I don't understand. Ahmed . . . beware of him, Azadeh.'

'Yes,' Azadeh said slowly. 'Did Father send the mullah to the village?'

'I don't know. I think he did. I heard him ask the Soviet to dispose of Mahmud, ah, yes, that was that false mullah's name. Perhaps His Highness sent him there to torment you and the saboteur, and also sent him to his own death – but God intervened. I heard the Soviet agree to send men after this Mahmud.'

Azadeh said casually, 'How did you hear that?'

Aysha nervously gathered the chador closer around her and knelt on the edge of the bath. 'The palace is a honeycomb of listening holes and spy holes, Azadeh. He . . . His Highness trusted no one, spied on everyone, even me. I think we should be friends, allies, you and I, we're defenceless – even you, perhaps you more than any of us and unless we help each other we're all lost. I can help you, protect you.' Beads of sweat were on her forehead. 'I only ask you to protect my son, please. I can protect you.'

'Of course we should be friends,' Azadeh said, not believing that she was under any threat, but intrigued to know the secrets of the palace. 'You will show me these secret places and share your knowledge?'

'Oh, yes, yes, I will.' The girl's face lit up. 'I'll show you everything and the two years will pass quickly. Oh, yes, we'll be friends.'

'What two years?'

'While your husband is away, Azadeh.'

Azadeh jerked upright, filled with alarm. 'He's going away?'

Aysha stared at her. 'Of course. What else can he do?'

In the European Room: Hashemi was handing Robert Armstrong the scrawled message from Mzytryk that Hakim had just given him. Armstrong glanced at it: 'Sorry, Hashemi, I can't read Turkish.'

'Ah, sorry, I forgot.' Hashemi read it out in English. Both men saw Armstrong's disappointment. 'Next time, Robert, we'll get him. In-sha'Allah.'

Not to worry, Armstrong thought. It was a long shot anyway. I'll get Mzytryk another time. I'll get him, and I'll get you, old friend Hashemi, rotten of you to murder Talbot. Why did you do that? Revenge because he knew many of your secrets? He'd done you no harm, on the contrary he put lots of bones your way and smoothed lots of errors for you. Rotten! You didn't give him a chance, why should you have one? Soon as my passage out's arranged, you've had it. No reason to delay anymore now that Mzytryk knows I'm on to him and he's jeering from safety. Perhaps the Brass'll send Special Branch or a special team into Tbilisi now we know where he is – someone'll get the bastard. Even if I don't . . .

He was distracted by Hakim Khan saying, 'Colonel, what's this about Yazernov and Jaleh Cemetery?' and Hashemi answering smoothly, 'It's an invitation, Highness. Yazernov's an intermediary Mzytryk uses from time to time, acceptable to both sides, when something of importance to both sides has to be discussed.' Armstrong almost laughed. Hashemi knew as well as he that it was a promise of a personal vendetta and of course an immediate Section 16/a. Clever of Mzytryk to use the name Yazernov and not Rakoczy.

'As soon as convenient to meet Yazernov!' Hashemi said, 'I think, Highness, we'd better return to Tehran tomorrow.'

'Yes,' Hakim said. Coming back in the car from the hospital with Azadeh, Hakim had decided the only way to deal with Mzytryk's message and these two men was head-on. 'When will you come back to Tabriz?'

'If it pleases you, next week. Then we could discuss how to tempt Mzytryk here. With your help there's much to do in Azerbaijan. We've just had a report that the Kurds are in open rebellion nearer to Rezaiyeh, now heavily provisioned with money and guns by the Iraqis – may God consume them. Khomeini has ordered the army to put them down, once and for all time.'

'The Kurds?' Hakim smiled. 'Even he, God keep him safe, even he won't do that – not once and for all.'

'This time he might, Highness. He has fanatics to send against fanatics.'

'Green Bands can obey orders and die but they do not inhabit those mountains, they do not have Kurdish stamina nor their lust for earthly freedom en route to Paradise.'

1106

'With your permission I will pass on your advice, Highness.'

Hakim said sharply, 'Will it be given any more credence than my father's – or my grandfather's – whose advice was the same?'

'I would hope so, Highness. I would hope . . .' His words were drowned as the 212 fired up, coughed, held for a moment, then died again. Out of the window they saw Erikki unclip one of the engine covers and stare at the complexity inside with a flashlight. Hashemi turned back to the Khan who sat on a chair, stiffly upright. The silence became complicated, three men's minds racing, each as strong as the other, each bent on violence of some kind.

Hakim Khan said carefully, 'He cannot be arrested in my house or my domain. Even though he knows nothing of the telex, he knows he cannot stay in Tabriz, even Iran, nor may my sister go with him, even leave Iran for two years. He knows he must leave at once. His machine cannot fly. I hope he avoids arrest.'

'My hands are tied, Highness.' Hashemi's voice was apologetic and patently sincere. 'It is my duty to obey the law of the land.' Absently he noticed a piece of fluff on his sleeve and brushed it away. Armstrong got the signal at once. Brushing a left sleeve meant, 'I need to talk to this man privately, he won't talk in front of you. Make an excuse and wait for me outside.' Hashemi repeated with the perfect amount of sadness, 'It's our duty to obey the law.'

'I'm certain, quite certain, he was not part of any conspiracy, knows nothing about the flight of the others, and I would like him left alone to leave in peace.'

'I would be glad to inform SAVAMA of your wishes.'

'I would be glad if you would do what I suggest.'

Armstrong said, 'Highness, if you'll excuse me, the matter of the captain is not my affair, nor would I wish to rock any ship of state.'

'Yes, you may go, Superintendent. When do I have your report on new security possibilities?'

'It will be in your hands when the colonel returns.'

'Peace be with you.'

'And with you, Highness.' Armstrong walked out, then strolled along the corridors to the steps. Hashemi will roast the poor sod, he thought.

The evening was pleasant, nice nip on the air, a reddish tinge to the west. Red sky at night, shepherd's delight, red sky in the morning, shepherd's warning. ' 'Evening, Captain. Between you, me, and the gatepost, if your bus was working I'd suggest a quick trip to a border.'

Erikki's eyes narrowed. 'Why?'

Armstrong took out a cigarette. 'Climate's not very healthy around here, is it?' He cupped his hands around his lighter and flicked it.

'If you light a cigarette with all this petrol around here, your climate and mine'll not be very healthy permanently.' Erikki pressed the switch. The engine began winding up perfectly for twenty seconds, and again spluttered into silence. Erikki cursed.

Armstrong nodded politely and went back to the car. The driver opened the door for him. He settled back, lit the cigarette, and inhaled deeply, not sure if Erikki had got the message. Hope so. Can't give away the phony telex, or about Whirlwind or that'd put me against the nearest wall for treachery to Hashemi and the Khan for sticking my nose where it's clearly not invited – I was warned. Fair enough. It is internal politics.

Christ! I'm chocker with all this. I need a holiday. A long holiday. Where? I could go back to Hong Kong for a week or two, look up my old chums, the few who're left, or perhaps go up into the Pays d'Enhaut, the High Country, skiing. Haven't been skiing for years and I could use some good Swiss cooking, roesti and wurst and good coffee with thick cream and lots of wine. Lots! That's what I'll do. First Tehran, then Hashemi concluded, and off into the wild blue. Perhaps I'll meet someone nice . . .

But the likes of us don't come in from the cold, nor change. What the hell am I going to do for future money now that my Iranian pension's up the spout and my Hong Kong police pension's worth less and less every day? 'Hello, Hashemi, how'd it go?'

'Fine, Robert. Driver, go back to HQ.' The driver accelerated through the main gate and sped down the road towards the city. 'Erikki'll sneak off in the early hours, just before dawn. We follow him until it pleases us and then we take him, outside Tabriz.'

'With Hakim's blessing?'

'Private blessing, public outrage. Thanks.' Hashemi accepted the cigarette, clearly pleased with himself. 'By that time, the poor fellow will probably be no more.'

Armstrong wondered what deal had been struck. 'At Hakim's suggestion?'

'Of course.'

'Interesting.' That's not Hakim's idea. What's Hashemi up to now, Armstrong asked himself.

'Yes, interesting. After we've burned the mujhadins tonight and made sure that maniac Finn is netted, one way or another, we'll go back to Tehran.'

'Perfect.'

Tehran – at the Bakravan House: 8:06 P.M. Sharazad put the grenade and pistol into the shoulder bag and hid it under some clothes in the drawer of her bureau. The clothes she would wear under her chador later, ski jacket and heavy sweater and ski pants, were already chosen. Now she wore a pale green silk dress from Paris that enhanced her figure and long legs perfectly. Her makeup too was perfect. A last check of the room and then she went downstairs to join the reception for Daranoush Farazan, her husband-to-be.

'Ah, Sharazad!' Meshang met her at the door. He was perspiring and he covered his nervousness with pretended good humour, not knowing what to expect from her. When she had come back from the doctor's earlier, he had begun to harangue her and use dire threats, but, astonishingly, she had just dropped her eyes and said docilely, 'There is no need to say any more, Meshang. God has decided, please excuse me, I will go and change.' And now she was here, still docile.

And so she should be, he thought. 'His Excellency Farazan has been dying to greet you.' He took her arm and led her through the twenty or so people in the room, mostly cronies of his and their wives, Zarah and some of her friends, none of Sharazad's. She smiled at those she knew and then turned all her concentration to Daranoush Farazan.

'Greetings, Excellency,' she said politely and held out her hand. This was the first time she had ever been so close. He was shorter than she. She looked down on the few strands of dyed hair over his coarse pate, coarse skin, and even coarser hands, his bad breath infringing her space, his small black eyes glittering. 'Peace be with you,' she said.

'Greetings, Sharazad, and peace be with you, but please, please don't call me Excellency. How . . . how beautiful you are.'

'Thank you,' she said and watched herself take back her hand and smile and stand beside him and run to fetch him a soft drink, skirts flying, and bring it back as beautifully as it was possible to do, smiling at his droll pleasantries, greeting other guests, pretending to be oblivious of their stares and private laughter, never overdoing the performance, her mind centred on the riot at the university that had already begun, and upon the protest march that had been forbidden by Khomeini but would take place.

Across the room Zarah was watching Sharazad, astonished with the change but thanking God that she had accepted her lot and was going to obey which would make all their lives easier. What else could she do? Nothing! And nothing for me to do but accept that Meshang has a fourteen-year-old whore who already has her fangs out, boasting that soon she'll become his second wife.

'Zarah!'

'Oh! Yes, Meshang, my dear.'

'The evening's perfect, perfect.' Meshang mopped his brow and accepted a soft drink from the tray that also contained glasses of champagne for those who cared for it. 'I'm delighted that Sharazad got her senses back, for of course it's a perfect match for her.'

'Perfect,' Zarah said agreeably. I suppose we should be thankful he arrived alone and did not bring one of his fancy boys – it's true, he really does smell of the ordure he sells. 'You've arranged everything perfectly, darling Meshang.'

'Yes. Yes, it is. It's working out just as I planned.'

Near Jaleh: To reach the small grass airstrip, once the home of an impoverished aero club, now disused, Lochart had skirted the city and kept low to come under any radar. All the way in from D'Arcy 1908 he had tuned his radio to Tehran International but the airwaves were silent, the airport closed down for Holy Day, no flights permitted. He had been careful to arrive at sunset. When he cut the engine and heard the muezzins he was pleased. So far so good.

The hangar door was rusty. With some difficulty he managed to open it and wheeled the 206 inside. Then he reshut the door and began the long walk. He wore his flight clothes and, if he was stopped, he planned to say that he was an airline pilot whose car had broken down and was going to spend the night with friends.

As he reached Tehran's outskirts, the roads became more and more crowded, people going home or coming from the mosques, no colour or laughter among them, only a brooding apprehension.

There was not much traffic except army vehicles crammed with Green Bands. No troops or uniformed police. Traffic wardens were young Green Bands. The city was coming back into order. Never a woman in western dress, all chadors.

A few curses followed him, not many. A few greetings – his pilot's uniform gave him standing. Deeper into the city he found a good place to wait for a taxi near the street market. While he waited he bought a bottled soft drink, took a wedge of warm fresh bread and munched it. The night wind picked up a little but the brazier was cheerful and inviting.

'Greetings. Your papers, please.'

The Green Bands were youths, polite, some with the beginnings of beards. Lochart showed them his ID that was stamped and current and they handed it back to him after some discussion. 'Where are you going, may we ask?'

Deliberately in atrocious Farsi he said, 'Visit friends, near bazaar. Car break down. Insha'Allah.' He heard them talking among themselves, saying that pilots were safe, that this one was Canadian – isn't that part of the Great Satan? No, I don't think so. 'Peace be with you,' they said and wandered off.

He went to the corner and watched the traffic, the smell of the city strong – petrol, spices, rotting fruits, urine, body odour, and death. His sharp eyes saw a taxi with only two men in the back and one in the front at an intersection now blocked by a truck making a turn. Without hesitation he ducked through the cars, shouldered another man out of the way, jerked the back door open, and crammed himself inside, apologising profusely in good Farsi, and begged the occupants to allow him to accompany them. After some cursing, some haggling, the driver discovered the bazaar was directly on the route that he had arranged with the others, all individual travellers who had also fought their way in. 'With the Help of God, yours will be the second stop, Excellency.'

I've made it, he told himself exultantly, then allowed the other thought to surface: hope the others made it too. Duke and Scrag, Rudi, all of them, Freddy and good old Mac.

Bahrain – International Airport: 8:50 P.M. Jean-Luc stood at the helipad and trained his binoculars on the two 212s that were over the end of the apron now, navigation lights winking. They had been cleared for a straight-in and approached fast. Beside him was Mathias, also using binoculars. Nearby, was an ambulance, a doctor, and the Immigration officer, Yusuf. The sky was clear and star-filled, the night good with a warm fine wind.

The lead 212 turned slightly and now Jean-Luc could read the registration letters. G-UVX. British. Thank God, they had time at Jellet, he thought, recognised Pettikin in the cockpit, then turned his glasses back to the other 212 and saw Ayre and Kyle, the mechanic.

Touchdown for Pettikin. Mathias and Jean-Luc converged, Mathias for Pettikin and Jean-Luc for the cabin door. He swung it open. 'Hello, Genny, how is he?'

'He can't seem to breathe.' Her face was white.

Jean-Luc caught a glimpse of McIver stretched out on the floor, a life

1111

jacket under his head. Twenty minutes before, Pettikin had reported to Bahrain Tower that one of his crew, McIver, seemed to be having a heart attack, urgently requested a doctor and ambulance to meet them. The tower had cooperated instantly.

The doctor hurried past him into the cabin and knelt beside McIver. One look was sufficient. He used the hypodermic he had prepared. 'This will settle him quickly and we'll have him in the hospital in a few minutes.' In Arabic he called to the paramedics and they came on the run. He helped Genny down into the light, Jean-Luc now with them. 'I'm Dr. Lanoire, please tell me what happened.'

'Is it a heart attack?' she asked.

'Yes, yes, it is. Not a bad one,' the doctor said, wanting to gentle her. He was half-French, half-Bahraini, very good, and they had been fortunate to get him at such short notice. Behind them the paramedics had McIver on a stretcher and were easing him gently out of the helicopter.

'He . . . my husband, he suddenly gasped and sort of croaked, "I can't breathe," then doubled over in pain and fainted.' She wiped the sweat off her upper lip and continued in the same flat voice: 'I thought it must be a heart attack and I didn't know what to do, then I remembered what old Doc Nutt had said when he gave all us wives a lecture once and I loosened Duncan's Collar and we put him on the floor, then I found the . . . the capsules he'd given us and put one under his nose and crushed it . . . .'

'Ammonal nitrate?'

'Yes, yes that was it. Doc Nutt gave us each two of them and told us to keep them safe and secret and how to use them. It smelled awful but Duncan groaned and half came around then went off again. But he was breathing, kind of breathing. It was hard to hear or to see in the cabin but I thought he stopped breathing once and then I used the last capsule and that seemed to make it better again.'

The doctor had been watching the stretcher. As soon as it was safely in the ambulance, he said to Jean-Luc, 'Captain, please bring Madame McIver to the hospital in half an hour, here's my card, they'll know where I am.'

Genny said quickly, 'Don't you think that th –'

The doctor said firmly, 'You'll help more by letting us do our job for half an hour. You're done yours, you've saved his life, I think.' He rushed off.

Tehran – At the Bakravan House. 8:59 P.M. Zarah was at the dining table, making a last check that all was ready. Plates and cutlery and napkins of white linen, bowls of various horisht, meats and vegetables, fresh breads and fresh fruits, sweetmeats and condiments. Only the rice left to arrive and that would be brought when she called for dinner. 'Good,' she said to the servants and went into the other room.

Their guests were still chattering but she saw that now Sharazad was standing by herself, near Daranoush who was deep in conversation with Meshang. Hiding her sadness, she went over to her. 'My darling, you look so tired. Are you feeling all right?'

'Of course she's all right,' Meshang called out with loud, brittle humour.

Sharazad put a smile on a face that had become very pale. 'It's the excitement, Zarah, just all the excitement.' Then to Farazan, 'If you don't mind, Excellency Daranoush, I won't join you for dinner to-night.'

'Why, what's the matter?' Meshang said sharply. 'Are you sick?'

1113

'Oh, no, dearest brother, it's just the excitement.' Sharazad put her attention back on the little man. 'Perhaps I may be allowed to see you tomorrow? Perhaps dinner tomorrow?'

Before Meshang could answer for him, Daranoush said, 'Of course, my dear,' and went closer, and kissed her hand, and it took all of her willpower not to heave. 'We'll have dinner tomorrow. Perhaps you and Excellency Meshang and Zarah will honour my poor house.' He chuckled. His face became even more grotesque. '*Our* poor house.'

'Thank you, I will treasure the thought. Good night, peace be with you.'

'And with you.'

She was equally polite with her brother and Zarah, then turned and left them. Daranoush watched her walk away, the sway of her boyish hips and her buttocks. By God, look at her, he told himself with relish, imagining her naked, cavorting for him. I've made an even better arrangement than I imagined. By God, when Meshang proposed the marriage I was only persuaded by the dowry along with the promises of political partnership in the bazaar – both substantial, which of course they should be for a woman pregnant with a foreigner's child. But now, by God, I don't think it will be so difficult to bed her, have her service me as I want to be served, and sometimes to make children of my own. Who knows, perhaps it will be as Meshang said, 'Perhaps she'll lose the one she carries.' Perhaps she will, perhaps she will.

He scratched absently until she left the room. 'Now, where were we, Meshang?'

'About my suggestion for a new bank . . .'

Sharazad closed the door and ran lightly up the stairs. Jari was in her room, dozing in the big chair. 'Oh Princess, how d –'

'I'm going to bed now, Jari. You can leave now and I'm not to be disturbed, Jari, by anyone for any reason. We'll talk at breakfast.'

'But, Princess, I'll sleep in the chair and b –'

Sharazad stamped her foot, vexed. 'Good *night*! And I am not to be disturbed!' Loudly she locked the door after her, kicked off her shoes, then, very quietly, changed quickly. Now the veil and chador. Cautiously she opened the French doors to the balcony and slipped out. Stairs went down to a patio garden and from there a passageway led to a back door. She eased off the bolts. The hinges creaked. Then she was out into the alley and had wedged the door shut. As she hurried away, her chador billowed out behind her like a great black wing.

* * *

In the reception room Zarah glanced at her watch and walked over to Meshang. 'Darling, would you like dinner to be served now?'

'In a moment, can't you see His Excellency and I are busy?'

Zarah sighed, then went off to talk to a friend, but stopped as she saw the doorkeeper come in anxiously, look around the room for Meshang, then hurry over to him and whisper. Blood drained out of Meshang's face. Daranoush Farazan gasped. She rushed over to them. 'What on earth is it?'

Meshang's mouth worked but no sound came out. In the sudden hush, the frightened servant blurted out, 'Green Bands're here, Highness, Green Bands with a . . . with a mullah. They want to see His Excellency at once.'

In the great silence everyone remembered Paknouri's arrest and Jared's summons and all the other arrests, executions, and rumours of more terror, more komitehs, jails filled with friends and customers and relations. Daranoush was almost spitting with rage that he was here in this house at this time, wanting to rend his clothes because he had foolishly agreed to ally himself with the Bakravan family, already damned because of Jared's usury – the same usury that all bazaari moneylenders were guilty of but Jared was caught! Son of a burnt father and I've agreed publicly to the marriage and agreed in private to participate in Meshang's plans, plans I can see now oh God protect me that are dangerously modern, dangerously Western, and clearly against the Imam's dictates and wishes! Son of a burnt father, there must be a back way out of this house of the damned.

Four Green Bands and the mullah were in the reception room the servant had shown them into, sitting cross-legged and leaning against the silk cushions; they had taken off their shoes and left them beside the door. The youths were wide-eyed at the richness of their surroundings, their guns on the carpets beside them. The mullah wore fine robes and a fine white turban and was an imposing man in his sixties with a white beard and heavy dark eyebrows, a strong face and dark eyes.

The door opened. Meshang tottered into the room like an automaton. He was pasty, and his head ached with the strength of his terror. 'Greetings . . . greetings, Excellency . . .'

'Greetings. You are Excellency Meshang Bakravan?' Meshang nodded mutely. 'Ah, then again greetings and peace be with you, Excellency, please excuse me that I arrive so late but I am the mullah Sayani and I come from the komiteh. We have just discovered about Excellency Jared Bakravan and I have come to tell you that though it

1115

was God's Will, His Excellency was never condemned according to the law, was mistakenly shot, his property mistakenly appropriated, and that it will all be returned at once.'

Meshang gaped at him, speechless.

'Islamic government is committed to uphold God's law.' The mullah's brow darkened as he continued: 'God knows we cannot control all zealots or simple-minded, misguided people. God knows there are some who through zeal make errors. And God knows too there are many who use the revolution for evil, hiding under the cloak of "patriot", many who twist Islam for their own filthy purposes, many who will not obey the Word of God, many who scheme to bring us into disrepute, even many who falsely wear the turban, many who do not merit the turban, even some ayatollahs, even them, but with the help of God we will tear off their turbans, cleanse Islam, and stamp out the evil, whoever they are . . .'

The words were not reaching Meshang. His mind was exploding with hope. 'He . . . my father . . . I get our . . . our property back?'

'Our Islamic government is the government of Law. Sovereignty belongs to God alone. The law of Islam has absolute authority over everyone – including the Islamic government. Even the Most Noble Messenger, upon whom be peace, was subject to the law that God alone revealed, alone expounded by the tongue of the Koran.' The mullah got up. 'It was the Will of God but Excellency Jared Bakravan was not judged according to the law.'

'It's . . . it's true?'

'Yes, the Will of God, Excellency. Everything will be returned to you. Didn't your father support us lavishly? How can Islamic government flourish without bazaari help and support, how can we exist without bazaaris to fight the enemies of Islam, the enemies of Iran and the Infidel . . .'

Outside the Bazaar: The taxi stopped in the crowded square. Lochart got out and paid the driver as two of a mass of would-be passengers, a woman and a man, fought their way into the space he had vacated. The square was full of people streaming into and out of the mosque and the bazaar and surrounding the street stalls. They paid little attention to him, his uniform and cap giving him free passage. The night was chill and overcast. The wind had picked up again and guttered the flames of the oil lamps of street vendors. Across the square was the street of the Bakravan house and he walked briskly, rounded the corner, and stepped aside to let the mullah Sayani and the Green Bands pass, then went on again.

At the door in the high wall he stopped, took a deep breath, and knocked loudly. Then knocked again. Then again. He heard footsteps, saw an eye behind the spy hole. 'Doorkeeper, it's me, Excellency Captain Lochart,' he called out happily.

The door swung open. 'Greetings, Excellency,' the doorkeeper said, still not over the shock of the abrupt arrival and departure of the mullah and Green Bands – bowed out humbly by Excellency Foul Temper himself, he thought in awe, who the very second the door was bolted had jumped up and down like a madman, drummed his feet on the ground, and rushed back silently into the house, and now here's another apparition, by God, the Infidel who once was married to the betrothed of Excellency Piss.

A squall blew dead leaves across the patio. Another pop-eyed servant stood at the open main door. 'Greetings, Excellency,' he mumbled, 'I'll . . . I'll tell Excellency Meshang you've arrived.'

'Wait!' Now Lochart could hear the excited buzz of voices coming from the dining salon, glasses clinking, laughter of a party. 'Is my wife in there?'

'Your wife?' The servant collected himself with difficulty. 'The, er, Her Highness, Captain Excellency, she's gone to bed.'

Lochart's anxiety soared. 'Is she sick?'

'She did not appear sick, Excellency, she went just before dinner. I'll tell Excellency Meshang that –'

'No need to disturb him and his guests,' he said, delighted with the opportunity of seeing her alone first, 'I'll see her, then come down and announce myself later.'

The servant watched him go up the stairs, two at a time, waited until he was out of sight, then hurried to find Meshang.

Lochart went along a corridor into another. He forced himself to walk, relishing how surprised she would be and so happy and then they would see Meshang and Meshang would listen to the plan. At last he was at their door and turned the handle. When the door did not open, he tapped and called out softly, 'Sharazad, it's me, Tommy.' His spirit sang while he waited. 'Sharazad?' Waiting. Knocking. Waiting. Then knocking a little louder. 'Sharazad!'

'Excellency!'

'Oh, hello, Jari,' he said, in his impatience not noticing that she was trembling. 'Sharazad, darling, unlock the door, it's me, Tommy!'

'Her Highness said she was not to be disturbed.'

'She didn't mean me, of course not! She's taken a sleeping pill?'

'Oh no, Excellency.'

He put all of his attention on her. 'What're you so frightened about?'

'Me? I'm not frightened, Excellency, why should I be frightened?'

Something's wrong, he thought. Impatiently he turned back to the door. 'Sharazad!' Waiting waiting waiting. 'This is ridiculous!' he muttered. '*Sharazad!*' Before he knew what he was doing he was hammering on the door. 'Open the door, for crissake!'

'*What are you doing here?*'

It was Meshang, raw with rage. At the far end of the corridor, Lochart saw Zarah come into view and stop. 'Good . . . good evening, Meshang,' he said, his heart pounding, trying to sound reasonable and polite and why the hell doesn't she open the door and this isn't the way it's supposed to happen. 'I came back to see my wife.'

'She's not your wife, she's divorced, now get out!'

Lochart stared at him blankly. 'Of course she's my wife!'

'By God, are you simple? She *was* your wife. Now leave my house!'

'You're crazy, you can't divorce her just like that!'

'GET OUT!'

'Get stuffed!' Again Lochart hammered on the door. 'Sharazad!'

Meshang whirled on Zarah. 'Go and get some Green Bands! Go on, get some Green Bands! They'll throw this madman out!'

'But Meshang, isn't it dangerous to involve them in ou –'

'Get them!'

Lochart's temper snapped. His shoulder went into the door. It shuddered but did not give so he raised his foot, slammed his heel against the lock. The lock shattered and the door burst open.

'Get Green Bands!' Meshang shrieked. 'Don't you understand they're on our side now, we're reinstated . . .' Then he rushed through the door too. Blankly he also saw the room was empty, bed empty, bathroom empty, nowhere else she could be. Both he and Lochart turned on Jari who stood at the doorway, staring with disbelief, Zarah cautiously behind her in the hall. 'Where is she?' Meshang shouted.

'I don't know, Excellency, she never left here, my room is next door and I'm a light sleeper . . .' Jari howled as Meshang belted her across the mouth, the blow sending her reeling on to her hands and knees.

'Where's she gone?'

'I don't know, Excellency, I thought she was in be—' She shrieked as Meshang's toe went into her side. 'By God, I don't know I don't know I don't know!'

Lochart was at the French doors. They opened easily, already unlatched. At once he was out on to the balcony, down the stairs, and to the back door. He came back slowly, in turmoil. Meshang and

1118

Zarah watched him from the balcony. 'The back door was unlocked. She must've gone out this way.'

'Gone where?' Meshang was flushed with rage, and Zarah turned on Jari who was still on her hands and knees in the bedroom, moaning and weeping with fear and pain. 'Shut up you dog or I'll whip you. Jari! If you don't know where she's gone, where do you think she's gone?'

'I . . . I don't know, Highness,' the old woman sobbed.

'Thinkkkk!' Zarah shrieked and slapped her.

Jari howled. 'I don't knowwww! She's been strange all day, Excellencies, strange, she sent me away this afternoon and went off by herself and I met her near 7 o'clock and we came back together but she said nothing, nothing, nothing . . .'

'By God, why didn't you tell me?' Meshang shouted.

'What was there to tell, Excellency? Please don't kick me again, please!'

Meshang groped for a chair. The violent pendulum from total terror when the mullah and Green Bands were announced to total euphoria at his reprieve and reinstatement to fury finding Lochart here and Sharazad gone, had momentarily unhinged him. His mouth moved but there was no sound and he saw Lochart questioning Jari but could not understand the words.

When he had rushed back into the dining room to stutter the God-given news there had been rejoicing, Zarah had wept with happiness and embraced him and so did the women, and the men had warmly wrung his hand. All except Daranoush. Daranoush was no longer there. He had fled. Out the back door. 'He's gone?'

'Like a bag full of fart!' someone had called out.

Everyone had started laughing, their private relief that they were no longer in any immediate danger of guilt by association, together with Meshang's totally unexpected rocket back to wealth and power, making them light-headed. Someone had shouted, 'You really can't have Daranoush the Daring as a brother-in-law, Meshang!'

'No, no, by God,' he remembered saying, quaffing a glass of champagne. 'How could you trust such a man?'

'Not even with a bucket of piss! By the Prophet, I've always thought Dirty Daranoush overcharged for his services. The bazaar should rescind his contract!'

Another cheer and general agreement and Meshang had drunk a second glass of champagne, gloating over the glorious new possibilities opened up before him: the new contract for the bazaar's waste which he as the injured party would of course have, a new syndicate to finance the government under his guidance and greater profit, new associations with more important ministers than Ali Kia – where is that son of a dog? – new deals in the oil fields, monopolies to manoeuvre, a new match for Sharazad, so easy now for who would not want to be part of his family, *the* bazaari family? No need now to pay out a usurious dowry I agreed to only under duress. All my property back, the estate on the Caspian shores, streets of houses in Jaleh, apartments in the northern suburbs, lands and orchards and fields and villages, all of it back.

Then the servant destroying his elation, whispering that Lochart had returned, was already in his house, already upstairs. Rushing upstairs, and now helplessly watching the man he hated so much questioning Jari, Zarah listening as intently.

With an effort he concentrated. Jari was saying between sobs, '. . . I'm not sure, Excellency, she . . . she only . . . she only told me the young man that saved her life at the first Women's Protest was a university student.'

'Did she ever meet him alone?'

'Oh, no, Excellency, no, as I said we met him at the march and he asked us to take coffee to recover,' Jari said. She was petrified of being caught in the lie but more petrified of telling what had really happened. God protect us, she prayed. Where has she gone, where?

'What was his name, Jari?'

'I don't know, Excellencies, it might have been Ibrahim or . . . or Ishmael, I don't know. I already told you, he had no importance.'

Lochart's head was pounding. No clue, nothing. Where would she have gone? To a friend's? To the university? Another protest march? Don't forget the rumours in the market about university students rioting again, more explosions expected tonight, more marches and countermarches, Green Bands versus the leftists, but all non-Imam-sponsored marches forbidden by the Komiteh and the Komiteh's patience ended. 'Jari, you must have some idea, some way of helping us!'

Meshang said gutturally, 'Whip her, she knows!'

'I don't I don't . . .' Jari wailed.

'Shut up, Jari!' Lochart turned on Meshang, his face pale and violence absolute, 'I don't know where she's gone but I know the why: you forced the divorce, and I swear by the Lord God if she comes to harm, any harm, *you will pay!*'

Meshang blustered, 'You left her, you left her penniless, you abandoned her and you're divorced, yo –'

'Remember, you will pay! And if you bar me from this house whenever I come back or she comes back, by God be that on your head too!' On the edge of madness, Lochart stalked towards the French doors.

Zarah said quickly, 'Where are you going?'

'I don't know . . . I . . . To the university. Perhaps she's gone to join another march though why she'd run off to do that . . .' Lochart could not bring himself to articulate his real terror: that her revolt was so extreme that her mind was unhinged and she would kill herself – oh, not suicide, but how many times in the past has she said, 'Never worry about me, Tommy. I am a Believer, I always try to do God's work and so long as I die doing God's work with God's name on my lips I will go to Paradise.'

But what about our child-to-be? A mother wouldn't, couldn't, could she, someone like Sharazad?

The room was very still. For an eternity he stood there. Then, all at once, his being swept him into new waters. In a strange clear voice he said, 'Bear witness for me: I attest that there is no other God but God and Mohammed is the Prophet of God . . . I attest that there is no other God but God and Mohammed is the Prophet of God . . .' and the third and last time. Now it was done. He was at peace with himself. He saw them staring at him. Stunned.

Meshang broke the silence, no longer in anger. 'Allah-u Akbar! Welcome. But saying the Shahada is not enough, not by itself.'

'I know. But it is the beginning.'

They watched him vanish into the night, all of them spellbound that they had witnessed a soul being saved, an unbeliever transmuted into a Believer, so unexpectedly. All of them were filled with joy, degrees of joy. 'God is Great!'

Zarah murmured, 'Meshang, doesn't this change everything?'

'Yes, yes and no. But now he will go to Paradise. As God wants.' Suddenly he was very tired. His eyes went to Jari, and she began to tremble again. 'Jari,' he said with the same calm, 'you are going to be whipped until you tell me all the truth or you are in hell. Come along, Zarah, we mustn't forget our guests.'

'And Sharazad?'

'As God wills.'

Near the University: 9:48 P.M. Sharazad turned into the main road where Green Bands and their supporters were collecting. Thousands of them. The vast majority were men. All armed. Mullahs marshalled them, exhorting them to maintain discipline, not to fire on the leftists until they were fired upon, to try to persuade them from their evil. 'Don't forget they're Iranians, not satanic foreigners. God is Great . . . God is Great . . .'

'Welcome, child,' an old mullah said gently, 'peace be upon you.'

'And upon you,' she said. 'We're marching against the anti-God?'

'Oh, yes, in a little while, there's plenty of time.'

'I have a gun,' she said proudly, showing it to him. 'God is Great.'

'God is Great. But better that the killing should cease and the misguided should recognise the Truth, renounce their heresies, obey the Imam, and come back to Islam.' The old man saw her youth and resolution and was uplifted, and saddened. 'Better the killing should cease but if those of the Left Hand do not cease to oppose the Imam, God's peace on him, then with the Help of God we will hurry them into hell . . .'

Tabriz – At the Palace: 10:05 P.M. The three of them were sitting in front of the wood fire drinking after-dinner coffee and watching the flames, the room small and richly brocaded, warm and intimate, one of Hakim's guards beside the door. But there was no peace between them, though all pretended otherwise, now and during the evening. The flames held their attention, each seeing different pictures therein. Erikki was watching the fork in the road, always the fork, one way the flames leading to loneliness, the other to fulfilment – perhaps and perhaps not. Azadeh watched the future, trying not to watch it.

Hakim Khan took his eyes off the fire and threw down the gauntlet. 'You've been distracted all evening, Azadeh,' he said.

'Yes. I think we all are.' Her smile was not real. 'Do you think we could talk in private, the three of us?'

'Of course.' Hakim motioned to the guard. 'I'll call if I need you.' The man obeyed and closed the door after him. Instantly the mood of the room changed. Now all three were adversaries, all aware of it, all on guard and all ready. 'Yes, Azadeh?'

'Is it true that Erikki must leave at once?'

'Yes.'

'There must be a solution. I cannot endure two years without my husband.'

'With the Help of God the time will pass quickly.' Hakim Khan sat stiffly upright, the pain eased by the codeine.

'I cannot endure two years,' she said again.

'Your oath cannot be broken.'

Erikki said, 'He's right, Azadeh. You gave the oath freely, Hakim is Khan and the price . . . fair. But all the killings – I must leave, the fault's mine, not yours or Hakim's.'

'You did nothing wrong, nothing, you were forced into protecting me and yourself, they were carrion bent on murdering us, and as to the raid . . . you did what you thought best, you had no way of knowing the ransom was part paid or Father was dead . . . he should not have ordered the messenger killed.'

'That changes nothing. I have to go tonight. We can accept it, and leave it at that,' Erikki said, watching Hakim. 'Two years will pass quickly.'

'If you live, my darling.' Azadeh turned to her brother who looked back at her, his smile still the same, eyes the same.

Erikki glanced from brother to sister, so different and yet so similar. What's changed her, why has she precipitated that which should not have been precipitated?

'Of course if I live,' he said, outwardly calm.

An ember fell into the hearth and he reached forward and moved it to safety. He saw that Azadeh had not taken her gaze off Hakim, nor he off her. The same calm, same polite smile, same inflexibility.

'Yes, Azadeh?' Hakim said.

'A mullah could absolve me from my oath.'

'Not possible. Neither a mullah nor I could do that, not even the Imam would agree.'

'I can absolve myself. This is between me and God, I can ab –'

'You cannot, Azadeh. You cannot and live at peace with yourself.'

'I can. I can and be at peace.'

'Not and remain Muslim.'

'Yes,' she said simply, 'I agree.'

Hakim gasped. 'You don't know what you say.'

'Oh, but I do, I've considered even that.' Her voice was toneless. 'I've considered that solution and found it bearable. I will not endure two years of separation, nor will I endure any attempt on my husband's life,

1124

or forgive it.' She sat back and left the lists for the moment, nauseous but glad she had brought the matter into the open but frightened all the same. Once more she blessed Aysha for forewarning her.

'I will not allow you to renounce Islam under any circumstances,' Hakim said.

She just looked back at the flames.

The minefield was all around them, all mines triggered, and though Hakim was concentrating on her, his senses probed Erikki, He of the Knife, knowing the man was waiting too, playing a different game now that the problem was before them. Should I have dismissed the guard, he asked himself, outraged by her threat, the smell of danger filling his nostrils. 'Whatever you say, Azadeh, whatever you try, for the sake of your soul I would be forced to prevent an apostasy – in any way I could. That's unthinkable.'

'Then please help me. You're very wise. You're Khan and we have been through much together. I beg you, remove the threat to my soul and to my husband.'

'I don't threaten your soul or your husband.' Hakim looked at Erikki directly. 'I don't.'

Erikki said, 'What were those dangers you mentioned?'

'I can't tell you, Erikki,' Hakim said.

'Would you excuse us, Highness? We must get ready to leave.' Azadeh got up. So did Erikki.

'You must stay where you are!' Hakim was furious. 'Erikki, you'd allow her to forswear Islam, her heritage, and her chance of life everlasting?'

'No, that's not part of my plan,' he said. Both of them stared at him, bewildered. 'Please tell me what dangers, Hakim.'

'What plan? You have a plan? To do what?'

'The dangers, first tell me what dangers. Azadeh's Islam is safe with me, by my own gods I swear it. What dangers?'

It had never been part of Hakim's strategy to tell them, but now he was rocked by her intractability, aghast that she would consider committing the ultimate heresy, and further disoriented by this strange man's sincerity. So he told them about the telex and the pilots and airplanes fleeing, and his conversation with Hashemi, noticing that though Azadeh was as aghast as Erikki, her surprise did not seem real. It's almost as though she already knew, had been present, both times, but how could she possibly know? He rushed on: 'I told him you could not be taken in my house or domain or in Tabriz, that I would give you a car, that I hoped you'd escape arrest, and that you would leave just before dawn.'

Erikki was shattered. The telex's changed everything, he thought. 'So they'll be waiting for me.'

'Yes. But I did not tell Hashemi I had another plan, that I've already sent a car into Tabriz, that the moment Azadeh was asleep I wo –'

'You'd've left me, Erikki?' Azadeh was appalled. 'You'd've left me without telling me, without asking me?'

'Perhaps. What were you saying, Hakim; please finish what you were saying.'

'The moment Azadeh was asleep I planned to smuggle you out of the palace into Tabriz where the car is and point you towards the border, the Turkish border. I have friends in Khvoy and they would help you across it, with the Help of God,' Hakim added automatically, enormously relieved that he had had the foresight to arrange this alternative plan – just in case it was needed. And now it's happened, he thought. 'You have a plan?'

'Yes.'

'What is it?'

'If you don't like it, Hakim Khan, what then?'

'In that case I would refuse to allow it and try to stop it.'

'I would prefer not to risk your displeasure.'

'Without my help, you cannot leave.'

'I'd like your help, that's true.' Erikki was no longer confident. With Mac and Charlie and the rest gone – how in hell could they do it so fast? Why the hell didn't it happen while we were in Tehran but thank all gods Hakim's Khan now and can protect Azadeh – it's clear what SAVAK'll do to me if they catch me, when they catch me. 'You were right about the danger. You think I could sneak out as you said?'

'Hashemi left two policemen on the gate. I think you could be smuggled out – somehow it should be possible to distract them – I don't know if there're others on the road down to the city but there may be, more than likely there would be. If they're vigilant and you're intercepted . . . that's God's will.'

Azadeh said, 'Erikki, they're expecting you to go alone, and the colonel agreed not to touch you inside Tabriz. If we were hidden in the back of an old truck – we only need a little luck to avoid them.'

'You cannot leave,' Hakim said impatiently, but she did not hear him. Her mind had leaped to Ross and Gueng and the previous escape, and how difficult those two had found it even though they were trained saboteurs and fighters. Poor Gueng. A chill went through her. The road north's as difficult as the one south, so easy to ambush us, so easy to put up roadblocks. Not so far in miles to Khvoy, and past Khvoy to the

1126

frontier, but a million miles in time and with my bad back . . . I doubt if I could walk even one of them.'

'Never mind,' she muttered. 'We'll get there all right. With the Help of God we'll escape.'

Hakim flared, 'By God and the Prophet, what about your oath, Azadeh?'

Her face was very pale now and she held on to her fingers to stop the tremble. 'Please forgive me, Hakim, I've told you. And if I'm prevented from leaving with Erikki now, or if Erikki won't take me with him, I'll escape somehow, I will, I swear it, I swear it.'

She glanced at Erikki, 'If Mac and all the others have fled, you could be used as a hostage.'

'I know. I have to get out as fast as I can. But you have to stay. You can't give up your religion just because of the two years, much as I loathe leaving you.'

'Would Tom Lochart leave Sharazad for two years?'

'That's not the point,' Erikki said carefully. 'You're not Sharazad, you're the sister of a Khan and you swore to stay.'

'That's between me and God. Tommy wouldn't leave Sharazad,' Azadeh said stubbornly, 'Sharazad wouldn't leave her Tommy, she lov –'

'Erikki, I must know your plan.' Hakim interrupted coldly.

'Sorry, I trust no one in this.'

The Khan's eyes narrowed to slits, and it took all of his will not to call the guard. 'So there's an impasse. Azadeh, pour me some coffee, please.' At once she obeyed. He looked at the huge man who stood with his back to the fire. 'Isn't there?'

'Please solve it, Hakim Khan,' Erikki said. 'I know you to be a wise man and I would do you no harm, or Azadeh harm.'

Hakim accepted the coffee and thanked her, watched the fire, weighing and sifting, needing to know what Erikki had in his mind, wanting an end to all this and Erikki gone and Azadeh here and as she always was before, wise and gentle and loving and obedient – and Muslim. But he knew her too well to be sure she would not do as she threatened, and he loved her too much to allow her to carry out the threat.

'Perhaps this would satisfy you, Erikki: I swear by God I will assist you, providing your plan does not negate my sister's oath, does not force her to apostatise, does not put her in spiritual danger or political danger . . .' He thought a moment, '. . . does not harm her or harm me – and has a chance of success.'

1127

Azadeh bridled angrily, 'That's no help, how can Erikki possib –'

'Azadeh!' Erikki said curtly. 'Where are your manners? Keep quiet. The Khan was talking to me, not you. It's my plan he wants to know, not yours.'

'Sorry, please excuse me,' she said at once, meaning it. 'Yes, you're right. I apologise to both of you, please excuse me.'

'When we were married, you swore to obey me. Does that still apply?' he asked harshly, furious that she had almost ruined his plan, for he had seen Hakim's eyes cross with rage and he needed him calm, not agitated.

'Yes, Erikki,' she told him immediately, still shocked by what Hakim had said, for that closed every path except the one she had chosen – and that choice petrified her. 'Yes, without reservation, provided you don't leave me.'

'Without reservation – yes or no?'

Pictures of Erikki flashed through her mind, his gentleness and love and laughter and all the good things, along with the brooding violence that had never touched her but would touch anyone who threatened her or stood in his way, Abdollah, Johnny, even Hakim – particularly Hakim.

Without reservation, yes, she wanted to say, except against Hakim, except if you leave me. His eyes were boring into her. For the first time she was afraid of him. She muttered, 'Yes, without any reservation. I beg you not to leave me.'

Erikki turned his attention to Hakim: 'I accept what you said, thank you.' He sat down again. Azadeh hesitated, then knelt beside him, resting her arm on his knees, wanting the contact, hoping it would help to push away her fear and anger with herself for losing her temper. I must be going mad, she thought. God help me . . .

'I accept the rules you've set, Hakim Khan,' Erikki was saying quietly. 'Even so I'm still not going to tell you my pl – Wait, wait, wait! You swore you'd help if I didn't put you at risk, and I won't. Instead,' he said carefully, 'instead I'll give you a hypothetical approach to a plan that might satisfy all your conditions.' Unconsciously his hand began stroking her hair and her neck. She felt the tension leaving her. Erikki watched Hakim, both men ready to explode. 'All right so far?'

'Go on.'

'Say hypothetically my chopper was in perfect shape, that I'd been pretending I couldn't start her properly to throw everyone off, and to get everyone used to the idea of the engines starting and stopping, say

I'd lied about the fuel and there was enough for an hour's flight, easily enough to get to the border and –'

'Is there?' Hakim said involuntarily, the idea opening a new avenue.

'For the sake of this hypothetical story, yes.' Erikki felt Azadeh's grip tighten on his knee but pretended not to notice. 'Say in a minute or two, before we all went to bed, I told you I wanted to start her again. Say I did just that, the engines caught and held enough to warm her and then died, no one'd worry – the Will of God. Everyone'd think the madman won't leave well alone, why doesn't he quit and let us sleep in peace? Then say I started her, pushed on all power and pulled her into the sky. Hypothetically I could be away in seconds – provided the guards didn't fire on me, and provided there were no hostiles, Green Bands, or police with guns on the gate or outside the walls.'

The breath escaped from Hakim's lips. Azadeh shifted a little. The silk of her dress rustled. 'I pray that such a make-believe could come to pass,' she said.

Hakim said, 'It would be a thousand times better than a car, ten thousand times better. You could fly all the way by night?'

'I could, providing I had a map. Most pilots who've spent time in an area keep a good map in their heads – of course, this is all make-believe.'

'Yes, yes it is. Well, then, so far so good with your make-believe plan. You could escape this way, if you could neutralise the hostiles in the forecourt. Now, hypothetically, what about my sister?'

'My wife isn't in on any escape, real or hypothetical. Azadeh has no choice: she must stay of her own accord and wait the two years,' Erikki saw Hakim's astonishment and felt Azadeh's instant rebellion under his fingers. But he did not allow his fingers to cease their rhythm on her hair and neck, soothing her, coaxing her, and he continued smoothly, 'She is committed to stay in obedience to her oath. She cannot leave. No one who loves her, most of all me, would allow her to give up Islam because of two years. In fact, Azadeh, make-believe or not, *it is forbidden*. Understand?'

'I hear what you say, husband,' she said through her teeth, so angry she could hardly speak and cursing herself for falling into his trap.

'You are bound by your oath for two years, then you can leave freely. It's ordered!'

She looked up at him, and said darkly, 'Perhaps after two years I might not wish to leave.'

Erikki rested his great hand on her shoulder, his fingers lightly around her neck. 'Then, woman, I shall come back and drag you out by

1129

your hair.' He said it so quietly with such venom that it froze her. In a moment she dropped her eyes and looked at the fire, still leaning against his legs. He kept his hand on her shoulder. She made no move to remove it. But he knew she was seething, hating him. Still he knew it was necessary to say what he had said.

'Please excuse me a moment,' she said, her voice like ice.

The two men watched her leave.

When they were alone, Hakim said, 'Will she obey?'

'No,' Erikki said. 'Not unless you lock her up and even then . . . No. Her mind's made up.'

'I will never, never allow her to break her oath and renounce Islam, you must understand that, even . . . even if I have to kill her.'

Erikki looked at him. 'If you harm her, you're a dead man – if I'm alive.'

At the Northern Slums of Tabriz City: 10:36 P.M. In the darkness the first wave of Green Bands rushed the door in the high wall, blew the locks off, and went into the inner patio with guns blazing. Hashemi and Robert Armstrong were across the square in the comparative safety of a parked truck. Other men lurked in the alley to cut off any retreat.

'Now!' Hashemi said into his walkie-talkie. At once the enemy side of the square was bathed in light from searchlights mounted on camouflaged trucks. Men were fleeing out of other doors but police and Green Bands opened up and the battle began. 'Come on, Robert,' Hashemi said and led a careful rush closer.

Informers had whispered that tonight there would be a high-level meeting of Islamic-Marxist leaders here and that this building was connected to others on either side by a rabbit warren of secret doors and passages. With Hakim Khan's assistance Hashemi had precipitated this first of a series of raids to de-activate extensive leftist opposition to the government, to seize the leaders and make a public example of them – for his own purposes.

The first group of Green Bands had cleared the ground floor, and were charging up the stairs careless of their safety. The defenders, now that they were over their surprise, fought back with equal ferocity, well armed and well trained.

Outside in the square there was a lull, no more defenders wishing to run the gauntlet or to join those pinned down helplessly among the cars, some already on fire. The alley behind the building was ominously quiet, police and Green Bands blocking both ends, well-entrenched behind their vehicles. 'Why do we wait here like stinking, cowardly

Iraqis?' one of the Green Bands said truculently. 'Why don't we carry the battle to them?'

'You wait because that's what the colonel ordered,' the sergeant of police said, 'you wait because we can kill all the dogs safely and th –'

'I'm not subject to any dog colonel, only to God! God is greattttt!' With that the youth cocked his rifle and rushed out of ambush towards the back door of the target building. Others followed him. The sergeant cursed them and ordered them back, but his words were buried by the fusillade that came down on the youths from small windows high in the walls and slaughtered them.

Hashemi and others had heard the firing in the alley and presumed that a breakout had been attempted. 'The dogs can't escape that way, Robert,' Hashemi shouted gleefully, 'they're trapped!' From where he was he could see that the attack on the main tenement was held up. He clicked on the sender: 'Second wave into the HQ building.' Immediately a mullah and another bunch of youths shrieked their battle cry and rushed across the square – Robert Armstrong appalled that Hashemi would order them out like that, floodlit, such easy targets. 'Don't interfere, Robert! By God, I'm tired of you interfering,' Hashemi had said coldly when he had made some suggestions on how to contain the raid before the attack had started. 'Keep your advice to yourself, this is internal, nothing to do with you!'

'But, Hashemi, not all the buildings are hostile or Marxist, there're bound to be families, perhaps hundreds of innocen –'

'Keep quiet or, by God, I'll consider it treason!'

'Then I'll stay behind. I'll go back and watch the palace.'

'I've said you'll come on the raid! You think you British're the only ones who can handle a few revolutionaries? You'll stay beside me where I can see you – but first give me your gun!'

'But, Hashem –'

'Your gun! By the Prophet, I don't trust you anymore. Your gun!'

So he had given it to him and then Hashemi had come out of his rage and had seemed to relax and laughed the encounter off. But he had not returned the gun and Armstrong felt naked in the night, afraid that somehow he had been betrayed. He glanced at him, saw again the strangeness in Fazir's eyes and the way his mouth was working, a little saliva at the corners.

A burst of heavy firing pulled his attention back to the tenement. The automatic fire was coming from the upper windows against the new attack. Many youths were cut down but some got inside, the mullah among them, to reinforce those fighters still alive. Together they pulled away the bodies blocking the stairs, and fought their way up on to the next floor.

In the square Hashemi was now ducked down behind a car, consumed with excitement and his sense of power. 'More men into the HQ building!'

Never before had he been in control of a battle or even part of one. All his previous work had been secret, undercover, just a few men involved on each operation – even with his Group Four assassins all he had ever done was to give orders in safety and wait in safety, far from the action. Except the once that he had personally detonated the car bomb that had obliterated his SAVAMA enemy, General Janan. By God and the Prophet, his mind was shouting, this is what I was born for: battle and war!

'General assault!' he shouted into the walkie-talkie and then stood up and bellowed as loud as he could, 'General assault!'

Men charged out of the night. Grenades over walls into patios and into windows indiscriminately. Explosions and billowing smoke, more firing, rifle and automatic and more explosions and then a giant explosion in the leftist headquarters as an ammunition and petrol cache detonated, blowing off the top storey and most of the façade. The wave of heat tore at Hashemi's clothes, knocked Armstrong down, and Mzytryk who had been watching through binoculars from the safety of an upstairs window on the other side of the square saw them clearly in the floodlighting and decided the time was perfect.

'Now!' he said in Russian.

The sharpshooter beside him was already centred on the target through his telescopic sight, the rifle barrel resting on the window ledge. At once he flattened his index finger above the trigger guard, felt Mzytryk's finger on the trigger, and began the countdown as ordered: 'Three . . . two . . . one . . . fire!' Mzytryk squeezed the trigger. Both men saw the dumdum bullet go into Hashemi's lower back, slam him spread-eagled against the car in front, then sprawling into the dirt.

'Good,' Mzytryk muttered grimly, regretting only that his own eyes and hands were not good enough to deal with his son's murderers by himself.

'Three . . . two . . . one . . .' The gunsight wavered. Both of them cursed, for they had seen Armstrong whirl around, look in their direction for an instant, then hurl himself through a gap in the cars and disappear behind one of them.

'He's near the front wheel. He can't escape. Be patient – fire when you can!' Mzytryk hurried out of the room to the stairwell and shouted in Turkish to the men waiting below, 'Go!' then rushed back again. As he came through the doorway, he saw the sharpshooter fire. 'God him,' the man said with an obscenity. Mzytryk trained his binoculars but could not see Armstrong. 'Where is he?'

'Behind the black car – he stuck his head around the front wheel for a second and I got him.'

'Did you kill him?'

'No, Comrade General. I was very careful, just as you ordered.'

'You're sure?'

'Yes, Comrade General, I got him in the shoulder, perhaps the chest.'

The headquarters building burning furiously now, firing from the adjoining tenements sporadic, just pockets of resistance, attackers heavily outnumbering defenders, all of them whipped into a frenzy of brutality. Barbarians, Mzytryk thought contemptuously, then looked back at the sprawled body of Hashemi twitching and jerking and twitching again, half in and half out of the joub. Don't die too quickly, *matyeryebyets*. 'Can you see him, the Englishman?'

'No, Comrade General, but I've both sides covered.'

Then Mzytryk saw the broken-down ambulance arriving and men with Red Cross armbands fan out with stretchers to begin picking up the wounded, the battle mostly over now. I'm glad I came tonight, he thought, his rage not yet assuaged. He had decided to direct the retaliation personally the moment Hakim Khan's message had arrived yesterday. The barely disguised 'summons' – together with Pahmudi's secret report of the manner of his son's death at the hands of Hashemi and Armstrong – had sent him into a paroxysm of rage.

Simple to arrange a helicopter and set down just outside Tabriz last night, simple to arrange a counterattack to ambush the two murderers. Simple to plan his vengeance that would cement relations with Pahmudi by removing his enemy Hashemi Fazir for him and at the same time save both his mujhadin and Tudeh much future trouble. And Armstrong, the elusive MI6 agent, another long-overdue elimination – curse that fornicator for appearing like a ghost after all those years.

'Comrade General!'

'Yes, I see them.' Mzytryk watched the Red Cross men put Hashemi on a stretcher and carry him off towards the ambulance. Others went behind the car. The crossed lines of telescopic sight followed them. Mzytryk's excitement soared. The sharpshooter waited patiently. When the men reappeared, they were half carrying, half dragging Armstrong between them. 'I knew I'd hit the bastard,' the sharpshooter said.

*　　*　　*

At the Palace: 11:04 P.M. Silently the phosphorescent, red night-flying lights of the massed instrument panel came to life. Erikki's finger pressed Engine Start. The jets caught, coughed, caught, hesitated as he eased the circuit breakers carefully in and out. Then he shoved them home. The engines began a true warm-up.

Floodlights at half power were on in the forecourt. Azadeh and Hakim Khan, heavy-coated against the night cold, stood just clear of the turning blades, watching him. At the front gate a hundred yards or so away two guards and Hashemi's two police also watched but idly. Their cigarettes glowed. The two policemen shouldered their Kalashnikovs and strolled nearer.

Once more the engines spluttered and Hakim Khan called out over the noise, 'Erikki, forget it for tonight!' But Erikki did not hear him. Hakim moved away from the noise, nearer to the gate, Azadeh following him reluctantly. His walk was ponderous and awkward, and he cursed, unused to his crutches.

'Greetings, Highness,' the policemen said politely.

'Greetings. Azadeh,' Hakim said irritably, 'your husband's got no patience, he's losing his senses. What's the matter with him? It's ridiculous to keep trying the engines. What good would it do even if he could start them?'

'I don't know, Highness.' Azadeh's face was white in the pale light and she was very uneasy. 'He's . . . since the raid he's been very strange, very difficult, difficult to understand – he frightens me.'

'I don't wonder! He's enough to frighten the Devil.'

'Please excuse me, Highness,' Azadeh said apologetically, 'but in normal times he's . . . he's not frightening.'

Politely the two policemen turned away, but Hakim stopped them. 'Have you noticed any difference in the pilot?'

'He's very angry, Highness. He's been angry for hours. Once I saw him kick the machine – but different or not is difficult to say. I've never been near to him before.' The corporal was in his forties and wanted no trouble. The other man was younger and even more afraid. Their orders were to watch and wait until the pilot left by car, or any car left, not to hinder its leaving but to report to HQ at once by their car radio. Both of them realised the danger of their position – the arm of the Gorgon Khan had a very long reach. Both knew of the servants and guards of the late Khan accused by him of treason still rotting in police dungeons. But both also knew the reach of Inner Intelligence was more certain.

'Tell him to stop it, Azadeh, to stop the engines.'

'He's never before been so . . . so angry with me, and tonight . . .' Her eyes almost crossed in her rage. 'I don't think I can obey him.'

'You will!'

After a pause she muttered, 'When he's even a little angry, I can do nothing with him.'

The policemen saw her paleness and were sorry for her but more sorry for themselves – they had heard what had happened on the mountainside. God protect us from He of the Knife! What must it be like to marry such a barbarian who everyone knows drank the blood of the tribesmen he slaughtered, worships forest spirits against the law of God, and rolls naked in the snow, forcing her to do the same.

The engines spluttered and began to die and they saw Erikki bellow with rage and smash his great fist on the side of the cockpit, denting the aluminium with the force of his blow.

'Highness, with your permission I will go to bed – I think I will take a sleeping pill and hope that tomorrow is a better . . .' Her words trailed off.

'Yes. A sleeping pill is a good idea. Very good. I'm afraid I'll have to take two, my back hurts terribly and now I can't sleep without them.' Hakim added angrily, 'It's his fault! If it wasn't for him I wouldn't be in pain.' He turned to his bodyguard, 'Fetch my guards on the gate, I want to give them instructions. Come along, Azadeh.'

Painfully he walked off, Azadeh obediently and sullenly at his side. The engines started shrieking again. Irritably Hakim Khan turned and snapped at the policemen, 'If he doesn't stop in five minutes, order him to stop in my name! Five minutes, by God!'

Uneasily the two men watched them leave, the bodyguard with the two gate guards hurrying after them up the steps. 'If Her Highness can't deal with him, what can we do?' the older policeman said.

'With the Help of God the engines will continue until the barbarian is satisfied, or he stops them himself.'

The lights in the forecourt went out. After six minutes the engines were still starting and stopping. 'We'd better obey.' The young policeman was very nervous. 'The Khan said five. We're late.'

'Be prepared to run and don't irritate him unnecessarily. Take your safety catch off.' Nervously they went closer. 'Pilot!' But the pilot still had his back to them and was half inside the cockpit. Son of a dog! Closer, now up to the whirling blades. 'Pilot!' the corporal said loudly.

'He can't hear you, who can hear anything? You go forward, I'll cover you.'

The corporal nodded, commended his soul to God, and ducked into the wash of air. 'Pilot!' He had to go very close, and touch him. 'Pilot!' Now the pilot turned, his face grim, said something in barbarian that he did not understand. With a forced smile and forced politeness, he said, 'Please, Pilot Excellency, we would consider it an honour if you would stop the engines, His Highness the Khan has ordered it.' He saw the blank look, remembered that He of the Knife could not speak any civilised language, so he repeated what he had said, speaking louder and slower and using signs. To his enormous relief, the pilot nodded apologetically, turned some switches, and now the engines were slowing and the blades were slowing.

Praise be to God! Well done, how clever you are, the corporal thought, gratified. 'Thank you, Excellency Pilot. Thank you.' Very pleased with himself he imperiously peered into the cockpit. Now he saw the pilot making signs to him, clearly wishing to please him – as so he should, by God – inviting him to get into the pilot's seat. Puffed with pride, he watched the barbarian politely lean into the cockpit and move the controls and point at instruments.

Not able to contain his curiosity the younger policeman came under the blades that were circling slower and slower, up to the cockpit door. He leaned in to see better, fascinated by the banks of switches and dials that glowed in the darkness.

'By God, Corporal, have you ever seen so many dials and switches? You look as though you belong in that seat!'

'I wish I was a pilot,' the corporal said. 'I th—' He stopped, astonished, as his words were swallowed by a blinding red fog that sucked the breath out of his lungs and made the darkness complete.

Erikki had rammed the younger man's head against the corporal's, stunning both of them. Above him the rotors stopped. He looked around. No movement in the darkness, just a few lights on in the palace. No alien eyes or presence that he could sense. Quickly he stowed their guns behind the pilot's seat. It took only seconds to carry the two men to the cabin and lay them inside, force their mouths open, put in the sleeping pills that he had stolen from Azadeh's cabinet, and gag them. A moment to collect his breath, before he went forward and checked that all was ready for instant departure. Then he came back to the cabin. The two men had not moved. He leaned against the doorway ready to silence them again if need be. His throat was dry. Sweat beaded him. Waiting. Then he heard dogs and the sound of chain leashes. Quietly he readied the Sten gun. The wandering patrol of two armed guards and the Doberman pinschers passed around the palace but did not come near him. He watched the palace, his arm no longer in the sling.

In the Northern Slums: The ramshackle, canvas-covered ambulance trundled through the potholed streets. In the back were two medics and three stretchers and Hashemi lay on one, howling, haemorrhaging, most of the front of his loin torn out.

'In the Name of God, give him morphine,' Armstrong gasped through his own pain. He was slumped on his stretcher, half propped against the swaying side, holding a surgical dressing tightly against the bullet hole in his upper chest, quite oblivious of the blood pumping from the wound in his back that was soaking the crude dressing one of the medics had stuffed through the rent in his trenchcoat. 'Give him morphine. Hurry!' he told them again, cursing them in Farsi and English, hating them for their stupidity and rough handling – still in shock from the suddenness of the bullet and the attack that had come out of nowhere. Why why why?

'What can I do, Excellency?' came out of the darkness. 'We have none of this morphine. It's God's Will.' The man switched on a flashlight and almost blinded him, turned it on to Hashemi, then to the third stretcher. The youth there was already dead. Armstrong saw they had not bothered to close his eyes. Another burbling scream came from Hashemi.

'Put out the light, Ishmael,' the other medic said. 'You want to get us shot?'

Idly, Ishmael obeyed. Once more in darkness, he lit a cigarette, coughed, and cleared his throat noisily, pulled the canvas side screen aside for a moment to get his bearings. 'Only a few more minutes, with the Help of God.' He leaned down and shook Hashemi out of his unconscious peace into waking hell. 'Only a few more minutes, Excellency Colonel. Don't die yet,' he said helpfully. 'Only a few more minutes and you'll get proper treatment.'

They all lurched as a wheel went into a pothole. Pain blazed through Armstrong. When he felt the ambulance stop, he almost wept with relief. Other men pulled away the canvas tail cover and scrambled in. Rough hands grabbed his feet and dragged him down on to the stretcher and bound him with the safety straps. Through the hell mist of pain he saw Hashemi's stretcher being carried off into the night, then men lifted him carelessly, the pain was too much, and he fainted.

*   *   *

1137

The stretcher bearers stepped over the joub and went through the doorway in the high wall, into the sleazy corridor and along it, down a flight of stairs, and into a large cellar that was lit with oil lamps. Mzytryk said, 'Put him there!' He pointed to the second table. Hashemi was already on the first one, also strapped to his stretcher. Leisurely Mzytryk examined Armstrong's wounds, then Hashemi's, both men still unconscious.

'Good,' he said. 'Wait for me upstairs, Ishmael.'

Ishmael took off the grimy Red Cross armband and threw it into a corner with the others. 'Many of our people were martyred in the building. I doubt if any escaped.'

'Then you were wise not to join the meeting.'

Ishmael clomped upstairs to rejoin his friends who were noisily congratulating themselves on their success in grabbing the enemy leader and his running dog, the foreigner. All were trusted, hard-core Islamic-Marxist fighters, not a medic among them.

Mzytryk waited until he was alone, then took a small penknife and probed Hashemi deeply. The bellowing scream pleased him. When it subsided he lifted the pail of icy water and dashed it into the colonel's face. The eyes opened and the terror and pain therein pleased him even more. 'You wanted to see me, Colonel? You murdered my son, Fedor. I'm General Petr Oleg Mzytryk.' He used the knife again. Hashemi's face became grotesque and he howled, screaming and babbling incoherently, trying to fight out of his bonds.

'This's for my son . . . and this for my son . . . and this for my son . . .'

Hashemi's heart was strong, and he lasted minutes, begging for mercy, begging for death, the One God for death and for vengeance. He died badly.

For a moment Mzytryk stood over him, his nostrils rebelling against the stench. But he did not need to force himself to remember what these two had done to his son to drag him down to the third level. Pahmudi's report had been explicit. 'Hashemi Fazir, you're repaid, you shiteater,' he said and spat in his face. Then he turned and stopped. Armstrong was awake and watching him from the stretcher on the other side of the cellar. Cold blue eyes. Bloodless face. The lack of fear astonished him. I'll soon change that, he thought and took out the penknife. Then he noticed Armstrong's right arm was out of the straps, but before he could do anything Armstrong had reached up for the lapel of his trenchcoat and now held the tip and the hidden cyanide capsule it contained near his mouth. 'Don't move!' Armstrong warned.

Mzytryk was too seasoned to consider rushing him, the distance too far. In his side pocket was an automatic but before he could get it out he was sure that Armstrong's teeth would crush the capsule and three seconds left was not nearly enough time for vengeance. His only hope was that Armstrong's pain would make him faint, or lose concentration. He leaned back against the other table and cursed him.

When the stretcher-bearers had tightened Armstrong's straps in the darkness of the ambulance, he had instinctively used his strength against the straps to give himself just enough space to pull out his arm – in case the pain became too much for him. Another capsule was secreted in his shirt collar. He had trembled through Hashemi's dying, thanking God for the respite that had allowed him to drag his arm free, the effort terrible. But once he had touched the capsule, his terror had left him and with it, much of his pain. He had made peace with himself at the edge of death where life is so utterly sublime.

'We're . . . we're professionals,' he said. 'We didn't murder your . . . your son. He was alive when . . . when General Janan took him away for Pahmudi.'

'Liar!' Mzytryk heard the weakness in the voice and knew he would not have to wait much longer. He readied.

'Read the official . . . official documents . . . SAVAMA must have made some . . . and those of your God-cursed KGB.'

'You think I'm such a fool you can set me against Pahmudi before you die?'

'Read the reports, ask questions, you could get the truth. But you KGB bastards never like the truth. I tell you he was alive when SAVAMA took him.'

Mzytryk was put off balance. It wouldn't be normal for a professional like Armstrong – near death, one way or another, to waste time suggesting such an investigation without being certain of the outcome. 'Where are the tapes?' he said, watching him carefully, seeing the eyes beginning to flicker, great tiredness from loss of blood. Any second now. 'Where are the tapes?'

'There weren't any. Not . . . not from the third level.' Armstrong's strength was ebbing. The pain had gone now – along with time. It took a bigger and bigger effort every second to concentrate. But the tapes must be protected, a copy already safely en route to London along with a special report. 'Your son was brave and strong and gave away nothing to us. What . . . what Pahmudi hacked . . . hacked out of him I don't know . . . Pahmudi's thugs . . . it was them or your own scum. He was al . . . alive when your lot took him. Pahmudi told Hashemi.'

That's possible, Mzytryk thought uneasily. Those incompetent, motherless shiteaters in Tehran messed up our Iran operations for years, misread the Shah for years, and befouled our work of generations. 'I'll find out. By my son's head I'll find out but that won't help you – comrade!'

'One favour deserves . . . one deserves ano . . . another. You knocked off Roger, Roger Crosse, eh?'

Mzytryk laughed, happy to taunt him and exploit the waiting. 'I arranged it, yes. And AMG, remember him? And Talbot, but I told Pahmudi to use this shiteater Fazir for that 16/a.' He watched the cold blue eyes narrow and wondered what was behind them.

Armstrong was searching his memory. AMG? Ah, yes, Alan Medford Grant: born 1905, dean of their counter intelligence agents. In 1963, as Ian Dunross's secret informant, he fingered a mole in the Noble House. And another in my Special Branch who turned out to be my best friend.

'Liar! AMG was killed in a motorcycle accident in '63.'

'It was assisted. We'd had a 16/a out on that traitor for a year or more – and his Jap wife.'

'He wasn't married.'

'You bastards know nothing. Special Branch? Turd-heads. She was Jap Intelligence. She had an accident in Sydney the same year.'

Armstrong allowed himself a little smile. The AMG motorcycle 'accident' had been organised by the KGB but had been restaged by MI6. The death certificate was genuine, someone else's, and Alan Medford Grant still operates successfully though with a different face and different cover that even I don't know. But a wife? Japanese? Was that another smoke screen, or another secret? Wheels within wheels within . . .

The past beckoned Armstrong. With an effort he put his mind on what he truly wanted to know, to check if he was right or wrong, no time to waste anymore, none. 'Who's the fourth man – our arch traitor?'

The question hung in the cellar. Mzytryk was startled and then he smiled for Armstrong had given him the key to have his revenge psychologically. He told him the name and saw the shock. And the name of the fifth man, even the sixth. 'MI6's riddled with our agents, not just moles, so's MI5, most of your trade unions – Ted Everly's one of ours, Broadhurst and Lord Grey – remember him from Hong Kong? – not just Labour though they're our best seeding ground. Names?' he said gloating, knowing he was safe. 'Look in *Who's Who*! High up in the banks, the City, in the Foreign Office – Henley's another of ours and I've already had a copy of your report – up to Cabinets, perhaps even into Downing Street. We've half a thousand professionals of our own in Britain, not counting your own traitors.' His laugh was cruel.

'And Smedley-Taylor?'

'Oh, yes, him too an—' Abruptly Mzytryk's gloating ceased, his guard slammed shut. 'How do you know about him? If you know about him . . . Eh?'

Armstrong was satisfied. Fedor Rakoczy had not lied. All those names on the tapes already gone, already safe, Henley never trusted, not even Talbot. He was content and sad, sorry that he would not be around to catch them himself. Someone will. AMG will.

His eyes fluttered, his hand slid away from his lapel. Instantly Mzytryk rushed the space, moving very fast for such a big man, and pinioned the arm between the table and his leg, ripped the lapel away, and now Armstrong was powerless and at his mercy. 'Wake up, *matyeryebyets*!' he said exultantly, the pocket knife out. 'How did you know about Smedley?'

But Armstrong did not answer. Death had come quietly.

Mzytryk was enraged, his heart thundering. 'Never mind, he's gone, no need to waste time,' he muttered out loud. The mother-eating bastard went into hell knowing he was the tool of traitors, some of them. But how did he know about Smedley-Taylor? To hell with him, what if he told the truth about my son?

In the corner of the cellar was a can of kerosene. He began to slop it over the bodies, his rage dissipating. 'Ishmael!' he called up the stairs. When he had finished with the kerosene he threw the can into the corner. Ishmael and another man came down into the cellar. 'Are you ready to leave?' Mzytryk asked them.

'Yes, with the Help of God.'

'And with the help of ourselves too,' Mzytryk said lightly. He wiped his hands, tired but satisfied with the way the day and the night had gone. Now just a short ride to the outskirts of Tabriz to his helicopter. An hour – less – to the Tbilisi dacha and Vertinskya. In a few weeks the young puppy Hakim will arrive, with or without my pishkesh, Azadeh. If it's without, it will be expensive for him. 'Start the fire,' he said crisply, 'and we'll be going.'

'Here, Comrade General!' Cheerfully Ishmael threw him some matches. 'It's your privilege to finish that which you began.'

Mzytryk had caught the matches. 'Good,' he said. The first did not light. Nor the second. The third did. He backed to the stairs and carefully threw it. Flames gushed to the ceiling and to the wooden rafters. Then Ishmael's foot went into his back and sent him sprawling, head first, into the outskirts of the fire. In panic, Mzytryk screamed and beat at the flames and he whirled and scuttled on his blackening hands and knees back towards the stairs, stopped a moment beating at his fur lapels, coughing and choking in the billowing black smoke and smell of burning flesh. Somehow he lurched to his feet. The first bullet smashed his kneecap, he howled and reeled backwards into the fire, the second broke his other leg and hurled him down. Impotently he beat at the flames, his screams drowned by the gathering roar of the inferno. And he became a torch.

Ishmael and the other man jumped back up the stairs to the first landing, almost colliding with others who had rushed down. They gaped at the twitching body of Mzytryk, the flames now eating his boots. 'What you do that for?' one of them said, aghast.

'My brother was martyred at the house, so was your cousin.'

'As God wants, but Ishmael, the comrade general? God protect us, he supplied us with money and arms and explosives – why kill him?'

'Why not? Wasn't the son of a dog an arrogant, ill-mannered Satanist? He wasn't even a Person of the Book,' Ishmael said contemptuously. 'Dozens more where they came from, thousands. They need us, we don't need them. He deserved to die. Didn't he come alone, tempting me?' He spat towards the body. 'Important persons should have bodyguards.'

A shaft of flames reached for them. They retreated hastily. The fire caught the wooden stairs and was spreading rapidly. In the street they all piled into the truck, no longer an ambulance. Ishmael looked back at the flames gutting the house and laughed uproariously. 'Now that dog's a burnt father! May all Infidels perish as quickly.'

In the Palace Forecourt: Erikki was leaning against the 212 when he saw the lights in the Khan's quarters on the second floor go out. A careful check on the two drugged policemen fast asleep in the cabin reassured him. Quietly he slid the cabin door closed, eased his knife under his belt and picked up the Sten. With the skill of a night hunter he moved noiselessly towards the palace. The Khan's guards on the gate did not notice him go – why should they bother to watch him? The Khan had given them clear orders to leave the pilot alone and not agitate him, that surely he would soon tire of playing with the machine. 'If he takes a car, let him. If the police want trouble, that's their problem.'

'Yes, Highness,' they had both told him, glad they were not responsible for He of the Knife.

Erikki slipped through the front door and along the dimly lit corridor to the stairs leading to the north wing, well away from the Khan's area. Noiselessly up the stairs and along another corridor. He saw a shaft of light under the door of their suite. Without hesitation he went into the anteroom, closing the door silently after him. Across the room to their bedroom door and swung it open. To his shock Mina, Azadeh's maid, was there too. She was kneeling on the bed where she had been massaging Azadeh who was fast asleep.

'Oh, your pardon,' she stuttered, terrified of him like all the servants. 'I didn't hear Your Excellency. Her Highness asked . . . asked me to continue as long as I could with . . . with the massage, then to sleep here.'

Erikki face was a mask, the oil streaks on his cheeks and on the taped bandage over his ear making him appear more dangerous. 'Azadeh!'

'Oh you won't wake her, Excellency, she took a . . . she took two sleeping pills and asked me to apologise for her if you c –'

'Dress her!' he hissed.

Mina blanched. 'But, Excellency!' Her heart almost stopped as she saw a knife appear in his hand.

'Dress her quickly and if you make a sound I'll gut you. *Do it*!' He saw her grab the dressing gown. 'Not that, Mina! Warm clothes, ski clothes – by all the gods, it doesn't matter which but be quick!' He watched her, positioning himself between her and the door so she couldn't bolt. On the bedside table was the sheathed kukri. A twinge went through him and he tore his eyes away, and when he was sure Mina was obeying he took Azadeh's purse from the dressing table. All her papers were in it, ID, passport, driver's licence, birth certificate, everything. Good, he thought, and blessed Aysha for the gift that Azadeh had told him about before dinner and thanked his ancient gods for giving him the plan this morning. Ah, my darling, did you think I'd really leave you?

Also in the purse was her soft silk jewellery bag which seemed heavier than normal. His eyes widened at the emeralds and diamonds and pearl necklaces and pendants that it now contained. The rest of Najoud's, he thought, the same that Hakim had used to barter with the tribesmen and that I retrieved from Bayazid. In the mirror he saw Mina gaping at the wealth he held in his hand, Azadeh inert and almost dressed. 'Hurry up!' he grated at her reflection.

* * *

At the Ambush Roadblock below the Palace: Both the sergeant of police and his driver in the car waiting beside the road were staring up at the palace four hundred yards away, the sergeant using binoculars. Just the dim lights on the outside of the vast gatehouse, no sign of any guards, or of his own two men. 'Drive up there,' the sergeant said uneasily. 'Something's wrong, by God! They're either asleep or dead. Go slowly and quietly.' He reached into the scabbard beside him and put a shell into the breech of the M16. The driver gunned the engine and eased out into the empty roadway.

At the Main Gate: Babak, the guard, was leaning against a pillar inside the massive iron gate that was closed and bolted. The other guard was curled up nearby on some sacking, fast asleep. Through the bars of the gate could be seen the snowbanked road that wound down to the city. Beyond the empty fountain in the forecourt, a hundred yards away, was the helicopter. The icy wind moved the blades slightly.

He yawned and stamped his feet against the cold, then began to relieve himself through the bars, absently waving the stream this way and that. Earlier when they had been dismissed by the Khan and had come back to their post, they had found that the two policemen had gone. 'They're off to scrounge some food, or to have a sleep,' he had said. 'God curse all police.'

Babak yawned, looking forward to the dawn when he would be off duty for a few hours. Only the pilot's car to usher through just before dawn, then relock the gate, and soon he would be in bed with a warm body. Automatically he scratched his genitals, feeling himself stir and harden. Idly he leaned back, playing with himself, his eyes checking that the gate's heavy bolt was in place and the small side gate also locked. Then the edge of his eyes caught a movement. He centered it. The pilot was slinking out of a side door of the palace with a large bundle over his shoulder, his arm no longer in the sling and carrying a gun. Hastily Babak buttoned up, slipped his rifle off his shoulder, moved farther out of view. Cautiously he kicked the other guard who awoke soundlessly. 'Look,' he whispered, 'I thought the pilot was still in the cabin of the helicopter.'

Wide-eyed, they watched Erikki keep to the shadows, then silently dart across the open space to the far side of the helicopter. 'What's he carrying? What's the bundle?'

'It looked like a carpet, a rolled-up carpet,' the other whispered. Sound of the far cockpit door opening.

'But why? In all the Names of God, what's he doing?'

1144

There was barely enough light but their vision was good and hearing good. They heard an approaching car but were at once distracted by the sound of the far cabin door sliding open. They waited, hardly breathing, then saw him dump what appeared to be two similar bundles under the belly of the helicopter, then duck under the tail boom and reappear on their side. For a moment he stood there, looking towards them but not seeing them, then eased the cockpit door open, and got in with the gun, the carpet bundle now propped on the opposite seat.

Abruptly the jets began and both guards jumped. 'God protect us, what do we do?'

Nervously Babak said, 'Nothing. The Khan told us exactly: "Leave the pilot alone, whatever he does, he's dangerous," that's what he told us, didn't he? "When the pilot takes the car near dawn let the pilot leave." ' Now he had to talk loudly over the rising scream. 'We do nothing.'

'But we weren't told he would start his engines again, the Khan didn't say that, or sneak out with bundles of carpets.'

'You're right. As God wants, but you're right.' Their nervousness increased. They had not forgotten the guards jailed and flogged by the old Khan for disobedience or failure, or those banished by the new one. 'The engines sound good now, don't you think?' They both looked up as lights came on at the second floor, the Khan's floor, then they jerked around as the police car came swirling to a stop outside the gate. The sergeant jumped out, a flashlight in his hand. 'What's going on, by God?' the sergeant shouted. 'Open the gate, by God! Where're my men?'

Babak rushed for the side gate and pulled the bolt back. In the cockpit Erikki's hands were moving as quickly as possible, the wound in his arm inhibiting him. The sweat ran down his face and mixed with a trickle of blood from his ear where the taped bandages had become displaced. His breath came in great pants from the long run from the north wing with Azadeh bundled in the carpet, drugged and helpless, and he was cursing the needles to rise quicker. He had seen the lights go on in Hakim's apartments and now heads were peering out. Before he had left their suite he had carefully knocked Mina unconscious, hoping he had not hurt her, to protect her as well as himself so she would not sound an alarm or be accused of collusion, had wrapped Azadeh in the carpet and attached the kukri to his belt.

'Come on,' he snarled at the needles, then glimpsed two men at the main gate in police uniforms. Suddenly the helicopter was bathed in a shaft of light from the flashlight and his stomach turned over. Without thinking, he grabbed his Sten, shoved the nose through the pilot's window, and pulled the trigger, aiming high.

The four men scattered for cover as bullets ricocheted off the gate masonry. In his panic the sergeant dropped the flash, but not before all had seen two crumpled, inert bodies of the corporal and the other policeman sprawled on the ground and presumed them dead. As the burst stopped, the sergeant scrambled for the side gate and his car and his M16.

'Fire, by God,' the driver policeman shouted. Whipped by the excitement, Babak squeezed the trigger, the shots going wild. Incautiously, the driver moved into the open to retrieve the flash. Another burst from the helicopter and he leaped backward, 'Son of a burnt father . . .' The three of them cowered in safety. Another burst at the flashlight danced it, then smashed it.

Erikki saw his escape plan in ruins, the 212 a helpless target on the ground. Time had run out for him. For a split second he considered closing down. The needles were far too low. Then he emptied his Sten at the gate with a howling battle-cry, slammed the throttles forward, and let out another primeval scream that chilled those who heard it. The jets went to full power, shrieked under the strain as he put the stick forward and dragged her airborne a few inches and now, tail high, she lurched ahead, skids screeching on the forecourt as she bounced and rose and fell back and bounced again and now was airborne but lumbering badly. At the main gate the driver tore the gun from a guard and went to the pillar, peered around it to see the helicopter escaping, and pulled the trigger.

On the second floor of the palace Hakim was blearily leaning out of his bedroom window, grasped from drugged sleep by the noise. His bodyguard, Margol, was beside him. They saw the 212 almost collide with a small wooden outhouse, her skids ripping away part of the roof, then struggle onward in a drunken climb. Outside the walls was the police car, the sergeant silhouetted in the beam of its headlights. Hakim watched him aim and willed the bullets to miss.

Erikki heard bullets zinging off metal, prayed they had touched nothing vital, and banked dangerously away from the exposed outer wall towards some space where he could slip behind the safety of the palace. In the wild turn the bundled carpet containing Azadeh toppled over and tangled with the controls. For a moment he was lost, then he used his massive strength to shove her away. The wound in his forearm split open.

Now he swerved behind the north wing, the chopper still only a few feet high and heading towards the other perimeter wall near the hut where Ross and Gueng had been hidden. Still only a few feet high, a stray bullet punctured his door, hacked into the instrument panel, exploding glass.

When the helicopter had disappeared from Hakim's view, he had hobbled across the huge bedroom, past the wood fire that blazed merrily, out into the corridor to the windows there. 'Can you see him?' he asked, panting from the exertion.

'Yes, Highness,' Margol said, and pointed excitedly. 'There!'

The 212 was just a black shape against more blackness, then the perimeter floodlights came on and Hakim saw her stagger over the wall with only inches to spare and dip down. A few seconds later she had reappeared, gaining speed and altitude. At that moment Aysha came running along the corridor, crying out hysterically, 'Highness, Highness . . . Azadeh's gone, she's gone . . . that devil's kidnapped her and Mina's been knocked unconscious . . .'

It was hard for Hakim to concentrate against the pills, his eyelids never so heavy. 'What are you talking about?'

'Azadeh's gone, your sister's gone, he wrapped her in a carpet and he's kidnapped her, taken her with him . . .' She stopped, afraid, seeing the look on Hakim's face, ashen in this bleak light, eyes drooping – not knowing about the sleeping pills. 'He's kidnapped her!'

'But that . . . that's not possible . . . not poss –'

'Oh, but it is, she's kidnapped and Mina's unconscious!'

Hakim blinked at her, then stuttered, 'Sound the alarm, Aysha! If she's kidnapped . . . by God, sound . . . sound the alarm! I've taken sleeping pills and they . . . I'll deal with that devil tomorrow, by God, I can't now, not now, but send someone . . . to the police . . . to the Green Bands . . . spread the alarm, there's a Khan's ransom on his head! Margol, help me back to my room.'

Frightened servants and guards were collecting at the end of the corridor and Aysha ran tearfully back to them, telling them what had happened and what the Khan had ordered.

Hakim groped for his bed and lay back, exhausted. 'Margol, tell the . . . tell guards to arrest those fools on the gate. How could they have let that happen?'

'They can't have been vigilant, Highness.' Margol was sure they would be blamed – someone had to be blamed – even though he had been present when the Khan had told them not to interfere with the pilot. He gave the order and came back. 'Are you all right, Highness?'

'Yes, thank you. Don't leave the room . . . wake me at dawn. Keep the fire going and wake me at dawn.'

Gratefully Hakim let himself go into the sleep that beckoned so seductively, his back no longer paining him, his mind focused on Azadeh and on Erikki. When she had walked out of the small room and left him alone with Erikki, he had allowed his grief to show: 'There's no way out of the trap, Erikki. We're trapped, all of us, you, Azadeh, and me. I still can't believe she'd renounce Islam, at the same time I'm convinced she won't obey me or you. I've no wish to hurt her but I've no alternative, her immortal soul is more important than her temporary life.'

'I could save her soul, Hakim. With your help.'

'How?' He had seen the tension in Erikki, his face tight, eyes strange.

'Remove her need to destroy it.'

'How?'

'Say, hypothetically, this madman of a pilot was not Muslim but barbarian and so much in love with his wife that he goes a little more mad and instead of just escaping by himself, he suddenly knocks her out, kidnaps her, flies her out of her own country against her will, and refuses to allow her to return. In most countries a husband can . . . can take extreme measures to hold on to his wife, even to force her obedience and curb her. This way she won't have broken her oath, she'll never need to give up Islam, you'll never need to harm her, and I'll keep my woman.'

'It's a cheat,' Hakim had said, bewildered. 'It's a cheat.'

'It's not, it's make-believe, hypothetical, all of it, only make-believe, but hypothetically it fulfils the rules you swore to abide by, and no one'd ever believe the sister of the Gorgon Khan would willingly break her oath and renounce Islam over a barbarian. No one. Even now you don't know for certain she would, do you?'

Hakim had tried to find the flaws. There's none, he had thought, astonished. And it would solve most of . . . wouldn't it solve everything if it came to pass? If Erikki was to do this without her knowledge and help . . . Kidnap her! It's true, no one'd ever believe she'd willingly break her oath. Kidnapped! I could deplore it publicly and rejoice for her in secret, if I want her to leave, and him to live. But I have to, it's the only way: to save her soul I have to save him.

In the peace of the bedroom he opened his eyes briefly. Flame shadows danced on the ceiling. Erikki and Azadeh were there. God will forgive me, he thought, swooping into sleep. I wonder if I'll ever see her again?

CHAPTER

69

Tehran – Near the University: 11:58 P.M. In the chill darkness Sharazad stood with the phalanx of Green Bands protecting the front of the massed, shouting Islamics. They were packed together, chanting 'Al-lahhhh-u Akbarrrrr' in unison, a living barrier against the two to three thousand roaring, leftist students and agitators approaching down the road. Flashlights and burning torches, some cars on fire, guns, sticks, wooden clubs. Her fingers gripped the automatic in her pocket, grenade ready in her other pocket. 'God is Great!' she shrieked.

The enemy was closing fast and Sharazad saw their clenched fists, the tumult growing on both sides, shouts more hoarse, nerves more stretched, anticipation rocketing – 'There is no other God but God . . .' Now their enemies were so near she could see individual faces. Suddenly she realised they were not massed satanic revolutionaries, not all of them, but the vast majority students, men and women of her own age, the women bravely not chadored and shouting for women's rights, the vote, and all the sensible, God-given, hard-fought-for, never-turning-back things.

1149

She was transported back to the heady excitement of the Women's March, all of them in their best clothes, hair free, as free as their hair, with freedom and justice for all in their great new Islamic republic where she and her son-to-be and Tommy would live happily ever after. But there again in front of her was the knife-wielding fanatic tearing the future away, but that didn't matter for her. Ibrahim had stopped him, Ibrahim, the student leader, he was there to save her. Oh, Ibrahim, are you here tonight, leading them now as you did with us? Are you here once more fighting for freedom and justice and women's rights or were you martyred in Kowiss as you wanted, killing your evil, two-faced mullah who murdered your father as mine was also murdered?

But . . . but Father was killed by Islamics, not leftists, she thought bewildered. And the Imam's still implacably for everything as it was in the Prophet's time . . . And Meshang . . . And Tommy forced out. And forced divorce and forced marriage to that foul old man and no rights!

'What am I doing here?' She gasped in the pandemonium. 'I should be over there with them, I should be over there with them, not here . . . no, no, not there either! What about my child, my son-to-be, it's dangerous for him an –'

Somewhere a gun went off, then others and mayhem became general, those in the fore trying to retreat and those behind trying to get to the fight. Around Sharazad there was a mindless surge. She felt herself being crushed and carried forward, her feet hardly touching the ground. A woman beside her screamed and went under the feet. An old man stumbled, and vanished below mumbling the Shahada, almost bringing her down. Someone's elbow went into her stomach, she cried out in pain and her fear became terror. 'Tommyyy! Help meeeee . . .' she shrieked.

A hundred yards or so ahead Tom Lochart was pressed against a shop front by the student marchers, his coat torn, peaked cap gone, more desperate than he had ever been. For hours he had been searching the groups of students hoping against hope to find her, sure she was somewhere among them. Where else would she go? Surely not to this student's apartment, the one Jari said she met. This Ibrahim or whatever his name was, who meant nothing. Better she's there than here, he thought in despair. Oh, God, let me find her.

Chanting women passed, most in Western dress, jeans, jackets, and then he saw her. He fought alongside but once more he had made a mistake and he apologised and shoved his way to the side again, a few curses shouted after him. Then he thought he saw her on the far side of the roadway but again he was mistaken. The girl wore similar ski clothes to Sharazad and had the same hairstyle and was about her age. But she carried a Marxist-Islamic banner and, scourged by his disappointment, he cursed her, hating her for her stupidity. The shouts and countershouts were reaching him too, agitating him, and he wanted to pick up the cudgel and smash the evil out of them.

Oh, God, help me find her. 'God IS great,' he muttered, and though he was frantic with worry for her, at the same time his heart was soaring. Becoming Muslim will make all the difference. Now they will accept me, I'm one of them, I can go on the Hajj to Mecca, I can worship in any mosque, colour or race means nothing to God. Only belief. I believe in God and that Mohammed was the Prophet of God. I won't be fundamentalist, or Shi'a. I'll be orthodox Sunni. I'll find a teacher and study and learn Arabic. And I'll fly for IranOil and the new regime and we will be happy, Sharazad and I . . .

A gun went off nearby, fires of a burning tyre barricade soared into the air as small groups of screaming students were throwing themselves at the ranks of the Green Bands, other guns began firing, and now the whole street erupted into shouting, heaving bodies, the weak crushed underfoot. A berserk phalanx of youths dragged him with them towards the fighting.

Eighty yards away Sharazad was screaming, fighting for her life, trying to shove and kick and push her way to the side where there would be comparative safey. Her chador was torn away, her scarf vanished. She was bruised, pain in her stomach. Those around her were a mob now, hacking at those opposing it, all for themselves but wrapped into the mob beast. The battle waged back and forth, no one knowing who was friend or enemy, except mullahs and Green Bands who shouted, trying to control the riot. With an earsplitting roar, the Islamic mob hesitated a moment, then advanced. The weak fell and were crushed. Men, women. Screams and shouts and pandemonium, all calling on their own version of God.

Desperately the students fought back but they were swamped. Relentlessly. Many went down. Feet trampled them. Now the rest broke, the rout began, and the sides intermixed.

Lochart used his superior height and strength to batter his way to the side and now stood between two cars, protected by them for the moment. A few yards away he saw a small, half-hidden alleyway that led towards a broken-down mosque where there would be sanctuary. Ahead was a huge explosion as a car tank exploded, scattering flames. The fortunate were killed instantly, the wounded began to scream. In the flame light he thought he caught a glimpse of her, then a group of fleeing youths swarmed over him, a fist went into his back, others pummelled him out of the way, and he fell under their boots.

Sharazad was only thirty yards away, hair awry, clothes torn, still locked into the press of the mob, still pulled along by the juggernaut, still screaming for help, no one hearing or caring. 'Tommyyy . . . help meeeee . . .'

The crowd parted momentarily. She darted for the opening, squeezing her way towards the barred and locked shops and parked cars. The tumult was lessening. Arms pushed for breathing space, hands wiped sweat and filth off, and men saw their neighbours. 'You God-cursed communist harlot,' the man in her path shouted, eyes almost out of his sockets with rage.

'I'm not, I'm not, I'm Muslim,' she gasped, but his hands had caught her ski jacket – the zipper wrecked – his hand went in and grabbed her breast.

'Harlot! Muslim women don't flaunt themselves, Muslim women wear chad –'

'I lost it – it was torn off me,' she shrieked.

'Harlot! God curse you! Our women wear chador.'

'I lost it – it was torn off me,' she shrieked again and tried to pull away, 'There is no oth –'

'Harlot! Whore! Satanist!' he shouted, his ears closed to her, the madness on him and the feel of her breast through her silk shirt and undershirt further inflaming him. His fingers clawed at the silk and ripped it away and now he held her roundness, his other hand dragging her closer to subdue her and strangle her as she kicked and screamed. Those nearby jostled them, or tried to move out of the way, hard to see in the darkness that was only rent by the light from fires, not knowing what was going on except someone had caught a leftist whore here in the ranks of the Godly. 'By God she's not a leftist, I heard her shouting for Imam . . .' someone called out but cries ahead overrode him, another pocket of fighting flared up and men shoved forward to help or elbowed space to retreat and they left her and him together.

She fought him with her nails and feet and voice, his breath and obscenities choking her. With a final effort she called on God for help, hacked upwards and missed and remembered her gun. Her hand grasped it, shoved it into him, and pulled the trigger. The man screamed, most of his genitals blown off, and he collapsed howling. There was a sudden hush around her. And space. Her hand came out of the pocket still holding the gun. A man near her grabbed it.

1152

Blankly she stared down at her attacker who twisted and moaned in the dirt.

'God is Great,' she stuttered, then noticed her disarray and pulled her jacket together, looked up and saw the hatred surrounding her. 'He was attacking me . . . God is Great, God is Great . . .'

'She's just saying that, she's a leftist . . .' a woman screeched.

'Look at her clothes, she's not one of us . . .'

Just a few yards away, Lochart was picking himself out of the dirt, head hurting, ears ringing, hardly able to see or to hear. With a great effort he stood upright, then shouldered his way forward towards the mouth of the alley and safety. Others had had the same thought and already the entrance was clogged. Then her voice, mingled with shouting, reached him and he turned back.

He saw her at bay, backed against a wall, a mob around her, clothes half torn off, the sleeve of her jacket ripped away, eyes staring, grenade in her hand. At that second a man made a move at her, she pulled the pin out, the man froze, everyone began to back off. Lochart burst through the cordon to reach her and seized the grenade, keeping the lever down. 'Get away from her,' he roared in Farsi and stood in front of her, protecting her. 'She's Muslim, you sons of dogs. She's Muslim and my wife and I'm Muslim!'

'You're a foreigner and she's a leftist by God!'

Lochart darted at the man and his fist now armoured with the grenade crushed the man's mouth in, shattering his jaw. 'God is Great,' Lochart bellowed. Others took up the shout and those who disbelieved him did nothing, afraid of him but more afraid of the grenade. Holding her tightly with his free arm, half guiding, half carrying her, Lochart went at the first rank, grenade ready. 'Please let us pass, God is Great, peace be with you.' The first rank parted, then the next, and he shoved through, muttering 'God is Great . . . Peace be with you,' continually until he had broken out of the cordon and into the crowded alley, stumbling in the filth and potholes, bumping people here and there in the darkness. A few lights were on outside the mosque ahead. At the fountain he stopped, he broke the ice, and with one hand scooped some water into his face, the torrent in his brain still raging, 'Christ,' he muttered and used more water.

'Oh, Tommyyyy!' Sharazad cried out, her voice far off and strange, near breaking. 'Where did you come from, where, oh I . . . I was so afraid, so afraid.'

'So was I,' he stammered, the words hard to get out. 'I've been searching for hours for you, my darling.' He pulled her to him. 'You all right?'

'Oh, yes, yes.' Her arms were tight around him, her face buried in his shoulder.

Sudden firing, more shrieks back towards the street. Instinctively he held her tighter but sensed no danger here. Just half-seen crowds passing in the semi-darkness, the firing becoming more distant and the noise of the riot decreasing.

We're safe at last. No, not yet, there's still the grenade – no pin to make it safe, no way to make it safe. Over her head and those of the passers-by, he saw a burnt-out building by the side of the mosque across the little square. I can get rid of it there safely, he persuaded himself, not thinking clearly yet, holding on to her and gathering strength from her embrace. The crowds had increased, now packing the alley. Until their numbers lessened it would be difficult and dangerous to dispose of the grenade across the square so he moved her closer to the fountain where the darkness was deeper. 'Don't worry. We'll wait a second, then go on.' They were talking English, softly – so much to tell, so much to ask. 'You sure you're all right?'

'Yes, oh, yes. How did you find me? How? When did you get back? How did you find me?'

'I . . . I flew back tonight and went to the house but you'd gone.' Then he burst out, 'Sharazad, I've become Muslim.'

She gaped at him. 'But . . . but that was just a trick, a trick to get away from them!'

'No, I swear it! I really have. I swear it. I said the Shahada in front of three witnesses, Meshang and Zarah and Jari, and I believe. I do believe. Everything's going to be all right now.'

Her disbelief vanished seeing the joy in him, his voice telling her over and over what had happened. 'Oh, how wonderful, Tommy,' she said, beyond herself with happiness, at the same time utterly certain that, for them, nothing would change. Nothing will change Meshang, she thought. Meshang will find a way to destroy us whether Tommy's a Believer or not. Nothing will change, the divorce will stay, the marriage will stay. Unless . . .

Her fears vanished. 'Tommy, can we leave Tehran tonight? Can we run away tonight, my darling?'

'There's no need for that, not now. I've wonderful plans. I've quit S-G. Now that I'm Muslim I can stay and fly for IranOil, don't you see?' Both were oblivious of the crowds passing, packed more tightly, anxious to be home. 'No need to worry, Sharazad.'

Someone stumbled and jostled him, then another, a pileup beginning that encroached on their little sanctuary. She saw him shove a man away and other began to curse. Quickly she took his hand, and pulled him into the mainstream. 'Let's go home, husband,' she said loudly in coarsened Farsi, cautioning him, holding on tightly, then whispered, 'Speak Farsi,' then a little louder, 'We're not safe here and we can talk better at home.'

'Yes, yes, woman. Better we go home.' Walking was better and safer and Sharazad was here and tomorrow would solve tomorrow, tonight there would be a bath and sleep and food and sleep and no dreams or only happy ones.

'If we wanted to leave tonight secretly, could we? Could we, Tommy?'

Tiredness washed over him and he almost shouted at her that didn't she understand what he had just told her? Instead he held back the anger and just said, 'There's no need to escape now.'

'You're quite right, husband, as always. But could we?'

'Yes, yes, I suppose so,' he said wearily and told how, stopping and starting again with the rest of the pedestrians as the alley narrowed, more claustrophobic every moment.

Now she was aglow, quite sure she could convince him. Tomorrow they would leave. Tomorrow morning I'll collect my jewels, we'll pretend to Meshang we'll meet him in the bazaar at lunchtime, but by then we will be flying south in Tommy's plane. He can fly in the Gulf states or Canada or anywhere, there you can be Muslim and Canadian without harm, they told me when I went to the embassy. And soon, in a month or so we'll come home to Iran and live here for ever.

Contentedly she went even closer to him, hidden in the crowd and by the darkness, not afraid anymore, certain their future would be grand. Now that he's a Believer he will go to Paradise, God is Great, God is Great, and so will I, together, with the Help of God, we will leave sons and daughters behind us. And then, when we are old, if he dies first, on the fortieth day I will make sure his spirit is remembered perfectly, and then, afterwards, I will curse his younger wife or wives and their children, then put my affairs in order and peacefully wait to join him – in God's time. 'Oh, I do love you, Tommy, I'm so sorry that you've had so much trouble . . . trouble over me . . .'

Now they were breaking out of the alley into a street. The crowds were even heavier, swarming all over the roadway and in the traffic. But there was a lightness on them all, men, women, mullahs, Green Bands, young and old, the night well spent doing God's work. 'Allah-u Akbar!' someone shouted, the words echoed and re-echoed by a thousand throats. Ahead an impatient car lurched, bumped into some pedestrians who bumped into others who brought down others amid curses and laughter, Sharazad and Lochart among them, no one hurt. He had caught her safely and, laughing together, they rested on the ground a moment, the grenade still tight in his hand. They did not hear its warning hiss – without knowing it in falling he had slackened the lever an instant, but just enough. For an infinity of time he smiled at her and she at him. 'God is Great,' she said joyously and he echoed her just as confidently. And, the same instant, they died.

Saturday
March 3, 1979

Al Shargaz: 6:34 A.M. The tip of the sun crested the horizon and turned black desert into a crimson sea, staining the old port city and dhows in the Gulf beyond. From the minaret loudspeakers muezzins began but the music in their voices did not please Gavallan or any of the other S-G personnel on the veranda of the Oasis Hotel, finishing a hurried breakfast. 'It gets to you, Scrag, doesn't it?' Gavallan said.

'Right you are, sport,' Scragger said. He, Rudi Lutz and Pettikin shared Gavallan's table, all of them tired and dispirited. Whirlwind's almost complete success was turning into a disaster. Dubois and Fowler still missing – in Bahrain, McIver not yet out of danger. Tom Lochart back in Tehran, God knows where. No news of Erikki and Azadeh. No sleep for most of them last night. And sunset today still their deadline.

From the moment yesterday when the 212s had started landing, they had all helped to strip them, removing rotors and tail booms for storing on the jumbo freighters when they arrived, if they arrived. Last night Roger Newbury had returned from the Al Shargaz palace meeting with the foreign minister in a foul humour: 'Not a bloody thing I can do, Andy. The minister said he and the Sheik had been asked to make a personal inspection of the airport by the new Iranian representative or ambassador who had seen eight or nine strange 212s at the airport, claiming them to be their "hijacked" Iran registereds. The Minister said that of course His Highness, the Sheik, had agreed – how could he refuse? The inspection's at sunset with the ambassador, I'm "cordially invited" as the British rep for a thorough check of IDs, and if any're found to be suspect, old boy, tough titty!'

Gavallan had been up all night trying to bring the arrival of the freighters forward, or to get substitutions from every international source he could conjure up. None were available. The best his present charterers could do was 'perhaps' to bring forward the ETA to noon tomorrow, Sunday. 'Bloody people,' he muttered and poured some more coffee. 'When you've got to have a couple of 747s there're none – and usually with a single phone call you can get fifty.'

Pettikin was equally worried, also about McIver in Bahrain hospital.

No news was expected until noon today about the seriousness of McIver's heart attack. '*Pas de problème*,' Jean-Luc had said last night. 'They've let Genny stay in the next room at the hospital, the doctor's the best in Bahrain, and I'm here. I've cancelled my early flight home and I'll wait, but send me some money tomorrow to pay the bills.'

Pettikin toyed with his coffee cup, his breakfast untouched. All yesterday and last night helping to get the helicopters ready so no chance to see Paula and she was off again to Tehran this morning still evacuating Italian nationals, and would not be back for at least two days. Gavallan had ordered an immediate retreat of all Whirlwind participants out of the Gulf area pending review. 'We can't be too careful,' he had told them all. 'Everyone's got to go for the time being.'

Later Pettikin had said, 'You're right, Andy, but what about Tom and Erikki? We should leave someone here – I'd be glad to volun –'

'For Christ's sake, Charlie, give over,' Gavallan had flared. 'You think I'm not worried sick about them? And Fowler and Dubois? We have to do it one step at a time. Everyone who's not necessary is out before sunset and you're one of them!' That had been about 1:00 a.m. this morning in the office when Pettikin had come to relieve Scot who was still blearily manning the HF. The rest of the night he had sat there. No calls. At 5:00 a.m. Nogger Lane had relieved him and he had come here for breakfast, Gavallan, Rudi and Scragger already seated. 'Any luck with the freighters, Andy?'

'No, Charlie, it's still tomorrow noon at the earliest,' Gavallán had said. 'Sit down, have some coffee.' Then had come the dawn and the muezzins. Now their singsong ceased. Some of the violence left the veranda.

Scragger poured himself another cup of tea, his stomach still upset. Another sudden chill zapped up from his bowels and he hurried to the bathroom. The spasm passed quickly with very little to show for it, but there was no blood therein, and Doc Nutt had said he didn't think it was dysentery: 'Just take it easy for a few days, Scrag. I'll have the result of all the tests tomorrow.' He had told Doc Nutt about the blood in his urine and the pain in his stomach over the last few days. To hide it would have been unforgivable added danger, both to his passengers and to his chopper. 'Scrag, best you stay here in hospital for a few days,' Doc Nutt had said.

'Get stuffed, old cock! There's things to do and mountains to conquer.'

Going back to the table he saw the brooding gloom upon everyone and hated it, but had no solution. Nothing to do except wait. No way to transit out because they would have to go through Saudi, Emirate, or Oman airspace and no possibility of a clearance for a few days. He had suggested, jokingly, they reassemble the helicopters, find out when the next British supertanker was outbound through Hormuz and then take off and land on her: '. . . and we just sail off into the wild blue and get off in Mombasa, or sail on around Africa to Nigeria.'

'Hey, Scrag,' Vossi had said in admiration, 'that's wild-assed. I could use a cruise. How about it, Andy?'

'We'd be arrested and in the brig before the rotors had begun.'

Scragger sat down and waved a fly away. The sun's birth colour was less red now and all of them were wearing dark glasses against the glare.

Gavallan finished his coffee. 'Well, I'm off to the office in case I can do something. If you want me I'm there. How soon'll you be finished, Rudi?'

Rudi was in charge of getting the choppers ready for transshipment. 'Your target was noon today. It'll be noon.' He swallowed the last of his coffee and got up. 'Time to leave, *meine Kinder!*' Groans and catcalls from the others but mostly good-natured through their fatigue. A general exodus to transport waiting outside.

'Andy,' Scragger said, 'I'll come along with you if it's okay.'

'Good idea, Scrag. Charlie, no need for you to be on Rudi's team as we're ahead of schedule. Why don't you come over to the office later?'

Pettikin smiled at him. 'Thanks.' Paula was not due to leave her hotel until 10:00 a.m. Now he would have plenty of time to see her. To say what? he asked himself, waving them goodbye.

Gavallan drove out of the gates. The airport was still partially in shadow. Already a few jets with their navigation lights on, engines winding up. The Iran evacuation was still priority. He glanced at Scragger, saw the grimace. 'You all right?'

'Sure, Andy. Just a touch of gippy tummy. Had it bad in New Guinea – so I've always been careful. If I could get some of old Dr. Collis Brown's Elixir I'd be raring to go!' This was a marvellous and highly effective tincture invented by Dr. Collis Brown, an English army surgeon, to combat the dysentery that tens of thousands of soldiers were dying of during the Crimean War. 'Six drops of the old magic and Bob's your unbloody uncle!'

'You're right, Scrag,' Gavallan said absently, wondering if Pan Am Freighting had had any cancellations. 'I never travel without Collis . . . wait a minute!' He suddenly beamed. 'My survival kit! There's some there. Liz always sticks it into my briefcase. Collis Brown's, Tiger Balm, aspirins, a golden sovereign, and a can of sardines.'

'Eh? Sardines?'

'In case I get hungry.' Gavallan was glad to talk to take his mind off the looming disaster. 'Liz and I have a mutual friend we met years ago in Hong Kong, fellow called Marlowe, a writer. He always carried a can with him, iron rations in case of famine – and Liz and I, we always laughed about it. It became kind of a symbol to remind ourselves how lucky we really are.'

'Peter Marlowe? The one who wrote *Changi* – about the POW camp in Singapore?'

'Yes. Do you know him?'

'No. But I read that book, not the others, but I read that one.' Scragger was suddenly reminded about his own war against the Japanese and then about Kasigi and Iran-Toda. Last night he had called other hotels to track Kasigi down and eventually had found him registered at the International and had left a message but as yet had not heard back. Probably he's chocker I let him down, he told himself, because we can't help him at Iran-Toda. Stone the crows! Bandar-e Delam and Iran-Toda seem a couple of years ago instead of just a couple of days. Even so, if it weren't for him, I'd still be handcuffed to that bleeding bed.

'Pity we don't all have our can of sardines, Andy,' he said. 'We really do forget our luck, don't we? Look how lucky we were to get out of Lengeh in one piece. What about old Duke? Soon he'll be fit as a fiddle.

1162

A fraction of an inch and he'd be dead but he isn't. Scot the same. What about Whirlwind! All the lads're out and so're our birds. Erikki's safe. Mac'll be all right, you wait and see! Dubois and Fowler? It's got to happen sometime, but it hasn't yet, so far as we know, so we can still hope. Tom? Well, he chose that and he'll get out.'

Near the Iran-Turkish Border: 7:59 A.M. Some seven hundred miles northwards, Azadeh shielded her eyes against the rising sun. She had seen something glint in the valley below. Was that light reflected off a gun, or harness? She readied the M16, picked up the binoculars. Behind her Erikki lay sprawled on some blankets in the 212's open cabin, heavily asleep. His face was pale and he had lost a lot of blood but she thought he was all right. Through the lenses she saw nothing move. Down there the countryside was snow-locked and sparsely treed. Desolate. No villages and no smoke. The day was good but very cold. No clouds and the wind had dropped in the night. Slowly she searched the valley. A few miles away was a village she had not noticed before.

The 212 was parked in rough mountainous country on a rocky plateau. Last night after the escape from the palace, because a bullet had smashed some instrumentation, Erikki had lost his way. Afraid to exhaust all his fuel, and unable to fly and at the same time staunch the flow of blood from his arm, he had decided to risk landing and wait for dawn. Once on the ground, he had pulled the carpet out of the cockpit and unrolled it. Azadeh was still sleeping peacefully. He had tied up his wound as best he could, then rewrapped her in the carpet for warmth, brought out some of the guns and leaned against the skid on guard. But much as he tried he could not keep his eyes open.

He had awakened suddenly. False dawn was touching the sky. Azadeh was still huddled down in the carpet but now she was watching him. 'So. You've kidnapped me!' Then her pretended coldness vanished and she scrambled into his arms, kissing him and thanking him for solving the dilemma for all three of them with such wisdom, saying the speech she had rehearsed: 'I know a wife can do little against a husband, Erikki, hardly anything at all. Even in Iran where we're civilised, even here, a wife's almost a chattel and the Imam is very clear on wifely duties, and in the Koran,' she added, 'in the Koran and Sharia her duties are oh so clear. Also I know I'm married to a non-Believer, and I openly swear I will try to escape at least once a day to try to go back to fulfil my oath, and though I'll be petrified and know you'll catch me every time and will keep me without money or beat me and I have to obey whatever you order, I will do it.' Her eyes were

1163

brimming with happy tears. 'Thank you, my darling, I was so afraid . . .'

'Would you have done that? Given up your God?'

'Erikki, oh, how I prayed God would guide you.'

'Would you?'

'There's no need now even to think the unthinkable, is there, my love?'

'Ah,' he said, understanding. 'Then you knew, didn't you? You knew that this was what I had to do!'

'I only know I'm your wife, I love you, I must obey you, you took me away without my help and against my will. We need never discuss it again. Please?'

Blearily he peered at her, disoriented, and could not understand how she could seem to be strong and have come out of the drugged sleep so easily. Sleep! 'Azadeh, I've got to have an hour of proper sleep. Sorry, I can't go on. Without an hour or so, I can't. We should be safe enough here. You guard, we should be safe enough.'

'Where are we?'

'Still in Iran, somewhere near the border.' He gave her a loaded M16, knowing she could use it accurately. 'One of the bullets smashed my compass.' She saw him stagger as he went for the cabin, grope for some blankets, and lie down. Instantly he was asleep. While she waited for the daylight she thought about their future and about the past. Still Johnny to settle. Nothing else. How strange life is. I thought I would scream a thousand times closed up in that vile carpet, pretending to be drugged. As if I would be so stupid as to drug myself in case I would have to help defend us! So easy to dupe Mina and my darling Erikki and even Hakim, no longer my darling: 'Her everlasting spirit's more important than her temporary body!' He would have killed me. Me! His beloved sister! But I tricked him.

She was very pleased with herself and with Aysha who had whispered about the secret listening places so that when she had stormed out of the room in pretended rage and left Hakim and Erikki alone, she had scurried to overhear what they were saying. Oh, Erikki, I was petrified you and Hakim weren't going to believe that I'd really break my oath – and frantic in case the clues I'd placed before you all evening wouldn't add up to your perfect stratagem. But you went one better than me – you even arranged the helicopter. Oh, how clever you were, I was, we were together. I even made sure you brought my handbag and jewel bag with Najoud's loot that I wheedled out of Hakim so now we're rich as well as safe, if only we can get out of this God-lost country.

'It is God-lost, my darling,' Ross had said the last time she had seen him in Tehran, just before he had left her – she could not endure parting without saying goodbye so she had gone to Talbot to inquire after him and then, a few hours later, he had knocked on her door, the apartment empty but for them. 'It's best you leave Iran, Azadeh. Your beloved Iran is once again bereft. This revolution's the same as all of them: a new tyranny replaces the old. Your new rulers will implant their law, their version of God's law, as the Shah implanted his. Your ayatollahs will live and die as popes live and die, some good men, some bad and some evil. In God's time the world'll get a little better, the beast in men that needs to bite and hack and kill and torment and torture will become a little more human and a little more restrained. It's only people that bugger up the world, Azadeh. Men mostly. You know I love you?'

'Yes. You said it in the village. You know I love you?'

'Yes.'

So easy to swoop back into the womb of time as when they were young. 'But we're not young now and there's a great sadness on me, Azadeh.'

'It'll pass, Johnny,' she had said, wanting his happiness. 'It'll pass as Iran's troubles will pass. We've had terrible times for centuries but they've passed.' She remembered how they had sat together, not touching now, yet possessed, one with the other. Then later he had smiled and raised his hand in his devil-may-care salute and he had left silently.

Again the glint in the valley. Anxiety rushed back into her. Now a movement through the trees and she saw them. 'Erikki!' He was instantly awake. 'Down there. Two men on horseback. They look like tribesmen.' She handed him the binoculars.

'I see them.' The men were armed and cantering along the valley bed, dressed as hill people would dress, keeping to cover where there was cover. Erikki focused on them. From time to time he saw them look up in their direction. 'They can probably see the chopper but I doubt if they can see us.'

'They're heading up here?'

Through his aching and tiredness he had heard the fear in her voice. 'Perhaps. Probably yes. It'd take them half an hour to get up here, we've plenty of time.'

'They're looking for us.' Her face was white and she moved closer to Erikki. 'Hakim will have alerted everywhere.'

'He won't have done that. He helped me.'

'That was to escape.' Nervously she looked around the plateau and the tree line and the mountains, then back at the two men. 'Once you escaped he'd act like a Khan. You don't know Hakim, Erikki. He's my brother but before that he's Khan.'

Through the binoculars he saw the half-hidden village beside the road in the middle distance. Sun glinted off telephone lines. His own anxiety increased. 'Perhaps they're just villagers and curious about us. But we won't wait to find out.' Wearily he smiled at her. 'Hungry?'

'Yes, but I'm fine.' Hastily she began bundling the carpet that was ancient, priceless, and one of her favourites. 'I'm thirsty more than hungry.'

'Me too but I feel better now. The sleep helped.' His eyes ranged the mountains, setting what he saw against his remembrance of the map. A last look at the men still far below. No danger for a while, unless there are others around, he thought, then went for the cockpit. Azadeh shoved the carpet into the cabin and tugged the door closed. There were bullet holes in it that she had not noticed before. Another spark of sunlight off metal in the forest, much closer, that neither saw.

Erikki's head ached and he felt weak. He pressed the starting button. Wind up, immediate and correct. A quick check of his instruments. Rev counter shattered, no compass, no ADF. No need for some instruments – the sound of the engines would tell him when the needles would be in the Green. But needles on the fuel gauges were stuck at a quarter full. No time to check on them or any other damage and if there was damage, what could he do? All gods great and small, old and new, living or dead or yet to be born, be on my side today, I'll need all the help you can give me. His eyes saw the kukri that he remembered vaguely shoving in the seat pocket. Without conscious effort his fingers reached out and touched it. The feel of it burned.

Azadeh hurried for the cockpit, turbulence from the rotors picking up speed clawing at her, chilling her even more. She climbed into the seat and locked the door, turning her eyes away from the mess of dried blood on the seat and floor. Her smile died, noticing his brooding concentration and the strangeness, his hand almost near the kukri but not quite. Again she wondered why he had brought it.

'Are you all right, Erikki?' she asked, but he did not appear to have heard her. Insha'Allah. It's God's will he is alive and I'm alive, that we're together and almost safe. But now it's up to me to carry the burden and to keep us safe. He's not my Erikki yet, neither in looks nor in spirit. I can almost hear the bad thoughts pounding in his head. Soon the bad will again overpower the good. God protect us. 'Thank you,

Erikki,' she said, accepting the headset he handed her, mentally girding herself for battle.

He made sure she was strapped in and adjusted the volume for her. 'You can hear me, all right?'

'Oh, yes, my darling. Thank you.'

Part of his hearing was concentrated on the sound of the engines, a minute or two yet before they could take off. 'We've not enough fuel to get to Van which's the nearest airfield in Turkey – I could go south to the hospital in Rezaiyeh for fuel but that's too dangerous. I'm going north a little. I saw a village that way and a road. Perhaps that's the Khvoy-Van road.'

'Good, let's hurry, Erikki, I don't feel safe here. Are there any airfields near here? Hakim's bound to have alerted the police and they'll have alerted the air force. Can we take off?'

'Just a few more seconds, engines're almost ready.' He saw the anxiety and her beauty and once more the picture of her and John Ross together tumbled into his mind. He forced it away. 'I think there are airfields in the border sector. We'll go as far as we can. I think we've enough fuel to get over the border.' He made an effort to be light. 'Maybe we can find a gas station. Do you think they'd take a credit card?'

She laughed nervously and lifted up her bag, winding the strap around her wrist. 'No need for credit cards, Erikki. We're rich – you're rich. I can speak Turkish and if I can't beg, buy, or bribe our way through I'm not of the tribe Gorgon! But through to where? Istanbul? You're overdue a fabulous holiday, Erikki. We're safe only because of you, you did everything, thought of everything!'

'No, Azadeh, you did.' You and John Ross, he wanted to shout and looked back at his instruments to hide. But without Ross, Azadeh'd be dead and therefore I'd be dead and I can't live with the thought of you and him together. I'm sure you lov –

At that moment his disbelieving eyes saw the groups of riders break out of the forest a quarter of a mile away on both sides of him, police among them, and begin galloping across the rocky space to head them off. His ears told him the engines were in the Green. At once his hands shoved full throttle. Time slowing. Creeping off the ground, no way that the attackers could not shoot them down. A million years of time for them to rein in, aim and fire, any one of the dozen men. Look, the gendarme in the middle, the sergeant, he's pulling the M16 out of his saddle holster!

Abruptly time came back at full speed and Erikki swung away and fled from them, weaving this way and that, expecting every second to be the last, then they were over the side, roaring down into the ravine at treetop level.

'Hold your fire,' the sergeant shouted to the overexcited tribesmen who were at the lip, aiming and firing, their horses cavorting. 'In the Name of God I told you we were ordered to capture them, to save her and kill him, not kill her!' Reluctantly the others obeyed and when he came up to them he saw the 212 was well away down in the valley. He pulled out the walkie-talkie and switched on: 'HQ. This is Sergeant Zibri. The ambush failed. His engines were going before we got into position. But he's flushed out of his hiding place.'

'Which way is he heading?'

'He's turning north towards the Khvoy-Van road.'

'Did you see Her Highness?'

'Yes. She looked petrified. Tell the Khan we saw the kidnapper strap her into the seat and it looked as though the kidnapper also had a strap around her wrist. She . . .' The sergeant's voice picked up excitedly. 'Now the helicopter's turned eastward, it's keeping about two or three kilometres south of the road.'

'Good. Well done. We'll alert the air force . . .'

Tehran – At Inner Intelligence HQ: 9:54 A.M. Group Four assassin Suliman al Waili tried to stop his fingers from trembling as he took the telex from the SAVAMA colonel: 'Chief of Inner Intelligence Colonel Hashemi Fazir was killed last night, bravely leading the charge that overran the leftist mujhadin HQ, together with the English adviser Armstrong. Both men were consumed by fire when the traitors blew up the building. (signed) Chief of Police, Tabriz.'

Suliman was not yet over his fright at the sudden summons, petrified that this official had already found incriminating papers in Fazir's safe about Group Four assassins – the safe open and empty behind him. Surely my Master wouldn't have been that careless, not here in his own office! 'The Will of God, Excellency,' he said, handing the telex back and hiding his fury. 'The Will of God. Are you the new leader of Inner Intelligence, Excellency?'

'Yes. What were your duties?'

'I'm an agent, Excellency,' Suliman told him, fawning as would be expected, disregarding the past tense. His fear began to leave him. If these dogs suspected anything, I wouldn't be standing here, he reasoned, his confidence growing, I'd be in a dungeon screaming. These incompetent sons of dogs don't deserve to live in the world of men. 'The

1168

colonel ordered me to live in Jaleh and keep my ears and eyes open and smoke out communists.' He kept his eyes blank, despising this lean-faced, pompous man who sat at Fazir's desk.

'How long have you been employed?'

'Three or four years, I don't remember exactly, Excellency, it's on my card. Perhaps it's five, I don't remember. It should be on my card, Excellency. About four years and I work hard and will serve you with all my power.'

'SAVAMA is absorbing Inner Intelligence. From now on you will report to me. I'll want copies of your reports since you began.'

'As God wants, Excellency, but I can't write, at least I write very badly and Excellency Fazir never required written reports,' Suliman lied guilelessly. He waited in the silence, shuffling his feet and acting dull-witted. SAVAK or SAVAMA, they're all liars and more than likely they arranged my Master's murder. God curse them – these dogs've ruined my Master's plan. They've done me out of my perfect job! My perfect job with real money and real power and real future. These dogs are thieves, they've stolen my future and my safety. Now I've no job, no pinpointed enemies of God to slay. No future, no safety, no protec – Unless!

Unless I use my wits and skills and take over where my Master was stopped!

Son of a burnt father, why not? It's the Will of God that he's dead and I'm alive, that he's the sacrifice and I'm not. Why not induct more teams? I know the Master's techniques and part of his plan. Even better, why not raid his house and empty the safe in the cellar he never knew I knew about. Not even his wife knows about that one. Now that he's dead it should be easy. Yes, and better I go tonight, get there first before these turd eaters of the Left Hand do it. What riches that safe could contain – should contain! Money, papers, lists – my Master loved lists like a dog loves shit! May I be sacrificed if the safe doesn't contain a list of the other Group Fours. Didn't my late Master plan to be today's al-Sabbah? Why not me instead? With assassins, real assassins who are already fearless of death and seek martyrdom as their guaranteed passport to Paradise . . .

He almost laughed aloud. To cover it he belched. 'Sorry, Excellency, I'm not feeling well, can I leave, pl –'

'Where did Colonel Fazir keep his papers?'

'Papers, Excellency? May I be your sacrifice, Excellency, but what should a man like me know about papers? I'm just an agent, I reported to him and he sent me away, most times with a boot and a curse – it will be grand to work for a real man.' He waited confidently. Now what would Fazir have wanted me to do? Certainly to be avenged which is clearly to dispose of Pahmudi who's responsible for his death – and this dog who dares to sit at his desk. Why not? But not until I've emptied the real safe. 'Please can I go, Excellency? My bowels are overfull and I've the parasite disease.'

Distastefully, the colonel looked up from the card that told him nothing. No files in the safe, just money. A marvellous pishkesh for me, he thought, but where are his files? Fazir must have kept files somewhere. His home? 'Yes, you can go,' he said irritably, 'but report to me once a week. Personally to me. And don't forget, unless you do a good job . . . we don't intend to employ malingerers.'

'Yes, Excellency, certainly, Excellency, thank you, Excellency, I'll do my best for God and the Imam, but when should I report?'

'The day after Holy Day, every week.' Testily the colonel waved him away. Suliman shuffled out, promised himself that before the next reporting day this colonel would be no more. Son of a dog, why not? Already my power reaches to Beirut and to Bahrain.

Bahrain: 12:50 P.M. Due south, almost seven hundred miles away, Bahrain was balmy and sunny, the beaches full with weekend vacationers, windsurfers off shore enjoying the fine breeze, hotel terrace tables filled with men and women, scantily dressed to bask in the fine spring sunshine. One of these was Sayada Bertolin.

She wore a filmy sundress over her bikini and sipped a citron pressé and sat alone, her table shaded by a green umbrella. Idly she watched the bathers and the children playing in the shallows – one small boy a pattern of her own son. It'll be so good to be home again, she thought, to hold my son in my arms again and yes, yes, even to see my husband again. It's been such a long time away from civilisation, from good food and good talk from good coffee and croissants and wine, from newspapers and radio and TV and all the wonderful things we take for granted. Though not me. I've always appreciated them and have always worked for a better world and justice in the Middle East.

But now? Her joy left her.

Now I'm not just a PLO sympathiser and courier but a secret agent for Lebanese Christian militia, their Israeli overlords and their CIA overlords – thank God I was fortunate to overhear *them* whispering together when they thought I had already left after getting their orders to return to Beirut. Still no names, but enough to pinpoint their origin. Dogs! Filthy vile dogs! Christians! Betrayers of Palestine! There's still

1170

Teymour to be revenged. Dare I tell my husband who'll tell others in the Council? I daren't. *They* know too much.

Her attention focused out to sea and she was startled. Among the windsurfers she recognised Jean-Luc, hurtling shorewards, beautifully balanced on the precarious board, leaning elegantly against the wind. At the very last second, he twisted into the wind, stepped off in the shallows, and allowed the sail to collapse. She smiled at such perfection.

Ah, Jean-Luc, how you do love yourself! But I admit you had flair. In many things you're superb, as a chef, as a lover – ah, yes, but only from time to time, you're not varied enough or experimental enough for us Middle Easterners who understand eroticism, and you're too concerned with your own beauty. 'I'll admit you're beautiful,' she murmured, moistening pleasantly at the thought. In lovemaking you're above average, *chéri*, but no more. You're not the best. My first husband was the best, perhaps because he was the first. Then Teymour. Teymour was unique. Ah, Teymour, I'm not afraid to think of you now, now that I'm out of Tehran. There I couldn't. I won't forget you, or what they did. I'll take revenge for you on Christian militia one day.

Her eyes were watching Jean-Luc, wondering what he was doing here, elated he was here, hoping he would see her, not wanting to make the first move to tempt fate but ready to wait and see what fate had in store. She glanced in her hand mirror, added a touch of gloss to her lips, perfume behind her ears. Again she waited. He started up from the beach. She pretended to concentrate on her glass, watching hm in its reflection, leaving it up to chance.

'Sayada! *Mon Dieu, chérie!* What are you doing here?'

She was suitably astonished and then he was kissing her and she tasted the sea salt and smelled the sun oil and sweat and decided this afternoon would be perfect after all. 'I just arrived, *chéri*. I arrived last night from Tehran,' she said breathlessly, letting her desire fill her. 'I'm wait-listed on Middle Eastern's noon flight to Beirut tomorrow – but what are you doing here, it's like a miracle!'

'It is, how lucky we are! But you can't go tomorrow, tomorrow's Sunday. Tomorrow we'll have a barbecue, lobsters and oysters!'

He was completely confident and Gallic and charmingly persuasive and she thought, why not? Beirut can wait, I've waited so long, one more day won't matter.

And he was thinking, how perfect! The weekend was going to be a disaster but now love this afternoon, then siesta. Later I'll choose a perfect dinner, then we'll dance a little and love tenderly and sleep soundly, ready for another perfect day tomorrow. '*Chérie*, I'm desolate but I must leave you for almost an hour,' he said with the perfect touch of sadness. 'We will lunch here – you stay at this hotel? Perfect, so do I: 1623. About one-thirty, quarter to two? Don't change, you look perfect. *C'est bon*?' He bent down and kissed her and let his hand stray to her breast, felt her tremor and was pleased.

At the Hospital: 1:16 P.M. 'Good morning, Dr. Lanoire. Captain McIver, is it good or bad?' Jean-Luc said, speaking French to him – Anton Lanoire's father came from Cannes, his mother was Bahraini, a Sorbonne-trained daughter of an illiterate fisherman who still fished as he had always done, still lived in a hovel though he was a multi-millionaire owner of oil wells.

'It's middling.'

'How middling is that?'

The doctor steepled his fingers. He was a distinguished man in his late thirties, trained in Paris and London, trilingual, Arabic, French and English. 'We won't know with much accuracy for a few days: we still have to make several tests. We'll know the real good or bad when he has an angiogram a month from now, but in the meantime Captain McIver's responding to treatment and is not in pain.'

'But is he going to be all right?'

'Angina is quite ordinary, usually. I understand from his wife he's been under very great stress for the last few months, and even worse for the last few days on this Whirlwind exercise of yours – and no wonder. What courage! I salute him and you and all those who took part. At the same time I'd strongly advise that all pilots and crews be given two or three months off.'

Jean-Luc beamed. 'May I have that in writing, please? Of course the three months sick leave should be with full pay – and allowances.'

'Of course. What a magnificent job all of you did for your company, risking your lives – you should all get a well-deserved bonus! I wonder why more of you don't have heart attacks. The two months is to recuperate, Jean-Luc – it's essential you have a careful checkup before you continue flying.'

Jean-Luc was perplexed. 'We can all expect heart attacks?'

'Oh, no, no, not at all.' Lanoire smiled. 'But it would be very wise to be checked thoroughly – just in case. You know angina's caused by a sudden blockage of blood? A stroke's when the same happens to the brain. Arteries get clogged and that's it! Insha'Allah. It can happen anytime.'

'It can?' Jean-Luc's discomfort increased. Piece of shit! It'd just be my luck to have a heart attack.

'Oh, yes,' the doctor continued helpfully. 'I've known patients in their thirties and early forties with perfectly normal blood pressure, normal cholesterol, and normal ECGs – electrocardiograms – and poof!' He parodied with his hands expressively. 'Within a few hours – poof!'

'Poof! Just like that?' Jean-Luc sat down uneasily.

'I can't fly but I would imagine flying creates a lot of stress, especially somewhere like the North Sea. And stress is perhaps the biggest cause of angina, when part of the heart dies an –'

'My God, old Mac's heart died?' Jean-Luc was shocked.

'Oh, no, just a part. Every time you have an attack of angina, however mild, a part's lost for ever. Dead.' Dr. Lanoire smiled. 'Of course you can go on quite a long time before you run out of tissue.'

Mon Dieu, Jean-Luc thought squeamishly, I don't like this at all. North Sea? Bucket of shit, I'd better apply for a transfer before I even go there! 'How long will Mac be in the hospital?'

'Four or five days. I would suggest you leave him today and visit tomorrow, but don't tax him. He must have a month's leave, then some further tests.'

'What are his chances?'

'That's up to God.'

Upstairs on the veranda of a pleasant room overlooking the blue waters, Genny was dozing in a chair, today's London *Times* brought by BA's early flight, open on her lap. McIver lay comfortably in the starched clean bed. The breeze came off the sea and touched him and he woke up. Wind's changed, he thought. It's back to the standard northeasterly. Good. He moved to see better out into the Gulf. The slight movement awakened her instantly. She folded the paper and got up.

'How're you feeling, luv?'

'Fine. I'm fine now. No pain. Just a bit tired. Vaguely heard you talking to the Doc, what did he say?'

'Everything seems fine. The attack wasn't bad. You'll have to take it easy for a few days, then a month off and then some more tests – he was very encouraging because you don't smoke, you're ever so fit, considering.' Genny stood over the bed, against the light, but he could see her face and read the truth thereon. 'You can't fly anymore – as a pilot,' she said and smiled.

'That's a bugger,' he said drily. 'Have you been in touch with Andy?'

'Yes. I called last night and this morning and will check again in an hour or so. Nothing yet on young Marc Dubois and Fowler but all our birds are safe at Al Shargaz and being stripped for freighting out tomorrow. Andy was so proud of you – and Scrag. I talked to him this morning too.'

The shadow of a smile. 'It'll be good to see old Scrag. You're okay?'

'Oh, yes.' She touched his shoulder. 'I'm ever so glad you're better – you did give me a turn.'

'I gave me a turn, Gen.' He smiled and held out his hand and said gruffly, 'Thanks, Mrs. McIver.'

She took it and put it to her cheek, then bent down and touched his lips with hers, warmed by the enormity of the affection in his face. 'You did give me such a turn,' she said again.

He noticed the newspaper. 'That today's, Gen?'

'Yes, dear.'

'Seems years since I saw one. What's new?'

'More of the usual.' She folded the paper and put it aside carelessly, not wanting him to see the section she had been reading in case it worried him: 'Stock market collapse in Hong Kong.' That'll certainly affect Struan's and that bastard Linbar, she thought, but will it touch S-G and Andy? Nothing Duncan can do, so never mind. 'Strikes, Callaghan's messing up poor old Britain more than ever. They say he might call a snap election this year, and if he does Maggie Thatcher's got a good chance. Wouldn't that be super? Be a change to have someone sensible in charge.'

'Because she's a woman?' He smiled wryly. 'That'd certainly set the cat among the chickens. Christ Almighty, a woman PM! Don't know how she ever wangled the leadership away from Heath in the first place . . . she must have iron-plated knickers! If only the bloody Liberals'd stayed out of the way . . .' His voice trailed off and she saw him look out to sea, some passing dhows beautiful.

Quietly she sat down and waited, wanting to let him drift back to sleep, or talk a little, whatever pleased him. He must be getting better if he's already taking off after the Libs, she thought, bemused, letting herself drift, watching the sea. Her hair was moved by the breeze that smelled of sea salt. It was pleasant just sitting, knowing that he was all right now, 'responding to treatment. No need to worry, Mrs. McIver.' Easy to say, hard not to do.

There'll be a huge change in our lives, has to be, apart from losing Iran and all our stuff there, lot of old rubbish, most of it, that I won't miss. Now that Whirlwind's over – I must've been mad to suggest it, but oh it worked so well! Now we've most of our lads out safely – can't

think of Tom or Marc or Fowler, Erikki or Azadeh or Sharazad, God
bless them all – and our best equipment and our face so we're still in
business, our stake in S-G's got to be worth something. We won't be
penniless and that's a blessing. I wonder how much we could get for our
shares? I suppose we do have a share? But what about the 'stock market
collapse'? I hope that hasn't buggered us again.

It would be nice to have a little money but I don't care so long as
Duncan gets better. Perhaps he'll retire and perhaps he won't. I
wouldn't want him to retire really, it would kill him. Where should
we live? Near Aberdeen? Or Edinburgh near Sarah and Trevor, or
London near Hamish and Kathy? Not London, nasty down there, and
we shouldn't live too near either of the kids, don't want to bother them
though it'd be ever so nice to be able to drop by from time to time, even
baby-sit. Don't want to become the boring mother-in-law to Trevor or
to young Kathy – such a lovely girl. Kathy, Kathleen, Kathy: Andrew
and Kathy, and sometimes going to Castle Avisyard, and now Andrew
and Maureen and tiny Electra. I wouldn't want to be alone, don't want
Duncan to . . .

Don't want to relive the horror, the pounding, rattling darkness, not
being able to see, jets howling, stink of petrol – my God, how do they
stand the noise and the bouncing around hour after hour – and all the
time Duncan gasping, not knowing if he was alive or dead, twice crying
out, 'He's dead, he's dead,' but no one hearing and no one to help
anyway and dear old Charlie flying here as fast as he could, the other
man, the Iranian sergeant, what was his name, ah, yes, Wazari, Wazari
nice but useless. Oh, God that was awful, and lasted for ever . . . but
now it's all right and thank God I was there. Duncan will be all right.
He will be. He must be.

Wonder what'll happen to Wazari? He looked so frightened when the
police took him off. Wait a moment, didn't Jean-Luc say he had heard
they would probably release him into Andy's custody as a political exile
if Andy guaranteed to take him out of Bahrain and give him a job?

Bloody revolution! Bloody nuisance I couldn't get back to collect
some of my things. There was that old frying pan that'd never stick, and
Grannie's teapot that made such a good cup of tea even out of teabags
and Tehran water. Ugh! Water! Soon no more squatting and using
water instead of good soft paper. Ugh! If I never have to squat again it
will be too soon . . .

'What are you smiling about, Gen?'

'Oh, let me think! Oh, yes, I was thinking about having to squat,
about all the bums in the early morning over the joubs and their bottles

1175

of water, poor people. It always looked so awful and at the same time funny. Poor people. No more squatting for us, me lad, it's back to Blighty.' She saw his eyes change and her anxiety returned. 'That's not bad, Duncan. Going home. It won't be, I promise.'

After a pause, he nodded, half to himself. 'We'll wait and see, Gen. We won't make any decision yet. No need to decide what we'll do for a month or two. First I'll get fit and then we'll decide. Don't worry, eh?'

'I'm not worried now.'

'Good, no need to worry.' Once more his attention strayed to the sea. I'm not going to spend the rest of my life battling bloody British weather, that'd be awful. Retire? Christ, I'll have to think of something. If I've got to stop working I'll go mad. Maybe we could get a little place by the sea to winter in Spain or the south of France. I'll be buggered if I'm going to let Gen freeze and get old and bent before her time – that bloody awful salt-heavy wind off the North Sea! Never by God. We'll have more than enough money now Whirlwind's a success. Nine out of ten 212s! Wonderful! Can't think about Dubois or Fowler or Tom or Erikki, Azadeh or Sharazad.

His anxiety came back and with it a twinge that increased his anxiety that brought a bigger twinge . . .

'What're you thinking, Duncan?'

'That it's a beautiful day.'

'Yes, yes, it is.'

'Will you try Andy for me, Gen?'

'Of course.' She picked up the phone and dialled, knowing it would be better for him to talk awhile. 'Hello? Oh, hello, Scot, how're you – it's Genny.' She listened then said. 'That's good. Is your dad there?' Listening again, then, 'No, just tell him I called for Duncan – he's fine and can be reached on extension 455 here. He just wants to say hello. Will you ask Andy to call when he comes back? Thanks, Scot . . . no he's really fine, tell Charlie too. 'Bye.'

Thoughtfully she replaced the phone on its cradle. 'Nothing new. Andy's out at the International with Scrag. They're seeing that Jap – you know the one from Iran-Toda – sorry, I wouldn't call him one to his face but that's what he is. Still can't forgive them for what they did in the war.'

McIver frowned. 'You know, Gen, perhaps it's time we did. Kasigi certainly helped old Scrag. The old "sins of the fathers" bit doesn't add up. Perhaps we should start the new era. That's what we've got, Gen, like it or not, a New Era. Eh?'

She saw his smile and it brought tears near again. Mustn't cry, all's going to be well, the New Era will be good and he's going to get better, must get better – oh, Duncan, I'm so afraid. 'Tell you what, me lad,' she said brightly, 'when you're super fit we'll go to Japan on holiday and then we'll see.'

'That's a deal. We could even visit Hong Kong again.' He took her hand and squeezed it and both hid their fear of the future, fear for the other.

Al Shargaz – International Hotel: 1:55 P.M. Kasigi was weaving through the busy tables on the immaculate terrace overlooking the swimming pool. 'Ah, Mr. Gavallan, Captain Scragger, so sorry to be late.'

'No problem, Mr. Kasigi, please sit down.'

'Thank you.' Kasigi wore a light tropical suit and looked cool though he was not. 'So sorry, I loathe being late but in the Gulf it's almost impossible to be on time. I had to come from Dubai and the traffic . . . I believe congratulations are in order. I hear your Whirlwind was almost a complete success.'

'We're still short one chopper with two crew, but we were very lucky, all in all,' Gavallan said, no joy in him or in Scragger. 'Would you care for lunch or a drink?' Their lunch appointment requested by Kasigi had been for 12:30. By pre-arrangement, Gavallan and Scragger had not waited and were already on coffee.

'A brandy and mineral water, tall, please, and mineral water on the side. No lunch, thank you, I'm not hungry.' Kasigi lied politely, not wanting to embarrass himself by eating when they were finished. He smiled at Scragger. 'So! I'm pleased to see you're safe with your airplanes and crew out. Congratulations!'

'Sorry I had to duck your questions but, well, now you'll understand.'

'The moment I heard, I understood, of course. Health!' Kasigi drank the mineral water thirstily. 'Now that Whirlwind's out of the way, Mr. Gavallan, perhaps you can help me solve my problems at Iran-Toda?'

'I'd like to, of course, but I can't. I'm very sorry but we can't. It's not possible. Just not possible, that must be obvious now.'

'Perhaps it can be made possible.' Kasigi's eyes did not waver. 'I've heard that sunset tonight is a firm deadline to have your airplanes out or they will be impounded.'

Politely Gavallan gestured with his hand. 'Let's hope it's just another rumour.'

'One of your embassy officials informed our ambassador that this was definite. It would be a tragedy to lose all your aircraft after so much success.'

'Definite? You're certain?' Gavallan felt empty.

'My ambassador was certain.' Kasigi put on a nice smile. 'Say I could get your deadline extended from sunset tonight to sunset tomorrow, could you solve my problems at Iran-Toda?'

Both men stared at him. 'Can you extend our deadline, Mr. Kasigi?'

'I can't but our ambassador might be able to. I have an appointment with him in an hour. I will ask him – perhaps he could influence the Iranian ambassador, or the Sheik, or both.' Kasigi saw Gavallan's immediate interest and let that hang in the air, far too experienced a fisherman in Western waters not to know the bait. 'I'm in Captain Scragger's debt. I haven't forgotten he saved my life, and went out of his way to fly me to Bandar-e Delam. Friends shouldn't forget friends, should they? At ambassador level . . . perhaps it could be done.'

The Japanese ambassador? My God, would it be possible – Gavallan's heart was racing with hope at the unexpected avenue. 'There's no way ours can do anything, my contact was quite clear. I'd appreciate any help I could get, I certainly would. You think he'd help?'

'If he wanted to, I think he could.' Kasigi sipped the brandy. 'As you can help us. My chairman asked to be remembered to you and mentioned your mutual friend Sir Ian Dunross.' He saw Gavallan's eyes react and added, 'They had dinner together two nights ago.'

'If I can help . . . just exactly what are your problems?' And where's the catch and what's the cost? Gavallan thought. And where's Ian? Three times I've tried to reach him and failed.

'I need three 212s and two 206s at Iran-Toda as soon as possible, under contract for a year. It's essential the plant gets completed and the local komiteh has promised me full cooperation – if we start at once. If not at once it will be disastrous.'

Last night Chief Engineer Watanabe at Iran-Toda had sent him a coded telex: 'Komiteh chief Zataki is like a mad shark over the S-G hijacking. His ultimatum: either we resume construction at once – for which we must have helicopters – or the whole plant will face immediate possession and nationalisation and "all foreigners here will face retribution for treason." D hour is after sunset prayers Sunday 4th, when I am to appear before the komiteh. Please advise.'

Urgent telephone calls most of the night to Osaka and Tokyo had only served to increase Kasigi's rage. 'Yoshi, my dear friend,' his cousin and overlord Hiro Toda had said with devastating politeness, 'I've consulted the Syndicate. We all agree we're fortunate you're there on the spot. It's up to you. We're completely confident that you will solve these problems – before you leave.'

The message was quite clear: Solve it or don't come back.

He had spent the rest of the night trying to find a way out of his dilemma. Then, with the dawn, he had remembered a chance remark that the Japanese ambassador had made about the new Iranian ambassador that gave him a possible means to solve Gavallan's deadline and his own problem. 'To be quite blunt and open, Mr Gavallan,' he said and almost laughed aloud at so stupid a remark – but so necessary in Western negotiations, 'I need a plan by tomorrow sunset and answers by tomorrow sunset.'

'Why then, may I ask?'

'Because I made commitments to a friend that I must honour which of course you'd understand,' Kasigi said. 'So we both have a deadline, the same one.' Then he judged the time correct and struck hard to make sure the hook was firm. 'If you can help me, I would for ever appreciate it. Of course I'll do everything to persuade my ambassador to help you anyway.'

'There's no point in offering any of our birds, they'd be impounded instantly, no point in offering you the 206s we left behind – they're sure to be *hors de combat* too. S-G's totally out, so's Bell, Guerney, or any of the other companies. Could you get Japanese nationals who're helicopter pilots?'

'No. There're none trained.' Not yet, Kasigi thought, again furious

1180

with the Syndicate for not having the foresight to train their own trustworthy people for the job. 'The personnel will have to be foreign. My ambassador could smooth visas, and so forth – of course you know Iran-Toda's a National Project,' he added, the exaggeration not bothering him. It soon will be when all the information I have gets into the right hands. 'What about French or German crews?'

With an effort Gavallan tore his mind off how Ambassador Level could lead to his own men and choppers being safe, how he would then be out of Linbar's trap and free to deal with Imperial Helicopters in the North Sea, the Hong Kong crisis, the early retirement of Linbar and positioning Scot for a future takeover. 'So many wonderful possibilities,' he said involuntarily, then covered himself quickly and concentrated on solving Iran-Toda. 'There are two parts to the problem. First, equipment and spares: if you could provide a letter of credit at our usual monthly rate, renewable as long as you keep the planes – wherever I can get them from – with a guarantee that if the Iran authorities impound them you'll assume all lease payments in dollars outside of Iran and reimburse the owners against a total loss, I could get them to Iran-Toda within . . . within a week.'

Kasigi said at once, 'Our bankers are the Sumitomo; I could arrange a meeting with them here this evening. That's no problem. Where would you get the airplanes?'

'Germany or France – can't use British or American, same for the pilots. Probably France's better because of their help to Khomeini. I might be able to get them through some friends at Aerospatiale. What about insurance? It'll be impossible for me to get you insurance in Iran.'

'Perhaps I could do that from Japan.'

'Good. I'd hate to fly uninsured birds. Next: Scrag, say we can get the aircraft, how many pilots and mecs'd you need?'

'Well, Andy, if you could get them, you'd best have eight to ten pilots, rostering, and ten to fourteen mecs, based outside Iran but close by.'

'Who'd pay them, Mr. Kasigi? In what currency and where?'

'Whatever currency they wanted, wherever and however. Standard rates?'

'I'd think you'd have to offer a "danger cost of living bonus", Iran being what it is.'

'Would you consider arranging the whole matter for me, Mr. Gavallan, the equipment and the personnel for say a ten percent override?'

'Forget percentages and remember our involvement'd have to be

1181

kept very quiet. I'd suggest this: your operation should be controlled – logistics, spares, and repairs – from Kuwait or Bahrain.'

'Bahrain'd be better, Andy,' Scragger said.

'Kuwait's much closer,' Kasigi said.

'Yes,' Scragger said, 'so more liable for pressure from Iran or Iran-sponsored unrest. This side of the Gulf's due for a battering, I think. Too many Shi'as who're usually poor, too many sheiks who're Sunni. Short term or long term you're better off in Bahrain.'

'Then Bahrain,' Kasigi said. 'Mr. Gavallan, can I have Captain Scragger's services for a year to run the operation – if it comes to fruition – at double his present salary?' He saw Scragger's eyes narrow and wondered if he'd gone too far too fast, so he added lightly, 'If I ask you to give up your first love, my friend, it's only right you should be compensated.'

'That's a great offer, but, well, I don't know. Andy?'

Gavallan hesitated. 'It'd mean you'd have to quit S-G, Scrag, and quit flying. You couldn't run five ships and fly – and anyway you could never go back to Iran, no way.'

That's right. Quit flying? So I'm at a crossroads too, Scragger was thinking. Don't try to pretend Mac's bad luck didn't give you a shaft to end all shafts. And why did I faint yesterday? Doc Nutt said it was just exhaustion. Balls, I've never fainted in my life before and what do doctors know anyways? A year in Bahrain? That's better than a few months in the North Sea always bucking the next medical. No flying? My Gawd! Wait a minute, I could keep current and my hand in with a little local joyriding. 'I'd have to think about that, but thanks for the offer, Mr. Kasigi.'

'Meanwhile, Mr. Gavallan, could you organise the first month or so?'

'Yes. With a certain amount of luck, within the week I could get enough birds and crew there to get you started, the balance in a week or two for a renewable three-month contract.' Gavallan added as delicately as he could, 'So long as we beat our deadline.'

Kasigi kept his satisfaction covered. 'Good. Shall we meet here at nine? I'll bring Mr. Umura, who's president of the Sumitomo for the Gulf, to arrange the letters of credit in the form you want, Mr. Gavallan.'

'Nine o'clock on the dot. Perhaps you could mention to your ambassador even if tonight's sunset deadline passes, my freighters won't arrive till noon tomorrow and I won't be able to get them loaded and off before tomorrow sunset.'

1182

'You will keep "Ambassador Level" just between us?'

'Of course. You have my word. Scrag?'

Kasigi heard Scrag say the same and was, as always, astounded that Westerners could be so naive as to rely on someone's 'word' – word of honour, whose honour, what honour? Hasn't it ever been that a secret shared is no secret and never will be again? Like Whirlwind, it had been so easy to smoke that one out. 'Perhaps we could plan it this way: we settle finances and letters of credit tonight: you begin to arrange the helicopters and spares and crew, and how to manage the operation from Bahrain, warehousing and so on – everything subject to confirmation tomorrow sunset. If you've successfully extracted your own equipment by then, you guarantee Iran-Toda will have its helicopters within the week.'

'You seem very confident you can eliminate our deadline.'

'My ambassador can, perhaps. I'll phone and tell you what he says the moment I've left him. Captain Scragger, would it be possible for you to run a trainee programme for Japanese pilots?'

'Easy, providing they speak English and have at least a hundred chopper hours. I'd have to get a training captain and . . .' Scragger stopped. It had suddenly occurred to him this was the perfect solution. 'That's a beaut idea. I could be examiner – I can sign them out in type and that way I'd get enough flying under the right circs. Bonza!' He beamed. 'Tell you what, sport, if Andy can fix it, I'm in.' He stuck out his hand and Kasigi shook it.

'Thank you. Perfect. So Mr. Gavallan, do we "give her a try"?'

'Why not?' Gavallan put out his hand and felt Kasigi's iron-hard grip and for the first time really believed there was a chance. Kasigi's smart. Very. Now he's got the modern Japanese company standard operating procedure in place: get foreign experts to train Japanese personnel on site, or to create the market in their own countries, then move in the trainees. We get the short-term profit, they get the long-term market. They're doing to us in business what they failed to do at war. In spades. So what? It is fair trading. And if Kasigi and his ambassador can extract me from my disaster, it's no skin off my nose to help him out of his. 'We'll give her a try.'

Kasigi smiled properly for the first time. 'Thank you. I'll phone the moment I have any news.' He half bowed, then strode off.

'You think he'll do it, Andy?' Scragger asked hopefully.

'Honest to God I don't know.' Gavallan waved at a waiter for the bill.

'How you going to solve him in time?'

1183

Gavallan started to answer and stopped. He had just noticed Pettikin and Paula at a table by the swimming pool, their heads close together. 'I thought Paula was off to Tehran this morning.'

'She was. Maybe the flight was cancelled or she took a sickie,' Scragger said absently, afraid to be grounded.

'What?'

'That's Aussie. If it's a nice day and a sheila suddenly wants the afternoon off to swim or make love or just goof off, she calls into the office during her lunch break and says she's feeling proper horrible. Sick. Sickie.' Scragger's eyebrows soared. 'Sheilas down under are very accommodating sometimes. That Paula's something else – Charlie's a gonner.'

Gavallan saw the pleasure on their faces under the umbrella, oblivious of the world. Apart from worry over Dubois, Erikki, and the others, he had read the piece in the morning's papers about the sudden stock market crash in Hong Kong; 'Many of the major companies, headed by Struan's, Rothwell-Gornt, Par-Con of China, lost 30 percent of their value or more in the day, with the whole market plunging and no end in sight. The statement issued by the Taipan, Mr. Linbar Struan, saying that this was just a seasonal hiccup brought a slashing rebuff from the government and his rivals. The more sensational press was rife with widely circulated rumours of insider trading among the Big Four and manipulation by selling short to bring prices tumbling from their record high.' That's got to be why I can't get hold of Ian. Has he gone to Hong Kong? Bloody Linbar! His balance sheet this year'll be red top to bottom.

With an effort he put brakes on his mind. He saw Pettikin reach over and cover Paula's hand. She did not take it away. 'You think he'll pop the question, Scrag?'

'If he doesn't he's a mug.'

'I agree.' Gavallan sighed and got up. 'Scrag, I'm not going to wait, you sign the bill, then go down and get Charlie, say I'm sorry but he's got to meet me in the office for an hour, then he's got the rest of the day off, then get hold of Willi and Rudi, I'll phone Jean-Luc, and between us we'll come up with what Kasigi needs, if he can deliver. Don't tell 'em why, just say it's urgent and to keep their mouths closed tighter than a gnat's bum.' He walked off. 'Hey, Mr. Gavallan!' stopped him. It was the American Wesson who jovially got up from his table and stuck out his hand. 'You got time for a drink and to visit awhile?'

'Oh, hello, Mr. Wesson, thanks, but, er, can I take a rain-check? I'm in a bit of a hurry.'

'Hell, yes, anytime.' Wesson grinned at him and leaned closer, dropping his voice to a good-natured conspiratorial whisper, and for the first time Gavallan noticed the small hearing aid in the man's left ear. 'Only wanted to say congratulations, you sure as hell showed those jokers your heels!'

'We, er, we just got lucky. Sorry, got to dash. 'Bye.'

'Sure, see you.' Thoughtfully Wesson picked up his pen and put it in his pocket. So Kasigi is gonna try and bail out Gavallan, he thought, meandering towards the lobby. I'd never've figured that one. Shit, there's no way the new regime'll cooperate. Kasigi's a pipe dreamer. Poor bastard must be going crazy, Iran-Toda's a mess, and hell, even if they start now it'll take years for that plant to be in production, and everyone knows Iran's oil spigot'll stay turned off, losing Japan 70 percent of her energy supply; there's gotta be another soar in world prices, more inflation . . . Japan's our only ally in the Pacific and the poor bastards're going to be nailed.

Jesus, with Gavallan's Lengeh op closed down, isn't the whole Siri field in jeopardy? How'll de Plessey operate Siri without chopper support? Ambassador, huh? Interesting. How's that gonna work? Who does what to whom? And how much do I pass on to old Aaron? The lot, that old bastard'll figure where it all fits if anyone can.

He wandered through the lobby and out to his car and did not notice Kasigi in a phone booth to one side.

'. . . I quite agree, Ishii-san.' Kasigi was speaking deferentially in Japanese, sweat on his brow. 'Please inform His Excellency we'll get our equipment and crew, I'm sure of it – if you can arrange the rest.' He kept the nervousness out of his voice.

'Ah, is that so? Excellent,' Ishii from the embassy said. 'I'll inform His Excellency at once. Now, what about the Iranian ambassador? Have you heard from him?'

The bottom dropped out of Kasigi's bottom. 'He hasn't accepted the invitation?'

'No, so sorry, not yet, and it's almost three o'clock. Very distressing. Please join the meeting as we agreed. Thank you, Kasigi-san.'

'Thank you, Ishii-san,' he said, wanting to scream. Gently he replaced the phone.

In the air-conditioned lobby he felt a little better and went to the reception desk. There he collected his messages – two from Hiro Toda to phone – and went upstairs to his room and locked the door. He crushed the messages into a ball, threw them into the toilet, and began to urinate on them. 'Dear stupid cousin Hiro,' he said aloud in

Japanese, 'if I save your stupid neck which I have to do to save my own,' then added a stream of English obscenities as there were none in Japanese, 'your family will be in debt to mine for eight generations for all the trouble you're causing me.'

He flushed the messages away, took off his clothes, showered, and lay naked on the bed in the cool breeze, wanting to gather energy and restore his tranquility to prepare for the meeting.

The Japanese ambassador's chance remark that had initiated his whole scheme had been made to Roger Newbury at a British embassy reception a couple of days ago. The ambassador had mentioned that the new Iranian ambassador had been bewailing the closure of Iran-Toda that would have given the new Islamic state a tremendous position of economic power throughout the whole Gulf region.

'His name's Abadani, university trained, majored in economics, of course fundamentalist but not rabidly so. He's quite young and not too experienced but he's a career officer, speaks good English, and was in the Kabul embassy . . .'

At the time the remarks had meant very little to Kasigi. Then Whirlwind happened. Tehran's telexes had spread throughout the Gulf, and then rumours of Abadani's demand for an inspection of Gavallan's helicopters – an inspection fixed for this evening that would obviously prove they had been Iranian registered: '. . . and that, Kasigi-san, will create an international incident,' Ishii had told him late last night, 'because now Kuwait, Saudi, Bahrain will be implicated – and that, I can assure you, one and all would prefer to avoid, most of all our Sheik.'

In the dawn he had gone to see Abadani and had explained about Zataki and starting construction again, adding in great secrecy that the Japanese government was rearranging Iran-Toda as a National Project – therefore covering all future financing – and that with Excellency Abadani's cooperation he could also start work again in Bandar-e Delam immediately.

'National Project? God be thanked! If your government is behind it formally, that would solve all financing for ever. God be thanked. What can I do? Anything!'

'To restart immediately I need helicopters and expatriate pilots and crew. The only way I can get them quickly is with the help of S-G Helicopters and Mr. Gavall –'

Abadani had exploded. After listening politely and seemingly agreeably to a tirade about air piracy and enemies of Iran, Kasigi had obliquely returned to the attack.

'You're quite right, Excellency,' he had said, 'but I had to choose between risking your displeasure by bringing it to your attention, or failing in my duty to your Great Country. Our choice is simple: if I don't get helicopters I cannot restart. I've tried Guerney's and others with no success and now I know I can only get them quickly through this dreadful man – of course only for a few months as a stopgap until I can make my own arrangements for Japanese personnel. If I don't restart at once that will precipitate this man Zataki, I assure you he and his Abadan komiteh is a law into itself, making good his threat. That will shock and embarrass my government and cause them to delay implementation of total National Project financing and then . . .' He had shrugged. 'My government will order Iran-Toda abandoned and start a new petrochemical plant in a safe area like Saudi Arabia, Kuwait, or Iraq.'

'Safe? Iraq? Those thieves? Saudi or Kuwait? By God, they're decadent sheikdoms ripe for overthrow by the people. Dangerous to attempt a long-term business with the sheiks, very dangerous. They don't obey God's law. Iran does now. Iran is in balance now. The Imam, God's peace on him, has rescued us. He has ordered oil to flow. There must be some other way of getting helicopters and crews! Gavallan and his mob of pirates have our property. I can't assist pirates to escape. Do you want pirates to escape?'

'Heaven forbid, I would never suggest that. Of course we don't know they are pirates, Excellency. I heard that these are just foul rumours spread by more enemies who want Iran hurt even more. Even if it were true, would you equate nine used airplanes against $3.1 billion already spent and another 1.1 billion my government might be persuaded to commit?'

'Yes. Piracy is piracy, the law is the law, the Sheik has agreed to the inspection, the truth is the truth. Insha'Allah.'

'I totally agree, Excellency, but you know that truth is relative and a postponement until after sunset tomorrow would be in your national interests . . .' He had bitten back a curse and corrected his slip quickly, 'in the interests of the Imam and your Islamic state.'

'God's truth is not relative.'

'Yes, yes, of course,' Kasigi said, outwardly calm but inwardly gnashing his teeth. How can anyone deal with these lunatics who use their beliefs as a coverall and 'God' whenever they wish to close a legitimate line of logic? They're all mad, blinkered! They won't under-stand as we Japanese do you've got to be tolerant about other people's beliefs, and that life is from nothing into nothing, and heaven and hell and god merely opium smoke from an aberrated brain – until *proven* otherwise!

'Of course you're right, Excellency. But they won't be his airplanes or crews – I just need his temporary connections.' Wearily he had waited and cajoled and listened, then played his penultimate card: 'I'm sure the Sheik and the foreign minister would consider it an immense favour if you'd postpone the inspection until tomorrow so they could go to my ambassador's special reception at eight this evening.'

'Reception, Mr. Kasigi?'

'Yes, it's sudden but terribly important – I happen to know you're invited as the most important guest.' Kasigi had dropped his voice even more. 'I beg you not to mention where you got the knowledge but, again in private, I can tell you that my government is seeking long-term oil contracts that would prove astoundingly profitable to you if Iran can continue to supply us. It would be a perfect moment t –'

'Long-term contracts? I agree the Shah-negotiated contracts are no good, one-sided, and must go. But we value Japan as a customer. Japan's never tried to exploit us. I'm sure your ambassador would not mind delaying his reception an hour until after the inspection. The Sheik, the foreign minister, Newbury, and I could go directly from the airport.'

Kasigi was not sure how far he dared go. But, Mister Excuse-for-an-Ambassador, he thought, if you don't postpone your inspection I will be revenged because you will have made me commit the only sin we acknowledge: failure. 'It's fortunate Iran's so well represented here.'

'I will certainly come to the reception, Mr. Kasigi, after the inspection.'

Kasigi's ultimate card had then been delivered with all the elegance needed: 'I have a feeling, Excellency, you will soon be personally invited to my country to meet the most important, *most important* leaders there – for you of course realise how vital your Islamic state is to Japan – and to inspect facilities that would be valuable to Iran.'

'We . . . we certainly need untainted friends,' Abadani said.

Kasigi had watched him carefully and had seen no reaction, still the same pitiless eyes and inflexibility. 'In these troubled times it's essential to look after friends, isn't it? You never know when disaster may strike you, whoever you are. Do you?'

'That's in the Hand of God. Only His.' There had been a long pause, then Abadani had said, 'As God wants. I will consider what you have said.'

Now in the privacy of his hotel bedroom, Kasigi was very afraid. It's only essential to look after yourself. However wise or careful you are, you never know when disaster will strike, whoever you are. If gods exist, they exist only to torment you.

Just Inside Turkey: 4:23 P.M. They had landed just outside the village this morning barely a mile inside Turkey. Erikki would have preferred to have gone farther into safey but his tanks were dry. He had been intercepted and ambushed again, this time by two fighters and two Huey gunships and had had to endure them for more than a quarter of an hour before he could duck across the line. The two Hueys had not ventured after him but remained circling in station just their side of the border.

'Forget them, Azadeh,' he had said joyously. 'We're safe now.'

But they were not. The villagers had surrounded them and the police had arrived. Four men, a sergeant, and three others, all in uniform – crumpled and ill fitting – with holstered revolvers. The sergeant wore dark glasses against the glare of the sun off the snow. None of them spoke English. Azadeh had greeted them according to the plan she and Erikki had concocted, explaining that Erikki, a Finnish citizen, had been employed by a British company under contract to Iran-Timber, that in the Azerbaijan riots and fighting near Tabriz his life had been threatened by leftists, that she, his wife, had been equally threatened, so they had fled.

'Ah, the Effendi is Finnish but you're Iranian?'

'Finnish by marriage, Sergeant Effendi, Iranian by birth. Here are our papers.' She had given him her Finnish passport which did not include references to her late father, Abdollah Khan. 'May we use the telephone, please? We can pay, of course. My husband would like to call our embassy, and also his employer in Al Shargaz.'

'Ah, Al Shargaz.' The sergeant nodded pleasantly. He was heavyset, close-shaven, even so the blue-black of his beard showed through his golden skin. 'Where's that?'

She told him, very conscious of the way she and Erikki looked. Erikki with the filthy, bloodstained bandage on his arm and the crude adhesive over his damaged ear, she with her hair matted and dirty clothes and face. Behind her the two Hueys circled. The sergeant watched them thoughtfully. 'Why would they dare to send fighters into our airspace and helicopters after you?'

'The Will of God, Sergeant Effendi. I'm afraid that on that side of the border many strange things are happening now.'

'How are things over the border?' He motioned the other policeman

1189

towards the 212 and began to listen attentively. The three policemen wandered over, peered into the cockpit. Bullet holes and dried blood and smashed instruments. One of them opened the cabin door. Many automatic weapons. More bullet holes. 'Sergeant!'

The sergeant acknowledged but waited politely until Azadeh had finished. Villagers listened wide-eyed, not a chador or veil among them. Then he pointed to one of the crude village huts. 'Please wait over there in the shade.' The day was cold, the land snowbound, the sun bright off the snow. Leisurely the sergeant examined the cabin and the cockpit. He picked up the kukri, half pulled it out of the scabbard, and shoved it home again. The he beckoned Azadeh and Erikki with it. 'How do you explain the guns, Effendi?'

Uneasily Azadeh translated the question for Erikki.

'Tell him they were left in my plane by tribesmen who were attempting to hijack her.'

'Ah, tribesmen,' the sergeant said. 'I'm astonished tribesmen would leave such wealth for you to fly away with. Can you explain that?'

'Tell him they were all killed by loyalists, and I escaped in the melee.'

'Loyalists, Effendi? What loyalists?'

'Police. Tabrizi police,' Erikki said, uncomfortably aware that each question would pull them deeper into the quicksand. 'Ask him if I can use the telephone, Azadeh.'

'Telephone? Certainly. In due time.' The sergeant studied the circling Hueys for a moment. Then he turned his hard brown eyes back to Erikki. 'I'm glad the police were loyal. Police have a duty to the state, to the people, and to uphold the law. Gunrunning is against the law. Fleeing from police upholding the law is a crime. Isn't it?'

'Yes, but we're not gunrunners, Sergeant Effendi, nor fleeing from police upholding the law,' Azadeh had said, even more afraid now. The border was so close, to close. For her the last part of their escape had been terrifying. Obviously Hakim had alerted the border area: no one but he had the power to arrange such an intercept so fast, both on the ground and in the air.

'Are you armed?' the sergeant asked politely.

'Just a knife.'

'May I have it please?' The sergeant accepted it. 'Please follow me.'

They had gone to the police station, a small brick building with cells and a few offices and telephones near the mosque in the little village square. 'Over the last months we've had many refugees of all sorts passing along our road, Iranians, British, Europeans, Americans, many Azerbaijanis, many – but no Soviets.' He laughed at his own joke.

'Many refugees, rich, poor, good, bad, many criminals among them. Some were sent back, some went on. Insha'Allah, eh? Please wait there.'

'There' was not a cell but a room with a few chairs and a table and bars on the windows, many flies and no way out. But it was warm and relatively clean. 'Could we have some food and drink and use the telephone, please?' Azadeh asked. 'We can pay, Sergeant Effendi.'

'I will order some for you from the hotel here. The food is good and not expensive.'

'My husband asks, can he use the telephone, please?'

'Certainly – in due course.'

That had been this morning, and now it was late afternoon. In the intervening time the food had arrived, rice and mutton stew and peasant bread and Turkish coffee. She had paid with rials and was not overcharged. The sergeant had allowed them to use the foul-smelling hole in the ground squatter, and water from a tank and an old basin to wash in. There were no medical supplies, just iodine. Erikki had cleaned his wounds as best he could, gritting his teeth at the sudden pain, still weak and exhausted. Then, with Azadeh close beside him, he had propped himself on a chair, his feet on another, and had drifted off. From time to time the door would open and one or other of the policemen would come in, then go out again. '*Matyeryebyets*,' Erikki muttered. 'Where can we run to?'

She had gentled him and stayed close and kept a steel gate on her own fear. I must carry him, she thought over and over. She was feeling better now with her hair combed and flowing, her face clean, her cashmere sweater tidy. Through the door she could hear muttered conversation, occasionally a telephone ringing, cars and trucks going past on the road from and to the border, flies droning. Her tiredness took her and she slept fitfully, her dreams bad: noise of engines and firing and Hakim mounted like a Cossack charging them, both she and Erikki buried up to their necks in the earth, hooves just missing them, then somehow free, rushing for the border that was acres of massed barbed wire, the false mullah Mahmud and the butcher suddenly between them and safety and th –

The door opened. Both of them awoke, startled. A major in immaculate uniform stood there, glowering, flanked by the sergeant and another policeman. He was a tall, hard-faced man. 'Your papers, please,' he said to Azadeh.

'I, I gave them to the sergeant, Major Effendi.'

'You gave him a Finnish passport. Your Iranian papers.' The major held out his hand. She was too slow. At once the sergeant went forward and grabbed her shoulder bag and spilled the contents on to the table. Simultaneously, the other policeman stalked over to Erikki, his hand on the revolver in his open holster, waved him into a corner against the wall. The major flicked some dirt off a chair and sat down, accepted her Iranian ID from the sergeant, read it carefully, then looked at the contents on the table. He opened the jewel bag. His eyes widened. 'Where did you get these?'

'They're mine. Inherited from my parents.' Azadeh was frightened, not knowing what he knew or how much, and she had seen the way his eyes covered her. So had Erikki. 'May my husband please use the telephone? He wish –'

'In due course! You have been told that many times. In due course is in due course.' The major zipped up the bag and put it on the table in front of him. His eyes strayed to her breasts. 'Your husband doesn't speak Turkish?'

'No, no he doesn't, Major Effendi.'

The officer turned on Erikki and said in good English, 'There's a warrant out for your arrest from Tabriz. For attempted murder and kidnapping.'

Azadeh blanched and Erikki held on to his panic as best he could. 'Kidnapping who, sir?'

A flash of irritability washed over the major. 'Don't try to play with me. This lady. Azadeh, sister to Hakim, the Gorgon Khan.'

'She's my wife. How can a hus –'

'I know she's your wife and you'd better tell me the truth, by God. The warrant says you took her against her will and flew off in an Iranian helicopter.' Azadeh started to answer but the major snapped, 'I asked him, not you. Well?'

'It was without her consent and the chopper is British not Iranian.' The major stared at him, then turned to Azadeh. 'Well?'

'It . . . it was without my consent . . .' The words trailed off. 'But what?'

Azadeh felt sick. Her head ached and she was in despair. Turkish police were known for their inflexibility, their great personal power and toughness. 'Please, Major Effendi, perhaps we may talk in private, explain in private?'

'We're in private now, madam,' the major said curtly, then seeing her anguish and appreciating her beauty, added, 'English is more private than Turkish. Well?'

So, haltingly, choosing her words carefully, she told him about her oath to Abdollah Khan and about Hakim and the dilemma, unable to leave, unable to stay and how Erikki, of his own volition and wisdom, had cut through the Gordian knot. Tears streaked her cheeks. 'Yes, it was without my consent but in a way it was with the consent of my brother who helped Er –'

'If it was with Hakim Khan's consent then why has he put a huge reward on this man's head, alive or dead,' the major said, disbelieving her, 'and had the warrant issued in his name, demanding immediate extradition if necessary?'

She was so shocked she almost fainted. Without thinking Erikki moved towards her, but the revolver went into his stomach. 'I was only going to help her,' he gasped.

'Then stay where you are!' In Turkish the officer said, 'Don't kill him.' In English he said, 'Well, Lady Azadeh? Why?'

She could not answer. Her mouth moved but made no sound. Erikki said for her, 'What else could a Khan do, Major? A Khan's honour, his face is involved. Publicly he would have to do that, wouldn't he, whatever he approved in private?'

'Perhaps, but certainly not so quickly, no, not so quickly, not alerting fighters and helicopters – why should he do that if he wanted you to escape? It's a miracle you weren't forced down, didn't fall down with all those bullet holes. It sounds like a pack of lies – perhaps she's so frightened of you she'll say anything. Now, your so-called escape from the palace: exactly what happened?'

Helplessly Erikki told him. Nothing more to do, he thought. Tell him the truth and hope. Most of his concentration was on Azadeh, seeing the blank horror pervading her, yet of course Hakim would react the way he had – of course dead or alive – wasn't the blood of his father strong in his veins?

'And the guns?'

Once more Erikki told it exactly, about being forced to fly the KGB, about Sheik Bayazid and his kidnap and ransom and the attack on the palace, having to fly them off and then their breaking their oaths and so having to kill them somehow.

'How many men?'

'I don't remember exactly. Half a dozen, perhaps more.'

'You enjoy killing, eh?'

'No, Major, I hate it, but please believe us, we've been caught up in a web not of our seeking, all we want to do is be let go, please let me call my embassy . . . they can vouch for us . . . we're a threat to no one.'

The major just looked at him. 'I don't agree, your story's too far fetched. You're wanted for kidnapping and attempted murder. Please go with the sergeant,' he said and repeated it in Turkish. Erikki did not move, his fists bunched, and he was near exploding. At once the sergeant's gun was out, both police converged on him dangerously, and the major said harshly, 'It's a very serious offence to disobey police in this country. Go with the sergeant! Go with him.'

Azadeh tried to say something, couldn't. Erikki thrust off the sergeant's hand, contained his own impotent panic-rage, and tried to smile to encourage her. 'It's all right,' he muttered and followed the sergeant.

Azadeh's panic and terror had almost overwhelmed her. Now her fingers and knees were trembling, but she wanted so much to sit tall and be tall, knowing she was defenceless and the major was sitting there opposite her watching her, the room empty but for the two of them. Insha'Allah, she thought and looked at him, hating him.

'You have nothing to fear,' he said, his eyes curious. Then he reached over and picked up her jewel bag. 'For safekeeping,' he said thinly and stalked for the door, closed it after him, and went down the passageway.

The cell at the end was small and dirty, more like a cage than a room, with a cot, bars on the tiny window, chains attached to a huge bolt in one wall, a foul-smelling bucket in a corner. The sergeant slammed the door and locked it on Erikki. Through the bars the major said, 'Remember, the Lady Azadeh's . . . "comfort" depends on your docility.' He went away.

Now, alone, Erikki started prowling the cage, studying the door, lock, bars, floor, ceiling, walls, chains – seeking a way out.

Al Shargaz – At the Airport: 5:40 P.M. A thousand miles away, southeast across the Gulf, Gavallan was in an HQ office anxiously waiting near the phone, an hour yet for sunset. Already he had a promise of one 212 from a Paris company and two 206s from a friend at Aerospatiale at reasonable rates. Scot was in the other office monitoring the HF, with Pettikin on the other phone there. Rudi, Willi Nurchtreiter and Scragger were at the hotel on more phones tracing down possible crews, arranging possible logistics in Bahrain. No word yet from Kasigi.

The phone rang. Gavallan grabbed it, hoping against hope for news about Dubois and Fowler, or that it was Kasigi. 'Hello?'

'Andy, it's Rudi. We've three pilots from Lufttransportgesellschaft and they also promise two mecs. Ten percent over scale, one month on, two off. Hang on . . . a call on the other line, I'll call you back, 'bye.'

Gavallan made a notation on his pad, his anxiety giving him heart-burn, and that made him think of McIver. When he had talked to him earlier he had not mentioned any of the deadline problems, not wanting to worry him further, promising that as soon as their choppers were safely out he would be on the next connection to Bahrain to see him. 'Nothing to worry about, Mac, can't thank you and Genny enough for all you've done . . .'

Through the window he could see the lowering sun. The airport was busy. He saw an Alitalia jumbo landing and that reminded him of Pettikin and Paula; no opportunity yet to ask him what was what. Near the far end of the runway in the freight area, his eight 212s looked raped and skeletal without their rotors and rotor columns, mechanics still crating some of them. Where the hell's Kasigi, for God's sake? He had tried to call him several times at the hotel but he was out and no one knew where he was or when he would return.

The door opened. 'Dad,' Scot said, 'Linbar Struan's on our phone.'

'Tell him to get stuffed . . . hold it,' Gavallan said quickly. 'Just say I'm still out, but you're sure I'll call him the moment I return.' He muttered a string of Chinese obscenities. Scot hurried away. Again the phone rang. 'Gavallan.'

'Andrew, this is Roger Newbury, how are you?'

Gavallan began to sweat. 'Hello, Roger, what's new?'

'Sunset's still the deadline. The Iranian insisted on coming by here to pick me up first so I'm standing by – we're supposed to go together to meet the Sheik at the airport. We'll arrive a few minutes early, then the three of us will go to the freight area to wait for His Nibs.'

'What about the reception at the Japanese ambassador's?'

'We're all supposed to go after the inspection – God only knows what'll happen then but . . . well, ours not to reason. Sorry about all this but our hands are tied. See you soon. 'Bye.'

Gavallan thanked him, put down the phone. and wiped his brow. Again the phone. Kasigi? He picked it up. 'Hello?'

'Andy? Ian – Ian Dunross.'

'My God, Ian.' Gavallan's cares dropped away. 'I'm so glad to hear from you, tried to reach you a couple of times.'

'Yes, sorry I wasn't available. How's it going?'

Gavallan told him guardedly. And about Kasigi. 'We've about an hour to sunset.'

'That's one reason I called. Damned bad luck about Dubois, Fowler and McIver, I'll keep my fingers crossed. Lochart sounds as though he cracked, but then when love's involved.' Gavallan heard his sigh and did not know how to interpret it. 'You remember Hiro Toda, Toda Shipping?'

'Of course, Ian.'

'Hiro told me about Kasigi and their problem at Iran-Toda. They're in a hell of a bind, so anything, anything you can do to help, please do.'

'Got it. I've been working on it all day. Did Toda tell you Kasigi's idea about their ambassador?'

'Yes. Hiro called personally – he said they're more than anxious to help but it's an Iranian problem, and to be honest, they don't expect very much as the Iranians would be quite within their rights.' Gavallan's face mirrored his dismay. 'Help them all you can. If Iran-Toda gets taken over . . . well, strictly between us . . .' Dunross switched to Shanghainese for a moment: 'The underbelly of a nobly thought of company would be slashed mortally.' Then in English again. 'Forget I mentioned it.'

Though Gavallan had forgotten most of his Shanghainese he understood and his eyes almost crossed. He had had no idea that Struan's was involved – Kasigi had never even implied it. 'Kasigi'll get his choppers and crew even if we miss our deadline and are impounded.'

'Let's hope you're not. Next, did you see the papers about the Hong Kong stock exchange crash?'

'Yes.'

'It's bigger than they're reporting. Someone's pulling some very rough stuff and Linbar's back is to the sea. If you get the 212s out and are still in business, you'll still have to cancel the X63s.'

Gavallan's temperature went up a notch. 'But, Ian, with those I can bust Imperial's hold by giving clients better service and better safety, an –'

'I agree, old chum. But if we can't pay for them you can't have them. Sorry, but there it is. The stock market's gone mad, worse than usual, it's bleeding over to Japan and we cannot afford to have Toda crash here either.'

'Perhaps we'll get lucky. I'm not going to lose my X63s. By the way did you hear Linbar's giving Profitable a seat in the Inner Office?'

'Yes. An interesting idea.' It was said flat and Gavallan could read neither positive nor negative. 'I heard their side of the meeting in a roundabout way. If today's a success, you're planning to be in London Monday?'

'Yes. I'll know better by sunset, or tomorrow sunset. If all goes well I'll drop by and see Mac in Bahrain, then head for London. Why?'

'I may want you to cancel London and meet me in Hong Kong.

Something very bloody curious has come up – about Nobunaga Mori, the other witness with Profitable Choy when David MacStruan died. Nobunaga was burned to death a couple of days ago at his home at Kanazawa, that's in the country just outside Tokyo, in rather strange circumstances. In today's mail I got a very curious letter. Can't discuss it on the phone but it's plenty bloody interesting.'

Gavallan held his breath. 'Then David . . . it wasn't an accident?'

'Have to wait and see on that one, Andy, until we meet – either Tokyo or London, the very soonest. By the way Hiro and I had planned to stay at Kanazawa the night Nobunaga died, but couldn't make it at the last moment.'

'My God, that was lucky.'

'Yes. Well, got to go. Is there anything I can do for you?'

'Nothing, unless you can give me an extension till Sunday night.'

'I'm still working on that, never fear. Damned sorry about Dubois, Fowler, and McIver . . . that Tokyo number will take messages till Monday . . .'

They said goodbye. Gavallan stared at the phone. Scot came in with more news about possible pilots and planes but he hardly heard his son. Was it murder after all? Christ! Goddam Linbar and his back to the wall and bad investments. Somehow or another I've got to have the X63s, got to.'

Again the phone. The connection was bad and the accent of the caller heavy: 'Long distance collect call for Effendi Gavallan.'

His heart surged. Erikki? 'This is Effendi Gavallan, I will accept the charge. Can you speak up, please, I can hardly hear you. Who is the call from?'

'One moment please . . .' As he waited impatiently he looked at the gate near the end of the runway that the Sheik and the others would use if Kasigi failed and the inspection took place. His breath almost stopped as he saw a big limousine with a Shargazi flag on its bumper approaching, but the car passed by in a cloud of dust and a voice on the other end of the phone he could hardly hear said, 'Andy, it's me, Marc, Marc Dubois . . .'

'Marc? Marc Dubois?' he stuttered and almost dropped the phone, cupped his hand over one ear to hear better. 'Christ Almighty! Marc? Are you all right, where the hell are you, is Fowler all right? Where the hell are you?' The answer was gibberish. He had to strain to hear. 'Say again!'

'We're at Kor al Amaya . . .' Kor al Amaya was Iraq's huge, half-mile-long, deep-sea-oil-terminal platform at the far end of the Gulf, off the mouth of the Shatt-al-Arab waterway that divided Iraq and Iran, about five hundred miles northwest. 'Can you hear me, Andy? Kor al Amaya . . .'

At the Kor al Amaya Platform: Marc Dubois also had one hand cupped over his ear and was trying to be guarded and not to shout down the phone. The phone was in the office of the platform manager, plenty of Iraqi and expats in the office outside able to overhear. 'This line's not private . . . *vous comprenez?*'

'Got it, but for God's sake, what the hell happened? You were picked up?'

Dubois made sure he was not being overheard and said carefully. 'No, *mon vieux*, I was running out of fuel and, *voilà*, the tanker *Oceanrider* appeared out of the *merde* so I landed on her, perfectly, of course. We're both fine, Fowler and me. *Pas de problème*! What about everyone, Rudi and Sandor and Pop?'

'They're all here in Al Shargaz, everyone, your lot, Scrag's, Mac, Freddy, though Mac's in Bahrain at the moment. With you safe Whirlwind's got ten out of ten – Erikki and Azadeh are safe in Tabriz though . . .' Gavallan was going to say Tom's risking his life to stay in Iran. But there was nothing he or Dubois could do so instead he said happily, 'How wonderful you're safe, Marc. Are you serviceable?'

'Of course, I, er, I just need fuel and instructions.'

'Marc, you're British registry now . . . hang on a sec . . . it's G-HKVC. Dump your old numbers and put the new ones on. There's been hell to pay and our late hosts have splattered the Gulf with telexes asking governments to impound us. Don't go ashore anywhere.'

Dubois's bonhomie had left him. 'GolfHotelKilo VictorCharlie, got it. Andy, *le bon Dieu* was with us because *Oceanrider*'s Liberian registry and her skipper's British. One of the first things I asked for was a pot of paint, paint . . . understand?'

'Got it, bloody marvellous. Go on!'

'As he was inbound Iraq I thought it best to keep quiet and stay with her until I talked with you and this is the first mo—' Through the half opened door Dubois saw the Iraqi manager approaching. Much more loudly now and in a slightly different voice, he said, 'This assignment with *Oceanrider*'s perfect, Mr. Gavallan, and I'm glad to tell you the captain's very content.'

'Okay, Marc, I'll ask the questions. When is she due to finish loading and what's her next port of call?'

'Probably tomorrow,' he nodded politely to the Iraqi who sat behind his desk. 'We should be in Amsterdam as scheduled.' Both men were having difficulty hearing.

'Do you think you could stay with her all the way? Of course we'd pay charges.'

'I don't see why not. I think you'll find this experiment will become a permanent assignment. The captain found the convenience of being able to lie offshore and yet get into port for a quick visit worthwhile but frankly the owners made an error ordering a 212. A 206'd be much better. I think they'll want a rebate.' He heard Gavallan's laugh and it made him happy too. 'I better get off the phone, just wanted to report in. Fowler sends his best and if possible I'll give you a call on the ship to shore as we pass by.'

'With any luck we won't be here. The birds'll be freighted off tomorrow. Don't worry, I'll monitor *Oceanrider* all the way home. Once you're through Hormuz and clear of Gulf waters, ask the captain to radio or telex contact us in Aberdeen. All right? I'm assigning everyone to the North Sea until we're sorted out. Oh, you're sure to be out of money, just sign for everything and I'll reimburse the captain. What's his name?'

'Tavistock, Brian Tavistock.'

'Got it. Marc, you don't know how happy I am.'

'Me too. *A bientôt.*' Dubois replaced the phone and thanked the manager.

'A pleasure, Captain,' the man said thoughtfully. 'Are all big tankers going to have their own chopper support?'

'I don't know, m'sieur. It would be wise for some. No?'

The manager smiled faintly, a tall middle-aged man, his accent and training American. 'There's an Iranian patrol boat standing off in their waters watching *Oceanrider*. Curious, huh?'

'Yes.'

'Fortunately they stay in their waters, we stay in ours. Iranians think they own the Arabian Gulf, along with us, the Shatt, and the waters of the Tigris and Euphrates back to their source – a thousand and almost two thousand miles.'

'The Euphrates is that long?' Dubois asked, his caution increasing.

'Yes. It's born in Turkey. Have you been to Iraq before?'

'No, m'sieur. Unfortunately. Perhaps on my next trip.'

'Baghdad's great, ancient, modern – so's the rest of Iraq, well worth a visit. We've got 9 billion metric tons of proven oil reserves and twice that waiting to be discovered. We're much more valuable than Iran. France should support us, not Israel.'

'Me, m'sieur, I'm just a pilot,' Dubois said. 'No politics for me.'

'For us that's not possible. Politics is life – we've discovered that the hard way. Even in the Garden of Eden – did you know people have been living around here for 60,000 years. The Garden of Eden was barely a hundred miles away: just upstream the Shatt where the Tigris and Euphrates join. Our people discovered fire, invented the wheel, mathematics, writing, wine, gardening, farming . . . the Hanging Gardens of Babylon were here. Scheherazade spun her tales to the Calif Harun al-Rashid, whose only equal was your Charlemagne, and here were the mightiest of the ancient civilisation, Babylonia and Assyria. Even the Flood began here. We've survived Sumerians, Greeks, Romans, Arabs, Turks, British and Persians,' he almost spat the word out. 'We'll continue to survive them.'

Dubois nodded warily. Captain Tavistock had warned him: 'We're in Iraqi waters, the platform's Iraqi territory, young fellow. The moment you leave my gangplank, you're on your own, I've no jurisdiction, understand?'

'I only want to make a phone call. I have to.'

'What about using my ship to shore when we pass by Al Shargaz on the way back?'

'There won't be any problem,' Dubois had told him, perfectly confident. 'Why should there be? I'm French.' When he had made the forced landing on the deck, he had had to tell the captain about Whirlwind and the reasons for it. The old man had just grunted. 'I know nothing about that, young fellow. You haven't told me. First you'd better paint out your Iran numbers and put G in front of whatever you like instead – I'll get my ship's painter to help. As far as I'm concerned if anyone asks me you're a one-shot experiment the owners foisted on me – you came aboard in Cape Town and I don't like you a bit and we hardly ever talk. All right?' The captain had smiled. 'Happy to have you aboard – I was in PT boats during the war, operating all over the Channel – my wife's from the Île d'Ouessant, near Brest – we used to sneak in there from time to time for wine and brandy just like my pirate ancestors used to do. Scratch an Englishman, find a pirate. Welcome aboard.'

Dubois waited now and watched the Iraqi manager. 'Perhaps I could use the phone tomorrow again, before we leave?'

'Of course. Don't forget us. Everything began here – it will end here. Salaam!' The manager smiled strangely and put out his hand. 'Good landings.'

'Thanks, see you soon.'

Dubois went out and down the stairs and out on to the deck, anxious to be back aboard *Oceanrider*. A few hundred yards north he saw the Iranian patrol boat, a small frigate, wallowing in the swell. '*Espèce de con*,' he muttered and set off, his mind buzzing.

It took Dubois almost fifteen minutes to walk back to his ship. He saw Fowler waiting for him and told him the good news. 'Effing good about the lads, effing bloody good, but all the way to Amsterdam in this old bucket?' Grumpily Fowler began to curse, but Dubois just walked to the bow and leaned on the gunwale.

Everyone safe! Never thought we'd all make it, never, he thought joyously. What a fantastic piece of luck! Andy and Rudi'll think it was planning but it wasn't. It was luck. Or God. God timed the *Oceanrider* perfectly to within a couple of minutes. Shit, that was another close one but over, so no need to remember it. Now what? So long as we don't run into bad weather and I get seasick, or this old bucket sinks, it'll be grand to have two to three weeks with nothing to do, just to think and eat and sleep and play a little bridge and sleep and think and plan. Then Aberdeen and the North Sea and laughing with Jean-Luc, Tom Lochart and Duke, and the other guys, then off to . . . off to where? It's time I got married. Shit, I don't want to get married yet. I'm only thirty and I've avoided it so far. It'd just be my bad luck to meet this Parisienne witch in angel's clothing who'll use her wiles to make me so smitten that she'll destroy my defences and ruin my resolve! Life's too good, far too good, and dredging too much fun!

He turned and looked west. The sun, hazed by the vast pollution, was settling towards the land horizon that was dull and flat and boring. Wish I was at Al Shargaz with the guys.

Al Shargaz – International Hospital: 6:01 P.M. Starke sat on the second-floor veranda, also watching the lowering sun, but here it was beautiful over a calm sea below a cloudless sky, the great bar of reflected light making him squint even though he was using dark glasses. He wore pyjama bottoms and his chest was strapped up and healing well and though he was still weak, he was trying to think and plan. So much to think about – if we get our birds out or if we don't.

In the room behind him he could hear Manuela chattering away in a patois of Spanish and Texan to her father and mother in far away Lubbock. He had already talked to them – and talked to his own folks and the children, Billyjoe, little Conroe, and Sarita: 'Gee, Daddy, when ya coming home? I got me a new horse and school's great and today's hotter'n a bowl of Chiquita's double chili peppers!'

Starke half smiled but could not pull himself out of his ocean of apprehension. Such a long way from there to here, everything alien, even in Britain. Next Aberdeen and the North Sea? I don't mind just a month or two but that's not for me, or the kids, or Manuela. It's clear the kids want Texas, want home, so does Manuela now. Too much's happened to frighten her, too much too quick too soon. And she's right but hell, I don't know where I want to go or what I want to do. Have to keep flying, that's all I'm trained for, want to keep flying. Where? Not the North Sea or Nigeria which're Andy's key areas now. Maybe one of his small ops in South America, Indonesia, Malaya or Borneo? I'd like to stay with him if I could but what about the kids and school and Manuela?

Maybe forget overseas and go Stateside? No. Too long abroad, too long here.

His eyes were reaching beyond the old city into the far distance of the desert. He was remembering the times he had gone out past the threshold of the desert by night, sometimes with Manuela, sometimes alone, going there just to listen. To listen to what? To the silence, to the night, or to the stars calling one to another? To nothing? 'You listen to God,' the mullah Hussain had said. 'How can an Infidel do that? You listen to God.'

'Those are your words, mullah, not mine.'

Strange man, saving my life, me saving his, almost dead because of him then saved again, then all of us at Kowiss freed – hell, he knew we were leaving Kowiss for good, I'm sure of it. Why did he let us go, us the Great Satan? And why did he keep on telling me to go and see Khomeini? *Imam*'s not right, not right at all.

What is it about all this that's got to me?

It's the out there, the something of the desert that exists for me. Utter peace. The absolute. It's just for me – not for the kids or Manuela or my folks or anyone else – just me . . . I can't explain it to anyone, Manuela most of all, anymore'n I could explain what happened in the mosque at Kowiss, or at the questioning.

I'd better get the hell out or I'm lost. The simplicity of Islam seems to make everything so simple and clear and better and, yet . . .

I'm Conroe Starke, Texan, chopper pilot with a great wife and great kids and that should be enough, by God, shouldn't it?

Troubled, he looked back at the old city, its minarets and walls already reddening from the setting sun. Beyond the city was the desert and beyond that Mecca. He knew that was the way to Mecca because he had seen hospital staff, doctors and nurses and others, kneeling at prayers in that direction. Manuela came out on to the veranda again, distracting his thought pattern, sat down beside him, and brought him partially back to reality.

'They send their love and ask when we're coming home. It'd be good to visit, don't you think, Conroe?' She saw him nod, absently, not with her, then looked where he was looking, seeing nothing special. Just the sun going down. Goddam –! She hid her concern. He was mending perfectly, but he wasn't the same. 'Not to worry, Manuela,' Doc Nutt had said, 'it's probably the shock of being hit with a bullet, the first time's always a bit traumatic. It's that, and Dubois, Tom, Erikki, and all the waiting and worrying and the not knowing – we're all poised, you, me, everyone, but we still don't quite know for what – it's got to all of us in different ways.'

Her worry was sinking her. To hide it she leaned on the railing, looking at the sea and the boats. 'While you were sleeping, I found Doc Nutt. He says you can leave in a few days, tomorrow if it was real important but you've got to take it easy for a month or two. At breakfast, Nogger told me the rumour is we'll all get at least a month vacation, with pay, isn't that great? With that and the sick leave we got lots of time to go home, huh?'

'Sure. Good idea.'

She hesitated, then turned and looked at him. 'What's troubling you, Conroe?'

'I'm not sure, honey. I feel fine. Not my chest. I don't know.'

'Doc Nutt said it's bound to be real strange for a bitty, darlin', and Andy said there's a good chance there'll be no inspection and the freighters are definite for noon tomorrow, nothing we can do, nothing more you can do . . .' The phone in the room rang and she went to answer it, still talking, '. . . nothing any of us can do more'n we're doing. If we can get out, us and our choppers, I know Andy'll get Kasigi's choppers and the crews then . . . Hello? Oh, hi, darlin' . . .'

Starke heard the sudden gasp and silence, his heart tweaked, then her explosion of excitement and she was calling out to him, 'It's Andy, Conroe, it's Andy, he's got a call from Marc Dubois and he's in Iraq on some ship, he and Fowler, they force-landed with no sweat on some tanker an' they're in Iraq and safe . . . Oh, Andy, that's goddam great! What? Oh, sure, he's fine and I'll . . . but what about Kasigi? . . . Wait a mo – . . . Yes, but . . . Sure.' She replaced the phone and hurried back. 'Nothing from Kasigi yet, Andy said he was in a rush and he'd call back. Oh, Conroe . . .' Now she was on her knees beside him, her arms around his neck, hugging him but very carefully, her happiness spilling

1203

tears. 'I've been so worried about Marc'nd old Fowler, I was so afraid they were lost.'

'Me too . . . me too.' He could feel her heart pounding and his was too and some of the weight on his spirit lifted – his good arm holding her tightly. 'Goddam,' he muttered, also hardly able to talk. 'Come on, Kasigi . . . come on, Kasigi . . .'

Al Shargaz H.Q. International Airport: 6:18 P.M. Gavallan was at the office window watching Newbury's official car with the small Union Jack fluttering swing through the gate. The car hurried along the perimeter road towards the front of his building – uniformed chauffeur, two figures in the back. He half nodded to himself. From the tap on the hand basin he splashed a little cold water into his face and dried it.

The door opened. Scot came in, beside him Charlie Pettikin. Both were pale. 'Not to worry,' Gavallan said, 'come on in.' He strolled back to the window, trying to appear calm and stood there, drying his hands. The sun was near the horizon. 'No need to wait here, we'll go to meet them.' Firmly he led the way out into the corridor. 'Great about Marc and Fowler, isn't it?'

'Wonderful,' Scot said, his voice flat in spite of his resolve. 'Ten birds out of ten, Dad. Can't do better than that. Ten out of ten.'

Along the corridor and out into the foyer. 'How's Paula, Charlie?'

'Oh, she . . . she's fine, Andy.' Pettikin was astounded by Gavallan's sangfroid and not a little envious. 'She . . . she took off for Tehran an hour ago, doesn't think she'll be back until Monday, though maybe tomorrow.' God curse Whirlwind, he thought in misery, it's ruined everything. I know a faint heart never won a fair lady, but what the hell can I do? If they grab our choppers S-G's down the sink, there's no job, no pension, I've almost no savings. I'm so much older than she is and . . . sod everything! In a sick, stupid way I'm glad – now I can't screw up her life and anyway she'd be crazy to say yes. 'Paula's fine, Andy.'

'She's a nice girl.'

The foyer was crowded. Across it and out of the cool air-conditioning to the sunset's warmth and on to the entrance steps. Gavallan stopped, astonished. Every one of the S-G contingent was there: Scragger, Vossi, Willi, Rudi, Pop Kelly, Sandor, Freddy Ayre and all the others and all the mechanics. All were motionless, watching the approaching car. It swung up to them.

Newbury got out. 'Hello, Andrew,' he said, but now they were all transfixed for Kasigi stood beside him, not the Iranian, and Kasigi was beaming, Newbury saying in a perplexed voice, 'Really don't quite understand what's happening but the ambassador, the Iranian ambassador, cancelled at the last minute, so did the Sheik, and Mr. Kasigi called for me to go to the Japanese reception so there'll be no inspection tonight . . .'

Gavallan let out a cheer and then they were all pummelling Kasigi, thanking him, talking, laughing, stumbling over each other and Kasigi said, '. . . and there won't be an inspection tomorrow even if we have to kidnap him . . .' and more laughter and cheers and Scragger was dancing a hornpipe. 'Hooray for Kasigi . . .'

Gavallan fought his way through to Kasigi and gave him a bear hug, and shouted over the bedlam, 'Thanks, thanks, by God. You'll have some of your birds in three days, the rest at the weekend . . .' then added incoherently, 'Christ Almighty, give me a second, Christ Almighty I've got to tell Mac, Duke and the others . . . celebration's on me . . .'

Kasigi watched him hurry away. Then he smiled to himself.

At the Hospital: 6:32 P.M. Shakily Starke put down the phone, glowing with happiness, and came back on to the veranda. 'Goddam, Manuela, goddam, we made it, no inspection! Whirlwind made it: Andy doesn't know how Kasigi did it but he did it and . . . Goddam!' He put his arm around her and leaned against the balustrade. 'Whirlwind made it, now we're safe, now we'll get out and now we can plan. Goddam! Kasigi, the sonofabitch, he did it! Allah-u Akbar,' he added triumphantly without thinking.

The sun touched the horizon. From the city a muezzin began, just one, the voice peerless, beckoning. And the sound filled his ears and his being and he listened, all else forgotten, his relief and joy mingled with the words and the beckoning and the Infinite, – and he went away from her. Helplessly she waited, alone. There in the going down of the sun she waited, afraid for him, sad for him, sensing the future was in balance. She waited as only a woman can.

The beckoning ceased. Now it was very quiet, very still. His eyes saw the old city in all its ancient splendour, the desert beyond, infinity beyond the horizon, he saw it for what it was. Sound of a jet taking off and seabirds calling. Then the puttputt of a chopper somewhere and he decided.

'Thou,' he said to her in Farsi, 'thou, I love thee.'

'Thou, I love thee for ever,' she murmured, near tears. Then she heard him sigh and knew they were together again.

'Time to go home, my darlin'.' He gathered her into his arms. 'Time for all of us to go home.'

'Home's where you are,' she said, not afraid anymore.

At the Oasis Hotel: 11:52 P.M. In the darkness the telephone jangled discordantly, jerking Gavallan out of a deep sleep. He groped for it, switching on his sidetable light. 'Hello?'

'Hello, Andrew, this is Roger Newbury, sorry to call so late but th –'

'Oh, that's all right, I said to call up till midnight, how did it go?' Newbury had promised to phone and tell him what happened at the reception. Normally Gavallan would have been awake but tonight he had excused himself from the celebration just after ten and within seconds was asleep. 'What about tomorrow?'

'Delighted to tell you His Excellency Abadani's accepted an invitation from the Sheik to spend the day hawking at Al Sal oasis, so it looks very good, he'll be isolated all day. Personally, I don't trust him, Andrew, and we strongly advise you to get your planes and all personnel out as quickly and discreetly as possible, also to close down here for a month or two till we can give you the word. All right?'

'Yes, great news. Thanks.' Gavallan lay back, a new man, the bed seductive, sleep beckoning. 'I'd already planned to close down,' he said with a mighty yawn. 'Everyone's confirmed out before sunset.' He had heard the nervousness in Newbury's voice but put it down to all the excitement, stifled another yawn and added, 'Scragger and I will be the last – we're on the plane to Bahrain with Kasigi to see McIver.'

'Good. How the hell you managed Abadani I don't know – and I don't want to know either – but our collective hat's off to you. Now, er, now hate to bring bad tidings along with the good but we've just had a telex from Henley in Tabriz.'

Sleep vanished from Gavallan. 'Trouble?'

'Afraid so. It sounds bizarre but this's what it says.' There was a rustle of paper, then, 'Henley says "We hear there was some sort of attack yesterday or last night on Hakim Khan's life, Captain Yokkonen is supposed to be implicated. Last night he fled for the Turkish border in his helicopter, taking his wife Azadeh with him, against her will. A warrant for attempted murder and kidnapping has been issued in Hakim Khan's name. A great deal of fighting between rival factions is presently going on in Tabriz which is making accurate reporting somewhat difficult. Further details will be sent immediately they are available." That's all there is. Astonishing, what?' Silence. 'Andrew? Are you there?'

'Yes . . . yes, I am. Just . . . just, er, trying to collect my wits. There's no chance there'd be a mistake?'

'I doubt that. I've sent an urgent signal for more details. We might get something tomorrow. I suggest you contact the Finnish ambassador in London, alert him. The embassy number is 01-766 8888. Sorry about all this.'

Gavallan thanked him and, dazed, replaced the phone.

Sunday
March 4, 1979

At the Turkish Village: 10:20 A.M. Azadeh awoke with a start. For a moment she could not remember where she was, then the room came into focus – small, drab, two windows, the straw mattress of the bed hard, clean but coarse sheets and blankets – and she recalled that this was the village hotel and last night at sunset, in spite of her protests and not wanting to leave Erikki, she had been escorted here by the major and a policeman. The major had brushed aside her excuses and insisted on dining with her in the tiny restaurant that had emptied immediately they had arrived. 'Of course you must eat something to keep up your strength. Please sit down. I will order whatever you eat for your husband and have them send it to him. Would you like that?'

'Yes, please,' she said, also in Turkish, and sat down, understanding the implied threat, the hackles on her neck twisting. 'I can pay for it.'

The barest touch of a smile moved his full lips. 'As you wish.'

'Thank you, Major Effendi. When can my husband and I leave, please?'

'I will discuss that with you tomorrow, not tonight.' He motioned to

1211

the policeman to stand guard on the door. 'Now we will speak English,' he said, offering her his silver cigarette case.

'No, thank you. I don't smoke. When can I have my jewellery back, please, Major Effendi?'

He selected a cigarette and began tapping the end on the case, watching her. 'As soon as it is safe. My name is Abdul Ikail. I'm stationed at Van and responsible for this whole region, up to the border.' He used his lighter, exhaled smoke, his eyes never leaving her. 'Have you been to Van before?'

'No, no I haven't.'

'It's a sleepy little place. It was,' he corrected himself, 'before your revolution though it's always been difficult on the border.' Another deep intake of smoke. 'Undesirables on both sides wanting to cross or to flee. Smugglers, drug dealers, arms dealers, thieves, all the carrion you can think of.' He said it casually, wisps of smoke punctuating the words. The air was heavy in the little room and smelled of old cooking, humans, and stale tobacco. She was filled with foreboding. Her fingers began to toy with the strap of her shoulder bag.

'Have you been to Istanbul?' he asked.

'Yes. Yes, once for a few days when I was a little girl. I went with my father, he had business there and I, I was put on a plane for school in Switzerland.'

'I've never been to Switzerland. I went to Rome once on a holiday. And to Bonn on a police course, and another one in London, but never Switzerland.' He smoked a moment, lost in thought, then stubbed out the cigarette in a chipped ashtray and beckoned the hotel owner who stood abjectly by the door, waiting to take his order. The food was primitive but good and served with great, nervous humility that further unsettled her. Clearly the village was not used to such an august presence.

'No need to be afraid, Lady Azadeh, you're not in danger,' he told her as though reading her mind. 'On the contrary. I'm glad to have the opportunity to talk to you, it's rare a person of your . . . your quality passes this way.' Throughout dinner, patiently and politely, he questioned her about Azerbaijan and Hakim Khan, volunteering little, refusing to discuss Erikki or what was going to happen. 'What will happen will happen. Please tell me your story again.'

'I've . . . I've already told it to you, Major Effendi. It's the truth, it's not a story. I told you the truth, so did my husband.'

'Of course,' he said eating hungrily. 'Please tell it to me again.'

So she had, afraid, reading his eyes and the desire therein though he

1212

was always punctilious and circumspect. 'It's the truth,' she said, hardly touching the food in front of her, her appetite vanished. 'We've committed no crime, my husband only defended himself and me – before God.'

'Unfortunately God cannot testify on your behalf. Of course, in your case, I accept what you say as what you believe. Fortunately here we're more of this world, we're not fundamentalist, there's a separation between Islam and state, no self-appointed men get between us and God, and we're only fanatic to keep our own way of life as we want it – and other people's beliefs or laws from being crammed down our throats.' He stopped, listening intently. Walking here in the falling light they had heard distant firing and some heavy mortars. Now, in the silence of the restaurant, they heard more. 'Probably Kurds defending their homes in the mountains.' His lips curled disgustedly. 'We hear Khomeini is sending your army, and Green Bands, against them.'

'Then it's another mistake,' she said. 'That's what my brother says.'

'I agree. My family is Kurd.' He got up. 'A policeman will be outside your door all night. For your protection,' he said with the same curious half smile that greatly perturbed her. 'For your protection. Please stay in your room until I . . . I come for you or send for you. Your compliance assists your husband. Sleep well.'

So she had gone to the room she had been given and then, seeing there was no lock or bolt on the door, had jammed a chair under the knob. The room was cold, the water in the jug icy. She washed and dried herself, then prayed, adding a special prayer for Erikki, and sat on the bed.

With great care she slipped out the six-inch, steel hatpin that was secreted in the binding of her shoulder bag, studied it for a second. The point was needle sharp, the head small but big enough to grip for a thrust. She slid it into the underside of the pillow as Ross had shown her: 'Then it's no danger to you,' he had said with a smile, 'a hostile wouldn't notice it, and you can get it easily. A beautiful young girl like you should always be armed, just in case.'

'Oh, but, Johnny, I'd never be able to . . . never.'

'You will when – if – the time ever comes, and you should be prepared to. So long as you're armed, know how to use the weapon whatever it is, and accept that you may have to kill to protect yourself, then you'll never, ever, need to be afraid.' Over those beautiful months in the High Lands he had shown her how to use it. 'Just an inch in the right place is more than enough, it's deadly enough . . .' She had carried it ever since, but never once had had to use it – not even in the village. The village. Leave the village to the night, not to the day.

Her fingers touched the head of the weapon. Perhaps tonight, she thought. Insha'Allah! What about Erikki? Insha'Allah! Then she was reminded of Erikki saying, ' "Insha'Allah's" fine, Azadeh, and a great excuse, but God by any name needs a helping earthly hand from time to time.'

Yes. I promise you I'm prepared, Erikki. Tomorrow is tomorrow and I will help, my darling. I'll get you out of this somehow.

Reassured she blew out the candle, curled up under the sheets and covers still dressed in sweater and ski pants. Moonlight came through the windows. Soon she was warm. Warmth and exhaustion and youth led her into sleep that was dreamless.

In the night she was suddenly awake. The doorknob was turning softly. Her hand went to the spike and she lay there, watching the door. The handle went to the limit, the door moved a fraction but did not budge, held tightly closed by the chair that now creaked under the strain. In a moment the knob turned quietly back to its resting place. Again silence. No footsteps or breathing. Nor did the knob move again. She smiled to herself. Johnny had also showed her how to place the chair. Ah, my darling, I hope you find the happiness you seek, she thought, and slept again, facing the door.

Now she was awake and rested and knew that she was much stronger than yesterday, more ready for the battle that would soon begin. Yes, by God, she told herself, wondering what had brought her out of sleep. Sounds of traffic and street vendors. No, not those. Then again a knock on the door.

'Who is it, please?'

'Major Ikail.'

'One moment, please.' She pulled on her boots, straightened her sweater and her hair. Deftly she disengaged the chair. 'Good morning, Major Effendi.'

He glanced at the chair, amused. 'You were wise to jam the door. Don't do it again – without permission.' Then he scrutinised her. 'You seem rested. Good. I've ordered coffee and fresh bread for you. What else would you like?'

'Just to be let go, my husband and I.'

'So?' He came into the room and closed the door and took the chair and sat down, his back to the sunlight that streamed in from the window. 'With your cooperation that might be arranged.'

When he had moved into the room, without being obvious she had retreated and now sat on the edge of the bed, her hand within inches of the pillow. 'What cooperation, Major Effendi?'

'It might be wise not to have a confrontation,' he said curiously. 'If you cooperate . . . and go back to Tabriz of your own free will this evening, your husband will remain in custody tonight and be sent to Istanbul tomorrow.'

She heard herself say, 'Sent where in Istanbul?'

'First to prison – for safekeeping – where his ambassador will be able to see him and, if it's God's will, to be released.'

'Why should he be sent to prison, he's done noth –'

'There's a reward on his head. Dead or alive.' The major smiled thinly. 'He needs protection – there are dozens of your nationals in the village and near here, all on the edge of starvation. Don't you need protection too? Wouldn't you be a perfect kidnap victim, wouldn't the Khan ransom his only sister at once and lavishly? Eh?'

'Gladly I'll go back if that will help my husband,' she said at once. 'But if I go back, what . . . what guarantee do I have that my husband will be protected and be sent to Istanbul, Major Effendi?'

'None.' He got up and stood over her. 'The alternative is if you don't cooperate of your own free will, you'll be sent to the border today and he . . . he will have to take his chances.'

She did not get up, nor take her hand away from the pillow. Nor look up at him. I'd do that gladly but once I'm gone Erikki's defenceless. Cooperate? Does that mean bed this man of my own free will? 'How must I cooperate? What do you want me to do?' she asked and was furious that her voice seemed smaller than before.

He half laughed and said sardonically, 'To do what all women have difficulty in doing: to be obedient, to do what they're told without argument, and to stop trying to be clever.' He turned on his heel. 'You will stay here in the hotel. I will return later. I hope by then you'll be prepared . . . to give me the correct answer.' He shut the door after him.

If he tries to force me, I will kill him, she thought. I cannot bed him as a barter – my husband would never forgive me, nor could I forgive myself, for we both know the act would not guarantee his freedom or mine, and even if it did he could not live with the knowledge and would seek revenge. Nor could I live with myself.

She got up and went to the window and looked out at the busy village, snow-covered mountains around it, the border over there, such a little way.

'The only chance Erikki has is for me to go back,' she muttered. 'But I can't, not without the major's approval. And even then . . .'

At the Police Station: 11:58 A.M. Gripped by Erikki's great fists, the lower end of the central iron bar in the window came free with a small shower of cement. Hastily he pushed it back into its hole, looked out of the cage door and down the corridor. No jailer appeared. Quickly he stuffed small pieces of cement and rubble back around the base camouflaging it – he had been working on this bar most of the night, worrying it as a dog would a bone. Now he had a weapon and a lever to bend the other bars out of shape.

It'll take me half an hour, no more, he thought, and sat back on his bunk, satisfied. After bringing the food last evening the police had left him alone, confident in the strength of their cage. This morning they had brought him coffee that had tasted vile and a hunk of rough bread and had stared at him without understanding when he asked for the major and for his wife. He did not know the Turkish for 'major' nor had he the officer's name, but when he pointed to his lapel, miming the man's rank, they had understood him and had just shrugged, spoken more Turkish that he did not understand, and gone away again. The sergeant had not reappeared.

Each of us knows what to do, he thought, Azadeh and I, each of us is at risk, each will do the best we can. But if she's touched, or hurt, no god will help him who touched her while I live. I swear it.

The door at the end of the corridor opened. The major strode towards him. 'Good morning,' he said, his nostrils crinkling at the foul smell.

'Good morning, Major. Where's my wife, please, and when are you letting us go?'

'Your wife is in the village, quite safe, rested. I've seen her myself.' The major eyed him thoughtfully, noticed the dirt on his hands, glanced keenly at the lock on the cage, the window bars, the floor, and the ceiling. 'Her safety and treatment are dependent on you. You do understand?'

'Yes, yes, I do understand. And I hold you as the senior policeman here responsible for her.'

The major laughed. 'Good,' he said sardonically, then the smile vanished. 'It seems best to avoid a confrontation. If you cooperate you will stay here tonight, tomorrow I'll send you under guard to Istanbul – where your ambassador can see you if he wants – to stand trial for the crimes you're accused of, or to be extradited.'

Erikki dismissed his own problems. 'I brought my wife here against her will. She's done nothing wrong, she should go home. Can she be escorted?'

The major watched him. 'That depends on your cooperation.'

'I will ask her to go back. I'll insist, if that's what you mean.'

'She could be sent back,' the major said, taunting him. 'Oh, yes. But of course it's possible that on the way to the border or even from the hotel, she could be "kidnapped" again, this time by bandits, Iranian bandits, bad ones, to be held in the mountains for a month or two, eventually to be ransomed to the Khan.'

Erikki was ashen. 'What do you want me to do?'

'Not far away is the railway. Tonight you could be smuggled out of here and taken safely to Istanbul. The charges against you could be quashed. You could be given a good job, flying, training our fliers – for two years. In return you agree to become a secret agent for us, you supply us with information about Azerbaijan, particularly about this Soviet you mentioned, Mzytryk, information about Hakim Khan, where and how he lives, how to get into the palace – and anything else that is wanted.'

'What about my wife?'

'She stays in Van of her own free will, hostage to your behaviour . . . for a month or two. Then she can join you, wherever you are.'

'Provided she's escorted back to Hakim Khan today, safely, unharmed and it's proved to me she's safe and unharmed, I will do what you ask.'

'Either you agree or you don't,' the major said impatiently. 'I'm not here to bargain with you!'

'Please, she's nothing to do with any crimes of mine. Please let her go. Please.'

'You think we're fools? Do you agree or don't you?'

'Yes! But first I want her safe. First!'

'Perhaps first you'd like to watch her spoiled. First.'

Erikki lunged for him through the bars and the whole cage door shuddered under the impact. But the major stood there just out of range and laughed at the great hand clawing for him impotently. He had judged the distance accurately, far too practised to be caught unawares, far too experienced an investigator not to know how to taunt and threaten and tempt, how to jeer and exaggerate and use the prisoner's own fears and terrors, how to twist truths to break through the curtain of inevitable lies and half-truths – to get at the real truth.

His superiors had left it up to him to decide what to do about both of them. Now he had decided. Without hurrying he pulled out his revolver and pointed it at Erikki's face. And cocked the pistol. Erikki did not back off, just held the bars with his huge hands, his breath coming in great pants.

'Good,' the major said calmly, holstering the gun. 'You have been warned your behaviour gauges her treatment.' He walked away. When Erikki was alone again, he tried to tear the cage door off its hinges. The door groaned but held firm.

Al Shargaz International Airport: 4:39 P.M. From the driver's seat of his car Gavallan watched the loading hatch of a 747 freighter close on half the 212s, crates of spares and rotors. Pilots and mechanics were feverishly loading the second jumbo, just one more 212 carcass to get aboard, a dozen crates and piles of suitcases. 'We're on schedule, Andy,' Rudi, the loading master, said, pretending not to notice his friend's pallor. 'Half an hour.'

'Good.' Gavallan handed him some papers. 'Here are clearances for all mechanics to go with her.'

'No pilots?'

'No. All pilots're on the BA flight. But make sure they're in Immigration by 6.10 tonight. BA can't hold the flight. Make sure everyone's there, Rudi. They've got to be on that flight – I guaranteed it.'

'Don't worry. What about Duke and Manuela?'

'They've already gone. Doc Nutt went with them, so they're launched. I . . . that's about all.' Gavallan was finding it hard to think.

'You and Scrag're still on the 6.35 to Bahrain?'

'Yes. Jean-Luc'll meet us. We're taking Kasigi to set up his op and get ready for his Iran-Toda birds. I'll see you all off.'

'See you in Aberdeen.' Rudi shook his hand firmly and rushed away. Gavallan let in the clutch, ground the gears and cursed, then went back to the office.

'Anything, Scrag?'

'No, no, not yet, sport. Kasigi called. I told him he's in business, gave him the chopper registrations, names of pilots and mecs. He said he's booked on our flight to Kuwait tonight then he'll catch a ride to Abadan, then to Iran-Toda.' Scragger was as perturbed as the others about the way Gavallan looked. 'Andy, you've covered every possibility.'

'Have I? I doubt it, Scrag, I haven't got Erikki and Azadeh out.' During the night, till very late London time, Gavallan had contacted everyone of importance he could think of. The Finnish ambassador had been shocked: 'But it's impossible! One of our nationals couldn't possibly be involved in such an affair. Impossible! Where will you be this time tomorrow?' Gavallan had told him and had watched the night turn into dawn. No way to contact Hakim Khan other than through Newbury and Newbury was handling that possibility. 'It's a bitch, Scrag, but there you are.' Numbly he picked up the phone, put it down again. 'Are you all checked out?'

'Yes, Kasigi'll meet us at the gate. I've sent all our bags to the terminal and had them checked in. We can stay here till the last moment and go straight over.'

Gavallan stared at the airport. Busy, normal, gentle day. 'I don't know what to do, Scrag. I just don't know what to do anymore.'

At the Police Station in the Turkish Village: 5:18 P.M. '. . . just as you say, Effendi. You will make the necessary arrangements?' the major said deferentially into the phone. He was sitting at the only desk in the small, scruffy office, the sergeant standing nearby, the kukri and Erikki's knife on the desktop. '. . . Good. Yes . . . yes, I agree. Salaam.' He replaced the phone, lit a cigarette, and got up. 'I'll be at the hotel.'

'Yes, Effendi.' The sergeant's eyes glinted with amusement but, carefully, he kept it off his face. He watched the major straighten his jacket and hair and put on his fez, envying him his rank and power. The phone rang. 'Police, yes? . . . oh, hello, sergeant.' He listened with growing astonishment. 'But . . . yes . . . yes, very well.' Blankly he put the phone back on its hook. 'It . . . it was Sergeant Kurbel at the border, Major Effendi. There's an Iran Air Force truck with Green Bands and a mullah coming to take the helicopter and the prisoner and her back to Ir –'

The major exploded. 'In the Name of God who allowed hostiles over our border without authority? There're standing orders about mullahs and revolutionaries!'

'I don't know, Effendi,' the sergeant said, frightened by the sudden rage. 'Kurbel just said they were waving official papers and insisted – everyone knows about the Iranian helicopter so he just let them through.'

'Are they armed?'

'He didn't say, Effendi.'

'Get your men, all of them, with submachine guns.'

'But . . . but what about the prisoner?'

'Forget him!' the major said and stormed out cursing.

* * *

1219

On the Outskirts of the Village: 5:32 P.M. The Iran Air Force truck was a four-wheel drive, part tanker and part truck and it turned off the side road that was little more than a track on to the snow, changed gears, and headed for the 212. Nearby, the police sentry went to meet it.

Half a dozen armed youths wearing green armbands jumped down, then three unarmed uniformed Iran Air Force personnel, and a mullah. The mullah slung his Kalashnikov. 'Salaam. We're here to take possession of our property in the name of the Imam and the people,' the mullah said importantly. 'Where is the kidnapper and the woman?'

'I . . . I don't know anything about this.' The policeman was flustered. His orders were clear: Stand guard and keep everyone away until you're told otherwise. 'You'd better go to the police station first and ask there.' He saw one of the air force personnel open the cockpit door and lean into the cockpit, the other two were reeling out refuelling hoses. 'Hey, you three, you're not allowed near the helicopter without permission!'

The mullah stood in his path. 'Here is our authority!' He waved papers in the policeman's face and that rattled him even more, for he could not read.

'You better go to the station first . . .' he stammered, then with vast relief saw the station police car hurtling along the little road towards them from the direction of the village. It swerved off into the snow, trundled a few yards and stopped. The major, sergeant and two policemen got out, riot guns in their hands. Surrounded by his Green Bands, the mullah went towards them, unafraid.

'Who're you?' the major said harshly.

'Mullah Ali Miandiry of the Khvoy komiteh. We have come to take possession of our property, the kidnapper and the woman, in the name of the Imam and the people.'

'Woman? You mean Her Highness, the sister of Hakim Khan?'

'Yes. Her.'

' "Imam"? Imam who?'

'Imam Khomeini, peace be on him.'

'Ah, Ayatollah Khomeini,' the major said, affronted by the title. 'What "people"?'

Just as toughly the mullah shoved some papers towards him. 'The People of Iran. Here is our authority.'

The major took the papers, scanned them rapidly. There were two of them, hastly scrawled in Farsi. The sergeant and his two men had spread out, surrounding the truck, submachine guns in their hands. The mullah and Green Bands watched them contemptuously.

'Why isn't it on the correct legal form?' the major said. 'Where's the police seal and the signature of the Khvoy police chief?'

'We don't need one. It's signed by the komiteh.'

'What komiteh? I know nothing about komitehs.'

'The revolutionary komiteh of Khvoy has authority over this area and the police.'

'This area? This area's Turkey!'

'I meant authority over the area up to the border.'

'By whose authority? Where is your authority? Show it to me!'

A current went through the youths. 'The mullah's shown it to you,' one of them said truculently. 'The komiteh signed the paper.'

'Who signed it? You?'

'I did,' the mullah said. 'It's legal. Perfectly legal. The komiteh is the authority.' He saw the air force personnel staring at him. 'What are you waiting for? Get the helicopter refuelled!'

Before the major could say anything, one of them said deferentially, 'Excuse me, Excellency, the panel's in a mess, some of the instruments are broken. We can't fly her until she's checked out. It'd be safer to g –'

'The Infidel flew it all the way from Tabriz safely by night and by day, landed it safely, why can't you fly it during the day?'

'It's just that it'd be safer to check before flying, Excellency.'

'Safer? Why safer?' one of the Green Bands said roughly, walking over to him. 'We're in God's hands doing God's work. Do you want to delay God's work and leave the helicopter here?'

'Of course not, of co –'

'Then obey our mullah and refuel it! Now!'

'Yes, yes, of course,' the pilot said lamely. 'As you wish.' Hastily the three of them hurried to comply – the major shocked to see that the pilot, a captain, allowed himself to be overridden so easily by the young thug who now stared back at him with flat, challenging eyes.

'The komiteh has jurisdiction over the police, agha,' the mullah was saying. 'Police served the Satan Shah and are suspect. Where is the kidnapper and the . . . the sister of the Khan?'

'Where's your authority to come over the border and ask for anything?' The major was coldly furious.

'In the Name of God, this is authority enough!' The mullah stabbed his finger at the papers. One of the youths cocked his gun.

'Don't,' the major warned him. 'If you pull a single trigger on our soil, our forces will come over your border and burn everything between here and Tabriz!'

'If it's the Will of God!' The mullah stared back, dark eyes and dark

1221

beard and just as resolved, despising the major and the loose regime the man and uniform represented to him. War now or later was all the same to him, he was in God's hands and doing God's work and the Word of the Imam would sweep them to victory – over all borders. But now was not the time for war, too much to do in Khvoy, leftists to overcome, revolts to put down, the Imam's enemies to destroy, and for that, in these mountains, every helicopter was priceless.

'I . . . I ask for possession of our property,' he said, more reasonably. He pointed at the markings. 'There are our registrations, that's proof that it is our property. It was stolen from Iran – you must know there was no permission to leave Iran, legally it is still our property. The warrant,' he pointed to the papers in the major's hand, 'the warrant is legal, the pilot kidnapped the woman, so we will take possession of them too. Please.'

The major was in an untenable situation. He could not possibly hand over the Finn and his wife to illegals because of an illegal piece of paper – that would be a gross dereliction of duty and would, correctly, cost him his head. If the mullah forced the issue he would have to resist and defend the police station, but obviously he had insufficient men to do so, obviously he would fail in the confrontation. Equally he was convinced that the mullah and Green Bands were prepared to die this very minute as he himself was not.

He decided to gamble. 'The kidnapper and the Lady Azadeh were sent to Van this morning. To extradite them you have to apply to Army HQ, not to me. The . . . the importance of the Khan's sister meant that the army took possession of both of them.'

The mullah's face froze. One of the Green Bands said sullenly, 'How do we know that's not a lie?' The major whirled on him, the youth jumped back a foot, Green Bands behind the truck aimed, the unarmed airmen dropped to the ground aghast, the major's hand went for his revolver.

'Stop!' the mullah said. He was obeyed, even by the major who was furious with himself for allowing pride and reflexes to overcome his self-discipline. The mullah thought a moment, considering possibilities. Then he said, 'We will apply to Van. Yes, we will do that. But not today. Today we will take our property and we will leave.' He stood there, legs slightly apart, assault rifle over his shoulder, supremely confident.

The major fought to hide his relief. The helicopter had no value to him or his superiors and was an extreme embarrassment. 'I agree they're your markings,' he said shortly. 'As to ownership, I don't know. If you sign a receipt leaving ownership open, you may take it and leave.'

'I will sign a receipt for our helicopter.'

On the back of the warrant the major scrawled what would satisfy him and perhaps satisfy the mullah. The mullah turned and scowled at the airmen who hurriedly began reeling in the fuel hoses, and the pilot stood beside the cockpit once more, brushing the snow off. 'Are you ready now, pilot?'

'Any moment, Excellency.'

'Here,' the major said to the mullah, handing him the paper.

With barely concealed derision the mullah signed it without reading it. 'Are you ready now, pilot?' he said.

'Yes, Excellency, yes.' The young captain looked at the major and the major saw – or thought he saw – the misery in his eyes and the unspoken plea for asylum that was impossible to grant. 'Can I start up?'

'Start up,' the mullah said imperiously. 'Of course start up.' In seconds the engines began winding up sweetly, rotors picking up speed. 'Ali and Abrim, you go with the truck back to the base.'

Obediently the two young men got in with the air force driver. The mullah motioned them to leave and the others to board the helicopter. The rotors were thrashing the air and he waited until everyone was in the cabin, then unslung his gun, sat beside the pilot and pulled the door closed.

Engines building, an awkward liftoff, the 212 started trundling away. Angrily the sergeant aimed his submachine gun. 'I can blow the motherless turds out of the sky, Major.'

'Yes, yes, we could.' The major took out his cigarette case. 'But we'll leave that to God. Perhaps God will do that for us.' He used the lighter shakily, inhaled, and watched the truck and the helicopter grinding away. 'Those dogs will have to be taught manners and a lesson.' He walked over to the car and got in. 'Drop me at the hotel.'

At the Hotel: Azadeh was leaning out of the window, searching the sky. She had heard the 212 start up and take off and was filled with impossible hope that Erikki had somehow escaped. 'Oh, God, let it be true . . .'

Villagers were also looking up at the sky and now she too saw the chopper well on its way back to the border. Her insides turned over. Has he bartered his freedom for mine? Oh, Erikki . . .

Then she saw the police car come into the square, stop outside the

1223

hotel, and the major get out, straighten his uniform. Her face drained. Resolutely she closed the window and sat on the chair facing the door, near the pillow. Waiting. Waiting. Now footsteps. The door opened. 'Follow me,' he said. 'Please.'

For a moment she did not understand. 'What?'

'Follow me. Please.'

'Why?' she asked suspiciously, expecting a trap and not wanting to leave the safety of the hidden spike. 'What's going on? Is my husband flying the helicopter? It's going back. Have you sent him back?' She felt her courage leaving her fast, her anxiety that Erikki had given himself up in return for her safety making her frantic. 'Is he flying it?'

'No, your husband's in the police station. Iranians came for the helicopter, for him and you.' Now that the crisis was over, the major felt very good. 'The airplane was Iran-registered, had no clearance to leave Iran, so therefore they still had a right to it. Now, follow me.'

'Where to, please?'

'I thought you might like to see your husband.' The major enjoyed looking at her, enjoyed the danger, wondering where her secret weapon was. These women always have a weapon or venom of some kind, death of some kind lurking for the unwary rapist. Easy to overcome if you're ready, if you watch their hands and don't sleep. 'Well?'

'There are . . . there are Iranians at the police station?'

'No. This is Turkey, not Iran, no alien is waiting for you. Come along, you've nothing to fear.'

'I'll . . . I'll be right down. At once.'

'Yes, you will – at once,' he said. 'You don't need a bag, just your jacket. Be quick before I change my mind.' He saw the flash of fury and it further amused him. But this time she obeyed, seething, put on her jacket and went down the stairs, hating her helplessness. Across the square beside him, eyes watching them. Into the station and the room, the same one as before. 'Please wait here.'

Then he closed the door and went into the office. The sergeant held out the phone for him. 'I have Captain Tanazak, Border Station duty officer for you, sir.'

'Captain? Major Ikail. The border's closed to all mullahs and Green Bands until further orders. Arrest the sergeant who let some through a couple of hours ago and send him to Van in great discomfort. An Iranian truck's coming back. Order it harassed for twenty hours, and the men in it. As for you, you're subject to court-martial for failing to ensure standing instructions about armed men!' He put the phone down, glanced at his watch. 'Is the car ready, Sergeant?'

'Yes, Effendi.'

'Good.' The major went through the door, down the corridor to the cage, the sergeant following him. Erikki did not get up. Only his eyes moved. 'Now, Mr. Pilot, if you're prepared to be calm, controlled, and no longer stupid, I'm going to bring your wife to see you.'

Erikki's voice grated. 'If you or anyone touches her I swear I'll kill you, I'll tear you to pieces.'

'I agree it must be difficult to have such a wife. Better to have an ugly one than one such as her – unless she's kept in purdah. Now do you want to see her or not?'

'What do I have to do?'

Irritably the major said, 'Be calm, controlled and no longer stupid.' To the sergeant he said in Turkish, 'Go and fetch her.'

Erikki's mind was expecting disaster or a trick. Then he saw her at the end of the corridor, and that she was whole, and he almost wept with relief, and so did she.

'Oh, Erikki . . .'

'Both of you listen to me,' the major said curtly. 'Even though you've both caused us a great deal of inconvenience and embarrassment, I've decided you were both telling the truth. You will be sent at once with a guard to Istanbul, discreetly, and handed over to your ambassador, discreetly – to be expelled, discreetly.'

They stared at him, dumbfounded. 'We're to be freed?' she said, holding on to the bars.

'At once. We expect your discretion – and that's part of the bargain. You will have to agree formally in writing. Discretion. That means no leaks, no public or private crowing about your escape or escapades. You agree?'

'Oh, yes, yes, of course,' Azadeh said. 'But there's, there's no trick?'

'No.'

'But . . . but why? Why after . . . why're you letting us go?' Erikki stumbled over the words, still not believing him.

'Because I tested both of you, you both passed the tests, you committed no crimes that we would judge crimes – your oaths are between you and God and not subject to any court – and, fortunately for you, the warrant was illegal and therefore unacceptable. Komiteh!' he muttered disgustedly, then noticed the way they were looking at each other. For a moment he was awed. And envious.

Curious that Hakim Khan allowed a komiteh to issue a warrant and sign it, not the police who would have made extradition legal. He motioned to the sergeant. 'Let him out. I'll wait for you both in the office. Don't forget I still have your jewellery to return to you. And the two knives.' He strode off.

The cage gate opened noisily. The sergeant hesitated, then left. Neither Erikki nor Azadeh noticed him go or the foulness of the cell, only each other, she just outside, still holding on to the bars, he just inside, holding on to the bars of the door. They did not move. Just smiled.

'Insha'Allah?' she said.

'Why not?' And then, still disoriented by their deliverance by an honest man whom Erikki would have torn apart as the epitome of evil a moment ago, Erikki remembered what the major had said about purdah, how desirable she was. In spite of his wish not to wreck the miracle of the good he blurted out, 'Azadeh, I'd like to leave all the bad here. Can we? What about John Ross?'

Her smile did not alter and she knew that they were at the abyss. With confidence she leaped into it, glad for the opportunity. 'Long ago in our beginning I told you that once upon a time I knew him when I was very young,' she said, her voice tender, belying her anxiety. 'In the village and at the base he saved my life. When I meet him again, if I meet him, I will smile at him and be happy. I beg you to do the same. The past is the past and should stay the past.'

Accept it and him, Erikki, now and for ever, she was willing him, or our marriage will end quickly, not of my volition but because you'll unman yourself, you'll make your life unbearable and you'll not want me near you. Then I'll go back to Tabriz and begin another life, sadly it's true, but that's what I've decided to do. I won't remind you of your promise to me before we were married, I don't want to humiliate you – but how rotten of you to forget; I forgive you only because I love you. Oh, God, men are so strange, so difficult to understand, please remind him of his oath at once!

'Erikki,' she murmured, 'let the past stay with the past. Please?' With her eyes she begged him as only a woman can beg.

But he avoided her look, devastated by his own stupidity and jealousy. Azadeh's right, he was shouting at himself. That's past. Azadeh told me about him honestly and I promised her freely that I could live with that and he did save her life. She's right, but even so I'm sure she loves him.

Tormented he looked down at her and into her eyes, a door slammed inside his head, he locked it and cast away the key. The old warmth pervaded him, cleansing him. 'You're right and I agree! You're right! I love you – and Finland for ever!' He lifted her off the ground and kissed

1226

her and she kissed him back, then held on to him as, more happy than he had ever been, he carried her effortlessly up the corridor. 'Do they have sauna in Istanbul, do you think he'll let us make a phone call, just one, do you think . . .'

But she was not listening. She was smiling to herself.

Bahrain – the International Hospital: 6:03 P.M. The muted phone rang in Mac's bedroom and Genny came out of her pleasing reverie on the veranda, Mac dozing in an easy chair beside her in the shade. She slipped out of her chair, not making a sound, not wanting to awaken him, and picked it up. 'Captain McIver's room,' she said softly.

'Oh, sorry to bother you, is Captain McIver free for a moment? This is Mr. Newbury's assistant at Al Shargaz.'

'Sorry, he's sleeping, this is Mrs. McIver, can I take a message for him?'

The voice hesitated. 'Perhaps you'd ask him to call me. Bertram Jones.'

'If it's important, you'd better give it to me.'

Again a hesitation, then, 'Very well. Thank you. It's a telex from our HQ in Tehran for him. It says: "Please advise Captain D. McIver, managing director of IHC, that one of his pilots, Thomas Lochart, and his wife have been reported accidentally killed during a demonstration". ' The voice picked up a little. 'Sorry for the bad news, Mrs. McIver.'

'Th – that's all right. Thank you. I'll see my, my husband gets it. Thank you.' Quietly she replaced the phone. She caught sight of herself in a mirror. Her face was colourless, naked in its misery.

Oh, my God, I can't let Duncan see me or know or he'll ha –

'Who was it, Gen?' McIver said from outside, still half asleep.

'It . . . it'll wait, luvey. Go back to sleep.'

'Good about the tests, wasn't it?' The results had been excellent.

'Wonderful . . . I'll be back in a second.' She went to the bathroom and closed the door and splashed water on her face. Can't tell him, just can't . . . got to protect him. Should I call Andy? A glance at her watch. Can't, Andy'll be at the airport already. I'll . . . I'll wait till he arrives, that's what I'll do . . . I'll go to meet him with Jean-Luc and . . . nothing to do till then . . . oh God oh God, poor Tommy, poor Sharazad . . . poor loves . . .

The tears poured out of her and she turned on the taps to hide the sound. When she came back on to the veranda McIver was contentedly asleep. She sat and looked at the sunset, not seeing it.

*   *   *

1227

Al Shargaz International Airport: Sunset. Rudi Lutz, Scragger and all the others were waiting at their exit barrier, anxiously staring off towards the crowded foyer, arriving and departing passengers milling about. 'Final call for BA 532 to Rome and London. Will all passengers board now, please.'

Through the huge, plate-glass windows they could see the sun almost at the horizon. All were nervous. 'Andy should've kept Johnny and the 125 as backup for God's sake,' Rudi muttered testily to no one in particular.

'He had to send it to Nigeria,' Scot said defensively. 'The Old Man had no choice, Rudi.' But he saw Rudi was not listening, so he half shrugged, absently said to Scragger, 'You really going to give up flying, Scrag?'

The lined old face twisted. 'For a year, only for a year – Bahrain's great for me, Kasigi's a beaut, and I won't give up flying completely, oh dear no. Can't, me son, gives me the creeps to think about it.'

'Me too. Scrag, if you were my age would y—' He stopped as an irritable BA official came through Security and strode up to Rudi: 'Captain Lutz, absolutely your last call! She's already five minutes late. We can't hold her any longer! You've just got to board the rest of your party at once or we'll leave without you!'

'All right,' Rudi said. 'Scrag, tell Andy we waited as long as possible. If Charlie doesn't make it, throw him in the *Gottverdamsticker* brig! Goddam Alitalia for being early. Everyone on.' He handed his boarding pass to the attractive flight attendant and went through the barrier and stood on the other side, checking them through, Freddy Ayre, Pop Kelly, Willi, Ed Vossi, Sandor, Nogger Lane, Scot last and dawdling until he could wait no longer. 'Hey, Scrag, tell the Old Man okay for me.'

'Sure, sport.' Scragger waved as he vanished into Security, then turned away, heading for his own gate the other side of the terminal, Kasigi waiting there already, brightened as he saw Pettikin running through the crowd, hand in hand with Paula, Gavallan twenty paces behind. Pettikin gave her a hurried embrace and rushed for the barrier.

'For Gawd's sake, Charlie . . .'

'Don't give me a hard time, Scrag, had to wait for Andy,' Charlie said, almost out of breath. He handed over his boarding pass, blew a beaming kiss to Paula, went through the barrier, and was gone.

'Hi, Paula, what's cooking?'

Paula was breathless too but radiant. She put her arm through his, gave him a little shrug: 'Charlie asked me to spend his leave with him, *caro*, in South Africa – I've relations near Cape Town, a sister and her family, so I said why not?'

'Why not indeed! Does that mean th –'

'Sorry, Scrag!' Gavallan called out, joining them. He was puffing but twenty years younger. 'Sorry, been on the phone for half an hour, looks like we've lost the bloody ExTex Saudi contract and part of the North Sea but to hell with that – great news!' He beamed and another ten years fell away, behind him the sun touched the horizon. 'Erikki called as I was half out the door, he's safe, so's Azadeh, they're safe in Turkey and . . .'

'Hallelujah!' Scragger burst out over him, and from the depths of the waiting area past Security there was a vast cheer from the others, the news given them by Pettikin.

'. . . and then I had a call from a friend in Japan. How much time have we?'

'Plenty, twenty minutes, why? You just missed Scot, he said to give you a message: "Tell the Old Man okay." '

Gavallan smiled. 'Good. Thanks.' Now he had regained his breath. 'I'll catch you up, Scrag. Wait for me, Paula, won't be a moment.' He went over to the JAL information counter. ''Evening, could you tell me, please, when's your next flight out of Bahrain for Hong Kong?'

The receptionist tapped the keys of the computer. '11.42 tonight, Sayyid.'

'Excellent.' Gavallan took out his tickets. 'Cancel me off BA's London flight tonight and put me on th—' Loudspeakers came to life and drowned him out with the all-pervading call to prayer. An immediate hush fell on the airport.

And high up in the vast reaches of the Zagros Mountains, five hundred miles northward, Hussain Kowissi slid off his horse, then helped his young son to make the camel kneel. He wore a Kash'kai belted sheepskin coat over his black robes, a white turban, his Kalashnikov slung on his back. Both were solemn, the little boy's face puffy from all the tears. Together they tethered the animals, found their prayer mats, faced Mecca, and began. A chill wind whined around them, blowing snow from the high drifts. The half-obscured sunset snowed through a narrow band of sky under the encroaching, nimbus-filled overcast that was again heavy with storm and with snow. Prayers were soon said.

'We'll camp here tonight, my son.'

'Yes, Father.' Obediently the little boy helped with the unloading, a spill of tears again on his cheeks. Yesterday his mother had died. 'Father, will Mother be in Paradise when we get there?'

'I don't know, my son. Yes, I think so.' Hussain kept the grief off his face. The birthing had been long and cruel, nothing he could do to help her but hold her hand and pray that she and the child would be spared and that the midwife was skilled. The midwife was skilled but the child was still-born, the haemorrhaging would not stop and what was ordained came to pass.

As God wants, he had said. But for once that did not help him. He had buried her and the still-born child. In great sadness he had gone to his cousin – also a mullah – had given him and his wife his two infant sons to rear, and his place at the mosque until the congregation chose his successor. Then, with his remaining son, he had turned his back on Kowiss.

'Tomorrow we will be down in the plains, my son. It will be warmer.'

'I'm very hungry, Father,' the little boy said.

'So am I, my son,' he said kindly. 'Was it ever different?'

'Will we be martyred soon?'

'In God's time.'

The little boy was six and he found many things hard to understand but not that. In God's time we get to Paradise where it's warm and green and there's more food than you can eat and cool clean water to drink. But what about . . . 'Are there joubs in Paradise?' he asked in his piping little voice, snuggling against his father for greater warmth.

Hussain put his arm around him. 'No, my son, I don't think so. No joubs or the need for them.' Awkwardly he continued cleaning the action of his gun with a piece of oiled cloth. 'No need for joubs.'

'That'll be very strange, Father, very strange. Why did we leave home? Where are we going?'

'At first northwest, a long way, my son. The Imam has saved Iran but Muslims north, south, east and west are beset with enemies. They need help and guidance and the Word.'

'The Imam, God's peace on him, has he sent you?'

'No, my son. He orders nothing, just guides. I go to do God's work freely, of my own choice, a man is free to choose what he must do.' He saw the little boy's frown and he gave him a little hug, loving him. 'Now we are soldiers of God.'

'Oh, good, I will be a good soldier. Will you tell me again why you let those Satanists go, the ones at our base, and let them take away our air machines?'

'Because of the leader, the captain,' Hussain said patiently. 'I think

1230

he was an instrument of God, he opened my eyes to God's message that I should seek life and not martyrdom, to leave the time of martyrdom to God. And also because he gave into my hands an invincible weapon against the enemies of Islam – Christians and Jews: the knowledge that they regard individual human life sacrosanct.'

The little boy stifled a yawn. 'What's sacrosanct mean?'

'They believe the life of an individual is priceless, any individual. We know all life comes from God, belongs to God, returns to God and any life only has value doing God's work. Do you understand, my son?'

'I think so,' the little boy said, very tired now. 'So long as we do God's work we go to Paradise and Paradise is for ever.'

'Yes, my son. Using what the pilot taught, one Believer can put his foot on the neck of ten millions. We will spread this word, you and I . . .' Hussain was very content that his purpose was clear. Curious, he thought, that the man Starke showed me the path. 'We are neither Eastern, nor Western, only Islam. Do you understand, my son?'

But there was no answer. The little boy was fast asleep. Hussain cradled him, watching the dying sun. The tip vanished. 'God is Great,' he said to the mountains and to the sky and to the night. 'There is no other God but God . . .'